KU-316-650

IN SEARCH OF
LOST TIME

———

CONTENTS OF
VOLUME TWO

———

Numerals in the text refer the reader to explanatory notes, while asterisks indicate the position of textual addenda. The notes and the addenda follow the text.

WITHIN A BUDDING GROVE

PLACE-NAMES · THE PLACE

I had arrived at a state of almost complete indifference to Gilberte when, two years later, I went with my grandmother to Balbec. When I succumbed to the attraction of a new face, when it was with the help of some other girl that I hoped to discover the Gothic cathedrals, the palaces and gardens of Italy, I said to myself sadly that this love of ours, in so far as it is a love for one particular creature, is not perhaps a very real thing, since, though associations of pleasant or painful musings can attach it for a time to a woman to the extent of making us believe that it has been inspired by her in a logically necessary way, if on the other hand we detach ourselves deliberately or unconsciously from those associations, this love, as though it were in fact spontaneous and sprang from ourselves alone, will revive in order to bestow itself on another woman. At the time, however, of my departure for Balbec, and during the earlier part of my stay there, my indifference was still only intermittent. Often, our life being so careless of chronology, interpolating so many anachronisms into the sequence of our days, I found myself living in those—far older days than yesterday or last week—when I still loved Gilberte. And then no longer seeing her became suddenly painful, as it would have been at that time. The self that had loved her, which another self had already almost entirely supplanted, would reappear, stimulated far more often by a trivial than by an important event. For instance, if I may anticipate for a moment my arrival in Normandy, I heard someone who passed me on the sea-front at Balbec refer to "the head of the Ministry of Posts and his family." Now, since I as yet knew nothing of the influence which that family was to have on my life, this remark ought to have passed unheeded; instead, it gave me at once an acute twinge, which a self that had for the most part long since been outgrown in me felt at being parted from Gilberte. For I had never given another thought to a conversation which Gilberte had had with her father in my hearing, in which allusion was made to the Secretary to the Ministry of Posts and his family.

Now the memories of love are no exception to the general laws of memory, which in turn are governed by the still more general laws of Habit. And as Habit weakens everything, what best reminds us of a person is precisely what we had forgotten (because it was of no importance, and we therefore left it in full possession of its strength). That is why the better part of our memories exists outside us, in a blatter of rain, in the smell of an unaired room or of the first crackling brushwood fire in a cold grate: wherever, in short, we happen upon what our mind, having no use for it, had rejected, the last treasure that the past has in store, the richest, that which, when all our flow of tears seems to have dried at the source, can make us weep again. Outside us? Within us, rather, but hidden from our eyes in an oblivion more or less prolonged. It is thanks to this oblivion alone that we can from time to time recover the person that we were, place ourselves in relation to things as he was placed, suffer anew because we are no longer ourselves but he, and because he loved what now leaves us indifferent. In the broad daylight of our habitual memory the images of the past turn gradually pale and fade out of sight, nothing remains of them, we shall never recapture it. Or rather we should never recapture it had not a few words (such as this "head of the Ministry of Posts") been carefully locked away in oblivion, just as an author deposits in the National Library a copy of a book which might otherwise become unobtainable.

But this pain and this recrudescence of my love for Gilberte lasted no longer than such things last in a dream, and this time, on the contrary, because at Balbec the old Habit was no longer there to keep them alive. And if these effects of Habit appear to be incompatible, that is because Habit is bound by a diversity of laws. In Paris I had grown more and more indifferent to Gilberte, thanks to Habit. The change of habit, that is to say the temporary cessation of Habit, completed Habit's work when I set out for Balbec. It weakens, but it stabilises; it leads to disintegration but it makes the scattered elements last indefinitely. Day after day, for years past, I had modelled my state of mind as best I could upon that of the day before. At Balbec a strange bed, to the side of which a tray was brought in the morning that differed from my Paris breakfast tray, could no longer sustain the thoughts upon which my love for Gilberte had fed: there are cases (fairly rare, it is true) where, one's days being paralysed by a sedentary life, the best way to gain time is to change one's place of residence. My journey to Balbec was like the first outing of a convalescent who needed only that to convince him that he was cured.

The journey was one that would now no doubt be made by motor-car, with a view to making it more agreeable. We shall see that, accomplished in such a way, it would even be in a sense more real, since one would be following more closely, in a more intimate contiguity, the various gradations by which the surface of the earth is diversified. But after all the specific attraction of a journey lies not in our being able to alight at places on the way and to stop altogether as soon as we grow tired, but in its making the difference between departure and arrival not as imperceptible but as intense as possible, so that we are conscious of it in its totality, intact, as it existed in us when our imagination bore us from the place in which we were living right to the very heart of a place we longed to see, in a single sweep which seemed miraculous to us not so much because it covered a certain distance as because it united two distinct individualities of the world, took us from one name to another name, and which is schematised (better than in a form of locomotion in which, since one can disembark where one chooses, there can scarcely be said to be any point of arrival) by the mysterious operation performed in those peculiar places, railway-stations, which scarcely form part of the surrounding town but contain the essence of its personality just as upon their signboards they bear its painted name.

But in this respect as in every other, our age is infected with a mania for showing things only in the environment that properly belongs to them, thereby suppressing the essential thing, the act of the mind which isolated them from that environment. A picture is nowadays "presented" in the midst of furniture, ornaments, hangings of the same period, stale settings which the hostess who but yesterday was so crassly ignorant but who now spends her time in archives and libraries excels at composing in the houses of today, and in the midst of which the masterpiece we contemplate as we dine does not give us the exhilarating delight that we can expect from it only in a public gallery, which symbolises far better, by its bareness and by the absence of all irritating detail, those innermost spaces into which the artist withdrew to create it.

Unhappily those marvellous places, railway-stations, from which one sets out for a remote destination, are tragic places also, for if in them the miracle is accomplished whereby scenes which hitherto have had no existence save in our minds are about to become the scenes among which we shall be living, for that very reason we must, as we emerge from the waiting-room, abandon any thought of presently finding ourselves once more in the familiar room which but a moment ago still housed us. We must lay aside all hope of going home to sleep in our own bed, once we have decided to penetrate into the pestiferous cavern through which we gain access to the mystery, into one of those vast, glass-roofed sheds, like that of Saint-Lazare into which I went to find the train for Balbec, and which extended over the eviscerated city one of those bleak and boundless skies, heavy with an accumulation of dramatic menace, like certain skies painted with an almost Parisian modernity by Mantegna or Veronese, beneath which only some terrible and solemn act could be in process, such as a departure by train or the erection of the Cross.

So long as I had been content to look out from the warmth of my own bed in Paris at the Persian church of Balbec, shrouded in driving sleet, no sort of objection to this journey had been offered by my body. Its objections began only when it realised that it would be of the party, and that on the evening of my arrival I should be shown to "my" room which would be unknown to it. Its revolt was all the more profound in that on the very eve of my departure I learned that my mother would not be coming with us, my father, who would be kept busy at the Ministry until it was time for him to set off for Spain with M. de Norpois, having preferred to take a house in the neighbourhood of Paris. On the other hand, the contemplation of Balbec seemed to me none the less desirable because I must purchase it at the price of a discomfort which, on the contrary, seemed to me to symbolise and to guarantee the reality of the impression which I was going there to seek, an impression which no allegedly equivalent spectacle, no "panorama" which I might have gone to see without being thereby precluded from returning home to sleep in my own bed, could possibly have replaced. It was not for the first time that I felt that those who love and those who enjoy are not always the same. I believed that I hankered after Balbec just as much as the doctor who was treating me and who said to me on the morning of our departure, surprised to see me looking so unhappy: "I don't mind telling you that if I could only manage a week to go down and get a blow by the sea, I shouldn't have to be asked twice. You'll be having races, regattas, it will be delightful." But I had already learned the lesson—long before I was taken to see Berma—that, whatever it might be that I loved, it would never be attained, save at the end of a long and painful pursuit, in the course of which I should have first to sacrifice my pleasure to that paramount good instead of seeking it therein.

My grandmother, naturally enough, looked upon our exodus from a somewhat different point of view, and (anxious as ever that the presents which were made me should take some artistic form) had planned, in order to offer me a "print" of this journey that was old in part, for us to repeat, partly by rail and partly by road, the itinerary that Mme de Sévigné had followed when she went from Paris to "L'Orient" by way of Chaulnes and "the Pont-Audemer." But my grandmother had been obliged to abandon this project at the instance of my father, who knew, whenever she organised any expedition with a view to extracting from it the utmost intellectual benefit that it was capable of yielding, what could be anticipated in missed trains, lost luggage, sore throats and broken rules. She was free at least to rejoice in the thought that never, when the time came for us to sally forth to the beach, would we be exposed to the risk of being kept indoors by the sudden appearance of what her beloved Sévigné calls a "beast of a coachload," since we should know not a soul at Balbec, Legrandin having refrained from offering us a letter of introduction to his sister. (This abstention had not been so well appreciated by my aunts Céline and Flora, who, having known that lady as a girl and always hitherto referred to her, to commemorate this early intimacy, as "Renée de Cambremer," and still possessing a number of gifts from her, the kind which continue to ornament a room or a conversation but to which the present reality no longer corresponds, imagined themselves to be avenging the insult by never uttering the name of her daughter again, when they called upon Mme Legrandin senior, confining themselves to mutual congratulations, once they were safely out of the house, such as: "I made no reference to you know whom. I think it went home!")

And so we were simply to leave Paris by that 1.22 train which I had too often beguiled myself by looking up in the railway time-table, where it never failed to give me the emotion, almost the illusion of departure, not to feel that I already knew it. As the delineation in our minds of the features of any form of happiness depends more on the nature of the longings that it inspires in us than on the accuracy of the information which we have about it, I felt that I already knew this happiness in all its details, and had no doubt that I should feel in my compartment a special delight as the day began to cool, should contemplate this or that view as the train approached one or another station; so much so that this train, which always brought to my mind's eye the images of the same towns which I swathed in the light of those afternoon hours through which it sped, seemed to me to be different from every other train; and I had ended—as we are apt to do with a person whom we have never seen but whose friendship we like to believe that we have won—by giving a distinct and unalterable cast of countenance to the fair, artistic traveller who would thus have taken me with him upon his journey, and to whom I should bid farewell beneath the Cathedral of Saint-Lô before he disappeared towards the setting sun.

As my grandmother could not bring herself to go "purely and simply" to Balbec, she was to break the journey half-way, staying the night with one of her friends, from whose house I was to proceed the same evening, so as not to be in the way there and also in order that I might arrive by daylight and see Balbec church, which, we had learned, was at some distance from Balbec–Plage, and which I might not have a chance to visit later on, when I had begun my course of bathing. And perhaps it was less painful for me to feel that the admirable goal of my journey stood between me and that cruel first night on which I should have to enter a new habitation and consent to dwell there. But I had had first to leave the old; my mother had arranged to move in that very afternoon at Saint-Cloud, and had made, or pretended to make, all the arrangements for going there directly after she had seen us off at the station, without having to call again at our own house, to which she was afraid that I might otherwise feel impelled to return with her at the last moment, instead of going to Balbec. In fact, on the pretext of having so much to see to in the house which she had just taken and of being pressed for time, but in reality so as to spare me the cruel ordeal of a long-drawn parting, she had decided not to wait with us until the moment of the train's departure when, concealed amidst comings and goings and preparations that involve no final commitment, a separation suddenly looms up, impossible to endure when it is no longer possible to avoid, concentrated in its entirety in one enormous instant of impotent and supreme lucidity.

For the first time I began to feel that it was possible that my mother might live another kind of life, without me, otherwise than for me. She was going to live on her own with my father, whose existence it may have seemed to her that my ill-health, my nervous excitability, made somewhat complicated and gloomy. This separation made me all the more wretched because I told myself that for my mother it was probably the outcome of the successive disappointments which I had caused her, of which she had never said a word to me but which had made her realise the difficulty of our taking our holidays together; and perhaps also a preliminary trial for a form of existence to which she was beginning, now, to resign herself for the future, as the years crept on for my father and herself, an existence in which I should see less of her, in which (a thing that not even in my nightmares had yet been revealed to me) she would already have become something of a stranger to me, a lady who might be seen going home by herself to a house in which I should not be, asking the concierge whether there was a letter for her from me.

I could scarcely answer the porter who offered to take my bag. My mother tried to comfort me by the methods which seemed to her most efficacious. Thinking it useless to appear not to notice my unhappiness, she gently teased me about it: "Well, and what would Balbec church say if it knew that people pulled long faces like that when they were going to see it? Surely this is not the enraptured traveller Ruskin speaks of. In any case I shall know if you have risen to the occasion, even when we're miles apart I shall still be with my little man. You shall have a letter tomorrow from your Mamma."

"My dear," said my grandmother, "I picture you like Mme de Sévigné, your eyes glued to the map, and never losing sight of us for an instant."

Then Mamma sought to distract me by asking what I thought of having for dinner and drawing my attention to Françoise, whom she complimented on a hat and coat which she did not recognise, although they had horrified her long ago when she first saw them, new, upon my great-aunt, the one with an immense bird towering over it, the other decorated with a hideous pattern and jet beads. But the cloak having grown too shabby to wear, Françoise had had it turned, exposing an "inside" of plain cloth and quite a good colour. As for the bird, it had long since come to grief and been discarded. And just as it is disturbing, sometimes, to find the effects which the most conscious artists have to strive for in a folk-song or on the wall of some peasant's cottage where above the door, at precisely the right spot in the composition, blooms a white or yellow rose—so with the velvet band, the loop of ribbon that would have delighted one in a portrait by Chardin or Whistler, which Françoise had set with simple but unerring taste upon the hat, which was now charming.

To take a parallel from an earlier age, the modesty and integrity which often gave an air of nobility to the face of our old servant having extended also to the clothes which, as a discreet but by no means servile woman, who knew how to hold her own and to keep her place, she had put on for the journey so as to be fit to be seen in our company without at the same time seeming or wishing to make herself conspicuous, Françoise, in the faded cherry-coloured cloth of her coat and the discreet nap of her fur collar, brought to mind one of those miniatures of Anne of Brittany painted in Books of Hours by an old master, in which everything is so exactly in the right place, the sense of the whole is so evenly distributed throughout the parts, that the rich and obsolete singularity of the costume expresses the same pious gravity as the eyes, the lips and the hands.

Of thought, in relation to Françoise, one could hardly speak. She knew nothing, in that absolute sense in which to know nothing means to understand nothing, except the rare truths to which the heart is capable of directly attaining. The vast world of ideas did not exist for her. But when one studied the clearness of her gaze, the delicate lines of the nose and the lips, all those signs lacking from so many cultivated people in whom they would have signified a supreme distinction, the noble detachment of a rare mind, one was disquieted, as one is by the frank, intelligent eyes of a dog, to which nevertheless one knows that all our human conceptions are alien, and one might have been led to wonder whether there may not be, among those other humbler brethren, the peasants, individuals who are as it were the élite of the world of the simple-minded, or rather who, condemned by an unjust fate to live among the simple-minded, deprived of enlightenment and yet more naturally, more essentially akin to the chosen spirits than most educated people, are members as it were, dispersed, strayed, robbed of their heritage of reason, of the sacred family, kinsfolk, left behind in infancy, of the loftiest minds, in whom—as is apparent from the unmistakable light in their eyes, although it is applied to nothing—there has been lacking, to endow them with talent, only the gift of knowledge.

My mother, seeing that I was having difficulty in keeping back my tears, said to me: "'Regulus was in the habit, when things looked grave . . .' Besides, it isn't very nice for your Mamma! What does Mme de Sévigné say? Your grandmother will tell you: 'I shall be obliged to draw upon all the courage that you lack.'" And remembering that affection for another distracts one's attention from selfish griefs, she endeavoured to beguile me by telling me that she expected the removal to Saint-Cloud to go without a hitch, that she was pleased with the cab, which she had kept waiting, that the driver seemed civil and the seats comfortable. I made an effort to smile at these trifles, and bowed my head with an air of acquiescence and contentment. But they helped me only to picture to myself the more accurately Mamma's imminent departure, and it was with a heavy heart that I gazed at her as though she were already torn from me, beneath that wide-brimmed straw hat which she had bought to wear in the country, in a flimsy dress which she had put on in view of the long drive through the sweltering midday heat; hat and dress making her someone else, someone who belonged already to the Villa Montretout, in which I should not see her.

To prevent the suffocating fits which the journey might bring on, the doctor had advised me to take a stiff dose of beer or brandy at the moment of departure, so as to begin the journey in a state of what he called "euphoria," in which the nervous system is for a time less vulnerable. I had not yet made up my mind whether to do this, but I wished at least that my grandmother should acknowledge that, if I did so decide, I should have wisdom and authority on my side. I spoke about it therefore as if my hesitation were concerned only with where I should go for my drink, to the platform buffet or to the bar on the train. But immediately, at the air of reproach which my grandmother's face assumed, an air of not wishing even to entertain such an idea for a moment, "What!" I cried, suddenly resolving upon this action of going to get a drink, the performance of which became necessary as a proof of my independence since the verbal announcement of it had not succeeded in passing unchallenged, "What! You know how ill I am, you know what the doctor ordered, yet look at the advice you give me!"

When I had explained to my grandmother how unwell I felt, her distress, her kindness were so apparent as she replied, "Run along then, quickly; get yourself some beer or a liqueur if it will do you good," that I flung myself upon her and smothered her with kisses. And if after that I went and drank a great deal too much in the bar of the train it was because I felt that otherwise I should have too violent an attack, which was what would distress her most. When at the first stop I clambered back into our compartment I told my grandmother how pleased I was to be going to Balbec, that I felt that everything would go off splendidly, that after all I should soon grow used to being without Mamma, that the train was most comfortable, the barman and the attendants so friendly that I should like to make the journey often so as to have the opportunity of seeing them again. My grandmother, however, did not appear to be quite so overjoyed at all these good tidings. She answered, without looking me in the face: "Why don't you try to get a little sleep?" and turned her eyes to the window, the blind of which, though we had lowered it, did not completely cover the glass, so that the sun could shed on the polished oak of the door and the cloth of the seat (like a far more persuasive advertisement for a life shared with nature than those hung high up on the wall of the compartment by the railway company, representing land-scapes whose names I could not make out from where I sat) the same warm and slumbrous light which drowsed in the forest glades.

But when my grandmother thought that my eyes were shut I could see her now and again, from behind her spotted veil, steal a glance at me, then withdraw it, then look back again, like a person trying to make himself perform some exercise that hurts him in order to get into the habit.

Thereupon I spoke to her, but that did not seem to please her. And yet to myself the sound of my own voice was agreeable, as were the most imperceptible, the innermost movements of my body. And so I endeavoured to prolong them. I allowed each of my inflexions to linger lazily upon the words, I felt each glance from my eyes pause pleasurably on the spot where it came to rest and remain there beyond its normal time. "Now, now, sit still and rest," said my grandmother. "If you can't manage to sleep, read something." And she handed me a volume of Mme de Sévigné which I opened, while she buried herself in the *Mémoires de Madame de Beausergent*.[1] She never travelled anywhere without a volume of each. They were her two favourite authors. Unwilling to move my head for the moment, and experiencing the greatest pleasure from maintaining a position once I was in it, I sat holding the volume of Mme de Sévigné without looking at it, without even lowering my eyes, which were confronted with nothing but the blue window-blind. But the contemplation of this blind appeared to me an admirable thing, and I should not have troubled to answer anyone who might have sought to distract me from contemplating it. The blue of this blind seemed to me, not perhaps by its beauty but by its intense vividness, to efface so completely all the colours that had passed before my eyes from the day of my birth up to the moment when I had gulped down the last of my drink and it had begun to take effect, that compared with this blue they were as drab, as null, as the darkness in which he has lived must be in retrospect to a man born blind whom a subsequent operation has at length enabled to see and to distinguish colours. An old ticket-collector came to ask for our tickets. I was charmed by the silvery gleam that shone from the metal buttons of his tunic. I wanted to ask him to sit down beside us. But he passed on to the next carriage, and I thought with longing of the life led by rail-waymen for whom, since they spent all their time on the line, hardly a day could pass without their seeing this old collector. The pleasure that I found in staring at the blind, and in feeling that my mouth was half-open, began at length to diminish. I became more mobile; I shifted in my seat; I opened the book that my grand-mother had given me and turned its pages casually, reading what-ever caught my eye. And as I read I felt my admiration for Mme de Sévigné grow.

One must not be taken in by purely formal characteristics, idioms of the period or social conventions, the effect of which is that certain people believe that they have caught the Sévigné manner when they have said: "Acquaint me, my dear," or "That count struck me as being a man of parts," or "Haymaking is the sweetest thing in the world." Mme de Simiane imagines already that she resembles her grandmother because she can write: "M. de la Boulie is flourishing, sir, and in perfect condition to hear the news of his death," or "Oh, my dear Marquis, how your letter enchanted me! What can I do but answer it?" or "Meseems, sir, that you owe me a letter, and I owe you some boxes of bergamot. I discharge my debt to the number of eight; others shall follow...Never has the soil borne so many—evidently for your gratification." And she writes in this style also her letter on bleeding, on lemons and so forth, supposing it to be typical of the letters of Mme de Sévigné. But my grandmother, who had come to the latter from within, from love of her family and of nature, had taught me to enjoy the real beauties of her correspondence, which are altogether different. They were soon to strike me all the more forcibly inasmuch as Mme de Sévigné is a great artist of the same family as a painter whom I was to meet at Balbec and who had such a profound influence on my way of seeing things: Elstir. I realised at Balbec that it was in the same way as he that she presented things to her readers, in the order of our perception of them, instead of first explaining them in relation to their several causes. But already that afternoon in the railway carriage, on re-reading that letter in which the moonlight appears—"I could not resist the temptation: I put on all my bonnets and cloaks, though there is no need of them, I walk along this mall, where the air is as sweet as that of my chamber; I find a thousand phantasms, *monks white and black, nuns grey and white, linen cast here and there on the ground, men enshrouded upright against the tree-trunks*"—I was enraptured by what, a little later, I should have described (for does not she draw landscapes in the same way as he draws characters?) as the Dostoievsky side of Mme de Sévigné's Letters.

When, that evening, after having accompanied my grandmother to her destination and spent some hours in her friend's house, I had returned by myself to the train, at any rate I found nothing to distress me in the night which followed; this was because I did not have to spend it imprisoned in a room whose somnolence would have kept me awake; I was surrounded by the soothing activity of all those movements of the train which kept me company, offered to stay and talk to me if I could not sleep, lulled me with their sounds which I combined—like the chime of the Combray bells—now in one rhythm, now in another (hearing as the whim took me first four equal semi-quavers, then one semi-quaver furiously dashing against a crotchet); they neutralised the centrifugal force of my insomnia by exerting on it contrary pressures which kept me in equilibrium and on which my immobility and presently my drowsiness seemed to be borne with the same sense of relaxation that I should have felt had I been resting under the protecting vigilance of powerful forces in the heart of nature and of life, had I been able for a moment to metamorphose myself into a fish that sleeps in the sea, carried along in its slumber by the currents and the waves, or an eagle outstretched upon the buoyant air of the storm.

Sunrise is a necessary concomitant of long railway journeys, like hard-boiled eggs, illustrated papers, packs of cards, rivers upon which boats strain but make no progress. At a certain moment, when I was counting over the thoughts that had filled my mind during the preceding minutes, so as to discover whether I had just been asleep or not (and when the very uncertainty which made me ask myself the question was about to furnish me with an affirmative answer), in the pale square of the window, above a small black wood, I saw some ragged clouds whose fleecy edges were of a fixed, dead pink, not liable to change, like the colour that dyes the feathers of a wing that has assimilated it or a pastel on which it has been deposited by the artist's whim. But I felt that, unlike them, this colour was neither inertia nor caprice, but necessity and life. Presently there gathered behind it reserves of light. It brightened; the sky turned to a glowing pink which I strove, glueing my eyes to the window, to see more clearly, for I felt that it was related somehow to the most intimate life of Nature, but, the course of the line altering, the train turned, the morning scene gave place in the frame of the window to a nocturnal village, its roofs still blue with moonlight, its pond encrusted with the opalescent sheen of night, beneath a firmament still spangled with all its stars, and I was lamenting the loss of my strip of pink sky when I caught sight of it anew, but red this time, in the opposite window which it left at a second bend in the line; so that I spent my time running from one window to the other to reassemble, to collect on a single canvas the intermittent, antipodean fragments of my fine, scarlet, ever-changing morning, and to obtain a comprehensive view and a continuous picture of it.

The scenery became hilly and steep, and the train stopped at a little station between two mountains. Far down the gorge, on the edge of a hurrying stream, one could see only a solitary watch-house, embedded in the water which ran past on a level with its windows. If a person can be the product of a soil to the extent of embodying for us the quintessence of its peculiar charm, more even than the peasant girl whom I had so desperately longed to see appear when I wandered by myself along the Méséglise way, in the woods of Roussainville, such a person must have been the tall girl whom I now saw emerge from the house and, climbing a path lighted by the first slanting rays of the sun, come towards the station carrying a jar of milk. In her valley from which the rest of the world was hidden by these heights, she must never see anyone save in these trains which stopped for a moment only. She passed down the line of windows, offering coffee and milk to a few awakened passengers. Flushed with the glow of morning, her face was rosier than the sky. I felt on seeing her that desire to live which is reborn in us whenever we become conscious anew of beauty and of happiness. We invariably forget that these are individual qualities, and, mentally substituting for them a conventional type at which we arrive by striking a sort of mean among the different faces that have taken our fancy, among the pleasures we have known, we are left with mere abstract images which are lifeless and insipid because they lack precisely that element of novelty, different from anything we have known, that element which is peculiar to beauty and to happiness. And we deliver on life a pessimistic judgment which we suppose to be accurate, for we believed that we were taking happiness and beauty into account, whereas in fact we left them out and replaced them by syntheses in which there is not a single atom of either. So it is that a well-read man will at once begin to yawn with boredom when one speaks to him of a new "good book," because he imagines a sort of composite of all the good books that he has read, whereas a good book is something special, something unforeseeable, and is made up not of the sum of all previous masterpieces but of something which the most through assimilation of every one of them would not enable him to discover, since it exists not in their sum but beyond it. Once he has become acquainted with this new work, the well-read man, however jaded his palate, feels his interest awaken in the reality which it depicts. So, completely unrelated to the models of beauty which I was wont to conjure up in my mind when I was by myself, this handsome girl gave me at once the taste for a certain happiness (the sole form, always different, in which we may acquire a taste for happiness), for a happiness that would be realised by my staying and living there by her side. But in this again the temporary cessation of Habit played a great part. I was giving the milk-girl the benefit of the fact that it was the whole of my being, fit to taste the keenest joys, which confronted her. As a rule it is with our being reduced to a minimum that we live; most of our faculties lie dormant because they can rely upon Habit, which knows what there is to be done and has no need of their services. But on this morning of travel, the interruption of the routine of my existence, the unfamiliar place and time, had made their presence indispensable. My habits, which were sedentary and not matutinal, for once were missing, and all my faculties came hurrying to take their place, vying with one another in their zeal, rising, each of them, like waves, to the same unaccustomed level, from the basest to the most exalted, from breath, appetite, the circulation of my blood to receptivity and imagination. I cannot say whether, in making me believe that this girl was unlike the rest of women, the rugged charm of the locality added to her own, but she was equal to it. Life would have seemed an exquisite thing to me if only I had been free to spend it, hour after hour, with her, to go with her to the stream, to the cow, to the train, to be always at her side, to feel that I was known to her, had my place in her thoughts. She would have initiated me into the delights of country life and of early hours of the day. I signalled to her to bring me some of her coffee. I felt the need to be noticed by her. She did not see me; I called to her. Above her tall figure, the complexion of her face was so burnished and so glowing that it was as if one were seeing her through a lighted window. She retraced her steps. I could not take my eyes from her face which grew larger as she approached, like a sun which it was somehow possible to stare at and which was coming nearer and nearer, letting itself be seen at close quarters, dazzling you with its blaze of red and gold. She fastened on me her penetrating gaze, but doors were being closed and the train had begun to move. I saw her leave the station and go down the hill to her home; it was broad daylight now; I was speeding away from the dawn. Whether my exaltation had been produced by this girl or had on the other hand been responsible for most of the pleasure that I had found in her presence, in either event she was so closely associated with it that my desire to see her again was above all a mental desire not to allow this state of excitement to perish utterly, not to be separated for ever from the person who, however unwittingly, had partici-pated in it. It was not only that this state was a pleasant one. It was above all that (just as increased tension upon a string or the accelerated vibration of a nerve produces a different sound or colour) it gave another tonality to all that I saw, introduced me as an actor upon the stage of an unknown and infinitely more interesting universe; that handsome girl whom I still could see, as the train gathered speed, was like part of a life other than the life I knew, separated from it by a clear boundary, in which the sensations aroused in me by things were no longer the same, from which to emerge now would be, as it were, to die to myself.

To have the consolation of feeling that I had at least an attachment to this new life, it would suffice that I should live near enough to the little station to be able to come to it every morning for a cup of coffee from the girl. But alas, she must be for ever absent from the other life towards which I was being borne with ever increasing speed, a life which I could resign myself to accept only by weaving plans that would enable me to take the same train again some day and to stop at the same station, a project which had the further advantage of providing food for the selfish, active, practical, mechanical, indolent, centrifugal tendency which is that of the human mind, for it turns all too readily aside from the effort which is required to analyse and probe, in a general and disinterested manner, an agreeable impression which we have received. And since, at the same time, we wish to continue to think of that impression, the mind prefers to imagine it in the future tense, to continue to bring about the circumstances which may make it recur—which, while giving us no clue as to the real nature of the thing, saves us the trouble of re-creating it within ourselves and allows us to hope that we may receive it afresh from without.

Certain names of towns, Vézelay or Chartres, Bourges or Beauvais, serve to designate, by abbreviation, their principal churches. This partial acceptation comes at length—if the names in question are those of places that we do not yet know—to mould the name as a whole which henceforth, whenever we wish to introduce into it the idea of the town—the town which we have never seen—will impose on it the same carved outlines, in the same style, will make of it a sort of vast cathedral. It was, however, in a railway-station, above the door of a refreshment-room in white letters on a blue panel, that I read the name—almost Persian in style—of Balbec. I strode buoyantly through the station and across the avenue that led up to it, and asked the way to the shore, so as to see nothing in the place but its church and the sea. People seemed not to understand what I meant. Old Balbec, Balbec-en-Terre, at which I had arrived, had neither beach nor harbour. True, it was indeed in the sea that the fishermen, according to the legend, had found the miraculous Christ, a discovery recorded in a window in the church a few yards away from me; it was indeed from cliffs battered by the waves that the stone of its nave and towers had been quarried. But this sea, which for those reasons I had imagined as coming to expire at the foot of the window, was twelve miles away and more, at Balbec-Plage, and, rising beside its cupola, that steeple which, because I had read that it was itself a rugged Norman cliff round which the winds howled and the sea-birds wheeled, I had always pictured to myself as receiving at its base the last dying foam of the uplifted waves, stood on a square which was the junction of two tramway routes, opposite a café which bore, in letters of gold, the legend "Billiards," against a background of houses with the roofs of which no upstanding mast was blended. And the church—impinging on my attention at the same time as the café, the passing stranger of whom I had had to ask my way, the station to which presently I should have to return—merged with all the rest, seemed an accident, a by-product of this summer afternoon, in which the mellow and distended dome against the sky was like a fruit of which the same light that bathed the chimneys of the houses ripened the pink, glowing, luscious skin. But I wished only to consider the eternal significance of the carvings when I recognised the Apostles, of which I had seen casts in the Trocadéro museum, and which on either side of the Virgin, before the deep bay of the porch, were awaiting me as though to do me honour. With their benign, blunt, mild faces and bowed shoulders they seemed to be advancing upon me with an air of welcome, singing the Alleluia of a fine day. But it was evident that their expression was as unchanging as that of a corpse, and altered only if one walked round them. I said to myself: "Here I am: this is the Church of Balbec. This square, which looks as though it were conscious of its glory, is the only place in the world that possesses Balbec Church. All that I have seen so far have been photographs of this church—and of these famous Apostles, this Virgin of the Porch, mere casts only. Now it is the church itself, the statue itself, they, the only ones—this is something far greater."

It was also something less, perhaps. As a young man on the day of an examination or of a duel feels the question that he has been asked, the shot that he has fired, to be very insignificant when he thinks of the reserves of knowledge and of valour that he would like to have displayed, so my mind, which had lifted the Virgin of the Porch far above the reproductions that I had had before my eyes, invulnerable to the vicissitudes which might threaten them, intact even if they were destroyed, ideal, endowed with a universal value, was astonished to see the statue which it had carved a thousand times, reduced now to its own stone semblance, occu-pying, in relation to the reach of my arm, a place in which it had for rivals an election poster and the point of my stick, fettered to the square, inseparable from the opening of the main street, powerless to hide from the gaze of the café and of the omnibus office, receiving on its face half of the ray of the setting sun (and presently, in a few hours' time, of the light of the street lamp) of which the savings bank received the other half, invaded simultaneously with that branch office of a loan society by the smells from the pastry-cook's oven, subjected to the tyranny of the Particular to such a point that, if I had chosen to scribble my name upon that stone, it was she, the illustrious Virgin whom until then I had endowed with a general existence and an intangible beauty, the Virgin of Balbec, the unique (which meant, alas, the only one), who, on her body coated with the same soot as defiled the neighbouring houses, would have displayed—powerless to rid herself of them—to all the admiring strangers come there to gaze upon her, the marks of my piece of chalk and the letters of my name, and it was she, finally, the immortal work of art so long desired, whom I found transformed, as was the church itself, into a little old woman in stone whose height I could measure and whose wrinkles I could count. But time was passing; I must return to the station, where I was to wait for my grandmother and Françoise, so that we should all go on to Balbec-Plage together. I reminded myself of what I had read about Balbec, of Swann's saying: "It's exquisite; as beautiful as Siena." And casting the blame for my disappointment upon various accidental causes, such as the state of my health, my exhaustion after the journey, my incapacity for looking at things properly, I endeavoured to console myself with the thought that other towns still remained intact for me, that I might soon, perhaps, be making my way, as into a shower of pearls, into the cool babbling murmur of watery Quimperlé, or traversing the roseate glow in which verdant Pont-Aven was bathed; but as for Balbec, no sooner had I set foot in it than it was as though I had broken open a name which ought to have been kept hermetically closed, and into which, seizing at once the opportunity that I had imprudently given them, expelling all the images that had lived in it until then, a tramway, a café, people crossing the square, the branch of the savings bank, irresistibly propelled by some external pressure, by a pneumatic force, had come surging into the interior of those two syllables which, closing over them, now let them frame the porch of the Persian church and would henceforth never cease to contain them.

I found my grandmother in the little train of the local railway which was to take us to Balbec-Plage, but found her alone—for she had had the idea of sending Françoise on ahead of her, so that everything should be ready before we arrived, but having given her the wrong instructions, had succeeded only in sending her off in the wrong direction, so that Françoise at that moment was being carried down all unsuspectingly at full speed to Nantes, and would probably wake up next morning at Bordeaux. No sooner had I taken my seat in the carriage, which was filled with the fleeting light of sunset and with the lingering heat of the afternoon (the former enabling me, alas, to see written clearly upon my grandmother's face how much the latter had tired her), than she began: "Well, and Balbec?" with a smile so brightly illuminated by her expectation of the great pleasure which she supposed me to have experienced that I dared not at once confess to her my disappointment. Besides, the impression which my mind had been seeking occupied it steadily less as the place to which my body would have to become accustomed drew nearer. At the end—still more than an hour away—of this journey I was trying to form a picture of the manager of the hotel at Balbec, for whom I, at that moment, did not exist, and I should have liked to be presenting myself to him in more impressive company than that of my grandmother, who would be certain to ask for a reduction of his terms. He appeared to me to be endowed with an indubitable haughtiness, but its contours were very vague.

Every few minutes the little train brought us to a standstill at one of the stations which came before Balbec-Plage, stations the mere names of which (Incarville, Marcouville, Douville, Pont-à-Couleuvre, Arambouville, Saint-Mars-le-Vieux, Hermonville, Maineville) seemed to me outlandish, whereas if I had come upon them in a book I should at once have been struck by their affinity to the names of certain places in the neighbourhood of Combray. But to the ear of a musician two themes, substantially composed of the same notes, will present no similarity whatever if they differ in the colour of their harmony and orchestration. In the same way, nothing could have reminded me less than these dreary names, redolent of sand, of space too airy and empty, and of salt, out of which the suffix "ville" emerged like "fly" in "butterfly"— nothing could have reminded me less of those other names, Roussainville or Martinville, which, because I had heard them pronounced so often by my great-aunt at table, in the dining-room, had acquired a certain sombre charm in which were blended perhaps extracts of the flavour of preserves, the smell of the log fire and of the pages of one of Bergotte's books, or the colour of the sandstone front of the house opposite, and which even today, when they rise like a gaseous bubble from the depths of my memory, preserve their own specific virtue through all the successive layers of different environments which they must traverse before reaching the surface.

Overlooking the distant sea from the crests of their dunes or already settling down for the night at the foot of hills of a harsh green and a disagreeable shape, like that of the sofa in one's bedroom in an hotel at which one has just arrived, each composed of a cluster of villas whose line was extended to include a tennis court and occasionally a casino over which a flag flapped in the freshening, hollow, uneasy wind, they were a series of little wateringplaces which now showed me for the first time their denizens, but showed them only through their habitual exterior—tennis players in white hats, the station-master living there on the spot among his tamarisks and roses, a lady in a straw "boater" who, following the everyday routine of an existence which I should never know, was calling to her dog which had stopped to examine something in the road before going in to her bungalow where the lamp was already lighted—and which with these strangely ordinary and disdainfully familiar sights cruelly stung my unconsidered eyes and stabbed my homesick heart. But how much more were my sufferings increased when we had finally landed in the hall of the Grand Hotel at Balbec, and I stood there in front of the monumental staircase of imitation marble, while my grandmother, regardless of the growing hostility and contempt of the strangers among whom we were about to live, discussed "terms" with the manager, a potbellied figure with a face and a voice alike covered with scars (left by the excision of countless pustules from the one, and from the other of the divers accents acquired from an alien ancestry and a cosmopolitan upbringing), a smart dinner-jacket, and the air of a psychologist who, whenever the "omnibus" discharged a fresh load, invariably took the grandees for haggling skinflints and the flashy crooks for grandees! Forgetting, doubtless, that he himself was not drawing five hundred francs a month, he had a profound contempt for people to whom five hundred francs—or, as he preferred to put it, "twenty-five louis"—was "a lot of money," and regarded them as belonging to a race of pariahs for whom the

Grand Hotel was certainly not intended. It is true that even within its walls there were people who did not pay very much and yet had not forfeited the manager's esteem, provided that he was assured that they were watching their expenditure not from poverty so much as from avarice. For this could in no way lower their standing, since it is a vice and may consequently be found at every grade in the social hierarchy. Social position was the one thing by which the manager was impressed—social position, or rather the signs which seemed to him to imply that it was exalted, such as not taking one's hat off when one came into the hall, wearing knickerbockers or an overcoat with a waist, and taking a cigar with a band of purple and gold out of a crushed morocco case—to none of which advantages could I, alas, lay claim. He would also adorn his business conversation with choice expressions, to which, as a rule, he gave the wrong meaning.

While I heard my grandmother, who betrayed no sign of annoyance at his listening to her with his hat on his head and whistling through his teeth, ask him in an artificial tone of voice "And what are . . . your charges? . . . Oh! far too high for my little budget," waiting on a bench, I took refuge in the innermost depths of my being, strove to migrate to a plane of eternal thoughts, to leave nothing of myself, nothing living, on the surface of my body—anaesthetised like those of certain animals, which, by inhibition, feign death when they are wounded—so as not to suffer too keenly in this place, my total unfamiliarity with which was impressed upon me all the more forcibly by the familiarity with it that seemed to be evinced at the same moment by a smartly dressed lady to whom the manager showed his respect by taking liberties with the little dog that followed her across the hall, the young dandy with a feather in his hat who came in asking if there were "any letters," all these people for whom climbing those imitation marble stairs meant going home. And at the same time the triple stare of Minos, Æacus and Rhadamanthus (into which I plunged my naked soul as into an unknown element where there was nothing now to protect it) was bent sternly upon me by a group of gentlemen who, though little versed perhaps in the art of receiving, yet bore the title "reception clerks," while beyond them again, behind a glass partition, were people sitting in a reading-room for the description of which I should have had to borrow from Dante alternately the colours in which he paints Paradise and Hell, according as I was thinking of the happiness of the elect who had the right to sit and read there undisturbed, or of the terror which my grandmother would have inspired in me if, in her insensibility to this sort of impression, she had asked me to go in there.

My sense of loneliness was further increased a moment later. When I had confessed to my grandmother that I did not feel well, that I thought that we should be obliged to return to Paris, she had offered no protest, saying merely that she was going out to buy a few things which would be equally useful whether we left or stayed (and which, I afterwards learned, were all intended for me, Françoise having gone off with certain articles which I might need). While I waited for her I had taken a turn through the streets, which were packed with a crowd of people who imparted to them a sort of indoor warmth, and in which the hairdresser's shop and the pastry-cook's were still open, the latter filled with customers eating ices opposite the statue of Duguay-Trouin. This crowd gave me just about as much pleasure as a photograph of it in one of the "illustrateds" might give a patient who was turning its pages in the surgeon's waiting-room. I was astonished to find that there were people so different from myself that this stroll through the town had actually been recommended to me by the manager as a diversion, and also that the torture-chamber which a new place of residence is could appear to some people a "delightful abode," to quote the hotel prospectus, which might perhaps exaggerate but was none the less addressed to a whole army of clients to whose tastes it must appeal. True, it invoked, to make them come to the Grand Hotel, Balbec, not only the "exquisite fare" and the "magical view across the Casino gardens," but also the "ordinances of Her Majesty Queen Fashion, which no one may violate with impunity without being taken for a philistine, a charge that no well-bred man would willingly incur."

The need that I now felt for my grandmother was enhanced by my fear that I had shattered another of her illusions. She must be feeling discouraged, feeling that if I could not stand the fatigue of this journey there was no hope that any change of air could ever do me good. I decided to return to the hotel and to wait for her there; the manager himself came forward and pressed a button, where-upon a personage whose acquaintance I had not yet made, known as "lift" (who at the highest point in the building, where the skylight would be in a Norman church, was installed like a photographer behind his curtain or an organist in his loft) began to descend towards me with the agility of a domestic, industrious and captive squirrel. Then, gliding upwards again along a steel pillar, he bore me aloft in his wake towards the dome of this temple of Mammon. On each floor, on either side of a narrow communicating stair, a range of shadowy galleries opened out fanwise, along one of which came a chambermaid carrying a bolster. I applied to her face, which was blurred in the twilight, the mask of my most impassioned dreams, but read in her eyes as they turned towards me the horror of my own nonentity. Meanwhile, to dissipate, in the course of this interminable ascent, the mortal anguish which I felt in traversing in silence the mystery of this chiaroscuro so devoid of poetry, lighted by a single vertical line of little windows which were those of the solitary water-closet on each landing, I addressed a few words to the young organist, artificer of my journey and my partner in captivity, who continued to manipulate the registers of his instrument and to finger the stops. I apologised for taking up so much room, for giving him so much trouble, and asked whether I was not obstructing him in the practice of an art in regard to which, in order to flatter the virtuoso, more than displaying curiosity, I confessed my strong attachment. But he vouchsafed no answer, whether from aston-ishment at my words, preoccupation with his work, regard for etiquette, hardness of hearing, respect for holy ground, fear of danger, slowness of understanding, or the manager's orders.

There is perhaps nothing that gives us so strong an impression of the reality of the external world as the difference in the position, relative to ourselves, of even a quite unimportant person before we have met him and after. I was the same man who had taken, that afternoon, the little train from Balbec to the coast; I carried in my body the same consciousness. But on that consciousness, in the place where at six o'clock there had been, together with the impossibility of forming any idea of the manager, the Grand Hotel or its staff, a vague and timorous anticipation of the moment at which I should reach my destination, were to be found now the pustules excised from the face of the cosmopolitan manager (he was, in fact, a naturalised Monegasque, although—as he himself put it, for he was always using expressions which he thought distinguished without noticing that they were incorrect—"of Romanian originality"), his action in ringing for the lift, the lift-boy himself, a whole frieze of puppet-show characters issuing from that Pandora's box which was the Grand Hotel, undeniable, irremovable, and, like everything that is realised, jejune. But at least this change which I had done nothing to bring about proved to me that something had happened which was external to myself—however devoid of interest that thing might be in itself—and I was like a traveller who, having had the sun in his face when he started, concludes that he has been for so many hours on the road when he finds the sun behind him. I was half dead with exhaustion, I was burning with fever; I would gladly have gone to bed, but I had no night-things. I should have liked at least to lie down for a little while on the bed, but to what purpose, since I should not have been able to procure any rest for that mass of sensations which is for each of us his conscious if not his physical body, and since the unfamiliar objects which encircled that body, forcing it to place its perceptions on the permanent footing of a vigilant defensive, would have kept my sight, my hearing, all my senses in a position as cramped and uncomfortable (even if I had stretched out my legs) as that of Cardinal La Balue in the cage in which he could neither stand nor sit? It is our noticing them that puts things in a room, our growing used to them that takes them away again and clears a space for us. Space there was none for me in my bedroom (mine in name only) at Balbec; it was full of things which did not know me, which flung back at me the distrustful glance I cast at them, and, without taking any heed of my exist-ence, showed that I was interrupting the humdrum course of theirs. The clock—whereas at home I heard mine tick only a few seconds in a week, when I was coming out of some profound meditation—continued without a moment's interruption to utter, in an unknown tongue, a series of observations which must have been most uncomplimentary to myself, for the violet curtains listened to them without replying, but in an attitude such as people adopt who shrug their shoulders to indicate that the sight of a third person irritates them. They gave to this room with its lofty ceiling a quasi-historical character which might have made it a suitable place for the assassination of the Duc de Guise, and afterwards for parties of tourists personally conducted by one of Thomas Cook's guides, but for me to sleep in—no. I was tormented by the presence of some little book-cases with glass fronts which ran along the walls, but especially by a large cheval-glass which stood across one corner and before the departure of which I felt there could be no possibility of rest for me there. I kept raising my eyes—which the things in my room in Paris disturbed no more than did my eyelids themselves, for they were merely extensions of my organs, an enlargement of myself—towards the high ceiling of this belvedere planted upon the summit of the hotel which my grandmother had chosen for me; and deep down in that region more intimate than that in which we see and hear, in that region where we experience the quality of smells, almost in the very heart of my inmost self, the scent of flowering grasses next launched its offensive against my last feeble line of trenches, an offensive against which I opposed, not without exhausting myself still further, the futile and unremitting riposte of an alarmed sniffling. Having no world, no room, no body now that was not menaced by the enemies thronging round me, penetrated to the very bones by fever, I was alone, and longed to die. Then my grandmother came in, and to the expansion of my constricted heart there opened at once an infinity of space.

She was wearing a loose cambric dressing-gown which she put on at home whenever any of us was ill (because she felt more comfortable in it, she used to say, for she always ascribed selfish motives to her actions), and which was, for tending us, for watching by our beds, her servant's smock, her nurse's uniform, her nun's habit. But whereas the attentions of servants, nurses and nuns, their kindness to us, the merits we find in them and the gratitude we owe them, increase the impression we have of being, in their eyes, someone else, of feeling that we are alone, keeping in our own hands the control over our thoughts, our will to live, I knew, when I was with my grandmother, that however great the misery that there was in me, it would be received by her with a pity still more vast, that everything that was mine, my cares, my wishes, would be buttressed, in my grandmother, by a desire to preserve and enhance my life that was altogether stronger than was my own; and my thoughts were continued and extended in her without undergoing the slightest deflection, since they passed from my mind into hers without any change of atmosphere or of personality. And—like a man who tries to fasten his tie in front of a glass and forgets that the end which he sees reflected is not on the side to which he raises his hand, or like a dog that chases along the ground the dancing shadow of an insect in the air—misled by her appearance in the body as we are apt to be in this world where we have no direct perception of people's souls, I threw myself into the arms of my grandmother and pressed my lips to her face as though

I were thus gaining access to that immense heart which she opened to me. And when I felt my mouth glued to her cheeks, to her brow, I drew from them something so beneficial, so nourishing, that I remained as motionless, as solemn, as calmly gluttonous as a babe at the breast.

Afterwards I gazed inexhaustibly at her large face, outlined like a beautiful cloud, glowing and serene, behind which I could discern the radiance of her tender love. And everything that received, in however slight a degree, any share of her sensations, everything that could be said to belong in any way to her was at once so spiritualised, so sanctified that with outstretched hands I smoothed her beautiful hair, still hardly grey, with as much respect, precaution and gentleness as if I had actually been caressing her goodness. She found such pleasure in taking any trouble that saved me one, and in a moment of immobility and rest for my weary limbs something so exquisite, that when, having seen that she wished to help me undress and go to bed, I made as though to stop her and to undress myself, with an imploring gaze she arrested my hands as they fumbled with the top buttons of my jacket and my boots.

"Oh, do let me!" she begged. "It's such a joy for your Granny. And be sure you knock on the wall if you want anything in the night. My bed is just on the other side, and the partition is quite thin. Just give a knock now, as soon as you're in bed, so that we shall know where we are."

And, sure enough, that evening I gave three knocks—a signal which, a week later, when I was ill, I repeated every morning for several days, because my grandmother wanted me to have some milk early. Then, when I thought that I could hear her stirring—so that she should not be kept waiting but might, the moment she had brought me the milk, go to sleep again—I would venture three little taps, timidly, faintly, but for all that distinctly, for if I was afraid of disturbing her in case I had been mistaken and she was still asleep, neither did I wish her to lie awake listening for a summons which she had not at once caught and which I should not have the heart to repeat. And scarcely had I given my taps than I heard three others, in a different tone from mine, stamped with a calm authority, repeated twice over so that there should be no mistake, and saying to me plainly: "Don't get agitated; I've heard you; I shall be with you in a minute!" and shortly afterwards my grandmother would appear. I would explain to her that I had been afraid she would not hear me, or might think that it was someone in the room beyond who was tapping; at which she would smile: "Mistake my poor pet's knocking for anyone else's! Why, Granny could tell it a mile away! Do you suppose there's anyone else in the world who's such a silly-billy, with such febrile little knuckles, so afraid of waking me up and of not making me understand? Even if it just gave the tiniest scratch, Granny could tell her mouse's sound at once, especially such a poor miserable little mouse as mine is. I could hear it just now, trying to make up its mind, and rustling the bedclothes, and going through all its tricks."

She would push open the shutters, and where a wing of the hotel jutted out at right angles to my window, the sun would already have settled on the roof, like a slater who is up betimes, and starts early and works quietly so as not to rouse the sleeping town whose stillness makes him seem more agile. She would tell me what time it was, what sort of day it would be, that it was not worth while my getting up and coming to the window, that there was a mist over the sea, whether the baker's shop had opened yet, what the vehicle was that I could hear passing—that whole trifling curtain-raiser, that insignificant *introit* of a new day which no one attends, a little scrap of life which was only for our two selves, but which I should have no hesitation in evoking, later on, to Françoise or even to strangers, speaking of the fog "which you could have cut with a knife" at six o'clock that morning, with the ostentation of one who was boasting not of a piece of knowledge that he had acquired but of a mark of affection shown to himself alone; sweet morning moment which opened like a symphony with the rhythmical dialogue of my three taps, to which the thin wall of my bedroom, steeped in love and joy, grown melodious, incorporeal, singing like the angelic choir, responded with three other taps, eagerly awaited, repeated once and again, in which it contrived to waft to me the soul of my grandmother, whole and perfect, and the promise of her coming, with the swiftness of an annunciation and a musical fidelity. But on this first night after our arrival, when my grandmother had left me, I began again to suffer as I had suffered the day before, in Paris, at the moment of leaving home. Perhaps this fear that I had—and that is shared by so many others—of sleeping in a strange room, perhaps this fear is only the most humble, obscure, organic, almost unconscious form of that great and desperate resistance put up by the things that constitute the better part of our present life against our mentally acknowledging the possibility of a future in which they are to have no part; a resistance which was at the root of the horror that I had so often been made to feel by the thought that my parents would die some day, that the stern necessity of life might oblige me to live far from Gilberte, or simply to settle permanently in a place where I should never see any of my old friends; a resistance which was also at the root of the difficulty that I found in imagining my own death, or a survival such as Bergotte used to promise to mankind in his books, a survival in which I should not be allowed to take with me my memories, my frailties, my character, which did not easily resign themselves to the idea of ceasing to be, and desired for me neither extinction nor an eternity in which they would have no part.

When Swann had said to me in Paris one day when I felt particularly unwell: "You ought to go off to one of those glorious islands in the Pacific; you'd never come back again if you did," I should have liked to answer: "But then I shall never see your daughter again, I shall be living among people and things she has never seen." And yet my reason, my better judgment whispered: "What difference can that make, since you won't be distressed by it? When M. Swann tells you that you won't come back he means by that that you won't want to come back, and if you don't want to that is because you'll be happier out there." For my reason was aware that Habit—Habit which was even now setting to work to make me like this unfamiliar lodging, to change the position of the mirror, the shade of the curtains, to stop the clock—undertakes as well to make dear to us the companions whom at first we disliked, to give another appearance to their faces, to make the sound of their voices attractive, to modify the inclinations of their hearts. It is true that these new friendships for places and people are based upon forgetfulness of the old; my reason precisely thought that I could envisage without dread the prospect of a life in which I should be for ever separated from people all memory of whom I should lose, and it was by way of consolation that it offered my heart a promise of oblivion which in fact succeeded only in sharpening the edge of its despair. Not that the heart, too, is not bound in time, when separation is complete, to feel the analgesic effect of habit; but until then it will continue to suffer. And our dread of a future in which we must forgo the sight of faces and the sound of voices which we love and from which today we derive our dearest joy, this dread, far from being dissipated, is intensified, if to the pain of such a privation we feel that there will be added what seems to us now in anticipation more painful still: not to feel it as a pain at all—to remain indifferent; for then our old self would have changed, it would then be not merely the charm of our family, our mistress, our friends that had ceased to environ us, but our affection for them would have been so completely eradicated from our hearts, of which today it is so conspicuous an element, that we should be able to enjoy a life apart from them, the very thought of which today makes us recoil in horror; so that it would be in a real sense the death of the self, a death followed, it is true, by resurrection, but in a different self, to the love of which the elements of the old self that are condemned to die cannot bring themselves to aspire. It is they—even the meanest of them, such as our obscure attachments to the dimensions, to the atmosphere of a bedroom—that take fright and refuse, in acts of rebellion which we must recognise to be a secret, partial, tangible and true aspect of our resistance to death, of the long, desperate, daily resistance to the fragmentary and continuous death that insinuates itself throughout the whole course of our life, detaching from us at each moment a shred of ourself, dead matter on which new cells will multiply and grow. And for a neurotic nature such as mine—one, that is to say, in which the intermediaries, the nerves, perform their functions badly, fail to arrest on its way to the consciousness, allow indeed to reach it, distinct, exhausting, innumerable and distressing, the plaints of the most humble elements of the self which are about to disappear—the anxiety and alarm which I felt as I lay beneath that strange and too lofty ceiling were but the protest of an affection that survived in me for a ceiling that was familiar and low. Doubtless this affection too would disappear, another having taken its place (when death, and then another life, had, in the guise of Habit, performed their double task); but until its annihilation, every night it would suffer afresh, and on this first night especially, confronted with an irreversible future in which there would no longer be any place for it, it rose in revolt, it tortured me with the sound of its lamentations whenever my straining eyes, powerless to turn from what was wounding them, endeavoured to fasten themselves upon that inaccessible ceiling.

But next morning!—after a servant had come to call me and to bring me hot water, and while I was washing and dressing myself and trying in vain to find the things that I needed in my trunk, from which I extracted, pell-mell, only a lot of things that were of no use whatever, what a joy it was to me, thinking already of the pleasure of lunch and a walk along the shore, to see in the window, and in all the glass fronts of the book-cases, as in the portholes of a ship's cabin, the open sea, naked, unshadowed, and yet with half of its expanse in shadow, bounded by a thin, fluctuating line, and to follow with my eyes the waves that leapt up one behind another like jumpers on a trampoline. Every other moment, holding in my hand the stiff starched towel with the name of the hotel printed upon it, with which I was making futile efforts to dry myself, I returned to the window to have another look at that vast, dazzling, mountainous amphitheatre, and at the snowy crests of its emerald waves, here and there polished and translucent, which with a placid violence and a leonine frown, to which the sun added a faceless smile, allowed their crumbling slopes to topple down at last. It was at this window that I was later to take up my position every morning, as at the window of a stage-coach in which one has slept, to see whether, during the night, a longed-for mountain range has come nearer or receded—only here it was those hills of the sea which, before they come dancing back towards us, are apt to withdraw so far that often it was only at the end of a long, sandy plain that I would distinguish, far off, their first undulations in a transparent, vaporous, bluish distance, like the glaciers that one sees in the backgrounds of the Tuscan Primitives. On other mornings it was quite close at hand that the sun laughed upon those waters of a green as tender as that pre-served in Alpine pastures (among mountains on which the sun displays himself here and there like a giant who may at any moment come leaping gaily down their craggy sides) less by the moisture of the soil than by the liquid mobility of the light. Moreover, in that breach which the shore and the waves open up in the midst of the rest of the world for the passage or the accumulation of light, it is above all the light, according to the direction from which it comes and along which our eyes follow it, it is the light that displaces and situates the undulations of the sea. Diversity of lighting modifies no less the orientation of a place, erects no less before our eyes new goals which it inspires in us the yearning to attain, than would a distance in space actually traversed in the course of a long journey. When, in the morning, the sun came from behind the hotel, disclosing to me the sands bathed in light as far as the first bastions of the sea, it seemed to be showing me another side of the picture, and to be inviting me to pursue, along the winding path of its rays, a motionless but varied journey amid all the fairest scenes of the diversified landscape of the hours. And on this first morning, it pointed out to me far off, with a jovial finger, those blue peaks of the sea which bear no name on any map, until, dizzy with its sublime excursion over the thundering and chaotic surface of their crests and avalanches, it came to take shelter from the wind in my bedroom, lolling across the unmade bed and scattering its riches over the splashed surface of the basin-stand and into my open trunk, where, by its very splendour and misplaced luxury, it added still further to the general impression of disorder. Alas for that sea-wind: an hour later, in the big dining-room—while we were having lunch, and from the leathern gourd of a lemon were sprinkling a few golden drops on to a pair of soles which presently left on our plates the plumes of their picked skeletons, curled like stiff feathers and resonant as citherns—it seemed to my grandmother a cruel deprivation not to be able to feel its life-giving breath on her cheek, on account of the glass partition, transparent but closed, which, like the front of a glass case in a museum, separated us from the beach while allowing us to look out upon its whole expanse, and into which the sky fitted so completely that its azure had the effect of being the colour of the windows and its white clouds so many flaws in the glass. Imagining that I was "sitting on the mole" or at rest in the "boudoir" of which Baudelaire speaks, I wondered whether his "sun's rays upon the sea" were not—a very different thing from the evening ray, simple and superficial as a tremulous golden shaft—just what at that moment was scorching the sea topaz-yellow, fermenting it, turning it pale and milky like beer, frothy like milk, while now and then there hovered over it great blue shadows which, for his own amusement, some god seemed to be shifting to and fro by moving a mirror in the sky. Unfortunately, it was not only in its outlook that this dining-room at Balbec—bare-walled, filled with a sun-light green as the water in a pond, while a few feet away from it the high tide and broad daylight erected as though before the gates of the heavenly city an indestructible and mobile rampart of emerald and gold—differed from our dining-room at Combray which gave on to the houses across the street. At Combray, since we were known to everyone, I took heed of no one. In seaside life one does not know one's neighbours. I was not yet old enough, and was still too sensitive to have outgrown the desire to find favour in the sight of other people and to possess their hearts. Nor had I acquired the more noble indifference which a man of the

world would have felt towards the people who were eating in the
dining-room or the boys and girls who strolled past the window,
with whom I was pained by the thought that I should never be
allowed to go on expeditions, though not so pained as if my
grandmother, contemptuous of social formalities and concerned
only with my health, had gone to them with the request, humi-
liating for me, that they should consent to allow me to accompany
them. Whether they were returning to some villa beyond my ken,
or had emerged from one, racquet in hand, on their way to a tennis
court, or were riding horses whose hooves trampled my heart, I
gazed at them with a passionate curiosity, in that blinding light of
the beach by which social distinctions are altered, I followed all
their movements through the transparency of that great bay of
glass which allowed so much light to flood the room. But it
intercepted the wind, and this was a defect in the eyes of my
grandmother, who, unable to endure the thought that I was losing
the benefit of an hour in the open air, surreptitiously opened a
pane and at once sent flying, together with the menus, the newspapers, veils and hats of all the people at the other tables, while she
herself, fortified by the celestial draught, remained calm and smiling like Saint Blandina amid the torrent of invective which,
increasing my sense of isolation and misery, those contemptuous,
dishevelled, furious visitors combined to pour on us.

To a certain extent—and this, at Balbec, gave to the population,
as a rule monotonously rich and cosmopolitan, of that sort of
"grand" hotel a quite distinctive local character—they were composed of eminent persons from the departmental capitals of that
region of France, a senior judge from Caen, a president of the
Cherbourg bar, a notary public from Le Mans, who annually,
when the holidays came round, starting from the various points
over which, throughout the working year, they were scattered
like snipers on a battlefield or draughtsmen upon a board, concentrated their forces in this hotel. They always reserved the same
rooms, and with their wives, who had pretensions to aristocracy,
formed a little group which was joined by a leading barrister and a
leading doctor from Paris, who on the day of their departure
would say to the others: "Oh, yes, of course; you don't go by
our train. You're privileged, you'll be home in time for lunch."

"Privileged, you say? You who live in the capital, in Paris, while
I have to live in a wretched county town of a hundred thousand
souls (it's true we managed to muster a hundred and two thousand

at the last census, but what is that compared to your two and a half millions?), going back, too, to asphalt streets and all the glamour of Paris life."

They said this with a rustic burring of their "r"s, without acrimony, for they were leading lights each in his own province, who could like others have gone to Paris had they chosen—the senior judge from Caen had several times been offered a seat on the Court of Appeal—but had preferred to stay where they were, from love of their native towns, or of obscurity, or of fame, or because they were reactionaries, and enjoyed being on friendly terms with the country houses of the neighbourhood. Besides, several of them were not going back at once to their county towns.

For—inasmuch as the Bay of Balbec was a little world apart in the midst of the great, a basketful of the seasons in which good days and bad, and the successive months, were clustered in a ring, so that not only on days when one could make out Rivebelle, which was a sign of storm, could one see the sunlight on the houses there while Balbec was plunged in darkness, but later on, when the cold weather had reached Balbec, one could be certain of finding on that opposite shore two or three supplementary months of warmth—those of the regular visitors to the Grand Hotel whose holidays began late or lasted long gave orders, when the rains and the mists came and autumn was in the air, for their boxes to be packed and loaded on to a boat, and set sail across the bay to find the summer again at Rivebelle or Costedor. This little group in the Balbec hotel looked at each new arrival with suspicion, and, while affecting to take not the least interest in him, hastened, all of them, to interrogate their friend the head waiter about him. For it was the same head waiter—Aimé—who returned every year for the season, and kept their tables for them; and their lady-wives, having heard that his wife was expecting a baby, would sit after meals each working on a part of the layette, while weighing up through their lorgnettes my grandmother and myself because we were eating hard-boiled eggs in salad, which was considered common and was not done in the best society of Alençon. They affected an attitude of contemptuous irony with regard to a Frenchman who was called "His Majesty" and who had indeed proclaimed himself king of a small island in the South Seas peopled only by a few savages. He was staying in the hotel with his pretty mistress, whom, as she crossed the beach to bathe, the little boys would greet with "Long live the Queen!" because she would reward them with a shower of small silver. The judge and the president went so far as to pretend not to see her, and if any of their friends happened to look at her, felt bound to warn him that she was only a little shop-girl.

"But I was told that at Ostend they used the royal bathing-hut."

"Well, and why not? It's on hire for twenty francs. You can take it yourself, if you care for that sort of thing. Anyhow, I know for a fact that the fellow asked for an audience with the King, who sent back word that he wasn't interested in pantomime princes."

"Really, that's interesting! What queer people there are in the world, to be sure!"

And no doubt all this was true; but it was also from resentment of the thought that, to many of their fellow-visitors, they were themselves simply solid middle-class citizens who did not know this king and queen who were so prodigal with their small change, that the notary, the judge, the president, when what they were pleased to call the "Carnival" went by, felt so much annoyance and expressed aloud an indignation that was quite understood by their friend the head waiter who, obliged to show proper civility to these generous if not authentic sovereigns, would nevertheless, as he took their orders, glance across the room at his old patrons and give them a meaningful wink. Perhaps there was also something of the same resentment at being erroneously supposed to be less "smart" and unable to explain that they were more, at the bottom of the "Fine specimen!" with which they referred to a young toff, the consumptive and dissipated son of an industrial magnate, who appeared every day in a new suit of clothes with an orchid in his buttonhole, drank champagne at luncheon, and then went off to the Casino, pale, impassive, a smile of complete indifference on his lips, to throw away at the baccarat table enormous sums "which he could ill afford to lose," as the notary said with a knowing air to the senior judge, whose wife had it "on good authority" that this "decadent" young man was bringing his parents' grey hair in sorrow to the grave.

Furthermore, the president and his friends were inexhaustibly sarcastic on the subject of a wealthy old lady of title, because she never moved anywhere without taking her whole household with her. Whenever the wives of the notary and the judge saw her in the dining-room at meal-times, they put up their lorgnettes and gave her an insolent scrutiny, as meticulous and distrustful as if she had been some dish with a pretentious name but a suspicious appearance which, after the adverse result of a systematic study, is sent away with a lofty wave of the hand and a grimace of disgust.

No doubt by this behaviour they meant only to show that, if there were things in the world which they themselves lacked—in this instance, certain prerogatives which the old lady enjoyed, and the privilege of her acquaintance—it was not because they could not, but because they did not choose to acquire them. But they had ended up by convincing themselves that this really was what they felt; and the suppression of all desire for, of all curiosity about, ways of life which are unfamiliar, of all hope of endearing oneself to new people, for which, in these women, had been substituted a feigned contempt, a spurious jubilation, had the disagreeable effect of obliging them to label their discontent satisfaction and to lie everlastingly to themselves, two reasons why they were unhappy. But everyone else in the hotel was no doubt behaving in a similar fashion, though under different forms, and sacrificing, if not to self-esteem, at any rate to certain inculcated principles or mental habits, the disturbing thrill of being involved in an unfamiliar way of life. Of course the microcosm in which the old lady isolated herself was not poisoned with virulent rancour, as was the group in which the wives of the notary and the judge sat sneering with rage. It was indeed embalmed with a delicate and old-world fragrance which, however, was no less artificial. For at heart the old lady would probably have discovered, in attracting, in attaching to herself (and, in doing so, renewing herself) the mysterious sympathy of new people, a charm which is altogether lacking from the pleasure that is to be derived from mixing only with the people of one's own world, and reminding oneself that, this being the best of all possible worlds, the ill-informed contempt of others may be disregarded. Perhaps she felt that if she arrived incognito at the Grand Hotel, Balbec, she would, in her black woollen dress and old-fashioned bonnet, bring a smile to the lips of some old reprobate, who from the depths of his rocking chair would glance up and murmur, "What a scarecrow!" or, still worse, to those of some worthy man who had, like the judge, kept between his pepper-and-salt whiskers a fresh complexion and a pair of sparkling eyes such as she liked to see, and who would at once bring the magnifying lens of the conjugal glasses to bear upon so quaint a phenomenon; and perhaps it was in unconscious apprehension of those first few minutes which one knows will be brief but which are none the less dreaded—like one's first header into the sea—

that this lady sent a servant down in advance to inform the hotel of the personality and habits of his mistress, and, cutting short the manager's greetings with an abruptness in which there was more shyness than pride, made straight for her room, where her own curtains, replacing those that draped the hotel windows, her own screens and photographs, set up so effectively between her and the outside world, to which otherwise she would have had to adapt herself, the barrier of her private life and habits, that it was her home (in the cocoon of which she had remained) that travelled rather than herself.

Thenceforward, having placed, between herself on the one hand and the hotel staff and the tradesmen on the other, her own servants who bore instead of her the shock of contact with all this strange humanity and kept up the familiar atmosphere around their mistress, having set her prejudices between herself and the other visitors, indifferent whether or not she gave offence to people whom her friends would not have had in their houses, it was in her own world that she continued to live, by correspond-ence with her friends, by memories, by her intimate awareness of her own position, the quality of her manners, the adroitness of her courtesy. And every day, when she came downstairs to go for a drive in her own carriage, the lady's-maid who came after her carrying her wraps, and the footman who preceded her, seemed like sentries who, at the gate of an embassy, flying the flag of the country to which she belonged, assured to her upon foreign soil the privilege of extra-territoriality. She did not leave her room until the middle of the afternoon on the day after our arrival, so that we did not see her in the dining-room, into which the manager, since we were newcomers, conducted us at the lunch hour, taking us under his wing, as a corporal takes a squad of recruits to the master-tailor to have them fitted; we did however see a moment later a country squire and his daughter, of an obscure but very ancient Breton family, M. and Mlle de Stermaria, whose table had been allotted to us in the belief that they had gone out and would not be back until the evening. Having come to Balbec only to see various owners of manors whom they knew in that neighbourhood, they spent in the hotel dining-room, what with the invitations they accepted and the visits they paid, only such time as was strictly unavoidable. It was their haughtiness that preserved them intact from all human sympathy, from arousing the least interest in the strangers seated round about them, among whom M. de Stermaria kept up the glacial, preoccupied, distant, stiff, touchy and ill-intentioned air that we assume in a railway refreshment-room in the midst of fellow-passengers whom we have never seen before and will never see again, and with whom we can conceive of no other relations than to defend from their onslaught our cold chicken and our corner seat in the train. No sooner had we begun our lunch than we were asked to leave the table on the instructions of M. de Stermaria who had just arrived and, without the faintest attempt at an apology to us, requested the head waiter in our hearing to see that such a mistake did not occur again, for it was repugnant to him that "people whom he did not know" should have taken his table.

And certainly the feeling which impelled a young actress (better known in fact for her smart clothes, her wit, her collection of German porcelain, than for the occasional parts that she had played at the Odéon), her lover, an immensely rich young man for whose sake she had acquired her culture, and two sprigs of the aristocracy at that time much in the public eye, to form an exclusive group, to travel only together, to come down to luncheon—when at Balbec—very late, after everyone else had finished, to spend the whole day in their sitting-room playing cards, reflected no sort of ill-will towards the rest of us but simply the requirements of the taste that they had formed for a certain type of witty conversation, for certain refinements of good living, which made them find pleasure in spending their time, in taking their meals, only by themselves, and would have rendered intolerable a life in common with people who had not been initiated. Even at a dinner-table or a card table, each of them had to be certain that in the diner or partner who sat opposite to him there were, latent and in abeyance, a certain brand of knowledge which would enable him to identify the rubbish which so many houses in Paris boast of as genuine mediaeval or Renaissance "pieces" and, whatever the subject of discussion, criteria common to them all wherewith to distinguish the good from the bad. No doubt by now, at such moments, it was merely by some rare and amusing interjection flung into the general silence of meal or game, or by the new and charming frock which the young actress had put on for lunch or for poker, that the special kind of existence in which these four friends desired everywhere to remain plunged was made apparent. But by engulfing them thus in a system of habits which they knew by heart it sufficed to protect them from the mystery of the life that was going on all round them. All the long afternoon, the sea was suspended there before their eyes only as a canvas of attractive colouring might hang on the wall of a wealthy bachelor's flat, and it was only in the intervals between hands that one of the players, finding nothing better to do, raised his eyes to it to seek some indication of the weather or the time, and to remind the others that tea was ready. And at night they did not dine in the hotel, where, hidden springs of electricity flooding the great dining-room with light, it became as it were an immense and wonderful aquarium against whose glass wall the working population of Balbec, the fishermen and also the tradesmen's families, clustering invisibly in the outer darkness, pressed their faces to watch the luxurious life of its occupants gently floating upon the golden eddies within, a thing as extraordinary to the poor as the life of strange fishes or molluscs (an important social question, this: whether the glass wall will always protect the banquets of these weird and wonderful creatures, or whether the obscure folk who watch them hungrily out of the night will not break in some day to gather them from their aquarium and devour them). Meanwhile, perhaps, amid the dumbfounded stationary crowd out there in the dark, there may have been some writer, some student of human ichthyology, who, as he watched the jaws of old feminine mon-strosities close over a mouthful of submerged food, was amusing himself by classifying them by race, by innate characteristics, as well as by those acquired characteristics which bring it about that an old Serbian lady whose buccal appendage is that of a great sea-fish, because from her earliest years she has moved in the fresh waters of the Faubourg Saint-Germain, eats her salad for all the world like a La Rochefoucauld.

At that hour the three young men in dinner-jackets could be observed waiting for the young woman, who was as usual late but presently, wearing a dress that was almost always different and one of a series of scarves chosen to gratify some special taste in her lover, after having rung for the lift from her landing, would emerge from it like a doll coming out of its box. And then all four, finding that the international phenomenon of the "de luxe" hotel, having taken root at Balbec, had blossomed there in material luxury rather than in food that was fit to eat, climbed into a carriage and went off to dine a mile away in a little restaurant of repute where they held endless discussions with the cook about the composition of the menu and the cooking of its various dishes.

During their drive, the road bordered with apple-trees that led out of Balbec was no more to them than the distance that must be traversed—barely distinguishable in the darkness from that which separated their homes in Paris from the Café Anglais or the Tour d'Argent—before they arrived at the fashionable little restaurant where, while the rich young man's friends envied him because he had such a smartly dressed mistress, the latter's scarves hung before the little company a sort of fragrant, flowing veil, but one that kept it apart from the outer world.

Alas for my peace of mind, I had none of the detachment that all these people showed. To many of them I gave constant thought; I should have liked not to pass unobserved by a man with a receding forehead and eyes that dodged between the blinkers of his prejudices and his upbringing, the grandee of the district, who was none other than the brother-in-law of Legrandin. He came every now and then to see somebody at Balbec, and on Sundays, by reason of the weekly garden-party that his wife and he gave, robbed the hotel of a large number of its occupants, because one or two of them were invited to these entertainments and the others, so as not to appear not to have been invited, chose that day for an expedition to some distant spot. He had had, as it happened, an exceedingly bad reception at the hotel on the first day of the season, when the staff, freshly imported from the Riviera, did not yet know who or what he was. Not only was he not wearing white flannels, but, with old-fashioned French courtesy and in his ignorance of the ways of grand hotels, on coming into the hall in which there were ladies sitting, he had taken off his hat at the door, with the result that the manager had not so much as raised a finger to his own in acknowledgement, concluding that this must be someone of the most humble extraction, what he called "sprung from the ordinary." The notary's wife alone had felt attracted to the stranger, who exhaled all the starched vulgarity of the really respectable, and she had declared, with the unerring discernment and the indisputable authority of a person for whom the highest society of Le Mans held no secrets, that one could see at a glance that one was in the presence of a gentleman of great distinction, of perfect breeding, a striking contrast to the sort of people one usually saw at Balbec, whom she condemned as impossible to know so long as she did not know them. This favourable judgment which she had pronounced on Legrandin's brother-in-law was based perhaps on the lacklustre appearance of a man about whom there was nothing to intimidate anyone; perhaps also she had recognised in this gentleman farmer with the look of a sacristan the Masonic signs of her own clericalism.

Even though I knew that the young men who went past the hotel every day on horseback were the sons of the shady proprietor of a fancy goods shop whom my father would never have dreamed of knowing, the glamour of "seaside life" exalted them in my eyes to equestrian statues of demi-gods, and the best thing that I could hope for was that they would never allow their proud gaze to fall upon the wretched boy who was myself, who left the hotel dining-room only to sit upon the sands. I should have been glad to arouse some response even from the adventurer who had been king of a desert island in the South Seas, even from the young consumptive, of whom I liked to think that he concealed beneath his insolent exterior a shy and tender heart, which might perhaps have lavished on me, and on me alone, the treasures of its affection. Besides (contrary to what is usually said about travelling acquaintances) since being seen in certain company can invest us, in a watering-place to which we shall return another year, with a coefficient that has no equivalent in real social life, there is nothing that, far from keeping resolutely at a distance, we cultivate with such assiduity after our return to Paris as the friendships that we have formed by the sea. I was concerned about the impression I might make on all these temporary or local celebrities whom my tendency to put myself in the place of other people and to re-create their state of mind made me place not in their true rank, that which they would have occupied in Paris for instance and which would have been quite low, but in that which they must imagine to be theirs and which indeed was theirs at Balbec, where the want of a common denominator gave them a sort of relative superiority and unwonted interest. Alas, none of these people's contempt was so painful to me as that of M. de Stermaria.

For I had noticed his daughter the moment she came into the room, her pretty face, her pallid, almost bluish complexion, the distinctiveness in the carriage of her tall figure, in her gait, which suggested to me, with reason, her heredity, her aristocratic upbringing, all the more vividly because I knew her name—like those expressive themes invented by musicians of genius which paint in splendid colours the glow of fire, the rush of water, the peace of fields and woods, to audiences who, having glanced through the programme in advance, have their imaginations trained in the right direction. "Pedigree," by adding to Mlle de Stermaria's charms the idea of their origin, made them more intelligible, more complete. It made them more desirable also, advertising their inaccessibility as a high price enhances the value of a thing that has already taken our fancy. And its stock of heredity gave to her complexion, in which so many selected juices had been blended, the savour of an exotic fruit or of a famous vintage.

Now, chance had suddenly put into our hands, my grandmother's and mine, the means of acquiring instantaneous prestige in the eyes of all the other occupants of the hotel. For on that first afternoon, at the moment when the old lady came downstairs from her room, producing, thanks to the footman who preceded her and the maid who came running after her with a book and a rug that she had forgotten, a marked effect upon all who beheld her and arousing in each of them a curiosity from which it was evident that none was so little immune as M. de Stermaria, the manager leaned across to my grandmother and out of kindness (as one might point out the Shah or Queen Ranavalo to an obscure onlooker who could obviously have no sort of connexion with such mighty potentates, but might all the same be interested to know that he had been standing within a few feet of one) whispered in her ear, "The Marquise de Villeparisis!" while at the same moment the old lady, catching sight of my grandmother, could not repress a start of pleased surprise.

It may be imagined that the sudden appearance, in the guise of a little old woman, of the most powerful of fairies would not have given me more pleasure, destitute as I was of any means of access to Mlle de Stermaria, in a strange place where I knew no one: no one, that is to say, for any practical purpose. Aesthetically, the number of human types is so restricted that we must constantly, wherever we may be, have the pleasure of seeing people we know, even without looking for them in the works of the old masters, like Swann. Thus it happened that in the first few days of our visit to Balbec I had succeeded in encountering Legrandin, Swann's hall-porter, and Mme Swann herself, transformed respectively into a waiter, a foreign visitor whom I never saw again, and a bathing superintendent. And a sort of magnetisation attracts and retains so inseparably, one beside another, certain characteristics of physiognomy and mentality, that when Nature thus introduces a person into a new body she does not mutilate him unduly. Legrandin turned waiter kept intact his stature, the outline of his nose, part of his chin; Mme Swann, in the masculine gender and the calling of a bathing superintendent, had been accompanied not only by her familiar features but even by certain mannerisms of speech. Only she could be of little if any more use to me, standing upon the beach there in the red sash of her office, and hoisting at the first gust of wind the flag which forbade us to bathe (for these super-intendents are prudent men, seldom knowing how to swim), than she would have been in that fresco of the *Life of Moses* in which Swann had long ago identified her in the person of Jethro's daughter. Whereas this Mme de Villeparisis was her real self; she had not been the victim of a magic spell which had robbed her of her power, but was capable, on the contrary, of putting at the disposal of mine a spell which would multiply it a hundredfold, and thanks to which, as though I had been swept through the air on the wings of a fabulous bird, I was about to cross in a few moments the infinitely wide social gulf which separated me—at least at Balbec—from Mlle de Stermaria.

Unfortunately, if there was one person who, more than anyone else, lived shut up in a world of her own, it was my grandmother. She would not even have despised me, she would simply not have understood what I meant, if she had known that I attached importance to the opinions, that I felt an interest in the persons, of people the very existence of whom she never noticed and of whom, when the time came to leave Balbec, she would not remember the names. I dared not confess to her that if these same people had seen her talking to Mme de Villeparisis, I should have been immensely gratified, because I felt that the Marquise enjoyed some prestige in the hotel and that her friendship would have given us status in the eyes of Mlle de Stermaria. Not that my grandmother's friend represented to me, in any sense of the word, a member of the aristocracy: I was too accustomed to her name, which had been familiar to my ears before my mind had begun to consider it, when as a child I had heard it uttered in conversation at home; while her title added to it only a touch of quaintness, as some uncommon Christian name would have done, or as in the names of streets, among which we can see nothing more noble in the Rue Lord Byron, in the plebeian and even squalid Rue Rochechouart, or in the Rue de Gramont that in the Rue Léonce-Reynaud or the Rue Hippolyte-Lebas. Mme de Villeparisis no more made me think of a person who belonged to a special social world than did her cousin MacMahon, whom I did not clearly distinguish from M. Carnot, likewise President of the Republic, or from Raspail, whose photograph Françoise had bought with that of Pius IX. It was one of my grandmother's principles that, when away from home, one should cease to have any social intercourse, that one did not go to the seaside to meet people, having plenty of time for that sort of thing in Paris, that they would make one waste in polite exchanges, in pointless conversation, the precious time which ought all to be spent in the open air, beside the waves; and finding it convenient to assume that this view was shared by everyone else, and that it authorised, between old friends whom chance brought face to face in the same hotel, the fiction of a mutual incognito, on hearing her friend's name from the manager she merely looked the other way and pretended not to see Mme de Villeparisis, who, realising that my grandmother did not want to be recognised, likewise gazed into space. She went past, and I was left in my isolation like a ship-wrecked mariner who has seen a vessel apparently approaching, which has then vanished under the horizon.

She, too, had her meals in the dining-room, but at the other end of it. She knew none of the people who were staying in the hotel or who came there to call, not even M. de Cambremer; indeed, I noticed that he gave her no greeting one day when, with his wife, he had accepted an invitation to lunch with the president, who, intoxicated with the honour of having the nobleman at his table, avoided his habitual friends and confined himself to a distant twitch of the eyelid, so as to draw their attention to this historic event but so discreetly that his signal could not be interpreted as an invitation to join the party.

"Well, I hope you've done yourself proud, I hope you feel smart enough," the judge's wife said to him that evening.

"Smart? Why should I?" asked the president, concealing his rapture in an exaggerated astonishment. "Because of my guests, do you mean?" he went on, feeling that it was impossible to keep up the farce any longer. "But what is there smart about having a few friends to lunch? After all, they must feed somewhere!"

"Of course it's smart! They were the de Cambremers, weren't they? I recognised them at once. She's a Marquise. And quite genuine, too. Not through the females."

"Oh, she's a very simple soul, she's charming, no stand-offish-ness about her. I thought you were coming to join us. I was making signals to you...I would have introduced you!" he asserted, tempering with a hint of irony the vast generosity of the offer, like Ahasuerus when he says to Esther: "Of all my Kingdom must I give you half?"

"No, no, no, no! We lie hidden, like the modest violet."

"But you were quite wrong, I assure you," replied the president, emboldened now that the danger point was passed. "They weren't going to eat you. I say, aren't we going to have our little game of bezique?"

"Why, of course! We didn't dare suggest it, now that you go about entertaining marquises."

"Oh, get along with you; there's nothing so very wonderful about them. Why, I'm dining there tomorrow. Would you care to go instead of me? I mean it. Honestly, I'd just as soon stay here."

"No, no! I should be removed from the bench as a reactionary," cried the senior judge, laughing till the tears came to his eyes at his own joke. "But you go to Féterne too, don't you?" he went on, turning to the notary.

"Oh, I go there on Sundays—in one door and out the other. But they don't come and have lunch with me as they do with the president."

M. de Stermaria was not at Balbec that day, to the president's great regret. But he managed to say a word in season to the head waiter:

"Aimé, you can tell M. de Stermaria that he's not the only nobleman you've had in here. You saw the gentleman who was with me today at lunch? Eh? A small moustache, looked like a military man. Well, that was the Marquis de Cambremer!"

"Was it indeed? I'm not surprised to hear it."

"That will show him that he's not the only man who's got a title. That'll teach him! It's not a bad thing to take 'em down a peg or two, those noblemen. I say, Aimé, don't say anything to him unless you want to. I mean to say, it's no business of mine; besides, they know each other already."

And next day M. de Stermaria, who remembered that the president had once represented one of his friends, came up and introduced himself.

"Our friends in common, the de Cambremers, were anxious that we should meet, the days didn't fit—I don't know quite what went wrong," said the president who, like most liars, imagined that other people do not take the trouble to investigate an unimportant detail which, for all that, may be sufficient (if chance puts you in possession of the humble facts of the case, and they contradict it) to show the liar in his true colours and to inspire a lasting mistrust.

As usual, but more easily now that her father had left her to talk to the president, I was gazing at Mlle de Stermaria. No less than the bold and always graceful distinctiveness of her attitudes, as when, leaning her elbows on the table, she raised her glass in both hands over her fore-arms, the dry flame of a glance at once extinguished, the ingrained, congenital hardness that one could sense, ill-concealed by her own personal inflexions, in the depths of her voice, and that had shocked my grandmother, a sort of atavistic ratchet to which she returned as soon as, in a glance or an intonation, she had finished expressing her own thoughts—all this brought the thoughts of the observer back to the long line of ancestors who had bequeathed to her that inadequacy of human sympathy, those gaps in her sensibility, a lack of fullness in the stuff of which she was made. But from a certain look which flooded for a moment the wells—instantly dry again—of her eyes, a look in which one sensed that almost humble docility which the predominance of a taste for sensual pleasures gives to the proudest of women, who will soon come to recognise but one form of personal magic, that which any man will enjoy in her eyes who can make her feel those pleasures, an actor or a mountebank for whom, perhaps, she will one day leave her husband, and from a certain pink tinge, warm and sensual, which flushed her pallid cheeks, like the colour that stained the hearts of the white water-lilies in the Vivonne, I thought I could discern that she might readily have consented to my coming to seek in her the savour of that life of poetry and romance which she led in Brittany, a life to which, whether from over-familiarity or from innate superiority, or from disgust at the penury or the avarice of her family, she seemed to attach no great value, but which, for all that, she held enclosed in her body. In the meagre stock of will-power that had been transmitted to her, and gave her expression a hint of weakness, she would not perhaps have found the strength to resist. And, crowned by a feather that was a trifle old-fashioned and pretentious, the grey felt hat which she invariably wore at meals made her all the more attractive to me, not because it was in harmony with her silver and rose complexion, but because, by making me suppose her to be poor, it brought her closer to me. Obliged by her father's presence to adopt a conventional attitude, but already bringing to the perception and classification of the people who passed before her eyes other principles than his, perhaps she saw in me not my humble rank, but the right sex and age. If one day M. de Stermaria had gone out leaving her behind, if, above all, Mme de Villeparisis, by coming to sit at our table, had given her an opinion of me which might have emboldened me to approach her, perhaps then we might have contrived to exchange a few words, to arrange a meeting, to form a closer tie. And for a whole month during which she would be left alone without her parents in her romantic Breton castle, we should perhaps have been able to wander by ourselves at evening, she and I together in the twilight through which the pink flowers of the bell heather would glow more softly above the darkening water, beneath oak-trees beaten and stunted by the pounding of the waves. Together we should have roamed that island impregnated with so intense a charm for me because it had enclosed the everyday life of Mlle de Stermaria and was reflected in the memory of her eyes. For it seemed to me that I should truly have possessed her only there, when I had traversed those regions which enveloped her in so many memories—a veil which my desire longed to tear aside, one of those veils which nature interposes between woman and her pursuers (with the same intention as when, for all of us, she places the act of reproduction between ourselves and our keenest pleasure, and for insects, places before the nectar the pollen which they must carry away with them) in order that, tricked by the illusion of possessing her thus more completely, they may be forced to occupy first the scenes among which she lives and which, of more service to their imagination than sensual pleasure can be, yet would not without that pleasure have sufficed to attract them.

But I was obliged to take my eyes from Mlle de Stermaria, for already, considering no doubt that making the acquaintance of an important person was an odd, brief act which was sufficient in itself and, to bring out all the interest that was latent in it, required only a handshake and a penetrating stare, without either immediate conversation or any subsequent relations, her father had taken leave of the president and returned to sit down facing her, rubbing his hands like a man who has just made a valuable acquisition. As for the president, once the first emotion of this interview had subsided, he could be heard, as on other days, addressing the head waiter every other minute: "But I'm not a king, Aimé; go and attend to the king! I say, Chief, those little trout don't look at all bad, do they? We must ask Aimé to let us have some. Aimé, that little fish you have over there looks to me highly commendable: will you bring us some, please, Aimé, and don't be sparing with it."

He repeated the name "Aimé" all the time, with the result that when he had anyone to dinner the guest would remark "I can see you're quite at home in this place," and would feel himself obliged to keep on saying "Aimé" also, from that tendency, combining elements of timidity, vulgarity and silliness, which many people have, to believe that it is smart and witty to imitate slavishly the people in whose company they happen to be. The president repeated the name incessantly, but with a smile, for he wanted to exhibit at one and the same time his good relations with the head waiter and his own superior station. And the head waiter, whenever he caught the sound of his own name, smiled too, as though touched and at the same time proud, showing that he was conscious of the honour and could appreciate the joke.

Intimidating as I always found these meals, in that vast restaurant, generally full, of the Grand Hotel, they became even more so when there arrived for a few days the proprietor (or he may have been the general manager, appointed by a board of directors) not only of this palace but of seven or eight more besides, situated at all the four corners of France, in each of which, shuttling from one to the other, he would spend a week now and again. Then, just after dinner had begun, there appeared every evening at the entrance to the dining-room this small man with the white hair and a red nose, astonishingly neat and impassive, who was known, it appeared, as well in London as at Monte Carlo, as one of the leading hoteliers in Europe. Once when I had gone out for a moment at the beginning of dinner, as I came in again I passed close by him, and he bowed to me, no doubt to acknowledge that he was my host, but with a coldness in which I could not distinguish whether it was attributable to the reserve of a man who could never forget what he was, or to his contempt for a customer of so little importance. To those, on the other hand, whose importance was considerable, the general manager would bow with quite as much coldness but more deeply, lowering his eyelids with a sort of bashful respect, as though he had found himself confronted, at a funeral, with the father of the deceased or with the Blessed Sacrament. Except for these icy and infrequent salutations, he made not the slightest movement, as if to show that his glittering eyes, which appeared to be starting out of his head, saw everything, controlled everything, ensured for the "Dinner at the Grand Hotel" perfection in every detail as well as overall harmony. He felt, evidently, that he was more than the producer, more than the conductor, nothing less than the generalissimo. Having decided that a contemplation raised to the maximum degree of intensity would suffice to assure him that everything was in readiness, that no mistake had been made which could lead to disaster, and enable him at last to assume his responsibilities, he abstained not merely from any gesture but even from moving his eyes, which, petrified by the intensity of their gaze, took in and directed operations as a whole. I felt that even the movements of my spoon did not escape him, and were he to vanish after the soup, for the whole of dinner, the inspection he had held would have taken away my appetite. His own was exceedingly good, as one could see at luncheon, which he took like an ordinary guest of the hotel at the same hour as everyone else in the public dining-room. His table had this peculiarity only, that by his side, while he was eating, the other manager, the resident one, remained standing all the time making conversation. For, being subordinate to the general manager, he was anxious to please a man of whom he lived in constant fear. My own fear of him diminished during these luncheons, for being then lost in the crowd of visitors he would exercise the discretion of a general sitting in a restaurant where there are also private soldiers, in not seeming to take any notice of them. Nevertheless when the porter, from the midst of his cluster of bell-hops, announced to me: "He leaves tomorrow morning for Dinard. Then he's going down to Biarritz, and after that to Cannes," I began to breathe more freely.

My life in the hotel was rendered not only gloomy because I had made no friends there but uncomfortable because Françoise had made many. It might be thought that they would have made things easier for us in various respects. Quite the contrary. The proletariat, if they succeeded only with great difficulty in being treated as people she knew by Françoise, and could not succeed at all unless they fulfilled certain exacting conditions of politeness towards her, were, on the other hand, once they had reached that point, the only people who mattered to her. Her time-honoured code taught her that she was in no way beholden to the friends of her employers, that she might, if she was busy, shut the door without ceremony in the face of a lady who had come to call on my grandmother. But towards her own acquaintance, that is to say the select handful of the lower orders whom she admitted to her fastidious friendship, her actions were regulated by the most subtle and most stringent of protocols. Thus Françoise, having made the acquaintance of the man in the coffee-shop and of a young lady's-maid who did dressmaking for a Belgian lady, no longer went upstairs immediately after lunch to get my grandmother's things ready, but came an hour later, because the coffee-man had wanted to make her a cup of coffee or a tisane in his shop, or the maid had invited her to go and watch her sew, and to refuse either of them would have been impossible, one of those things that were not done. Moreover, particular regard was due to the little sewing-maid, who was an orphan and had been brought up by strangers to whom she still went occasionally for a few days' holiday. Her situation aroused Françoise's pity, and also her benevolent con-tempt. She who had a family, a little house that had come to her from her parents, with a field in which her brother kept a few cows, could not regard so uprooted a creature as her equal. And since this girl hoped, on Assumption Day, to be allowed to pay her benefactors a visit, Françoise kept on repeating: "She does make me laugh! She says, 'I hope to be going home for the Assumption.' Home, says she! It isn't just that it's not her own place, it's people as took her in from nowhere, and the creature says 'home' just as if it really was her home. Poor thing! What a misery it must be, not to know what it is to have a home." Still, if Françoise had associated only with the ladies'-maids brought to the hotel by other visitors, who fed with her in the "service" quarters and, seeing her grand lace cap and her fine profile, took her perhaps for some lady of noble birth, whom reduced circumstances or a personal attach-ment had driven to serve as companion to my grandmother, if in a word Françoise had known only people who did not belong to the hotel, no great harm would have been done, since she could not have prevented them from being of some service to us, for the simple reason that in no circumstances, even without her know-ledge, would it have been possible for them to be of service to us at all. But she had formed connexions also with one of the wine waiters, with a man in the kitchen, and with the head chamber-maid of our landing. And the result of this in our everyday life was that Françoise—who on the day of her arrival, when she still did not know anyone, would set all the bells jangling for the slightest thing, at hours when my grandmother and I would never have dared to ring, and if we offered some gentle admonition would answer: "Well, we're paying enough for it, aren't we?" as though it were she herself that would have to pay—now that she had made friends with a personage in the kitchen, which had appeared to us to augur well for our future comfort, were my grandmother or I to complain of cold feet, Françoise, even at an hour that was quite normal, dared not ring, assuring us that it would give offence because they would have to relight the boilers, or because it would interrupt the servants' dinner and they would be annoyed. And she ended with a formula that, in spite of the dubious way in which she pronounced it, was none the less clear and put us plainly in the wrong: "The fact is . . ." We did not insist, for fear of bringing upon ourselves another, far more serious: "It's a bit much . . . !" So that what it amounted to was that we could no longer have any hot water because Françoise had become a friend of the person who heated it.

In the end we too made a social connexion, in spite of but through my grandmother, for she and Mme de Villeparisis collided one morning in a doorway and were obliged to accost each other, not without having first exchanged gestures of surprise and hesitation, performed movements of withdrawal and uncertainty, and finally broken into protestations of joy and greeting, as in certain scenes in Molière where two actors who have been delivering long soliloquies each on his own account, a few feet apart, are supposed not yet to have seen each other, and then suddenly catching sight of each other, cannot believe their eyes, break off what they are saying, and then simultaneously find their tongues again (the chorus meanwhile having kept the dialogue going) and fall into each other's arms. Mme de Villeparisis tactfully made as if to leave my grandmother to herself after the first greetings, but my grandmother insisted on staying to talk to her until lunch-time, being anxious to discover how her friend managed to get her letters earlier than we got ours, and to get such nice grilled dishes (for Mme de Villeparisis, who took a keen interest in her food, had the poorest opinion of the hotel kitchen which served us with meals that my grandmother, still quoting Mme de Sévigné, described as "of a sumptuousness to make you die of hunger"). And the Marquise formed the habit of coming every day, while waiting to be served, to sit down for a moment at our table in the dining-room, insisting that we should not rise from our chairs or in any way put ourselves out. At the most we would occasionally linger, after finishing our lunch, to chat to her, at that sordid moment when the knives are left littering the table-cloth among crumpled napkins. For my own part, in order to preserve (so that I might be able to enjoy Balbec) the idea that I was on the uttermost promontory of the earth, I compelled myself to look further afield, to notice only the sea, to seek in it the effects described by Baudelaire and to let my gaze fall upon our table only on days when there was set on it some gigantic fish, some marine monster, which unlike the knives and forks was contemporary with the primitive epochs in which the Ocean first began to teem with life, at the time of the Cimmerians, a fish whose body with its numberless vertebrae, its blue and pink veins, had been constructed by nature, but according to an architectural plan, like a polychrome cathedral of the deep.

As a barber, seeing an officer whom he is accustomed to shave with special deference and care recognise a customer who has just entered the shop and stop for a moment to talk to him, rejoices in the thought that these are two men of the same social order, and cannot help smiling as he goes to fetch the bowl of soap, for he knows that in his establishment, to the vulgar routine of a mere barber's-shop are being added social, not to say aristocratic pleasures, so Aimé, seeing that Mme de Villeparisis had found in us old friends, went to fetch our finger-bowls with the proudly modest and knowingly discreet smile of a hostess who knows when to leave her guests to themselves. He suggested also a pleased and loving father who watches silently over the happy pair who have plighted their troth at his hospitable board. Besides, it was enough merely to utter the name of a person of title for Aimé to appear pleased, unlike Françoise, in whose presence you could not mention Count So-and-so without her face darkening and her speech becoming dry and curt, which meant that she cherished the aristocracy not less than Aimé but more. But then Françoise had that quality which in others she condemned as the worst possible fault: she was proud. She was not of that amenable and good-natured race to which Aimé belonged. They feel and they exhibit an intense delight when you tell them a piece of news which may be more or less sensational but is at any rate new, and not to be found in the papers. Françoise would refuse to appear surprised. You might have announced in her hearing that the Archduke Rudolf—not that she had the least suspicion of his having ever existed—was not, as was generally supposed, dead, but alive and kicking, and she would have answered only "Yes," as though she had known it all the time. It may, however, have been that if, even from our own lips, from us whom she so meekly called her masters and who had so nearly succeeded in taming her, she could not hear the name of a nobleman without having to restrain an impulse of anger, this was because the family from which she had sprung occupied in its own village a comfortable and independent position, unlikely to be disturbed in the consideration which it enjoyed save by those same nobles in whose households, meanwhile, from his boyhood, an Aimé would have been domiciled as a servant, if not actually brought up by their charity. Hence, for Françoise, Mme de Villeparisis had to make amends for being noble. But (in France, at any rate) that is precisely the talent, in fact the sole occupation of the aristocracy. Françoise, following the common tendency of servants, who pick up incessantly from the conversation of their masters with other people fragmentary observations from which they are apt to draw erroneous conclusions—as humans do with respect to the habits of animals—was constantly discovering that somebody had slighted us, a conclusion to which she was easily led not so much, perhaps, by her extravagant love for us as by the delight that she took in being disagreeable to us. But having once established, without possibility of error, the endless consideration and kindness shown to us, and shown to herself also, by Mme de Villeparisis, Françoise forgave her for being a marquise, and, as she had never ceased to admire her for being one, preferred her thenceforward to all our other friends. It must be added that no one else took the trouble to be so continually nice to us. Whenever my grandmother remarked on a book that Mme de Villeparisis was reading, or said she had been admiring the fruit which someone had just sent to our friend, within an hour the footman would come to our rooms with book or fruit. And the next time we saw her, in response to our thanks she would simply say, as though trying to find an excuse for her present in some special use to which it might be put: "It's nothing wonderful, but the newspapers come so late here; one must have something to read," or "It's always wiser to have fruit one can be quite certain of, at the seaside."

"But I don't believe I've ever seen you eating oysters," she said to us one day (increasing the sense of disgust which I felt at that moment, for the living flesh of oysters revolted me even more than the viscosity of the stranded jelly-fish defiled the Balbec beach for me). "They're quite delicious down here! Oh, let me tell my maid to fetch your letters when she goes for mine. What, your daughter writes to you *every day*? But what on earth can you find to say to each other?"

My grandmother was silent, but it may be assumed that her silence was due to disdain, for she used to repeat, when she wrote to Mamma, the words of Mme de Sévigné: "As soon as I have received a letter, I want another at once; I sigh for nothing else. There are few who are worthy to understand what I feel." And I was afraid that she might apply to Mme de Villeparisis the conclusion: "I seek out those who are of this chosen few, and I avoid the rest." She fell back upon praise of the fruit which Mme de Villeparisis had sent us the day before. And it had indeed been so fine that the manager, in spite of the jealousy aroused by our neglect of his official offerings, had said to me: "I am like you; I am sweeter for fruit than any other kind of dessert." My grandmother told her friend that she had enjoyed them all the more because the fruit which we got in the hotel was generally horrid. "I cannot," she went on, "say with Mme de Sévigné that if we should take a sudden fancy for bad fruit we should be obliged to order it from Paris." "Oh yes, of course, you read Mme de Sévigné. I've seen you with her letters ever since the day you came." (She forgot that she had never officially seen my grandmother in the hotel before meeting her in that doorway.) "Don't you find it rather exaggerated, her constant anxiety about her daughter? She refers to it too often to be really sincere. She's not very natural." My grandmother felt that any discussion would be futile, and so as not to be obliged to speak of the things she loved to a person incapable of understanding them, concealed the *Mémoires de Madame de Beausergent* by laying her bag upon them.

Were she to encounter Françoise at the moment (which Françoise called "the noon") when, wearing her fine cap and surrounded with every mark of respect, she was coming downstairs to "feed with the service," Mme Villeparisis would stop her to ask after us. And Françoise, when transmitting to us the Marquise's message: "She said to me, 'You'll be sure and bid them good day,' she said," would counterfeit the voice of Mme de Villeparisis, whose exact words she imagined herself to be quoting textually, whereas in fact she was distorting them no less than Plato distorts the words of Socrates or St John the words of

Jesus. Françoise was naturally deeply touched by these attentions. Only she did not believe my grandmother, but supposed that she must be lying in the interests of class (the rich always supporting one another) when she assured us that Mme de Villeparisis had been lovely as a young woman. It was true that of this loveliness only the faintest trace remained, from which no one—unless he happened to be a great deal more of an artist than Françoise— would have been able to reconstitute her ruined beauty. For in order to understand how beautiful an elderly woman may once have been one must not only study but translate every line of her face.

"I must remember some time to ask her whether I'm not right, after all, in thinking that there's some connexion with the Guermantes," said my grandmother, to my great indignation. How could I be expected to believe in a common origin uniting two names which had entered my consciousness, one through the low and shameful gate of experience, the other by the golden gate of imagination?

We had several times, in the last few days, seen driving past us in a stately equipage, tall, red-haired, handsome, with a rather prom-inent nose, the Princesse de Luxembourg, who was staying in the neighbourhood for a few weeks. Her carriage had stopped outside the hotel, a footman had come in and spoken to the manager, had gone back to the carriage and had reappeared with the most amazing armful of fruit (which combined a variety of seasons in a single basket, like the bay itself) with a card: "La Princesse de Luxembourg," on which were scrawled a few words in pencil. For what princely traveller, sojourning here incognito, could they be intended, those plums, glaucous, lumi-nous and spherical as was at that moment the circumfluent sea, those transparent grapes clustering on the shrivelled wood, like a fine day in autumn, those pears of a heavenly ultramarine? For it could not be on my grandmother's friend that the Princess had meant to pay a call. And yet on the following evening Mme de Villeparisis sent us the bunch of grapes, cool, liquid, golden, and plums and pears which we remembered too, though the plums had changed, like the sea at our dinner-hour, to a dull purple, and in the ultramarine of the pears there floated the shapes of a few pink clouds.

A few days later we met Mme de Villeparisis as we came away from the symphony concert that was given every morning on the beach. Convinced that the music that I heard there (the Prelude to *Lohengrin*, the Overture to *Tannhäuser* and suchlike) expressed the loftiest of truths, I tried to raise myself in so far as I could in order to reach and grasp them, I drew from myself, in order to understand them, and put back into them all that was best and most profound in my own nature at that time. But, as we came out of the concert, and, on our way back to the hotel, had stopped for a moment on the front, my grandmother and I, to exchange a few words with Mme de Villeparisis who told us that she had ordered some *croque-monsieurs* and a dish of creamed eggs for us at the hotel, I saw, in the distance, coming in our direction, the Princesse de Luxembourg, half leaning upon a parasol in such a way as to impart to her tall and wonderful form that slight inclination, to make it trace that arabesque, so dear to the women who had been beautiful under the Empire and knew how, with drooping shoulders, arched backs, concave hips and taut legs, to make their bodies float as softly as a silken scarf about the rigid armature of an invisible shaft which might be supposed to have transfixed it. She went out every morning for a stroll on the beach almost at the time when everyone else, after bathing, was coming home to lunch, and as hers was not until half-past one she did not return to her villa until long after the hungry bathers had left the scorching beach a desert. Mme de Villeparisis introduced my grandmother and was about to introduce me, but had first to ask me my name, which she could not remember. She had perhaps never known it, or if she had must have forgotten years ago to whom my grandmother had married her daughter. The name appeared to make a sharp impression on Mme de Villeparisis. Meanwhile the Princesse de Luxembourg had offered us her hand and from time to time, while she chatted to the Marquise, turned to bestow a kindly glance on my grandmother and myself, with that embryonic kiss which we put into our smiles when they are addressed to a baby out with its "Nana." Indeed, in her anxiety not to appear to be enthroned in a higher sphere than ours, she had probably miscalculated the distance, for by an error in adjustment her eyes became infused with such benevolence that I foresaw the moment when she would put out her hand and stroke us like two lovable beasts who had poked our heads out at her through the bars of our cage in the Zoo. And immediately, as it happened, this idea of caged animals and the Bois de Boulogne received striking confirmation. It was the time of day when the beach is crowded by itinerant and clamorous vendors, hawking cakes and sweets and biscuits. Not knowing quite what to do to show her affection for us, the Princess hailed the next one to come by; he had nothing left but a loaf of rye bread, of the kind one throws to the ducks. The Princess took it and said to me: "For your grandmother." And yet it was to me that she held it out, saying with a friendly smile, "You shall give it to her yourself," thinking that my pleasure would thus be more complete if there were no intermediary between myself and the animals. Other vendors came up, and she stuffed my pockets with everything that they had, tied up in packets, comfits, sponge-cakes, sugar-sticks. "You will eat some yourself," she told me, "and give some to your grandmother," and she had the vendors paid by the little negro page, dressed in red satin, who followed her every-where and was a nine days' wonder on the beach. Then she said good-bye to Mme de Villeparisis and held out her hand to us with the intention of treating us in the same way as she treated her friend, as people whom she knew, and of bringing herself within our reach. But this time she must have reckoned our level as not quite so low in the scale of creation, for her equality with us was indicated by the Princess to my grandmother by that tender and maternal smile which one bestows upon a little boy when one says good-bye to him as though to a grown-up person. By a miraculous stride in evolution, my grandmother was no longer a duck or an antelope, but had already become what Mme Swann would have called a "*baby.*" Finally, having taken leave of us all, the Princess resumed her stroll along the sunlit esplanade, curving and inflecting her splendid form, which, like a serpent coiled about a wand, twined itself round the white parasol patterned in blue which she carried unopened in her hand. She was my first Royalty—I say my first, for the Princesse Mathilde was not at all royal in her ways. The second, as we shall see in due course, was to astonish me no less by her graciousness. One aspect of the benevolence of the nobility, kindly intermediaries between commoners and kings, was revealed to me next day when Mme de Villeparisis reported: "She thought you quite charming. She is a woman of the soundest judgment, the warmest heart. Not like so many queens and highnesses. She has real merit." And Mme de Villeparisis added in a tone of conviction, and quite thrilled to be able to say it to us: "I think she would be delighted to see you again."

But on that previous morning, after we had parted from the Princesse de Luxembourg, Mme de Villeparisis said a thing which impressed me far more and was not prompted merely by friendly feeling.

"Are you," she had asked me, "the son of the Permanent Secretary at the Ministry? Indeed! I'm told your father is a most charming man. He is having a splendid holiday just now."

A few days earlier we had heard, in a letter from Mamma, that my father and his travelling-companion M. de Norpois had lost their luggage.

"It has been found, or rather it was never really lost. I can tell you what happened," explained Mme de Villeparisis, who, without our knowing how, seemed to be far better informed than ourselves about my father's travels. "I think your father is now planning to come home earlier, next week, in fact, as he will probably give up the idea of going to Algeciras. But he's anxious to spend a day longer in Toledo, since he's an admirer of a pupil of Titian—I forget the name—whose work can only be seen properly there."

And I wondered by what strange accident, in the impartial telescope through which Mme de Villeparisis considered, from a safe distance, the minuscule, perfunctory, vague agitation of the host of people whom she knew, there had come to be inserted at the spot through which she observed my father a fragment of glass of prodigious magnifying power which made her see in such high relief and in the fullest detail everything that was agreeable about him, the contingencies that obliged him to return home, his difficulties with the customs, his admiration for El Greco, and, altering the scale of her vision, showed her this one man, so large among all the rest so small, like that Jupiter to whom Gustave Moreau, when he portrayed him by the side of a weak mortal, gave a superhuman stature.

My grandmother bade Mme de Villeparisis good-bye, so that we might stay and imbibe the fresh air for a little while longer outside the hotel, until they signalled to us through the glazed partition that our lunch was ready. There were sounds of uproar. The young mistress of the King of the Cannibal Island had been down to bathe and was now coming back to the hotel.

"Really and truly, it's a perfect plague, it's enough to make one decide to emigrate!" cried the president in a towering rage as he crossed her path.

Meanwhile the notary's wife was following the bogus queen with eyes that seemed ready to start from their sockets.

"I can't tell you how angry Mme Blandais makes me when she stares at those people like that," said the president to the judge, "I feel I want to slap her. That's just the way to make the wretches appear important, which is of course the very thing they want. Do ask her husband to tell her what a fool she's making of herself. I swear I won't go out with them again if they stop and gape at those masqueraders."

As to the coming of the Princesse de Luxembourg, whose carriage, on the day she had left the fruit, had drawn up outside the hotel, it had not passed unobserved by the little group of wives, the notary's, the president's and the judge's, who had already for some time past been extremely anxious to know whether that Mme de Villeparisis whom everyone treated with so much respect—which all these ladies were burning to hear that she did not deserve—was a genuine marquise and not an adventuress. Whenever Mme de Villeparisis passed through the hall the judge's wife, who scented irregularities everywhere, would lift her nose from her needlework and stare at the intruder in a way that made her friends die with laughter.

"Oh, well, you know," she proudly explained, "I always begin by believing the worst. I will never admit that a woman is properly married until she has shown me her birth certificate and her marriage lines. But never fear—just wait till I've finished my little investigation."

And so day after day the ladies would come together and laughingly ask: "Any news?"

But on the evening of the Princesse de Luxembourg's call the judge's wife laid a finger on her lips.

"I've discovered something."

"Oh, isn't Mme Poncin simply wonderful? I never saw . . . But do tell us! What's happened?"

"Just listen to this. A woman with yellow hair and six inches of paint on her face and a carriage which reeked of harlot a mile away—which only a creature like that would dare to have—came here today to call on the so-called Marquise!"

"Oh-yow-yow! Crash bang! Did you ever! Why, it must be the woman we saw—you remember, President—we said at the time we didn't at all like the look of her, but we didn't know that it was the 'Marquise' she'd come to see. A woman with a nigger-boy, you mean?"

"That's the one."

"You don't say! Do you happen to know her name?"

"Yes, I made a mistake on purpose. I picked up her card. She *trades* under the name of the 'Princesse de Luxembourg'! Wasn't I right to have my doubts about her? It's a nice thing to have to fraternise with a Baronne d'Ange like that?"[2]

The president quoted Mathurin Régnier's *Macette* to the judge.

It must not, however, be supposed that this misunderstanding was merely temporary, like those that occur in the second act of a farce to be cleared up before the final curtain. Mme de Luxembourg, a niece of the King of England and of the Emperor of Austria, and Mme de Villeparisis, when one called to take the other for a drive, always appeared like two "old trots" of the kind one has always such difficulty in avoiding at a watering-place. Nine tenths of the men of the Faubourg Saint-Germain appear to a large section of the middle classes as crapulous paupers (which, individually, they not infrequently are) whom no respectable person would dream of asking to dinner. The middle classes pitch their standards in this respect too high, for the failings of these men would never prevent their being received with every mark of esteem in houses which they themselves will never enter. And so fondly do the aristocracy imagine that the middle classes know this that they affect a simplicity in speaking of themselves, a disparagement of friends of theirs who are particularly "on their beam-ends," that compounds the misunderstanding. If, by chance, a man of the fashionable world has dealings with the petty bourgeoisie because, having more money than he knows what to do with, he finds himself elected chairman of all sorts of important financial concerns, his business associates who at last see a nobleman worthy to be ranked with the professional classes, would take their oaths that such a man would not consort with the Marquis ruined by gambling whom the said business associates assume to be all the more destitute of friends the more friendly he makes himself. And they cannot get over their surprise when the duke who is Chairman of the Board of Directors of the colossal undertaking arranges a marriage for his son with the daughter of that very marquis, who may be a gambler but who bears the oldest name in France, just as a sovereign would sooner see his son marry the daughter of a dethroned king than that of a president still in office. In other words, the two worlds have as fanciful a view of one another as the inhabitants of the resort situated at one end of

Balbec Bay have of the resort at the other end: from Rivebelle you can just see Marcouville-l'Orgueilleuse; but even that is deceptive, for you imagine that you are seen from Marcouville, where, as a matter of fact, the splendours of Rivebelle are almost wholly invisible.

The Balbec doctor, called in to cope with a sudden feverish attack, gave the opinion that I ought not to stay out all day on the beach in the blazing sun during the hot weather, and wrote out various prescriptions for me. My grandmother took these with a show of respect in which I could at once discern her firm resolve to ignore them all, but did pay attention to the advice on the question of hygiene, and accepted an offer from Mme de Villeparisis to take us for drives in her carriage. After this I would spend the mornings going to and fro between my own room and my grandmother's. Hers did not look out directly on the sea, as mine did, but was open on three of its four sides—on to a strip of the esplanade, a courtyard, and a view of the country inland—and was furnished differently from mine, with armchairs embroidered with metallic filigree and pink flowers from which the cool and pleasant odour that greeted one on entering seemed to emanate. And at that hour when the sun's rays, drawn from different exposures and, as it were, from different hours of the day, broke the angles of the wall, projected on to the chest of drawers, side by side with a reflection of the beach, a festal altar as variegated as a bank of field-flowers, hung on the fourth wall the folded, quivering, warm wings of a radiance ready at any moment to resume its flight, warmed like a bath a square of provincial carpet before the window overlooking the courtyard which the sun festooned and patterned like a climbing vine, and added to the charm and complexity of the room's furniture by seeming to pluck and scatter the petals of the silken flowers on the chairs and to make their silver threads stand out from the fabric, this room in which I lingered for a moment before going to get ready for our drive suggested a prism in which the colours of the light that shone outside were broken up, a hive in which the sweet juices of the day which I was about to taste were distilled, scattered, intoxicating and visible, a garden of hope which dissolved in a quivering haze of silver threads and rose petals. But before all this I had drawn back my own curtains, impatient to know what Sea it was that was playing that morning by the shore, like a Nereid. For none of those Seas ever stayed with us longer than a day. The next day

there would be another, which sometimes resembled its predecessor. But I never saw the same one twice.

There were some that were of so rare a beauty that my pleasure
on catching sight of them was enhanced by surprise. By what
privilege, on one morning rather than another, did the window on
being uncurtained disclose to my wondering eyes the nymph
Glauconome, whose lazy beauty, gently breathing, had the transparency of a vaporous emerald through which I could see teeming
the ponderable elements that coloured it? She made the sun join in
her play, with a smile attenuated by an invisible haze which was no
more than a space kept vacant about her translucent surface,
which, thus curtailed, was rendered more striking, like those
goddesses whom the sculptor carves in relief upon a block of
marble the rest of which he leaves unchiselled. So, in her matchless
colour, she invited us out over those rough terrestrial roads, from
which, sitting with Mme de Villeparisis in her barouche, we
should glimpse, all day long and without ever reaching it, the
coolness of her soft palpitation.

Mme de Villeparisis used to order her carriage early, so that we
should have time to reach Saint-Mars-le-Vêtu, or the rocks of
Quetteholme, or some other goal which, for a somewhat lumber-
ing vehicle, was far enough off to require the whole day. In my joy
at the thought of the long drive we were going to take I would
hum some tune that I had heard recently as I strolled up and down
until Mme de Villeparisis was ready. If it was Sunday, hers would
not be the only carriage drawn up outside the hotel; several hired
cabs would be waiting there, not only for the people who had
been invited to Féterne by Mme de Cambremer, but for those
who, rather than stay at home all day like children in disgrace,
declared that Sunday was always quite impossible at Balbec and set
off immediately after lunch to hide themselves in some neighbouring watering-place or to visit one of the "sights" of the
neighbourhood. And indeed whenever (which was often) Mme
Blandais was asked if she had been to the Cambremers', she would
answer emphatically: "No, we went to the Falls of the Bec," as
though that were the sole reason for her not having spent the day
at Féterne. And the president would charitably remark: "I envy
you. I wish I had gone there instead. They must be well worth
seeing."

Beside the row of carriages, in front of the porch in which I
stood waiting, was planted, like some shrub of a rare species, a

young page who attracted the eye no less by the unusual and harmonious colouring of his hair than by his plant-like epidermis. Inside, in the hall, corresponding to the narthex, or Church of the Catechumens in a primitive basilica, through which the persons who were not staying in the hotel were entitled to pass, the comrades of the "outside" page did not indeed work much harder than he but did at least execute certain movements. It is probable that in the early morning they helped with the cleaning. But in the afternoon they stood there only like a chorus who, even when there is nothing for them to do, remain upon the stage in order to strengthen the representation. The general manager, the same who had so terrified me, reckoned on increasing their number considerably next year, for he had "big ideas." And this prospect greatly afflicted the manager of the hotel, who found that all these boys were simply "busybodies," by which he meant that they got in the visitors' way and were of no use to anyone. But between lunch and dinner at least, between the exits and entrances of the visitors, they did fill an otherwise empty stage, like those pupils of Mme de Maintenon who, in the garb of young Israelites, carry on the action whenever Esther or Joad "goes off." But the outside page, with his delicate tints, his slender, fragile frame, in proximity to whom I stood waiting for the Marquise to come down, preserved an immobility mixed with a certain melancholy, for his elder brothers had left the hotel for more brilliant careers elsewhere, and he felt isolated upon this alien soil. At last Mme de Villeparisis appeared. To stand by her carriage and to help her into it ought perhaps to have been part of the young page's duties. But he knew that a person who brings her own servants to an hotel expects them to wait on her and is not as a rule lavish with her tips, and that the same was true also of the nobility of the old Faubourg Saint-Germain. Mme de Villeparisis belonged to both these categories. The arborescent page concluded therefore that he could expect nothing from her, and leaving her own maid and footman to pack her and her belongings into the carriage, he continued to dream sadly of the enviable lot of his brothers and preserved his vegetable immobility.

We would set off; some time after rounding the railway-station, we came into a country road which soon became as familiar to me as the roads round Combray, from the bend where it took off between charming orchards to the turning at which we left it where there were tilled fields on either side. Among these we could see here and there an apple-tree, stripped it was true of its blossom and bearing no more than a fringe of pistils, but sufficient even so to enchant me since I could imagine, seeing those inimitable leaves, how their broad expanse, like the ceremonial carpet spread for a wedding that was now over, had been only recently swept by the white satin train of their blushing flowers.

How often in Paris, during the month of May of the following year, was I to bring home a branch of apple-blossom from the florist and afterwards to spend the night in company with its flowers in which bloomed the same creamy essence that still powdered with its froth the burgeoning leaves and between whose white corollas it seemed almost as though it had been the florist who, from generosity towards me, from a taste for invention too and as an effective contrast, had added on either side the supplement of a becoming pink bud: I sat gazing at them, I grouped them in the light of my lamp—for so long that I was often still there when the dawn brought to their whiteness the same flush with which it must at that moment have been tingeing their sisters on the Balbec road—and I sought to carry them back in my imagination to that roadside, to multiply them, to spread them out within the frame prepared for them, on the canvas already primed, of those fields and orchards whose outline I knew by heart, which I so longed to see, which one day I must see, again, at the moment when, with the exquisite fervour of genius, spring covers their canvas with its colours.

Before getting into the carriage, I had composed the sea-scape which I was going to look out for, which I hoped to see with Baudelaire's "radiant sun" upon it, and which at Balbec I could distinguish only in too fragmentary a form, broken by so many vulgar adjuncts that had no place in my dream—bathers, cabins, pleasure yachts. But when, Mme de Villeparisis's carriage having reached the top of a hill, I caught a glimpse of the sea through the leafy boughs of the trees, then no doubt at such a distance those temporal details which had set it apart, as it were, from nature and history disappeared, and I could try to persuade myself as I looked down upon its waters that they were the same which Leconte de Lisle describes for us in his *Orestie*, where "like a flight of birds of prey, at break of day" the long-haired warriors of heroic Hellas "with oars a hundred thousand sweep the resounding deep." But on the other hand I was no longer near enough to the sea, which seemed to me not alive but congealed, I no longer felt any power beneath its colours, spread like those of a picture between the leaves, through which it appeared as insubstantial as the sky and only of an intenser blue.

Mme de Villeparisis, seeing that I was fond of churches, promised me that we should visit several of them, and especially the church at Carqueville "quite buried in all its old ivy," as she said with a gesture of her hand which seemed tastefully to be clothing the absent façade in an invisible and delicate screen of foliage. Mme de Villeparisis would often, with this little descriptive gesture, find just the right word to define the charm and distinctiveness of an historic building, always avoiding technical terms, but incapable of concealing her thorough understanding of the things to which she referred. She appeared to seek an excuse for this erudition in the fact that one of her father's country houses, the one in which she had lived as a girl, was situated in a region where there were churches similar in style to those round Balbec, so that it would have been shameful if she had not acquired a taste for architecture, this house being, incidentally, one of the finest examples of that of the Renaissance. But as it was also a regular museum, as moreover Chopin and Liszt had played there, Lamartine recited poetry, all the most famous artists for fully a century written thoughts, dashed off melodies, made sketches in the family album, Mme de Villeparisis ascribed, whether from delicacy, good breeding, true modesty or want of speculative intelligence, only this purely material origin to her acquaintance with all the arts, and had seemingly come to regard painting, music, literature, and philosophy as the appanage of a young lady brought up on the most aristocratic lines in an historic building that was classified and starred. One got the impression that for her there were no other pictures than those that have been inherited. She was pleased that my grandmother liked a necklace which she wore, and which hung over her dress. It appeared in the portrait of an ancestress of hers, by Titian, which had never left the family. So that one could be certain of its being genuine. She would not hear a word about pictures bought, heaven knew where, by a Croesus; she was persuaded in advance that they were fakes, and had no desire to see them. We knew that she herself painted flowers in water-colour, and my grandmother, who had heard these praised, spoke to her of them. Mme de Villeparisis modestly changed the subject, but without showing any more surprise or pleasure than would an artist of established reputation to whom compliments mean nothing. She said merely that it was a delightful pastime because, even if the flowers that sprang from the brush were nothing wonderful, at least the work made you live in the company of real flowers, of the beauty of which, especially when you were obliged to study them closely in order to draw them, you could never grow tired. But at Balbec Mme de Villeparisis was giving herself a holiday, in order to rest her eyes.

We were astonished, my grandmother and I, to find how much more "liberal" she was than even the majority of the middle class. She did not understand how anyone could be scandalised by the expulsion of the Jesuits, saying that it had always been done, even under the Monarchy, in Spain even. She defended the Republic, reproaching it for its anti-clericalism only to this extent: "I should find it just as bad to be prevented from going to mass when I wanted to, as to be forced to go to it when I didn't!" and even startled us with such remarks as: "Oh! the aristocracy in these days, what does it amount to?" or, "To my mind, a man who doesn't work doesn't count!"—perhaps only because she sensed how much they gained in spice and piquancy, how memorable they became, on her lips.

When we heard these advanced opinions—though never so far advanced as to amount to socialism, which Mme de Villeparisis held in abhorrence—expressed so frequently and with so much frankness precisely by one of those people in consideration of whose intelligence our scrupulous and timid impartiality would refuse to condemn outright the ideas of conservatives, we came very near, my grandmother and I, to believing that in the pleasant companion of our drives was to be found the measure and the pattern of truth in all things. We took her word for it when she pronounced judgment on her Titians, the colonnade of her country house, the conversational talent of Louis-Philippe. But—like those learned people who hold us spellbound when we get them on to Egyptian painting or Etruscan inscriptions, and yet talk so tritely about modern work that we wonder whether we have not overestimated the interest of the sciences in which they are versed since they do not betray therein the mediocrity of mind which they must have brought to those studies just as much as to their fatuous essays on Baudelaire—Mme de Villeparisis, questioned by me about Chateaubriand, about Balzac, about Victor Hugo, each of whom in his day had been the guest of her parents and had been glimpsed by her, smiled at my reverence, told amusing anecdotes about them such as she had just been telling us about dukes and statesmen, and severely criticised those writers precisely because they had been lacking in that modesty, that self-effacement, that sober art which is satisfied with a single precise stroke and does not over-emphasise, which avoids above all else the absurdity of grandiloquence, in that aptness, those qualities of moderation, of judgment and simplicity to which she had been taught that real greatness aspired and attained. It was evident that she had no hesitation in placing above them men who might after all, perhaps, by virtue of those qualities, have had the advantage over a Balzac, a Hugo, a Vigny in a drawing-room, an academy, a cabinet council, men like Molé, Fontanes, Vitrolles, Bersot, Pasquier, Lebrun, Salvandy or Daru.

"Like those novels of Stendhal which you seem to admire. You would have given him a great surprise, I assure you, if you had spoken to him in that tone. My father, who used to meet him at M. Mérimée's—now he was a man of talent, if you like—often told me that Beyle (that was his real name) was appallingly vulgar, but quite good company at dinner, and not in the least conceited about his books. Why, you must have seen for yourself how he just shrugged his shoulders at the absurdly extravagant compliments of M. de Balzac. There at least he showed that he knew how to behave like a gentleman."

She possessed the autographs of all these great men, and seemed, presuming on the personal relations which her family had had with them, to think that her judgment of them must be better founded than that of young people who, like myself, had had no opportunity of meeting them. "I think I have a right to speak about them, since they used to come to my father's house; and as M. Sainte-Beuve, who was a most intelligent man, used to say, in forming an estimate you must take the word of people who saw them close to and were able to judge more exactly their real worth."

Sometimes, as the carriage laboured up a steep road through ploughlands, making the fields more real, adding to them a mark of authenticity like the precious floweret with which certain of the old masters used to sign their pictures, a few hesitant cornflowers, like those of Combray, would follow in our wake. Presently the horses outdistanced them, but a little way on we would glimpse another which while awaiting us had pricked up its azure star in front of us in the grass. Some made so bold as to come and plant themselves by the side of the road, and a whole constellation began to take shape, what with my distant memories and these domesticated flowers.

We began to go down the hill; and then we would meet, climbing it on foot, on a bicycle, in a cart or carriage, one of those creatures—flowers of a fine day but unlike the flowers of the field, for each of them secretes something that is not to be found in another and that will prevent us from gratifying with any of her peers the desire she has aroused in us—a farm-girl driving her cow or reclining on the back of a waggon, a shopkeeper's daughter taking the air, a fashionable young lady erect on the back seat of a landau, facing her parents. Certainly Bloch had been the means of opening a new era and had altered the value of life for me on the day when he had told me that the dreams which I had entertained on my solitary walks along the Méséglise way, when I hoped that some peasant girl might pass whom I could take in my arms, were not a mere fantasy which corresponded to nothing outside myself but that all the girls one met, whether villagers or "young ladies," were alike ready and willing to give heed to such yearnings. And even if I were fated, now that I was ill and did not go out by myself, never to be able to make love to them, I was happy all the same, like a child born in a prison or a hospital who, having long supposed that the human organism was capable of digesting only dry bread and medicines, has learned suddenly that peaches, apricots and grapes are not simply part of the decoration of the country scene but delicious and easily assimilated food. Even if his gaoler or his nurse does not allow him to pluck those tempting fruits, still the world seems to him a better place and existence in it more clement. For a desire seems to us more attractive, we repose on it with more confidence, when we know that outside ourselves there is a reality which conforms to it, even if, for us, it is not to be realised. And we think more joyfully of a life in which (on condition that we eliminate for a moment from our mind the tiny obstacle, accidental and special, which prevents us personally from doing so) we can imagine ourselves to be assuaging that desire. As to the pretty girls who went past, from the day on which I had first known that their cheeks could be kissed, I had became curious about their souls. And the universe had appeared to me more interesting.

Mme de Villeparisis's carriage moved fast. I scarcely had time to see the girl who was coming in our direction; and yet—since the beauty of human beings is not like the beauty of things, and we feel that it is that of a unique creature, endowed with consciousness and free-will—as soon as her individuality, a soul still vague, a will unknown to me, presented a tiny picture of itself, enormously reduced but complete, in the depths of her indifferent eyes, at once, by a mysterious response of the pollen ready in me for the pistils that should receive it, I felt surging through me the embryo, equally vague, equally minute, of the desire not to let this girl pass without forcing her mind to become aware of my person, without preventing her desires from wandering to someone else, without insinuating myself into her dreams and taking possession of her heart. Meanwhile our carriage had moved on; the pretty girl was already behind us; and as she had—of me—none of those notions which constitute a person in one's mind, her eyes, which had barely seen me, had forgotten me already. Was it because I had caught but a momentary glimpse of her that I had found her so attractive? It may have been. In the first place, the impossibility of stopping when we meet a woman, the risk of not meeting her again another day, give her at once the same charm as a place derives from the illness or poverty that prevents us from visiting it, or the lustreless days which remain to us to live from the battle in which we shall doubtless fall. So that, if there were no such thing as habit, life must appear delightful to those of us who are continually under the threat of death—that is to say, to all mankind. Then, if our imagination is set going by the desire for what we cannot possess, its flight is not limited by a reality perceived in these casual encounters in which the charms of the passing stranger are generally in direct ratio to the swiftness of our passage. If night is falling and the carriage is moving fast, whether in town or country, there is not a single torso, disfigured like an antique marble by the speed that tears us away and the dusk that blurs it, that does not aim at our heart, from every crossing, from the lighted interior of every shop, the arrows of Beauty, that Beauty of which we are sometimes tempted to ask ourselves whether it is, in this world, anything more than the complementary part that is added to a fragmentary and fugitive stranger by our imagination, overstimulated by regret.

Had I been free to get down from the carriage and to speak to the girl whom we were passing, I might perhaps have been disillusioned by some blemish on her skin which from the carriage I had not distinguished. (Whereupon any attempt to penetrate into her life would have seemed suddenly impossible. For beauty is a sequence of hypotheses which ugliness cuts short when it bars the way that we could already see opening into the unknown.) Perhaps a single word which she might have uttered, or a smile, would have furnished me with an unexpected key or clue with which to read the expression on her face, to interpret her bearing, which would at once have become commonplace. It is possible, for I have never in real life met any girls so desirable as on days when I was with some solemn person from whom, despite the myriad pretexts that I invented, I could not tear myself away: some years after the one in the course of which I went for the first time to Balbec, as I was driving through Paris with a friend of my father, and had caught sight of a woman walking quickly along the dark street, I felt that it was unreasonable to forfeit, for a purely conventional scruple, my share of happiness in what may very well be the only life there is, and jumping from the carriage without a word of apology I went in search of the stranger, lost her at the junction of two streets, caught up with her again in a third, and arrived at last, breathless, beneath a street lamp, face to face with old Mme Verdurin whom I had been carefully avoiding for years, and who, in her delight and surprise, exclaimed: "But how very nice of you to have run all this way just to say how d'ye do to me!"

That year at Balbec, on the occasion of such encounters, I would assure my grandmother and Mme de Villeparisis that I had so severe a headache that the best thing for me would be to go home alone on foot. But they would never let me get out of the carriage. And I must add the pretty girl (far harder to find again than an historic monument, for she was nameless and had the power of locomotion) to the collection of all those whom I promised myself that I would examine more closely at a later date. One of them, however, happened to pass more than once before my eyes in circumstances which allowed me to believe that I should be able to get to know her as fully as I wished. This was a milk-girl who came from a farm with an additional supply of cream for the hotel. I fancied that she had recognised me also; and she did indeed look at me with an attentiveness which was perhaps due only to the surprise which my attentiveness caused her. And next day, a day on which I had been resting all morning, when Françoise came in about noon to draw my curtains, she handed me a letter which had been left for me downstairs. I knew no one at Balbec. I had no doubt that the letter was from the milk-girl. Alas, it was only from Bergotte who, as he happened to be passing, had tried to see me, but on hearing that I was asleep had scribbled a few charming lines for which the lift-boy had addressed an envelope which I had supposed to have been written by the milk-girl. I was bitterly disappointed, and the thought that it was more difficult and more flattering to get a letter from Bergotte did not in the least console me for this one's not being from her. As for the girl, I never came across her again, any more than I came across those whom I had seen only from Mme de Villeparisis's carriage. Seeing and then losing them all thus increased the state of agitation in which I was living, and I found a certain wisdom in the philosophers who recommend us to set a limit to our desires (if, that is, they refer to our desire for people, for that is the only kind that leads to anxiety, having for its object something unknown but conscious. To suppose that philosophy could be referring to the desire for wealth would be too absurd). At the same time I was inclined to regard this wisdom as incomplete, for I told myself that these encounters made me find even more beautiful a world which thus caused to grow along all the country roads flowers at once rare and common, fleeting treasures of the day, windfalls of the drive, of which the contingent circumstances that might not, perhaps, recur had alone prevented me from taking advantage, and which gave a new zest to life.

But perhaps in hoping that, one day, with greater freedom, I should be able to find similar girls on other roads, I was already beginning to falsify what is exclusively individual in the desire to live in the company of a woman whom one has found attractive, and by the mere fact that I admitted the possibility of bringing it about artificially, I had implicitly acknowledged its illusoriness.

On the day when Mme de Villeparisis took us to Carqueville to see the ivy-covered church of which she had spoken to us and which, built upon rising ground, dominated both the village and the river that flowed beneath it with its little mediaeval bridge, my grandmother, thinking that I would like to be left alone to study the building at my leisure, suggested to her friend that they should go on and wait for me at the pastry-cook's, in the village square which was clearly visible from where we were and beneath its mellow patina seemed like another part of a wholly ancient object. It was agreed that I should join them there later. In the mass of verdure in front of which I was left standing I was obliged, in order to recognise a church, to make a mental effort which involved my grasping more intensely the idea "Church." In fact, as happens to schoolboys who gather more fully the meaning of a sentence when they are made, by translating or by paraphrasing it, to divest it of the forms to which they are accustomed, I was obliged perpetually to refer back to this idea of "Church," which as a rule I scarcely needed when I stood beneath steeples that were recognisable in themselves, in order not to forget, here that the arch of this clump of ivy was that of a Gothic window, there that the salience of the leaves was due to the carved relief of a capital. Then came a breath of wind, sending a tremor through the mobile porch, which was traversed by eddies flickering and spreading like light; the leaves unfurled against one another; and, quivering, the arboreal façade bore away with it the undulant, rustling, fugitive pillars.

As I came away from the church I saw by the old bridge a cluster of girls from the village who, probably because it was Sunday, were standing about in their best clothes, hailing the boys who went past. One of them, a tall girl not so well dressed as the others but seeming to enjoy some ascendancy over them—for she scarcely answered when they spoke to her—with a more serious and a more self-willed air, was sitting on the parapet of the bridge with her feet hanging down, and holding on her lap a bowl full of fish which she had presumably just caught. She had a tanned complexion, soft eyes but with a look of disdain for her surroundings, and a small nose, delicately and attractively modelled. My eyes alighted upon her skin; and my lips, at a pinch, might have believed that they had followed my eyes. But it was not only to her body that I should have liked to attain; it was also the person that lived inside it, and with which there is but one form of contact, namely to attract its attention, but one sort of penetration, to awaken an idea in it.

And this inner being of the handsome fisher-girl seemed to be still closed to me; I was doubtful whether I had entered it, even after I had seen my own image furtively reflected in the twin mirrors of her gaze, following an index of refraction that was as unknown to me as if I had been placed in the field of vision of a doe. But just as it would not have sufficed that my lips should find pleasure in hers without giving pleasure to them too, so I could have wished that the idea of me which entered this being and took hold in it should bring me not merely her attention but her admiration, her desire, and should compel her to keep me in her memory until the day when I should be able to meet her again. Meanwhile I could see, within a stone's-throw, the square in which Mme de Villeparisis's carriage must be waiting for me. I had not a moment to lose; and already I could feel that the girls were beginning to laugh at the sight of me standing there before them. I had a five-franc piece in my pocket. I drew it out, and, before explaining to the girl the errand on which I proposed to send her, in order to have a better chance of her listening to me I held the coin for a moment before her eyes.

"Since you seem to belong to the place," I said to her, "I wonder if you would be so good as to take a message for me. I want you to go to a pastry-cook's—which is apparently in a square, but I don't know where that is—where there is a carriage waiting for me. One moment! To make quite sure, will you ask if the carriage belongs to the Marquise de Villeparisis? But you can't miss it; it's a carriage and pair."

That was what I wished her to know, so that she should regard me as someone of importance. But when I had uttered the words "Marquise" and "carriage and pair," suddenly I had a sense of enormous assuagement. I felt that the fisher-girl would remember me, and together with my fear of not being able to see her again, a part of my desire to do so evaporated too. It seemed to me that I had succeeded in touching her person with invisible lips, and that I had pleased her. And this forcible appropriation of her mind, this immaterial possession, had robbed her of mystery as much as physical possession would have done.

We came down towards Hudimesnil; and suddenly I was over-whelmed with that profound happiness which I had not often felt since Combray, a happiness analogous to that which had been given me by—among other things—the steeples of Martinville. But this time it remained incomplete. I had just seen, standing a little way back from the hog's-back road along which we were travelling, three trees which probably marked the entry to a covered driveway and formed a pattern which I was not seeing for the first time. I could not succeed in reconstructing the place from which they had been as it were detached, but I felt that it had been familiar to me once; so that, my mind having wavered between some distant year and the present moment, Balbec and its surroundings began to dissolve and I wondered whether the whole of this drive were not a make-believe, Balbec a place to which I had never gone except in imagination, Mme de

Villeparisis a character in a story and the three old trees the reality
which one recaptures on raising one's eyes from the book which
one has been reading and which describes an environment
into which one has come to believe that one has been bodily
transported.

I looked at the three trees; I could see them plainly, but my
mind felt that they were concealing something which it could not
grasp, as when an object is placed out of our reach, so that our
fingers, stretched out at arm's-length, can only touch for a
moment its outer surface, without managing to take hold of anything. Then we rest for a little while before thrusting out our arm
with renewed momentum, and trying to reach an inch or two
further. But if my mind was thus to collect itself, to gather
momentum, I should have to be alone. What would I not have
given to be able to draw aside as I used to do on those walks along
the Guermantes way, when I detached myself from my parents!
I felt indeed that I ought to do so. I recognised that kind of pleasure
which requires, it is true, a certain effort on the part of the mind,
but in comparison with which the attractions of the indolence
which inclines us to renounce that pleasure seem very slight. That
pleasure, the object of which I could only dimly feel, which I must
create for myself, I experienced only on rare occasions, but on
each of these it seemed to me that the things that had happened in
the meantime were of little importance, and that in attaching
myself to the reality of that pleasure alone could I at length begin
to lead a true life. I put my hand for a moment across my eyes, so as
to be able to shut them without Mme de Villeparisis's noticing.
I sat there thinking of nothing, then with my thoughts collected,
compressed and strengthened I sprang further forward in the
direction of the trees, or rather in that inner direction at the end
of which I could see them inside myself. I felt again behind them
the same object, known to me and yet vague, which I could not
bring nearer. And yet all three of them, as the carriage moved on,
I could see coming towards me. Where had I looked at them
before? There was no place near Combray where an avenue
opened off the road like that. Nor was there room for the site
which they recalled to me in the scenery of the place in Germany
where I had gone one year with my grandmother to take the
waters. Was I to suppose, then, that they came from years already
so remote in my life that the landscape which surrounded them
had been entirely obliterated from my memory and that, like the

pages which, with a sudden thrill, we recognise in a book that we imagined we had never read, they alone survived from the forgotten book of my earliest childhood? Were they not rather to be numbered among those dream landscapes, always the same, at least for me in whom their strange aspect was only the objectivation in my sleeping mind of the effort I made while awake either to penetrate the mystery of a place beneath the outward appearance of which I was dimly conscious of there being something more, as had so often happened to me on the Guermantes way, or to try to put mystery back into a place which I had longed to know and which, from the day when I had come to know it, had seemed to me to be wholly superficial, like Balbec? Or were they merely an image freshly extracted from a dream of the night before, but already so worn, so faded that it seemed to me to come from somewhere far more distant? Or had I indeed never seen them before, and did they conceal beneath their surface, like certain trees on tufts of grass that I had seen beside the Guermantes way, a meaning as obscure, as hard to grasp, as is a distant past, so that, whereas they were inviting me to probe a new thought, I imagined that I had to identify an old memory? Or again, were they concealing no hidden thought, and was it simply visual fatigue that made me see them double in time as one sometimes sees double in space? I could not tell. And meanwhile they were coming towards me; perhaps some fabulous apparition, a ring of witches or of Norns who would propound their oracles to me. I chose rather to believe that they were phantoms of the past, dear companions of my childhood, vanished friends who were invoking our common memories. Like ghosts they seemed to be appealing to me to take them with me, to bring them back to life. In their simple and passionate gesticulation I could discern the helpless anguish of a beloved person who has lost the power of speech, and feels that he will never be able to say to us what he wishes to say and we can never guess. Presently, at a cross-roads, the carriage left them. It was bearing me away from what alone I believed to be true, what would have made me truly happy; it was like my life.

I watched the trees gradually recede, waving their despairing arms, seeming to say to me: "What you fail to learn from us today, you will never know. If you allow us to drop back into the hollow of this road from which we sought to raise ourselves up to you, a whole part of yourself which we were bringing to you will vanish for ever into thin air." And indeed if, in the course of time, I did discover the kind of pleasure and disquiet which I had just felt once again, and if one evening—too late, but then for all time—I fastened myself to it, of those trees themselves I was never to know what they had been trying to give me nor where else I had seen them. And when, the road having forked and the carriage with it, I turned my back on them and ceased to see them, while Mme de Villeparisis asked me what I was dreaming about, I was as wretched as if I had just lost a friend, had died to myself, had broken faith with the dead or repudiated a god.

It was time to be thinking of home. Mme de Villeparisis, who had a certain feeling for nature, colder than that of my grandmother but capable of recognising, even outside museums and noblemen's houses, the simple and majestic beauty of certain old and venerable things, told her coachman to take us back by the old Balbec road, a road little used but planted with old elm-trees which we thought magnificent.

Once we had got to know this road, for a change we would return—unless we had taken it on the outward journey—by another which ran through the woods of Chantereine and Canteloup. The invisibility of the numberless birds that took up one another's song close beside us in the trees gave me the same sense of being at rest that one has when one shuts one's eyes. Chained to my flap-seat like Prometheus on his rock, I listened to my Oceanides. And whenever I caught a glimpse of one of those birds as it flitted from one leaf to another, there was so little apparent connexion between it and the songs I heard that I could not believe I was beholding their cause in that little body, fluttering, startled and blank.

This road was like many others of the same kind which are to be found in France, climbing on a fairly steep gradient and then gradually descending over a long stretch. At that particular moment, I found no great attraction in it; I was only glad to be going home. But it became for me later on a frequent source of joy by remaining in my memory as a lure to which all the similar roads that I was to take, on walks or drives or journeys, would at once attach themselves without breach of continuity and would be able, thanks to it, to communicate immediately with my heart. For as soon as the carriage or the motor-car turned into one of these roads that seemed to be the continuation of the road along which I had driven with Mme de Villeparisis, what I found my present consciousness immediately dwelling upon, as upon the most recent event in my past, would be (all the intervening years being quietly obliterated) the impressions that I had had on those bright summer afternoons and evenings, driving in the neighbourhood of Balbec, when the leaves smelt good, the mist was rising from the ground, and beyond the nearby village one could see through the trees the sun setting as though it had been some place further along the road, distant and forested, which we should not have time to reach that evening. Linked up with those I was experiencing now in another place, on a similar road, surrounded by all the incidental sensations of breathing fresh air, of curiosity, indolence, appetite, gaiety which were common to them both, and excluding all others, these impressions would be reinforced, would take on the consistency of a particular type of pleasure, and almost of a framework of existence which, as it happened, I rarely had the luck to come across, but in which these awakened memories introduced, amid the reality that my senses could perceive, a large enough element of evoked, dreamed, unseizable reality to give me, among these regions through which I was passing, more than an aesthetic feeling, a fleeting but exalted ambition to stay and live there for ever. How often since then, at a mere whiff of green leaves, has not being seated on a folding-seat opposite Mme de Villeparisis, meeting the Princesse de Luxembourg who waved a greeting to her from her own carriage, coming back to dinner at the Grand Hotel, appeared to me as one of those ineffable moments of happiness which neither the present nor the future can restore to us and which we taste only once in a lifetime!

Often dusk would have fallen before we reached the hotel. Shyly I would quote to Mme de Villeparisis, pointing to the moon in the sky, some memorable expression of Chateaubriand or Vigny or Victor Hugo: "She shed all around her that ancient secret of melancholy" or "Weeping like Diana by the brink of her streams" or "The shadows nuptial, solemn and august."

"And you think that good, do you?" she would ask, "inspired, as you call it. I must confess that I am always surprised to see people taking things seriously nowadays which the friends of those gentlemen, while giving them full credit for their qualities, were the first to laugh at. People weren't so free then with the word 'genius' as they are now, when if you say to a writer that he has talent he takes it as an insult. You quote me a fine phrase of M. de Chateaubriand's about moonlight. You shall see that I have my own reasons for being resistant to it. M. de Chateaubriand used often to come to see my father. He was quite a pleasant person when you were alone with him, because then he was simple and amusing, but the moment he had an audience he would begin to pose, and then he became absurd. Once, in my father's presence, he claimed that he had flung his resignation in the King's face, and that he had controlled the Conclave, forgetting that he had asked my father to beg the King to take him back, and that my father had heard him make the most idiotic forecasts of the Papal election. You ought to have heard M. de Blacas on that famous Conclave; he was a very different kind of man from M. de Chateaubriand. As for his fine phrases about the moon, they had quite simply become a family joke. Whenever the moon was shining, if there was anyone staying with us for the first time he would be told to take M. de Chateaubriand for a stroll after dinner. When they came in, my father would take his guest aside and say: 'Well, and was M. de Chateaubriand very eloquent?'—'Oh, yes.' 'He talked to you about the moonlight.'—'Yes, how did you know?'—'One moment, didn't he say—' and then my father would quote the phrase. 'He did; but how in the world . . .?'—'And he spoke to you of the moonlight on the Roman Campagna?'—'But, my dear sir, you're a magician.' My father was no magician, but M. de Chateaubriand had the same little speech about the moon which he served up every time."

At the mention of Vigny she laughed: "The man who said: 'I am the Comte Alfred de Vigny!' One is either a count or one isn't; it is not of the slightest importance."

And then perhaps she discovered that it was, after all, of some slight importance, for she went on: "For one thing I'm by no means sure that he was, and in any case he was of very inferior stock, that gentleman who speaks in his verses of his 'esquire's crest.' In such charming taste, is it not, and so interesting to his readers! Like Musset, a plain citizen of Paris, who laid so much stress on 'The golden falcon that surmounts my helm.' As if you would ever hear a real gentleman say a thing like that! At least Musset had some talent as a poet. But except for *Cinq-Mars*, I've never been able to read a thing by M. de Vigny. I get so bored that the book falls from my hands. M. Molé, who had all the wit and tact that were wanting in M. de Vigny, put him properly in his place when he welcomed him to the Academy. What, you don't know the speech? It's a masterpiece of irony and impertinence."

She found fault with Balzac, whom she was surprised to find her nephews admiring, for having presumed to describe a society "in which he was never received" and of which his descriptions were wildly improbable. As for Victor Hugo, she told us that M. de Bouillon, her father, who had friends among the young Romantics thanks to whom he had attended the first performance of *Hernani*, had been unable to sit through it, so ridiculous had he found the verse of that gifted but extravagant writer who had acquired the title of "major poet" only by virtue of having struck a bargain, and as a reward for the not disinterested indulgence that he showed towards the dangerous aberrations of the socialists.

We had now come in sight of the hotel, with its lights, so hostile that first evening on our arrival, now protective and kind, speaking to us of home. And when the carriage drew up outside the door, the porter, the bell-hops, the lift-boy, attentive, clumsy, vaguely uneasy at our lateness, massed on the steps to receive us, were numbered, now that they had grown familiar, among those beings who change so many times in the course of our lives, as we ourselves change, but in whom, when they are for the time being the mirror of our habits, we find comfort in the feeling that we are being faithfully and amicably reflected. We prefer them to friends whom we have not seen for some time, for they contain more of what we are at present. Only the outside page, exposed to the sun all day, had been taken indoors for protection from the cold night air and swaddled in thick woollen garments which, combined with the orange effulgence of his locks and the curiously red bloom of his cheeks, made one, seeing him there in the glassed-in hall, think of a hothouse plant muffled up for protection from the frost. We got out of the carriage with the help of a great many more servants than were required, but they were conscious of the importance of the scene and each felt obliged to take some part in it. I was always very hungry. And so, often, in order not to keep dinner waiting, I would not go upstairs to the room which had succeeded in becoming so really mine that to catch sight of its long violet curtains and low book-cases was to find myself alone again with that self of which things, like people, gave me a reflected image; and we would all wait together in the hall until the head waiter came to tell us that our dinner was ready. This gave us another opportunity of listening to Mme de Villeparisis.

"But you must be tired of us by now," my grandmother would protest.

"Not at all! Why, I'm delighted, what could be nicer?" replied her friend with a winning smile, drawing out, almost intoning her words in a way that contrasted markedly with her customary simplicity of speech.

And indeed at such moments as this she was not natural; her mind reverted to her early training, to the aristocratic manner in which a great lady is supposed to show commoners that she is glad to be with them, that she is not at all arrogant. And her one and only failure in true politeness lay in this excess of politeness— which it was easy to identify as the professional bent of a lady of the Faubourg Saint-Germain, who, always seeing in her humbler friends the latent discontent that she must one day arouse in their bosoms, greedily seizes every possible opportunity to estab- lish in advance, in the ledger in which she keeps her social account with them, a credit balance which will enable her presently to enter on the debit side the dinner or reception to which she will not invite them. And so, having long ago taken effect in her once and for all, and oblivious of the fact that now both the circum- stances and the people concerned were different, and that in Paris she would wish to see us often at her house, the spirit of her caste was urging Mme de Villeparisis on with feverish ardour, as if the time that was allowed her for being amiable to us was limited, to step up, while we were at Balbec, her gifts of roses and melons, loans of books, drives in her carriage and verbal effusions. And for that reason, quite as much as the dazzling splendour of the beach, the many-coloured flamboyance and subaqueous light of the rooms, as much even as the riding-lessons by which tradesmen's sons were deified like Alexander of Macedon, the daily kindnesses shown us by Mme de Villeparisis, and also the unaccustomed, momentary, holiday ease with which my grandmother accepted them, have remained in my memory as typical of life at the seaside.

"Give them your coats to take upstairs."

My grandmother handed them to the manager, and because he had been so nice to me I was distressed by this want of considera- tion, which seemed to pain him.

"I think you've hurt his feelings," said the Marquise. "He probably fancies himself too great a gentleman to carry your wraps. I remember the Duc de Nemours, when I was still quite little, coming to see my father who was living then on the top floor of the Hôtel Bouillon, with a fat parcel under his arm, and letters and newspapers. I can see the Prince now, in his blue coat, framed

in our doorway, which had such pretty panelling—I think it was
Bagard who used to do it—you know those fine laths that they
used to cut, so supple that the joiner would twist them sometimes
into little shells and flowers, like the ribbons round a nosegay.
'Here you are, Cyrus,' he said to my father, 'look what your
porter's given me to bring you. He said to me: Since you're
going up to see the Count, it's not worth my while climbing all
those stairs; but take care you don't break the string.'—Now that
you've got rid of your things, why don't you sit down," she said to
my grandmother, taking her by the hand. "Here, take this chair."

"Oh, if you don't mind, not that one! It's too small for two, and
too big for me by myself. I shouldn't feel comfortable."

"You remind me, for it was exactly like this one, of an armchair
I had for many years, until at last I couldn't keep it any longer,
because it had been given to my mother by the unfortunate
Duchesse de Praslin. My mother, though she was the simplest
person in the world, really, had ideas that belonged to another
generation, which even in those days I could scarcely understand;
and at first she had not been at all willing to let herself be introduced to Mme de Praslin, who had been plain Mlle Sebastiani,
while she, because she was a Duchess, felt that it was not for her to
be introduced to my mother. And really, you know," Mme de
Villeparisis went on, forgetting that she herself did not understand
these fine shades of distinction, "even if she had just been Mme de
Choiseul, there was a good deal to be said for her claim. The
Choiseuls are everything you could want; they spring from a sister
of Louis the Fat; they were real sovereigns down in Bassigny.
I admit that we beat them in marriages and in distinction, but
the seniority is pretty much the same. This little matter of precedence gave rise to several comic incidents, such as a luncheon-
party which was kept waiting a whole hour or more before one of
these ladies could make up her mind to let herself be introduced to
the other. In spite of which they became great friends, and she
gave my mother a chair like this one, in which people always
refused to sit, as you've just done, until one day my mother heard a
carriage drive into the courtyard. She asked a young servant who it
was. 'The Duchesse de La Rochefoucauld, ma'am.' 'Very well, say
that I am at home.' A quarter of an hour passed; no one came.
'What about the Duchesse de La Rochefoucauld?' my mother
asked, 'where is she?' 'She's on the stairs, ma'am, getting her
breath,' said the young servant, who had not been long up from

the country, where my mother had the excellent habit of getting all her servants. Often she had seen them born. That's the only way to get really good ones. And they're the rarest of luxuries. And sure enough the Duchesse de La Rochefoucauld had the greatest difficulty in getting upstairs, for she was an enormous woman, so enormous, indeed, that when she did come into the room my mother was quite at a loss for a moment to know where to put her. And then the seat that Mme de Praslin had given her caught her eye. 'Won't you sit down?' she said, bringing it forward. And the Duchess filled it from side to side. She was quite a pleasant woman, for all her . . . imposingness. 'She still creates a certain effect when she comes in,' one of our friends said once. 'She certainly creates an effect when she goes out,' said my mother, who was rather more free in her speech than would be thought proper nowadays. Even in Mme de La Rochefoucauld's own drawing-room people didn't hesitate to make fun of her to her face (and she was always the first to laugh at it) over her ample proportions. 'But are you all alone?' my mother once asked M. de La Rochefoucauld, when she had come to pay a call on the Duchess, and being met at the door by him had not seen his wife who was in an alcove at the other end of the room. 'Is Mme de La Rochefoucauld not at home? I don't see her.'—'How charming of you!' replied the Duke, who had about the worst judgment of any man I have ever known, but was not altogether lacking in humour."

After dinner, when I had gone upstairs with my grandmother, I said to her that the qualities which attracted us in Mme de Villeparisis, her tact, her shrewdness, her discretion, her self-effacement, were not perhaps of very great value since those who possessed them in the highest degree were merely people like Molé and Loménie, and that if the want of them can make everyday social relations disagreeable yet it did not prevent conceited fellows who had no judgment—whom it was easy to deride, like Bloch—from becoming Chateaubriand, Vigny, Hugo, Balzac . . . But at the name of Bloch, my grandmother expostulated. And she proceeded to sing the praises of Mme de Villeparisis. As we are told that it is the preservation of the species which guides our individual preferences in love and, so that the child may be constituted in the most normal fashion, sends fat men in pursuit of lean women and vice versa, so in some dim way it was the requirements of my happiness, threatened by my disordered nerves, by my morbid tendency to melancholy and solitude, that made her allot the highest place to the qualities of balance and judgment, peculiar not only to Mme de Villeparisis but to a society in which I might find distraction and assuagement—a society similar to the one in which our ancestors saw the minds of a Doudan, a M. de Rémusat flourish, not to mention a Beausergent, a Joubert, a Sévigné, a type of mind that invests life with more happiness, with greater dignity than the converse refinements which had led a Baudelaire, a Poe, a Verlaine, a Rimbaud to sufferings, to a disrepute such as my grandmother did not wish for her daughter's child. I interrupted her with a kiss and asked her if she had noticed such and such a remark Mme de Villeparisis had made which seemed to point to a woman who thought more of her noble birth than she was prepared to admit. In this way I used to submit my impressions of life to my grandmother, for I was never certain what degree of respect was due to anyone until she had pointed it out to me. Every evening I would come to her with the mental sketches that I had made during the day of all those non-existent people who were not her.

Once I said to her: "I couldn't live without you."

"But you mustn't speak like that," she replied in a troubled voice. "We must be a bit pluckier than that. Otherwise, what would become of you if I went away on a journey? But I hope that you would be quite sensible and quite happy."

"I could manage to be sensible if you went away for a few days, but I should count the hours."

"But if I were to go away for months . . . " (at the mere thought my heart turned over) " . . . for years . . . for . . . "

We both fell silent. We dared not look one another in the face. And yet I was suffering more keenly from her anguish than from my own. And so I walked across to the window and said to her distinctly, with averted eyes:

"You know what a creature of habit I am. For the first few days after I've been separated from the people I love best, I'm miserable. But though I go on loving them just as much, I get used to their absence, my life becomes calm and smooth. I could stand being parted from them for months, for years . . . "

I was obliged to stop speaking and look straight out of the window. My grandmother left the room for a moment. But next day I began to talk to her about philosophy, and, speaking in the most casual tone but at the same time taking care that my grandmother should pay attention to my words, I remarked what a curious thing it was that, according to the latest scientific discoveries, the materialist position appeared to be crumbling, and what was again most likely was the immortality of souls and their future reunion.

Mme de Villeparisis gave us warning that presently she would not be able to see so much of us. A young nephew who was preparing for Saumur, and was meanwhile stationed in the neighbourhood, at Doncières, was coming to spend a few weeks' leave with her, and she would be devoting most of her time to him. In the course of our drives together she had spoken highly of his intelligence and above all his kind-heartedness, and already I imagined that he would take a liking to me, that I should be his best friend; and when, before his arrival, his aunt gave my grandmother to understand that he had unfortunately fallen into the clutches of an appalling woman with whom he was infatuated and who would never let him go, since I was persuaded that that sort of love was doomed to end in mental derangement, crime and suicide, thinking how short a time was reserved for our friendship, already so great in my heart although I had not yet set eyes on him, I wept for that friendship and for the misfortunes that were in store for it, as we weep for someone we love when we learn that he is seriously ill and that his days are numbered.

One afternoon of scorching heat I was in the dining-room of the hotel, plunged in semi-darkness to shield it from the sun, which gilded the drawn curtains through the gaps between which twinkled the blue of the sea, when along the central gangway leading from the beach to the road I saw approaching, tall, slim, bare-necked, his head held proudly erect, a young man with penetrating eyes whose skin was as fair and his hair as golden as if they had absorbed all the rays of the sun. Dressed in a suit of soft, whitish material such as I could never have believed that any man would have the audacity to wear, the thinness of which suggested no less vividly than the coolness of the dining-room the heat and brightness of the glorious day outside, he was walking fast. His eyes, from one of which a monocle kept dropping, were the colour of the sea. Everyone looked at him with interest as he passed, knowing that this young Marquis de Saint-Loup-en-Bray was famed for his elegance. All the newspapers had described the suit in which he had recently acted as second to the young Duc d'Uzès in a duel. One felt that the distinctive quality of his hair, his eyes, his skin, his bearing, which would have marked him out in a crowd like a precious vein of opal, azure-shot and luminous, embedded in a mass of coarser substance, must correspond to a life different from that led by other men. So that when, before the attachment which Mme de Villeparisis had been deploring, the prettiest women in society had disputed the possession of him, his presence, at a watering-place for instance, in the company of the beauty of the season to whom he was paying court, not only brought her into the limelight, but attracted every eye fully as much to himself. Because of his "tone," because he had the insolent manner of a young "blood," above all because of his extraordinary good looks, some even thought him effeminate-looking, though without holding it against him since they knew how virile he was and how passionately fond of women. This was the nephew about whom Mme de Villeparisis had spoken to us. I was delighted at the thought that I was going to enjoy his company for some weeks, and confident that he would bestow on me all his affection. He strode rapidly across the whole width of the hotel, seeming to be in pursuit of his monocle, which kept darting away in front of him like a butterfly. He was coming from the beach, and the sea which filled the lower half of the glass front of the hall made a background against which he stood out full-length, as in certain portraits whose painters attempt, without in any way falsifying the most accurate observation of contemporary life, but by choosing for their sitter an appropriate setting—a polo ground, golf links, a race-course, the bridge of a yacht—to furnish a modern equivalent of those canvases on which the old masters used to present the human figure in the foreground of a landscape. A carriage and pair awaited him at the door; and, while his monocle resumed its gambollings on the sunlit road, with the elegance and mastery which a great pianist contrives to display in the simplest stroke of execution, where it did not seem possible that he could reveal his superiority to a performer of the second class, Mme de Villeparisis's nephew, taking the reins that were handed him by the coachman, sat down beside him and, while opening a letter which the manager of the hotel brought out to him, started up his horses.

How disappointed I was on the days that followed, when, each time that I met him outside or in the hotel—his head erect, perpetually balancing the movements of his limbs round the fugitive and dancing monocle which seemed to be their centre of gravity—I was forced to acknowledge that he had evidently no desire to make our acquaintance, and saw that he did not bow to us although he must have known that we were friends of his aunt. And calling to mind the friendliness that Mme de Villeparisis, and before her M. de Norpois, had shown me, I thought that perhaps they were only mock aristocrats and that there must be a secret article in the laws that govern the nobility which allowed women, perhaps, and certain diplomats to discard, in their relations with commoners, for a reason which was beyond me, the haughtiness which must, on the other hand, be pitilessly maintained by a young marquis. My intelligence might have told me the opposite. But the characteristic feature of the ridiculous age I was going through—awkward indeed but by no means infertile—is that we do not consult our intelligence and that the most trivial attributes of other people seem to us to form an inseparable part of their personality. In a world thronged with monsters and with gods, we know little peace of mind. There is hardly a single action we perform in that phase which we would not give anything, in later life, to be able to annul. Whereas what we ought to regret is that we no longer possess the spontaneity which made us perform them. In later life we look at things in a more practical way, in full conformity with the rest of society, but adolescence is the only period in which we learn anything.

This insolence which I surmised in M. de Saint-Loup, and all that it implied of innate hardness, received confirmation from his attitude whenever he passed us, his body as inflexibly erect as ever, his head held as high, his gaze as impassive, not to say as implacable, devoid of that vague respect which one has for the rights of other people, even if they do not know one's aunt, in accordance with which I did not behave in quite the same way towards an old lady as towards a gas-lamp. These frigid manners were as far removed from the charming letters which, only a few days before, I had still imagined him writing to me to express his regard as, from the enthusiasm of the Chamber and of the populace which he has pictured himself rousing by an imperishable speech, is the humble, dull, obscure position of the dreamer who, after rehearsing it thus by himself, for himself, aloud, finds himself, once the imaginary applause has died away, just the same Tom, Dick or Harry as before. When Mme de Villeparisis, doubtless in an attempt to counteract the bad impression that had been made on us by an exterior indicative of an arrogant and unfriendly nature, spoke to us again of the inexhaustible kindness of her great-nephew (he was

the son of one of her nieces, and a little older than myself),
I marvelled how the gentry, with an utter disregard of truth,
ascribe tenderness of heart to people whose hearts are in reality
so hard and dry, provided only that they behave with common
courtesy to the brilliant members of their own set. Mme de
Villeparisis herself confirmed, though indirectly, my diagnosis,
which was already a conviction, of the essential points of her
nephew's character one day when I met them both coming
along a path so narrow that she could not do otherwise than
introduce me to him. He seemed not to hear that a person's
name was being announced to him; not a muscle of his face
moved; his eyes, in which there shone not the faintest gleam of
human sympathy, showed merely, in the insensibility, in the
inanity of their gaze an exaggeration failing which there would
have been nothing to distinguish them from lifeless mirrors. Then,
fastening on me those hard eyes as though he wished to examine
me before returning my salute, with an abrupt gesture which
seemed to be due rather to a reflex action of his muscles than to
an exercise of will, keeping between himself and me the greatest
possible interval, he stretched his arm out to its full extension and,
at the end of it, offered me his hand. I supposed that it must mean,
at the very least, a duel when, next day, he sent me his card. But he
spoke to me when we met only of literature, and declared after a
long talk that he would like immensely to spend several hours with
me every day. He had not only, in this encounter, given proof of
an ardent zest for the things of the mind; he had shown a regard for
me which was little in keeping with his greeting of the day before.
After I had seen him repeat the same process every time someone
was introduced to him, I realised that it was simply a social usage
peculiar to his branch of the family, to which his mother, who had
seen to it that he should be perfectly brought up, had moulded his
limbs; he went through those motions without thinking about
them any more than he thought about his beautiful clothes or hair;
they were a thing devoid of the moral significance which I had at
first ascribed to them, a thing purely acquired, like that other habit
that he had of at once demanding an introduction to the family of
anyone he knew, which had become so instinctive in him that,
seeing me again the day after our meeting, he bore down on me
and without further ado asked to be introduced to my grandmother who was with me, with the same feverish haste as if the
request had been due to some instinct of self-preservation, like the

act of warding off a blow or of shutting one's eyes to avoid a stream of boiling water, without the protection of which it would have been dangerous to remain a moment longer.

The first rites of exorcism once performed, as a cantankerous fairy discards her preliminary guise and assumes all the most enchanting graces, I saw this disdainful creature become the most friendly, the most considerate young man that I had ever met. "Right," I said to myself, "I've been mistaken about him once already. I was the victim of a mirage. But I've got over the first only to fall for a second, for he must be a dyed-in-the-wool grandee who's trying to hide it." As a matter of fact it was not long before all the exquisite breeding, all the friendliness of Saint-Loup were indeed to let me see another person, but one very different from what I had suspected.

This young man who had the air of a disdainful aristocrat and sportsman had in fact no respect or curiosity except for the things of the mind, and especially those modern manifestations of literature and art which seemed so ridiculous to his aunt; he was imbued, moreover, with what she called "socialistic spoutings," was filled with the most profound contempt for his caste, and spent long hours in the study of Nietzsche and Proudhon. He was one of those "intellectuals" easily moved to admiration, who shut themselves up in a book and are interested only in the higher thought. Indeed in Saint-Loup the expression of this highly abstract tendency, which removed him so far from my customary preoccupations, while it seemed to me touching, also annoyed me a little. I may say that when I fully realised who his father had been, on days when I had been reading memoirs rich in anecdotes of that famous Comte de Marsantes in whom were embodied the special graces of a generation already remote, my mind full of speculations, and anxious to obtain fuller details of the life that M. de Marsantes had led, I was infuriated that Robert de Saint-Loup, instead of being content to be the son of his father, instead of being able to guide me through the old-fashioned romance which his father's existence had been, had raised himself to a passion for Nietzsche and Proudhon. His father would not have shared my regret. He had been himself a man of intelligence, who had transcended the narrow confines of his life as a man of the world. He had hardly had time to know his son, but had hoped that he would prove a better man than himself. And I dare say that, unlike the rest of the family, he would have admired his son, would have rejoiced at his abandoning what had been his own small diversions for austere meditations, and without saying a word, in his modesty as a nobleman of wit, would have read in secret his son's favourite authors in order to appreciate how far Robert was superior to himself.

There was, however, this rather painful consideration: that if M. de Marsantes, with his extremely open mind, would have appreciated a son so different from himself, Robert de Saint-Loup, because he was one of those people who believe that merit is attached only to certain forms of art and of life, had an affectionate but slightly contemptuous memory of a father who had spent all his time hunting and racing, who yawned at Wagner and raved over Offenbach. Saint-Loup was not intelligent enough to understand that intellectual worth has nothing to do with adhesion to any one aesthetic formula, and regarded the "intellect-uality" of M. de Marsantes with much the same sort of scorn as might have been felt for Boieldieu or Labiche by sons of Boieldieu or Labiche who had become adherents of the most extreme symbolist literature and the most complicated music. "I scarcely knew my father," he used to say. "He seems to have been a charming man. His tragedy was the deplorable age in which he lived. To have been born in the Faubourg Saint-Germain and to have to live in the days of *La Belle Hélène* would be enough to wreck any existence. Perhaps if he'd been some little shop-keeper mad about the *Ring* he'd have turned out quite different. Indeed they tell me that he was fond of literature. But it's impossible to know, because literature to him meant only the most antiquated stuff." And in my own case, if I found Saint-Loup a trifle earnest, he could not understand why I was not more earnest still. Never judging anything except by its intellectual weightiness, never perceiving the magic appeal to the imagination that I found in things which he condemned as frivolous, he was astonished that I—to whom he imagined himself to be so utterly inferior—could take any interest in them.

From the first Saint-Loup made a conquest of my grandmother, not only by the incessant kindness which he went out of his way to show to us both, but by the naturalness which he put into it as into everything else. For naturalness—doubtless because through the artifice of man it allows a feeling of nature to permeate—was the quality which my grandmother preferred to all others, whether in gardens, where she did not like there to be, as in our Combray garden, too formal flower-beds, or in cooking, where she detested those dressed-up dishes in which you can hardly detect the food-stuffs that have gone to make them, or in piano-playing, which she did not like to be too finicking, too polished, having indeed had a special weakness for the discords, the wrong notes of Rubinstein. This naturalness she found and appreciated even in the clothes that Saint-Loup wore, of a loose elegance, with nothing "swagger" or "dressed-up" about them, no stiffness or starch. She appreciated this rich young man still more highly for the free and careless way that he had of living in luxury without "smelling of money," without giving himself airs; she even discovered the charm of this naturalness in the incapacity which Saint-Loup had kept—though as a rule it is outgrown with childhood, at the same time as certain physiological peculiarities of that age—for preventing his face from at once reflecting every emotion. Something, for instance, that he wanted to have but had not expected, if only a compliment, induced in him a pleasure so quick, so glowing, so volatile, so expansive that it was impossible for him to contain and to conceal it; a grin of delight seized irresistible hold of his face, the too delicate skin of his cheeks allowed a bright red glow to shine through them, his eyes sparkled with confusion and joy; and my grandmother was infinitely touched by this charming show of innocence and frankness, which indeed in Saint-Loup—at any rate at the time of our first friendship—was not misleading. But I have known another person, and there are many such, in whom the physiological sincerity of that fleeting blush in no way excluded moral duplicity; as often as not it proves nothing more than the intensity with which pleasure may be felt—to the extent of disarming them and forcing them publicly to confess it—by natures capable of the vilest treachery. But where my grandmother especially adored Saint-Loup's naturalness was in his way of con-fessing without the slightest reservation his affection for me, to give expression to which he found words than which she herself, she told me, could not have thought of any more appropriate, more truly loving, words to which "Sévigné and Beausergent" might have set their signatures. He was not afraid to make fun of my weaknesses—which he had discerned with a shrewdness that made her smile—but as she herself would have done, affection-ately, at the same time extolling my good qualities with a warmth, an impulsive freedom that showed no sign of the reserve, the coldness by means of which young men of his age are apt to suppose that they give themselves importance. And he evinced, in anticipating my every discomfort, however slight, in covering my legs if the day had turned cold without my noticing it, in arranging (without telling me) to stay later with me in the evening if he thought I was sad or gloomy, a vigilance which, from the point of view of my health, for which a more hardening discipline would perhaps have been better, my grandmother found almost excess- ive, though as a proof of his affection for me she was deeply touched by it.

It was promptly settled between us that he and I were to be great friends for ever, and he would say "our friendship" as though he were speaking of some important and delightful thing which had an existence independent of ourselves, and which he soon called—apart from his love for his mistress—the great joy of his life. These words filled me with a sort of melancholy and I was at a loss for an answer, for I felt when I was with him, when I was talking to him—and no doubt it would have been the same with anyone else—none of that happiness which it was possible for me to experience when I was by myself. Alone, at times, I felt surging from the depths of my being one or other of those impressions which gave me a delicious sense of well-being. But as soon as I was with someone else, as soon as I was talking to a friend, my mind as it were faced about, it was towards this interlocutor and not towards myself that it directed its thoughts, and when they fol- lowed this outward course they brought me no pleasure. Once I had left Saint-Loup, I managed, with the help of words, to put some sort of order into the confused minutes that I had spent with him; I told myself that I had a good friend, that a good friend was a rare thing, and I savoured, when I felt myself surrounded by assets that were difficult to acquire, what was precisely the opposite of the pleasure that was natural to me, the opposite of the pleasure of having extracted from myself and brought to light something that was hidden in my inner darkness. If I had spent two or three hours in conversation with Saint-Loup and he had expressed his admira- tion of what I had said to him, I felt a sort of remorse, or regret, or weariness at not having remained alone and settled down to work at last. But I told myself that one is not intelligent for oneself alone, that the greatest of men have wanted to be appreciated, that hours in which I had built up a lofty idea of myself in my friend's mind could not be considered wasted. I had no difficulty in persuading myself that I ought to be happy in consequence, and I hoped all the more keenly that this happiness might never be taken from me because I had not actually felt it. We fear more than the loss of anything else the disappearance of possessions that have remained outside ourselves, because our hearts have not taken possession of them. I felt that I was capable of exemplifying the virtues of friendship better than most people (because I should always place the good of my friends before those personal interests to which other people are devoted but which did not count for me), but not of finding happiness in a feeling which, instead of increasing the differences that there were between my nature and those of other people—as there are between all of us—would eliminate them. On the other hand there were moments when my mind distinguished in Saint-Loup a personality more generalised than his own, that of the "nobleman," which like an indwelling spirit moved his limbs, ordered his gestures and his actions; then, at such moments, although in his company, I was alone, as I should have been in front of a landscape the harmony of which I could understand. He was no more then than an object the properties of which, in my musings, I sought to explore. The discovery in him of this pre-existent, this immemorial being, this aristocrat who was precisely what Robert aspired not to be, gave me intense joy, but a joy of the mind rather than the feelings. In the moral and physical agility which gave so much grace to his kindnesses, in the ease with which he offered my grandmother his carriage and helped her into it, in the alacrity with which he sprang from the box when he was afraid that I might be cold, to spread his own cloak over my shoulders, I sensed not only the inherited litheness of the mighty hunters who had been for generations the ancestors of this young man who had no pretensions except to intellectuality, their scorn of wealth which, subsisting in him side by side with his enjoyment of it simply because it enabled him to entertain his friends more lavishly, made him so carelessly shower his riches at their feet; I sensed in it above all the certainty or the illusion in the minds of those great lords of being "better than other people," thanks to which they had not been able to hand down to Saint-Loup that anxiety to show that one is "just as good as the next man," that dread of seeming too assiduous of which he was indeed wholly innocent and which mars with so much stiffness and awkwardness the most sincere plebeian civility. Sometimes I reproached myself for thus taking pleasure in considering my friend as a work of art, that is to say in regarding the play of all the parts of his being as harmoniously ordered by a general idea from which they depended but of which he was unaware and which consequently added nothing to his own qualities, to that personal value, intellectual and moral, which he prized so highly.

And yet that idea was to a certain extent their determining cause. It was because he was a gentleman that that mental activity, those socialist aspirations, which made him seek the company of arrogant and ill-dressed young students, connoted in him something really pure and disinterested which was not to be found in them. Looking upon himself as the heir of an ignorant and selfish caste, he was sincerely anxious that they should forgive in him that aristocratic origin which they, on the contrary, found irresistibly attractive and on account of which they sought his acquaintance while simulating coldness and indeed insolence towards him. He was thus led to make advances to people from whom my parents, faithful to the sociological theories of Combray, would have been stupefied at his not turning away in disgust. One day when we were sitting on the sands, Saint-Loup and I, we heard issuing from a canvas tent against which we were leaning a torrent of imprecation against the swarm of Jews that infested Balbec. "You can't go a yard without meeting them," said the voice. "I am not in principle irremediably hostile to the Jewish race, but here there is a plethora of them. You hear nothing but, 'I thay, Apraham, I've chust theen Chacop.' You would think you were in the Rue d'Aboukir." The man who thus inveighed against Israel emerged at last from the tent, and we raised our eyes to behold this anti-semite. It was my old friend Bloch. Saint-Loup at once asked me to remind him that they had met each other at the *concours général*, when Bloch had carried off the prize of honour, and since then at a people's university course.[3]

At the most I may have smiled now and then, to discover in Robert the marks of his Jesuit schooling in the embarrassment which the fear of hurting people's feelings at once provoked in him whenever one of his intellectual friends made a social error or did something silly to which Saint-Loup himself attached no importance but felt that the other would have blushed if anybody had noticed it. And it was Robert who used to blush as though he were the guilty party, for instance on the day when Bloch, after promising to come and see him at the hotel, went on: "As I cannot endure to be kept waiting among all the false splendour of these great caravanserais, and the Hungarian band would make me ill, you must tell the 'lighft-boy' to make them shut up, and to let you know at once."

Personally, I was not particularly anxious that Bloch should come to the hotel. He was at Balbec, not by himself, unfortunately, but with his sisters, and they in turn had innumerable relatives and friends staying there. Now this Jewish colony was more picturesque than pleasing. Balbec was in this respect like such countries as Russia or Romania, where the geography books teach us that the Jewish population does not enjoy the same esteem and has not reached the same stage of assimilation as, for instance, in Paris. Always together, with no admixture of any other element, when the cousins and uncles of Bloch or their co-religionists male or female repaired to the Casino, the ladies to dance, the gentlemen branching off towards the baccarat-tables, they formed a solid troop, homogeneous within itself, and utterly dissimilar to the people who watched them go by and found them there again every year without ever exchanging a word or a greeting, whether these were the Cambremer set, or the senior judge's little group, professional or "business" people, or even simple corn-chandlers from Paris, whose daughters, handsome, proud, mocking and French as the statues at Rheims, would not care to mix with that horde of ill-bred sluts who carried their zeal for "seaside fashions" so far as to be always apparently on their way home from shrimping or out to dance the tango. As for the men, despite the brilliance of their dinner-jackets and patent-leather shoes, the exaggeration of their type made one think of the so-called "bright ideas" of those painters who, having to illustrate the Gospels or the Arabian Nights, consider the country in which the scenes are laid, and give to St Peter or to Ali Baba the identical features of the heaviest "punter" at the Balbec tables. Bloch introduced his sisters, who, though he silenced their chatter with the utmost rudeness, screamed with laughter at the mildest sallies of this brother who was their blindly worshipped idol. Although it is probable that this set of people contained, like every other, perhaps more than any other, plenty of attractions, qualities and virtues, in order to experience these one would first have had to penetrate it. But it was not popular, it sensed this, and saw there the mark of an anti-semitism to which it presented a bold front in a compact and closed phalanx into which, as it happened, no one dreamed of trying to force his way.

As regards the word "lighft," I had all the less reason to be surprised at Bloch's pronunciation in that, a few days before, when he had asked me why I had come to Balbec (although it seemed to him perfectly natural that he himself should be there) and whether it had been "in the hope of making grand friends," and I had explained to him that this visit was a fulfilment of one of my earliest longings, though one not so deep as my longing to see Venice, he had replied: "Yes, of course, to sip iced drinks with the pretty ladies, while pretending to read the *Stones of Venighce* by Lord John Ruskin, a dreary bore, in fact one of the most tedious old prosers you could find." Thus Bloch evidently thought that in England not only were all the inhabitants of the male sex called "Lord," but the letter "i" was invariably pronounced "igh." As for Saint-Loup, this mistake in pronunciation seemed to him all the more venial inasmuch as he saw in it pre-eminently a want of those almost "society" notions which my new friend despised as fully as he was versed in them. But the fear lest Bloch, discovering one day that one says "Venice" and that Ruskin was not a lord, should retrospectively imagine that Robert had thought him ridiculous, made the latter feel as guilty as if he had been found wanting in the indulgence with which, as we have seen, he overflowed, so that the blush which would doubtless one day dye the cheek of Bloch on the discovery of his error, Robert already, by anticipation and reversibility, could feel mounting to his own. For he assumed that Bloch attached more importance than he to this mistake—an assumption which Bloch confirmed some days later, when he heard me pronounce the word "lift," by breaking in with: "Oh, one says 'lift,' does one?" And then, in a dry and lofty tone: "Not that it's of the slightest importance." A phrase that is like a reflex action, the same in all proud and susceptible men, in the gravest circumstances as well as in the most trivial, betraying there as clearly as on this occasion how important the thing in question seems to him who declares that it is of no importance; a tragic phrase at times, the first to escape (and then how heart-breakingly) the lips of any man who is at all proud from whom we have just removed the last hope to which he still clung by refusing to do him a service: "Oh, well, it's not of the slightest importance; I shall make some other arrangement": the other arrangement which it is not of the slightest importance that he should be driven to adopt being sometimes suicide.

Thereupon Bloch made me the prettiest speeches. He was certainly anxious to be on the best of terms with me. And yet he asked me: "Is it because you've taken a fancy to the minor aristocracy that you run after de Saint-Loup-en-Bray? You must be suffering from a severe attack of snobbery. Tell me, are you a snob? I think so, what?" Not that his desire to be friendly had suddenly changed. But what is called in not too correct language "ill breeding" was his defect, therefore the defect which he was bound to overlook, and *a fortiori* the defect by which he did not believe that other people could be shocked.

In the human race, the frequency of the virtues that are identical in us all is not more wonderful than the multiplicity of the defects that are peculiar to each one of us. Undoubtedly, it is not common sense that is "the commonest thing in the world"; it is human kindness. In the most distant, the most desolate corners of the earth, we marvel to see it blossom of its own accord, as in a remote valley a poppy like all the poppies in the rest of the world, which it has never seen as it has never known anything but the wind that occasionally stirs the folds of its lonely scarlet cloak. Even if this human kindness, paralysed by self-interest, is not put into practice, it exists none the less, and whenever there is no selfish motive to restrain it, for example when reading a novel or a newspaper, it will blossom, even in the heart of one who, cold-blooded in real life, has retained a tender heart as a lover of serial romances, and turn towards the weak, the just and the persecuted. But the variety of our defects is no less remarkable than the similarity of our virtues. The most perfect person in the world has a certain defect which shocks us or makes us angry. One man is of rare intelligence, sees everything from the loftiest viewpoint, never speaks ill of anyone, but will pocket and forget letters of supreme importance which he himself asked you to let him post for you, and so make you miss a vital engagement without offering you any excuse, with a smile, because he prides himself upon never knowing the time. Another is so refined, so gentle, so delicate in his conduct that he never says anything to you about yourself that you would not be glad to hear, but you feel that he suppresses, that he keeps buried in his heart, where they turn sour, other, quite different opinions, and the pleasure that he derives from seeing you is so dear to him that he will let you faint with exhaustion sooner than leave you to yourself. A third has more sincerity, but carries it so far that he feels bound to let you know, when you have pleaded the state of your health as an excuse for not having been to see him, that you were seen going to the theatre and were reported to be looking well, or else that he has not been able to turn to full advantage the step you took on his behalf, which in any case three other people had already offered to take, so that he is only moderately indebted to you. In similar circumstances the previous friend would have pretended not to know that you had gone to the theatre, or that other people could have done him the same service. But this last friend feels himself obliged to repeat or to reveal to somebody the very thing that is most likely to give offence; is delighted with his own frankness and tells you, emphatically: "I am like that." While others infuriate you by their exaggerated curiosity, or by a want of curiosity so absolute that you can speak to them of the most sensational happenings without their knowing what it is all about; and others again take months to answer you if your letter has been about something that concerns yourself and not them, or else, if they write that they are coming to ask you for something and you dare not leave the house for fear of missing them, do not appear, but leave you in suspense for weeks because, not having received from you the answer which their letter did not in the least call for, they have concluded that you must be cross with them. And others, considering their own wishes and not yours, talk to you without letting you get a word in if they are in good spirits and want to see you, however urgent the work you may have in hand, but if they feel exhausted by the weather or out of humour, you cannot drag a word out of them, they greet your efforts with an inert languor and no more take the trouble to reply, even in monosyllables, to what you say to them than if they had not heard you. Each of our friends has his defects, to such an extent that to continue to love him we are obliged to console ourselves for them—by thinking of his talent, his kindness, his affection—or rather by ignoring them, for which we need to deploy all our good will. Unfortunately our obliging obstinacy in refusing to see the defect in our friend is surpassed by the obstinacy with which he persists in that defect, from his own blindness to it or the blindness that he attributes to other people. For he does not notice it himself or imagines that it is not noticed. Since the risk of giving offence arises principally from the difficulty of appreciating what does and what does not pass unnoticed, we ought at least, from prudence, never to speak of ourselves, because that is a subject on which we may be sure that other people's views are never in accordance with our own. If, when we discover the true lives of other people, the real world beneath the world of appearance, we get as many surprises as on visiting a house of plain exterior which inside is full of hidden treasures, torture-chambers or skeletons, we are no less surprised if, in place of the image that we have of ourselves as a result of all the things that people have said to us, we learn from the way they speak of us in our absence what an entirely different image they have been carrying in their minds of us and of our lives. So that whenever we have spoken about ourselves, we may be sure that our inoffensive and prudent words, listened to with apparent politeness and hypocritical approbation, have given rise afterwards to the most exasperated or the most mirthful, but in either case the least favourable comments. At the very least we run the risk of irritating people by the disproportion between our idea of ourselves and the words that we use, a disproportion which as a rule makes people's talk about themselves as ludicrous as the performances of those self-styled music-lovers who when they feel the need to hum a favourite tune compensate for the inadequacy of their inarticulate murmurings by a strenuous mimicry and an air of admiration which is hardly justified by what they let us hear. And to the bad habit of speaking about oneself and one's defects there must be added, as part of the same thing, that habit of denouncing in other people defects precisely analogous to one's own. For it is always of those defects that one speaks, as though it were a way of speaking of oneself indirectly, and adding to the pleasure of absolving oneself the pleasure of confession. Moreover it seems that our attention, always attracted by what is characteristic of ourselves, notices it more than anything else in other people. One short-sighted man says of another: "But he can scarcely open his eyes!"; a consumptive has his doubts as to the pulmonary integrity of the most robust; an unwashed man speaks only of the baths that other people do not take; an evil-smelling man insists that other people smell; a cuckold sees cuckolds everywhere, a light woman light women, a snob snobs. Then, too, every vice, like every profession, requires and develops a special knowledge which we are never loath to display. The invert sniffs out inverts; the tailor asked out to dine has hardly begun to talk to you before he has already appraised the cloth of your coat, which his fingers are itching to feel; and if after a few words of conversation you were to ask a dentist what he really thought of you, he would tell you how many of your teeth wanted filling. To him nothing appears more important, or to you, who have noticed his, more absurd. And it is not only when we speak of ourselves that we imagine other people to be blind; we behave as though they were. Each one of us has a special god in attendance who hides from him or promises him the concealment of his defect from other people, just as he closes the eyes and nostrils of people who do not wash to the streaks of dirt which they carry in their ears and the smell of sweat that emanates from their armpits, and assures them that they can with impunity carry both of these about a world that will notice nothing. And those who wear artificial pearls, or give them as presents, imagine that people will take them to be genuine.

Bloch was ill-bred, neurotic and snobbish, and since he belonged to a family of little repute, had to support, as on the floor of the ocean, the incalculable pressures imposed on him not only by the Christians at the surface but by all the intervening layers of Jewish castes superior to his own, each of them crushing with its contempt the one that was immediately beneath it. To pierce his way through to the open air by raising himself from Jewish family to Jewish family would have taken Bloch many thousands of years. It was better to seek an outlet in another direction.

When Bloch spoke to me of the attack of snobbery from which I must be suffering, and bade me confess that I was a snob, I might well have replied: "If I were, I shouldn't be going about with you." I said merely that he was not being very polite. Then he wanted to apologise, but in the way that is typical of the ill-bred man who is only too happy, in retracting his words, to find an opportunity to aggravate his offence. "Forgive me," he would now say to me whenever we met, "I've distressed you, tormented you, I've been wantonly mischievous. And yet—man in general and your friend in particular is so singular an animal—you cannot imagine the affection that I, I who tease you so cruelly, have for you. It brings me often, when I think of you, to the verge of tears." And he gave an audible sob.

What astonished me more in Bloch than his bad manners was to find how the quality of his conversation varied. This youth, so hard to please that of authors who were at the height of their fame he would say: "He's a dismal fool; he's a sheer imbecile," would every now and then recount with immense gusto anecdotes that were simply not funny or would instance as a "really remarkable person" someone who was completely insignificant. This double scale of measuring the wit, the worth, the interest of people continued to puzzle me until I was introduced to M. Bloch, senior.

I had not supposed that we should ever be allowed to meet him, for Bloch junior had spoken ill of me to Saint-Loup and of Saint-Loup to me. In particular, he had said to Robert that I was (still) a frightful snob. "Yes, really, he's thrilled to know M. LLLLegrandin." This trick of Bloch's of isolating a word was a sign at once of irony and literature. Saint-Loup, who had never heard the name Legrandin, was bewildered: "But who is he?" "Oh, he's a *very distinguished* person," Bloch replied with a laugh, thrusting his hands into his pockets as though for warmth, convinced that he was at that moment engaged in contemplation of the picturesque aspect of an extraordinary country gentleman compared to whom those of Barbey d'Aurevilly were as nothing. He consoled himself for his inability to portray M. Legrandin by giving him a string of capital L's and smacking his lips over the name as over a wine of the finest vintage. But these subjective enjoyments remained hidden from other people. If he spoke ill of me to Saint-Loup he made up for it by speaking no less ill of Saint-Loup to me. We had each of us learned these slanders in detail the very next day, not that we had repeated them to each other, a thing which would have seemed to us very wrong but to Bloch appeared so natural and almost inevitable that in his natural anxiety, in the certainty moreover that he would be telling us only what each of us was bound sooner or later to learn, he preferred to anticipate the disclosure and, taking Saint-Loup aside, admitted that he had spoken ill of him, on purpose, so that it might be repeated to him, swore to him "by Zeus Kronion, binder of oaths" that he loved him dearly, that he would lay down his life for him, and wiped away a tear. The same day, he contrived to see me alone, made his confession, declared that he had acted in my interest, because he felt that a certain kind of social intercourse was fatal to me and that I was "worthy of better things." Then, clasping me by the hand with the sentimentality of a drunkard, although his drunkenness was purely nervous: "Believe me," he said, "and may the black Ker seize me this instant and bear me across the portals of Hades, hateful to men, if yesterday, when I thought of you, of Combray, of my boundless affection for you, of afternoon hours in class which you do not even remember, I did not lie awake sobbing all night long. Yes, all night long, I swear it, and alas, I know—for I know the human soul—you will not believe me." I did indeed "not believe" him, and to these words which I felt he was making up on the spur of the moment and developing as he went on, his swearing "by Ker" added no great weight, the Hellenic cult being in Bloch purely literary. Besides, whenever he began to get emotional over a falsehood and wanted one to share his emotion, he would say "I swear it," more for the hysterical pleasure of lying than to make one think that he was speaking the truth. I did not believe what he was saying, but I bore him no ill-will on that account, for I had inherited from my mother and grandmother their incapacity for rancour even against far worse offenders, and their habit of never condemning anyone.

Besides, Bloch was not altogether a bad fellow: he was capable of being extremely nice. And now that the race of Combray, the race from which sprang creatures as absolutely unspoiled as my grandmother and my mother, seems almost extinct, since I no longer have much choice except between decent brutes, frank and insensitive, the mere sound of whose voices shows at once that they take absolutely no interest in your life—and another kind of men who so long as they are with you understand you, cherish you, grow sentimental to the point of tears, then make up for it a few hours later with some cruel joke at your expense, but come back to you, always just as understanding, as charming, as in tune with you for the moment, I think that it is of this latter sort that I prefer, if not the moral worth, at any rate the society.

"You cannot imagine my grief when I think of you," Bloch went on. "Actually, I suppose it's a rather Jewish side of my nature coming out," he added ironically, contracting his pupils as though measuring out under the microscope an infinitesimal quantity of "Jewish blood," as a French nobleman might (but never would) have said who among his exclusively Christian ancestry nevertheless numbered Samuel Bernard, or further back still, the Blessed Virgin from whom, it is said, the Lévy family claim descent. "I rather like," he continued, "to take into account the element in my feelings (slight though it is) which may be ascribed to my Jewish origin." He made this statement because it seemed to him at once clever and courageous to speak the truth about his race, a truth which at the same time he managed to water down to a remarkable extent, like misers who decide to discharge their debts but cannot bring themselves to pay more than half of them. This

kind of deceit which consists in having the boldness to proclaim
the truth, but only after mixing with it an ample measure of lies
which falsify it, is commoner than people think, and even among
those who do not habitually practise it certain crises in life,
especially those in which a love affair is involved, give them
occasion to indulge in it.

All these confidential diatribes by Bloch to Saint-Loup against
me and to me against Saint-Loup ended in an invitation to dinner.
I am by no means sure that he did not first make an attempt to
secure Saint-Loup by himself. It would have been so like Bloch to
do so that probably he did; but if so, success did not crown his
effort, for it was to myself and Saint-Loup both that he said one
day: "Dear master, and you, O horseman beloved of Ares, de
Saint-Loup-en-Bray, tamer of horses, since I have encountered
you by the shore of Amphitrite, resounding with foam, hard by
the tents of the swift-shipped Meniers, will both of you come to
dinner one day this week with my illustrious sire, of blameless
heart?" He proffered this invitation because he desired to attach
himself more closely to Saint-Loup who would, he hoped, secure
him the right of entry into aristocratic circles. Formed by me, for
myself, this ambition would have seemed to Bloch the mark of the
most hideous snobbery, quite in keeping with the opinion that he
already held of a whole side of my nature which he did not
regard—or at least had not hitherto regarded—as the most important side; but the same ambition in himself seemed to him the proof
of a finely developed curiosity in a mind anxious to carry out
certain social explorations from which he might perhaps glean
some literary benefit. M. Bloch senior, when his son had told him
that he was going to bring one of his friends in to dinner, and had
in a sarcastic but self-satisfied tone enunciated the name and title of
that friend: "The Marquis de Saint-Loup-en-Bray," had been
thrown into great commotion. "The Marquis de Saint-Loup-
en-Bray! I'll be jiggered!" he had exclaimed, using the oath
which was with him the strongest indication of social deference.
And he gazed at a son capable of having formed such an acquaintance with an admiring look which seemed to say: "He really is
astounding. Can this prodigy be indeed a child of mine!" which
gave my friend as much pleasure as if his monthly allowance had
been increased by fifty francs. For Bloch was not in his element at
home and felt that his father treated him like a black sheep because
of his inveterate admiration for Leconte de Lisle, Heredia and

other "Bohemians." But to have got to know Saint-Loup-en-Bray, whose father had been chairman of the Suez Canal board ("I'll be jiggered!") was an indisputable "score." What a pity that they had left the stereoscope in Paris for fear of its being broken on the journey. M. Bloch senior alone had the skill, or at least the right, to manipulate it. He did so, moreover, on rare occasions only, and then to good purpose, on evenings when there was a full-dress affair, with hired waiters. So that from these stereoscope sessions there emanated, for those who were present, as it were a special distinction, a privileged position, and for the master of the house who gave them, a prestige such as talent confers on a man—which could not have been greater had the pictures been taken by M. Bloch himself and the machine his own invention. "You weren't invited to Solomon's yesterday?" one of the family would ask another. "No! I wasn't one of the elect. What was on?" "Oh, a great how-d'ye-do, the stereoscope, the whole box of tricks!" "Indeed! If they had the stereoscope I'm sorry I wasn't there; they say Solomon is quite amazing when he works it."

"Ah, well," said M. Bloch now to his son, "it's a mistake to let him have everything at once. Now he'll have something else to look forward to."

He had actually thought, in his paternal affection and in the hope of touching his son's heart, of sending for the instrument. But it was not "physically possible" in the time, or rather they had thought it would not be; for we were obliged to put off the dinner because Saint-Loup could not leave the hotel, where he was expecting an uncle who was coming to spend a few days with Mme de Villeparisis. Since he was greatly addicted to physical culture, and especially to long walks, it was largely on foot, spending the night in wayside farms, that this uncle was to make the journey from the country house in which he was staying, and the precise moment of his arrival at Balbec was somewhat uncertain. Indeed Saint-Loup, afraid to stir out of doors, even entrusted me with the duty of taking to Incarville, where the nearest tele-graph-office was, the messages that he sent every day to his mistress. The uncle in question was called Palamède, a Christian name that had come down to him from his ancestors the Princes of Sicily. And later on, when I found, in the course of my historical reading, belonging to this or that Podestà or Prince of the Church, the same Christian name, a fine Renaissance medal—some said a genuine antique—that had always remained in the family, having passed from generation to generation, from the Vatican cabinet to the uncle of my friend, I felt the pleasure that is reserved for those who, unable from lack of means to start a medal collection or a picture gallery, look out for old names (names of localities, instructive and picturesque as an old map, a bird's-eye view, a sign-board or an inventory of customs; baptismal names whose fine French endings echo the defect of speech, the intonation of an ethnic vulgarity, the corrupt pronunciation whereby our ancestors made Latin and Saxon words undergo lasting mutilations which in due course became the august law-givers of our grammar books) and, in short, by drawing upon these collections of ancient sonorities, give themselves concerts like the people who acquire violas da gamba and violas d'amore to perform the music of the past on old instruments. Saint-Loup told me that even in the most exclusive aristocratic society his uncle Palamède stood out as being particularly unapproachable, scornful, obsessed with his nobility, forming with his brother's wife and a few other chosen spirits what was known as the Phoenix Club. Even there his insolence was so dreaded that it had happened more than once that society people who had been anxious to meet him and had applied to his own brother for an introduction had met with a refusal: "Really, you mustn't ask me to introduce you to my brother Palamède. Even if my wife and the whole lot of us put ourselves to the task it would be no good. Or else you'd run the risk of his being rude to you, and I shouldn't like that." At the Jockey Club he had, with a few of his friends, marked a list of two hundred members whom they would never allow to be introduced to them. And in the Comte de Paris's circle he was known by the nickname of "The Prince" because of his elegance and his pride.

Saint-Loup told me about his uncle's early life, now long since past. Every day he used to take women to a bachelor establishment which he shared with two of his friends, as good-looking as himself, on account of which they were known as "the three Graces."

"One day, a man who is now one of the brightest luminaries of the Faubourg Saint-Germain, as Balzac would have said, but who at a rather unfortunate stage of his early life displayed bizarre tastes, asked my uncle to let him come to this place. But no sooner had he arrived than it was not to the ladies but to my uncle Palamède that he began to make overtures. My uncle pretended not to understand, and took his two friends aside on some pretext or other.

They reappeared on the scene, seized the offender, stripped him, thrashed him till he bled, and then in ten degrees of frost kicked him outside where he was found more dead than alive; so much so that the police started an inquiry which the poor devil had the greatest difficulty in getting them to abandon. My uncle would never go in for such drastic methods now—in fact you can't imagine the number of working men he takes under his wing, only to be repaid quite often with the basest ingratitude—though he's so haughty with society people. It may be a servant who has looked after him in a hotel, for whom he will find a place in Paris, or a farm-labourer whom he will pay to have taught a trade. It's a really rather nice side of his character, in contrast to his social side." For Saint-Loup belonged to that type of young men of fashion, situated at an altitude at which it has been possible to cultivate such expressions as "what is really rather nice about him," "his nicer side," previous seeds which produce very rapidly a way of looking at things in which one counts oneself as nothing and the "people" as everything; the exact opposite, in a word, of plebeian pride. "I'm told it was quite extraordinary to what extent he set the tone, to what extent he laid down the law for the whole of society when he was a young man. As far as he was concerned, in any circumstance he did whatever seemed most agreeable or most convenient to himself, but immediately it was imitated by all the snobs. If he felt thirsty at the theatre, and had a drink brought to him in his box, a week later the little sitting-rooms behind all the boxes would be filled with refreshments. One wet summer when he had a touch of rheumatism, he ordered an overcoat of a loose but warm vicuna wool, which is generally used for travelling rugs, and insisted on the blue and orange stripes. The big tailors at once received orders from their customers for blue overcoats, fringed and shaggy. If for some reason he wanted to remove every aspect of ceremony from a dinner in a country house where he was spending the day, and to underline the distinction had come without evening clothes and sat down to table in the suit he had been wearing that afternoon, it became the fashion not to dress for dinner in the country. If instead of taking a spoon to eat a pudding he used a fork, or a special implement of his own invention which he had had made for him by a silversmith, or his fingers, it was no longer permissible to eat it in any other way. He wanted once to hear some Beethoven quartets again (for with all his preposterous ideas he is far from being a fool and has great gifts) and arranged for some musicians to come and play them to him and a few friends once a week. The ultra-fashionable thing that season was to give quite small parties with chamber music. I should say he's not done at all badly out of life. With his looks, he must have had any number of women! I couldn't tell you exactly which, because he's very discreet. But I do know that he was thoroughly unfaithful to my poor aunt. Which doesn't mean that he wasn't always perfectly charming to her, that she didn't adore him, and that he didn't go on mourning her for years. When he's in Paris, he still goes to the cemetery nearly every day."

The morning after Robert had told me all these things about his uncle while waiting for him (as it happened in vain), as I was passing the Casino alone on my way back to the hotel, I had the sensation of being watched by somebody who was not far off. I turned my head and saw a man of about forty, very tall and rather stout, with a very black moustache, who, nervously slapping the leg of his trousers with a switch, was staring at me, his eyes dilated with extreme attentiveness. From time to time these eyes were shot through by a look of restless activity such as the sight of a person they do not know excites only in men in whom, for whatever reason, it inspires thoughts that would not occur to anyone else—madmen, for instance, or spies. He darted a final glance at me that was at once bold, prudent, rapid and profound, like a last shot which one fires at an enemy as one turns to flee, and, after first looking all round him, suddenly adopting an absent and lofty air, with an abrupt revolution of his whole person he turned towards a playbill in the reading of which he became absorbed, while he hummed a tune and fingered the moss-rose in his button-hole. He drew from his pocket a note-book in which he appeared to be taking down the title of the performance that was announced, looked at his watch two or three times, pulled down over his eyes a black straw hat the brim of which he extended with his hand held out over it like an eye-shade, as though to see whether someone was coming at last, made the perfunctory gesture of annoyance by which people mean to show that they have waited long enough, although they never make it when they are really waiting, then pushing back his hat and exposing a scalp cropped close except at the sides where he allowed a pair of waved "pigeon's-wings" to grow quite long, he emitted the loud panting breath that people exhale not when they are too hot but when they wish it to be thought that they are too hot. He gave me the impression of a hotel crook who, having been watching my grandmother and myself for some days, and planning to rob us, had just discovered that I had caught him in the act of spying on me. Perhaps he was only seeking by his new attitude to express abstractedness and detachment in order to put me off the scent, but it was with an exaggeration so aggressive that his object appeared to be—at least as much as the dissipating of the suspicions he might have aroused in me—to avenge a humiliation which I must unwittingly have inflicted on him, to give me the idea not so much that he had not seen me as that I was an object of too little importance to attract his attention. He threw back his shoulders with an air of bravado, pursed his lips, twisted his moustache, and adjusted his face into an expression that was at once indifferent, harsh, and almost insulting. So much so that I took him at one moment for a thief and at another for a lunatic. And yet his scrupulously ordered attire was far more sober and far more simple than that of any of the summer visitors I saw at Balbec, and reassured me as to my own suit, so often humiliated by the usual dazzling whiteness of their holiday garb. But my grandmother was coming towards me, we took a turn together, and I was waiting for her, an hour later, outside the hotel into which she had gone for a moment, when I saw emerge from it Mme de Villeparisis with Robert de Saint-Loup and the stranger who had stared at me so intently outside the Casino. Swift as a lightning-flash his look shot through me, just as at the moment when I had first noticed him, and returned, as though he had not seen me, to hover, slightly lowered, before his eyes, deadened, like the neutral look which feigns to see nothing without and is incapable of reporting anything to the mind within, the look which expresses merely the satisfaction of feeling round it the eyelids which it keeps apart with its beatific roundness, the devout and sanctimonious look that we see on the faces of certain hypocrites, the smug look on those of certain fools. I saw that he had changed his clothes. The suit he was wearing was darker even than the other; and no doubt true elegance lies nearer to simplicity than false; but there was something more: from close at hand one felt that if colour was almost entirely absent from these garments it was not because he who had banished it from them was indifferent to it but rather because for some reason he forbade himself the enjoyment of it. And the sobriety which they displayed seemed to be of the kind that comes from obedience to a rule of diet rather than from lack of appetite. A dark green thread harmonised, in the stuff of his trousers, with the stripe on his socks, with a refinement which betrayed the vivacity of a taste that was everywhere else subdued, to which this single concession had been made out of tolerance, while a spot of red on his tie was imperceptible, like a liberty which one dares not take.

"How are you? Let me introduce my nephew, the Baron de Guermantes," Mme de Villeparisis said to me, while the stranger, without looking at me, muttering a vague "Charmed!" which he followed with a "H'm, h'm, h'm," to make his affability seem somehow forced, and crooking his little finger, forefinger and thumb, held out to me his middle and ring fingers, destitute of rings, which I clasped through his suede glove; then, without lifting his eyes to my face, he turned towards Mme de Villeparisis.

"Good gracious, I shall be forgetting my own name next!" she exclaimed with a laugh. "Here am I calling you Baron de Guermantes. Let me introduce the Baron de Charlus. But after all, it's not a very serious mistake," she went on, "for you're a thorough Guermantes all the same."

By this time my grandmother had reappeared, and we all set out together. Saint-Loup's uncle declined to honour me not only with a word but with so much as a look in my direction. If he stared strangers out of countenance (and during this short excursion he two or three times hurled his terrible and searching scrutiny like a sounding-lead at insignificant people of the most humble extraction who happened to pass), on the other hand he never for a moment, if I was to judge by myself, looked at persons whom he knew—as a detective on a secret mission might except his personal friends from his professional vigilance. Leaving my grandmother, Mme de Villeparisis and him to talk to one another, I fell behind with Saint-Loup.

"Tell me, am I right in thinking I heard Mme de Villeparisis say just now to your uncle that he was a Guermantes?"

"Of course he is: Palamède de Guermantes."

"Not the same Guermantes who have a place near Combray, and claim descent from Geneviève de Brabant?"

"Most certainly: my uncle, who is the very last word in heraldry and all that sort of thing, would tell you that our 'cry,' our war-cry, that is to say, which was changed afterwards to 'Passavant' was originally 'Combraysis,'" he said, smiling so as not to appear to be priding himself on this prerogative of a "cry," which only the quasi-royal houses, the great chiefs of feudal bands, enjoyed. "It's his brother who has the place now."

So she was related, and very closely, to the Guermantes, this Mme de Villeparisis who had for so long been for me the lady who had given me a duck filled with chocolates when I was small, more remote then from the Guermantes way than if she had been shut up somewhere on the Méséglise way, less brilliant, less highly placed by me than was the Combray optician, and who now suddenly went through one of those fantastic rises in value, parallel to the no less unforeseen depreciations of other objects in our possession, which—rise and fall alike—introduce in our youth, and in those periods of our life in which a trace of youth persists, changes as numerous as the Metamorphoses of Ovid.*

"Haven't they got the busts of all the old lords of Guermantes down there?"

"Yes, and a lovely sight they are!" Saint-Loup was ironical. "Between you and me, I look on all that sort of thing as rather a joke. But what they have got at Guermantes, which is a little more interesting, is quite a touching portrait of my aunt by Carrière. It's as fine as Whistler or Velázquez," went on Saint-Loup, who in his neophyte zeal was not always very exact about degrees of greatness. "There are also some stunning pictures by Gustave Moreau. My aunt is the niece of your friend Mme de Villeparisis; she was brought up by her, and married her cousin, who was a nephew, too, of my aunt Villeparisis, the present Duc de Guermantes."

"Then what is your uncle?"

"He bears the title of Baron de Charlus. Strictly, when my great-uncle died, my uncle Palamède ought to have taken the title of Prince des Laumes, which was that of his brother before he became Duc de Guermantes—in that family they change their names as often as their shirts. But my uncle has peculiar ideas about all that sort of thing. And as he feels that people are rather apt to overdo the Italian Prince and Grandee of Spain business nowadays, and although he had half-a-dozen princely titles to choose from, he has remained Baron de Charlus, as a protest, and with an apparent simplicity which really covers a good deal of pride. 'In these days,' he says, 'everybody is a prince; one really must have something to distinguish one; I shall call myself Prince when I wish to travel incognito.' According to him there is no older title than the Charlus barony; to prove to you that it's earlier than the Montmorency title, though they used to claim, quite wrongly,

to be the premier barons of France when they were only premier
in the Ile-de-France, where their fief was, my uncle will hold forth
to you for hours on end and enjoy doing so because, although he's
a most intelligent man, really gifted, he regards that sort of thing as
quite a live topic of conversation." Saint-Loup smiled again. "But
as I'm not like him, you mustn't ask me to talk pedigrees. I know
nothing more deadly, more outdated; really, life's too short."

I now recognised in the hard look which had made me turn
round outside the Casino the same that I had seen fixed on me at
Tansonville at the moment when Mme Swann had called Gilberte
away.

"Wasn't Mme Swann one of the numerous mistresses you told
me your uncle M. de Charlus had had?"

"Good lord, no! That is to say, my uncle's a great friend of
Swann, and has always stood up for him. But no one has ever
suggested that he was his wife's lover. You would cause the utmost
astonishment in Parisian society if people thought you believed
that."

I dared not reply that it would have caused even greater astonishment in Combray society if people had thought that I did not
believe it.

My grandmother was delighted with M. de Charlus. No doubt
he attached an extreme importance to all questions of birth and
social position, and my grandmother had remarked this, but without any trace of that severity which as a rule embodies a secret envy
and irritation, at seeing another person enjoy advantages which
one would like but cannot oneself possess. Since, on the contrary,
my grandmother, content with her lot and not for a moment
regretting that she did not move in a more brilliant sphere,
employed only her intellect in observing the eccentricities of
M. de Charlus, she spoke of Saint-Loup's uncle with that detached,
smiling, almost affectionate benevolence with which we reward
the object of our disinterested observation for the pleasure that it
has given us, all the more so because this time the object was a
person whose pretensions, if not legitimate at any rate picturesque,
made him stand out in fairly vivid contrast to the people whom she
generally had occasion to see. But it was above all in consideration
of his intelligence and sensibility, qualities which it was easy to see
that M. de Charlus, unlike so many of the society people whom
Saint-Loup derided, possessed in a marked degree, that my grandmother had so readily forgiven him his aristocratic prejudice. And

yet this prejudice had not been sacrificed by the uncle, as it had been by the nephew, to higher qualities. Rather, M. de Charlus had reconciled it with them. Possessing, by virtue of his descent from the Ducs de Nemours and the Princes de Lamballe, documents, furniture, tapestries, portraits painted for his ancestors by Raphael, Velázquez, Boucher, justified in saying that he was "visiting" a museum and a matchless library when he was merely going over his family mementoes, he still placed the whole heritage of the aristocracy in the high position from which Saint-Loup had toppled it. Perhaps also, being less ideological than Saint-Loup, less satisfied with words, a more realistic observer of men, he did not care to neglect an essential element of prestige in their eyes which, if it gave certain disinterested pleasures to his imagination, could often be a powerfully effective aid to his utilitarian activities. No agreement can ever be reached between men of his sort and those who obey an inner ideal which drives them to rid themselves of such advantages so that they may seek only to realise that ideal, resembling in that respect the painters and writers who renounce their virtuosity, the artistic people who modernise themselves, the warrior people who initiate universal disarmament, the absolute governments which turn democratic and repeal their harsh laws, though as often as not the sequel fails to reward their noble efforts; for the artists lose their talent, the nations their age-old predominance; pacifism often breeds wars and tolerance criminality. If Saint-Loup's strivings towards sincerity and emancipation could not but be regarded as extremely noble, to judge by their visible result, one could still be thankful that they had failed to bear fruit in M. de Charlus, who had transferred to his own home much of the admirable furniture from the Hôtel Guermantes instead of replacing it, like his nephew, with Art Nouveau furniture, pieces by Lebourg or Guillaumin. It was none the less true that M. de Charlus's ideal was highly artificial, and, if the epithet can be applied to the word ideal, as much social as artistic. In certain women of great beauty and rare culture whose ancestresses, two centuries earlier, had shared in all the glory and grace of the old order, he found a distinction which made him capable of taking pleasure in their society alone, and doubtless his admiration for them was sincere, but countless reminiscences, historical and artistic, evoked by their names played a considerable part in it, just as memories of classical antiquity are one of the reasons for the pleasure which a literary man finds in reading an ode by Horace that is perhaps inferior to poems of our own day which would leave him cold. Any of these women by the side of a pretty commoner was for him what an old picture is to a contemporary canvas representing a procession or a wedding—one of those old pictures the history of which we know, from the Pope or King who ordered them, through the hands of the eminent persons whose acquisition of them, by gift, purchase, conquest or inheritance, recalls to us some event or at least some alliance of historic interest, and consequently some knowledge that we ourselves have acquired, gives it new meaning, increases our sense of the richness of the possessions of our memory or of our erudition. M. de Charlus was thankful that a prejudice similar to his own, by preventing these few great ladies from mixing with women whose blood was less pure, presented them for his veneration intact, in their unadulterated nobility, like some eighteenth-century façade supported on its flat columns of pink marble, in which the passage of time has wrought no change.

M. de Charlus extolled the true "nobility" of mind and heart which characterised these women, playing upon the word in a double sense by which he himself was taken in, and in which lay the falsehood of this bastard conception, of this medley of aristocracy, generosity and art, but also its seductiveness, dangerous to people like my grandmother, to whom the less refined but more innocent prejudice of a nobleman who cared only about quarterings and took no thought for anything besides would have appeared too silly for words, whereas she was defenceless as soon as a thing presented itself under the externals of an intellectual superiority, so much so, indeed, that she regarded princes as enviable above all other men because they were able to have a La Bruyère or a Fénelon as their tutors.

Outside the Grand Hotel the three Guermantes left us; they were going to luncheon with the Princesse de Luxembourg. While my grandmother was saying good-bye to Mme de Villeparisis and Saint-Loup to my grandmother, M. de Charlus, who up till then had not addressed a single word to me, drew back from the group and arriving at my side, said to me: "I shall be taking tea this evening after dinner in my aunt Villeparisis's room. I hope that you will give me the pleasure of seeing you there with your grandmother." With which he rejoined the Marquise.

Although it was Sunday, there were no more carriages waiting outside the hotel now than at the beginning of the season. The notary's wife, in particular, had decided that it was not worth the expense of hiring one every time simply because she was not going to the Cambremers', and simply stayed in her room.

"Is Mme Blandais not well?" her husband was asked. "We haven't seen her all morning."

"She has a slight headache—the heat, you know, this thundery weather. The least thing upsets her. But I expect you'll see her this evening. I've told her she ought to come down. It can do her nothing but good."

I had supposed that in thus inviting us to take tea with his aunt, whom I never doubted that he would have warned of our coming, M. de Charlus wished to make amends for the impoliteness which he had shown me during our walk that morning. But when, on our entering Mme de Villeparisis's room, I attempted to greet her nephew, for all that I walked right round him while in shrill accents he was telling a somewhat spiteful story about one of his relatives, I could not succeed in catching his eye. I decided to say "Good evening" to him, and fairly loud, to warn him of my presence; but I realised that he had observed it, for before ever a word had passed my lips, just as I was beginning to bow to him, I saw his two fingers held out for me to shake without his having turned to look at me or paused in his story. He had evidently seen me, without letting it appear that he had, and I noticed then that his eyes, which were never fixed on the person to whom he was speaking, strayed perpetually in all directions, like those of certain frightened animals, or those of street hawkers who, while delivering their patter and displaying their illicit merchandise, keep a sharp look-out, though without turning their heads, on the different points of the horizon from which the police may appear at any moment. At the same time I was a little surprised to find that Mme de Villeparisis, while glad to see us, did not seem to have been expecting us, and I was still more surprised to hear M. de Charlus say to my grandmother: "Ah! what a capital idea of yours to come and pay us a visit! Charming of them, is it not, my dear aunt?" No doubt he had noticed his aunt's surprise at our entry and thought, as a man accustomed to set the tone, that it would be enough to transform that surprise into joy were he to show that he himself felt it, that it was indeed the feeling which our arrival there ought to prompt. In which he calculated wisely; for Mme de Villeparisis, who had a high opinion of her nephew and knew how difficult it was to please him, appeared suddenly to have found new attractions in my grandmother and welcomed her with open arms. But I failed to understand how M. de Charlus could, in the space of a few hours, have forgotten the invitation—so curt but apparently so intentional, so premeditated—which he addressed to me that same morning, or why he called a "capital idea" on my grandmother's part an idea that had been entirely his own. With a regard for accuracy which I retained until I had reached the age at which I realised that it is not by questioning him that one learns the truth of what another man has had in his mind, and that the risk of a misunderstanding which will probably pass unobserved is less than that which may come from a purblind insistence: "But, Monsieur," I reminded him, "you remember, surely, that it was you who asked me if we would come round this evening?" Not a sound, not a movement betrayed that M. de Charlus had so much as heard my question. Seeing which, I repeated it, like diplomats or like young men after a misunderstanding who endeavour, with untiring and unrewarded zeal, to obtain an explanation which their adversary is determined not to give them. Still M. de Charlus answered me not a word. I seemed to see hovering upon his lips the smile of those who from a great height pass judgment on the character and breeding of their inferiors.

Since he refused all explanation, I tried to provide one for myself, but succeeded only in hesitating between several, none of which might have been the right one. Perhaps he did not remember, or perhaps it was I who had failed to understand what he had said to me that morning . . . More probably, in his pride, he did not wish to appear to have sought the company of people he despised, and preferred to cast upon them the responsibility for their intrusion. But then, if he despised us, why had he been so anxious that we should come, or rather that my grandmother should come, for of the two of us it was to her alone that he spoke that evening, and never once to me? Talking with the utmost animation to her, as also to Mme de Villeparisis, hiding, so to speak, behind them as though he were seated at the back of a theatre-box, he merely turned from them every now and then the searching gaze of his penetrating eyes and fastened it on my face, with the same gravity, the same air of preoccupation, as if it had been a manuscript difficult to decipher.

No doubt, had it not been for those eyes, M. de Charlus's face would have been similar to the faces of many good-looking men.

And when Saint-Loup, speaking to me of various other Guermantes, said on a later occasion: "Admittedly, they don't have that thoroughbred air, that look of being noblemen to their finger-tips, that uncle Palamède has," confirming my suspicion that a thoroughbred air and aristocratic distinction were not something mysterious and new but consisted in elements which I had recognised without difficulty and without receiving any particular impression from them, I was to feel that another of my illusions had been shattered. But however much M. de Charlus tried to seal hermetically the expression on that face, to which a light coating of powder lent a faintly theatrical aspect, the eyes were like two crevices, two loop-holes which alone he had failed to block, and through which, according to one's position in relation to him, one suddenly felt oneself in the path of some hidden weapon which seemed to bode no good, even to him who, without being altogether master of it, carried it within himself in a state of precarious equilibrium and always on the verge of explosion; and the circumspect and unceasingly restless expression of those eyes, with all the signs of exhaustion which the heavy pouches beneath them stamped upon his face, however carefully he might compose and regulate it, made one think of some incognito, some disguise assumed by a powerful man in danger, or merely by a dangerous—but tragic—individual. I should have liked to divine what was this secret which other men did not carry in their breasts and which had already made M. de Charlus's stare seem to me so enigmatic when I had seen him that morning outside the Casino. But with what I now knew of his family I could no longer believe that it was that of a thief, nor, after what I had heard of his conversation, of a madman. If he was so cold towards me, while making himself so agreeable to my grandmother, this did not perhaps arise from any personal antipathy, for in general, to the extent that he was kindly disposed towards women, of whose faults he spoke without, as a rule, departing from the utmost tolerance, he displayed towards men, and especially young men, a hatred so violent as to suggest that of certain misogynists for women. Of two or three "gigolos," relatives or intimate friends of Saint-Loup, who happened to mention their names, M. de Charlus remarked with an almost ferocious expression in sharp contrast to his usual coldness: "Young scum!" I gathered that the particular fault which he found in the young men of the day was their effeminacy. "They're nothing but women," he said with scorn. But what life would not have appeared effeminate beside that which he expected a man to lead, and never found energetic or virile enough? (He himself, when he walked across country, after long hours on the road would plunge his heated body into frozen streams.) He would not even concede that a man should wear a single ring.

But this obsession with virility did not prevent his having also the most delicate sensibilities. When Mme de Villeparisis asked him to describe to my grandmother some country house in which Mme de Sévigné had stayed, adding that she could not help feeling that there was something rather "literary" about that lady's distress at being parted from "that tiresome Mme de Grignan":

"On the contrary," he retorted, "I can think of nothing more genuine. Besides, it was a time in which feelings of that sort were thoroughly understood. The inhabitant of La Fontaine's Monomotapa, running round to see his friend who had appeared to him in a dream looking rather sad, the pigeon finding that the greatest of evils is the absence of the other pigeon, seem to you perhaps, my dear aunt, as exaggerated as Mme de Sévigné's impatience for the moment when she will be alone with her daughter. It's so beautiful, what she says when she leaves her: 'This parting gives a pain to my soul which I feel like an ache in my body. In absence one is liberal with the hours. One anticipates a time for which one is longing.'"

My grandmother was delighted to hear the Letters thus spoken of, exactly as she would have spoken of them herself. She was astonished that a man could understand them so well. She found in M. de Charlus a delicacy, a sensibility that were quite feminine. We said to each other afterwards, when we were by ourselves and discussed him together, that he must have come under the strong influence of a woman—his mother, or in later life his daughter if he had any children. "A mistress," I thought to myself, remembering the influence which Saint-Loup's seemed to have had over him and which enabled me to realise the degree to which men can be refined by the women with whom they live.

"Once she was with her daughter, she had probably nothing to say to her," put in Mme de Villeparisis.

"Most certainly she had: if it was only what she calls 'things so slight that nobody else would notice them but you and I.' And anyhow she was with her. And La Bruyère tells us that that is everything: 'To be with the people one loves, to speak to them, not to speak to them, it is all the same.' He is right: that is the only true happiness," added M. de Charlus in a mournful voice, "and alas, life is so ill arranged that one very rarely experiences it. Mme de Sévigné was after all less to be pitied than most of us. She spent a great part of her life with the person whom she loved."

"You forget that it wasn't 'love' in her case, since it was her daughter."

"But what matters in life is not whom or what one loves," he went on, in a judicial, peremptory, almost cutting tone, "it is the fact of loving. What Mme de Sévigné felt for her daughter has a far better claim to rank with the passion that Racine described in *Andromaque* or *Phèdre* than the commonplace relations young Sévigné had with his mistresses. It's the same with a mystic's love for his God. The hard and fast lines with which we circumscribe love arise solely from our complete ignorance of life."

"You like *Andromaque* and *Phèdre* that much?" Saint-Loup asked his uncle in a faintly contemptuous tone.

"There is more truth in a single tragedy of Racine than in all the dramatic works of Monsieur Victor Hugo," replied M. de Charlus.

"Society people really are appalling," Saint-Loup murmured in my ear. "Say what you like, to prefer Racine to Victor is a bit thick!" He was genuinely distressed by his uncle's words, but the satisfaction of saying "say what you like" and better still "a bit thick" consoled him.

In these reflexions upon the sadness of having to live apart from those one loves (which were to lead my grandmother to say to me that Mme de Villeparisis's nephew understood certain things a great deal better than his aunt, and moreover had something about him that set him far above the average clubman) M. de Charlus not only revealed a refinement of feeling such as men rarely show; his voice itself, like certain contralto voices in which the middle register has not been sufficiently cultivated, so that when they sing it sounds like an alternating duet between a young man and a woman, mounted, when he expressed these delicate sentiments, to its higher notes, took on an unexpected sweetness and seemed to embody choirs of betrothed maidens, of sisters, pouring out their fond feelings. But the bevy of young girls whom M. de Charlus in his horror of every kind of effeminacy would have been so distressed to learn that he gave the impression of sheltering thus within his voice did not confine themselves to the interpretation, the modulation of sentimental ditties. Often while M. de Charlus was talking one could hear their laughter, the shrill, fresh laughter of schoolgirls or coquettes twitting their companions with all the mischievousness of sharp tongues and quick wits.

He told us about a house that had belonged to his family, in which Marie-Antoinette had slept, with a park laid out by Le Nôtre, which now belonged to the Israels, the wealthy financiers, who had bought it. "Israel—at least that is the name these people go by, though it seems to me a generic, an ethnic term rather than a proper name. One cannot tell; possibly people of that sort do not have names, and are designated only by the collective title of the tribe to which they belong. It is of no importance! To have been the abode of the Guermantes and to belong to the Israels!!!" His voice rose. "It reminds me of a room in the Château of Blois where the caretaker who was showing me round said to me: 'This is where Mary Stuart used to say her prayers. I use it to keep my brooms in.' Naturally I wish to know no more of this house that has disgraced itself, any more than of my cousin Clara de Chimay who has left her husband. But I keep a photograph of the house, taken when it was still unspoiled, just as I keep one of the Princess before her large eyes had learned to gaze on anyone but my cousin. A photograph acquires something of the dignity which it ordinarily lacks when it ceases to be a reproduction of reality and shows us things that no longer exist. I could give you a copy, since you are interested in that style of architecture," he said to my grandmother. At that moment, noticing that the embroidered handkerchief which he had in his pocket was exhibiting its coloured border, he thrust it sharply down out of sight with the scandalised air of a prudish but far from innocent lady concealing attractions which, by an excess of scrupulosity, she regards as indecent.

"Would you believe it?" he went on. "The first thing these people did was to destroy Le Nôtre's park, which is as bad as slashing a picture by Poussin. For that alone, these Israels ought to be in prison. It is true," he added with a smile, after a moment's silence, "that there are probably plenty of other reasons why they should be there! In any case, you can imagine the effect of an English garden with that architecture."

"But the house is in the same style as the Petit Trianon," said Mme de Villeparisis, "and Marie-Antoinette had an English garden laid out there."

"Which, after all, ruins Gabriel's façade," replied M. de Charlus. "Obviously, it would be an act of vandalism now to destroy the Hameau. But whatever may be the spirit of the age, I beg leave to doubt whether, in that respect, a whim of Mme Israels has the same justification as the memory of the Queen."

Meanwhile my grandmother had been making signs to me to go up to bed, in spite of the urgent appeals of Saint-Loup who, to my utter shame, had alluded in front of M. de Charlus to the depression which used often to come upon me at night before I went to sleep, and which his uncle must regard as betokening a sad want of virility. I lingered a few moments still, then went upstairs, and was greatly surprised when, a little later, having heard a knock at my bedroom door and asked who was there, I heard the voice of M. de Charlus saying dryly: "It is Charlus. May I come in, Monsieur? Monsieur," he continued in the same tone as soon as he had shut the door, "my nephew was saying just now that you were apt to be a little upset at night before going to sleep, and also that you were an admirer of Bergotte's books. As I had one here in my luggage which you probably do not know, I have brought it to you to while away these moments during which you are unhappy."

I thanked M. de Charlus warmly and told him that I had been afraid that what Saint-Loup had said to him about my distress at the approach of night would have made me appear in his eyes even more stupid than I was.

"Not at all," he answered in a gentler voice. "You have not, perhaps, any personal merit—I've no idea, so few people have! But for a time at least you have youth, and that is always an attraction. Besides, Monsieur, the greatest folly of all is to mock or to condemn in others what one does not happen to feel oneself. I love the night, and you tell me that you dread it. I love the scent of roses, and I have a friend whom it throws into a fever. Do you suppose that for that reason I consider him inferior to me? I try to understand everything and I take care to condemn nothing. In short, you must not be too sorry for yourself; I do not say that these moods of depression are not painful, I know how much one can suffer from things which others would not understand. But at least you have placed your affection wisely in your grandmother. You see a great deal of her. And besides, it is a legitimate affection, I mean one that is repaid. There are so many of which that cannot be said!"

He walked up and down the room, looking at one thing, picking up another. I had the impression that he had something to tell me, and could not find the right words to express it.

"I have another volume of Bergotte here. I will have it fetched for you," he went on, and rang the bell. Presently a page came. "Go and find me your head waiter. He is the only person here who is capable of performing an errand intelligently," said M. de Charlus stiffly. "Monsieur Aimé, sir?" asked the page. "I cannot tell you his name. Ah yes, I remember now, I did hear him called Aimé. Run along, I'm in a hurry." "He won't be a minute, sir, I saw him downstairs just now," said the page, anxious to appear efficient. A few minutes went by. The page returned. "Sir, M. Aimé has gone to bed. But I can take a message." "No, you must get him out of bed." "But I can't do that, sir; he doesn't sleep here." "Then you can leave us alone."

"But, Monsieur," I said when the page had gone, "you are too kind; one volume of Bergotte will be quite enough."

"That is just what I was thinking, after all." M. de Charlus continued to walk up and down the room. Several minutes passed in this way, then after a few moments' hesitation and several false starts, he swung sharply round and, in his earlier biting tone of voice, flung at me: "Good night, Monsieur!" and left the room.

After all the lofty sentiments which I had heard him express that evening, next day, which was the day of his departure, on the beach in the morning, as I was on my way down to bathe, when M. de Charlus came across to tell me that my grandmother was waiting for me to join her as soon as I left the water, I was greatly surprised to hear him say, pinching my neck as he spoke with a familiarity and a laugh that were frankly vulgar: "But he doesn't care a fig for his old grandmother, does he, eh? Little rascal!"

"What, Monsieur! I adore her!"

"Monsieur," he said stepping back a pace, and with a glacial air, "you are still young; you should profit by your youth to learn two things: first, to refrain from expressing sentiments that are too natural not to be taken for granted; and secondly not to rush into speech in reply to things that are said to you before you have penetrated their meaning. If you had taken this precaution a moment ago you would have saved yourself the appearance of speaking at cross-purposes like a deaf man, thereby adding a second absurdity to that of having anchors embroidered on your bathing-dress. I have lent you a book by Bergotte which I require. See that it is brought to me within the next hour by that head waiter with the absurd and inappropriate name, who, I suppose, is not in bed at this time of day. You make me realise that I was premature in speaking to you last night of the charms of youth. I should have done you a greater service had I pointed out to you its thoughtlessness, its inconsequence, and its want of comprehension. I hope, Monsieur, that this little douche will be no less salutary to you than your bathe. But don't let me keep you standing: you may catch cold. Good day, Monsieur."

No doubt he felt remorse for this speech, for some time later I received—in a morocco binding on the front of which was inlaid a panel of tooled leather representing in demi-relief a spray of forget-me-nots—the book which he had lent me, and which I had sent back to him, not by Aimé who was apparently off duty, but by the lift-boy.

M. de Charlus having gone, Robert and I were free at last to dine with Bloch. And I realised during this little party that the stories too readily admitted by our friend as funny were favourite stories of M. Bloch senior, and that the son's "really remarkable person" was always one of his father's friends whom he had so classified. There are a certain number of people whom we admire in our childhood, a father who is wittier than the rest of the family, a teacher who acquires credit in our eyes from the philosophy he reveals to us, a schoolfellow more advanced than we are (which was what Bloch had been to me) who despises the Musset of the *Espoir en Dieu* when we still admire it, and when we have reached Leconte or Claudel will be raving only about

> At Saint-Blaise, at the Zuecca
> You were well, you were well pleased . . .

to which he will add:

> Padua is a place to adore
> Where very great doctors of law . . .
> But I prefer the polenta . . .
> Goes past in her cloak of velour
> La Toppatelle,

and of all the *Nuits* will remember only:

At Le Havre, facing the Atlantic,
At Venice, in the Lido's gloom,
Where on the grass above a tomb
Comes to die the pale Adriatic.

So, whenever we confidently admire anyone, we collect from him and quote with admiration sayings vastly inferior to the sort which, left to our own judgment, we would sternly reject, just as the writer of a novel puts into it, on the pretext that they are true, "witticisms" and characters which in the living context are like a dead weight, mere padding. Saint-Simon's portraits, composed by himself evidently without any self-admiration, are admirable, whereas the strokes of wit of the clever people he knew which he cites as being delightful are frankly mediocre when they have not become meaningless. He would have scorned to invent what he reports as so acute or so colourful when said by Mme Cornuel or Louis XIV, a point which is to be remarked also in many other writers, and is capable of various interpretations, of which it is enough to note but one for the present: namely, that in the state of mind in which we "observe" we are a long way below the level to which we rise when we create.

There was, then, embedded in my friend Bloch, a father Bloch who lagged forty years behind his son and told preposterous stories at which he laughed as loudly, inside my friend's being, as did the real, visible, authentic Bloch senior, since to the laugh which the latter emitted, not without several times repeating the last word so that his audience might taste the full flavour of the story, was added the braying laugh with which the son never failed, at table, to greet his father's anecdotes. Thus it came about that after saying the most intelligent things Bloch junior, manifesting the portion that he had inherited from his family, would tell us for the thirtieth time some of the gems which Bloch senior brought out only (together with his swallow-tail coat) on the solemn occasions on which Bloch junior brought someone to the house on whom it was worth while making an impression: one of his masters, a "chum" who had taken all the prizes, or, this evening, Saint-Loup and myself. For instance: "A military critic of great insight, who had brilliantly worked out, supporting them with infallible proofs, the reasons for which, in the Russo-Japanese war, the Japanese must inevitably be beaten and the Russians victorious," or else: "He is an eminent gentleman who passes for a great financier in political circles and for a great politician in financial circles." These stories were interchangeable with one about the Baron de Rothschild and one about Sir Rufus Israels, who were brought into the conversation in an equivocal manner which might let it be supposed that M. Bloch knew them personally.

I myself was taken in, and from the way in which M. Bloch spoke of Bergotte I assumed that he too was an old friend. In fact, all the famous people M. Bloch claimed to know he knew only "without actually knowing them," from having seen them at a distance in the theatre or in the street. He imagined, moreover, that his own appearance, his name, his personality were not unknown to them, and that when they caught sight of him they had often to repress a furtive inclination to greet him. People in society, because they know men of talent in the flesh, because they have them to dinner in their houses, do not on that account understand them any better. But when one has lived to some extent in society, the silliness of its inhabitants makes one too desirous to live, makes one suppose too high a standard of intelligence, in the obscure circles in which people know only "without actually knowing." I was to discover this when I introduced the topic of Bergotte.

M. Bloch was not alone in being a social success at home. My friend was even more so with his sisters, whom he continually twitted in hectoring tones, burying his face in his plate, and making them laugh until they cried. They had adopted their brother's language, and spoke it fluently, as if it had been obligatory and the only form of speech that intelligent people could use. When we arrived, the eldest sister said to one of the younger ones: "Go, tell our sage father and our venerable mother!" "Whelps," said Bloch, "I present to you the cavalier Saint-Loup, hurler of javelins, who is come for a few days from Doncières to the dwellings of polished stone, fruitful in horses." And, since he was as vulgar as he was literate, his speech ended as a rule in some pleasantry of a less Homeric kind: "Come, draw closer your pepla with the fair clasps. What's all this fandangle? Does your mother know you're out?" And the misses Bloch collapsed in a tempest of laughter. I told their brother how much pleasure he had given me by recommending me to read Bergotte, whose books I had loved.

M. Bloch senior, who knew Bergotte only by sight, and Bergotte's life only from what was common gossip, had a manner quite as indirect of making the acquaintance of his books, by the help of judgments that were by way of being literary. He lived in the world of approximations, where people salute in a void and criticise in error, a world where assurance, far from being tempered by ignorance and inaccuracy, is increased thereby. It is the propitious miracle of self-esteem that, since few of us can have brilliant connexions or profound attainments, those to whom they are denied still believe themselves to be the best endowed of men, because the optics of our social perspective make every grade of society seem the best to him who occupies it and who regards as less favoured than himself, ill-endowed, to be pitied, the greater men whom he names and calumniates without knowing them, judges and despises without understanding them. Even in cases where the multiplication of his modest personal advantages by self-esteem would not suffice to assure a man the share of happiness, superior to that accorded to others, which is essential to him, envy is always there to make up the balance. It is true that if envy finds expression in scornful phrases, we must translate "I have no wish to know him" by "I have no means of knowing him." That is the intellectual meaning. But the emotional meaning is indeed, "I have no wish to know him." The speaker knows that it is not true, but he does not, all the same, say it simply to deceive; he says it because it is what he feels, and that is sufficient to bridge the gulf, that is to say to make him happy.

Self-centredness thus enabling every human being to see the universe spread out in descending tiers beneath himself who is its lord, M. Bloch afforded himself the luxury of being a pitiless one when in the morning, as he drank his chocolate, seeing Bergotte's signature at the foot of an article in the newspaper which he had scarcely opened, he disdainfully granted him a hearing which was soon cut short, pronounced sentence upon him, and gave himself the comforting pleasure of repeating after every mouthful of the scalding brew: "That fellow Bergotte has become unreadable. My word, what a bore the brute can be. I really must stop my subscription. It's such a rigmarole—stodgy stuff!" And he helped himself to another slice of bread.

This illusory importance of M. Bloch senior did, however, extend some little way beyond the radius of his own perceptions. In the first place his children regarded him as a superior person.

Children have always a tendency either to depreciate or to exalt their parents, and to a good son his father is always the best of fathers, quite apart from any objective reasons there may be for admiring him. Now, such reasons were not altogether lacking in the case of M. Bloch, who was an educated man, shrewd, affectionate towards his family. In his most intimate circle they were all the more proud of him because if, in "society," people are judged, in accordance with a standard scale which is incidentally absurd and a series of false but fixed rules, by comparison with the aggregate of all the other fashionable people, in the subdivisions of middle-class life on the other hand, dinner-parties and family reunions turn upon certain people who are pronounced agreeable and amusing but who in "society" would not survive a second evening. Moreover in this social environment where the artificial values of the aristocracy do not exist, their place is taken by even more stupid distinctions. Thus it was that in his family circle, and even to a fairly remote degree of consanguinity, an alleged similarity in his way of wearing his moustache and in the bridge of his nose led to M. Bloch's being called "the Duc d'Aumale's double." (In the world of club bell-hops, is not the one who wears his cap on one side and his tunic tightly buttoned so as to give himself the appearance, he imagines, of a foreign officer, also a personage of a sort to his colleagues?)

The resemblance was of the faintest, but it seemed almost to confer a title. Whenever he was mentioned, it was always: "Bloch? Which one? The Duc d'Aumale?" as people say "Princesse Murat? Which one? The Queen (of Naples)?" And together with certain other minor indications it combined to give him, in the eyes of the cousinhood, an acknowledged claim to distinction. Not going to the lengths of having a carriage of his own, M. Bloch used on special occasions to hire an open victoria with a pair of horses from the Company, and would drive through the Bois de Boulogne, reclining indolently, two fingers on his temple, two others under his chin, and if people who did not know him concluded that he was an "old humbug," they were convinced in the family that in point of elegance Uncle Solomon could have taught Gramont-Caderousse a thing or two. He was one of those people who when they die, because for years they have shared a table in a restaurant on the boulevard with its editor, are described in the social column of the *Radical* as "well-known Paris figures." M. Bloch told Saint-Loup and me that Bergotte knew so well why he, M. Bloch, always cut him that as soon as he caught sight of him, at the theatre or in the club, he avoided his eye. Saint-Loup blushed, for it occurred to him that this club could not be the Jockey, of which his father had been president. On the other hand it must be a fairly exclusive club, for M. Bloch had said that Bergotte would never have got into it if he had come up now. So it was not without the fear that he might be "underrating his adversary" that Saint-Loup asked whether the club in question were that of the Rue Royale, which was considered "degrading" by his own family, and to which he knew that certain Jews were admitted. "No," replied M. Bloch in a tone at once careless, proud and ashamed, "it is a small club, but far more agreeable: the Ganaches. We're very strict there, don't you know." "Isn't Sir Rufus Israels the president?" Bloch junior asked his father, so as to give him the opportunity for a glorious lie, unaware that the financier had not the same eminence in Saint-Loup's eyes as in his. The fact of the matter was that the Ganaches club boasted not Sir Rufus Israels but one of his staff. But as this man was on the best of terms with his employer, he had at his disposal a stock of the financier's cards, and would give one to M. Bloch whenever he wished to travel on a line of which Sir Rufus was a director, so that old Bloch was able to say: "I'm just going round to the Club to ask for a letter of introduction from Sir Rufus." And the card enabled him to dazzle the guards on the trains.

The misses Bloch were more interested in Bergotte and, reverting to him rather than pursue the subject of the Ganaches, the youngest asked her brother, in the most serious tone imaginable, for she believed that there existed, for the designation of men of talent, no other terms than those which he was in the habit of using:

"Is he a really amazing cove, this Bergotte? Is he in the category of the great johnnies, chaps like Villiers and Catulle?"

"I've met him several times at dress rehearsals," said M. Nissim Bernard. "He is an uncouth creature, a sort of Schlemihl."

There was nothing very serious in this allusion to Chamisso's story, but the epithet "Schlemihl" formed part of that dialect, half-German, half-Jewish, which delighted M. Bloch in the family circle, but struck him as vulgar and out of place in front of strangers. And so he cast a reproving glance at his uncle.

"He has talent," said Bloch.

"Ah!" said his sister gravely, as though to imply that in that case there was some excuse for me.

"All writers have talent," said M. Bloch scornfully.

"In fact it appears," went on his son, raising his fork and screwing up his eyes with an air of diabolical irony, "that he is going to put up for the Academy."

"Go on. He hasn't enough to show them," replied his father, who seemed not to have for the Academy the same contempt as his son and daughters. "He hasn't the necessary calibre."

"Besides, the Academy is a salon, and Bergotte has no polish," declared the uncle (from whom Mme Bloch had expectations), a mild and inoffensive person whose surname, Bernard, might perhaps by itself have quickened my grandfather's powers of diagnosis, but would have appeared too little in harmony with a face which looked as if it had been brought back from Darius's palace and restored by Mme Dieulafoy, had not his first name, Nissim, chosen by some collector desirous of giving a crowning touch of orientalism to this figure from Susa, set hovering above it the pinions of an androcephalous bull from Khorsabad. But M. Bloch never stopped insulting his uncle, either because he was inflamed by the unresisting good-humour of his butt, or because, the rent of the villa being paid by M. Nissim Bernard, the beneficiary wished to show that he retained his independence and above all scorned to seek by flattery to make sure of the rich inheritance to come.

"Of course, whenever there's a chance of saying something pompous and stupid, one can be quite certain that you won't miss it. You'd be the first to lick his boots if he were in the room!" shouted M. Bloch, while M. Nissim Bernard in sorrow lowered over his plate the ringleted beard of King Sargon. (My schoolfriend, since he had begun to grow a beard, which also was blue-black and crimped, looked very like his great-uncle.)

What most hurt the old man was being treated so rudely in front of his manservant. He murmured an unintelligible sentence of which all that could be made out was: "When the meschores are in the room." "Meschores," in the Bible, means "the servant of God." In the family circle the Blochs used the word to refer to the servants, and were always delighted by it, because their certainty of not being understood either by Christians or by the servants themselves enhanced in M. Nissim Bernard and M. Bloch their twofold distinction of being "masters" and at the same time "Jews." But this latter source of satisfaction became a source of displeasure when there was "company." At such times M. Bloch, hearing his uncle say "meschores," felt that he was over-exposing his oriental side, just as a harlot who has invited some of her sisters to meet her respectable friends is annoyed if they allude to their profession or use objectionable words. Hence, far from being mollified by his uncle's plea, M. Bloch, beside himself with rage, could contain himself no longer. He let no opportunity pass of scarifying the wretched old man.

"What! Are you the son of the Marquis de Marsantes? Why, I knew him very well," said M. Nissim Bernard to Saint-Loup. I supposed that he meant the word "knew" in the sense in which Bloch's father had said that he knew Bergotte, namely by sight. But he went on: "Your father was a great friend of mine." Meanwhile, Bloch had turned very red, his father was looking intensely cross, and the misses Bloch were choking with sup-pressed laughter. The fact was that in M. Nissim Bernard the love of ostentation, which in M. Bloch and his children was held in check, had engendered the habit of perpetual lying. For instance, if he was staying in an hotel, M. Nissim Bernard, as M. Bloch equally might have done, would have his newspapers brought to him by his valet in the dining-room in the middle of lunch, when everybody was there, so that they should see that he travelled with a valet. But to the people with whom he made friends in the hotel the uncle used to say, what the nephew would never have said, that he was a senator. For all that he was certain that they would sooner or later discover that the title was usurped, he could not, at the critical moment, resist the temptation to assume it. M. Bloch suffered acutely from his uncle's lies and from all the embarrassments that they caused him. "Don't pay any attention to him, he's a terrible old yarn-spinner," he whis-pered to Saint-Loup, whose interest was whetted all the more, for he was curious to explore the psychology of liars. "A greater liar even than the Ithacan Odysseus, albeit Athene called him the greatest liar among mortals," his son completed the indictment. "Well, upon my word!" cried M. Nissim Bernard, "If I'd known that I was going to sit down to dinner with my old friend's son! Why, I have a photograph still of your father at home in Paris, and any number of letters from him. He used always to call me 'uncle,' nobody ever knew why. He was a charming man, sparkling. I remember so well a dinner I gave at Nice: there was Sardou,

Labiche, Augier" . . . "Molière, Racine, Corneille," M. Bloch
added sarcastically, while his son completed the list of guests
with "Plautus, Menander, Kalidasa." M. Nissim Bernard, cut to
the quick, stopped short in his reminiscence, and, ascetically
depriving himself of a great pleasure, remained silent until the
end of dinner.

"Saint-Loup with helm of bronze," said Bloch, "have a piece
more of this duck with thighs heavy with fat, over which the
illustrious sacrificer of birds has poured numerous libations of red
wine."

As a rule, after bringing out from his store for one of his son's
distinguished fellow-students his anecdotes of Sir Rufus Israels and
others, M. Bloch, feeling that he had succeeded in touching and
melting his son's heart, would withdraw, in order not to
"demean" himself in the eyes of a "schoolkid." If, however,
there was an absolutely compelling reason, as for instance on the
night when his son passed the *agrégation*, M. Bloch would add to
the usual string of anecdotes the following ironical reflexion
which he ordinarily reserved for his own personal friends and
which the young Bloch was extremely proud to see produced
for his: "The Government have acted unpardonably. They have
forgotten to consult M. Coquelin! M. Coquelin has let it be
known that he is displeased." (M. Bloch prided himself on being
a reactionary, and contemptuous of theatrical people.)

But the misses Bloch and their brother blushed to the tips of
their ears, so impressed were they when Bloch senior, to show that
he could be regal to the last in his entertainment of his son's two
"chums," gave the order for champagne to be served, and
announced casually that, as a "treat" for us, he had taken three
stalls for the performance which a company from the Opéra-
Comique was giving that evening at the Casino. He was sorry
that he had not been able to get a box. They had all been taken. In
any case, he had often been in the boxes, and really one saw and
heard better in the stalls. However, if the failing of his son, that is to
say the failing which his son believed to be invisible to other
people, was coarseness, the father's was avarice. And so it was in
a decanter that we were served, under the name of champagne,
with a light sparkling wine, while under that of orchestra stalls he
had taken three in the pit, which cost half as much, miraculously
persuaded by the divine intervention of his failing that neither at
table nor in the theatre (where the boxes were all empty) would

the difference be noticed. When M. Bloch had invited us to moisten our lips in the flat glasses which his son dignified with the style and title of "craters with deeply hollowed flanks," he showed us a picture to which he was so much attached that he always brought it with him to Balbec. He told us that it was a Rubens. Saint-Loup asked innocently if it was signed. M. Bloch replied, blushing, that he had had the signature cut off to make it fit the frame, but that it made no difference, as he had no intention of selling the picture. Then he hurriedly bade us good night, in order to bury himself in the *Journal Officiel*, back numbers of which littered the house and which, he informed us, he was obliged to read carefully on account of his "parliamentary position," as to the precise nature of which he gave us no enlightenment.

"I shall take a muffler," said Bloch, "for Zephyrus and Boreas are vying with each other over the fish-teeming sea, and should we but tarry a little after the show is over, we shall not be home before the first flush of Eos, the rosy-fingered.* By the way," he asked Saint-Loup when we were outside (and I trembled, for I realised at once that it was of M. de Charlus that Bloch spoke in tones of sarcasm), "who was that splendid old card dressed in black that I saw you walking with the day before yesterday on the beach?"

"That was my uncle," replied Saint-Loup, somewhat ruffled.

Unfortunately, a "gaffe" was far from seeming to Bloch a thing to be avoided. He shook with laughter. "Heartiest congratulations. I ought to have guessed: he has a lot of style, and the most priceless dial of an old dotard of the highest lineage."

"You are absolutely mistaken: he's an extremely clever man," retorted Saint-Loup, now furious.

"I'm sorry about that; it makes him less complete. All the same, I should very much like to know him, for I flatter myself I could write some highly adequate pieces about old buffers like that. He's killing when you see him go by. But I should disregard the caricaturable aspect of his mug, which really is hardly worthy of an artist enamoured of the plastic beauty of phrases, although (you'll forgive me) it had me doubled up for quite a while with joyous laughter, and I should bring out the aristocratic side of your uncle, who on the whole makes a tip-top impression, and when one has finished laughing, does strike one with his considerable sense of style. But," he went on, addressing me this time, "there is something in a completely different connexion about which I have been meaning to question you, and every time we are together, some god, some blessed denizen of Olympus, makes me completely forget to ask for a piece of information which might before now have been and is sure some day to be of the greatest use to me. Tell me, who was the lovely lady I saw you with in the Zoological Gardens accompanied by a gentleman whom I seem to know by sight and a girl with long hair?"

It had been quite plain to me at the time that Mme Swann did not remember Bloch's name, since she had referred to him by another, and had described my friend as being on the staff of some Ministry, as to which I had never since then thought of finding out whether he had joined it. But how came it that Bloch, who, according to what she then told me, had got himself introduced to her, was ignorant of her name? I was so astonished that I paused for a moment before answering.

"Whoever she is," he went on, "hearty congratulations. You can't have been bored with her. I picked her up a few days before that on the Zone railway, where, speaking of zones, she was so kind as to undo hers for the benefit of your humble servant. I've never had such a time in my life, and we were just going to make arrangements to meet again when somebody she knew had the bad taste to get in at the last station but one."

My continued silence did not appear to please Bloch. "I was hoping," he said, "thanks to you, to learn her address, so as to go there several times a week to taste in her arms the delights of Eros, dear to the gods; but I do not insist since you seem pledged to discretion with respect to a professional who gave herself to me three times running, and in the most rarefied manner, between Paris and the Point-du-Jour. I'm bound to see her again some night."

I called upon Bloch after his dinner; he returned my call, but I was out and he was seen asking for me by Françoise, who, as it happened, although he had visited us at Combray, had never set eyes on him before. So that she knew only that one of "the gentlemen" I knew had looked in to see me, she did not know "with what effect," dressed in a nondescript way which had not made any particular impression upon her. Now though I knew quite well that certain of Françoise's social ideas must for ever remain impenetrable to me, based as they were, perhaps, partly upon confusions between words and names which she had once and for all time mistaken for one another, I could not refrain, for all that I had long since abandoned the quest for enlightenment in such cases, from seeking—though in vain—to discover what could be the immense significance that the name of Bloch had for Françoise. For no sooner had I mentioned to her that the young man whom she had seen was M. Bloch than she took several paces backwards so great were her stupor and disappointment. "What! Is that M. Bloch?" she cried, thunderstruck, as if so portentous a personage ought to have been endowed with an appearance which "made you realise" as soon as you saw him that you were in the presence of one of the great ones of the earth; and, like someone who has discovered that an historical character is not up to the level of his reputation, she repeated in an awed tone of voice, in which I could detect the latent seeds of a universal scepticism: "So that's M. Bloch! Well, really, you would never think it, to look at him." She seemed also to bear me a grudge, as if I had always "overdone" the praise of Bloch to her. At the same time she was kind enough to add: "Well, he may be M. Bloch, and all that, but at least Monsieur can say he's every bit as good."

She had presently, with respect to Saint-Loup, whom she worshipped, a disillusionment of a different kind and of shorter duration: she discovered that he was a Republican. For although, when speaking for instance of the Queen of Portugal, she would say with that disrespect which is, among the people, the supreme form of respect: "Amélie, Philippe's sister," Françoise was a Royalist. But above all a marquis, a marquis who had dazzled her at first sight, and who was for the Republic, seemed no longer real. And it aroused in her the same ill-humour as if I had given her a box which she had believed to be made of gold, and had thanked me for it effusively, and then a jeweller had revealed to her that it was only plated. She at once withdrew her esteem from Saint-Loup, but soon afterwards restored it to him, having reflected that he could not, being the Marquis de Saint-Loup, be a Republican, that he was just pretending, out of self-interest, for with the Government we had it might be a great advantage to him. From that moment her coldness towards him and her resentment towards me ceased. And when she spoke of Saint-Loup she said: "He's a hypocrite," with a broad and kindly smile which made it clear that she "considered" him again just as much as when she first knew him, and that she had forgiven him.

In fact, Saint-Loup was obviously sincere and disinterested, and it was this intense moral purity which, unable to find entire satisfaction in a selfish emotion such as love, and moreover not finding in him the impossibility (which existed in me, for instance) of gaining spiritual nourishment elsewhere than in oneself, rendered him truly capable (to the extent that I was incapable) of friendship.

Françoise was no less mistaken about Saint-Loup when she said that he "just pretended" not to look down on the common people: you had only to see him when he was in a temper with his groom. It had indeed sometimes happened that Robert would scold his groom with a certain amount of brutality, which was proof in him of a sense not so much of the difference as of the equality between the classes. "But," he said when I reproached him for having treated the man rather harshly, "why should I go out of my way to speak politely to him? Isn't he my equal? Isn't he just as near to me as any of my uncles and cousins? You seem to think I ought to treat him with respect, as an inferior. You talk like an aristocrat!" he added scornfully.

And indeed if there was a class to which he showed himself prejudiced and hostile, it was the aristocracy, so much so that he found it as hard to believe in the superior qualities of a man of the world as he found it easy to believe in those of a man of the people. When I mentioned the Princesse de Luxembourg, whom I had met with his aunt:

"An old trout," was his comment. "Like all that lot. She's a sort of cousin of mine, by the way."

Having a strong prejudice against the people who frequented it, he went rarely into "society," and the contemptuous or hostile attitude which he adopted towards it served to intensify, among all his closest relatives, the painful impression made by his liaison with a woman of the theatre, a liaison which, they declared, would be his ruin, blaming it specially for having bred in him that spirit of denigration, that rebelliousness, for having "led him astray," until it was only a matter of time before he dropped out altogether. And so, many easy-going men of the Faubourg Saint-Germain were without compunction when they spoke of Robert's mistress. "Whores do their job," they would say, "they're as good as anybody else. But not that one! We can't forgive her. She has done too much harm to a fellow we're fond of." Of course, he was not the first to be thus ensnared. But the others amused themselves like men of the world, continued to think like men of the world about politics and everything else. Whereas Saint-Loup's family found him "soured." They failed to realise that for many young men of fashion who would otherwise remain uncultivated mentally, rough in their friendships, without gentleness or taste, it is very often their mistresses who are their real masters, and liaisons of this sort the only school of ethics in which they are initiated into a superior culture, where they learn the value of disinterested relations. Even among the lower orders (who in point of coarseness so often remind us of high society) the woman, more sensitive, more fastidious, more leisured, is driven by curiosity to adopt certain refinements, respects certain beauties of sentiment and of art which, though she may not understand them, she nevertheless places above what has seemed most desirable to the man, above money or position. Now whether it concerns the mistress of a young blood (such as Saint-Loup) or a young workman (electricians, for instance, must now be included in our truest order of Chivalry) her lover has too much admiration and respect for her not to extend them also to what she herself respects and admires; and for him the scale of values is thereby overturned. Her very sex makes her weak; she suffers from nervous troubles, inexplicable things which in a man, or even in another woman—an aunt or cousin of his—would bring a smile to the lips of this robust young man. But he cannot bear to see the woman he loves suffer. The young nobleman who, like Saint-Loup, has a mistress acquires the habit, when he takes her out to dine, of carrying in his pocket the valerian drops which she may need, of ordering the waiter, firmly and with no hint of sarcasm, to see that he shuts the doors quietly and does not put any damp moss on the table, so as to spare his companion those little ailments which he himself has never felt, which compose for him an occult world in whose reality she has taught him to believe, ailments for which he now feels sympathy without needing to understand them, for which he will still feel sympathy when women other than she are the sufferers. Saint-Loup's mistress—as the first monks of the Middle Ages taught Christendom—had taught him to be kind to animals, for which she had a passion, never going anywhere without her dog, her canaries, her parrots; Saint-Loup looked after them with motherly devotion and regarded those who were unkind to animals as brutes. At the same time an actress, or so-called actress, like the woman who was living with him—whether she was intelligent or not, and as to that I had no knowledge—by making him find society women boring, and look upon having to go out to a party as a painful duty, had saved him from snobbishness and cured him of frivolity. Thanks to her, social relations filled a smaller place in the life of her young lover, but whereas, if he had been simply a man about town, vanity or self-interest would have dictated his choice of friends as rudeness would have characterised his treatment of them, his mistress had taught him to bring nobility and refinement into his friendships. With her feminine instinct, with a keener appreciation of certain qualities of sensibility in men which her lover might perhaps, without her guidance, have misunderstood and mocked, she had always been quick to distinguish from among the rest of Saint-Loup's friends the one who had a real affection for him, and to make that one her favourite. She knew how to persuade him to feel grateful to that friend, to show his gratitude, to notice what things gave his friend pleasure and what pain. And presently Saint-Loup, without any more need for her to prompt him, began to think of these things by himself, and at Balbec, where she was not with him, for me whom she had never seen, whom he had perhaps not yet so much as mentioned in his letters to her, of his own accord would pull up the window of a carriage in which I was sitting, take out of the room the flowers that made me feel unwell, and when he had to say good-bye to several people at once would contrive to do so before it was actually time for him to go, so as to be left alone and last with me, to make that distinction between them and me, to treat me differently from the rest. His mistress had opened his mind to the invisible, had brought an element of seriousness into his life, of delicacy into his heart, but all this escaped his sorrowing family who repeated: "That creature will be the death of him, and meanwhile she's doing what she can to disgrace him."

It is true that he had already drawn from her all the good that she was capable of doing him; and that she now caused him only incessant suffering, for she had taken an intense dislike to him and tormented him in every possible way. She had begun, one fine day, to regard him as stupid and absurd because the friends that she had among the younger writers and actors had assured her that he was, and she duly repeated what they had said with that passion, that lack of reserve which we show whenever we receive from without, and adopt as our own, opinions or customs of which we previously knew nothing. She readily professed, like her actor friends, that between Saint-Loup and herself there was an unbridgeable gulf, because they were of a different breed, because she was an intellectual and he, whatever he might claim, by birth an enemy of the intellect. This view of him seemed to her profound, and she sought confirmation of it in the most insignificant words, the most trivial actions of her lover. But when the same friends had further convinced her that she was destroying the great promise she had shown in company so ill-suited to her, that her lover's influence would finally rub off on her, that by living with him she was ruining her future as an artist, to her contempt for Saint-Loup was added the sort of hatred that she would have felt for him if he had insisted upon inoculating her with a deadly germ. She saw him as seldom as possible, at the same time postponing a definite rupture, which seemed to me a highly improbable event. Saint-Loup made such sacrifices for her that unless she was ravishingly beautiful (but he had always refused to show me her photograph, saying: "For one thing, she's not a beauty, and besides she always takes badly. They're only some snapshots that I took myself with my Kodak; they would give you a false impression of her") it seemed unlikely that she would find another man prepared to do the same. I never reflected that a fancy to make a name for oneself even when one has no talent, that the admiration, merely the privately expressed admiration, of people by whom one is impressed, can (although it may not perhaps have been the case with Saint-Loup's mistress), even for a little prostitute, be motives more determining than the pleasure of making money. Without quite understanding what was going on in his mistress's mind, Saint-Loup did not believe her to be completely sincere either in her unfair reproaches or in her promises of undying love, but nevertheless at certain moments had the feeling that she would break with him whenever she could, and accordingly, impelled no doubt by an instinctive desire to preserve his love that was perhaps more clear-sighted than he was himself, and incidentally bringing into play a practical capacity for business which was compatible in him with the loftiest and blindest impulses of the heart, had refused to settle any capital on her, had borrowed an enormous sum so that she should want nothing, but made it over to her only from day to day. And no doubt, assuming that she really did think of leaving him, she was calmly waiting until she had "feathered her nest," a process which, with the money given her by Saint-Loup, would not perhaps take very long, but would all the same be an extra lease of time to prolong the happiness of my new friend—or his misery.

This dramatic period of their liaison—which had now reached its most acute, its cruellest state for Saint-Loup, for she had forbidden him to remain in Paris, where his presence exasperated her, and had forced him to spend his leave at Balbec, within easy reach of his regiment—had begun one evening at the house of one of his aunts, on whom he had prevailed to allow his mistress to come there, before a large party, to recite some fragments of a symbolist play in which she had once appeared in an avant-garde theatre, and for which she had brought him to share the admiration that she herself professed.

But when she appeared in the room, with a large lily in her hand, and wearing a costume copied from the *Ancilla Domini* which she had persuaded Saint-Loup was an absolute "vision of beauty," her entrance had been greeted, in that assemblage of clubmen and duchesses, with smiles which the monotonous tone of her sing-song, the oddity of certain words and their frequent repetition, had changed into fits of giggles, stifled at first but presently so uncontrollable that the wretched reciter had been unable to go on. Next day Saint-Loup's aunt had been universally censured for having allowed so grotesque an actress to appear in her drawing-room. A well-known duke made no bones about telling her that she had only herself to blame if she found herself criticised. "Damn it all, people really don't come to see turns like that! If the woman had talent, even; but she has none and never will have any. 'Pon my soul, Paris is not so stupid as people make out. Society does not consist exclusively of imbeciles. This little lady evidently believed that she was going to take Paris by surprise. But Paris is not so easily surprised as all that, and there are still some things that they can't make us swallow."

As for the actress, she left the house with Saint-Loup, exclaiming: "What do you mean by letting me in for those old hens, those uneducated bitches, those oafs? I don't mind telling you, there wasn't a man in the room who hadn't leered at me or tried to paw me, and it was because I wouldn't look at them that they were out to get their revenge."

Words which had changed Robert's antipathy for society people into a horror that was altogether more profound and distressing, and was provoked in him most of all by those who least deserved it, devoted kinsmen who, on behalf of the family, had sought to persuade his mistress to break with him, a move which she represented to him as inspired by their desire for her.

Robert, although he had at once ceased to see them, used to imagine when he was separated from his mistress as he was now, that they or others like them were profiting by his absence to return to the charge and had possibly enjoyed her favours. And when he spoke of the lechers who betrayed their friends, who sought to corrupt women, tried to make them come to houses of assignation, his whole face radiated suffering and hatred.

"I'd kill them with less compunction than I'd kill a dog, which is at least a decent, honest and faithful beast. They're the ones who deserve the guillotine if you like, far more than poor wretches who've been led into crime by poverty and by the cruelty of the rich."

He spent the greater part of his time sending letters and telegrams to his mistress. Every time that, while still preventing him from returning to Paris, she found an excuse to quarrel with him by post, I read the news at once on his tormented face. Since she never told him in what way he was at fault, he suspected that she did not know herself, and had simply had enough of him; but he nevertheless longed for an explanation and would write to her: "Tell me what I've done wrong. I'm quite ready to acknowledge my faults," the grief that overpowered him having the effect of persuading him that he had behaved badly.

But she kept him waiting indefinitely for answers which, when they came, were utterly meaningless. And so it was almost always with a furrowed brow and often empty-handed that I would see Saint-Loup returning from the post-office, where, alone in all the hotel, he and Françoise went to fetch or to hand in letters, he from a lover's impatience, she with a servant's mistrust of others. (His telegrams obliged him to make a much longer journey.)

When, some days after our dinner with the Blochs, my grandmother told me with a joyful air that Saint-Loup had just asked her whether she would like him to take a photograph of her before he left Balbec, and when I saw that she had put on her nicest dress for the purpose and was hesitating between various hats, I felt a little annoyed at this childishness, which surprised me on her part. I even wondered whether I had not been mistaken in my grandmother, whether I did not put her on too lofty a pedestal, whether she was as unconcerned about her person as I had always supposed, whether she was entirely innocent of the weakness which I had always thought most alien to her, namely vanity.

Unfortunately, the displeasure that was aroused in me by the prospect of this photographic session, and more particularly by the delight with which my grandmother appeared to be looking forward to it, was sufficiently apparent for Françoise to notice it and to do her best, unintentionally, to increase it by making me a sentimental, gushing speech by which I refused to appear moved.

"Oh, Monsieur, my poor Madame will be so pleased at having her likeness taken. She's going to wear the hat that her old Françoise has trimmed for her: you must let her."

I persuaded myself that it was not cruel of me to mock Françoise's sensibility, by reminding myself that my mother and grandmother, my models in all things, often did the same. But my grandmother, noticing that I seemed put out, said that if her sitting for her photograph offended me in any way she would give up the idea. I would not hear of it. I assured her that I saw no harm in it, and let her adorn herself, but, thinking to show how shrewd and forceful I was, added a few sarcastic and wounding words calculated to neutralise the pleasure which she seemed to find in being photographed, with the result that, if I was obliged to see my grandmother's magnificent hat, I succeeded at least in driving from her face that joyful expression which ought to have made me happy. Alas, it too often happens, while the people we love best are still alive, that such expressions appear to us as the exasperating manifestation of some petty whim rather than as the precious form of the happiness which we should dearly like to procure for them. My ill-humour arose more particularly from the fact that, during that week, my grandmother had appeared to be avoiding me, and I had not been able to have her to myself for a moment, either by night or day. When I came back in the afternoon to be alone with her for a little I was told that she was not in the hotel; or else she would shut herself up with Françoise for endless confabulations which I was not permitted to interrupt. And when, after being out all evening with Saint-Loup, I had been thinking on the way home of the moment at which I should be able to go to my grandmother and embrace her, I waited in vain for her to give the three little knocks on the party wall which would tell me to go in and say good night to her. At length I would go to bed, a little resentful of her for depriving me, with an indifference so new and strange in her, of a joy on which I had counted so much, and I would lie there for a while, my heart throbbing as in my childhood, listening to the wall which remained silent, until I cried myself to sleep.

That day, as for some days past, Saint-Loup had been obliged to go to Doncières, where, until he returned there for good, he would be on duty now until late every afternoon. I was sorry that he was not at Balbec. I had seen some young women, who at a distance had seemed to me lovely, alighting from carriages and entering either the ball-room of the Casino or the ice-cream shop. I was going through one of those phases of youth, devoid of any particular love, as it were in abeyance, in which at all times and in all places—as a lover the woman by whose charms he is smitten—we desire, we seek, we see Beauty. Let but a single flash of reality—the glimpse of a woman from afar or from behind—enable us to project the image of Beauty before our eyes, and we imagine that we have recognised it, our hearts beat, and we will always remain half-persuaded that it was She, provided that the woman has vanished: it is only if we manage to overtake her that we realise our mistake.

Moreover, as I was becoming more and more unwell, I was inclined to overrate the simplest pleasures because of the very difficulty of attaining them. I seemed to see charming women all round me, because I was too tired, if it was on the beach, too shy if it was in the Casino or at a pastry-cook's, to go anywhere near them. And yet, if I was soon to die, I should have liked to know beforehand what the prettiest girls that life had to offer looked like at close quarters, in reality, even if it should be another than myself or no one at all who was to take advantage of that offer (I did not, in fact, realise that a desire for possession underlay my curiosity). I should have had the courage to enter the ball-room if Saint-Loup had been with me. Left by myself, I was simply hanging about in front of the Grand Hotel until it was time for me to join my grandmother, when, still almost at the far end of the esplanade, along which they projected a striking patch of colour, I saw five or six young girls as different in appearance and manner from all the people one was accustomed to see at Balbec as would have been a flock of gulls arriving from God knows where and performing with measured tread upon the sands—the dawdlers flapping their wings to catch up with the rest—a parade the purpose of which seems as obscure to the human bathers whom they do not appear to see as it is clearly determined in their own birdish minds.

One of these unknown girls was pushing a bicycle in front of her; two others carried golf-clubs; and their attire generally was in striking contrast to that of the other girls at Balbec, some of whom, it was true, went in for sports, but without adopting a special outfit.

It was the hour at which ladies and gentlemen came out every day for a stroll along the front, exposed to the merciless fire of the lorgnette fastened upon them, as if they had each borne some disfigurement which she felt it her duty to inspect in its minutest details, by the senior judge's wife, proudly seated there with her back to the band-stand, in the middle of that dread line of chairs on which presently they too, actors turned critics, would come and establish themselves, to scrutinise in their turn the passing crowds. All these people who paced up and down the esplanade, lurching as heavily as if it had been the deck of a ship (for they could not lift a leg without at the same time waving their arms, turning their eyes, squaring their shoulders, compensating by a balancing movement on one side for the movement they had just made on the other, and puffing out their faces), pretending not to see, so as to let it be thought that they were not interested in them, but covertly eyeing, for fear of running into them, the people who were walking beside or coming towards them, did in fact bump into them, became entangled with them, because each was mutually the object of the same secret attention veiled beneath the same apparent disdain—love, and consequently fear, of the crowd being one of the most powerful motives in all human beings, whether they seek to please other people or to impress them, or to show that they despise them; and in the case of the solitary, even if his seclusion is absolute and lifelong it is often based on a deranged love of the crowd which so far overrides every other feeling that, unable to win the admiration of his hall-porter, of the passers-by, of the cabman he hails, he prefers not to be seen by them at all, and with that object abandons every activity that would oblige him to go out of doors.

In the midst of all these people, some of whom were pursuing a train of thought, but then betrayed its instability by a fitfulness of gesture, an aberrancy of gaze as inharmonious as the circumspect titubation of their neighbours, the girls whom I had noticed, with the control of gesture that comes from the perfect suppleness of one's own body and a sincere contempt for the rest of humanity, were advancing straight ahead, without hesitation or stiffness, performing exactly the movements that they wished to perform, each of their limbs completely independent of the others, the rest of the body preserving that immobility which is so noticeable in good waltzers. They were now quite near me. Although each was of a type absolutely different from the others, they all had beauty; but to tell the truth I had seen them for so short a time, and without venturing to look hard at them, that I had not yet individualised any of them. Except for one, whose straight nose and dark complexion singled her out from the rest, like the Arabian king in a Renaissance picture of the Epiphany, they were known to me only by a pair of hard, obstinate and mocking eyes, for instance, or by cheeks whose pinkness had a coppery tint reminiscent of geraniums; and even these features I had not yet indissolubly attached to any one of these girls rather than to another; and when (according to the order in which the group met the eye, marvellous because the most different aspects were juxtaposed, because all the colour scales were combined in it, but confused as a piece of music in which I was unable to isolate and identify at the moment of their passage the successive phrases, no sooner distinguished than forgotten) I saw a pallid oval, black eyes, green eyes, emerge, I did not know if these were the same that had already charmed me a moment ago, I could not relate them to any one girl whom I had set apart from the rest and identified. And this want, in my vision, of the demarcations which I should presently establish between them permeated the group with a sort of shimmering harmony, the continuous transmutation of a fluid, collective and mobile beauty.

It was not perhaps mere chance in life that, in forming this group of friends, had chosen them all so beautiful; perhaps these girls (whose demeanour was enough to reveal their bold, hard and frivolous natures), extremely aware of everything that was ludicrous or ugly, incapable of yielding to an intellectual or moral attraction, had naturally felt a certain repulsion for all those among the companions of their own age in whom a pensive or sensitive disposition was betrayed by shyness, awkwardness, constraint, by what they would regard as antipathetic, and from such had held aloof; while attaching themselves, conversely, to others to whom they were drawn by a certain blend of grace, suppleness and physical elegance, the only form in which they were able to picture a straightforward and attractive character and the promise of pleasant hours in one another's company. Perhaps, too, the class to which they belonged, a class which I should not have found it easy to define, was at that point in its evolution when, thanks either to its growing wealth and leisure, or to new sporting habits, now prevalent even among certain elements of the working class, and a physical culture to which had not yet been added the culture of the mind, a social group comparable to the smooth and prolific schools of sculpture which have not yet gone in for tortured expression, produces naturally, and in abundance, fine bodies, fine legs, fine hips, wholesome, serene faces, with an air of agility and guile. And were they not noble and calm models of human beauty that I beheld there, outlined against the sea, like statues exposed to the sunlight on a Grecian shore?

Just as if, within their little band, which progressed along the esplanade like a luminous comet, they had decided that the surrounding crowd was composed of beings of another race not even whose sufferings could awaken in them any sense of fellowship, they appeared not to see them, forced those who had stopped to talk to step aside, as though from the path of a machine which had been set going by itself and which could not be expected to avoid pedestrians; and if some terrified or furious old gentleman whose existence they did not even acknowledge and whose contact they spurned took precipitate and ludicrous flight, they merely looked at one another and laughed. They had, for whatever did not form part of their group, no affectation of contempt; their genuine contempt was sufficient. But they could not set eyes on an obstacle without amusing themselves by clearing it, either in a running jump or with both feet together, because they were all brimming over with the exuberance that youth so urgently needs to expend that even when it is unhappy or unwell, obedient rather to the necessities of age than to the mood of the day, it can never let pass an opportunity to jump or to slide without indulging in it conscientiously, interrupting and interspersing even the slowest walk—as Chopin his most melancholy phrase—with graceful deviations in which caprice is blended with virtuosity. The wife of an elderly banker, after hesitating between various possible exposures for her husband, had settled him in a deck-chair facing the esplanade, sheltered from wind and sun by the band-stand. Having seen him comfortably installed there, she had gone to buy a newspaper which she would read aloud to him by way of diversion, one of her little absences which she never prolonged for more than five minutes, which seemed to her quite long enough but which she repeated at fairly frequent intervals so that this old husband on whom she lavished an attention that she took care to conceal should have the impression that he was still quite alive and like other people and was in no need of protection. The platform of the band-stand provided, above his head, a natural and tempting springboard across which, without a moment's hesitation, the eldest of the little band began to run; she jumped over the terrified old man, whose yachting cap was brushed by her nimble feet, to the great delight of the other girls, especially of a pair of green eyes in a doll-like face, which expressed, for that bold act, an admiration and a merriment in which I seemed to discern a trace of shyness, a shamefaced and blustering shyness which did not exist in the others. "Oh, the poor old boy, I feel sorry for him; he looks half dead," said a girl in a rasping voice, with more sarcasm than sympathy. They walked on a little way, then stopped for a moment in the middle of the road, oblivious of the fact that they were impeding the passage of other people, in an agglomerate that was at once irregular in shape, compact, weird and shrill, like an assembly of birds before taking flight; then they resumed their leisurely stroll along the esplanade, against the background of the sea.

By this time their charming features had ceased to be indistinct and jumbled. I had dealt them like cards into so many heaps to compose (failing their names, of which I was still ignorant): the tall one who had jumped over the old banker; the little one sil-houetted against the horizon of sea with her plump and rosy cheeks and green eyes; the one with the straight nose and dark complexion who stood out among the rest; another, with a face as white as an egg in which a tiny nose described an arc of a circle like a chicken's beak—a face such as one sometimes sees in the very young; yet another, also tall, wearing a hooded cape (which gave her so shabby an appearance and so contradicted the elegance of the figure beneath that the explanation which suggested itself was that this girl must have parents of high position who valued their self-esteem so far above the visitors to Balbec and the sartorial elegance of their own children that it was a matter of the utmost indifference to them that their daughter should stroll on the front dressed in a way which humbler people would have considered too modest); a girl with brilliant, laughing eyes and plump, matt cheeks, a black polo-cap crammed on her head, who was pushing a bicycle with such an uninhibited swing of the hips, and using slang terms so typical of the gutter and shouting so loudly when I passed her (although among her expressions I caught that tiresome phrase "living one's own life") that, abandoning the hypothesis which her friend's hooded cape had prompted me to formulate, I concluded instead that all these girls belonged to the population which frequents the velodromes, and must be the very juvenile mistresses of racing cyclists. In any event, none of my suppositions embraced the possibility of their being virtuous. At first sight—in the way in which they looked at one another and laughed, in the insistent stare of the one with the matt complexion—I had grasped that they were not. Besides, my grandmother had always watched over me with a delicacy too tremulous for me not to believe that the sum total of the things one ought not to do is indivisible and that girls who are lacking in respect for their elders would not suddenly be stopped short by scruples at the prospect of pleasures more tempting than that of jumping over an octogenarian.

Though they were now separately identifiable, still the inter-play of their eyes, animated with self-assurance and the spirit of comradeship and lit up from one moment to the next either by the interest or the insolent indifference which shone from each of them according to whether her glance was directed at her friends or at passers-by, together with the consciousness of knowing one another intimately enough always to go about together in an exclusive "gang," established between their independent and separate bodies, as they slowly advanced, an invisible but harmon-ious bond, like a single warm shadow, a single atmosphere, making of them a whole as homogeneous in its parts as it was different from the crowd through which their procession gradually wound.

For an instant, as I passed the dark one with the plump cheeks who was wheeling a bicycle, I caught her smiling, sidelong glance, aimed from the centre of that inhuman world which enclosed the life of this little tribe, an inaccessible, unknown world wherein the idea of what I was could certainly never penetrate or find a place. Wholly occupied with what her companions were saying, had she seen me—this young girl in the polo-cap pulled down very low over her forehead—at the moment in which the dark ray emanat-ing from her eyes had fallen on me? If she had seen me, what could I have represented to her? From the depths of what universe did she discern me? It would have been as difficult for me to say as, when certain distinguishing features in a neighbouring planet are made visible thanks to the telescope, it is to conclude therefrom that human beings inhabit it, and that they can see us, and to guess what ideas the sight of us can have aroused in their minds.

If we thought that the eyes of such a girl were merely two glittering sequins of mica, we should not be athirst to know her and to unite her life to ours. But we sense that what shines in those reflecting discs is not due solely to their material composition; that it is the dark shadows, unknown to us, of the ideas that the person cherishes about the people and places she knows—the turf of race-courses, the sand of cycling tracks over which, pedalling on past fields and woods, she would have drawn me after her, that little peri, more seductive to me than she of the Persian paradise—the shadows, too, of the home to which she will presently return, of the plans that she is forming or that others have formed for her; and above all that it is she, with her desires, her sympathies, her revulsions, her obscure and incessant will. I knew that I should never possess this young cyclist if I did not possess also what was in her eyes. And it was consequently her whole life that filled me with desire; a sorrowful desire because I felt that it was not to be fulfilled, but an exhilarating one because, what had hitherto been my life having ceased of a sudden to be my whole life, being no more now than a small part of the space stretching out before me which I was burning to cover and which was composed of the lives of these girls, it offered me that prolongation, that possible multiplication of oneself, which is happiness. And no doubt the fact that we had, these girls and I, not one habit—as we had not one idea—in common must make it more difficult for me to make friends with them and to win their regard. But perhaps, also, it was thanks to those differences, to my consciousness that not a single element that I knew or possessed entered into the composition of the nature and actions of these girls, that satiety had been suc-ceeded in me by a thirst—akin to that with which a parched land burns—for a life which my soul, because it had never until now received one drop of it, would absorb all the more greedily, in long draughts, with a more perfect imbibition.

I had looked so closely at the dark cyclist with the bright eyes that she seemed to notice my attention, and said to the tallest of the girls something that I could not hear but that made her laugh. Truth to tell, this dark-haired one was not the one who attracted me most, simply because she was dark and because (since the day on which, from the little path by Tansonville, I had seen Gilberte) a girl with reddish hair and a golden skin had remained for me the inaccessible ideal. But had I not loved Gilberte herself principally because she had appeared to me haloed with that aureole of being the friend of Bergotte, of going to look at cathedrals with him? And in the same way could I not rejoice at having seen this dark girl look at me (which made me hope that it would be easier for me to get to know her first), for she would introduce me to the pitiless one who had jumped over the old man's head, to the cruel one who had said "I feel sorry for the poor old boy," to all these girls in turn of whom she enjoyed the prestige of being the inseparable companion? And yet the supposition that I might some day be the friend of one or other of these girls, that these eyes, whose incomprehensible gaze struck me from time to time and played unwittingly upon me like an effect of sunlight on a wall, might ever, by some miraculous alchemy, allow the idea of my existence, some affection for my person, to interpenetrate their ineffable particles, that I myself might some day take my place among them in the evolution of their course by the sea's edge—that supposition appeared to me to contain within it a contradiction as insoluble as if, standing before some Attic frieze or a fresco representing a procession, I had believed it possible for me, the spectator, to take my place, beloved of them, among the divine participants.

Was, then, the happiness of knowing these girls unattainable? Certainly it would not have been the first of its kind that I had renounced. I had only to recall the numberless strangers whom, even at Balbec, the carriage bowling away from them at full speed had forced me for ever to abandon. And indeed the pleasure I derived from the little band, as noble as if it had been composed of Hellenic virgins, arose from the fact that it had something of the fleetingness of the passing figures on the road. This evanescence of persons who are not known to us, who force us to cast off from our habitual life in which the women whose society we frequent have all, in course of time, laid bare their blemishes, urges us into that state of pursuit in which there is no longer anything to stem the tide of imagination. To strip our pleasures of imagination is to reduce them to their own dimensions, that is to say to nothing. Offered me by one of those procuresses whose good offices, as has been seen, I by no means always scorned, withdrawn from the element which gave them so many nuances, such impreciseness, these girls would have enchanted me less. We need imagination, awakened by the uncertainty of being unable to attain its object, to create a goal which hides the other goal from us, and by substituting for sensual pleasures the idea of penetrating another life, prevents us from recognising that pleasure, from tasting its true savour, from restricting it to its own range. We need, between us and the fish which, if we saw it for the first time cooked and served on a table, would not appear worth the endless shifts and wiles required to catch it, the intervention, during our afternoons with the rod, of the rippling eddy to whose surface come flashing, without our quite knowing what we intend to do with them, the bright gleam of flesh, the hint of a form, in the fluidity of a transparent and mobile azure.

These girls benefited also by that alteration of social proportions characteristic of seaside life. All the advantages which, in our ordinary environment, extend and enhance us, we there find to have become invisible, in fact eliminated; while on the other hand the people whom we suppose, without reason, to enjoy similar advantages appear to us amplified to artificial dimensions. This made it easier for unknown women in general, and today for these girls in particular, to acquire an enormous importance in my eyes, and impossible to make them aware of such importance as I might myself possess.

But if the parade of the little band could be said to be but an excerpt from the endless flight of passing women, which had always disturbed me, that flight was here reduced to a movement so slow as to approach immobility. And the very fact that, in a phase so far from rapid, faces no longer swept away in a whirlwind, but calm and distinct, still seemed to me beautiful, prevented me from thinking, as I had so often thought when Mme de Villeparisis's carriage bore me away, that at closer quarters, if I had stopped for a moment, certain details, a pock-marked skin, a flaw in the nostrils, a gawping expression, a grimace of a smile, an ugly figure, might have been substituted, in the face and body of the woman, for those that I had doubtless imagined; for no more than a pretty outline, the glimpse of a fresh complexion, had sufficed for me to add, in entire good faith, a ravishing shoulder, a delicious glance of which I carried in my mind for ever a memory or a preconceived idea, these rapid decipherings of a person whom we momentarily glimpse exposing us thus to the same errors as those too rapid readings in which, on the basis of a single syllable and without waiting to identify the rest, we replace

the word that is in the text by a wholly different word with which
our memory supplies us. It could not be so with me now. I had
looked at their faces long and carefully; I had seen each of them,
not from every angle and rarely in full face, but all the same in two
or three aspects different enough to enable me to make the
necessary correction or verification to "prove" the difficult suppositions of line and colour that are hazarded at first sight, and to
see subsist in them, through successive expressions, something
unalterably material. I could say to myself with conviction that
neither in Paris nor at Balbec, on the most favourable assumption
of what, even if I had been able to stop and talk to them, the
passing women who had caught my eye would have been like, had
there ever been any whose appearance, followed by their disappearance without my having got to know them, had left me with
more regret than would these, had given me the idea that their
friendship could be so intoxicating. Never, among actresses or
peasants or convent girls, had I seen anything so beautiful, impregnated with so much that was unknown, so inestimably precious, so
apparently inaccessible. They were, of the unknown and potential
happiness of life, an illustration so delicious and in so perfect a state
that it was almost for intellectual reasons that I was sick with
despair at the thought of being unable to sample, in unique
conditions which left no room for any possibility of error, all
that is most mysterious in the beauty which we desire, and
which we console ourselves for never possessing by demanding
pleasure—as Swann had always refused to do before Odette's
day—from women whom we have not desired, so that we die
without ever having known what that other pleasure was. It might
well be, of course, that it was not in reality an unknown pleasure,
that on close inspection its mystery would dissolve, that it was no
more than a projection, a mirage of desire. But in that case I had
only to blame the compulsion of a law of nature—which if it
applied to these girls would apply to all—and not the imperfection
of the object. For it was the one that I would have chosen above all
others, convinced as I was, with a botanist's satisfaction, that it was
not possible to find gathered together rarer specimens than these
young flowers that at this moment before my eyes were breaking
the line of the sea with their slender hedge, like a bower of
Pennsylvania roses adorning a cliffside garden, between whose
blooms is contained the whole tract of ocean crossed by some
steamer, so slow in gliding along the blue, horizontal line that

stretches from one stem to the next that an idle butterfly, dawdling in the cup of a flower which the ship's hull has long since passed, can wait, before flying off in time to arrive before it, until nothing but the tiniest chink of blue still separates the prow from the first petal of the flower towards which it is steering.

I went indoors because I was to dine at Rivebelle with Robert, and my grandmother insisted that on those evenings, before going out, I must lie down for an hour on my bed, a rest which the Balbec doctor presently ordered me to extend to all other evenings too.

As it happened, there was no need, when one went indoors, to leave the esplanade and to enter the hotel by the hall, that is to say from the back. By virtue of an alteration of the clock which reminded me of those Saturdays when, at Combray, we used to have lunch an hour earlier, now with summer at the full the days had become so long that the sun was still high in the heavens, as though it were only tea-time, when the tables were being laid for dinner in the Grand Hotel. And so the great sliding windows remained open on to the esplanade. I had only to step across a low wooden sill to find myself in the dining-room, through which I walked to take the lift.

As I passed the reception desk I addressed a smile to the manager, and without the slightest twinge of distaste collected one in return from a face which, since I had been at Balbec, my comprehensive study had impregnated and transformed like a natural history specimen. His features had become familiar to me, charged with a meaning that was of no importance but none the less intelligible like a script which one can read, and had ceased in any way to resemble those strange and repellent characteristics which his face had presented to me on that first day, when I had seen before me a personage now forgotten, or, if I succeeded in recalling him, unrecognisable, difficult to identify with this insignificant and polite individual of which the other was but a caricature, a hideous and rapid sketch. Without either the shyness or the sadness of the evening of my arrival, I rang for the lift attendant, who no longer stood in silence while I rose by his side as in a mobile thoracic cage propelled upwards along its ascending pillar, but repeated to me:

"There aren't the people now as there was a month back. They're beginning to go now; the days are drawing in." He said this not because there was any truth in it but because, having an

engagement, presently, on a warmer part of the coast, he would
have liked us all to leave as soon as possible so that the hotel could
be shut up and he have a few days to himself before "rejoining" his
new place. "Rejoin" and "new" were not, as it happened, incompatible terms, since, for the lift-boy, "rejoin" was the usual form of
the verb "to join." The only thing that surprised me was that he
condescended to say "place," for he belonged to that modern
proletariat which seeks to eliminate from its speech every trace
of a career in service. And a moment later indeed he informed me
that in the "situation" which he was about to "rejoin," he would
have a smarter "tunic" and a better "salary," the words "livery"
and "wages" sounding to him obsolete and unseemly. And since,
by an absurd contradiction, the vocabulary has survived the conception of inequality among the "masters," I was always failing to
understand what the lift-boy said. For instance, the only thing that
interested me was to know whether my grandmother was in the
hotel. Now, forestalling my questions, the lift-boy would say to
me: "That lady has just come out of your rooms." I was invariably
taken in; I supposed that he meant my grandmother. "No, that
lady who I think is an employee of yours." Since, in the traditional
vocabulary of the upper classes which ought indeed to be done
away with, a cook is not called an employee, I thought for a
moment: "But he must have made a mistake. We don't own a
factory; we haven't any employees." Suddenly I remembered that
the title of "employee," like the wearing of a moustache among
waiters, is a sop to their self-esteem given to servants, and realised
that this lady who had just gone out must be Françoise (probably
on a visit to the coffee-maker, or to watch the Belgian lady's-maid
at her sewing), though even this sop did not satisfy the lift-boy, for
he would say quite naturally, speaking pityingly of his own class,
"the working man" or "the small man," using the same singular
form as Racine when he speaks of "the poor man." But as a rule,
for my zeal and timidity of the first evening were now things of the
past, I no longer spoke to the lift-boy. It was he now who stood
there and received no answer during the short journey on which
he threaded his way through the hotel, which, hollowed out
inside like a toy, deployed around us, floor by floor, the ramifications of its corridors in the depths of which the light grew velvety,
lost its tone, blurred the communicating doors or the steps of the
service stairs which it transformed into that amber haze, unsub-
stantial and mysterious as a twilight, in which Rembrandt picks

out here and there a window-sill or a well-head. And on each landing a golden light reflected from the carpet indicated the setting sun and the lavatory window.

I wondered whether the girls I had just seen lived at Balbec, and who they could be. When our desire is thus concentrated upon a little tribe of humanity which it singles out from the rest, everything that can be associated with that tribe becomes a spring of emotion and then of reflexion. I had heard a lady say on the esplanade: "She's a friend of the Simonet girl" with that self-important air of inside knowledge, as who should say: "He's the inseparable companion of young La Rochefoucauld." And immediately she had detected on the face of the person to whom she gave this information a curiosity to see more of the favoured person who was "a friend of the Simonet girl." A privilege, obviously, that did not appear to be granted to all the world. For aristocracy is a relative thing. And there are plenty of out-of-the-way places where the son of an upholsterer is the arbiter of fashion and reigns over a court like any young Prince of Wales. I have often since then sought to recall how it first sounded to me there on the beach, that name of Simonet, still uncertain in its form, which I had not clearly distinguished, and also in its significance, its designation of such and such a person as opposed to another; instinct, in short, with that vagueness and novelty which we find so moving in the sequel, when a name whose letters are every moment engraved more deeply on our hearts by our incessant thought of them has become (though this was not to happen to me with the name of the "Simonet girl" until several years had passed) the first coherent sound that comes to our lips, whether on waking from sleep or on recovering from a fainting fit, even before the idea of what time it is or of where we are, almost before the word "I," as though the person whom it names were more "us" than we are ourselves, and as though after a brief spell of unconsciousness the phase that is the first to dissolve were that in which we were not thinking of her. I do not know why I said to myself from the first that the name Simonet must be that of one of the band of girls; from that moment I never ceased to wonder how I could get to know the Simonet family, get to know them, moreover, through people whom they would consider superior to themselves (which ought not to be difficult if they were only common little wenches) so that they might not form a disdainful idea of me. For one cannot have a perfect knowledge, one cannot effect the complete absorption of a person who disdains one, so long as one has not overcome that disdain. And since, whenever the idea of women who are so different from us penetrates our minds, unless we are able to forget it or the competition of other ideas eliminates it, we know no rest until we have converted these aliens into something that is compatible with ourselves, the mind being in this respect endowed with the same kind of reaction and activity as our physical organism, which cannot abide the infusion of any foreign body into its veins without at once striving to digest and assimilate it. The Simonet girl must be the prettiest of them all—she who, I felt moreover, might yet become my mistress, for she was the only one who, two or three times half-turning her head, had appeared to take cognisance of my fixed stare. I asked the lift-boy whether he knew of any people at Balbec called Simonet. Not liking to admit that there was anything he did not know, he replied that he seemed to have heard the name somewhere. When we reached the top floor I asked him to send me up the latest list of visitors.

I stepped out of the lift, but instead of going to my room I made my way further along the corridor, for before my arrival the valet in charge of the landing, despite his horror of draughts, had opened the window at the end, which instead of looking out to the sea faced the hill and valley inland, but never allowed them to be seen because its panes, which were made of clouded glass, were generally closed. I made a brief halt in front of it, time enough just to pay my devotions to the view which for once it revealed beyond the hill immediately behind the hotel, a view that contained only a single house situated at some distance, to which the perspective and the evening light, while preserving its mass, gave a gem-like precision and a velvet casing, as though to one of those architectural works in miniature, tiny temples or chapels wrought in gold and enamel, which serve as reliquaries and are exposed only on rare and solemn days for the veneration of the faithful. But this moment of adoration had already lasted too long, for the valet, who carried in one hand a bunch of keys and with the other saluted me by touching his sacristan's skull cap, though without raising it on account of the pure, cool evening air, came and drew together, like those of a shrine, the two sides of the window, and so shut off the minute edifice, the glistening relic from my adoring gaze.

I went into my room. Gradually, as the season advanced, the picture that I found there in my window changed. At first it was

broad daylight, and dark only if the weather was bad: and then, in
the greenish glass which it distended with the curve of its rounded
waves, the sea, set between the iron uprights of my casement
window like a piece of stained glass in its leads, ravelled out over
all the deep rocky border of the bay little plumed triangles of
motionless foam etched with the delicacy of a feather or a
downy breast from Pisanello's pencil, and fixed in that white,
unvarying, creamy enamel which is used to depict fallen snow in
Gallé's glass.

Presently the days grew shorter and at the moment when
I entered the room the violet sky seemed branded with the stiff,
geometrical, fleeting, effulgent figure of the sun (like the representation of some miraculous sign, of some mystical apparition)
lowering over the sea on the edge of the horizon like a sacred
picture over a high altar, while the different parts of the western
sky exposed in the glass fronts of the low mahogany book-cases
that ran along the walls, which I carried back in my mind to the
marvellous painting from which they had been detached, seemed
like those different scenes executed long ago for a confraternity by
some old master on a reliquary, whose separate panels are now
exhibited side by side in a gallery, so that the visitor's imagination
alone can restore them to their place on the predella of the reredos.

A few weeks later, when I went upstairs, the sun had already set.
Like the one that I used to see at Combray, behind the Calvary,
when I came home from a walk and was getting ready to go down
to the kitchen before dinner, a band of red sky above the sea,
compact and clear-cut as a layer of aspic over meat, then, a little
later, over a sea already cold and steel-blue like a grey mullet, a sky
of the same pink as the salmon that we should presently be
ordering at Rivebelle, reawakened my pleasure in dressing to go
out to dinner. Close to the shore, patches of vapour, soot-black
but with the burnish and consistency of agate, visibly solid and
palpable, were trying to rise one above another over the sea in ever
wider tiers, so that the highest of them, poised on top of the
twisted column and overreaching the centre of gravity of those
which had hitherto supported them, seemed on the point of
bringing down in ruin this lofty structure already half-way up
the sky, and precipitating it into the sea. The sight of a ship
receding like a nocturnal traveller gave me the same impression
that I had had in the train of being set free from the necessity of
sleep and from confinement in a bedroom. Not that I felt myself a

prisoner in the room in which I now was, since in another hour I should be leaving it to drive away in a carriage. I threw myself down on the bed; and, just as if I had been lying in a berth on board one of those steamers which I could see quite near me and which at night it would be strange to see stealing slowly through the darkness, like shadowy and silent but unsleeping swans, I was surrounded on all sides by pictures of the sea.

But as often as not they were, indeed, only pictures; I forgot that below their coloured expanse lay the sad desolation of the beach, swept by the restless evening breeze whose breath I had so anxiously felt on my arrival at Balbec; besides, even in my room, being wholly taken up with thoughts of the girls I had seen go by, I was no longer in a sufficiently calm or disinterested state of mind to receive any really profound impression of beauty. The anticipation of dinner at Rivebelle made my mood more frivolous still, and my mind, dwelling at such moments upon the surface of the body which I was about to dress up in order to try to appear as pleasing as possible to the feminine eyes which would scrutinise me in the well-lit restaurant, was incapable of putting any depth behind the colour of things. And if, beneath my window, the soft, unwearying flight of swifts and swallows had not arisen like a playing fountain, like living fireworks, jointing the intervals between their soaring rockets with the motionless white streaming lines of long horizontal wakes—without the charming miracle of this natural and local phenomenon which brought into touch with reality the scenes that I had before my eyes—I might easily have believed that they were no more than a selection, made afresh every day, of paintings which were shown quite arbitrarily in the place in which I happened to be and without having any necessary connexion with that place. At one time it was an exhibition of Japanese colour-prints: beside the neat disc of sun, red and round as the moon, a yellow cloud seemed a lake against which black swords were outlined like the trees upon its shore, while a bar of a tender pink which I had never seen since my first paint-box swelled out like a river on either bank of which boats seemed to be waiting high and dry for someone to push them down and set them afloat. And with the contemptuous, bored and frivolous glance of an amateur or a woman hurrying through a picture gallery between two social engagements, I would say to myself: "Curious sunset, this; it's different, but after all I've seen them just as delicate, just as remarkable as this." I had more pleasure on evenings when a ship, absorbed and liquefied by the horizon, appeared so much the same colour as its background, as in an Impressionist picture, that it seemed to be also of the same substance, as though its hull and the rigging in which it tapered into a slender filigree had simply been cut out from the vaporous blue of the sky. Sometimes the ocean filled almost the whole of my window, raised as it was by a band of sky edged at the top only by a line that was of the same blue as the sea, so that I supposed it to be still sea, and the change in colour due only to some effect of lighting. Another day the sea was painted only in the lower part of the window, all the rest of which was filled with so many clouds, packed one against another in horizontal bands, that its panes seemed, by some premeditation or predilection on the part of the artist, to be presenting a "Cloud Study," while the fronts of the various book-cases showing similar clouds but in another part of the horizon and differently coloured by the light, appeared to be offering as it were the repetition—dear to certain contemporary masters—of one and the same effect caught at different hours but able now in the immobility of art to be seen all together in a single room, drawn in pastel and mounted under glass. And sometimes to a sky and sea uniformly grey a touch of pink would be added with an exquisite delicacy, while a little butterfly that had gone to sleep at the foot of the window seemed to be appending with its wings at the corner of this "Harmony in Grey and Pink" in the Whistler manner the favourite signature of the Chelsea master. Then even the pink would vanish; there was nothing now left to look at. I would get to my feet and, before lying down again, close the inner curtains. Above them I could see from my bed the ray of light that still remained, growing steadily fainter and thinner, but it was without any feeling of sadness, without any regret for its passing, that I thus allowed the hour at which as a rule I was seated at table to die above the curtains, for I knew that this day was of another kind from ordinary days, longer, like those arctic days which night interrupts for a few minutes only; I knew that from the chrysalis of this twilight, by a radiant metamorphosis, the dazzling light of the Rivebelle restaurant was preparing to emerge. I said to myself: "It's time"; I stretched myself on the bed, and rose, and finished dressing; and I found a charm in these idle moments, relieved of every material burden, in which, while the others were dining down below, I was employing the forces accumulated during the inactivity of this late evening hour only in drying my washed body, in putting on a dinner-jacket, in tying my tie, in making all those gestures which were already dictated by the anticipated pleasure of seeing again some woman whom I had noticed at Rivebelle last time, who had seemed to be watching me, had perhaps left the table for a moment only in the hope that I would follow her; it was with joy that I embellished myself with all these allurements so as to give myself, fresh, alert and whole-hearted, a new life, free, without cares, in which I would lean my hesitations upon the calm strength of Saint-Loup and would choose, from among the different species of animated nature and the produce of every land, those which, composing the unfamiliar dishes that my companion would at once order, might have tempted my appetite or my imagination.

And then at the end of the season came the days when I could no longer go straight in from the front through the dining-room; its windows stood open no more, for it was night now outside and the swarm of poor folk and curious idlers, attracted by the blaze of light which was beyond their reach, hung in black clusters, chilled by the north wind, on the luminous sliding walls of that buzzing hive of glass.

There was a knock at my door; it was Aimé who had come upstairs in person with the latest list of visitors.

Aimé could not go away without telling me that Dreyfus was guilty a thousand times over. "It will all come out," he assured me, "not this year, but next. It was a gentleman who's very thick with the General Staff who told me. I asked him if they wouldn't decide to bring it all to light at once, before the year is out. He laid down his cigarette," Aimé went on, acting the scene for my benefit, and shaking his head and his forefinger as his informant had done, as much as to say: "We mustn't be too impatient."—" 'Not this year, Aimé,' he said to me, putting his hand on my shoulder, 'It isn't possible. But next Easter, yes!' " And Aimé tapped me gently on the shoulder, saying, "You see, I'm showing you exactly what he did," whether because he was flattered at this act of familiarity by a distinguished person or so that I might better appreciate, with a full knowledge of the facts, the weight of the argument and our grounds for hope.

It was not without a slight pang that on the first page of the list I caught sight of the words "Simonet and family." I had in me a store of old dream-memories dating from my childhood, in which all the tenderness that existed in my heart but, being felt by my heart, was not distinguishable from it, was brought to me by a being as different as possible from myself. Once again I fashioned such a being, utilising for the purpose the name Simonet and the memory of the harmony that had reigned between the young bodies which I had seen deployed on the beach in a sportive procession worthy of Greek art or of Giotto. I did not know which of these girls was Mlle Simonet, if indeed any of them was so named, but I did know that I was loved by Mlle Simonet and that with Saint-Loup's help I was going to try to get to know her. Unfortunately, having on that condition only obtained an extension of his leave, he was obliged to report for duty every day at Doncières: but to make him commit a breach of his military obligations I had felt that I might count, more even than on his friendship for myself, on that same curiosity as a human naturalist which I myself had so often felt—even without having seen the person mentioned, and simply on hearing it said that there was a pretty cashier at a fruiterer's—to become acquainted with a new variety of feminine beauty. But I had been wrong in hoping to excite that curiosity in Saint-Loup by speaking to him of my band of girls. For it had been and would remain paralysed in him by his love for the actress whose lover he was. And even if he had felt it lightly stirring within him he would have repressed it, from an almost superstitious belief that on his own fidelity might depend that of his mistress. And so it was without any promise from him that he would take an active interest in my girls that we set off to dine at Rivebelle.

On the first few occasions, when we arrived there, the sun would just have set, but it was light still; in the garden outside the restaurant, where the lamps had not yet been lighted, the heat of the day was falling and settling, as though in a vase along the sides of which the transparent, dusky jelly of the air seemed of such consistency that a tall rose-tree, fastened against the dim wall which it veined with pink, looked like the arborescence that one sees at the heart of an onyx. Presently it was after nightfall when we alighted from the carriage, often indeed when we started from Balbec if the weather was bad and we had put off sending for the carriage in the hope of a lull. But on those days it was with no sense of gloom that I listened to the wind howling, for I knew that it did not mean the abandonment of my plans, imprisonment in my bedroom, I knew that in the great dining-room of the restaurant which we would enter to the sound of the music of the gipsy band, the innumerable lamps would triumph easily over the darkness and the cold, by applying to them their broad cauteries of molten gold, and I climbed light-heartedly after Saint-Loup into the closed carriage which stood waiting for us in the rain.

For some time past the words of Bergotte, when he pronounced himself positive that, in spite of all I might say, I had been created to enjoy pre-eminently the pleasures of the mind, had restored to me, with regard to what I might succeed in achieving later on, a hope that was disappointed afresh every day by the boredom I felt on settling down before a writing-table to start work on a critical essay or a novel. "After all," I said to myself, "perhaps the pleasure one feels in writing it is not the infallible test of the literary value of a page; perhaps it is only a secondary state which is often superadded, but the want of which can have no prejudicial effect on it. Perhaps some of the greatest masterpieces were written while yawning." My grandmother set my doubts at rest by telling me that I should be able to work, and to enjoy working, as soon as I was well. And, our doctor having thought it only prudent to warn me of the grave risks to which my state of health might expose me, and having outlined all the hygienic precautions that I ought to take to avoid any accident, I subordinated all my pleasures to an object which I judged to be infinitely more important than them, that of becoming strong enough to be able to bring into being the work which I had, possibly, within me, and had been exercising over myself, ever since I had come to Balbec, a scrupulous and constant control. Nothing would have induced me to touch the cup of coffee which would have robbed me of the night's sleep that was necessary if I was not to be tired next day. But when we arrived at Rivebelle, immediately—what with the excitement of a new pleasure, and finding myself in that different zone into which the exceptional introduces us after having cut the thread, patiently spun throughout so many days, that was guiding us towards wisdom—as though there were never to be any such thing as tomorrow, nor any lofty aims to be realised, all that precise machinery of prudent hygiene which had been working to safeguard them vanished. A waiter was offering to take my coat, whereupon Saint-Loup asked: "You're sure you won't be cold? Perhaps you'd better keep it: it's not very warm in here."

"No, no," I assured him, and perhaps I did not feel the cold; but however that might be, I no longer knew the fear of falling ill, the necessity of not dying, the importance of work. I gave up my coat; we entered the dining-room to the sound of some warlike march played by the gipsy band, we advanced between two rows of tables laid for dinner as along an easy path of glory, and, feeling a happy glow imparted to our bodies by the rhythms of the band which conferred on us these military honours, this unmerited triumph, we concealed it beneath a grave and frozen mien, beneath a languid, casual gait, so as not to be like those music-hall "mashers" who, wedding a ribald verse to a patriotic air, come running on to the stage with the martial countenance of a victorious general.

From that moment I was a new man, who was no longer my grandmother's grandson and would remember her only when it was time to get up and go, but the brother, for the time being, of the waiters who were going to bring us our dinner.

The dose of beer, and *a fortiori* of champagne, which at Balbec I should not have ventured to take in a week, albeit to my calm and lucid consciousness the savour of those beverages represented a pleasure clearly appreciable if easily sacrificed, I now imbibed at a sitting, adding to it a few drops of port which I was too bemused to be able to taste, and I gave the violinist who had just been playing the two louis which I had been saving up for the last month with a view to buying something, I could not remember what. Several of the waiters, let loose among the tables, were flying along at full speed, each carrying on his outstretched palm a dish which it seemed to be the object of this kind of race not to let fall. And in fact the chocolate soufflés arrived at their destination unspilled, the potatoes *à l'anglaise*, in spite of the gallop that must have given them a shaking, arranged as at the start round the Pauillac lamb. I noticed one of these waiters, very tall, plumed with superb black locks, his face dyed in a tint that suggested certain species of rare birds rather than a human being, who, running without pause (and, one would have said, without purpose) from one end of the room to the other, recalled one of those macaws which fill the big aviaries in zoological gardens with their gorgeous colouring and incomprehensible agitation. Presently the spectacle settled down, in my eyes at least, into an order at once more noble and more calm. All this dizzy activity became fixed in a quiet harmony. I looked at the round tables whose innumerable assemblage filled the restaurant like so many planets, as the latter are represented in old allegorical pictures. Moreover, there seemed to be some irresistible force of attraction at work among these various stars, and at each table the diners had eyes only for the tables at which they were not sitting, with the possible exception of some wealthy Amphitryon who, having managed to secure a famous author, was endeavouring to extract from him, thanks to the magic properties of the turning-table, a few insignificant remarks at which the ladies marvelled. The harmony of these astral tables did not prevent the incessant revolution of the countless waiters who, because instead of being seated like the diners they were on their feet, performed their gyrations in a more exalted sphere. No doubt they were running, one to fetch the hors d'œuvre, another to change the wine or to bring clean glasses. But despite these special reasons, their perpetual course among the round tables yielded, after a time, to the observer the law of its dizzy but ordered circulation. Seated behind a bank of flowers, two horrible cashiers, busy with endless calculations, seemed two witches occupied in forecasting by astrological signs the disasters that might from time to time occur in this celestial vault fashioned according to the scientific conceptions of the Middle Ages.

And I rather pitied all the diners because I felt that for them the round tables were not planets and that they had not cut through the scheme of things in such a way as to be delivered from the bondage of habitual appearances and enabled to perceive analogies. They thought that they were dining with this or that person, that the dinner would cost roughly so much, and that tomorrow they would begin all over again. And they appeared absolutely indifferent to the progress through their midst of a train of young waiters who, having probably at that moment no urgent duty, advanced processionally bearing rolls of bread in baskets. Some of these, the youngest, stunned by the cuffs which the head waiters administered to them as they passed, fixed melancholy eyes upon a distant dream and were consoled only if some visitor from the Balbec hotel in which they had once been employed, recognising them, said a few words to them, telling them in person to take away the champagne which was not fit to drink, an order that filled them with pride.

I could hear the twanging of my nerves, in which there was a sense of well-being independent of the external objects that might have produced it, and which the least shifting of my body or of my attention was enough to make me feel, just as to a closed eye a slight compression gives the sensation of colour. I had already drunk a good deal of port, and if I now asked for more it was not so much with a view to the well-being which the additional glasses would bring me as an effect of the well-being produced by the glasses that had gone before. I allowed the music itself to guide my pleasure from note to note, and, meekly following, it rested on each in turn. If, like one of those chemical industries by means of which compounds are produced in large quantities which in a state of nature are encountered only by accident and very rarely, this restaurant at Rivebelle assembled at one and the same moment more women to tempt me with beckoning vistas of happiness than I should have come across in the course of walks or travels in a whole year, at the same time this music that greeted our ears— arrangements of waltzes, of German operettas, of music-hall songs, all of them quite new to me—was itself like an ethereal pleasure-dome superimposed upon the other and more intoxicating still. For these tunes, each as individual as a woman, did not reserve, as she would have done, for some privileged person the voluptuous secret which they contained: they offered it to me, ogled me, came up to me with wayward or wanton movements, accosted me, caressed me as if I had suddenly become more seductive, more powerful, richer. Certainly I found in these tunes an element of cruelty; because any such thing as a disinterested feeling for beauty, a gleam of intelligence, was unknown to them; for them physical pleasure alone existed. And they are the most merciless of hells, the most firmly sealed, for the jealous wretch to whom they present that pleasure—that pleasure which the woman he loves is enjoy-ing with another—as the only thing that exists in the world for her who is all the world to him. But while I was humming softly to myself the notes of this tune and returning its kiss, the pleasure peculiar to itself which it made me feel became so dear to me that I would have left my father and mother to follow it through the singular world which it constructed in the invisible, in lines alter-nately filled with languor and vivacity. Although such a pleasure as this is not calculated to enhance the value of the person to whom it comes, for it is perceived by him alone, and although whenever, in the course of our lives, we have failed to attract a woman who has caught sight of us, she did not know whether at that moment we possessed this inward and subjective felicity which, consequently, could in no way have altered the judgment that she passed on us, I felt myself more powerful, almost irresistible. It seemed to me that my love was no longer something unattractive, at which people might smile, but had precisely the touching beauty, the seductiveness, of this music, itself comparable to a congenial atmosphere in which she whom I loved and I would have met, suddenly grown intimate.

This restaurant was not frequented solely by women of easy virtue, but also by people of the very best society, who came there for afternoon tea or gave big dinner-parties there. The tea-parties were held in a long gallery, glazed and narrow, shaped like a funnel, which led from the entrance hall to the dining-room and was bounded on one side by the garden, from which it was separated (but for a few stone pillars) only by its wall of glass which opened here and there. The result of which, apart from ubiquitous draughts, was sudden and intermittent bursts of sunshine, a dazzling and changeable light that made it almost impossible to see the tea-drinkers, so that when they were installed there, at tables crowded pair after pair the whole way along the narrow gully, shimmering and sparkling with every movement they made in drinking their tea or in greeting one another, it resembled a giant fish-tank or bow-net in which a fisherman has collected all his glittering catch, which, half out of water and bathed in sunlight, coruscate before one's eyes in an ever-changing iridescence.

A few hours later, during dinner, which, naturally, was served in the dining-room, the lights would be turned on, even when it was still quite light out of doors, so that one saw before one's eyes, in the garden, among summer-houses glimmering in the twilight like pale spectres of evening, arbours whose glaucous verdure was pierced by the last rays of the setting sun and which, from the lamp-lit room in which one was dining, appeared through the glass no longer—as one would have said of the ladies drinking tea in the afternoon along the blue and gold corridor—caught in a glittering and dripping net, but like the vegetation of a pale and green aquarium of gigantic size lit by a supernatural light. People began to rise from the table; and if each party, while their dinner lasted, although they spent the whole time examining, recognising, naming the party at the next table, had been held in perfect cohesion about their own, the magnetic force that had kept them gravitating round their host of the evening lost its power at the moment when they repaired for coffee to the same corridor that had been used for the tea-parties; so that it often happened that in its passage from place to place some party on the march dropped one or more of its human corpuscles who, having come under the irresistible attraction of the rival party, detached themselves for a moment from their own, in which their places were taken by

ladies or gentlemen who had come across to speak to friends
before hurrying off with an "I really must get back to my host
Monsieur X..." And for the moment one was reminded of two
separate bouquets that had exchanged a few of their flowers. Then
the corridor too began to empty. Often, since even after dinner
there might still be a little light left outside, this long corridor was
left unlighted, and, skirted by the trees that overhung it on the
other side of the glass, it suggested a pleached alley in a wooded
and shady garden. Sometimes, in the gloom, a fair diner would be
lingering there. As I passed through it one evening on my way out
I saw, sitting among a group of strangers, the beautiful Princesse de
Luxembourg. I raised my hat without stopping. She recognised
me, and nodded to me with a smile; in the air, far above her
salutation, but emanating from the movement, rose melodiously a
few words addressed to myself, which must have been a somewhat
amplified good-evening, intended not to stop me but simply to
complete the gesture, to make it a spoken greeting. But her words
remained so indistinct and the sound which was all that I caught
was prolonged so sweetly and seemed to me so musical that it was
as if, among the dim branches of the trees, a nightingale had begun
to sing.

   If it so happened that, to finish the evening with a party of his
friends whom we had met, Saint-Loup decided to go on to the
Casino of a neighbouring resort, and, taking them with him, put
me in a carriage by myself, I would urge the driver to go as fast as
he possibly could, so that the minutes might pass less slowly which
I must spend without having anyone at hand to exempt me from
furnishing my own sensibility—reversing the engine, so to speak,
and emerging from the passivity in which I was caught and held as
in a mesh—with those modifications which, since my arrival at
Rivebelle, I had been receiving from other people. The risk of
collision with a carriage coming the other way along those lanes
where there was barely room for one and it was dark as pitch; the
instability of the surface, crumbling in many places, at the cliff's
edge; the proximity of its vertical drop to the sea—none of these
things exerted on me the slight stimulus that would have been
required to bring the vision and the fear of danger within the orbit
of my reason. For just as it is not the desire to become famous but
the habit of being industrious that enables us to produce a finished
work, so it is not the activity of the present moment but wise
reflexions from the past that help us to safeguard the future. But if

already, before this point, on my arrival at Rivebelle, I had flung irretrievably away from me those crutches of reason and self-control which help our infirmity to follow the right road, if I now found myself the victim of a sort of moral ataxia, the alcohol that I had drunk, in stretching my nerves exceptionally, had given to the present moment a quality, a charm, which did not have the effect of making me more competent or indeed more resolute to defend it; for in making me prefer it a thousand times to the rest of my life, my exaltation isolated it therefrom; I was enclosed in the present, like heroes and drunkards; momentarily eclipsed, my past no longer projected before me that shadow of itself which we call our future; placing the goal of my life no longer in the realisation of the dreams of the past, but in the felicity of the present moment, I could see no further than it. So that, by a contradiction which was only apparent, it was at the very moment in which I was experiencing an exceptional pleasure, in which I felt that my life might yet be happy, in which it should have become more precious in my sight, it was at this very moment that, delivered from the anxieties which it had hitherto inspired in me, I unhesitatingly abandoned it to the risk of an accident. But after all, I was doing no more than concentrate in a single evening the carelessness that, for most men, is diluted throughout their whole existence, in which every day they face unnecessarily the dangers of a sea-voyage, of a trip in an aeroplane or motor-car, when there is waiting for them at home the person whom their death would shatter, or when the book whose eventual publication is the sole reason for their existence is still stored in the fragile receptacle of their brain. And so too in the Rivebelle restaurant, on evenings when we stayed there after dinner, if anyone had come in with the intention of killing me, since I no longer saw, save in a distance too remote to have any reality, my grandmother, my life to come, the books I might write, since I now clung body and soul to the scent of the woman at the next table, to the politeness of the waiters, to the contours of the waltz that the band was playing, since I was glued to the sensation of the moment, with no extension beyond its limits, nor any object other than not to be separated from it, I should have died in and with that sensation, I should have let myself be slaughtered without offering any resistance, without a movement, a bee drugged with tobacco smoke that had ceased to take any thought for preserving the accumulation of its labours and the hopes of its hive.

I ought here to add that this insignificance into which the most serious matters relapsed, by contrast with the violence of my exaltation, came in the end to include Mlle Simonet and her friends. The enterprise of knowing them seemed to me easy now but a matter of indifference, for my immediate sensation, thanks to its extraordinary intensity, to the joy that its slightest modifications, its mere continuity provoked, alone had any importance for me; all the rest, parents, work, pleasures, girls at Balbec, weighed no more than a flake of foam in a strong wind that will not let it find a resting place, existed no longer save in relation to this internal power: inebriation brings about for an hour or two a state of subjective idealism, pure phenomenalism; everything is reduced to appearances and exists only as a function of our sublime self. This is not to say that a genuine love, if we have one, cannot subsist in such a state. But we feel so unmistakably, as though in a new atmosphere, that unknown pressures have altered the dimensions of that love, that we can no longer consider it in the old way. It is indeed still there, but somehow displaced, no longer weighing upon us, satisfied by the sensation which the present affords it, a sensation that is sufficient for us, since for what is not the here and now we take no thought. Unfortunately the coefficient which thus alters our values alters them only during that hour of intoxication. The people who were no longer of any importance, whom we scattered with our breath like soap-bubbles, will tomorrow resume their density; we shall have to try afresh to settle down to work which had ceased to have any meaning. A more serious matter still, these mathematics of the morrow, the same as those of yesterday, in whose problems we shall find ourselves inexorably involved, govern us even during those hours, and we alone are unconscious of their rule. If there is a hostile or virtuous woman in our vicinity, that question so difficult an hour ago—to know whether we should succeed in finding favour with her—seems to us now a million times easier of solution without having become easier in any respect, for it is only in our eyes, in our own inward eyes, that we have altered. And she is as displeased with us at this moment for having taken a liberty with her as we shall be with ourselves next day at the thought of having given a hundred francs to the bell-hop, and for the same reason, which in our case has merely been delayed, namely the absence of intoxication.

I knew none of the women who were at Rivebelle and who, because they were part and parcel of my intoxication just as its reflexions are part and parcel of a mirror, appeared to me a thousand times more desirable than the less and less existent Mlle Simonet. One of them, young, fair, alone, with a sad expression on a face framed in a straw hat trimmed with field-flowers, gazed at me for a moment with a dreamy air and struck me as being attractive. Then it was the turn of another, and of a third; finally of a dark one with glowing cheeks. Almost all of them were known, if not to myself, to Saint-Loup.

He had, in fact, before he made the acquaintance of his present mistress, lived so much in the restricted world of amorous adventure that of all the women who were dining on those evenings at Rivebelle, where many of them had appeared quite by chance, having come to the coast some to join their lovers, others in the hope of finding lovers, there was scarcely one that he did not know from having spent—he himself, or one or other of his friends—at least one night with her. He did not greet them if they were with men, and they, although they looked more at him than at anyone else because the indifference which he was known to feel towards every woman who was not his actress gave him in their eyes a special glamour, appeared not to know him. But you could hear them whispering: "That's young Saint-Loup. It seems he's still quite gone on that tart of his. It's true love! What a handsome fellow he is! I think he's just wonderful. And what style! Some women have all the luck, don't they? And he's so nice in every way. I saw a lot of him when I was with d'Orléans. They were quite inseparable, those two. He was going the pace in those days. But he's given it all up now, she can't complain. Ah! she can certainly consider herself lucky. I wonder what in the world he sees in her. He must be a bit of a chump, when all's said and done. She's got feet like boats, whiskers like an American, and her undies are filthy. I can tell you, a little shop-girl would be ashamed to be seen in her knickers. Do just look at his eyes a moment: you'd go to hell for a man like that. Hush, don't say a word; he's seen me; look, he's smiling. Oh, he knew me all right. Just you mention my name to him, and see what he says!" Between these women and him I caught a glance of mutual understanding. I should have liked him to introduce me to them, so that I might ask them for assignations which they would grant me, even if I was unable to keep them. For otherwise each of their faces would remain for all time devoid, in my memory, of that part of itself—just as though it had been hidden by a veil—which varies in every woman, which we cannot imagine in any woman until we have actually seen it in her, and which appears only in the look she gives us that acquiesces in our desire and promises that it shall be satisfied. And yet, even thus reduced, their faces meant far more to me than those of women whom I knew to be virtuous, and did not seem to me to be flat, like theirs, with nothing behind them, fashioned in one piece with no depth or solidity. It was not, of course, for me what it must be for Saint-Loup who, by an act of memory, beneath the indifference, transparent to him, of the motionless features which affected not to know him, or beneath the dull formality of the greeting that might equally well have been addressed to anyone else, could recall, could see, dishevelled locks, a convulsed mouth, a pair of half-closed eyes, a whole silent picture like those that painters, to deceive the bulk of their visitors, drape with a decent covering. For me, who felt that nothing of my personality had penetrated the surface of any one of these women, or would be borne by her upon the unknown ways which she would tread through life, these faces remained sealed. But it was enough for me to know that they did open in order for them to seem to me to be more precious than I should have thought them had they been only handsome medals instead of lockets within which memories of love were hidden. As for Robert, scarcely able to keep his seat at table, concealing beneath a courtier's smile his warrior's thirst for action—when I looked at him closely I could see to what extent the vigorous bone structure of his triangular face must have been modelled on that of his ancestors, a face designed rather for an ardent bowman than for a sensitive man of letters. Beneath the delicate skin the bold construction, the feudal architecture were apparent. His head reminded one of those old castle keeps on which the disused battlements are still to be seen, although inside they have been converted into libraries.

On the way back to Balbec, of this or that charmer to whom he had introduced me I would repeat to myself without a moment's interruption, and yet almost unconsciously: "What a delightful woman!" as one sings a refrain. True, these words were prompted rather by over-excitement than by any lasting judgment. It was nevertheless true that if I had had a thousand francs on me and if there had still been a jeweller's shop open at that hour, I should have bought the unknown a ring. When the successive hours of our lives unfold as though on too widely disparate planes, we find that we give away too much of ourselves to all sorts of people who next day will not interest us in the least. But we feel that we are still responsible for what we said to them overnight, and that we must honour our promises.

Since, on those evenings, I came back late, it was a pleasure to be reunited, in a room no longer hostile, with the bed in which, on the day of my arrival, I had supposed that it would always be impossible for me to find any rest, whereas now my weary limbs longed for its support; so that, one after the other, my thighs, my hips and my shoulders sought to adhere at every point to the sheets that covered its mattress, as if my fatigue, like a sculptor, had wished to take a cast of an entire human body. But I could not get to sleep; I sensed the approach of morning; peace of mind, health of body were no longer mine. In my distress it seemed to me that I should never recapture them. I should have had to sleep for a long time if I were to find them again. But then, had I begun to doze, I must in any event be awakened in a couple of hours by the symphony concert on the beach. Suddenly I fell asleep, plunged into that deep slumber in which vistas are opened to us of a return to childhood, the recapture of past years, and forgotten feelings, of disincarnation, the transmigration of souls, the evoking of the dead, the illusions of madness, retrogression towards the most elementary of the natural kingdoms (for we say that we often see animals in our dreams, but we forget that almost always we are ourselves animals therein, deprived of that reasoning power which projects upon things the light of certainty; on the contrary we bring to bear on the spectacle of life only a dubious vision, extinguished anew every moment by oblivion, the former reality fading before that which follows it as one projection of a magic lantern fades before the next as we change the slide), all those mysteries which we imagine ourselves not to know and into which we are in reality initiated almost every night, as into the other great mystery of extinction and resurrection. Rendered more vagabond by the difficulty of digesting my Rivebelle dinner, the successive and flickering illumination of shadowy zones of my past made of me a person for whom the supreme happiness would have been to meet Legrandin, with whom I had just been talking in my dream.

And then, even my own life was entirely hidden from me by a new scene, like the drop lowered right at the front of the stage before which, while the scene shifters are busy behind, actors appear in an interim turn. The turn in which I was now playing a part was in the manner of oriental tales; I retained no knowledge of my past or of myself, on account of the extreme proximity of this interposed scenery; I was merely a character receiving the bastinado and undergoing various punishments for a crime the nature of which I could not make out, though it was actually that of having drunk too much port. Suddenly I awoke and discovered that, thanks to a long sleep, I had not heard a note of the concert. It was already afternoon; I verified this by my watch after several efforts to sit up in bed, efforts fruitless at first and interrupted by backward falls on to my pillow, brief falls of the kind that are a sequel of sleep as of other forms of intoxication, whether due to wine or to convalescence; in any case, even before I had looked at the time, I was certain that it was past midday. Last night I had been nothing more than an empty vessel, weightless, and (since one must have been lying down in order to be able to sit up, and have been asleep to be able to keep silent) had been unable to refrain from moving about and talking, no longer had any stability, any centre of gravity; I had been set in motion and it seemed that I might have continued on my dreary course until I reached the moon. But if, while I slept, my eyes had not seen the time, my body had nevertheless contrived to calculate it, had measured the hours not on a dial superficially decorated with figures, but by the steadily growing weight of all my replenished forces which, like a powerful clock, it had allowed, notch by notch, to descend from my brain into the rest of my body where they now accumulated as far as the top of my knees the unimpaired abundance of their store. If it is true that the sea was once upon a time our native element, in which we must plunge our blood to recover our strength, it is the same with oblivion, with mental nothingness; we seem then to absent ourselves for a few hours from time, but the forces which have gathered in that interval without being expended measure it by their quantity as accurately as the pendulum of the clock or the crumbling hillocks of the hour-glass. Moreover, one does not emerge more easily from such a sleep than from a prolonged spell of wakefulness, so strongly does everything tend to persist; and if it is true that certain narcotics make us sleep, to have slept for a long time is an even more potent narcotic, after which we have great difficulty in making ourselves wake up. Like a sailor who sees plainly the quay where he can moor his boat, still tossed by the waves, I had every intention of looking at the time and of getting up, but my body was constantly cast back upon the tide of sleep;

the landing was difficult, and before I attained a position in which I could reach my watch and confront its time with that indicated by the wealth of accumulated materials which my exhausted limbs had at their disposal, I fell back two or three times more upon my pillow.

At length I could reach and read it: "Two o'clock in the afternoon!" I rang, but at once I plunged back into a sleep which this time must have lasted infinitely longer if I was to judge by the refreshment, the vision of an immense night outlived, which I experienced on awakening. And yet, since my awakening was caused by the entry of Françoise, and since her entry had been prompted by my ringing the bell, this second sleep which, it seemed to me, must have been longer than the other and had brought me so much well-being and forgetfulness, could not have lasted for more than half a minute.

My grandmother opened the door of my bedroom, and I asked her countless questions about the Legrandin family.

It is not enough to say that I had returned to tranquillity and health, for it was more than a mere interval of space that had divided them from me the day before; I had had all night long to struggle against a contrary tide, and then I not only found myself again in their presence, but they had once more entered into me. At certain definite and still somewhat painful points beneath the surface of my empty head which would one day be broken, letting my ideas dissolve for ever, those ideas had once again taken their proper place and resumed that existence by which hitherto, alas, they had failed to profit.

Once again I had escaped from the impossibility of sleeping, from the deluge, the shipwreck of my nervous storms. I no longer feared the threats that had loomed over me the evening before, when I was deprived of rest. A new life was opening before me; without making a single movement, for I was still shattered, although quite alert and well, I savoured my weariness with a light heart; it had isolated and broken the bones of my legs and arms, which I could feel assembled before me, ready to come together again, and which I would rebuild merely by singing, like the architect in the fable.[4]

Suddenly I remembered the fair girl with the sad expression whom I had seen at Rivebelle and who had looked at me for a moment. Many others, in the course of the evening, had seemed to me attractive; now she alone arose from the depths of my memory. I felt that she had noticed me, and expected one of the Rivebelle waiters to come to me with a whispered message from her. Saint-Loup did not know her and believed that she was respectable. It would be very difficult to see her, to see her constantly. But I was prepared to make any sacrifice: I thought now only of her. Philosophy distinguishes often between free and necessary acts. Perhaps there is none to the necessity of which we are more completely subjected than that which, by virtue of a climbing power held in check during the act itself, brings back (once our mind is at rest) a memory until then levelled down with all the rest by the oppressive force of bemusement and makes it spring to the surface because unknown to us it contained more than any of the others a charm of which we do not become aware until the following day. And perhaps, too, there is no act so free, for it is still unprompted by habit, by that sort of mental obsession which, in matters of love, encourages the invariable reappearance of the image of one particular person.

That day, as it happened, was the day after the one on which I had seen the beautiful procession of young girls advancing along the sea-front. I questioned a number of the visitors in the hotel about them, people who came almost every year to Balbec. They could tell me nothing. Later on, a photograph showed me why. Who could now have recognised in them, scarcely and yet quite definitely beyond the age at which one changes so completely, an amorphous, delicious mass, still utterly childish, of little girls who, only a few years back, might have been seen sitting in a ring on the sand round a tent: a sort of vague, white constellation in which one would have distinguished a pair of eyes that sparkled more than the rest, a mischievous face, flaxen hair, only to lose them again and to confound them almost at once in the indistinct and milky nebula.

No doubt, in those earlier years that were still so comparatively recent, it was not, as it had been yesterday when they appeared for the first time before me, the impression of the group but the group itself that had been lacking in clearness. Then those children, still mere babies, had been at that elementary stage in their development when personality has not yet stamped its seal on each face. Like those primitive organisms in which the individual barely exists by itself, is constituted by the polypary rather than by each of the polyps that compose it, they were still pressed one against another. Sometimes one pushed her neighbour over, and then a giggle, which seemed the sole manifestation of their personal life, convulsed them all together, obliterating, merging those imprecise and grinning faces in the congealment of a single cluster, scintillating and tremulous. In an old photograph of themselves, which they were one day to give me, and which I have kept ever since, their childish troupe already presents the same number of participants as, later, their feminine procession; one can sense from it that their presence must even then have made on the beach an unusual impression which forced itself on the attention, but one cannot recognise them individually save by a process of reasoning, making allowances for all the transformations possible during girlhood, up to the point at which these reconstituted forms would begin to encroach upon another individuality which must be identified also, and whose handsome face, owing to the concomitance of a tall build and curly hair, may quite possibly have been, long ago, that wizened and impish little grin which the photograph album presents to us; and the distance traversed in a short interval of time by the physical characteristics of each of these girls making of them a criterion too vague to be of any use, and moreover what they had in common and, so to speak, collectively, being therefore very pronounced, it sometimes happened that even their most intimate friends mistook one for another in this photograph, so much so that the question could in the last resort be settled only by some detail of costume which one of them was certain to have worn to the exclusion of the others. Since those days, so different from the day on which I had just seen them strolling along the front, so different and yet so close in time, they still gave way to fits of laughter, as I had observed the previous afternoon, but to laughter of a kind that was no longer the intermittent and almost automatic laughter of childhood, a spasmodic explosion which, in those days, had continually sent their heads dipping out of the circle, as the clusters of minnows in the Vivonne used to scatter and vanish only to gather again a moment later; each of their physiognomies was now mistress of itself, their eyes were fixed on the goal they were pursuing; and it had taken, yesterday, the tremulous uncertainty of my first impression to make me confuse vaguely (as their childish hilarity and the old photograph had confused) the spores, now individualised and disjoined, of the pale madrepore.

Doubtless often enough before, when pretty girls went by, I had promised myself that I would see them again. As a rule, people

PLACE-NAMES · THE PLACE 175

thus seen do not appear a second time; moreover our memory, which speedily forgets their existence, would find it difficult to recall their features; our eyes would not recognise them, perhaps, and in the meantime we have seen others go by, whom we shall not see again either. But at other times, and this was what was to happen with the pert little band at Balbec, chance brings them back insistently before our eyes. Chance seems to us then a good and useful thing, for we discern in it as it were the rudiments of organisation, of an attempt to arrange our lives; and it makes it easy, inevitable, and sometimes—after interruptions that have made us hope that we may cease to remember—painful for us to retain in our minds images for the possession of which we shall come in time to believe that we were predestined, and which but for chance we should from the very first have managed to forget, like so many others, so easily.

Presently Saint-Loup's visit drew to an end. I had not seen those girls again on the beach. He was too little at Balbec in the afternoons to have time to pay attention to them and attempt, in my interest, to make their acquaintance. In the evenings he was freer, and continued to take me regularly to Rivebelle. There are, in such restaurants, as there are in public gardens and railway trains, people enclosed in a quite ordinary appearance, whose names astonish us when, having happened to ask, we discover that they are not the mere inoffensive strangers whom we supposed but no less than the Minister or the Duke of whom we have so often heard. Two or three times already, in the Rivebelle restaurant, when everyone else was getting ready to leave, Saint-Loup and I had seen a man of large stature, very muscular, with regular features and a grizzled beard, come in and sit down at a table, where his pensive gaze remained fixed with concentrated attention upon the void. One evening, on our asking the landlord who this obscure, solitary and belated diner was, "What!" he exclaimed, "do you mean to say you don't know the famous painter Elstir?" Swann had once mentioned his name to me, I had entirely forgotten in what connexion; but the omission of a particular memory, like that of part of a sentence when we are reading, leads sometimes not to uncertainty but to the birth of a premature certainty. "He's a friend of Swann's, and a very well-known artist, extremely good," I told Saint-Loup. Immediately the thought swept through us both like a thrill of emotion, that Elstir was a great artist, a celebrated man, and that, confounding us with the rest of the diners, he had no suspicion of the excitement into which we were plunged by the idea of his talent. Doubtless, his unconsciousness of our admiration and of our acquaintance with Swann would not have troubled us had we not been at the seaside. But since we were still at an age when enthusiasm cannot keep silence, and had been transported into a life where anonymity is suffocating, we wrote a letter, signed with both our names, in which we revealed to Elstir in the two diners seated within a few feet of him two passionate admirers of his talent, two friends of his great friend Swann, and asked to be allowed to pay our homage to him in person. A waiter undertook to convey this missive to the celebrity.

A celebrity Elstir was perhaps not yet at this period quite to the extent claimed by the landlord, though he was to reach the height of his fame within a very few years. But he had been one of the first to frequent this restaurant when it was still only a sort of farm-house, and had brought to it a whole colony of artists (who had all, as it happened, migrated elsewhere as soon as the farm, where they used to feed in the open air under a lean-to roof, had become a fashionable centre; Elstir himself had returned to Rivebelle this evening on account of the temporary absence of his wife, with whom he lived not far away). But great talent, even when its existence is not yet recognised, will inevitably provoke a few quirks of admiration, such as the landlord had managed to detect in the questions asked by more than one English lady visitor, athirst for information as to the life led by Elstir, or in the number of letters that he received from abroad. Then the landlord had further remarked that Elstir did not like to be disturbed when he was working, that he would rise in the middle of the night and take a young model down to the sea-shore to pose for him, nude, if the moon was shining, and had told himself that so much labour was not in vain, nor the admiration of the tourist unjustified, when he had recognised in one of Elstir's pictures a wooden cross which stood by the roadside on the way into Rivebelle.

"That's it all right," he would repeat with stupefaction, "there are all the four beams! Oh, he does take a lot of trouble!"

And he did not know whether a little *Sunrise over the Sea* which Elstir had given him might not be worth a fortune.

We watched him read our letter, put it in his pocket, finish his dinner, begin to ask for his things, get up to go; and we were so convinced that we had offended him by our overture that we

would now have hoped (as keenly as at first we had dreaded) to
make our escape without his noticing us. What did not cross our
minds for a single instant was a consideration which should have
seemed to us of cardinal importance, namely that our enthusiasm
for Elstir, on the sincerity of which we would not have allowed the
least doubt to be cast, which we could indeed have confirmed
with the evidence of our bated breath, our desire to do no matter
what that was difficult or heroic for the great man, was not, as we
imagined it to be, admiration, since neither of us had ever seen
anything that he had painted; our feeling might have as its object
the hollow idea of a "great artist," but not a body of work which
was unknown to us. It was, at most, admiration in the abstract, the
nervous envelope, the sentimental framework of an admiration
without content, that is to say a thing as indissolubly attached to
boyhood as are certain organs which no longer exist in the adult
man; we were still boys. Elstir meanwhile was approaching the
door when suddenly he turned and came towards us. I was
overcome by a delicious thrill of terror such as I could not have
felt a few years later, because, as age diminishes the capacity,
familiarity with the world meanwhile destroys in us any inclination to provoke such strange encounters, to feel that kind of
emotion.

In the course of the few words that Elstir came to say to us,
sitting down at our table, he never replied to me on the several
occasions on which I spoke to him of Swann. I began to think that
he did not know him. He nevertheless asked me to come and see
him at his Balbec studio, an invitation which he did not extend to
Saint-Loup, and which I had earned, as I might not, perhaps, from
Swann's recommendation had Elstir been a friend of his (for the
part played by disinterested motives is greater than we are inclined
to think in people's lives), by a few words which made him think
that I was devoted to the arts. He lavished on me a friendliness
which was as far above that of Saint-Loup as the latter's was above
the affability of a shop-keeper. Compared with that of a great
artist, the friendliness of a great nobleman, however charming it
may be, seems like play-acting, like simulation. Saint-Loup sought
to please; Elstir loved to give, to give himself. Everything that he
possessed, ideas, works, and the rest which he counted for far less,
he would have given gladly to anyone who understood him. But,
for lack of congenial company, he lived in an unsociable isolation
which fashionable people called pose and ill-breeding, the

authorities a recalcitrant spirit, his neighbours madness, his family selfishness and pride.

And no doubt at first he had thought with pleasure, even in his solitude, that, thanks to his work, he was addressing from a distance, was imbuing with a loftier idea of himself, those who had misunderstood or offended him. Perhaps, in those days, he lived alone not from indifference but from love of his fellows, and, just as I had renounced Gilberte in order to appear to her again one day in more attractive colours, dedicated his work to certain people as a sort of new approach to them whereby, without actually seeing him, they would be brought to love him, admire him, talk about him; a renunciation is not always total from the start, when we decide upon it in our original frame of mind and before it has reacted upon us, whether it be the renunciation of an invalid, a monk, an artist or a hero. But if he had wished to produce with certain people in his mind, in producing he had lived for himself, remote from society, to which he had become indifferent; the practice of solitude had given him a love for it, as happens with every big thing which we have begun by fearing, because we know it to be incompatible with smaller things which we prize and which it does not so much deprive us of as detach us from. Before we experience it, our whole preoccupation is to know to what extent we can reconcile it with certain pleasures which cease to be pleasures as soon as we have experienced it.

Elstir did not stay talking to us for long. I made up my mind that I would go to his studio during the next few days, but on the following afternoon, after I had accompanied my grandmother to the far end of the sea-front, near the cliffs of Canapville, on the way back, at the corner of one of the little streets which ran down at right angles to the beach, we passed a girl who, hanging her head like an animal that is being driven reluctant to its stall, and carrying golf-clubs, was walking in front of an authoritarian-looking person, in all probability her or one of her friends' "Miss," who suggested a portrait of Jeffreys by Hogarth, with a face as red as if her favourite beverage were gin rather than tea, on which a dried smear of tobacco at the corner of her mouth prolonged the curve of a moustache that was grizzled but abundant. The girl who preceded her resembled the member of the little band who, beneath a black polo-cap, had shown in an inexpressive chubby face a pair of laughing eyes. However, though this one had also a black polo-cap, she struck me as being even prettier than the other; the line of her nose was straighter, the curve of the nostrils fuller and more fleshy. Besides, the other had seemed a proud, pale girl, this one a child well-disciplined and of rosy complexion. And yet, since she was pushing a bicycle just like the other's, and was wearing the same kid gloves, I concluded that the differences arose perhaps from the angle and the circumstances in which I now saw her, for it was hardly likely that there could be at Balbec a second girl with a face that was on the whole so similar and combining the same details in her accoutrement. She flung a rapid glance in my direction. During the next few days, when I saw the little band again on the beach, and indeed long afterwards when I knew all the girls who composed it, I could never be absolutely certain that any of them—even the one who resembled her most, the girl with the bicycle—was indeed the one that I had seen that evening at the corner of the street at the end of the esplanade, a girl who was scarcely but still just perceptibly different from the one I had noticed in the procession.

From that moment, whereas for the last few days my mind had been occupied chiefly by the tall one, it was the one with the golf-clubs, presumed to be Mlle Simonet, who began once more to absorb my attention. When walking with the others she would often stop, forcing her friends, who seemed greatly to respect her, to stop also. Thus it is, coming to a halt, her eyes sparkling beneath her polo-cap, that I still see her again today, silhouetted against the screen which the sea spreads out behind her, and separated from me by a transparent sky-blue space, the interval of time that has elapsed since then—the first impression, faint and tenuous in my memory, desired, pursued, then forgotten, then recaptured, of a face which I have many times since projected upon the cloud of the past in order to be able to say to myself, of a girl who was actually in my room: "It is she!"

But it was perhaps yet another, the one with geranium cheeks and green eyes, whom I should have liked most to know. And yet, whichever of them it might be, on any given day, that I preferred to see, the others, without her, were sufficient to excite my desire which, concentrated now chiefly on one, now on another, con-tinued—as, on the first day, my confused vision had done—to combine and blend them, to make of them the little world apart, animated by a life in common, which indeed they doubtless imagined themselves to form; and in becoming a friend of one of them I should have penetrated—like a cultivated pagan or a meticulous Christian going among barbarians—a youthful society in which thoughtlessness, health, sensual pleasure, cruelty, unintellectuality and joy held sway.

My grandmother, whom I had told of my meeting with Elstir and who rejoiced at the thought of all the intellectual profit that I might derive from his friendship, considered it absurd and none too polite of me not to have yet gone to pay him a visit. But I could think only of the little band, and being uncertain of the hour at which the girls would be passing along the front, I dared not absent myself. My grandmother was astonished, too, at the elegance of my attire, for I had suddenly remembered suits which had been lying all this time at the bottom of my trunk. I put on a different one every day, and had even written to Paris ordering new hats and new ties.

It adds a great charm to life in a watering-place like Balbec if the face of a pretty girl, a vendor of shells, cakes or flowers, painted in vivid colours in our mind, is regularly, from early morning, the purpose of each of those leisured, luminous days which we spend on the beach. They become then, and for that reason, albeit idle, as alert as working-days, pointed, magnetised, raised slightly to meet an approaching moment, that in which, while we purchase shortbread, roses, ammonites, we will delight in seeing, on a feminine face, colours displayed as purely as on a flower. But at least one can speak to these young vendors, and this dispenses one from having to construct with one's imagination those aspects which a mere visual perception fails to provide, and to re-create their life, magnifying its charm, as in front of a portrait; moreover, precisely because one speaks to them, one can learn where and at what time it will be possible to see them again. Now I had none of these advantages when it came to the little band. Since their habits were unknown to me, when on certain days I failed to catch a glimpse of them, not knowing the cause of their absence I sought to discover whether it was something fixed and regular, if they were to be seen only every other day, or in certain kinds of weather, or if there were days on which they were not to be seen at all. I imagined myself already friends with them, and saying: "But you weren't there the other day?" "Weren't we? Oh, no, of course not; it was a Saturday. On Saturdays we don't ever come, because . . ." If only it were simply a matter of knowing that on black Saturday it was useless to torment oneself, that one might range the beach from end to end, sit down outside the pastry-cook's and pretend to be nibbling an éclair, poke into the curio shop, wait for bathing time, the concert, high tide, sunset, night, all without seeing the longed-for little band. But the fatal day did not, perhaps, come once a week. It did not, perhaps, of necessity fall on a Saturday. Perhaps certain atmospheric conditions influenced it or were entirely unconnected with it. How many observations, patient but not at all serene, must one accumulate of the movements, to all appear-ance irregular, of these unknown worlds before being able to be sure that one has not allowed oneself to be led astray by mere coincidence, that one's forecasts will not be proved wrong, before deducing the incontrovertible laws, acquired at the cost of so much painful experience, of that passionate astronomy!

Remembering that I had not yet seen them on some particular day of the week, I assured myself that they would not be coming, that it was useless to wait any longer on the beach. And at that very moment I caught sight of them. And yet on another day which, in so far as I had been able to conjecture that there were laws that guided the return of those constellations, must, I had calculated, prove an auspicious day, they did not come. But to this primary uncertainty as to whether I should see them or not that day, there was added another, more disquieting: whether I should ever set eyes on them again, for I had no reason, after all, to know that they were not about to set sail for America, or return to Paris. This was enough to make me begin to love them. One can feel an attraction towards a particular person. But to release that fount of sorrow, that sense of the irreparable, those agonies which prepare the way for love, there must be—and this is perhaps, more than a person, the actual object which our passion seeks so anxiously to embrace—the risk of an impossibility. Thus already they were acting upon me, those influences which recur in the course of our successive love affairs (which can moreover occur, but then rather in the life of big cities, in relation to working-girls of whose half-holidays we are uncertain and whom we are alarmed not to have seen at the factory exit), or which at least have recurred in the course of mine. Perhaps they are inseparable from love; perhaps everything that formed a distinctive feature of our first love comes to attach itself to those that follow, by virtue of recollection, suggestion, habit, and, through the successive periods of our life, gives to its different aspects a general character.

I seized every pretext for going down to the beach at the hours when I hoped to succeed in finding them there. Having caught sight of them once while we were at lunch, I now invariably came in late for it, waiting interminably on the esplanade for them to pass; spending the whole of my brief stay in the dining-room interrogating with my eyes its azure wall of glass; rising long before dessert, so as not to miss them should they have gone out at a different hour, and chafing with irritation at my grandmother when, with unwitting malevolence, she made me stay with her past the hour that seemed to me propitious. I tried to prolong the horizon by changing the position of my chair, and if by chance I did catch sight of one or other of the girls, since they all partook of the same special essence, it was as if I had seen projected before my face in a shifting, diabolical hallucination a little of the unfriendly and yet passionately coveted dream which, but a moment ago, had existed only—stagnating permanently there—in my brain.

I loved none of them, loving them all, and yet the possibility of meeting them was in my daily life the sole element of delight, alone aroused in me those hopes for which one would break down every obstacle, hopes ending often in fury if I had not seen them. For the moment, these girls eclipsed my grandmother in my affection; the longest journey would at once have seemed attractive to me had it been to a place in which they might be found. It was to them that my thoughts agreeably clung when I supposed myself to be thinking of something else or of nothing. But when, even without knowing it, I thought of them, they, more unconsciously still, were for me the mountainous blue undulations of the sea, the outline of a procession against the sea. It was the sea that I hoped to find, if I went to some town where they had gone. The most exclusive love for a person is always a love for something else.

Meanwhile my grandmother, because I now showed a keen interest in golf and tennis and was letting slip an opportunity of seeing at work and hearing talk an artist whom she knew to be one of the greatest of his time, evinced for me a scorn which seemed to me to be based on somewhat narrow views. I had guessed long ago in the Champs-Elysées, and had verified since, that when we are in love with a woman we simply project on to her a state of our own soul; that consequently the important thing is not the worth of the woman but the profundity of the state; and that the emotions which a perfectly ordinary girl arouses in us can enable us to bring to the surface of our consciousness some of the innermost parts of our being, more personal, more remote, more quintessential than any that might be evoked by the pleasure we derive from the conversation of a great man or even from the admiring contemplation of his work.

I finally had to comply with my grandmother's wishes, all the more reluctantly in that Elstir lived at some distance from the front in one of the newest of Balbec's avenues. The heat of the day obliged me to take the tramway which passed along the Rue de la Plage, and I endeavoured, in order to persuade myself that I was in the ancient realm of the Cimmerians, in the country, perhaps, of King Mark, or on the site of the Forest of Broceliande, not to look at the gimcrack splendour of the buildings that extended on either hand, among which Elstir's villa was perhaps the most sumptuously hideous, in spite of which he had taken it because, of all that there were to be had at Balbec, it was the only one that provided him with a really big studio.

It was with averted eyes that I crossed the garden, which had a lawn (similar, on a smaller scale, to that of any suburban villa round Paris), a statuette of an amorous gardener, glass balls in which one saw one's distorted reflexion, beds of begonias, and a little arbour beneath which rocking chairs were drawn up round an iron table. But after all these preliminaries stamped with urban ugliness, I took no notice of the chocolate mouldings on the plinths once I was in the studio; I felt perfectly happy, for, with the help of all the sketches and studies that surrounded me, I foresaw the possibility of raising myself to a poetical understanding, rich in delights, of manifold forms which I had not hitherto isolated from the total spectacle of reality. And Elstir's studio appeared to me like the laboratory of a sort of new creation of the world in which, from the chaos that is everything we see, he had extracted, by painting them on various rectangles of canvas that were placed at all angles, here a sea-wave angrily crashing its lilac foam on to the sand, there a young man in white linen leaning on the rail of a ship. The young man's jacket and the splashing wave had acquired a new dignity from the fact that they continued to exist, even though they were deprived of those qualities in which they might be supposed to consist, the wave being no longer able to wet or the jacket to clothe anyone.

At the moment at which I entered, the creator was just finishing, with the brush which he had in his hand, the outline of the setting sun.

The blinds were closed almost everywhere round the studio, which was fairly cool and, except in one place where daylight laid

against the wall its brilliant but fleeting decoration, dark; one small
rectangular window alone was open, embowered in honeysuckle
and giving on to an avenue beyond a strip of garden; so that the
atmosphere of the greater part of the studio was dusky, transparent
and compact in its mass, but liquid and sparkling at the edges
where the sunlight encased it, like a lump of rock crystal of
which one surface, already cut and polished, gleams here and
there like a mirror with iridescent rays. While Elstir, at my request,
went on painting, I wandered about in the half-light, stopping to
examine first one picture, then another.

Most of those that covered the walls were not what I should
chiefly have liked to see of his work, paintings in what an English
art journal which lay on the reading-room table in the Grand
Hotel called his first and second manners, the mythological manner and the manner in which he showed signs of Japanese influence, both admirably represented, it was said, in the collection of
Mme de Guermantes. Naturally enough, what he had in his studio
were almost all sea-scapes done here at Balbec. But I was able to
discern from these that the charm of each of them lay in a sort of
metamorphosis of the objects represented, analogous to what in
poetry we call metaphor, and that, if God the Father had created
things by naming them, it was by taking away their names or
giving them other names that Elstir created them anew. The
names which designate things correspond invariably to an intellectual notion, alien to our true impressions, and compelling us to
eliminate from them everything that is not in keeping with that
notion.

Sometimes, at my window in the hotel at Balbec, in the morning when Françoise undid the blankets that shut out the light, or in
the evening when I was waiting until it was time to go out with
Saint-Loup, I had been led by some effect of sunlight to mistake
what was only a darker stretch of sea for a distant coastline, or to
gaze delightedly at a belt of liquid azure without knowing whether
it belonged to sea or sky. But presently my reason would re-
establish between the elements the distinction which my first
impression had abolished. In the same way from my bedroom in
Paris I would sometimes hear a dispute, almost a riot, in the street
below, until I had traced back to its cause—a carriage for instance
that was rattling towards me—that noise from which I now
eliminated the shrill and discordant vociferations which my ear
had really heard but which my reason knew that wheels did not

produce. But the rare moments in which we see nature as she is, poetically, were those from which Elstir's work was created. One of the metaphors that occurred most frequently in the sea-scapes which surrounded him here was precisely that which, comparing land with sea, suppressed all demarcation between them. It was this comparison, tacitly and untiringly repeated on a single canvas, which gave it that multiform and powerful unity, the cause (not always clearly perceived by themselves) of the enthusiasm which Elstir's work aroused in certain collectors.

It was, for instance, for a metaphor of this sort—in a picture of the harbour of Carquethuit, a picture which he had finished only a few days earlier and which I stood looking at for a long time—that Elstir had prepared the mind of the spectator by employing, for the little town, only marine terms, and urban terms for the sea. Whether because its houses concealed a part of the harbour, a dry dock, or perhaps the sea itself plunging deep inland, as constantly happened on the Balbec coast, on the other side of the promontory on which the town was built the roofs were over-topped (as they might have been by chimneys or steeples) by masts which had the effect of making the vessels to which they belonged appear town-bred, built on land, an impression reinforced by other boats moored along the jetty but in such serried ranks that you could see men talking across from one deck to another without being able to distinguish the dividing line, the chink of water between them, so that this fishing fleet seemed less to belong to the water than, for instance, the churches of Criquebec which, in the distance, surrounded by water on every side because you saw them without seeing the town, in a powdery haze of sunlight and crumbling waves, seemed to be emerging from the waters, blown in alabaster or in sea-foam, and, enclosed in the band of a variegated rainbow, to form an ethereal, mystical tableau. On the beach in the foreground the painter had contrived that the eye should discover no fixed boundary, no absolute line of demarcation between land and sea. The men who were pushing down their boats into the sea were running as much through the waves as along the sand, which, being wet, reflected the hulls as if they were already in the water. The sea itself did not come up in an even line but followed the irregularities of the shore, which the perspective of the picture increased still further, so that a ship actually at sea, half-hidden by the projecting works of the arsenal, seemed to be sailing through the middle of the town; women gathering shrimps

among the rocks had the appearance, because they were surrounded by water and because of the depression which, beyond
the circular barrier of rocks, brought the beach (on the two sides
nearest the land) down to sea-level, of being in a marine grotto
overhung by ships and waves, open yet protected in the midst of
miraculously parted waters. If the whole picture gave this impression of harbours in which the sea penetrated the land, in which the
land was already subaqueous and the population amphibian, the
strength of the marine element was everywhere apparent; and
round about the rocks, at the mouth of the harbour where the
sea was rough, one sensed, from the muscular efforts of the fishermen and the slant of the boats leaning over at an acute angle,
compared with the calm erectness of the warehouse, the church,
the houses in the town to which some of the figures were returning and from which others were setting out to fish, that they were
riding bareback on the water as though on a swift and fiery animal
whose rearing, but for their skill, must have unseated them. A
party of holiday-makers were putting gaily out to sea in a boat that
tossed like a jaunting-car on a rough road; their boatmen, blithe
but none the less attentive, trimmed the bellying sail, everyone
kept in his place in order not to unbalance and capsize the boat,
and so they went scudding through sunlit fields and shady places,
rushing down the slopes. It was a fine morning in spite of the
recent storm. Indeed, one could still feel the powerful impulses
that must first be neutralised in order to attain the easy balance of
the boats that lay motionless, enjoying sunshine and breeze, in
parts where the sea was so calm that the reflections had almost
more solidity and reality than the floating hulls, vaporised by an
effect of the sunlight and made to overlap one another by the
perspective. Or rather one would not have called them other parts
of the sea. For between those parts there was as much difference as
there was between one of them and the church rising from the
water, or the ships behind the town. One's reason then set to work
to make a single element of what was in one place black beneath a
gathering storm, a little further all of one colour with the sky and as
brightly burnished, and elsewhere so bleached by sunshine, haze
and foam, so compact, so terrestrial, so circumscribed with houses
that one thought of some white stone causeway or of a field of
snow, up the slope of which one was alarmed to see a ship come
climbing high and dry, as a carriage climbs dripping from a
ford, but which a moment later, when you saw on the raised,

uneven surface of the solid plain boats drunkenly heaving, you understood, identical in all these different aspects, to be still the sea.

Although it is rightly said that there can be no progress, no discovery in art, but only in the sciences, and that each artist starting afresh on an individual effort cannot be either helped or hindered therein by the efforts of any other, it must none the less be acknowledged that, in so far as art brings to light certain laws, once an industry has popularised them, the art that was first in the field loses retrospectively a little of its originality. Since Elstir began to paint, we have grown familiar with what are called "wonderful" photographs of scenery and towns. If we press for a definition of what their admirers mean by the epithet, we shall find that it is generally applied to some unusual image of a familiar object, an image different from those that we are accustomed to see, unusual and yet true to nature, and for that reason doubly striking because it surprises us, takes us out of our cocoon of habit, and at the same time brings us back to ourselves by recalling to us an earlier impression. For instance, one of these "magnificent" photographs will illustrate a law of perspective, will show us some cathedral which we are accustomed to see in the middle of a town, taken instead from a selected vantage point from which it will appear to be thirty times the height of the houses and to be thrusting out a spur from the bank of the river, from which it is actually at some distance. Now the effort made by Elstir to reproduce things not as he knew them to be but according to the optical illusions of which our first sight of them is composed, had led him precisely to bring out certain of these laws of perspective, which were thus all the more striking, since art had been the first to disclose them. A river, because of the windings of its course, a bay because of the apparent proximity to one another of the cliffs on either side of it, would seem to have hollowed out in the heart of the plain or of the mountains, a lake absolutely landlocked on every side. In a picture of a view from Balbec painted upon a scorching day in summer an inlet of the sea, enclosed between walls of pink granite, appeared not to be the sea, which began further out. The continuity of the ocean was suggested only by the gulls which, wheeling over what seemed to be solid rock, were as a matter of fact sniffing the moist vapour of the shifting tide. Other laws emerged from the same canvas, as, at the foot of immense cliffs, the lilliputian grace of white sails on the blue mirror on whose surface they looked like sleeping butterflies, and certain contrasts between the depth of the shadows and the paleness of the light. This play of light and shade, which photography has also rendered commonplace, had interested Elstir so much that at one time he had delighted in painting what were almost mirages, in which a castle crowned with a tower appeared as a completely circular castle extended by a tower at its summit, and at its foot by an inverted tower, either because the exceptional purity of the atmosphere on a fine day gave the shadow reflected in the water the hardness and brightness of stone, or because the morning mists rendered the stone as vaporous as the shadow. And similarly, beyond the sea, behind a line of woods, another sea began, roseate with the light of the setting sun, which was in fact the sky. The light, fashioning as it were new solids, thrust back the hull of the boat on which it fell behind the other hull that was still in shadow, and arranged as it were the steps of a crystal staircase on what was in reality the flat surface, broken only by the play of light and shade, of the morning sea. A river running beneath the bridges of a town was caught from such an angle that it appeared entirely dislocated, now broadening into a lake, now narrowing into a rivulet, broken elsewhere by the interposition of a hill crowned with trees among which the townsman would repair at evening to breathe the cool air; and even the rhythm of this topsy-turvy town was assured only by the rigid vertical of the steeples which did not rise but rather, in accordance with the plumbline of the pendulum of gravity beating time as in a triumphal march, seemed to hold suspended beneath them the blurred mass of houses that rose in terraces through the mist along the banks of the crushed, disjointed stream. And (since Elstir's earliest works belonged to the time in which a painter would embellish his landscape by inserting a human figure), on the cliff's edge or among the mountains, the path too, that half-human part of nature, underwent, like river or ocean, the eclipses of perspective. And whether a mountain ridge, or the spray of a waterfall, or the sea prevented the eye from following the continuity of the path, visible to the traveller but not to us, the little human figure in old-fashioned clothes, lost in those solitudes, seemed often to be stopped short on the edge of a precipice, the path which he had been following ending there, while, a thousand feet above him in those pine-forests, it was with a fond eye and a relieved heart that we saw reappear the threadlike whiteness of its sandy surface, grateful to the wayfarer's feet, though the mountainside had concealed from us its intervening bends as it skirted the waterfall or the gulf.

The effort made by Elstir to strip himself, when face to face with reality, of every intellectual notion, was all the more admirable in that this man who made himself deliberately ignorant before sitting down to paint, forgot everything that he knew in his honesty of purpose (for what one knows does not belong to oneself), had in fact an exceptionally cultivated mind. When I confessed to him the disappointment I had felt on seeing the porch at Balbec:

"What!" he exclaimed, "you were disappointed by the porch! Why, it's the finest illustrated Bible that the people have ever had. That Virgin and all the bas-reliefs telling the story of her life—it's the most loving, the most inspired expression of that endless poem of adoration and praise in which the Middle Ages extolled the glory of the Madonna. If you only knew, side by side with the most scrupulous accuracy in rendering the sacred text, what exquisite *trouvailles* came to the old carver, what profound thoughts, what delicious poetry! The idea of that great sheet in which the angels carry the body of the Virgin, too sacred for them to venture to touch it with their hands" (I mentioned to him that this theme had been treated also at Saint-André-des-Champs; he had seen photographs of the porch there, and agreed, but pointed out that the eagerness of those little peasant figures, all scurrying together round the Virgin, was not at all the same thing as the gravity of those two great angels, almost Italian, so slender, so gentle); "and the angel who carries away the Virgin's soul, to reunite it with her body; or in the meeting of the Virgin with Elizabeth, Elizabeth's gesture when she touches the Virgin's womb and marvels to feel that it is swollen; and the outstretched arm of the midwife who had refused, without touching, to believe in the Virgin Birth; and the loincloth thrown by the Virgin to St Thomas to give him proof of the Resurrection; that veil, too, which the Virgin tears from her own breast to cover the nakedness of her son, whose blood, the wine of the Eucharist, the Church collects from one side of him, while on the other the Synagogue, its kingdom at an end, has its eyes bandaged, holds a half-broken sceptre and lets fall, together with the crown that is slipping from its head, the tables of the old law. And the husband who, on the Day of Judgment, as he helps his young wife to rise from her grave, lays her hand against his own heart to reassure her, to prove to her that it is indeed beating, isn't that also rather a stunning idea, really inspired? And the angel who is taking away the sun and the moon which are no longer needed since it is written that the Light of the Cross will be seven times brighter than the light of the firmament; and the one who is dipping his hand into Jesus's bath, to see whether the water is warm enough; and the one emerging from the clouds to place the crown on the Virgin's brow; and all the angels leaning from the vault of heaven, between the balusters of the New Jerusalem, and throwing up their arms in horror or joy at the sight of the torments of the wicked or the bliss of the elect! Because it's all the circles of heaven, a whole gigantic poem full of theology and symbolism that you have there. It's prodigious, it's divine, it's a thousand times better than anything you will see in Italy, where for that matter this very tympanum has been carefully copied by sculptors with far less genius. Because, you know, it's all a question of genius. There never was a time when everybody had genius, that's all nonsense, it would be more extraordinary than the golden age. The chap who carved that façade, take my word for it, was every bit as good, had just as profound ideas, as the men you admire most at the present day. I could show you what I meant if we went there together. There are certain passages from the Office of the Assumption which have been conveyed with a subtlety that not even a Redon could equal."

And yet, when my eager eyes had opened before the façade of Balbec church, it was not this vast celestial vision of which he spoke to me that I had seen, not this gigantic theological poem which I understood to have been inscribed there in stone. I spoke to him of those great statues of saints mounted on stilts which formed a sort of avenue on either side.

"It starts from the mists of antiquity to end in Jesus Christ," he explained. "You see on one side his ancestors after the spirit, on the other the Kings of Judah, his ancestors after the flesh. All the ages are there. And if you looked more closely at what you took for stilts you would have been able to give names to the figures standing on them. Under the feet of Moses you would have recognised the golden calf, under Abraham's the ram, and under Joseph's the demon counselling Potiphar's wife."

I told him also that I had gone there expecting to find an almost Persian building, and that this had doubtless been one of the chief factors in my disappointment. "Not at all," he assured me, "it's perfectly true. Some parts of it are quite oriental. One of the capitals reproduces so exactly a Persian subject that you cannot simply explain it by the persistence of oriental traditions. The carver must have copied some casket brought from the East by navigators." And indeed he was later to show me the photograph of a capital on which I saw dragons that were almost Chinese devouring one another, but at Balbec this little piece of sculpture had passed unnoticed by me in the general effect of the building which did not conform to the pattern traced in my mind by the words "an almost Persian church."

The intellectual pleasures which I was enjoying in this studio did not in the least prevent me from being aware, although they enveloped us as it were in spite of ourselves, of the warm glazes, the sparkling penumbra of the room itself and, through the little window framed with honeysuckle, in the rustic avenue, the resilient dryness of the sun-parched earth, veiled only by the diaphanous gauze woven of distance and the shade of the trees. Perhaps the unconscious well-being induced by this summer day came like a tributary to swell the flood of joy that had surged in me at the sight of Elstir's *Carquethuit Harbour*.

I had supposed Elstir to be a modest man, but I realised my mistake on seeing his face cloud with melancholy when, in a little speech of thanks, I uttered the word "fame." Men who believe that their works will last—as was the case with Elstir—form the habit of placing them in a period when they themselves will have crumbled into dust. And thus, by obliging them to reflect on their own extinction, the idea of fame saddens them because it is inseparable from the idea of death. I changed the subject in the hope of dispelling the cloud of ambitious melancholy with which I had unwittingly shadowed Elstir's brow. "Someone advised me once," I said, thinking of the conversation we had had with Legrandin at Combray, as to which I was glad of an opportunity of learning Elstir's views, "not to visit Brittany, because it would not be wholesome for a mind with a natural inclination towards day-dreams." "Not at all," he replied. "When a mind has a tendency towards day-dreams, it's a mistake to shield it from them, to ration them. So long as you divert your mind from its day-dreams, it will not know them for what they are; you will be the victim of all sorts of appearances because you will not have grasped their true nature. If a little day-dreaming is danger-ous, the cure for it is not to dream less but to dream more, to dream all the time. One must have a thorough understanding of one's day-dreams if one is not to be troubled by them; there is a way of separating one's dreams from one's life which so often produces good results that I wonder whether one oughtn't to try it just in case, simply as a preventative, as certain surgeons suggest that, to avoid the risk of appendicits later on, we ought all to have our appendixes taken out when we're children."

Elstir and I had meanwhile been walking towards the end of the studio, and had reached the window that looked across the garden on to a narrow side-street that was almost a country lane. We had gone there to breathe the cooler air of the late afternoon. I supposed myself to be nowhere near the girls of the little band, and it was only by sacrificing for once the hope of seeing them that I had yielded to my grandmother's entreaties and had gone to see Elstir. For we do not know the whereabouts of what we are seeking, and often we avoid for a long time the place to which, for quite different reasons, everyone has been asking us to go; but we never suspect that we shall there see the very person of whom we are thinking. I looked out vaguely over this rustic path which passed quite close to the studio but did not belong to Elstir. Suddenly there appeared on it, coming towards us at a rapid pace, the young cyclist of the little band, with her polo-cap pulled down over her dark hair towards her plump cheeks, her eyes gay and slightly challenging; and on that auspicious path, miraculously filled with the promise of delights, I saw her, beneath the trees, address to Elstir the smiling greeting of a friend, a rainbow that bridged for me the gulf between our terraqueous world and regions which I had hitherto regarded as inaccessible. She even came up to shake hands with the painter, though without stopping, and I saw that she had a tiny beauty spot on her chin. "Do you know that girl, Monsieur?" I asked Elstir, realising that he might introduce me to her, invite her to his house. And this peaceful studio with its rural horizon was at once filled with a surfeit of delight such as a child might feel in a house where he was already happily playing when he learned that, in addition, out of that bounteousness which enables lovely things and noble hosts to increase their gifts beyond all measure, a sumptuous meal was being prepared for him. Elstir told me that she was called Albertine Simonet, and gave me the names also of her friends, whom I described to him with sufficient accuracy for him to identify them almost without hesitation. I had made a mistake with regard to their social position, but not the mistake that

I usually made at Balbec. I was always ready to take the sons of shopkeepers for princes when they appeared on horseback. This time I had placed in a shady milieu the daughters of middle-class people, extremely rich, belonging to the world of trade and industry. It was the class which, at first sight, interested me least since it held for me none of the mystery either of the people or of a society such as that of the Guermantes. And no doubt if a preliminary glamour which they would never now lose had not been conferred on them, in my dazzled eyes, by the glaring vacuity of seaside life, I should perhaps not have succeeded in resisting and overcoming the idea that they were the daughters of prosperous merchants. I could not help marvelling at what a wonderful workshop the French middle class was for sculpture of the most varied kind. What unexpected types, what richness of invention in the character of the faces, what firmness, what freshness, what simplicity in the features! The shrewd old burghers from whom these Dianas and these nymphs had sprung seemed to me to have been the greatest of statuaries. Scarcely had I had time to register the social metamorphosis of the little band—for these discoveries of a mistake, these modifications of the notion one has of a person, have the instantaneousness of a chemical reaction—than the idea had already established itself behind the guttersnipe ways of these girls, whom I had taken for the mistresses of racing cyclists or prize-fighters, that they might easily be connected with the family of some lawyer or other whom we knew. I was barely conscious of who Albertine Simonet was. She had certainly no conception of what she was one day to mean to me. Even the name, Simonet, which I had already heard spoken on the beach, I should have spelt with a double "n" had I been asked to write it down, never dreaming of the importance which this family attached to there being only one. The further we descend the social scale the more we find that snobbery fastens on to mere trifles which are perhaps no more null than the distinctions observed by the aristocracy, but, being more obscure, more peculiar to each individual, surprise us more. Possibly there had been Simonnets who had done badly in business, or worse still. The fact remains that the Simonets never failed, it appeared, to be annoyed if anyone doubled their "n." They were as proud, perhaps, of being the only Simonets in the world with one "n" instead of two as the Montmorencys of being the premier barons of France. I asked Elstir whether these girls lived at Balbec; yes, he told me, some of them at any rate. The villa in which one of them lived was precisely at the far end of the beach, where the cliffs of Canapville began. Since this girl was a great friend of Albertine Simonet, this was one more reason for me to believe that it was indeed the latter whom I had met that day when I was with my grandmother. There were of course so many of those little streets running down to the beach, and all at the same angle, that I could not have specified exactly which of them it had been. One would like to remember a thing accurately, but at the time one's vision is always clouded. And yet that Albertine and the girl whom I had seen going to her friend's house were one and the same person was a practical certainty. In spite of this, whereas the countless images that have since been presented to me by the dark young golfer, however different they may be, are superimposed one upon the other (because I know that they all belong to her), and by retracing my memories I can, under cover of that identity and as if through an internal passageway, run through all those images in turn without losing my grasp of one and the same person; if, on the other hand, I wish to go back to the girl whom I passed that day when I was with my grandmother, I have to emerge into the open air. I am convinced that it is Albertine whom I find there, the same who used often to come to a halt in the midst of her friends during their walks against the backdrop of the sea; but all those more recent images remain separate from that earlier one because I am unable to confer on her retrospectively an identity which she did not have for me at the moment she caught my eye; whatever assurance I may derive from the law of probabilities, that girl with the plump cheeks who stared at me so boldly from the corner of the little street and from the beach, and by whom I believe that I might have been loved, I have never, in the strict sense of the words, seen again.

Was it my hesitation between the different girls of the little band, all of whom retained something of the collective charm which had disturbed me from the first, that, combined with those other reasons, allowed me later on, even at the time of my greater—my second—love for Albertine, a sort of intermittent and all too brief liberty to abstain from loving her? From having strayed among all her friends before it finally concentrated on her, my love kept for some time between itself and the image of Albertine a certain "play" which enabled it, like ill-adjusted stage lighting, to flit over others before returning to focus upon her; the connexion between the pain which I felt in my heart and the memory of Albertine did not seem to me a necessary one; I might perhaps have been able to co-ordinate it with the image of another person. And this enabled me, in a momentary flash, to banish the reality altogether, not only the external reality, as in my love for Gilberte (which I had recognised to be an inner state wherein I drew from myself alone the particular quality, the special character of the person I loved, everything that rendered her indispensable to my happiness), but even the other reality, internal and purely subjective.

"Not a day passes but one or other of them comes by here, and looks in for a minute or two," Elstir told me, plunging me into despair at the thought that if I had gone to see him at once, when my grandmother had begged me to do so, I should in all probability have made Albertine's acquaintance long since.

She had continued on her way; from the studio she was no longer in sight. I supposed that she had gone to join her friends on the front. If I could have been there with Elstir, I should have got to know them. I thought up endless pretexts to induce him to take a stroll with me on the beach. I no longer had the same feeling of serenity as before the apparition of the girl in the frame of the little window, so charming until then in its fringe of honeysuckle and now so drearily empty. Elstir caused me a joy that was mixed with torture when he agreed to walk a few steps with me but said that he must first finish the piece of work on which he was engaged. It was a study of some flowers, but not those of which I would rather have commissioned a portrait from him than one of a person, so that I might learn from the revelation of his genius what I had so often sought in vain from the flowers themselves—hawthorn white and pink, cornflowers, apple-blossom. Elstir as he worked talked botany to me, but I scarcely listened; he was no longer sufficient in himself, he was now only the necessary intermediary between these girls and me; the prestige which, only a few moments ago, his talent had still given him in my eyes was now worthless except in so far as it might confer a little on me also in the eyes of the little band to whom I should be introduced by him.

I paced up and down the room, impatient for him to finish what he was doing; I picked up and examined various sketches, quantities of which were stacked against the walls. It was thus that I happened to bring to light a water-colour which evidently belonged to a much earlier period in Elstir's life, and gave me that particular kind of enchantment which is diffused by works of

art not only delightfully executed but representing a subject so
singular and so seductive that it is to it that we attribute a great deal
of their charm, as if that charm were something that the painter
had merely to discover and observe, realised already in a material
form by nature, and to reproduce. The fact that such objects can
exist, beautiful quite apart from the painter's interpretation of
them, satisfies a sort of innate materialism in us, against which
our reason contends, and acts as a counterpoise to the abstractions
of aesthetic theory. It was—this water-colour—the portrait of a
young woman, by no means beautiful but of a curious type, in a
close-fitting hat not unlike a bowler, trimmed with a ribbon of
cerise silk; in one of her mittened hands was a lighted cigarette,
while the other held at knee level a sort of broad-brimmed garden
hat, no more than a screen of plaited straw to keep off the sun. On
a table by her side, a tall vase filled with pink carnations. Often
(and it was the case here) the singularity of such works is due
principally to their having been executed in special conditions, so
that it is not immediately clear to us whether, for instance, the
strange attire of a female model is her costume for a fancy dress
ball, or whether, conversely, the scarlet cloak which an elderly
man looks as though he had put on in response to some whim of
the painter's is his professor's or alderman's gown or his cardinal's
cape. The ambiguous character of the person whose portrait now
confronted me arose, without my understanding it, from the fact
that it was a young actress of an earlier generation half dressed up as
a man. But the bowler beneath which the hair was fluffy but short,
the velvet jacket, without lapels, opening over a white shirt-front,
made me hesitate as to the period of the clothes and the sex of the
model, so that I did not know exactly what I had before my eyes,
except that it was a most luminous piece of painting. And the
pleasure which it afforded me was troubled only by the fear that
Elstir, by delaying further, would make me miss the girls, for the
declining sun now hung low in the little window. Nothing in this
water-colour was merely set down there as a fact and painted
because of its practical relevance to the scene, the costume because
the young woman must be wearing something, the vase to hold
the flowers. The glass of the vase, cherished for its own sake,
seemed to be holding the water in which the stems of the carnations were dipped in something as limpid, almost as liquid as itself;
the woman's clothes enveloped her in a material that had an
independent, fraternal charm, and, if the products of industry

can compete in charm with the wonders of nature, as delicate, as pleasing to the touch of the eye, as freshly painted as the fur of a cat, the petals of a flower, the feathers of a dove. The whiteness of the shirt-front, as fine as soft hail, with its gay pleats gathered into little bells like lilies of the valley, was spangled with bright gleams of light from the room, themselves sharply etched and subtly shaded as if they were flowers stitched into the linen. And the velvet of the jacket, with its brilliant sheen, had something rough, frayed and shaggy about it here and there that recalled the crumpled bright-ness of the carnations in the vase. But above all one felt that Elstir, heedless of any impression of immorality that might be given by this transvestite costume worn by a young actress for whom the talent she would bring to the role was doubtless of less importance than the titillation she would offer to the jaded or depraved senses of some of her audience, had on the contrary fastened upon this equivocal aspect as on an aesthetic element which deserved to be brought into prominence, and which he had done everything in his power to emphasise. Along the lines of the face, the latent sex seemed to be on the point of confessing itself to be that of a somewhat boyish girl, then vanished, and reappeared further on with a suggestion rather of an effeminate, vicious and pensive youth, then fled once more and remained elusive. The dreamy sadness in the expression of the eyes, by its very contrast with the accessories belonging to the world of debauchery and the stage, was not the least disturbing element in the picture. One imagined moreover that it must be feigned, and that the young person who seemed ready to submit to caresses in this provoking costume had probably thought it intriguing to enhance the provocation with this romantic expression of a secret longing, an unspoken grief. At the foot of the picture was inscribed: "*Miss Sacripant*, October, 1872." I could not contain my admiration. "Oh, it's nothing, only a rough sketch I did when I was young: it was a costume for a variety show. It's all ages ago now." "And what has become of the model?" A bewilderment provoked by my words preceded on Elstir's face the indifferent, absent-minded air which, a moment later, he displayed there. "Quick, give it to me!" he said, "I hear Madame Elstir coming, and though, I assure you, the young person in the bowler hat never played any part in my life, still there's no point in my wife's coming in and finding the picture staring her in the face. I've kept it only as an amusing sidelight on the theatre of those days." And, before putting it away behind the pile, Elstir, who perhaps had not set eyes on the sketch for years, gave it a careful scrutiny. "I must keep just the head," he murmured, "the lower part is really too shockingly bad, the hands are a beginner's work." I was miserable at the arrival of Mme Elstir, who could only delay us still further. The window-sill was already aglow. Our excursion would be a pure waste of time. There was no longer the slightest chance of our seeing the girls, and consequently it mattered now not at all how quickly Mme Elstir left us. In fact she did not stay very long. I found her most tedious; she might have been beautiful at twenty, driving an ox in the Roman Campagna, but her dark hair was streaked with grey and she was common without being simple, because she believed that a pompous manner and a majestic pose were required by her statuesque beauty, which, however, advancing age had robbed of all its charm. She was dressed with the utmost simplicity. And it was touching but at the same time surprising to hear Elstir exclaim, whenever he opened his mouth, and with a respectful gentleness, as if merely uttering the words moved him to tenderness and veneration: "My beautiful Gabrielle!" Later on, when I had become familiar with Elstir's mythological paintings, Mme Elstir acquired beauty in my eyes also. I understood then that to a certain ideal type illustrated by certain lines, certain arabesques which reappeared incessantly throughout his work, to a certain canon of art, he had attributed a character that was almost divine, since he had dedicated all his time, all the mental effort of which he was capable, in a word his whole life, to the task of distinguishing those lines as clearly and of reproducing them as faithfully as possible. What such an ideal inspired in Elstir was indeed a cult so solemn, so exacting, that it never allowed him to be satisfied with what he had achieved; it was the most intimate part of himself; and so he had never been able to look at it with detachment, to extract emotion from it, until the day on which he encountered it, realised outside himself, in the body of a woman, the body of the woman who had in due course become Mme Elstir and in whom he had been able (as is possible only with something that is not oneself) to find it meritorious, moving, divine. How restful, moreover, to be able to place his lips upon that ideal Beauty which hitherto he had been obliged so laboriously to extract from within himself, and which now, mysteriously incarnate, offered itself to him in a series of communions, filled with saving grace. Elstir at this period was no longer at that youthful age in which we look only to the power of the mind for the realisation of our ideal. He was nearing the age at which we count on bodily satisfactions to stimulate the force of the brain, at which mental fatigue, by inclining us towards materialism, and the diminution of our energy, towards the possibility of influences passively received, begin to make us admit that there may indeed be certain bodies, certain callings, certain rhythms that are specially privileged, realising so naturally our ideal that even without genius, merely by copying the movement of a shoulder, the tension of a neck, we can achieve a masterpiece; it is the age at which we like to caress Beauty with our eyes objectively, outside ourselves, to have it near us, in a tapestry, in a beautiful sketch by Titian picked up in a second-hand shop, in a mistress as lovely as Titian's sketch. When I understood this I could no longer look at Mme Elstir without a feeling of pleasure, and her body began to lose its heaviness, for I filled it with an idea, the idea that she was an immaterial creature, a portrait by Elstir. She was one for me, and doubtless for him too. The particulars of life do not matter to the artist; they merely provide him with the opportunity to lay bare his genius. One feels unmistakably, when one sees side by side ten portraits of different people painted by Elstir, that they are all, first and foremost, Elstirs. Only, after that rising tide of genius which sweeps over and submerges an artist's life, when the brain begins to tire, gradually the balance is disturbed and, like a river that resumes its course after the counterflow of a spring tide, it is life that once more takes the upper hand. But, while the first period lasted, the artist has gradually evolved the law, the formula of his unconscious gift. He knows what situations, if he is a novelist, what scenes, if he is a painter, provide him with the material, unimportant in itself but essential to his researches, as a laboratory might be or a workshop. He knows that he has created his masterpieces out of effects of attenuated light, out of the action of remorse upon consciousness of guilt, out of women posed beneath trees or half-immersed in water, like statues. A day will come when, owing to the erosion of his brain, he will no longer have the strength, faced with those materials which his genius was wont to use, to make the intellectual effort which alone can produce his work, and yet will continue to seek them out, happy to be near them because of the spiritual pleasure, the allurement to work, that they arouse in him; and, surrounding them besides with an aura of superstition as if they were superior to all things else, as if there dwelt in them already a great part of the work of art which they might be said to carry within them ready-made, he will confine himself to the company, to the adoration of his models. He will hold endless conversations with the repentant criminals whose remorse and regeneration once formed the subject of his novels; he will buy a house in a countryside where mists attenuate the light, he will spend long hours looking at women bathing; he will collect sumptuous stuffs. And thus the beauty of life, an expression somehow devoid of meaning, a stage this side of art at which I had seen Swann come to rest, was that also which, by a slackening of creative ardour, idolatry of the forms which had inspired it, a tendency to take the line of least resistance, must gradually undermine an Elstir's progress.

At last he had applied the final brush-stroke to his flowers. I sacrificed a minute to look at them. There was no merit in my doing so, for I knew that there was no chance now of our finding the girls on the beach; and yet, had I believed them to be still there, and that these wasted moments would make me miss them, I should have stopped to look none the less, for I should have told myself that Elstir was more interested in his flowers than in my meeting with the girls. My grandmother's nature, a nature that was the exact opposite of my complete egoism, was nevertheless reflected in certain aspects of my own. In circumstances in which someone to whom I was indifferent, for whom I had always feigned affection or respect, ran the risk merely of some unpleasantness whereas I was in real danger, I could not have done otherwise than commiserate with him on his vexation as though it had been something important, and treat my own danger as nothing, because I would feel that these were the proportions in which he must see things. To be quite accurate, I would go even further and not only not complain of the danger in which I myself stood but go half-way to meet it, and with respect to one that threatened other people, try, on the contrary, at the risk of being endangered myself, to avert it from them. The reasons for this are several, none of them to my credit. One is that if, as long as I was simply applying my reason to the matter, I felt that I cherished life above all else, whenever in the course of my existence I have found myself obsessed by mental worry or merely by nervous anxieties, sometimes so puerile that I would not dare to reveal them, if an unforeseen circumstance then arose, involving for me the risk of being killed, this new preoccupation was so trivial in comparison with the others that I welcomed it with a sense of relief, almost of joy. Thus I find that I have experienced, although the least courageous of men, a feeling which has always seemed to me, in my reasoning moods, so foreign to my nature, so inconceivable: the intoxication of danger. But even if, when a danger arose, however mortal, I were going through an entirely calm and happy phase, I could not, were I with another person, refrain from sheltering him behind me and choosing for myself the post of danger. When a sufficient number of experiences had taught me that I invariably acted and enjoyed acting thus, I discovered—and was deeply ashamed by the discovery—that it was because, contrary to what I had always believed and asserted, I was extremely sensitive to the opinion of others. Not that this kind of unconfessed self-esteem has anything to do with vanity or conceit. For what might satisfy one or other of those failings would give me no pleasure, and I have always refrained from indulging them. But with the people in whose company I have succeeded in concealing most effectively the minor assets a knowledge of which might have given them a less paltry idea of me, I have never been able to deny myself the pleasure of showing them that I take more trouble to avert the risk of death from their path than from my own. As my motive is then self-esteem and not virtue, I find it quite natural that in any crisis they should act differently. I am far from blaming them for it, as I should perhaps do if I had been moved by a sense of duty, a duty which would seem to me in that case to be as incumbent upon them as upon myself. On the contrary, I feel that it is eminently sensible of them to safeguard their lives, while at the same time being unable to prevent myself from pushing my own safety into the background, which is particularly absurd and culpable of me since I have come to realise that the lives of many of the people in front of whom I plant myself when a bomb bursts are more valueless even than my own.

However, on the day of this first visit to Elstir, the time was still distant at which I was to become conscious of this difference in value, and there was no question of danger, but simply—a premonitory sign of that pernicious self-esteem—the question of my not appearing to attach to the pleasure which I so ardently desired more importance than to the work which the painter had still to finish. It was finished at last. And, once we were out of doors, I discovered that—so long were the days still at this season—it was not so late as I had supposed. We strolled down to the front. What stratagems I employed to keep Elstir standing at the spot where I thought that the girls might still come past! Pointing to the cliffs that towered beside us, I kept on asking him to tell me about them, so as to make him forget the time and stay there a little longer. I felt that we had a better chance of waylaying the little band if we moved towards the end of the beach.

"I should like to look at those cliffs with you from a little nearer," I said to him, having noticed that one of the girls was in the habit of going in that direction. "And as we go, do tell me about Carquethuit. I should so like to see Carquethuit," I went on, without thinking that the novel character which manifested itself with such force in Elstir's *Carquethuit Harbour* might belong perhaps rather to the painter's vision than to any special quality in the place itself. "Since I've seen your picture, I think that is where I should most like to go, there and to the Pointe du Raz, but of course that would be quite a journey from here."

"Yes, and besides, even if it weren't nearer, I should advise you perhaps all the same to visit Carquethuit," he replied. "The Pointe du Raz is magnificent, but after all it's simply another of those high cliffs of Normandy or Brittany which you know already. Carquethuit is quite different, with those rocks on a low shore. I know nothing in France like it, it reminds me rather of certain aspects of Florida. It's very curious, and moreover extremely wild. It's between Clitourps and Nehomme; you know how desolate those parts are; the sweep of the coastline is exquisite. Here, the coastline is pretty ordinary, but along there I can't tell you what grace it has, what softness."

Dusk was falling; it was time to be turning homewards. I was accompanying Elstir back to his villa when suddenly, as it were Mephistopheles springing up before Faust, there appeared at the end of the avenue—like a simple objectification, unreal and dia-bolical, of the temperament diametrically opposed to my own, of the semi-barbarous and cruel vitality of which I, in my weakness, my excess of tortured sensibility and intellectuality, was so desti-tute—a few spots of the essence impossible to mistake for anything else, a few spores of the zoophytic band of girls, who looked as though they had not seen me but were unquestionably engaged in passing a sarcastic judgment on me. Feeling that a meeting between them and us was now inevitable, and that Elstir would be certain to call me, I turned my back like a bather preparing to meet the shock of a wave; I stopped dead and, leaving my illustrious companion to pursue his way, remained where I was, stooping, as if I had suddenly become engrossed in it, towards the window of the antique shop which we happened to be passing at that moment. I was not sorry to give the appearance of being able to think of something other than these girls, and I was already dimly aware that when Elstir did call me up to introduce me to them I should wear that sort of inquiring expression which betrays not surprise but the wish to look surprised—such bad actors are we all, or such good mind-readers our fellow-men—that I should even go so far as to point a finger to my breast, as who should ask "Are you calling me?" and then run to join him, my head lowered in compliance and docility and my face coldly masking my annoyance at being torn from the study of old pottery in order to be introduced to people whom I had no wish to know. Meanwhile I contemplated the window and waited for the moment when my name, shouted by Elstir, would come to strike me like an expected and innocuous bullet. The certainty of being introduced to these girls had had the effect of making me not only feign indifference to them, but actually feel it. Henceforth inevitable, the pleasure of knowing them began at once to contract, to shrink, appeared smaller to me than the pleasure of talking to Saint-Loup, of dining with my grandmother, of making excursions in the vicinity which I would regret being probably forced to abandon in consequence of my relations with people who could scarcely be much interested in old buildings. Moreover, what diminished the pleasure which I was about to feel was not merely the imminence but the incoherence of its realisation. Laws as precise as those of hydrostatics maintain the relative position of the images which we form in a fixed order, which the proximity of the event at once upsets. Elstir was about to call me. This was not at all the way in which I had so often, on the beach, in my bedroom, imagined myself making the acquaintance of these girls. What was about to happen was a different event, for which I was not prepared. I recognised in it neither my desire nor its object; I regretted almost that I had come out with Elstir. But, above all, the shrinking of the pleasure that I had previously expected to feel was due to the certainty that nothing now could take it from me. And it recovered, as though by some latent elasticity in itself, its full extent when it ceased to be subjected to the pressure of that certainty, at the moment when, having decided to turn my head, I saw Elstir, standing a few feet away with the girls, bidding them good-bye. The face of the girl who stood nearest to him, round and plump and glittering with the light in her eyes, reminded me of a cake on the top of which a place has been kept for a morsel of blue sky. Her eyes, even when fixed on an object, gave the impression of mobility, as on days of high wind the air, though invisible, lets us perceive the speed with which it is coursing between us and the sky. For a moment her eyes met mine, like those travelling skies on stormy days which approach a slower cloud, touch it, overtake it, pass it. But they do not know one another, and are soon driven far apart. So, now, our looks were for a moment confronted, each ignorant of what the celestial continent that lay before it held by way of promises or threats for the future. Only at the moment when her gaze was directly coincident with mine, without slackening its pace it clouded over slightly. So on a clear night the wind-swept moon passes behind a cloud and veils its brightness for a moment, but soon reappears. But already Elstir had left the girls without having summoned me. They disappeared down a side-street; he came towards me. My whole plan was wrecked.

I have said that Albertine had not seemed to me that day to be the same as on previous days, and that each time I saw her she was to appear different. But I felt at that moment that certain modifications in the appearance, the importance, the stature of a person may also be due to the variability of certain states of consciousness interposed between that person and ourselves. One of those that play the most considerable part in this respect is belief (that evening my belief, then the vanishing of my belief, that I was about to know Albertine had, with a few seconds' interval only, rendered her almost insignificant, then infinitely precious, in my eyes; some years later, the belief, then the disappearance of the belief, that Albertine was faithful to me, brought about similar changes).

Of course, long ago at Combray, I had seen how, according to the time of day, according to whether I was entering one or the other of the two dominant moods that governed my sensibility in turn, my grief at not being with my mother would lessen or grow, as imperceptible all afternoon as is the moon's light when the sun is shining, and then, when night had come, reigning alone in my anxious heart in place of recent memories now obliterated. But on that day at Balbec, when I saw that Elstir was leaving the girls without having called me, I learned for the first time that the variations in the importance which a pleasure or a sorrow has in our eyes may depend not merely on this alternation of two moods, but on the displacement of invisible beliefs, such, for example, as make death seem to us of no account because they bathe it in a glow of unreality, and thus enable us to attach importance to our attending a musical evening which would lose much of its charm if, on the announcement that we were sentenced to be guillotined, the belief that had bathed the evening in its warm glow suddenly evaporated. It is true that something in me was aware of this role that beliefs play: namely, my will; but its knowledge is vain if one's intelligence and one's sensibility continue in ignorance; these last are sincere when they believe that we are anxious to forsake a mistress to whom our will alone knows that we are still attached. This is because they are clouded by the belief that we shall see her again at any moment. But let this belief be shattered, let them suddenly become aware that this mistress has gone from us for ever, and our intelligence and sensibility, having lost their focus, run mad, the most infinitesimal pleasure becomes infinitely great.

Variation of a belief, annulment also of love, which, pre-exist-ent and mobile, comes to rest on the image of a woman simply because that woman will be almost impossible of attainment. Thenceforward we think not so much of the woman, whom we have difficulty in picturing to ourselves, as of the means of getting to know her. A whole series of agonies develops and is sufficient to fix our love definitely upon her who is its almost unknown object. Our love becomes immense, and we never dream how small a place in it the real woman occupies. And if suddenly, as at the moment when I had seen Elstir stop to talk to the girls, we cease to be uneasy, to suffer anguish, since it is this anguish that is the whole of our love, it seems to us as though our love had abruptly vanished at the moment when at length we grasp the prey to whose value we had not given enough thought before. What did I know of Albertine? One or two glimpses of a profile against the sea, less beautiful, assuredly, than those of Veronese's women whom I ought, had I been guided by purely aesthetic reasons, to have preferred to her. By what other reasons could I be guided, since, my anxiety having subsided, I could recapture only those mute profiles, possessing nothing else? Since my first sight of Albertine I had thought about her endlessly, I had carried on with what I called by her name an interminable inner dialogue in which I made her question and answer, think and act, and in the infinite series of imaginary Albertines who followed one after the other in my fancy hour by hour, the real Albertine, glimpsed on the beach, figured only at the head, just as the actress who "creates" a role, the star, appears, out of a long series of performances, in the few first alone. That Albertine was scarcely more than a silhouette, all that had been superimposed upon her being of my own invention, to such an extent when we love does the contribution that we ourselves make outweigh—even in terms of quantity alone— those that come to us from the beloved object. And this is true of loves that have been realised in actuality. There are loves that can not only develop but survive on very little—and this even among those that have achieved their carnal fulfilment. An old drawing-master who had taught my grandmother had been presented by some obscure mistress with a daughter. The mother died shortly after the birth of the child, and the drawing-master was so broken-hearted that he did not long survive her. In the last months of his life my grandmother and some of the Combray ladies, who had never liked to make any allusion in his presence to the woman with whom in any case he had not officially lived and had had comparatively sparse relations, took it into their heads to ensure the little girl's future by clubbing together to provide her with an annuity. It was my grandmother who suggested this; several of her friends jibbed; after all, was the child really such a very interesting case? Was she even the child of her reputed father? With women like that, one could never be sure. Finally, everything was settled. The child came to thank the ladies. She was plain, and so absurdly like the old drawing-master as to remove every shadow of doubt. Since her hair was the only nice thing about her, one of the ladies said to her father, who had brought her: "What pretty hair she has." And thinking that now, the guilty woman being dead and the old man only half alive, a discreet allusion to that past of which they had always pretended to know nothing could do no harm, my grandmother added: "It must run in the family. Did her mother have pretty hair like that?" "I don't know," was the old man's quaint answer, "I never saw her except with a hat on."

Before rejoining Elstir, I caught sight of myself in a glass. To add to the disaster of my not having been introduced to the girls, I noticed that my tie was all crooked, and my hat left long wisps of hair showing, which did not become me; but it was a piece of luck, all the same, that they should have seen me, even thus attired, in Elstir's company, and so could not forget me; also that I should have put on that morning, at my grandmother's suggestion, my smart waistcoat, when I might so easily have been wearing one that was simply hideous, and that I was carrying my best stick. For while an event for which we are longing never happens quite in the way we have been expecting, failing the advantages on which we supposed that we might count, others present themselves for which we never hoped, and make up for our disappointment; and we have been so dreading the worst that in the end we are inclined to feel that, taking one thing with another, chance has, on the whole, been rather kind to us.

"I did so much want to know them," I said as I rejoined Elstir. "Then why did you stand a mile away?" These were his actual words, uttered not because they expressed what was really in his mind, since, if his desire had been to gratify mine, he could quite easily have called me, but perhaps because he had heard phrases of this sort, in familiar use among vulgar people when they are caught in the wrong, and because even great men are in certain respects much the same as vulgar people, and take their everyday excuses from the same common stock just as they get their daily bread from the same baker; or it may be that such remarks (which ought, one might almost say, to be read backwards, since their literal meaning is the opposite of the truth) are the instantaneous effect, the negative exposure of a reflex action. "They were in a hurry." It struck me that of course they must have stopped him from summoning a person who did not greatly attract them; otherwise he would not have failed to do so, after all the questions that I had put to him about them, and the interest which he must have seen that I took in them.

"We were speaking just now of Carquethuit," he said to me as we walked towards his villa. "I've done a little sketch in which you can see the curve of the beach much better. The painting is not too bad, but it's different. If you will allow me, as a souvenir of our friendship, I'd like to give you the sketch," he went on, for the people who refuse us the objects of our desire are always ready to offer us something else.

"I should very much like, if you have such a thing, a photograph of the little portrait of Miss Sacripant. By the way, that's not a real name, surely?"

"It's the name of a character the sitter played in a stupid little musical comedy."

"But, I assure you, Monsieur, that I've never set eyes on her; you look as though you thought that I knew her."

Elstir was silent. "It couldn't be Mme Swann before she was married?" I hazarded, in one of those sudden fortuitous stumblings upon the truth, which are rare enough in all conscience, and yet suffice, after the event, to give a certain cumulative support to the theory of presentiments, provided that one takes care to forget all the wrong guesses that would invalidate it.

Elstir did not reply. The portrait was indeed that of Odette de Crécy. She had preferred not to keep it for many reasons, some of them only too obvious. But there were others less apparent. The portrait dated from before the point at which Odette, disciplining her features, had made of her face and figure that creation the broad outlines of which her hairdressers, her dressmakers, she herself—in her way of holding herself, of speaking, of smiling, of moving her hands and eyes, of thinking—were to respect throughout the years to come. It required the vitiated taste of a surfeited lover to make Swann prefer to all the countless photographs of the "definitive" Odette who was his charming wife the little photograph which he kept in his room and in which, beneath a straw hat trimmed with pansies, one saw a thin young woman, fairly plain, with bunched-out hair and drawn features.

But in any case, even if the portrait had been, not anterior, like Swann's favourite photograph, to the systematisation of Odette's features into a new type, majestic and charming, but subsequent to it, Elstir's vision would have sufficed to discompose that type. Artistic genius acts in a similar way to those extremely high temperatures which have the power to split up combinations of atoms which they proceed to combine afresh in a diametrically opposite order, corresponding to another type. All that artificial harmony which a woman has succeeded in imposing upon her features, the maintenance of which she oversees in her mirror every day before going out, relying on the angle of her hat, the smoothness of her hair, the vivacity of her expression, to ensure its continuity, that harmony the keen eye of the great painter instantly destroys, substituting for it a rearrangement of the woman's features such as will satisfy a certain pictorial ideal of femininity which he carries in his head. Similarly it often happens that, after a certain age, the eye of a great scientist will find every-where the elements necessary to establish those relations which alone are of interest to him. Like those craftsmen, those players who, instead of making a fuss and asking for what they cannot have, content themselves with whatever comes to hand, the artist might say of anything, no matter what, that it will serve his purpose. Thus a cousin of the Princesse de Luxembourg, a beauty of the most queenly type, having taken a fancy to a form of art which was new at that time, had asked the leading painter of the naturalist school to do her portrait. At once the artist's eye found what he had been seeking everywhere. And on his canvas there appeared, in place of the proud lady, a street-girl, and behind her a vast, sloping, purple background which reminded one of the Place Pigalle. But even without going so far as that, not only will the portrait of a woman by a great artist not seek in the least to give satisfaction to various demands on the woman's part—such as, for instance, when she begins to age, make her have herself photo-graphed in dresses that are almost those of a little girl which bring out her still youthful figure and make her appear like the sister or even the daughter of her own daughter, who, if need be, is tricked out for the occasion as a "perfect fright" beside her. It will, on the contrary, emphasise those very blemishes which she seeks to hide, and which (as for instance a sickly, almost greenish complexion) are all the more tempting to him since they show "character," though they are enough to destroy the illusions of the ordinary beholder who sees crumble into dust the ideal of which the woman so proudly sustained the figment, and which set her, in her unique, irreducible form, so far outside, so far above the rest of humanity. Fallen now, situated outside her own type in which she sat unassailably enthroned, she is now just an ordinary woman, in the legend of whose superiority we have lost all faith. We are so accustomed to incorporating in this type not only the beauty of an Odette but her personality, her identity, that standing before the portrait which has thus stripped her of it we are inclined to protest not simply "How plain he has made her!" but "Why, it isn't the least bit like her!" We find it hard to believe that it can be she. We do not recognise her. And yet there is a person there on the canvas whom we are quite conscious of having seen before. But that person is not Odette; the face of the person, her body, her general appearance seem familiar. They recall to us not this particular woman who never held herself like that, whose natural pose never formed any such strange and teasing arabesque, but other women, all the women whom Elstir has ever painted, women whom invariably, however they may differ from one another, he has chosen to plant thus, in full face, with an arched foot thrust out from under the skirt, a large round hat in one hand, symmetrically corresponding, at the level of the knee which it covers, to that other disc, higher up in the picture, the face. And furthermore, not only does a portrait by the hand of genius dislocate a woman's type, as it has been defined by her coquetry and her selfish conception of beauty, but if it is also old, it is not content with ageing the original in the same way as a photograph ages its sitter, by showing her dressed in the fashions of long ago. In a portrait, it is not only the manner the woman then had of dressing that dates her, it is also the manner the artist had of painting. And this, Elstir's earliest manner, was the most devastating of birth certificates for Odette because it not only established her, as did her photographs of the same period, as the younger sister of various well-known courtesans, but made her portrait contemporary with the countless portraits that Manet or Whistler had painted of all those vanished models, models who already belonged to oblivion or to history.

It was along this train of thought, silently ruminated over by Elstir's side as I accompanied him to his door, that I was being led by the discovery that I had just made of the identity of his model, when this first discovery caused me to make a second, more disturbing still, concerning the identity of the artist. He had painted the portrait of Odette de Crécy. Could it possibly be that this man of genius, this sage, this recluse, this philosopher with his marvellous flow of conversation, who towered over everyone and everything, was the ridiculous, depraved painter who had at one time been adopted by the Verdurins? I asked him if he had known them, and whether by any chance it was he that they used to call M. Biche. He answered me in the affirmative, with no trace of embarrassment, as if my question referred to a period in his life that was already somewhat remote and he had no suspicion of the extraordinary disillusionment he was causing me. But, looking up, he read it on my face. His own assumed an expression of annoyance. And, as we were now almost at the gate of his house, a man of less distinction of heart and mind might simply have said good-bye to me a trifle dryly and taken care to avoid seeing me again. This however was not Elstir's way with me; like the master that he was—and it was, perhaps, from the point of view of pure creativity, his one fault that he was a master in that sense of the word, for an artist, if he is to be absolutely true to the life of the spirit, must be alone, and not squander his ego, even upon disciples—from every circumstance, whether involving himself or other people, he sought to extract, for the

better edification of the young, the element of truth that it contained. He chose therefore, instead of the words that might have
avenged the injury to his pride, those that could prove instructive
to me. "There is no man," he began, "however wise, who has not
at some period of his youth said things, or lived a life, the memory
of which is so unpleasant to him that he would gladly expunge it.
And yet he ought not entirely to regret it, because he cannot be
certain that he has indeed become a wise man—so far as it is
possible for any of us to be wise—unless he has passed through
all the fatuous or unwholesome incarnations by which that
ultimate stage must be preceded. I know that there are young
people, the sons and grandsons of distinguished men, whose
masters have instilled into them nobility of mind and moral
refinement from their schooldays. They may perhaps have
nothing to retract from their past lives; they could publish a signed
account of everything they have ever said or done; but they are
poor creatures, feeble descendants of doctrinaires, and their
wisdom is negative and sterile. We do not receive wisdom, we
must discover it for ourselves, after a journey through the wild-
erness which no one else can make for us, which no one can spare
us, for our wisdom is the point of view from which we come at last
to regard the world. The lives that you admire, the attitudes that
seem noble to you, have not been shaped by a paterfamilias or a
schoolmaster, they have sprung from very different beginnings,
having been influenced by everything evil or commonplace that
prevailed round about them. They represent a struggle and a
victory. I can see that the picture of what we were at an earlier
stage may not be recognisable and cannot, certainly, be pleasing to
contemplate in later life. But we must not repudiate it, for it is a
proof that we have really lived, that it is in accordance with the
laws of life and of the mind that we have, from the common
elements of life, of the life of studios, of artistic groups—assuming
one is a painter—extracted something that transcends them."

Meanwhile we had reached his door. I was disappointed at not
having met the girls. But after all there was now the possibility of
meeting them again later on; they had ceased merely to be
silhouetted against a horizon where I had been ready to suppose
that I should never see them reappear. Around them no longer
swirled that sort of great eddy which had separated me from them,
which had been merely the expression of the perpetually active
desire, mobile, urgent, fed ever on fresh anxieties, which was

aroused in me by their inaccessibility, their flight from me, possibly for ever. I could now set my desire for them at rest, hold it in
reserve, among all those other desires the realisation of which, as
soon as I knew it to be possible, I would cheerfully postpone. I
took leave of Elstir; I was alone once again. Then all of a sudden,
despite my recent disappointment, I saw in my mind's eye all that
chain of coincidences which I had not supposed could possibly
come about: that Elstir should be a friend of those very girls, that
they, who only that morning had been to me merely figures in a
picture with the sea for background, had seen me, had seen me
walking in friendly intimacy with a great painter, who was now
informed of my secret longing and would no doubt do what he
could to assuage it. All this had been a source of pleasure to me, but
that pleasure had remained hidden; it was like one of those visitors
who wait before letting us know that they are in the room until
everyone else has gone and we are by ourselves. Then only do we
catch sight of them, and can say to them, "I am at your service,"
and listen to what they have to tell us. Sometimes between the
moment at which these pleasures have entered our consciousness
and the moment at which we are free to entertain them, so many
hours have passed, we have in the meantime seen so many people,
that we are afraid lest they should have grown tired of waiting. But
they are patient, they do not grow tired, and as soon as the crowd
has gone we find them there ready for us. Sometimes, then, it is we
ourselves who are so exhausted that it seems as though our weary
mind will no longer have the strength to seize and retain those
memories, those impressions for which our frail self is the one
habitable place, the sole means of realisation. And we should regret
that failure, for existence is of little interest save on days when the
dust of realities is mingled with magic sand, when some trivial
incident becomes a springboard for romance. Then a whole
promontory of the inaccessible world emerges from the twilight
of dream and enters our life, our life in which, like the sleeper
awakened, we actually see the people of whom we had dreamed
with such ardent longing that we had come to believe that we
should never see them except in our dreams.

    The assuagement brought about by the probability of my now
being able to meet the little band whenever I chose was all the
more precious to me because I should not have been able to keep
watch for them during the next few days, which were taken up
with preparations for Saint-Loup's departure. My grandmother

was anxious to offer my friend some token of her gratitude for all the kindnesses that he had shown to her and myself. I told her that he was a great admirer of Proudhon, and this put it into her head to send for a collection of autograph letters by that philosopher which she had once bought. Saint-Loup came to the hotel to look at them on the day of their arrival, which was also his last day at Balbec. He read them eagerly, fingering each page with reverence, trying to get the sentences by heart; and then, rising from the table, was beginning to apologise to my grandmother for having stayed so long, when he heard her say: "No, no, take them with you, they are for you to keep. That was why I sent for them, to give them to you."

He was overwhelmed by a joy which he could no more control than we can a physical condition that arises without the intervention of our will. He blushed scarlet as a child who has just been punished, and my grandmother was far more touched to see all the efforts he made (without success) to contain the joy that convulsed him than she would have been to hear any words of thanks that he could have uttered. But he, fearing that he had failed to show his gratitude properly, begged me to make his excuses to her again, next day, leaning from the window of the little local train which was to take him back to his regiment. The distance was, as a matter of fact, nothing. He had thought of going by road, as he had frequently done that summer, when he was to return the same evening and was not encumbered with baggage. But this time he would in any case have had to put all his heavy luggage in the train. And he found it simpler to take the train himself too, following the advice of the manager who, on being consulted, replied that "Carriage or train, it was more or less equivocal." He meant it to be understood that they were equivalent (in fact, very much what Françoise would have expressed as "coming to the same as makes no difference"). "Very well," Saint-Loup had decided, "I shall take the 'little crawler.'" I should have taken it too, had I not been tired, and gone with my friend to Doncières; failing this, I kept on promising, all the time we waited in Balbec station—the time, that is to say, which the driver of the little train spent waiting for unpunctual friends, without whom he refused to start, and also in seeking some refreshment for himself—to go over there and see him several times a week. As Bloch had also come to the station— much to Saint-Loup's disgust—the latter, seeing that our companion could hear him begging me to come to luncheon, to dinner, to stay altogether at Doncières, finally turned to him and, in the most forbidding tone, intended to counteract the forced civility of the invitation and to prevent Bloch from taking it seriously: "If you ever happen to be passing through Doncières any afternoon when I'm off duty, you might ask for me at the barracks; but I hardly ever am off duty." Perhaps, also, Robert was afraid that I might not come alone, and, thinking that I was more intimate with Bloch than I made out, was providing me in this way with a travelling companion, one who would urge me on.

I was afraid that this tone, this manner of inviting a person while advising him not to come, might have wounded Bloch, and felt that Saint-Loup would have done better to say nothing. But I was mistaken, for after the train had gone, while we were walking back together as far as the cross-roads where we had to separate, one road going to the hotel, the other to the Blochs' villa, he never stopped asking me on what day we should go to Doncières, for after "all the civility that Saint-Loup had shown" him, it would be "too rude" on his part not to accept his invitation. I was glad that he had not noticed, or was so little displeased as to wish to let it be thought that he had not noticed, in what a less than pressing, indeed barely polite, tone the invitation had been issued. At the same time I should have liked Bloch, for his own sake, to refrain from making a fool of himself by going over at once to Doncières. But I dared not offer a piece of advice which could only have offended him by hinting that Saint-Loup had been less pressing than he himself was impressed. He was a great deal too ready to respond, and even if all his faults of this nature were atoned for by remarkable qualities which others, with more reserve than he, would never have possessed, he carried tactlessness to a pitch that was almost maddening. According to him, the week must not pass without our going to Doncières (he said "our" for I think that he counted to some extent on my presence there as an excuse for his own). All the way home, opposite the gymnasium in its grove of trees, opposite the tennis courts, the mayor's office, the shell-fish stall, he stopped me, imploring me to fix a day, and, as I did not, left me in anger, saying: "As your lordship pleases. For my part, I am obliged to go since he has invited me."

Saint-Loup was still so afraid of not having thanked my grand-mother properly that he charged me once again to express his gratitude to her a day or two later in a letter I received from him from the town in which he was quartered, a town which seemed, on the envelope where the post-mark had stamped its name, to be hastening to me across country, to tell me that within its walls, in the Louis XVI cavalry barracks, he was thinking of me. The paper was embossed with the arms of Marsantes, in which I could make out a lion surmounting a coronet closed by the cap of a peer of France.

"After a journey which," he wrote, "passed pleasantly enough, with a book I bought at the station, by Arvède Barine[5] (a Russian author, I fancy; it seemed to me remarkably well written for a foreigner, but you shall give me your critical opinion, since you are bound to know all about it, you who are a fount of knowledge and have read everything), here I am again in the thick of this debased existence, where, alas, I feel a sad exile, not having here what I left behind at Balbec; this life in which I can find no affectionate memory, no intellectual attraction; an environment which you would no doubt despise yet which has a certain charm. Everything seems to have changed since I left it, for in the interval one of the most important periods in my life, that from which our friendship dates, has begun. I hope that it may never come to an end. I have spoken of our friendship, of you, to one person only, to the friend I told you of, who has just paid me a surprise visit here. She would very much like to know you, and I feel that you would get on well together, for she too is extremely literary. Otherwise, to go over in my mind all our talks, to relive those hours which I never shall forget, I have shut myself off from my comrades, excellent fellows, but altogether incapable of understanding that sort of thing. This remembrance of the moments I spent with you I should almost have preferred, on my first day here, to conjure up for my own solitary enjoyment, without writing to you. But I was afraid lest, with your subtle mind and ultra-sensitive heart, you might needlessly torment yourself if you did not hear from me, if, that is to say, you still condescend to occupy your thoughts with this blunt trooper whom you will have a hard task to polish and refine and make a little more subtle and worthier of your company."

On the whole this letter, in its affectionate spirit, was not at all unlike those which, when I did not yet know Saint-Loup, I had imagined that he would write to me, in those day-dreams from which the coldness of his first greeting had shaken me by bringing me face to face with an icy reality which was not, however, to last. Once I had received this letter, every time the post was brought in, at lunch-time, I could tell at once when it was from him that a letter came, for it had always that second face which a person assumes when he is absent, in the features of which (the characters of the handwriting) there is no reason why we should not suppose that we can detect an individual soul just as much as in the line of a nose or the inflexions of a voice.

I would now happily remain at the table while it was being cleared, and, if it was not a moment at which the girls of the little band might be passing, it was no longer solely towards the sea that I would turn my eyes. Since I had seen such things depicted in water-colours by Elstir, I sought to find again in reality, I cherished as though for their poetic beauty, the broken gestures of the knives still lying across one another, the swollen convexity of a discarded napkin into which the sun introduced a patch of yellow velvet, the half-empty glass which thus showed to greater advantage the noble sweep of its curved sides and, in the heart of its translucent crystal, clear as frozen daylight, some dregs of wine, dark but glittering with reflected lights, the displacement of solid objects, the transmutation of liquids by the effect of light and shade, the shifting colours of the plums which passed from green to blue and from blue to golden yellow in the half-plundered dish, the promenade of the antiquated chairs that came twice daily to take their places round the white cloth spread on the table as on an altar at which were celebrated the rites of the palate, and where in the hollows of the oyster-shells a few drops of lustral water had remained as in tiny holy-water stoups of stone; I tried to find beauty there where I had never imagined before that it could exist, in the most ordinary things, in the profundities of "still life."

When, some days after Saint-Loup's departure, I had succeeded in persuading Elstir to give a small party at which I should meet Albertine, the freshness of appearance and elegance of attire, both quite momentary, which were to be observed in me at the moment of my starting out from the Grand Hotel (and which were due respectively to a longer rest than usual and to special pains over my toilet) were such that I regretted my inability to reserve them (and also the credit accruing from Elstir's friendship) for the captivation of some other, more interesting person, I regretted having to use them all up on the simple pleasure of making Albertine's acquaintance. My brain assessed this pleasure at a very low value now that it was assured. But, inside, my will did not for a moment share this illusion, that will which is the persevering and unalterable servant of our successive personalities; hidden away in the shadow, despised, downtrodden, untiringly faithful, toiling incessantly, and with no thought for the variability of the self, to ensure that the self may never lack what is needed. While, at the moment when we are about to start on an eagerly awaited journey, our intelligence and our sensibility begin to ask themselves whether it is really worth the trouble, the will, knowing that those lazy masters would at once begin to consider that journey the most wonderful experience if it became impossible for us to undertake it, leaves them arguing outside the station, vying with each other in their hesitations; but it busies itself with buying the tickets and putting us into the carriage before the train starts. It is as invariable as the intelligence and the sensibility are fickle, but since it is silent, gives no account of its actions, it seems almost non-existent; it is by its dogged determination that the other constituent parts of our personality are led, but without seeing it, whereas they distinguish clearly all their own uncertainties. So my intelligence and my sensibility began a discussion as to the real value of the pleasure that there would be in knowing Albertine, while I studied in the glass vain and perishable attractions which they would have preserved intact for use on some other occasion. But my will would not let the hour pass at which I must start, and it was Elstir's address that it called out to the driver. My intelligence and my sensibility were at liberty, now that the die was cast, to think this a pity. If my will had given the man a different address, they would have been properly had.

When I arrived at Elstir's a few minutes later, I thought at first that Mlle Simonet was not in the studio. There was certainly a girl sitting there in a silk frock, bareheaded, but one whose marvellous hair, whose nose, whose complexion, meant nothing to me, in whom I did not recognise the human entity that I had extracted from a young cyclist in a polo-cap strolling past between myself and the sea. Nevertheless it was Albertine. But even when I knew it to be her, I gave her no thought. On entering any social gathering, when one is young, one loses consciousness of one's old self, one becomes a different man, every drawing-room being a fresh universe in which, coming under the sway of a new moral perspective, we fasten our attention, as if they were to matter to us for all time, on people, dances, card-tables, all of which we shall have forgotten by the morning. Obliged to follow, if I was to arrive at the goal of conversation with Albertine, a route in no way of my own planning, which first brought me to a halt in front of Elstir, passed by other groups of guests to whom I was presented, then along the buffet table, at which I was offered, and where I ate, a strawberry tart or two, while I listened, motionless, to the music that had begun in another part of the room, I found myself giving to these various incidents the same importance as to my introduction to Mlle Simonet, an introduction which was now nothing more than one among several such incidents, having entirely forgotten that it had been, but a few minutes since, my sole object in coming there. But is it not thus, in the bustle of daily life, with every true happiness, every great sorrow? In a room full of other people we receive from the woman we love the answer, auspicious or fatal, which we have been awaiting for the last year. But we must go on talking, ideas come flocking one after another, unfolding a smooth surface which is pricked now and then at the very most by a dull throb from the memory, infinitely more profound but very narrow, that misfortune has come upon us. If, instead of misfortune, it is happiness, it may be that not until many years have elapsed will we recall that the most important event in our emotional life occurred without our having time to give it any prolonged attention, or even to become aware of it almost, at a social gathering to which we had gone solely in expectation of that event.

When Elstir asked me to come with him so that he might introduce me to Albertine, who was sitting a little further down the room, I first of all finished eating a coffee éclair and, with a show of keen interest, asked an old gentleman whose acquaintance I had just made (and to whom I thought that I might offer the rose in my buttonhole which he had admired) to tell me more about the old Norman fairs. This is not to say that the introduction which followed did not give me any pleasure and did not assume a certain solemnity in my eyes. But so far as the pleasure was concerned, I was naturally not conscious of it until some time later, when, back at the hotel, and in my room alone, I had become myself again. Pleasure in this respect is like photography. What we take, in the presence of the beloved object, is merely a negative, which we develop later, when we are back at home, and have once again found at our disposal that inner darkroom the entrance to which is barred to us so long as we are with other people.

If my consciousness of the pleasure it had brought me was thus retarded by a few hours, the gravity of this introduction made itself felt at once. At the moment of introduction, for all that we feel ourselves to have been suddenly rewarded, to have been furnished with a pass that will admit us henceforward to pleasures which we have been pursuing for weeks past, we realise only too clearly that this acquisition puts an end for us not merely to hours of toilsome search—a relief that can only fill us with joy—but also to the existence of a certain person, the person whom our imagination had wildly distorted, whom our anxious fear that we might never become known to her had magnified. At the moment when our name rings out on the lips of the introducer, especially if the latter amplifies it, as Elstir now did, with a flattering commentary—that sacramental moment, as when in a fairy-tale the magician commands a person suddenly to become someone else—she to whose presence we have been longing to attain vanishes: indeed, how could she remain the same when—by reason of the attention which she is obliged to pay to the announcement of our name and the sight of our person—in the eyes that only yesterday were situated at an infinite distance (where we supposed that ours, wandering, unsteady, desperate, divergent, would never succeed in meeting them) the conscious gaze, the incommunicable thought which we were seeking have just been miraculously and quite simply replaced by our own image painted in them as in a smiling mirror? If this incarnation of ourselves in the person who seemed to differ most from us is what does most to modify the appearance of the person to whom we have just been introduced, the form of that person still remains quite vague; and we may wonder whether it will turn out to be a god, a table or a basin. But, as nimble as the wax-modellers who will fashion a bust before our eyes in five minutes, the few words which the stranger is now going to say to us will substantiate that form and give it something positive and final that will exclude all the hypotheses in which our desire and our imagination had been indulging. Doubtless, even before coming to this party, Albertine had ceased to be for me simply that phantom fit to haunt the rest of our lives which a passing stranger of whom we know nothing and have caught but the barest glimpse remains. Her relationship to Mme Bontemps had already restricted the scope of those marvellous hypotheses, by stopping one of the channels along which they might have spread. As I drew closer to the girl and began to know her better, this

knowledge developed by a process of subtraction, each constituent of imagination and desire giving place to a notion which was
worth infinitely less, a notion to which, it is true, there was added
presently a sort of equivalent, in the domain of real life, of what
joint stock companies give one, after repaying one's original
investment, and call dividend shares. Her name, her family connections, had been the first limit set to my suppositions. Her
friendly greeting as, standing close beside her, I once again saw
the tiny mole on her cheek, below her eye, marked another stage;
finally, I was surprised to hear her use the adverb "perfectly," in
place of "completely," of two people whom she mentioned,
saying of one, "She's perfectly mad, but very nice all the same,"
and of the other, "He's perfectly common and perfectly boring."
However little to be commended this use of "perfectly" may be, it
indicates a degree of civilisation and culture which I could never
have imagined as having been attained by the bacchante with the
bicycle, the orgiastic muse of the golf-course. Nor did it mean that
after this first metamorphosis Albertine was not to change again for
me, many times. The qualities and defects which a person presents
to us, exposed to view on the surface of his or her face, rearrange
themselves in a totally different order if we approach them from a
new angle—just as, in a town, buildings that appear strung in
extended order along a single line, from another viewpoint are
disposed in depth and their relative heights altered. To begin with,
Albertine struck me as somewhat shy instead of implacable; she
seemed to me more proper than ill-bred, judging by the descriptions, "she has bad manners" or "she has peculiar manners," which
she applied to each in turn of the girls of whom I spoke to her;
finally, she presented as a target for my line of vision a temple that
was somewhat inflamed and by no means attractive to the eye, and
no longer the curious look which I had always associated with her
until then. But this was merely a second impression and there were
doubtless others through which I would successively pass. Thus it
can be only after one has recognised, not without some tentative
stumblings, the optical errors of one's first impression that one can
arrive at an exact knowledge of another person, supposing such
knowledge to be ever possible. But it is not; for while our original
impression of him undergoes correction, the person himself, not
being an inanimate object, changes for his part too: we think that
we have caught him, he shifts, and, when we imagine that at last
we are seeing him clearly, it is only the old impressions which we

had already formed of him that we have succeeded in clarifying, when they no longer represent him.

And yet, whatever the inevitable disappointments that it must bring in its train, this movement towards what we have only glimpsed, what we have been free to dwell upon and imagine at our leisure, this movement is the only one that is wholesome for the senses, that whets their appetite. How drearily monotonous must be the lives of people who, from indolence or timidity, drive in their carriages straight to the doors of friends whom they have got to know without having first dreamed of knowing them, without ever daring, on the way, to stop and examine what arouses their desire!

I returned home thinking of that party, of the coffee éclair which I had finished eating before I let Elstir take me up to Albertine, the rose which I had given the old gentleman, all the details selected unbeknown to us by the circumstances of the occasion, which compose for us, in a special and quite fortuitous order, the picture that we retain of a first meeting. But I had the impression that I was seeing this picture from another angle of vision, very far removed from myself, realising that it had not existed only for me, when some months later, to my great surprise, on my speaking to Albertine about the day on which I had first met her, she reminded me of the éclair, the flower that I had given away, all those things which I had supposed to have been, I cannot say of importance only to myself, but perceived only by myself, and which I now found thus transcribed, in a version of which I had never suspected the existence, in the mind of Albertine. On this first day itself, when, on my return to the hotel, I was able to visualise the memory which I had brought away with me, I realised what a conjuring trick had been performed, and with what consummate sleight of hand, and how I had talked for a moment or two with a person who, thanks to the skill of the conjurer, without actually embodying anything of that other person whom I had for so long been following as she paced beside the sea, had been substituted for her. I might, for that matter, have guessed as much in advance, since the girl on the beach was a fabrication of my own. In spite of which, since I had, in my conversations with Elstir, identified her with Albertine, I felt myself in honour bound to fulfil to the real the promises of love made to the imagined Albertine. We betroth ourselves by proxy, and then feel obliged to marry the intermediary. Moreover, if there had disappeared from my life, provisionally at any rate, an anguish that the memory of polite manners, the expression "perfectly common" and an inflamed temple had sufficed to assuage, that memory awakened in me another kind of desire which, though placid and in no way painful, resembling a brotherly feeling, might in the long run become fully as dangerous by making me feel at every moment a compelling need to kiss this new person whose good manners, whose shyness, whose unexpected accessibility, arrested the futile course of my imagination but gave birth to a tender gratitude. And then, since memory begins at once to record photographs independent of one another, eliminates every link, any kind of sequence between the scenes portrayed in the collection which it exposes to our view, the most recent does not necessarily destroy or cancel those that came before. Confronted with the commonplace and touching Albertine to whom I had spoken that afternoon, I still saw the other mysterious Albertine outlined against the sea. These were now memories, that is to say pictures neither of which now seemed to me any truer than the other. Finally, to conclude this account of my first introduction to Albertine, when trying to recapture that little beauty spot on her cheek, just under the eye, I remembered that, looking from Elstir's window when Albertine had gone by, I had seen it on her chin. In fact, when I saw her I noticed that she had a beauty spot, but my errant memory made it wander about her face, fixing it now in one place, now in another.

Whatever my disappointment in finding in Mlle Simonet a girl so little different from those that I knew already, just as my disillusionment when I saw Balbec church did not prevent me from wishing still to go to Quimperlé, Pont-Aven and Venice, I comforted myself with the thought that through Albertine at any rate, even if she herself was not all that I had hoped, I might make the acquaintance of her comrades of the little band.

I thought at first that I should fail in this. As she was to be staying (and I too) for a long time still at Balbec, I had decided that the best thing was not to make my efforts to meet her too apparent, but to wait for an accidental encounter. But even if this should occur every day it was greatly to be feared that she would confine herself to acknowledging my greeting from a distance, and such meetings, repeated day after day throughout the whole season, would benefit me not at all.

Shortly after this, one morning when it had been raining and was almost cold, I was accosted on the front by a girl wearing a little toque and carrying a muff, so different from the girl whom I had met at Elstir's party that to recognise in her the same person seemed an operation beyond the power of the human mind; mine was, however, successful in performing it, but after a moment's surprise which did not, I think, escape Albertine's notice. On the other hand, remembering the "well-bred" manners which had so impressed me before, I now experienced a converse astonishment at her rude tone and manners typical of the "little band." Moreover, her temple had ceased to be the reassuring optical centre of her face, either because I was now on her other side, or because her toque hid it, or else possibly because its inflammation was not a constant thing.

"What weather!" she began. "Really the perpetual summer of Balbec is all stuff and nonsense. Don't you do anything here? We never see you playing golf, or dancing at the Casino. You don't ride either. You must be bored stiff. You don't find it too deadly, idling about on the beach all day? Ah, so you like basking in the sun like a lizard? You must have plenty of time on your hands. I can see you're not like me; I simply adore all sports. You weren't at the Sogne races? We went in the 'tram,' and I can quite understand that you wouldn't see any fun in going in an old rattletrap like that. It took us two whole hours! I could have gone there and back three times on my bike."

I who had admired Saint-Loup when, in the most natural manner in the world, he had called the little local train the "crawler," because of the ceaseless windings of its line, was daunted by the glibness with which Albertine spoke of it as the "tram" and the "rattletrap." I could sense her mastery of a mode of nomenclature in which I was afraid of her detecting and despising my inferiority. And the full wealth of the synonyms that the little band possessed to designate this railway had not yet been revealed to me. In speaking, Albertine kept her head motionless and her nostrils pinched, and scarcely moved her lips. The result of this was a drawling, nasal sound, into the composition of which there entered perhaps a provincial heredity, a juvenile affectation of British phlegm, the teaching of a foreign governess and a con-gestive hypertrophy of the mucus of the nose. This enunciation which, as it happened, soon disappeared when she knew people better, giving place to a natural girlish tone, might have been thought unpleasant. But to me it was peculiarly delightful. Whenever I had gone for several days without seeing her, I would refresh my spirit by repeating to myself: "We don't ever see you playing golf," with the nasal intonation in which she had uttered the words, point blank, without moving a muscle of her face. And I thought then that there was no one in the world so desirable.

We formed, that morning, one of those couples who dotted the front here and there with their conjunction, their stopping together just long enough to exchange a few words before break-ing apart, each to resume separately his or her divergent stroll. I took advantage of this immobility to look again and discover once and for all where exactly the little mole was placed. Then, just as a phrase of Vinteuil which had delighted me in the sonata, and which my recollection allowed to wander from the andante to the finale, until the day when, having the score in my hands, I was able to find it and to fix it in my memory in its proper place, in the scherzo, so this mole, which I had visualised now on her cheek, now on her chin, came to rest for ever on her upper lip, just below her nose. In the same way, too, we are sometimes amazed to come upon lines that we know by heart in a play in which we never dreamed that they were to be found.

At that moment, as if in order that the rich decorative ensemble formed by the lovely train of maidens, at once pink and golden, baked by the sun and wind, might freely proliferate before the sea in all the variety of its forms, Albertine's friends, with their shapely limbs, their supple figures, but so different one from another, came into sight in a cluster that spread out as it advanced in our direc-tion, but closer to the sea, in a parallel line. I asked Albertine's permission to walk for a little way with her. Unfortunately, all she did was to wave her hand to them in greeting. "But your friends will be disappointed if you don't go with them," I hinted, hoping that we might all walk together.

A young man with regular features, carrying a bag of golf-clubs, sauntered up to us. It was the baccarat-player whose fast ways so enraged the senior judge's wife. In a frigid, impassive tone, which he evidently regarded as an indication of the highest distinction, he bade Albertine good day. "Been playing golf, Octave?" she asked. "How did it go? Were you in form?" "Oh, it's too sickening; I'm a wash-out," he replied. "Was Andrée playing?" "Yes, she went round in seventy-seven." "Why, that's a record!" "I went round in eighty-two yesterday." He was the son of an immensely rich manufacturer who was to take an important part in the organisation of the coming World's Fair. I was struck by the extreme degree to which, in this young man and the other very rare male friends of the band of girls, the knowledge of everything that pertained to clothes and how to wear them, cigars, English drinks, horses—a knowledge which he displayed down to its minutest details with a haughty infallibility that approached the reticent modesty of the true expert—had been developed in complete isolation, unaccompanied by the least trace of any intellectual culture. He had no hesitation as to the right time and place for dinner-jacket or pyjamas, but had no notion of the circumstances in which one might or might not employ this or that word, or even of the simplest rules of grammar. This disparity between the two forms of culture must have existed also in his father, the President of the Householders' Association of Balbec, for, in an open letter to the electors which he had recently had posted on all the walls, he announced: "I desired to see the Mayor, to chat to him about it, but he would not listen to my just grievances." Octave, at the Casino, took prizes in all the dancing competitions, for the boston, the tango, and what-not, an accomplishment that would enable him, if he chose, to make a fine marriage in that seaside society where it is not figuratively but literally that the girls are "wedded" to their "dancing partners." He lit a cigar with a "D'you mind?" to Albertine, as one who asks permission to finish an urgent piece of work while going on talking. For he was one of those people who can never be "doing nothing," although there was nothing, in fact, that he could ever be said to do. And since complete inactivity in the end has the same effect as prolonged overwork, in the mental sphere as much as in the life of the body and the muscles, the steadfast intellectual nullity that reigned behind Octave's meditative brow had ended by giving him, despite his air of unruffled calm, an ineffectual itch to think which kept him awake at night, for all the world like an overwrought philosopher.

Thinking that if I knew their male friends I should have more opportunities of seeing the girls, I had been on the point of asking for an introduction to Octave. I told Albertine this, as soon as he had left us, still muttering "I'm a wash-out," thinking to put into her head the idea of doing it next time.

"Come, come," she exclaimed, "I can't introduce you to a gigolo! This place simply swarms with them. But what on earth would they have to say to you? This one plays golf quite well, and that's all there is to him. I know what I'm talking about; you'd find he wasn't at all your sort."

"Your friends will be cross with you if you desert them like this," I repeated, hoping that she would then suggest my joining the party.

"Oh, no, they don't need me."

We passed Bloch, who directed at me a subtle, insinuating smile, and, embarrassed by the presence of Albertine, whom he did not know, or, rather, knew "without knowing" her, lowered his head towards his neck in a stiff, ungainly motion. "Who's that weird customer?" Albertine asked. "I can't think why he should bow to me since he doesn't know me. So I didn't respond."

I had no time to explain to her, for, bearing straight down upon us, "Excuse me," he began, "for interrupting you, but I must tell you that I'm going to Doncières tomorrow. I cannot put it off any longer without discourtesy; indeed, I wonder what de Saint-Loup-en-Bray must think of me. I just came to let you know that I shall take the two o'clock train. At your service."

But I thought now only of seeing Albertine again, and of trying to get to know her friends, and Doncières, since they were not going there, and my going would bring me back too late to see them still on the beach, seemed to me to be situated at the other end of the world. I told Bloch that it was impossible.

"Oh, very well, I shall go alone. In the fatuous alexandrines of Master Arouet, I shall say to Saint-Loup, to beguile his clericalism:

My duty stands alone, by his in no way bound;
Though he should choose to fail, yet faithful I'll be found."

"I admit he's not a bad-looking boy," said Albertine, "but he makes me feel quite sick."

I had never thought that Bloch might be "not a bad-looking boy"; and yet in fact he was. With his rather prominent forehead, his very aquiline nose, and his air of being extremely clever and of being convinced of his cleverness, he had a pleasing face. But he could not succeed in pleasing Albertine. This was perhaps to some extent due to the bad side of her, to the hardness, the insensitivity of the little band, its rudeness towards everything that was not itself. And later on, when I introduced them, Albertine's antipathy for him did not diminish. Bloch belonged to a social group in which, between scoffing at high society and at the same time showing the due regard for polite manners which a man is supposed to show who "does not soil his hands," a sort of special compromise has been reached which differs from the manners of the fashionable world but is none the less a peculiarly odious form of worldliness. When he was introduced to anyone he would bow with a sceptical smile, and at the same time with an exaggerated show of respect, and, if it was to a man, would say: "Pleased to meet you, sir," in a voice which ridiculed the words that it was uttering, though with a consciousness of belonging to someone who was not a boor. Having sacrificed this first moment to a custom which he at once followed and derided (just as on the first of January he would say: "The compliments of the season to you!"), he would adopt an air of infinite cunning, and would "proffer subtle words" which were often true enough but "got on" Albertine's nerves. When I told her on this first day that his name was Bloch, she exclaimed: "I would have betted anything he was a Yid. Typical of their creepy ways!" In fact, Bloch was destined to give Albertine other grounds for annoyance later on. Like many intellectuals, he was incapable of saying a simple thing in a simple way. He would find some precious qualifier for every statement, and would sweep from the particular to the general. It irritated Albertine, who was never too well pleased at other people's paying attention to what she was doing, that when she had sprained her ankle and was lying low, Bloch said of her: "She is outstretched on her couch, but in her ubiquity has not ceased to frequent simultaneously vague golf-courses and dubious tennis courts." He was simply being "literary," of course, but in view of the difficulties which Albertine felt that it might create for her with friends whose invitations she had declined on the plea that she was unable to move, it was quite enough to make her take a profound dislike to the face and the sound of the voice of the young man who said these things.

We parted, Albertine and I, after promising each other to go out together one day. I had talked to her without being any more conscious of where my words were falling, of what became of them, than if I were dropping pebbles into a bottomless pit. That our words are, as a general rule, filled by the people to whom we address them with a meaning which those people derive from their own substance, a meaning widely different from that which we had put into the same words when we uttered them, is a fact which is perpetually demonstrated in daily life. But if in addition we find ourselves in the company of a person whose education (as Albertine's was to me) is inconceivable, her taste, her reading, her principles unknown to us, we cannot tell whether our words have aroused in her anything that resembles their meaning, any more than in an animal to which we had to make ourselves understood. So that trying to make friends with Albertine seemed to me like entering into contact with the unknown, if not the impossible, an occupation as arduous as breaking in a horse, as restful as keeping bees or growing roses.

I had thought, a few hours before, that Albertine would acknowledge my greeting only from a distance. We had now left one another after planning to make an excursion soon together. I vowed that when I next met Albertine I would treat her with greater boldness, and I had sketched out in advance a plan of all that I would say to her, and even (being now quite convinced that she was not strait-laced) of all the favours that I would demand of her. But the mind is subject to external influences, as plants are, and cells and chemical elements, and the medium which alters it if we immerse it therein is a change of circumstances, or new surroundings. Changed by the mere fact of her presence, when I found myself once again in Albertine's company, I said to her quite different things from what I had planned. Then, remembering her flushed temple, I asked myself whether she might not appreciate more keenly a polite attention which she knew to be disinterested. Finally, I was embarrassed by some of her looks and her smiles. They might equally well signify a laxity of morals and the rather silly merriment of a high-spirited girl who was at heart thoroughly respectable. A single expression, of face or speech, being susceptible of sundry interpretations, I wavered like a schoolboy faced by the difficulties of a piece of Greek prose.

On this occasion we met almost immediately the tall one, Andrée, the one who had jumped over the old banker, and Albertine was obliged to introduce me. Her friend had extraordinarily bright eyes, like a glimpse, through an open door in a dark house, of a room into which the sun is shining with a greenish reflexion from the glittering sea.

A group of five men passed by whom I had come to know very well by sight during my stay at Balbec. I had often wondered who they were. "They're nothing very wonderful," said Albertine with a contemptuous snigger. "The little old one with dyed hair and yellow gloves—isn't he a weird-looking specimen, quite an eyeful, what?—that's the Balbec dentist. He's a good sort. The fat one is the Mayor, not the tiny little fat one, you must have seen him before, he's the dancing-master, and he's pretty awful too—he can't stand us, because we make such a row at the Casino and smash his chairs and want to have the carpet up when we dance, which is why he never gives us prizes, though we're the only ones who know how to dance. The dentist is a nice man—I would have said how d'ye do to him, just to make the dancing-master mad, but I couldn't because they've got M. de Sainte-Croix with them—he's a county councillor, and he comes of a very good family, but he's joined the Republicans, for money, so no decent people ever speak to him now. He knows my uncle, because they're both in the Government, but the rest of my family always cut him. The thin one in the waterproof is the conductor of the orchestra. What, you don't know him! Oh, he plays divinely. You haven't been to *Cavalleria Rusticana*? Ah, I think it's marvellous! He's giving a concert this evening, but we can't go because it's to be in the town hall. In the Casino it wouldn't matter, but in the town hall, where they've taken down the crucifix, Andrée's mother would have a fit if we went there. You're going to say that my aunt's husband is in the Government. But what difference does that make? My aunt is my aunt, but that's no reason why I should like her. The only thing she's ever wanted to do is get rid of me. No, the person who has really been a mother to me, and all the more credit to her because she's no relation at all, is a friend of mine whom I love just as much as if she was my mother. I'll show you her photo."

We were joined for a moment by the golf champion and baccarat-player, Octave. I thought I had discovered a bond between us, for I learned in the course of our conversation that he was some sort of relative of the Verdurins, who were quite fond of him. But he spoke contemptuously of the famous Wednesdays, adding that M. Verdurin had never even heard of dress-clothes, which made it a horrid bore when one ran into him in certain "music-halls" where one would very much rather not be greeted with "Well, you young rascal" by an old fellow in a jacket and black tie, like a village notary.

Octave left us, and soon it was Andrée's turn, when we came to her villa, into which she vanished without having uttered a single word to me during the whole of our walk. I regretted her departure all the more because, while I was complaining to Albertine how cold her friend had been towards me, and was comparing in my mind this difficulty which Albertine seemed to find in bringing me into contact with her friends with the hostility that Elstir, in attempting to fulfil my wish, seemed to have encountered on that first afternoon, two girls came by to whom I lifted my hat, the misses d'Ambresac, whom Albertine greeted also.

I felt that my position in relation to Albertine would be improved by this meeting. They were the daughters of a kinswoman of Mme de Villeparisis, who was also a friend of Mme de Luxembourg. M. and Mme d'Ambresac, who had a small villa at Balbec and were immensely rich, led the simplest of lives, and always went about in the same clothes, he in the same jacket, she in a dark dress. Both of them used to make sweeping bows to my grandmother, which never led to anything further. The daughters, who were very pretty, were dressed more elegantly, but it was an elegance more suited to Paris than to the seaside. With their long skirts and large hats, they seemed to belong to a different race from Albertine. She, I discovered, knew all about them.

"Oh, so you know the little d'Ambresacs, do you? Well, well, you do have some grand friends. But they're very simple really," she went on as though the two things were mutually exclusive. "They're very nice, but so well brought up that they aren't allowed near the Casino, mainly because of us, because we're too badly behaved. You find them attractive, do you? Well, it all depends on what you like. They're real goody-goodies. Perhaps there's a certain charm in that. If you like goody-goodies, they're all that you could wish for. There must be some attraction, because one of them has got engaged already to the Marquis de Saint-Loup. Which was a cruel blow to the younger one, who was madly in love with that young man. As far as I'm concerned, the way they purse their lips when they talk is enough to madden me. And then they dress in the most absurd way. Fancy going to play golf in silk frocks! At their age, they dress more pretentiously than grown-up women who really know about clothes. Look at Mme Elstir. There's a well-dressed woman if you like." I answered that she had struck me as being dressed with the utmost simplicity. Albertine laughed.

"She's very simply turned out, I admit, but she dresses wonderfully, and to get what you call simplicity costs her a fortune."

Mme Elstir's elegance passed unnoticed by anyone who had not a sober and unerring taste in matters of dress. This I lacked. Elstir possessed it in a supreme degree, so Albertine told me. I had not suspected this, nor that the beautiful but quite simple objects which littered his studio were treasures long desired by him which he had followed from sale-room to sale-room, knowing all their history, until he had made enough money to be able to acquire them. But as to this Albertine, being as ignorant as myself, could not enlighten me. Whereas when it came to clothes, prompted by a coquettish instinct and perhaps by the regretful longing of a penniless girl who is able to appreciate with greater disinterestedness, more delicacy and discrimination, in the rich things that she will never be able to afford for herself, she spoke very interestingly about the refinement of Elstir's taste, so difficult to satisfy that all women appeared to him badly dressed and, attaching infinite importance to proportions and shades of colour, he would have specially made for his wife, at fabulous prices, the sunshades, hats and coats whose charm he had taught Albertine to appreciate and which a person wanting in taste would no more have noticed than I had. Apart from this, Albertine, who had done a little painting, though without, she confessed, having any "gift" for it, felt a boundless admiration for Elstir, and, thanks to his precept and example, showed a judgment of pictures which was in marked contrast to her enthusiasm for *Cavalleria Rusticana*. The truth was that, though as yet it was hardly apparent, she was highly intelligent, and that in the things that she said the stupidity was not her own but that of her environment and her age. Elstir's had been a good but only a partial influence. All the branches of her intelligence had not reached the same stage of development. Her taste in pictures had almost caught up with her taste in clothes and all forms of elegance, but had not been followed by her taste in music, which was still a long way behind.

Albertine might know all about the Ambresacs; but as he who can achieve great things is not necessarily capable of small, I did not find her, after I had greeted those young ladies, any more disposed to make me known to her friends. "It's very good of you to attach importance to them. You shouldn't take any notice of them; they don't count. What on earth can a lot of kids like them mean to a man like you? Now Andrée, I must say, is remarkably clever. She's a good girl, though perfectly weird at times, but the others are really dreadfully stupid."

When I had left Albertine, I felt suddenly a keen regret that Saint-Loup should have concealed his engagement from me and that he should be doing anything so improper as to choose a wife before breaking with his mistress. And then, some days later, I met Andrée, and as she went on talking to me for some time I seized the opportunity to tell her that I would very much like to see her again next day; but she replied that this was impossible, because her mother was not at all well and she did not want to leave her alone. Two days later I went to see Elstir, who told me that Andrée had taken a great liking to me. When I protested that it was I who had taken a liking to her from the start, and had asked her to meet me again next day but she couldn't, "Yes, I know, she told me all about that," was his reply, "she was very sorry, but she had promised to go for a picnic somewhere miles from here. They were to drive over in a break, and it was too late for her to get out of it." Although this falsehood was of no real significance since Andrée knew me so slightly, I ought not to have continued to seek the company of a person who was capable of it. For what people have once done they will go on doing indefinitely, and if you go every year to see a friend who, the first few times, was unable to keep an appointment with you, or was in bed with a chill, you will find him in bed with another chill which he has just caught, you will miss him again at another meeting-place where he has failed to appear, for a single and unalterable reason in place of which he supposes himself to have various reasons, according to the circumstances.

One morning, not long after Andrée had told me that she would be obliged to stay beside her mother, I was taking a short stroll with Albertine, whom I had found on the beach tossing up and catching again at the end of a string a weird object which gave her a look of Giotto's "Idolatry"; it was called, as it happened, a "diabolo," and has so fallen into disuse now that, when they come upon the picture of a girl playing with one, the commentators of future generations will solemnly discuss, as it might be in front of the allegorical figures in the Arena Chapel, what it is that she is holding. A moment later their friend with the penurious and hard appearance, the one who on that first day had sneered so malevolently: "I do feel sorry for him, poor old boy," when she saw the old gentleman's head brushed by the flying feet of Andrée, came up to Albertine and said: "Good morning. Am I disturbing you?" She had taken off her hat for comfort, and her hair, like a strange and fascinating plant, lay over her brow, displaying all the delicate tracery of its foliation. Albertine, perhaps irritated at seeing the other bare-headed, made no reply, and preserved a frigid silence in spite of which the girl stayed with us, kept apart from me by Albertine who arranged at one moment to be alone with her, at another to walk with me leaving her to follow. I was obliged, to secure an introduction, to ask for it in the girl's hearing. Then, as Albertine uttered my name, the face and the blue eyes of this girl, whose expression I had thought so cruel when I heard her say: "Poor old boy, I do feel sorry for him," lit up with a cordial and affectionate smile, and she held out her hand to me. Her hair was golden, and not her hair only; for if her cheeks were pink and her eyes blue, it was like the still roseate morning sky which sparkles everywhere with dazzling points of gold.

Instantly aroused, I said to myself that this was a child who when in love grew shy, that it was for my sake, for love of me that she had remained with us despite Albertine's rebuffs, and that she must have rejoiced in the opportunity to confess to me at last, by that smiling, friendly look, that she would be as gentle to me as she was ferocious to other people. Doubtless she had noticed me on the beach when I did not yet know her, and had been thinking of me ever since; perhaps it was to win my admiration that she had mocked at the old gentleman, and because she had not succeeded in getting to know me that on the following days she had appeared so morose. I had often seen her from the hotel, walking by herself on the beach in the evenings. It was probably in the hope of meeting me. And now, hindered as much by Albertine's presence as she would have been by that of the whole band, she had evidently attached herself to us, in spite of the increasing coldness of her friend's attitude, only in the hope of outstaying her, of being left alone with me, when she might make a rendezvous with me for some time when she would find an excuse to slip away without either her family or her friends knowing that she had gone, and would meet me in some safe place before church or after golf. It was all the more difficult to see her because Andrée had quarrelled with her and now detested her. "I've put up quite long enough," she told me, "with her appalling duplicity, her baseness, and all the dirty tricks she's played on me. I've stood it all because of the others. But her latest effort was really too much!" And she told me of some piece of malicious gossip that this girl had perpetrated, which might indeed have injurious consequences for Andrée.

But those private words promised me by Gisèle's confiding eyes for the moment when Albertine should have left us by ourselves were destined never to be spoken, because after Albertine, stubbornly planted between us, had continued to reply with increasing curtness, and had finally ceased to reply at all, to her friend's remarks, Gisèle at length abandoned the attempt and turned back. I reproached Albertine for having been so disagreeable. "It will teach her to be more tactful. She's not a bad kid, but she's so boring. She's got no business, either, to come poking her nose into everything. Why should she fasten herself on to us without being asked? In another minute I'd have told her to go to blazes. Besides, I can't stand her going about with her hair like that; it's such bad form."

I gazed at Albertine's cheeks as she spoke, and asked myself what might be the perfume, the taste of them: that day she was not fresh and cool but smooth, with a uniform pinkness, violet-tinted, creamy, like certain roses whose petals have a waxy gloss. I felt a passionate longing for them such as one feels sometimes for a particular flower. "I hadn't noticed it," was all that I said.

"You stared at her hard enough; anyone would have thought you wanted to paint her portrait," she replied, not at all mollified by the fact that it was at herself that I was now staring so fixedly. "I don't believe you would care for her, though. She's not in the least a flirt. You like girls who flirt, I suspect. Anyhow, she won't have another chance of sticking to us and having to be shaken off. She's going back to Paris later today."

"Are the rest of your friends going too?"

"No, only she and 'Miss,' because she's got to take her exams again; she'll have to swot for them, poor kid. It's not much fun, I don't mind telling you. Of course, you may be set a good subject, you never know. It's such a matter of luck. One girl I know was given: *Describe an accident that you have witnessed.* That was a piece of luck. But I know another girl who had to discuss, in writing too: *Which would you rather have as a friend, Alceste or Philinte?* I'm sure I should have dried up altogether! Apart from everything else, it's not a question to set to girls. Girls go about with other girls; they're not supposed to have gentlemen friends." (This announcement, which showed that I had small chance of being admitted to the little band, made me quake.) "But in any case, even if it was set for boys, what on earth would you expect them to find to say about it? Several parents wrote to the *Gaulois*, to complain of the difficulty of questions like that. The joke of it is that in a collection of prize-winning essays there were two which treated the question in absolutely opposite ways. You see, it all depends on the examiner. One wanted you to say that Philinte was a two-faced socialite flatterer, the other that you couldn't help admiring Alceste, but that he was too cantankerous, and that as a friend you ought to choose Philinte. How can you expect a lot of unfortunate candidates to know what to say when the professors themselves don't agree? But that's nothing. It gets more difficult every year. Gisèle will have to pull a string or two if she's to get through."

I returned to the hotel. My grandmother was not there. I waited for her some time, and when at last she appeared, I begged her to allow me, in quite unexpected circumstances, to make an expedition which might keep me away for a couple of days. I had lunch with her, ordered a carriage and drove to the station. Gisèle would not be surprised to see me there. After we had changed at Doncières, in the Paris train there would be a carriage with a corridor, along which, while the governess dozed, I should be able to lead Gisèle into a dark corner and make an appointment to meet her on my return to Paris, which I would then try to put forward to the earliest possible date. I would travel with her as far as Caen or Evreux, whichever she preferred, and would take the next train back to Balbec. And yet, what would she have thought of me had she known that I had hesitated for a long time between her and her friends, that quite as much as with her I had contemplated falling in love with Albertine, with the girl with the bright eyes, with Rosemonde. I felt a pang of remorse, now that a bond of mutual affection was going to unite me with Gisèle. I could, however, truthfully have assured her that Albertine no longer attracted me. I had seen her that morning as she swerved aside, almost turning her back on me, to speak to Gisèle. Her head was sulkily lowered, and the hair at the back, which was different and darker still, glistened as though she had just been bathing. Like a wet hen, I had thought to myself, and this view of her hair had induced me to embody in Albertine a different soul from that implied hitherto by her violet face and mysterious gaze. That shining cataract of hair at the back of her head had been for a moment or two all that I was able to see of her, and continued to be all that I saw in retrospect. Our memory is like one of those shops in the window of which is exposed now one, now another photograph of the same person. And as a rule the most recent exhibit remains for some time the only one to be seen. While the coachman whipped on his horse I sat there listening to the words of gratitude and tenderness that Gisèle was murmuring in my ear, all of them born of her friendly smile and outstretched hand; for the fact was that in those periods of my life in which I was not actually in love but desired to be, I carried in my mind not only a physical ideal of beauty which, as the reader has seen, I recognised from a distance in every passing woman far enough away from me for her indistinct features not to belie the identification, but also the mental phantom—ever ready to become incarnate—of the woman who was going to fall in love with me, to take up her cues in the amorous comedy which I had had all written out in my mind from my earliest boyhood, and in which every attractive girl seemed to me to be equally desirous of playing, provided that she had also some of the physical qualifications required. In this play, whoever the new star might be whom I invited to create or to revive the leading part, the plot, the incidents, the lines themselves preserved an unalterable form.

Within the next few days, in spite of the reluctance that Albertine had shown to introduce me to them, I knew all the little band of that first afternoon (except Gisèle, whom, owing to a prolonged delay at the level crossing by the station and a change in the time-table, I had not succeeded in meeting on the train, which had left some minutes before I arrived, and to whom in any case I never gave another thought), and two or three other girls as well to whom at my request they introduced me. And thus, my expecta- tion of the pleasure which I should find in a new girl springing from another through whom I had come to know her, the latest was like one of those new varieties of rose which gardeners get by using first a rose of another species. And as I passed from corolla to corolla along this chain of flowers, the pleasure of knowing a different one would send me back to the one to whom I was indebted for it, with a gratitude mixed with as much desire as my new hope. Presently I was spending all my time among these girls.

Alas! in the freshest flower it is possible to discern those just perceptible signs which to the instructed mind already betray what will, by the desiccation or fructification of the flesh that is today in bloom, be the ultimate form, immutable and already predestined, of the autumnal seed. The eye follows with delight a nose like a wavelet that deliciously ripples the surface of the water at day-break, and seems motionless, capturable by the pencil, because the sea is so calm that one does not notice its tidal flow. Human faces seem not to change while we are looking at them, because the revolution they perform is too slow for us to perceive it. But one had only to see, by the side of any of these girls, her mother or her aunt, to realise the distance over which, obeying the internal gravitation of a type that was generally frightful, these features would have travelled in less than thirty years, until the hour when the looks have begun to wane, until the hour when the face, having sunk altogether below the horizon, catches the light no more. I knew that, as deep, as ineluctable as Jewish patriotism or Christian atavism in those who imagine themselves to be the most emancipated of their race, there dwelt beneath the rosy inflores-cence of Albertine, Rosemonde, Andrée, unknown to them-selves, held in reserve until the occasion should arise, a coarse nose, a protruding jaw, a paunch which would create a sensation when it appeared, but which was actually in the wings, ready to come on, unforeseen, inevitable, just as it might be a burst of Dreyfusism or clericalism or patriotic, feudal heroism, emerging suddenly in answer to the call of circumstance from a nature anterior to the individual himself, through which he thinks, lives, evolves, gains strength or dies, without ever being able to distinguish that nature from the particular motives he mistakes for it. Even mentally, we depend a great deal more than we think upon natural laws, and our minds possess in advance, like some cryptogamous plant, the characteristic that we imagine ourselves to be selecting. For we grasp only the secondary ideas, without detecting the primary cause (Jewish blood, French birth or whatever it may be) that inevitably produced them, and which we manifest when the time comes. But perhaps, while the one may appear to us to be the result of deliberate thought, the other of an imprudent disregard for our own health, we take from our family, as the papilionaceae take the form of their seed, as well the ideas by which we live as the malady from which we shall die.

As in a nursery plantation where the flowers mature at different seasons, I had seen them, in the form of old ladies, on this Balbec shore, those shrivelled seed-pods, those flabby tubers, which my new friends would one day be. But what matter? For the moment it was their flowering-time. And so when Mme de Villeparisis asked me to go for a drive, I sought an excuse to avoid doing so. I no longer visited Elstir unless accompanied by my new friends. I could not even spare an afternoon to go to Doncières, to pay the visit I had promised Saint-Loup. Social engagements, serious discussions, even a friendly conversation, had they usurped the place allotted to my outings with these girls, would have had the same effect on me as if, at lunch-time, one were taken not to eat but to look at an album. The men, the youths, the women, old or mature, in whose society we think to take pleasure, exist for us only on a flat, one-dimensional surface, because we are conscious of them only through visual perception restricted to its own limits; whereas it is as delegates from our other senses that our eyes direct themselves towards young girls; the senses follow, one after another, in search of the various charms, fragrant, tactile, savorous, which they thus enjoy even without the aid of hands and lips; and able, thanks to the arts of transposition, the genius for synthesis in which desire excels, to reconstruct beneath the hue of cheeks or bosom the feel, the taste, the contact that is forbidden them, they give to these girls the same honeyed consistency as they create when they go foraging in a rose-garden, or in a vine whose clusters their eyes devour.

If it rained, although the weather had no power to daunt Albertine, who was often to be seen in her waterproof spinning on her bicycle through the showers, we would spend the day in the Casino, where on such days it would have seemed to me impossible not to go. I had the greatest contempt for the Ambresac sisters, who had never set foot in it. And I willingly joined my new friends in playing tricks on the dancing-master. As a rule we had to listen to admonitions from the manager, or from some of his staff usurping directorial powers, because my friends— even Andrée whom on that account I had regarded when I first saw her as so Dionysiac a creature whereas in reality she was delicate, intellectual and this year far from well, in spite of which her actions were responsive less to the state of her health than to the spirit of that age which sweeps everything aside and mingles in a general gaiety the weak with the strong—could not go from the hall to the ball-room without breaking into a run, jumping over all the chairs, and sliding along the floor, their balance maintained by a graceful poise of their outstretched arms, singing the while, mingling all the arts, in that first bloom of youth, in the manner of those poets of old for whom the different genres were not yet separate, so that in an epic poem they would mix agricultural precepts with theological doctrine.

This Andrée, who had struck me when I first saw her as the coldest of them all, was infinitely more refined, more affectionate, more sensitive than Albertine, to whom she displayed the caressing, gentle tenderness of an elder sister. At the Casino she would come across the floor to sit down beside me and was prepared, unlike Albertine, to forgo a waltz or even, if I was tired, to give up the Casino and come to me instead at the hotel. She expressed her friendship for me, for Albertine, in terms that were evidence of the most exquisite understanding of the things of the heart, which may have been partly due to her delicate health. She had always a gay smile of excuse for the childish behaviour of Albertine, who expressed with naïve violence the temptation held out to her by the parties and pleasures which she was incapable of resisting, as Andrée could, in order to stay and talk to me. When the time came for her go to off to a tea-party at the golf-club, if we were all three together at that moment she would get ready to leave and then, coming up to Andrée, would say: "Well, Andrée, what are you waiting for? You know we're having tea at the golf-club." "No, I'm going to stay and talk to him," Andrée would reply, pointing to me. "But you know Mme Durieux invited you," Albertine would cry, as if Andrée's intention to remain with me could be explained only by ignorance on her part as to whether or not she had been invited. "Come, my sweet, don't be such an idiot," Andrée would chide her, and Albertine would not insist, for fear that she might be asked to stay too. She would toss her head and say "Just as you like," in the tone one uses to an invalid who is deliberately killing himself by inches. "Anyway I must fly; I'm sure your watch is slow," and off she would go. "She's a dear girl, but quite impossible," Andrée would say, enveloping her friend in a smile at once caressing and critical. If in this craze for amusement Albertine might be said to echo something of the old original Gilberte, that is because a certain similarity exists, although the type evolves, between all the women we successively love, a similarity that is due to the fixity of our own temperament, which chooses them, eliminating all those who would not be at once our opposite and our complement, apt, that is to say, to gratify our senses and to wring our hearts. They are, these women, a product of our temperament, an image, an inverted projection, a negative of our sensibility. So that a novelist might, in relating the life of his hero, describe his successive love affairs in almost exactly similar terms, and thereby give the impression not that he was repeating himself but that he was creating, since an artificial novelty is never so effective as a repetition that manages to suggest a fresh truth. He ought, moreover, to note in the character of the lover an index of variation which becomes apparent as the story moves into fresh regions, into different latitudes of life. And perhaps he would be expressing yet another truth if, while investing all the other dramatis personae with distinct characters, he refrained from giving any to the beloved. We understand the characters of people to whom we are indifferent, but how can we ever grasp that of a person who is an intimate part of our existence, whom after a while we no longer distinguish from ourselves, whose motives provide us with an inexhaustible source of anxious hypotheses, continually revised? Springing from somewhere beyond our intellect, our curiosity about the woman we love overleaps the bounds of that woman's character, at which, even if we could stop, we probably never would. The object of our anxious investigation is something more basic than those details of character comparable to the tiny particles of epidermis whose varied combinations form the florid originality of human flesh. Our intuitive radiography pierces them, and the images which it brings back, far from being those of a particular face, present rather the joyless universality of a skeleton.

Andrée, being herself extremely rich while the other was penniless and an orphan, with real generosity lavished on Albertine the full benefit of her wealth. As for her feelings towards Gisèle, they were not quite what I had been led to suppose. News soon reached us of the young student, and when Albertine handed round the letter she had received from her, a letter intended by Gisèle to give an account of her journey and to report her safe arrival to the little band, apologising for her laziness in not yet having written to the others, I was surprised to hear Andrée, whom I imagined to be at daggers drawn with her, say: "I shall write to her tomorrow, because if I wait for her to write I may have to wait for ages, she's such a slacker." And turning to me she added: "You mightn't see much in her, but she's a jolly nice girl, and besides I'm really very fond of her." From which I concluded that Andrée's quarrels were apt not to last very long.

Except on these rainy days, as we always arranged to go on our bicycles along the cliffs, or on an excursion inland, an hour or so before it was time to start I would go upstairs to make myself smart and would complain if Françoise had not laid out all the things that I wanted. Now even in Paris, at the first word of reproach she would proudly and angrily straighten a back which the years had begun to bend, she so humble, modest and charming when her self-esteem was flattered. As this was the mainspring of Françoise's life, her satisfaction and her good humour were in direct ratio to the difficulty of the tasks imposed on her. Those which she had to perform at Balbec were so easy that she displayed an almost continual dissatisfaction which was suddenly multiplied a hundred-fold and combined with an ironic air of offended dignity when I complained, on my way down to join my friends, that my hat had not been brushed or my ties sorted. She who was capable of taking such endless pains and would think nothing of it, on my simply remarking that a coat was not in its proper place would not only boast of the care with which she had "shut it away sooner than let it go gathering the dust," but, paying a formal tribute to her own labours, lamented that it was little enough of a holiday that she was getting at Balbec, and that we would not find another person in the whole world who would consent to put up with such treatment. "I can't think how people can leave things lying about the way you do; you just try and get anyone else to find what you want in such a pell and mell. The devil himself couldn't make head nor tail of it." Or else she would adopt a regal mien, scorching me with her fiery glance, and preserve a silence that was broken as soon as she had fastened the door behind her and had set off down the corridor, which would then reverberate with utterances which I guessed to be abusive, though they remained as indistinct as those of characters in a play whose opening lines are spoken in the wings, before they appear on the stage. But even if nothing was missing and Françoise was in a good temper, still she made herself quite intolerable when I was getting ready to go out with my friends. For, drawing upon a store of jokes which, in my need to talk about these girls, I had told her at their expense, she took it upon herself to reveal to me what I should have known better than she if it had been accurate, which it never was, Françoise having misunderstood what she had heard. She had, like everyone else, her own peculiar character, which in no one resembles a straight highway, but surprises us with its strange, unavoidable windings which other people do not see and which it is painful to have to follow. Whenever I arrived at the stage of

"Where is my hat?" or uttered the name of Andrée or Albertine, I was forced by Françoise to stray into endless and absurd side-tracks which greatly delayed my progress. So too when I ordered the cheese or salad sandwiches or sent out for the cakes which I would eat on the cliff with the girls, and which they "might very well have taken turns to provide, if they hadn't been so close-fisted," declared Françoise, to whose aid there came at such moments a whole heritage of atavistic peasant rapacity and coarse-ness, and for whom one would have said that the divided soul of her late enemy Eulalie had been reincarnated, more becomingly than in St Eloi, in the charming bodies of my friends of the little band. I listened to these accusations with a dull fury at finding myself brought to a standstill at one of those places beyond which the rustic and familiar path that was Françoise's character became impassable, though fortunately never for very long. Then, my hat or coat found and the sandwiches ready, I went to join Albertine, Andrée, Rosemonde, and any others there might be, and we would set out on foot or on our bicycles.

In the old days I should have preferred our excursions to be made in bad weather. For then I still looked to find in Balbec "the land of the Cimmerians," and fine days were a thing that had no right to exist there, an intrusion of the vulgar summer of seaside holiday-makers into that ancient region swathed in eternal mist. But everything that I had hitherto despised and thrust from my sight, not only the effects of sunlight upon sea and shore, but even regattas and race-meetings, I now sought out with ardour, for the same reason which formerly had made me wish only for stormy seas: namely, that they were now associated in my mind, as the others had once been, with an aesthetic idea. For I had gone several times with my new friends to visit Elstir, and, on the days when the girls were there, what he had selected to show us were drawings of pretty women in yachting dress, or else a sketch made on a race-course near Balbec. I had at first shyly admitted to Elstir that I had not felt inclined to go to the meetings that had been held there. "You were wrong," he told me, "it's such a pretty sight, and so strange too. For one thing, that peculiar creature the jockey, on whom so many eyes are fastened, and who sits there in the paddock so gloomy and grey-faced in his bright jacket, reining in the rearing horse that seems to be one with him: how interesting to analyse his professional movements, the bright splash of colour he makes, with the horse's coat blending in it, against the background of the course! What a transformation of every visible object in that luminous vastness of a race-course where one is constantly surprised by fresh lights and shades which one sees only there! How pretty the women can look there, too! The first meeting in particular was delightful, and there were some extremely elegant women there in the misty, almost Dutch light in which you could feel the piercing cold of the sea even in the sun itself. I've never seen women arriving in carriages, or standing with glasses to their eyes in so extraordinary a light, which was due, I suppose, to the moisture from the sea. Ah! how I should have loved to paint it. I came back from those races wild with enthusiasm and longing to get to work!" After which he waxed more enthusiastic still over the yacht-races, and I realised that regattas, and race-meetings where well-dressed women might be seen bathed in the greenish light of a marine race-course, might be for a modern artist as interesting a subject as the festivities which they so loved to depict were for a Veronese or a Carpaccio. When I suggested this to Elstir, "Your comparison is all the more apt," he replied, "since because of the nature of the city in which they painted, those festivities were to a great extent aquatic. Except that the beauty of the shipping in those days lay as a rule in its solidity, in the complication of its structure. They had water-tournaments, as we have here, held generally in honour of some Embassy, such as Carpaccio shows us in his *Legend of Saint Ursula*. The ships were massive, built like pieces of architecture, and seemed almost amphibious, like lesser Venices set in the heart of the greater, when, moored to the banks by gangways decked with crimson satin and Persian carpets, they bore their freight of ladies in cerise brocade and green damask close under the balconies incrusted with multicoloured marble from which other ladies leaned to gaze at them, in gowns with black sleeves slashed with white, stitched with pearls or bordered with lace. You couldn't tell where the land finished and the water began, what was still the palace or already the ship, the caravel, the galley, the Bucentaur."

Albertine listened with passionate interest to these details of costume, these visions of elegance that Elstir described to us. "Oh, I should so like to see that lace you speak of; it's so pretty, Venetian lace," she exclaimed, "and I should love to see Venice." "You may, perhaps, before very long," Elstir informed her, "be able to gaze at the marvellous stuffs which they used to wear. One used only to be able to see them in the works of the Venetian painters, or very rarely among the treasures of old churches, or now and then when a specimen turned up in the sale-room. But I hear that a Venetian artist, called Fortuny, has rediscovered the secret of the craft, and that in a few years' time women will be able to parade around, and better still to sit at home, in broacades as sumptuous as those that Venice adorned for her patrician daughters with patterns brought from the Orient. But I don't know whether I should much care for that, whether it wouldn't be too much of an anachronism for the women of today, even when they parade at regattas, for, to return to our modern pleasure-craft, the times have completely changed since 'Venice, Queen of the Adriatic.' The great charm of a yacht, of the furnishings of a yacht, of yachting clothes, is their simplicity, as things of the sea, and I do so love the sea. I must confess that I prefer the fashions of today to those of Veronese's and even of Carpaccio's time. What is so attractive about our yachts—and the medium-sized yachts especially, I don't like the huge ones, they're too much like ships; and the same goes for hats, there must be some sense of proportion—is the uniform surface, simple, gleaming, grey, which in a blush haze takes on a creamy softness. The cabin ought to make us think of a little café. And it's the same with women's clothes on board a yacht; what's really charming are those light garments, uniformly white, cotton or linen or nankeen or drill, which in the sunlight and against the blue of the sea show up with as dazzling a whiteness as a spread sail. Actually, there are very few women who know how to dress, though some of them are quite wonderful. At the races, Mlle Léa had a little white hat and a little white sunshade that were simply enchanting. I don't know what I wouldn't give for that little sunshade."

I should have liked very much to know in what respect this little sunshade differed from any other, and for other reasons, reasons of feminine coquetry, Albertine was still more curious. But, just as Françoise used to explain the excellence of her soufflés by saying simply: "It's a knack," so here the difference lay in the cut. "It was tiny and round, like a Chinese parasol," Elstir said. I mentioned the sunshades carried by various women, but none of them would do. Elstir found them all quite hideous. A man of exquisite taste, singularly hard to please, he would isolate some minute detail which was the whole difference between what was worn by three-quarters of the women he saw, and which he abominated, and a thing which enchanted him by its prettiness; and—in contrast to its effect on myself, for whom every kind of luxury was stultifying—stimulated his desire to paint "so as to make something as attractive."

"Here you see a young lady who has guessed what the hat and sunshade were like," he said to me, pointing to Albertine, whose eyes shone with covetousness.

"How I should love to be rich and to have a yacht!" she said to the painter. "I should come to you for advice on how to do it up. What lovely trips I'd make! And what fun it would be to go to Cowes for the regatta! And a motor-car! Tell me, do you think women's fashions for motoring pretty?"

"No," replied Elstir, "but that will come in time. You see, there are very few good couturiers at present, one or two only, Callot—although they go in rather too freely for lace—Doucet, Cheruit, Paquin sometimes. The others are all ghastly."

"So there's a vast difference between a Callot dress and one from any ordinary shop?" I asked Albertine.

"Why, an enormous difference, my little man! Oh, sorry! Only, alas! what you get for three hundred francs in an ordinary shop will cost two thousand there. But there can be no comparison; they look the same only to people who know nothing at all about it."

"Quite so," put in Elstir, "though I wouldn't go so far as to say that it's as profound as the difference between a statue from Rheims Cathedral and one from Saint-Augustin. By the way, talking of cathedrals," he went on, addressing himself exclusively to me, because what he was saying referred to an earlier conversation in which the girls had not taken part, and which for that matter would in no way have interested them, "I spoke to you the other day of Balbec church as a great cliff, a huge breakwater built of the stone of the country, but conversely," he went on, showing me a water-colour, "look at these cliffs (it's a sketch I did near here, at the Creuniers); don't those rocks, so powerfully and delicately modelled, remind you of a cathedral?"

And indeed one would have taken them for soaring red arches. But, painted on a scorching hot day, they seemed to have been reduced to dust, volatilised by the heat which had drunk up half the sea so that it had almost been distilled, over the whole surface of the picture, into a gaseous state. On this day when the sunlight had, so to speak, destroyed reality, reality concentrated itself in certain dusky and transparent creatures which, by contrast, gave a more striking, a closer impression of life: the shadows. Thirsting for coolness, most of them, deserting the torrid sea, had taken shelter at the foot of the rocks, out of reach of the sun; others, swimming gently upon the tide, like dolphins, kept close under the sides of occasional moving boats, whose hulls they extended upon the pale surface of the water with their glossy blue forms. It was perhaps the thirst for coolness which they conveyed that did most to give me the sensation of the heat of that day and made me exclaim how much I regretted not knowing the Creuniers. Albertine and Andrée were positive that I must have been there hundreds of times. If so I had been there without knowing it, never suspecting that one day the sight of these rocks would arouse in me such a thirst for beauty, not perhaps precisely natural beauty such as I had sought hitherto among the cliffs of Balbec, but architectural rather. Especially since, having come here to visit the kingdom of the storms, I had never found, on any of my drives with Mme de Villeparisis, when often we saw it only from afar, painted in a gap between the trees, that the sea was sufficiently real or sufficiently liquid or gave a sufficient impression of hurling its massed forces against the shore, and would have liked to see it lie motionless only under a wintry shroud of fog, I could never have believed that I should now be dreaming of a sea which was no more than a whitish vapour that had lost both consistency and colour. But of such a sea Elstir, like the people who sat musing on board those vessels drowsy with the heat, had felt so intensely the enchantment that he had succeeded in transcribing, in fixing for all time upon his canvas, the imperceptible ebb of the tide, the throb of one happy moment; and at the sight of this magic portrait, one could think of nothing else than to range the wide world, seeking to recapture the vanished day in its instantaneous, slumbering beauty.

So that if, before these visits to Elstir—before I had set eyes on one of his sea-pictures in which a young woman in a dress of white serge or linen, on the deck of a yacht flying the American flag, put into my imagination the spiritual "carbon copy" of a white linen dress and coloured flag which at once bred in me an insatiable desire to see there and then with my own eyes white linen dresses and flags against the sea, as if no such experience had ever yet befallen me—I had always striven, when I stood before the sea, to expel from my field of vision, as well as the bathers in the fore-ground and the yachts with their too dazzling sails that were like seaside costumes, everything that prevented me from persuading myself that I was contemplating the immemorial ocean which had already been pursuing the same mysterious life before the appearance of the human race, and had grudged even the days of radiant sunshine which seemed to me to invest with the trivial aspect of universal summer this coast of fog and tempest, to mark simply a pause, equivalent to what in music is known as a silent bar—now on the contrary it was bad weather that appeared to me to be some baleful accident, no longer worthy of a place in the world of beauty: I felt a keen desire to go out and recapture in reality what had so powerfully aroused my imagination, and I hoped that the weather would be propitious enough for me to see from the summit of the cliff the same blue shadows as in Elstir's picture.

Nor, as I went along, did I still screen my eyes with my hands as in the days when, conceiving nature to be animated by a life anterior to the first appearance of man and in opposition to all those wearisome improvements of industrial civilisation which had hitherto made me yawn with boredom at universal exhibitions or milliners' windows, I endeavoured to see only that section of the sea over which there was no steamer passing, so that I might picture it to myself as immemorial, still contemporary with the ages when it had been divorced from the land, or at least contemporary with the early centuries of Greece, which enabled me to repeat in their literal meaning the lines of "old man Leconte" of which Bloch was so fond:

> Gone are the kings, their ships pierced by rams,
> Vanished upon the raging deep, alas,
> The long-haired warriors of heroic Hellas.

I could no longer despise the milliners, now that Elstir had told me that the delicate gesture with which they give a last refinement, a supreme caress to the bows or feathers of a hat after it is finished, would be as interesting to him to paint as that of the jockeys (a statement which had delighted Albertine). But I must wait until I had returned—for milliners, to Paris, for regattas and races to Balbec, where there would be no more now until next year. Even a yacht with women in white linen was not to be found.

Often we encountered Bloch's sisters, to whom I was obliged to bow since I had dined with their father. My new friends did not know them. "I'm not allowed to play with Israelites," Albertine announced. Her way of pronouncing the word—"Issraelites" instead of "Izraelites"—would in itself have sufficed to show, even if one had not heard the rest of the sentence, that it was no feeling of friendliness towards the chosen race that inspired these young bourgeoises, brought up in God-fearing homes, and quite ready to believe that the Jews were in the habit of butchering Christian children. "Besides, they're shocking bad form, your friends," said Andrée with a smile which implied that she knew very well that they were no friends of mine. "Like everything to do with the tribe," added Albertine, in the sententious tone of one who spoke from personal experience. To tell the truth, Bloch's sisters, at once overdressed and half naked, with their languid, brazen, ostentatious, slatternly air, did not create the best impression. And one of their cousins, who was only fifteen, scandalised the Casino by her unconcealed admiration for Mlle Léa, whose talent as an actress M. Bloch senior rated very high, but whose tastes were understood not to be primarily directed towards gentlemen.

There were days when we picnicked at one of the outlying farms which catered for visitors. These were the farms known as Les Ecorres, Marie-Thérèse, La Croix d'Heuland, Bagatelle, Californie and Marie-Antoinette. It was the last that had been adopted by the little band.

But at other times, instead of going to a farm, we would climb to the highest point of the cliff, and, when we had reached it and were seated on the grass, would undo our parcel of sandwiches and cakes. My friends preferred the sandwiches, and were surprised to see me eat only a single chocolate cake, sugared with Gothic tracery, or an apricot tart. This was because, with the sandwiches of cheese or salad, a form of food that was novel to me and was ignorant of the past, I had nothing in common. But the cakes understood, the tarts were talkative. There was in the former an insipid taste of cream, in the latter a fresh taste of fruit which knew all about Combray, and about Gilberte, not only the Gilberte of Combray but the Gilberte of Paris, at whose tea-parties I had come across them again. They reminded me of those cake-plates with the Arabian Nights pattern, the subjects on which so diverted my aunt Léonie when Françoise brought her up, one day Aladdin and his Wonderful Lamp, another day Ali Baba, or the Sleeper Awakes or Sinbad the Sailor embarking at Bassorah with all his treasures. I should dearly have liked to see them again, but my grandmother did not know what had become of them and thought moreover that they were just common plates that had been bought in the village. No matter, in grey, rustic Combray they were a multi-coloured inset, as in the dark church were the flickering jewels of the stained-glass windows, as in the twilight of my bedroom were the projections cast by the magic lantern, as in front of the railway-station and the little local line the buttercups from the Indies and the Persian lilacs, as was my great-aunt's collection of old porcelain in the sombre dwelling of an elderly lady in a country town.

Stretched out on the cliff I would see before me nothing but grassy meadows and beyond them not the seven heavens of the Christian cosmogony but two stages only, one of a deeper blue, the sea, and above it another, paler one. We ate our food, and if I had brought with me also some little keepsake which might appeal to one or other of my friends, joy sprang with such sudden violence into their translucent faces, flushed in an instant, that their lips had not the strength to hold it in, and, to allow it to escape, parted in a burst of laughter. They were gathered close round me, and between their faces, which were not far apart, the air that separated them traced azure pathways such as might have been cut by a gardener wishing to create a little space so as to be able himself to move freely through a thicket of roses.

When we had finished eating we would play games which until then I should have thought boring, sometimes such childish games as King of the Castle, or Who Laughs First; not for a kingdom would I have renounced them now; the aurora of adolescence with which the faces of these girls still glowed, and from which I, young as I was, had already emerged, shed its light on everything around them and, like the fluid painting of certain Primitives, brought out in relief the most insignificant details of their daily lives against a golden background. Their faces were for the most part blurred with this misty effulgence of a dawn from which their actual features had not yet emerged. One saw only a charming glow of colour beneath which what in a few years' time would be a profile was not discernible. The profile of today had nothing definitive about it, and could be only a momentary resemblance to some deceased member of the family to whom nature had paid this commemorative courtesy. It comes so soon, the moment when there is nothing left to wait for, when the body is fixed in an immobility which holds no fresh surprise in store, when one loses all hope on seeing—as on a tree in the height of summer one sees leaves already brown—round a face still young hair that is growing thin or turning grey; it is so short, that radiant morning time, that one comes to like only the very youngest girls, those in whom the flesh, like a precious leaven, is still at work. They are no more than a stream of ductile matter, continuously moulded by the fleeting impression of the moment. It is as though each of them was in turn a little statuette of gaiety, of childish earnestness, of cajolery, of surprise, shaped by an expression frank and complete, but fugitive. This plasticity gives a wealth of variety and charm to the pretty attentions which a young girl pays to us. Of course, such attentions are indispensable in the mature woman also, and one who is not attracted to us, or who does not show that she is attracted to us, tends to assume in our eyes a somewhat tedious uniformity. But even these endearments, after a certain age, cease to send gentle ripples over faces which the struggle for existence has hardened, has rendered unalterably militant or ecstatic. One—owing to the prolonged strain of the obedience that subjects wife to husband—will seem not so much a woman's face as a soldier's; another, carved by the sacrifices which a mother has consented to make, day after day, for her children, will be the face of an apostle. A third is, after a stormy passage through the years, the face of an ancient mariner, upon a body of which its garments alone indicate the sex. Certainly the attentions that a woman pays us can still, so long as we are in love with her, endue with fresh charms the hours that we spend in her company. But she is not then for us a series of different women. Her gaiety remains external to an unchanging face. Whereas adolescence precedes this complete solidification, and hence we feel, in the company of young girls, the refreshing sense that is afforded us by the spectacle of forms undergoing an incessant process of change, a play of unstable forces which recalls that perpetual re-creation of the primordial elements of nature which we contemplate when we stand before the sea.

It was not merely a social engagement, a drive with Mme de Villeparisis, that I was prepared to sacrifice to the hide-and-seek or guessing games of my new friends. More than once, Robert de Saint-Loup had sent word that, since I had failed to come to see him at Doncières, he had applied for twenty-four hours' leave which he would spend at Balbec. Each time I wrote back to say that he was on no account to come, offering the excuse that I should be obliged to be away myself that very day, having some duty call to pay with my grandmother on family friends in the neighbourhood. No doubt he thought ill of me when he learned from his aunt in what the "duty call" consisted, and who

the persons were who combined to play the part of my grandmother. And yet, perhaps I was not wrong in sacrificing the
pleasures not only of society but of friendship to that of spending
the whole day in this green garden. People who have the capacity
to do so—it is true that such people are artists, and I had long been
convinced that I should never be that—also have a duty to live for
themselves. And friendship is a dispensation from this duty, an
abdication of self. Even conversation, which is friendship's mode
of expression, is a superficial digression which gives us nothing
worth acquiring. We may talk for a lifetime without doing more
than indefinitely repeat the vacuity of a minute, whereas the
march of thought in the solitary work of artistic creation proceeds
in depth, in the only direction that is not closed to us, along which
we are free to advance—though with more effort, it is true—
towards a goal of truth. And friendship is not merely devoid of
virtue, like conversation, it is fatal to us as well. For the sense of
boredom which those of us whose law of development is purely
internal cannot help but feel in a friend's company (when, that is to
say, we must remain on the surface of ourselves, instead of pursuing our voyage of discovery into the depths)—that first impression
of boredom our friendship impels us to correct when we are alone
again, to recall with emotion the words which our friend said to
us, to look upon them as a valuable addition to our substance,
when the fact is that we are not like buildings to which stones can
be added from without, but like trees which draw from their own
sap the next knot that will appear on their trunks, the spreading
roof of their foliage. I was lying to myself, I was interrupting the
process of growth in the direction in which I could indeed truly
develop and be happy, when I congratulated myself on being liked
and admired by so good, so intelligent, so rare a person as Saint-
Loup, when I focused my mind, not upon my own obscure
impressions which it should have been my duty to unravel, but
on the words of my friend, in which, by repeating them to
myself—by having them repeated to me by that other self who
dwells in us and on to whom we are always so ready to unload the
burden of taking thought—I strove to find a beauty very different
from that which I pursued in silence when I was really alone, but
one that would enhance the merit not only of Robert, but of
myself and of my life. In the life which such a friend provided
for me, I seemed to myself to be cosily preserved from solitude,
nobly desirous of sacrificing myself for him, in short incapable of

realising myself. With the girls, on the other hand, if the pleasure which I enjoyed was selfish, at least it was not based on the lie which seeks to make us believe that we are not irremediably alone and prevents us from admitting that, when we chat, it is no longer we who speak, that we are fashioning ourselves then in the likeness of other people and not of a self that differs from them. The words exchanged between the girls of the little band and myself were of little interest; they were, moreover, few, broken by long spells of silence on my part. This did not prevent me from taking as much pleasure in listening to them as in looking at them, in discovering in the voice of each one of them a brightly coloured picture. It was with delight that I listened to their pipings. Loving helps us to discern, to discriminate. The bird-lover in a wood at once distinguishes the twittering of the different species, which to ordinary people sound the same. The devotee of girls knows that human voices vary even more. Each one possesses more notes than the richest instrument of music. And the combinations in which it groups those notes are as inexhaustible as the infinite variety of personalities. When I talked with any one of my young friends I was conscious that the original, the unique portrait of her individuality had been skilfully traced, tyrannically imposed on my mind as much by the inflexions of her voice as by those of her face, and that they were two separate spectacles which expressed, each on its own plane, the same singular reality. No doubt the lines of the voice, like those of the face, were not yet finally fixed; the voice had still to break, as the face to change. Just as infants have a gland the secretion of which enables them to digest milk, a gland which is not found in adults, so there were in the twitterings of these girls notes which women's voices no longer contain. And on this more varied instrument they played with their lips, with all the application and the ardour of Bellini's little angel musicians, qualities which also are an exclusive appanage of youth. Later on these girls would lose that note of enthusiastic conviction which gave a charm to their simplest utterances, whether it were Albertine who, in a tone of authority, repeated puns to which the younger ones listened with admiration, until a paroxysm of giggles took hold of them with the irresistible violence of a sneezing fit, or Andrée who spoke of their school work, even more childish seemingly than the games they played, with an essentially puerile gravity; and their words varied in tone, like the strophes of anti- quity when poetry, still hardly differentiated from music, was declaimed on different notes. In spite of everything, the voices of these girls already gave a quite clear indication of the attitude that each of these young people had adopted towards life, an attitude so individual that it would be speaking in far too general terms to say of one: "She treats everything as a joke," of another: "She jumps from assertion to assertion," of a third: "She lives in a state of expectant hesitancy." The features of our face are hardly more than gestures which force of habit has made permanent. Nature, like the destruction of Pompeii, like the metamorphosis of a nymph, has arrested us in an accustomed movement. Similarly, our intonation embodies our philosophy of life, what a person invariably says to himself about things. No doubt these characteristics did not belong only to these girls. They were those of their parents. The individual is steeped in something more general than himself. By this reckoning, our parents furnish us not only with those habitual gestures which are the outlines of our face and voice, but also with certain mannerisms of speech, certain favourite expressions, which, almost as unconscious as our intonation, almost as profound, indicate likewise a definite point of view towards life. It is true that in the case of girls there are certain of these expressions which their parents do not hand on to them until they have reached a certain age, as a rule not before they are women. They are kept in reserve. Thus, for instance, if one were to speak of the pictures of one of Elstir's friends, Andrée, whose hair was still "down," could not yet personally make use of the expression which her mother and elder sister employed: "It appears the *man* is quite charming!" But that would come in due course, when she was allowed to go to the Palais-Royal. And not long after her first communion, Albertine had begun to say, like a friend of her aunt: "It sounds to me pretty awful." She had also inherited the habit of making one repeat whatever one said to her, so as to appear to be interested, and to be trying to form an opinion of her own. If you said that an artist's work was good, or his house nice, "Oh, his painting's good, is it?" "Oh, his house is nice, is it?" Finally, and more general still than the family heritage, was the rich layer imposed by the native province from which they derived their voices and of which their inflexions smacked. When Andrée sharply plucked a solemn note she could not prevent the Périgordian string of her vocal instrument from giving back a resonant sound quite in harmony, moreover, with the meridional purity of her features; while to the incessant japing of Rosemonde the substance of her northern face and voice responded willy-nilly in the accent of her province. Between the province and the temperament of the girl that dictated these inflexions, I perceived a charming dialogue. A dialogue, not in any sense a discord. No discord can possibly separate a young girl and her native place. She is herself, and she is still it. Moreover this reaction of local materials on the genius who utilises them and to whose work it imparts an added vigour, does not make the work any less individual, and whether it be that of an architect, a cabinet-maker or a composer, it reflects no less minutely the most subtle shades of the artist's personality, because he has been compelled to work in the mill-stone of Senlis or the red sandstone of Strasbourg, has respected the knots peculiar to the ash-tree, has borne in mind, when writing his score, the resources and limits of the sonority and range of the flute and the viola.

All this I realised, and yet we talked so little! Whereas with Mme de Villeparisis or Saint-Loup I should have displayed by my words a great deal more pleasure than I should actually have felt, for I was worn out on leaving them, when, on the other hand, I was lying on the grass among these girls, the plenitude of what I felt infinitely outweighed the paucity, the infrequency of our speech, and brimmed over from my immobility and silence in waves of happiness that rippled up to die at the feet of these young roses.

For a convalescent who rests all day long in a flower-garden or an orchard, a scent of flowers or fruit does not more completely pervade the thousand trifles that compose his idle hours than did for me that colour, that fragrance in search of which my eyes kept straying towards the girls, and the sweetness of which finally became incorporated in me. So it is that grapes sweeten in the sun. And by their slow continuity these simple little games had gradually wrought in me also, as in those who do nothing else all day but lie outstretched by the sea, breathing the salt air and sunning themselves, a relaxation, a blissful smile, a vague dazzle-ment that had spread from brain to eyes.

Now and then a pretty attention from one or another of them would stir in me vibrations which dissipated for a time my desire for the rest. Thus one day Albertine suddenly asked: "Who has a pencil?" Andrée provided one, Rosemonde the paper. Albertine warned them: "Now, young ladies, I forbid you to look at what I write." After carefully tracing each letter, supporting the paper on her knee, she passed it to me, saying: "Take care no one sees."

Whereupon I unfolded it and read her message, which was: "I like you."

"But we mustn't sit here scribbling nonsense," she cried, turning with an impulsive and serious air to Andrée and Rosemonde, "I ought to show you the letter I got from Gisèle this morning. What an idiot I am; I've had it in my pocket all this time—and to think how useful it can be to us!"

Gisèle had been moved to copy out for her friend, so that it might be passed on to the others, the essay which she had written in her examination. Albertine's fears as to the difficulty of the subjects set had been more than justified by the two from which Gisèle had had to choose. The first was: "Sophocles, from the Shades, writes to Racine to console him for the failure of *Athalie*"; the other: "Suppose that, after the first performance of *Esther*, Mme de Sévigné is writing to Mme de La Fayette to tell her how much she regretted her absence." Now Gisèle, in an excess of zeal which must have touched the examiners' hearts, had chosen the first and more difficult of these two subjects, and had handled it with such remarkable skill that she had been given fourteen marks and had been congratulated by the board. She would have received a "distinction" if she had not "dried up" in the Spanish paper. The essay of which Gisèle had sent a copy to Albertine was immediately read aloud to us by the latter, who, having presently to take the same examination, was anxious to have Andrée's opinion, since she was by far the cleverest of them all and might be able to give her some good tips.

"She did have a bit of luck," Albertine observed. "It's the very subject her French mistress made her swot up while she was here."

The letter from Sophocles to Racine, as drafted by Gisèle, ran as follows:

"My dear friend, you must pardon me the liberty of addressing you when I have not the honour of your personal acquaintance, but your latest tragedy, *Athalie*, shows, does it not, that you have made a thorough study of my own modest works. You have not only put poetry in the mouths of the protagonists, or principal persons of the drama, but you have written other, and, let me tell you without flattery, charming verses for the chorus, a feature which did not work too badly, from what one hears, in Greek tragedy, but is a veritable novelty in France. In addition, your talent, so fluent, so dainty, so seductive, so fine, so delicate, has here acquired an energy on which I congratulate you. Athalie, Joad—these are figures which your rival Corneille could have wrought no better. The characters are virile, the plot simple and strong. You have given us a tragedy in which love is not the keynote, and on this I must offer you my sincerest compliments. The most familiar precepts are not always the truest. I will give you an example:

> This passion treat, which makes the poet's art
> Fly, as on wings, straight to the listener's heart.

You have shown us that the religious sentiment in which your chorus is steeped is no less capable of moving us. The general public may have been baffled, but true connoisseurs must give you your due. I have felt myself impelled to offer you all my congratulations, to which I would add, my dear brother poet, the expression of my very highest esteem."

Albertine's eyes never ceased to sparkle while she was reading this to us. "Really, you'd think she must have cribbed it somewhere!" she exclaimed when she reached the end. "I'd never have believed Gisèle could cook up an essay like that! And the poetry she brings in! Where on earth can she have pinched that from?"

Albertine's admiration, with a change, it is true, of object, but with no loss—an increase, rather—of intensity, combined with the closest attention to what was being said, continued to make her eyes "start from her head" all the time that Andrée (consulted as being the biggest and cleverest) first of all spoke of Gisèle's essay with a certain irony, then, with a levity of tone which failed to conceal her underlying seriousness, proceeded to reconstruct the letter in her own way.

"It's not bad," she said to Albertine, "but if I were you and had the same subject set me, which is quite likely, as they set it very often, I shouldn't do it in that way. This is how I would tackle it. In the first place, if I had been Gisèle, I shouldn't have got carried away and I'd have begun by making a rough sketch of what I was going to write on a separate piece of paper. First and foremost, the formulation of the question and the exposition of the subject; then the general ideas to be worked into the development; finally, appreciation, style, conclusion. In that way, with a summary to refer to, you know where you are. But at the very start, with the exposition of the subject, or, if you like, Titine, since it's a letter, with the preamble, Gisèle has made a bloomer. Writing to a person of the seventeenth century, Sophocles ought never to have said 'My dear friend.'"

"Why, of course, she ought to have said 'My dear Racine,'" came impetuously from Albertine. "That would have been much better."

"No," replied Andrée, with a trace of mockery in her tone, "She ought to have put 'Sir.' In the same way, to end up, she ought to have thought of something like, 'Allow me, Sir,' (at the very most, 'Dear Sir') 'to inform you of the high esteem with which I have the honour to be your servant.' Then again, Gisèle says that the chorus in *Athalie* is a novelty. She is forgetting *Esther*, and two tragedies that are not much read now but happen to have been analysed this year by the teacher himself, so that you need only mention them, since they're his hobby-horse, and you're bound to pass. I mean *Les Juives* by Robert Garnier, and Montchrestien's *Aman*."

Andrée quoted these titles without managing quite to conceal a secret sense of benevolent superiority, which found expression in a rather charming smile. Albertine could contain herself no longer.

"Andrée, you really are staggering," she cried. "You must write down those names for me. Just fancy, what luck it would be if I got on to that, even in the oral, I should quote them at once and make a colossal impression."

But in the days that followed, every time that Albertine asked Andrée to tell her again the names of those two plays so that she might write them down, her erudite friend seemed to have forgotten them, and never recalled them for her.

"And another thing," Andrée went on with the faintest note of scorn for companions more childish than herself, though relishing their admiration and attaching to the manner in which she herself would have composed the essay a greater importance than she wished to reveal, "Sophocles in the Shades must be well-informed about all that goes on. He must therefore know that it was not before the general public but before the Sun King and a few privileged courtiers that *Athalie* was first played. What Gisèle says in this connexion of the esteem of the connoisseurs is not at all bad, but she might have gone a little further. Sophocles, now that he is immortal, may quite well have the gift of prophecy and announce that, according to Voltaire, *Athalie* will be the supreme achievement not only of Racine but of the human mind."

Albertine was drinking in every word. Her eyes blazed. And it was with the utmost indignation that she rejected Rosemonde's suggestion that they should have a game.

"Finally," Andrée concluded in the same detached, airy tone, a trifle mocking and at the same time fairly warmly convinced, "if Gisèle had first calmly noted down the general ideas that she was going to develop, it might perhaps have occurred to her to do what I myself should have done, point out what a difference there is between the religious inspiration of Racine's choruses and those of Sophocles. I should have made Sophocles remark that if Racine's choruses are impregnated with religious feeling like those of the Greek tragedians, the gods are not the same. The god of Joad has nothing in common with the god of Sophocles. And that brings us quite naturally, when we have finished developing the subject, to our conclusion: What does it matter if beliefs are different? Sophocles would hesitate to insist upon this point. He would be afraid of wounding Racine's convictions, and so, slipping in a few appropriate words on his masters at Port-Royal, he prefers to congratulate his disciple on the loftiness of his poetic genius."

Admiration and attention had made Albertine so hot that she was sweating profusely. Andrée preserved the unruffled calm of a female dandy. "It would not be a bad thing, either, to quote some of the opinions of famous critics," she added, before they began their game.

"Yes," put in Albertine, "so I've been told. The best ones to quote, on the whole, are Sainte-Beuve and Merlet, aren't they?"

"Well, you're not absolutely wrong," Andrée told her. "Merlet and Sainte-Beuve would do no harm. But above all you ought to mention Deltour and Gascq-Desfossés."

Meanwhile I had been thinking of the little page torn from a scribbling block which Albertine had handed me. "I like you," she had written. And an hour later, as I scrambled down the paths which led back, a little too vertically for my liking, to Balbec, I said to myself that it was with her that I would have my romance.

The state of being characterised by the presence of all the signs by which we are accustomed to recognise that we are in love, such as the orders which I left in the hotel not to wake me whoever might ask to see me, unless it were one or other of the girls, the throbbing of my heart while I waited for them (whichever of them it might be that I was expecting), and, on those mornings, my fury if I had not succeeded in finding a barber to shave me, and would make an unsightly appearance before Albertine, Rosemonde or Andrée, no doubt this state, recurring for each of them in turn, was as different from what we call love as is from human life the life of the zoophytes, in which existence, individuality if we may so term it, is divided up among several organisms. But natural history teaches us that such an organisation of animal life is indeed to be observed, and that our own life, provided we have outgrown the first phase, is no less positive as to the reality of states hitherto unsuspected by us through which we have to pass, even though we abandon them later. Such was for me this state of love divided among several girls at once. Divided, or rather undivided, for more often than not what was so delicious to me, different from the rest of the world, what was beginning to become so precious to me that the hope of encountering it again the next day was the greatest joy of my life, was rather the whole of the group of girls, taken as they were all together on those afternoons on the cliffs, during those wind-swept hours, upon the strip of grass on which were laid those forms, so exciting to my imagination, of Albertine, of Rosemonde, of Andrée; and that without my being able to say which of them it was that made those scenes so precious to me, which of them I most wanted to love. At the start of a new love as at its ending, we are not exclusively attached to the object of that love, but rather the desire to love from which it will presently arise (and, later on, the memory it leaves behind) wanders voluptuously through a zone of interchangeable charms— simply natural charms, it may be, gratification of appetite, enjoyment of one's surroundings—which are harmonious enough for it not to feel at a loss in the presence of any one of them. Besides, as my perception of them was not yet dulled by familiarity, I still had the faculty of seeing them, that is to say of feeling a profound astonishment every time that I found myself in their presence.

No doubt this astonishment is to some extent due to the fact that the other person on such occasions presents some new facet; but so great is the multiformity of each individual, so abundant the wealth of lines of face and body, so few of which leave any trace, once we are no longer in the presence of the other person, on the arbitrary simplicity of our recollection, since the memory has selected some distinctive feature that had struck us, has isolated it, exaggerated it, making of a woman who has appeared to us tall a sketch in which her figure is elongated out of all proportion, or of a woman who has seemed to be pink-cheeked and golden-haired a pure "Harmony in pink and gold," that the moment this woman is once again standing before us, all the other forgotten qualities which balance that one remembered feature at once assail us, in their confused complexity, diminishing her height, paling her cheeks, and substituting for what we came exclusively to seek other features which we remember having noticed the first time and fail to understand why we so little expected to find them again. We remembered, we anticipated a peacock, and we find a peony. And this inevitable astonishment is not the only one; for side by side with it comes another, born of the difference, not now between the stylisations of memory and the reality, but between the person whom we saw last time and the one who appears to us today from another angle and shows us a new aspect. The human face is indeed, like the face of the God of some oriental theogony, a whole cluster of faces juxtaposed on different planes so that one does not see them all at once.

But to a great extent our astonishment springs from the fact that the person presents to us also a face that is the same as before. It would require so immense an effort to reconstruct everything that has been imparted to us by things other than ourselves—were it only the taste of a fruit—that no sooner is the impression received than we begin imperceptibly to descend the slope of memory and, without realising it, in a very short time we have come a long way from what we actually felt. So that every fresh glimpse is a sort of rectification, which brings us back to what we in fact saw. Already we no longer had any recollection of it, to such an extent does what we call remembering a person consist really in forgetting him. But as long as we can still see, as soon as the forgotten feature appears we recognise it, we are obliged to correct the straying line, and thus the perpetual and fruitful surprise which made so salutary and invigorating for me these daily outings with the charming damsels of the sea shore consisted fully as much in recollection as in discovery. When there is added to this the agitation aroused by what these girls were to me, which was never quite what I had supposed, and meant that my expectancy of our next meeting resembled not so much my expectancy the time before as the still vibrant memory of our last encounter, it will be realised that each of our excursions brought about a violent change in the course of my thoughts and not at all in the direction which, in the solitude of my own room, I had traced for them at my leisure. That plotted course was forgotten, had ceased to exist, when I returned home buzzing like a bee-hive with remarks which had disturbed me and were still echoing in my brain. Every person is destroyed when we cease to see him; after which his next appearance is a new creation, different from that which immediately preceded it, if not from them all. For the minimum variation that is to be found in these creations is twofold. Remembering a strong and searching glance, a bold manner, it is inevitably, next time, by an almost languid profile, a sort of dreamy gentleness, overlooked by us in our previous impression, that at the next encounter we shall be astonished, that is to say almost uniquely struck. In confronting our memory with the new reality it is this that will mark the extent of our disappointment or surprise, will appear to us like a revised version of the reality by notifying us that we had not remembered correctly. In its turn, the facial aspect neglected the time before, and for that very reason the most striking this time, the most real, the most corrective, will become a matter for day-dreams and memories. It is a languorous and rounded profile, a gentle, dreamy expression which we shall now desire to see again. And then once more, next time, such resolution, such strength of character as there may be in the piercing eyes, the pointed nose, the tight lips, will come to correct the discrepancy between our desire and the object to which it has supposed itself to correspond. Of course, this fidelity to the first and purely physical impressions experienced anew at each encounter with my young friends did not only concern their facial appearance, since the reader has seen that I was sensitive also to their voices, more disturbing still, perhaps (for not only does a voice offer the same strange and sensuous surfaces as a face, it issues from that unknown, inaccessible region the mere thought of which sets the mind swimming with unattainable kisses), those voices, like the unique sound of a little instrument into which each of them put all of herself and which belonged to her alone. Traced by a casual inflexion, a sudden deep chord in one of these voices would surprise me when I recognised it after having forgotten it. So much so that the corrections which after every fresh meeting I was obliged to make so as to ensure absolute accuracy were as much those of a tuner or singing-master as of a draughtsman.

As for the harmonious cohesion into which, by the resistance that each brought to bear against the expansion of the others, the several waves of feeling induced in me by these girls had become neutralised, it was broken in Albertine's favour one afternoon when we were playing the game of "ferret."[6] It was in a little wood on the cliff. Stationed between two girls, strangers to the little band, whom the band had brought in its train because we wanted that day to have a bigger party than usual, I gazed enviously at Albertine's neighbour, a young man, saying to myself that if I had been in his place I could have been touching my beloved's hands during those unhoped-for moments which perhaps would never recur and which might have taken me a long way. Already, in itself, and even without the consequences which it would probably have involved, the contact of Albertine's hands would have been delicious to me. Not that I had never seen prettier hands than hers. Even in the group of her friends, those of Andrée, slender and far more delicate, had as it were a private life of their own, obedient to the commands of their mistress, but independent, and would often stretch out before her like thoroughbred greyhounds, with lazy pauses, languid reveries, sudden flexings of a finger-joint, seeing which Elstir had made a number of studies of these hands; and in one of them, in which Andrée was to be seen warming them at the fire, they had, with the light behind them, the golden diaphanousness of two autumn leaves. But, plumper than these, Albertine's hands would yield for a moment, then resist the pressure of the hand that clasped them, giving a sensation that was quite peculiar to themselves. The act of pressing Albertine's hand had a sensual sweetness which was in keeping somehow with the pink, almost mauve colouring of her skin. This pressure seemed to allow you to penetrate into the girl's being, to plumb the depths of her senses, like the ringing sound of her laughter, indecent in the way that the cooing of doves or certain animal cries can be. She was one of those women with whom shaking hands affords so much pleasure that one feels grateful to civilisation for having made of the hand-clasp a lawful act between boys and girls when they meet. If the arbitrary code of good manners had replaced the hand-shake by some other gesture, I should have gazed, day after day, at the untouchable hands of Albertine with a curiosity to know the feel of them as ardent as was my curiosity to learn the savour of her cheeks. But in the pleasure of holding her hand unrestrictedly in mine, had I been next to her at "ferret," I did not envisage that pleasure alone; what avowals, what declarations silenced hitherto by my bashfulness, I could have conveyed by certain pressures of hand on hand; for her part, how easy it would have been, in responding by other pressures, to show me that she accepted; what complicity, what a vista of sensual delight stood open! My love would be able to make more progress in a few minutes spent thus by her side than it had yet made in all the time that I had known her. Feeling that they would last but a short time, were rapidly nearing their end, since presumably we were not going on much longer with this game, and that once it was over it would be too late, I could not stay in my place for another moment. I let myself deliberately be caught with the ring, and, once in the middle, when the ring passed I pretended not to see it but followed its course with my eyes, waiting for the moment when it should come into the hands of the young man next to Albertine, who herself, convulsed with laughter, and in the excitement and pleasure of the game, was flushed pink. "Why, we really are in the Fairy Wood," said Andrée to me, pointing to the trees all round us, with a smile in her eyes which was meant only for me and seemed to pass over the heads of the other players, as though we two alone were intelligent and detached enough to make, in connexion with the game we were playing, a remark of a poetic nature. She even carried the delicacy of her fancy so far as to sing half-unconsciously: "The ferret of the Wood has passed this way, sweet ladies; he has passed by this way, the ferret of Fairy Wood!" like those people who cannot visit Trianon without getting up a party in Louis XVI costume, or think it amusing to have a song sung to its original setting. I should no doubt have been saddened not to see any charm in this realisation, had I had time to think about it. But my thoughts were all elsewhere. The players began to show surprise at my stupidity in never getting the ring. I was looking at Albertine, so pretty, so indifferent, so gay, who, though she little knew it, would be my neighbour when at last I should catch the ring in the right hands, thanks to a stratagem which she did not suspect, and would certainly have resented if she had. In the heat of the game her long hair had become loosened, and fell in curling locks over her cheeks on which it served to intensify, by its dry brownness, the carnation pink. "You have the tresses of Laura Dianti, of Eleanor of Guyenne, and of her descendant so beloved of Chateaubriand. You ought always to wear your hair half down like that," I murmured in her ear as an excuse for drawing close to her. Suddenly the ring passed to her neighbour. I sprang upon him at once, forced open his hands and seized it; he was obliged now to take my place inside the circle, while I took his beside Albertine. A few minutes earlier I had been envying this young man, when I saw that his hands as they slipped over the string were constantly brushing against hers. Now that my turn had come, too shy to seek, too agitated to savour this contact, I no longer felt anything but the rapid and painful beating of my heart. At one moment Albertine leaned her round pink face towards me with an air of complicity, pretending thus to have the ring in order to deceive the ferret and prevent him from looking in the direction in which it was being passed. I realised at once that it was to this ruse that the insinuations of Albertine's look applied, but I was excited to see thus kindle in her eyes the image—simulated purely for the purposes of the game—of a secret understanding between her and myself which did not exist but which from that moment seemed to me to be possible and would have been divinely sweet. While I was still enraptured by this thought, I felt a slight pressure of Albertine's hand against mine, and her caressing finger slip under my finger along the cord, and I saw her, at the same moment, give me a wink which she tried to make imperceptible to the others. At once, a multitude of hopes, invisible hitherto, crystallised within me. "She's taking advantage of the game to make it clear to me that she likes me," I thought to myself in a paroxysm of joy from which I instantly relapsed on hearing Albertine mutter furiously: "Why can't you take it? I've been shoving it at you for the last hour." Stunned with grief, I let go the cord, the ferret saw the ring and swooped down on it, and I had to go back into the middle, where I stood helpless, in despair, looking at the unbridled rout which continued to circle round me, stung by the jeers of all the players, obliged, in reply, to laugh when I had so little mind for laughter, while Albertine kept on repeating: "People shouldn't play if they won't pay attention and spoil the game for the others. We shan't ask him again when we're going to play, Andrée, or else I shan't come." Andrée, with a mind above the game, still chanting her "Fairy Wood" which, in a spirit of imitation, Rosemonde had taken up too, without conviction, sought to take my mind off Albertine's reproaches by saying to me: "We're quite close to those old Creuniers you wanted so much to see. Look, I'll take you there by a pretty little path, while these idiots play at eight-year-olds." Since Andrée was extremely nice to me, as we went along I said to her everything about Albertine that seemed calculated to endear me to the latter.

Andrée replied that she too was very fond of Albertine, and thought her charming; nevertheless my compliments about her friend did not seem altogether to please her. Suddenly, in the little sunken path, I stopped short, touched to the heart by an exquisite memory of my childhood. I had just recognised, from the fretted and glossy leaves which it thrust out towards me, a hawthorn-bush, flowerless, alas, now that spring was over. Around me floated an atmosphere of far-off Months of Mary, of Sunday afternoons, of beliefs, of errors long since forgotten. I wanted to seize hold of it. I stood still for a moment, and Andrée, with a charming divination of what was in my mind, left me to converse with the leaves of the bush. I asked them for news of the flowers, those hawthorn flowers that were like merry little girls, head-strong, provocative, pious. "The young ladies have been gone from here for a long time now," the leaves told me. And perhaps they thought that, for the great friend of those young ladies that I pretended to be, I seemed to have singularly little knowledge of their habits. A great friend, but one who had never been to see them again for all these years, despite his promises. And yet, as Gilberte had been my first love among girls, so these had been my first love among flowers. "Yes, I know, they leave about the middle of June," I answered, "but I'm delighted to see the place where they lived when they were here. They came to see me at Combray, in my room; my mother brought them when I was ill in bed. And we used to meet again on Saturday evenings, at the Month of Mary devotions. Can they go to them here?" "Oh, of course! Why, they make a special point of having our young ladies at Saint-Denis du Désert, the church near here." "So if I want to see them now?" "Oh, not before May next year." "But can I be sure that they will be here?" "They come regularly every year." "Only I don't know whether I'll be able to find the place." "Oh, dear, yes! They are so gay, the young ladies, they stop laughing only to sing hymns together, so that you can't possibly miss them, you can recognise their scent from the other end of the path."

I caught up with Andrée, and began again to sing Albertine's praises. It was inconceivable to me that she would not repeat what I said in view of the emphasis I put into it. And yet I never heard that Albertine had been told. Andrée had, nevertheless, a far greater understanding of the things of the heart, a refinement of sweetness; finding the look, the word, the action that could most ingeniously give pleasure, keeping to herself a remark that might possibly cause pain, making a sacrifice (and making it as though it were no sacrifice at all) of an afternoon's play, or it might be an "at home" or a garden-party, in order to stay with a friend who was feeling sad, and thus show him or her that she preferred the simple company of a friend to frivolous pleasures: such were her habitual kindnesses. But when one knew her a little better one would have said it was with her as with those heroic poltroons who wish not to be afraid and whose bravery is especially meritorious; one would have said that deep down in her nature there was none of that kindness which she constantly displayed out of moral distinction, or sensibility, or a noble desire to show herself a true friend. When I listened to all the charming things she said to me about a possible attachment between Albertine and myself it seemed as though she were bound to do everything in her power to bring it to pass. Whereas, by chance perhaps, not even of the slightest opportunity which she had at her command and which might have proved effective in uniting me to Albertine did she ever make use, and I would not swear that my effort to make myself loved by Albertine did not—if not provoke in her friend secret stratagems calculated to thwart it—at any rate arouse in her an anger which however she took good care to hide and against which, out of delicacy of feeling, she may herself have fought. Of the countless refinements of affectionate kindness which Andrée showed, Albertine would have been incapable, and yet I was not certain of the underlying goodness of the former as I was to be later of the latter's. Showing herself always tenderly indulgent towards the exuberant frivolity of Albertine, Andrée greeted her with words and smiles that were those of a friend; better still, she acted towards her as a friend. I have seen her, day after day, in order to give this penniless friend the benefit of her own wealth, in order to make her happy, without any possibility of advantage to herself, take more pains than a courtier seeking to win his sovereign's favour. She was charmingly gentle and sympathetic, and spoke in sweet and sorrowful terms, when one expressed pity for Albertine's poverty, and took infinitely more trouble on her behalf than she would have taken for a rich friend. But if anyone were to hint that Albertine was perhaps not quite so poor as people made out, a just discernible cloud would overshadow Andrée's eyes and brow; she seemed out of temper. And if one went on to say that after all Albertine might perhaps be less difficult to marry off than people supposed, she would vehemently contradict one, repeating almost angrily: "Oh dear, no, she'll be quite unmarriageable! I'm certain of it, and I feel so sorry for her." As far as I myself was concerned, Andrée was the only one of the girls who would never have repeated to me anything at all disagreeable that might have been said about me by a third person; more than that, if it was I who told her what had been said she would make a pretence of not believing it, or would furnish some explanation which made the remark inoffensive. It is the aggregate of these qualities that goes by the name of tact. It is the attribute of those people who, if we fight a duel, congratulate us and add that there was no necessity to do so, in order to enhance still further in our own eyes the courage of which we have given proof without having been forced. They are the opposite of the people who in similar circumstances say: "It must have been a horrid nuisance for you to have to fight a duel, but on the other hand you couldn't possibly swallow an insult like that—there was nothing else to be done." But as there are pros and cons in everything, if the pleasure or at least the indifference shown by our friends in repeating something offensive that they have heard said about us proves that they do not exactly put themselves inside our skin at the moment of speaking, but thrust in the pin-point, turn the knife-blade as though it were gold-beater's skin and not human, the art of always keeping hidden from us what might be disagreeable to us in what they have heard said about our actions or in the opinion which those actions have led the speakers themselves to form, proves that there is in the other category of friends, in the friends who are so full of tact, a strong vein of dissimulation. It does no harm if indeed they are incapable of thinking ill of us, and if the ill that is said by other people only makes them suffer as it would make us. I supposed this to be the case with Andrée, without, however, being absolutely sure.

We had left the little wood and had followed a network of unfrequented paths through which Andrée managed to find her way with great skill. "Look," she said to me suddenly, "there are your famous Creuniers, and what's more you're in luck, it's just the time of day and the light is the same as when Elstir painted them." But I was still too wretched at having fallen, during the game of "ferret," from such a pinnacle of hopes. And so it was not with the pleasure which otherwise I should doubtless have felt that I suddenly discerned at my feet, crouching among the rocks for protection against the heat, the marine goddesses for whom Elstir had lain in wait and whom he had surprised there, beneath a dark glaze as lovely as Leonardo would have painted, the marvellous Shadows, sheltering furtively, nimble and silent, ready at the first glimmer of light to slip behind the stone, to hide in a cranny, and prompt, once the menacing ray had passed, to return to the rock or the sea-weed over whose torpid slumbers they seemed to be keeping vigil, beneath the sun that crumbled the cliffs and the etiolated ocean, motionless lightfoot guardians darkening the water's surface with their viscous bodies and the attentive gaze of their deep blue eyes.

We went back to the wood to pick up the other girls and go home together. I knew now that I was in love with Albertine; but, alas! I did not care to let her know it. This was because, since the days of the games with Gilberte in the Champs-Elysées, my conception of love had become different, even if the persons to whom my love was successively assigned remained almost identical. For one thing, the avowal, the declaration of my passion to her whom I loved no longer seemed to be one of the vital and necessary stages of love, nor love itself an external reality, but simply a subjective pleasure. And I felt that Albertine would do what was necessary to sustain that pleasure all the more readily if she did not know that I was experiencing it.

As we walked home, the image of Albertine, bathed in the light that streamed from the other girls, was not the only one that existed for me. But as the moon, which is no more than a tiny white cloud of a more definite and fixed shape than other clouds during the day, assumes its full power as soon as daylight fades, so when I was once more in the hotel it was Albertine's sole image that rose from my heart and began to shine. My room seemed to me to have become suddenly a new place. Of course, for a long time past, it had not been the hostile room of my first night in it. All our lives, we go on patiently modifying the surroundings in which we live; and gradually, as habit dispenses us from feeling them, we suppress the noxious elements of colour, shape and smell which objectified our uneasiness. Nor was it any longer the room, still with sufficient power over my sensibility, not certainly to make me suffer, but to give me joy, the well of summer days, like a marble basin in which, half-way up its polished sides, they mirrored an azure surface steeped in light over which glided for an instant, impalpable and white as a wave of heat, the fleeting reflexion of a cloud; nor the purely aesthetic room of the pictorial evening hours; it was the room in which I had been now for so many days that I no longer saw it. And now I was beginning again to open my eyes to it, but this time from the selfish angle which is that of love. I liked to feel that the fine slanting mirror, the handsome glass-fronted book-cases, would give Albertine, if she came to see me, a good impression of me. Instead of a place of transit in which I would stay for a few minutes before escaping to the beach or to Rivebelle, my room became real and dear to me again, fashioned itself anew, for I looked at and appreciated each article of its furniture with the eyes of Albertine.

A few days after the game of "ferret," when, having allowed ourselves to wander rather too far afield, we had been fortunate in finding at Maineville a couple of little "governess-carts" with two seats in each which would enable us to be back in time for dinner, the intensity, already considerable, of my love for Albertine had the effect of making me suggest successively that Andrée and Rosemonde should come with me, and never once Albertine, and then, while still inviting Andrée or Rosemonde for preference, of bringing everyone round, in virtue of secondary considerations connected with time, route, coats and so forth, to decide, as though against my wishes, that the most practical policy after all was that I should take Albertine, to whose company I pretended to resign myself willy-nilly. Unfortunately, since love tends to the complete assimilation of a person, and none is comestible by way of conversation alone, for all that Albertine was as nice as possible on our way home, when I had deposited her at her own door she left me happy but more famished for her even than I had been at the start, and reckoning the moments that we had just spent together as only a prelude, of little importance in itself, to those that were still to come. Nevertheless it had that initial charm which is not to be found again. I had not yet asked anything of Albertine. She could imagine what I wanted, but, not being certain of it, surmise that I was aiming only at relations with no precise objective, in which my beloved would find that delicious vagueness, rich in expected surprises, which is romance.

In the week that followed I scarcely attempted to see Albertine. I made a show of preferring Andrée. Love is born; we wish to remain, for the one we love, the unknown person whom she may love in turn, but we need her, we need to make contact not so much with her body as with her attention, her heart. We slip into a letter some unkind remark which will force the indifferent one to ask for some little kindness in compensation, and love, following

an infallible technique, tightens up with an alternating movement
the cog-wheels in which we can no longer not love or be loved.
I gave to Andrée the hours spent by the others at a party which
I knew that she would sacrifice for my sake with pleasure, and
would have sacrificed even with reluctance, from moral nicety, in
order not to give either the others or herself the idea that she
attached any importance to a relatively frivolous amusement.
I arranged in this way to have her entirely to myself every evening,
not with the intention of making Albertine jealous, but of enhancing my prestige in her eyes, or at any rate not imperilling it by
letting Albertine know that it was herself and not Andrée that
I loved. Nor did I confide this to Andrée either, lest she should
repeat it to her friend. When I spoke of Albertine to Andrée
I affected a coldness by which she was perhaps less deceived than
I, from her apparent credulity. She made a show of believing in my
indifference to Albertine, and of desiring the closest possible union
between Albertine and myself. It is probable that, on the contrary,
she neither believed in the one nor wished for the other. While I
was saying to her that I did not care very greatly for her friend, I
was thinking of one thing only, how to become acquainted with
Mme Bontemps, who was staying for a few days near Balbec, and
whom Albertine was shortly to visit for a few days. Naturally I did
not disclose this desire to Andrée, and when I spoke to her of
Albertine's family, it was in the most careless manner possible.
Andrée's direct answers did not appear to throw any doubt on my
sincerity. Why then did she blurt out suddenly one day: "Oh, by
the way, I happen to have seen Albertine's aunt"? It is true that she
had not said in so many words: "I could see through your casual
remarks all right that the one thing you were really thinking of was
how you could get to know Albertine's aunt." But it was clearly to
the presence in Andrée's mind of some such idea which she felt it
more becoming to keep from me that the phrase "happen to"
seemed to point. It was of a kind with certain glances, certain
gestures which, although they have no logical rational form
directly devised for the listener's intelligence, reach him nevertheless in their true meaning, just as human speech, converted into
electricity in the telephone, is turned into speech again when it
strikes the ear. In order to remove from Andrée's mind the idea
that I was interested in Mme Bontemps, I spoke of her thenceforth
not only absent-mindedly but with downright malice, saying that
I had once met that idiot of a woman, and trusted I should never

have that experience again. Whereas I was seeking by every means in my power to meet her.

I tried to induce Elstir (but without mentioning to anyone else that I had asked him) to speak to her about me and to bring us together. He promised to introduce me to her, though he seemed greatly surprised at my wishing it, for he regarded her as a contemptible woman, a born intriguer, as uninteresting as she was self-interested. Reflecting that if I did see Mme Bontemps, Andrée would be sure to hear of it sooner or later, I thought it best to warn her in advance. "The things one tries hardest to avoid are those one finds one cannot escape," I told her. "Nothing in the world could bore me so much as meeting Mme Bontemps again, and yet I can't get out of it. Elstir has arranged to invite us together." "I've never doubted it for a single instant," exclaimed Andrée in a bitter tone, while her eyes, enlarged and altered by her annoyance, focused themselves upon some invisible object. These words of Andrée's were not the most reasoned statement of a thought which might be expressed thus: "I know that you're in love with Albertine, and that you're moving heaven and earth to get to know her family." But they were the shapeless fragments, capable of reconstitution, of that thought which I had caused to explode, by striking it, against Andrée's will. Like her "happen to," these words had no meaning save at one remove, that is to say they were words of the sort which (rather than direct assertions) inspire in us respect or distrust for another person, and lead to a rupture.

If Andrée had not believed me when I told her that Albertine's family left me indifferent, it was because she thought that I was in love with Albertine. And probably she was none too happy in the thought.

She was generally present as a third party at my meetings with her friend. There were however days when I was to see Albertine by herself, days to which I looked forward with feverish impatience, which passed without bringing me any decisive result, without any of them having been that cardinal day whose role I immediately entrusted to the following day, which would prove no more apt to play it; thus there rose and toppled one after another, like waves, those peaks at once replaced by others.

About a month after the day on which we had played "ferret" together, I learned that Albertine was going away next morning to spend a couple of days with Mme Bontemps, and, since she would have to take an early train, was coming to spend the night at the Grand Hotel, from which, by taking the omnibus, she would be able, without disturbing the friends with whom she was staying, to catch the first train in the morning. I mentioned this to Andrée. "I don't believe a word of it," she replied with a look of annoyance. "Anyhow it won't help you at all, for I'm quite sure Albertine won't want to see you if she goes to the hotel by herself. It would be against 'protocol,'" she added, employing an expression which had recently come into favour with her, in the sense of "what is done." "I tell you this because I understand Albertine. What difference do you suppose it makes to me whether you see her or not? Not the slightest, I can assure you!"

We were joined by Octave who had no hesitation in telling Andrée the number of strokes he had gone round in, the day before, at golf, then by Albertine, who came along swinging her diabolo like a nun her rosary. Thanks to this pastime she could remain alone for hours on end without getting bored. As soon as she joined us I became conscious of the impish tip of her nose, which I had omitted from my mental picture of her during the last few days; beneath her dark hair the vertical line of her forehead controverted—and not for the first time—the blurred image that I had preserved of her, while its whiteness made a vivid splash in my field of vision; emerging from the dust of memory, Albertine was built up afresh before my eyes.

Golf gives one a taste for solitary pleasures. The pleasure to be derived from diabolo is undoubtedly one of these. And yet, after she had joined us, Albertine continued to play with it, just as a lady on whom friends have come to call does not on their account stop working at her crochet. "I gather that Mme de Villeparisis," she remarked to Octave, "has been complaining to your father." (I could hear, underlying the "I gather," one of those notes that were peculiar to Albertine; every time I realised that I had forgotten them, I would remember having already caught a glimpse behind them of Albertine's determined and Gallic mien. I could have been blind and yet have detected certain of her qualities, alert and slightly provincial, in those notes just as plainly as in the tip of her nose. They were equivalent and might have been substituted for one another, and her voice was like what we are promised in the photo-telephone of the future: the visual image was clearly outlined in the sound.) "She hasn't written only to your father, either, she wrote to the Mayor of Balbec at the same time, to say that we must stop playing diabolo on the front as somebody hit her in the face with a ball."

"Yes, I was hearing about that," said Octave. "It's ridiculous. There's little enough to do here as it is."

Andrée did not join in the conversation; she was not acquainted, any more than was Albertine or Octave, with Mme de Villeparisis. She did, however, remark: "I can't think why this lady should make such a song about it. Old Mme de Cambremer got hit in the face, and she never complained."

"I'll explain the difference," replied Octave gravely, striking a match as he spoke. "It's my belief that Mme de Cambremer is a society lady, and Mme de Villeparisis is just an upstart. Are you playing golf this afternoon?" And he left us, followed by Andrée. I was alone now with Albertine. "You see," she began, "I'm wearing my hair now the way you like—look at my ringlet. They all laugh at it and nobody knows who I'm doing it for. My aunt will laugh at me too. But I shan't tell her why, either." I had a sidelong view of Albertine's cheeks, which often appeared pale, but, seen thus, were flushed with unclouded blood which lighted them up, gave them that brightness of certain winter mornings when the stones catching the sun seem blocks of pink granite and radiate joy. The joy I felt at this moment at the sight of Albertine's cheeks was as keen, but led to another desire which was not the desire for a walk but for a kiss. I asked her if the report of her plans which I had heard was correct. "Yes," she told me, "I shall be sleeping at your hotel tonight, and in fact as I've got a bit of a cold I shall be going to bed before dinner. You can come and sit by my bed and watch me eat, if you like, and afterwards we'll play at anything that you choose. I should have liked you to come to the station tomorrow morning, but I'm afraid it might look rather odd, I don't say to Andrée who is a sensible person, but to the others who will be there; if my aunt got to know, I should never hear the last of it. But we can spend the evening together, at any rate. My aunt will know nothing about that. I must go and say good-bye to Andrée. Till we meet again then. Come early, so that we can have a nice long time together," she added, smiling.

At these words I was swept back past the days when I loved Gilberte to those when love seemed to me not simply an external entity but one that could be realised. Whereas the Gilberte whom I used to see in the Champs-Elysées was a different Gilberte from the one I found within me when I was alone again, suddenly in the

real Albertine, the one I saw every day, whom I supposed to be
stuffed with middle-class prejudices and entirely frank with her
aunt, the imaginary Albertine had just been embodied, she whom,
when I did not yet know her, I had suspected of casting furtive
glances at me on the front, she who had worn an air of being
reluctant to go home when she saw me making off in the other
direction.

I went into dinner with my grandmother. I felt within me a
secret which she could never guess. Similarly with Albertine;
tomorrow her friends would be with her, not knowing what
new experience she and I had in common; and when she kissed
her niece on the forehead Mme Bontemps would never imagine
that I stood between them, in the shape of that hair arrangement
which had for its object, concealed from all the world, to give
pleasure to me, to me who had until then so greatly envied Mme
Bontemps because, being related to the same people as her niece,
she had the same occasions to put on mourning, the same family
visits to pay; and now I found myself being more to Albertine than
was the aunt herself. When she was with her aunt, it was of me that
she would be thinking. What was going to happen that evening,
I scarcely knew. In any event, the Grand Hotel and the evening no
longer seemed empty to me; they contained my happiness. I rang
for the lift-boy to take me up to the room which Albertine had
engaged, a room that looked over the valley. The slightest movements, such as that of sitting down on the bench in the lift, were
sweet to me, because they were in direct relation to my heart; I saw
in the ropes that drew the cage upwards, in the few stairs that I had
still to climb, only the machinery, the materialised stages of my joy.
I now had only two or three steps to take along the corridor before
coming to that room in which was enshrined the precious substance of that rosy form—that room which, even if there were to
be done in it delicious things, would keep that air of changeless-
ness, of being, to a chance visitor who knew nothing of its history,
just like any other room, which makes of inanimate things the
obstinately mute witnesses, the scrupulous confidants, the inviolable depositaries of our pleasure. Those few steps from the landing
to Albertine's door, those few steps which no one could stop, I
took with rapture but with prudence, as though plunged in a new
and strange element, as if in going forward I had been gently
displacing a liquid stream of happiness, and at the same time
with a strange feeling of omnipotence, and of entering at last

into an inheritance which had belonged to me from time immemorial. Then suddenly I reflected that I was wrong to be in any doubt; she had told me to come when she was in bed. It was as clear as daylight; I pranced for joy, I nearly knocked over Françoise who was standing in my way, and I ran, with sparkling eyes, towards my beloved's room.

I found Albertine in bed. Leaving her throat bare, her white nightdress altered the proportions of her face, which, flushed by being in bed or by her cold or by dinner, seemed pinker; I thought of the colours I had had beside me a few hours earlier on the front, the savour of which I was now at last to taste; her cheek was traversed by one of those long, dark, curling tresses which, to please me, she had undone altogether. She looked at me and smiled. Beyond her, through the window, the valley lay bright beneath the moon. The sight of Albertine's bare throat, of those flushed cheeks, had so intoxicated me (that is to say had so shifted the reality of the world for me away from nature into the torrent of my sensations which I could scarcely contain), that it had destroyed the equilibrium between the immense and indestructible life which circulated in my being and the life of the universe, so puny in comparison. The sea, which was visible through the window as well as the valley, the swelling breasts of the first of the Maineville cliffs, the sky in which the moon had not yet climbed to the zenith—all this seemed less than a feather-weight on my eyeballs, which between their lids I could feel dilated, resistant, ready to bear far greater burdens, all the mountains of the world, upon their fragile surface. Their orb no longer found even the sphere of the horizon adequate to fill it. And all the life-giving energy that nature could have brought me would have seemed to me all too meagre, the breathing of the sea all too short to express the immense aspiration that was swelling my breast. I bent over Albertine to kiss her. Death might have struck me down in that moment and it would have seemed to me a trivial, or rather an impossible thing, for life was not outside me but in me; I should have smiled pityingly had a philosopher then expressed the idea that some day, even some distant day, I should have to die, that the eternal forces of nature would survive me, the forces of that nature beneath whose godlike feet I was no more than a grain of dust; that, after me, there would still remain those rounded, swelling cliffs, that sea, that moonlight and that sky! How could it have been possible; how could the world have lasted longer than myself, since I was not lost in its vastness, since it was the world that was enclosed in me, in me whom it fell far short of filling, in me who, feeling that there was room to store so many other treasures, flung sky and sea and cliffs contemptuously into a corner. "Stop it or I'll ring the bell!" cried Albertine, seeing that I was flinging myself upon her to kiss her. But I told myself that not for nothing does a girl invite a young man to her room in secret, arranging that her aunt should not know, and that boldness, more-over, rewards those who know how to seize their opportunities; in the state of exaltation in which I was, Albertine's round face, lit by an inner flame as by a night-light, stood out in such relief that, imitating the rotation of a glowing sphere, it seemed to me to be turning, like those Michelangelo figures which are being swept away in a stationary and vertiginous whirlwind. I was about to discover the fragrance, the flavour which this strange pink fruit concealed. I heard a sound, abrupt, prolonged and shrill. Albertine had pulled the bell with all her might.

I had supposed that my love for Albertine was not based on the hope of carnal possession. And yet, when the lesson to be drawn from my experience that evening was, apparently, that such pos-session was impossible; when, after having had no doubt, that first day on the beach, that Albertine was licentious, and having passed through various intermediate assumptions, it seemed to me to be established that she was absolutely virtuous; when on her return from her aunt's a week later, she greeted me coldly with: "I forgive you; in fact I'm sorry to have upset you, but you must never do it again"—then in contrast to what I had felt on learning from Bloch that one could have all the women one wanted, and as if, instead of a real girl, I had known a wax doll, my desire to penetrate into her life, to follow her through the places in which she had spent her childhood, to be initiated by her into the sporting life, gradually detached itself from her; my intellectual curiosity as to thoughts on this subject or that did not survive my belief that I might kiss her if I chose. My dreams abandoned her as soon as they ceased to be nourished by the hope of a possession of which I had supposed them to be independent. Thenceforward they found themselves once more at liberty to transfer themselves—according to the attraction that I had found in her on any particular day, above all according to the chances I seemed to detect of my being possibly loved by her—to one or other of Albertine's friends, and to

Andrée first of all. And yet, if Albertine had not existed, perhaps I should not have had the pleasure which I began to feel more and more strongly during the days that followed in the kindness that was shown me by Andrée. Albertine told no one of the rebuff which I had received at her hands. She was one of those pretty girls who, from their earliest youth, on account of their beauty, but especially of an attraction, a charm which remains somewhat mysterious and has its source perhaps in reserves of vitality to which others less favoured by nature come to quench their thirst, have always—in their home circle, among their friends, in society—been more sought after than other more beautiful and richer girls; she was one of those people from whom, before the age of love and much more still after it is reached, more is asked than they themselves ask, more even than they are able to give. From her childhood Albertine had always had round her in an adoring circle four or five little girl friends, among them Andrée who was so far her superior and knew it (and perhaps this attraction which Albertine exerted quite involuntarily had been the origin, had laid the foundations of the little band). This attraction was still potent even at a great social distance, in circles quite brilliant by comparison, where, if there was a pavane to be danced, Albertine would be sent for rather than another girl of better family. The consequence was that, not having a penny to her name, living, not very well, at the expense of M. Bontemps who was said to be a shady individual and was anyhow anxious to be rid of her, she was nevertheless invited, not only to dine but to stay, by people who in Saint-Loup's eyes might not have had much distinction, but to Rosemonde's mother or Andrée's, women who though very rich themselves did not know these people, represented something quite extraordinary. Thus Albertine spent a few weeks every year with the family of one of the Governors of the Bank of France, who was also Chairman of the Board of Directors of a railway company. The wife of this financier entertained prominent people, and had never mentioned her "day" to Andrée's mother, who thought her wanting in politeness, but was nevertheless prodigiously interested in everything that went on in her house. Accordingly she encouraged Andrée every year to invite Albertine down to their villa, because, she said, it was a charitable act to offer a holiday by the sea to a girl who had not herself the means to travel and whose aunt did so little for her. Andrée's mother was probably not prompted by the thought that the banker and his wife, learning that Albertine was made much of by her and her daughter, would form a high opinion of them both; still less did she hope that Albertine, kind and clever as she was, would manage to get her invited, or at least to get Andrée invited, to the financier's garden-parties. But every evening at the dinner-table, while assuming an air of indifference and disdain, she was fascinated by Albertine's accounts of everything that had happened at the big house while she was staying there, and the names of the other guests, almost all of them people whom she knew by sight or by name. Even the thought that she knew them only in this indirect fashion, that is to say did not know them at all (she called this kind of acquaintance knowing people "all my life"), gave Andrée's mother a touch of melancholy while she plied Albertine with questions about them in a lofty and distant tone, with pursed lips, and might have left her doubtful and uneasy as to the importance of her own social position had she not been able to reassure herself, to return safely to the "realities of life," by saying to the butler: "Please tell the chef that his peas aren't soft enough." She then recovered her serenity. And she was quite determined that Andrée was to marry nobody but a man, of the best family of course, rich enough for her too to be able to keep a chef and a couple of coachmen. That was the reality, the practical proof of "position." But the fact that Albertine had dined at the banker's country house with this or that great lady, and that the said great lady had invited her to stay with her next winter, invested the girl, in the eyes of Andrée's mother, with a peculiar esteem which went very well with the pity and even contempt aroused by her lack of fortune, a contempt increased by the fact that M. Bontemps had betrayed his flag and—being even vaguely Panamist, it was said—had rallied to the Government. Not that this deterred Andrée's mother, in her passion for abstract truth, from withering with her scorn the people who appeared to believe that Albertine was of humble origin. "What's that you say? Why, they're one of the best families in the country. Simonet with a single 'n,' you know!" Certainly, in view of the class of society in which all this went on, in which money plays so important a part, and mere charm makes people ask you out but not marry you, an "acceptable" marriage did not appear to be for Albertine a practical outcome of the so distinguished patronage which she enjoyed but which would not have been held to compensate for her poverty. But even in themselves, and with no prospect of any matrimonial consequence, Albertine's "successes" excited the envy of certain spiteful mothers, furious at seeing her received "like one of the family" by the banker's wife, even by Andrée's mother, whom they scarcely knew. They therefore went about telling mutual friends of theirs and of those two ladies that the latter would be very angry if they knew the truth, which was that Albertine repeated to each of them everything that the intimacy to which she was rashly admitted enabled her to spy out in the household of the other, countless little secrets which it must be infinitely unpleasant to the interested party to have made public. These envious women said this so that it might be repeated and might get Albertine into trouble with her patrons. But, as often happens, their machinations met with no success. The spite that prompted them was too apparent, and their only result was to make the women who had perpetrated them appear rather more contemptible than before. Andrée's mother was too firm in her opinion of Albertine to change her mind about her now. She looked upon her as "unfortunate," but the best-natured girl living, and one who was incapable of making anything up except to give pleasure.

If this sort of popularity to which Albertine had attained did not seem likely to lead to any practical result, it had stamped Andrée's friend with the distinctive characteristic of people who, being always sought after, have never any need to offer themselves, a characteristic (to be found also, and for analogous reasons, at the other end of the social scale, among the smartest women) which consists in their not making any display of the successes they have scored, but rather keeping them to themselves. She would never say of anyone: "So-and-so is anxious to meet me," would speak of everyone with the greatest good-nature, and as if it was she who ran after, who sought to know other people. If someone mentioned a young man who, a few minutes earlier, had been in private conversation with her, heaping the bitterest reproaches upon her because she had refused him an assignation, so far from proclaiming this in public or betraying any resentment she would stand up for him: "He's such a nice boy!" Indeed it quite annoyed her to be so attractive to people, since it obliged her to disappoint them, whereas her natural instinct was always to give pleasure. So much did she enjoy giving pleasure that she had come to employ a particular kind of falsehood peculiar to certain utilitarians and men who have "arrived." Existing, incidentally, in an embryonic state in a vast number of people, this form of insincerity consists in not being able to confine the pleasure arising out of a single act of politeness to a single person. For instance, if Albertine's aunt wished her niece to accompany her to a not very amusing party, Albertine by going to it might have found it sufficient to extract from the incident the moral profit of having given pleasure to her aunt. But, being courteously welcomed by her host and hostess, she preferred to say to them that she had been wanting to see them for so long that she had finally seized this opportunity and begged her aunt to take her to their party. Even this was not enough: at the same party there might happen to be one of Albertine's friends who was very unhappy. Albertine would say to her: "I didn't like the thought of your being here by yourself. I felt it might do you good to have me with you. If you would rather leave the party, go somewhere else, I'm ready to do anything you like. What I want above all is to see you look less unhappy" (which, as it happened, was true also). Sometimes it happened however that the fictitious aim destroyed the real one. Thus Albertine, having a favour to ask on behalf of one of her friends, would go to see a certain lady who could help her. But on arriving at the house of this lady—a kind and sympathetic soul—the girl, unconsciously following the principle of the multiple utilisation of a single action, would think it more affectionate to appear to have come there solely on account of the pleasure she knew she would derive from seeing the lady again. The lady would be deeply touched that Albertine should have taken a long journey out of pure friendship. Seeing her almost overcome by emotion, Albertine liked the lady even more. Only, there was this awkward consequence: she now felt so keenly the pleasure of friendship which she pretended to have been her motive in coming, that she was afraid of making the lady suspect the genuineness of sentiments which were actually quite sincere if she now asked her to do the favour for her friend. The lady would think that Albertine had come for that purpose, which was true, but would conclude also that Albertine had no disinterested pleasure in seeing her, which was false. With the result that she came away without having asked the favour, like a man sometimes who has been so kind to a woman, in the hope of winning her favours, that he refrains from declaring his passion in order not to deprive his kindness of its appearance of nobility. In other instances it would be wrong to say that the true object was sacrificed to the subordinate and subsequently conceived idea, but the two were so incompatible that if the person to whom Albertine endeared herself by stating the second had known of the existence of the first, her pleasure would at once have been turned into the deepest pain. At a much later point in this story, we shall have occasion to see this kind of contradiction expressed in clearer terms. Suffice it to say for the present, borrowing an example from a completely different context, that they occur very frequently in the most divergent situations that life has to offer. A husband has established his mistress in the town where he is quartered with his regiment. His wife, left by herself in Paris, and with an inkling of the truth, grows more and more miserable, and writes her husband letters embittered by jealousy. Then the mistress is obliged to go to Paris for the day. The husband cannot resist her entreaties to him to accompany her, and applies for a twenty-four-hour leave. But since he is a good-natured fellow, and hates making his wife unhappy, he goes to see her and tells her, shedding a few quite genuine tears, that, dismayed by her letters, he has found the means of getting away from his duties to come to her and to console her in his arms. He has thus contrived by a single journey to furnish wife and mistress alike with proofs of his love. But if the wife were to learn the reason for which he has come to Paris, her joy would doubtless be turned into grief, unless her pleasure in seeing the faithless wretch outweighed, in spite of everything, the pain that his infidelities had caused her. Among the men who have struck me as practising most consistently this system of killing several birds with one stone must be included M. de Norpois. He would now and then agree to act as intermediary between two of his friends who had quarrelled, and this led to his being called the most obliging of men. But it was not sufficient for him to appear to be doing a service to the friend who had come to him to request it; he would represent to the other the steps which he was taking to effect a reconciliation as undertaken not at the request of the first friend but in the interest of the second, a notion of which he never had any difficulty in persuading an interlocutor influenced in advance by the idea that he had before him the "most obliging of men." In this way, playing both ends against the middle, what in stage parlance is known as "doubling" two parts, he never allowed his influence to be in the slightest degree imperilled, and the services which he rendered constituted not an expenditure of capital but a dividend upon some part of his credit. At the same time every service, seemingly rendered twice over, correspondingly enhanced his reputation as an obliging friend, and, better still, a friend whose interventions were efficacious, one who did not simply beat the air, whose efforts were always justified by success, as was shown by the gratitude of both parties. This duplicity in obligingness was—allowing for disappointments such as are the lot of every human being—an important element in M. de Norpois's character. And often at the Ministry he would make use of my father, who was a simple soul, while making him believe that it was he, M. de Norpois, who was being useful to my father.

Pleasing people more easily than she wished, and having no need to trumpet her conquests abroad, Albertine kept silent about the scene she had had with me by her bedside, which a plain girl would have wished the whole world to know. And yet for her attitude during that scene I could not arrive at any satisfactory explanation. As regards the supposition that she was absolutely chaste (a supposition to which I had first of all attributed the violence with which Albertine had refused to let herself be taken in my arms and kissed, though it was by no means essential to my conception of the kindness, the fundamentally honourable character of my beloved), I could not accept it without a copious revision of its terms. It ran so entirely counter to the hypothesis which I had constructed that day when I saw Albertine for the first time. Then, so many different acts of affectionate sweetness towards myself (a sweetness that was caressing, at times uneasy, alarmed, jealous of my predilection for Andrée) came up on all sides to challenge the brutal gesture with which, to escape from me, she had pulled the bell. Why then had she invited me to come and spend the evening by her bedside? Why did she speak all the time in the language of affection? What is the basis of the desire to see a friend, to be afraid that he may be fonder of someone else than of you, to seek to please him, to tell him, so romantically, that no one else will ever know that he has spent the evening in your room, if you refuse him so simple a pleasure and if it is no pleasure to you? I could not believe, after all, that Albertine's virtue went as far as that, and I came to wonder whether her violence might not have been due to some reason of vanity, a disagreeable odour, for instance, which she suspected of lingering about her person, and by which she was afraid that I might be repelled, or else of cowardice—if for instance she imagined, in her ignorance of the facts of love, that my state of nervous debility was due to something contagious, communicable to her in a kiss.

She was genuinely distressed by her failure to gratify me, and gave me a little gold pencil, with the virtuous perverseness of people who, touched by your kindness but not prepared to grant what it clamours for, nevertheless want to do something on your behalf—the critic, an article from whose pen would so gratify the novelist, who asks him to dinner instead; the duchess who does not take the snob with her to the theatre but lends him her box on an evening when she will not be using it herself. To such an extent are those who do the minimum, and might easily do nothing, driven by conscience to do something!

I told Albertine that in giving me this pencil she was giving me great pleasure, and yet not so great as I should have felt if, on the night she had spent at the hotel, she had permitted me to kiss her: "It would have made me so happy! What possible harm could it have done you? I'm amazed that you should have refused me."

"What amazes me," she retorted, "is that you should find it amazing. I wonder what sort of girls you must know if my behaviour surprised you."

"I'm sorry to have annoyed you, but even now I cannot say that I think I was in the wrong. What I feel is that all that sort of thing is of no importance really, and I can't understand a girl who could so easily give pleasure not consenting to do so. Let's be quite clear about it," I went on, throwing a sop of sorts to her moral scruples as I recalled how she and her friends had scarified the girl who went about with the actress Léa, "I don't mean to say that a girl can behave exactly as she likes and that there's no such thing as immorality. Take, for example, what you were saying the other day about a girl who's staying at Balbec and her relations with an actress. I call that unspeakable, so unspeakable that I feel sure it must all have been made up by some enemies of the girl and that there can't be any truth in the story. It strikes me as improbable, impossible. But to allow oneself to be kissed, or even more, by a friend—since you say that I'm your friend . . ."

"So you are, but I've had other friends before now, I've known lots of young men who were every bit as friendly, I can assure you. Well, not one of them would ever have dared to do such a thing. They know they'd get their ears boxed if they tried it on. Besides, they never dreamed of doing so. We would shake hands in a straightforward, friendly sort of way, like good pals, but there was never a word said about kissing, and yet we weren't any the less friends for that. Why, if it's my friendship you're after, you've nothing to complain of; I must be jolly fond of you to forgive you. But I'm sure you don't care two hoots about me, really. Own up now, it's Andrée you're in love with. Besides, you're quite right; she's ever so much nicer than I am, and absolutely ravishing! Oh, you men!"

Despite my recent disappointment, these words so frankly uttered, by giving me a great respect for Albertine, made a very agreeable impression on me. And perhaps this impression was to have serious and vexatious consequences for me later on, for it was around it that there began to form that feeling almost of brotherly intimacy, that moral core which was always to remain at the heart of my love for Albertine. Such a feeling may be the cause of the greatest suffering. For in order really to suffer at the hands of a woman one must have believed in her completely. For the moment, that embryo of moral esteem, of friendship, was left embedded in my soul like a stepping-stone in a stream. It could have availed nothing, by itself, against my happiness if it had remained there without growing, in an inertia which it was to retain the following year, and still more during the final weeks of this first visit to Balbec. It dwelt in me like one of those foreign bodies which it would be wiser when all is said to expel, but which we leave where they are without disturbing them, so harmless for the present does their weakness, their isolation amid a strange environment render them.

My longings were now once more at liberty to concentrate on one or another of Albertine's friends, and returned first of all to Andrée, whose attentions might perhaps have touched me less had I not been certain that they would come to Albertine's ears. Undoubtedly the preference that I had long pretended to feel for Andrée had furnished me—in habits of conversation and declarations of affection—with, so to speak, the material for a ready-made love for her which had hitherto lacked only the complement of a genuine feeling, which my heart, being once more free, was now in a position to supply. But Andrée was too intellectual, too neurotic, too sickly, too like myself for me really to love her. If Albertine now seemed to me to be void of substance, Andrée was filled with something which I knew only too well. I had thought, that first day, that what I saw on the beach was the mistress of some racing cyclist, passionately interested in sport, and now Andrée told me that if she had taken it up, it was on orders from her doctor, to cure her neurasthenia, her digestive troubles, but that her happiest hours were those which she spent translating one of George Eliot's novels. My disappointment, due to an initial mistake as to what Andrée was, had not, in fact, the slightest importance for me. But the mistake was one of the kind which, if they allow love to be born and are not recognised as mistakes until it has ceased to be modifiable, become a cause of suffering. Such mistakes—which may be quite different from mine with regard to Andrée, and even its exact opposite—are frequently due (and this was especially the case here) to the fact that people take on the aspect and the mannerisms of what they are not but would like to be sufficiently to create an illusion at first sight. To the outward appearance, affectation, imitation, the longing to be admired, whether by the good or by the wicked, add misleading similarities of speech and gesture. There are cynicisms and cruelties which, when put to the test, prove no more genuine than certain apparent virtues and generosities. Just as we often discover a vain miser beneath the cloak of a man famed for his charity, so her flaunting of vice leads us to surmise a Messalina in a respectable girl with middle-class prejudices. I had thought to find in Andrée a healthy, primitive creature, whereas she was merely a person in search of health, as perhaps were many of those in whom she herself had thought to find it, and who were in reality no more healthy than a burly arthritic with a red face and in white flannels is necessarily a Hercules. Now there are circumstances in which it is not immaterial to our happiness that the person we have loved for what appeared to be so healthy about her is in reality only one of those invalids who receive such health as they possess from others, as the planets borrow their light, as certain bodies are only conductors of electricity.

No matter, Andrée, like Rosemonde and Gisèle, indeed more than they, was, when all was said, a friend of Albertine, sharing her life, imitating her ways, to the point that, on the first day, I had not at once distinguished them from one another. Among these girls, rose-sprigs whose principal charm was that they were silhouetted against the sea, the same indivisibility prevailed as at the time when I did not know them, when the appearance of no matter which of them had caused me such violent emotion by heralding the fact that the little band was not far off. And even now the sight of one of them filled me with a pleasure in which was included, to an extent which I should not have found it easy to define, that of seeing the others follow her in due course, and, even if they did not come that day, of speaking about them, and of knowing that they would be told that I had been on the beach.

It was no longer simply the attraction of those first days, it was a genuine wish to love that wavered between them all, to such an extent was each the natural substitute for the others. My greatest sadness would not have been to be abandoned by whichever of these girls I loved best, but I should at once have loved best, because I should have fastened on to her the sum total of the melancholy longings which had been floating vaguely among them all, the one who had abandoned me. It would, moreover, in that event, be the loss of all her friends, in whose eyes I should speedily have forfeited whatever prestige I might possess, that I should, in losing her, have unconsciously regretted, having pledged to them that sort of collective love which the politician and the actor feel for the public for whose desertion of them after they have enjoyed all its favours they can never be consoled. Even those favours which I had failed to win from Albertine I would hope suddenly to receive from one or other who had left me in the evening with a word or glance of ambiguous meaning, thanks to which it was towards her that, for the next day or so, my desire would turn.

It strayed among them all the more voluptuously in that upon those volatile faces a comparative fixity of features had now begun, and had been carried far enough for the eye to distinguish—even if it were to change yet further—each malleable and elusive effigy. The differences that existed between these faces doubtless bore little relation to equivalent differences in the length and breadth of their features, any of which, dissimilar as the girls appeared, might perhaps almost have been lifted from one face and imposed at random upon any other. But our knowledge of faces is not mathematical. In the first place, it does not begin by measuring the parts, it takes as its starting-point an expression, a sum total. In Andrée, for instance, the fineness of her gentle eyes seemed to go with the thinness of her nose, as slender as a mere curve which one could imagine having been traced in order to pursue along a single line the notion of delicacy divided higher up between the dual smile of her twin gaze. A line equally fine cut through her hair, as pliant and as deep as the line with which the wind furrows the sand. And there it must have been hereditary; for the snow-white hair of Andrée's mother rippled in the same way, forming here a swelling, there a depression like a snow-drift that rises or sinks according to the irregularities of the land. Certainly, when compared with the fine delineation of Andrée's, Rosemonde's nose seemed to present broad surfaces, like a high tower resting upon massive foundations. Although expression may suffice to make us believe in enormous differences between things that are separated by infinitely little—although that infinitely little may by itself create an expression that is absolutely unique, an individuality—it was not only the infinitely little of its lines and the originality of its expression that made these faces appear irreducible to one another. Between my friends' faces their colouring established a separation wider still, not so much by the varied beauty of the tones with which it provided them, so contrasted that I felt when I looked at Rosemonde—suffused with a sulphurous pink that was further modified by the greenish light of her eyes—and then at Andrée—whose white cheeks derived such austere distinction from her black hair—the same kind of pleasure as if I had been looking alternately at a geranium growing by a sunlit sea and a camellia in the night; but principally because the infinitely small differences of their lines were enlarged out of all proportion, the relations between one and another surface entirely changed by this new element of colour which, in addition to being the dispenser of tints, is a great generator or at least modifier of dimensions. So that faces which were perhaps constructed on not dissimilar lines, according as they were lit, by the flames of a shock of red hair, with a pinkish hue, or, by white light, with a matt pallor, grew sharper or broader, became something else, like those properties used in the Russian ballet, consisting sometimes, when they are seen in the light of day, of a mere paper disc, out of which the genius of a Bakst, according to the blood-red or moonlit lighting in which he plunges his stages, makes a hard incrustation, like a turquoise on a palace wall, or something softly blooming, like a Bengal rose in an eastern garden. And so when studying faces, we do indeed measure them, but as painters, not as surveyors.

The same was true of Albertine as of her friends. On certain days, thin, with a grey complexion, a sullen air, a violet transparency slanting across her eyes such as we notice sometimes on the sea, she seemed to be feeling the sorrows of exile. On other days her face, smoother and glossier, drew one's desires on to its varnished surface and prevented them from going further; unless I caught a sudden glimpse of her from the side, for her matt cheeks, like white wax on the surface, were visibly pink beneath, which was what made one so long to kiss them, to reach that different tint which was so elusive. At other times, happiness bathed those cheeks with a radiance so mobile that the skin, grown fluid and vague, gave passage to a sort of subcutaneous glaze which made it appear to be of another colour but not of another substance than the eyes; sometimes, when one looked without thinking at her face punctuated with tiny brown marks among which floated what were simply two larger, bluer stains, it was as though one were looking at a goldfinch's egg, or perhaps at an opalescent agate cut and polished in two places only, where, at the heart of the brown stone, there shone, like the transparent wings of a sky-blue butterfly, the eyes, those features in which the flesh becomes a mirror and gives us the illusion of enabling us, more than through the other parts of the body, to approach the soul. But most often it too showed more colour, and was then more animated; sometimes in her white face only the tip of her nose was pink, and as delicate as that of a mischievous kitten with which one would have liked to play; sometimes her cheeks were so glossy that one's glance slipped, as over the surface of a miniature, over their pink enamel, which was made to appear still more delicate, more private, by the enclosing though half-opened lid of her black hair; or it might happen that the tint of her cheeks had deepened to the mauvish pink of cyclamen, and sometimes even, when she was flushed or feverish, with a suggestion of unhealthiness which lowered my desire to something more sensual and made her glance expressive of something more perverse and unwholesome, to the deep purple of certain roses, a red that was almost black; and each of these Albertines was different, as is each appearance of the dancer whose colours, form, character, are transmuted according to the endlessly varied play of a spotlight. It was perhaps because they were so diverse, the persons whom I used to contemplate in her at this period, that later I developed the habit of becoming myself a different person, according to the particular Albertine to whom my thoughts had turned; a jealous, an indifferent, a voluptuous, a melancholy, a frenzied person, created anew not merely by the accident of the particular memory that had risen to the surface, but in proportion also to the strength of the belief that was lent to the support of one and the same memory by the varying manner in which I appreciated it. For this was the point to which I invariably had to return, to those beliefs which for most of the time occupy our souls unbeknown to us, but which for all that are of more importance to our happiness than is the person whom we see, for it is through them that we see him, it is they that impart his moment-ary grandeur to the person seen. To be quite accurate, I ought to give a different name to each of the selves who subsequently thought about Albertine; I ought still more to give a different name to each of the Albertines who appeared before me, never the same, like those seas—called by me simply and for the sake of convenience "the sea"—that succeeded one another and against which, a nymph likewise, she was silhouetted. But above all, in the same way as, in telling a story (though to far greater purpose here), people mention what the weather was like on such and such a day, I ought always to give its name to the belief that reigned over my soul and created its atmosphere on any given day on which I saw Albertine, the appearance of people, like that of the sea, being dependent on those clouds, themselves barely visible, which change the colour of everything by their concentration, their mobility, their dissemination, their flight—like that cloud which Elstir had rent one evening by not introducing me to these girls with whom he had stopped to talk, and whose images had sud-denly appeared to me more beautiful when they moved away—a cloud that had formed again a few days later when I did get to know them, veiling their brightness, interposing itself frequently between my eyes and them, opaque and soft, like Virgil's Leucothea.

No doubt, all their faces had assumed quite new meanings for me since the manner in which they were to be read had been to some extent indicated to me by their talk, talk to which I could ascribe a value all the greater in that, by questioning them, I could prompt it whenever I chose, could vary it like an experimenter who seeks by corroborative proofs to establish the truth of his theory. And it is, after all, as good a way as any of solving the problem of existence to get near enough to the things and people that have appeared to us beautiful and mysterious from a distance to be able to satisfy ourselves that they have neither mystery nor beauty. It is one of the systems of mental hygiene among which we are at liberty to choose our own, a system which is perhaps not to be recommended too strongly, but gives us a certain tranquillity with which to spend what remains of life, and also—since it enables us to regret nothing, by assuring us that we have attained to the best, and that the best was nothing out of the ordinary—with which to resign ourselves to death.

For the contempt for chastity, for the memory of casual every-day affairs, I had substituted, in the minds of these girls, upright principles, liable perhaps to falter, but principles which had hitherto kept unscathed those who had acquired them in their middle-class homes. And yet, when one has been mistaken from the start, even in trifling details, when an error of assumption or recollection makes one seek for the author of a malicious slander, or for the place where one has lost something, in the wrong direction, it frequently happens that one discovers one's error only to substitute for it not the truth but a fresh error. I drew, as regards their manner of life and the conduct to be observed towards them, all the possible conclusions from the word "inno-cence" which I had read, in talking familiarly with them, upon their faces. But perhaps I had carelessly misread it, and it was no more written there than was the name of Jules Ferry on the programme of the performance at which I had seen Berma for the first time, an omission which had not prevented me from maintaining to M. de Norpois that Jules Ferry, beyond any poss-ibility of doubt, was a person who wrote curtain-raisers.

No matter which of my friends of the little band I thought of, how could the last face that she had shown me not have been the only one that I could recall, since, of our memories with respect to a person, the mind eliminates everything that does not concur with the immediate purpose of our daily relations (even, and especially, if those relations are impregnated with an element of love which, ever unsatisfied, lives always in the moment that is about to come)? It allows the chain of spent days to slip away, holding on only to the very end of it, often of a quite different metal from the links that have vanished in the night, and in the journey which we make through life, counts as real only the place in which we are at present. My very earliest impressions, already so remote, could not find any remedy in my memory against the daily distortion to which they were subjected; during the long hours which I spent in talking, eating, playing with these girls, I did not even remember that they were the same pitiless and sensual virgins whom I had seen, as in a fresco, file past between me and the sea.

Geographers or archaeologists may conduct us over Calypso's island, may excavate the Palace of Minos. Only, Calypso becomes then a mere woman, Minos a mere king with no semblance of divinity. Even the qualities and defects which history then teaches us to have been the attributes of those quite real personages often differ widely from those which we had ascribed to the fabulous beings who bore the same names as they. Thus had there faded and vanished all the lovely oceanic mythology which I had composed in those first days. But it is not altogether a matter of indifference that we do succeed, at any rate now and then, in spending our time in familiar intercourse with what we thought to be unattainable and longed to possess. In our later dealings with people whom at first we found disagreeable there persists always, even amid the factitious pleasure which we have come at length to enjoy in their society, the lingering taint of the defects which they have succeeded in hiding. But, in relations such as I enjoyed with Albertine and her friends, the genuine pleasure which was there at the start leaves that fragrance which no artifice can impart to hothouse fruits, to grapes that have not ripened in the sun. The supernatural creatures which for a little time they had been to me still introduced, even without my being aware of it, a miraculous element into the most commonplace dealings I might have with them, or rather prevented such dealings from ever becoming in the least commonplace. My desire had sought so avidly to learn the meaning of eyes which now knew and smiled at me, but which, that first day, had crossed mine like rays from another universe, it had distributed colour and fragrance so generously, so carefully, so minutely, over the fleshly surfaces of these girls who now, stretched out on the cliff-top, simply offered me sandwiches or played guessing-games, that often, in the afternoon, while I lay there among them—like those painters who, seeking to match the grandeurs of antiquity in modern life, give to a woman cutting her toe-nail the nobility of the *Thorn Puller*, or, like Rubens, make goddesses out of women they know to people some mythological scene—I would gaze at those lovely forms, dark and fair, so dissimilar in type, scattered around me on the grass, without emptying them, perhaps, of all the mediocre content with which my everyday experience had filled them, and yet (without expressly recalling their celestial origin) as if, like young Hercules or Telemachus, I had been playing amid a band of nymphs.

Then the concerts ended, the bad weather began, my friends left Balbec, not all at once, like the swallows, but all in the same week. Albertine was the first to go, abruptly, without any of her friends understanding, then or afterwards, why she had returned suddenly to Paris whither neither her work nor any amusement summoned her. "She said neither why nor wherefore, and with that she left!" muttered Françoise, who, for that matter, would have liked us to do the same. We were, she thought, inconsiderate towards the staff, now greatly reduced in number, but retained on account of the few visitors who were still staying on, and towards the manager who was "just eating up money." It was true that the hotel, which would very soon be closed for the winter, had long since seen most of its patrons depart, and never had it been so agreeable. This view was not shared by the manager; from end to end of the rooms in which we sat shivering, and at the doors of which no page now stood on guard, he paced the corridors, wearing a new frock-coat, so well tended by the barber that his insipid face appeared to be made of some composition in which, for one part of flesh, there were three of cosmetics, and incessantly changing his neckties. (These refinements cost less than having the place heated and keeping on the staff, just as a man who is no longer able to subscribe ten thousand francs to a charity can still parade his generosity without inconvenience to himself by tipping the boy who brings him a telegram with five.) He appeared to be inspecting the empty air, to be seeking, by the smartness of his personal appearance, to give a provisional splendour to the desolation that could now be felt in this hotel where the season had not been good, and walked like the ghost of a monarch who returns to haunt the ruins of what was once his palace. He was particularly annoyed when the little local railway company, finding the supply of passengers inadequate, discontinued its trains until the following spring. "What is lacking here," said the manager, "is the means of commotion." In spite of the deficit which his books showed, he was making plans for the future on a lavish scale. And as he was, after all, capable of retaining an exact memory of fine phrases when they were directly applicable to the hotel-keeping industry and had the effect of enhancing its importance: "I was not adequately supported, although in the dining-room I had an efficient squad," he explained, "but the pages left something to be desired. You will see, next year, what a phalanx I shall convene." In the meantime the suspension of the services of the little railway obliged him to send for letters and occasionally to dispatch visitors in a carriole. I would often ask leave to sit by the driver, and in this way I managed to be out in all weathers, as in the winter I had spent at Combray.

Sometimes, however, the driving rain kept my grandmother and me, the Casino being closed, in rooms almost completely deserted, as in the hold of a ship when a storm is raging; and there, day by day, as in the course of a sea-voyage, a new person from among those in whose company we had spent three months without getting to know them, the senior judge from Caen, the president of the Cherbourg bar, an American lady and her daughters, came up to us, engaged us in conversation, thought up some way of making the time pass less slowly, revealed some talent, taught us a new game, invited us to drink tea or to listen to music, to meet them at a certain hour, to plan together some of those diversions which contain the true secret of giving ourselves pleasure, which is not to aspire to it but merely to help ourselves to pass the time less boringly—in a word, formed with us, at the end of our stay at Balbec, ties of friendship which, in a day or two, their successive departures from the place would sever. I even made the acquaintance of the rich young man, of one of his pair of aristocratic friends and of the actress, who had reappeared for a few days; but their little society was composed now of three persons only, the other friend having returned to Paris. They asked me to come out to dinner with them at their restaurant. I think they were just as well pleased that I did not accept. But they had issued the invitation in the most friendly way imaginable, and although it came in fact from the rich young man, since the others were only his guests, as the friend who was staying with him, the Marquis Maurice de Vaudémont, came of a very good family indeed, instinctively the actress, in asking me whether I would not come, said, to flatter my vanity: "It will give Maurice such pleasure."

And when I met them all three together in the hall of the hotel, it was M. de Vaudémont (the rich young man effacing himself) who said to me: "Won't you give us the pleasure of dining with us?"

On the whole I had derived very little benefit from Balbec, but this only strengthened my desire to return there. It seemed to me that I had not stayed there long enough. This was not the opinion of my friends in Paris, who wrote to ask whether I meant to stay there for the rest of my life. And when I saw that it was the name "Balbec" which they were obliged to put on the envelope, as my window looked out not over a landscape or a street but on to the plains of the seas, as through the night I heard its murmur, to which, before going to sleep, I had entrusted the ship of my dreams, I had the illusion that this life of promiscuity with the waves must effectively, without my knowledge, pervade me with the notion of their charm, like those lessons which one learns by heart while one is asleep.

The manager offered to reserve better rooms for me next year, but I had now become attached to mine, into which I went without ever noticing the scent of vetiver, while my mind, which had once found such difficulty in rising to fill its space, had come now to take its measurements so exactly that I was obliged to submit it to a reverse process when I had to sleep in Paris, in my own room, the ceiling of which was low.

For we had had to leave Balbec at last, the cold and the damp having become too penetrating for us to stay any longer in an hotel which had neither fireplaces in the rooms nor central heating. Moreover, I forgot almost immediately these last weeks of our stay. What I saw almost invariably in my mind's eye when I thought of Balbec were the hours which, every morning during the fine weather, since I was due to go out in the afternoon with Albertine and her friends, my grandmother, following the doctor's orders, insisted on my spending lying down with the room darkened. The manager gave instructions that no noise was to be made on my landing, and came up himself to see that they were obeyed. Because the light outside was so strong, I kept drawn for as long as possible the big violet curtains which had adopted so hostile an attitude towards me the first evening. But since, in spite of the pins with which Françoise fastened them every night so that the light should not enter, and which she alone knew how to unfasten, in spite of the rugs, the red cretonne table-cover, the various fabrics collected here and there which she fitted into her defensive scheme, she never succeeded in making them meet exactly, the darkness was not complete, and they spilled over the carpet as it were a scarlet shower of anemone-petals, which I could not resist the temptation to trample for a moment with my bare feet. And on the wall which faced the window and so was partially lighted, a cylinder of gold with no visible support was placed vertically and moved slowly along like the pillar of fire which went before the Hebrews in the desert. I went back to bed; obliged to taste without moving, in imagination only, and all at once, the pleasures of games, bathing, walks which the morning prompted, joy made my heart beat thunderingly like a machine set going at full speed but fixed to the ground, which can spend its energy only by turning over on itself.

I knew that my friends were on the front, but I did not see them as they passed before the links of the sea's uneven chain, at the far end of which, perched amid its bluish peaks like an Italian citadel, could occasionally be distinguished, in clear weather, the little town of Rivebelle, picked out in minutest detail by the sun. I did not see my friends, but (while there mounted to my belvedere the shout of the newsboys, the "journalists" as Françoise used to call them, the shouts of the bathers and of children at play, punctuating like the cries of sea-birds the sough of the gently breaking waves) I guessed their presence, I heard their laughter enveloped like the laughter of the Nereids in the soft surge of sound that rose to my ears. "We looked up," said Albertine in the evening, "to see if you were coming down. But your shutters were still closed when the concert began." At ten o'clock, sure enough, it broke out beneath my windows. In the intervals between the blare of the instruments, if the tide were high, the gliding surge of a wave would be heard again, slurred and continuous, seeming to enfold the notes of the violin in its crystal spirals and to be spraying its foam over the intermittent echoes of a submarine music. I grew impatient because no one had yet come with my things, so that I might get up and dress. Twelve o'clock struck, and Françoise arrived at last. And for months on end, in this Balbec to which I had so looked forward because I imagined it only as battered by storms and buried in the mist, the weather had been so dazzling and so unchanging that when she came to open the window I could always, without once being wrong, expect to see the same patch of sunlight folded in the corner of the outer wall, of an unalterable colour which was less moving as a sign of summer than depressing as the colour of a lifeless and factitious enamel. And when Françoise removed the pins from the top of the window-frame, took down the cloths, and drew back the curtains, the summer day which she disclosed seemed as dead, as immemorial, as a sumptuous millenary mummy from which our old servant had done no more than cautiously unwind the linen wrappings before displaying it, embalmed in its vesture of gold.

THE GUERMANTES WAY

PART ONE

THE twittering of the birds at daybreak sounded insipid to Françoise. Every word uttered by the maids upstairs made her jump; disturbed by all their running about, she kept asking herself what they could be doing. In other words, we had moved. True, the servants had made no less commotion in the attics of our old home; but she knew them, she had made of their comings and goings something friendly and familiar. Now she listened to the very silence with painful attentiveness. And as our new neighbourhood appeared to be as quiet as the boulevard on to which we had hitherto looked had been noisy, the song (distinct even at a distance, when it was still quite faint, like an orchestral motif) of a passer-by brought tears to the eyes of the exiled Françoise. Hence, if I had been tempted to scoff at her when, in her misery at having to leave a house in which one was "so well respected on all sides," she had packed her trunks weeping, in accordance with the rites of Combray, and declaring superior to all possible houses that which had been ours, on the other hand, finding it as hard to assimilate the new as I found it easy to abandon the old, I felt myself drawn towards our old servant when I saw that moving into a building where she had not received from the concierge, who did not yet know us, the marks of respect necessary to her spiritual well-being, had brought her positively to the verge of prostration. She alone could understand what I was feeling; certainly her young footman was not the person to do so; for him, who was as unlike the Combray type as it was possible to conceive, moving house, going to live in another neighbourhood, was like taking a holiday in which the novelty of one's surroundings gave one the same sense of refreshment as if one had actually travelled; he felt he was in the country; and a cold in the head afforded him, as though he had been sitting in a draughty railway carriage, the delicious sensation of having seen something of the world; at each fresh sneeze he rejoiced that he had found so "posh" a situation, having always longed to work for people who travelled a lot. And so, without giving him a thought, I went straight to Françoise, who, in return for my having laughed at her tears over a departure which had left me cold, now showed an icy indifference to my sorrow, because she shared it. The alleged "sensitivity" of neurotic people is matched by their egotism; they cannot abide the flaunting by others of the sufferings to which they pay an ever-increasing attention in themselves. Françoise, who would not allow the least of her own ailments to pass unnoticed, if I were in pain would turn her head away so that I should not have the satisfaction of seeing my sufferings pitied, or so much as observed. It was the same as soon as I tried to speak to her about our new house. Moreover, having been obliged, a day or two later, to return to the house we had just left, to retrieve some clothes which had been overlooked in our removal, while I, as a result of it, still had a "temperature," and like a boa constrictor that has just swallowed an ox felt myself painfully distended by the sight of a long sideboard which my eyes had still to digest, Françoise, with true feminine inconstancy, came back saying that she had really thought she would stifle on our old boulevard, that she had found it quite a day's journey to get there, that never had she seen such stairs, that she would not go back to live there for a king's ransom, not if you were to offer her millions—gratuitous hypotheses—and that *everything* (everything, that is to say, to do with the kitchen and "usual offices") was much better fitted up in our new home. Which, it is high time now that the reader should be told—and told also that we had moved into it because my grandmother, not having been at all well (though we took care to keep this reason from her), was in need of better air—was a flat forming part of the Hôtel de Guermantes.

At the age when Names, offering us an image of the unknowable which we have poured into their mould, while at the same moment connoting for us also a real place, force us accordingly to identify one with the other to such a point that we set out to seek in a city for a soul which it cannot enshrine but which we have no longer the power to expel from its name, it is not only to towns and rivers that they give an individuality, as do allegorical paintings, it is not only the physical universe which they speckle with differences, people with marvels, it is the social universe also; and so every historic house, in town or country, has its lady or its fairy, as every forest has its genie, every stream its deity. Sometimes, hidden in the heart of its name, the fairy is transformed to suit the life of our imagination, by which she lives; thus it was that the atmosphere in which Mme de Guermantes existed in me, after having been for years no more than the reflexion of a magic lantern slide and of a stained-glass window, began to lose its colours when quite other dreams impregnated it with the bubbling coolness of swift-flowing streams.

However, the fairy languishes if we come in contact with the real person to whom her name corresponds, for the name then begins to reflect that person, who contains nothing of the fairy; the fairy may revive if we absent ourselves from the person, but if we remain in the person's presence the fairy ultimately dies and with her the name, as happened to the family of Lusignan which was fated to become extinct on the day when the fairy Mélusine should disappear. Then the Name, beneath the successive retouchings of which we may end by finding the original handsome portrait of a strange woman whom we have never met, becomes no more than the mere identity card photograph to which we refer in order to decide whether we know, whether or not we ought to bow to a person who passes us in the street. But should a sensation from a bygone year—like those recording instruments which preserve the sound and the manner of the various artists who have sung or played into them—enable our memory to make us hear that name with the particular ring with which it then sounded in our ears, we feel at once, though the name itself has apparently not changed, the distance that separates the dreams which at different times its same syllables have meant to us. For a moment, from the clear echo of its warbling in some distant spring-time, we can extract, as from the little tubes used in painting, the exact, forgotten, mysterious, fresh tint of the days which we had believed ourselves to be recalling, when, like a bad painter, we were giving to the whole of our past, spread out on the same canvas, the conventional and undifferentiated tones of voluntary memory. Whereas, on the contrary, each of the moments that composed it employed, for an original creation, in a unique harmony, the colours of that time which are now lost to us and which, for example, still suddenly enrapture me if by some chance the name "Guermantes," resuming for a moment after all these years the sound, so different from its sound today, which it had for me on the day of Mlle Percepied's marriage, brings back to me that mauve—so soft and smooth but almost too bright, too new—with which the billowy scarf of the young Duchess glowed, and, like two inaccessible, ever-flowering periwinkles, her eyes, sunlit with an azure smile. And the name Guermantes of those days is also like one of those little balloons which have been filled with oxygen or some other gas; when I come to prick it, to extract its contents from it, I breathe the air of the Combray of that year, of that day, mingled with a fragrance of hawthorn-blossom blown by the wind from the corner of the square, harbinger of rain, which now sent the sun packing, now let it spread itself over the red woollen carpet of the sacristy, clothing it in a bright geranium pink and in that, so to speak, Wagnerian sweetness and solemnity in joy that give such nobility to a festive occasion. But even apart from rare moments such as these, in which suddenly we feel the original entity quiver and resume its form, carve itself out of syllables now dead, if in the dizzy whirl of daily life, in which they serve only the most practical purpose, names have lost all their colour, like a prismatic top that spins too quickly and seems only grey, when, on the other hand, we reflect upon the past in our day-dreams and seek, in order to recapture it, to slacken, to suspend the perpetual motion by which we are borne along, gradually we see once more appear, side by side but entirely distinct from one another, the tints which in the course of our existence have been successively presented to us by a single name.

What shape was projected in my mind's eye by this name Guermantes when my wet-nurse—knowing no more, probably, than I know today in whose honour it had been composed—sang me to sleep with that old ditty, *Gloire à la Marquise de Guermantes*, or when, some years later, the veteran Maréchal de Guermantes, making my nursery-maid's bosom swell with pride, stopped in the Champs-Elysées to remark: "A fine child, that!" and gave me a chocolate drop from his pocket bonbonnière, I cannot, of course, now say. Those years of my earliest childhood are no longer a part of myself; they are external to me; I can learn nothing of them save—as we learn things that happened before we were born—from the accounts given me by other people. But more recently I find in the period of that name's occupation of me seven or eight different figures. The earliest were the most beautiful: gradually my day-dream, forced by reality to abandon a position that was no longer tenable, established itself anew in one slightly less advanced until it was obliged to retire still further. And, together with Mme de Guermantes, her dwelling was simultaneously transformed; itself also the offspring of that name, fertilised from year to year by some word or other that came to my ears and modified my reveries, that dwelling of hers mirrored them in its very stones, which had become reflectors, like the surface of a cloud or of a lake. A two-dimensional castle, no more indeed than a strip of orange light, from the summit of which the lord and his lady disposed of the lives and deaths of their vassals, had given place—right at the end of that "Guermantes way" along which, on so many summer afternoons, I followed with my parents the course of the Vivonne—to that land of bubbling streams where the Duchess taught me to fish for trout and to know the names of the flowers whose red and purple clusters adorned the walls of the neighbouring gardens; then it had been the ancient heritage, the poetic domain from which the proud race of Guermantes, like a mellow, crenellated tower that traverses the ages, had risen already over France, at a time when the sky was still empty at those points where later were to rise Notre-Dame of Paris and Notre-Dame of Chartres; a time when on the summit of the hill of Laon the nave of its cathedral had not yet been poised like the Ark of the Deluge on the summit of Mount Ararat, crowded with Patriarchs and Judges anxiously leaning from its windows to see whether the wrath of God has yet subsided, carrying with it specimens of the plants that will multiply on the earth, brimming over with animals which have even climbed out through the towers, between which oxen grazing calmly on the roof look down over the plains of Champagne; when the traveller who left Beauvais at the close of day did not yet see, following him and turning with his road, the black, ribbed wings of the cathedral spread out against the golden screen of the western sky. It was, this "Guermantes," like the setting of a novel, an imaginary landscape which I could with difficulty picture to myself and longed all the more to discover, set in the midst of real lands and roads which all of a sudden would become alive with heraldic details, within a few miles of a railway-station; I recalled the names of the places round it as if they had been situated at the foot of Parnassus or of Helicon, and they seemed precious to me as the physical conditions—in the realm of topographical science—required for the production of an unaccountable phenomenon. I saw again the escutcheons blazoned beneath the windows of Combray church; their quarters filled, century after century, with all the fiefs which, by marriage or conquest, this illustrious house had appropriated to itself from all the corners of Germany, Italy and France; vast territories in the North, powerful cities in the South, assembled there to group themselves in Guermantes, and, losing their material quality, to inscribe allegorically their sinople keep or castle triple-towered argent upon its azure field. I had heard of the famous tapestries of Guermantes, and could see them, mediaeval and blue, a trifle coarse, stand out like floating clouds against the legendary, amaranthine name at the edge of the ancient forest in which Childebert so often went hunting; and it seemed to me that, as effectively as by travelling to see them, I might penetrate the secrets of the mysterious reaches of these lands, these vistas of the centuries, simply by coming in contact for a moment in Paris with Mme de Guermantes, the princess paramount of the place and lady of the lake, as if her face and her speech must possess the local charm of forest groves and streams, and the same time-honoured characteristics as the old customs recorded in her archives. But then I had met Saint-Loup; he had told me that the castle had borne the name of Guermantes only since the seventeenth century, when his family had acquired it. They had lived, until then, in the neighbourhood, but their title did not come from those parts. The village of Guermantes had received its name from the manor round which it had been built, and so that it should not destroy the manorial view, a servitude that was still in force had traced the line of its streets and limited the height of its houses. As for the tapestries, they were by Boucher, bought in the nineteenth century by a Guermantes with a taste for the arts, and hung, interspersed with a number of mediocre sporting pictures which he himself had painted, in a hideous drawing-room upholstered in "adrianople" and plush. By these revelations, Saint-Loup had introduced into the castle elements foreign to the name of Guermantes which made it impossible for me to continue to extract solely from the resonance of the syllables the stone and mortar of its walls. Then in the depths of this name the castle mirrored in its lake had faded, and what now became apparent to me, surrounding Mme de Guermantes as her dwelling, had been her house in Paris, the Hôtel de Guermantes, limpid like its name, for no material and opaque element intervened to interrupt and occlude its transparency. As the word church signifies not only the temple but also the assembly of the faithful, this Hôtel de Guermantes comprised all those who shared the life of the Duchess, but these intimates on whom I had never set eyes were for me only famous and poetic names, and, knowing exclusively persons who themselves too were only names, served to enhance and protect the mystery of the Duchess by extending all round her a vast halo which at the most declined in brilliance as its circumference increased.

In the entertainments which she gave, since I could not imagine the guests as possessing bodies, moustaches, boots, as making any utterance that was commonplace, or even original in a human and rational way, this vortex of names, introducing less material substance than would a phantom banquet or a spectral ball, round that statuette in Dresden china which was Mme de Guermantes, gave her mansion of glass the transparency of a showcase. Then, after Saint-Loup had told me various anecdotes about his cousin's chaplain, her gardeners and the rest, the Hôtel de Guermantes had become—as the Louvre might have been in days gone by—a kind of palace surrounded, in the very heart of Paris, by its own domains, acquired by inheritance, by virtue of an ancient right that had quaintly survived, over which she still enjoyed feudal privileges. But this last dwelling had itself vanished when we came to live near Mme de Villeparisis in one of the apartments adjoining that occupied by Mme de Guermantes in a wing of the Hôtel. It was one of those old town houses, a few of which for all I know may still be found, in which the main courtyard was flanked— alluvial deposits washed there by the rising tide of democracy, perhaps, or a legacy from a more primitive time when the different trades were clustered round the overlord—by little shops and workrooms, a shoemaker's, for instance, or a tailor's, such as we see nestling between the buttresses of those cathedrals which the aesthetic zeal of the restorer has not swept clear of such accretions, and a porter who also did cobbling, kept hens, grew flowers—and, at the far end, in the main house, a "Countess" who, when she drove out in her old carriage and pair, flaunting on her hat a few nasturtiums which seemed to have escaped from the plot by the lodge (with, by the coachman's side on the box, a footman who got down to leave cards at every aristocratic mansion in the neighbourhood), dispensed smiles and little waves of the hand impartially to the porter's children and to any bourgeois tenants who might happen to be passing and whom, in her disdainful affability and her egalitarian arrogance, she found indistinguishable from one another.

In the house in which we had now come to live, the great lady at the end of the courtyard was a Duchess, elegant and still young. She was, in fact, Mme de Guermantes and, thanks to Françoise,

I soon came to know all about her household. For the Guermantes (to whom Françoise regularly alluded as the people "below," or "downstairs") were her constant preoccupation from the first thing in the morning when, as she did Mamma's hair, casting a forbidden, irresistible, furtive glance down into the courtyard, she would say: "Look at that, now, a pair of holy Sisters: they'll be for downstairs, surely"; or, "Oh! just look at the fine pheasants in the kitchen window. No need to ask where they've become from: the Duke's been out with his gun!"—until the last thing at night when, if her ear, while she was putting out my night-things, caught the sound of a piano or a few notes of a song, she would conclude: "They're having company down below; gay goings-on"; whereupon, in her symmetrical face, beneath her snow-white hair, a smile from her young days, sprightly but proper, would for a moment set each of her features in its place, arranging them in a prim and prepared order, as though for a quadrille.

But the moment in the life of the Guermantes which excited the keenest interest in Françoise, gave her the most complete satisfaction and at the same time the sharpest annoyance, was that at which, the carriage gates having been flung open, the Duchess stepped into her barouche. It was generally a little while after our servants had finished celebrating that sort of solemn passover which none might disturb, called their midday dinner, during which they were so far "taboo" that my father himself would not have taken the liberty of ringing for them, knowing moreover that none of them would have paid any more attention to the fifth peal than to the first, and that he would thus have committed this impropriety to no purpose, though not without detriment to himself. For Françoise (who, in her old age, lost no opportunity of standing upon her dignity) would not have failed to present him, for the rest of the day, with a face covered with the tiny red cuneiform hieroglyphs by which she made visible—though by no means legible—to the outer world the long tale of her grievances and the underlying causes of her displeasure. She would enlarge upon them, too, in a running "aside," but not so that we could catch her words. She called this practice—which, she imagined, must be shattering for us, "mortifying," "vexing," as she put it—saying "low masses" to us the whole blessed day.

The last rites accomplished, Françoise, who was at one and the same time, as in the primitive church, the celebrant and one of the faithful, helped herself to a final glass, undid the napkin from her throat, folded it after wiping from her lips the vestiges of watered wine and coffee, slipped it into its ring, turned a doleful eye to thank "her" young footman who, to show his zeal in her service, was saying: "Come, ma'am, a few more grapes—they're d'li-cious," and went straight across to the window, which she flung open, protesting that it was too hot to breathe in "this wretched kitchen." Dexterously casting, as she turned the latch and let in the fresh air, a glance of studied indifference into the courtyard below, she furtively ascertained that the Duchess was not yet ready to start, gazed for a moment with scornful and impassioned eyes at the waiting carriage, and, this meed of attention once paid to the things of the earth, raised them towards the heavens, whose purity she had already divined from the sweetness of the air and the warmth of the sun; and let them rest on a corner of the roof, at the place where, every spring, there came to nest, immediately over the chimney of my bedroom, a pair of pigeons like those she used to hear cooing from her kitchen at Combray.

"Ah! Combray, Combray!" she cried. And the almost singing tone in which she declaimed this invocation might, taken with the Arlesian purity of her features, have prompted a stranger to sur-mise that she was of Southern origin and that the lost homeland she was lamenting was no more than a land of adoption. If so, he would have been wrong, for it seems that there is no province that has not its own South-country; do we not indeed constantly meet Savoyards and Bretons in whose speech we find all those pleasing transpositions of longs and shorts that are characteristic of the Southerner? "Ah, Combray, when will I see you again, poor old place? When will I spend the whole blessed day among your hawthorns, under our own poor lilac-trees, hearing the finches sing and the Vivonne making a little noise like someone whisper-ing, instead of that wretched bell from our young master, who can never stay still for half an hour on end without having me run the length of that confounded corridor. And even then he makes out I don't come quick enough; you'd need to hear the bell before he rung it, and if you're a minute late, he flies into the most horrible rage. Ah, poor Combray! maybe I'll only see you when I'm dead, when they drop me like a stone into a hole in the ground. And so, nevermore will I smell your lovely hawthorns, so white. But in the sleep of death I dare say I shall still hear those three peals of the bell which will already have driven me to damnation in this world."

Her soliloquy was interrupted by the voice of the waistcoat-maker in the courtyard below, the same who had so pleased my grandmother once, long ago, when she had gone to pay a call on Mme de Villeparisis, and now occupied no less high a place in Françoise's affections. Having raised his head when he heard our window open, he had already been trying for some time to attract his neighbour's attention, in order to bid her good day. The coquetry of the young girl that Françoise had once been softened and refined for M. Jupien the querulous face of our old cook, dulled by age, ill-temper and the heat of the kitchen stove, and it was with a charming blend of reserve, familiarity and modesty that she bestowed a gracious salutation on the waistcoat-maker, but without making any audible response, for if she infringed Mamma's injunctions by looking into the courtyard, she would never have dared to go the length of talking from the window, which would have been quite enough (according to her) to bring down on her "a whole chapter" from the Mistress. She pointed to the waiting carriage, as who should say: "A fine pair, eh!" though what she actually muttered was: "What an old rattletrap!"—but principally because she knew that he would be bound to answer, putting his hand to his lips so as to be audible without having to shout: "*You* could have one too if you liked, as good as they have and better, I dare say, only you don't care for that sort of thing."

And Françoise, after a modest, evasive and delighted signal, the meaning of which was, more or less: "Tastes differ, you know; simplicity's the rule in this house," shut the window again in case Mamma should come in. The "you" who might have had more horses than the Guermantes were ourselves, but Jupien was right in saying "you" since, except for a few purely personal self-gratifications (such as, when she coughed all day long without ceasing and everyone in the house was afraid of catching her cold, that of insisting, with an irritating little titter, that she had not got a cold), Françoise, like those plants that an animal to which they are wholly attached keeps alive with food which it catches, eats and digests for them and of which it offers them the ultimate and easily assimilable residue, lived with us in a symbiotic relationship; it was we who, with our virtues, our wealth, our style of living, must take on ourselves the task of concocting those little sops to her vanity out of which was formed—with the addition of the recognised right to practise freely the cult of the midday dinner according to the traditional custom, which included a gulp of air at the

window when the meal was finished, a certain amount of loitering
in the street when she went out to do her marketing, and a holiday
on Sundays when she paid a visit to her niece—the portion of
contentment indispensable to her existence. So it can be understood why Françoise pined in those first days of our migration, a
prey—in a house where my father's claims to distinction were not
yet known—to a malady which she herself called "ennui," ennui
in the strong sense in which the word is employed by Corneille,
or in the letters of soldiers who end by taking their own lives
because they are pining after[7] their sweethearts or their native
villages. Françoise's ennui had soon been cured by none other
than Jupien, for he at once procured her a pleasure no less keen and
more refined than she would have felt if we had decided to keep a
carriage. "Very good class, those Juliens" (for Françoise readily
assimilated new names to those with which she was already familiar), "very decent people; you can see it written on their faces."
Jupien was indeed able to understand, and to inform the world,
that if we did not keep a carriage it was because we had no wish
to do so.

This new friend of Françoise's was seldom at home, having
obtained a post in a Government office. A waistcoat-maker first of
all, with the "chit of a girl" whom my grandmother had taken for
his daughter, he had lost all interest in the exercise of that calling
after the girl (who, when still little more than a child, had shown
great skill in darning a torn skirt, that day when my grandmother
had gone to call on Mme de Villeparisis) had turned to ladies'
fashions and become a skirt-maker. A prentice hand, to begin
with, in a dressmaker's workroom, employed to stitch a seam, to
sew up a flounce, to fasten a button or a press-stud, to fix a
waistband with hooks and eyes, she had quickly risen to be second
and then chief assistant, and having formed a clientele of her own
among ladies of fashion, now worked at home, that is to say in our
courtyard, generally with one or two of her young friends from
the workroom, whom she had taken on as apprentices. After this,
Jupien's presence had become less essential. No doubt the little girl
(a big girl by this time) had often to cut out waistcoats still. But
with her friends to assist her she needed no one besides. And so
Jupien, her uncle, had sought employment outside. He was free at
first to return home at midday; then, when he had definitely
succeeded the man whose assistant only he had begun by being,
not before dinner-time. His appointment to the "regular

establishment" was, fortunately, not announced until some weeks after our arrival, so that his amiability could be brought to bear on Françoise long enough to help her through the first, most difficult phase without undue pain. At the same time, and without under-rating his value to Françoise as, so to speak, an interim sedative, I am bound to say that my first impression of Jupien had been far from favourable. From a few feet away, entirely destroying the effect that his plump cheeks and florid complexion would other-wise have produced, his eyes, brimming with a compassionate, mournful, dreamy gaze, led one to suppose that he was seriously ill or had just suffered a great bereavement. Not only was this not so, but as soon as he spoke (quite perfectly as it happened) he was inclined rather to be cold and mocking. There resulted from this discord between his look and his speech a certain falsity which was not attractive, and by which he himself had the air of being made as uncomfortable as a guest who arrives in day clothes at a party where everyone else is in evening dress, or as someone who, having to speak to a royal personage, does not know exactly how he ought to address him and gets round the difficulty by cutting down his remarks to almost nothing. Jupien's (here the comparison ends) were, on the contrary, charming. Indeed, cor-responding perhaps to that inundation of the face by the eyes (which one ceased to notice when one came to know him), I soon discerned in him a rare intelligence, one of the most spon-taneously literary that it has been my privilege to come across, in the sense that, probably without education, he possessed or had assimilated, with the help only of a few books hastily perused, the most ingenious turns of speech. The most gifted people that I had known had died young. And so I was convinced that Jupien's life would soon be cut short. He was kind and sympathetic, and had the most delicate and the most generous feelings.

His role in Françoise's life had soon ceased to be indispensable. She had learned to stand in for him. Even when a tradesman or servant came to our door with a parcel or message, while seeming to pay no attention to him and merely pointing vaguely to an empty chair, Françoise so skilfully put to the best advantage the few moments that he spent in the kitchen while he waited for Mamma's answer, that it was very seldom that he went away without having ineradicably engraved in his mind the conviction that, if we "did not have" any particular thing, it was because we had "no wish" for it. If she made such a point of other people's knowing that we "had money"[8] (for she knew nothing of what Saint-Loup used to call partitive articles, and said simply "have money," "fetch water"), of their knowing us to be rich, it was not because wealth with nothing else besides, wealth without virtue, was in her eyes the supreme good; but virtue without wealth was not her ideal either. Wealth was for her, so to speak, a necessary condition failing which virtue would lack both merit and charm. She distinguished so little between them that she had come in time to invest each with the other's attributes, to expect some material comfort from virtue, to discover something edifying in wealth.

As soon as she had shut the window again, fairly quickly—otherwise Mamma would, it appeared, have heaped on her "every imaginable insult"—Françoise began with many groans and sighs to put the kitchen table straight.

"There's some Guermantes who stay in the Rue de la Chaise," began my father's valet. "I had a friend used to work there; he was their second coachman. And I know a fellow, not my old pal but his brother-in-law, who did his time in the Army with one of the Baron de Guermantes's grooms. 'And after all, he ain't my father,'"[9] added the valet, who was in the habit, just as he used to hum the popular airs of the season, of peppering his conversation with all the latest witticisms.

Françoise, with the tired eyes of an ageing woman, eyes which moreover saw everything from Combray, in a hazy distance, perceived, not the witticism that underlay these words, but the fact that there must be something witty in them since they bore no relation to the rest of the observation and had been uttered with considerable emphasis by one whom she knew to be a joker. She therefore smiled with an air of dazzled benevolence, as who should say: "Always the same, that Victor!" And she was genuinely pleased, knowing that listening to smart sayings of this sort was akin—if remotely—to those reputable social pleasures for which, in every class of society, people make haste to dress themselves in their best and run the risk of catching cold. Furthermore, she believed the valet to be a friend after her own heart, for he never ceased to denounce with fierce indignation the appalling measures which the Republic was about to enforce against the clergy. Françoise had not yet learned that our cruellest adversaries are not those who contradict and try to convince us, but those who magnify or invent reports which are liable to distress us, taking care not to give them any appearance of justification which might lessen our pain and perhaps give us some slight regard for an attitude which they make a point of displaying to us, to complete our torment, as being at once terrible and triumphant.

"The Duchess must be allianced with all that lot," said Françoise, taking up the conversation again at the Guermantes of the Rue de la Chaise, as one resumes a piece of music at the andante. "I can't recall who it was told me one of them married a cousin of the Duke. It's the same kindred, anyway. Ay, they're a great family, the Guermantes!" she added, in a tone of respect, founding the greatness of the family at once on the number of its branches and the brilliance of its connexions, as Pascal founds the truth of Religion on Reason and on the authority of the Scriptures. For since she had only the single word "great" to express both meanings, it seemed to her that they formed a single idea, her vocabulary, like certain cut stones, showing thus on certain of its facets a flaw which projected a ray of darkness into the recesses of her mind.

"I wonder now if it wouldn't be them that have their castle at Guermantes, not a score of miles from Combray; then they must be kin to their cousin in Algiers, too." (My mother and I had wondered for a long time who this cousin in Algiers could be until finally we discovered that Françoise meant by the name "Algiers" the town of Angers. What is far off may be more familiar to us than what is quite near. Françoise, who knew the name "Algiers" from some particularly unpleasant dates that used to be given us at the New Year, had never heard of Angers. Her language, like the French language itself, and especially its toponymy, was thickly strewn with errors.) "I meant to talk to their butler about it . . . What is it now they call him?" She broke off as though putting to herself a question of protocol, which she went on to answer with: "Oh, of course, it's Antoine they call him!" as though Antoine had been a title. "He's the one could tell me, but he's quite the gentleman, he is, a great pedant, you'd think they'd cut his tongue out, or that he'd forgotten to learn to speak. He makes no reply when you talk to him," went on Françoise, who said "make reply" like Mme de Sévigné. "But," she added, quite untruthfully, "so long as I know what's boiling in my pot I don't bother my head about what's in other people's. In any case it's not Catholic. And what's more, he's not a courageous man." (This criticism might have led one to suppose that Françoise had changed her mind about physical bravery which according to her, in Combray days, lowered men to the level of wild beasts. But it was not so. "Courageous" meant simply hard-working.) "They do say, too, that he's thievish as a magpie, but it doesn't do to believe all you hear. The staff never stay long there because of the lodge; the porters are jealous and set the Duchess against them. But it's safe to say that he's a real idler, that Antoine, and his Antoinesse is no better," concluded Françoise, who, in furnishing the name "Antoine" with a feminine suffix that would designate the butler's wife, was inspired, no doubt, in her act of word-formation by an unconscious memory of the words *chanoine* and *chanoinesse*. If so, she was not far wrong. There is still a street near Notre-Dame called Rue Chanoinesse, a name which must have been given to it (since it was inhabited only by canons) by those Frenchmen of olden days of whom Françoise was in reality the contemporary. She proceeded, moreover, at once to furnish another example of this way of forming feminines, for she added: "But one thing sure and certain is that it's the Duchess that has Guermantes Castle. And it's she that is the Lady Mayoress down in those parts. That's something."

"I should think it *is* something," said the footman with conviction, having failed to detect the irony.

"You think so, do you, my boy, you think it's something? Why, for folk like them to be Mayor and Mayoress, it's just thank you for nothing. Ah, if it was mine, that Guermantes Castle, you wouldn't see me setting foot in Paris, I can tell you. I'm sure a family who've got something to go on with, like Monsieur and Madame here, must have queer ideas to stay on in this wretched town sooner than get away down to Combray the moment they're free to start, and no one hindering them. Why do they put off retiring when they've got everything they want? Why wait till they're dead? Ah, if only I had a crust of dry bread to eat and a faggot to keep me warm in winter, I'd have been back home long since in my brother's poor old house at Combray. Down there at least you feel you're alive; you don't have all these houses stuck up in front of you, and there's so little noise at night-time you can hear the frogs singing five miles off and more."

"That must be really nice, Madame," exclaimed the young footman with enthusiasm, as though this last attraction had been as peculiar to Combray as the gondola is to Venice. A more recent arrival in the household than my father's valet, he used to talk to Françoise about things which might interest not himself so much as her. And Françoise, whose face wrinkled up in disgust when she was treated as a mere cook, had for the young footman, who referred to her always as the "housekeeper," that peculiar tenderness which certain princes of the second rank feel towards the well-intentioned young men who dignify them with a "Highness."

"At any rate you know what you're about there, and what time of year it is. It isn't like here where you won't find one wretched buttercup flowering at holy Easter any more than you would at Christmas, and I can't hear so much as the tiniest angelus ring when I lift my old bones out of bed in the morning. Down there, you can hear every hour. It's only a poor old bell, but you say to yourself: 'My brother will be coming in from the fields now,' and you watch the daylight fade, and the bell rings to bless the fruits of the earth, and you have time to take a turn before you light the lamp. But here it's day-time and it's night-time, and you go to bed, and you can't say any more than the dumb beasts what you've been about."

"They say Méséglise is a fine place, too, Madame," broke in the young footman, who found that the conversation was becoming a little too abstract for his liking, and happened to remember having heard us, at table, mention Méséglise.

"Oh! Méséglise, is it?" said Françoise with the broad smile which one could always bring to her lips by uttering any of those names—Méséglise, Combray, Tansonville. They were so intimate a part of her life that she felt, on meeting them outside it, on hearing them used in conversation, a hilarity more or less akin to that which a teacher excites in his class by making an allusion to some contemporary personage whose name the pupils had never supposed could possibly greet their ears from the height of the academic rostrum. Her pleasure arose also from the feeling that these places meant something to her which they did not to the rest of the world, old companions with whom one has shared many an outing; and she smiled at them as if she found in them something witty, because there was in them a great part of herself.

"Yes, you may well say so, son, it's a pretty enough place is Méséglise," she went on with a tinkling laugh, "but how did you ever come to hear tell of Méséglise?"

"How did I hear of Méséglise? But it's a well-known place. People have told me about it oftentimes," he assured her with that criminal inexactitude of the informant who, whenever we attempt to form an impartial estimate of the importance that a thing which matters to us may have for other people, makes it impossible for us to do so.

"Ah! I can tell you it's better down there under the cherry-trees than standing in front of the kitchen stove all day."

She spoke to them even of Eulalie as a good person. For since Eulalie's death Françoise had completely forgotten that she had loved her as little in her lifetime as she loved anyone whose cupboard was bare, who was "perishing poor" and then came, like a good for nothing, thanks to the bounty of the rich, to "put on airs." It no longer pained her that Eulalie had so skilfully managed, Sunday after Sunday, to secure her "tip" from my aunt. As for the latter, Françoise never ceased to sing her praises.

"So it was at Combray itself that you used to be, with a cousin of Madame?" asked the young footman.

"Yes, with Mme Octave—ah, a real saintly woman, I can tell you, and a house where there was always more than enough, and all of the very best—a good woman, and no mistake, who didn't spare the partridges, or the pheasants, or anything. You might turn up five to dinner or six, it was never the meat that was lacking, and of the first quality too, and white wine, and red wine, and everything you could wish." (Françoise used the word "spare" in the same sense as La Bruyère.)[10] "It was she that always paid the damages, even if the family stayed for months and years." (This reflexion was not really meant as a slur upon us, for Françoise belonged to an epoch when the word "damages" was not restricted to a legal use and meant simply expense.) "Ah, I can tell you people didn't go away empty from that house. As his reverence the Curé impressed on us many's the time, if there ever was a woman who could count on going straight before the Throne of God, it was her. Poor Madame, I can still hear her saying, in that faint little voice of hers: 'You know, Françoise, I can eat nothing myself, but I want it all to be just as nice for the others as if I could.' They weren't for her, the victuals, you may be quite sure. If you'd only seen her, she weighed no more than a bag of cherries; there wasn't that much of her. She would never listen to a word I said, she'd never send for the doctor. Ah, it wasn't in that house that you'd have to gobble down your dinner. She liked her servants to be fed properly. Here, it's been just the same again today; we've hardly had time for a snack. Everything has to be done on the run."

What exasperated her more than anything were the slices of thin toast that my father used to eat. She was convinced that he indulged in them simply to give himself airs and to keep her "dancing." "I can tell you frankly," the young footman assured her, "that I never saw the like." He said this as if he had seen everything, and as if for him the range of an inexhaustible experience extended over all countries and their customs, among which was nowhere to be found the custom of eating slices of toast. "Yes, yes," the butler muttered, "but that may all be changed; the workers are going on strike in Canada, and the Minister told Monsieur the other evening that he's clearing two hundred thousand francs out of it." There was no note of censure in his tone, not that he was not himself entirely honest, but since he regarded all politicians as shady, the crime of peculation seemed to him less serious than the pettiest larceny. He did not even stop to ask himself whether he had heard this historic utterance aright, and seemed not to have been struck by the improbability that such a thing should have been said by the guilty party himself to my father without my father's immediately turning him out of the house. But the philosophy of Combray made it impossible for Françoise to expect that the strikes in Canada could have any repercussion on the consumption of toast. "Ah, well, as long as the world goes round, there'll be masters to keep us on the trot, and servants to do their bidding." In disproof of this theory of perpetual trotting, for the last quarter of an hour my mother (who probably did not employ the same measures of time as Françoise in reckoning the duration of the latter's dinner) had been saying: "What on earth can they be doing? They've been at table for at least two hours." And she rang timidly three or four times. Françoise, "her" footman and the butler heard the bell ring, not as a summons to themselves, and with no thought of answering it, but rather as the first sounds of the instruments being tuned when the next part of a concert will soon begin, and one knows that there will be only a few minutes more of interval. And so, when the peals were repeated and became more urgent, our servants began to pay attention, and, judging that they had not much time left and that the resumption of work was at hand, at a peal somewhat louder than the rest gave a collective sigh and went their several ways, the footman slipping downstairs to smoke a cigarette outside the door, Françoise, after a string of reflexions on ourselves, such as: "They've got the jumps today all right," going up to tidy her attic, while the butler, having supplied himself first with notepaper from my bedroom, polished off the arrears of his private correspondence.

Despite the arrogant air of their butler, Françoise had been in a position, from the first, to inform me that the Guermantes occupied their mansion by virtue not of an immemorial right but of a quite recent tenancy, and that the garden over which it looked on the side that I did not know was quite small and just like all the neighbouring gardens, and I realised at last that there were not to be seen there pit and gallows or fortified mill, secret chamber, pillared dovecot, manorial bakehouse, tithe-barn or fortress, drawbridge or fixed bridge or even flying or toll bridge, charters, muniments, ramparts or commemorative mounds. But just as Elstir, when the bay of Balbec, losing its mystery, had become for me simply a portion, interchangeable with any other, of the total quantity of salt water distributed over the earth's surface, had suddenly restored to it a personality of its own by telling me that it was the gulf of opal painted by Whistler in his *Harmonies in Blue and Silver*, so the name Guermantes had seen the last of the dwellings that had issued from its syllables perish under Françoise's blows, when one day an old friend of my father said to us, speaking of the Duchess: "She has the highest position in the Faubourg Saint-Germain; hers is the leading house in the Faubourg Saint-Germain." No doubt the most exclusive drawing-room, the leading house in the Faubourg Saint-Germain was little or nothing after all those other mansions of which in turn I had dreamed. And yet this one too (and it was to be the last of the series), however humble it was, possessed something, quite apart from its material components, that amounted to an obscure differentiation.

And it became all the more essential that I should be able to explore in the "salon" of Mme de Guermantes, among her friends, the mystery of her name, since I did not find it in her person when I saw her leave the house in the morning on foot, or in the afternoon in her carriage. Once before, indeed, in the church at Combray, she had appeared to me in the blinding flash of a transfiguration, with cheeks that were irreducible to, impervious to the colour of the name Guermantes and of afternoons on the banks of the Vivonne, taking the place of my shattered dream, like a swan or a willow into which a god or nymph has been changed, and which henceforward, subjected to natural laws, will glide over the water or be shaken by the wind. And yet scarcely had I left her presence than those glittering fragments had reassembled like the green and roseate reflexions of the sunset behind the oar that has broken them, and in the solitude of my thoughts the name had quickly appropriated to itself my impression of the face. But now, frequently, I saw her at her window, in the courtyard, in the street, and for myself at least, if I did not succeed in integrating into the living woman the name Guermantes, in thinking of her as Mme de Guermantes, I could cast the blame on the impotence of my mind to carry through the act that I demanded of it; but she herself, our neighbour, seemed to commit the same error, commit it without discomfiture moreover, without any of my scruples, without even suspecting that it was an error. Thus Mme de Guermantes showed in her dresses the same anxiety to follow the fashion as if, believing herself to have become a woman like any other, she had aspired to that elegance in her attire in which ordinary women might equal and perhaps surpass her; I had seen her in the street gaze admiringly at a well-dressed actress; and in the morning, before she sallied forth on foot, as if the opinion of the passers-by, whose vulgarity she accentuated by parading familiarly through their midst her inaccessible life, could be a tribunal competent to judge her, I would see her in front of the glass playing, with a conviction free from all pretence or irony, with passion, with ill-humour, with conceit, like a queen who has consented to appear as a servant-girl in theatricals at court, the role, so unworthy of her, of a fashionable woman; and in this mythological obliviousness of her native grandeur, she checked whether her veil was hanging properly, smoothed her cuffs, adjusted her cloak, as the divine swan performs all the movements natural to his animal species, keeps his eyes painted on either side of his beak without putting into them any glint of life, and darts suddenly after a button or an umbrella, as a swan would, without remembering that he is a god. But as the traveller, disappointed by his first impression of a strange town, tells himself that he will doubtless succeed in penetrating its charm if he visits its museums and galleries, strikes up an acquaintance with its people, works in its libraries, so I assured myself that, had I been given the right of entry into Mme de Guermantes's house, were I one of her friends, were I to penetrate into her life, I should then know what, within its glowing amber envelope, her name enclosed in reality, objectively, for other people, since, after all, my father's friend had said that the Guermantes set was in a class of its own in the Faubourg Saint-Germain.

The life which I supposed them to lead there flowed from a source so different from anything in my experience, and must, I felt, be so out of the ordinary, that I could not have imagined the presence at the Duchess's parties of people in whose company I myself had already been, of people who really existed. For, not being able suddenly to change their nature, they would have carried on conversations there of the sort that I knew; their partners would perhaps have stooped to reply to them in the same human speech; and, in the course of an evening spent in the leading house in the Faubourg Saint-Germain, there would have been moments identical with moments that I had already lived. Which was impossible. It is true that my mind was perplexed by certain difficulties, and the presence of the body of Jesus Christ in the host seemed to me no more obscure a mystery than this leading house in the Faubourg being situated on the right bank of the river and so near that from my bedroom in the morning I could hear its carpets being beaten. But the line of demarcation that separated me from the Faubourg Saint-Germain seemed to me all the more real because it was purely ideal; I sensed that it was already part of the Faubourg when I saw, spread out on the other side of that Equator, the Guermantes door-mat of which my mother had ventured to say, having like myself caught a glimpse of it one day when their door stood open, that it was in a shocking state. Besides, how could their dining-room, their dim gallery upholstered in red plush, into which I could see sometimes from our kitchen window, have failed to possess in my eyes the mysterious charm of the Faubourg Saint-Germain, to form an essential part of it, to be geographically situated within it, since to have been entertained to dinner in that dining-room was to have gone into the Faubourg Saint-Germain, to have breathed its atmosphere, since the people who, before going to table, sat down beside Mme de Guermantes on the leather-covered sofa in that gallery were all of the Faubourg Saint-Germain? No doubt elsewhere than in the Faubourg, at certain parties, one might see now and then, majestically enthroned amid the vulgar herd of fashion, one of those men who are no more than names and who alternately assume, when one tries to picture them to oneself, the aspect of a tourney or of a royal forest. But here, in the leading salon in the Faubourg Saint-Germain, in the dim gallery, there was no one but them. They were the columns, wrought of precious materials, that upheld the temple. Even for small and intimate gatherings it was from among them only that Mme de Guermantes could choose her guests, and in the dinners for twelve, assembled around the dazzling napery and plate, they were like the golden statues of the apostles in the Saint-Chapelle, symbolic, dedicative pillars before the Lord's Table. As for the tiny strip of garden that stretched between high walls at the back of the house, where in summer Mme de Guermantes had liqueurs and orangeade brought out after dinner, how could I not have felt that to sit there of an evening, between nine and eleven, on its iron chairs—endowed with a magic as potent as the leather sofa—without inhaling at the same time the breezes peculiar to the Faubourg Saint-Germain, was as impossible as to take a siesta in the oasis of Figuig without thereby being necessarily in Africa? Only imagination and belief can differentiate from the rest certain objects, certain people, and create an atmosphere. Alas, those picturesque sites, those natural features, those local curiosities, those works of art of the Faubourg Saint-Germain, doubtless I should never be permitted to set my feet among them. And I must content myself with a shiver of excitement as I sighted from the open sea (and without the least hope of ever landing there), like a prominent minaret, like the first palm, like the first signs of some exotic industry or vegetation, the well-trodden door-mat of its shore.

But if the Hôtel de Guermantes began for me at its hall-door, its dependencies must be regarded as extending a long way further, in the estimation of the Duke, who, looking on all the tenants as peasants, yokels, appropriators of national assets, whose opinion was of no account, shaved himself every morning in his nightshirt at the window, came down into the courtyard, according to the warmth or coldness of the day, in his shirt-sleeves, in pyjamas, in a plaid jacket of startling colours with a shaggy nap, in little light-coloured topcoats shorter than his jacket, and made one of his grooms lead past him at a trot some horse that he had just bought. More than once, indeed, the horse damaged Jupien's shop-front, whereupon Jupien, to the Duke's indignation, demanded compensation. "If it were only in consideration of all the good that Madame la Duchesse does in the house here and in the parish," said M. de Guermantes, "it's an outrage on this fellow's part to claim a sou from us." But Jupien had stuck to his guns, apparently not having the faintest idea what "good" the Duchess had ever done. And yet she did do good, but—since one cannot do good to everybody at once—the memory of the benefits that we have heaped on one person is a valid reason for our abstaining from helping another, whose discontent we thereby arouse the more. From other points of view than that of philanthropy, the quarter appeared to the Duke—and this over a considerable area—to be merely an extension of his courtyard, a longer track for his horses. After seeing how a new acquisition trotted by itself he would have it harnessed and taken through all the neighbouring streets, the groom running beside the carriage holding the reins, making it pass to and fro before the Duke who stood on the pavement, erect, gigantic, enormous in his vivid clothes, a cigar between his teeth, his head in the air, his eyeglass quizzical, until the moment when he sprang on to the box, drove the horse up and down for a little to try it, then set off with his new turn-out to pick up his mistress in the Champs-Elysées. M. de Guermantes would bid good day in the courtyard to two couples who belonged more or less to his world: the first, some cousins of his who, like working-class parents, were never at home to look after their children, since every morning the wife went off to the Schola Cantorum to study counterpoint and fugue, and the husband to his studio to carve wood and tool leather; and then the Baron and Baronne de Norpois, always dressed in black, she like a pew-opener and he like an undertaker, who emerged several times daily on their way to church. They were the nephew and niece of the old Ambassador whom we knew, and whom my father had in fact met at the foot of the staircase without realising where he was coming from; for my father supposed that so considerable a personage, one who had come in contact with the most eminent men in Europe and was probably quite indifferent to the empty distinctions of social rank, was hardly likely to frequent the society of these obscure, clerical and narrow-minded nobles. They had not been long in the place; Jupien, who had come out into the courtyard to say a word to the husband just as he was greeting M. de Guermantes, called him "M. Norpois," not being certain of his name.

"Monsieur Norpois, indeed! Oh, that really is good! Just wait a little! This individual will be calling you Citizen Norpois next!" exclaimed M. de Guermantes, turning to the Baron. He was at last able to vent his spleen against Jupien who addressed him as "Monsieur" instead of "Monsieur le Duc."

One day when M. de Guermantes required some information upon a matter of which my father had professional knowledge, he had introduced himself to him with great courtesy. After that, he had often some neighbourly service to ask of my father and, as soon as he saw him coming downstairs, his mind occupied with his work and anxious to avoid any interruption, the Duke, leaving his stable-boys, would come up to him in the courtyard, straighten the collar of his greatcoat with the obliging deftness inherited from a line of royal body-servants, take him by the hand, and, holding it in his own, stroking it even, to prove to him, with the shameless-ness of a courtesan, that he did not begrudge him the privilege of contact with the ducal flesh, would steer him, extremely irked and thinking only how he might escape, through the carriage entrance out into the street. He had given us a sweeping bow one day when he had passed us as he was setting out in the carriage with his wife; he was bound to have told her my name, but what likelihood was there of her remembering it, or my face either? And besides, what a feeble recommendation to be pointed out simply as being one of her tenants! Another, more valuable, would have been to meet the Duchess at the house of Mme de Villeparisis, who, as it happened, had sent word by my grandmother that I was to go and see her, and, remembering that I had been intending to go in for literature, had added that I should meet several authors there. But my father felt that I was still a little young to go into society, and as the state of my health continued to cause him disquiet he was reluctant to allow me unnecessary occasions for renewed outings.

As one of Mme de Guermantes's footmen was in the habit of gossiping with Françoise, I picked up the names of several of the houses which she frequented, but formed no impression of any of them: the moment they were a part of her life, of that life which I saw only through the veil of her name, were they not incon-ceivable?

"Tonight there's a big party with a shadow-theatre show at the Princesse de Parme's," said the footman, "but we shan't be going, because at five o'clock Madame is taking the train to Chantilly, to spend a few days with the Duc d'Aumale; but it'll be the lady's-maid and valet that go with her. I'm to stay here. She won't be at all pleased, the Princesse de Parme won't, that's four times already she's written to Madame la Duchesse."

"Then you won't be going down to Guermantes Castle this year?"

"It's the first time we shan't be going there: it's because of Monsieur le Duc's rheumatics, the doctor says he's not to go there till the radiators are in, but we've been there every year till now, right on to January. If the radiators aren't ready, perhaps Madame will go for a few days to Cannes to the Duchesse de Guise, but nothing's settled yet."

"And do you ever go to the theatre?"

"We go now and then to the Opéra, usually on the evenings when the Princesse de Parme has her box, that's once a week. It seems it's a fine show they give there, plays, operas, everything. Madame refused to rent a box herself, but we go all the same to the boxes Madame's friends take, now one, now another, often the Princesse de Guermantes, the Duke's cousin's lady. She's sister to the Duke of Bavaria . . . And so you've got to run upstairs again now, have you?" went on the footman, who, though identified with the Guermantes, looked upon "masters" in general as a political estate, a view which allowed him to treat Françoise with as much respect as if she too were in service with a duchess. "You enjoy good health, ma'am."

"Oh, if it wasn't for these cursed legs of mine! On the plain I can still get along" ("on the plain" meant in the courtyard or in the streets, where Françoise was not averse from walking, in other words on flat ground), "but it's these confounded stairs. Good day to you. Perhaps we'll meet again this evening."

She was all the more anxious to continue her conversations with the footman after learning from him that the sons of dukes often bore a princely title which they retained until their fathers were dead. Evidently the cult of the nobility, blended with and accommodating itself to a certain spirit of revolt against it, must, springing hereditarily from the soil of France, be very strongly implanted still in her people. For Françoise, to whom you might speak of the genius of Napoleon or of wireless telegraphy without succeeding in attracting her attention, and without her pausing for a moment in the job she was doing, whether clearing the grate or laying the table, if she learnt of these peculiarities and that the younger son of the Duc de Guermantes was generally called the Prince d'Oléron, would exclaim: "Now isn't that nice!" and stand there bemused, as though in front of a stained-glass window.

Françoise learned also from the Prince d'Agrigente's valet, who had become friends with her by often calling round with notes for the Duchess, that he had been hearing a great deal of talk in society about the marriage of the Marquis de Saint-Loup to Mlle d'Ambresac, and that it was practically settled.

That villa, that opera-box, into which Mme de Guermantes transfused the current of her life, must, it seemed to me, be places no less magical than her home. The names of Guise, of Parme, of Guermantes-Bavière, differentiated from all possible others the holiday places to which the Duchess resorted, the daily festivities which the track of her carriage wheels linked to her mansion. If they told me that the life of Mme de Guermantes consisted of a succession of such holidays and such festivities, they brought no further light to bear on it. Each of them gave to the life of the Duchess a different determination, but merely brought it a change of mystery without allowing any of its own mystery to evaporate, so that it simply floated, protected by a watertight covering, enclosed in a bell, amid the waves of others' lives. The Duchess might have lunch on the shore of the Mediterranean at Carnival time, but in the villa of Mme de Guise, where the queen of Parisian society was no more, in her white piqué dress, among numberless princesses, than a guest like any other, and on that account more moving still to me, more herself by being thus made new, like a star of the ballet who in the intricacies of a dance figure takes the place of each of her humbler sisters in succession; she might look at shadow-theatre shows, but at a party given by the Princesse de Parme; listen to tragedy or opera, but from the Princesse de Guermantes's box.

Since we localise in the body of a person all the potentialities of his or her life, the memory of the people he or she knows and has just left or is on the way to join, if, having learned from Françoise that Mme de Guermantes was going on foot to luncheon with the Princesse de Parme, I saw her emerge from the house about midday in a gown of flesh-coloured satin above which her face was of the same shade, like a cloud at sunset, it was all the pleasures of the Faubourg Saint-Germain that I saw before me, contained in that small compass, as though between the glossy pearl-pink valves of a shell.

My father had a friend at the Ministry, one A. J. Moreau, who, to distinguish himself from the other Moreaus, took care always to prefix his name with these two initials, with the result that people called him "A.J." for short. For some reason or other, this A.J. found himself in possession of a stall for a gala night at the Opéra. He sent the ticket to my father, and since Berma, whom I had not seen again since my first disappointment, was to give an act of *Phèdre*, my grandmother persuaded my father to pass it on to me.

Truth to tell, I set little store by this opportunity of seeing and hearing Berma which, a few years earlier, had plunged me in such a state of agitation. And it was not without a sense of melancholy that I registered to myself my indifference to what at one time I had put before health, comfort, everything. It was not that there had been any diminution in my desire to be able to contemplate at first hand the precious particles of reality which my imagination envisioned. But it no longer located them in the diction of a great actress; since my visits to Elstir, it was on to certain tapestries, certain modern paintings that I had transferred the inner faith I had once had in the acting, the tragic art of Berma; my faith and my desire no longer coming forward to pay incessant worship to the diction and the presence of Berma, the "double" that I possessed of them in my heart had gradually shrivelled, like those other "doubles" of the dead in ancient Egypt which had to be fed continually in order to maintain their originals in eternal life. That art had become a poor and pitiable thing. It was no longer inhabited by a deep-rooted soul.

That evening, as, armed with the ticket my father had received from his friend, I was climbing the grand staircase of the Opéra, I saw in front of me a man whom I took at first for M. de Charlus, whose bearing he had; when he turned his head to ask some question of an attendant I saw that I had been mistaken, but I nevertheless had no hesitation in placing the stranger in the same class of society, from the way not only in which he was dressed but in which he spoke to the man who took the tickets and to the box-openers who were keeping him waiting. For, apart from individual characteristics, there was still at this period a very marked difference between any rich and well-dressed man of that section of the aristocracy and any rich and well-dressed man of the world of finance or "big business." Where one of the latter would have thought he was giving proof of his exclusiveness by adopting a sharp and haughty tone in speaking to an inferior, the nobleman, affable and mild, gave the impression of considering, of practising an affectation of humility and patience, a pretence of being just an ordinary member of the audience, as a prerogative of his good breeding. It is probable that on seeing him thus dissemble behind a smile overflowing with good-nature the inaccessible threshold of the little world apart which he carried in his person, more than one wealthy banker's son, entering the theatre at that moment, would have taken this nobleman for a person of humble condition if he had not remarked in him an astonishing resemblance to the portrait that had recently appeared in the illustrated papers of a nephew of the Austrian Emperor, the Prince of Saxony, who happened to be in Paris at the time. I knew him to be a great friend of the Guermantes. As I myself reached the ticket attendant I heard the Prince of Saxony (or his double) say with a smile: "I don't know the number. My cousin told me I had only to ask for her box."

He may well have been the Prince of Saxony; it was perhaps the Duchesse de Guermantes (whom, in that event, I should be able to watch in the process of living one of the moments of her unimaginable life in her cousin's box) that he saw in his mind's eye when he referred to "my cousin who told me I had only to ask for her box," so much so that that distinctive smiling gaze and those so simple words caressed my heart (far more than any abstract reverie would have done) with the alternative antennae of a possible happiness and a vague glamour. At least, in uttering this sentence to the attendant, he grafted on to a commonplace evening in my everyday life a potential entry into a new world; the passage to which he was directed after having spoken the word "box" and along which he now proceeded was moist and fissured and seemed to lead to subaqueous grottoes, to the mythological kingdom of the water-nymphs. I had before me a gentleman in evening dress who was walking away from me, but I kept playing upon and around him, as with a badly fitting projector, without ever succeeding in focusing it on him exactly, the idea that he was the Prince of Saxony and was on his way to join the Duchesse de Guermantes. And for all that he was alone, that idea, external to himself, impalpable, immense, unsteady as a searchlight beam, seemed to precede and guide him like that deity, invisible to the rest of mankind, who stands beside the Greek warrior in the hour of battle.

I took my seat, trying to recapture a line from *Phèdre* which I could not quite remember. In the form in which I repeated it to myself it did not have the right number of feet, but as I made no attempt to count them, between its unwieldiness and a classical line of poetry it seemed as though no common measure could exist. It would not have surprised me to learn that I must subtract at least half a dozen syllables from that portentous phrase to reduce it to alexandrine dimensions. But suddenly I remembered it, the irremediable asperities of an inhuman world vanished as if by magic; the syllables of the line at once filled up the requisite measure, and what there was in excess floated off with the ease, the dexterity of a bubble of air that rises to burst on the surface of the water. And, after all, this excrescence with which I had been struggling consisted of only a single foot.

A certain number of orchestra stalls had been offered for sale at the box office and bought, out of snobbishness or curiosity, by such as wished to study the appearance of people whom they might not have another opportunity of seeing at close quarters. And it was indeed a fragment of their true social life, ordinarily concealed, that one could examine here in public, for, the Princesse de Parme having herself distributed among her friends the seats in stalls, balconies and boxes, the house was like a drawing-room in which everyone changed places, went to sit here or there, next to friends.

Next to me were some vulgar people who, not knowing the regular seat-holders, were anxious to show that they were capable of identifying them and named them aloud. They went on to remark that these "regulars" behaved there as though they were in their own drawing-rooms, meaning that they paid no attention to what was being played. In fact it was the opposite that took place. A budding genius who has taken a stall in order to see Berma thinks only of not soiling his gloves, of not disturbing, of conciliating the neighbour whom chance has put beside him, of pursuing with an intermittent smile the fleeting glance, and avoiding with apparent want of politeness the intercepted glance, of a person of his acquaintance whom he has discovered in the audience and to whom, after endless indecisions, he makes up his mind to go and talk just as the three knocks from the stage, resounding before he has had time to reach his friend, force him to take flight, like the Hebrews in the Red Sea, through a heaving tide of spectators and spectatresses whom he has forced to rise to their feet and whose dresses he tears and boots he crushes as he passes. On the other hand, it was because the society people sat in their boxes (behind the tiered circle) as in so many little suspended drawing-rooms, the fourth walls of which had been removed, or in so many little cafés to which one might go for refreshment without letting oneself be intimidated by the mirrors in gilt frames or the red plush seats, in the Neapolitan style, of the establishment—it was because they rested an indifferent hand on the gilded shafts of the columns which upheld this temple of the lyric art—it

was because they remained unmoved by the extravagant honours which seemed to be being paid them by a pair of carved
figures which held out towards the boxes branches of palm and
laurel, that they alone would have had the equanimity of mind to
listen to the play, if only they had had minds.

At first there were only vague shadows, in which one suddenly
caught—like the gleam of a precious stone which one cannot
see—the phosphorescence of a pair of famous eyes, or, like a
medallion of Henri IV on a dark background, the bent profile of
the Duc d'Aumale, to whom an invisible lady was exclaiming
"Your Royal Highness must allow me to take his coat," to which
the Prince replied, "Oh, come, come! Really, Madame
d'Ambresac." She took it, in spite of this vague demurral, and
was envied by one and all for being thus honoured.

But in the other boxes, almost everywhere, the white deities
who inhabited those sombre abodes had taken refuge against their
shadowy walls and remained invisible. Gradually, however, as the
performance went on, their vaguely human forms detached themselves languidly one after the other from the depths of the night
which they embroidered, and, raising themselves towards the
light, allowed their half-naked bodies to emerge into the chiaroscuro of the surface where their gleaming faces appeared behind
the playful, frothy undulations of their ostrich-feather fans,
beneath their hyacinthine, pearl-studded headdresses which
seemed to bend with the motion of the waves. Beyond began
the orchestra stalls, abode of mortals for ever separated from the
sombre and transparent realm to which here and there, in their
smooth liquid surface, the limpid, reflecting eyes of the water-
goddesses served as frontier. For the folding seats on its shore and
the forms of the monsters in the stalls were mirrored in those eyes
in simple obedience to the laws of optics and according to their
angle of incidence, as happens with those two sections of external
reality to which, knowing that they do not possess any soul,
however rudimentary, that can be considered analogous to our
own, we should think ourselves insane to address a smile or a
glance: namely, minerals and people to whom we have not been
introduced. Within the boundaries of their domain, however, the
radiant daughters of the sea were constantly turning round to smile
up at the bearded tritons who clung to the anfractuosities of the
cliff, or towards some aquatic demi-god whose skull was a
polished stone on to which the tide had washed a smooth covering

of sea-weed, and his gaze a disc of rock crystal. They leaned towards these creatures, offering them sweetmeats; from time to time the flood parted to admit a new nereid who, belated, smiling, apologetic, had just floated into blossom out of the shadowy depths; then, the act ended, having no further hope of hearing the melodious sounds of earth which had drawn them to the surface, plunging back all at once, the several sisters vanished into the night. But of all these retreats to the thresholds of which their frivolous desire to behold the works of man brought the curious goddesses who let none approach them, the most famous was the cube of semi-darkness known to the world as the stage box of the Princesse de Guermantes.

Like a tall goddess presiding from afar over the frolics of the lesser deities, the Princess had deliberately remained somewhat in the background on a sofa placed sideways in the box, red as a coral reef, beside a large vitreous expanse which was probably a mirror and suggested a section, perpendicular, opaque and liquid, cut by a ray of sunlight in the dazzling crystal of the sea. At once plume and corolla, like certain subaqueous growths, a great white flower, downy as the wing of a bird, hung down from the Princess's forehead along one of her cheeks, the curve of which it followed with coquettish, amorous, vibrant suppleness, as if half enclosing it like a pink egg in the softness of a halcyon's nest. Over her hair, reaching in front to her eyebrows and caught back lower down at the level of her throat, was spread a net composed of those little white shells which are fished up in certain southern seas and which were intermingled with pearls, a marine mosaic barely emerging from the waves and at moments plunged back again into a darkness in the depths of which even then a human presence was revealed by the glittering motility of the Princess's eyes. The beauty which set her far above all the other fabulous daughters of the twilight was not altogether materially and comprehensively inscribed in the nape of her neck, in her shoulders, her arms, her waist. But the exquisite, unfinished line of the last was the exact starting-point, the inevitable focus of invisible lines into which the eye could not help prolonging them—lines marvellously engendered round the woman like the spectre of an ideal figure projected against the darkness.

"That's the Princesse de Guermantes," said my neighbour to the gentleman beside her, taking care to begin the word "Princesse" with a string of "P"s, to show that the designation was absurd. "She hasn't been sparing with her pearls. I'm sure if I had as many as that I wouldn't make such a display of them; it doesn't look at all genteel to my mind."

And yet, when they caught sight of the Princess, all those who were looking round to see who was in the audience felt the rightful throne of beauty rise up in their hearts. The fact was that, with the Duchesse de Luxembourg, with Mme de Morienval, with Mme de Saint-Euverte, with any number of others, what enabled one to identify their faces would be the juxtaposition of a big red nose and a hare-lip, or of a pair of wrinkled cheeks and a faint moustache. These features were moreover sufficient in themselves to charm the eye, since, having merely the conventional value of a specimen of handwriting, they gave one to read a famous and impressive name; but also, in the long run, they gave one the idea that ugliness had something aristocratic about it, and that it was immaterial whether the face of a great lady, provided it possessed distinction, was beautiful as well. But like certain artists who, instead of the letters of their names, set at the foot of their canvases a figure that is beautiful in itself, a butterfly, a lizard, a flower, so it was the figure of a delicious face and body that the Princess affixed at the corner of her box, thereby showing that beauty can be the noblest of signatures; for the presence there of Mme de Guermantes-Bavière, who brought to the theatre only such persons as at other times formed part of her intimate circle, was in the eyes of connoisseurs of the aristocracy the best possible certificate of the authenticity of the picture which her box presented, a sort of evocation of a scene from the intimate and exclusive life of the Princess in her palaces in Munich and in Paris.

Our imagination being like a barrel-organ out of order, which always plays some other tune than that shown on its card, every time I had heard any mention of the Princesse de Guermantes-Bavière, a recollection of certain sixteenth-century masterpieces had begun singing in my brain. I was obliged to rid myself of this association now that I saw her engaged in offering crystallised fruit to a stout gentleman in tails. Certainly I was very far from concluding that she and her guests were mere human beings like the rest of the audience. I understood that what they were doing there was only a game, and that as a prelude to the acts of their real life (of which, presumably, this was not where they lived the important part) they had arranged, in obedience to a ritual unknown to me, to pretend to offer and decline sweets, a gesture robbed of its ordinary significance and regulated beforehand like the steps of a dancer who alternately raises herself on her toes and circles around a scarf. For all I knew, perhaps at the moment of offering him her sweets, the goddess was saying, with that note of irony in her voice (for I saw her smile): "Will you have a sweet?" What did it matter to me? I should have found a delicious refinement in the deliberate dryness, in the style of Mérimée or Meilhac, of these words addressed by a goddess to a demi-god who knew what sublime thoughts they both had in their minds, in reserve, doubtless, for the moment when they would begin again to live their real life, and, joining in the game, answered with the same mysterious playfulness: "Thanks, I should like a cherry." And I should have listened to this dialogue with the same avidity as to a scene from *Le Mari de la Débutante*, where the absence of poetry, of lofty thoughts, things which were so familiar to me and which, I suppose, Meilhac would have been eminently capable of putting into it, seemed to me in itself a refinement, a conventional refinement and therefore all the more mysterious and instructive.

"That fat fellow is the Marquis de Ganançay," came in a knowing tone from the man next to me, who had not quite caught the name whispered in the row behind.

The Marquis de Palancy, his face bent downwards at the end of his long neck, his round bulging eye glued to the glass of his monocle, moved slowly around in the transparent shade and appeared no more to see the public in the stalls than a fish that drifts past, unconscious of the press of curious gazers, behind the glass wall of an aquarium. Now and again he paused, venerable, wheezing, moss-grown, and the audience could not have told whether he was in pain, asleep, swimming, about to spawn, or merely taking breath. No one aroused in me so much envy as he, on account of his apparent familiarity with this box and the indifference with which he allowed the Princess to hold out to him her box of sweets, throwing him as she did so a glance from her fine eyes, cut from a diamond which at such moments intelligence and friendliness seemed to liquefy, whereas, when they were in repose, reduced to their purely material beauty, to their mineral brilliance alone, if the least reflected light displaced them ever so slightly, they set the depths of the pit ablaze with their inhuman, horizontal and resplendent fires. But now, because the act of *Phèdre* in which Berma was playing was due to start, the

Princess came to the front of the box; whereupon, as if she herself were a theatrical apparition, in the different zone of light which she traversed, I saw not only the colour but the material of her adornments change. And in the box, now drained dry, emergent, no longer a part of the watery realm, the Princess, ceasing to be a nereid, appeared turbaned in white and blue like some marvellous tragic actress dressed for the part of Zaïre, or perhaps of Orosmane; then, when she had taken her place in the front row, I saw that the halcyon's nest which tenderly shielded the pearly pink of her cheeks was an immense bird of paradise, soft, glittering and velvety.

But now my gaze was diverted from the Princesse de Guermantes's box by an ill-dressed, plain little woman who came in, her eyes ablaze with indignation, followed by two young men, and sat down a few seats away from me. Then the curtain rose. I could not help being saddened by the reflexion that there remained now no trace of my former predispositions in regard to Berma and the dramatic art, at the time when, in order to miss nothing of the extraordinary phenomenon which I would have gone to the ends of the earth to see, I kept my mind prepared like the sensitive plates which astronomers take out to Africa or the West Indies with a view to the scrupulous observation of a comet or an eclipse; when I trembled for fear lest some cloud (a fit of ill-humour on the artist's part or an incident in the audience) should prevent the spectacle from taking place with the maximum of intensity; when I should not have believed that I was watching it in the best conditions had I not gone to the very theatre which was consecrated to her like an altar, in which I then felt to be an inseparable if accessory part of her appearance from behind the little red curtain, the officials with their white carnations appointed by her, the vaulted balcony over a pit filled with a shabbily dressed crowd, the women selling programmes bearing her photograph, the chestnut-trees in the square outside, all those companions, those confidants of my impressions of those days which seemed to me to be inseparable from them. *Phèdre*, the "Declaration Scene," Berma, had had then for me a sort of absolute existence. Standing aloof from the world of current experience, they existed by themselves, I must go out to meet them, I would penetrate what I could of them, and if I opened my eyes and my soul to their fullest extent I would still absorb only too little of them. But how pleasant life seemed to me! The insignificance of the form of it that I myself was leading mattered nothing, no more than the time we spend on dressing, on getting ready to go out, since beyond it there existed in an absolute form, difficult to approach, impossible to possess in their entirety, those more solid realities, *Phèdre* and the way in which Berma spoke her lines. Steeped in these dreams of perfection in the dramatic art (a strong dose of which anyone who had at that time subjected my mind to analysis at any moment of the day or even the night would have been able to extract from it), I was like a battery that accumulates and stores up electricity. And a time had come when, ill as I was, even if I had believed that I should die of it, I should still have been compelled to go and hear Berma. But now, like a hill which from a distance seems azure-clad but as we draw nearer returns to its place in our commonplace vision of things, all this had left the world of the absolute and was no more than a thing like other things, of which I took cognisance because I was there; the actors were people of the same substance as the people I knew, trying to declaim as well as possible these lines of *Phèdre* which themselves no longer formed a sublime and individual essence, distinct from everything else, but were simply more or less effective lines ready to slip back into the vast corpus of French poetry, of which they were merely a part. I felt a despondency that was all the more profound in that, if the object of my headstrong and active desire no longer existed, on the other hand the same tendency to indulge in an obsessional day-dream, which varied from year to year but led me always to sudden impulses, regardless of danger, still persisted. The evening on which I rose from my bed of sickness and set out to see a picture by Elstir or a mediaeval tapestry in some country house or other was so like the day on which I ought to have set out for Venice, or that on which I had gone to see Berma or left for Balbec, that I felt in advance that the immediate object of my sacrifice would leave me cold after a very short while, that then I might pass close by the place without stopping even to look at that picture or those tapestries for which I would at this moment risk so many sleepless nights, so many hours of pain. I discerned in the instability of its object the vanity of my effort, and at the same time its immensity, which I had not noticed before, like one of those neurasthenics whose exhaustion is doubled when it is pointed out to them that they are exhausted. In the meantime my musings gave a certain glamour to anything that might be related to them. And even in my most carnal desires, orientated always in a particular direction, concentrated round a single dream, I might have recognised as their primary motive an idea, an idea for which I would have laid down my life, at the innermost core of which, as in my day-dreams while I sat reading all afternoon in the garden at Combray, lay the notion of perfection.

I no longer felt the same indulgence as on the former occasion for the scrupulous efforts to express tenderness or anger which I had then remarked in the delivery and gestures of Aricie, Ismène and Hippolyte. It was not that the players—they were the same—did not still seek, with the same intelligent application, to impart now a caressing inflexion or a calculated ambiguity to their voices, now a tragic amplitude or a suppliant gentleness to their movements. Their tones bade the voice: "Be gentle, sing like a nightingale, caress," or on the contrary: "Make yourself furious," and then hurled themselves upon it, trying to carry it along with them in their frenzy. But it, mutinous, independent of their diction, remained unalterably their natural voice with its material defects or charms, its everyday vulgarity or affectation, and thus presented a complex of acoustic or social phenomena which the sentiment contained in the lines they were declaiming was powerless to alter.

Similarly the gestures of the players said to their arms, to their garments: "Be majestic." But the unsubmissive limbs allowed a biceps which knew nothing of the part to flaunt itself between shoulder and elbow; they continued to express the triviality of everyday life and to bring into prominence, instead of fine shades of Racinian meaning, mere muscular relationships; and the draperies which they held up fell back again along vertical lines in which the natural law that governs falling bodies was challenged only by an inspid textile pliancy. At this point the little woman who was sitting near me exclaimed:

"Not a clap! And did you ever see such a get-up? She's too old; she can't do it any more; she ought to give up."

Amid a sibilant protest from their neighbours the two young men with her quietened her down and her fury raged now only in her eyes. This fury could be prompted only by the notion of success and fame, for Berma, who had earned so much money, was overwhelmed with debts. Since she was always making business or social appointments which she was prevented from keeping, she had messengers flying with apologies along every street in Paris, hotel suites booked in advance which she would never occupy, oceans of scent to bathe her dogs, heavy penalties for

breaches of contract with all her managers. Failing any more
serious expenses, and being less voluptuous than Cleopatra, she
would have found the means of squandering provinces and kingdoms on telegrams and hired carriages. But the little woman was
an actress who had never tasted success, and had vowed a deadly
hatred against Berma. The latter had just come on to the stage.
And then, miraculously, like those lessons which we have
laboured in vain to learn overnight and find intact, got by heart,
on waking up next morning, and like those faces of dead friends
which the impassioned efforts of our memory pursue without
recapturing and which, when we are no longer thinking of
them, are there before our eyes just as they were in life, the talent
of Berma, which had evaded me when I sought so greedily to
grasp its essence, now, after these years of oblivion, in this hour of
indifference, imposed itself on my admiration with the force of
self-evidence. Formerly, in my attempts to isolate this talent,
I deducted, so to speak, from what I heard, the part itself, a part,
the common property of all the actresses who appeared as Phèdre,
which I myself had studied beforehand so that I might be capable
of subtracting it, of gleaning as a residuum Mme Berma's talent
alone. But this talent which I sought to discover outside the part
itself was indissolubly one with it. So with a great musician (it
appears that this was the case with Vinteuil when he played the
piano), his playing is that of so fine a pianist that one is no longer
aware that the performer is a pianist at all, because (by not interposing all that apparatus of digital effort, crowned here and there
with brilliant effects, all that spattering shower of notes in which at
least the listener who does not quite know where he is thinks that
he can discern talent in its material, tangible reality) his playing has
become so transparent, so imbued with what he is interpreting,
that one no longer sees the performer himself—he is simply a
window opening upon a great work of art. I had been able to
distinguish the intentions underlying the voices and the mime of
Aricie, Ismène and Hippolyte, but Phèdre had interiorised hers,
and my mind had not succeeded in wresting from her diction and
attitudes, in apprehending in the miserly simplicity of their unbroken surfaces, those inventions, those effects of which no sign
emerged, so completely had they been absorbed into it. Berma's
voice, in which there subsisted not one scrap of inert matter
refractory to the mind, betrayed no visible sign of that surplus of
tears which, because they had been unable to soak into it, one

could feel trickling down the voice of Aricie or of Ismène, but had been delicately refined down to its smallest cells like the instrument of a master violinist in whom, when one says that he produces a beautiful sound, one means to praise not a physical peculiarity but a superiority of soul; and, as in the classical landscape where in the place of a vanished nymph there is an inanimate spring, a discernible and concrete intention had been transformed into a certain limpidity of tone, strange, appropriate and cold. Berma's arms, which the lines of verse themselves, by the same emissive force that made the voice issue from her lips, seemed to raise on to her bosom like leaves displaced by a gush of water; her stage presence, her poses, which she had gradually built up, which she was to modify yet further, and which were based upon reasonings altogether more profound than those of which traces could be seen in the gestures of her fellow-actors, but reasonings that had lost their original deliberation, had melted into a sort of radiance whereby they sent throbbing, round the person of the heroine, rich and complex elements which the fascinated spectator nevertheless took not for a triumph of dramatic artistry but for a manifestation of life; those white veils themselves, which, tenuous and clinging, seemed to be of a living substance and to have been woven by the suffering, half-pagan, half-Jansenist, around which they drew themselves like a frail and shrinking cocoon—all these, voice, posture, gestures, veils, round this embodiment of an idea which a line of poetry is (an embodiment that, unlike our human bodies, is not an opaque screen, but a purified, spiritualised garment), were merely additional envelopes which, instead of concealing, showed up in greater splendour the soul that had assimilated them to itself and had spread itself through them, lava-flows of different substances, grown translucent, the superimposition of which causes only a richer refraction of the imprisoned, central ray that pierces through them, and makes more extensive, more precious and more beautiful the flame-drenched matter in which it is enshrined. So Berma's interpretation was, around Racine's work, a second work, quickened also by genius.

My impression, to tell the truth, though more agreeable than on the earlier occasion, was not really different. Only, I no longer confronted it with a pre-existent, abstract and false idea of dramatic genius, and I understood now that dramatic genius was precisely this. It had just occurred to me that if I had not derived any pleasure from my first encounter with Berma, it was because, as earlier still when I used to meet Gilberte in the Champs-Elysées, I had come to her with too strong a desire. Between my two disappointments there was perhaps not only this resemblance, but another, deeper one. The impression given us by a person or a work (or an interpretation of a work) of marked individuality is peculiar to that person or work. We have brought with us the ideas of "beauty," "breadth of style," "pathos" and so forth which we might at a pinch have the illusion of recognising in the banality of a conventional face or talent, but our critical spirit has before it the insistent challenge of a form of which it possesses no intellectual equivalent, in which it must disengage the unknown element. It hears a sharp sound, an oddly interrogative inflexion. It asks itself: "Is that good? Is what I am feeling now admiration? Is that what is meant by richness of colouring, nobility, strength?" And what answers it again is a sharp voice, a curiously questioning tone, the despotic impression, wholly material, caused by a person whom one does not know, in which no scope is left for "breadth of interpretation." And for this reason it is the really beautiful works that, if we listen to them with sincerity, must disappoint us most keenly, because in the storehouse of our ideas there is none that responds to an individual impression.

This was precisely what Berma's acting showed me. This was indeed what was meant by nobility, by intelligence of diction. Now I could appreciate the merits of a broad, poetical, powerful interpretation, or rather it was to this that those epithets were conventionally applied, but only as we give the names of Mars, Venus, Saturn to planets which have nothing mythological about them. We feel in one world, we think, we give names to things in another; between the two we can establish a certain correspondence, but not bridge the gap. It was to some extent this gap, this fault, that I had to cross when, that afternoon on which I first went to see Berma, having strained my ears to catch every word, I had found some difficulty in correlating my ideas of "nobility of interpretation," of "originality," and had broken out in applause only after a moment of blankness and as if my applause sprang not from my actual impression but was connected in some way with my preconceived ideas, with the pleasure that I found in saying to myself: "At last I am listening to Berma." And the difference which exists between a person or a work of art that are markedly individual and the idea of beauty exists just as much between what they make us feel and the idea of love or of admiration. Wherefore we fail to recognise them. I had found no pleasure in listening to Berma (any more than, when I loved her, in seeing Gilberte). I had said to myself: "Well, I don't admire her." But meanwhile I was thinking only of mastering the secret of Berma's acting, I was preoccupied with that alone, I was trying to open my mind as wide as possible to receive all that her acting contained. I realised now that that was precisely what admiration meant.

Was this genius, of which Berma's interpretation was only the revelation, solely the genius of Racine?

I thought so at first. I was soon to be undeceived, when the act from *Phèdre* came to an end, after enthusiastic curtain-calls during which my furious old neighbour, drawing her little body up to its full height, turning sideways in her seat, stiffened the muscles of her face and folded her arms over her bosom to show that she was not joining the others in their applause, and to make more notice-able a protest which to her appeared sensational though it passed unperceived. The piece that followed was one of those novelties which at one time I had expected, since they were not famous, to be inevitably trivial and of no general application, devoid as they were of any existence outside the performance that was being given of them at the moment. But also I did not have, as with a classic, the disappointment of seeing the eternity of a masterpiece occupy no more space or time than the width of the footlights and the length of a performance which would accomplish it as effect-ively as an occasional piece. Then at each set speech which I felt that the audience liked and which would one day be famous, in the absence of the celebrity it could not have won in the past I added the fame it would enjoy in the future, by a mental process the converse of that which consists in imagining masterpieces on the day of their first frail appearance, when it seemed inconceiv-able that a title which no one had ever heard before could one day be set, bathed in the same mellow light, beside those of the author's other works. And this role would eventually figure in the list of her finest impersonations, next to that of Phèdre. Not that in itself it was not destitute of all literary merit; but Berma was as sublime in it as in *Phèdre*. I realised then that the work of the playwright was for the actress no more than the raw material, more or less irrelevant in itself, for the creation of her masterpiece of interpretation, just as the great painter whom I had met at Balbec, Elstir, had found the inspiration for two pictures of equal merit in a school building devoid of character and a cathedral which was itself a work of art. And as the painter dissolves houses, carts, people, in some broad effect of light which makes them homogeneous, so Berma spread out great sheets of terror or tenderness over the words which were equally blended, all planed down or heightened, and which a lesser artist would have carefully detached from one another. Of course each of them had an inflexion of its own, and Berma's diction did not prevent one from distinguishing the lines. Is it not already a first element of ordered complexity, of beauty, when, on hearing a rhyme, that is to say something that is at once similar to and different from the preceding rhyme, which is prompted by it, but introduces the variety of a new idea, one is conscious of two systems overlapping each other, one intellectual, the other prosodic? But Berma at the same time made the words, the lines, whole speeches even, flow into an ensemble vaster than themselves, at the margins of which it was a joy to see them obliged to stop, to break off; thus it is that a poet takes pleasure in making the word which is about to spring forth pause for a moment at the rhyming point, and a composer in merging the various words of the libretto in a single rhythm which runs counter to them and yet sweeps them along. Thus into the prose of the modern playwright as into the verse of Racine, Berma contrived to introduce those vast images of grief, nobility, passion, which were the masterpieces of her own personal art, and in which she could be recognised as, in the portraits which he has made of different sitters, we recognise a painter.

I had no longer any desire, as on the former occasion, to be able to arrest Berma's poses, or the beautiful effect of colour which she gave for a moment only in a beam of limelight which at once faded never to reappear, or to make her repeat a single line a hundred times over. I realised that my original desire had been more exacting than the intentions of the poet, the actress, the great decorative artist who directed the production, and that the charm which floated over a line as it was spoken, the shifting poses perpetually transformed into others, the successive tableaux, were the fleeting result, the momentary object, the mobile masterpiece which the art of the theatre intended and which the attentiveness of a too-enraptured audience would destroy by trying to arrest. I did not even wish to come back another day and hear Berma again; I was satisfied with her; it was when I admired too keenly not to be disappointed by the object of my admiration, whether that object was Gilberte or Berma, that I demanded in advance, of the impression to be received on the morrow, the pleasure that yesterday's impression had denied me. Without seeking to analyse the joy which I had just felt, and might perhaps have turned to some more profitable use, I said to myself, as in the old days some of my schoolfellows used to say: "Certainly, I put Berma first," not without a confused feeling that Berma's genius was not perhaps very accurately represented by this affirmation of my preference and this award to her of a "first" place, whatever the peace of mind that they might incidentally restore to me.

Just as the curtain was rising on this second play I looked up at Mme de Guermantes's box. The Princess, with a movement that called into being an exquisite line which my mind pursued into the void, had just turned her head towards the back of her box; the guests were all on their feet, and also turned towards the door, and between the double hedge which they thus formed, with all the triumphant assurance, the grandeur of the goddess that she was, but with an unwonted meekness due to her feigned and smiling embarrassment at arriving so late and making everyone get up in the middle of the performance, the Duchesse de Guermantes entered, enveloped in white chiffon. She went straight up to her cousin, made a deep curtsey to a young man with fair hair who was seated in the front row, and turning towards the amphibian monsters floating in the recesses of the cavern, gave to these demi-gods of the Jockey Club—who at that moment, and among them all M. de Palancy in particular, were the men I should most have liked to be—the familiar "good evening" of an old friend, an allusion to her day-to-day relations with them during the last fifteen years. I sensed but could not decipher the mystery of that smiling gaze which she addressed to her friends, in the azure brilliance with which it glowed while she surrendered her hand to them one after another, a gaze which, could I have broken up its prism, analysed its crystallisations, might perhaps have revealed to me the essence of the unknown life which was apparent in it at that moment. The Duc de Guermantes followed his wife, the gay flash of his monocle, the gleam of his teeth, the whiteness of his carnation or of his pleated shirt-front relegating, to make room for their light, the darkness of his eyebrows, lips and coat; with a wave of his outstretched hand which he let fall on to their shoulders, vertically, without moving his head, he commanded the inferior monsters who were making way for him to resume their seats, and made a deep bow to the fair young man. It was as though the Duchess had guessed that her cousin, of whom, it was rumoured, she was inclined to make fun for what she called her "exaggerations" (a noun which, from her point of view, so wittily French and restrained, was instantly applicable to the poetry and enthusiasm of the Teuton), would be wearing this evening one of those costumes in which the Duchess considered her "dressed up," and that she had decided to give her a lesson in good taste. Instead of the wonderful downy plumage which descended from the crown of the Princess's head to her throat, instead of her net of shells and pearls, the Duchess wore in her hair only a simple aigrette which, surmounting her arched nose and prominent eyes, reminded one of the crest on the head of a bird. Her neck and shoulders emerged from a drift of snow-white chiffon, against which fluttered a swansdown fan, but below this her gown, the bodice of which had for its sole ornament innumerable spangles (either little sticks and beads of metal, or brilliants), moulded her figure with a precision that was positively British. But different as their two costumes were, after the Princess had given her cousin the chair in which she herself had previously been sitting, they could be seen turning to gaze at one another in mutual appreciation.

Perhaps Mme de Guermantes would smile next day when she referred to the headdress, a little too complicated, which the Princess had worn, but certainly she would declare that the latter had been none the less quite lovely and marvellously got up; and the Princess, whose own tastes found something a little cold, a little austere, a little "tailor-made" in her cousin's way of dressing, would discover in this strict sobriety an exquisite refinement. Moreover, the harmony that existed between them, the universal and pre-established gravitational pull of their upbringing, neutralised the contrasts not only in their apparel but in their attitude. At those invisible magnetic longitudes which the refinement of their manners traced between them, the natural expansiveness of the Princess died away, while towards them the formal correctness of the Duchess allowed itself to be attracted and loosened, turned to sweetness and charm. As, in the play which was now being performed, to realise how much personal poetry Berma extracted from it one had only to entrust the part which she was playing, which she alone could play, to any other actress, so the spectator who raised his eyes to the balcony would have seen in two smaller boxes there how an "arrangement" intended to suggest that of the

Princesse de Guermantes simply made the Baronne de Morienval appear eccentric, pretentious and ill-bred, while an effort as painstaking as it must have been costly to imitate the clothes and style of the Duchesse de Guermantes only made Mme de Cambremer look like some provincial schoolgirl, mounted on wires, rigid, erect, desiccated, angular, with a plume of raven's feathers stuck vertically in her hair. Perhaps this lady was out of place in a theatre in which it was only with the brightest stars of the season that the boxes (even those in the highest tier, which from below seemed like great hampers studded with human flowers and attached to the ceiling of the auditorium by the red cords of their plush-covered partitions) composed an ephemeral panorama which deaths, scandals, illnesses, quarrels would soon alter, but which this evening was held motionless by attentiveness, heat, dizziness, dust, elegance and boredom, in the sort of eternal tragic instant of unconscious expectancy and calm torpor which, in retrospect, seems always to have preceded the explosion of a bomb or the first flicker of a fire.

The explanation for Mme de Cambremer's presence on this occasion was that the Princesse de Parme, devoid of snobbishness as are most truly royal personages, and by contrast eaten up with a pride in and passion for charity which rivalled her taste for what she believed to be the Arts, had bestowed a few boxes here and there upon women like Mme de Cambremer who were not numbered among the highest aristocratic society but with whom she was in communication with regard to charitable undertakings. Mme de Cambremer never took her eyes off the Duchesse and Princesse de Guermantes, which was all the easier for her since, not being actually acquainted with either, she could not be suspected of angling for a sign of recognition. Inclusion in the visiting lists of these two great ladies was nevertheless the goal towards which she had been striving for the last ten years with untiring patience. She had calculated that she might possibly reach it in five years more. But having been smitten by a fatal disease, the inexorable character of which—for she prided herself upon her medical knowledge—she thought she knew, she was afraid that she might not live so long. This evening she was happy at least in the thought that all these women whom she scarcely knew would see in her company a man who was one of their own set, the young Marquis de Beausergent, Mme d'Argencourt's brother, who moved impartially in both worlds and whom the women of the second were very keen to parade before the eyes of those of the first. He was seated behind Mme de Cambremer on a chair placed at an angle, so that he might be able to scan the other boxes. He knew everyone in them and to bow to his friends, with the exquisite elegance of his delicately arched figure, his fine features and fair hair, he half-raised his upright torso, a smile brightening his blue eyes, with a blend of deference and detachment, a picture etched with precision in the rectangle of the oblique plane in which he was placed, like one of those old prints which portray a great nobleman in his courtly pride. He often accepted these invitations to go to the theatre with Mme de Cambremer. In the auditorium, and, on the way out, in the lobby, he stood gallantly by her side amid the throng of more brilliant friends whom he saw about him, and to whom he refrained from speaking, to avoid any awkwardness, just as though he had been in doubtful company. If at such moments the Princesse de Guermantes swept by, lightfoot and fair as Diana, trailing behind her the folds of an incomparable cloak, making every head turn round and followed by all eyes (and, most of all, by Mme de Cambremer's), M. de Beausergent would become engrossed in conversation with his companion, acknowledging the friendly and dazzling smile of the Princess only with constraint, and with the well-bred reserve, the considerate coldness of a person whose friendliness might have become momentarily embarrassing.

Had not Mme de Cambremer known already that the box belonged to the Princess, she could still have told that the Duchesse de Guermantes was the guest from the air of greater interest with which she was surveying the spectacle of stage and auditorium, out of politeness to her hostess. But simultaneously with this centrifugal force, an equal and opposite force generated by the same desire to be sociable drew her attention back to her own attire, her plume, her necklace, her bodice and also to that of the Princess herself, whose subject, whose slave her cousin seemed to proclaim herself, come there solely to see her, ready to follow her elsewhere should the titular holder of the box have taken it into her head to get up and go, and regarding the rest of the house as composed merely of strangers, worth looking at simply as curiosities, though she numbered among them many friends to whose boxes she regularly repaired on other evenings and with regard to whom she never failed on those occasions to demonstrate a similar loyalty, exclusive, relativistic and weekly. Mme de

Cambremer was surprised to see her there that evening. She knew that the Duchess stayed on very late at Guermantes, and had supposed her to be there still. But she had been told that some-times, when there was some special function in Paris which she considered it worth her while to attend, Mme de Guermantes would order one of her carriages to be brought round as soon as she had taken tea with the guns, and, as the sun was setting, drive off at a spanking pace through the gathering darkness of the forest, then along the high road, to join the train at Combray and so be in Paris the same evening. "Perhaps she has come up from Guermantes especially to see Berma," thought Mme de Cambremer, and marvelled at the thought. And she remembered having heard Swann say in that ambiguous jargon which he shared with M. de Charlus: "The Duchess is one of the noblest souls in Paris, the cream of the most refined, the choicest society." For myself, who derived from the names Guermantes, Bavaria and Condé what I imagined to be the lives and the thoughts of the two cousins (I could no longer do so from their faces, having seen them), I would rather have had their opinion of *Phèdre* than that of the greatest critic in the world. For in his I should have found merely intelligence, an intelligence superior to my own but similar in kind. But what the Duchesse and Princesse de Guermantes might think, an opinion which would have furnished me with an invaluable clue to the nature of these two poetic creatures, I imagined with the aid of their names, I endowed with an irrational charm, and, with the thirst and the longing of a fever-stricken patient, what I demanded that their opinion of *Phèdre* should yield to me was the charm of the summer afternoons that I had spent wandering along the Guermantes way.

Mme de Cambremer was trying to make out how exactly the two cousins were dressed. For my own part, I never doubted that their garments were peculiar to themselves, not merely in the sense in which the livery with red collar or blue facings had once belonged exclusively to the houses of Guermantes and Condé, but rather as for a bird its plumage which, as well as being a heighten-ing of its beauty, is an extension of its body. The costumes of these two ladies seemed to me like the materialisation, snow-white or patterned with colour, of their inner activity, and, like the gestures which I had seen the Princesse de Guermantes make and which, I had no doubt, corresponded to some latent idea, the plumes which swept down from her forehead and her cousin's dazzling and spangled bodice seemed to have a special meaning, to be to each of these women an attribute which was hers, and hers alone, the significance of which I should have liked to know: the bird of paradise seemed inseparable from its wearer as her peacock is from Juno, and I did not believe that any other woman could usurp that spangled bodice, any more than the fringed and flashing shield of Minerva. And when I turned my eyes to their box, far more than on the ceiling of the theatre, painted with lifeless allegories, it was as though I had seen, thanks to a miraculous break in the custom-ary clouds, the assembly of the Gods in the act of contemplating the spectacle of mankind, beneath a crimson canopy, in a clear lighted space, between two pillars of Heaven. I gazed on this momentary apotheosis with a perturbation which was partly soothed by the feeling that I myself was unknown to the Immortals; the Duchess had indeed seen me once with her hus-band, but could surely have kept no memory of that, and I was not distressed that she should find herself, owing to the position that she occupied in the box, gazing down upon the nameless, collect-ive madrepores of the audience in the stalls, for I was happily aware that my being was dissolved in their midst, when, at the moment in which, by virtue of the laws of refraction, the blurred shape of the protozoon devoid of any individual existence which was myself must have come to be reflected in the impassive current of those two blue eyes, I saw a ray illumine them: the Duchess, goddess turned woman, and appearing in that moment a thousand times more lovely, raised towards me the white-gloved hand which had been resting on the balustrade of the box and waved it in token of friendship; my gaze was caught in the spontaneous incandescence of the flashing eyes of the Princess, who had unwit-tingly set them ablaze merely by turning her head to see who it might be that her cousin was thus greeting; and the latter, who had recognised me, poured upon me the sparkling and celestial shower of her smile.

Now, every morning, long before the hour at which she left her house, I went by a devious route to post myself at the corner of the street along which she generally came, and, when the moment of her arrival seemed imminent, I strolled back with an air of being absorbed in something else, looking the other way, and raised my eyes to her face as I drew level with her, but as though I had not in the least expected to see her. Indeed, for the first few mornings, so as to be sure of not missing her, I waited in front of the house. And every time the carriage gate opened (letting out one after another so many people who were not the one for whom I was waiting) its grinding rattle prolonged itself in my heart in a series of oscillations which took a long time to subside. For never was devotee of a famous actress whom he does not know, kicking his heels outside the stage door, never was angry or idolatrous crowd, gathered to insult or to carry in triumph through the streets the condemned assassin or the national hero whom it believes to be on the point of coming whenever a sound is heard from the inside of the prison or the palace, never were these so stirred by emotion as I was, awaiting the emergence of this great lady who in her simple attire was able, by the grace of her movements (quite different from the gait she affected on entering a drawing-room or a box), to make of her morning walk—and for me there was no one in the world but she out walking—a whole poem of elegant refinement and the loveliest ornament, the rarest flower of the season. But after the third day, so that the porter should not discover my stratagem, I betook myself much further afield, to some point upon the Duchess's usual route. Often before that evening at the theatre I had made similar little excursions before lunch, when the weather was fine; if it had been raining, at the first gleam of sunshine I would hasten downstairs to take a stroll, and if, suddenly, coming towards me along the still wet pavement, changed by the sun into a golden lacquer, in the transformation scene of a cross-roads powdered with mist which the sun tanned and bleached, I caught sight of a schoolgirl followed by her governess or of a dairy-maid with her white sleeves, I stood motionless, my hand pressed to my heart which was already leaping towards an unexplored life; I tried to bear in mind the street, the time, the number of the door through which the girl (whom I followed sometimes) had vanished and failed to reappear. Fortunately the fleeting nature of these cherished images, which I promised myself that I would make an effort to see again, prevented them from fixing themselves with any vividness in my memory. No matter, I was less depressed now at the thought of my own ill-health, of my never having summoned up the energy to set to work, to begin a book, for the world appeared to me a pleasanter place to live in, life a more interesting experience to go through, now that I had learned that the streets of Paris, like the roads round Balbec, were in bloom with those unknown beauties whom I had so often sought to conjure from the woods of Méséglise, each of whom aroused a voluptuous longing which she alone seemed capable of assuaging.

On coming home from the Opéra, I had added for the following morning, to those whom for some days past I had been hoping to meet again, the image of Mme de Guermantes, tall, with her high-piled crown of silky, golden hair, with the tenderness promised by the smile which she had directed at me from her cousin's box. I would follow the route which Françoise had told me that the Duchess generally took, and I would try at the same time, in the hope of meeting two girls whom I had seen a few days earlier, not to miss the coming out of a class or a catechism. But meanwhile, from time to time, the scintillating smile of Mme de Guermantes, and the warm feeling it had engendered, came back to me. And without exactly knowing what I was doing, I tried to find a place for them (as a woman studies the effect a certain kind of jewelled buttons that have just been given her might have on a dress) beside the romantic ideas which I had long held and which Albertine's coldness, Gisèle's premature departure, and before them my deliberate and too long sustained separation from Gilberte had set free (the idea for instance of being loved by a woman, of having a life in common with her); then it was the image of one or other of the two girls seen in the street that I coupled with those ideas, to which immediately afterwards I tried to adapt my memory of the Duchess. Compared with those ideas, the memory of Mme de Guermantes at the Opéra was a very insignificant thing, a tiny star twinkling beside the long tail of a blazing comet; moreover I had been quite familiar with the ideas long before I came to know Mme de Guermantes; whereas the memory of her I possessed but imperfectly; at moments it escaped me; it was during the hours when, from floating vaguely in my mind in the same way as the images of various other pretty women, it gradually developed into a unique and definitive association—exclusive of every other feminine image—with those romantic ideas of mine which were of so much longer standing than itself, it was during those few hours in which I remembered it most clearly, that I ought to have taken steps to find out exactly what it was; but I did not then know the importance it was to assume for me; I cherished it simply as a first private meeting with Mme de Guermantes inside myself; it was the first, the only accurate sketch, the only one made from life, the only one that was really Mme de Guermantes; during the few hours in which

I was fortunate enough to retain it without giving it any consciou
thought, it must have been charming, though, that memory, sinc
it was always to it, freely still at that moment, without haste
without strain, without the slightest compulsion or anxiety, tha
my ideas of love returned; then, as gradually those ideas fixed
more permanently, it acquired from them a greater strength bu
itself became more vague; presently I could no longer recapture i
and in my dreams I no doubt distorted it completely, for wheneve
I saw Mme de Guermantes I realised the disparity—always, as :
happened, different—between what I had imagined and wha
I saw. True, every morning now, at the moment when Mme d
Guermantes emerged from her doorway at the top of the stree
I saw again her tall figure, her face with its bright eyes and crown c
silken hair—all the things for which I was waiting there; but, o
the other hand, a minute or two later, when, having first turne
my eyes away so as to appear not to be expecting this encounte
which I had come to seek, I raised them to look at the Duchess a
the moment in which we converged, what I saw then were re
patches (as to which I did not know whether they were due to th
fresh air or to a blotchy skin) on a sullen face which with the curtes
of nods, a long way removed from the affability of the *Phèdr*
evening, acknowledged the greeting which I addressed to he
daily with an air of surprise and which did not seem to pleas
her. And yet, after a few days during which the memory of the tw
girls fought against heavy odds for the mastery of my amorou
feelings with that of Mme de Guermantes, it was in the end th
latter which, as though of its own accord, generally prevaile
while its competitors withdrew; it was to it that I finally foun
myself, on the whole voluntarily still and as though from choic
and with pleasure, to have transferred all my thoughts of love.
had ceased to dream of the little girls coming from their catechism
or of a certain dairy-maid; and yet I had also lost all hope c
encountering in the street what I had come to seek, either th
affection promised to me at the theatre in a smile, or the profile
the bright face beneath its pile of golden hair which were so onl
when seen from afar. Now I should not even have been able to sa
what Mme de Guermantes was like, what I recognised her by, fo
every day, in the picture which she presented as a whole, the fac
was as different as were the dress and the hat.

Why, on such and such a morning, when I saw advancing
towards me beneath a violet hood a sweet, smooth face whos

charms were symmetrically arranged about a pair of blue eyes and into which the curve of the nose seemed to have been absorbed, did I gauge from a joyous commotion in my breast that I was not going to return home without having caught a glimpse of Mme de Guermantes? Why did I feel the same perturbation, affect the same indifference, turn away my eyes with the same abstracted air as on the day before, at the appearance in profile in a side-street, beneath a navy-blue toque, of a beak-like nose alongside a red cheek with a piercing eye, like some Egyptian deity? Once it was not merely a woman with a bird's beak that I saw but almost the bird itself; Mme de Guermantes's outer garments, even her toque, were of fur, and since she thus left no cloth visible, she seemed naturally furred, like certain vultures whose thick, smooth, tawny, soft plumage looks like a sort of animal's coat. In the midst of this natural plumage, the tiny head arched out its beak and the bulging eyes were piercing and blue.

One day I would be pacing up and down the street for hours on end without seeing Mme de Guermantes when suddenly, inside a dairy shop tucked in between two of the mansions of this aristocratic and plebeian quarter, there would emerge the vague and unfamiliar face of a fashionably dressed woman who was asking to see some *petits suisses*, and before I had had time to distinguish her I would be struck, as by a flash of light reaching me sooner than the rest of the image, by the glance of the Duchess; another time, having failed to meet her and hearing midday strike, realising that it was not worth my while to wait for her any longer, I would be mournfully making my way homewards absorbed in my disappointment and gazing absent-mindedly at a receding carriage, when suddenly I realised that the nod which a lady had given through the carriage window was meant for me, and that this lady, whose features, relaxed and pale, or alternatively tense and vivid, composed, beneath a round hat or a towering plume, the face of a stranger whom I had supposed that I did not know, was Mme de Guermantes, by whom I had let myself be greeted without so much as an acknowledgement. And sometimes I would come upon her as I entered the carriage gate, standing outside the lodge where the detestable porter whose inquisitive eyes I loathed was in the act of making her a profound obeisance and also, no doubt, his daily report. For the entire staff of the Guermantes household, hidden behind the window curtains, would tremble with fear as they watched a conversation which they were unable to overhear, but which meant as they very well knew that one or other of them would certainly have his day off stopped by the Duchess to whom this Cerberus had betrayed him.

In view of the succession of different faces which Mme de Guermantes displayed thus one after another, faces that occupied a relative and varying expanse, sometimes narrow, sometimes large, in her person and attire as a whole, my love was not attached to any particular one of those changeable elements of flesh and fabric which replaced one another as day followed day, and which she could modify and renew almost entirely without tempering my agitation because beneath them, beneath the new collar and the strange cheek, I felt that it was still Mme de Guermantes. What I loved was the invisible person who set all this outward show in motion, the woman whose hostility so distressed me, whose approach threw me into a turmoil, whose life I should have liked to make my own, chasing away her friends. She might flaunt a blue feather or reveal an inflamed complexion, and her actions would still lose none of their importance for me.

I should not myself have felt that Mme de Guermantes was irritated at meeting me day after day, had I not learned it indirectly by reading it on the face, stiff with coldness, disapproval and pity, which Françoise wore when she was helping me to get ready for these morning walks. The moment I asked her for my outdoor things I felt a contrary wind arise in her worn and shrunken features. I made no attempt to win her confidence, for I knew that I should not succeed. She had a power, the nature of which I have never been able to fathom, for at once becoming aware of anything unpleasant that might happen to my parents and myself. Perhaps it was not a supernatural power, but could have been explained by sources of information that were peculiar to herself: as it may happen that the news which often reaches a savage tribe several days before the post has brought it to the European colony has really been transmitted to them not by telepathy but from hill-top to hill-top by beacon fires. Thus, in the particular instance of my morning walks, possibly Mme de Guermantes's servants had heard their mistress say how tired she was of running into me every day without fail wherever she went, and had repeated her remarks to Françoise. My parents might, it is true, have attached some servant other than Françoise to my person, but I should have been no better off. Françoise was in a sense less of a servant than the others. In her way of feeling things, of being kind and compassionate, harsh and disdainful, shrewd and narrow-minded, of combining a white skin with red hands, she was still the village girl whose parents had had "a place of their own" but having come to grief had been obliged to put her into service. Her presence in our household was the country air, the social life of a farm of fifty years ago transported into our midst by a sort of holiday journey in reverse whereby it is the countryside that comes to visit the traveller. As the glass cases in a local museum are filled with specimens of the curious handiwork which the peasants still carve or embroider in certain parts of the country, so our flat in Paris was decorated with the words of Françoise, inspired by a traditional and local sentiment and governed by extremely ancient laws. And she could trace her way back as though by clues of coloured thread to the birds and cherry-trees of her childhood, to the bed in which her mother had died, and which she still saw. But in spite of all this wealth of background, once she had come to Paris and had entered our service she had acquired—as, *a fortiori*, anyone else would have done in her place—the ideas, the system of interpretation used by the servants on the other floors, compensating for the respect which she was obliged to show to us by repeating the rude words that the cook on the fourth floor had used to her mistress, with a servile gratification so intense that, for the first time in our lives, feeling a sort of solidarity with the detestable occupant of the fourth-floor flat, we said to ourselves that possibly we too were employers after all. This alteration in Françoise's character was perhaps inevitable. Certain ways of life are so abnormal that they are bound to produce certain characteristic faults; such was the life led by the King at Versailles among his courtiers, a life as strange as that of a Pharaoh or a Doge—and, far more even than his, the life of his courtiers. The life led by servants is probably of an even more monstrous abnormality, which only its familiarity can prevent us from seeing. But it was actually in details more intimate still that I should have been obliged, even if I had dismissed Françoise, to keep the same servant. For various others were to enter my service in the years to come; already endowed with the defects common to all servants, they underwent nevertheless a rapid transformation with me. As the laws of attack govern those of riposte, in order not to be worsted by the asperities of my character, all of them effected in their own an identical withdrawal, always at the same point, and to make up for this took advantage of the gaps in my line to thrust out advanced posts. Of these gaps I knew nothing, any more than of the salients to which they gave rise, precisely because they were gaps. But my servants, by gradually becoming spoiled, taught me of their existence. It was from the defects which they invariably acquired that I learned what were my own natural and invariable short-comings; their character offered me a sort of negative of my own. We had always laughed, my mother and I, at Mme Sazerat, who used, in speaking of servants, to say "that race," "that species." But I am bound to admit that what made it useless to think of replacing Françoise by anyone else was that her successor would inevitably have belonged just as much to the race of servants in general and to the class of my servants in particular.

To return to Françoise, I never in my life experienced a humi-liation without having seen beforehand on her face the signs of ready-made condolences, and when in my anger at the thought of being pitied by her I tried to pretend that on the contrary I had scored a distinct success, my lies broke feebly against the wall of her respectful but obvious unbelief and the consciousness that she enjoyed of her own infallibility. For she knew the truth. She refrained from uttering it, and made only a slight movement with her lips as if she still had her mouth full and was finishing a tasty morsel. She refrained from uttering it? So at least I long believed, for at that time I still supposed that it was by means of words that one communicated the truth to others. Indeed the words that people said to me recorded their meaning so unalterably on the sensitive plate of my mind that I could no more believe it possible that someone who had professed to love me did not love me than Françoise herself could have doubted when she had read in the paper that some priest or gentleman or other was prepared, on receipt of a stamped envelope, to furnish us free of charge with an infallible remedy for every known com-plaint or with the means of multiplying our income a hundredfold. (If, on the other hand, our doctor were to prescribe for her the simplest cure for a cold in the head, she, so stubborn to endure the keenest suffering, would complain bitterly of what she had been made to sniff, insisting that it tickled her nose and that life was not worth living.) But she was the first person to prove to me by her example (which I was not to understand until long afterwards, when it was given me afresh and more painfully, as will be seen in the later volumes of this work, by a person who was dearer to me) that the truth has no need to be uttered to be made apparent, and that one may perhaps gather it with more certainty, without waiting for words and without even taking any account of them, from countless outward signs, even from certain invisible phenomena, analogous in the sphere of human character to what atmospheric changes are in the physical world. I might perhaps have suspected this, since it frequently occurred to me at that time to say things myself in which there was no vestige of truth, while I made the real truth plain by all manner of involuntary confidences expressed by my body and in my actions (which were only too accurately interpreted by Françoise); I ought perhaps to have suspected it, but to do so I should first have had to be conscious that I myself was occasionally mendacious and deceitful. Now mendacity and deceitfulness were with me, as with most people, called into being in so immediate, so contingent a fashion, in the defence of some particular interest, that my mind, fixed on some lofty ideal, allowed my character to set about those urgent, sordid tasks in the darkness below and did not look down to observe them.

When Françoise, in the evening, was nice to me, and asked my permission to sit in my room, it seemed to me that her face became transparent and that I could see the kindness and honesty that lay beneath. But Jupien, who had lapses into indiscretion of which I learned only later, revealed afterwards that she had told him that I was not worth the price of a rope to hang me, and that I had tried to do her every conceivable harm. These words of Jupien's set up at once before my eyes, in new and strange colours, a print of my relations with Françoise so different from the one which I often took pleasure in contemplating and in which, without the least shadow of doubt, Françoise adored me and lost no opportunity of singing my praises, that I realised that it is not only the physical world that differs from the aspect in which we see it; that all reality is perhaps equally dissimilar from what we believe ourselves to be directly perceiving and which we compose with the aid of ideas that do not reveal themselves but are none the less efficacious, just as the trees, the sun and the sky would not be the same as what we see if they were apprehended by creatures having eyes differently constituted from ours, or else endowed for that purpose with organs other than eyes which would furnish equivalents of trees and sky and sun, though not visual ones. However that might be, this sudden glimpse that Jupien afforded me of the real world appalled me. And yet it concerned only Françoise, about whom I cared little. Was it the same with all one's social relations? And into what depths of despair might this not some day plunge me, if it were the same with love? That was the future's secret. For the present only Françoise was concerned. Did she sincerely believe what she had said to Jupien? Had she said it to embroil Jupien with me, possibly so that we should not appoint Jupien's girl as her successor? At any rate I realised the impossibility of obtaining any direct and certain knowledge of whether Françoise loved or hated me. And thus it was she who first gave me the idea that a person does not, as I had imagined, stand motionless and clear before our eyes with his merits, his defects, his plans, his intentions with regard to ourselves (like a garden at which we gaze through a railing with all its borders spread out before us), but is a shadow which we can never penetrate, of which there can be no such thing as direct knowledge, with respect to which we form count-less beliefs, based upon words and sometimes actions, neither of which can give us anything but inadequate and as it proves contra-dictory information—a shadow behind which we can alternately imagine, with equal justification, that there burns the flame of hatred and of love.

I was genuinely in love with Mme de Guermantes. The greatest happiness that I could have asked of God would have been that he should send down on her every imaginable calamity, and that ruined, despised, stripped of all the privileges that separated her from me, having no longer any home of her own or people who would condescend to speak to her, she should come to me for asylum. I imagined her doing so. And indeed on those evenings when some change in the atmosphere or in my own state of health brought to the surface of my consciousness some forgotten scroll on which were recorded impressions of other days, instead of profiting by the forces of renewal that had been generated in me, instead of using them to unravel in my own mind thoughts which as a rule escaped me, instead of setting myself at last to work, I preferred to relate aloud, to excogitate in a lively, external manner, with a flow of invention as useless as was my declamation of it, a whole novel crammed with adventure, in which the Duchess, fallen upon misfortune, came to implore assistance from me—who had become, by a converse change of circum-stances, rich and powerful. And when I had thus spent hours on end imagining the circumstances, rehearsing the sentences with which I should welcome the Duchess beneath my roof, the situa-tion remained unaltered; I had, alas, in reality, chosen to love the woman who in her own person combined perhaps the greatest possible number of different advantages; in whose eyes, accordingly, I could not hope to cut any sort of figure; for she was as rich as the richest commoner—and noble also; not to mention that personal charm which set her at the pinnacle of fashion, made her among the rest a sort of queen.

I felt that I displeased her by crossing her path every morning; but even if I had had the heart to refrain from doing so for two or three days consecutively, Mme de Guermantes might not have noticed that abstention, which would have represented so great a sacrifice on my part, or might have attributed it to some obstacle beyond my control. And indeed I could not have brought myself to cease to dog her footsteps except by arranging that it should be impossible for me to do so, for the perpetually recurring need to meet her, to be for a moment the object of her attention, the person to whom her greeting was addressed, was stronger than my fear of arousing her displeasure. I should have had to go away for some time; and for that I had not the heart. I did think of it more than once. I would then tell Françoise to pack my boxes, and immediately afterwards to unpack them. (And as the spirit of imitation, the desire not to appear behind the times, alters the most natural and most positive form of oneself, Françoise, borrowing the expression from her daughter's vocabulary, used to remark that I was "dippy.") She did not approve of my tergiversations; she said that I was always "balancing," for when she was not aspiring to rival the moderns, she employed the very language of Saint-Simon. It is true that she liked it still less when I spoke to her authoritatively. She knew that this was not natural to me, and did not suit me, a condition which she expressed in the phrase "where there isn't a will." I should never have had the heart to leave Paris except in a direction that would bring me closer to Mme de Guermantes. This was by no means an impossibility. Would I not indeed find myself nearer to her than I was in the morning, in the street, solitary, humiliated, feeling that not a single one of the thoughts which I should have liked to convey to her ever reached her, in that weary marking time of my daily walks, which might go on indefinitely without getting me any further, if I were to go miles away from Mme de Guermantes, but to someone of her acquaintance, someone whom she knew to be particular in the choice of his friends and who appreciated me, who might speak to her about me, and if not obtain from her at least make her aware of what I wanted, someone thanks to whom at all events, simply because I should discuss with him whether or not it would be possible for him to convey this or that message to her, I should give to my solitary and silent meditations a new form, spoken, active, which would seem to me an advance, almost a realisation? What she did during the mysterious daily life of the "Guermantes" that she was—this was the constant object of my thoughts; and to break into that life, even by indirect means, as with a lever, by employing the services of a person who was not excluded from the Duchess's house, from her parties, from prolonged conversation with her, would not that be a contact more distant but at the same time more effective than my contemplation of her every morning in the street?

The friendship and admiration that Saint-Loup had shown me seemed to me undeserved and had hitherto left me unmoved. All at once I set great store by them; I would have liked him to disclose them to Mme de Guermantes, was quite prepared even to ask him to do so. For when we are in love, we long to be able to divulge to the woman we love all the little privileges we enjoy, as the deprived and the tiresome do in everyday life. We are distressed by her ignorance of them and we seek to console ourselves with the thought that precisely because they are never visible she has perhaps added to the opinion which she already has of us this possibility of further undisclosed virtues.

Saint-Loup had not for a long time been able to come to Paris, either, as he himself claimed, because of his military duties, or, as was more likely, because of the trouble he was having with his mistress, with whom he had twice now been on the point of breaking off. He had often told me what a pleasure it would be to him if I came to visit him in that garrison town the name of which, a couple of days after his leaving Balbec, had caused me so much joy when I had read it on the envelope of the first letter I had received from my friend. Not so far from Balbec as its wholly inland surroundings might have led one to think, it was one of those little fortified towns, aristocratic and military, set in a broad expanse of country over which on fine days there floats so often in the distance a sort of intermittent blur of sound which—as a screen of poplars by its sinuosities outlines the course of a river which one cannot see—indicates the movements of a regiment on manoeuvre that the very atmosphere of its streets, avenues and squares has been gradually tuned to a sort of perpetual vibrancy, musical and martial, and the most commonplace sound of cartwheel or tramway is prolonged in vague trumpet calls, indefinitely repeated, to the hallucinated ear, by the silence. It was not too far away from Paris for me to be able, if I took the express, to return to my mother and grandmother and sleep in my own bed. As soon as I realised this, troubled by a painful longing, I had too little will-power to decide not to return to Paris but rather to stay in the little town; but also too little to prevent a porter from carrying my luggage to a cab and not to adopt, as I walked behind him, the destitute soul of a traveller looking after his belongings with no grandmother in attendance, not to get into the carriage with the complete detachment of a person who, having ceased to think of what it is that he wants, has the air of knowing what he wants, and not to give the driver the address of the cavalry barracks. I thought that Saint-Loup might come and sleep that night in the hotel at which I should be staying, in order to make the first shock of contact with this strange town less painful for me. One of the guard went to find him, and I waited at the barracks gate, in front of that huge ship of stone, booming with the November wind, out of which, every moment, for it was now six o'clock, men were emerging in pairs into the street, staggering as if they were coming ashore in some exotic port where they found themselves temporarily anchored.

Saint-Loup appeared, moving like a whirlwind, his monocle spinning in the air before him. I had not given my name, and was eager to enjoy his surprise and delight.

"Oh, what a bore!" he exclaimed, suddenly catching sight of me, and blushing to the tips of his ears. "I've just had a week's leave, and I shan't be off duty again for another week."

And, preoccupied by the thought of my having to spend this first night alone, for he knew better than anyone my bed-time agonies, which he had often noticed and soothed at Balbec, he broke off his lamentation to turn and look at me, coax me with little smiles, with tender though unsymmetrical glances, half of them coming directly from his eye, the other half through his monocle, but both sorts alike testifying to the emotion that he felt on seeing me again, testifying also to that important matter which I still did not understand but which now vitally concerned me, our friendship.

"I say, where are you going to sleep? Really, I can't recommend the hotel where we mess; it's next to the Exhibition ground, where there's a show just starting; you'll find it beastly crowded. No, you'd better go to the Hôtel de Flandre; it's a little eighteenth-century palace with old tapestries. It's quite the (*ça fait assez*) 'old historical dwelling.'"

Saint-Loup employed in every connexion the verb *faire* for "have the air of," because the spoken language, like the written, feels from time to time the need of these alterations in the meanings of words, these refinements of expression. And just as journalists often have not the least idea what school of literature the "turns of phrase" they use originate from, so the vocabulary, the very diction of Saint-Loup were formed in imitation of three different aesthetes none of whom he knew but whose modes of speech had been indirectly inculcated into him. "Besides," he concluded, "the hotel I mean is more or less adapted to your auditory hyperaesthesia. You will have no neighbours. I quite see that it's a slender advantage, and as, after all, another guest may arrive tomorrow, it would not be worth your while to choose that particular hotel on such precarious grounds. No, it's for its appearance that I recommend it. The rooms are rather attractive, all the furniture is old and comfortable; there's something reassuring about it." But to me, less of an artist than Saint-Loup, the pleasure that an attractive house might give one was superficial, almost non-existent, and could not calm my incipient anguish, as painful as that which I used to feel long ago at Combray when my mother did not come upstairs to say good night, or that which I felt on the evening of my arrival at Balbec in the room with the unnaturally high ceiling, which smelt of vetiver. Saint-Loup read all this in my fixed stare.

"A lot you care, though, about this charming palace, my poor fellow; you're quite pale; and here am I like a great brute talking to you about tapestries which you won't even have the heart to look at. I know the room they'll put you in; personally I find it most cheerful, but I can quite understand that it won't have the same effect on you with your sensitive nature. You mustn't think I don't understand you. I don't feel the same myself, but I can put myself in your place."

At that moment a sergeant who was exercising a horse on the square, entirely absorbed in making the animal jump, disregarding the salutes of passing troopers, but hurling volleys of oaths at such as got in his way, turned with a smile to Saint-Loup and, seeing that he had a friend with him, saluted us. But his horse, frothing, at once reared. Saint-Loup flung himself at its head, caught it by the bridle, succeeded in quieting it and returned to my side.

"Yes," he resumed, "I assure you that I fully understand and sympathise with what you are going through. I feel wretched," he went on, laying his hand affectionately on my shoulder, "when I think that if I could have stayed with you tonight, I might have been able, by chatting to you till morning, to relieve you of a little of your unhappiness. I could lend you some books, but you won't want to read if you're feeling like that. And I shan't be able to get anyone else to stand in for me here: I've done it twice running because my girl came down to see me."

And he knitted his brows with vexation and also in the effort to decide, like a doctor, what remedy he might best apply to my disease.

"Run along and light the fire in my quarters," he called to a trooper who passed by. "Hurry up; get a move on!"

Then, once more, he turned towards me, and once more his monocle and his peering, myopic gaze testified to our great friendship.

"No, really, you here, in these barracks where I've thought so much about you, I can scarcely believe my eyes, I feel I must be dreaming! But how is your health on the whole? A little better, I hope. You must tell me all about yourself presently. We'll go up to my room; we mustn't hang about too long on the square, there's the devil of a wind. I don't feel it now myself, but you aren't accustomed to it, I'm afraid of your catching cold. And what about your work? Have you settled down to it yet? No? You are an odd fellow! If I had your talent I'm sure I should be writing morning, noon and night. It amuses you more to do nothing. What a pity it is that it's the second-raters like me who are always ready to work, while the ones who could, don't want to! There, and I've clean forgotten to ask you how your grandmother is. Her Proudhon never leaves me."

A tall, handsome, majestic officer emerged with slow and solemn steps from the foot of a staircase. Saint-Loup saluted him and arrested the perpetual mobility of his body for the time it took him to hold his hand against the peak of his cap. But he had flung himself into the action with such force, straightening himself with so sharp a movement, and, the salute ended, brought his hand down with so abrupt a release, altering all the positions of shoulder, leg and monocle, that this moment was one not so much of immobility as of a vibrant tension in which the excessive movements which he had just made and those on which he was about to embark were neutralised. Meanwhile the officer, without coming any nearer, calm, benevolent, dignified, imperial, representing, in short, the direct opposite of Saint-Loup, also raised his hand, but unhurriedly, to the peak of his cap.

"I must just say a word to the Captain," whispered Saint-Loup. "Be a good fellow, and go and wait for me in my room. It's the second on the right, on the third floor. I'll be with you in a minute."

And setting off at the double, preceded by his monocle which fluttered in every direction, he made straight for the slow and stately captain whose horse had just been brought round and who, before preparing to mount, was giving orders with a studied nobility of gesture as in some historical painting, and as though he were setting forth to take part in some battle of the First Empire, whereas he was simply going to ride home, to the house which he had taken for the period of his service at Doncières, and which stood in a square that was named, as though in an ironical anticipation of the arrival of this Napoleonid, Place de la République. I started to climb the staircase, nearly slipping on each of its nail-studded steps, catching glimpses of barrack-rooms, their bare walls bordered with a double line of beds and kits. I was shown Saint-Loup's room. I stood for a moment outside its closed door, for I could hear movement—something stirring, something being dropped. I felt the room was not empty, that there was somebody there. But it was only the freshly lighted fire beginning to burn. It could not keep quiet; it kept shifting its logs about, and very clumsily. As I entered the room, it let one roll into the fender and set another smoking. And even when it was not moving, like an ill-bred person it made noises all the time, which, from the moment I saw the flames rising, revealed themselves to me as noises made by a fire, although if I had been on the other side of a wall I should have thought that they came from someone who was blowing his nose and walking about. I sat down in the room and waited. Liberty hangings and old German stuffs of the eighteenth century preserved it from the smell exuded by the rest of the building, a coarse, stale, mouldy smell like that of wholemeal bread. It was here, in this charming room, that I could have dined and slept with a calm and happy mind. Saint-Loup seemed almost to be present in it by reason of the text-books which littered his table, between his photographs, among which I recognised my own and that of the Duchesse de Guermantes, by reason of the fire which had at length grown accustomed to the grate, and, like an animal crouching in an ardent, noiseless, faithful watchfulness, merely let fall now and then a smouldering log which crumbled into sparks, or licked with a tongue of flame the sides of the chimney. I heard the tick of Saint-Loup's watch, which could not be far away. This tick changed place every moment, for I could not see the watch; it seemed to come from behind, from in front of me, from my right, from my left, sometimes to die away as though it were a long way off. Suddenly I caught sight of the watch on the table. Then I heard the tick in a fixed place from which it did not move again. That is to say, I thought I heard it at this place; I did not hear it there, I saw it there, for sounds have no position in space. At least we associate them with movements, and in that way they serve the purpose of warning us of those movements, of appearing to make them necessary and natural. True, it sometimes happens that a sick man whose ears have been stopped with cotton-wool ceases to hear the noise of a fire such as was crackling at that moment in Saint-Loup's fireplace, labouring at the formation of brands and cinders, which it then dropped into the fender, nor would he hear the passage of the tram-cars whose music rose at regular intervals over the main square of Doncières. Then, if the sick man reads, the pages will turn silently as though fingered by a god. The ponderous rumble of a bath being filled becomes thin, faint and distant, like a celestial twittering. The withdrawal of sound, its dilution, rob it of all its aggressive power; alarmed a moment ago by hammer-blows which seemed to be shattering the ceiling above our head, we take pleasure now in receiving them, light, caressing, distant, like the murmur of leaves playing by the roadside with the passing breeze. We play games of patience with cards which we do not hear, so much so that we imagine that we have not touched them, that they are moving of their own accord, and, anticipating our desire to play with them, have begun to play with us. And in this connexion we may wonder whether, in the case of love (to which we may even add the love of life and the love of fame, since there are, it appears, persons who are acquainted with these latter sentiments), we shouldn't act like those who, when a noise disturbs them, instead of praying that it may cease, stop their ears; and, in emulation of them, bring our attention, our defences, to bear on ourselves, give them as an object to subdue not the external being whom we love, but our capacity for suffering through that being.

To return to the problem of sound, we have only to thicken the wads which close the aural passages, and they confine to a pianissimo the girl who has been playing a boisterous tune overhead; if we go further, and steep one of these wads in grease, at once the whole household must obey its despotic rule; its laws extend even beyond our portals. Pianissimo is no longer enough; the wad instantly closes the piano and the music lesson is abruptly ended; the gentleman who was walking up and down in the room above breaks off in the middle of his beat; the movement of carriages and trams is interrupted as though a sovereign were expected to pass. And indeed this attenuation of sounds sometimes disturbs our sleep instead of protecting it. Only yesterday the incessant noise in our ears, by describing to us in a continuous narrative all that was happening in the street and in the house, succeeded at length in sending us to sleep like a boring book; today, on the surface of silence spread over our sleep, a shock louder than the rest manages to make itself heard, gentle as a sigh, unrelated to any other sound, mysterious; and the demand for an explanation which it exhales is sufficient to awaken us. On the other hand, take away for a moment from the sick man the cotton-wool that has been stopping his ears and in a flash the broad daylight, the dazzling sun of sound dawns afresh, blinding him, is born again in the universe; the multitude of exiled sounds comes hastening back; we are present, as though it were the chanting of choirs of angels, at the resurrection of the voice. The empty streets are filled for a moment with the whirr of the swift and recurrent wings of the singing tram-cars. In the bedroom itself the sick man has created, not, like Prometheus, fire, but the sound of fire. And when we increase or reduce the wads of cotton-wool, it is as though we were pressing alternately one and then the other of the two pedals which we have added to the sonority of the outer world.

Only there are also suppressions of sound which are not temporary. The man who has become completely deaf cannot even heat a pan of milk by his bedside without having to keep an eye open to watch, on the tilted lid, for the white hyperborean reflexion, like that of a coming snowstorm, which is the premonitory sign it is wise to obey by cutting off (as the Lord stilled the

waves) the electric current; for already the fitfully swelling egg of
the boiling milk is reaching its climax in a series of sidelong
undulations, puffs out and fills a few drooping sails that had been
puckered by the cream, sending a nacreous spinnaker bellying out
in the hurricane, until the cutting off of the current, if the electric
storm is exorcised in time, will make them all twirl round on
themselves and scatter like magnolia petals. But should the sick
man not have been quick enough in taking the necessary precautions, presently, his drowned books and watch scarcely emerging
from the milky tidal wave, he will be obliged to call the old nurse,
who, for all that he is an eminent statesman or a famous writer, will
tell him that he has no more sense than a child of five. At other
times in the magic chamber, standing inside the closed door, a
person who was not there a moment ago will have made his
appearance; it is a visitor who has entered unheard, and who
merely gesticulates, like a figure in one of those little puppet
theatres, so restful for those who have taken a dislike to the spoken
tongue. And for this stone-deaf man, since the loss of a sense adds
as much beauty to the world as its acquisition, it is with ecstasy that
he walks now upon an earth become almost an Eden, in which
sound has not yet been created. The highest waterfalls unfold for
his eyes alone their sheets of crystal, stiller than the glassy sea, pure
as the cascades of Paradise. Since sound was for him, before his
deafness, the perceptible form which the cause of a movement
assumed, objects moved soundlessly now seem to be moved without cause; deprived of the quality of sound, they show a spontaneous activity, seem to be alive. They move, halt, become alight of
their own accord. Of their own accord they vanish in the air like
the winged monsters of prehistory. In the solitary and neighbour-
less house of the deaf man, the service which, before his infirmity
was complete, was already showing more reserve, was being
executed silently, is now carried out, with a sort of surreptitious
deftness, by mutes, as at the court of a fairy-tale king. And again as
on the stage, the building which the deaf man looks out on from
his window—whether barracks, church, or town hall—is only so
much scenery. If one day it should fall to the ground, it may emit a
cloud of dust and leave visible ruins; but, less substantial even than
a palace on the stage, though it has not the same exiguity, it will
subside in the magic universe without letting the fall of its heavy
blocks of stone tarnish the chastity of the prevailing silence with
the vulgarity of noise.

The silence, altogether more relative, which reigned in the little barrack-room where I sat waiting was now broken. The door opened and Saint-Loup rushed in, dropping his monocle.

"Ah, Robert, how comfortable it is here," I said to him. "How good it would be if one were allowed to dine and sleep here."

And indeed, had it not been against the regulations, what repose untinged by sadness I could have enjoyed there, guarded by that atmosphere of tranquillity, vigilance and gaiety which was maintained by a thousand ordered and untroubled wills, a thousand carefree minds, in that great community called a barracks where, time having taken the form of action, the sad bell that tolled the hours outside was replaced by the same joyous clarion of those martial calls, the ringing memory of which was kept perpetually alive in the paved streets of the town, like the dust that floats in a sunbeam—a voice sure of being heard, and musical because it was the command not only of authority to obedience but of wisdom to happiness.

"So you'd rather stay with me and sleep here, would you, than go to the hotel by yourself?" Saint-Loup asked me, smiling.

"Oh, Robert, it's cruel of you to be sarcastic about it," I answered. "You know it's not possible, and you know how wretched I shall be over there."

"Well, you flatter me!" he replied. "Because it actually occurred to me that you'd rather stay here tonight. And that is precisely what I went to ask the Captain."

"And he has given you leave?" I cried.

"He hadn't the slightest objection."

"Oh! I adore him!"

"No, that would be going too far. But now, let me just get hold of my batman and tell him to see about our dinner," he went on, while I turned away to hide my tears.

We were several times interrupted by the entry of one or other of Saint-Loup's comrades. He drove them all out again.

"Get out of here. Buzz off!"

I begged him to let them stay.

"No, really, they would bore you stiff. They're absolutely uncouth people who can talk of nothing but racing or stable shop. Besides, I don't want them here either; they would spoil these precious moments I've been looking forward to. Mind you, when I tell you that these fellows are brainless, it isn't that everything military is devoid of intellectuality. Far from it. We have a major here who's an admirable man. He's given us a course in which military history is treated like a demonstration, like a problem in algebra. Even from the aesthetic point of view there's a curious beauty, alternately inductive and deductive, about it which you couldn't fail to appreciate."

"That's not the officer who's given me leave to stay here tonight?"

"No, thank God! The man you 'adore' for so very trifling a service is the biggest fool that ever walked the face of the earth. He's perfect at looking after messing, and at kit inspections; he spends hours with the senior sergeant and the master-tailor. There you have his mentality. Besides, he has a vast contempt, like everyone here, for the excellent major in question, whom no one speaks to because he's a freemason and doesn't go to confession. The Prince de Borodino would never have an outsider like that in his house. Which is pretty fair cheek, when all's said and done, from a man whose great-grandfather was a small farmer, and who would probably be a small farmer himself if it hadn't been for the Napoleonic wars. Not that he isn't a little aware of his own rather ambiguous position in society, neither flesh nor fowl. He hardly ever shows his face at the Jockey, it makes him feel so deuced awkward, this so-called Prince," added Robert, who, having been led by the same spirit of imitation to adopt the social theories of his teachers and the worldly prejudices of his relatives, unconsciously combined a democratic love of humanity with a contempt for the nobility of the Empire.

I looked at the photograph of his aunt, and the thought that, since Saint-Loup had this photograph in his possession, he might perhaps give it to me, made me cherish him all the more and long to do him a thousand services, which seemed to me a very small exchange for it. For this photograph was like a supplementary encounter added to all those that I had already had with Mme de Guermantes; better still, a prolonged encounter, as if, by a sudden stride forward in our relations, she had stopped beside me, in a garden hat, and had allowed me for the first time to gaze at my leisure at that rounded cheek, that arched neck, that tapering eyebrow (veiled from me hitherto by the swiftness of her passage, the bewilderment of my impressions, the imperfection of memory); and the contemplation of them, as well as the bare throat and arms of a woman whom I had never seen save in a high-necked and long-sleeved dress, was to me a voluptuous discovery, a

priceless favour. Those forms, which had seemed to me almost a
forbidden spectacle, I could study there as in a text-book of the
only geometry that had any value for me. Later on, looking at
Robert, it struck me that he too was a little like the photograph of
his aunt, by a mysterious process which I found almost as moving,
since, if his face had not been directly produced by hers, the two
had nevertheless a common origin. The features of the Duchesse
de Guermantes, which were pinned to my vision of Combray, the
nose like a falcon's beak, the piercing eyes, seemed to have served
also as a pattern for the cutting out—in another copy analogous
and slender, with too delicate a skin—of Robert's face, which
might almost be superimposed upon his aunt's. I looked longingly
at those features of his so characteristic of the Guermantes, of that
race which had remained so individual in the midst of a world in
which it remained isolated in its divinely ornithological glory, for
it seemed to have sprung, in the age of mythology, from the union
of a goddess with a bird.

Robert, without being aware of its cause, was touched by my
evident affection. This was moreover increased by the sense of
well-being inspired in me by the heat of the fire and by the
champagne which simultaneously bedewed my forehead with
beads of sweat and my eyes with tears; it washed down some
young partridges which I ate with the wonderment of a layman,
of whatever sort he may be, who finds in a way of life with which
he is not familiar what he has supposed it to exclude—the wonderment, for instance, of an atheist who sits down to an exquisitely
cooked dinner in a presbytery. And next morning, when I awoke,
I went over to Saint-Loup's window, which being at a great height
overlooked the whole countryside, curious to make the acquaintance of my new neighbour, the landscape which I had not been
able to see the day before, having arrived too late, at an hour when
it was already sleeping beneath the outspread cloak of night. And
yet, early as it had awoken, I could see it, when I opened the
window and looked out, only as though from the window of a
country house overlooking the lake, shrouded still in its soft white
morning gown of mist which scarcely allowed me to make out
anything at all. But I knew that, before the troopers who were
busy with their horses in the square had finished grooming them, it
would have cast its gown aside. In the meantime, I could see only a
bare hill, raising its lean and rugged flanks, already swept clear of
darkness, over the back of the barracks. Through the translucent

screen of hoarfrost I could not take my eyes from this stranger who was looking at me too for the first time. But when I had formed the habit of coming to the barracks, my consciousness that the hill was there, more real, consequently, even when I did not see it, than the hotel at Balbec, than our house in Paris, of which I thought as of absent—or dead—friends, that is to say scarcely believing any longer in their existence, caused its reflected form, even without my realising it, to be silhouetted against the slightest impressions that I formed at Doncières, and among them, to begin with this first morning, the pleasing impression of warmth given me by the cup of chocolate, prepared by Saint-Loup's batman in this comfortable room, which seemed like a sort of optical centre from which to look out at the hill—the idea of doing anything else but just gaze at it, the idea of actually climbing it, being rendered impossible by this same mist. Imbued with the shape of the hill, associated with the taste of hot chocolate and with the whole web of my fancies at that particular time, this mist, without my having given it the least thought, came to infuse all my thoughts of that time, just as a massive and unmelting lump of gold had remained allied to my impressions of Balbec, or as the proximity of the outside steps of sandstone gave a greyish background to my impressions of Combray. It did not, however, persist late into the day; the sun began by hurling at it in vain a few darts which sprinkled it with brilliants, then finally overcame it. The hill might expose its grizzled rump to the sun's rays, which, an hour later, when I went into the town, gave to the russet tints of the autumn leaves, to the reds and blues of the election posters pasted on the walls, an exaltation which raised my spirits also and made me stamp, singing as I went, on the paving-stones from which I could hardly keep myself from jumping in the air for joy.

But after that first night I had to sleep at the hotel. And I knew beforehand that I was doomed to find sadness there. It was like an unbreathable aroma which all my life long had been exhaled for me by every new bedroom, that is to say by every bedroom—for in the one which I usually occupied I was not present, my mind remained elsewhere and sent mere Habit to take its place. But I could not employ this servant, less sensitive than myself, to look after things for me in a new place, where I preceded him, where I arrived alone, where I must bring into contact with its environment that "Self" which I rediscovered only at year-long intervals, but always the same, not having grown at all since Combray, since my first arrival at Balbec, weeping inconsolably on the edge of an unpacked trunk.

As it happened, I was mistaken. I had no time to be sad, for I was not alone for an instant. The fact of the matter was that there remained of the old palace a surplus refinement of structure and decoration, out of place in a modern hotel, which, released from any practical assignment, had in its long spell of leisure acquired a sort of life: passages winding about in all directions, which one was continually crossing in their aimless wanderings, lobbies as long as corridors and as ornate as drawing-rooms, which had the air rather of dwelling there themselves than of forming part of the dwelling, which could not be induced to enter and settle down in any of the rooms but roamed about outside mine and came up at once to offer me their company—neighbours of a sort, idle but never noisy, menial ghosts of the past who had been granted the privilege of staying quietly by the doors of the rooms which were let to visitors, and who whenever I came across them greeted me with a silent deference. In short, the idea of a lodging, a mere container for our present existence, simply shielding us from the cold and from the sight of other people, was absolutely inapplicable to this dwelling, an assembly of rooms, as real as a colony of people, living, it was true, in silence, but which one was obliged to encounter, to avoid, to greet when one came in. One tried not to disturb, and one could not look at without respect, the great drawing-room which had formed, far back in the eighteenth century, the habit of stretching itself at its ease among its hangings of old gold beneath the clouds of its painted ceiling. And one was seized with a more personal curiosity as regards the smaller rooms which, without the least concern for symmetry, ran all round it, innumerable, startled, fleeing in disorder as far as the garden, to which they had so easy an access down three broken steps.

If I wished to go out or come in without taking the lift or being seen on the main staircase, a smaller private staircase, no longer in use, offered me its steps so skilfully arranged, one close above another, that there seemed to exist in their gradation a perfect proportion of the same kind as those which, in colours, scents, savours, often arouse in us a peculiar sensuous pleasure. But the pleasure to be found in going up and downstairs was one I had had to come here to learn, as once in an alpine resort I had found that the act—as a rule not noticed—of breathing can be a perpetual delight. I received that dispensation from effort which is granted to

us only by the things to which long use has accustomed us, when I
set my feet for the first time on those steps, familiar before ever
I knew them, as if they possessed, stored up, incorporated in them
perhaps by the masters of old whom they used to welcome every
day, the prospective charm of habits which I had not yet contracted and which indeed could only dwindle once they had
become my own. I went into a room; the double doors closed
behind me, the hangings let in a silence in which I felt myself
invested with a sort of exhilarating royalty; a marble fireplace with
ornaments of wrought brass—of which one would have been
wrong to think that its sole idea was to represent the art of the
Directory—offered me a fire, and a little easy chair on short
legs helped me to warm myself as comfortably as if I had been
sitting on the hearthrug. The walls held the room in a close
embrace, separating it from the rest of the world and, to let into
it, to enclose in it what made it complete, parted to make way for
the book-case, reserved a place for the bed, on either side of which
columns airily upheld the lofty ceiling of the alcove. And the room
was prolonged in depth by two closets as wide as itself, one of
which had hanging from its wall, to scent the occasion on which
one had recourse to it, a voluptuous rosary of orris-roots; the
doors, if I left them open when I withdrew into this innermost
retreat, were not content with tripling its dimensions without
spoiling its harmonious proportions, and not only allowed my
eyes to enjoy the delights of extension after those of concentration, but added further to the pleasure of my solitude—which,
while still inviolable, was no longer shut in—the sense of liberty.
This closet gave on to a courtyard, a solitary fair stranger whom I
was glad to have for a neighbour when next morning my eyes fell
on her, a captive between her high walls in which no other
window opened, with nothing but two yellowing trees which
contrived to give a mauve softness to the pure sky above.

Before going to bed I left the room to explore the whole of my
enchanted domain. I walked down a long gallery which displayed
to me successively all that it had to offer me if I could not sleep, an
armchair placed in a corner, a spinet, a blue porcelain vase filled
with cinerarias on a console table, and, in an old frame, the
phantom of a lady of long ago with powdered hair mingled with
blue flowers, holding in her hand a bunch of carnations. When
I came to the end, the bare wall in which no door opened said to
me simply: "Now you must go back, but you see, you are at home

here," while the soft carpet, not to be outdone, added that if I could not sleep that night I could perfectly well come in my bare feet, and the unshuttered windows looking out over the countryside assured me that they would keep a sleepless vigil and that, at whatever hour I chose to come, I need not be afraid of disturbing anyone. And behind a hanging curtain I came upon a little closet which, stopped by the outer wall and unable to escape, had hidden itself there shamefacedly and gave me a frightened stare from its little round window, glowing blue in the moonlight. I went to bed, but the presence of the eiderdown, of the slim columns, of the little fireplace, by screwing up my attention to a pitch beyond that of Paris, prevented me from surrendering to the habitual routine of my musings. And as it is this particular state of attention that enfolds our slumbers, acts upon them, modifies them, brings them into line with this or that series of past impressions, the images that filled my dreams that first night were borrowed from a memory entirely distinct from that on which I was in the habit of drawing. If I had been tempted while asleep to let myself be swept back into my usual current of remembrance, the bed to which I was not accustomed, the careful attention which I was obliged to pay to the position of my limbs when I turned over, were sufficient to adjust or maintain the new thread of my dreams. It is the same with sleep as with our perception of the external world. It needs only a modification in our habits to make it poetic, it is enough that while undressing we should have dozed off involuntarily on top of the bed for the dimensions of sleep to be altered and its beauty felt. We wake up, look at our watch and see "four o'clock"; it is only four o'clock in the morning, but we imagine that the whole day has gone by, so vividly does this unsolicited nap of a few minutes appear to have come down to us from heaven, by virtue of some divine right, huge and solid as an Emperor's orb of gold. In the morning, worried by the thought that my grandfather was ready and they were waiting for me to set out for our walk along the Méséglise way, I was awakened by the blare of a regimental band which passed every day beneath my windows. But two or three times—and I say this because one cannot properly describe human life unless one bathes it in the sleep into which it plunges night after night and which sweeps round it as a promontory is encircled by the sea—the intervening layer of sleep was resistant enough to withstand the impact of the music and I heard nothing. On other mornings it gave way for a moment; but my consciousness, still muffled from sleep (like those organs by which, after a preliminary anaesthetic, a cauterisation, not perceived at first, is felt only at the very end and then as a faint smarting), was touched only gently by the shrill points of the fifes which caressed it with a vague, cool, matutinal warbling; and after this fragile interruption in which the silence had turned to music it relapsed into my slumber before even the dragoons had finished passing, depriving me of the last blossoming sheafs of the surging bouquet of sound. And the zone of my consciousness which its springing stems had brushed was so narrow, so circumscribed with sleep that later on, when Saint-Loup asked me whether I had heard the band, I was not certain that the sound of its brasses had not been as imaginary as that which I heard during the day echoing, after the slightest noise, from the paved streets of the town. Perhaps I had heard it only in my dreams, prompted by my fear of being awakened, or else of not being awakened and so not seeing the regiment march past. For often when I remained asleep at the moment when on the contrary I had supposed that the noise would awaken me, for the next hour I imagined that I was awake, while still dozing, and I enacted to myself with tenuous shadow-shapes on the screen of my slumber the various scenes of which it deprived me but at which I had the illusion of looking on.

Indeed, what one has meant to do during the day it turns out, sleep intervening, that one accomplishes only in one's dreams, that is to say after it has been diverted by drowsiness into following a different path from that which one would have chosen when awake. The same story branches off and has a different ending. When all is said, the world in which we live when we are asleep is so different that people who have difficulty in going to sleep seek first of all to escape from the waking world. After having desperately, for hours on end, with their eyes closed, revolved in their minds thoughts similar to those which they would have had with their eyes open, they take heart again on noticing that the preceding minute has been weighted down by a line of reasoning in strict contradiction to the laws of logic and the reality of the present, this brief "absence" signifying that the door is now open through which they may perhaps presently be able to escape from the perception of the real, to advance to a resting-place more or less remote from it, which will mean their having a more or less "good" night. But already a great stride has been made when we turn our backs on the real, when we reach the outer caves in which "auto-suggestions" prepare—like witches—the hell-broth of imaginary illnesses or of the recurrence of nervous disorders, and watch for the hour when the spasms which have been building up during the unconsciousness of sleep will be unleashed with sufficient force to make sleep cease.

Not far thence is the secret garden in which the kinds of sleep, so different one from another, induced by datura, by Indian hemp, by the multiple extracts of ether—the sleep of belladonna, of opium, of valerian—grow like unknown flowers whose petals remain closed until the day when the predestined stranger comes to open them with a touch and to liberate for long hours the aroma of their peculiar dreams for the delectation of an amazed and spellbound being. At the end of the garden stands the convent with open windows through which we hear voices repeating the lessons learned before we went to sleep, which we shall know only at the moment of awakening; while, presaging that moment, our inner alarm-clock ticks away, so well regulated by our preoccupation that when our housekeeper comes in and tells us it is seven o'clock she will find us awake and ready. The dim walls of that chamber which opens upon our dreams and within which the sorrows of love are wrapped in that oblivion whose incessant toil is interrupted and annulled at times by a nightmare heavy with reminiscences, but quickly resumed, are hung, even after we are awake, with the memories of our dreams, but they are so murky that often we catch sight of them for the first time only in the broad light of the afternoon when the ray of a similar idea happens by chance to strike them; some of them, clear and harmonious while we slept, already so distorted that, having failed to recognise them, we can but hasten to lay them in the earth, like corpses too quickly decomposed or relics so seriously damaged, so nearly crumbling into dust that the most skilful restorer could not give them back a shape or make anything of them.

Near the gate is the quarry to which our heavier slumbers repair in search of substances which coat the brain with so unbreakable a glaze that, to awaken the sleeper, his own will is obliged, even on a golden morning, to smite him with mighty blows, like a young Siegfried. Beyond this, again, are nightmares, of which the doctors foolishly assert that they tire us more than does insomnia, whereas on the contrary they enable the thinker to escape from the strain of thought—nightmares with their fantastic picture-books in which our relatives who are dead are shown meeting with serious accidents which at the same time do not preclude their speedy recovery. Until then we keep them in a little rat-cage, in which they are smaller than white mice and, covered with big red spots out of each of which a feather sprouts, regale us with Ciceronian speeches. Next to this picture-book is the revolving disc of awakening, by virtue of which we submit for a moment to the tedium of having to return presently to a house which was pulled down fifty years ago, the image of which is gradually effaced by a number of others as sleep recedes, until we arrive at the image which appears only when the disc has ceased to revolve and which coincides with the one we shall see with opened eyes.

Sometimes I had heard nothing, being in one of those slumbers into which we fall as into a pit from which we are heartily glad to be drawn up a little later, heavy, overfed, digesting all that has been brought to us (as by the nymphs who fed the infant Hercules) by those agile vegetative powers whose activity is doubled while we sleep.

We call that a leaden sleep, and it seems as though, even for a few moments after such a sleep is ended, one has oneself become a simple figure of lead. One is no longer a person. How then, searching for one's thoughts, one's personality, as one searches for a lost object, does one recover one's own self rather than any other? Why, when one begins again to think, is it not a personality other than the previous one that becomes incarnate in one? One fails to see what dictates the choice, or why, among the millions of human beings one might be, it is on the being one was the day before that unerringly one lays one's hand. What is it that guides us, when there has been a real interruption—whether it be that our unconsciousness has been complete or our dreams entirely different from ourselves? There has indeed been death, as when the heart has ceased to beat and a rhythmical traction of the tongue revives us. No doubt the room, even if we have seen it only once before, awakens memories to which other, older memories cling, or perhaps some were dormant in us, of which we now become conscious. The resurrection at our awakening—after that beneficent attack of mental alienation which is sleep—must after all be similar to what occurs when we recall a name, a line, a refrain that we had forgotten. And perhaps the resurrection of the soul after death is to be conceived as a phenomenon of memory.

When I had finished sleeping, tempted by the sunlit sky but held back by the chill of those last autumn mornings, so luminous and so cold, which herald winter, in order to look at the trees on which the leaves were indicated now only by a few strokes of gold or pink which seemed to have been left in the air, on an invisible web, I raised my head from the pillow and stretched my neck, keeping my body still hidden beneath the bedclothes; like a chrysalis in the process of metamorphosis, I was a dual creature whose different parts were not adapted to the same environment; for my eyes colour was sufficient, without warmth; my chest on the other hand was anxious for warmth and not for colour. I got up only after my fire had been lighted, and studied the picture, so delicate and transparent, of the pink and golden morning, to which I had now added by artificial means the element of warmth that it lacked, poking my fire which burned and smoked like a good pipe and gave me, as a pipe would have given me, a pleasure at once coarse because it was based upon a material comfort and delicate because behind it were the soft outlines of a pure vision. The walls of my dressing-room were papered in a violent red, sprinkled with black and white flowers to which it seemed that I should have some difficulty in growing accustomed. But they succeeded only in striking me as novel, in forcing me to enter not into conflict but into contact with them, in modulating the gaiety and the songs of my morning ablutions; they succeeded only in imprisoning me in the heart of a sort of poppy, out of which to look at a world which I saw quite otherwise than in Paris, from the gay screen which was this new dwelling-place, of a different aspect from the house of my parents, and into which flowed a purer air.

On certain days, I was agitated by the desire to see my grand-mother again or by the fear that she might be ill, or else by the memory of some business left half-finished in Paris, which seemed to have made no progress, or sometimes, again, by some difficulty in which, even here, I had managed to become involved. One or other of these anxieties would have prevented me from sleeping, and I would be powerless to face up to my depression, which in an instant would fill the whole of my existence. Then I would send a messenger from the hotel to the barracks with a note for Saint-Loup, telling him that if it was physically possible—I knew that it was extremely difficult for him—I should be most grateful if he would look in for a minute. An hour later he would arrive; and on hearing his ring at the door I felt myself liberated from my obsessions. I knew that, if they were stronger than I, he was stronger than they, and my attention was diverted from them and turned

towards him, who would know how to settle them. On entering
the room he would at once envelop me in the fresh air in which
from early morning he had been active and busy, a vital atmosphere very different from that of my room, to which I at once
adapted myself by appropriate reactions.

"I hope you weren't angry with me for bothering you. There is
something that's worrying me, as you probably guessed."

"Not at all. I just supposed you wanted to see me, and
I thought it very nice of you. I was delighted that you sent for
me. But what's the trouble? Things not going well? What can I do
to help?"

He would listen to my explanations, and give precise answers;
but before he uttered a word he would have transformed me to his
own likeness; compared with the important occupations which
kept him so busy, so alert, so happy, the worries which a moment
ago I had been unable to endure for another instant seemed to me
as negligible as they did to him. I was like a man who, having been
unable to open his eyes for some days, sends for a doctor, who
neatly and gently raises his eyelid, removes from beneath it a grain
of sand, and shows it to him; the sufferer is healed and comforted.
All my cares resolved themselves in a telegram which Saint-Loup
undertook to dispatch. Life seemed to me so different, so delightful, I was flooded with such a surfeit of strength, that I longed for
action.

"What are you doing now?" I asked him.

"I must leave you, I'm afraid. We're going on a route march in
three quarters of an hour, and I have to be on parade."

"Then it's been a great bother to you, coming here?"

"No, no bother at all, the Captain was very good about it. He
told me that if it was for you I must go at once. But I don't like to
seem to be abusing the privilege."

"But if I got up and dressed quickly and went by myself to the
place where you'll be training, it would interest me immensely,
and I could perhaps talk to you during the breaks."

"I shouldn't advise you to do that. You've been lying awake,
fretting about something that I assure you is not of the
slightest importance, but now that it has ceased to worry you,
you should turn over and go to sleep—you'll find it an excellent
antidote to the demineralisation of your nerve-cells. Only you
mustn't go to sleep too soon, because our band-boys will be
coming along under your windows. But as soon as they've passed

I think you'll be left in peace, and we shall meet again this evening at dinner."

But soon I was constantly going to see the regiment doing field manoeuvres, when I began to take an interest in the military theories which Saint-Loup's friends used to expound over the dinner-table, and when it had become the chief desire of my life to see at close quarters their various leaders, just as a person who makes music his principal study and spends his life in the concert halls finds pleasure in frequenting the cafés in which one can share the life of the members of the orchestra. To reach the training-ground I used to have to make long journeys on foot. In the evening after dinner the longing for sleep made my head droop every now and then as in a fit of vertigo. Next morning I realised that I had not heard the band any more than, at Balbec, after the evenings on which Saint-Loup had taken me to dinner at Rivebelle, I used to hear the concert on the beach. And when I wanted to get up I had a delicious sensation of being incapable of doing so; I felt myself fastened to a deep, invisible soil by the articulations (of which my tiredness made me conscious) of muscular and nutritious roots. I felt myself full of strength; life seemed to extend more amply before me; for I had reverted to the healthy tiredness of my childhood at Combray on mornings after the days when we had taken the Guermantes walk. Poets claim that we recapture for a moment the self that we were long ago when we enter some house or garden in which we used to live in our youth. But these are most hazardous pilgrimages, which end as often in disappointment as in success. It is in ourselves that we should rather seek to find those fixed places, contemporaneous with different years. And great fatigue followed by a good night's rest can to a certain extent help us to do so. For in order to make us descend into the most subterranean galleries of sleep, where no reflexion from overnight, no gleam of memory comes to light up the interior monologue—if the latter does not itself cease—fatigue followed by rest will so thoroughly turn over the soil and penetrate the bedrock of our bodies that we discover down there, where our muscles plunge and twist in their ramifications and breathe in new life, the garden where we played in our childhood. There is no need to travel in order to see it again; we must dig down inwardly to discover it. What once covered the earth is no longer above but beneath it; a mere excursion does not suffice for a visit to the dead city: excavation is necessary also. But we shall see how certain

fugitive and fortuitous impressions carry us back even more effectively to the past, with a more delicate precision, with a more light-
winged, more immaterial, more headlong, more unerring, more
immortal flight, than these organic dislocations.

Sometimes my exhaustion was greater still. I had followed the
manoeuvres for several days on end without being able to go to
bed. How blissful then was my return to the hotel! As I got into
bed I seemed to have escaped at last from the hands of enchanters
and sorcerers like those who people the "romances" beloved of
our forebears in the seventeenth century. My sleep that night and
the lazy morning that followed it were no more than a charming
fairy-tale. Charming; beneficent perhaps also. I reminded myself
that the worst sufferings have their place of sanctuary, that one can
always, when all else fails, find rest. These thoughts carried me far.

On days when, although there was no parade, Saint-Loup had
to stay in barracks, I used often to go and visit him there. It was a
long way; I had to leave the town and cross the viaduct, from
either side of which I had an immense view. A strong breeze blew
almost always over this high ground, and swept round the buildings erected on three sides of the barrack-square, which howled
incessantly like a cave of the winds. While I waited for Robert—
he being engaged on some duty or other—outside the door of his
room or in the mess, talking to some of his friends to whom he had
introduced me (and whom later I came to see from time to time,
even when he was not going to be there), looking down from the
window at the countryside three hundred feet below me, bare
now except where recently sown fields, often still soaked with rain
and glittering in the sun, showed a few strips of green, of the
brilliance and translucent limpidity of enamel, I often heard him
discussed by the others, and I soon learned what a popular favourite he was. Among many of the volunteers, belonging to other
squadrons, sons of rich business or professional men who looked at
aristocratic high society only from outside and without penetrating its enclosure, the attraction which they naturally felt towards
what they knew of Saint-Loup's character was reinforced by the
glamour that attached in their eyes to the young man whom, on
Saturday evenings, when they went on pass to Paris, they had seen
supping in the Café de la Paix with the Duc d'Uzès and the Prince
d'Orléans. And on that account they associated his handsome face,
his casual way of walking and saluting, the perpetual dance of his
monocle, the jaunty eccentricity of his service dress—the caps

always too high, the breeches of too fine a cloth and too pink a shade—with a notion of elegance and "tone" which, they averred, was lacking in the best turned-out officers in the regiment, even the majestic Captain to whom I had been indebted for the privilege of sleeping in barracks, who seemed, in comparison, too pompous and almost common.

One of them mentioned that the Captain had bought a new horse. "He can buy as many horses as he likes. I passed Saint-Loup on Sunday morning in the Allée des Acacias. He's got altogether more style on a horse!" replied his companion with the knowledge of experience, for these young men belonged to a class which, if it does not frequent the same houses and know the same people, yet, thanks to money and leisure, does not differ from the nobility in its experience of all those refinements of life which money can procure. At most their elegance, in the matter of clothes, for instance, had something more studied, more impeccable about it than that relaxed and careless elegance which had so delighted my grandmother in Saint-Loup. It gave quite a thrill to these sons of big stockbrokers or bankers, as they sat eating oysters after the theatre, to see Sergeant Saint-Loup at an adjoining table. And what a tale there was to tell in barracks on Monday night, after a week-end leave, by one of them who was in Robert's squadron, and to whom he had said how d'ye do "most civilly," while another, who was not in the same squadron, was quite positive that in spite of this Saint-Loup had recognised him, for two or three times he had put up his monocle and stared in the speaker's direction.

"Yes, my brother saw him at the Paix," said another, who had been spending the day with his mistress. "Apparently his dress coat was cut too loose and didn't fit him."

"What was the waistcoat like?"

"He wasn't wearing a white waistcoat; it was purple, with sort of palms on it—smashing!"

To the "old soldiers" (sons of the soil who had never heard of the Jockey Club and simply put Saint-Loup in the category of ultra-rich non-commissioned officers, in which they included all those who, whether bankrupt or not, lived in a certain style, whose income or debts ran into several figures, and who were generous towards their men), the gait, the monocle, the breeches, the caps of Saint-Loup, even if they saw in them nothing particularly aristocratic, furnished nevertheless just as much interest and meaning. They recognised in these peculiarities the character, the style which they had assigned once and for all to this most popular of the "stripes" in the regiment, manners like no one else's, scornful indifference to what his superior officers might think, which seemed to them the natural corollary of his kindness to his subordinates. The morning cup of coffee in the canteen, the afternoon rest in the barrack-room, seemed pleasanter when some old soldier fed the greedy and idle squad with some savoury tit-bit about a cap of Saint-Loup's.

"It was the height of my pack."

"Come off it, old chap, you're having us on, it couldn't have been the height of your pack," interrupted a young college graduate who hoped by using these slang terms not to appear a greenhorn, and by venturing on this contradiction to obtain confirmation of a fact which enchanted him.

"Oh, so it wasn't the height of my pack, wasn't it? You measured it, I suppose! I tell you this much, the CO glared at him as if he'd have liked to put him in clink. But you needn't think the great Saint-Loup was rattled, oh no, he came and he went, and down with his head and up with his head, and always that trick with the monocle. We'll see what the Cap'n has to say when he hears. Oh, very likely he'll say nothing, but you may be sure he won't be pleased. But there's nothing so wonderful about that cap. I hear he's got thirty of 'em and more at home in town."

"How come you heard about it, old man? From our blasted Corp?" asked the young graduate, pedantically displaying the new grammatical forms which he had only recently acquired and with which he took a pride in garnishing his conversation.

"How come I heard it? From his batman of course!"

"Ah, there's a bloke who knows when he's well off!"

"I should think so! He's got more brass than I have, that's for sure! And besides he gives him all his own belongings and everything. He wasn't getting enough grub in the canteen, he says. So along comes de Saint-Loup and gives cooky hell: 'I want him to be properly fed, d'you hear,' he says, 'and I don't care what it costs.'"

The old soldier made up for the triviality of the words quoted by the emphasis of his tone, in a feeble imitation of the speaker which had an immense success.

On leaving the barracks I would take a stroll, and then, to fill up the time before I went, as I did every evening, to dine with

Saint-Loup at the hotel in which he and his friends had established their mess, I walked back to my own, as soon as the sun went down, so as to have a couple of hours in which to rest and read. In the square, the evening sky bedecked the pepper-pot turrets of the castle with little pink clouds which matched the colour of the bricks, and completed the harmony by softening the tone of the latter with a sunset glow. So strong a current of vitality coursed through my veins that no movement on my part could exhaust it; each step I took, after touching a paving-stone of the square, rebounded off it. I seemed to have the wings of Mercury growing on my heels. One of the fountains was filled with a ruddy glow, while in the other the moonlight had already begun to turn the water opalescent. Between them were children at play, uttering shrill cries, wheeling in circles, obeying some necessity of the hour, like swifts or bats. Next door to the hotel, the old law-courts and the Louis XVI orangery, in which were now installed the savings bank and the Army Corps headquarters, were lit from within by the palely gilded globes of their gas-jets which, already aglow though it was still daylight outside, suited those vast, tall, eighteenth-century windows from which the last gleams of the setting sun had not yet departed, as a headdress of yellow tortoise-shell might suit a complexion heightened with rouge, and per-suaded me to seek out my fireside and the lamp which, alone in the shadowy façade of my hotel, was striving to resist the gathering darkness, and for the sake of which I went indoors before it was quite dark, for pleasure, as to an appetising meal. I retained, in my lodgings, the same fullness of sensation that I had felt outside. It gave such an apparent convexity of surface to things which as a rule seem flat and insipid—to the yellow flame of the fire, the coarse blue paper of the sky on which the setting sun had scribbled corkscrews and whirligigs like a schoolboy with a piece of red chalk, the curiously patterned cloth on the round table on which a ream of essay paper and an inkpot lay in readiness for me together with one of Bergotte's novels—that ever since then these things have continued to seem to me to abound in a richly particular form of existence which I feel that I should be able to extract from them if it were granted me to set eyes on them again. I thought with joy of the barracks I had just left and of its weather-cock turning with every wind that blew. Like a diver breathing through a pipe which rises above the surface of the water, I felt that I was in some sense linked to a healthy, open-air life through my connexion with those barracks, that towering observatory dominating a countryside furrowed with strips of green enamel, into whose various buildings I esteemed it a priceless privilege, which I hoped would last, to be free to go whenever I chose, always certain of a welcome.

At seven o'clock I dressed and went out again to dine with Saint-Loup at the hotel where he took his meals. I liked to go there on foot. It was by now pitch dark, and after the third day of my visit, as soon as night had fallen an icy wind began blowing which seemed a harbinger of snow. As I walked, I ought not, one might have supposed, to have ceased for a moment to think of Mme de Guermantes; it was only in an attempt to draw nearer to her that I had come to visit Robert's garrison. But memories and griefs are fleeting things. There are days when they recede so far that we are barely conscious of them, we think that they have gone for ever. Then we pay attention to other things. And the streets of this town had not yet become for me what streets are in the place where one is accustomed to live, simply means of getting from one place to another. The life led by the inhabitants of this unknown world must, it seemed to me, be a thing of wonder, and often the lighted windows of some dwelling kept me standing for a long while motionless in the dark by laying before my eyes the actual and mysterious scenes of an existence into which I might not penetrate. Here the fire-spirit displayed to me in a crimson tableau a chestnut-seller's booth in which a couple of non-commissioned officers, their belts slung over the backs of chairs, were playing cards, never dreaming that a magician's wand was conjuring them out of the night like an apparition on the stage and presenting them as they actually were at that very moment to the eyes of a spellbound passer-by whom they could not see. In a little curio shop a half-spent candle, projecting its warm glow over an engraving, reprinted it in sanguine, while, battling against the darkness, the light of a big lamp bronzed a scrap of leather, inlaid a dagger with glittering spangles, spread a film of precious gold like the patina of time or the varnish of an old master on pictures which were only bad copies, made in fact of the whole hovel, in which there was nothing but pinchbeck rubbish, a marvellous composition by Rembrandt. Sometimes I lifted my eyes to gaze at some huge old dwelling-house whose shutters had not been closed and in which amphibious men and women, adapting themselves anew each evening to living in a different element from their daytime one, floated slowly to and fro in the rich liquid that after nightfall rose incessantly from the wells of the lamps to fill the rooms to the very brink of their outer walls of stone and glass, the displacement of their bodies sending oleaginous golden ripples through it. I proceeded on my way, and often, in the dark alley that ran past the cathedral, as long ago on the road to Méséglise, the force of my desire caught and held me; it seemed that a woman must be on the point of appearing, to satisfy it; if, in the darkness, I suddenly felt a skirt brush past me, the violence of the pleasure which I then felt made it impossible for me to believe that the contact was accidental and I attempted to seize in my arms a terrified stranger. This Gothic alley meant for me something so real that if I had been successful in picking up and enjoying a woman there, it would have been impossible for me not to believe that it was the ancient charm of the place that was bringing us together, even if she were no more than a common street-walker, stationed there every evening, whom the wintry night, the strange place, the darkness, the mediaeval atmosphere had invested with their mysterious glamour. I thought of what might be in store for me; to try to forget Mme de Guermantes seemed to me to be painful, but sensible, and for the first time possible, even perhaps easy. In the absolute quiet of this neighbourhood I could hear ahead of me shouted words and laughter which must come from tipsy revellers staggering home. I waited to see them; I stood peering in the direction from which I had heard the noise. But I was obliged to wait for some time, for the surrounding silence was so intense that it had allowed sounds that were still a long way off to penetrate it with the utmost clarity and force. Finally the revellers did appear; not, as I had supposed, in front of me, but far behind. Whether because the intersection of side-streets and the interposition of buildings had, by reverberation, brought about this acoustic error, or because it is very difficult to locate a sound when its position is unknown to us, I had been as mistaken about direction as about distance.

The wind grew stronger. It was grainy and bristling with coming snow. I returned to the main street and jumped on board the little tram, from the platform of which an officer was acknowledging, without seeming to see them, the salutes of the uncouth soldiers who trudged past along the pavement, their faces daubed crimson by the cold, reminding me, in this little town which the sudden leap from autumn into early winter seemed to have transported further north, of the rubicund faces which Breughel gives to his merry, junketing, frostbound peasants.

And indeed at the hotel where I was to meet Saint-Loup and his friends and to which the festive season now beginning attracted a number of people from near and far, I found, as I hurried across the courtyard with its glimpses of glowing kitchens in which chickens were turning on spits, pigs were roasting, lobsters were being flung alive into what the landlord called the "everlasting fire," an influx (worthy of some *Numbering of the People at Bethlehem* such as the Old Flemish masters used to paint) of new arrivals who assembled there in groups, asking the landlord or one of his staff (who, if they did not like the look of them, would recommend lodgings elsewhere in the town) for bed and board, while a scullion hurried past holding a struggling fowl by the neck. And similarly, in the big dining-room which I passed through on the first day before coming to the little room where my friend was waiting for me, it was of some Biblical repast portrayed with mediaeval naïvety and Flemish exaggeration that one was reminded by the quantity of fish, chickens, grouse, woodcock, pigeons, brought in dressed and garnished and piping hot by breathless waiters who slid along the polished floor for greater speed and set them down on the huge sideboard where they were carved at once, but where—for many diners were finishing when I arrived—they piled up untouched, as though their profusion and the haste of those who brought them were inspired far less by a desire to meet the requirements of the diners than by respect for the sacred text, scrupulously followed in the letter but naïvely illustrated with real details borrowed from local custom, and by an aesthetic and religious anxiety to make evident to the eye the splendour of the feast by the profusion of the victuals and the assiduity of the servers. One of these stood lost in thought by a sideboard at the far end of the room; and to find out from him, who alone appeared calm enough to be capable of answering me, in which room our table had been laid, I made my way forward among the chafing-dishes that had been lighted here and there to keep the late-comers' plates from growing cold (which did not, however, prevent the dessert, in the centre of the room, from being piled in the outstretched hands of a huge mannikin, sometimes supported on the wings of a duck, apparently of crystal but really of ice, carved afresh every day with a hot iron by a sculptor-cook, quite in the Flemish manner), and, at the risk of being knocked down by his colleagues, went straight

towards this servitor in whom I felt I recognised a character traditionally present in these sacred subjects, for he reproduced with
scrupulous accuracy the simple, snub-nosed, ill-drawn features and
dreamy expression, already half aware of the miracle of a divine
presence which the others have not yet begun to suspect. In addition—doubtless in view of the coming festivities—the cast was
reinforced by a celestial contingent recruited entirely from a reserve
of cherubim and seraphim. A young angel musician, with fair hair
framing a fourteen-year-old face, was not, it was true, playing an
instrument, but stood musing before a gong or a pile of plates, while
other less infantile angels flew swiftly across the boundless expanse
of the room, beating the air with the ceaseless fluttering of
the napkins which dangled from them like the wings in primitive
paintings, with pointed ends. Fleeing those ill-defined regions,
screened by a hedge of palms, from which the angelic servitors
looked, at a distance, as though they had floated down out of the
empyrean, I forced my way through to the smaller room in which
Saint-Loup's table was laid. I found there several of his friends who
dined with him regularly, nobles except for one or two commoners
in whom the young nobles had, as early as their school-days,
detected likely friends, and with whom they readily fraternised,
proving thereby that they were not in principle hostile to the
middle classes, even if they were Republican, provided they had
clean hands and went to mass. On the first of these evenings, before
we sat down to dinner, I drew Saint-Loup into a corner and, in front
of all the rest but so that they should not hear me, said to him:

"Robert, this is hardly the time or the place for what I am going
to say, but I shan't be a second. I keep forgetting to ask you when
I'm in the barracks: isn't that Mme de Guermantes's photograph
that you have on your table?"

"Why, yes, she's my dear aunt."

"Of course she is; what a fool I am. I used to know that, but I'd
never thought about it. I say, your friends will be getting impatient, we must be quick, they're looking at us. Or another time
will do; it isn't at all important."

"That's all right, carry on. They can wait."

"No, no, I do want to be polite to them; they're so nice.
Besides, it doesn't really matter in the least, I assure you."

"Do you know the worthy Oriane, then?"

This "worthy Oriane," as he might have said "the good
Oriane," did not imply that Saint-Loup regarded Mme de

Guermantes as especially good. In this instance the words "good," "excellent," "worthy," are mere reinforcements of the definite article indicating a person who is known to both parties and of whom the speaker does not quite know what to say to someone outside the family circle. The word "good" does duty as a stop-gap and keeps the conversation going for a moment until the speaker has hit upon "Do you see much of her?" or "I haven't set eyes on her for months," or "I shall be seeing her on Tuesday," or "She must be getting on, now, you know."

"I can't tell you how funny it is that it should be her photograph, because we're living in her house now, and I've been hearing the most astounding things about her" (I should have been hard put to it to say what) "which have made me immensely interested in her, only from a literary point of view, you understand, from a—how shall I put it—from a Balzacian point of view. You're so clever you can see what I mean without my having to explain. But we must hurry up. What on earth will your friends think of my manners?"

"They'll think absolutely nothing. I've told them you're sublime, and they're a great deal more nervous than you are."

"You really are too kind. But listen, what I want to say is this: I suppose Mme de Guermantes hasn't any idea that I know you, has she?"

"I can't say. I haven't seen her since the summer, because I haven't had any leave since she's been in town."

"The fact of the matter is, I've been told that she regards me as an absolute idiot."

"That I do not believe. Oriane isn't exactly a genius, but all the same she's by no means stupid."

"You know that as a rule I'm not at all keen on your advertising the good opinion you're kind enough to hold of me; I'm not conceited. That's why I'm sorry you should have said flattering things about me to your friends here (whom we'll join in two seconds). But Mme de Guermantes is different. If you could let her know—even with a bit of exaggeration—what you think of me, you would give me great pleasure."

"Why, of course I will. If that's all you want me to do, it's not very difficult. But what difference can it possibly make to you what she thinks of you? I suppose you think her no end of a joke, really. Anyhow, if that's all you want we can discuss it in front of the others or when we're by ourselves; I'm afraid of your tiring

yourself if you stand talking, especially in such awkward conditions, when we have heaps of opportunities of being alone
together."

It was precisely these awkward conditions that had given me
courage to approach Robert; the presence of the others was for me
a pretext that justified my giving my remarks a brief and disjointed
form, under cover of which I could more easily dissemble the
falsehood of my saying to my friend that I had forgotten his
connexion with the Duchess, and also for not giving him time
to frame—with regard to my reasons for wishing Mme de
Guermantes to know that I was his friend, was clever, and so
forth—questions which would have been all the more disturbing
in that I should not have been able to answer them.

"Robert, I'm surprised that a man of your intelligence should
fail to understand that one doesn't discuss the things that will give
one's friends pleasure; one does them. Now I, if you were to ask
me no matter what—and indeed I only wish you would ask me to
do something for you—I can assure you I shouldn't demand any
explanations. I've gone further than I really meant; I have no
desire to know Mme de Guermantes, but just to test you I ought
to have said that I was anxious to dine with Mme de Guermantes
and I'm sure you would never have done it."

"Not only would I have done it, but I will do it."

"When?"

"Next time I'm in Paris, three weeks from now, I expect."

"We shall see. I dare say she won't want to see me, though.
I can't tell you how grateful I am."

"Not at all, it's nothing."

"Don't say that; it's tremendous, because now I can see what a
friend you are. Whether what I ask you to do is important or not,
disagreeable or not, whether I mean it truly or only to test you, it
makes no difference: you say you will do it, and there you show
the fineness of your mind and heart. A stupid friend would have
argued."

This was exactly what he had just been doing; but perhaps
I wanted to flatter his self-esteem; perhaps also I was sincere, the
sole touchstone of merit seeming to me to be the extent to which a
friend could be useful in respect of the one thing that seemed to
me to have any importance, my love. Then I added, perhaps out of
duplicity, perhaps in a genuine access of affection inspired by
gratitude, by self-interest, and by all the similarities with Mme

de Guermantes's very features which nature had reproduced in her nephew Robert:

"But now we must really join the others, and I've mentioned only one of the two things I wanted to ask you, the less important; the other is more important to me, but I'm afraid you'll never consent. Would it annoy you if we were to call each other *tu*?"

"Annoy me? My dear fellow! *Joy! Tears of joy! Undreamed-of happiness!*"[11]

"How can I thank you? . . . After you! It's such a pleasure to me that you needn't do anything about Mme de Guermantes if you'd rather not, saying *tu* and *toi* is enough."

"I can do both."

"I say, Robert! Listen to me a minute," I said to him later during dinner. "Oh, it's really too absurd, this conversation in fits and starts, I can't think why—you remember the lady I was speaking to you about just now."

"Yes."

"You're quite sure you know who I mean?"

"Why, what do you take me for, a village idiot?"

"You wouldn't care to give me her photograph, I suppose?"

I had meant to ask him only for the loan of it. But as I was about to speak I was overcome with shyness, feeling that the request was indiscreet, and in order to hide my confusion I formulated it more bluntly and amplified it, as if it had been quite natural.

"No, I should have to ask her permission first," was his answer.

He blushed as he spoke. I could see that he had a reservation in his mind, that he attributed one to me as well, that he would further my love only partially, subject to certain moral principles, and for this I hated him.

At the same time I was touched to see how differently Saint-Loup behaved towards me now that I was no longer alone with him, and that his friends formed an audience. His increased affability would have left me cold had I thought that it was deliberately assumed; but I could feel that it was spontaneous and simply consisted of all that he was wont to say about me in my absence and refrained as a rule from saying when I was alone with him. True, in our private conversations I could detect the pleasure that he found in talking to me, but that pleasure almost always remained unexpressed. Now, at the same remarks of mine which ordinarily he enjoyed without showing it, he watched from the corner of his eye to see whether they produced on his friends the

effect on which he had counted and which evidently corresponded to what he had promised them beforehand. The mother
of a debutante could be no more anxiously attentive to her
daughter's repartee and to the attitude of the audience. If I had
made some remark at which, alone in my company, he would
merely have smiled, he was afraid that the others might not have
seen the point, and kept saying "What? What?" to make me repeat
what I had said, to attract their attention, and turning at once to his
friends with a hearty laugh, making himself willy-nilly the fugle-
man of their laughter, presented me for the first time with the
opinion that he had of me and must often have expressed to them.
So that I caught sight of myself suddenly from the outside, like
someone who reads his name in a newspaper or sees himself in
a mirror.

It occurred to me on one of these evenings to tell a mildly
amusing story about Mme Blandais, but I stopped at once,
remembering that Saint-Loup knew it already, and that when
I had started to tell it to him the day after my arrival he had
interrupted me with: "You told me that before, at Balbec." I was
surprised, therefore, to find him begging me to go on and assuring
me that he did not know the story and that it would amuse him
immensely. "You've forgotten it for the moment," I said to him,
"but you'll soon remember." "No, really, I swear to you, you're
mistaken. You've never told it to me. Do go on." And throughout
the story he kept his feverish and enraptured gaze fixed alternately
on myself and on his friends. I realised only after I had finished,
amid general laughter, that it had struck him that this story would
give his comrades a good idea of my wit, and that it was for this
reason that he had pretended not to know it. Such is the stuff of
friendship.

On the third evening, one of his friends, to whom I had not had
an opportunity of speaking before, conversed with me at great
length; and at one point I overheard him telling Saint-Loup how
much he was enjoying himself. And indeed we sat talking together
almost the entire evening, leaving our glasses of Sauterne
untouched on the table before us, separated, sheltered from the
others by the imposing veils of one of those instinctive likings
between men which, when they are not based on physical attraction, are the only kind that is altogether mysterious. Of such an
enigmatic nature had seemed to me to be, at Balbec, the feeling
which Saint-Loup had for me, a feeling not to be confused with

the interest of our conversations, free from any material association, invisible, intangible, and yet of whose presence in himself
like a sort of combustible gas he had been sufficiently conscious to
refer to with a smile. And perhaps there was something more
surprising still in this fellow-feeling born here in a single evening,
like a flower that had blossomed in a few minutes in the warmth of
this little room.

I could not help asking Robert when he spoke to me about
Balbec whether it was really settled that he was to marry Mlle
d'Ambresac. He assured me that not only was it not settled, but
that there had never been any question of such a match, that he
had never seen her, that he did not know who she was. If at that
moment I had happened to see any of the social gossips who
had told me of this coming event, they would promptly have
announced the engagement of Mlle d'Ambresac to someone who
was not Saint-Loup and that of Saint-Loup to someone who was
not Mlle d'Ambresac. I should have surprised them greatly had
I reminded them of their incompatible and still so recent predictions. In order that this little game should continue, and should
multiply false reports by attaching the greatest possible number to
every name in turn, nature has furnished those who play it with a
memory as short as their credulity is long.

Saint-Loup had spoken to me of another of his comrades who
was present also, one with whom he was on particularly good
terms since in this environment they were the only two to champion the reopening of the Dreyfus case.

"That fellow? Oh, he's not like Saint-Loup, he's a tub-thum-
per," my new friend told me. "He's not even sincere. At first he
used to say: 'Just wait a little, there's a man I know well, a very
shrewd and kind-hearted fellow, General de Boisdeffre; you need
have no hesitation in accepting his opinion.' But as soon as he
heard that Boisdeffre had pronounced Dreyfus guilty, Boisdeffre
ceased to count: clericalism, the prejudices of the General Staff,
prevented him from forming a candid opinion, although there is,
or rather was, before this Dreyfus business, no one as clerical as our
friend. Next he told us that in any event we were to get the truth,
because the case had been put in the hands of Saussier, and he, a
Republican soldier (our friend coming of an ultra-monarchist
family, if you please), was a man of steel, with a stern unyielding
conscience. But when Saussier pronounced Esterhazy innocent,
he found fresh reasons to account for the verdict, reasons

damaging not to Dreyfus but to General Saussier. Saussier was blinded by the militarist spirit (and our friend, by the way, is as militarist as he is clerical, or at least was; I don't know what to make of him any more). His family are broken-hearted at seeing him possessed by such ideas."

"Don't you think," I suggested, half turning towards Saint-Loup so as not to appear to be cutting myself off from him, and in order to bring him into the conversation, "that the influence we ascribe to environment is particularly true of an intellectual environment. Each of us is conditioned by an idea. There are far fewer ideas than men, therefore all men with similar ideas are alike. As there is nothing material in an idea, the people who are only materially connected to the man with an idea in no way modify it."

At this point I was interrupted by Saint-Loup, because another of the young soldiers had leaned across to him with a smile and, pointing to me, exclaimed: "Duroc! Duroc all over!" I had no idea what this might mean, but I felt the expression on the shy young face to be more than friendly.

Saint-Loup was not satisfied with this comparison. In an ecstasy of joy, no doubt intensified by the joy he felt in making me shine before his friends, with extreme volubility, he reiterated, stroking and patting me as though I were a horse that had just come first past the post: "You're the cleverest man I know, do you hear?" He corrected himself, and added: "Together with Elstir.—You don't mind my bracketing him with you, I hope? Scrupulous accuracy, don't you know. As one might have said to Balzac, for example: 'You're the greatest novelist of the century—together with Stendhal.' Scrupulous to a fault, you see, but nevertheless, immense admiration. No? You don't agree about Stendhal?" he went on, with a naïve confidence in my judgment which found expression in a charming, smiling, almost childish glance of inter-rogation from his green eyes. "Oh, good! I see you're on my side. Bloch can't stand Stendhal. I think it's idiotic of him. The *Chartreuse* is after all a stunning work, don't you think? I'm so glad you agree with me. What is it you like best in the *Chartreuse*? Answer me," he urged with boyish impetuosity. And the menace of his physical strength made the question almost terrifying. "Mosca? Fabrice?" I answered timidly that Mosca reminded me a little of M. de Norpois. Whereupon there were peals of laughter from the young Siegfried Saint-Loup. And no sooner had I added:

"But Mosca is far more intelligent, not so pedantic," than I heard Robert exclaim "Bravo," actually clapping his hands, and, helpless with laughter, gasp: "Oh, perfect! Admirable! You really are astounding."

While I was speaking, even the approbation of the others seemed supererogatory to Saint-Loup; he insisted on silence. And just as a conductor stops his orchestra with a rap from his baton because someone has made a noise, so he rebuked the author of this disturbance: "Gibergue, you must be silent when people are speaking. You can tell us about it afterwards." And to me: "Please go on."

I gave a sigh of relief, for I had been afraid that he was going to make me begin all over again.

"And as an idea," I went on, "is a thing that cannot partake of human interests and would be incapable of deriving any benefit from them, the men who are governed by an idea are not swayed by self-interest."

When I had finished speaking, "That stops your gob, doesn't it, my boys," exclaimed Saint-Loup, who had been following me with his eyes with the same anxious solicitude as if I had been walking a tight-rope. "What were you going to say, Gibergue?"

"I was just saying that your friend reminded me of Major Duroc. I could almost hear him speaking."

"Why, I've often thought so myself," replied Saint-Loup. "They have several points in common, but you'll find that this one has all kinds of qualities Duroc hasn't."

Just as a brother of this friend of Saint-Loup, who had been trained at the Schola Cantorum, thought about every new musical work not at all what his father, his mother, his cousins, his clubmates thought, but exactly what the other students at the Schola thought, so this non-commissioned nobleman (of whom Bloch formed an extraordinary opinion when I told him about him, because, touched to hear that he was on the same side as himself, he nevertheless imagined him, on account of his aristocratic birth and religious and military upbringing, to be as different as possible, endowed with the romantic attraction of a native of a distant country) had a "mentality," as people were now beginning to say, analogous to that of the whole body of Dreyfusards in general and of Bloch in particular, on which the traditions of his family and the interests of his career could retain no hold whatever. (Similarly, one of Saint-Loup's cousins had married a young

Eastern princess who was said to write poetry quite as fine as Victor Hugo's or Alfred de Vigny's, and in spite of this was presumed to have a different type of mind from what could normally be imagined, the mind of an Eastern princess immured in an *Arabian Nights* palace. It was left to the writers who had the privilege of meeting her to savour the disappointment, or rather the joy, of listening to conversation which gave the impression not of Scheherazade but of a person of genius of the type of Alfred de Vigny or Victor Hugo.)[12]

I took a particular pleasure in talking to my new friend, as for that matter to all Robert's comrades and to Robert himself, about the barracks, the officers of the garrison, and the Army in general. Thanks to the immensely exaggerated scale on which we see the things, however petty they may be, in the midst of which we eat, and talk, and lead our real life; thanks to that formidable enlargement which they undergo, and the effect of which is that the rest of the world, not being present, cannot compete with them, and assumes in comparison the insubstantiality of a dream, I had begun to take an interest in the various personalities of the barracks, in the officers whom I saw in the square when I went to visit Saint-Loup, or, if I was awake then, when the regiment passed beneath my windows. I should have liked to know more about the major whom Saint-Loup so greatly admired, and about the course in military history which would have appealed to me "even aesthetically." I knew that all too often Robert indulged in a rather hollow verbalism, but at other times gave evidence of the assimilation of profound ideas which he was fully capable of grasping. Unfortunately, in respect of Army matters Robert was chiefly preoccupied at this time with the Dreyfus case. He spoke little about it, since he alone of the party at table was a Dreyfusard; the others were violently opposed to the idea of a fresh trial, except my other neighbour, my new friend, whose opinions appeared to be somewhat wavering. A firm admirer of the colonel, who was regarded as an exceptionally able officer and had denounced the current agitation against the Army in several of his regimental orders which had earned him the reputation of being an anti-Dreyfusard, my neighbour had heard that his commanding officer had let fall certain remarks leading to suppose that he had his doubts as to the guilt of Dreyfus and retained his admiration for Picquart. On this last point at any rate, the rumour of the colonel's relative Dreyfusism was ill-founded, as are all the rumours,

springing from no one knows where, which float around any great
scandal. For, shortly afterwards, this colonel having been detailed
to interrogate the former Chief of the Intelligence Branch, had
treated him with a brutality and contempt the like of which had
never been known before. However this might be (and although
he had not taken the liberty of making a direct inquiry of the
colonel), my neighbour had been kind enough to tell Saint-
Loup—in the tone in which a Catholic lady might tell a Jewish
lady that her parish priest denounced the pogroms in Russia and
admired the generosity of certain Jews—that their colonel was
not, with regard to Dreyfusism—to a certain kind of Dreyfusism,
at least—the fanatical, narrow opponent that he had been made
out to be.

"I'm not surprised," was Saint-Loup's comment, "as he's a
sensible man. But in spite of everything he's blinded by the
prejudices of his caste, and above all, by his clericalism. By the
way," he turned to me, "Major Duroc, the lecturer on military
history I was telling you about—there's a man who is whole-
heartedly in support of our views, or so I'm told. And I should
have been surprised to hear that he wasn't, for he's not only a
brilliantly clever man, but a Radical-Socialist and a freemason."

Partly out of courtesy to his friends, to whom Saint-Loup's
professions of Dreyfusard faith were painful, and also because the
subject was of more interest to me, I asked my neighbour if it were
true that this major gave a demonstration of military history which
had a genuine aesthetic beauty.

"It's absolutely true."

"But what do you mean by that?"

"Well, all that you read, let us say, in the narrative of a military
historian, the smallest facts, the most trivial happenings, are only
the outward signs of an idea which has to be elucidated and which
often conceals other ideas, like a palimpsest. So that you have a
field of study as intellectual as any science you care to name, or any
art, and one that is satisfying to the mind."

"Give me an example or two, if you don't mind."

"It's not very easy to explain," Saint-Loup broke in. "You read,
let us say, that this or that corps has tried . . . but before we go any
further, the serial number of the corps, its order of battle, are not
without their significance. If it isn't the first time that the operation
has been attempted, and if for the same operation we find a
different corps being brought up, it's perhaps a sign that the

previous corps has been wiped out or has suffered heavy casualties in the said operation, that it's no longer in a fit state to carry it through successfully. Next, we must ask ourselves what this corps which is now out of action consisted of; if it was made up of shock troops, held in reserve for big attacks, a fresh corps of inferior quality will have little chance of succeeding where the first has failed. Furthermore, if we are not at the start of a campaign, this fresh corps may itself be a composite formation of odds and ends drawn from other corps, and this provides an indication of the strength of the forces the belligerent still has at its disposal, and the proximity of the moment when its forces will definitely be inferior to the enemy's, which puts the operation on which this corps is about to engage in a different perspective, because, if it is no longer in a condition to make good its losses, its successes themselves will, with arithmetical certainty, only bring it nearer to its ultimate destruction. Moreover, the serial number of the corps that it has facing it is of no less significance. If, for instance, it is a much weaker unit, which has already accounted for several important units of the attacking force, the whole nature of the operation is changed, since, even if it should end in the loss of the position which the defending force has been holding, simply to have held it for any length of time may be a great success if a very small defending force has been sufficient to destroy considerable forces on the other side. You can understand that if, in the analysis of the various corps engaged on both sides, there are all these points of importance, the study of the position itself, of the roads and railways which it commands, of the supply lines which it protects, is of even greater consequence. One must study what I may call the whole geographical context," he added with a laugh. (And indeed he was so delighted with this expression that, every time he employed it, even months afterwards, it was always accompanied by the same laugh.) "While the operation is being prepared by one of the belligerents, if you read that one of its patrols has been wiped out in the neighbourhood of the position by the other belligerent, one of the conclusions which you are entitled to draw is that one side was attempting to reconnoitre the defensive works with which the other intended to resist the attack. An exceptional burst of activity at a given point may indicate the desire to capture that point, but equally well the desire to hold the enemy in check there, not to retaliate at the point at which he has attacked you; or it may indeed be only a feint, intended to cover by an intensification of activity withdrawals of troops in that sector. (This was a classic feint in Napoleon's wars.) On the other hand, to appreciate the significance of a manoeuvre, its probable object, and, as a corollary, other manoeuvres by which it will be accompanied or followed, it is not immaterial to consult, not so much the announcements issued by the High Command, which may be intended to deceive the enemy, to mask a possible setback, as the manual of field operations in use in the country in question. We are always entitled to assume that the manoeuvre which an army has attempted to carry out is that prescribed by the rules in force for analogous circumstances. If, for instance, the rules lay down that a frontal attack should be accompanied by a flank attack and if, this flank attack having failed, the High Command claims that it had no connexion with the main attack and was merely a diversion, there is a strong likelihood that the truth will be found by consulting the field regulations rather than the statements issued from Headquarters. And there are not only the regulations governing each army to be considered, but their traditions, their habits, their doctrines. The study of diplomatic activity, which is constantly acting or reacting upon military activity, must not be neglected either. Incidents apparently insignificant, misinterpreted at the time, will explain to you how the enemy, counting on support which these incidents prove to have been denied him, was able to carry out only a part of his strategic plan. So that, if you know how to read your military history, what is a confused jumble for the ordinary reader becomes a chain of reasoning as rational as a painting is for the picture-lover who knows how to look and can see what the person portrayed is wearing, what he has in his hands, whereas the average visitor to a gallery is bewildered by a blur of colour which gives him a headache. But just as with certain pictures it isn't enough to observe that the figure is holding a chalice, but one must know why the painter chose to place a chalice in his hands, what it's intended to symbolise, so these military operations, quite apart from their immediate objective, are habitually modelled, in the mind of the general who is directing the campaign, on earlier battles which represent, so to speak, the past, the literature, the learning, the etymology, the aristocracy of the battles of today. Mind you, I'm not speaking for the moment of the local, the (what shall I call it?) spatial identity of battles. That exists also. A battlefield has never been, and never will be throughout the centuries, simply the ground upon which a single battle has been fought. If it has been a battlefield, that was because it combined certain conditions of geographical position, of geological formation, even of certain defects calculated to hinder the enemy (a river, for instance, cutting it in two), which made it a good battlefield. And so what it has been it will continue to be. You don't make an artist's studio out of any old room; so you don't make a battlefield out of any old piece of ground. There are predestined sites. But, once again, that's not what I was talking about so much as the type of battle a general takes as his model, a sort of strategic carbon copy, a tactical pastiche, if you like. Battles like Ulm, Lodi, Leipzig, Cannae. I don't know whether there'll ever be another war, or what nations will fight in it, but, if a war does come, you may be sure that it will include (and deliberately, on the commander's part) a Cannae, an Austerlitz, a Rossbach, a Waterloo, to mention a few. Some people make no bones about it. Marshal von Schlieffen and General von Falkenhausen have planned in advance a Battle of Cannae against France, in the Hannibal style, pinning their enemy down along his whole front, and advancing on both flanks, especially on the right through Belgium, while Bernhardi prefers the oblique advance of Frederick the Great, Leuthen rather than Cannae. Others expound their views less crudely, but I can tell you one thing, my boy, and that is that Beauconseil, the squadron commander I introduced you to the other day and who's an officer with a very great future before him, has swotted up a little Pratzen attack of his own which he knows inside out and is keeping up his sleeve, and if he ever has an opportunity to put it into practice he won't miss the boat but will let us have it good and proper. The breakthrough in the centre at Rivoli, too—that will crop up again if there's ever another war. It's no more obsolete than the *Iliad*. I may add that we're more or less condemned to frontal attacks, because we can't afford to repeat the mistake we made in '70; we must assume the offensive, nothing but the offensive. The only thing that troubles me is that although I see only the slower, more antiquated minds among us opposing this splendid doctrine, nevertheless one of the youngest of my masters, who is a genius, I mean Mangin, feels that there ought to be a place, provisional of course, for the defensive. It isn't very easy to answer him when he cites the example of Austerlitz, where the defensive was simply a prelude to attack and victory."

The enunciation of these theories by Saint-Loup was cheering. They gave me to hope that perhaps I was not being led astray, in my life at Doncières, with regard to these officers whom I heard being discussed as I sat sipping a Sauterne which bathed them in its charming golden glint, by the same magnifying power that had blown up to such huge dimensions in my eyes, while I was at Balbec, the King and Queen of the South Seas, the little group of the four gastronomes, the young gambler, and Legrandin's brother-in-law, who were now so shrunken as to appear non-existent. What gave me pleasure today would not perhaps leave me indifferent tomorrow, as had always happened hitherto; the person that I still was at this moment was not perhaps doomed to imminent destruction, since to the ardent and fugitive passion which I felt on these few evenings for everything that concerned the military life, Saint-Loup, by what he had just been saying to me about the art of war, added an intellectual foundation, of a permanent character, capable of gripping me so strongly that I could believe, without any attempt at self-deception, that after I had left Doncières I should continue to take an interest in the work of my friends there, and should not be long in coming to pay them another visit. However, in order to be quite sure that this art of war was indeed an art in the artistic sense of the word, I said to Saint-Loup:

"You interest me enormously. But tell me, there's one point that puzzles me. I feel that I could become passionately involved in the art of war, but first I should want to be sure that it is not so very different from the other arts, that knowing the rules is not everything. You tell me that battles are reproduced. I do find something aesthetic, just as you said, in seeing beneath a modern battle the plan of an older one; I can't tell you how attractive the idea sounds. But then, does the genius of the commander count for nothing? Does he really do no more than apply the rules? Or, granted equal knowledge, are there great generals as there are great surgeons, who, when the symptoms exhibited by two cases of illness are identical to the outward eye, nevertheless feel, for some infinitesimal reason, founded perhaps on their experience, but interpreted afresh, that in one case they ought to do this, in another case that; that in one case it is better to operate, in another to wait?"

"But of course! You'll find Napoleon not attacking when all the rules demanded that he should attack, but some obscure divination warned him not to. For instance, look at Austerlitz, or, in 1806, his instructions to Lannes. But you will find certain generals slavishly imitating one of Napoleon's manoeuvres and arriving at a diametrically opposite result. There are a dozen examples of that in 1870. But even as regards the interpretation of what the enemy *may* do, what he actually does is only a symptom which may mean any number of different things. Each of them has an equal chance of being the right one, if you confine yourself to logic and science, just as in certain difficult cases all the medical science in the world will be powerless to decide whether the invisible tumour is malignant or not, whether or not the operation ought to be performed. It is his flair, his divination, his crystal-gazing (if you know what I mean) which decides, in the case of the great general as of the great doctor. Thus I explained to you, to take one instance, what a reconnaissance on the eve of a battle might signify. But it may mean a dozen other things, such as making the enemy think you're going to attack him at one point whereas you intend to attack him at another, putting up a screen which will prevent him from seeing the preparations for your real operation, forcing him to bring up fresh troops, to fix them there, to immobilise them in a different place from where they are needed, forming an estimate of the forces at his disposal, sounding him out, forcing him to show his hand. Sometimes, even, the fact that you deploy an immense number of troops in an operation is by no means a proof that that is your true objective; for you may carry it out in earnest, even if it is only a feint, so that the feint may have a better chance of deceiving the enemy. If I had time now to go through the Napoleonic wars from this point of view, I assure you that these simple classic movements which we study here, and which you'll come and see us practising in the field, just for the pleasure of an outing, you young rotter (no, I know you're not well, I'm sorry!), well, in a war, when you feel behind you the vigilance, the judgment, the profound study of the High Command, you're as moved by them as by the beam of a lighthouse, a purely physical light but none the less an emanation of the mind, sweeping through space to warn ships of danger. In fact I may perhaps be wrong in speaking to you only of the literature of war. In reality, as the formation of the soil, the direction of wind and light tell us which way a tree will grow, so the conditions in which a campaign is fought, the features of the country through which you manoeuvre, prescribe, to a certain extent, and limit the number of the plans among which the general has to choose. Which means that along a mountain range, through a system of valleys, over certain plains, it's almost with the inevitability and the grandiose beauty of an avalanche that you can predict the line of an army on the march."

"Now you deny me that freedom of choice in the commander, that power of divination in the enemy who is trying to read his intentions, which you allowed me a moment ago."

"Not at all. You remember that book of philosophy we read together at Balbec, the richness of the world of possibilities compared with the real world. Well, it's exactly the same with the art of war. In a given situation there will be four plans that apply and among which the general may choose, as a disease may take various courses for which the doctor has to be prepared. And there again human weakness and human greatness are fresh causes of uncertainty. For of these four plans let us assume that contingent reasons (such as the attainment of minor objectives, or the time factor, or numerical inferiority and inadequate supplies) lead the general to prefer the first, which is less perfect but less costly and swifter to execute, and has for its terrain a richer country for feeding his troops. He may, after having begun with this plan, which the enemy, uncertain at first, will soon detect, find that success lies beyond his grasp, the difficulties being too great (that is what I call the element of human weakness), abandon it and try the second or third or fourth. But it may equally be that he has tried the first plan (and this is what I call human greatness) merely as a feint to pin down the enemy, so as to surprise him later at a point where he has not been expecting an attack. Thus at Ulm, Mack, who expected the enemy to attack from the west, was encircled from the north where he thought he was perfectly safe. My example is not a very good one, as a matter of fact. Actually Ulm is a better example of the battle of encirclement, which the future will see reproduced because it is not only a classic example from which generals will draw inspiration, but a form that is to some extent logically necessary (like several others, thus leaving room for choice and variety) like a type of crystallisation. But it doesn't much matter really, because these conditions are after all artificial. To go back to our philosophy book; it's like the rules of logic or scientific laws, reality conforms to them more or less, but remember the great mathematician Poincaré: he's by no means certain that mathematics is a rigorously exact science. As to the rules themselves, which I mentioned to you, they are of secondary importance really, and besides they're altered from time to time. We cavalrymen, for instance, live by the *Field Service* of 1895, which may be said to be out of date since it is based on the old and obsolete doctrine which maintains that cavalry action has little more than a psychological effect by creating panic in the enemy ranks. Whereas the more intelligent of our teachers, all the best brains in the cavalry, and particularly the major I was telling you about, consider on the contrary that the issue will be decided in a real free-for-all with sabre and lance and the side that can hold out longer will be the winner, not merely psychologically, by creating panic, but physically."

"Saint-Loup is quite right, and it's likely that the next *Field Service* will reflect this new school of thought," my neighbour observed.

"I'm glad to have your support, since your opinions seem to make more impression upon my friend than mine," said Saint-Loup with a smile, whether because the growing liking between his comrade and myself annoyed him slightly or because he thought it graceful to solemnise it with this official acknowledgement. "Perhaps I may have underestimated the importance of the rules. They do change, that must be admitted. But in the meantime they control the military situation, the plans of campaign and troop concentration. If they reflect a false conception of strategy they may be the initial cause of defeat. All this is a little too technical for you," he remarked to me. "Always remember that, when all's said and done, what does most to accelerate the evolution of the art of war is wars themselves. In the course of a campaign, if it is at all long, you will see one belligerent profiting by the lessons provided by the enemy's successes and mistakes, perfecting the methods of the latter, who will improve on them in turn. But all that is a thing of the past. With the terrible advance of artillery, the wars of the future, if there are to be any more wars, will be so short that, before we have had time to think of putting our lessons into practice, peace will have been signed."

"Don't be so touchy," I told Saint-Loup, reverting to the first words of this speech. "I was listening to you quite avidly!"

"If you will kindly not take offence, and will allow me to speak," his friend went on, "I shall add to what you've just been saying that if battles reproduce themselves indistinguishably it isn't merely due to the mind of the commander. It may happen that a mistake on his part (for instance, his failure to appreciate the strength of the enemy) will lead him to call upon his men for extravagant sacrifices, sacrifices which certain units will make with an abnegation so sublime that the part they play will be analogous to that of some other unit in some other battle, and they'll be quoted in history as interchangeable examples: to stick to 1870, we have the Prussian Guard at Saint-Privat, and the Turcos at Froeschviller and Wissembourg."

"Ah, interchangeable; precisely! Excellent! The lad has brains," was Saint-Loup's comment.

I was not insensible to these last examples, as always when, beneath the particular instance, I was afforded a glimpse of the general law. What really interested me, however, was the genius of the commander; I was anxious to discover in what it consisted, how, in given circumstances, when the commander who lacked genius could not withstand the enemy, the inspired commander would set about restoring his jeopardised position, which, according to Saint-Loup, was quite possible and had been done several times by Napoleon. And to understand what good generalship meant I asked for comparisons between the various commanders whom I knew by name, which of them had most markedly the character of a leader, the gifts of a tactician—at the risk of boring my new friends, who however showed no signs of boredom, but continued to answer me with an inexhaustible good-nature.

I felt cut off—not only from the great icy darkness which stretched out into the distance and in which we could hear from time to time the whistle of a train which only accentuated the pleasure of being there, or the chimes of an hour still happily distant from that at which these young men would have to buckle on their sabres and go—but also from all external preoccupations, almost from the memory of Mme de Guermantes, by the kindness of Saint-Loup, to which that of his friends, reinforcing it, gave, so to speak, a greater solidity; by the warmth, too, of that little dining-room, by the savour of the exquisite dishes that were set before us. These gave as much pleasure to my imagination as to my palate; sometimes the little piece of nature from which they had been extracted, the rugged holy-water stoup of the oyster in which lingered a few drops of brackish water, or the gnarled stem, the yellowed branches of a bunch of grapes, still enveloped them, inedible, poetic and distant as a landscape, evoking as we dined successive images of a siesta in the shade of a vine or of an excursion on the sea; on other evenings it was the cook alone who brought out these original properties of the viands, presenting them in their natural setting, like works of art, and a fish cooked in a court-bouillon was brought in on a long earthenware platter, on which, standing out in relief on a bed of bluish herbs, intact but still contorted from having been dropped alive into boiling water, surrounded by a ring of satellite shell-fish, of animalcules, crabs, shrimps and mussels, it had the appearance of a ceramic dish by Bernard Palissy.

"I'm furiously jealous," Saint-Loup said to me, half laughing, half in earnest, alluding to the interminable conversations apart which I had been having with his friend. "Is it because you find him more intelligent than me? Do you like him better than me? Ah, well, I suppose he's everything now, and no one else is to have a look in!" (Men who are enormously in love with a woman, who live in a society of woman-lovers, allow themselves pleasantries which others, seeing less innocence in them, would never dare to contemplate.)

When the conversation became general, the subject of Dreyfus was avoided for fear of offending Saint-Loup. A week later, however, two of his friends remarked how curious it was that, living in so military an environment, he was so keen a Dreyfusard, almost an anti-militarist. "The reason is," I suggested, not wishing to enter into details, "that the influence of environment is not so important as people think . . ." I intended of course to stop at this point, and not to reiterate the observations which I had made to Saint-Loup a week earlier. Since, however, I had made this particular remark almost word for word, I was about to excuse myself by adding: "Just as I was saying the other day . . ." But I had reckoned without the reverse side of Robert's cordial admiration for myself and certain other people. That admiration was complemented by so entire an assimilation of their ideas that after a day or two, he would have completely forgotten that those ideas were not his own. And so, in the matter of my modest thesis, Saint-Loup, for all the world as though it had always dwelt in his own brain, and as though I was merely poaching on his preserves, felt it incumbent upon him to greet my discovery with warm approval.

"Why, yes; environment is of no importance."

And with as much vehemence as if he were afraid I might interrupt or fail to understand him:

"The real influence is that of the intellectual environment! One is conditioned by an idea!"

He paused for a moment, with the satisfied smile of one who has digested his dinner, dropped his monocle, and, fixing me with a gimlet-like stare, said to me challengingly:

"All men with similar ideas are alike."

No doubt he had completely forgotten that I myself had said to him only a few days earlier what on the other hand he had remembered so well.

I did not arrive at Saint-Loup's restaurant every evening in the same state of mind. If a memory, or a sorrow that weighs on us, are capable of leaving us, to the extent that we no longer notice them, they can also return and sometimes remain with us for a long time. There were evenings when, as I passed through the town on my way to the restaurant, I felt so keen a longing for Mme de Guermantes that I could scarcely breathe; it was as though part of my breast had been cut out by a skilled anatomist and replaced by an equal part of immaterial suffering, by its equivalent in nostalgia and love. And however neatly the wound may have been stitched together, one lives rather uncomfortably when regret for the loss of another person is substituted for one's entrails; it seems to be occupying more room than they; one feels it perpetually; and besides, what a contradiction in terms to be obliged to *think* a part of one's body. Only it seems that we are worth more, somehow. At the whisper of a breeze we sigh, with oppression but also with languor. I would look up at the sky. If it was clear, I would say to myself: "Perhaps she is in the country; she's looking at the same stars; and, for all I know, when I arrive at the restaurant Robert may say to me: 'Good news! I've just heard from my aunt. She wants to meet you, she's coming down here.'" It was not the firmament alone that I associated with the thought of Mme de Guermantes. A passing breath of air, more fragrant than the rest, seemed to bring me a message from her, as, long ago, from Gilberte in the wheatfields of Méséglise. We do not change; we introduce into the feeling which we associate with a person many slumbering elements which it awakens but which are foreign to it. Besides, with these feelings for particular people, there is always something in us that strives to give them a larger truth, that is to say, to absorb them in a more general feeling, common to the whole of humanity, with which individuals and the suffering that they cause us are merely a means to enable us to communicate. What mixed a certain pleasure with my pain was that I knew it to be a tiny fragment of universal love. True, from the fact that I seemed to recognise the same sorts of sadness that I had felt on Gilberte's account, or else when in the evenings at Combray Mamma did not stay in my room, and also the memory of certain pages of Bergotte, in the suffering which I now felt and to which Mme de Guermantes, her coldness, her absence, were not clearly linked as cause is to effect in the mind of a philosopher, I did not conclude that Mme de Guermantes was not that cause. Is there not such a thing as a diffused bodily pain, extending, radiating out into other parts, which, however, it leaves, to vanish altogether, if the practitioner lays his finger on the precise spot from which it springs? And yet, until that moment, its extension made it seem to us so vague and sinister that, powerless to explain or even to locate it, we imagined that there was no possibility of its being healed. As I made my way to the restaurant I said to myself: "A fortnight already since I last saw Mme de Guermantes" (a fortnight, which did not appear so enormous an interval except to me, who, where Mme de Guermantes was concerned, counted in minutes). For me it was no longer the stars and the breeze alone, but the arithmetical divisions of time that assumed a dolorous and poetic aspect. Each day now was like the mobile crest of an indistinct hill, down one side of which I felt that I could descend towards forgetfulness, but down the other was carried along by the need to see the Duchess again. And I was continually inclining one way or the other, having no stable equilibrium. One day I said to myself: "Perhaps there'll be a letter tonight"; and on entering the dining-room I found courage to ask Saint-Loup:

"You don't happen to have had any news from Paris?"

"Yes," he replied gloomily, "bad news."

I breathed a sigh of relief when I realised that it was only he who had cause for unhappiness, and that the news was from his mistress. But I soon saw that one of its consequences would be to prevent Robert for a long time from taking me to see his aunt.

I learned that a quarrel had broken out between him and his mistress, through the post presumably, unless she had come down to pay him a flying visit between trains. And the quarrels, even when relatively slight, which they had previously had, had always seemed as though they must prove insoluble. For she had a violent temper, and would stamp her foot and burst into tears for reasons as incomprehensible as those that make children shut themselves into dark cupboards, not come out for dinner, refuse to give any explanation, and only redouble their sobs when, our patience exhausted, we give them a slap.

To say that Saint-Loup suffered terribly from this estrangement would be an oversimplification, would give a false impression of his grief. When he found himself alone, with nothing else to think about but his mistress parting from him with the respect for him which she had felt on seeing him so full of energy and vigour, the agony he had experienced during the first few hours at first gave way before the irreparable, and the cessation of pain is such a relief that the rupture, once it was certain, assumed for him something of the same kind of charm as a reconciliation. What he began to suffer from a little later was a secondary and accidental grief, the tide of which flowed incessantly from within himself, at the idea that perhaps she would have been glad to make it up, that it was not inconceivable that she was waiting for a word from him, that in the meantime, by way of revenge, she would perhaps on a certain evening, in a certain place, do a certain thing, and that he had only to telegraph to her that he was coming for it not to happen, that others perhaps were taking advantage of the time which he was letting slip, and that in a few days it would be too late to get her back, for she would be already bespoken. Among all these possibilities he was certain of nothing; his mistress preserved a silence which wrought him up to such a frenzy of grief that he began to ask himself whether she might not be in hiding at Doncières, or have set sail for the Indies.

It has been said that silence is strength; in a quite different sense it is a terrible strength in the hands of those who are loved. It increases the anxiety of the one who waits. Nothing so tempts us to approach another person as what is keeping us apart; and what barrier is so insurmountable as silence? It has been said also that silence is torture, capable of goading to madness the man who is condemned to it in a prison cell. But what an even greater torture than that of having to keep silence it is to have to endure the silence of the person one loves! Robert said to himself: "What can she be doing, to keep so silent as this? Obviously she's being unfaithful to me with others." He also said to himself: "What have I done that she should be so silent? Perhaps she hates me, and will go on hating me for ever." And he reproached himself. Thus silence indeed drove him mad with jealousy and remorse. Besides, more cruel than the silence of prisons, that kind of silence is in itself a prison. It is an intangible enclosure, true, but an impenetrable one, this interposed slice of empty atmosphere through which nevertheless the visual rays of the abandoned lover cannot pass. Is there a more terrible form of illumination than that of silence, which shows us not one absent love but a thousand, and shows us each of them in the act of indulging in some new betrayal? Sometimes, in a sudden slackening of tension, Robert would imagine that this silence was about to cease, that the letter was on its way. He saw it, it had arrived, he started at every sound, his thirst was already quenched, he murmured: "The letter! The letter!" After this glimpse of a phantom oasis of tenderness, he found himself once more toiling across the real desert of a silence without end.

He suffered in anticipation, without missing a single one, all the griefs and pains of a rupture which at other moments he fancied he might somehow contrive to avoid, like people who put all their affairs in order with a view to an expatriation which will never take place, and whose minds, no longer certain where they will find themselves living next day, flutter momentarily, detached from them, like a heart that is taken out of a dying man and continues to beat, though separated from the rest of his body. At all events, this hope that his mistress would return gave him courage to persevere in the rupture, as the belief that one may return alive from the battle helps one to face death. And inasmuch as habit is, of all the plants of human growth, the one that has least need of nutritious soil in order to live, and is the first to appear on the most seemingly barren rock, perhaps had he begun by thinking of the rupture as a feint he would in the end have become genuinely accustomed to it. But his uncertainty kept him in a state which, linked with the memory of the woman herself, was akin to love. He forced himself, nevertheless, not to write to her, thinking perhaps that it was a less cruel torment to live without his mistress than with her in certain conditions, or else that, after the way in which they had parted, it was essential to wait for her apologies if she was to retain what he believed her to feel for him in the way, if not of love, at any rate of esteem and regard. He contented himself with going to the telephone, which had recently been installed at Doncières, and asking for news from, or giving instructions to, a lady's-maid whom he had hired for his mistress. These communications were complicated and time-consuming, since, influenced by what her literary friends preached to her about the ugliness of the capital, but principally for the sake

of her animals, her dogs, her monkey, her canaries and her para-
keet, whose incessant din her Paris landlord had ceased to tolerate,
Robert's mistress had taken a little house in the neighbourhood of
Versailles. Meanwhile he, at Doncières, no longer slept a wink all
night. Once, in my room, overcome by exhaustion, he dozed off
for a while. But suddenly he began to speak, tried to get up and run
to stop something from happening, said: "I hear her; you
shan't . . . you shan't . . ." He awoke. He had been dreaming, he
told me, that he was in the country with the senior sergeant. His
host had tried to keep him away from a certain part of the house.
Saint-Loup had discovered that the senior sergeant had staying
with him a subaltern, extremely rich and extremely vicious,
whom he knew to have a violent passion for his mistress. And
suddenly in his dream he had distinctly heard the intermittently
regular cries which his mistress was in the habit of uttering at the
moment of gratification. He had tried to force the senior sergeant
to take him to the room in which she was. And the other had held
on to him to keep him from going there, with an air of annoyance
at such a want of discretion in a guest which, Robert said, he
would never be able to forget.

"It was an idiotic dream," he concluded, still quite out of
breath.

All the same I could see that, during the hour that followed, he
was more than once on the point of telephoning to his mistress to
beg for a reconciliation. My father now had the telephone, but
I doubt whether that would have been of much use to Saint-Loup.
Besides, it hardly seemed to me quite proper to make my parents,
or even a mechanical instrument installed in their house, play
pander between Saint-Loup and his mistress, however ladylike
and high-minded the latter might be. His bad dream began to
fade from his memory. With a fixed and absent stare, he came to
see me on each of those cruel days which traced in my mind as they
followed one after the other the splendid sweep of a staircase
painfully forged, from the steps of which Robert stood asking
himself what decision his beloved was going to take.

At length she wrote to ask whether he would consent to forgive
her. As soon as he realised that a definite rupture had been avoided
he saw all the disadvantages of a reconciliation. Besides, he had
already begun to suffer less acutely, and had almost accepted a grief
of which, in a few months perhaps, he would have to suffer the
sharp bite again if their liaison were to be resumed. He did not

hesitate for long. And perhaps he hesitated only because he was now certain of being able to recover his mistress, of being able to do so and therefore of doing so. However, she asked him, so that she might have time to recover her equanimity, not to come to Paris at the New Year. And he did not have the heart to go to Paris without seeing her. On the other hand, she had declared her willingness to go abroad with him, but for that he would need to make a formal application for leave, which Captain de Borodino was unwilling to grant.

"I'm sorry about it because of our visit to my aunt, which will have to be put off. I dare say I shall be in Paris at Easter."

"We shan't be able to call on Mme de Guermantes then, because I shall have gone to Balbec. But, really, it doesn't matter in the least, I assure you."

"To Balbec? But you didn't go there till August."

"I know, but next year I'm being sent there earlier, for my health."

His main fear was that I might form a bad impression of his mistress after what he had told me. "She is violent simply because she's too frank, too headstrong in her feelings. But she's a sublime creature. You can't imagine the poetic delicacy there is in her. She goes every year to spend All Souls' Day at Bruges. Rather good, don't you think? If you ever meet her you'll see what I mean: she has a sort of greatness . . . " And, as he was infected with certain of the linguistic mannerisms current in the literary circles in which the lady moved: "There's something astral about her, in fact something vatic. You know what I mean, the poet merging into the priest."

I searched all through dinner for a pretext which would enable Saint-Loup to ask his aunt to see me without my having to wait until he came to Paris. Such a pretext was finally furnished me by the desire I cherished to see some more pictures by Elstir, the famous painter whom Saint-Loup and I had met at Balbec— a pretext behind which there was, moreover, an element of truth, for if, on my visits to Elstir, I had asked of his painting that it should lead me to the understanding and love of things better than itself, a real thaw, an authentic square in a country town, live women on a beach (at most I would have commissioned from him portraits of realities I had not been able to fathom, such as a hedge of hawthorns, not so much that it might perpetuate their beauty for me as that it might reveal that beauty to me), now, on the contrary, it was the originality, the seductive attraction of those paintings that aroused my desire, and what I wanted above all else was to look at other pictures by Elstir.

It seemed to me, moreover, that the least of his pictures were something quite different from the masterpieces even of greater painters than himself. His work was like a realm apart, with impenetrable frontiers, peerless in substance. Eagerly collecting the infrequent periodicals in which articles on him and his work had appeared, I had learned that it was only recently that he had begun to paint landscape and still life, and that he had started with mythological subjects (I had seen photographs of two of these in his studio), and had then been for long under the influence of Japanese art.

Several of the works most characteristic of his various manners were scattered about the provinces. A certain house at Les Andelys, in which there was one of his finest landscapes, seemed to me as precious, gave me as keen a desire to go there, as might a village near Chartres among whose millstone walls was enshrined a glorious stained-glass window; and towards the possessor of this treasure, towards the man who, inside his rough-hewn house, on the main street, closeted like an astrologer, sat questioning one of those mirrors of the world which Elstir's pictures were, and who had perhaps bought it for many thousands of francs, I felt myself borne by that instinctive sympathy which joins the very hearts, the inmost natures of those who think alike upon a vital subject. Now three important works by my favourite painter were described in one of these articles as belonging to Mme de Guermantes. So that it was on the whole quite sincerely that, on the evening on which Saint-Loup told me of his lady's projected visit to Bruges, I was able, during dinner, in front of his friends, to say to him casually, as though on the spur of the moment:

"I say, if you don't mind, just one last word on the subject of the lady we were speaking about. You remember Elstir, the painter I met at Balbec?"

"Why, of course I do."

"You remember how much I admired his work?"

"I do, very well; and the letter we sent him."

"Well, one of the reasons—not one of the chief reasons, an incidental reason—why I should like to meet the said lady—you do know who I mean, don't you?"

"Of course I do. All these digressions!"

"Is that she has in her house at least one very fine picture by Elstir."

"Really, I never knew that."

"Elstir will probably be at Balbec at Easter; you know he now spends almost the entire year on that coast. I should very much like to have seen this picture before I leave Paris. I don't know whether you're on sufficiently intimate terms with your aunt: but couldn't you manage, somehow, giving her so good an impression of me that she won't refuse, to ask her to let me come and see the picture without you, since you won't be there?"

"Certainly. I'll answer for her; leave it to me."

"Oh, Robert, I do like you."

"It's very nice of you to like me, but it would be equally nice if you were to call me *tu*, as you promised, and as you began to do."

"I hope it's not your departure that you two are plotting together," one of Robert's friends said to me. "You know, if Saint-Loup does go on leave, it needn't make any difference, we shall still be here. It will be less amusing for you, perhaps, but we'll do all we can to make you forget his absence!"

The fact was that, just when it had been generally assumed that Robert's mistress would be going to Bruges alone, the news came that Captain de Borodino, hitherto obdurate in his refusal, had given authority for Sergeant Saint-Loup to proceed on long leave to Bruges. What had happened was this. The Prince, extremely proud of his luxuriant head of hair, was an assiduous customer of the principal hairdresser in the town, who had started life as an apprentice to Napoleon III's barber. Captain de Borodino was on the best of terms with the hairdresser, being, in spite of his majestic airs, extremely simple in his dealings with his inferiors. But the hairdresser, through whose books the Prince's account had been running without payment for at least five years, swollen no less by bottles of "Portugal" and "Eau des Souverains," curling-tongs, razors, and strops, than by the ordinary charges for shampooing, haircutting and the like, had a greater respect for Saint-Loup, who always paid on the nail and kept several carriages and saddle-horses. Having learned of Saint-Loup's vexation at not being able to go with his mistress, he had spoken warmly about it to the Prince at a moment when he was trussed up in a white surplice with his head held firmly over the back of the chair and his throat menaced by a razor. This account of a young man's amatory adventures won from the princely Captain a smile of Bonapartist indulgence. It is hardly probable that he thought of his unpaid bill, but the barber's recommendation inclined him to good humour as much as a duke's would have inclined him to bad. While his chin was still smothered in soap, the leave was promised and the warrant was signed that evening. As for the hairdresser, who was in the habit of boasting incessantly, and in order to be able to do so laid claim, with an astonishing faculty for lying, to exploits that were entirely fictitious, having for once rendered a signal service to Saint-Loup, not only did he refrain from publicly claiming credit for it, but, as if vanity were obliged to lie, and when there is no call to do so gives way to modesty, he never mentioned the matter to Robert again.

All Robert's friends assured me that, as long as I stayed at Doncières, or if I should come there again at any time, even though Robert was away, their horses, their quarters, their free time would be at my disposal, and I felt that it was with the greatest cordiality that these young men put their comfort and youth and strength at the service of my weakness.

"Why at any rate," they went on after insisting that I should stay, "don't you come down here every year? You see how our humble life appeals to you! Besides, you're so keen about everything that goes on in the regiment: quite the old soldier."

For I continued to ask them eagerly to classify the different officers whose names I knew according to the degree of admiration which they felt them to deserve, just as, in the old days, I used to make my school-friends classify the actors of the Théâtre-Français. If, in the place of one of the generals whom I had always heard mentioned at the head of the list, such as Galliffet or Négrier, one of Saint-Loup's friends remarked, "But Négrier is one of the feeblest of our general officers," and put in the new, untarnished, appetising name of Pau or Geslin de Bourgogne, I felt the same happy surprise as long ago when the outworn names of Thiron or Febvre were ousted by the sudden blossoming of the unfamiliar name of Amaury. "Better even than Négrier? But in what respect? Give me an example." I should have liked there to exist profound differences even among the junior officers of the regiment, and I hoped, in the reason for these differences, to grasp the essence of what constituted military superiority. One of those whom I should have been most interested to hear discussed, because he was the one whom I had most often seen, was the

Prince de Borodino. But neither Saint-Loup nor his friends, while giving him credit for being a fine officer who kept his squadron up to an incomparable pitch of efficiency, liked the man. Without speaking of him, naturally, in the same tone as of certain other officers, rankers and freemasons, who did not fraternise much with the rest and had, in comparison, an uncouth, barrack-room manner, they seemed not to include M. de Borodino among the other officers of noble birth, from whom indeed he differed considerably in his attitude even towards Saint-Loup. These, taking advantage of the fact that Robert was only an NCO, and that therefore his influential relatives might be grateful were he invited to the houses of superior officers on whom otherwise they would have looked down, lost no opportunity of having him to dine when any bigwig was expected who might be of use to a young cavalry sergeant. Captain de Borodino alone confined himself to his official relations (which for that matter were always excellent) with Robert. The fact was that the Prince, whose grandfather had been made a Marshal and a Prince-Duke by the Emperor, into whose family he had subsequently married, and whose father had then married a cousin of Napoleon III and had twice been a minister after the coup d'état, felt that in spite of all this he did not count for much with Saint-Loup and the Guermantes set, who in turn, since he did not look at things from the same point of view as they, counted for very little with him. He suspected that, for Saint-Loup, he—a kinsman of the Hohenzollerns—was not a true noble but the grandson of a farmer, but at the same time he regarded Saint-Loup as the son of a man whose countship had been confirmed by the Emperor—one of what were known in the Faubourg Saint-Germain as "touched-up" counts—and who had besought him first for a Prefecture, then for some other post a long way down the list of subordinates to His Highness the Prince de Borodino, Minister of State, who was styled on his letters "Monseigneur" and was a nephew of the sovereign.

More than a nephew, possibly. The first Princesse de Borodino was reputed to have bestowed her favours on Napoleon I, whom she followed to the Isle of Elba, and the second hers on Napoleon III. And if, in the Captain's placid countenance, one caught a trace of Napoleon I—if not his actual features, at least the studied majesty of the expression—the officer had, particularly in his melancholy and kindly gaze, in his drooping moustache, something that reminded one also of Napoleon III; and this in so striking a fashion that, when he asked leave, after Sedan, to join the Emperor in captivity, and was shown the door by Bismarck, before whom he had been brought, the latter, happening to look up at the young man who was preparing to leave the room, was instantly struck by the likeness and, reconsidering his decision, recalled him and gave him the authorisation which, in common with everyone else, he had just been refused.

If the Prince de Borodino was not prepared to make overtures either to Saint-Loup or to the other representatives of the Faubourg Saint-Germain in the regiment (whereas he frequently invited two subalterns of plebeian origin who were pleasant companions) it was because, looking down on them all from the height of his Imperial grandeur, he drew between these two classes of inferiors the distinction that one set consisted of inferiors who knew themselves to be such and with whom he was delighted to consort, being beneath his outward majesty of a simple, jovial nature, and the other of inferiors who thought themselves his superiors, a claim which he could not allow. And so, while all the other officers of the regiment made much of Saint-Loup, the Prince de Borodino, to whom the young man had been recommended by Marshal X——, confined himself to being kindly towards him in the matter of military duty, where Saint-Loup was in fact exemplary, but never had him to his house, except on one special occasion when he found himself practically compelled to invite him, and, since this occurred during my stay at Doncières, asked him to bring me too. I had no difficulty that evening, as I watched Saint-Loup sitting at his Captain's table, in distinguishing, in their respective manners and refinements, the difference that existed between the two aristocracies: the old nobility and that of the Empire. The product of a caste whose faults, even if he repudiated them with all the force of his intellect, had been absorbed into his blood, a caste which, having ceased to exert any real authority for at least a century, no longer saw in the patronising affability which was part and parcel of its education anything more than an exercise, like horsemanship or fencing, cultivated without any serious purpose, as a diversion, Saint-Loup, on meeting representatives of that middle class which the old nobility so far despised as to believe that they were flattered by its intimacy and would be honoured by its informality, would cordially shake hands with any bourgeois to whom he was introduced, and whose name he had probably failed to catch, and as he talked to him (constantly crossing and uncrossing his legs, flinging himself back in his chair in an attitude of abandon, one foot in the palm of his hand) would call him "my dear fellow." Belonging, on the other hand, to a nobility whose titles still preserved their meaning, possessed as they still were of the rich emoluments given in reward for glorious services and bringing to mind the record of high offices in which one is in command of numberless men and must know how to deal with men, the Prince de Borodino—not perhaps very distinctly or in the personal awareness of his conscious mind, but at any rate in his body, which revealed it by its attitudes and manners—regarded his rank as a prerogative that was still effective; those same commoners whom Saint-Loup would have slapped on the shoulder and taken by the arm he addressed with a majestic affability, in which a reserve instinct with grandeur tempered the smiling good-fellowship that came naturally to him, in a tone marked at once by a genuine kindliness and a stiffness deliberately assumed. This was due, no doubt, to his being not so far removed from the chancelleries and the Court itself, at which his father had held the highest posts, and where the manners of Saint-Loup, his elbow on the table and his foot in his hand, would not have been well received; but principally it was due to the fact that he was less contemptuous of the middle class since it was the great reservoir from which the first Emperor had chosen his marshals and his nobles and in which the second had found a Rouher or a Fould.

Son or grandson of an Emperor though he might be, with nothing more important to do than to command a squadron, the preoccupations of his putative father and grandfather could not, of course, for want of an object on which to fasten themselves, survive in any real sense in the mind of M. de Borodino. But as the spirit of an artist continues, for many years after he is dead, to model the statue which he carved, so those preoccupations had taken shape in him, were materialised, incarnate in him, it was them that his face reflected. It was with the sharpness of the first Emperor in his voice that he addressed a reprimand to a corporal, with the dreamy melancholy of the second that he exhaled a puff of cigarette-smoke. When he passed in plain clothes through the streets of Doncières, a certain glint in his eyes, issuing from under the brim of his bowler hat, surrounded the Captain with the aura of a regal incognito; people trembled when he strode into the senior sergeant's office, followed by the sergeant-major and the quartermaster, as though by Berthier and Masséna. When he chose the cloth for his squadron's breeches, he fastened on the master-tailor a look capable of baffling Talleyrand and deceiving Alexander; and at times, in the middle of a kit inspection, he would pause, a dreamy look in his handsome blue eyes, and twist his moustache with the air of one building up a new Prussia and a new Italy. But a moment later, reverting from Napoleon III to Napoleon I, he would point out that the equipment was not properly polished, and insist on tasting the men's rations. And at home, in his private life, it was for the wives of middle-class officers (provided they were not freemasons) that he would bring out not only a dinner-service of royal blue Sèvres, fit for an ambassador (which had been given to his father by Napoleon, and appeared even more priceless in the commonplace house he inhabited on the avenue, like those rare porcelains which tourists admire with a special delight in the rustic china-cupboard of some old manor that has been converted into a comfortable and prosperous farmhouse), but other gifts of the Emperor also: those noble and charming manners, which too would have done wonders in a diplomatic post abroad (if for some it did not mean a lifelong condemnation to the most unjust form of ostracism merely to have a "name"), the easy gestures, the kindness, the grace, and, enclosing images of glory in an enamel that was also royal blue, the mysterious, illuminated, living reliquary of his gaze.

And in regard to the social relations with the middle classes which the Prince had at Doncières, it may be appropriate to add the following. The lieutenant-colonel played the piano beautifully; the senior medical officer's wife sang like a Conservatoire medallist. This latter couple, as well as the lieutenant-colonel and his wife, used to dine every week with M. de Borodino. They were certainly flattered, knowing that when the Prince went to Paris on leave he dined with Mme de Pourtalès, with the Murats and suchlike. "But," they said to themselves, "he's just a captain, after all; he's only too glad to get us to come. Still, he's a real friend to us." But when M. de Borodino, who had long been pulling every possible wire to secure an appointment nearer Paris, was posted to Beauvais, he packed up and went, and forgot the two musical couples as completely as he forgot the Doncières theatre and the little restaurant to which he used often to send out for his lunch, and, to their great indignation, neither the lieutenant-colonel nor the senior medical officer, who had so often sat at his table, ever had so much as a single word from him for the rest of their lives.

One morning, Saint-Loup confessed to me that he had written to my grandmother to give her news of me and to suggest to her that, since there was a telephone service functioning between Paris and Doncières, she might make use of it to speak to me. In short, that very day she was to give me a call, and he advised me to be at the post-office at about a quarter to four. The telephone was not yet at that date as commonly in use as it is today. And yet habit requires so short a time to divest of their mystery the sacred forces with which we are in contact, that, not having had my call at once, my immediate thought was that it was all very long and very inconvenient, and I almost decided to lodge a complaint. Like all of us nowadays, I found too slow for my liking, in its abrupt changes, the admirable sorcery whereby a few moments are enough to bring before us, invisible but present, the person to whom we wish to speak, and who, while still sitting at his table, in the town in which he lives (in my grandmother's case, Paris), under another sky than ours, in weather that is not necessarily the same, in the midst of circumstances and preoccupations of which we know nothing and of which he is about to inform us, finds himself suddenly transported hundreds of miles (he and all the surroundings in which he remains immured) within reach of our ear, at the precise moment which our fancy has ordained. And we are like the person in the fairy-tale for whom a sorceress, at his express wish, conjures up, in a supernatural light, his grandmother or his betrothed in the act of turning over a book, of shedding tears, of gathering flowers, close by the spectator and yet very far away, in the place where she actually is at the moment. We need only, so that the miracle may be accomplished, apply our lips to the magic orifice and invoke—occasionally for rather longer than seems to us necessary, I admit—the Vigilant Virgins to whose voices we listen every day without ever coming to know their faces and who are our guardian angels in the dizzy realm of darkness whose portals they so jealously guard; the All-Powerful by whose intervention the absent rise up at our side, without our being permitted to set eyes on them; the Danaïds of the unseen who incessantly empty and fill and transmit to one another the urns of sound; the ironic Furies who, just as we were murmuring a confidence to a loved one, in the hope that no one could hear us, cry brutally: "I'm listening!"; the ever-irritable handmaidens of the Mystery, the umbrageous priestesses of the Invisible, the Young Ladies of the Telephone.

And as soon as our call has rung out, in the darkness filled with apparitions to which our ears alone are unsealed, a tiny sound, an abstract sound—the sound of distance overcome—and the voice of the dear one speaks to us.

It is she, it is her voice that is speaking, that is there. But how far away it is! How often have I been unable to listen without anguish, as though, confronted by the impossibility of seeing, except after long hours of travel, the woman whose voice was so close to my ear, I felt more clearly the illusoriness in the appearance of the most tender proximity, and at what a distance we may be from the persons we love at the moment when it seems that we have only to stretch out our hands to seize and hold them. A real presence, perhaps, that voice that seemed so near—in actual separation! But a premonition also of an eternal separation! Many are the times, as I listened thus without seeing her who spoke to me from so far away, when it has seemed to me that the voice was crying to me from the depths out of which one does not rise again, and I have felt the anxiety that was one day to wring my heart when a voice would thus return (alone and attached no longer to a body which I was never to see again), to murmur in my ear words I longed to kiss as they issued from lips for ever turned to dust.

That afternoon, alas, at Doncières, the miracle did not occur. When I reached the post-office, my grandmother's call had already been received. I stepped into the booth; the line was engaged; someone was talking who probably did not realise that there was nobody to answer him, for when I raised the receiver to my ear, the lifeless piece of wood began to squeak like Punchinello; I silenced it, as one silences a puppet, by putting it back on its hook, but, like Punchinello, as soon as I picked it up again it resumed its gabblings. At length, giving up in despair and hanging up the receiver once and for all, I stifled the convulsions of this vociferous stump which kept up its chatter until the last moment, and went in search of the telephonist, who told me to wait a while; then I spoke, and after a few seconds of silence, suddenly I heard that voice which I mistakenly thought I knew so well; for always until then, every time that my grandmother had talked to me, I had been accustomed to follow what she said on the open score of her face, in which the eyes figured so largely; but her voice itself I was hearing this afternoon for the first time. And because that voice appeared to me to have altered in its proportions from the moment that it was a whole, and reached me thus alone and without the accompaniment of her face and features, I discovered for the first time how sweet that voice was; perhaps indeed it had never been so sweet as it was now, for my grandmother, thinking of me as being far away and unhappy, felt that she might abandon herself to an outpouring of tenderness which, in accordance with her principles of upbringing, she usually restrained and kept hidden. It was sweet, but also how sad it was, first of all on account of its very sweetness, a sweetness drained almost—more than any but a few human voices can ever have been—of every element of hardness, of resistance to others, of selfishness! Fragile by reason of its delicacy, it seemed constantly on the verge of breaking, of expiring in a pure flow of tears; then, too, having it alone beside me, seen without the mask of her face, I noticed in it for the first time the sorrows that had cracked it in the course of a lifetime.

Was it, however, solely the voice that, because it was alone, gave me this new impression which tore my heart? Not at all; it was rather that this isolation of the voice was like a symbol, an evocation, a direct consequence of another isolation, that of my grandmother, for the first time separated from me. The commands or prohibitions which she constantly addressed to me in the ordinary course of life, the tedium of obedience or the fire of rebellion which neutralised the affection that I felt for her, were at this moment eliminated and indeed might be eliminated for ever (since my grandmother, no longer insisting on having me with her under her control, was in the act of expressing her hope that I would stay at Doncières altogether, or would at any rate extend my visit for as long as possible, since both my health and my work might benefit by the change); and so, what I held compressed in this little bell at my ear was our mutual affection, freed from the conflicting pressures which had daily counteracted it, and henceforth irresistible, uplifting me entirely. My grandmother, by telling me to stay, filled me with an anxious, an insensate longing to return. This freedom she was granting me henceforward, and to which I had never dreamed that she would consent, appeared to me suddenly as sad as my freedom of action might be after her death (when I should still love her and she would for ever have abandoned me). "Granny!" I cried to her, "Granny!" and I longed to kiss her, but I had beside me only the voice, a phantom as impalpable as the one that would perhaps come back to visit me when my grandmother was dead. "Speak to me!" But then, suddenly, I ceased to hear the voice, and was left even more alone. My grandmother could no longer hear me; she was no longer in communication with me; we had ceased to be close to each other, to be audible to each other; I continued to call her, groping in the empty darkness, feeling that calls from her must also be going astray. I quivered with the same anguish which I had felt once before in the distant past, when, as a little child, I had lost her in a crowd, an anguish due less to my not finding her than to the thought that she must be searching for me, must be saying to herself that I was searching for her, an anguish not unlike that which I was later to feel, on the day when we speak to those who can no longer reply and when we long for them at least to hear all the things we never said to them, and our assurance that we are not unhappy. It seemed to me as though it was already a beloved ghost that I had allowed to lose herself in the ghostly world, and, standing alone before the instrument, I went on vainly repeating: "Granny! Granny!" as Orpheus, left alone, repeats the name of his dead wife. I decided to leave the post-office, and go and find Robert at his restaurant in order to tell him that, as I was half expecting a telegram which would oblige me to return to Paris, I wanted, just in case, to know the times of the trains. And yet, before reaching this decision, I felt I must make one more attempt to invoke the Daughters of the Night, the Messengers of the Word, the faceless divinities; but the capricious Guardians had not deigned once again to open the miraculous portals, or, more probably, had been unable to do so; untiringly though they invoked, as was their custom, the venerable inventor of printing and the young prince, collector of Impressionist paintings and driver of motor-cars (who was Captain de Borodino's nephew), Gutenberg and Wagram, those telephone exchanges, left their supplications unanswered, and I came away, feeling that the Invisible would continue to turn a deaf ear.

When I joined Robert and his friends, I withheld the confession that my heart was no longer with them, that my departure was now irrevocably fixed. Saint-Loup appeared to believe me, but I learned afterwards that he had from the first moment realised that my uncertainty was feigned and that he would not see me again next day. While he and his friends, letting their plates grow cold, searched through the time-table for a train which would take me to Paris, and while the whistling of the locomotives in the cold,

starry night could be heard on the line, I certainly no longer felt
the same peace of mind as on so many evenings I had derived from
the friendship of the former and the latter's distant passage. And yet
they did not fail, this evening, to perform the same office in a
different form. My departure oppressed me less when I was no
longer obliged to think of it alone, when I felt that the more
normal and healthy exertions of my energetic friends, Robert's
brothers-in-arms, were being applied to what was to be done, and
of those other strong creatures, the trains, whose comings and
goings, morning and night, between Doncières and Paris, broke
up in retrospect what had been too compact and unendurable in
my long isolation from my grandmother into daily possibilities of
return.

"I don't doubt the truth of what you say, and that you aren't
thinking of leaving us just yet," said Saint-Loup, smiling, "but
pretend you are going, and come and say good-bye to me tomorrow morning early, otherwise there's a risk of my not seeing you.
I'm going out to lunch, I've got leave from the Captain, but I shall
have to be back in barracks by two, as we are to be on the march all
afternoon. I suppose the man to whose house I'm going, a couple
of miles out, will manage to get me back in time."

Scarcely had he uttered these words than a messenger came for
me from my hotel: the post-office had asked for me on the
telephone. I ran there, for it was nearly closing time. The word
"trunks" recurred incessantly in the answers given me by the
clerks. I was in a fever of anxiety, for it was my grandmother
who had asked for me. The post-office was closing for the night.
Finally I got my connexion. "Is that you, Granny?" A woman's
voice, with a strong English accent, answered: "Yes, but I don't
recognise your voice." Neither did I recognise the voice that was
speaking to me; besides, my grandmother called me *tu*, and not
vous. And then all was explained. The young man for whom his
grandmother had called on the telephone had a name almost
identical with mine, and was staying in an annex of my hotel.
This call coming on the very day on which I had been telephoning
to my grandmother, I had never for a moment doubted that it was
she who was asking for me. Whereas it was by pure coincidence
that the post-office and the hotel had combined to make a twofold
error.

The following morning I was late, and failed to catch Saint-
Loup, who had already left for the country house where he was

invited to lunch. About half-past one, having decided to go to the
barracks so as to be there as soon as he returned, I was crossing one
of the avenues on the way there when I noticed, coming behind
me in the same direction as myself, a tilbury which, as it overtook
me, obliged me to jump out of its way. An NCO was driving it,
wearing a monocle; it was Saint-Loup. By his side was the friend
whose guest he had been at lunch, and whom I had met once
before at the hotel where we dined. I did not dare shout to Robert
since he was not alone, but, in the hope that he would stop and
pick me up, I attracted his attention with a sweep of my hat which
was by way of being motivated by the presence of a stranger.
I knew that Robert was short-sighted, but I should have supposed
that if he saw me at all he could not fail to recognise me. He did
indeed see my salute, and returned it, but without stopping;
driving on at full speed, without a smile, without moving a muscle
of his face, he confined himself to keeping his hand raised for a
minute to the peak of his cap, as though he were acknowledging
the salute of a trooper whom he did not know. I ran to the
barracks, but it was a long way; when I arrived, the regiment
was forming up on the square, where I was not allowed to remain,
and I was heart-broken at not having been able to say good-bye to
Saint-Loup. I went up to his room, but there was no sign of him.
I inquired after him from a group of sick troopers—recruits who
had been excused route marches, the young graduate, one of the
"old soldiers," who were watching the regiment form up.

"You haven't seen Sergeant Saint-Loup, by any chance?" I
asked.

"He's already gone down, sir," said the old soldier.

"I never saw him," said the graduate.

"You never saw him," exclaimed the old soldier, losing all
interest in me, "you never saw our famous Saint-Loup, the figure
he's cutting with his new breeches! When the Cap'n sees that,
officer's cloth, my word!"

"Oh, that's a good one, officer's cloth," replied the young
graduate, who, having reported sick, was excused marching and
ventured, not without some trepidation, to make bold with the
veterans. "It isn't officer's cloth, it's just ordinary cloth."

"Monsieur?" inquired the old soldier angrily.

He was indignant that the young graduate should question his
assertion that the breeches were made of officer's cloth, but, being
a Breton, born in a village that went by the name of Penguern-

Stereden, and having learned French with as much difficulty as if it had been English or German, whenever he felt himself overcome by emotion he would go on saying "Monsieur?" to give himself time to find words, then, after this preparation, let loose his eloquence, confining himself to the repetition of certain words which he knew better than others, but without haste, taking every precaution to gloss over his unfamiliarity with the pronunciation.

"Ah! so it's just ordinary cloth?" he broke out eventually with a fury whose intensity increased in direct proportion to the sluggishness of his speech. "Ah! so it's just ordinary cloth! When I tell you that it is officer's cloth, when-I-tell-you, since-I-tell-you, it's because I know, I would think. You'd better not spin your cock-and-bull yarns here."

"Oh, well, if you say so," replied the young graduate, overcome by the force of this argument.

"There, look, there's the Cap'n coming along. No, but just look at Saint-Loup, the way he throws his leg out, and his head. Would you call that a non-com? And his eyeglass—it's all over the shop."

I asked these troopers, who did not seem at all embarrassed by my presence, whether I too might look out of the window. They neither objected to my doing so nor moved to make room for me. I saw Captain de Borodino go majestically by, putting his horse into a trot, and seemingly under the illusion that he was taking part in the Battle of Austerlitz. A few loiterers had stopped by the gate to see the regiment file out. Erect on his charger, his face rather plump, his cheeks of an Imperial fullness, his eye clear-sighted, the Prince must have been the victim of some hallucination, as I was myself whenever, after the tram-car had passed, the silence that followed its rumble seemed to me crossed and striated by a vaguely musical palpitation.

I was wretched at having failed to say good-bye to Saint-Loup, but I went nevertheless, for my only concern was to return to my grandmother; always until then, in this little country town, when I thought of what my grandmother must be doing by herself, I had pictured her as she was when with me, but eliminating myself without taking into account the effects on her of such an elimination; now, I had to free myself at the first possible moment, in her arms, from the phantom, hitherto unsuspected and suddenly called into being by her voice, of a grandmother really separated from me, resigned, having (something I had never yet thought of her as having) a definite age, who had just received a letter from me in the empty house in which I had already imagined Mamma when I had left her to go to Balbec.

Alas, it was this phantom that I saw when, entering the drawing-room before my grandmother had been told of my return, I found her there reading. I was in the room, or rather I was not yet in the room since she was not aware of my presence, and, like a woman whom one surprises at a piece of needlework which she will hurriedly put aside if anyone comes in, she was absorbed in thoughts which she had never allowed to be seen by me. Of myself—thanks to that privilege which does not last but which gives one, during the brief moment of return, the faculty of being suddenly the spectator of one's own absence—there was present only the witness, the observer, in travelling-coat and hat, the stranger who does not belong to the house, the photographer who has called to take a photograph of places which one will never see again. The process that automatically occurred in my eyes when I caught sight of my grandmother was indeed a photograph. We never see the people who are dear to us save in the animated system, the perpetual motion of our incessant love for them, which, before allowing the images that their faces present to reach us, seizes them in its vortex and flings them back upon the idea that we have always had of them, makes them adhere to it, coincide with it. How, since into the forehead and the cheeks of my grandmother I had been accustomed to read all the most delicate, the most permanent qualities of her mind, how, since every habitual glance is an act of necromancy, each face that we love a mirror of the past, how could I have failed to overlook what had become dulled and changed in her, seeing that in the most trivial spectacles of our daily life, our eyes, charged with thought, neglect, as would a classical tragedy, every image that does not contribute to the action of the play and retain only those that may help to make its purpose intelligible. But if, instead of our eyes, it should happen to be a purely physical object, a photographic plate, that has watched the action, then what we see, in the courtyard of the Institute, for example, instead of the dignified emergence of an Academician who is trying to hail a cab, will be his tottering steps, his precautions to avoid falling on his back, the parabola of his fall, as though he were drunk or the ground covered in ice. So it is when some cruel trick of chance prevents our intelligent and pious tenderness from coming forward in time to hide from our eyes what they ought never to behold, when it is forestalled by our eyes, and they, arriving first in the field and having it to themselves, set to work mechanically, like films, and show us, in place of the beloved person who has long ago ceased to exist but whose death our tenderness has always hitherto kept concealed from us, the new person whom a hundred times daily it has clothed with a loving and mendacious likeness. And—like a sick man who, not having looked at his own reflexion for a long time, and regularly composing the features which he never sees in accordance with the ideal image of himself that he carries in his mind, recoils on catching sight in the glass, in the middle of an arid desert of a face, of the sloping pink protuberance of a nose as huge as one of the pyramids of Egypt—I, for whom my grandmother was still myself, I who had never seen her save in my own soul, always in the same place in the past, through the transparency of contiguous and overlapping memories, suddenly, in our drawing-room which formed part of a new world, that of Time, that which is inhabited by the strangers of whom we say "He's begun to age a good deal," for the first time and for a moment only, since she vanished very quickly, I saw, sitting on the sofa beneath the lamp, red-faced, heavy and vulgar, sick, day-dreaming, letting her slightly crazed eyes wander over a book, an overburdened old woman whom I did not know.

My request to be allowed to inspect the Elstirs in Mme de Guermantes's collection had been met by Saint-Loup with: "I'll answer for her." And indeed, unfortunately, it was he and he alone who did answer. We answer readily enough for other people when, setting our mental stage with the little puppets that represent them, we manipulate these to suit our fancy. No doubt even then we take into account the difficulties due to another person's nature being different from our own, and we do not fail to appeal to motives with the power to influence that nature—self-interest, persuasion, emotion—which will neutralise any contrary tendencies. But it is still our own nature which imagines these divergences from our nature; it is we who remove these difficulties; it is we who measure these compelling motives. And when we wish to see the other person perform in real life the actions which in our mind's eye we have made him rehearse, the case is altered, we come up against unseen resistances which may prove insuperable. One of the strongest is doubtless that which may be developed in a woman who does not love, by the rank and unconquerable repulsion she feels for the man who loves her: during the long weeks in which Saint-Loup still did not come to Paris, his aunt, to whom I had no doubt of his having written begging her to do so, never once asked me to call at her house to see the Elstirs.

I perceived signs of coldness on the part of another occupant of the building. This was Jupien. Did he consider that I ought to have gone in and said good-day to him, on my return from Doncières, before even going upstairs to our own flat? My mother said that it was nothing to be surprised about. Françoise had told her that he was like that, subject to sudden fits of ill-humour, without any cause. These invariably passed off after a while.

Meanwhile the winter was drawing to an end. One morning, after several weeks of showers and storms, I heard in my chimney—instead of the formless, elastic, sombre wind which stirred in me a longing to go to the sea—the cooing of the pigeons, nesting in the wall outside; shimmering and unexpected like a first hyacinth gently tearing open its nutritious heart to release its flower of sound, mauve and satin-soft, letting into my still dark and shuttered bedroom as through an opened window the warmth, the brightness, the fatigue of a first fine day. That morning, I caught myself humming a music-hall tune which had never entered my head since the year when I had been due to go to Florence and Venice—so profoundly, and so unpredictably, does the atmosphere act on our organism and draw from dim reserves where we had forgotten them the melodies written there which our memory has failed to decipher. Presently a more conscious dreamer accompanied this musician to whom I was listening inside myself, without even having recognised at first what he was playing.

I realised that it was not for any reason peculiar to Balbec that on my arrival there I had failed to find in its church the charm which it had had for me before I knew it; that in Florence or Parma or Venice my imagination could no more take the place of my eyes when I looked at the sights there. I realised this; similarly, one New Year's evening at nightfall, standing before a column of playbills, I had discovered the illusion that lies in our thinking that certain feast-days differ essentially from the other days in the calendar. And yet I could not prevent my memory of the time during which I had looked forward to spending Easter in Florence from continuing to make that festival the atmosphere, so to speak, of the City of Flowers, to give at once to Easter Day something Florentine and to Florence something paschal. Easter was still a long way off; but in the range of days that stretched out before me the days of Holy Week stood out more clearly at the end of those that came between. Touched by a ray, like certain houses in a village which one sees from a distance when the rest are in shadow, they had caught and kept all the sun.

The weather had now become milder. And my parents themselves, by urging me to take more exercise, gave me an excuse for continuing my morning walks. I had wanted to give them up, since they meant my meeting Mme de Guermantes. But it was for that very reason that I kept thinking all the time of those walks, and this induced me to go on finding fresh reasons for taking them, reasons which had no connexion with Mme de Guermantes and which easily convinced me that, had she never existed, I should still have gone for a walk at that hour every morning.

Alas, if for me meeting any person other than herself would have been a matter of indifference, I felt that, for her, meeting anyone in the world except myself would have been only too endurable. It happened that, in the course of her morning walks, she received the salutations of plenty of fools whom she regarded as such. But the appearance of these in her path seemed to her, if not to hold out any promise of pleasure, to be at any rate the result of mere accident. And she stopped them at times, for there are moments in which one wants to escape from oneself, to accept the hospitality offered by the soul of another, provided always that this soul, however modest and plain it may be, is a different soul, whereas in my heart she felt with exasperation that what she would have found was herself. And so, even when I had another reason for taking the same route than my desire to see her, I trembled like a guilty man as she came past; and sometimes, in order to neutralise what might seem to be excessive in my overtures, I would barely acknowledge her salute, or would stare at her without raising my hat, and succeed only in irritating her even more and making her begin to regard me as insolent and ill-bred besides.

She was now wearing lighter, or at any rate brighter clothes, and would come strolling down the street in which already, as though it were spring, in front of the narrow shops that were squeezed in between the spacious fronts of the old aristocratic mansions, over the booths of the butter-woman and the fruit-woman and the vegetable-woman, awnings were spread to protect them from the sun. I told myself that the woman whom I could see in the distance, walking, opening her sunshade, crossing the street, was, in the opinion of those best qualified to judge, the greatest living exponent of the art of performing those movements and of making of them something exquisite. Meanwhile she advanced towards me, and, unconscious of this widespread reputation, her narrow, refractory body, which had absorbed nothing of it, was arched forward under a scarf of violet silk; her clear, sullen eyes looked absently in front of her, and had perhaps caught sight of me; she was biting the corner of her lip; I watched her adjust her muff, give alms to a beggar, buy a bunch of violets from a flower-seller, with the same curiosity that I should have felt in watching the brush-strokes of a great painter. And when, as she passed me, she gave me a bow that was accompanied sometimes by a faint smile, it was as though she had sketched for me, adding a personal dedication, a water-colour that was a masterpiece of art. Each of her dresses seemed to me her natural and necessary setting, like the projection of a particular aspect of her soul. On one of these Lenten mornings, when she was on her way out to lunch, I met her wearing a dress of bright red velvet, cut slightly low at the neck. Her face appeared dreamy beneath its pile of fair hair. I was less sad than usual because the melancholy of her expression, the sort of claustration which the startling hue of her dress set between her and the rest of the world, made her seem somehow lonely and unhappy, and this comforted me. The dress struck me as being the materialisation round about her of the scarlet rays of a heart which I did not recognise in her and might perhaps have been able to console; sheltered in the mystical light of the garment with its soft folds, she reminded me of some saint of the early ages of Christianity. After which I felt ashamed of inflicting my presence on this holy martyr. "But, after all, the streets belong to every-body."

The streets belong to everybody, I repeated to myself, giving a different meaning to the words, and marvelling that indeed in the crowded street, often soaked with rain, which gave it a precious lustre like the streets, at times, in the old towns of Italy, the Duchesse de Guermantes mingled with the public life of the world moments of her own secret life, showing herself thus in all her mystery to everyone, jostled by all and sundry, with the splendid gratuitousness of the greatest works of art. As I often went out in the morning after staying awake all night, in the afternoon my parents would tell me to lie down for a little and try to get some sleep. There is no need, when one is trying to find sleep, to give much thought to the quest, but habit is very useful, and even the absence of thought. But in these afternoon hours I lacked both. Before going to sleep, I devoted so much time to thinking that I should be unable to do so that even after I was asleep a little of my thought remained. It was no more than a glimmer in the almost total darkness, but it was enough to cast a reflexion in my sleep, first of the idea that I could not sleep, and then, a reflexion of this reflexion, that it was in my sleep that I had had the idea that I was not asleep, then, by a further refraction, my awakening . . . to a fresh doze in which I was trying to tell some friends who had come into my room that, a moment earlier, when I was asleep, I had imagined that I was not asleep. These shadows were barely distinguishable; it would have required a keen—and quite useless—delicacy of perception to seize them. Similarly, in later years, in Venice, long after the sun had set, when it seemed to be quite dark, I have seen, thanks to the echo, itself imperceptible, of a last note of light held indefinitely on the surface of the canals as though by the effect of some optical pedal, the reflexions of the palaces displayed as though for all time in a darker velvet on the crepuscular greyness of the water. One of my dreams was the synthesis of what my imagination had often sought to depict, in my waking hours, of a certain seagirt place and its mediaeval past. In my sleep I saw a Gothic city rising from a sea whose waves were stilled as in a stained-glass window. An arm of the sea divided the town in two; the green water stretched to my feet; on the opposite shore it washed round the base of an oriental church, and beyond it houses which existed already in the fourteenth century, so that to go across to them would have been to ascend the stream of time. This dream in which nature had learned from art, in which the sea had turned Gothic, this dream in which I longed to attain, in which I believed that I was attaining to the impossible, was one that I felt I had often dreamed before. But as it is the nature of what we imagine in sleep to multiply itself in the past, and to appear, even when new, to be familiar, I supposed that I was mistaken. I noticed, however, that I did indeed frequently have this dream.

The diminutions, too, that characterise sleep were reflected in mine, but in a symbolic manner; I could not in the darkness make out the faces of the friends who were in the room, for we sleep with our eyes shut; I, who could carry on endless verbal arguments with myself while I dreamed, as soon as I tried to speak to these friends felt the words stick in my throat, for we do not speak distinctly in our sleep; I wanted to go to them, and I could not move my limbs, for we do not walk when we are asleep either; and, suddenly, I was ashamed to be seen by them, for we sleep without our clothes. So, my eyes blinded, my lips sealed, my limbs fettered, my body naked, the image of sleep which my sleep itself projected had the appearance of those great allegorical figures where Giotto has portrayed Envy with a serpent in her mouth, and which Swann had given me.

Saint-Loup came to Paris for a few hours only. While affirming that he had not yet had an opportunity of speaking to his cousin, "She's not at all nice, Oriane," he told me with innocent self-betrayal. "She's not my old Oriane any longer, they've gone and changed her, I assure you it's not worth while bothering your head about her. You pay her far too great a compliment. You wouldn't care to meet my cousin Poictiers?" he went on, without stopping to reflect that this could not possibly give me any pleasure. "There's an intelligent young woman whom you'd like. She's married to my cousin, the Duc de Poictiers, who is a good fellow, but a bit slow for her. I've told her about you. She said I was to bring you to see her. She's much prettier than Oriane, and younger, too. She's a really nice person, you know, a really excellent person." Then there were expressions newly—and all the more ardently—adopted by Robert, which meant that the person in question had a delicate nature. "I don't go so far as to say she's a Dreyfusard, you must remember her background; still, she did say to me: 'If he was innocent, how ghastly for him to have been shut up on Devil's Island.' You see what I mean, don't you? And then she's the sort of woman who does a tremendous lot for her old governesses; she's given orders that they're never to be made to use the servants' staircase. She's a very good sort, I assure you. Oriane doesn't really like her because she feels she's more intelligent."

Although completely absorbed in the pity which she felt for one of the Guermantes footmen—who could not go to see his girl, even when the Duchess was out, because it would immediately have been reported to her from the lodge—Françoise was heart-broken at not having been in the house at the moment of Saint-Loup's visit, but this was because now she herself paid visits too.

She never failed to go out on the days when I most needed her. It was always to see her brother, her niece and, more particularly, her own daughter, who had recently come to live in Paris. The family nature of these visits itself increased the irritation that I felt at being deprived of her services, for I foresaw that she would speak of them as being among those duties which could not be avoided, according to the laws laid down at Saint-André-des-Champs. And so I never listened to her excuses without an ill-humour which was highly unjust to her, and was brought to a head by Françoise's way of saying not: "I've been to see my brother," or "I've been to see my niece," but: "I've been to see the brother," "I just looked in to say good-day to the niece" (or "to my niece the butcheress"). As for her daughter, Françoise would have been glad to see her return to Combray. But the latter, who went in for abbreviations like a woman of fashion, though hers were of a vulgar kind, protested that the week she was shortly going to spend at Combray would seem quite long enough without so much as a sight of "the *Intran*."[13] She was even less willing to go to Françoise's sister, who lived in a mountainous region, for "moun-tains aren't really interesting," said the daughter, giving to the adjective a new and terrible meaning. She could not make up her mind to go back to Méséglise, where "the people are so stupid," where in the market the gossips at their stalls would claim cousinhood with her and say "Why, it's never poor Bazireau's daughter?" She would sooner die than go back and bury herself down there, now that she had "tasted the life of Paris," and Françoise, traditionalist as she was, smiled complacently nevertheless at the spirit of innovation embodied in this new "Parisian" when she said: "Very well, mother, if you don't get your day off, you've only to send me a wire."

The weather had turned chilly again. "Go out? What for? To catch your death?" said Françoise, who preferred to remain in the house during the week which her daughter and brother and the butcher-niece had gone to spend at Combray. Being, moreover, the last adherent in whom survived obscurely the doctrine of my aunt Léonie in matters of natural philosophy, Françoise would add, speaking of this unseasonable weather: "It's the remains of the wrath of God!" But I responded to her complaints only with a languid smile; all the more indifferent to these predictions in that whatever happened it would be fine for me; already, I could see the morning sun shining on the slope of Fiesole, and I warmed myself smilingly in its rays; their strength obliged me to half-open and half-shut my eyelids, which, like alabaster lamps, were filled with a roseate glow. It was not only the bells that came from Italy, Italy had come with them. My faithful hands would not lack flowers to honour the anniversary of the pilgrimage which I ought to have made long ago, for since, here in Paris, the weather had turned cold again as in another year at the time of our preparations for departure at the end of Lent, in the liquid, freezing air which bathed the chestnuts and planes on the boulevards and the tree in the courtyard of our house, the narcissi, the jonquils, the anemones of the Ponte Vecchio were already opening their petals as in a bowl of pure water.

My father had informed us that he now knew, through his friend A.J., where M. de Norpois went when he met him about the place.

"It's to see Mme de Villeparisis. They're great friends; I never knew anything about it. It seems she's a delightful person, a most superior woman. You ought to go and call on her," he told me. "Another thing that surprised me very much: he spoke to me of M. de Guermantes as a most distinguished man; I'd always taken him for a boor. It seems he knows an enormous amount, and has perfect taste, only he's very proud of his name and his connexions. But as a matter of fact, according to Norpois, he has a tremendous position, not only here but all over Europe. It appears the Austrian Emperor and the Tsar treat him just like one of themselves. Old Norpois told me that Mme de Villeparisis had taken quite a fancy to you, and that you meet all sorts of interesting people in her house. He praised you very highly. You'll see him if you go there, and he may have some good advice for you even if you are going to be a writer. For I can see you won't do anything else. It might turn out quite a good career; it's not what I should have chosen for you myself, but you'll be a man in no time now, we shan't always be here to look after you, and we mustn't prevent you from following your vocation."

If only I had been able to start writing! But, whatever the conditions in which I approached the task (as, too, alas, the undertakings not to touch alcohol, to go to bed early, to sleep, to keep fit), whether it was with enthusiasm, with method, with pleasure, in depriving myself of a walk, or postponing it and keeping it in reserve as a reward for industry, taking advantage of an hour of good health, utilising the inactivity forced on me by a day's illness, what always emerged in the end from all my efforts was a virgin page, undefiled by any writing, ineluctable as that forced card which in certain tricks one invariably is made to draw, however carefully one may first have shuffled the pack. I was merely the instrument of habits of not working, of not going to bed, of not sleeping, which must somehow be realised at all costs; if I offered them no resistance, if I contented myself with the pretext they seized from the first opportunity that the day afforded them of acting as they chose, I escaped without serious harm, I slept for a few hours after all towards morning, I read a little, I did not over-exert myself; but if I attempted to thwart them, if I decided to go to bed early, to drink only water, to work, they grew restive, they adopted strong measures, they made me really ill, I was obliged to double my dose of alcohol, did not lie down in bed for two days and nights on end, could not even read, and I vowed that another time I would be more reasonable, that is to say less wise, like the victim of an assault who allows himself to be robbed for fear, should he offer resistance, of being murdered.

My father, in the meantime, had met M. de Guermantes once or twice, and, now that M. de Norpois had told him that the Duke was a remarkable man, had begun to pay more attention to what he said. As it happened, they met in the courtyard and discussed Mme de Villeparisis. "He tells me she's his aunt; 'Viparisi,' he pronounces it. He tells me, too, she's an extraordinarily able woman. In fact he said she kept a School of Wit," my father added, impressed by the vagueness of this expression, which he had indeed come across now and then in volumes of memoirs, but without attaching to it any definite meaning. My mother had so much respect for him that when she saw that he did not dismiss as of no importance the fact that Mme de Villeparisis kept a School of Wit, she decided that this must be of some consequence. Although she had always known through my grandmother the Marquise's intellectual worth, it was immediately enhanced in her eyes. My grandmother, who was not very well just then, was not in favour at first of the suggested visit, and afterwards lost interest in the matter. Since we had moved into our new flat, Mme de Villeparisis had several times asked my grandmother to call upon her. And invariably my grandmother had replied that she was not going out just at present, in one of those letters which, by a new habit of hers which we did not understand, she no longer sealed herself but employed Françoise to stick down for her. As for myself, without any very clear picture in my mind of this School of Wit, I should not have been greatly surprised to find the old lady from Balbec installed behind a desk, as, for that matter, I eventually did.

My father would in addition have been glad to know whether the Ambassador's support would be worth many votes to him at the *Institut*, for which he had thoughts of standing as an independent candidate. To tell the truth, while he did not venture to doubt that he would have M. de Norpois's support, he was by no means certain of it. He had thought it merely malicious gossip when he was told at the Ministry that M. de Norpois, wishing to be himself the only representative there of the *Institut*, would put every possible obstacle in the way of my father's candidature, which would moreover embarrass him at the moment since he was supporting another candidate. And yet, when M. Leroy-Beaulieu had first advised him to stand, and had calculated his chances, my father had been struck by the fact that, among the colleagues upon whom he could count for support, the eminent economist had not mentioned M. de Norpois. He dared not ask the Ambassador point-blank, but hoped that I would return from my visit to Mme de Villeparisis with his election as good as secured. This visit was now imminent. M. de Norpois's endorsement, capable of ensuring my father the votes of at least two thirds of the Academy,[14] seemed to him all the more probable since the Ambassador's willingness to oblige was proverbial, those who liked him least admitting that no one else took such pleasure in being of service. And besides, at the Ministry, his patronage was extended to my father far more markedly than to any other official.

My father had another encounter about this time, which caused him extreme indignation as well as astonishment. One day he ran into Mme Sazerat, whose life in Paris was restricted by her comparative poverty to occasional visits to a friend. There was no one who bored my father quite so intensely as did Mme Sazerat, so much so that Mamma was obliged, once a year, to intercede with him in sweet and suppliant tones: "My dear, I really must invite Mme Sazerat to the house, just once; she won't stay long"; and even: "Listen, dear, I'm going to ask you to make a great sacrifice; do go and call on Mme Sazerat. You know I hate bothering you, but it would be so nice of you." He would laugh, raise various objections, and go to pay the call. And so, for all that Mme Sazerat did not appeal to him, on catching sight of her in the street my father went towards her, doffing his hat; but to his profound astonishment Mme Sazerat confined her greeting to the frigid bow enforced by politeness towards a person who is guilty of some disgraceful action or has been condemned to live henceforth in another hemisphere. My father had come home speechless with rage. Next day my mother met Mme Sazerat in someone's house. She did not offer my mother her hand, but merely smiled at her with a vague and melancholy air as one smiles at a person with whom one used to play as a child, but with whom one has since severed all connexions because she has led an abandoned life, has married a jailbird or (what is worse still) a divorced man. Now, from time immemorial my parents had accorded to Mme Sazerat, and inspired in her, the most profound respect. But (and of this my mother was ignorant) Mme Sazerat, alone of her kind at Combray, was a Dreyfusard. My father, a friend of M. Méline,[15] was convinced that Dreyfus was guilty. He had sharply sent about their business those colleagues who had asked him to sign a petition for a retrial. He refused to speak to me for a week after learning that I had chosen to take a different line. His opinions were well known. He came near to being looked upon as a Nationalist. As for my grandmother, who alone of the family seemed likely to be stirred by a generous doubt, whenever anyone spoke to her of the possible innocence of Dreyfus, she gave a shake of her head the meaning of which we did not at the time understand, but which was like the gesture of a person who has been interrupted while thinking of more serious things. My mother, torn between her love for my father and her hope that I might turn out to have brains, preserved an impartiality which she expressed by silence. Finally my grandfather, who adored the Army (albeit his duties with the National Guard had been the bugbear of his riper years), could never see a regiment march past the garden railings at Combray without baring his head as the colonel and the colours passed. All this was quite enough to make Mme Sazerat, who was thoroughly aware of the disinterestedness and integrity of my father and grandfather, regard them as pillars of Injustice. We forgive the crimes of individuals, but not their participation in a collective crime. As soon as she knew my father to be an anti-Dreyfusard she put continents and centuries between herself and him. Which explains why, across such an interval of time and space, her greeting had been imperceptible to my father, and why it had not occurred to her to shake hands or to say a few words

which would never have carried across the worlds that lay
between.

Saint-Loup, who was due to come to Paris, had promised to
take me to Mme de Villeparisis's, where I hoped, though I had not
said so to him, that we might meet Mme de Guermantes. He
invited me to lunch in a restaurant with his mistress, whom we
were afterwards to accompany to a rehearsal. We were to go out in
the morning and call for her at her home on the outskirts of Paris.

I had asked Saint-Loup if the restaurant to which we went for
lunch (in the lives of young noblemen with money to spend the
restaurant plays as important a part as do bales of merchandise in
Arabian tales) could for preference be the one to which Aimé had
told me that he would be going as head waiter until the Balbec
season opened. It was a great attraction to me who dreamed of so
many journeys and made so few to see again someone who formed
part not merely of my memories of Balbec but of Balbec itself,
who went there year after year and, when ill-health or my studies
compelled me to stay in Paris, would be watching just the same,
during the long July afternoons while he waited for the guests to
come in to dinner, the sun creep down the sky and set in the sea,
through the glass panels of the great dining-room behind which, at
the hour when the light died, the motionless wings of vessels,
smoky blue in the distance, looked like exotic and nocturnal
butterflies in a show-case. Himself magnetised by his contact
with the powerful lodestone of Balbec, this head waiter became
in turn a magnet for me. I hoped by talking to him to enter in
advance into communication with Balbec, to have realised here in
Paris something of the delights of travel.

I set out first thing, leaving Françoise at home to moan over the
affianced footman who had once again been prevented, the evening before, from going to see his betrothed. Françoise had found
him in tears; he had been itching to go and strike the porter, but
had restrained himself, for he valued his place.

Before reaching Saint-Loup's, where he was to be waiting for
me at the door, I ran into Legrandin, of whom we had lost sight
since our Combray days, and who, though now quite grey, had
preserved his air of youthful candour. Seeing me, he stopped.

"Ah! so it's you," he exclaimed, "a man of fashion, and in a
frock-coat too! That is a livery in which my independent spirit
would be ill at ease. It is true that you are a man of the world,
I suppose, and go out paying calls! In order to go and meditate, as

I do, beside some half-ruined tomb, my bow-tie and jacket are not out of place. You know how I admire the charming quality of your soul; that is why I tell you how deeply I regret that you should go forth and betray it among the Gentiles. By being capable of remaining for a moment in the nauseating atmosphere of the salons—for me, unbreathable—you pronounce on your own future the condemnation, the damnation of the Prophet. I can see it all: you frequent the frivolous-minded, the gracious livers—that is the vice of our contemporary bourgeoisie. Ah, those aristocrats! The Terror was greatly to blame for not cutting the heads off every one of them. They are all disreputable scum, when they are not simply dreary idiots. Still, my poor boy, if that sort of thing amuses you! While you are on your way to some *tea-party* your old friend will be more fortunate than you, for alone in an outlying suburb he will be watching the pink moon rise in a violet sky. The truth is that I scarcely belong to this earth upon which I feel myself such an exile; it takes all the force of the law of gravity to hold me here, to keep me from escaping into another sphere. I belong to a different planet. Good-bye; do not take amiss the old-time frankness of the peasant of the Vivonne, who has also remained a peasant of the Danube. To prove my sincere regard for you, I shall send you my latest novel. But you will not care for it; it is not deliquescent enough, not *fin de siècle* enough for you; it is too frank, too honest. What you want is Bergotte, you have confessed it, gamy stuff for the jaded palates of refined voluptuaries. I suppose I am looked upon, in your set, as an old stick-in-the-mud; I make the mistake of putting my heart into what I write: that is no longer done; besides, the life of the people is not distinguished enough to interest your little snobbicules. Go, get you gone, try to recall at times the words of Christ: 'This do, and thou shalt live.' Farewell, friend."

It was not with any particular ill-humour against Legrandin that I parted from him. Certain memories are like friends in common, they can bring about reconciliations; set down amid fields of buttercups strewn with the ruins of feudal battlements, the little wooden bridge still joined us, Legrandin and me, as it joined the two banks of the Vivonne.

After coming out of a Paris in which, although spring had begun, the trees on the boulevards had hardly put on their first leaves, it was a marvel to Saint-Loup and myself, when the circle train had set us down at the suburban village in which his mistress was living, to see each little garden decked with the huge festal altars of the fruit-trees in blossom. It was like one of those peculiar, poetic, ephemeral, local festivals which people travel long distances to attend on certain fixed occasions, but this one was given by Nature. The blossom of the cherry-tree is stuck so close to its branches, like a white sheath, that from a distance, among the other trees that showed as yet scarcely a flower or leaf, one might on this day of sunshine that was still so cold have taken it for snow that had remained clinging there, having melted everywhere else. But the tall pear-trees enveloped each house, each modest courtyard, in a more spacious, more uniform, more dazzling whiteness, as if all the dwellings, all the enclosed spaces in the village, were on their way to make their first communion on the same solemn day.

These villages in the environs of Paris still have at their gates parks of the seventeenth and eighteenth centuries which were the "follies" of the stewards and mistresses of the great. A market gardener had utilised one of these, which was situated on low ground beside the road, for his fruit-trees (or had simply, perhaps, preserved the plan of an immense orchard of former days). Laid out in quincunxes, these pear-trees, more spaced-out and less advanced than those that I had seen, formed great quadrilaterals—separated by low walls—of white blossom, on each side of which the light fell differently, so that all these airy roofless chambers seemed to belong to a Palace of the Sun, such as one might find in Crete; and they reminded one also of the different ponds of a reservoir, or of those parts of the sea which man has subdivided for some fishery, or to plant oyster-beds, when one saw, according to their orientation, the light play upon the espaliers as upon springtime waters, and coax into unfolding here and there, gleaming amid the open-work, azure-panelled trellis of the branches, the foaming whiteness of a creamy, sunlit flower.

It had been a country village, and still had its old *mairie*, sun-burned and mellow, in front of which, in the place of maypoles and streamers, three tall pear-trees were elegantly beflagged with white satin as though for some local civic festival.

Never had Robert spoken to me more tenderly of his mistress than he did during this journey. She alone had taken root in his heart; to his future career in the Army, his position in society, his family, he was not, of course, indifferent, but they counted for nothing beside the smallest thing that concerned his mistress. That alone had any importance in his eyes, infinitely more importance than the Guermantes and all the kings of the earth put together. I do not know whether he formulated to himself the notion that she was of a superior essence to the rest of the world, but he was exclusively preoccupied and concerned with what affected her. Through her and for her he was capable of suffering, of being happy, perhaps of killing. There was really nothing that interested, that could excite him except what his mistress wanted, what she was going to do, what was going on, discernible at most in fleeting changes of expression, in the narrow expanse of her face and behind her privileged brow. So nice-minded in all else, he looked forward to the prospect of a brilliant marriage, solely in order to be able to continue to maintain and keep her. If one had asked oneself what was the value that he set on her, I doubt whether one could ever have imagined a figure high enough. If he did not marry her, it was because a practical instinct warned him that as soon as she had nothing more to expect from him she would leave him, or would at least live as she pleased, and that he must retain his hold on her by keeping her in expectation. For he admitted the possibility that she did not love him. No doubt the general malady called love must have forced him—as it forces all men—to believe at times that she did. But in his heart of hearts he felt that her love for him was not inconsistent with her remaining with him only on account of his money, and that as soon as she had nothing more to expect from him she would make haste (the dupe of her literary friends and their theories, and yet still loving him, he thought) to leave him.

"Today, if she's nice," he confided to me, "I'm going to give her a present that will make her very happy. It's a necklace she saw at Boucheron's. It's rather too much for me just at present—thirty thousand francs. But, poor puss, she doesn't have much pleasure in her life. She will be jolly pleased with it, I know. She mentioned it to me and told me she knew somebody who would perhaps give it to her. I don't believe it's true, but just in case, I arranged with Boucheron, who is our family jeweller, to reserve it for me. I'm so happy to think that you're going to meet her. She's nothing so very wonderful to look at, you know" (I could see that he thought just the opposite and had said this only to make my admiration the greater). "What she has above all is marvellous judgment: she'll perhaps be afraid to talk much in front of you, but I rejoice in advance over what she'll say to me about you afterwards. You know she says things one can go on thinking about for hours; there's really something about her that's quite Pythian."

On our way to her house we passed a row of little gardens, and I was obliged to stop, for they were all dazzlingly aflower with pear and cherry blossom; as empty, no doubt, and lifeless only yesterday as a house that is still to let, they were suddenly peopled and adorned by these newcomers, arrived overnight, whose beautiful white garments could be seen through the railings along the garden paths.

"I'll tell you what—I can see you'd rather stop and look at all that and be poetical," said Robert, "so don't budge from here, will you—my friend's house is quite close, and I'll go and fetch her."

While I waited I strolled up and down the road, past these modest gardens. If I raised my head I could see now and then girls sitting at the windows, but outside, in the open air, at the height of a half-landing, dangling here and there among the foliage, light and pliant in their fresh mauve frocks, clusters of young lilacs swayed in the breeze without heeding the passer-by who raised his eyes towards their green arbour. I recognised in them the purple-clad platoons posted at the entrance to M. Swann's park in the warm spring afternoons, like an enchanting rustic tapestry. I took a path which led me into a meadow. A cold wind swept through it, as at Combray, but in the middle of this rich, moist, rural land, which might have been on the banks of the Vivonne, there had nevertheless arisen, punctual at the trysting place like all its band of brothers, a great white pear-tree which waved smilingly in the sun's face, like a curtain of light materialised and made palpable, its flowers shaken by the breeze but polished and glazed with silver by the sun's rays.

Suddenly Saint-Loup appeared, accompanied by his mistress, and then, in this woman who was for him the epitome of love, of all the sweet things of life, whose personality, mysteriously enshrined as in a tabernacle, was the object that occupied incessantly his toiling imagination, whom he felt that he would never really know, as to whom he asked himself what could be her secret self, behind the veil of eyes and flesh—in this woman I recognised instantaneously "Rachel when from the Lord," she who, but a few years since (women change their situation so rapidly in that world, when they do change) used to say to the procuress: "Tomorrow evening, then, if you want me for someone, you'll send round for me, won't you?"

And when they had "come round" for her, and she found herself alone in the room with the "someone," she knew so well what was required of her that after locking the door, as a womanly precaution or a ritual gesture, she would quickly remove all her clothes, as one does before the doctor who is going to examine one, and did not pause in the process unless the "someone," not caring for nudity, told her that she might keep on her shift, as specialists do sometimes, who, having an extremely fine ear and being afraid of their patient's catching a chill, are satisfied with listening to his breathing and the beating of his heart through his shirt. I sensed that on this woman—whose whole life, whose every thought, whose entire past and all the men by whom at one time or another she had been had, were to me so utterly unimportant that if she had told me about them I should have listened only out of politeness and scarcely have heard—the anxiety, the torment, the love of Saint-Loup had been concentrated in such a way as to make, out of what was for me a mechanical toy, the cause of endless suffering, the very object and reward of existence. Seeing these two elements separately (because I had known "Rachel when from the Lord" in a house of ill-fame), I realised that many women for the sake of whom men live, suffer, take their own lives, may be in themselves or for other people what Rachel was for me. The idea that anyone could be tormented by curiosity with regard to her life amazed me. I could have told Robert of any number of her unchastities, which seemed to me the most uninteresting things in the world. And how they would have pained him! And what had he not given to learn them, without avail!

I realised then how much a human imagination can put behind a little scrap of a face, such as this woman's was, if it is the imagination that has come to know it first; and conversely into what wretched elements, crudely material and utterly valueless, something that had been the inspiration of countless dreams might be decomposed if, on the contrary, it had been perceived in the opposite manner, by the most casual and trivial acquaintance. I saw that what had appeared to me to be not worth twenty francs when it had been offered to me for twenty francs in the brothel, where it was then for me simply a woman desirous of earning twenty francs, might be worth more than a million, more than family affection, more than all the most coveted positions in life, if one had begun by imagining her as a mysterious being, interesting to know, difficult to seize and to hold. No doubt it was the same thin and narrow face that we saw, Robert and I. But we had arrived at it by two opposite ways which would never converge, and we would never both see it from the same side. That face, with its looks, its smiles, the movements of its mouth, I had known from the outside as being that of a woman of the sort who for twenty francs would do anything that I asked. And so her looks, her smiles, the movements of her mouth had seemed to me expressive merely of generalised actions with no individual quality, and beneath them I should not have had the curiosity to look for a person. But what to me had in a sense been offered at the start, that consenting face, had been for Robert an ultimate goal towards which he had made his way through endless hopes and doubts, suspicions and dreams. Yes, he had given more than a million francs in order to have, in order that others should not have, what had been offered to me, as to all and sundry, for twenty. That he too should not have had her at that price may have been due to the chance of a moment, the instant in which she who seemed ready to give herself suddenly jibs, having perhaps an assignation else-where, some reason which makes her more difficult of access that day. If the man in question is a sentimentalist, then, even if she has not noticed it, but infinitely more if she has, the direst game begins. Unable to swallow his disappointment, to make himself forget about the woman, he pursues her afresh, she rebuffs him, until a mere smile for which he no longer dared to hope is bought at a thousand times what should have been the price of the last favours. It sometimes even happens in such a case, when a man has been led by a mixture of naïvety of judgment and cowardice in the face of suffering to commit the crowning folly of making an inaccessible idol of a whore, that he never obtains these ultimate favours, or even the first kiss, and no longer even ventures to ask for them in order not to belie his assurances of Platonic love. And it is then a bitter anguish to leave the world without ever having experienced the embraces of the woman one has most passionately loved. As for Rachel's favours, however, Saint-Loup had fortu-nately succeeded in winning them all. True, if he had now learned that they had been offered to all the world for a louis, he would have suffered terribly, but would still have given a million francs to keep them, for nothing that he might have learned could have diverted him (what is beyond man's power can only happen in spite of him, through the action of some great natural law) from the path he had taken and from which that face could appear to him only through the web of the dreams that he had already spun. The immobility of that thin face, like that of a sheet of paper subjected to the colossal pressure of two atmospheres, seemed to me to be held in equilibrium by two infinites which converged on her without meeting, for she held them apart. Indeed, looking at her, Robert and I, the two of us did not see her from the same side of the mystery.

It was not "Rachel when from the Lord," who seemed to me of little significance, it was the power of the human imagination, the illusion on which were based the pains of love, that I found so striking. Robert noticed that I seemed moved. I turned my eyes to the pear- and cherry-trees of the garden opposite, so that he might think that it was their beauty that had touched me. And it did touch me in somewhat the same way; it also brought close to me things of the kind which we not only see with our eyes but feel also in our hearts. In likening those trees that I had seen in the garden to strange deities, had I not been mistaken like Magdalene when, in another garden, on a day whose anniversary was soon to come, she saw a human form, "supposing him to be the gardener"? Treasurers of our memories of the golden age, keepers of the promise that reality is not what we suppose, that the splendour of poetry, the wonderful radiance of innocence may shine in it and may be the recompense which we strive to earn, were they not, these great white creatures miraculously bowed over that shade so propitious for rest, for angling or for reading, were they not rather angels? I exchanged a few words with Saint-Loup's mistress. We cut across the village. Its houses were sordid. But by each of the most wretched, of those that looked as though they had been scorched and branded by a rain of brimstone, a mysterious traveller, halting for a day in the accursed city, a resplendent angel, stood erect, stretching over it the dazzling protection of his widespread wings of innocence in flower: it was a pear-tree. Saint-Loup drew me a little way ahead to explain:

"I should have liked you and me to have been able to stay together, in fact I'd much rather have had lunch just with you, and stayed with you until it was time to go to my aunt's. But this poor girl of mine here, it gives her so much pleasure, and she's so nice to me, don't you know, I hadn't the heart to refuse her. In any case you'll like her, she's literary, so responsive, and besides it's such a pleasure to be with her in a restaurant, she's so charming, so simple, always delighted with everything."

I fancy nevertheless that, on that precise morning, and probably for the first and only time, Robert detached himself for a moment from the woman whom out of successive layers of tenderness he had gradually created, and suddenly saw at some distance from himself another Rachel, the double of his but entirely different, who was nothing more nor less than a little whore. We had left the blossoming orchard and were making for the train which was to take us back to Paris when, at the station, Rachel, who was walking by herself, was recognised and hailed by a pair of common little "tarts" like herself, who first of all, thinking that she was alone, called out: "Hello, Rachel, why don't you come with us? Lucienne and Germaine are in the train, and there's room for one more. Come on, we'll all go to the rink together." They were just going to introduce to her two counter-jumpers, their lovers, who were accompanying them, when, noticing that she seemed a little ill at ease, they looked up and beyond her, caught sight of us, and with apologies bade her a good-bye to which she responded in a somewhat embarrassed but none the less friendly tone. They were two poor little tarts with collars of sham otter-skin, looking more or less as Rachel must have looked when Saint-Loup first met her. He did not know them, or their names even, and seeing that they appeared to be on intimate terms with his mistress, he could not help wondering whether she too might not once have had, had not still, perhaps, her place in an unsuspected life, utterly different from the life she led with him, a life in which one had women for a louis apiece. He not only glimpsed this life, but saw also in the thick of it a Rachel quite different from the one he knew, a Rachel like those two little tarts, a twenty-franc Rachel. In short, Rachel had for the moment duplicated herself in his eyes; he had seen, at some distance from his own Rachel, the little tart Rachel, the real Rachel, if it can be said that Rachel the tart was more real than the other. It may then have occurred to Robert that from the hell in which he was living, with the prospect and the necessity of a rich marriage, of the sale of his name, to enable him to go on giving Rachel a hundred thousand francs a year, he might easily perhaps have escaped, and have enjoyed the favours of his mistress, as the two counter-jumpers enjoyed those of their girls, for next to nothing. But how was it to be done? She had done nothing blameworthy. Less generously rewarded, she would be less nice to him, would stop saying and writing the things that so deeply touched him, things which he would quote, with a touch of boastfulness, to his comrades, taking care to point out how nice it was of her to say them, but omitting to mention that he was maintaining her in the most lavish fashion, or even that he ever gave her anything at all, that these inscriptions on photographs, or tender greetings at the end of telegrams, were but the transmutation of gold in its most exiguous but most precious form. If he took care not to admit that these rare kindnesses on Rachel's part were handsomely paid for, it would be wrong to say—and yet this oversimplification is applied, absurdly, to every lover who has to pay cash, and to a great many husbands—that this was from self-esteem or vanity. Saint-Loup was intelligent enough to realise that all the pleasures of vanity were freely available to him in society, thanks to his historic name and handsome face, and that his liaison with Rachel had on the contrary tended to cut him off from society, had led to his being less sought after. No; this pride which seeks to appear to be getting for nothing the apparent marks of predilection of the woman one loves is simply a consequence of love, the need to figure in one's own eyes and in other people's as being loved by the person whom one loves so much. Rachel rejoined us, leaving the two tarts to get into their compartment; but, no less than their sham otter-skins and the self-conscious appearance of their young men, the names Lucienne and Germaine kept the new Rachel alive for a moment longer. For a moment Robert imagined a Place Pigalle existence with unknown associates, sordid pick-ups, afternoons spent in simple pleasures, in that Paris in which the sunny brightness of the streets from the Boulevard de Clichy onwards did not seem the same as the solar radiance in which he himself strolled with his mistress, for love, and suffering that is inseparable from it, have, like intoxication, the power to differentiate things for us. It was almost another Paris in the heart of Paris itself that he suspected; his liaison appeared to him like the exploration of a strange life, for if when with him Rachel was somewhat similar to himself, it was nevertheless a part of her real life that she lived with him, indeed the most precious part in view of his reckless expenditure on her, the part that made her so greatly envied by her friends and would enable her one day to retire to the country or to establish herself in the leading theatres, when she had made her pile. Robert longed to ask her who Lucienne and Germaine were, what they would have said to her if she had joined them in their compartment, how they would all have spent a day which would perhaps have ended, as a supreme diversion, after the pleasures of the skating-rink, at the Olympia Tavern, if Robert and I had not been there. For a moment the purlieus of the Olympia, which until then had seemed to him deadly dull, stirred his curiosity and anguish, and the sunshine of this spring day beating down on the Rue Caumartin where, possibly, if she had not known Robert, Rachel might have gone that afternoon and have earned a louis, filled him with a vague longing. But what would be the use of plying Rachel with questions when he already knew that her answer would be merely silence, or a lie, or something extremely painful for him to hear, which would yet explain nothing. The porters were shutting the doors; we hurriedly climbed into a first-class carriage; Rachel's magnificent pearls reminded Robert that she was a woman of great price; he caressed her, restored her to her place in his heart where he could contemplate her, interiorised, as he had always done hitherto—save during this brief instant in which he had seen her in the Place Pigalle of an Impressionist painter—and the train moved off.

It was true that she was "literary." She never stopped talking to me about books, Art Nouveau and Tolstoyism, except to rebuke Saint-Loup for drinking too much wine:

"Ah! if you could live with me for a year, we'd see a fine change. I should keep you on water and you'd be much better for it."

"Right you are. Let's go away."

"But you know quite well I have a great deal of work to do" (for she took her dramatic art very seriously). "Besides, what would your family say?"

And she began to abuse his family to me in terms which seemed to me highly justified, and with which Saint-Loup, while disobeying Rachel in the matter of champagne, entirely concurred. I, who was so afraid of the effect of wine on him, and felt the good influence of his mistress, was quite prepared to advise him to let his family go hang. Tears sprang to the young woman's eyes when I was rash enough to mention Dreyfus.

"The poor martyr!" she almost sobbed; "it will be the death of him in that dreadful place."

"Don't upset yourself, Zézette, he'll come back, he'll be acquitted all right, they'll admit they made a mistake."

"But long before then he'll be dead! Ah well, at least his children will bear a stainless name. But just think of the agony he must be going through: that's what I can't stand! And would you believe that Robert's mother, a pious woman, says that he ought to be left on Devil's Island even if he's innocent. Isn't that appalling?"

"Yes, it's absolutely true, she does say that," Robert assured me. "She's my mother, I can't contradict her, but it's quite clear she hasn't got a sensitive nature like Zézette."

In reality these luncheons which were said to be "such a pleasure" always led to trouble. For as soon as Saint-Loup found himself in a public place with his mistress, he would imagine that she was looking at every other man in the room, and his brow would darken; she would notice his ill-humour, which she perhaps took pleasure in fanning, but which more probably, out of stupid pride, feeling wounded by his tone, she did not wish to appear to be seeking to disarm; she would pretend not to be able to take her eyes off some man or other, and indeed this was not always purely for fun. In fact the man who happened to be sitting next to them in a theatre or a café, or, to go no further, the driver of the cab they had engaged, need only have something attractive about him, and Robert, his perception quickened by jealousy, would have noticed it before his mistress; he would see in him immediately one of those foul creatures whom he had denounced to me at Balbec, who corrupted and dishonoured women for their own amusement, and would beg his mistress to avert her eyes from the man, thereby drawing her attention to him. And sometimes she found that Robert had shown such good taste in his suspicions that after a while she even left off teasing him in order that he might calm down and consent to go off by himself on some errand which would give her time to enter into conversation with the stranger, often to make an assignation, sometimes even to bring matters to a head there and then.

I could see as soon as we entered the restaurant that Robert was looking troubled. For he had at once observed—what had escaped our notice at Balbec—that among his coarser colleagues Aimé exuded not only a modest distinction but, quite unconsciously of course, that air of romance which emanates for a certain number of years from fine hair and a Grecian nose, features thanks to which he stood out among the crowd of other waiters. These, almost all of them well on in years, presented a series of types, extraordinarily

ugly and pronounced, of hypocritical priests, sanctimonious con-
fessors, more numerously of actors of the old school whose sugar-
loaf foreheads are scarcely to be seen nowadays outside the
collections of portraits that hang in the humbly historic green-
rooms of antiquated little theatres, where they are represented in
the roles of servants or pontiffs, though this restaurant seemed,
thanks to selective recruiting and perhaps to some system of
hereditary nomination, to have preserved their solemn type in a
sort of College of Augurs. As ill luck would have it, Aimé having
recognised us, it was he who came to take our order, while the
procession of operatic high-priests swept past us to other tables.
Aimé inquired after my grandmother's health; I asked for news of
his wife and children. He gave it to me with feeling, for he was a
family man. He had an intelligent and vigorous but respectful air.
Robert's mistress began to gaze at him with a strange attentiveness.
But Aimé's sunken eyes, to which a slight short-sightedness gave a
sort of veiled depth, betrayed no sign of awareness in his still face.
In the provincial hotel in which he had served for many years
before coming to Balbec, the charming sketch, now a trifle dis-
coloured and faded, which was his face, and which, for all those
years, like some engraved portrait of Prince Eugène, had been
visible always in the same place, at the far end of a dining-room
that was almost always empty, had probably not attracted many
curious looks. He had thus for long remained, doubtless for want
of connoisseurs, in ignorance of the artistic value of his face, and
moreover but little inclined to draw attention to it, for he was
temperamentally cold. At most some passing Parisian lady, stopping for some reason in the town, had raised her eyes to his, had
asked him perhaps to serve her in her room before she took the
train again, and, in the pellucid, monotonous, profound void of
the existence of this good husband and provincial hotel servant,
had buried the secret of a short-lived whim which no one would
ever bring to light. And yet Aimé must have been conscious of the
insistence with which the eyes of the young actress were fastened
upon him now. At all events it did not escape Robert, beneath
whose skin I saw a flush begin to gather, not vivid like that which
burned his cheeks when he felt sudden emotion, but faint and
diffused.

"Anything specially interesting about that waiter, Zézette?" he
inquired, after sharply dismissing Aimé. "One would think you
were making a study of him."

"There we go again; I knew it would happen!"

"You knew what would happen, my dear girl? If I was mistaken, I'm quite prepared to take it all back. But I have after all the right to warn you against that flunkey whom I know all about from Balbec (otherwise I shouldn't give a damn), and who is the biggest scoundrel that ever walked the face of the earth."

She seemed anxious to pacify Robert and began to engage me in a literary conversation in which he joined. I did not find her boring to talk to, for she had a thorough knowledge of the works I admired, and her opinion of them agreed more or less with mine; but since I had heard Mme de Villeparisis declare that she had no talent, I attached little importance to this evidence of culture. She discoursed wittily on all manner of topics, and would have been genuinely entertaining had she not affected to an irritating degree the jargon of the coteries and studios. She extended it, moreover, to everything under the sun; for instance, having acquired the habit of saying of a picture, if it were Impressionist, or an opera, if Wagnerian, "Ah! that's *good*," one day when a young man had kissed her on the ear, and, touched by her pretence of being thrilled, had affected modesty, she said: "But really, as a sensation I call it distinctly *good*." But what most surprised me was that the expressions peculiar to Robert (which in any case had probably come to him from literary men whom she knew) were used by her to him and by him to her as though they had been a necessary form of speech, and without any conception of the pointlessness of an originality that is universal.

She was so clumsy with her hands when eating that one felt she must appear extremely awkward on the stage. She recovered her dexterity only when making love, with that touching prescience of women who love the male so intensely that they immediately guess what will give most pleasure to that body which is yet so different from their own.

I ceased to take part in the conversation when it turned upon the theatre, for on that topic Rachel was too malicious for my liking. She did, it was true, take up in a tone of commiseration—against Saint-Loup, which proved that he was accustomed to hearing Rachel attack her—the defence of Berma, saying: "Oh, no, she's a remarkable woman really. Of course, the things she does no longer appeal to us, they don't correspond quite to what we're after, but one must think of her at the time when she made her first appearance; we owe her a great deal. She has done good work, you know. And, besides she's such a splendid woman, she has such a good heart. Naturally she doesn't care about the things that interest us, but in her time she had, as well as a rather moving face, quite a shrewd intelligence." (Our fingers, by the way, do not play the same accompaniment to all our aesthetic judgments. If it is a picture that is under discussion, to show that it is a fine piece of work, painted with a full brush, it is enough to stick out one's thumb. But the "shrewd intelligence" is more exacting. It requires two fingers, or rather two fingernails, as though one were trying to flick away a particle of dust.) But, with this single exception, Saint-Loup's mistress spoke of the best-known actresses in a tone of ironical superiority which annoyed me because I believed—quite mistakenly, as it happened—that it was she who was inferior to them. She was clearly aware that I must regard her as an indifferent actress and conversely have a great regard for those she despised. But she showed no resentment, because there is in all great talent while it is still, as hers was then, unrecognised, however sure it may be of itself, a vein of humility, and because we make the consideration that we expect from others proportionate not to our latent powers but to the position to which we have attained. (An hour or so later, at the theatre, I was to see Saint-Loup's mistress show a great deal of deference towards those very artists whom she now judged so harshly.) And so, however little doubt my silence may have left her in, she insisted none the less on our dining together that evening, assuring me that never had anyone's conversation delighted her so much as mine. If we were not yet in the theatre, to which we were to go after lunch, we had the sense of being in a green-room hung with portraits of old members of the company, so markedly were the waiters' faces of a kind that seems to have perished with a whole generation of outstanding actors. They had a look, too, of Academicians: one of them, standing in front of a sideboard, was examining a dish of pears with the expression of detached curiosity that M. de Jussieu[16] might have worn. Others, on either side of him, were casting about the room the sort of gaze, instinct with curiosity and coldness, with which Members of the Institute who have arrived early scrutinise the audience, while they exchange a few murmured words which one fails to catch. They were faces well known to all the regular customers. One of them, however, was being pointed out, a newcomer with a wrinkled nose and sanctimonious lips who had an ecclesiastical air, and everyone gazed with interest at this newly elected candidate. But presently, perhaps to drive Robert away so that she might be alone with Aimé, Rachel began to make eyes at a young student who was lunching with a friend at a neighbouring table.

"Zézette, would you mind not looking at that young man like that," said Saint-Loup, on whose face the hesitant flush of a moment ago had gathered now into a scarlet cloud which dilated and darkened his swollen features. "If you must make an exhibition of us I shall go and lunch elsewhere and join you at the theatre afterwards."

At this point a messenger came up to tell Aimé that a gentleman wished him to go and speak to him at the door of his carriage. Saint-Loup, ever uneasy, and afraid now that it might be some message of an amorous nature that was to be conveyed to his mistress, looked out of the window and saw there, sitting in the back of his brougham, his hands tightly buttoned in white gloves with black seams and a flower in his buttonhole, M. de Charlus.

"There, you see!" he said to me in a low voice, "my family hunt me down even here. Will you, please—I can't very well do it myself—but since you know the head waiter well, ask him not to go to the carriage. He's certain to give us away. Ask him to send some other waiter who doesn't know me. I know my uncle; if they tell him I'm not known here, he'll never come inside to look for me, he loathes this sort of place. Really, it's pretty disgusting that an old womaniser like him, who's still at it, too, should be perpetually lecturing me and coming to spy on me!"

Aimé, on receiving my instructions, sent one of his underlings to explain that he was busy and could not come out at the moment, and (should the gentleman ask for the Marquis de Saint-Loup) that they did not know any such person. Presently the carriage departed. But Saint-Loup's mistress, who had failed to catch our whispered conversation and thought that it was about the young man whom Robert had been reproaching her for making eyes at, broke out in a torrent of abuse.

"Ah, so that's it! So it's the young man over there, now, is it? Thank you for telling me; it's a real pleasure to have this sort of thing with one's meals! Don't pay any attention to him," she added, turning to me, "he's a bit piqued today, and anyway he just says these things because he thinks it's smart and rather aristo-cratic to appear to be jealous."

And she began to drum her feet and her fingers in nervous irritation.

"But, Zézette, it's for me that it's unpleasant. You're making us ridiculous in the eyes of that fellow, who will begin to imagine you're making advances to him, and who looks an impossible bounder, too."

"Oh, no, I think he's charming. For one thing, he's got the most adorable eyes, and a way of looking at women—you can feel he must love them."

"If you've lost your senses, you can at least keep quiet until I've left the room," cried Robert. "Waiter, my things."

I did not know whether I was expected to follow him.

"No, I need to be alone," he told me in the same tone in which he had just been addressing his mistress, and as if he were quite as furious with me. His anger was like a single musical phrase to which in an opera several lines of dialogue are sung which are entirely different from one another in meaning and character in the libretto, but which the music gathers into a common senti-ment. When Robert had gone, his mistress called Aimé and asked him various questions. She then wanted to know what I thought of him.

"He has an amusing expression, hasn't he? You see, what would amuse me would be to know what he really thinks about things, to have him wait on me often, to take him travelling. But that would be all. If we were expected to love all the people we find attractive, life would be pretty ghastly, wouldn't it? It's silly of Robert to imagine things. It all begins and ends in my head: Robert has nothing to worry about." She was still gazing at Aimé. "Do look what dark eyes he has. I should love to know what goes on behind them."

Presently she received a message that Robert was waiting for her in a private room, to which he had gone by another door to finish his lunch without having to pass through the restaurant again. I thus found myself alone, until I too was summoned by Robert. I found his mistress stretched out on a sofa laughing under the kisses and caresses that he was showering on her. They were drinking champagne. "Hallo, you!" she said to him from time to time, having recently picked up this expression which seemed to her the last word in affection and wit. I had had little lunch, I was extremely uncomfortable, and, though Legrandin's words had no bearing on the matter, I was sorry to think that I was beginning this first afternoon of spring in a back room in a restaurant and would finish it in the wings of a theatre. Looking first at the time to see that she was not making herself late, Rachel offered me a glass of champagne, handed me one of her Turkish cigarettes and unpinned a rose for me from her bodice. Whereupon I said to myself: "I needn't regret my day too much, after all. These hours spent in this young woman's company are not wasted, since I have had from her—charming gifts which cannot be bought too dear— a rose, a scented cigarette and a glass of champagne." I told myself this because I felt that it would endow with an aesthetic character, and thereby justify and rescue, these hours of boredom. I ought perhaps to have reflected that the very need which I felt of a reason that would console me for my boredom was sufficient to prove that I was experiencing no aesthetic sensation. As for Robert and his mistress, they appeared to have no recollection of the quarrel which had been raging between them a few minutes earlier, or of my having been a witness to it. They made no allusion to it, offered no excuse for it, any more than for the contrast with it which their present conduct provided. By dint of drinking cham- pagne with them, I began to feel a little of the intoxication that had come over me at Rivebelle, though probably not quite the same. Not only every kind of intoxication, from that which we get from the sun or from travelling to that which is induced by exhaustion or wine, but every degree of intoxication—and each should have a different "reading," like fathoms on a chart—lays bare in us, at the precise depth which it has reached, a different kind of man. The room which Saint-Loup had taken was small, but the single mirror which decorated it was of such a kind that it seemed to reflect a score of others in an endless vista; and the electric bulb placed at the top of the frame must at night, when it was lit, followed by the procession of twenty or more reflexions similar to its own, give to the drinker, even when alone, the idea that the surrounding space was multiplying itself simultaneously with his sensations, height- ened by intoxication, and that, shut up by himself in this little cell, he was reigning nevertheless over something far more extensive in its indefinite luminous curve than a passage in the "Jardin de Paris." Being then myself at this moment the said drinker, sud- denly, looking for him in the glass, I caught sight of him, a hideous stranger, staring at me. The joy of intoxication was stronger than my disgust; from gaiety or bravado, I gave him a smile which he returned. And I felt myself so much under the ephemeral and potent sway of the minute in which our sensations are so strong, that I am not sure whether my sole regret was not at the thought that the hideous self whom I had just caught sight of in the glass was perhaps on his last legs, and that I should never meet that stranger again for the rest of my life.

Robert was annoyed only because I did not seem to want to shine more in the eyes of his mistress.

"What about that fellow you met this morning who combines snobbery with astronomy? Do tell her about him, I've forgotten the story," and he watched her out of the corner of his eye.

"But, my dear boy, there's nothing more to say than what you've just said."

"What a bore you are. Then tell her about Françoise in the Champs-Elysées. She'll enjoy that."

"Oh, do! Bobby has told me so much about Françoise." And taking Saint-Loup by the chin, she said once more, for want of anything more original, drawing the said chin nearer to the light: "Hallo, you!"

Since actors had ceased to be for me exclusively the depositaries, in their diction and playing, of an artistic truth, they had begun to interest me in themselves; I was amused, imagining that I was contemplating the characters in some old comic novel, to see the heroine of the play, struck by the new face of the young man who had just come into the stalls, listen abstractedly to the declaration of love which the juvenile lead was addressing to her, while he, through the running fire of his impassioned speech, still kept a gleaming eye fixed on an old lady seated in a stage box, whose magnificent pearls had caught his fancy; and thus, thanks mainly to the information that Saint-Loup had given me as to the private lives of actors, I saw another drama, mute but expressive, enacted beneath the words of the spoken drama which in itself, although of little merit, interested me too; for I could feel germinating and blossoming within it for an hour in the glare of the footlights, created out of the agglutination on the face of an actor of another face of grease-paint and pasteboard, and on his individual soul of the words of a part, those robust if ephemeral, and rather captivating, personalities which are the characters in a play, whom one loves, admires, pities, whom one would like to see again after one has left the theatre, but who by that time have already disintegrated into an actor who is no longer in the situation which was his in the play, into a text which no longer shows the actor's face, into a coloured powder which a handkerchief wipes off, who have returned, in short, to elements that contain nothing of them, because of their dissolution, effected as soon as the play is over—a dissolution which, like that of a loved one, causes one to doubt the reality of the self and to meditate on the mystery of death.

One number in the programme I found extremely painful. A young woman whom Rachel and some of her friends disliked was to make her debut with a recital of old songs—a debut on which she had based all her hopes for the future of herself and her family. This young woman was possessed of an unduly, almost grotesquely prominent rump and a pretty but too slight voice, reduced still further by her nervousness and in marked contrast to her muscular development. Rachel had posted among the audience a certain number of friends, male and female, whose business it was by their sarcastic comments to disconcert the novice, who was known to be timid, and to make her lose her head so that her recital should prove a complete fiasco, after which the manager would refuse to give her a contract. At the first notes uttered by the wretched woman, several of the male spectators, recruited for that purpose, began pointing to her hindquarters with jocular comments, several of the women who were also in the plot laughed out loud, and each fluty note from the stage increased the deliberate hilarity until it verged on the scandalous. The unhappy woman, sweating with anguish under her grease-paint, tried for a little longer to hold out, then stopped and gazed round the audience with a look of misery and rage which succeeded only in increasing the uproar. The instinct to imitate others, the desire to show off their own wit and daring, added to the party several pretty actresses who had not been forewarned but now exchanged with the others glances charged with malicious connivance, and gave vent to such violent peals of laughter that at the end of the second song, although there were still five more on the programme, the stage manager rang down the curtain. I did my utmost to pay no more heed to the incident than I had paid to my grandmother's sufferings when my great-uncle, to tease her, used to give my grandfather brandy, the idea of deliberate unkindness being too painful for me to bear. And yet, just as our pity for misfortune is perhaps not very precise since in our imagination we re-create a whole world of grief by which the unfortunate who has to struggle against it has no thought of being moved to self-pity, so unkindness has probably not in the minds of the unkind that pure and voluptuous cruelty which we find it so painful to imagine. Hatred inspires them, anger prompts them to an ardour and an activity in which there is no great joy; sadism is needed to extract any pleasure from it; whereas unkind people suppose themselves to be punishing someone equally unkind. Rachel certainly imagined that the actress whom she had tortured was far from being of interest to anyone, and that in any case, by having her hissed off the stage, she was herself avenging an outrage on good taste and teaching an unworthy colleague a lesson. Nevertheless, I preferred not to speak of this incident since I had had neither the courage nor the power to prevent it, and it would have been too embarrassing for me, by speaking well of their victim, to make the sentiments which animated the tormentors of the novice look like gratifications of cruelty.

But the beginning of this performance interested me in quite another way. It made me realise in part the nature of the illusion of which Saint-Loup was a victim with regard to Rachel, and which had set a gulf between the images that he and I respectively had of his mistress, when we saw her that morning among the blossoming pear-trees. Rachel had scarcely more than a walking-on part in the little play. But seen thus, she was another woman. She had one of those faces to which distance—and not necessarily that between stalls and stage, the world being merely a larger theatre—gives form and outline and which, seen from close to, crumble to dust. Standing beside her one saw only a nebula, a milky way of freckles, of tiny spots, nothing more. At a respectable distance, all this ceased to be visible and, from cheeks that withdrew, were reabsorbed into her face, there rose like a crescent moon a nose so fine and so pure that one would have liked to be the object of Rachel's attention, to see her again and again, to keep her near one, provided that one had never seen her differently and at close range. This was not my case, but it had been Saint-Loup's when he first saw her on the stage. Then he had asked himself how he might approach her, how get to know her, a whole miraculous world had opened up in his imagination—the world in which she lived—from which emanated an exquisite radiance but into which he could never penetrate. He had left the theatre in the little provincial town where this had happened several years before, telling himself that it would be madness to write to her, that she would not answer his letter, quite prepared to give his fortune and his name for the creature who now lived within him in a world so vastly superior to those too familiar realities, a world made beautiful by desire and dreams of happiness, when he saw emerging from the stage-door the gay and charmingly hatted band of actresses who had just been playing. Young men who knew them were waiting for them outside. The number of pawns on the human chessboard being less than the number of combinations that they are capable of forming, in a theatre from which all the people we know and might have expected to find are absent, there turns up one whom we never imagined that we should see again and who appears so opportunely that the coincidence seems to us providential, although no doubt some other coincidence would have occurred in its stead had we been not in that place but in some other, where other desires would have been born and another old acquaintance forthcoming to help us to satisfy them. The golden portals of the world of dreams had closed upon Rachel before Saint-Loup saw her emerge from the theatre, so that the freckles and spots were of little importance. They displeased him nevertheless, especially as, being no longer alone, he had not now the same power to dream as in the theatre. But she, for all that he could no longer see her, continued to dictate his actions, like those stars which govern us by their attraction even during the hours in which they are not visible to our eyes. And so his desire for the actress with the delicate features which were not now even present in Robert's memory caused him to fling himself at the old friend whom chance had brought to the spot and get himself introduced to the person with no features and with freckles, since she was the same person, telling himself that later on he would take care to find out which of the two the actress really was. She was in a hurry, she did not on this occasion address a single word to Saint-Loup, and it was only some days later that he finally induced her to leave her companions and allow him to escort her home. He loved her already. The need for dreams, the desire to be made happy by the woman one has dreamed of, ensure that not much time is required before one entrusts all one's chances of happiness to someone who a few days since was no more than a fortuitous, unknown, insignificant apparition on the boards of a theatre.

When, the curtain having fallen, we moved on to the stage, alarmed at finding myself there for the first time, I felt the need to begin a spirited conversation with Saint-Loup. In this way my demeanour, since I did not know which one to adopt in a setting that was new to me, would be entirely dominated by our talk, and people would think that I was so absorbed in it, so unobservant of my surroundings, that it was quite natural for me not to be wearing the facial expressions proper to a place in which, to judge by what I appeared to be saying, I was barely conscious of standing; and seizing, for the sake of speed, upon the first topic that came to my mind:

"You know," I said, "I did come to say good-bye to you the day I left Doncières. I've never had a chance to mention it. I waved to you in the street."

"Don't speak about it," he replied, "I was so sorry. I passed you just outside the barracks, but I couldn't stop because I was late already. I assure you I felt quite wretched about it."

So he had recognised me! I saw again in my mind the utterly impersonal salute which he had given me, raising his hand to his cap, without a glance to indicate that he knew me, without a gesture to show that he was sorry he could not stop. Evidently the fiction of not recognising me which he had adopted at that moment must have simplified matters for him greatly. But I was amazed that he had hit upon it so swiftly and before a reflex had betrayed his original impression. I had already observed at Balbec that, side by side with that childlike sincerity of his face, the skin of which by its transparency made visible the sudden surge of his emotions, his body had been admirably trained to perform a certain number of well-bred dissimulations, and that, like a consummate actor, he could, in his regimental and in his social life, play alternately quite different roles. In one of his roles he loved me tenderly, and behaved towards me almost as if he was my brother; my brother he had been, and was now again, but for a moment that day he had been another person who did not know me and who, holding the reins, his monocle screwed into his eye, without a look or a smile had lifted his disengaged hand to the peak of his cap to give me a correct military salute!

The stage sets, still in their place, among which I was passing, seen thus at close range and deprived of those effects of lighting and distance on which the eminent artist whose brush had painted them had calculated, were a depressing sight, and Rachel, when I came near her, was subjected to a no less destructive influence. The curves of her charming nostrils had remained in the perspective between auditorium and stage, like the relief of the scenery. It was no longer she: I recognised her only by her eyes, in which her identity had taken refuge. The form, the radiance of this young star, so brilliant a moment ago, had vanished. On the other hand—as though we were to look more closely at the moon so that it ceased to present the appearance of a disc of pink and gold—on this face that had seemed so smooth a surface I could now distinguish only protuberances, blemishes, hollows.

Yet in spite of the incoherence into which the woman's face and likewise the painted backdrops dissolved when seen from close to, I was happy to be there, to stroll among the sets, in surroundings which in the past my love of nature would have made me find tiresome and artificial, but to which Goethe's portrayal of them in *Wilhelm Meister* had given a certain beauty in my eyes. And I was delighted to observe, in the thick of a crowd of journalists or men of fashion, admirers of the actresses, who were greeting one another, talking, smoking, as though at a party in town, a young man in a black velvet cap and hortensia-coloured skirt, his cheeks chalked in red like a page from a Watteau album, who with smiling lips and eyes raised to the ceiling, describing graceful patterns with the palms of his hands and springing lightly into the air, seemed so entirely of another species from the sensible people in everyday clothes in the midst of whom he was pursuing like a madman the course of his ecstatic dream, so alien to the preoccupations of their life, so anterior to the habits of their civilisation, so enfranchised from the laws of nature, that it was as restful and refreshing a spectacle as watching a butterfly straying through a crowd to follow with one's eyes, between the flats, the natural arabesques traced by his winged, capricious, painted curvetings. But at that moment Saint-Loup conceived the notion that his mistress was paying undue attention to this dancer, who was now engaged in a final rehearsal of a dance-figure for the ballet performance in which he was about to appear, and his face darkened.

"You might look the other way," he said to her sombrely. "You know that those dancer-fellows are not worth the rope which one hopes they'll fall off and break their necks, and they're the sort of people who go about afterwards boasting that you've taken notice of them. Besides, you know very well you've been told to go to your dressing-room and change. You'll be missing your call again."

A group of men—journalists—noticing the look of fury on Saint-Loup's face, came nearer, amused, to listen to what was being said. And as the stage-hands had just set up some scenery on our other side we were forced into close contact with them.

"Oh, but I know him; he's a friend of mine," cried Saint-Loup's mistress, her eyes still fixed on the dancer. "Look how beautifully made he is; just watch those little hands of his dancing away by themselves like the rest of him!"

The dancer turned his head towards her, and his human person appeared beneath the sylph that he was endeavouring to be, the clear grey jelly of his eyes trembled and sparkled between eyelashes stiff with paint, and a smile extended the corners of his mouth in a face plastered with rouge; then, to amuse the young woman, like a singer who obligingly hums the tune of the song in which we have told her that we admired her singing, he began to repeat the movement of his hands, counterfeiting himself with the subtlety of a mime and the good humour of a child.

"Oh, it's too lovely, the way he mimics himself," cried Rachel, clapping her hands.

"I implore you, my dearest girl," Saint-Loup broke in, in a tone of utter misery, "don't make an exhibition of yourself, I can't stand it. I swear if you say another word I won't go with you to your room, I shall walk straight out. Come on, don't be nasty... You oughtn't to stand about in the cigar smoke like that, it'll make you ill," he added, turning to me, with the solicitude he had shown for me in our Balbec days.

"Oh! what bliss it would be if you did go."

"I warn you, if I do, I shan't come back."

"That's more than I should dare to hope."

"Look here, I promised you the necklace if you behaved nicely to me, but since you treat me like this..."

"Ah! that doesn't surprise me in the least. You gave me a promise, but I ought to have known you'd never keep it. You want the whole world to know you're made of money, but I'm not self-interested and money-grubbing like you. You can keep your blasted necklace; I know someone else who'll give it to me."

"No one else can possibly give it to you. I've told Boucheron he's to keep it for me, and I have his promise not to sell it to anyone else."

"So that's it! You wanted to blackmail me, so you took all your precautions in advance. It's just what they say: Marsantes, *Mater*

Semita, it smells of the race," retorted Rachel, quoting an etymology which was founded on a wild misinterpretation, for *Semita*
means "path" and not "Semite," but one which the Nationalists
applied to Saint-Loup on account of the Dreyfusard views for
which, as it happened, he was indebted to the actress. (She was less
justified than anyone in applying the appellation of Jewess to Mme
de Marsantes, in whom the ethnologists of society could succeed
in finding no trace of Jewishness apart from her kinship with the
Lévy-Mirepoix family.) "But this isn't the last of it, I can tell you.
An agreement like that isn't binding. You've behaved treacherously towards me. Boucheron shall be told of it and he'll be paid
twice as much for his necklace. You'll hear from me before long,
don't you worry."

Robert was in the right a hundred times over. But circumstances are always so entangled that the man who is in the right a
hundred times may have been once in the wrong. (Lord Derby
himself acknowledges that England does not always seem right *vis-
à-vis* Ireland.) And I could not help recalling that unpleasant and
yet quite innocent remark he had made at Balbec: "In that way
I keep a hold over her."

"You don't understand what I mean about the necklace. I made
no formal promise. Once you start doing everything you possibly
can to make me leave you, it's only natural, surely, that I shouldn't
give it to you. I fail to understand what treachery you can see in
that, or in what way I'm supposed to be self-interested. You can't
seriously maintain that I brag about my money, I'm always telling
you that I'm only a poor devil without a cent to my name. It's
foolish of you to take it that way, my sweet. How am I self-
interested? You know very well that my one interest in life is you."

"Yes, yes, please go on," she retorted ironically, with the
sweeping gesture of a barber wielding his razor.[17] And turning
towards the dancer:

"Isn't he too wonderful with his hands! I couldn't do the things
he's doing there, even though I'm a woman." She went closer to
him and, pointing to Robert's stricken face: "Look, he's hurt," she
murmured, in a momentary impulse of sadistic cruelty totally out
of keeping with her genuine feelings of affection for Saint-Loup.

"Listen; for the last time, I swear to you that you can try as hard
as you like, that in a week's time you can have all the regrets in the
world, but I shan't come back, I've had enough, do you hear, it's
irrevocable; you'll be sorry one day, when it's too late."

Perhaps he was sincere in saying this, and the torture of leaving his mistress may have seemed to him less cruel than that of remaining with her in certain circumstances.

"But, my dear boy," he added, addressing me, "you oughtn't to stay here, I tell you, you'll start coughing."

I pointed to the scenery which barred my way. He touched his hat and said to one of the journalists:

"Would you mind, sir, throwing away your cigar? The smoke is bad for my friend."

His mistress, not waiting for him to accompany her, was on her way to the dressing-room when she turned round and addressed the dancer from the back of the stage, in an artificially melodious tone of girlish innocence:

"Do they do those tricks with women too, those nice little hands? You look just like a woman yourself. I'm sure I could have a wonderful time with you and a girl I know."

"There's no rule against smoking that I know of," said the journalist. "If people aren't well, they have only to stay at home."

The dancer smiled mysteriously at the actress.

"Oh! Do stop! You're driving me crazy," she cried to him. "The larks we'll have!"

"In any case, sir, you are not very civil," observed Saint-Loup to the journalist, still in a mild and courteous tone, with the air of appraisal of a man judging retrospectively the rights and wrongs of an incident that is already closed.

At that moment I saw Saint-Loup raise his arm vertically above his head as if he were making a sign to someone I could not see, or like the conductor of an orchestra, and indeed—without any greater transition than when, at a simple stroke of a violin bow, in a symphony or a ballet, violent rhythms succeed a graceful andante—after the courteous words that he had just uttered, he brought down his hand with a resounding smack upon the journalist's cheek.

Now that to the measured conversations of the diplomats, to the smiling arts of peace, had succeeded the furious onthrust of war, since blows lead to blows, I should not have been surprised to see the combatants wading in one another's blood. But what I could not understand (like people who feel that it is not according to the rules for war to break out between two countries when up till then it has been a question merely of the rectification of a frontier, or for a sick man to die when there was talk of nothing more serious than a swelling of the liver) was how Saint-Loup had contrived to follow up those words, which implied a hint of affability, with a gesture which in no way arose out of them, which they had not foreshadowed, the gesture of that arm raised in defiance not only of international law but of the principle of causality, in a spontaneous generation of anger, a gesture created *ex nihilo*. Fortunately the journalist who, staggering back from the violence of the blow, had turned pale and hesitated for a moment, did not retaliate. As for his friends, one of them had promptly turned away his head and was staring fixedly into the wings at someone who was evidently not there; the second pretended that a speck of dust had got into his eye, and began rubbing and squeezing his eyelid with every sign of being in pain; while the third had rushed off, exclaiming: "Good heavens, I believe the curtain's going up; we shan't get into our seats."

I wanted to speak to Saint-Loup, but he was so full of his indignation with the dancer that it clung to the very surface of his eyeballs; like a subcutaneous integument it distended his cheeks, so that, his inner agitation expressing itself externally in total immobility, he had not even the elasticity, the "play" necessary to take in a word from me and to answer it. The journalist's friends, seeing that the incident was at an end, gathered round him again, still trembling. But, ashamed of having deserted him, they were absolutely determined that he should be made to suppose that they had noticed nothing. And so they expatiated, one upon the speck of dust in his eye, one upon the false alarm which had made him think that the curtain was going up, the third upon the astonishing resemblance between a man who had just gone by and the speaker's brother. Indeed they seemed quite to resent their friend's not having shared their several emotions.

"What, didn't it strike you? You must be going blind."

"What I say is that you're a pack of cowards," growled the journalist who had been struck.

Forgetting the fictions they had adopted, to be consistent with which they ought—but they did not think of it—to have pretended not to understand what he meant, they fell back on certain expressions traditional in the circumstances: "What's all the excitement? Keep your hair on, old chap. You seem to be rather het up."

I had realised that morning beneath the pear blossom how illusory were the grounds upon which Robert's love for

"Rachel when from the Lord" was based. On the other hand, I was no less aware how very real was the pain to which that love gave rise. Gradually the pain he had suffered without ceasing for the last hour receded, withdrew inside him, and a zone of accessibility appeared in his eyes. The two of us left the theatre and began to walk. I had stopped for a moment at a corner of the Avenue Gabriel from which I had often in the past seen Gilberte appear. I tried for a few seconds to recall those distant impressions, and was hurrying almost at the double to overtake Saint-Loup when I saw that a somewhat shabbily attired gentleman appeared to be talking to him confidentially. I concluded that this was a personal friend of Robert; meanwhile they seemed to be drawing even closer to one another; suddenly, as an astral phenomenon flashes through the sky, I saw a number of ovoid bodies assume with a dizzy swiftness all the positions necessary for them to compose a flickering constellation in front of Saint-Loup. Flung out like stones from a catapult, they seemed to me to be at the very least seven in number. They were merely, however, Saint-Loup's two fists, multiplied by the speed with which they were changing place in this—to all appearance ideal and decorative—arrangement. But this elaborate display was nothing more than a pummelling which Saint-Loup was administering, the aggressive rather than aesthetic character of which was first revealed to me by the aspect of the shabbily dressed gentleman who appeared to be losing at once his self-possession, his lower jaw and a quantity of blood. He gave mendacious explanations to the people who came up to question him, turned his head and, seeing that Saint-Loup had made off and was hastening to rejoin me, stood gazing after him with an offended, crushed, but by no means furious expression on his face. Saint-Loup, on the other hand, was furious, although he himself had received no blow, and his eyes were still blazing with anger when he reached me. The incident was in no way connected (as I had supposed) with the assault in the theatre. It was an impassioned loiterer who, seeing the handsome young soldier that Saint-Loup was, had made a proposition to him. My friend could not get over the audacity of this "clique" who no longer even waited for the shades of night to venture forth, and spoke of the proposition that had been made to him with the same indignation as the newspapers use in reporting an armed assault and robbery in broad daylight in the centre of Paris. And yet the recipient of his blows was excusable in one respect, for the trend of the downward slope brings desire so rapidly to the point of enjoyment that beauty in itself appears to imply consent. And that Saint-Loup was beautiful was beyond dispute. Castigation such as he had just administered has this value, for men of the type that had accosted him, that it makes them think seriously of their conduct, though never for long enough to enable them to mend their ways and thus escape correction at the hands of the law. And so, although Saint-Loup had administered the thrashing without much preliminary thought, all such punishments, even when they reinforce the law, are powerless to bring uniformity to morals.

These incidents, particularly the one that was weighing most on his mind, seemed to have prompted in Robert a desire to be left alone for a while. For after a time he asked me to leave him, and go by myself to call on Mme de Villeparisis. He would join me there, but preferred that we should not go in together, so that he might appear to have only just arrived in Paris instead of having spent half the day already with me.

As I had supposed before making the acquaintance of Mme de Villeparisis at Balbec, there was a vast difference between the world in which she lived and that of Mme de Guermantes. Mme de Villeparisis was one of those women who, born of an illustrious house, entering by marriage into another no less illustrious, do not for all that enjoy any great position in the social world, and, apart from a few duchesses who are their nieces or sisters-in-law, perhaps even a crowned head or two, old family connexions, have their drawing-rooms patronised only by third-rate people, drawn from the middle classes or from a nobility either provincial or tainted in some way, whose presence there has long since driven away all such smart and snobbish folk as are not obliged to come to the house by ties of blood or the claims of a friendship too old to be ignored. Certainly I had no difficulty after the first few minutes in understanding how Mme de Villeparisis, at Balbec, had come to be so well informed, better than ourselves even, as to the smallest details of the tour through Spain which my father was then making with M. de Norpois. It was impossible, for all that, to entertain the theory that the intimacy—of more than twenty years' standing— between Mme de Villeparisis and the Ambassador could have been responsible for the lady's loss of caste in a world where the smartest women boasted lovers far less respectable than him, quite apart from the fact that it was probably years since he had been

anything more to the Marquise than an old friend. Had Mme de
Villeparisis then had other adventures in the past? Being then of a
more passionate temperament than now, in a calm and pious old
age which nevertheless owed some of its mellow colouring to
those ardent, vanished years, had she somehow failed, in the
country neighbourhood where she had lived for so long, to
avoid certain scandals unknown to a younger generation which
merely noted their effect in the mixed and defective composition
of a visiting-list bound otherwise to have been among those least
tarnished by any base alloy? Had that "sharp tongue" which her
nephew ascribed to her made her enemies in those far-off days?
Had it driven her into taking advantage of certain successes with
men to avenge herself upon women? All this was possible; nor
could the exquisitely sensitive way in which—modulating so
delicately her choice of words as well as her tone of voice—
Mme de Villeparisis spoke of modesty or kindness be held to
invalidate this supposition; for the people who not only speak
with approval of certain virtues but actually feel their charm and
understand them admirably (who will be capable of painting a
worthy picture of them in their memoirs) are often sprung from,
but do not themselves belong to, the inarticulate, rough-hewn,
artless generation which practised them. That generation is
reflected but not continued in them. Instead of the character
which it possessed, one finds a sensibility, an intelligence which
are not conducive to action. And whether or not there had been in
the life of Mme de Villeparisis any of those scandals which the
lustre of her name had expunged, it was this intelligence, resembling rather that of a writer of the second rank than that of a
woman of position, that was undoubtedly the cause of her social
decline.

It is true that the qualities, such as level-headedness and moderation, which Mme de Villeparisis chiefly extolled were not
especially exalting; but in order to describe moderation in an
entirely convincing way, moderation will not suffice, and some
of the qualities of authorship which presuppose a quite immoderate exaltation are required. I had remarked at Balbec that the
genius of certain great artists was completely unintelligible to
Mme de Villeparisis, and that all she could do was to make delicate
fun of them and to express her incomprehension in a graceful and
witty form. But this wit and grace, in the degree to which they
were developed in her, became themselves—on another plane,

and even though they were employed to belittle the noblest masterpieces—true artistic qualities. Now the effect of such qualities on any social position is a morbid activity of the kind which doctors call elective, and so disintegrating that the most firmly established can hardly resist it for any length of time. What artists call intelligence seems pure presumption to the fashionable world which, incapable of adopting the angle of vision from which they, the artists, judge things, incapable of understanding the particular attraction to which they yield when they choose an expression or draw a parallel, feel in their company an exhaustion, an irritation, from which antipathy rapidly springs. And yet in her conversation, and the same may be said of the *Memoirs* which she afterwards published, Mme de Villeparisis showed nothing but a sort of graciousness that was eminently social. Having passed by great works without considering them deeply, sometimes without even noticing them, she had retained from the period in which she had lived, and which indeed she described with great aptness and charm, little but the most trivial things it had had to offer. But a piece of writing, even if it treats exclusively of subjects that are not intellectual, is still a work of the intelligence, and to give a consummate impression of frivolity in a book, or in a talk which is not dissimilar, requires a touch of seriousness which a purely frivolous person would be incapable of. In a certain book of memoirs written by a woman and regarded as a masterpiece, such and such a sentence that people quote as a model of airy grace has always made me suspect that, in order to arrive at such a degree of lightness, the author must once have been imbued with a rather weighty learning, a forbidding culture, and that as a girl she probably appeared to her friends an insufferable bluestocking. And between certain literary qualities and lack of social success the connexion is so inevitable that when we open Mme de Villeparisis's *Memoirs* today, on any page an apt epithet, a sequence of metaphors will suffice to enable the reader to reconstruct the deep but icy bow which must have been bestowed on the old Marquise on the staircase of an embassy by a snob such as Mme Leroi, who may perhaps have left a card on her when she went to call on the Guermantes, but never set foot in her house for fear of losing caste among all the doctors' or solicitors' wives whom she would find there. A bluestocking Mme de Villeparisis had perhaps been in her earliest youth, and, intoxicated with her learning, had perhaps been unable to resist applying to people in society, less intelligent and less educated than herself, those cutting taunts which the injured party never forgets.

Moreover, talent is not a separate appendage which can be artificially attached to those qualities which make for social success, in order to create from the whole what people in society call a "complete woman." It is the living product of a certain moral conformation from which as a rule many qualities are lacking and in which there predominates a sensibility of which other manifestations not discernible in a book may make themselves fairly acutely felt in the course of a life: certain curiosities for instance, certain whims, the desire to go to this place or that for one's own amusement and not with a view to the extension, the maintenance or even the mere exercise of one's social relations. I had seen Mme de Villeparisis at Balbec hemmed in by a bodyguard of her own servants and not even glancing at the people sitting in the hall of the hotel. But I had had a presentiment that this abstention was not due to indifference, and it seemed that she had not always confined herself to it. She would get a sudden craze to know such and such an individual who had no claim to be received in her house, sometimes because she had thought him good-looking, or merely because she had been told that he was amusing, or because he had struck her as different from the people she knew, who at this period, when she had not yet begun to appreciate them because she imagined that they would never abandon her, belonged, all of them, to the purest Faubourg Saint-Germain. To this bohemian or bourgeois intellectual whom she had marked out with her favour she was obliged to address her invitations, the value of which he was unable to appreciate, with an insistence that gradually depreciated her in the eyes of the snobs who were in the habit of judging a salon by the people whom its mistress excluded rather than by those whom she entertained. True, if at some point in her youth Mme de Villeparisis, surfeited with the satisfaction of belonging to the flower of the aristocracy, had somehow amused herself by scandalising the people among whom she lived, and deliberately impairing her own position in society, she had begun to attach importance to that position once she had lost it. She had wished to show the duchesses that she was better than they, by saying and doing all the things that they dared not say or do. But now that the latter, except for those who were closely related to her, had ceased to call, she felt herself diminished, and sought once more to reign, but with another sceptre than that of wit. She would have liked to attract to her house all those whom she had taken such pains to discard. How many women's lives, lives of which little enough is known (for we all live in different worlds according to our age, and the discretion of their elders prevents the young from forming any clear idea of the past and taking in the whole spectrum), have been divided thus into contrasting periods, the last being entirely devoted to the reconquest of what in the second has been so light-heartedly flung to the winds! Flung to the winds in what way? The young are all the less capable of imagining it, since they see before them an elderly and respectable Marquise de Villeparisis and have no idea that the grave memorialist of today, so dignified beneath her pile of snowy hair, can ever have been a gay midnight-reveller who was perhaps in those days the delight, who perhaps devoured the fortunes, of men now sleeping in their graves. That she should also have set to work, with a persevering and natural industry, to destroy the social position which she owed to her high birth does not in the least imply that even at that remote period Mme de Villeparisis did not attach great importance to her position. In the same way the web of isolation, of inactivity in which a neuras-thenic lives may be woven by him from morning to night without thereby seeming endurable, and while he is hastening to add another mesh to the net which holds him captive, it is possible that he is dreaming only of dancing, sport and travel. We strive all the time to give our life its form, but we do so by copying willy-nilly, like a drawing, the features of the person that we are and not of the person we should like to be. Mme Leroi's disdainful bows might to some extent be expressive of the true nature of Mme de Villeparisis; they in no way corresponded to her ambition.

No doubt at the same moment in which Mme Leroi was—to use an expression dear to Mme Swann—"cutting" the Marquise, the latter could seek consolation in remembering how Queen Marie-Amélie had once said to her: "You are just like a daughter to me." But such royal civilities, secret and unknown to the world, existed for the Marquise alone, as dusty as the diploma of an old Conservatoire medallist. The only real social advantages are those that create life, that can disappear without the person who has benefited by them needing to try to cling on to them or to make them public, because on the same day a hundred others will take their place. Remember as she might the words of the Queen, Mme de Villeparisis would have bartered them gladly for the permanent capacity for being invited everywhere which Mme Leroi possessed, just as, in a restaurant, a great but unknown artist whose genius is written neither in the lines of his shy face nor in the antiquated cut of his threadbare coat, would willingly change places with the young stock-jobber from the lowest ranks of society, who is sitting with a couple of actresses at a neighbouring table to which in an obsequious and incessant chain come hurrying owner, manager, waiters, bell-hops and even the scullions who file out of the kitchen to salute him, as in the fairy-tales, while the wine waiter advances, as dust-covered as his bottles, limping and dazed as if, on his way up from the cellar, he had twisted his foot before emerging into the light of day.

It must be remarked, however, that the absence of Mme Leroi from Mme de Villeparisis's salon, if it distressed the lady of the house, passed unperceived by the majority of her guests. They were entirely ignorant of the peculiar position which Mme Leroi occupied, a position known only to the fashionable world, and never doubted that Mme de Villeparisis's receptions were, as the readers of her *Memoirs* today are convinced that they must have been, the most brilliant in Paris.

On the occasion of this first call which, after leaving Saint-Loup, I went to pay on Mme de Villeparisis following the advice given by M. de Norpois to my father, I found her in a drawing-room hung with yellow silk, against which the settees and the admirable armchairs upholstered in Beauvais tapestry stood out with the almost purple redness of ripe raspberries. Side by side with the Guermantes and Villeparisis portraits were to be seen—gifts from the sitters themselves—those of Queen Marie-Amélie, the Queen of the Belgians, the Prince de Joinville and the Empress of Austria. Mme de Villeparisis herself, wearing an old-fashioned bonnet of black lace (which she preserved with the same shrewd instinct for local or historical colour as a Breton innkeeper who, however Parisian his clientele may have become, thinks it more astute to keep his maids dressed in coifs and wide sleeves), was seated at a little desk on which, as well as her brushes, her palette and an unfinished flower-piece in water-colour, were arranged— in glasses, in saucers, in cups—moss-roses, zinnias, maidenhair ferns, which on account of the sudden influx of callers she had just left off painting, and which gave the impression of being arrayed on a florist's counter in some eighteenth-century mezzo-tint. In this drawing-room, which had been slightly heated on

purpose because the Marquise had caught cold on the journey
from her house in the country, there were already, among those
present when I arrived, an archivist with whom Mme de
Villeparisis had spent the morning selecting the autograph letters
to herself from various historical personages which were to figure
in facsimile as documentary evidence in the *Memoirs* which she
was preparing for the press, and a solemn and tongue-tied historian, who, hearing that she had inherited and still possessed a
portrait of the Duchesse de Montmorency, had come to ask her
permission to reproduce it as a plate in his work on the Fronde—
guests who were presently joined by my old school-friend Bloch,
now a rising dramatist upon whom she counted to secure the
gratuitous services of actors and actresses at her next series of
afternoon parties. It was true that the social kaleidoscope was in
the act of turning and that the Dreyfus case was shortly to relegate
the Jews to the lowest rung of the social ladder. But, for one thing,
however fiercely the anti-Dreyfus cyclone might be raging, it is
not in the first hour of a storm that the waves are at their worst. In
the second place, Mme de Villeparisis, leaving a whole section of
her family to fulminate against the Jews, had remained entirely
aloof from the Affair and never gave it a thought. Lastly, a young
man like Bloch whom no one knew might pass unnoticed,
whereas leading Jews who were representative of their side were
already threatened. His chin was now decorated with a goatee
beard, he wore a pince-nez and a long frock-coat, and carried a
glove like a roll of papyrus in his hand. The Romanians, the
Egyptians, the Turks may hate the Jews. But in a French drawing-room the differences between those peoples are not so apparent, and a Jew making his entry as though he were emerging from
the desert, his body crouching like a hyena's, his neck thrust
forward, offering profound "salaams," completely satisfies a certain taste for the oriental. Only it is essential that the Jew in
question should not be actually "in" society, otherwise he will
readily assume the aspect of a lord and his manners become so
Gallicised that on his face a refractory nose, growing like a nas-
turtium in unexpected directions, will be more reminiscent of
Molière's Mascarille than of Solomon. But Bloch, not having been
limbered up by the gymnastics of the Faubourg, nor ennobled by a
crossing with England or Spain, remained for a lover of the exotic
as strange and savoury a spectacle, in spite of his European costume, as a Jew in a painting by Decamps. How marvellous the

power of the race which from the depths of the ages thrusts forwards even into modern Paris, in the corridors of our theatres, behind the desks of our public offices, at a funeral, in the street, a solid phalanx, setting their mark upon our modern ways of hair-dressing, absorbing, making us forget, disciplining the frock-coat which on the whole has remained almost identical with the gar-ment in which Assyrian scribes are depicted in ceremonial attire on the frieze of a monument at Susa before the gates of the Palace of Darius. (An hour later, Bloch was to feel that it was out of anti-semitic malice that M. de Charlus inquired whether his first name was Jewish, whereas it was simply from aesthetic interest and love of local colour.) But in any case to speak of racial persistence is to convey inaccurately the impression we receive from the Jews, the Greeks, the Persians, all those peoples whose variety is worth preserving. We know from classical paintings the faces of the ancient Greeks, we have seen Assyrians on the walls of a palace at Susa. And so we feel, on encountering in a Paris drawing-room Orientals belonging to such and such a group, that we are in the presence of supernatural creatures whom the forces of necro-mancy must have called into being. Hitherto we had only a superficial image; suddenly it has acquired depth, it extends into three dimensions, it moves. The young Greek lady, daughter of a rich banker and one of the latest society favourites, looks exactly like one of those dancers who in the chorus of a ballet at once historical and aesthetic symbolise Hellenic art in flesh and blood; but in the theatre the setting somehow vulgarises these images; whereas the spectacle to which the entry into a drawing-room of a Turkish lady or a Jewish gentleman admits us, by animating their features makes them appear stranger still, as if they really were creatures evoked by the efforts of a medium. It is the soul (or rather the pigmy thing which—up to the present, at any rate—the soul amounts to in this sort of materialisation), it is the soul, glimpsed by us hitherto in museums alone, the soul of the ancient Greeks, of the ancient Hebrews, torn from a life at once insignificant and transcendental, which seems to be enacting before our eyes this disconcerting pantomime. What we seek in vain to embrace in the shy young Greek is the figure admired long ago on the side of a vase. It struck me that if in the light of Mme de Villeparisis's drawing-room I had taken some photographs of Bloch, they would have given an image of Israel identical with those we find in spirit photographs—so disturbing because it does not appear to emanate from humanity, so deceptive because it none the less resembles humanity all too closely. There is nothing, to speak more generally, even down to the insignificance of the remarks made by the people among whom we spend our lives, that does not give us a sense of the supernatural, in our poor everyday world where even a man of genius from whom, gathered as though around a table at a séance, we expect to learn the secret of the infinite, simply utters these words, which had just issued from the lips of Bloch: "Take care of my top hat."

"Oh, ministers, my dear sir," Mme de Villeparisis was saying, addressing in particular my old school-friend and picking up the thread of a conversation which had been interrupted by my arrival, "ministers, nobody ever wanted to see them. I was only a child at the time, but I can well remember the King begging my grandfather to invite M. Decazes[18] to a rout at which my father was to dance with the Duchesse de Berry. 'It will give me pleasure, Florimond,' said the King. My grandfather, who was a little deaf, thought he had said M. de Castries, and found the request perfectly natural. When he understood that it was M. Decazes, he was furious at first, but he gave in, and wrote the same evening to M. Decazes, begging him to do him the honour of attending the ball which he was giving the following week. For we were polite in those days, and no hostess would have dreamed of simply sending her card and writing on it 'Tea' or 'Dancing' or 'Music.' But if we understood politeness, we were not incapable of impertinence either. M. Decazes accepted, but the day before the ball it was given out that my grandfather felt indisposed and had cancelled the ball. He had obeyed the King, but he had not had M. Decazes at his ball . . . Yes, indeed, I remember M. Molé very well, he was a man of wit—he showed that in his reception of M. de Vigny at the Academy—but he was very pompous, and I can see him now coming downstairs to dinner in his own house with his top hat in his hand."

"Ah! how evocative that is of what must have been a pretty perniciously philistine epoch, for it was no doubt a universal habit to carry one's hat in one's hand in one's own house," observed Bloch, anxious to make the most of so rare an opportunity of learning from an eyewitness details of the aristocratic life of another day, while the archivist, who was a sort of intermittent secretary to the Marquise, gazed at her tenderly as though he were saying to the rest of us: "There, you see what she's like, she knows everything, she has met everybody, you can ask her anything you like, she's quite amazing."

"Oh dear, no," replied Mme de Villeparisis, drawing towards her as she spoke the glass containing the maidenhair which presently she would continue painting. "It was simply a habit of M. de Molé's. I never saw my father carry his hat in the house, except of course when the King came, because the King being at home wherever he is, the master of the house is then only a visitor in his own drawing-room."

"Aristotle tells us in the second chapter of..." ventured M. Pierre, the historian of the Fronde, but so timidly that no one paid any attention. Having been suffering for some weeks from a nervous insomnia which resisted every attempt at treatment, he had given up going to bed, and, half-dead with exhaustion, went out only whenever his work made it imperative. Incapable of repeating too often these expeditions which, simple enough for other people, cost him as much effort as if he was obliged to come down from the moon, he was surprised to be brought up so frequently against the fact that other people's lives were not organised on a constant and permanent basis with a view to providing the maximum utility to the sudden eruptions of his own. He sometimes found closed a library which he had set out to visit only after planting himself artificially on his feet and in a frock-coat like the invisible man in a story by Wells. Fortunately he had found Mme de Villeparisis at home and was going to be shown the portrait.

Meanwhile he was cut short by Bloch. "Really," the latter observed, referring to what Mme de Villeparisis had said as to the etiquette for royal visits. "Do you know, I never knew that" (as though it were strange that he should not have known it).

"Talking of that sort of visit, do you know the stupid joke my nephew Basin played on me yesterday morning?" Mme de Villeparisis asked the librarian. "He told my people, instead of announcing him, to say that it was the Queen of Sweden who had called to see me."

"What! He made them tell you just like that! I say, he must have a nerve," exclaimed Bloch with a shout of laughter, while the historian smiled with a stately timidity.

"I was rather surprised, because I had only been back from the country a few days; I had given instructions, so as to be left in peace for a while, that no one was to be told that I was in Paris, and

I wondered how the Queen of Sweden could have heard so soon, and in any case didn't leave me a couple of days to get my breath," went on Mme de Villeparisis, leaving her guests under the impression that a visit from the Queen of Sweden was in itself nothing unusual for their hostess.

And it was true that if earlier in the day Mme de Villeparisis had been checking the documentation of her *Memoirs* with the archivist, she was now quite unconsciously trying out their effect on an average audience representative of that from which she would eventually have to recruit her readers. Hers might differ in many ways from a really fashionable salon from which many of the bourgeois ladies whom she entertained would have been absent and where one would have seen instead such brilliant leaders of fashion as Mme Leroi had in course of time managed to secure, but this distinction is not perceptible in her *Memoirs*, in which certain mediocre connexions of the author's have disappeared because there is no occasion to refer to them; while the absence of ladies who did not visit her leaves no gap because, in the necessarily restricted space at the author's disposal, only a few persons can appear, and if these persons are royal personages, historic personalities, then the maximum impression of elegance which any volume of memoirs can convey to the public is achieved. In the opinion of Mme Leroi, Mme de Villeparisis's salon was third-rate; and Mme de Villeparisis felt the sting of Mme Leroi's opinion. But hardly anyone today remembers who Mme Leroi was, her opinions have vanished into thin air, and it is the salon of Mme de Villeparisis, frequented as it was by the Queen of Sweden, and as it had been by the Duc d'Aumale, the Duc de Broglie, Thiers, Montalembert, Mgr. Dupanloup, which will be regarded as one of the most brilliant of the nineteenth century by that posterity which has not changed since the days of Homer and Pindar, and for which the enviable things are exalted birth, royal or quasi-royal, and the friendship of kings, of leaders of the people and other eminent men.

Now of all these Mme de Villeparisis had her share in her present salon and in the memories—sometimes slightly touched up—by means of which she extended it into the past. And then there was M. de Norpois who, while unable to restore his friend to any substantial position in society, on the other hand brought to her house such foreign or French statesmen as might have need of his services and knew that the only effective method of securing

them was to pay court to Mme de Villeparisis. Perhaps Mme Leroi
also knew these European celebrities. But, as an agreeable woman
who shunned anything that smacked of the bluestocking, she
would as little have thought of mentioning the Eastern Question
to a Prime Minister as of discussing the nature of love with a
novelist or a philosopher. "Love?" she had once replied to a
pretentious lady who had asked for her views on love, "I make it
often but I never talk about it." When she had any of these literary
or political lions in her house she contented herself, as did the
Duchesse de Guermantes, with setting them down to play poker.
They often preferred this to the serious conversations on general
ideas in which Mme de Villeparisis forced them to engage. But
these conversations, ridiculous as in the social sense they may have
been, have furnished the *Memoirs* of Mme de Villeparisis with
those admirable passages, those political dissertations which read
well in volumes of autobiography as they do in tragedies in the
style of Corneille. Furthermore, the salons of the Mme de
Villeparisis of this world are alone destined to be handed down
to posterity, because the Mme Lerois of this world cannot write,
and, if they could, would not have the time. And if the literary
dispositions of the Mme de Villeparisis are the cause of the disdain
of the Mme Lerois, in its turn the disdain of the Lerois does a
singular service to the literary dispositions of the Mme de
Villeparisis by affording those bluestocking ladies that leisure
which the career of letters requires. God, whose will it is that
there should be a few well-written books in the world, breathes
with that purpose such disdain into the hearts of the Mme Lerois,
for he knows that if these should invite the Mme Villeparisis to
dinner, the latter would at once rise from their writing-tables and
order their carriages to be round at eight.

Presently there entered with slow and solemn tread an old lady
of tall stature who, beneath the raised brim of her straw hat,
revealed a monumental pile of snowy hair in the style of Marie-
Antoinette. I did not then know that she was one of three women
still to be seen in Parisian society who, like Mme de Villeparisis,
while all of the noblest birth, had been reduced, for reasons which
were now lost in the mists of time and could have been explained
to us only by some old gallant of their period, to entertaining only
certain of the dregs of society who were not sought after elsewhere. Each of these ladies had her own "Duchesse de
Guermantes," the brilliant niece who came regularly to pay her

respects, but none of them could have succeeded in attracting to her house the "Duchesse de Guermantes" of either of the others. Mme de Villeparisis was on the best of terms with these three ladies, but she did not like them. Perhaps the similarity between their social position and her own gave her a disagreeable impression of them. Besides, soured bluestockings as they were, seeking, by the number and frequency of the dramatic entertainments which they arranged in their houses, to give themselves the illusion of a regular salon, there had grown up among them a rivalry which the erosion of their wealth in the course of somewhat tempestuous lives, obliging them to watch their expenditure, to count on the services of professional actors or actresses free of charge, transformed into a sort of struggle for existence. Furthermore, the lady with the Marie-Antoinette hair-style, whenever she set eyes on Mme de Villeparisis, could not help being reminded of the fact that the Duchesse de Guermantes did not come to her Fridays. Her consolation was that at these same Fridays she could always count on having, blood being thicker than water, the Princesse de Poix, who was her own personal Guermantes, and who never went near Mme de Villeparisis, albeit Mme de Poix was an intimate friend of the Duchess.

Nevertheless from the mansion on the Quai Malaquais to the drawing-rooms of the Rue de Tournon, the Rue de la Chaise and the Faubourg Saint-Honoré, a bond as compelling as it was hateful united the three fallen goddesses, as to whom I should have been interested to learn, from some dictionary of social mythology, what amorous adventure, what sacrilegious presumption, had brought about their punishment. The same illustrious origins, the same present decline, no doubt had much to do with the necessity which compelled them, while hating each other, to frequent one another's society. Besides, each of them found in the others a convenient way of impressing her guests. How should these fail to suppose that they had scaled the most inaccessible peak of the Faubourg when they were introduced to a lady with a string of titles whose sister was married to a Duc de Sagan or a Prince de Ligne? Especially as there was infinitely more in the newspapers about these sham salons than about the genuine ones. Indeed these old ladies' "swell" nephews—and Saint-Loup the foremost of them—when asked by a friend to introduce him into society would say: "I'll take you to my aunt Villeparisis's, or to my aunt X's—you meet interesting people there." They knew very well

that this would mean less trouble for themselves than trying to get
the said friend invited by the smart nieces or sisters-in-law of these
ladies. Certain very old men, and young women who had heard it
from those men, told me that if these ladies were no longer
received in society it was because of the extraordinary dissolute-
ness of their conduct, which, when I objected that dissolute
conduct was not necessarily a barrier to social success, was represented to me as having gone far beyond anything to be met with
today. The misconduct of these solemn dames who held themselves so erect assumed on the lips of those who hinted at it
something that I was incapable of imagining, something proportionate to the magnitude of prehistoric days, to the age of the
mammoth. In a word, these three Parcae with their white or blue
or pink hair had been the ruin of an incalculable number of
gentlemen. It struck me that the men of today exaggerated the
vices of those fabulous times, like the Greeks who created Icarus,
Theseus, Heracles out of men who had been but little different
from those who long afterwards deified them. But one does not
tabulate the sum of a person's vices until he has almost ceased to be
in a fit state to practise them, when from the magnitude of his
social punishment, which is then nearing the completion of its
term and which alone one can estimate, one measures, one imagines, one exaggerates the magnitude of the crime that has been
committed. In that gallery of symbolical figures which is "society,"
the really dissolute women, the true Messalinas, invariably present
the solemn aspect of a lady of at least seventy, with an air of lofty
distinction, who entertains everyone she can but not everyone she
would like to, to whose house women whose own conduct is not
above reproach refuse to go, to whom the Pope regularly sends his
Golden Rose, and who as often as not has written a book about
Lamartine's early years that has been crowned by the French
Academy.

"How d'ye do, Alix?" Mme de Villeparisis greeted the lady
with the Marie-Antoinette hair-style, which lady cast a searching
glance round the assembly to see whether there was not in this
drawing-room any item that might be a valuable addition to her
own, in which case she would have to discover it for herself, for
Mme de Villeparisis, she was sure, would be malevolent enough to
hide it from her. Thus Mme de Villeparisis took good care not
to introduce Bloch to the old lady for fear of his being asked to
produce the same play that he was arranging for her in the

drawing-room of the Quai Malaquais. Besides, it was only tit for tat. For the evening before the old lady had had Mme Ristori reciting verses, and had taken care that Mme de Villeparisis, from whom she had filched the Italian artist, should not hear of this function until it was over. So that she should not read it first in the newspapers and feel ruffled, the old lady had come in person to tell her about it, showing no sense of guilt. Mme de Villeparisis, judging that the introduction of myself was unlikely to have the same drawbacks as that of Bloch, made me known to the Marie-Antoinette of the Quai Malaquais. The latter, who sought, by making the fewest possible movements, to preserve in her old age those lines, as of a Coysevox goddess, which had years ago charmed the young men of fashion and which spurious poets still celebrated in rhyming couplets—and had acquired the habit of a lofty and compensating stiffness common to all those whom a personal uncomeliness obliges to be continually making advances—just perceptibly lowered her head with a frigid majesty, and, turning the other way, took no more notice of me than if I had not existed. Her dual-purpose attitude seemed to be saying to Mme de Villeparisis: "You see, I'm not as hard up for acquaintance as all that, and I'm not interested—in any sense of the word, you old cat—in young men." But when, twenty minutes later, she took her leave, taking advantage of the general hubbub she slipped into my ear an invitation to come to her box the following Friday with another of the three, whose high-sounding name—she had been born a Choiseul, moreover—made a prodigious impression on me.

"I understand, M'sieur, that you want to write somethin' about Mme la Duchesse de Montmorency," said Mme de Villeparisis to the historian of the Fronde in the gruff tone with which her genuine affability was furrowed by the shrivelled crotchiness, the physiological spleen of old age, as well as by the affectation of imitating the almost rustic speech of the old nobility. "I'll show you her portrait, the original of the copy they have in the Louvre."

She rose, laying down her brushes beside the flowers, and the little apron which then came into sight at her waist, and which she wore so as not to stain her dress with paint, added still further to the impression of an old peasant given by her bonnet and her big spectacles, and offered a sharp contrast to the luxury of her household, the butler who had brought in the tea and cakes, the liveried footman for whom she now rang to light up the portrait of the

Duchesse de Montmorency, abbess of one of the most famous chapters in the east of France. Everyone had risen. "What is rather amusin'," said our hostess, "is that in these chapters where our great-aunts were so often made abbesses, the daughters of the King of France would not have been admitted. They were very exclusive chapters." "The King's daughters not admitted!" cried Bloch in amazement, "why ever not?" "Why, because the House of France had not enough quarterin's after that misalliance." Bloch's bewilderment increased. "A misalliance? The House of France? When was that?" "Why, when they married into the Medicis," replied Mme de Villeparisis in the most natural tone in the world. "It's a fine picture, is it not, and in a perfect state of preservation," she added.

"My dear," said the lady with the Marie-Antoinette hair-style, "surely you remember that when I brought Liszt to see you he said that it was this one that was the copy."

"I shall bow to any opinion of Liszt's on music, but not on painting. Besides, he was already gaga, and I don't remember his ever saying anything of the sort. But it wasn't you who brought him here. I had met him any number of times at dinner at Princess Sayn-Wittgenstein's."

Alix's shot had misfired; she stood silent, erect and motionless. Plastered with layers of powder, her face had the appearance of stone. And, since the profile was noble, she seemed, on a triangular, moss-grown pedestal hidden by her cape, like a crumbling goddess in a park.

"Ah, I see another fine portrait," said the historian.

The door opened and the Duchesse de Guermantes entered the room.

"Oh, good evening," Mme de Villeparisis greeted her without even a nod of the head, taking from her apron-pocket a hand which she held out to the newcomer; and ceasing at once to pay any further attention to her niece, turned back to the historian: "That is the portrait of the Duchesse de La Rochefoucauld . . . "

A young servant with a bold manner and a charming face (but so finely chiselled to ensure its perfection that the nose was a little red and the rest of the skin slightly inflamed as though they were still smarting from the recent sculptural incision) came in bearing a card on a salver.

"It is that gentleman who has been several times to see Mme la Marquise."

"Did you tell him I was at home?"

"He heard the voices."

"Oh, very well then, show him in. It's a gentleman who was introduced to me," she explained. "He told me he was very anxious to come to my house. I certainly never said he might. But he's taken the trouble to call five times now, and it doesn't do to hurt people's feelings. Monsieur," she added to me, "and you, Monsieur," to the historian of the Fronde, "let me introduce my niece, the Duchesse de Guermantes."

The historian made a low bow, as I did too, and since he seemed to suppose that some friendly remark ought to follow this salute, his eyes brightened and he was preparing to open his mouth when he was chilled by the demeanour of Mme de Guermantes, who had taken advantage of the independence of her torso to throw it forward with an exaggerated politeness and bring it neatly back to a position of rest without letting face or eyes appear to have noticed that anyone was standing before them; after breathing a little sigh she contented herself with manifesting the nullity of the impression that had been made on her by the sight of the historian and myself by performing certain movements of her nostrils with a precision that testified to the absolute inertia of her unoccupied attention.

The importunate visitor entered the room, making straight for Mme de Villeparisis with an ingenuous, fervent air: it was Legrandin.

"Thank you so very much for letting me come and see you," he began, laying stress on the word "very." "It is a pleasure of a quality altogether rare and subtle that you confer on an old solitary. I assure you that its repercussion . . ."

He stopped short on catching sight of me.

"I was just showing this gentleman a fine portrait of the Duchesse de La Rochefoucauld, the wife of the author of the *Maxims*; it's a family heirloom."

Mme de Guermantes meanwhile had greeted Alix, with apologies for not having been able, that year as in every previous year, to go and see her. "I hear all about you from Madeleine," she added.

"She was at luncheon with me today," said the Marquise of the Quai Malaquais, with the satisfying reflexion that Mme de Villeparisis could never say the same.

Meanwhile I had been talking to Bloch, and fearing, from what I had been told of his father's change of attitude towards him, that he might be envying my life, I said to him that his must be happier. My remark was prompted simply by a desire to be friendly. But such friendliness readily convinces those who cherish a high opinion of themselves of their own good fortune, or gives them a desire to convince other people of it. "Yes, I do lead a delightful existence," Bloch assured me with a beatific smile. "I have three great friends—I do not wish for one more—and an adorable mistress; I am infinitely happy. Rare is the mortal to whom Father Zeus accords so much felicity." I fancy that he was anxious principally to congratulate himself and to make me envious. Perhaps, too, his optimism reflected a desire to be original. It was evident that he did not wish to reply with the usual banalities—"Oh, it was nothing, really," and so forth—when, to my question: "Was it nice?" apropos of an afternoon dance at his house to which I had been prevented from going, he replied in a level, careless tone, as if the dance had been given by someone else: "Why, yes, it was very nice, couldn't have been more successful. In fact it was really enchanting."

"What you have just told us interests me enormously," said Legrandin to Mme de Villeparisis, "for I was saying to myself only the other day that you showed a marked resemblance to him in the agile sharpness of your turn of phrase, in a quality which I will describe by two contradictory terms, concise rapidity and immortal instantaneousness. I should have liked this afternoon to take down all the things you say; but I shall remember them. They are, in a phrase which comes, I think, from Joubert, congenial to the memory. You have never read Joubert? Oh! he would have admired you so! I will take the liberty this very evening of sending you his works: it will be a privilege to make you a present of his mind. He had not your force. But he had a similar gracefulness."

I had wanted to go and greet Legrandin at once, but he kept as far away from me as he could, no doubt in the hope that I might not overhear the stream of flattery which, with a remarkable preciosity of expression, he kept pouring out to Mme de Villeparisis whatever the subject.

She shrugged her shoulders, smiling, as though he had been trying to make fun of her, and turned to the historian.

"And this is the famous Marie de Rohan, Duchesse de Chevreuse, who was previously married to M. de Luynes."

"My dear, Mme de Luynes reminds me of Yolande; she came to me yesterday evening, and if I had known that you weren't engaged I'd have sent round to ask you to come. Mme Ristori turned up quite by chance, and recited some poems by Queen Carmen Sylva[19] in the author's presence. It was too beautiful!"

"What treachery!" thought Mme de Villeparisis. "Of course that was what she was whispering about the other day to Mme de Beaulaincourt and Mme de Chaponay." . . . "I was free," she replied, "but I would not have come. I heard Ristori in her great days, she's a mere wreck now. Besides, I detest Carmen Sylva's poetry. Ristori came here once—the Duchess of Aosta brought her—to recite a canto of Dante's *Inferno*. In that sort of thing she's incomparable."

Alix bore the blow without flinching. She remained marble. Her gaze was piercing and blank, her nose proudly arched. But the surface of one cheek was flaking. A faint, strange vegetation, green and pink, was invading her chin. Perhaps another winter would finally lay her low.

"There, Monsieur, if you are fond of painting, look at the portrait of Mme de Montmorency," Mme de Villeparisis said to Legrandin to interrupt the flow of compliments which was beginning again.

Taking the opportunity of his back being turned, Mme de Guermantes pointed to him with an ironical, questioning look at her aunt.

"It's M. Legrandin," murmured Mme de Villeparisis. "He has a sister called Mme de Cambremer, not that will mean any more to you than it does to me."

"What! Oh, but I know her very well!" exclaimed Mme de Guermantes, clapping her hand to her mouth. "Or rather I don't know her, but for some reason or other Basin, who meets the husband heaven knows where, took it into his head to tell the wretched woman she might call on me. And she did. I can't tell you what it was like. She told me she had been to London, and gave me a complete catalogue of all the things in the British Museum. And just as you see me now, the moment I leave your house, I'm going to drop a card on the monster. And don't think it's as easy as all that, because on the pretext that she's dying of some disease she's always at home, no matter whether you arrive at seven at night or nine in the morning, she's ready for you with a plate of strawberry tarts. No, but seriously, you know, she is a monstrosity," Mme de Guermantes went on in reply to a questioning glance from her aunt. "She's an impossible person, she

talks about 'scriveners' and things like that." "What does 'scrivener' mean?" asked Mme de Villeparisis. "I haven't the slightest
idea!" cried the Duchess in mock indignation. "I don't want to
know. I don't speak that sort of language." And seeing that her
aunt really did not know what a scrivener was, to give herself the
satisfaction of showing that she was a scholar as well as a purist, and
to make fun of her aunt after having made fun of Mme de
Cambremer: "Why, of course," she said, with a half-laugh
which the last traces of her feigned ill-humour kept in check,
"everybody knows what it means; a scrivener is a writer, a person
who scribbles. But it's a horror of a word. It's enough to make
your wisdom teeth drop out. Nothing will ever make me use
words like that . . . And so that's the brother, is it? I can't get used to
the idea. But after all it's not inconceivable. She has the same
door-mat humility and the same mass of information like a
circulating library. She's just as much of a toady as he is, and just
as boring. Yes, I'm beginning to see the family likeness now quite
plainly."

"Sit down, we're just going to take a dish of tea," said Mme de
Villeparisis to her niece. "Help yourself; you don't want to look at
the pictures of your great-grandmothers, you know them as well
as I do."

Presently Mme de Villeparisis sat down again at her desk and
went on with her painting. The rest of the party gathered round
her, and I took the opportunity to go up to Legrandin and, seeing
no harm myself in his presence in Mme de Villeparisis's drawing-
room and never dreaming how much my words would at once
hurt him and make him believe that I had deliberately intended
to hurt him, say: "Well, Monsieur, I am almost excused for being
in a salon when I find you here too." M. Legrandin concluded
from these words (at least this was the opinion which he expressed
of me a few days later) that I was a thoroughly spiteful young
wretch who delighted only in doing mischief.

"You might at least have the civility to begin by saying how d'ye
do to me," he replied, without offering me his hand and in a coarse
and angry voice which I had never suspected him of possessing, a
voice which, having no rational connexion with what he ordinarily said, had another more immediate and striking connexion
with something he was feeling. For the fact of the matter is that,
since we are determined always to keep our feelings to ourselves,
we have never given any thought to the manner in which we

should express them. And suddenly there is within us a strange and obscene animal making itself heard, whose tones may inspire as much alarm in the person who receives the involuntary, elliptical and almost irresistible communication of one's defect or vice as would the sudden avowal indirectly and outlandishly proffered by a criminal who can no longer refrain from confessing to a murder of which one had never imagined him to be guilty. I knew, of course, that idealism, even subjective idealism, did not prevent great philosophers from still having hearty appetites or from presenting themselves with untiring perseverance for election to the Academy. But really Legrandin had no need to remind people so often that he belonged to another planet when all his uncontrollable impulses of anger or affability were governed by the desire to occupy a good position on this one.

"Naturally, when people pester me twenty times on end to go somewhere," he went on in lower tones, "although I am perfectly free to do what I choose, still I can't behave like an absolute boor."

Mme de Guermantes had sat down. Her name, accompanied as it was by her title, added to her physical person the duchy which cast its aura round about her and brought the shadowy, sunsplashed coolness of the woods of Guermantes into this drawingroom, to surround the pouf on which she was sitting. I was surprised only that the likeness of those woods was not more discernible on the face of the Duchess, about which there was nothing suggestive of vegetation, and on which the ruddiness of her cheeks—which ought, one felt, to have been emblazoned with the name Guermantes—was at most the effect, and not the reflexion, of long gallops in the open air. Later on, when I had become indifferent to her, I came to know many of the Duchess's distinctive features, notably (to stick for the moment only to those of which I already at this time felt the charm though without yet being able to identify it) her eyes, which captured as in a picture the blue sky of a French country afternoon, broadly expansive, bathed in light even when no sun shone; and a voice which one would have thought, from its first hoarse sounds, to be almost plebeian, in which there lingered, as over the steps of the church at Combray or the pastry-cook's in the square, the rich and lazy gold of a country sun. But on this first day I discerned nothing, my ardent attention volatilised at once the little that I might otherwise have been able to take in and from which I might have been able to grasp something of the name Guermantes. In any case, I told myself that it was indeed she who was designated for all the world by the title Duchesse de Guermantes: the inconceivable life which that name signified was indeed contained in this body; it had just introduced that life into the midst of a group of disparate people, in this room which enclosed it on every side and on which it produced so vivid a reaction that I felt I could see, where the extent of that mysterious life ceased, a fringe of effervescence outline its frontiers—in the circumference of the circle traced on the carpet by the balloon of her blue pekin skirt, and in the bright eyes of the Duchess at the point of intersection of the preoccupations, the memories, the incomprehensible, scornful, amused and curious thoughts which filled them from within and the outside images that were reflected on their surface. Perhaps I should have been not quite so deeply stirred had I met her at Mme de Villeparisis's at an evening party, instead of seeing her thus at one of the Marquise's "at homes," at one of those tea-parties which are for women no more than a brief halt in the course of their afternoon's outing, when, keeping on the hats in which they have been doing their shopping, they waft into a succession of salons the quality of the fresh air outside, and offer a better view of Paris in the late afternoon than do the tall open windows through which one can hear the rumble of victorias: Mme de Guermantes wore a straw hat trimmed with cornflowers, and what they recalled to me was not the sunlight of bygone years among the tilled fields round Combray where I had so often gathered them on the slope adjoining the Tansonville hedge, but the smell and the dust of twilight as they had been an hour ago when Mme de Guermantes had walked through them in the Rue de la Paix. With a smiling, disdainful, absent-minded air, and a pout on her pursed lips, she was tracing circles on the carpet with the point of her sunshade, as with the extreme tip of an antenna of her mysterious life; then, with that indifferent attention which begins by eliminating every point of contact between oneself and what one is considering, her gaze fastened upon each of us in turn, then inspected the settees and chairs, but softened now by that human sympathy which is aroused by the presence, however insignificant, of a thing one knows, a thing that is almost a person: these pieces of furniture were not like us, they belonged vaguely to her world, they were bound up with the life of her aunt; then from a Beauvais chair her gaze was carried back to the person sitting on it, and thereupon resumed the same air of perspicacity and that same disapproval

which the respect that Mme de Guermantes felt for her aunt
would have prevented her from expressing in words, but which
she would have felt had she noticed on the chairs, instead of our
presence, that of a spot of grease or a layer of dust.

The excellent writer G—— entered the room, having come to
pay a call on Mme de Villeparisis which he regarded as a tiresome
duty. The Duchess, although delighted to see him again, gave him
no sign of welcome, but instinctively he made straight for her, the
charm that she possessed, her tact, her simplicity making him look
upon her as a woman of intelligence. He was bound, in any case, in
common politeness to go and talk to her, for, since he was a
pleasant and distinguished man, Mme de Guermantes frequently
invited him to lunch even when her husband and herself were
alone, or, in the autumn, took advantage of this intimacy to have
him to dinner occasionally at Guermantes with royal personages
who were curious to meet him. For the Duchess liked to entertain
certain eminent men, on condition always that they were bachelors, a condition which, even when married, they invariably
fulfilled for her, for since their wives, who were always more or
less common, would have been a blot on a salon in which there
were never any but the most fashionable beauties of Paris, it was
always without them that their husbands were invited; and the
Duke, to forestall any hurt feelings, would explain to these
involuntary widowers that the Duchess never had women in the
house, could not endure feminine company, almost as though
this had been under doctor's orders, and as he might have said
that she could not stay in a room in which there were smells, or eat
over-salted food, or travel with her back to the engine, or wear
stays. It was true that these eminent men used to see at the
Guermantes' the Princesse de Parme, the Princesse de Sagan
(whom Françoise, hearing her constantly mentioned, had taken
to calling, in the belief that this feminine ending was required by
the laws of accidence, "the Sagante"), and plenty more, but their
presence was accounted for by the explanation that they were
relations, or such very old friends that it was impossible to exclude
them. Whether or not they were convinced by the explanations
which the Duc de Guermantes had given of the singular malady
that made it impossible for the Duchess to associate with other
women, the great men duly transmitted them to their wives. Some
of these thought that the malady was only an excuse to cloak her
jealousy, because the Duchess wished to reign alone over a court

of worshippers. Others more simple still thought that perhaps the Duchess had some peculiar habit, or even a scandalous past, so that women did not care to go to her house and that she gave the name of a whim to what was stern necessity. The better among them, hearing their husbands expatiate on the Duchess's wit, assumed that she must be so far superior to the rest of womankind that she found their society boring since they could not talk intelligently about anything. And it was true that the Duchess was bored by other women, if their princely rank did not give them an exceptional interest. But the excluded wives were mistaken when they imagined that she chose to entertain men only in order to be able to discuss with them literature, science, and philosophy. For she never spoke of these, at least with the great intellectuals. If, by virtue of a family tradition such as makes the daughters of great soldiers preserve a respect for military matters in the midst of their most frivolous distractions, she felt, as the granddaughter of women who had been on terms of friendship with Thiers, Mérimée and Augier, that a place must always be kept in her drawing-room for men of intellect, she had at the same time derived from the manner, at once condescending and familiar, in which those famous men had been received at Guermantes, the foible of looking on men of talent as family friends whose talent does not dazzle one, to whom one does not speak of their work, and who would not be at all interested if one did. Moreover the type of mind illustrated by Mérimée and Meilhac and Halévy, which was also hers, led her, by contrast with the verbal sentimentality of an earlier generation, to a style of conversation that rejects everything to do with fine language and the expression of lofty thoughts, so that she made it a sort of point of good breeding when she was with a poet or a musician to talk only of the food that they were eating or the game of cards to which they would afterwards sit down. This abstention had, on a third person not conversant with her ways, a disturbing effect which amounted to mystification. Mme de Guermantes having asked him if he would like to be invited with this or that famous poet, devoured by curiosity he arrived at the appointed hour. The Duchess would talk to the poet about the weather. They sat down to lunch. "Do you like this way of doing eggs?" she would ask the poet. On hearing his approval, which she shared, for everything in her own house appeared to her exquisite, down to a horrible cider which she imported from Guermantes: "Give Monsieur some more eggs," she would tell the butler, while the anxious fellow-guest sat waiting for what must surely have been the object of the occasion, since they had arranged to meet, in spite of every sort of difficulty, before the Duchess, the poet and he himself left Paris. But the meal went on, one after another the courses would be cleared away, not without having provided Mme de Guermantes with opportunities for clever witticisms or well-judged anecdotes. Meanwhile the poet went on eating without either the Duke or Duchess showing any sign of remembering that he was a poet. And presently the luncheon came to an end and the party broke up, without a word having been said about poetry which they nevertheless all admired but to which, by a reserve analogous to that of which Swann had given me a foretaste, no one referred. This reserve was simply a matter of good form. But for the fellow-guest, if he thought about the matter, there was something strangely melancholy about it all, and these meals in the Guermantes household were reminiscent of the hours which timid lovers often spend together in talking trivialities until it is time to part, without—whether from shyness, from modesty or from awkwardness—the great secret which they would have been happier to confess ever having succeeded in passing from their hearts to their lips. It must, however, be added that this silence with regard to deeper things which one was always waiting in vain to see broached, if it might pass as characteristic of the Duchess, was by no means absolute with her. Mme de Guermantes had spent her girlhood in a somewhat different environment, equally aristocratic but less brilliant and above all less futile than that in which she now lived, and one of wide culture. It had left beneath her present frivolity a sort of firmer bedrock, invisibly nutritious, to which indeed the Duchess would repair in search (very rarely, though, for she detested pedantry) of some quotation from Victor Hugo or Lamartine which, extremely appropriate, uttered with a look of true feeling from her fine eyes, never failed to surprise and charm her audience. Sometimes, even, unpretentiously, with pertinence and simplicity, she would give some dramatist and Academician a piece of sage advice, would make him modify a situation or alter an ending.

If, in the drawing-room of Mme de Villeparisis, as in the church at Combray on the day of Mlle Percepied's wedding, I had difficulty in rediscovering in the handsome but too human face of Mme de Guermantes the enigma of her name, I thought at least that, when she spoke, her conversation, profound, mysterious, would have the strangeness of a mediaeval tapestry or a Gothic window. But in order that I should not be disappointed by the words that I should hear uttered by a person who called herself Mme de Guermantes, even if I had not been in love with her, it would not have sufficed that those words should be shrewd, beautiful and profound, they would have had to reflect that amaranthine colour of the closing syllable of her name, that colour which on first seeing her I had been disappointed not to find in her person and had fancied as having taken refuge in her mind. True, I had already heard Mme de Villeparisis and Saint-Loup, people whose intelligence was in no way extraordinary, pronounce quite casually this name Guermantes, simply as that of a person who was coming to see them or with whom they were going to dine, without seeming to feel that there were latent in her name the glow of yellowing woods and a whole mysterious tract of country. But this must have been an affectation on their part, as when the classic poets give us no warning of the profound intentions which they nevertheless had, an affectation which I myself also strove to imitate, saying in the most natural tone: "The Duchesse de Guermantes," as though it were a name that was just like other names. Besides, everyone declared that she was a highly intelligent woman, a witty conversationalist, living in a small circle of most interesting people: words which became accomplices of my dream. For when they spoke of an intelligent group, of witty talk, it was in no way intelligence as I knew it that I imagined, not even that of the greatest minds; it was not at all with men like Bergotte that I peopled this group. No, by intelligence I understood an ineffable faculty gilded by the sun, impregnated with a sylvan coolness. Indeed, had she made the most intelligent remarks (in the sense in which I understood the word when it was used of a philosopher or critic), Mme de Guermantes would perhaps have disappointed even more keenly my expectation of so special a faculty than if, in the course of a trivial conversation, she had confined herself to discussing cooking recipes or the furnishing of a country house, to mentioning the names of neighbours or relatives of hers, which would have given me a picture of her life.

"I thought I should find Basin here. He was meaning to come and see you today," said Mme de Guermantes to her aunt.

"I haven't set eyes on your husband for some days," replied Mme de Villeparisis in a somewhat nettled tone. "In fact, I haven't seen him—well, perhaps once—since the charming joke he played on me of having himself announced as the Queen of Sweden."

Mme de Guermantes formed a smile by contracting the corners of her mouth as though she were biting her veil.

"We met her at dinner last night at Blanche Leroi's. You wouldn't know her now, she's positively enormous. I'm sure she must be ill."

"I was just telling these gentlemen that you said she looked like a frog."

Mme de Guermantes emitted a sort of raucous noise which meant that she was laughing for form's sake.

"I don't remember making such a charming comparison, but if she was one before, now she's the frog that has succeeded in swelling to the size of the ox. Or rather, it isn't quite that, because all her swelling is concentrated in her stomach: she's more like a frog in an interesting condition."

"Ah, I do find that funny," said Mme de Villeparisis, secretly proud that her guests should be witnessing this display of her niece's wit.

"It is purely *arbitrary*, though," answered Mme de Guermantes, ironically detaching this selected epithet, as Swann would have done, "for I must admit I never saw a frog in the family way. Anyhow, the frog in question, who, by the way, does not require a king, for I never saw her so skittish as she's been since her husband died, is coming to dine with us one day next week. I promised I'd let you know just in case."

Mme de Villeparisis gave vent to an indistinct growl, from which emerged: "I know she was dining with the Mecklenburgs the night before last. Hannibal de Bréauté was there. He came and told me about it, quite amusingly, I must say."

"There was a man there who's a great deal wittier than Babal," said Mme de Guermantes who, intimate though she was with M. de Bréauté-Consalvi, felt the need to advertise the fact by the use of this diminutive. "I mean M. Bergotte."

I had never imagined that Bergotte could be regarded as witty; moreover, I thought of him always as part of the intellectual section of humanity, that is to say infinitely remote from that mysterious realm of which I had caught a glimpse through the purple hangings of a theatre box behind which, making the Duchess laugh, M. de Bréauté had been holding with her, in the language of the gods, that unimaginable thing, a conversation between people of the Faubourg Saint-Germain. I was distressed to see the balance upset and Bergotte rise above M. de Bréauté. But above all I was dismayed to think that I had avoided Bergotte on the evening of *Phèdre*, that I had not gone up and spoken to him, when I heard Mme de Guermantes, in whom one could always, as at the turn of a mental tide, see the flow of curiosity with regard to well-known intellectuals sweep over the ebb of her aristocratic snobbishness, say to Mme de Villeparisis: "He's the only person I have any wish to know. It would be such a pleasure."

The presence of Bergotte by my side, which it would have been so easy for me to secure but which I should have thought liable to give Mme de Guermantes a bad impression of me, would no doubt, on the contrary, have resulted in her signalling to me to join her in her box, and inviting me to bring the eminent writer to lunch one day.

"I gather that he didn't behave very well. He was presented to M. de Cobourg, and never uttered a word to him," Mme de Guermantes went on, dwelling on this odd fact as she might have recounted that a Chinese had blown his nose on a sheet of paper. "He never once said 'Your Royal Highness' to him," she added, with an air of amusement at this detail, as important to her mind as the refusal of a Protestant, during an audience with the Pope, to go on his knees before His Holiness.

Interested by these idiosyncrasies of Bergotte's, she did not, however, appear to consider them reprehensible, and seemed rather to give him credit for them, though she would have been hard put to it to say why. Despite this unusual mode of appreciating Bergotte's originality, it was a fact which I was later to regard as not wholly negligible that Mme de Guermantes, greatly to the surprise of many of her friends, considered Bergotte wittier than M. de Bréauté. Thus it is that such judgments, subversive, isolated, and yet after all right, are delivered in the world of society by those rare people who are superior to the rest. And they sketch then the first rough outlines of the hierarchy of values as the next generation will establish it, instead of abiding eternally by the old standards.

The Comte d'Argencourt, Chargé d'Affaires at the Belgian Legation and a second cousin by marriage of Mme de Villeparisis, came in limping, followed presently by two young men, the Baron de Guermantes and H.H. the Duc de Châtellerault, whom Mme de Guermantes greeted with: "Good evening, my dear Châtellerault," with a nonchalant air and with-out moving from her pouf, for she was a great friend of the young Duke's mother, which had given him a deep and lifelong respect for her. Tall, slim, with golden hair and skin, thoroughly Guermantes in type, these two young men looked like a conden-sation of the light of the spring evening which was flooding the spacious room. Following a custom which was the fashion at that time, they laid their top hats on the floor beside them. The historian of the Fronde assumed that they must be embarrassed, like peasants coming into the mayor's office and not knowing what to do with their hats. Feeling that he ought in charity to come to the rescue of the awkwardness and timidity which he ascribed to them:

"No, no," he said, "don't leave them on the floor, they'll be trodden on."

A glance from the Baron de Guermantes, tilting the plane of his pupils, shot suddenly from them a wave of pure and piercing blue which froze the well-meaning historian.

"What is that person's name?" the Baron asked me, having just been introduced to me by Mme de Villeparisis.

"M. Pierre," I whispered.

"Pierre what?"

"Pierre: it's his name, he's a very distinguished historian."

"Really? You don't say so."

"No, it's a new fashion with these young men to put their hats on the floor," Mme de Villeparisis explained. "I'm like you, I can never get used to it. Still, it's better than my nephew Robert, who always leaves his in the hall. I tell him, when I see him come in like that, that he looks just like a clockmaker, and I ask him if he's come to wind the clocks."

"You were speaking just now, Madame la Marquise, of M. Molé's hat; we shall soon be able, like Aristotle, to compile a chapter on hats," said the historian of the Fronde, somewhat reassured by Mme de Villeparisis's intervention, but in so faint a voice that no one heard him except me.

"She really is astonishing, the little Duchess," said M. d'Argencourt, pointing to Mme de Guermantes who was talking to G——. "Whenever there's a prominent person in the room you're sure to find him sitting with her. Evidently that must be the lion of the party over there. It can't be M. de Borelli every day, or M. Schlumberger or M. d'Avenel. But then it's bound to be M. Pierre Loti or M. Edmond Rostand. Yesterday evening at the Doudeauvilles', where by the way she was looking splendid in her emerald tiara and a pink dress with a long train, she had M. Deschanel on one side and the German Ambassador on the other: she was holding forth to them about China. The general public, at a respectful distance where they couldn't hear what was being said, were wondering whether there wasn't going to be war. Really, you'd have said she was a queen holding her circle."

Everyone had gathered round Mme de Villeparisis to watch her painting.

"Those flowers are a truly celestial pink," said Legrandin, "I should say sky-pink. For there is such a thing as sky-pink just as there is sky-blue. But," he lowered his voice in the hope that he would not be heard by anyone but the Marquise, "I think I still plump for the silky, the living rosiness of your rendering of them. Ah, you leave Pisanello and Van Huysum a long way behind, with their meticulous, dead herbals."

An artist, however modest, is always willing to hear himself preferred to his rivals, and tries only to see that justice is done them.

"What gives you that impression is that they painted flowers of their time which we no longer know, but they did it with great skill."

"Ah! Flowers of their time! That is a most ingenious theory," exclaimed Legrandin.

"I see you're painting some fine cherry blossoms—or are they mayflowers?" began the historian of the Fronde, in some doubt as to the flower, but with a note of confidence in his voice, for he was beginning to forget the incident of the hats.

"No, they're apple blossom," said the Duchesse de Guermantes, addressing her aunt.

"Ah! I see you're a good countrywoman like me; you can tell one flower from another."

"Why yes, so they are! But I thought the season for apple blossom was over now," hazarded the historian, to cover his mistake.

"Not at all; on the contrary it's not out yet; it won't be out for another fortnight, or three weeks perhaps," said the archivist who, since he helped with the management of Mme de Villeparisis's estates, was better informed upon country matters.

"Yes, even round Paris, where they're very far forward," put in the Duchess. "Down in Normandy, don't you know, at his father's place," she pointed to the young Duc de Châtellerault, "where they have some splendid apple-trees close to the sea, like a Japanese screen, they're never really pink until after the twentieth of May."

"I never see them," said the young Duke, "because they give me hay fever. Such a bore."

"Hay fever? I never heard of that before," said the historian.

"It's the fashionable complaint just now," the archivist informed him.

"It all depends: you won't get it at all, probably, if it's a good year for apples. You know the Norman saying: 'When it's a good year for apples...'," put in M. d'Argencourt who, not being quite French, was always trying to give himself a Parisian air.

"You're quite right," Mme de Villeparisis said to her niece, "these are from the South. It was a florist who sent them round and asked me to accept them as a present. You're surprised, I dare say, Monsieur Vallenères," she turned to the archivist, "that a florist should make me a present of apple blossom. Well, I may be an old woman, but I'm not quite on the shelf yet, I still have a few friends," she went on with a smile that might have been taken as a sign of her simplicity but meant rather, I could not help feeling, that she thought it intriguing to pride herself on the friendship of a mere florist when she had such grand connexions.

Bloch rose and in his turn came over to look at the flowers which Mme de Villeparisis was painting.

"Never mind, Marquise," said the historian, sitting down again, "even if we were to have another of those revolutions which have stained so many pages of our history with blood—and, upon my soul, in these days one can never tell," he added with a circular and circumspect glance, as if to make sure that there were no "dissidents" in the room, though he did not suppose there were any, "with a talent like yours and your five languages you would be certain to get on all right."

The historian of the Fronde was feeling quite refreshed, for he had forgotten his insomnia. But he suddenly remembered that he had not slept for six nights, whereupon a crushing weariness, born of his mind, took hold of his legs and bowed his shoulders, and his melancholy face began to droop like an old man's.

Bloch wanted to express his admiration in an appropriate gesture, but only succeeded in knocking over the glass containing the spray of apple blossom with his elbow, and all the water was spilled on the carpet.

"You really have a fairy's touch," the historian said to the Marquise; having his back turned to me at that moment, he had not noticed Bloch's clumsiness.

But Bloch took the remark as a jibe at him, and to cover his shame with a piece of insolence, retorted: "It's not of the slightest importance; I'm not wet."

Mme de Villeparisis rang the bell and a footman came to wipe the carpet and pick up the fragments of glass. She invited the two young men to her theatricals, and also Mme de Guermantes, with the injunction:

"Remember to tell Gisèle and Berthe" (the Duchesses d'Auberjon and de Portefin) "to be here a little before two to help me," as she might have told hired waiters to come early to arrange the fruit-stands.

She treated her princely relatives, as she treated M. de Norpois, without any of the little courtesies which she showed to the historian, Cottard, Bloch and myself, and they seemed to have no interest for her beyond the possibility of serving them up as food for our social curiosity. This was because she knew that she need not put herself out to entertain people for whom she was not a more or less brilliant woman but the sister, touchy and used to tactful handling, of their father or uncle. There would have been no object in her trying to shine in front of them; she could never have deceived them as to the strength or weakness of her situation, for they knew her whole story only too well and respected the illustrious race from which she sprang. But, above all, they had ceased to be anything more for her than a dead stock that would never bear fruit again; they would never introduce her to their new friends, or share their pleasures with her. She could obtain from them only their occasional presence, or the possibility of speaking of them, at her five o'clock receptions as, later on, in her *Memoirs*, of which these receptions were only a sort of rehearsal, a preliminary reading aloud of the manuscript before a selected audience. And the society which all these noble kinsmen and kinswomen served to interest, to dazzle, to enthral, the society of the Cottards, of the Blochs, of well-known dramatists, historians of the Fronde and suchlike, it was this society that, for Mme

de Villeparisis—in the absence of that section of the fashionable
world which did not go to her house—represented movement,
novelty, entertainment and life; it was from people like these that
she was able to derive social advantages (which made it well worth
her while to let them meet, now and then, though without ever
getting to know her, the Duchesse de Guermantes): dinners with
remarkable men whose work had interested her, a light opera or a
pantomime staged complete by its author in her drawing-room,
boxes for interesting shows.

Bloch got up to go. He had said aloud that the incident of the
broken flower-glass was of no importance, but what he said under
his breath was different, more different still what he thought: "If
people can't train their servants to put vases where they won't risk
soaking and even injuring their guests, they oughtn't to go in for
such luxuries," he muttered angrily. He was one of those susceptible, highly-strung persons who cannot bear to have made a
blunder which, though they do not admit it to themselves, is
enough to spoil their whole day. In a black rage, he was just
making up his mind never to go into society again. He had reached
the point at which some distraction was imperative. Fortunately in
a moment Mme de Villeparisis would press him to stay. Either
because she was aware of the opinions of her friends and the rising
tide of anti-semitism, or simply from absent-mindedness, she had
not introduced him to any of the people in the room. He, however, being little used to society, felt that he ought to take leave of
them all before going, out of good manners, but without
warmth; he lowered his head several times, buried his bearded
chin in his stiff collar, and scrutinised each of the party in turn
through his glasses with a cold and peevish glare. But Mme de
Villeparisis stopped him; she had still to discuss with him the
little play which was to be performed in her house, and also she
did not wish him to leave before he had had the satisfaction of
meeting M. de Norpois (whose failure to appear surprised
her), although as an inducement to Bloch this introduction was
quite superfluous, he having already decided to persuade the two
actresses whose names he had mentioned to her to come and sing
for nothing in the Marquise's drawing-room, in the interest of
their careers, at one of those receptions to which the élite of
Europe thronged. He had even offered in addition a tragic actress
"with sea-green eyes, fair as Hera," who would recite lyrical prose
with a sense of plastic beauty. But on hearing this lady's name

Mme de Villeparisis had declined, for it was that of Saint-Loup's mistress.

"I have better news," she murmured in my ear. "I really believe it's on its last legs, and that before very long they'll have separated—in spite of an officer who has played an abominable part in the whole business," she added. (For Robert's family were beginning to look with a deadly hatred on M. de Borodino, who had given him leave, at the hairdresser's instance, to go to Bruges, and accused him of giving countenance to an infamous liaison.) "He's a very bad man," said Mme de Villeparisis with that virtuous accent common to all the Guermantes, even the most depraved. "Very, very bad," she repeated, emphasising the word "very" and rolling the "r"s. One felt that she had no doubt of the Prince's being present at all their orgies. But, as kindness of heart was the old lady's dominant quality, her expression of frowning severity towards the horrible captain, whose name she articulated with an ironical emphasis: "The Prince de Borodino!"—as a woman for whom the Empire simply did not count—melted into a gentle smile at myself with a mechanical twitch of the eyelid indicating a vague connivance between us.

"I was quite fond of de Saint-Loup-en-Bray," said Bloch, "dirty dog though he is, because he's extremely well-bred. I have a great admiration for well-bred people, they're so rare," he went on, without realising, since he was himself so extremely ill-bred, how displeasing his words were. "I will give you an example which I consider most striking of his perfect breeding. I met him once with a young man just as he was about to spring into his wheelèd chariot, after he himself had buckled their splendid harness on a pair of steeds nourished with oats and barley, who had no need of the flashing whip to urge them on. He introduced us, but I did not catch the young man's name—one never does catch people's names when one's introduced to them," he added with a laugh, this being one of his father's witticisms. "De Saint-Loup-en-Bray remained perfectly natural, made no fuss about the young man, seemed absolutely at his ease. Well, I found out by pure chance a day or two later that the young man was the son of Sir Rufus Israels!"

The end of this story sounded less shocking than its preface, for it remained quite incomprehensible to everyone in the room. The fact was that Sir Rufus Israels, who seemed to Bloch and his father an almost royal personage before whom Saint-Loup ought to tremble, was in the eyes of the Guermantes world a foreign upstart, tolerated in society, on whose friendship nobody would ever have dreamed of priding himself—far from it.

"I learned this," said Bloch, "from Sir Rufus Israels' agent, who is a friend of my father and a quite remarkable man. Oh, an absolutely wonderful individual," he added with that affirmative energy, that note of enthusiasm which one puts only into convictions that do not originate from oneself.

"But tell me," Bloch asked me, lowering his voice, "how much money do you suppose Saint-Loup has? Not that it matters to me in the least, you quite understand. I'm interested from the Balzacian point of view. You don't happen to know what it's in, French stocks, foreign stocks, or land or what?"

I could give him no information whatsoever. Suddenly raising his voice, Bloch asked if he might open the windows, and without waiting for an answer, went across the room to do so. Mme de Villeparisis said that it was out of the question, as she had a cold. "Oh, well, if it's bad for you!" Bloch was downcast. "But you can't say it's not hot in here." And breaking into a laugh, he swept a glance round the room in an appeal for support against Mme de Villeparisis. He received none, from these well-bred people. His blazing eyes, having failed to seduce any of the other guests, resignedly reverted to their former gravity of expression. He acknowledged his defeat with: "What's the temperature? Twenty-two at least, I should say. Twenty-five? I'm not surprised. I'm simply dripping. And I have not, like the sage Antenor, son of the river Alpheus, the power to plunge myself in the paternal wave to staunch my sweat before laying my body in a bath of polished marble and anointing my limbs with fragrant oils." And with that need which people feel to outline for the benefit of others medical theories the application of which would be beneficial to their own health: "Well, if you believe it's good for you! I must say, I think the opposite. It's exactly what gives you your cold."

Bloch had expressed delight at the idea of meeting M. de Norpois. He would like, he said, to get him to talk about the Dreyfus case.

"There's a mentality at work there which I don't altogether understand, and it would be rather intriguing to have an interview with this eminent diplomat," he said in a sarcastic tone, so as not to appear to be rating himself below the Ambassador.

Mme de Villeparisis was sorry that he had said this so loud, but minded less when she saw that the archivist, whose strong Nationalist views kept her, so to speak, on a leash, was too far off to have overheard. She was more shocked to hear Bloch, led on by that demon of ill breeding which made him permanently blind to the consequences of what he said, inquiring with a laugh at the paternal pleasantry:

"Haven't I read a learned treatise by him in which he sets forth a string of irrefutable arguments to prove that the Russo-Japanese war was bound to end in a Russian victory and a Japanese defeat? And isn't he a bit senile? I'm sure he's the one I've seen taking aim at his chair before sliding across the room to it, as if on casters."

"Good gracious, never!" the Marquise put in. "Just wait a minute. I don't know what he can be doing."

She rang the bell and, when the servant appeared, as she made no secret of, and indeed liked to advertise, the fact that her old friend spent the greater part of his time in her house: "Go and tell M. de Norpois to come," she ordered. "He's sorting some papers in my library; he said he would be twenty minutes, and I've been waiting now for an hour and three-quarters. He'll talk to you about the Dreyfus case, or anything else you like," she said grumpily to Bloch. "He doesn't much approve of what's happening."

For M. de Norpois was not on good terms with the ministry of the day, and Mme de Villeparisis, although he had never taken the liberty of bringing any governmental personalities to her house (she still preserved all the unapproachable dignity of a great lady of the aristocracy and remained outside and above the political relations which he was obliged to cultivate), was kept well informed by him of everything that went on. Equally, these politicians of the present regime would never have dared to ask M. de Norpois to introduce them to Mme de Villeparisis. But several of them had gone down to see him at her house in the country when they needed his advice or help at critical junctures. They knew the address. They went to the house. They did not see its mistress. But at dinner that evening she would say: "I hear they've been down here bothering you. Are things going better?"

"You're not in a hurry?" she now asked Bloch.

"No, not at all. I was thinking of going because I'm not very well; in fact there's a possibility of my taking a cure at Vichy for my gall bladder," he explained, articulating these words with a fiendish irony.

"Why, that's just where my nephew Châtellerault's got to go. You must fix it up together. Is he still here? He's a nice boy, you know," said Mme de Villeparisis, sincerely perhaps, thinking that two people whom she knew had no reason not to be friends with each other.

"Oh, I dare say he wouldn't care about that—I don't . . . I scarcely know him. He's over there," stammered Bloch, over-whelmed with delight.

The butler had evidently failed to deliver his mistress's message properly, for M. de Norpois, to give the impression that he had just come in from the street and had not yet seen his hostess, had picked up the first hat that he found in the vestibule, one which I thought I recognised, and came forward to kiss Mme de Villeparisis's hand with great ceremony, asking after her health with all the interest that people show after a long separation. He was not aware that the Marquise had removed in advance any semblance of verisimilitude from this charade, which indeed she eventually cut short by introducing him to Bloch. The latter, who had observed all the polite attentions that were being shown to a person whom he had not yet discovered to be M. de Norpois, and the formal, gracious, deep bows with which the Ambassador replied to them, evidently felt inferior to all this ceremonial and vexed to think that it would never be addressed to him, and said to me in order to appear at ease: "Who is that old idiot?" Perhaps, too, all this bowing and scraping by M. de Norpois had really shocked the better element in Bloch's nature, the freer and more straightforward manners of a younger generation, and he was partly sincere in condemning it as absurd. However that might be, it ceased to appear absurd and indeed delighted him the moment it was himself, Bloch, to whom the salutations were addressed.

"Monsieur l'Ambassadeur," said Mme de Villeparisis, "I should like you to meet this gentleman. Monsieur Bloch, Monsieur le Marquis de Norpois." She made a point, in spite of the way she bullied M. de Norpois, of addressing him always as "Monsieur l'Ambassadeur," as a point of etiquette as well as from an exaggerated respect for his ambassadorial rank, a respect which the Marquis had inculcated in her, and also with the intention of applying that less familiar, more ceremonious posture towards one particular man which, in the salon of a distinguished woman, in contrast to the freedom with which she treats her other regular guests, marks that man out instantly as her lover.

M. de Norpois sank his azure gaze in his white beard, bent his tall body deep down as though he were bowing before all the renowned and imposing connotations of the name Bloch, and murmured: "I'm delighted..." whereat his young interlocutor, moved, but feeling that the illustrious diplomat was going too far, hastened to correct him, saying: "Not at all! On the contrary, it is I who am delighted." But this ceremony, which M. de Norpois, out of friendship for Mme de Villeparisis, repeated for the benefit of every new person that his old friend introduced to him, did not seem to her adequate to the deserts of Bloch, to whom she said:

"Just ask him anything you want to know. Take him aside if it's more convenient; he will be delighted to talk to you. I think you wished to speak to him about the Dreyfus case," she went on, no more considering whether this would be agreeable to M. de Norpois than she would have thought of asking leave of the Duchesse de Montmorency's portrait before having it lighted up for the historian, or of the tea before offering a cup of it.

"You must speak loud," she warned Bloch, "he's a little deaf, but he will tell you anything you want to know; he knew Bismarck very well, and Cavour. That is so, isn't it?" she raised her voice, "you knew Bismarck well."

"Have you got anything on the stocks?" M. de Norpois asked me with a knowing air as he shook my hand warmly. I took the opportunity to relieve him politely of the hat which he had felt obliged to bring ceremonially into the room, for I saw that it was my own which he had picked up at random. "You showed me a somewhat laboured little thing in which you went in for a good deal of hair-splitting. I gave you my frank opinion; what you had written was not worth the trouble of putting on paper. Are you preparing something for us? You were greatly smitten with Bergotte, if I remember rightly." "You're not to say anything against Bergotte," put in the Duchess. "I don't dispute his pictorial talent; no one would, Duchess. He understands all about etching and engraving, if not brush-work on a large canvas like M. Cherbuliez. But it seems to me that in these days there is a tendency to mix up the genres and forget that the novelist's business is rather to weave a plot and edify his readers than to fiddle away at producing a frontispiece or tailpiece in drypoint.

I shall be seeing your father on Sunday at our good friend A.J.'s," he went on, turning again to me.

I had hoped for a moment, when I saw him talking to Mme de Guermantes, that he would perhaps afford me, for getting myself asked to her house, the help he had refused me for getting to Mme Swann's. "Another of my great favourites," I told him, "is Elstir. It seems the Duchesse de Guermantes has some wonderful examples of his work, particularly that admirable *Bunch of Radishes* which I remember at the Exhibition and should so much like to see again; what a masterpiece it is!" And indeed, if I had been a prominent person and had been asked to state what picture I liked best, I should have named this *Bunch of Radishes*.

"A masterpiece?" cried M. de Norpois with a surprised and reproachful air. "It makes no pretence of being even a picture, it's merely a sketch." (He was right.) "If you label a clever little thing of that sort 'masterpiece,' what will you say about Hébert's *Virgin* or Dagnan-Bouveret?"

"I heard you refusing to have Robert's woman," said Mme de Guermantes to her aunt, after Bloch had taken the Ambassador aside. "I don't think you'll miss much: she's a perfect horror, you know, without a vestige of talent, and besides she's grotesquely ugly."

"Do you mean to say you know her, Duchess?" asked M. d'Argencourt.

"Yes, didn't you know that she performed in my house before anyone else's—not that that's anything to be proud of," replied Mme de Guermantes with a laugh, glad nevertheless, since the actress was under discussion, to let it be known that she herself had had the first taste of her absurdities. "Hallo, I suppose I ought to go now," she added, without moving.

She had just seen her husband enter the room, and these words were an allusion to the absurdity of their appearing to be paying a call together like a newly married couple, rather than to the often strained relations that existed between her and the strapping individual she had married, who, despite his advancing years, still led the life of a gay bachelor. Casting over the considerable party that was gathered round the tea-table the affable, waggish gaze—dazzled a little by the slanting rays of the setting sun—of the little round pupils lodged in the exact centre of his eyes, like the "bulls" which the excellent marksman that he was could always target with such perfect precision, the Duke advanced with a

wondering, gingerly deliberation as though, alarmed by so brilliant a gathering, he was afraid of treading on ladies' skirts and
interrupting conversations. A permanent smile suggesting a
slightly tipsy "Good King Wenceslas," and a half-open hand
floating like a shark's fin by his side, which he allowed to be
clasped indiscriminately by his old friends and by the strangers
who were introduced to him, enabled him, without having to
make a single movement, or to interrupt his genial, lazy, royal
progress, to reward the alacrity of them all by simply murmuring:
"How do, my boy; how do, my dear fellow; charmed, Monsieur
Bloch; how do, Argencourt"; and, on coming to myself, who was
the most favoured of all when he had been told my name: "How
do, young neighbour, how's your father? What an admirable
man!" He made no great demonstration except to Mme de
Villeparisis, who greeted him with a nod of her head, drawing
one hand from a pocket of her little apron.

Being formidably rich in a world where people were becoming
steadily less so, and having adapted himself long since to the idea of
this enormous fortune, he had all the vanity of the great nobleman
combined with that of the man of means, the refinement and
breeding of the former only just managing to counterbalance the
smugness of the latter. One could understand, moreover, that his
success with women, which made his wife so unhappy, was not
due merely to his name and his wealth, for he was still remarkably
handsome, and his profile retained the purity, the firmness of
outline of a Greek god's.

"Do you mean to tell me she performed in your house?"
M. d'Argencourt asked the Duchess.

"Well, you know, she came to recite, with a bunch of lilies in
her hand, and more lilies on her *dwess*." (Mme de Guermantes
shared her aunt's affectation of pronouncing certain words in an
exceedingly rustic fashion, though she never rolled her "r"s like
Mme de Villeparisis.)

Before M. de Norpois, under constraint from his hostess, had
taken Bloch into the little recess where they could talk more
freely, I went up to the old diplomat for a moment and put in a
word about my father's academic chair. He tried first of all to
postpone the conversation to another day. I pointed out that I was
going to Balbec. "What? Going to Balbec again? Why, you're a
regular *globe-trotter*." Then he listened to what I had to say. At the
name of Leroy-Beaulieu, he looked at me suspiciously. I

conjectured that he had perhaps said something disparaging to M. Leroy-Beaulieu about my father and was afraid that the economist might have repeated it to him. All at once he seemed to be filled with a positive affection for my father. And after one of those decelerations in the flow of speech out of which suddenly a word explodes as though in spite of the speaker, whose irresistible conviction overcomes his stuttering efforts at silence: "No, no," he said to me with emotion, "your father *must not* stand. In his own interest he must not, for his own sake, out of respect for his merits, which are great, and which would be compromised by such an adventure. He is too big a man for that. If he were elected, he would have everything to lose and nothing to gain. He is not an orator, thank heaven. And that is the one thing that counts with my dear colleagues, even if you only talk platitudes. Your father has an important goal in life; he should march straight ahead towards it, and not beat about the bush, even the bushes (more thorny than flowery) of the groves of Academe. Besides, he would not get many votes. The Academy likes to keep a postulant waiting for some time before taking him to its bosom. For the present, there is nothing to be done. Later on, I can't say. But he must wait until the Society itself comes to seek him out. It observes with more fetishism than success the maxim *Farà da sé* of our neighbours across the Alps. Leroy-Beaulieu spoke to me about it all in a way I found highly displeasing. I should have said at a guess that he was hand in glove with your father? . . . I pointed out to him, a little sharply perhaps, that a man accustomed as he is to dealing with textiles and metals could not be expected to understand the part played by the imponderables, as Bismarck used to say. But, whatever happens, your father must on no account put himself forward as a candidate. *Principiis obsta.* His friends would find themselves placed in a delicate position if he presented them with a *fait accompli.* Indeed," he went on brusquely with an air of candour, fixing his blue eyes on my face, "I am going to tell you something that will surprise you coming from me, who am so fond of your father. Well, precisely because I am fond of him (we are known as the inseparables—*Arcades ambo*), precisely because I know the immense service that he can still render to his country, the reefs from which he can steer her if he remains at the helm; out of affection, out of high regard for him, out of patriotism, I would not vote for him. I fancy, moreover, that I have given him to understand that I wouldn't." (I seemed to discern in his eyes the stern Assyrian profile of Leroy-Beaulieu.) "So that to give him my vote now would be a sort of recantation on my part." M. de Norpois repeatedly dismissed his brother Academicians as old fossils. Other reasons apart, every member of a club or academy likes to ascribe to his fellow-members the type of character that is the direct converse of his own, less for the advantage of being able to say: "Ah! if it only rested with me!" than for the satisfaction of making the honour which he himself has managed to secure seem less accessible, a greater distinction. "I may tell you," he concluded, "that in the best interests of you all, I should prefer to see your father triumphantly elected in ten or fifteen years' time." Words which I assumed to have been dictated, if not by jealousy, at any rate by an utter lack of willingness to oblige, and which were later, in the event, to acquire a different meaning.

"You haven't thought of giving the *Institut* an address on the price of bread during the Fronde, I suppose," the historian of that movement timidly inquired of M. de Norpois. "It might be an enormous success" (which was to say, "give me a colossal advertisement"), he added, smiling at the Ambassador with an obsequious tenderness which made him raise his eyelids and reveal eyes as wide as the sky. I seemed to have seen this look before, though I had met the historian for the first time this afternoon. Suddenly I remembered having seen the same expression in the eyes of a Brazilian doctor who claimed to be able to cure breathless spasms of the kind from which I suffered by absurd inhalations of plant essences. When, in the hope that he would pay more attention to my case, I had told him that I knew Professor Cottard, he had replied, as though speaking in Cottard's interest: "Now this treatment of mine, if you were to tell him about it, would give him the material for a most sensational paper for the Academy of Medicine!" He had not ventured to press the matter but had stood gazing at me with the same air of interrogation, timid, suppliant and self-seeking, which I had just wonderingly observed on the face of the historian of the Fronde. Obviously the two men were not acquainted and had little or nothing in common, but psychological laws, like physical laws, have a more or less general application. And if the requisite conditions are the same, an identical expression lights up the eyes of different human animals, as an identical sunrise lights up places that are a long way apart and that have no connexion with one another. I did not hear the Ambassador's reply, for the whole party, with a good deal of commotion, had again gathered round Mme de Villeparisis to watch her at work.

"You know who we're talking about, Basin?" the Duchess asked her husband.

"I can make a pretty good guess," said the Duke. "As an actress she's not, I'm afraid, in what one would call the great tradition."

"You can't imagine anything more ridiculous," went on Mme de Guermantes to M. d'Argencourt.

"In fact, it was drolatic," put in M. de Guermantes, whose odd vocabulary enabled society people to declare that he was no fool and literary people, at the same time, to regard him as a complete imbecile.

"What I fail to understand," resumed the Duchess, "is how in the world Robert ever came to fall in love with her. Oh, of course I know one must never discuss that sort of thing," she added, with the charming pout of a philosopher and sentimentalist whose last illusion had long been shattered. "I know that anybody may fall in love with anybody else. And," she went on, for, though she might still make fun of modern literature, it had to some extent seeped into her, either through popularisation in the press or through certain conversations, "that is the really nice thing about love, because it's what makes it so 'mysterious.'"

"Mysterious! Oh, I must say, cousin, that's a bit beyond me," said the Comte d'Argencourt.

"Oh dear, yes, it's a very mysterious thing, love," declared the Duchess, with the sweet smile of a good-natured woman of the world, but also with the uncompromising conviction with which a Wagnerian assures a clubman that there is something more than just noise in the *Walküre*. "After all, one never does know what makes one person fall in love with another; it may not be at all what we think," she added with a smile, repudiating at once by this interpretation the idea she had just put forward. "After all, one never knows anything, does one?" she concluded with an air of weary scepticism. "So you see it's wiser never to discuss other people's choices in love."

But having laid down this principle she proceeded at once to violate it by criticising Saint-Loup's choice.

"All the same, don't you know, it's amazing to me that people can find any attraction in a ridiculous person."

Bloch, hearing Saint-Loup's name mentioned and gathering that he was in Paris, began to slander him so outrageously that everybody was shocked. He was beginning to nourish hatreds, and one felt that he would stop at nothing to gratify them. Having established the principle that he himself was of great moral integrity and that the sort of people who frequented La Boulie (a sporting-club which he supposed to be highly fashionable) deserved penal servitude, he regarded every injury he could do to them as praiseworthy. He once went so far as to threaten to bring a lawsuit against one of his La Boulie friends. In the course of the trial he proposed to give certain evidence which would be entirely false, though the defendant would be unable to disprove it. In this way Bloch (who never in fact put his plan into action) counted on tormenting and alarming him still further. What harm could there be in that, since the man he sought to injure was a man who was interested only in fashion, a La Boulie man, and against people like that any weapon was justified, especially in the hands of a saint such as Bloch himself?

"I say, though, what about Swann?" objected M. d'Argencourt, who having at last succeeded in grasping the point of his cousin's remarks, was impressed by their shrewdness and was racking his brains for instances of men who had fallen in love with women in whom he himself would have seen no attraction.

"Oh, but Swann's case was quite different," the Duchess protested. "It was a great surprise, I admit, because she was a bit of an idiot, but she was never ridiculous, and she was at one time pretty."

"Pooh!" muttered Mme de Villeparisis.

"You didn't find her pretty? Surely, she had some charming points, very fine eyes, good hair, and she used to dress and still dresses wonderfully. Nowadays, I quite agree, she's unspeakable, but she has been a lovely woman in her time. Not that that made me any less sorry when Charles married her, because it was so unnecessary."

The Duchess had not intended to say anything out of the common, but as M. d'Argencourt began to laugh she repeated these last words—either because she thought them amusing or because she thought it nice of him to laugh—and looked up at him with a caressing smile, to add the enchantment of her femininity to that of her wit. She went on:

"Yes, really, it wasn't worth the trouble, was it? Still, after all, she did have some charm and I can quite understand why people might fall for her, but if you saw Robert's young lady, I assure you

you'd simply die laughing. Oh, I know somebody's going to quote Augier at me: 'What matters the bottle so long as one gets drunk?'[20] Well, Robert may have got drunk all right, but he certainly hasn't shown much taste in his choice of a bottle! First of all, would you believe it, she actually expected me to fit up a staircase right in the middle of my drawing-room. Oh, a mere nothing—what?—and she announced that she was going to lie flat on her stomach on the steps. And then, if you'd heard the things she recited! I only remember one scene, but I'm sure nobody could imagine anything like it: it was called *The Seven Princesses*."

"*Seven Princesses*! Dear, dear, what a snob she must be!" cried M. d'Argencourt. "But, wait a minute, why, I know the whole play. The author sent a copy to the King, who couldn't understand a word of it and called on me to explain it to him."

"It isn't, by any chance, by Sâr Péladan?" asked the historian of the Fronde, meaning to make a subtle and topical illusion, but in such a low voice that his question passed unnoticed.

"So you know *The Seven Princesses*, do you?" said the Duchess. "I congratulate you! I only know one, but she's quite enough; I have no wish to make the acquaintance of the other six. If they're all like the one I've seen!"

"What a goose!" I thought to myself, irritated by her icy greeting. I found a sort of bitter satisfaction in this proof of her total incomprehension of Maeterlinck. "To think that's the woman I walk miles every morning to see. Really, I'm too kind. Well, it's my turn now to ignore her." Those were the words I said to myself, but they were the opposite of what I thought; they were purely conversational words such as we say to ourselves at those moments when, too excited to remain quietly alone with ourselves, we feel the need, for want of another listener, to talk to ourselves, without meaning what we say, as we talk to a stranger.

"I can't tell you what it was like," the Duchess went on. "It was enough to make you howl with laughter. Most people did, rather too much, I'm sorry to say, for the young person was not at all pleased and Robert has never really forgiven me. Though I can't say I'm sorry, actually, because if it had been a success the lady would perhaps have come again, and I don't think Marie-Aynard would have been exactly thrilled."

Marie-Aynard was the name given in the family to Robert's mother, Mme de Marsantes, the widow of Aynard de Saint-Loup, to distinguish her from her cousin, the Princesse de Guermantes-

Bavière, also a Marie, to whose Christian name her nephews and cousins and brothers-in-law added, to avoid confusion, either that of her husband or another of her own, making her Marie-Gilbert or Marie-Hedwige.

"To begin with, there was a sort of rehearsal the night before, which was a wonderful affair!" went on Mme de Guermantes in ironical pursuit of her theme. "Just imagine, she uttered a sentence, no, not so much, not a quarter of a sentence, and then she stopped; after which she didn't open her mouth—I'm not exaggerating—for a good five minutes."

"Oh, I say," cried M. d'Argencourt.

"With the utmost politeness I took the liberty of suggesting to her that this might seem a little unusual. And she said—I give you her actual words—'One ought always to recite a thing as though one were just composing it oneself.' It's really monumental, that reply, when you come to think of it!"

"But I understood she wasn't at all bad at reciting poetry," said one of the two young men.

"She hasn't the ghost of a notion what poetry is," replied Mme de Guermantes. "However, I didn't need to listen to her to tell that. It was quite enough to see her arriving with her lilies. I knew at once that she couldn't have any talent when I saw those lilies!"

Everybody laughed.

"I hope, my dear aunt, you weren't annoyed by my little joke the other day about the Queen of Sweden. I've come to ask your forgiveness."

"Oh, no, I'm not at all angry, I even give you leave to eat at my table, if you're hungry.—Come along, M. Vallenères, you're the daughter of the house," Mme de Villeparisis went on to the archivist, repeating a time-honoured pleasantry.

M. de Guermantes sat up in the armchair into which he had sunk, his hat on the carpet by his side, and examined with a satisfied smile the plate of cakes that was being held out to him.

"Why, certainly, now that I'm beginning to feel at home in this distinguished company, I will take a sponge-cake; they look excellent."

"This gentleman makes you an admirable daughter," commented M. d'Argencourt, whom the spirit of imitation prompted to keep Mme de Villeparisis's little joke in circulation.

The archivist handed the plate of cakes to the historian of the Fronde.

"You perform your functions admirably," said the latter, startled into speech, and hoping also to win the sympathy of the crowd. At the same time he cast a covert glance of connivance at those who had anticipated him.

"Tell me, my dear aunt," M. de Guermantes inquired of Mme de Villeparisis, "who was that rather handsome-looking gentleman who was leaving just now as I came in? I must know him, because he gave me a sweeping bow, but I couldn't place him at all; you know I never can remember names, it's such a nuisance," he added with a self-satisfied air.

"M. Legrandin."

"Oh, but Oriane has a cousin whose mother, if I'm not mistaken, was a Grandin. Yes, I remember quite well, she was a Grandin de l'Eprevier."

"No," replied Mme de Villeparisis, "no relation at all. These are plain Grandins. Grandins of nothing at all. But they'd be only too glad to be Grandins of anything you choose to name. This one has a sister called Mme de Cambremer."

"Why, Basin, you know quite well who my aunt means," cried the Duchess indignantly. "He's the brother of that great graminivorous creature you had the weird idea of sending to call on me the other day. She stayed a solid hour; I thought I'd go mad. But I began by thinking it was she who was mad when I saw a person I didn't know come browsing into the room looking exactly like a cow."

"Look here, Oriane; she asked me what afternoon you were at home; I couldn't very well be rude to her; and besides, you do exaggerate so, she's not in the least like a cow," he added in a plaintive tone, though not without a furtive smiling glance round the audience.

He knew that his wife's conversational zest needed the stimulus of contradiction, the contradiction of common sense which protests that one cannot, for instance, mistake a woman for a cow. It was in this way that Mme de Guermantes, improving on a preliminary notion, had been inspired to produce many of her wittiest sallies. And the Duke would come forward with feigned naïvety to help her to bring off her effects, like the unacknowledged partner of a three-card trickster in a railway carriage.

"I admit she doesn't look like *a* cow, she looks like several," exclaimed Mme de Guermantes. "I assure you, I didn't know what to do when I saw a herd of cattle come marching into my

drawing-room in a hat and asking me how I was. I had half a mind
to say: 'Please, herd of cattle, you must be making a mistake, you
can't possibly know me, because you're a herd of cattle,' but after
racking my brains I came to the conclusion that your Cambremer
woman must be the Infanta Dorothea, who had said she was
coming to see me one day and who is rather bovine too, so that
I was just on the point of saying 'Your Royal Highness' and using
the third person to a herd of cattle. She's also got the same sort of
dewlap as the Queen of Sweden. But actually this mass attack had
been prepared for by long-range artillery fire, according to all the
rules of war. For I don't know how long before, I was bombarded
with her cards; I used to find them lying about all over the house,
on all the tables and chairs, like prospectuses. I couldn't think what
they were supposed to be advertising. You saw nothing in the
house but 'Marquis and Marquise de Cambremer' with
some address or other which I've forgotten and which you may
be quite sure I shall never make use of."

"But it's very flattering to be taken for a queen," said the
historian of the Fronde.

"Good God, sir, kings and queens don't amount to much these
days," said M. de Guermantes, partly because he liked to be
thought broad-minded and modern, and also so as not to seem
to attach any importance to his own royal connexions, which he
valued highly.

Bloch and M. de Norpois had risen and were now in our
vicinity.

"Well, Monsieur," asked Mme de Villeparisis, "have you been
talking to him about the Dreyfus case?"

M. de Norpois raised his eyes to the ceiling, but with a smile, as
though calling on heaven to witness the enormity of the whims to
which his Dulcinea compelled him to submit. Nevertheless he
spoke to Bloch with great affability of the terrible, perhaps fatal
period through which France was passing. As this presumably
meant that M. de Norpois (to whom Bloch had confessed his
belief in the innocence of Dreyfus) was an ardent anti-Dreyfusard,
the Ambassador's geniality, his air of tacit admission that his interlocutor was in the right, of never doubting that they were both of
the same opinion, of joining forces with him to denounce the
Government, flattered Bloch's vanity and aroused his curiosity.
What were the important points which M. de Norpois never
specified but on which he seemed implicitly to affirm that he

was in agreement with Bloch? What opinion did he hold of the case that could bring them together? Bloch was all the more astonished at the mysterious unanimity which seemed to exist between him and M. de Norpois, in that it was not confined to politics, Mme de Villeparisis having spoken at some length to M. de Norpois of Bloch's literary work.

"You are not of your age," the former Ambassador told him, "and I congratulate you upon that. You are not of this age in which disinterested work no longer exists, in which writers offer the public nothing but obscenities or inanities. Efforts such as yours ought to be encouraged, and would be if we had a Government."

Bloch was flattered by this picture of himself swimming alone amid a universal shipwreck. But here again he would have been glad of details, would have liked to know what were the inanities to which M. de Norpois referred. Bloch had the feeling that he was working along the same lines as plenty of others; he had never supposed himself to be so exceptional. He returned to the Dreyfus case, but did not succeed in disentangling M. de Norpois's own views. He tried to induce him to speak of the officers whose names were appearing constantly in the newspapers at that time; they aroused more curiosity than the politicians who were involved in the affair, because they were not, like the politicians, well known already, but, wearing a special garb, emerging from the obscurity of a different kind of life and a religiously guarded silence, had only just appeared on the scene and spoken, like Lohengrin landing from a skiff drawn by a swan. Bloch had been able, thanks to a Nationalist lawyer of his acquaintance, to secure admission to several hearings of the Zola trial. He would arrive there in the morning and stay until the court rose, with a supply of sandwiches and a flask of coffee, as though for the final examination for a degree, and this change of routine stimulating a nervous excitement which the coffee and the emotional interest of the trial worked up to a climax, he would come away so enamoured of everything that had happened in court that when he returned home in the evening he longed to immerse himself again in the thrilling drama and would hurry out to a restaurant frequented by both parties in search of friends with whom he would go over the day's proceedings interminably and make up, by a supper ordered in an imperious tone which gave him the illusion of power, for the hunger and exhaustion of a day begun so early and unbroken by any interval for lunch. The human mind, hovering perpetually between the two planes of experience and imagination, seeks to fathom the ideal life of the people it knows and to know the people whose life it has had to imagine. To Bloch's questions M. de Norpois replied:

"There are two officers in the case now being tried of whom I remember hearing some time ago from a man whose judgment inspired me with the greatest confidence, and who had a high opinion of them both—I mean M. de Miribel. They are Lieutenant-Colonel Henry and Lieutenant-Colonel Picquart."

"But," exclaimed Bloch, "the divine Athena, daughter of Zeus, has put in the mind of each the opposite of what is in the mind of the other. And they are fighting against one another like two lions. Colonel Picquart had a splendid position in the Army, but his Moira has led him to the side that was not rightly his. The sword of the Nationalists will carve his tender flesh, and he will be cast out as food for the beasts of prey and the birds that feed on the fat of dead men."

M. de Norpois made no reply.

"What are those two palavering about over there?" M. de Guermantes asked Mme de Villeparisis, pointing to M. de Norpois and Bloch.

"The Dreyfus case."

"The devil they are. By the way, do you know who is a rabid supporter of Dreyfus? I give you a thousand guesses. My nephew Robert! I can tell you that when they heard of his goings-on at the Jockey there was a fine gathering of the clans, a regular outcry. And as he's coming up for election next week . . . "

"Of course," broke in the Duchess, "if they're all like Gilbert, who's always maintained that all the Jews ought to be sent back to Jerusalem . . . "

"Ah! then the Prince de Guermantes is quite of my way of thinking," put in M. d'Argencourt.

The Duke showed off his wife, but did not love her. Extremely self-important, he hated to be interrupted, and was moreover in the habit of being rude to her at home. Quivering with the twofold rage of a bad husband when his wife speaks to him, and a glib talker when he is not listened to, he stopped short and transfixed the Duchess with a glare which made everyone feel uncomfortable.

"What makes you think we want to hear about Gilbert and Jerusalem?" he said at last. "That's got nothing to do with it. But," he went on in a gentler tone, "you must admit that if one of our family were to be blackballed at the Jockey, especially Robert whose father was president for ten years, it would be the limit. What do you expect, my dear, it's caught 'em on the raw, those-fellows, it made them roll their eyes. I don't blame them, either; personally, you know that I have no racial prejudice, all that sort of thing seems to me out of date, and I do claim to move with the times; but damn it all, when one goes by the name of Marquis de Saint-Loup one isn't a Dreyfusard. I'm sorry, but there it is."

M. de Guermantes uttered the words "when one goes by the name of Marquis de Saint-Loup" with some emphasis. And yet he knew very well that it was a far greater thing to go by that of Duc de Guermantes. But if his self-esteem had a tendency to exaggerate if anything the superiority of the title Duc de Guermantes over all others, it was perhaps not so much the rules of good taste as the laws of imagination that prompted him thus to diminish it. Each of us sees in brighter colours what he sees at a distance, what he sees in other people. For the general laws which govern perspective in imagination apply just as much to dukes as to ordinary mortals. And not only the laws of imagination, but those of speech. Now, one or other of two laws of speech might apply here. One of them demands that we should express ourselves like others of our mental category and not of our caste. Under this law M. de Guermantes might, in his choice of expressions, even when he wished to talk about the nobility, be indebted to the humblest little tradesman, who would have said: "When one goes by the name of Duc de Guermantes," whereas an educated man, a Swann, a Legrandin, would not have said it. A duke may write novels worthy of a grocer, even about life in high society, titles and pedigrees being of no help to him there, and the writings of a plebeian may deserve the epithet "aristocratic." Who in this instance had been the inferior from whom M. de Guermantes had picked up "when one goes by the name," he had probably not the least idea. But another law of speech is that, from time to time, as diseases appear and then vanish of which nothing more is ever heard, there come into being, no one knows how, spontaneously perhaps or by an accident like that which introduced into France a certain weed from America the seeds of which, caught in the wool of a travel-ling rug, fell on a railway embankment, modes of expression which one hears in the same decade on the lips of people who have not in any way combined together to that end. So, just as in a certain year I heard Bloch say, referring to himself, that "the most charming people, the most brilliant, the best known, the most exclusive had discovered that there was only one man in Paris whom they felt to be intelligent and agreeable, whom they could not do without—namely Bloch," and heard the same remark used by countless other young men who did not know him and varied it only by substituting their own names for his, so I was often to hear this "when one goes by the name."

"What do you expect," the Duke went on, "with the attitude he's adopted, it's fairly understandable."

"It's more comic than anything else," said the Duchess, "when you think of his mother's attitude, how she bores us to tears with her *Patrie française*, morning, noon and night."

"Yes, but there's not only his mother to be thought of, you can't humbug us like that. There's a wench, a bed-hopper of the worst type; she has far more influence over him than his mother, and she happens to be a compatriot of Master Dreyfus. She has infected Robert with her way of thinking."

"You may not have heard, Duke, that there is a new word to describe that sort of attitude," said the archivist, who was Secretary to the Committee against Reconsideration. "One says 'mentality.' It means exactly the same thing, but it has the advantage that nobody knows what you're talking about. It's the *ne plus ultra* just now, the 'latest thing,' as they say."

Meanwhile, having heard Bloch's name, he watched him question M. de Norpois with misgivings which aroused others as strong though of a different order in the Marquise. Trembling before the archivist, and always acting the anti-Dreyfusard in his presence, she dreaded what he would say were he to find out that she had asked to her house a Jew more or less affiliated to the "Syndicate."[21]

"Indeed," said the Duke, "'mentality,' you say. I must make a note of that and trot it out one of these days." (This was no figure of speech, the Duke having a little pocket-book filled with "quotations" which he used to consult before dinner-parties.) "I like 'mentality.' There are a lot of new words like that which people suddenly start using, but they never last. Some time ago I read that a writer was 'talentuous.' Damned if I know what it means. And since then I've never come across the word again."

"But 'mentality' is more widely used than 'talentuous,'" the historian of the Fronde put in his oar. "I'm on a committee at the Ministry of Education where I've heard it used several times, as well as at my club, the Volney, and even at dinner at M. Emile Ollivier's."

"I who have not the honour to belong to the Ministry of Education," replied the Duke with a feigned humility but with a vanity so intense that his lips could not refrain from curving in a smile, nor his eyes from casting round his audience a glance sparkling with joy, the ironical scorn in which made the poor historian blush, "I who have not the honour to belong to the Ministry of Education," he repeated, relishing the sound of his own voice, "nor to the Volney Club. My only clubs are the Union and the Jockey—you aren't in the Jockey, I think, sir?" he asked the historian, who, reddening still further, scenting an insult and failing to understand it, began to tremble in every limb. "I who am not even invited to dine with M. Emile Ollivier, I must confess that I had never heard 'mentality.' I'm sure you're in the same boat, Argencourt... You know," he went on, "why they can't produce the proofs of Dreyfus's guilt. Apparently it's because he's the lover of the War Minister's wife, that's what people are saying on the sly."

"Ah! I thought it was the Prime Minister's wife," said M. d'Argencourt.

"I think you're all equally tiresome about this wretched case," said the Duchesse de Guermantes, who, in the social sphere, was always anxious to show that she did not allow herself to be led by anyone. "It can't make any difference to me so far as the Jews are concerned, for the simple reason that I don't know any of them and I intend to remain in that state of blissful ignorance. But on the other hand I do think it perfectly intolerable that just because they're supposed to be right-thinking and don't deal with Jewish tradesmen, or have 'Down with the Jews' written on their sunshades, we should have a swarm of Durands and Dubois and so forth, women we should never have known but for this business, forced down our throats by Marie-Aynard or Victurnienne. I went to see Marie-Aynard a couple of days ago. It used to be so nice there. Nowadays one finds all the people one has spent one's life trying to avoid, on the pretext that they're against Dreyfus, and others of whom you have no idea who they can be."

"No, it was the War Minister's wife; at least, that's the talk of the coffee-houses," went on the Duke, who liked to flavour his conversation with certain expressions which he imagined to be of the old school. "Personally, of course, as everyone knows, I take just the opposite view to my cousin Gilbert. I'm not feudal like him, I'd go about with a negro if he was a friend of mine, and I shouldn't care two straws what anybody thought; still, after all you must agree with me that when one goes by the name of Saint-Loup one doesn't amuse oneself by flying in the face of public opinion, which has more sense than Voltaire or even my nephew. Nor does one go in for what I may be allowed to call these acrobatics of conscience a week before one comes up for a club. It really is a bit stiff! No, it's probably that little tart of his who worked him up to it. I expect she told him he would be classed among the 'intellectuals.' The intellectuals, that's the shibboleth of those gentlemen. It's given rise, by the way, to a rather amusing pun, though a very naughty one."

And the Duke murmured, lowering his voice, for his wife's and M. d'Argencourt's benefit, "Mater Semita," which had already made its way into the Jockey Club, for, of all the flying seeds in the world, that to which are attached the most solid wings, enabling it to be disseminated at the greatest distance from its point of origin, is still a joke.

"We might ask this gentleman, who has a *nerudite* air, to explain it to us," he went on, pointing to the historian. "But it's better not to repeat it, especially as there's not a vestige of truth in the suggestion. I'm not so ambitious as my cousin Mirepoix, who claims that she can trace the descent of her family before Christ to the Tribe of Levi, and I'll guarantee to prove that there has never been a drop of Jewish blood in our family. Still it's no good shutting our eyes to the fact that my dear nephew's charming views are liable to make a considerable stir in Landerneau. Especially as Fezensac is ill just now, and Duras will be running the election; you know how he likes to draw the longbow," concluded the Duke, who had never succeeded in learning the exact meaning of certain phrases, and supposed drawing the long-bow to mean making complications.

"In any case, if this man Dreyfus is innocent," the Duchess broke in, "he hasn't done much to prove it. What idiotic, turgid letters he writes from his island! I don't know whether M. Esterhazy is any better, but at least he has more of a knack of phrase-making, a different tone altogether. That can't be very welcome to the supporters of M. Dreyfus. What a pity for them that they can't swap innocents."

Everyone burst out laughing. "Did you hear what Oriane said?" the Duc de Guermantes inquired eagerly of Mme de Villeparisis. "Yes, I thought it most amusing." This was not enough for the Duke: "Well, I don't know, I can't say that I thought it amusing; or rather it doesn't make the slightest difference to me whether a thing is amusing or not. I set no store by wit." M. d'Argencourt protested. "He doesn't believe a word he says," murmured the Duchess. "It's probably because I've been a Member of Parliament, where I've listened to brilliant speeches that meant absolutely nothing. I learned there to value logic more than anything else. That's probably why I wasn't re-elected. Amusing things leave me cold." "Basin, don't play the humbug like that, my sweet, you know quite well that no one admires wit more than you do." "Please let me finish. It's precisely because I'm unmoved by a certain type of humour that I appreciate my wife's wit. For you will find it based, as a rule, upon sound observation. She reasons like a man; she expresses herself like a writer."

Meanwhile Bloch was trying to pin M. de Norpois down on Colonel Picquart.

"There can be no question," replied M. de Norpois, "that the Colonel's evidence became necessary if only because the Government felt that there might well be something in the wind. I am well aware that, by maintaining this attitude, I have drawn shrieks of protest from more than one of my colleagues, but to my mind the Government were bound to let the Colonel speak. One can't get out of that sort of fix simply by performing a pirouette, or if one does there's always the risk of falling into a quagmire. As for the officer himself, his statement made a most excellent impression at the first hearing. When one saw him, looking so well in that smart Chasseur uniform, come into court and relate in a perfectly simple and frank tone what he had seen and what he had deduced, and say: 'On my honour as a soldier'" (here M. de Norpois's voice shook with a faint patriotic throb) "'such is my conviction,' it is impossible to deny that the impression he made was profound."

"There, he's a Dreyfusard, there's not the least doubt of it," thought Bloch.

"But where he entirely forfeited all the sympathy that he had managed to attract was when he was confronted with the registrar, Gribelin. When one heard that old public servant, a man of his word if ever there was one" (here M. de Norpois began to accentuate his words with the energy of sincere conviction), "when one saw him look his superior officer in the face, not afraid to hold his head up to him, and say to him in an unanswerable tone: 'Come, come, Colonel, you know very well that I have never told a lie, you know that at this moment, as always, I am speaking the truth,' the wind changed; M. Picquart might move heaven and earth at the subsequent hearings, but he came completely to grief."

"No, he's definitely an anti-Dreyfusard; it's quite obvious," said Bloch to himself. "But if he considers Picquart a traitor and a liar, how can he take his revelations seriously, and quote them as if he found them charming and believed them to be sincere? And if, on the other hand, he sees him as an honest man unburdening his conscience, how can he suppose him to have been lying when he was confronted with Gribelin?"

Perhaps the reason why M. de Norpois spoke thus to Bloch as though they were in agreement arose from the fact that he himself was so keen an anti-Dreyfusard that, finding the Government not anti-Dreyfusard enough, he was its enemy just as much as the Dreyfusards were. Perhaps it was because the object to which he devoted himself in politics was something more profound, situated on another plane, from which Dreyfusism appeared as an unimportant issue which did not deserve the attention of a patriot interested in large questions of foreign policy. Perhaps, rather, it was because, the maxims of his political wisdom being applicable only to questions of form, of procedure, of expediency, they were as powerless to solve questions of fact as, in philosophy, pure logic is powerless to tackle the problems of existence; or else because that very wisdom made him see danger in handling such subjects and so, in his caution, he preferred to speak only of minor circumstances. But where Bloch was mistaken was in assuming that M. de Norpois, even had he been less cautious by nature and of a less exclusively formal cast of mind, could, if he had wished, have told him the truth as to the part played by Henry, Picquart or du Paty de Clam, or as to any of the different aspects of the case. For Bloch had no doubt that M. de Norpois knew the truth as to all these matters. How could he fail to know it, seeing that he was a friend of all the ministers? Naturally, Bloch thought that the truth in politics could be approximately reconstructed by the most lucid minds, but he imagined, like the man in the street, that it resided permanently, beyond the reach of argument and in a material form, in the secret files of the President of the Republic and the Prime Minister, who imparted it to the Cabinet. Whereas, even when a political truth is enshrined in written documents, it is seldom that these have any more value than a radiographic plate on which the layman imagines that the patient's disease is inscribed in so many words, whereas in fact the plate furnishes simply one piece of material for study, to be combined with a number of others on which the doctor's reasoning powers will be brought to bear and on which he will base his diagnosis. Thus the truth in politics, when one goes to well-informed men and imagines that one is about to grasp it, eludes one. Indeed, later on (to confine ourselves to the Dreyfus case), when so startling an event occurred as Henry's confession, followed by his suicide, this fact was at once interpreted in opposite ways by the Dreyfusard ministers and by Cavaignac and Cuignet who had themselves made the discovery of the forgery and conducted the interrogation; more remarkable still, among the Dreyfusard ministers themselves, men of the same shade of opinion, judging not only from the same documents but in the same spirit, the part played by Henry was explained in two entirely opposite ways, one set seeing in him an accomplice of Esterhazy, the others assigning that role to du Paty de Clam, thus adopting a thesis of their opponent Cuignet and in complete opposition to their supporter Reinach. All that Bloch could elicit from M. de Norpois was that if it were true that the Chief of the General Staff, General de Boisdeffre, had had a secret communication sent to M. Rochefort, it was evident that a singularly regrettable irregularity had occurred.

"You may be quite sure that the War Minister must (*in petto* at any rate) have called down every curse on his Chief of Staff. An official disclaimer would not have been (to my mind) a work of supererogation. But the War Minister expresses himself very bluntly on the matter *inter pocula*. There are certain subjects, moreover, about which it is highly imprudent to create an agitation over which one cannot afterwards retain control."

"But those documents are obviously fake," said Bloch.

M. de Norpois made no reply to this, but declared that he did not approve of the public demonstrations of Prince Henri d'Orléans:[22]

"Besides, they can only ruffle the calm of the praetorium, and encourage disturbances which, looked at from either point of view, would be deplorable. Certainly we must put a stop to the anti-militarist intrigues, but neither can we tolerate a brawl encouraged by those elements on the Right who instead of serving the patriotic ideal themselves are hoping to make it serve them. Heaven be praised, France is not a South American replica, and the need has not yet been felt here for a military pronunciamento."

Bloch could not get him to pronounce on the question of Dreyfus's guilt, nor would he utter any forecast as to the judgment in the civil trial then proceeding. On the other hand, M. de Norpois seemed only too ready to expatiate on the consequences of the verdict.

"If it is a conviction," he said, "it will probably be quashed, for it is seldom that, in a case where there has been such a number of witnesses, there is not some flaw in the procedure which counsel can raise on appeal. To return to Prince Henri's outburst, I greatly doubt whether it met with his father's approval."

"You think Chartres is for Dreyfus?" asked the Duchess with a smile, her eyes rounded, her cheeks bright, her nose buried in her plate of petits fours, her whole manner deliciously scandalised.

"Not at all. I meant only that there runs through the whole family, on that side, a political sense of which we have seen the *ne plus ultra* in the admirable Princess Clémentine, and which her son, Prince Ferdinand, has kept as a priceless inheritance. You would never have found the Prince of Bulgaria clasping Major Esterhazy to his bosom."

"He would have preferred a private soldier," murmured Mme de Guermantes, who often met the Bulgarian at dinner at the Prince de Joinville's, and had said to him once, when he asked if she was not jealous: "Yes, Your Highness, of your bracelets."

"You aren't going to Mme de Sagan's ball this evening?" M. de Norpois asked Mme de Villeparisis, to cut short his conversation with Bloch.

The latter had made a not unpleasing impression on the Ambassador, who told us afterwards, with some naïvety, thinking no doubt of the traces that survived in Bloch's speech of the neo-Homeric manner which he had on the whole outgrown: "He is quite amusing, with his old-fashioned, rather solemn way of speaking. You expect him to come out with 'the Learned Sisters,' like Lamartine or Jean-Baptiste Rousseau. It has become quite rare in the youth of the present day, as it was indeed in the generation before them. We ourselves were inclined to be a bit romantic." But however interesting his interlocutor may have seemed to him, M. de Norpois considered that the conversation had lasted long enough.

"No, I don't go to balls any more," Mme de Villeparisis replied with a charming grandmotherly smile. "You're going, all of you, I suppose? You're the right age for that sort of thing," she added, embracing in a comprehensive glance M. de Châtellerault, his friend and Bloch. "I was asked too," she went on, coyly pretending to be flattered by the distinction. "In fact, they came specially to invite me." ("They" being the Princesse de Sagan.)

"I haven't had a card," said Bloch, thinking that Mme de Villeparisis would at once offer to procure him one, and that Mme de Sagan would be happy to welcome the friend of a woman on whom she had called in person to invite.

The Marquise made no reply, and Bloch did not press the point, for he had another, more serious matter to discuss with her, and, with that in view, had already asked her whether he might call again in a couple of days. Having heard the two young men say that they had both just resigned from the Rue Royale Club, which was letting in every Tom, Dick and Harry, he wished to ask Mme de Villeparisis to arrange for his election there.

"Aren't they rather bad form, rather stuck-up snobs, these Sagans?" he inquired in a sarcastic tone of voice.

"Not at all, they're the best we can do for you in that line," replied M. d'Argencourt, who adopted all the witticisms of Parisian society.

"Then," said Bloch, still half in irony, "I suppose it's one of the solemnities, the great social fixtures of the season."

Mme de Villeparisis turned merrily to Mme de Guermantes:

"Tell us, is it a great social solemnity, Mme de Sagan's ball?"

"It's no good asking me," answered the Duchess, "I have never yet succeeded in finding out what a social solemnity is. Besides, society isn't my forte."

"Oh, I thought it was just the opposite," said Bloch, who supposed Mme de Guermantes to have spoken seriously.

He continued, to the desperation of M. de Norpois, to ply him
with questions about the Dreyfus case. The Ambassador declared
that at first sight Colonel du Paty de Clam gave him the impression
of a somewhat woolly mind, which had perhaps not been very
happily chosen to conduct that delicate operation, which required
so much coolness and discernment, a judicial inquiry.

"I know that the Socialist Party are clamouring for his head on a
charger, as well as for the immediate release of the prisoner from
Devil's Island. But I trust that we are not yet reduced to the
necessity of going through the Caudine Forks of MM. Gérault-
Richard and company. So far, there's no making head or tail of the
case. I don't say that on both sides there isn't some pretty dirty
work to be hushed up. That certain of your client's more or less
disinterested patrons may have the best intentions I will not
attempt to deny. But you know that hell is paved with such
things," he added, with a look of great subtlety. "The great thing
is that the Government should make it clear that it is no more in
the hands of the factions of the Left than it is prepared to surrender,
bound hand and foot, to the demands of some praetorian guard or
other which, believe me, is not the same thing as the Army. It goes
without saying that, should any fresh evidence come to light, a
new trial would be ordered. It's as plain as a pikestaff; to demand
that is to push at an open door. When that day comes the
Government will speak out loud and clear—otherwise it would
forfeit what is its essential prerogative. Cock and bull stories will
no longer suffice. We must appoint judges to try Dreyfus. And that
will be an easy matter because, although we have acquired the
habit in our beloved France, where we love to speak ill of ourselves, of thinking or letting it be thought that in order to hear the
words Truth and Justice it is necessary to cross the Channel, which
is very often only a roundabout way of reaching the Spree, there
are judges to be found outside Berlin. But once the machinery of
Government has been set in motion, will you have ears for the
voice of authority? When it bids you perform your duty as a
citizen will you take your stand in the ranks of law and order?
When its patriotic appeal sounds, will you have the wisdom not to
turn a deaf ear but to answer: 'Present!'?"

M. de Norpois put these questions to Bloch with a vehemence
which, while it alarmed my old school-friend, flattered him also;
for the Ambassador seemed to be addressing a whole party in
Bloch's person, to be interrogating him as though he had been

in the confidence of that party and might be held responsible for the decisions which it would adopt. "Should you fail to disarm," M. de Norpois went on without waiting for Bloch's collective answer, "should you, before even the ink has dried on the decree ordering the retrial, obeying I know not what insidious word of command, fail, I say, to disarm, and band yourselves in a sterile opposition which seems to some minds the *ultima ratio* of policy, should you retire to your tents and burn your boats, you would be doing so to your own detriment. Are you the prisoner of those who foment disorder? Have you given them pledges?" Bloch was at a loss for an answer. M. de Norpois gave him no time. "If the negative be true, as I sincerely hope and trust, and if you have a little of what seems to me to be lamentably lacking in certain of your leaders and your friends, namely political sense, then, on the day when the Criminal Court assembles, if you do not allow yourselves to be dragooned by the fishers in troubled waters, you will have won the day. I do not guarantee that the whole of the General Staff is going to get away unscathed, but it will be so much to the good if some of them at least can save their faces without putting a match to the powder-barrel. It goes without saying, of course, that it rests with the Government to pronounce judgment and to close the list—already too long—of unpunished crimes, not, certainly, at the bidding of Socialist agitators, nor yet of any obscure military rabble," he added, looking Bloch in the eyes, perhaps with the instinct that leads all Conservatives to try to win support for themselves in the enemy's camp. "Government action is not to be dictated by the highest bid, wherever it may come from. The Government is not, thank heaven, under the orders of Colonel Driant, nor, at the other end of the scale, under M. Clemenceau's. We must curb the professional agitators and prevent them from raising their heads again. France, the vast majority here in France, desires only to be allowed to work in orderly conditions. As to that, there can be no question whatever. But we must not be afraid to enlighten public opinion; and if a few sheep, of the kind our friend Rabelais knew so well, should dash headlong into the water, it would be as well to point out to them that the water in question is troubled water, that it has been troubled deliberately by an agency not within our borders, in order to conceal the dangers lurking in its depths. And the Government must not give the impression that it is emerging from its passivity under duress when it exercises the right which is essentially its own and no one else's, I mean that of setting the wheels of justice in motion. The Government will accept all your suggestions. If there should prove to have been a judicial error, it can be assured of an overwhelming majority which would give it some elbow-room."

"You, sir," said Bloch, turning to M. d'Argencourt, to whom he had been introduced with the rest of the party on that gentleman's arrival, "you are a Dreyfusard, of course. Everyone is, abroad."

"It is a question that concerns only the French themselves, don't you think?" replied M. d'Argencourt with that peculiar form of insolence which consists in ascribing to the other person an opinion which one plainly knows that he does not share since he has just expressed one directly its opposite.

Bloch coloured; M. d'Argencourt smiled, looking round the room, and if this smile, so long as it was directed at the rest of the company, was charged with malice at Bloch's expense, he tempered it with cordiality when finally it came to rest on the face of my friend, so as to deprive him of any excuse for annoyance at the words he had just heard, though those words remained just as cruel. Mme de Guermantes muttered something in M. d'Argencourt's ear which I could not catch but which must have referred to Bloch's religion, for there flitted at that moment over the face of the Duchess that expression to which one's fear of being noticed by the person one is speaking of gives a certain hesitancy and falseness mixed with the inquisitive, malicious amusement inspired by a human group to which one feels oneself to be fundamentally alien. To retrieve himself, Bloch turned to the Duc de Châtellerault. "You, Monsieur, as a Frenchman, you must be aware that people abroad are all Dreyfusards, although everyone pretends that in France we never know what is going on abroad. Anyhow, I know I can talk freely to you; Saint-Loup told me so." But the young Duke, who felt that everyone was turning against Bloch, and was a coward as people often are in society, employing a mordant and precious form of wit which he seemed, by a sort of collateral atavism, to have inherited from M. de Charlus, replied: "Forgive me, Monsieur, if I don't discuss the Dreyfus case with you; it is a subject which, on principle, I never mention except among Japhetics." Everyone smiled, except Bloch, not that he was not himself in the habit of making sarcastic references to his Jewish origin, to that side of his ancestry which came from somewhere near Sinai. But instead of one of these remarks (doubtless because he did not have one ready) the trigger of his inner mechanism brought to Bloch's lips something quite different. And all one heard was: "But how on earth did you know? Who told you?" as though he had been the son of a convict. Whereas, given his name, which had not exactly a Christian sound, and his face, his surprise argued a certain naïvety.

What M. de Norpois had said to him not having completely satisfied him, he went up to the archivist and asked him whether M. du Paty de Clam or M. Joseph Reinach were not sometimes to be seen at Mme de Villeparisis's. The archivist made no reply; he was a Nationalist, and never ceased preaching to the Marquise that the social revolution might break out at any moment, and that she ought to show more caution in the choice of her acquaintances. He wondered whether Bloch might not be a secret emissary of the Syndicate, come to collect information, and went off at once to repeat to Mme de Villeparisis the questions that Bloch had put to him. She decided that he was ill-bred at best and that he might perhaps be in a position to compromise M. de Norpois. She also wished to give satisfaction to the archivist, who was the only person she was a little afraid of, and by whom she was being indoctrinated, though without much success (every morning he read her M. Judet's article in the *Petit Journal*). She decided, therefore, to make it plain to Bloch that he need not come to the house again, and had no difficulty in choosing from her social repertory the scene by which a great lady shows someone her door, a scene which does not in the least involve the raised finger and blazing eyes that people imagine. As Bloch came up to her to say good-bye, buried in her deep armchair she seemed only half-awakened from a vague somnolence. Her filmy eyes held only the faint and charming gleam of a pair of pearls. Bloch's farewells, barely unwrinkling the Marquise's face in a languid smile, drew from her not a word, and she did not offer him her hand. This scene left Bloch in utter bewilderment, but as he was surrounded by a circle of bystanders he felt that it could not be prolonged without embarrassment to himself, and, to force the Marquise, he himself thrust out the hand which she had just refused to shake. Mme de Villeparisis was shocked. But doubtless, while still bent on giving immediate satisfaction to the archivist and the anti-Dreyfus clan, she wished at the same time to insure against the future, and so contented herself with letting her eyelids droop over her half-closed eyes.

"I think she's asleep," said Bloch to the archivist who, feeling that he had the support of the Marquise, assumed an air of indignation. "Good-bye, Madame," shouted Bloch.

The old lady made the slight movement with her lips of a dying woman who wants to open her mouth but whose eyes betray no hint of recognition. Then she turned, overflowing with restored vitality, towards M. d'Argencourt, while Bloch took himself off, convinced that she must be "soft" in the head. Full of curiosity and anxious to clear up such a strange incident, he came to see her again a few days later. She received him in the most friendly fashion, because she was a good-natured woman, because the archivist was not there, because she was keen on the little play which Bloch was to put on in her house, and finally because she had staged the appropriate *grande dame* act which was universally admired and commented upon that very evening in various drawing-rooms, but in a version that had already ceased to bear the slightest relation to the truth.

"You were speaking just now of *The Seven Princesses*, Duchess. You know (not that it's anything to be proud of) that the author of that—what shall I call it?—that object is a compatriot of mine," said M. d'Argencourt with an irony blended with the satisfaction of knowing more than anyone else in the room about the author of a work which had been under discussion. "Yes, he's a Belgian, by nationality," he went on.

"Indeed? No, we don't accuse you of any responsibility for *The Seven Princesses*. Fortunately for yourself and your compatriots you are not like the author of that absurdity. I know several charming Belgians, yourself, your King, who is a little shy but full of wit, my Ligne cousins, and heaps of others, but none of you, I'm happy to say, speak the same language as the author of *The Seven Princesses*. Besides, if you want to know, it's not worth talking about, because really there is absolutely nothing in it. You know the sort of people who are always trying to seem obscure, and don't even mind making themselves ridiculous to conceal the fact that they haven't an idea in their heads. If there was anything behind it all, I may tell you that I'm not in the least afraid of a little daring," she added in a serious tone, "provided there's a little thought. I don't know if you've seen Borelli's play. Some people seem to have been shocked by it, but I must say, even if they stone me through the streets for saying it," she went on, without stopping to think that she ran no very great risk of such a punishment, "I found it immensely interesting. But *The Seven Princesses*! One of them may have a fondness for my nephew, but I can't carry family feeling quite . . ."

The Duchess broke off abruptly, for a lady came in who was the Comtesse de Marsantes, Robert's mother. Mme de Marsantes was regarded in the Faubourg Saint-Germain as a superior being, of a goodness and resignation that were positively angelic. So I had been told, and had had no particular reason to feel surprised, not knowing at the time that she was the sister of the Duc de Guermantes. Later, I was always taken aback when I learned, in that society, that melancholy, pure, self-sacrificing women, venerated like ideal saints in stained-glass windows, had flowered from the same genealogical stem as brothers who were brutal, debauched and vile. Brothers and sisters, when they are identical in features as were the Duc de Guermantes and Mme de Marsantes, ought (I felt) to have a single intellect in common, a similar heart, like a person who may have good or bad moments but in whom nevertheless one cannot expect to find a vast breadth of outlook if his mental range is narrow or a sublime abnegation if he is hard-hearted.

Mme de Marsantes attended Brunetière's lectures. She inspired the Faubourg Saint-Germain with enthusiasm and, by her saintly life, edified it as well. But the morphological link of handsome nose and piercing gaze none the less led me to classify Mme de Marsantes in the same intellectual and moral family as her brother the Duke. I could not believe that the mere fact of her being a woman, and perhaps of her having had an unhappy life and won everyone's high opinion, could make a person so different from the rest of her family, as in the mediaeval romances where all the virtues and graces are combined in the sister of wild and lawless brothers. It seemed to me that nature, less unfettered than the old poets, must make use almost exclusively of the elements common to the family, and I was unable to credit her with enough power of invention to construct, out of materials analogous to those that composed a fool and a lout, a lofty mind without the least strain of foolishness, a saint without the least taint of brutality. Mme de Marsantes was wearing a gown of white surah embroidered with large palms, on which stood out flowers of a different material, these being black. This was because, three weeks earlier, she had lost her cousin M. de Montmorency, a bereavement which did not prevent her from paying calls or even from going to small dinners, but always in mourning. She was a great lady. Atavism had filled her with the frivolity of generations of life at court, with all the superficial and rigorous duties that that implies. Mme de Marsantes had not had the strength to mourn her father and mother for any length of time, but she would not for anything in the world have appeared in colours in the month following the death of a cousin. She was more than friendly to me, both because I was Robert's friend and because I did not move in the same world as he. This friendliness was accompanied by a pretence of shyness, by a sort of intermittent withdrawal of the voice, the eyes, the mind, as though she were drawing in a wayward skirt, so as not to take up too much room, to remain stiff and erect even in her suppleness, as good breeding demands—a good breeding that must not, however, be taken too literally, many of these ladies lapsing very swiftly into moral licentiousness without ever losing the almost childlike correctness of their manners. Mme de Marsantes was a trifle irritating in conversation since, whenever she had occasion to speak of a commoner, as for instance Bergotte or Elstir, she would say, isolating the word, giving it its full value, intoning it on two different notes with a modulation peculiar to the Guermantes: "I have had the *honour*, the great *hon*-our of meeting Monsieur Bergotte," or "of making the acquaintance of Monsieur Elstir," either in order that her hearers might marvel at her humility, or from the same tendency evinced by M. de Guermantes to revert to obsolete forms as a protest against the slovenly usages of the present day, in which people never professed themselves sufficiently "honoured." Whichever of these was the true reason, one felt that when Mme de Marsantes said: "I have had the *honour*, the great *hon*-our," she felt she was fulfilling an important role and showing that she could take in the names of distinguished men as she would have welcomed the men themselves at her country seat had they happened to be in the neighbourhood. On the other hand, as her family was large, as she was devoted to all her relations, as, slow of speech and fond of explaining things at length, she was always trying to make clear the exact degrees of kinship, she found herself (without any desire to create an effect and while genuinely preferring to talk only about touching peasants and sublime gamekeepers) referring incessantly to all the families of Europe under the suzerainty of the Holy Roman

Empire, which people less brilliantly connected than herself could not forgive her and, if they were at all intellectual, derided as a sign of stupidity.

In the country, Mme de Marsantes was adored for the good that she did, but principally because the purity of a blood-line into which for many generations there had flowed only what was greatest in the history of France had rid her manner of everything that the lower orders call "airs" and had endowed her with perfect simplicity. She never shrank from embracing a poor woman who was in trouble, and would tell her to come up to the house for a cartload of wood. She was, people said, the perfect Christian. She was determined to find an immensely rich wife for Robert. Being a great lady means playing the great lady, that is to say, to a certain extent, playing at simplicity. It is a pastime which costs a great deal of money, all the more because simplicity charms people only on condition that they know that you are capable of not living simply, that is to say that you are very rich. Someone said to me afterwards, when I mentioned that I had seen her: "You saw of course that she must have been lovely as a young woman." But true beauty is so individual, so novel always, that one does not recognise it as beauty. I said to myself that afternoon only that she had a tiny nose, very blue eyes, a long neck and a sad expression.

"By the way," said Mme de Villeparisis to the Duchesse de Guermantes, "I'm expecting a woman at any moment whom you don't wish to know. I thought I'd better warn you, to avoid any unpleasantness. But you needn't be afraid, I shall never have her here again, only I was obliged to let her come today. It's Swann's wife."

Mme Swann, seeing the dimensions that the Dreyfus case had begun to assume, and fearing that her husband's racial origin might be used against herself, had besought him never again to allude to the prisoner's innocence. When he was not present she went further and professed the most ardent nationalism; in doing which she was only following the example of Mme Verdurin, in whom a latent bourgeois anti-semitism had awakened and grown to a positive fury. Mme Swann had won by this attitude the privilege of membership in several of the anti-semitic leagues of society women that were beginning to be formed and had succeeded in establishing relations with various members of the aristocracy. It may seem strange that, so far from following their example, the Duchesse de Guermantes, so close a friend of Swann, had on the contrary always resisted the desire which he had not concealed from her to introduce his wife to her. But we shall see in due course that this was an effect of the peculiar character of the Duchess, who held that she was not "bound to" do such and such a thing, and laid down with despotic force what had been decided by her social "free will," which was extremely arbitrary.

"Thank you for warning me," said the Duchess. "It would indeed be most disagreeable. But as I know her by sight I shall be able to get away in time."

"I assure you, Oriane, she is really quite nice; an excellent woman," said Mme de Marsantes.

"I have no doubt she is, but I feel no need to assure myself of it in person."

"Have you been invited to Lady Israel's?" Mme de Villeparisis asked the Duchess, to change the subject.

"Why, thank heaven, I don't know the woman," replied Mme de Guermantes. "You must ask Marie-Aynard. She knows her. I never could make out why."

"I did indeed know her at one time," said Mme de Marsantes. "I confess my sins. But I have decided not to know her any more. It seems she's one of the very worst of them, and makes no attempt to conceal it. Besides, we have all been too trusting, too hospitable. I shall never go near anyone of that race again. While we closed our doors to old country cousins, people of our own flesh and blood, we threw them open to Jews. And now we see what thanks we get from them. But alas, I've no right to speak; I have an adorable son who, young fool that he is, goes round talking the most utter nonsense," she went on, having caught some allusion by M. d'Argencourt to Robert. "But, talking of Robert, haven't you seen him?" she asked Mme de Villeparisis. "Since it's Saturday, I thought he might have come to Paris for twenty-four hours, and in that case would have been sure to pay you a visit."

As a matter of fact Mme de Marsantes thought that her son would not obtain leave that week; but knowing that, even if he did, he would never dream of coming to see Mme de Villeparisis, she hoped, by making herself appear to have expected to find him there, to make his susceptible aunt forgive him for all the visits that he had failed to pay her.

"Robert here! But I haven't even had a word from him. I don't think I've seen him since Balbec."

"He is so busy; he has so much to do," said Mme de Marsantes.

A faint smile made Mme de Guermantes's eyelashes quiver as she studied the circle which she was tracing on the carpet with the point of her sunshade. Whenever the Duke had been too openly unfaithful to his wife, Mme de Marsantes had always taken up the cudgels against her own brother on her sister-in-law's behalf. The latter had a grateful and bitter memory of this support, and was not herself seriously shocked by Robert's pranks. At this point the door opened again and Robert himself came in.

"Well, talk of the Saint!"[23] said Mme de Guermantes.

Mme de Marsantes, who had her back to the door, had not seen her son come in. When she caught sight of him, her motherly bosom was convulsed with joy as by the beating of a wing, her body half rose from her seat, her face quivered and she fastened on Robert eyes that glowed with wonderment.

"What, you've come! How delightful! What a surprise!"

"Ah! *talk of the Saint*—I see," cried the Belgian diplomat with a shout of laughter.

"Delicious, isn't it?" the Duchess retorted curtly, for she hated puns, and had ventured this one only with a pretence of self-mockery.

"Good evening, Robert," she said. "Well, so this is how we forget our aunt."

They talked for a moment, doubtless about me, for as Saint-Loup was leaving her to join his mother Mme de Guermantes turned to me:

"Good evening, how are you?" was her greeting.

She showered me with the light of her azure gaze, hesitated for a moment, unfolded and stretched towards me the stem of her arm, and leaned forward her body which sprang rapidly backwards like a bush that has been pulled down to the ground and, on being released, returns to its natural position. Thus she acted under the fire of Saint-Loup's eyes, which kept her under observation from a distance and made frantic efforts to obtain some further concession still from his aunt. Fearing that our conversation might dry up altogether, he came across to fuel it, and answered for me:

"He's not very well just now, he gets rather tired. I think he would be a great deal better, by the way, if he saw you more often, for I don't mind telling you that he enjoys seeing you very much."

"Oh, but that's very nice of him," said Mme de Guermantes in a deliberately trite tone, as if I had brought her her coat. "I'm most flattered."

"Look, I must go and talk to my mother for a minute; take my chair," said Saint-Loup, thus forcing me to sit down next to his aunt.

We were both silent.

"I catch sight of you sometimes in the morning," she said, as though she were giving me a piece of news and as though I for my part never saw her. "It's so good for one, a walk."

"Oriane," said Mme de Marsantes in a low voice, "you said you were going on to Mme de Saint-Ferréol's. Would you be so very kind as to tell her not to expect me to dinner. I shall stay at home now that I've got Robert. And might I ask you in passing to see that someone sends out at once for a box of the cigars Robert likes? 'Corona,' they're called. I've none in the house."

Robert came up to us. He had caught only the name of Mme de Saint-Ferréol.

"Who in the world is Mme de Saint-Ferréol?" he inquired in a tone of studied surprise, for he affected ignorance of everything to do with society.

"But, my darling boy, you know perfectly well," said his mother. "She's Vermandois's sister. It was she who gave you that nice billiard table you liked so much."

"What, she's Vermandois's sister, I had no idea. Really, my family are amazing," he went on, half-turning towards me and unconsciously adopting Bloch's intonation just as he borrowed his ideas, "they know the most unheard-of people, people called Saint-Ferréol" (emphasising the final consonant of each word) "or something like that; my family go to balls, they drive in victorias, they lead a fabulous existence. It's prodigious."

Mme de Guermantes made a slight, short, sharp sound in her throat as of an involuntary laugh choked back, which was intended to show that she acknowledged her nephew's wit to the degree which kinship demanded. A servant came in to say that the Prince von Faffenheim-Munsterburg-Weinigen sent word to M. de Norpois that he had arrived.

"Go and fetch him, Monsieur," said Mme de Villeparisis to the ex-Ambassador, who set off in quest of the German Prime Minister.

"Wait, Monsieur. Do you think I ought to show him the miniature of the Empress Charlotte?"

"Why, I'm sure he'll be delighted," said the Ambassador in a tone of conviction, as though he envied the fortunate Minister the favour that was in store for him.

"Oh, I know he's very *sound*," said Mme de Marsantes, "and that is so rare among foreigners. But I've found out all about him. He's anti-semitism personified."

The Prince's name preserved, in the boldness with which its opening syllables were—to borrow an expression from music—attacked, and in the stammering repetition that scanned them, the energy, the mannered simplicity, the heavy refinements of the Teutonic race, projected like green boughs over the "Heim" of dark blue enamel which glowed with the mystic light of a Rhenish window behind the pale and finely wrought gildings of the German eighteenth century. This name included, among the several names of which it was composed, that of a little German watering-place to which as a small child I had gone with my grandmother, under a mountain honoured by the feet of Goethe, from the vineyards of which we used to drink at the Kurhof the illustrious vintages with their compound and sonorous names like the epithets which Homer applies to his heroes. And so, scarcely had I heard it spoken than, before I had recalled the watering-place, the Prince's name seemed to shrink, to become imbued with humanity, to find large enough for itself a little place in my memory to which it clung, familiar, earthbound, pictur-esque, appetising, light, with something about it that was authorised, prescribed. Furthermore, M. de Guermantes, in explaining who the Prince was, quoted a number of his titles, and I recognised the name of a village traversed by a river on which, every evening, the cure finished for the day, I used to go boating amid the mosquitoes, and that of a forest far enough away for the doctor not to allow me to make the excursion to it. And indeed it was comprehensible that the suzerainty of the noble gentleman should extend to the surrounding places and associate afresh in the enumeration of his titles the names which one could read side by side on a map. Thus beneath the visor of the Prince of the Holy Roman Empire and Knight of Franconia it was the face of a beloved, smiling land, on which the rays of the evening sun had often lingered for me, that I saw, at any rate before the Prince, Rhinegrave and Elector Palatine, had entered the room. For I speedily learned that the revenues which he drew from the forest and the river peopled with gnomes and undines, and from the magic mountain on which rose the ancient Burg that still cherished memories of Luther and Louis the German, he employed in keeping five Charron motor-cars, a house in Paris and another in London, a box on Mondays at the Opéra and another for the "Tuesdays" at the "Français." He did not seem to me to be—nor did he himself seem to believe that he was—different from other men of similar wealth and age who had a less poetic origin. He had their culture, their ideals, he was proud of his rank but purely on account of the advantages it conferred on him, and had now only one ambition in life, to be elected a corresponding member of the Academy of Moral and Political Sciences, which was the reason of his coming to see Mme de Villeparisis.

If he, whose wife was a leader of the most exclusive set in Berlin, had solicited an introduction to the Marquise, it was not the result of any desire on his part for her acquaintance. Devoured for years past by this ambition to be elected to the *Institut*, he had unfortunately never been in a position to reckon above five the number of Academicians who seemed prepared to vote for him. He knew that M. de Norpois could by himself command at least a dozen votes, a number which he was capable, by skilful negotiations, of increasing still further. And so the Prince, who had known him in Russia when they were both there as ambassadors, had gone to see him and had done everything in his power to win him over. But in vain might he intensify his friendly overtures, procure for the Marquis Russian decorations, quote him in articles on foreign policy, he had been faced with a heartless ingrate, a man in whose eyes all these attentions appeared to count as nothing, who had not advanced the prospects of his candidature one inch, had not even promised him his own vote. True, M. de Norpois received him with extreme politeness, indeed begged him not to put himself out and "take the trouble to come so far out of his way," went himself to the Prince's residence, and when the Teutonic knight had launched his: "I should very much like to be your colleague," replied in a tone of deep emotion: "Ah! I should be most happy!" And no doubt a simpleton, a Dr Cottard, would have said to himself: "Well, here he is in my house; it was he who insisted on coming because he regards me as a more important person than himself; he tells me he'd be happy to see me in the Academy; words do have some meaning after all, damn it, so if he doesn't offer to vote for me it's probably because it hasn't occurred to him. He lays so much stress on influence that he must imagine the plums fall into my lap, that I have all the support I need and that's why he doesn't offer me his; but I've only to corner him here, just the two of us, and say to him: 'Very well, vote for me,' and he'll be obliged to do it."

But Prince von Faffenheim was no simpleton. He was what Dr Cottard would have called "a shrewd diplomat" and he knew that M. de Norpois was a no less shrewd one and a man who would have realised without needing to be told that he could confer a favour on a candidate by voting for him. The Prince, in his ambassadorial missions and as Foreign Minister, had conducted, on his country's behalf instead of, as in the present instance, his own, many of those conversations in which one knows beforehand just how far one is prepared to go and at what point one will decline to commit oneself. He was not unaware that in diplomatic parlance to talk means to offer. And it was for this reason that he had arranged for M. de Norpois to receive the Order of Saint Andrew. But if he had had to report to his Government the conversation which he had subsequently had with M. de Norpois, he would have stated in his dispatch: "I realised that I had taken the wrong tack." For as soon as he had returned to the subject of the *Institut*, M. de Norpois had repeated:

"I should like nothing better; nothing could be better for my colleagues. They ought, I consider, to feel genuinely honoured that you should have thought of them. It's a really interesting candidature, a little outside our normal practice. As you know, the Academy is very hidebound; it takes fright at anything that smacks of novelty. Personally, I deplore this. How often have I not had occasion to say as much to my colleagues! I cannot be sure, God forgive me, that I did not even once let the term 'stick-in-the-mud' escape my lips," he added with a scandalised smile in an undertone, almost an aside, as though on the stage, giving the Prince a rapid, sidelong glance from his blue eyes, like a veteran actor studying an effect on his audience. "You understand, Prince, that I should not care to allow a personality so eminent as yourself to embark on a venture which was hopeless from the start. So long as my colleagues' ideas linger so far behind the times, I consider that the wiser course will be to abstain. But you may rest assured that if I were ever to discern a slightly more modern, a slightly more lively spirit emerge in that college, which is tending to become a mausoleum, if I felt you had a genuine chance of success, I should be the first to inform you of it."

"The Order was a mistake," thought the Prince; "the negotiations have not advanced one step. That's not what he wanted. I have not yet laid my hand on the right key."

This was a kind of reasoning of which M. de Norpois, formed in the same school as the Prince, would also have been capable. One may mock at the pedantic silliness which makes diplomats of the Norpois type go into ecstasies over some piece of official wording which is to all intents and purposes meaningless. But their childishness has this compensation: diplomats know that, in the scales which ensure that balance of power, European or otherwise, which we call peace, good feeling, fine speeches, earnest entreaties weigh very little; and that the heavy weight, the true determinant consists in something else, in the possibility which the adversary enjoys, if he is strong enough, or does not enjoy, of satisfying a desire in exchange for something in return. With this order of truths, which an entirely disinterested person, such as my grandmother for instance, would not have understood, M. de Norpois and Prince von Faffenheim had frequently to deal. As an envoy in countries with which we had been within an ace of going to war, M. de Norpois, in his anxiety as to the turn which events were about to take, knew very well that it was not by the word "Peace," nor by the word "War," that it would be revealed to him, but by some other, apparently commonplace word, a word of terror or blessing, which the diplomat, by the aid of his cipher, would immediately know how to interpret and to which, to safeguard the dignity of France, he would respond in another word, quite as commonplace, but one beneath which the minister of the enemy nation would at once decipher: "War." Moreover, in accordance with a time-honoured custom, analogous to that which used to give to the first meeting between two young people promised to one another in marriage the form of a chance encounter at a performance in the Théâtre du Gymnase, the dialogue in the course of which destiny was to dictate the word "War" or the word "Peace" took place, as a rule, not in the ministerial sanctum but on a bench in a Kurgarten where the minister and M. de Norpois went independently to a thermal spring to drink at its source their little tumblers of some curative water. By a sort of tacit convention they met at the hour appointed for their cure, and began by taking together a short stroll which, beneath its benign appearance, the two interlocutors knew to be as tragic as an order for mobilisation. And so, in a private matter like this nomination for election to the Institute, the Prince had employed the same system of induction which had served him in the diplomatic service, the same method of reading beneath superimposed symbols.

And certainly it would be wrong to pretend that my grand-mother and the few who resembled her would have been alone in their failure to understand this kind of calculation. For one thing, the average run of humanity, practising professions the lines of which have been laid down in advance, approximate in their lack of intuition to the ignorance which my grandmother owed to her lofty disinterestedness. Often one has to come down to "kept" persons, male or female, before one finds the hidden spring of actions or words, apparently of the most innocent nature, in self-interest, in the necessity to keep alive. What man does not know that when a woman whom he is going to pay says to him: "Don't let's talk about money," the speech must be regarded as what is called in music "a silent bar" and that if, later on, she declares: "You make me too unhappy, you're always keeping things from me; I can't stand it any longer," he must interpret this as: "Someone else has been offering her more"? And yet this is only the language of the woman of easy virtue, not so far removed from society women. The ponce furnishes more striking examples. But M. de Norpois and the German prince, if ponces and their ways were unknown to them, had been accustomed to living on the same plane as nations, which are also, for all their grandeur, creatures of selfishness and cunning, which can be tamed only by force, by consideration of their material interests which may drive them to murder, a murder that is also often symbolic, since its mere hesitation or refusal to fight may spell for a nation the word "Perish." But since all this is not set forth in the various Yellow Books or elsewhere, the people as a whole are naturally pacific; if they are warlike, it is instinctively, from hatred, from a sense of injury, not for the reasons which have made up the mind of their ruler on the advice of his Norpois.

The following winter the Prince was seriously ill. He recovered, but his heart was permanently affected.

"The devil!" he said to himself, "I can't afford to lose any time over the *Institut*. If I wait too long, I may be dead before they elect me. That really would be disagreeable."

He wrote an essay for the *Revue des Deux Mondes* on European politics over the past twenty years, in which he referred more than once to M. de Norpois in the most flattering terms. The latter called upon him to thank him. He added that he did not know how to express his gratitude. The Prince said to himself, like a man who has just tried to fit another key into a stubborn lock: "Still not the right one!" and, feeling somewhat out of breath as he showed M. de Norpois to the door, thought: "Damn it, these fellows will see me in my grave before letting me in. We must hurry up."

That evening, he met M. de Norpois again at the Opéra.

"My dear Ambassador," he said to him, "you told me this morning that you did not know how to prove your gratitude to me. It's entirely superfluous, since you owe me none, but I am going to be so indelicate as to take you at your word."

M. de Norpois had a no less high esteem for the Prince's tact than the Prince had for his. He understood at once that it was not a request that Prince von Faffenheim was about to put to him, but an offer, and with a radiant affability he made ready to hear it.

"Well now, you will think me highly indiscreet. There are two people to whom I am greatly attached—in quite different ways, as you will understand in a moment—two people both of whom have recently settled in Paris, where they intend to live henceforth: my wife, and the Grand Duchess John. They are thinking of giving a few dinners, notably in honour of the King and Queen of England, and their dream would have been to be able to offer their guests the company of a person for whom, without knowing her, they both of them feel a great admiration. I confess that I did not know how I was going to gratify their wish when I learned just now, by the merest chance, that you were a friend of this person. I know that she lives a most retired life, and sees only a very few people—*happy few*—but if you were to give me your support, with the kindness you have always shown me, I am sure that she would allow you to present me to her so that I might convey to her the wish of the Grand Duchess and the Princess. Perhaps she would consent to come to dinner with the Queen of England, and then (who knows) if we don't bore her too much, to spend the Easter holidays with us at Beaulieu, at the Grand Duchess John's. This person is called the Marquise de Villeparisis. I confess that the hope of becoming an habitué of such a school of wit would console me, would make me contemplate without regret the abandoning of my candidature for the *Institut*. For in her house, too, I understand, there is intellectual intercourse and brilliant talk."

With an inexpressible sense of pleasure the Prince felt that the lock no longer resisted and that at last the key was turning.

"Such an alternative is wholly unnecessary, my dear Prince," replied M. de Norpois. "Nothing could be more in harmony with the *Institut* than the house you speak of, which is a regular breeding-ground of academicians. I shall convey your request to Mme la Marquise de Villeparisis: she will undoubtedly be flattered. As for her dining with you, she goes out very little, and that will perhaps be more difficult to arrange. But I shall introduce you to her and you will plead your cause in person. You must on no account give up the Academy; tomorrow fortnight, as it happens, I shall be having luncheon, before going on with him to an important meeting, with Leroy-Beaulieu, without whom nobody can be elected; I had already allowed myself in conversation with him to let fall your name, with which, naturally, he was perfectly familiar. He raised certain objections. But it so happens that he requires the support of my group at the next election, and I fully intend to return to the charge; I shall tell him frankly of the extremely cordial ties that unite us, I shall not conceal from him that, if you were to stand, I should ask all my friends to vote for you" (here the Prince breathed a deep sigh of relief), "and he knows that I have friends. I consider that if I were to succeed in obtaining his co-operation, your chances would become very real. Come that evening, at six, to Mme de Villeparisis's. I will introduce you, and at the same time will be able to give you an account of my morning meeting."

Thus it was that Prince von Faffenheim had been led to call upon Mme de Villeparisis. My profound disillusionment occurred when he spoke. It had never struck me that, whereas a period has features both particular and general which are stronger than those of a nationality, so that in an illustrated dictionary which goes so far as to include an authentic portrait of Minerva, Leibniz with his periwig and his neckerchief differs little from Marivaux or Samuel Bernard, a nationality has particular features stronger than those of a caste. In the present instance these found expression not in a discourse in which I had expected to hear the rustling of the elves and the dance of the kobolds, but by a transposition which certified no less plainly that poetic origin: the fact that as he bowed, short, red-faced and portly, over the hand of Mme de

Villeparisis, the Rhinegrave said to her: "Goot-tay, Matame la Marquise," in the accent of an Alsatian concierge.

"Won't you let me give you a cup of tea or a little of this tart, it's so good?" Mme de Guermantes asked me, anxious to have shown herself as friendly as possible. "I do the honours in this house just as if it was mine," she explained in an ironical tone which gave a slightly guttural sound to her voice, as though she were trying to stifle a hoarse laugh.

"Monsieur," said Mme de Villeparisis to M. de Norpois, "you won't forget that you have something to say to the Prince about the Academy?"

Mme de Guermantes lowered her eyes and gave a semi-circular turn to her wrist to look at the time.

"Gracious! It's time I said good-bye to my aunt if I'm to get to Mme de Saint-Ferréol's, and I'm dining with Mme Leroi."

And she rose without bidding me good-bye. She had just caught sight of Mme Swann, who appeared somewhat embarrassed at finding me in the room. Doubtless she remembered that she had been the first to assure me that she was convinced of Dreyfus's innocence.

"I don't want my mother to introduce me to Mme Swann," Saint-Loup said to me. "She's an ex-whore. Her husband's a Jew, and she comes here to pose as a Nationalist. Hallo, here's my uncle Palamède."

The arrival of Mme Swann had a special interest for me, owing to an incident which had occurred a few days earlier and which it is necessary to relate because of the consequences which it was to have at a much later date and which the reader will follow in detail in due course. A few days before this visit to Mme de Villeparisis, I had myself received a visitor whom I little expected, namely Charles Morel, the son, whom I did not know, of my great-uncle's old valet. This great-uncle (he in whose house I had met the lady in pink) had died the year before. His servant had more than once expressed his intention of coming to see me; I had no idea of the object of his visit, but should have been glad to see him, for I had learned from Françoise that he had a genuine veneration for my uncle's memory and made a pilgrimage regularly to the cemetery in which he was buried. But, being obliged for reasons of health to retire to his home in the country, where he expected to remain for some time, he had delegated the duty to his son. I was surprised to see a handsome young man of eighteen come into my room, dressed expensively rather than with taste, but looking, all the same, like anything but the son of a valet. He made a point, moreover, from the start, of emphasising his aloofness from the domestic class from which he sprang, by informing me with a complacent smile that he had won a first prize at the Conservatoire. The object of his visit to me was as follows: his father on going through the effects of my uncle Adolphe, had set aside some which he felt it unseemly to send to my parents but which he considered to be of a nature to interest a young man of my age. These were photographs of the famous actresses, the notorious courtesans whom my uncle had known, the last fading pictures of that gay life of a man about town which he kept separated by a watertight compartment from his family life. While the young Morel was showing them to me, I noticed that he affected to speak to me as to an equal. He derived from saying "you" to me as often and "sir" as seldom as possible the pleasure of one whose father had never ventured, when addressing my parents, upon anything but the third person. Almost all the photographs bore an inscription such as: "To my best friend." One actress, less grateful and more circumspect than the rest, had written: "To the best of friends," which enabled her (so I have been assured) to say afterwards that my uncle was in no sense and had never been her best friend but was merely the friend who had done the most small services for her, the friend she made use of, a good, kind man, in other words an old fool. In vain might young Morel seek to divest himself of his lowly origin, one felt that the shade of my uncle Adolphe, venerable and gigantic in the eyes of the old servant, had never ceased to hover, almost a sacred vision, over the childhood and youth of the son. While I was turning over the photographs Charles Morel examined my room. And as I was looking for somewhere to put them, "How is it," he asked me (in a tone in which the reproach had no need to be emphasised, so implicit was it in the words themselves), "that I don't see a single photograph of your uncle in your room?" I felt the blood rise to my cheeks and stammered: "Why, I don't believe I have one." "What, you haven't a single photograph of your uncle Adolphe, who was so fond of you! I'll send you one of the governor's—he's got stacks of them—and I hope you'll put it in the place of honour above that chest of drawers, which incidentally came to you from your uncle." It is true that, as I had not even a photograph of my father or mother in my room, there was nothing so very shocking in there not being one of my uncle Adolphe. But it was easy enough to see that for old Morel, who had trained his son in the same way of thinking, my uncle was the important person in the family, from whom my parents derived only a dim reflected glory. I was in higher favour, because my uncle used constantly to say to his valet that I was going to turn out a sort of Racine, or Vaulabelle, and Morel regarded me almost as an adopted son, as a favourite child of my uncle. I soon discovered that Morel's son was extremely "go-getting." Thus at this first meeting he asked me, being something of a composer as well and capable of setting short poems to music, whether I knew any poet who had a good position in "aristo" society. I mentioned one. He did not know the work of this poet and had never heard his name, of which he made a note. And I was to discover that shortly afterwards he wrote to the poet telling him that, being a fanatical admirer of his work, he, Morel, had composed a musical setting for one of his sonnets and would be grateful if the author would arrange for its performance at the Comtesse So-and-so's. This was going a little too fast and exposing his hand. The poet, taking offence, made no reply.

For the rest, Charles Morel seemed to possess, besides ambition, a strong leaning towards more concrete realities. He had noticed, as he came through the courtyard, Jupien's niece at work upon a waistcoat, and although he explained to me only that he happened to want a fancy waistcoat at that very moment, I felt that the girl had made a vivid impression on him. He had no hesitation in asking me to come downstairs and introduce him to her, "but not as a connexion of your family, you follow me, I rely on your discretion not to drag in my father, say just a distinguished artist of your acquaintance, you know how important it is to make a good impression on tradespeople." Although he had suggested to me that, not knowing him well enough to call him, he quite realised, "dear friend," I might address him, in front of the girl, in some such terms as "not dear master, of course ... although ... well, if you like, dear distinguished artist," I avoided "qualifying" him, as Saint-Simon would have said, in the shop and contented myself with returning his "you's." He picked out from several patterns of velvet one of the brightest red imaginable, so loud that, for all his bad taste, he was never able to wear the waistcoat when it was made. The girl settled down to work again with her two "apprentices," but it struck me that the impression had been mutual, and that Charles Morel, whom she regarded as of my "station" (only smarter and richer), had proved singularly attractive to her. As I had been greatly surprised to find among the photographs which his father had sent me one of the portrait of Miss Sacripant (otherwise Odette) by Elstir, I said to Charles Morel as I accompanied him to the carriage gateway: "I don't suppose you can tell me, but did my uncle know this lady well? I can't think what stage of his life she fits into exactly; and it interests me, because of M. Swann..." "Why, if I wasn't forgetting to tell you that my father asked me specially to draw your attention to that lady's picture. As a matter of fact, she was lunching with your uncle the last time you saw him. My father was in two minds whether to let you in. It seems you made a great impression on the wench, and she hoped to see you again. But just at that time there was a row in the family, from what my father tells me, and you never set eyes on your uncle again." He broke off to give Jupien's niece a smile of farewell across the courtyard. She gazed after him, doubtless admiring his thin but regular features, his fair hair and sparkling eyes. For my part, as I shook hands with him I was thinking of Mme Swann and saying to myself with amazement, so far apart, so different were they in my memory, that I should have henceforth to identify her with the "Lady in pink."

M. de Charlus was soon seated by the side of Mme Swann. At every social gathering at which he appeared, contemptuous towards the men, courted by the women, he promptly attached himself to the most elegantly dressed of the latter, by whose garments he felt himself to be embellished. The Baron's frock-coat or tails were reminiscent of a portrait by some great colourist of a man dressed in black but having by his side, thrown over a chair, the brilliant cloak which he is about to wear at some fancy dress ball. These tête-à-têtes, generally with some royal lady, secured for M. de Charlus various privileges which he cherished. For instance, one consequence of them was that his hostesses, at theatricals or recitals, allowed the Baron alone to have a front seat in a row of ladies, while the rest of the men jostled one another at the back of the room. Furthermore, completely absorbed, it seemed, in telling amusing stories to the enraptured lady at the top of his voice, M. de Charlus was dispensed from the necessity of going to shake hands with any of the others, was set free from all social duties. Behind the scented barrier which the chosen beauty provided for him, he was isolated in the middle of a crowded drawing-room, as, in a crowded theatre, behind the rampart of a box; and when anyone came up to greet him, through, as it were, the beauty of his companion, it was permissible for him to reply quite curtly and without interrupting his conversation with a lady. True, Mme Swann was scarcely of the rank of the persons with whom he liked thus to flaunt himself. But he professed admiration for her and friendship for Swann, knew that she would be flattered by his attentions, and was himself flattered at being compromised by the prettiest woman in the room.

Mme de Villeparisis meanwhile was not too well pleased to receive a visit from M. de Charlus. The latter, while admitting serious defects in his aunt's character, was genuinely fond of her. But every now and then in a fit of anger or imaginary grievance, he would sit down and write to her, without making the slightest attempt to resist his impulse, letters full of the most violent abuse, in which he made the most of trifling incidents which until then he seemed not even to have noticed. Among other examples I may instance the following, which my stay at Balbec brought to my knowledge: Mme de Villeparisis, fearing that she had not brought enough money with her to Balbec to enable her to prolong her holiday there, and not caring, since she was of a thrifty disposition and shrank from superfluous expenditure, to have money sent to her from Paris, had borrowed three thousand francs from M. de Charlus. A month later, annoyed with his aunt for some trivial reason, he asked her to repay him this sum by telegraphic money order. He received two thousand nine hundred and ninety-odd francs. Meeting his aunt a few days later in Paris, in the course of a friendly conversation he drew her attention, very mildly, to the mistake that her bank had made when sending the money. "But there was no mistake," replied Mme de Villeparisis, "the money order cost six francs seventy-five." "Ah, well, if it was intentional, that's fine," said M. de Charlus. "I mentioned it only in case you didn't know, because in that case, if the bank had done the same thing with anyone who didn't know you as well as I do, it might have led to unpleasantness." "No, no, there was no mistake." "Actually you were quite right," M. de Charlus concluded gaily, stooping to kiss his aunt's hand. And in fact he bore her no ill-will and was only amused at this little instance of her stinginess. But some time afterwards, imagining that, in a family matter, his aunt had been trying to cheat him and had "worked up a regular conspiracy" against him, as she rather foolishly took shelter behind the lawyers with whom he suspected her of having plotted to do him down, he had written her a letter boiling over with insolence and rage. "I shall not be satisfied with having my revenge," he added as a postscript, "I shall make you a laughing-stock. Tomorrow I shall tell everyone the story of the money order and the six francs seventy-five you kept back from me out of the three thousand I lent you. I shall disgrace you publicly." Instead of so doing, he had gone to his aunt the next day to apologise, having already regretted a letter in which he had used some really appalling language. In any case, to whom could he have told the story of the money order? Since he no longer sought vengeance but a sincere reconciliation, now would have been the time for him to keep silence. But he had already told the story everywhere, while still on the best of terms with his aunt, had told it without malice, as a joke, and because he was the soul of indiscretion. He had told the story, but without Mme de Villeparisis's knowledge. With the result that, having learned from his letter that he intended to disgrace her by divulging a transaction in which he had assured her personally that she had acted rightly, she concluded that he had deceived her then and had lied when he pretended to be fond of her. All this had now died down, but neither of them knew precisely what the other thought of him or her. This sort of intermittent quarrel is of course somewhat exceptional. Of a different order again were those of M. de Charlus, as we shall presently see, with people wholly unlike Mme de Villeparisis. In spite of this we must bear in mind that the opinions which we hold of one another, our relations with friends and family, far from being static, save in appearance, are as eternally fluid as the sea itself. Whence all the rumours of divorce between couples who have always seemed so perfectly united and will soon afterwards speak of one another with affection; all the terrible things said by one friend of another from whom we supposed him to be inseparable and with whom we shall find him once more reconciled before we have had time to recover from our surprise; all the reversals of alliances between nations after the briefest of spells.

"I say, things are hotting up between my uncle and Mme Swann," remarked Saint-Loup. "And look at Mamma in the innocence of her heart going across to disturb them. To the pure all things are pure!"

I studied M. de Charlus. The tuft of his grey hair, his twinkling eye, the brow of which was raised by his monocle, the red flowers in his buttonhole, formed as it were the three mobile apexes of a convulsive and striking triangle. I had not ventured to greet him, for he had given me no sign of recognition. And yet, though he was not facing in my direction, I was convinced that he had seen me; while he sat spinning some yarn to Mme Swann, whose sumptuous, pansy-coloured cloak floated over his knee, the Baron's roving eye, like that of a street hawker who is watching all the time for the "law" to appear, had certainly explored every corner of the room and taken note of all the people who were in it. M. de Châtellerault came up to say good evening to him without there being the slightest hint on M. de Charlus's face that he had seen the young Duke until he was actually standing in front of him. In this way, in fairly numerous gatherings such as this, M. de Charlus kept almost continuously on show a smile without determinate direction or particular object, which, thereby pre-existing the greetings of new arrivals, remained, when the latter entered its zone, devoid of any amiable implication towards them. Nevertheless, I felt obliged to go across and speak to Mme Swann. But as she was not certain whether I knew Mme de Marsantes and M. de Charlus, she was distinctly cold, fearing no doubt that I might ask her to introduce me to them. I then turned to M. de Charlus, and at once regretted it, for though he could not have helped seeing me he showed no sign of having done so. As I stood before him and bowed I found, at some distance from his body which it prevented me from approaching by the full length of his outstretched arm, a finger bereft, one would have said, of an episcopal ring, of which he appeared to be offering the consecrated site for the kiss of the faithful, and I was made to appear to have penetrated, without leave from the Baron and by an act of trespass for which he left me the entire responsibility, the unalterable, anonymous and vacant dispersion of his smile. This coldness was hardly of a kind to encourage Mme Swann to depart from hers.

"How tired and worried you look," said Mme de Marsantes to her son who had come up to greet M. de Charlus.

And indeed the expression in Robert's eyes seemed now and then to reach a depth from which it rose at once like a diver who has touched bottom. This bottom which hurt Robert so much when he touched it that he left it at once, to return to it a moment later, was the thought that he had broken with his mistress.

"Never mind," his mother went on, stroking his cheek, "never mind; it's good to see my little boy again."

This show of affection seeming to irritate Robert, Mme de Marsantes led her son away to the other end of the room where in an alcove hung with yellow silk a group of Beauvais armchairs massed their violet-hued tapestries like purple irises in a field of buttercups. Mme Swann, finding herself alone and having realised that I was a friend of Saint-Loup, beckoned me to come and sit beside her. Not having seen her for so long, I did not know what to talk to her about. I was keeping an eye on my hat among all those that littered the carpet, and I wondered with a vague curiosity to whom could belong one that was not the Duc de Guermantes's and yet in the lining of which a capital "G" was surmounted by a ducal coronet. I knew who everyone in the room was, and could not think of anyone whose hat this could possibly be.

"What a pleasant man M. de Norpois is," I said to Mme Swann, pointing him out to her. "It's true that Robert de Saint-Loup says he's a pest, but . . . "

"He's quite right," she replied.

Seeing from her face that she was thinking of something which she was keeping from me, I plied her with questions. Pleased, perhaps, to appear to be very taken up with someone in this room where she hardly knew anyone, she took me into a corner.

"I'm sure this is what M. de Saint-Loup meant," she began, "but you must never tell him I said so, for he would think me indiscreet, and I value his esteem very highly—I'm an 'honest Injun,' you know. The other day, Charlus was dining at the Princesse de Guermantes's, and for some reason or other your name was mentioned. It appears that M. de Norpois told them— it's all too silly for words, don't go and worry yourself to death over it, nobody paid any attention, they all knew only too well the mischievous tongue that said it—that you were a hysterical little flatterer."

I have recorded a long way back my stupefaction at the dis- covery that a friend of my father such as M. de Norpois was could have expressed himself thus in speaking of me. I was even more astonished to learn that my emotion on that evening long ago when I had spoken about Mme Swann and Gilberte was known to the Princess de Guermantes, whom I imagined never to have heard of my existence. Each of our actions, our words, our

attitudes is cut off from the "world," from the people who have
not directly perceived it, by a medium the permeability of which is
infinitely variable and remains unknown to ourselves; having
learned from experience that some important utterance which
we eagerly hoped would be disseminated (such as those so enthusiastic speeches which I used at one time to make to everyone and
at every opportunity on the subject of Mme Swann, thinking that
among so many scattered seeds one at least would germinate) has at
once, often because of our very anxiety, been hidden under a
bushel, how immeasurably less do we suppose that some tiny word
which we ourselves have forgotten, which may not even have
been uttered by us but formed along its way by the imperfect
refraction of a different word, could be transported, without ever
being halted in its progress, infinite distances—in the present
instance to the Princesse de Guermantes—and succeed in divert-
ing at our expense the banquet of the gods! What we remember of
our conduct remains unknown to our nearest neighbour; what we
have forgotten that we ever said, or indeed what we never did say,
flies to provoke hilarity in another planet, and the image that other
people form of our actions and demeanour no more resembles our
own than an inaccurate tracing, on which for the black line we
find an empty space and for a blank area an inexplicable contour,
resembles the original drawing. It may happen however that what
has not been transcribed is a non-existent feature which only our
purblind self-esteem reveals to us, and what seems to us to have
been added does indeed belong to us, but so quintessentially that it
escapes us. So that this strange print which seems to us to have so
little resemblance to us bears sometimes the same stamp of truth,
unflattering, certainly, but profound and useful, as an X-ray
photograph. Not that that is any reason why we should recognise
ourselves in it. A man who is in the habit of smiling in the glass at
his handsome face and stalwart figure will, if he is shown an X-ray
of them, have the same suspicion of error at the sight of this rosary
of bones labelled as being a picture of himself as the visitor to an art
gallery who, on coming to the portrait of a girl, reads in his
catalogue: "Dromedary resting." Later on, this discrepancy in
the picture of ourselves according to whether it is drawn by
one's own hand or another's was something I was to register in
the case of others than myself, living placidly in the midst of a
collection of photographs which they had taken of themselves
while round about them grinned frightful faces, invisible to them

as a rule, but stunning them with amazement if some chance revealed them to them, saying: "It's you."

A few years earlier I should have been only too glad to tell Mme Swann in what connexion I had behaved so tenderly towards M. de Norpois, since the connexion had been my desire to get to know her. But I no longer felt this desire, since I was no longer in love with Gilberte. At the same time I found it difficult to identify Mme Swann with the lady in pink of my childhood. Accordingly I spoke of the woman who was on my mind at the moment.

"Did you see the Duchesse de Guermantes just now?" I asked Mme Swann.

But since the Duchess did not greet Mme Swann when they met, the latter chose to appear to regard her as a person of no interest, whose presence in a room one did not even notice.

"I don't know; I didn't *realise* she was here," she replied sourly, using an expression borrowed from English.

I was anxious nevertheless for information with regard not only to Mme de Guermantes but to all the people who came in contact with her, and (for all the world like Bloch), with the tactlessness of people who seek in their conversations not to give pleasure to others but to elucidate, from sheer egoism, points that are of interest to themselves, in my effort to form an exact idea of the life of Mme de Guermantes I questioned Mme de Villeparisis about Mme Leroi.

"Oh, yes, I know who you mean," she replied with an affectation of contempt, "the daughter of those rich timber merchants. I've heard that she's begun to go about quite a lot lately, but I must explain to you that I'm rather old now to make new acquaintances. I've known such interesting, such delightful people in my time that really I don't believe Mme Leroi would add much to what I already have."

Mme de Marsantes, who was playing lady-in-waiting to the Marquise, presented me to the Prince, and scarcely had she finished doing so than M. de Norpois also presented me in the most glowing terms. Perhaps he found it opportune to pay me a compliment which could in no way damage his credit since I had just been introduced; perhaps it was that he thought that a foreigner, even so distinguished a foreigner, was unfamiliar with French society and might think that he was being introduced to a young man of fashion; perhaps it was to exercise one of his prerogatives, that of adding the weight of his personal recommendation as an ambassador, or in his taste for the archaic to revive in the Prince's honour the old custom, flattering to his rank, whereby two sponsors were necessary if one wished to be presented to a royal personage.

Mme de Villeparisis appealed to M. de Norpois, feeling it imperative that I should have his assurance that she had nothing to regret in not knowing Mme Leroi.

"Isn't it true, M. l'Ambassadeur, that Mme Leroi is of no interest, very inferior to all the people who come here, and that I'm quite right not to have cultivated her?"

Whether from independence or because he was tired, M. de Norpois replied merely in a bow full of respect but devoid of meaning.

"Do you know," went on Mme de Villeparisis with a laugh, "there are some absurd people in the world. Would you believe that I had a visit this afternoon from a gentleman who tried to persuade me that he found more pleasure in kissing my hand than a young woman's?"

I guessed at once that this was Legrandin. M. de Norpois smiled with a slight quiver of the eyelid, as though he felt that such a remark had been prompted by a concupiscence so natural that one could not feel any resentment against the person who had felt it, almost as though it were the beginning of a romance which he was prepared to forgive, even to encourage, with the perverse tolerance of a Voisenon or a Crébillon *fils*.

"Many young women's hands would be incapable of doing what I see there," said the Prince, pointing to Mme de Villeparisis's unfinished water-colours. And he asked her whether she had seen the flower paintings by Fantin-Latour which had recently been exhibited.

"They are first class, the work, as they say nowadays, of a fine painter, one of the masters of the palette," declared M. de Norpois. "Nevertheless, in my opinion, they cannot stand comparison with those of Mme de Villeparisis, which give a better idea of the colouring of the flower."

Even supposing that the partiality of an old lover, the habit of flattery, the prevailing opinions in a social circle, had dictated these words to the ex-Ambassador, they nevertheless proved on what a negation of true taste the judgment of society people is based, so arbitrary that the smallest trifle can make it rush to the wildest absurdities, on the way to which it comes across no genuinely felt impression to arrest it.

"I claim no credit for knowing about flowers, since I've lived all my life in the fields," replied Mme de Villeparisis modestly. "But," she added graciously, turning to the Prince, "if, when I was very young, I had some rather more serious notions about them than other country children, I owe it to a distinguished fellow-country-man of yours, Herr von Schlegel. I met him at Broglie, where I was taken by my aunt Cordelia (Marshal de Castellane's wife, don't you know?). I remember so well M. Lebrun, M. de Salvandy, M. Doudan, getting him to talk about flowers. I was only a little girl, and I couldn't understand all he said. But he liked playing with me, and when he went back to your country he sent me a beautiful botany book to remind me of a drive we took together in a phaeton to the Val Richer, when I fell asleep on his knee. I've always kept the book, and it taught me to observe many things about flowers which I should not have noticed otherwise. When Mme de Barante published some of Mme de Broglie's letters, charming and affected like herself, I hoped to find among them some record of those conversations with Herr von Schlegel. But she was a woman who only looked to nature for arguments in support of religion."

Robert called me away to the far end of the room where he and his mother were.

"How very nice you've been," I said to him, "I don't know how to thank you. Can we dine together tomorrow?"

"Tomorrow? Yes, if you like, but it will have to be with Bloch. I met him just now on the doorstep. He was rather stiff with me at first because I had quite forgotten to answer his last two letters (he didn't tell me that was what had offended him, but I guessed it), but after that he was so friendly to me that I simply can't disappoint him. Between ourselves, on his side at least, I feel it's a friendship for life."

I do not think that Robert was altogether mistaken. Furious detraction was often, with Bloch, the effect of a keen affection which he had supposed to be unrequited. And as he made little effort to imagine other people's lives, and never dreamed that one might have been ill, or away from home, or otherwise occupied, a week's silence was at once interpreted by him as arising from deliberate coldness. And so I never believed that his most violent outbursts as a friend, or in later years as a writer, went very deep.

They were exacerbated if one replied to them with an icy dignity, or with a platitude which encouraged him to redouble his onslaught, but yielded often to a warmly sympathetic response. "As for my being nice to you," went on Saint-Loup, "I haven't really been nice at all. My aunt tells me that it's you who avoid her, that you never utter a word to her. She wonders whether you have anything against her."

Fortunately for myself, if I had been taken in by these words, our departure for Balbec, which I believed to be imminent, would have prevented my making any attempt to see Mme de Guermantes again, to assure her that I had nothing against her, and so put her under the necessity of proving that it was she who had something against me. But I had only to remind myself that she had not even offered to let me see her Elstirs. Moreover, this was not a disappointment; I had never expected her to talk to me about them; I knew that I did not appeal to her, that I had no hope of ever making her like me; the most that I had been able to look forward to was that, since I should not be seeing her again before I left Paris, her kindness would afford me an entirely soothing impression of her, which I could take with me to Balbec indefinitely prolonged, intact, instead of a memory mixed with anxiety and gloom.

Mme de Marsantes kept on interrupting her conversation with Robert to tell me how often he had spoken to her about me, how fond he was of me; she treated me with a deference which I found almost painful because I felt it to be prompted by her fear of falling out because of me with this son whom she had not seen all day, with whom she must accordingly have supposed that the influence which she wielded was not equal to and must conciliate mine. Having heard me earlier asking Bloch for news of his uncle, M. Nissim Bernard, Mme de Marsantes inquired whether it was he who had at one time lived at Nice.

"In that case, he knew M. de Marsantes there before our marriage," she told me. "My husband used often to speak of him as an excellent man, with such a delicate, generous nature."

"To think that for once in his life he wasn't lying! It's incredible," Bloch would have thought.

All this time I should have liked to explain to Mme de Marsantes that Robert felt infinitely more affection for her than for myself, and that even if she had shown hostility towards me it was not in my nature to attempt to set him against her, to detach him from her. But now that Mme de Guermantes had gone I had more leisure to observe Robert, and it was only then that I noticed that a sort of fury seemed to have taken possession of him once more, rising to the surface of his stern and sombre features. I was afraid lest, remembering the scene in the theatre that afternoon, he might be feeling humiliated in my presence at having allowed himself to be treated so harshly by his mistress without making any rejoinder.

Suddenly he broke away from his mother, who had put her arm round his neck, and, coming towards me, led me behind the little flower-strewn counter at which Mme de Villeparisis had resumed her seat and beckoned me to follow him into the smaller drawing-room. I was hurrying after him when M. de Charlus, who may have supposed that I was leaving the house, turned abruptly from Prince von Faffenheim, to whom he had been talking, and made a rapid circuit which brought him face to face with me. I saw with alarm that he had taken the hat in the lining of which were a capital "G" and a ducal coronet. In the doorway into the small drawing-room he said without looking at me:

"As I see that you have taken to going into society, you must give me the pleasure of coming to see me. But it's a little complicated," he went on with a distracted but calculating air, as if the pleasure had been one that he was afraid of not securing again once he had let slip the opportunity of arranging with me the means by which it might be realised. "I am very seldom at home; you will have to write to me. But I should prefer to explain things to you more quietly. I shall be leaving soon. Will you walk a short way with me? I shall only keep you for a moment."

"You'd better take care, Monsieur," I warned him. "You have picked up the wrong hat by mistake."

"Do you want to prevent me from taking my own hat?"

I assumed, a similar mishap having recently occurred to myself, that, someone else having taken his hat, he had seized upon one at random so as not to go home bare-headed, and that I had placed him in a difficulty by exposing his stratagem. So I did not pursue the matter. I told him that I must say a few words to Saint-Loup. "He's talking to that idiotic Duc de Guermantes," I added. "That's a charming thing to say: I shall tell my brother." "Oh! you think that would interest M. de Charlus?" (I imagined that, if he had a brother, that brother must be called Charlus too. Saint-Loup had indeed explained his family tree to me at Balbec, but I had forgotten the details.) "Who's talking about M. de Charlus?" said the Baron in an insolent tone. "Go to Robert. I know that you took part this morning in one of those lunch-time orgies that he has with a woman who is disgracing him. You would do well to use your influence with him to make him realise the pain he is causing his poor mother and all of us by dragging our name in the dirt."

I should have liked to reply that at this degrading luncheon the conversation had been entirely about Emerson, Ibsen and Tolstoy, and that the young woman had lectured Robert to make him drink nothing but water. In the hope of bringing some balm to Robert, whose pride I thought had been wounded, I sought to excuse his mistress. I did not know that at that moment, in spite of his anger with her, it was on himself that he was heaping reproaches. But it always happens, in quarrels between a good man and a worthless woman and when the right is all on one side, that some trifle crops up which enables the woman to appear not to have been in the wrong on one point. And since she ignores all the other points, if the man feels the need of her, if he is upset by the separation, his weakness will make him exaggeratedly scrupulous, he will remember the absurd reproaches that have been flung at him and will ask himself whether they have not some foundation in fact.

"I've come to the conclusion that I was wrong about that necklace," Robert said to me. "Of course, I didn't do it with any ill intent, but I know very well that other people don't look at things in the same way as oneself. She had a very hard time when she was young. In her eyes I'm bound to appear the rich man who thinks he can get anything he wants with his money and against whom a poor person can't compete, whether in trying to influence Boucheron or in a lawsuit. Of course she has been horribly cruel to me, when I've never thought of anything but her good. But I do see clearly that she thinks I wanted to make her feel that one could keep a hold on her with money, and that's not true. And she's so fond of me—what must she be thinking? Poor darling, if you only knew how sweet and thoughtful she is, I simply can't tell you what adorable things she's often done for me. How wretched she must be feeling now! In any case, whatever happens I don't want to let her think me a cad; I shall dash off to Boucheron's and get the necklace. Who knows? Perhaps when she sees what I've done she'll admit that she's been partly in the wrong. You see, it's the idea that she's suffering at this moment that I can't bear. What one suffers oneself one knows—it's nothing. But to tell oneself that *she's* suffering and not to be able to form any idea of what she feels—I think I should go mad, I'd rather not see her ever again than let her suffer. All I ask is that she should be happy without me if need be. You know, for me everything that concerns her is enormously important, it becomes something cosmic; I shall run to the jeweller's and then go and ask her to forgive me. Until I get down there, what will she be thinking of me? If she could only know that I was on my way! Why don't you come to her house on the off chance; perhaps everything will be all right. Perhaps," he went on with a smile, as though hardly daring to believe in so idyllic a possibility, "we can all three dine together in the country. But one can't tell yet. I'm so bad at handling her; poor sweet, I may perhaps hurt her feelings again. Besides, her decision may be irrevocable."

Robert swept me back to his mother.

"Good-bye," he said to her. "I've got to go now. I don't know when I shall get leave again. Probably not for a month. I shall write to you as soon as I know."

Certainly Robert was not in the least the sort of son who, when he goes out with his mother, feels that an attitude of exasperation towards her ought to counterbalance the smiles and greetings which he bestows on strangers. Nothing is more prevalent than this odious form of vengeance on the part of those who appear to believe that rudeness to one's own family is the natural complement to ceremonial behaviour. Whatever the wretched mother may say, her son, as though he had been brought along against his will and wished to make her pay dearly for his presence, immediately refutes the timidly ventured assertion with a sarcastic, precise, cruel contradiction; the mother at once conforms, though without thereby disarming him, to the opinion of this superior being whose delightful nature she will continue to vaunt to all and sundry in his absence, but who, for all that, spares her none of his most wounding remarks. Saint-Loup was not at all like this; but the anguish which Rachel's absence provoked in him caused him for different reasons to be no less harsh with his mother than those other sons are with theirs. And as she listened to him I saw the same throb, like the beating of a wing, which Mme de Marsantes had been unable to repress when her son first entered the room, convulse her whole body once again; but this time it was an anxious face and woebegone eyes that she fastened on him.

"What, Robert, you're going off? Seriously? My little son—the one day I had a chance to see something of you!"

And then quite softly, in the most natural tone, in a voice from which she strove to banish all sadness so as not to inspire her son with a pity which would perhaps have been painful to him, or else useless and simply calculated to irritate him, as a simple common-sense assertion she added: "You know it's not at all nice of you."

But to this simplicity she added so much timidity, to show him that she was not trespassing on his freedom, so much affection, so that he should not reproach her for interfering with his pleasures, that Saint-Loup could not help but observe in himself as it were the possibility of a similar wave of affection, in other words an obstacle to his spending the evening with his mistress. And so he reacted angrily: "It's unfortunate, but, nice or not, that's how it is."

And he heaped on his mother the reproaches which no doubt he felt that he himself perhaps deserved; thus it is that egoists have always the last word; having posited at the start that their resolution is unshakeable, the more susceptible the feeling to which one appeals in them to make them abandon their resolution, the more reprehensible they find, not themselves who resist that appeal, but those who put them under the necessity of resisting it, so that their own harshness may be carried to the utmost degree of cruelty without having any effect in their eyes but to aggravate the culpability of the person who is so indelicate as to be hurt, to be in the right, and to cause them thus treacherously the pain of acting against their natural instinct of pity. But of her own accord Mme de Marsantes ceased to pursue the matter, for she sensed that she would be unable to dissuade him.

"Well, I'm off," he said to me, "but you're not to keep him long, Mamma, because he's got to go and pay a call elsewhere quite soon."

I was fully aware that my company could not afford any pleasure to Mme de Marsantes, but I was glad not to give her the impression by leaving with Robert that I was involved in these pleasures which deprived her of him. I should have liked to find some excuse for her son's conduct, less from affection for him than from pity for her. But it was she who spoke first:

"Poor boy," she began, "I'm sure I must have hurt him dreadfully. You see, Monsieur, mothers are such selfish creatures. After all, he hasn't many pleasures, he comes so seldom to Paris. Oh, dear, if he hadn't gone already I should have liked to stop him, not to keep him of course, but just to tell him that I'm not vexed with him, that I think he was quite right. Will you excuse me if I go and look over the staircase?"

I accompanied her there.

"Robert! Robert!" she called. "No, he's gone. It's too late."

At that moment I would as gladly have undertaken a mission to make Robert break with his mistress as, a few hours earlier, to make him go and live with her altogether. In the one case Saint-Loup would have regarded me as a false friend, in the other his family would have called me his evil genius. Yet I was the same man at an interval of a few hours.

We returned to the drawing-room. Seeing that Saint-Loup was not with us, Mme de Villeparisis exchanged with M. de Norpois one of those sceptical, mocking and not too compassionate glances with which people point out to one another an over-jealous wife or an over-fond mother (traditional laughing-stocks), as much as to say: "Well, well, there's been trouble."

Robert went to his mistress, taking with him the splendid ornament which, after what had passed between them, he ought not to have given her. But it came to the same thing, for she would not look at it, and even subsequently he could never persuade her to accept it. Certain of Robert's friends thought that these proofs of disinterestedness were deliberately calculated to bind him to her. And yet she was not greedy for money, except perhaps in order to be able to spend it freely. I often saw her lavish on people whom she believed to be in need the most extravagant largesse. "At this moment," Robert's friends would say to him, seeking to invalidate by their malicious words a disinterested action on Rachel's part, "at this moment she'll be in the promenade at the Folies-Bergère. She's an enigma, that Rachel, a regular sphinx." In any case, how many mercenary women, women who are kept by men, does one not see setting countless little limits to the generosity of their lovers out of a delicacy that flowers in the midst of that sordid existence!

Robert was ignorant of almost all the infidelities of his mistress, and tormented himself over what were mere nothings compared with the real life of Rachel, a life which began every day only after he had left her. He was ignorant of almost all these infidelities. One could have told him of them without shaking his confidence in

Rachel. For it is a charming law of nature, which manifests itself in the heart of the most complex social organisms, that we live in perfect ignorance of those we love. On the one hand the lover says to himself: "She is an angel, she will never give herself to me, I may as well die—and yet she loves me; she loves me so much that perhaps . . . but no, it can never possibly happen." And in the exaltation of his desire, in the anguish of his expectation, what jewels he flings at the feet of this woman, how he runs to borrow money to save her from financial worries! Meanwhile, on the other side of the glass screen, through which these conversations will no more carry than those which visitors exchange in front of an aquarium in a zoo, the public are saying: "You don't know her? You can count yourself lucky—she has robbed, in fact ruined, I don't know how many men, as girls go there's nothing worse. She's a swindler pure and simple. And crafty!" And perhaps this last epithet is not absolutely wrong, for even the sceptical man who is not really in love with the woman, who merely gets pleasure from her, says to his friends: "No, no, my dear fellow, she's not at all a whore. I don't say she hasn't had an adventure or two in her time, but she's not a woman one pays, she'd be a damned sight too expensive if she was. With her it's fifty thousand francs or nothing." The fact of the matter is that he himself has spent fifty thousand francs for the privilege of having her once, but she (finding a willing accomplice in the man himself, in the person of his self-esteem) has managed to persuade him that he is one of those who have had her for nothing. Such is society, where every being is double, and where the most thoroughly exposed, the most notorious, will be known to a certain other only as protected by a shell, by a sweet cocoon, as a charming natural curiosity. There were in Paris two thoroughly decent men whom Saint-Loup no longer greeted when he saw them and to whom he could not refer without a tremor in his voice, calling them exploiters of women: this was because they had both been ruined by Rachel.

"There's only one thing I blame myself for," Mme de Marsantes murmured in my ear, "and that is for telling him that he wasn't nice. Such an adorable, unique son, like no one else in the world—to have told him, the only time I see him, that he wasn't nice to me! I'd sooner have been given a beating, because I'm sure that whatever pleasure he may be having this evening, and he hasn't many, will be spoiled for him by that unfair word. But I mustn't keep you, Monsieur, since you're in a hurry."

Mme de Marsantes bade me good-bye anxiously. Those feelings concerned Robert, and she was sincere. But she ceased to be so on becoming a grand lady again: "I have been so *interested*, so *happy*, so *charmed* to have this little talk with you. Thank you! Thank you!"

And with a humble air she fastened on me a look of ecstatic gratitude, as though my conversation had been one of the keenest pleasures she had experienced in her life. This charming expression went very well with the black flowers on her white patterned skirt; they were those of a great lady who knew her business.

"I can't leave at once. I must wait for M. de Charlus. I'm going with him."

Mme de Villeparisis overheard these last words. They appeared to vex her. Had the matter not been one which couldn't involve a sentiment of that nature, it would have struck me that what seemed to be alarmed at that moment in Mme de Villeparisis was her sense of decency. But this hypothesis never even entered my mind. I was delighted with Mme de Guermantes, with Saint-Loup, with Mme de Marsantes, with M. de Charlus, with Mme de Villeparisis; I did not stop to reflect, and I spoke light-heartedly, and at random.

"You're leaving here with my nephew Palamède?" she asked me.

Thinking that it might produce a highly favourable impression on Mme de Villeparisis if she learned that I was on intimate terms with a nephew whom she esteemed so greatly, "He has asked me to walk home with him," I answered blithely. "I'm delighted. As a matter of fact, we're better friends than you think, and I've quite made up my mind that we're going to be better friends still."

From being vexed, Mme de Villeparisis seemed to have become worried. "Don't wait for him," she said to me with a preoccupied air. "He is talking to M. de Faffenheim. He's already forgotten what he said to you. You'd much better go now quickly while his back is turned."

I was not myself in any hurry to join Robert and his mistress. But Mme de Villeparisis seemed so anxious for me to go that, thinking perhaps that she had some important business to discuss with her nephew, I bade her good-bye. Next to her M. de Guermantes, superb and Olympian, was ponderously seated. One felt that the notion, omnipresent in all his limbs, of his vast riches, as though they had been smelted in a crucible into a single human ingot, gave an extraordinary density to this man who was worth so much. When I said good-bye to him he rose politely from his seat, and I sensed the inert and compact mass of thirty millions which his old-fashioned French breeding activated and raised up until it stood before me. I seemed to be looking at that statue of Olympian Zeus which Phidias is said to have cast in solid gold. Such was the power that a Jesuit education had over M. de Guermantes, over the body of M. de Guermantes at least, for it did not reign with equal mastery over the ducal mind. M. de Guermantes laughed at his own jokes, but did not even smile at other people's.

On my way downstairs I heard a voice calling out to me from behind: "So this is how you wait for me, is it?"

It was M. de Charlus.

"You don't mind if we go a little way on foot?" he asked dryly, when we were in the courtyard. "We'll walk until I find a cab that suits me."

"You wished to speak to me, Monsieur?"

"Ah, yes, as a matter of fact there were some things I wanted to say to you, but I'm not so sure now whether I shall. As far as you are concerned, I am sure that they could be the starting-point for inestimable benefits. But I can see also that they would bring into my existence, at an age when one begins to value tranquillity, a great deal of time-wasting, all sorts of inconvenience. I ask myself whether you are worth all the pains that I should have to take with you, and I have not the pleasure of knowing you well enough to be able to say. I found you very unsatisfactory at Balbec, even when allowances are made for the stupidity inseparable from the image of the 'bather' and the wearing of the objects called *espadrilles*. Perhaps in any case you are not sufficiently desirous of what I could do for you to make it worth my while, for I must repeat to you quite frankly, Monsieur, that for me it can mean nothing but trouble."

I protested that, in that case, he must not dream of it. This summary end to negotiations did not seem to be to his liking.

"That sort of politeness means nothing," he rebuked me coldly. "There is nothing so agreeable as to put oneself out for a person who is worth one's while. For the best of us, the study of the arts, a taste for old things, collections, gardens, are all mere ersatz, surrogates, alibis. From the depths of our tub, like Diogenes, we cry out for a man. We cultivate begonias, we trim yews, as a last resort, because yews and begonias submit to treatment. But we should prefer to give our time to a plant of human growth, if we were sure that he was worth the trouble. That is the whole question. You must know yourself a little. Are you worth my trouble or not?"

"I would not for anything in the world, Monsieur, be a cause of anxiety to you," I said to him, "but so far as I am concerned you may be sure that everything that comes to me from you will give me very great pleasure. I am deeply touched that you should be so kind as to take an interest in me in this way and try to help me."

Greatly to my surprise, it was almost with effusion that he thanked me for these words. Slipping his arm through mine with that intermittent familiarity which had already struck me at Balbec, and was in such contrast to the harshness of his tone, he went on:

"With the want of consideration common at your age, you are liable to say things at times which would open an unbridgeable gulf between us. What you have said just now, on the other hand, is exactly the sort of thing that is capable of touching me, and of inducing me to do a great deal for you."

As he walked arm in arm with me and uttered these words, which, though tinged with disdain, were so affectionate, M. de Charlus now fastened his gaze on me with that intense fixity, that piercing hardness which had struck me the first morning, when I saw him outside the casino at Balbec, and indeed many years before that, through the pink hawthorns, standing beside Mme Swann, whom I supposed then to be his mistress, in the park at Tansonville, now let it stray around him and examine the cabs which at this time of day were passing in considerable numbers, staring so insistently at them that several stopped, the drivers supposing that he wished to engage them. But M. de Charlus immediately dismissed them.

"None of them is suitable," he explained to me, "it's all a question of their lamps, and the direction they're going home in. I hope, Monsieur," he went on, "that you will not in any way misinterpret the purely disinterested and charitable nature of the proposal which I am going to make to you."

I was struck by the way, even more than at Balbec, his diction resembled Swann's.

"You are intelligent enough, I dare say, not to imagine that it is inspired by 'lack of connexions,' by fear of solitude and boredom. I need not speak to you of my family, for I assume that a youth of your age belonging to the lower middle class" (he accentuated the phrase in a tone of self-satisfaction) "must know the history of France. It is the people of my world who read nothing and are as ignorant as lackeys. In the old days the King's valets were recruited among the nobility; now the nobility are scarcely better than valets. But young bourgeois like you do read, and you must certainly know Michelet's fine passage about my family: 'I see them as being very great, these powerful Guermantes. And what is the poor little King of France beside them, shut up in his palace in Paris?' As for what I am personally, that, Monsieur, is a subject which I do not much care to talk about, but you may possibly have heard—it was alluded to in a leading article in *The Times*, which made a considerable impression—that the Emperor of Austria, who has always honoured me with his friendship, and is good enough to maintain cousinly relations with me, declared the other day in an interview which was made public that if the Comte de Chambord had had at his side a man as thoroughly conversant with the undercurrents of European politics as myself he would be King of France today. I have often thought, Monsieur, that there was in me, thanks not to my own humble gifts but to circumstances which you may one day have occasion to learn, a wealth of experience, a sort of secret dossier of inestimable value, of which I have not felt myself at liberty to make use for my own personal ends, which would be a priceless acquisition to a young man to whom I would hand over in a few months what it has taken me more than thirty years to acquire, and which I am perhaps alone in possessing. I do not speak of the intellectual enjoyment which you would find in learning certain secrets which a Michelet of our day would give years of his life to know, and in the light of which certain events would assume an entirely different aspect. And I do not speak only of events that have already occurred, but of the chain of circumstances." (This was a favourite expression of M. de Charlus's, and often, when he used it, he joined his hands as if in prayer, but with his fingers stiffened, as though by this complexus to illustrate the said circumstances, which he did not specify, and the links between them.) "I could give you an explanation that no one has dreamed of, not only of the past but of the future."

M. de Charlus broke off to question me about Bloch, whom he had heard discussed, though without appearing to be listening, in his aunt's drawing-room. And in that tone which he was so skilful at detaching from what he was saying that he seemed to be thinking of something else altogether, and to be speaking mechanically, simply out of politeness, he asked if my friend was young, good-looking and so forth. Bloch, if he had heard him, would have been more puzzled even than with M. de Norpois, but for very different reasons, to know whether M. de Charlus was for or against Dreyfus. "It is not a bad idea, if you wish to learn about life," went on M. de Charlus when he had finished questioning me about Bloch, "to have a few foreigners among your friends." I replied that Bloch was French. "Indeed," said M. de Charlus, "I took him to be a Jew." His assertion of this incompatibility made me suppose that M. de Charlus was more anti-Dreyfusard than anyone I had met. He protested, however, against the charge of treason levelled against Dreyfus. But his protest took this form: "I believe the newspapers say that Dreyfus has committed a crime against his country—so I understand; I pay no attention to the newspapers; I read them as I wash my hands, without considering it worth my while to take an interest in what I am doing. In any case, the crime is non-existent. This compatriot of your friend would have committed a crime if he had betrayed Judaea, but what has he to do with France?" I pointed out that if there should be a war the Jews would be mobilised just as much as anyone else. "Perhaps so, and I am not sure that it would not be an imprudence. If we bring over Senegalese or Malagasies, I hardly suppose that their hearts will be in the task of defending France, and that is only natural. Your Dreyfus might rather be convicted of a breach of the laws of hospitality. But enough of that. Perhaps you could ask your friend to allow me to attend some great festival in the Temple, a circumcision, or some Hebrew chants. He might perhaps hire a hall and give me some biblical entertainment, as the young ladies of Saint-Cyr performed scenes taken from the Psalms by Racine, to amuse Louis XIV. You might perhaps arrange that, and even some comic exhibitions. For instance a contest between your friend and his father, in which he would smite him as David smote Goliath. That would make quite an amusing farce. He might even, while he was about it, give his hag (or, as my old nurse would say, his 'haggart') of a mother a good thrashing. That would be an excellent show, and would not be unpleasing to us, eh, my young friend, since we like exotic spectacles, and to thrash that non-European creature would be giving a well-earned punishment to an old cow."

As he poured out these terrible, almost insane words, M. de Charlus squeezed my arm until it hurt. I reminded myself of all that his family had told me of his wonderful kindness to this old nurse, whose Molièresque vocabulary he had just recalled, and thought to myself that the connexions, hitherto, I felt, little studied, between goodness and wickedness in the same heart, various as they might be, would be an interesting subject for research.

I warned him that in any case Mme Bloch no longer existed, while as for M. Bloch, I questioned to what extent he would enjoy a sport which might easily result in his being blinded. M. de Charlus seemed annoyed. "That," he said, "is a woman who made a great mistake in dying. As for blinding him, surely the Synagogue is blind, since it does not perceive the truth of the Gospel. Besides, just think, at this moment when all those unhappy Jews are trembling before the stupid fury of the Christians, what an honour it would be for him to see a man like myself condescend to be amused by their sports."

At this point I caught sight of M. Bloch senior coming towards us, probably on his way to meet his son. He did not see us, but I offered to introduce him to M. de Charlus. I had no idea of the torrent of rage which my words were to let loose. "Introduce him to me! But you must have singularly little idea of social values! People do not get to know me as easily as that. In the present instance, the impropriety would be twofold, on account of the youth of the introducer and the unworthiness of the person introduced. At the most, if I am ever permitted to enjoy the Asiatic spectacle which I outlined to you, I might address to the frightful fellow a few affable words. But on condition that he should have allowed himself to be thoroughly thrashed by his son. I might go so far as to express my satisfaction."

In any event M. Bloch paid no attention to us. He was in the process of greeting Mme Sazerat with a sweeping bow, which was very favourably received. I was surprised at this, for in the old days at Combray she was so anti-semitic that she had been highly indignant with my parents for having young Bloch in the house. But Dreyfusism, like a strong gust of wind, had, a few days before this, borne M. Bloch to her feet. My friend's father had found Mme Sazerat charming and was particularly gratified by that lady's anti-semitism which he regarded as a proof of the sincerity of her faith and the soundness of her Dreyfusard opinions, and which also enhanced the value of the call which she had authorised him to pay her. He had not even been offended when she had said to him without thinking: "M. Drumont has the impudence to put the Reconsiderationists in the same bag as the Protestants and the Jews. A charming promiscuity!" "Bernard," he had said proudly to M. Nissim Bernard on returning home, "she has the prejudice, you know!" But M. Nissim Bernard had said nothing, raising his eyes to heaven in an angelic gaze. Saddened by the misfortunes of the Jews, remembering his old Christian friendships, grown mannered and precious with increasing years for reasons which the reader will learn in due course, he had now the air of a pre-Raphaelite grub on to which hair had been incongruously grafted, like threads in the heart of an opal.

"All this Dreyfus business," went on the Baron, still clasping me by the arm, "has only one drawback. It destroys society (I don't mean polite society; society has long ceased to deserve that laudatory epithet) by the influx of Mr and Mrs Cow and Cowshed and Cow-pat, whom I find even in the houses of my own cousins, because they belong to the Patriotic League, the Anti-Jewish League, or some such league, as if a political opinion entitled one to a social qualification."

This frivolity in M. de Charlus brought out his family likeness to the Duchesse de Guermantes. I remarked on the resemblance. As he appeared to think that I did not know her, I reminded him of the evening at the Opéra when he had seemed to be trying to avoid me. He assured me so forcefully that he had never seen me there that I should have ended by believing him if presently a trifling incident had not led me to think that M. de Charlus, in his excessive pride perhaps, did not care to be seen with me.

"Let us return to yourself," he said, "and my plans for you. There exists among certain men a freemasonry of which I cannot now say more than that it numbers in its ranks four of the reigning sovereigns of Europe. Now, the entourage of one of these, who is the Emperor of Germany, is trying to cure him of his fancy. That is a very serious matter, and may lead us to war. Yes, my dear sir, that is a fact. You remember the story of the man who believed that he had the Princess of China shut up in a bottle. It was a form of insanity. He was cured of it. But as soon as he ceased to be mad he became merely stupid. There are maladies which we must not seek to cure because they alone protect us from others that are more serious. A cousin of mine had a stomach ailment: he could digest nothing. The most learned stomach specialists treated him, to no avail. I took him to a certain doctor (another highly interesting man, by the way, of whom I could tell you a great deal). He guessed at once that the malady was nervous, persuaded his patient of this, advised him to eat whatever he liked unhesitatingly, and assured him that his digestion would stand it. But my cousin also had nephritis. What the stomach digested perfectly well the kidneys ceased after a time to be able to eliminate, and my cousin, instead of living to a fine old age with an imaginary disease of the stomach which obliged him to keep to a diet, died at forty with his stomach cured but his kidneys ruined. Given a very considerable lead over your contemporaries, who knows whether you may not perhaps become what some eminent man of the past might have been if a beneficent spirit had revealed to him, among a generation that knew nothing of them, the secrets of steam and electricity. Do not be foolish, do not refuse for reasons of tact and discretion. Try to understand that, if I do you a great service, I do not expect my reward from you to be any less great. It is many years now since people in society ceased to interest me. I have but one passion left, to seek to redeem the mistakes of my life by conferring the benefit of my knowledge on a soul that is still virgin and capable of being fired by virtue. I have had great sorrows, of which I may tell you perhaps some day; I have lost my wife, who was the loveliest, the noblest, the most perfect creature that one could dream of. I have young relatives who are not—I do not say worthy, but capable of accepting the intellectual heritage of which I have been speaking. Who knows but that you may be the person into whose hands it is to pass, the person whose life I shall be able to guide and to raise to so lofty a plane. My own would gain in return. Perhaps in teaching you the great secrets of diplomacy I might recover a taste for them myself, and begin at last to do things of real interest in which you would have an equal share. But before I can discover this I must see you often, very often, every day."

I was thinking of taking advantage of these unexpectedly ardent predispositions on M. de Charlus's part to ask him whether he could not arrange for me to meet his sister-in-law when suddenly I felt my arm violently jerked as though by an electric shock. It was M. de Charlus who had hurriedly withdrawn his arm from mine. Although as he talked he had allowed his eyes to wander in all directions, he had only just caught sight of M. d'Argencourt emerging from a side street. On seeing us, the Belgian Minister appeared annoyed and gave me a look of distrust, almost that look intended for a creature of another race with which Mme de Guermantes had scrutinised Bloch, and tried to avoid us. But it was as though M. de Charlus was determined to show him that he was not at all anxious not to be seen by him, for he called after him to tell him something of extreme insignificance. And fearing perhaps that M. d'Argencourt had not recognised me, M. de Charlus informed him that I was a great friend of Mme de Villeparisis, of the Duchesse de Guermantes, of Robert de Saint-Loup, and that he himself, Charlus, was an old friend of my grandmother, glad to be able to show her grandson a little of the affection that he felt for her. Nevertheless I observed that M. d'Argencourt, although I had barely been introduced to him at Mme de Villeparisis's and M. de Charlus had now spoken to him at great length about my family, was distinctly colder to me than he had been an hour ago, and thereafter, for a long time, he showed the same aloofness whenever we met. He examined me now with a curiosity in which there was no sign of friendliness, and seemed even to have to overcome an instinctive repulsion when, on leaving us, after a moment's hesitation, he held out a hand to me which he at once withdrew.

"I'm sorry about that," said M. de Charlus. "That fellow Argencourt, well born but ill bred, a worse than second-rate diplomat, an execrable husband and a womaniser, as double-faced as a villain in a play, is one of those men who are incapable of understanding but perfectly capable of destroying the things in life that are really great. I hope that our friendship will be one of them, if it is ever to be formed, and that you will do me the honour of keeping it—as I shall—well clear of the heels of any of those donkeys who, from idleness or clumsiness or sheer malice, trample on what seemed destined to endure. Unfortunately, that is the mould in which most society people have been cast."

"The Duchesse de Guermantes seems to be very intelligent. We were talking this afternoon about the possibility of war. It appears that she is especially knowledgeable on that subject."

"She is nothing of the sort," replied M. de Charlus tartly. "Women, and most men for that matter, understand nothing about what I wished to speak to you of. My sister-in-law is an agreeable woman who imagines that we are still living in the days of Balzac's novels, when women had an influence on politics. Association with her could at present only have a most unfortunate effect on you, as for that matter all social intercourse. That was one of the very things I was about to tell you when that fool interrupted me. The first sacrifice that you must make for me—I shall claim them from you in proportion to the gifts I bestow on you—is to give up going into society. It distressed me this afternoon to see you at that idiotic gathering. You will tell me that I was there myself, but for me it was not a social gathering, it was simply a family visit. Later on, when you are a man of established position, if it amuses you to stoop for a moment to that sort of thing, it may perhaps do no harm. And then I need not point out how invaluable I can be to you. The 'Open Sesame' to the Guermantes house, and any others that it is worth while throwing open the doors of to you, rests with me. I shall be the judge, and intend to remain in control of the situation. At present you are a catechumen. There was something scandalous about your presence up there. You must at all costs avoid impropriety."

Since M. de Charlus had mentioned this visit to Mme de Villeparisis's, I wanted to ask him his exact relationship to the Marquise, the latter's birth, and so on, but the question took another form on my lips than I had intended, and I asked him instead what the Villeparisis family was.

"Dear me, it's not an easy question to answer," M. de Charlus replied in a voice that seemed to skate over the words. "It's as if you had asked me to tell you what nothing was. My aunt, who is capable of anything, took it into her whimsical head to plunge the greatest name in France into oblivion by marrying for the second time a little M. Thirion. This Thirion thought that he could assume an extinct aristocratic name with impunity, as people do in novels. History doesn't relate whether he was tempted by La Tour d'Auvergne, whether he hesitated between Toulouse and Montmorency. At all events he made a different choice and became Monsieur de Villeparisis. Since there have been no Villeparisis since 1702, I thought that he simply meant to indicate modestly that he was a gentleman from Villeparisis, a little place near Paris, that he had a solicitor's practice or a barber's shop at Villeparisis. But my aunt didn't see things that way—as a matter of fact she's reaching the age when she can scarcely see at all. She tried to make out that such a marquisate existed in the family; she wrote to us all and wanted to put things on a proper footing, I don't know why. When one takes a name to which one has no right, it's best not to make too much fuss, like our excellent friend the so-called Comtesse de M. who, against the advice of Mme Alphonse Rothschild, refused to swell the coffers of the State for a title which would not have been made more authentic thereby. The joke is that ever since then my aunt has claimed a monopoly of all the paintings connected with the real Villeparisis family, to whom the late Thirion was in no way related. My aunt's country house has become a sort of repository for their portraits, genuine or not, under the rising flood of which several Guermantes and several Condés who are by no means small beer have had to disappear. The picture dealers manufacture new ones for her every year. And she even has in her dining-room in the country a portrait of Saint-Simon because of his niece's first marriage to a M. de Villeparisis, as if the author of the *Memoirs* hadn't perhaps other claims to the interest of visitors than not to have been the great-grandfather of M. Thirion."

Mme de Villeparisis being merely Mme Thirion completed the decline and fall in my estimation of her which had begun when I had seen the mixed composition of her salon. It seemed to me to be unfair that a woman whose title and name were of quite recent origin should be able thus to delude her contemporaries and might similarly delude posterity by virtue of her friendships with royal personages. Now that she had become once again what I had supposed her to be in my childhood, a person who had nothing aristocratic about her, these distinguished kinsfolk by whom she was surrounded struck me as somehow extraneous to her. She did not cease to be charming to us all. I went occasionally to see her and she sent me little presents from time to time. But I had never any impression that she belonged to the Faubourg Saint-Germain, and if I had wanted any information about it she was one of the last people to whom I should have applied.

"At present," M. de Charlus went on, "by going into society you will only damage your position, warp your intellect and character. Moreover, you must be particularly careful in choosing your friends. Keep mistresses if your family have no objection—that doesn't concern me, and indeed I can only encourage it, you young rascal—a young rascal who will soon have to start shaving," he added, touching my chin. "But your choice of men friends is more important. Eight out of ten young men are little bounders, little wretches capable of doing you an injury which you will never be able to repair. My nephew Saint-Loup, now, he might be a suitable companion for you at a pinch. As far as your future is

concerned, he can be of no possible use to you, but for that I will
suffice. And really, when all's said and done, as a person to go
about with, at times when you have had enough of me, he does
not seem to present any serious drawback that I know of. At least
he's a man, not one of those effeminate creatures one sees so many
of nowadays, who look like little rent boys and at any moment
may bring their innocent victims to the gallows." (I did not know
the meaning of this slang expression, "rent boy"; anyone who had
known it would have been as greatly surprised by his use of it as
myself. Society people always like talking slang, and people who
may be suspected of certain things like to show that they are not
afraid to mention them. A proof of innocence in their eyes. But
they have lost their sense of proportion, they are no longer capable
of realising the point beyond which a certain pleasantry will
become too technical, too flagrant, will be a proof rather of
corruption than of ingenuousness.) "He's not like the rest of
them: he's very nice, very serious."

I could not help smiling at this epithet "serious," to which the
intonation that M. de Charlus gave it seemed to impart the sense of
"virtuous," of "steady," as one says of a little shop-girl that she is
"serious." At that moment a cab passed, zigzagging along the
street. A young cabman, who had deserted his box, was driving
it from inside, where he lay sprawling on the cushions, apparently
half-tipsy. M. de Charlus instantly stopped him. The driver began
to parley:

"Which way are you going?"

"Yours." (This surprised me, for M. de Charlus had already
refused several cabs with similarly coloured lamps.)

"Well, I don't want to get up on the box. D'you mind if I stay
inside?"

"No, but lower the hood. Well, think over my proposal," said
M. de Charlus, preparing to leave me, "I give you a few days to
consider it. Write to me. I repeat, I shall need to see you every day,
and to receive from you guarantees of loyalty and discretion
which, I must admit, you do seem to offer. But in the course of
my life I have been so often deceived by appearances that I never
wish to trust them again. Damn it, it's the least I can expect that
before giving up a treasure I should know into what hands it is
going to pass. Anyway, bear in mind what I'm offering you. You
are like Hercules (though, unfortunately for yourself, you do not
appear to me to have quite his muscular development) at the

parting of the ways. Remember that you may regret for the rest of
your life not having chosen the way that leads to virtue. Hallo," he
turned to the cabman, "haven't you put the hood down? I'll do it
myself. I think, too, I'd better drive, seeing the state you appear to
be in."

He jumped in beside the cabman, and the cab set off at a brisk
trot.

As for myself, no sooner had I turned in at our gate than I came
across the pendant to the conversation which I had heard that
afternoon between Bloch and M. de Norpois, but in another
form, brief, inverted and cruel. This was a dispute between our
butler, who was a Dreyfusard, and the Guermantes', who was an
anti-Dreyfusard. The truths and counter-truths which contended
on high among the intellectuals of the rival Leagues, the Patrie
Française and the Droits de l'Homme, were fast spreading downwards into the subsoil of popular opinion. M. Reinach manipulated through their feelings people whom he had never seen,
whereas for him the Dreyfus case simply presented itself to his
reason as an irrefutable theorem which he "demonstrated" in the
sequel by the most astonishing victory for rational politics (a
victory against France, according to some) that the world has
ever seen. In two years he replaced a Billot ministry by a
Clemenceau ministry, revolutionised public opinion from top to
bottom, took Picquart from his prison to instal him, ungrateful, in
the Ministry of War. Perhaps this rationalist crowd-manipulator
was himself manipulated by his ancestry. When we find that the
systems of philosophy which contain the most truths were dictated
to their authors, in the last analysis, by reasons of sentiment, how
are we to suppose that in a simple affair of politics like the Dreyfus
case reasons of that sort may not, unbeknown to the reasoner, have
ruled his reason? Bloch believed himself to have been led by a
logical chain of reasoning to choose Dreyfusism, yet he knew that
his nose, his skin and his hair had been imposed on him by his race.
Doubtless the reason enjoys more freedom; yet it obeys certain
laws which it has not prescribed for itself. The case of the
Guermantes' butler and our own was peculiar. The waves of
the two currents of Dreyfusism and anti-Dreyfusism which now
divided France from top to bottom were, on the whole, silent, but
the occasional echoes which they emitted were sincere. When
you heard anyone in the middle of a talk which was being
deliberately kept off the Affair announce furtively some piece of

political news, generally false but always devoutly to be wished, you could induce from the nature of his predictions where his heart lay. Thus there came into conflict on certain points, on one side a timid apostolate, on the other a righteous indignation. The two butlers whom I heard arguing as I came in furnished an exception to the rule. Ours insinuated that Dreyfus was guilty, the Guermantes' that he was innocent. This was done not to conceal their personal convictions, but from cunning and competitive ruthlessness. Our butler, being uncertain whether the retrial would be ordered, wanted in case of failure to deprive the Duke's butler in advance of the joy of seeing a just cause vanquished. The Duke's butler thought that, in the event of a refusal to grant a retrial, ours would be more indignant at the detention of an innocent man on Devil's Island. The concierge looked on. I had the impression that it was not he who was the cause of dissension in the Guermantes household.

I went upstairs, and found my grandmother not at all well. For some time past, without knowing exactly what was wrong, she had been complaining of her health. It is in sickness that we are compelled to recognise that we do not live alone but are chained to a being from a different realm, from whom we are worlds apart, who has no knowledge of us and by whom it is impossible to make ourselves understood: our body. Were we to meet a brigand on the road, we might perhaps succeed in making him sensible of his own personal interest if not of our plight. But to ask pity of our body is like discoursing in front of an octopus, for which our words can have no more meaning than the sound of the tides, and with which we should be appalled to find ourselves condemned to live. My grandmother's ailments often passed unnoticed by her attention, which was always directed towards us. When they gave her too much pain, in the hope of curing them she tried in vain to understand them. If the morbid phenomena of which her body was the theatre remained obscure and beyond the reach of her mind, they were clear and intelligible to certain beings belonging to the same natural kingdom as themselves, beings to whom the human mind has learned gradually to have recourse in order to understand what its body is saying to it, as when a foreigner addresses us we try to find someone of his country who will act as interpreter. These can talk to our body, can tell us if its anger is serious or will soon be appeased. Cottard, who had been called in to examine my grandmother—and who had infuriated us by asking with a subtle smile, the moment we told him she was ill: "Ill? You're sure it's not what they call a diplomatic illness?"— tried to soothe his patient's restlessness by a milk diet. But incessant bowls of milk soup gave her no relief, because my grandmother sprinkled them liberally with salt, the injurious effects of which were then unknown (Widal not yet having made his discoveries). For, medicine being a compendium of the successive and contra- dictory mistakes of medical practitioners, when we summon the wisest of them to our aid the chances are that we may be relying on a scientific truth the error of which will be recognised in a few years' time. So that to believe in medicine would be the height of folly, if not to believe in it were not a greater folly still, for from this mass of errors a few truths have in the long run emerged. Cottard had told us to take her temperature. A thermometer was fetched. Almost throughout its entire length the tube was empty of mer- cury. One could scarcely make out, nestling at the bottom of its trough, the silver salamander. It seemed dead. The little glass pipe was slipped into my grandmother's mouth. We had no need to leave it there for long; the little sorceress had not been slow in casting her horoscope. We found her motionless, perched half- way up her tower and declining to move, showing us with preci- sion the figure that we had asked of her, a figure with which all the most careful thought that my grandmother's mind might have devoted to herself would have been incapable of furnishing her: 101°. For the first time we felt some anxiety. We shook the thermometer well, to erase the ominous sign, as though we were able thus to reduce the patient's fever simultaneously with the temperature indicated. Alas, it was only too clear that the little sibyl, bereft of reason though she was, had not pronounced judg- ment arbitrarily, for the next day, scarcely had the thermometer been inserted between my grandmother's lips when almost at once, as though with a single bound, exulting in her certainty and in her intuition of a fact that to us was imperceptible, the little prophetess had come to a halt at the same point, in an implacable immobility, and pointed once again to that figure 101 with the tip of her gleaming wand. She said nothing else; in vain had we longed, wished, prayed, she was deaf to our entreaties; it seemed as though this were her final word, a warning and a threat.

Then, in an attempt to constrain her to modify her response, we had recourse to another creature of the same kingdom, but more potent, a creature not content with questioning the body but capable of commanding it, a febrifuge of the same order as the modern aspirin, which had not then come into use. We had not brought the thermometer down below 99.5, in the hope that it would not have to rise from there. We made my grandmother swallow this drug and then replaced the thermometer in her mouth. Like an implacable warder to whom one presents a permit signed by a higher authority whose patronage one enjoys, and who, finding it to be in order, replies: "All right, I've nothing to say; if that's how it is you may pass," this time the vigilant out-sister did not move. But sullenly she seemed to be saying: "What good will it do you? Since you know quinine, she may give me the order not to go up once, ten times, twenty times. And then she'll grow tired of telling me, I know her, believe me. This won't last for ever. And then where will it have got you?"

Thereupon my grandmother felt the presence within her of a being who knew the human body better than she; the presence of a contemporary of the races that have vanished from the earth, the presence of earth's first inhabitant—far earlier than the creation of thinking man; she felt that primeval ally probing in her head, her heart, her elbow; he was reconnoitring the ground, organising everything for the prehistoric combat which began at once to be fought. In a moment, a crushed Python, the fever was vanquished by the potent chemical element to which my grandmother, across all the kingdoms, reaching out beyond all animal and vegetable life, would have liked to be able to give thanks. And she remained moved by this glimpse which she had caught, through the mists of so many centuries, of an element anterior to the creation even of plants. Meanwhile the thermometer, like one of the Parcae momentarily vanquished by a more ancient god, held its silver spindle motionless. Alas! other inferior creatures which man has trained to hunt the mysterious quarry which he himself is incapable of pursuing in the depths of his being, reported cruelly to us every day a certain quantity of albumin, not large, but constant enough for it also to appear to be related to some persistent malady which we could not detect. Bergotte had shaken that scrupulous instinct in me which made me subordinate my intellect when he spoke to me of Dr du Boulbon as of a physician who would not bore me, who would discover methods of treatment which, however strange they might appear, would adapt themselves to the singularity of my intelligence. But ideas transform themselves in us, overcome the resistance we put up to them at first, and feed upon rich intellectual reserves which were ready-made for them without our realising it. So, as happens whenever remarks we have heard made about someone we do not know have had the faculty of awakening in us the idea of great talent, of a sort of genius, in my inmost mind I now gave Dr du Boulbon the benefit of that unlimited confidence which is inspired in us by the man who, with an eye more penetrating than other men's, perceives the truth. I knew indeed that he was more of a specialist in nervous diseases, the man to whom Charcot before his death had predicted that he would reign supreme in neurology and psychiatry. "Ah, I don't know about that. It's quite possible," put in Françoise, who was in the room and who was hearing Charcot's name, as indeed du Boulbon's, for the first time. But this in no way prevented her from saying "It's possible." Her "possibles," her "perhapses," her "I don't knows" were peculiarly irritating at such moments. One wanted to say to her: "Naturally you didn't know, since you haven't the faintest idea what we are talking about. How can you even say whether it's possible or not, since you know nothing about it? Anyhow, you can't say now that you don't know what Charcot said to du Boulbon. You do know because we've just told you, and your 'perhapses' and 'possibles' are out of place, because it's a fact."

In spite of this more special competence in cerebral and nervous matters, as I knew that du Boulbon was a great physician, a superior man with a profound and inventive intellect, I begged my mother to send for him, and the hope that, by a clear perception of the malady, he might perhaps cure it, finally prevailed over the fear that we had that by calling in a consultant we would alarm my grandmother. What decided my mother was the fact that, unwittingly encouraged by Cottard, my grandmother no longer went out of doors, and scarcely rose from her bed. In vain might she answer us in the words of Mme de Sévigné's letter on Mme de La Fayette: "Everyone said she was mad not to wish to go out. I said to these persons so precipitate in their judgment: 'Mme de La Fayette is not mad!' and I stuck to that. It has taken her death to prove that she was quite right not to go out." Du Boulbon when he came decided against, if not Mme de Sévigné, whom we did not quote to him, at any rate my grandmother. Instead of sounding her chest, he gazed at her with his wonderful eyes, in which there was perhaps the illusion that he was making a profound scrutiny of his patient, or the desire to give her that illusion, which seemed spontaneous but must have become mechanical, or not to let her see that he was thinking of something quite different, or to establish his authority over her, and began to talk about Bergotte.

"Ah yes, indeed, Madame, he's splendid. How right you are to admire him! But which of his books do you prefer? Oh, really? Why, yes, perhaps that is the best after all. In any case it is the best composed of his novels. Claire is quite charming in it. Which of his male characters appeals to you most?"

I supposed at first that he was making her talk about literature because he himself found medicine boring, perhaps also to display his breadth of mind and even, with a more therapeutic aim, to restore confidence to his patient, to show her that he was not alarmed, to take her mind off the state of her health. But afterwards I realised that, being chiefly distinguished as an alienist and for his work on the brain, he had been seeking to ascertain by these questions whether my grandmother's memory was in good order. With seeming reluctance he began to inquire about her life, fixing her with a stern and sombre eye. Then suddenly, as though he had glimpsed the truth and was determined to reach it at all costs, with a preliminary rubbing of his hands to shake off any lingering hesitations which he himself might feel and any objections which we might have raised, looking down at my grandmother with a lucid eye, boldly and as though he were at last upon solid ground, punctuating his words in a quietly impressive tone, every inflexion of which was instinct with intelligence (his voice, indeed, throughout his visit remained what it naturally was, caressing, and under his bushy brows his ironical eyes were full of kindness), he said:

"You will be cured, Madame, on the day, whenever it comes—and it rests entirely with you whether it comes today—on which you realise that there is nothing wrong with you and resume your ordinary life. You tell me that you have not been eating, not going out?"

"But, Doctor, I have a temperature."

"Not just now at any rate. Besides, what a splendid excuse! Don't you know that we feed up tuberculosis patients with temperatures of 102 and keep them out in the open air?"

"But I have a little albumin as well."

"You ought not to know anything about that. You have what I have had occasion to call 'mental albumin.' We have all of us had, when we have not been very well, little albuminous phases which our doctor has done his best to prolong by calling our attention to them. For one disorder that doctors cure with medicaments (as I am assured that they do occasionally succeed in doing) they produce a dozen others in healthy subjects by inoculating them with that pathogenic agent a thousand times more virulent than all the microbes in the world, the idea that one is ill. A belief of that sort, which has a potent effect on any temperature, acts with special force on neurotic people. Tell them that a shut window is open behind their backs, and they will begin to sneeze; persuade them that you have put magnesia in their soup, and they will be seized with colic; that their coffee is stronger than usual, and they will not sleep a wink all night. Do you imagine, Madame, that I needed to do more than look you in the eyes, listen to the way in which you express yourself, observe, if I may say so, your daughter and your grandson who are so like you, to realise what was the matter with you?"

"Your grandmother might perhaps go and sit, if the doctor allows it, in some quiet path in the Champs-Elysées, near that clump of laurels where you used to play when you were little," said my mother to me, thus indirectly consulting Dr du Boulbon and her voice for that reason assuming a tone of timid deference which it would not have had if she had been addressing me alone. The doctor turned to my grandmother and, being a man of letters no less than a man of science, adjured her as follows:

"Go to the Champs-Elysées, Madame, to the clump of laurels which your grandson loves. The laurel will be beneficial to your health. It purifies. After he had exterminated the serpent Python, it was with a branch of laurel in his hand that Apollo made his entry into Delphi. He sought thus to guard himself from the deadly germs of the venomous monster. So you see that the laurel is the most ancient, the most venerable and, I may add—something that has its therapeutic as well as its prophylactic value—the most beautiful of antiseptics."

Inasmuch as a great part of what doctors know is taught them by the sick, they are easily led to believe that this knowledge which patients exhibit is common to them all, and they fondly imagine that they can impress the patient of the moment with some remark picked up at a previous bedside. Thus it was with the superior smile of a Parisian who, in conversation with a peasant, might hope to surprise him by using a word of the local dialect, that Dr du Boulbon said to my grandmother: "Probably a windy night will help to put you to sleep when the strongest soporifics would have no effect." "On the contrary, the wind always keeps me wide awake." But doctors are touchy people. "Ach!" muttered du Boulbon with a frown, as if someone had trodden on his toe, or as if my grandmother's sleeplessness on stormy nights were a personal insult to himself. He had not, however, an undue opinion of himself, and since, in his character as a "superior" person, he felt himself bound not to put any faith in medicine, he quickly recovered his philosophic serenity.

My mother, in her passionate longing for reassurance from Bergotte's friend, added in support of his verdict that a first cousin of my grandmother's, who suffered from a nervous complaint, had remained for seven years shut up in her bedroom at Combray, without getting up more than once or twice a week.

"You see, Madame, I didn't know that, and yet I could have told you."

"But, Doctor, I'm not in the least like her; on the contrary, my doctor complains that he cannot get me to stay in bed," said my grandmother, either because she was a little irritated by the doctor's theories, or because she was anxious to submit to him all the objections that might be made to them, in the hope that he would refute these and that, once he had gone, she would no longer have any doubts as to the accuracy of his encouraging diagnosis.

"Why, naturally, Madame, one cannot have—if you'll forgive the expression—every form of mental derangement. You have others, but not that particular one. Yesterday I visited a home for neurasthenics. In the garden, I saw a man standing on a bench, motionless as a fakir, his neck bent in a position which must have been highly uncomfortable. On my asking him what he was doing there, he replied without turning his head or moving a muscle: 'You see, Doctor, I am extremely rheumatic and catch cold very easily. I have just been taking a lot of exercise, and while I was foolishly getting too hot, my neck was touching my flannels. If I move it away from my flannels now before letting myself cool down, I'm sure to get a stiff neck and possibly bronchitis.' Which he would, in fact, have done. 'You're a real neurotic, that's what you are,' I told him. And do you know what argument he advanced to prove that I was mistaken? It was this: that while all the other patients in the establishment had a mania for testing their weight, so much so that the weighing-machine had to be pad- locked so that they shouldn't spend the whole day on it, he had to be lifted on to it bodily, so little did he care to be weighed. He prided himself on not sharing the mania of the others, oblivious of the fact that he had one of his own, and that it was this that saved him from another. You must not be offended by the comparison, Madame, for that man who dared not turn his neck for fear of catching a chill is the greatest poet of our day. That poor lunatic is the most lofty intellect that I know. Submit to being called a neurotic. You belong to that splendid and pitiable family which is the salt of the earth. Everything we think of as great has come to us from neurotics. It is they and they alone who found religions and create great works of art. The world will never realise how much it owes to them, and what they have suffered in order to bestow their gifts on it. We enjoy fine music, beautiful pictures, a thousand exquisite things, but we do not know what they cost those who wrought them in insomnia, tears, spasmodic laughter, urticaria, asthma, epilepsy, a terror of death which is worse than any of these, and which you perhaps have experienced, Madame," he added with a smile at my grandmother, "for confess now, when I came, you were not feeling very confident. You thought you were ill, dangerously ill, perhaps. Heaven only knows what disease you thought you had detected the symptoms of in yourself. And you were not mistaken; they were there. Neurosis has a genius for mimicry. There is no illness which it cannot counterfeit perfectly. It will produce lifelike imitations of the dilatations of dyspepsia, the nausea of pregnancy, the arythmia of the cardiac, the feverish-ness of the consumptive. If it is capable of deceiving the doctor, how should it fail to deceive the patient? Ah, do not think that I am mocking your sufferings. I should not undertake to cure them unless I understood them thoroughly. And, may I say, there is no good confession that is not reciprocal. I have told you that without nervous disorder there can be no great artist. What is more," he added, raising a solemn forefinger, "there can be no great scientist either. I will go further, and say that, unless he himself is subject to nervous trouble, he is not, I won't say a good doctor, but I do say the right doctor to treat nervous troubles. In the pathology of nervous diseases, a doctor who doesn't talk too much nonsense is a half-cured patient, just as a critic is a poet who has stopped writing verse and a policeman a burglar who has retired from practice. I, Madame, I do not, like you, fancy myself to be suffering from albuminuria, I have not your neurotic fear of food, or of fresh air, but I can never go to sleep without getting out of bed at least twenty times to see if my door is shut. And yesterday I went to that nursing-home, where I came across the poet who wouldn't move his neck, for the purpose of booking a room, for, between ourselves, I spend my holidays there looking after myself when I have aggravated my own troubles by wearing myself out in the attempt to cure those of others."

"But, Doctor, ought I to take a similar cure?" asked my grandmother, aghast.

"It is not necessary, Madame. The symptoms you betray here will vanish at my bidding. Besides, you have a very efficient person whom I appoint as your doctor from now onwards. That is your malady itself, your nervous hyperactivity. Even if I knew how to cure you of it, I should take good care not to. All I need do is to control it. I see on your table there one of Bergotte's books. Cured of your nervous diathesis, you would no longer care for it. Now, how could I take it upon myself to substitute for the joys that it procures you a nervous stability which would be quite incapable of giving you those joys? But those joys themselves are a powerful remedy, the most powerful of all perhaps. No, I have nothing to say against your nervous energy. All I ask is that it should listen to me; I leave you in its charge. It must reverse its engines. The force which it has been using to prevent you from going out, from taking sufficient food, must be directed towards making you eat, making you read, making you go out, and distracting you in every possible way. Don't tell me that you feel tired. Tiredness is the organic realisation of a preconceived idea. Begin by not thinking it. And if ever you have a slight indisposition, which is a thing that may happen to anyone, it will be just as if you hadn't, for your nervous energy will have endowed you with what M. de Talleyrand astutely called 'imaginary good health.' See, it has begun to cure you already. You've been sitting up in bed listening to me without once leaning back on your pillows, your eyes bright, colour in your cheeks. I've been talking to you for a good half-hour and you haven't noticed the time. Well, Madame, I shall now bid you good-day."

When, after seeing Dr du Boulbon to the door, I returned to the room in which my mother was alone, the anguish that had been weighing me down for several weeks suddenly lifted, I sensed that my mother was going to give vent to her joy and would observe mine too, and I felt that inability to endure the suspense of the coming moment when a person is about to be overcome with emotion in our presence, which *mutatis mutandis* is not unlike the thrill of fear that runs through one when one knows that some-body is going to come in and startle one by a door that is still closed. I tried to speak to Mamma but my voice broke, and, bursting into tears, I remained for a long time with my head on her shoulder, weeping, savouring, accepting, cherishing my grief, now that I knew that it had departed from my life, as we like to work ourselves up into a state of exaltation with virtuous plans which circumstances do not permit us to put into execution.

Françoise annoyed me by refusing to share in our joy. She was in a state of great excitement because there had been a terrible scene between the lovesick footman and the tale-bearing porter. It had required the Duchess herself, in her benevolence, to inter-vene, restore a semblance of calm, and forgive the footman. For she was a kind mistress, and it would have been the ideal "place" if only she didn't listen to "tittle-tattle."

During the last few days people had begun to hear of my grandmother's illness and to ask after her. Saint-Loup had written to me: "I do not wish to take advantage of a time when your dear grandmother is unwell to convey to you what is far more than mere reproach on a matter with which she has no concern. But I should not be speaking the truth were I to say to you, if only by preterition, that I shall ever forget the perfidy of your conduct, or that there can ever be any forgiveness for so scoundrelly a betrayal." But some other friends, supposing that my grandmother was not seriously ill, or not knowing that she was ill at all, had asked me to meet them next day in the Champs-Elysées, to go with them from there to pay a call together, ending up with a dinner in the country, the thought of which appealed to me. I had no longer any reason to forgo these two pleasures. When my grandmother had been told that it was now imperative, if she was to obey Dr du Boulbon's orders, that she should go out as much as possible, she had herself at once suggested the Champs-Elysées. It would be easy for me to escort her there; and, while she sat reading, to arrange with my friends where I should meet them later; and I should still be in time, if I made haste, to take the train with them to Ville d'Avray. When the time came, my grand-mother did not want to go out, saying that she felt tired. But my mother, acting on du Boulbon's instructions, had the strength of mind to be firm and to command obedience. She was almost in tears at the thought that my grandmother was going to relapse again into her nervous weakness and might not recover from it. Never had there been such a fine, warm day for an outing. The sun as it moved through the sky interposed here and there in the broken solidity of the balcony its insubstantial muslins, and gave to the freestone ledge a warm epidermis, an ill-defined halo of gold. As Françoise had not had time to send a "wire" to her daughter, she left us immediately after lunch. She considered it kind enough of her as it was to call first at Jupien's to get a stitch put in the cape which my grandmother was going to wear. Returning at that moment from my morning walk, I accompanied her into the shop. "Is it your young master who brings you here," Jupien asked Françoise, "is it you who have brought him to see me, or is it a fair wind and Dame Fortune that brings you both?" For all his want of education, Jupien respected the laws of syntax as instinctively as M. de Guermantes, in spite of every effort, broke them. With Françoise gone and the cape mended, it was time for my grandmother to get ready. Having obstinately refused to let Mamma stay in the room with her, left to herself she took an endlessly long time over her dressing, and now that I knew that she was not ill, with that strange indifference which we feel towards our relations so long as they are alive, and which makes us put everyone else before them, I thought it very selfish of her to take so long and to risk making me late when she knew that I had an appointment with my friends and was dining at Ville d'Avray. In my impatience I finally went downstairs without waiting for her, after I had twice been told that she was just ready. At last she joined me, without apologising to me as she generally did for having kept me waiting, flushed and bothered like a person who has come to a place in a hurry and has forgotten half her belongings, just as I was reaching the half-opened glass door which let in the liquid, humming, tepid air from outside, as though the sluices of a reservoir had been opened between the glacial walls of the house, without warming them.

"Oh, dear, if you're going to meet your friends I ought to have put on another cape. I look rather wretched in this one."

I was startled to see her so flushed, and supposed that having begun by making herself late she had had to hurry over her dressing. When we left the cab at the corner of the Avenue Gabriel, in the Champs-Elysées, I saw my grandmother turn away without a word and make for the little old pavilion with its green trellis at the door of which I had once waited for Françoise.

The same park-keeper who had been there then was still there beside the "Marquise" as, following my grandmother who, doubtless because she was feeling sick, had her hand in front of her mouth, I climbed the steps of the little rustic theatre erected there in the middle of the gardens. At the entrance, as in those travelling circuses where the clown, dressed for the ring and smothered in flour, stands at the door and takes the money himself for the seats, the "Marquise," at the receipt of custom, was still in her place with her huge, irregular face smeared with coarse paint and her little bonnet of red flowers and black lace surmounting her auburn wig. But I do not think she recognised me. The park-keeper, abandoning the supervision of the greenery, with the colour of which his uniform had been designed to harmonise, was sitting beside her chatting.

"So you're still here," he was saying. "You don't think of retiring?"

"And why should I retire, Monsieur? Will you tell me where I should be better off than here, where I'd be more comfy and snug? And then there's all the coming and going, plenty of distraction. My little Paris, I call it; my customers keep me in touch with everything that's going on. Just to give you an example, there's one of them went out not five minutes ago; he's a judge, a proper high-up. Well!" she exclaimed heatedly, as though prepared to maintain the truth of this assertion by violence, should the agent of civic authority show any sign of challenging its accuracy, "for the last eight years, do you hear me, every blessed day, regular on the stroke of three he comes here, always polite, never saying one word louder than another, never making any mess; and he stays half an hour and more to read his papers while seeing to his little needs. There was one day he didn't come. I never noticed it at the time, but that evening, all of a sudden I says to myself: 'Why, that gentleman never came today; perhaps he's dead!' And I came over all queer, seeing as how I get quite fond of people when they behave nicely. And so I was very glad when I saw him come in again next day, and I said to him: 'I hope nothing happened to you yesterday, sir?' And he told me nothing had happened to *him*, it was his wife that had died, and it had given him such a turn he hadn't been able to come. He looked sad, of course—well, you know, people who've been married five-and-twenty years—but he seemed pleased, all the same, to be back here. You could see that all his little habits had been quite upset. I did what I could to cheer him up. I said to him: 'You mustn't let go of things, sir. Just keep coming here the same as before, it will be a little distraction for you in your sorrow.'"

The "Marquise" resumed a gentler tone, for she had observed that the guardian of groves and lawns was listening to her good-naturedly and with no thought of contradiction, keeping harm-lessly in its scabbard a sword which looked more like a gardening implement or some horticultural emblem.

"And besides," she went on, "I choose my customers, I don't let everyone into my parlours, as I call them. Doesn't it just look like a parlour with all my flowers? Such friendly customers I have; there's always someone or other brings me a spray of nice lilac, or jasmine or roses; my favourite flowers, roses are."

The thought that we were perhaps viewed with disfavour by this lady because we never brought any sprays of lilac or fine roses to her bower made me blush, and in the hope of escaping physi-cally (or of being condemned only *in absentia*) from an adverse judgment, I moved towards the exit. But it is not always in this world the people who bring us fine roses to whom we are most friendly, for the "Marquise," thinking that I was bored, turned to me:

"You wouldn't like me to open a little cabin for you?"

And, on my declining:

"No? You're sure you won't?" she persisted, smiling. "You're welcome to it, but of course, not having to pay for a thing won't make you want to do it if you've got nothing to do."

At this moment a shabbily dressed woman hurried into the place who seemed to be feeling precisely the want in question. But she did not belong to the "Marquise's" world, for the latter, with the ferocity of a snob, said to her curtly:

"I've nothing vacant, Madame."

"Will they be long?" asked the poor lady, flushed beneath the yellow flowers in her hat.

"Well, ma'am, if you want my advice you'd better try some-where else. You see, there's still these two gentlemen waiting, and I've only one closet; the others are out of order."

"Looked like a bad payer to me," she explained when the other had gone. "That's not the sort we want here, either; they're not clean, don't treat the place with respect. It'd be me who'd have to spend the next hour cleaning up after her ladyship. I'm not sorry to lose her couple of sous."

At last, after a good half-hour, my grandmother emerged, and fearing that she might not seek to atone by a lavish gratuity for the indiscretion she had shown by remaining so long inside, I beat a retreat so as not to have to share in the scorn which the "Marquise" would no doubt heap on her, and strolled down a path, but slowly, so that my grandmother should not have to hurry to overtake me, as presently she did. I expected her to begin: "I'm afraid I've kept you waiting; I hope you'll still be in time for your friends," but she did not utter a single word, so much so that, feeling a little hurt, I was disinclined to speak first. Finally, looking up at her I noticed that as she walked beside me she kept her face turned the other way. I was afraid that she might be feeling sick again. I looked at her more closely and was struck by the disjointedness of her gait. Her hat was crooked, her cloak stained; she had the dishevelled and disgruntled appearance, the flushed, slightly dazed look of a person who has just been knocked down by a carriage or pulled out of a ditch.

"I was afraid you were feeling sick, Grandmamma; are you feeling better now?" I asked her.

Doubtless she thought that it would be impossible for her not to make some answer without alarming me.

"I heard the whole of the 'Marquise's' conversation with the keeper," she told me. "Could anything have been more typical of the Guermantes, or the Verdurins and their little clan? 'Ah! in what courtly terms those things were put!'"[24] And she added, with deliberate application, this from her own special Marquise, Mme de Sévigné: "As I listened to them I thought that they were preparing for me the delights of a farewell."

Such were the remarks that she addressed to me, remarks into which she had put all her critical delicacy, her love of quotation, her memory of the classics, more thoroughly even than she would normally have done, and as though to prove that she retained possession of all these faculties. But I guessed rather than heard what she said, so inaudible was the voice in which she mumbled her sentences, clenching her teeth more than could be accounted for by the fear of vomiting.

"Come!" I said lightly enough not to seem to be taking her illness too seriously, "since you're feeling a little sick I suggest we go home. I don't want to trundle a grandmother with indigestion about the Champs-Elysées."

"I didn't like to suggest it because of your friends," she replied. "Poor pet! But if you don't mind, I think it would be wiser."

I was afraid of her noticing the strange way in which she uttered these words.

"Come," I said to her brusquely, "you mustn't tire yourself talking when you're feeling sick—it's silly; wait till we get home."

She smiled at me sorrowfully and gripped my hand. She had realised that there was no need to hide from me what I had at once guessed, that she had had a slight stroke.

PART TWO

CHAPTER ONE

WE made our way back along the Avenue Gabriel through the strolling crowds. I left my grandmother to rest on a bench and went in search of a cab. She, in whose heart I always placed myself in order to form an opinion of the most insignificant person, she was now closed to me, had become part of the external world, and, more than from any casual passer-by, I was obliged to keep from her what I thought of her condition, to betray no sign of my anxiety. I could not have spoken of it to her with any more confidence than to a stranger. She had suddenly returned to me the thoughts, the griefs which, from my earliest childhood, I had entrusted to her for all time. She was not yet dead. But I was already alone. And even those allusions which she had made to the Guermantes, to Molière, to our conversations about the little clan, assumed a baseless, adventitious, fantastical air, because they sprang from this same being who tomorrow perhaps would have ceased to exist, for whom they would no longer have any meaning, from the non-being—incapable of conceiving them—which my grandmother would shortly be.

"Monsieur, I don't like to say no, but you have not made an appointment, you haven't a number. Besides, this is not my day for seeing patients. You surely have a doctor of your own. I cannot stand in for him, unless he calls me in for consultation. It's a question of professional etiquette . . ."

Just as I was signalling to a cabman, I had caught sight of the famous Professor E——, almost a friend of my father and grandfather, acquainted at any rate with them both, who lived in the Avenue Gabriel, and, on a sudden inspiration, had stopped him just as he was entering his house, thinking that he would perhaps be the very person to examine my grandmother. But, being evidently in a hurry, after collecting his letters he seemed anxious to get rid of me, and I could only speak to him by going up with him in the lift, of which he begged me to allow him to press the buttons himself, this being an idiosyncrasy of his.

"But Doctor, I'm not asking you to see my grandmother here; you will realise when I've explained to you that she isn't in a fit state; what I'm asking is that you should call at our house in half an hour's time, when I've taken her home."

"Call at your house! Really, Monsieur, you can't mean such a thing. I'm dining with the Minister of Commerce. I have a call to pay first. I must change at once, and to make matters worse my tail-coat is torn and the other one has no buttonhole for my decorations. Would you please oblige me by not touching the lift-buttons. You don't know how the lift works; one can't be too careful. Getting that buttonhole made means more delay. However, out of friendship for your family, if your grandmother comes here at once I'll see her. But I warn you I shan't be able to give her more than a quarter of an hour."

I had set off again at once, without even getting out of the lift, which Professor E—— had himself set in motion to take me down again, eyeing me distrustfully as he did so.

We may, indeed, say that the hour of death is uncertain, but when we say this we think of that hour as situated in a vague and remote expanse of time; it does not occur to us that it can have any connexion with the day that has already dawned and can mean that death—or its first assault and partial possession of us, after which it will never leave hold of us again—may occur this very afternoon, so far from uncertain, this afternoon whose time-table, hour by hour, has been settled in advance. One insists on one's daily outing so that in a month's time one will have had the necessary ration of fresh air; one has hesitated over which coat to take, which cabman to call; one is in the cab, the whole day lies before one, short because one must be back home early, as a friend is coming to see one; one hopes that it will be as fine again tomorrow; and one has no suspicion that death, which has been advancing within one on another plane, has chosen precisely this particular day to make its appearance, in a few minutes' time, more or less at the moment when the carriage reaches the Champs-Elysées. Perhaps those who are habitually haunted by the fear of the utter strangeness of death will find something reassuring in this kind of death—in this kind of first contact with death—because death thus assumes a known, familiar, everyday guise. A good lunch has preceded it, and the same outing that people take who are in perfect health. A drive home in an open carriage comes on top of its first onslaught; ill as my grandmother was, there were, after all, several people who could testify that at six o'clock, as we came home from the Champs-Elysées, they had bowed to her as she drove past in an open carriage, in perfect weather. Legrandin, making his way towards the Place de la Concorde, raised his hat to us, stopping to look after us with an air of surprise. I, who was not yet detached from life, asked my grandmother if she had acknowledged his greeting, reminding her of his touchiness. My grandmother, thinking me no doubt very frivolous, raised her hand in the air as though to say: "What does it matter? It's of no importance."

Yes, it might have been said that a few minutes earlier, while I was looking for a cab, my grandmother was resting on a bench in the Avenue Gabriel, and that a little later she had driven past in an open carriage. But would it have been really true? A bench, in order to maintain its position at the side of an avenue—although it may also be subject to certain conditions of equilibrium—has no need of energy. But in order for a living being to be stable, even when supported by a bench or in a carriage, there must be a tension of forces which we do not ordinarily perceive, any more than we perceive (because its action is multi-dimensional) atmospheric pressure. Perhaps if a vacuum were created within us and we were left to bear the pressure of the air, we should feel, in the moment that preceded our extinction, the terrible weight which there was now nothing else to neutralise. Similarly, when the abyss of sickness and death opens up within us, and we have nothing left to oppose to the tumult with which the world and our own body rush upon us, then to sustain even the thought of our muscles, even the shudder that pierces us to the marrow, then even to keep ourselves still, in what we ordinarily regard as no more than the simple negative position of a thing, demands, if one wants one's head to remain erect and one's demeanour calm, an expense of vital energy and becomes the object of an exhausting struggle.

And if Legrandin had looked back at us with that air of astonishment, it was because to him, as to the other people who passed us then, in the cab in which my grandmother was apparently sitting on the back seat, she had seemed to be foundering, slithering into the abyss, clinging desperately to the cushions which could scarcely hold back the headlong plunge of her body, her hair dishevelled, her eyes wild, no longer capable of facing the assault of the images which their pupils no longer had the strength to bear. She had appeared, although I was beside her, to be plunged in that unknown world in the heart of which she had already received the blows of which she bore the marks when I had looked up at her in the Champs-Elysées, her hat, her face, her coat deranged by the hand of the invisible angel with whom she had wrestled.

I have thought, since, that this moment of her stroke cannot have altogether surprised my grandmother, that indeed she had perhaps foreseen it a long time back, had lived in expectation of it. She had not known, naturally, when this fatal moment would come, had never been certain, any more than those lovers whom a similar doubt leads alternately to found unreasonable hopes and unjustified suspicions on the fidelity of their mistresses. But it is rare for these grave illnesses, such as that which now at last had struck her full in the face, not to take up residence in a sick person a long time before killing him, during which period they hasten, like a "sociable" neighbour or tenant, to make themselves known to him. A terrible acquaintance, not so much for the sufferings that it causes as for the strange novelty of the terminal restrictions which it imposes upon life. We see ourselves dying, in these cases, not at the actual moment of death but months, sometimes years before, when death has hideously come to dwell in us. We make the acquaintance of the Stranger whom we hear coming and going in our brain. True, we do not know him by sight, but from the sounds we hear him regularly make we can form an idea of his habits. Is he a malefactor? One morning, we can no longer hear him. He has gone. Ah! if only it were for ever! In the evening he has returned. What are his plans? The consultant, put to the question, like an adored mistress, replies with avowals that one day are believed, another day questioned. Or rather it is not the mistress's role but that of interrogated servants that the doctor plays. They are only third parties. The person whom we press for an answer, whom we suspect of being about to play us false, is Life itself, and although we feel it to be no longer the same, we believe in it still, or at least remain undecided until the day on which it finally abandons us.

I helped my grandmother into Professor E——'s lift and a moment later he came to us and took us into his consulting-room. But there, pressed for time though he was, his offensive manner changed, such is the force of habit, and his habit was to be friendly, not to say playful, with his patients. Since he knew that my grandmother was a great reader, and was himself one, he devoted the first few minutes to quoting various favourite passages of poetry appropriate to the glorious summer weather. He had placed her in an armchair and himself with his back to the light so as to have a good view of her. His examination was minute and thorough, even obliging me to leave the room for a moment. He continued it after my return, then, having finished, went on, although the quarter of an hour was almost at an end, repeating various quotations to my grandmother. He even made a few jokes, which were witty enough, though I should have preferred to hear them on some other occasion, but which completely reassured me by the tone of amusement in which he uttered them. I then remembered that M. Fallières, the President of the Senate, had, many years earlier, had a false seizure, and that to the consternation of his political rivals he had taken up his duties again a few days later and had begun, it was said, to prepare an eventual candidature for the Presidency of the Republic. My confidence in my grandmother's prompt recovery was all the more complete in that, just as I was recalling the example of M. Fallières, I was distracted from pursuing the parallel by a shout of laughter which served as conclusion to one of the Professor's jokes. After which he took out his watch, frowned feverishly on seeing that he was five minutes late, and while he bade us good-bye rang for his dress clothes to be brought to him at once. I waited until my grandmother had left the room, closed the door and asked him to tell me the truth.

"Your grandmother is doomed," he said to me. "It is a stroke brought on by uraemia. In itself, uraemia is not necessarily fatal, but this case seems to me hopeless. I need not tell you that I hope I am mistaken. At all events, with Cottard you're in excellent hands. Excuse me," he broke off as a maid came into the room with his tail-coat over her arm. "As I told you, I'm dining with the Minister of Commerce, and I have a call to pay first. Ah! life is not all a bed of roses, as one is apt to think at your age."

And he graciously offered me his hand. I had shut the door behind me, and a footman was ushering us into the hall, when my grandmother and I heard a great shout of rage. The maid had forgotten to cut and hem the buttonhole for the decorations. This would take another ten minutes. The Professor continued to storm while I stood on the landing gazing at my grandmother

who was doomed. Each of us is indeed alone. We set off homewards.

The sun was sinking; it burnished an interminable wall along
which our cab had to pass before reaching the street in which we
lived, a wall against which the shadow of horse and carriage cast by
the setting sun stood out in black on a ruddy background, like a
hearse on some Pompeian terra-cotta. At length we arrived at the
house. I sat the invalid down at the foot of the staircase in the hall,
and went up to warn my mother. I told her that my grandmother
had come home feeling slightly unwell, after an attack of giddi-
ness. As soon as I began to speak, my mother's face was convulsed
by a paroxysm of despair, a despair which was yet already so
resigned that I realised that for many years she had been holding
herself quietly in readiness for an indeterminate but inexorable
day. She asked me no questions; it seemed that, just as malevolence
likes to exaggerate the sufferings of others, she in her loving
tenderness did not want to admit that her mother was seriously
ill, especially with a disease which might have affected the brain.
Mamma shuddered, her eyes wept without tears, she ran to give
orders for the doctor to be fetched at once; but when Françoise
asked who was ill she could not reply, her voice stuck in her throat.
She came running downstairs with me, struggling to banish from
her face the sob that crumpled it. My grandmother was waiting
below on the settee in the hall, but as soon as she heard us coming
she drew herself up, rose to her feet, and waved her hand cheerfully at Mamma. I had partially wrapped her head in a white lace
shawl, telling her that this was to prevent her from catching cold
on the stairs. I had hoped that my mother might not immediately
notice the alteration in the face, the distortion of the mouth. My
precaution proved unnecessary: my mother went up to my grandmother, kissed her hand as though it were that of her God, raised
her up and supported her to the lift with an infinite care which
reflected, together with the fear of being clumsy and hurting her,
the humility of one who felt herself unworthy to touch what was
for her the most precious thing in the world, but not once did she
raise her eyes and look at the sufferer's face. Perhaps this was in
order that my grandmother should not be saddened by the
thought that the sight of her might have alarmed her daughter.
Perhaps from fear of a grief so piercing that she dared not face
it. Perhaps from respect, because she did not feel it permissible
for her without impiety to notice the trace of any mental

enfeeblement on those revered features. Perhaps to be better able to preserve intact in her memory the image of the true face of my grandmother, radiant with wisdom and goodness. So they went up side by side, my grandmother half-hidden in her shawl, my mother averting her eyes.

Meanwhile there was one person who never took hers from what could be discerned of my grandmother's altered features at which her daughter dared not look, a person who fastened on them a dumbfounded, indiscreet and ominous look: this was Françoise. Not that she was not sincerely attached to my grand-mother (indeed she had been disappointed and almost scandalised by the coldness shown by Mamma, whom she would have liked to see fling herself weeping into her mother's arms), but she had a certain tendency always to look at the worse side of things, and had retained from her childhood two characteristics which would seem to be mutually exclusive, but which, when combined, reinforce one another: the lack of restraint common among uneducated people who make no attempt to conceal the impres-sion, indeed the painful alarm aroused in them by the sight of a physical change which it would be more tactful to appear not to notice, and the unfeeling roughness of the peasant who tears the wings off dragonflies until she gets a chance to wring the necks of chickens, and lacks that sense of shame which would make her conceal the interest that she feels in the sight of suffering flesh.

When, thanks to the faultless ministrations of Françoise, my grandmother had been put to bed, she discovered that she could speak much more easily, the little rupture or obstruction of a blood-vessel which had produced the uraemia having apparently been quite slight. And at once she was anxious not to fail Mamma in her hour of need, to assist her in the most cruel moments through which she had yet to pass.

"Well, my child," she began, taking my mother's hand in one of hers, and keeping the other in front of her lips, in order thus to account for the slight difficulty which she still found in pronoun-cing certain words. "So this is all the pity you show your mother! You look as if you thought that indigestion was quite a pleasant thing!"

Then for the first time my mother's eyes gazed passionately into those of my grandmother, not wishing to see the rest of her face, and she replied, beginning the list of those false promises which we swear but are unable to keep:

"Mamma, you'll soon be quite well again, your daughter will see to that."

And gathering up all her most ardent love, all her determination that her mother should recover, she entrusted them to a kiss which she accompanied with her whole mind, with her whole being until it flowered upon her lips, and bent down to lay it humbly, reverently, on the beloved forehead.

My grandmother complained of a sort of alluvial deposit of bedclothes which kept gathering all the time in the same place, over her left leg, and which she could never manage to lift off. But she did not realise that she was herself the cause of this (so that day after day she accused Françoise unjustly of not "doing" her bed properly). By a convulsive movement she kept flinging to that side the whole flood of those billowing blankets of fine wool, which gathered there like the sand in a bay which is very soon transformed into a beach (unless a breakwater is built) by the successive deposits of the tide.

My mother and I (whose mendacity was exposed before we spoke by the obnoxious perspicaciousness of Françoise) would not even admit that my grandmother was seriously ill, as though such an admission might give pleasure to her enemies (not that she had any) and it was more loving to feel that she was not so bad as all that, in short from the same instinctive sentiment which had led me to suppose that Andrée pitied Albertine too much to be really fond of her. The same individual phenomena are reproduced in the mass, in great crises. In a war, the man who does not love his country says nothing against it, but regards it as doomed, pities it, sees everything in the blackest colours.

Françoise was infinitely helpful to us owing to her faculty of doing without sleep, of performing the most arduous tasks. And if, when she had gone to bed after several nights spent in the sick-room, we were obliged to call her a quarter of an hour after she had fallen asleep, she was so happy to be able to perform painful duties as if they had been the simplest things in the world that, far from baulking, she would show signs of satisfaction tinged with modesty. Only when the time came for mass, or for breakfast, even if my grandmother had been in her death throes, Françoise would have slipped away in order not to be late. She neither could nor would let her place be taken by her young footman. It was true that she had brought from Combray an extremely exalted idea of everyone's duty towards ourselves; she would not have tolerated that any of our servants should "fail" us. This doctrine had made her so noble, so imperious, so efficient an instructor that we had never had in our house any servants, however corrupt, who had not speedily modified and purified their conception of life so far as to refuse to touch the usual commissions from tradesmen and to come rushing—however little they might previously have sought to oblige—to take from my hands and not let me tire myself by carrying the smallest parcel. But at Combray Françoise had contracted also—and had brought with her to Paris—the habit of not being able to put up with any assistance in her work. The sight of anyone coming to help her seemed to her like a deadly insult, and servants had remained for weeks without receiving from her any response to their morning greeting, had even gone off on their holidays without her bidding them good-bye or their guessing her reason, which was simply and solely that they had offered to do a share of her work on some day when she had not been well. And at this moment when my grandmother was so ill, Françoise's duties seemed to her peculiarly her own. She would not allow herself, as the official incumbent, to be done out of her role in the ritual of these gala days. And so her young footman, discarded by her, did not know what to do with himself, and not content with having copied the butler's example and supplied himself with notepaper from my desk, had begun as well to borrow volumes of poetry from my bookshelves. He sat reading them for a good half of the day, out of admiration for the poets who had written them, but also in order, during the rest of his time, to sprinkle with quotations the letters which he wrote to his friends in his native village. True, his intention was to dazzle them. But since he was somewhat lacking in logic he had formed the notion that these poems, picked out at random from my shelves, were things of common currency to which it was customary to refer. So much so that in writing to these peasants whom he expected to impress, he interspersed his own reflexions with lines from Lamartine, just as he might have said "Who laughs last, laughs longest!" or merely "How are you keeping?"

Because of her acute pain my grandmother was given morphine. Unfortunately, if this relieved the pain it also increased the quantity of albumin. The blows which we aimed at the evil which had settled inside her were always wide of the mark, and it was she, it was her poor interposed body that had to bear them, without her ever uttering more than a faint groan by way of complaint. And the pain that we caused her found no compensation in any benefit that we were able to give her. The ferocious beast we were anxious to exterminate we barely succeeded in grazing; we merely enraged it even more, hastening perhaps the moment when the captive would be devoured. On certain days when the discharge of albumin had been excessive Cottard, after some hesitation, stopped the morphine. During these brief moments in which he deliberated, in which the relative dangers of one and another course of treatment fought it out between them in his mind until he arrived at a decision, this man who was so insignificant and so commonplace had something of the greatness of a general who, vulgar in all things else, moves us by his decisiveness when the fate of the country is at stake and, after a moment's reflexion, he decides upon what is from the military point of view the wisest course, and gives the order: "Advance eastwards." Medically, however little hope there might be of bringing this attack of uraemia to an end, it was important not to put a strain on the kidneys. But, on the other hand, when my grandmother was given no morphine, her pain became unbearable; she would perpetually attempt a certain movement which it was difficult for her to perform without groaning: to a great extent, pain is a sort of need on the part of the organism to take cognisance of a new state which is troubling it, to adapt its sensibility to that state. We can discern this origin of pain in the case of certain discomforts which are not such for everyone. Into a room filled with pungent smoke two men of coarse fibre will come and attend to their business; a third, more sensitively constituted, will betray an incessant discomfort. His nostrils will continue to sniff anxiously the odour which he ought, one would think, to try not to notice but which he will keep on attempting to accommodate, by a more exact apprehension of it, to his troubled sense of smell. Hence the fact that an intense preoccupation will prevent one from complaining of a toothache. When my grandmother was suffering thus the sweat trickled over the mauve expanse of her forehead, glueing her white locks to it, and if she thought that none of us was in the room she would cry out: "Oh, it's dreadful!"—but if she caught sight of my mother, at once she devoted all her energy to banishing from her face every sign of pain, or alternatively repeated the same plaints accompanying them with explanations which gave a different sense retrospectively to those which my mother might have overheard:

"Ah! my dear, it's dreadful to have to stay in bed on a beautiful sunny day like this when one wants to be out in the fresh air—I've been weeping with rage against your instructions."

But she could not get rid of the anguish in her eyes, the sweat on her forehead, the convulsive start, checked at once, of her limbs.

"I'm not in pain, I'm complaining because I'm not lying very comfortably, I feel my hair is untidy, I feel sick, I knocked my head against the wall."

And my mother, at the foot of the bed, riveted to that suffering as though, by dint of piercing with her gaze that pain-racked forehead, that body which contained the evil thing, she must ultimately succeed in reaching and removing it, my mother said:

"No, no, Mamma dear, we won't let you suffer like that, we'll find something to take it away, have patience just for a moment; let me give you a kiss, darling—no, you're not to move."

And stooping over the bed, with her knees bent, almost kneeling on the ground, as though by an exercise of humility she would have a better chance of making acceptable the impassioned gift of herself, she lowered towards my grandmother her whole life contained in her face as in a ciborium which she was holding out to her, adorned with dimples and folds so passionate, so sorrowful, so sweet that one could not have said whether they had been engraved on it by a kiss, a sob or a smile. My grandmother too tried to lift up her face to Mamma's. It was so altered that probably, had she been strong enough to go out, she would have been recognised only by the feather in her hat. Her features, as though during a modelling session, seemed to be straining, with an effort which distracted her from everything else, to conform to some particular model which we failed to identify. The work of the sculptor was nearing its end, and if my grandmother's face had shrunk in the process, it had at the same time hardened. The veins that traversed it seemed those not of marble, but of some more rugged stone. Permanently thrust forward by the difficulty that she found in breathing, and as permanently withdrawn into itself by exhaustion, her face, worn, diminished, terrifyingly expressive, seemed like the rude, flushed, purplish, desperate face of some wild guardian of a tomb in a primitive, almost prehistoric sculpture. But the work was not yet completed. Afterwards, the sculpture would have to be broken, and into that tomb—so painfully and tensely guarded—be lowered.

At one of those moments when, as the saying goes, we did not know which way to turn, since my grandmother was coughing and sneezing a good deal, we took the advice of a relative who assured us that if we sent for the specialist X—— the trouble would be over in a couple of days. Society people say that sort of thing about their own doctors, and their friends believe them just as Françoise always believed the advertisements in the newspapers. The specialist came with his bag packed with all the colds and coughs of his other patients, like Aeolus's goatskin. My grandmother refused point-blank to let herself be examined. And we, out of consideration for this doctor who had been put to trouble for nothing, deferred to the desire that he expressed to inspect each of our noses in turn, although there was nothing the matter with any of them. According to him, however, there was; everything, whether headache or colic, heart-disease or diabetes, was a disease of the nose that had been wrongly diagnosed. To each of us he said: "I should like to have another look at that little nozzle. Don't put it off too long. I'll soon clear it for you with a hot needle." Of course we paid no attention whatsoever. And yet we asked ourselves: "Clear it of what?" In a word, every one of our noses was infected; his mistake lay only in his use of the present tense. For by the following day his examination and provisional treatment had taken effect. Each of us had his or her catarrh. And when in the street he ran into my father doubled up with a cough, he smiled to think that an ignorant layman might suppose the attack to be due to his intervention. He had examined us at a moment when we were already ill.

My grandmother's illness gave occasion to various people to manifest an excess or deficiency of sympathy which surprised us quite as much as the sort of chance which led one or another of them to reveal to us connecting links of circumstances, or even of friendships, which we had never suspected. And the signs of interest shown by the people who called incessantly at the house to inquire revealed to us the gravity of an illness which, until then, we had not sufficiently detached from the countless painful impressions that we received by my grandmother's sickbed. Informed by telegram, her sisters declined to leave Combray. They had discovered a musician there who gave them excellent chamber recitals, in listening to which they felt they could enjoy better than by the invalid's bedside a contemplative melancholy, a sorrowful exaltation, the form of which was, to say the least of it, unusual. Mme Sazerat wrote to Mamma, but in the tone of a person whom the sudden breaking off of an engagement (the cause of the rupture being Dreyfusism) has separated from one for ever. Bergotte, on the other hand, came every day and spent several hours with me.

He had always enjoyed going regularly for some time to the same house where he had no need to stand on ceremony. But formerly it had been in order that he might talk without being interrupted; now it was so that he might sit for as long as he chose in silence, without being expected to talk. For he was very ill, some people said with albuminuria, like my grandmother, while according to others he had a tumour. He grew steadily weaker; it was with difficulty that he climbed our staircase, with greater difficulty still that he went down it. Even though he held on to the banisters he often stumbled, and he would, I believe, have stayed at home had he not been afraid of losing altogether the habit and the capacity of going out, he, the "man with the goatee" whom I remembered as being so alert not very long since. He was now quite blind, and often he even had trouble with his speech.

But at the same time, by a directly opposite process, the corpus of his work, known only to a few literary people at the period when Mme Swann used to patronise their timid efforts to disseminate it, now grown in stature and strength in the eyes of all, had acquired an extraordinary power of expansion among the general public. No doubt it often happens that only after his death does a writer become famous. But it was while he was still alive, and during his own slow progress towards approaching death, that this writer was able to watch the progress of his works towards Renown. A dead writer can at least be illustrious without any strain on himself. The effulgence of his name stops short at his gravestone. In the deafness of eternal sleep he is not importuned by Glory. But for Bergotte the antithesis was still incomplete. He existed still sufficiently to suffer from the tumult. He still moved about, though with difficulty, while his books, cavorting like daughters whom one loves but whose impetuous youthfulness and noisy pleasures tire one, brought day after day to his very bedside a crowd of fresh admirers.

The visits which he now began to pay us came for me several years too late, for I no longer had the same admiration for him as of old. This was in no sense incompatible with the growth of his reputation. A man's work seldom becomes completely understood and successful before that of another writer, still obscure, has begun, among a few more exigent spirits, to substitute a fresh cult for the one that has almost ceased to command observance. In Bergotte's books, which I constantly re-read, his sentences stood out as clearly before my eyes as my own thoughts, the furniture in my room and the carriages in the street. All the details were easily visible, not perhaps precisely as one had always seen them, but at any rate as one was accustomed to see them now. But a new writer had recently begun to publish work in which the relations between things were so different from those that connected them for me that I could understand hardly anything of what he wrote. He would say, for instance: "The hose-pipes admired the splendid upkeep of the roads" (and so far it was simple, I followed him smoothly along those roads) "which set out every five minutes from Briand and Claudel." At that point I ceased to understand, because I had expected the name of a place and was given that of a person instead. Only I felt that it was not the sentence that was badly constructed but I myself that lacked the strength and agility necessary to reach the end. I would start afresh, striving tooth and nail to reach the point from which I would see the new relationships between things. And each time, after I had got about half-way through the sentence, I would fall back again, as later on, in the Army, in my attempts at the exercises on the horizontal bar. I felt nevertheless for the new writer the admiration which an awkward boy who gets nought for gymnastics feels when he watches another more nimble. And from then onwards I felt less admiration for Bergotte, whose limpidity struck me as a deficiency. There was a time when people recognised things quite easily when it was Fromentin who had painted them, and could not recognise them at all when it was Renoir.

People of taste tell us nowadays that Renoir is a great eighteenth-century painter. But in so saying they forget the element of Time, and that it took a great deal of time, even at the height of the nineteenth century, for Renoir to be hailed as a great artist. To succeed thus in gaining recognition, the original painter or the original writer proceeds on the lines of the oculist. The course of treatment they give us by their painting or by their prose is not always pleasant. When it is at an end the practitioner says to us: "Now look!" And, lo and behold, the world around us (which was not created once and for all, but is created afresh as often as an original artist is born) appears to us entirely different from the old world, but perfectly clear. Women pass in the street, different from those we formerly saw, because they are Renoirs, those Renoirs we persistently refused to see as women. The carriages, too, are Renoirs, and the water, and the sky; we feel tempted to go for a walk in the forest which is identical with the one which when we first saw it looked like anything in the world except a forest, like for instance a tapestry of innumerable hues but lacking precisely the hues peculiar to forests. Such is the new and perishable universe which has just been created. It will last until the next geological catastrophe is precipitated by a new painter or writer of original talent.

The writer who had taken Bergotte's place in my affections wearied me not by the incoherence but by the novelty—perfectly coherent—of associations which I was unaccustomed to following. The point, always the same, at which I felt myself falter indicated the identity of each renewed feat of acrobatics that I must undertake. Moreover, when once in a thousand times I did succeed in following the writer to the end of his sentence, what I saw there always had a humour, a truthfulness and a charm similar to those which I had found long ago in reading Bergotte, only more delightful. I reflected that it was not so many years since a renewal of the world similar to that which I now expected his successor to produce had been wrought for me by Bergotte himself. And I was led to wonder whether there was any truth in the distinction which we are always making between art, which is no more advanced now than in Homer's day, and science with its continuous progress. Perhaps, on the contrary, art was in this respect like science; each new original writer seemed to me to have advanced beyond the stage of his immediate predecessor; and who was to say whether in twenty years' time, when I should be able to accompany without strain or effort the newcomer of today, another might not emerge in the face of whom the present one would go the way of Bergotte?

I spoke to the latter of the new writer. He put me off him not so much by assuring me that his art was uncouth, facile and vacuous, as by telling me that he had seen him and had almost mistaken him (so strong was the likeness) for Bloch. The latter's image thenceforth loomed over the printed pages, and I no longer felt under compulsion to make the effort necessary to understand them. If Bergotte had decried him to me it was less, I fancy, from jealousy of a success that was yet to come than from ignorance of his work.

He read scarcely anything. The bulk of his thought had long since passed from his brain into his books. He had grown thin, as though they had been extracted from him by a surgical operation. His reproductive instinct no longer impelled him to any activity, now that he had given an independent existence to almost all his thoughts. He led the vegetative life of a convalescent, of a woman after childbirth; his fine eyes remained motionless, vaguely dazed, like the eyes of a man lying on the sea-shore and in a vague day-dream contemplating only each little breaking wave. However, if it was less interesting to talk to him now than I should once have found it, I felt no compunction about that. He was so far a creature of habit that the simplest as well as the most luxurious habits, once he had formed them, became indispensable to him for a certain length of time. I do not know what made him come to our house the first time, but thereafter he came every day simply because he had been there the day before. He would turn up at the house as he might have gone to a café, in order that no one should talk to him, in order that he might—very rarely—talk himself, so that it would have been difficult on the whole to say whether he was moved by our grief or that he enjoyed my company, had one sought to draw any conclusion from such assiduity. But it did not fail to impress my mother, sensitive to everything that might be regarded as an act of homage to her invalid. And every day she reminded me: "See that you don't forget to thank him nicely."

We had also—a discreet feminine attention like the refreshments that are brought to one, between sittings, by a painter's mistress—as a supplement, free of charge, to those which her husband paid us professionally, a visit from Mme Cottard. She came to offer us her "waiting-woman," or, if we preferred the services of a man, she would "scour the country" for one, and on our declining, said that she did hope this was not just a "put-off" on our part, a word which in her world signified a false pretext for not accepting an invitation. She assured us that the Professor, who never referred to his patients when he was at home, was as sad about it as if it had been she herself who was ill. We shall see in due course that even if this had been true it would have meant at once very little and a great deal on the part of the most unfaithful and the most attentive of husbands.

Offers as helpful, and infinitely more touching in the way in which they were expressed (which was a blend of the highest intelligence, the warmest sympathy, and a rare felicity of expression), were addressed to me by the heir to the Grand Duchy of Luxembourg. I had met him at Balbec where he had come on a visit to one of his aunts, the Princesse de Luxembourg, being himself at that time merely Comte de Nassau. He had married, some months later, the beautiful daughter of another Luxembourg princess, extremely rich because she was the only daughter of a prince who was the proprietor of an immense flour-milling business. Whereupon the Grand Duke of Luxembourg, who had no children of his own and was devoted to his nephew Nassau, had obtained parliamentary approval for declaring the young man his heir. As with all marriages of this nature, the origin of the bride's fortune was the obstacle, as it was also the efficient cause. I remembered this Comte de Nassau as one of the most striking young men I had ever met, already devoured, at that time, by a dark and blazing passion for his betrothed. I was deeply touched by the letters which he wrote to me regularly during my grandmother's illness, and Mamma herself, in her emotion, quoted sadly one of her mother's expressions: "Sévigné would not have put it better."

On the sixth day Mamma, yielding to my grandmother's entreaties, left her for a little and pretended to go and lie down. I should have liked (so that Grandmamma should go to sleep) Françoise to stay quietly at her bedside. In spite of my supplications, she got up and left the room. She was genuinely devoted to my grandmother, and with her perspicacity and her natural pessimism she regarded her as doomed. She would therefore have liked to give her every possible care and attention. But word had just come that an electrician had arrived, a veteran member of his firm, the head of which was his brother-in-law, highly esteemed throughout the building, where he had been coming for many years, and especially by Jupien. This man had been sent for before my grandmother's illness. It seemed to me that he could have been sent away again, or asked to wait. But Françoise's code of manners would not permit this; it would have been to show a lack of courtesy towards this excellent man; my grandmother's condition ceased at once to matter. When, after waiting a quarter of an hour, I lost patience and went to look for her in the kitchen, I found her chatting to him on the landing of the back staircase, the door of which stood open, a device which had the advantage, should any of us come on the scene, of letting it be thought that they were just saying good-bye, but had also the drawback of sending a terrible draught through the house. Françoise tore herself from the workman, not without turning to shout down after him various greetings, forgotten in her haste, to his wife and his brother-in-law. This concern, characteristic of Combray, not to be found wanting in politeness was one which Françoise extended even to foreign policy. People foolishly imagine that the broad generalities of social phenomena afford an excellent opportunity to penetrate further into the human soul; they ought, on the contrary, to realise that it is by plumbing the depths of a single personality that they might have a chance of understanding those phenomena. Françoise had told the gardener at Combray over and over again that war was the most senseless of crimes, that life was the only thing that mattered. Yet, when the Russo-Japanese war broke out, she was quite ashamed, vis-à-vis the Tsar, that we had not gone to war to help the "poor Russians," "since," she reminded us, "we're allianced to them." She felt this abstention to be discourteous to Nicholas II, who had always "said such nice things about us"; it was a corollary of the same code which would have prevented her from refusing a glass of brandy from Jupien, knowing that it would "upset" her digestion, and which caused her, with my grandmother lying at death's door, to feel that, by failing to go in person to make her apologies to this trusty electrician who had been put to so much trouble, she would have been committing the same discourtesy of which she considered France guilty in remaining neutral between Russia and Japan.

Luckily, we were soon rid of Françoise's daughter, who was obliged to be away for some weeks. To the regular stock of advice which people at Combray gave to the family of an invalid: "You haven't tried a little excursion . . . the change of air, you know . . . pick up an appetite . . . etc.," she had added the almost unique idea, which she herself had thought up specially and which she repeated accordingly whenever we saw her, without fail, as though hoping by dint of reiteration to force it through the thickness of people's heads: "She ought to have looked after herself *radically* from the first." She did not recommend one particular kind of cure rather than another, provided it was "radical." As to Françoise herself, she noticed that my grandmother was not being given many medicaments. Since, according to her, they only upset the stomach, she was quite glad of this, but at the same time even more humiliated. She had, in the South of France, some relatively well-to-do cousins whose daughter, after falling ill in her adolescence, had died at twenty-three; for several years the father and mother had ruined themselves on drugs and cures, on different doctors, on pilgrimages from one thermal spa to another, until her decease. Now all this seemed to Françoise, for the parents in question, a kind of luxury, as though they had owned race-horses or a place in the country. They themselves, in the midst of their affliction, derived a certain pride from such lavish expenditure. They had now nothing left, least of all their most precious possession, their child, but they enjoyed telling people how they had done as much for her and more than the richest in the land. The ultra-violet rays to which the poor girl had been subjected several times a day for months on end particularly gratified them. The father, elated in his grief by the glory of it all, was so carried away as to speak of his daughter at times as though she had been an opera star for whose sake he had ruined himself. Françoise was not insensible to such a wealth of scenic effect; that which framed my grandmother's sickbed seemed to her a trifle meagre, suited rather to an illness on the stage of a small provincial theatre.

There was a moment when her uraemic trouble affected my grandmother's eyes. For some days she could not see at all. Her eyes were not at all like those of a blind person, but remained just the same as before. And I gathered that she could see nothing only from the strangeness of a certain smile of welcome which she assumed the moment one opened the door, until one had come up to her and taken her hand, a smile which began too soon and remained stereotyped on her lips, fixed, but always full-faced, and endeavouring to be visible from every quarter, because it could no longer rely on the eyes to regulate it, to indicate the right moment, the proper direction, to focus it, to make it vary according to the change of position or of facial expression of the person who had come in; because it was left isolated, without the accompanying smile in her eyes which would have diverted the attention of the visitor from it for a while, it assumed in its awkwardness an undue importance, giving an impression of exaggerated amiability. Then her sight was completely restored, and from her eyes the wandering affliction passed to her ears. For several days my grandmother was deaf. And as she was afraid of being taken by surprise by the sudden entry of someone whom she would not have heard come in, all day long (although she was lying with her face to the wall) she kept turning her head sharply towards the door. But the movement of her neck was awkward, for one cannot adapt oneself in a few days to this transposition of faculties, so as, if not actually to see sounds, at least to listen with one's eyes. Finally her pain grew less, but the impediment in her speech increased. We were obliged to ask her to repeat almost everything that she said.

And now my grandmother, realising that we could no longer understand her, gave up altogether the attempt to speak and lay perfectly still. When she caught sight of me she gave a sort of convulsive start like a person who suddenly finds himself unable to breathe, but could make no intelligible sound. Then, overcome by her sheer powerlessness, she let her head fall back on the pillows, stretched herself out flat on her bed, her face grave and stony, her hands motionless on the sheet or occupied in some purely mechanical action such as that of wiping her fingers with her handkerchief. She made no effort to think. Then came a state of perpetual agitation. She was incessantly trying to get up. But we restrained her so far as we could from doing so, for fear of her discovering how paralysed she was. One day when she had been left alone for a moment I found her out of bed, standing in her nightdress trying to open the window.

At Balbec, once, when a widow who had flung herself into the sea had been rescued against her will, my grandmother had told me (moved perhaps by one of those presentiments we discern at times in the mystery of our organic life which remains so obscure but in which nevertheless it seems that the future is foreshadowed) that she could think of nothing so cruel as to snatch a desperate woman away from the death that she had deliberately sought and restore her to her living martyrdom.

We were just in time to catch my grandmother; she put up an almost savage resistance to my mother, then, overpowered, seated forcibly in an armchair, she ceased to will, to regret, her face resumed its impassivity and she began laboriously to pick off the hairs that had been left on her nightdress by a fur coat which had been thrown over her shoulders.

The look in her eyes changed completely; often uneasy, plaintive, haggard, it was no longer the look we knew, it was the sullen expression of a senile old woman.

By dint of repeatedly asking her whether she would like her hair done, Françoise ended up by persuading herself that the request had come from my grandmother. She armed herself with brushes, combs, eau de Cologne, a wrapper. "It can't hurt Madame

Amédée," she said, "if I just comb her hair; nobody's ever too weak to be combed." In other words, one is never too weak for another person to be able, for her own satisfaction, to comb one's hair. But when I came into the room I saw between the cruel hands of Françoise, as blissfully happy as though she were in the act of restoring my grandmother to health, beneath aged straggling tresses which scarcely had the strength to withstand the contact of the comb, a head which, incapable of maintaining the position into which it had been forced, was rolling about in a ceaseless whirl in which sheer debility alternated with spasms of pain. I felt that the moment at which Françoise would have finished her task was approaching, and I dared not hasten it by suggesting to her: "That's enough," for fear of her disobeying me. But I did forcibly intervene when, in order that my grandmother might see whether her hair had been done to her liking, Françoise, with innocent brutality, brought her a mirror. I was glad for the moment that I had managed to snatch it from her in time, before my grandmother, whom we had carefully kept away from mirrors, caught even a stray glimpse of a face unlike anything she could have imagined. But alas, when, a moment later, I bent over her to kiss that beloved forehead which had been so harshly treated, she looked up at me with a puzzled, distrustful, shocked expression: she had not recognised me.

According to our doctor, this was a symptom that the congestion of her brain was increasing. It must be relieved in some way. Cottard was in two minds. Françoise hoped at first that they were going to apply "clarified cups." She looked up the effects of this treatment in my dictionary, but could find no reference to it. Even if she had said "scarified" instead of "clarified" she still would not have found any reference to this adjective, since she did not look for it under "C" any more than under "S"—she did indeed say "clarified" but she wrote (and consequently assumed that the printed word was) "esclarified." Cottard, to her disappointment, gave the preference, though without much hope, to leeches. When, a few hours later, I went into my grandmother's room, fastened to her neck, her temples, her ears, the tiny black reptiles were writing among her bloodstained locks, as on the head of Medusa. But in her pale and peaceful, entirely motionless face I saw her beautiful eyes, wide open, luminous and calm as of old (perhaps even more charged with the light of intelligence than they had been before her illness, since, as she could not speak and must not move, it was to her eyes alone that she entrusted her thought, that thought which can be reborn, as though by spontaneous generation, thanks to the withdrawal of a few drops of blood), her eyes, soft and liquid as oil, in which the rekindled fire that was now burning lit up for the sick woman the recaptured universe. Her calm was no longer the wisdom of despair but of hope. She realised that she was better, wanted to be careful and not to move, and made me the present only of a beautiful smile so that I should know that she was feeling better, as she gently pressed my hand.

I knew the disgust that my grandmother felt at the sight of certain animals, let alone at being touched by them. I knew that it was in consideration of a higher utility that she was enduring the leeches. And so it infuriated me to hear Françoise repeating to her with the little chuckle one gives to a baby one is trying to amuse: "Oh, look at the little beasties running all over Madame." This was moreover to treat our patient with a lack of respect, as though she had lapsed into second childhood. But my grandmother, whose face had assumed the calm fortitude of a stoic, did not even seem to hear her.

Alas! no sooner had the leeches been removed than the congestion returned and grew steadily worse. I was surprised to find that at this stage, when my grandmother was so ill, Françoise was constantly disappearing. The fact was that she had ordered herself a mourning-dress, and did not wish to keep the dressmaker waiting. In the lives of most women, everything, even the greatest sorrow, resolves itself into a question of "trying-on."

A few days later, while I was asleep in bed, my mother came to call me in the early hours of the morning. With that tender concern which in the gravest circumstances people who are overwhelmed by grief show for the comfort and convenience of others, "Forgive me for disturbing your sleep," she said to me.

"I wasn't asleep," I answered as I awoke.

I said this in good faith. The great modification which the act of awakening effects in us is not so much that of ushering us into the clear life of consciousness, as that of making us lose all memory of the slightly more diffused light in which our mind had been resting, as in the opaline depths of the sea. The tide of thought, half veiled from our perception, on which we were still drifting a moment ago, kept us in a state of motion perfectly sufficient to enable us to refer to it by the name of wakefulness. But then our actual awakenings produce an interruption of memory. A little later we describe these states as sleep because we no longer remember them. And when that bright star shines which at the moment of waking lights up behind the sleeper the whole expanse of his sleep, it makes him imagine for a few moments that it was not a sleeping but a waking state; a shooting star indeed, which blots out with the fading of its light not only the illusory existence but every aspect of our dream, and merely enables him who has awoken to say to himself: "I was asleep."

In a voice so gentle that it seemed to be afraid of hurting me, my mother asked whether it would tire me too much to get up, and, stroking my hands, went on:

"My poor child, you have only your Papa and Mamma to rely on now."

We went into the sickroom. Bent in a semi-circle on the bed, a creature other than my grandmother, a sort of beast that had put on her hair and crouched among her bedclothes, lay panting, whimpering, making the blankets heave with its convulsions. The eyelids were closed, and it was because they did not shut properly rather than because they opened that they disclosed a chink of eyeball, blurred, rheumy, reflecting the dimness of an organic vision and of an inward pain. All this agitation was not addressed to us, whom she neither saw nor knew. But if it was only a beast that was stirring there, where was my grandmother? Yes, I could recognise the shape of her nose, which bore no relation now to the rest of her face, but to the corner of which a beauty spot still adhered, and the hand that kept thrusting the blankets aside with a gesture which formerly would have meant that those blankets were oppressing her, but now meant nothing.

Mamma asked me to go for a little vinegar and water with which to sponge my grandmother's forehead. It was the only thing that refreshed her, thought Mamma, who saw that she was trying to push back her hair. But now one of the servants was signalling to me from the doorway. The news that my grandmother was *in extremis* had spread like wildfire through the house. One of those "extra helps" whom people engage at exceptional times to relieve the strain on their servants (a practice which gives deathbeds something of the air of social functions) had just opened the front door to the Duc de Guermantes, who was now waiting in the hall and had asked for me: I could not escape him.

"I have just, my dear sir, heard your macabre news. I should like, as a mark of sympathy, to shake your father by the hand."

I pleaded the difficulty of disturbing him for the moment. M. de Guermantes was like a caller who turns up just as one is about to set out on a journey. But he was so intensely aware of the importance of the courtesy he was showing us that it blinded him to all else, and he insisted upon being taken into the drawing-room. As a rule, he made a point of carrying out to the last letter the formalities with which he had decided to honour anyone, and took little heed that the trunks were packed or the coffin ready.

"Have you sent for Dieulafoy? No? That was a grave error. And if you had only asked me, I would have got him to come—he never refuses me anything, although he has refused the Duchesse de Chartres before now. You see, I set myself above a Princess of the Blood. However, in the presence of death we are all equal," he added, not in order to assure me that my grandmother was becoming his equal, but perhaps because he felt that a prolonged discussion of his power over Dieulafoy and his pre-eminence over the Duchesse de Chartres would not be in very good taste.

His advice did not in the least surprise me. I knew that, in the Guermantes family, the name of Dieulafoy was regularly quoted (only with slightly more respect) among those of other tradesmen who were "quite the best" in their respective lines. And the old Duchesse de Mortemart, *née* Guermantes (I never could understand, by the way, why the moment one speaks of a Duchess, one almost invariably says: "The old Duchess of So-and-so," or, alternatively, in a delicate Watteau tone, if she is still young, "The little Duchess of So-and-so") would prescribe almost automatically, with a droop of the eyelid, in serious cases: "Dieulafoy, Dieulafoy!" as, if one wanted a place for ices, she would advise "Poiré Blanche," or for cakes "Rebattet, Rebattet." But I was not aware that my father had, as a matter of fact, just sent for Dieulafoy.

At this point my mother, who was waiting impatiently for some cylinders of oxygen which would help my grandmother to breathe more easily, came out herself to the hall where she little expected to find M. de Guermantes. I should have liked to conceal him, no matter where. But convinced in his own mind that nothing was more essential, could be more gratifying to her or more indispensable to the maintenance of his reputation as a perfect gentleman, he seized me violently by the arm and, although I defended myself as though against an assault with repeated protestations of "Sir, Sir, Sir," dragged me across to Mamma, saying: "Will you do me the great honour of presenting me to your lady mother?", going slightly off pitch on the word "mother." And it was so plain to him that the honour was hers that he could not help smiling at her even while he was composing a grave face. I had no alternative but to effect the introduction, which triggered off a series of bowings and scrapings: he was about to begin the complete ritual of salutation, and even proposed to enter into conversation, but my mother, beside herself with grief, told me to come at once and did not reply to the speeches of M. de Guermantes who, expecting to be received as a visitor and finding himself instead left alone in the hall, would have been obliged to leave had he not at that moment caught sight of Saint-Loup who had arrived in Paris that morning and had come to us in haste to ask for news. "I say, this is a piece of luck!" cried the Duke joyfully, grabbing his nephew by a button which he nearly tore off, regardless of the presence of my mother who was again crossing the hall. Saint-Loup was not, I think, despite his genuine sympathy, altogether sorry to avoid seeing me, considering his attitude towards me. He left, dragged off by his uncle who, having had something very important to say to him and having very nearly gone down to Doncières on purpose to say it, was beside himself with joy at being able to save himself the trouble. "Upon my soul, if anybody had told me I had only to cross the courtyard to find you here, I should have thought they were pulling my leg. As your friend M. Bloch would say, it's rather droll." And as he disappeared down the stairs with his arm round Robert's shoulder: "All the same," he went on, "it's quite clear I must have touched the hangman's rope or something; I do have the devil's own luck." It was not that the Duc de Guermantes was bad-mannered; far from it. But he was one of those men who are incapable of putting themselves in the place of others, who resemble in that respect undertakers and the majority of doctors, and who, after having composed their faces and said "This is a very painful occasion," having embraced you at a pinch and advised you to rest, cease to regard a deathbed or a funeral as anything but a social gathering of a more or less restricted kind at which, with a joviality that has been checked for a moment only, they scan the room in search of the person whom they can talk to about their own little affairs, or ask to introduce them to someone else, or offer a lift in their carriage when it is time to go home. The Duc de Guermantes, while congratulating himself on the "good wind" that had blown him into the arms of his nephew, was still so surprised at the reception—natural as it was—that he had had from my mother that he declared later on that she was as disagreeable as my father was civil, that she had "aberrations" during which she seemed literally not to hear a word you said to her, and that in his opinion she was out of sorts and perhaps even not quite "all there." At the same time he was prepared (according to what I was told) to put it down partly at least to the "circumstances" and to aver that my mother had seemed to him greatly "affected" by the sad event. But his limbs were still twitching with all the residue of bows and heel-clickings and backings-out which he had been prevented from using up, and he had so little idea of the real nature of Mamma's grief that he asked me, the day before the funeral, if I was doing anything to distract her.

A brother-in-law of my grandmother's, who was a monk, and whom I had never seen, had telegraphed to Austria, where the head of his order was, and having as a special dispensation received permission, arrived that day. Bowed down with grief, he sat by the bedside reading prayers and meditations without, however, taking his gimlet eyes from the invalid's face. At one point when my grandmother was unconscious, the sight of the priest's grief began to upset me, and I looked at him tenderly. He appeared surprised by my pity, and then an odd thing happened. He joined his hands in front of his face like a man absorbed in sorrowful meditation, but, on the assumption that I would then cease to watch him, left, as I observed, a tiny chink between his fingers. And just as I was looking away, I saw his sharp eye, which had been taking advantage of the shelter of his hands to observe whether my sympathy was sincere. He was crouched there as in the shadow of a confessional. He saw that I had noticed him and at once shut tight the lattice which he had left ajar. I met him again later, but never was any reference made by either of us to that minute. It was tacitly agreed that I had not noticed that he was spying on me. With priests as with alienists, there is always an element of the examining magistrate. Besides, what friend is there, however dear to us, in whose past as in ours there has not been some such episode which we find it more convenient to believe that he must have forgotten?

The doctor gave my grandmother an injection of morphine, and to make her breathing less painful ordered cylinders of oxygen. My mother, the doctor, the nursing sister held these in their hands; as soon as one was exhausted another was put in its place.

I had left the room for a few minutes. When I returned I found myself in the presence of a sort of miracle. Accompanied by an incessant low murmur, my grandmother seemed to be singing us a long, joyous song which filled the room, rapid and musical. I soon realised that it was scarcely less unconscious than, as purely mechanical as, the hoarse rattle that I had heard before leaving the room. Perhaps to a slight extent it reflected some improvement brought about by the morphine. Principally it was the result (the air not passing quite in the same way through the bronchial tubes) of a change in the register of her breathing. Released by the twofold action of the oxygen and the morphine, my grandmother's breath no longer laboured, no longer whined, but, swift and light, glided like a skater towards the delicious fluid. Perhaps the breath, imperceptible as that of the wind in the hollow stem of a reed, was mingled in this song with some of those more human sighs which, released at the approach of death, suggest intimations of pain or happiness in those who have already ceased to feel, and came now to add a more melodious accent, but without changing its rhythm, to that long phrase which rose, soared still higher, then subsided, to spring up once more, from the alleviated chest, in pursuit of the oxygen. Then, having risen to so high a pitch, having been sustained with so much vigour, the chant, mingled with a murmur of supplication in the midst of ecstasy, seemed at times to stop altogether like a spring that has ceased to flow.

Françoise, in any great sorrow, felt the need, however futile—but did not possess the art, however simple—to give it expression. Realising that my grandmother was doomed, it was her own personal impressions that she felt impelled to communicate to us. And all that she could do was to repeat: "I feel quite upset," in the same tone in which she would say, when she had taken too large a plateful of cabbage broth: "I've got a sort of weight on my stomach," sensations both of which were more natural than she seemed to think. Though so feebly expressed, her grief was nevertheless very great, and was aggravated moreover by the fact that her daughter, detained at Combray (to which this young Parisian now disdainfully referred as "the back of beyond" and where she felt herself becoming a "country bumpkin"), would probably not be able to return in time for the funeral ceremony, which was certain, Françoise felt, to be a superb spectacle. Knowing that we were not inclined to be expansive, she had taken the precaution of bespeaking Jupien in advance for every evening that week. She knew that he would not be free at the time of the funeral. She was determined at least to "go over it all" with him on his return.

For several nights now my father, my grandfather and one of our cousins had been keeping vigil and no longer left the house. Their continuous devotion ended by assuming a mask of indifference, and their interminable enforced idleness around this deathbed made them indulge in the sort of small talk that is an inseparable accompaniment of prolonged confinement in a railway carriage. Besides, this cousin (a nephew of my great-aunt) aroused in me an antipathy as strong as the esteem which he deserved and generally enjoyed. He was always in the offing on such occasions, and was so assiduous in his attentions to the dying that their mourning families, on the pretext that he was delicate, despite his robust appearance, his bass voice and bristling beard, invariably besought him, with the customary euphemisms, not to come to the cemetery. I could tell already that Mamma, who thought of others in the midst of the most crushing grief, would soon be saying to him in different terms what he was in the habit of hearing said on all such occasions:

"Promise me that you won't come 'tomorrow.' Please, for 'her sake.' At any rate, you won't go 'all the way.' It's what she would have wished."

But it was no use; he was always the first to arrive "at the house," by reason of which he had been given, in another circle, the nickname (unknown to us) of "No flowers by request." And before attending "everything" he had always "attended to everything," which entitled him to the formula: "You, we don't even thank you."

"What's that?" came in a loud voice from my grandfather, who had grown rather deaf and had failed to catch something which our cousin had just said to my father.

"Nothing," answered the cousin. "I was just saying that I'd heard from Combray this morning. The weather is appalling down there, and here we've got almost too much sun."

"And yet the barometer is very low," put in my father.

"Where did you say the weather was bad?" asked my grandfather.

"At Combray."

"Ah! I'm not surprised; whenever the weather's bad here it's fine at Combray, and vice versa. Good gracious! Talking of Combray, has anyone remembered to tell Legrandin?"

"Yes, don't worry about that, it's been done," said my cousin, whose cheeks, bronzed by an irrepressible growth of beard, dimpled slightly with the satisfaction of having thought of it.

At this point my father hurried from the room. I supposed that a sudden change, for better or worse, had occurred. It was simply that Dr Dieulafoy had just arrived. My father went to receive him in the drawing-room, like the actor who is next to appear on the stage. He had been sent for not to cure but to certify, almost in a legal capacity. Dr Dieulafoy may indeed have been a great physician, a marvellous teacher; to the several roles in which he excelled, he added another, in which he remained for forty years without a rival, a role as original as that of the confidant, the clown or the noble father, which consisted in coming to certify that a patient was *in extremis*. His name alone presaged the dignity with which he would sustain the part, and when the servant announced: "M. Dieulafoy," one thought one was in a Molière play. To the dignity of his bearing was added, without being conspicuous, the litheness of a perfect figure. His exaggerated good looks were tempered by a decorum suited to distressing circumstances. In the sable majesty of his frock-coat the Professor would enter the room, melancholy without affectation, uttering not one word of condolence that could have been construed as insincere, nor being guilty of the slightest infringement of the rules of tact. At the foot of a deathbed it was he and not the Duc de Guermantes who was the great nobleman. Having examined my grandmother without tiring her, and with an excess of reserve which was an act of courtesy to the doctor in charge of the case, he murmured a few words to my father, and bowed respectfully to my mother, to whom I felt that my father had positively to restrain himself from saying: "Professor Dieulafoy." But already the latter had turned away, not wishing to seem intrusive, and made a perfect exit, simply accepting the sealed envelope that was slipped into his hand. He did not appear to have seen it, and we ourselves were left wondering for a moment whether we had really given it to him, with such a conjurer's dexterity had he made it vanish without sacrificing one iota of the gravity—which was if anything accentuated—of the eminent consultant in his long frock-coat with its silk lapels, his noble features engraved with the most dignified commiseration. His deliberation and his vivacity combined to show that, even if he had a hundred other calls to make, he did not wish to appear to be in a hurry. For he was the embodiment of tact, intelligence and kindness. The eminent man is no longer with us. Other physicians, other professors, may have rivalled, may indeed have surpassed him. But the "capacity" in which his knowledge, his physical endowments, his distinguished manners made him supreme exists no longer, for want of any successor capable of taking his place.

Mamma had not even noticed M. Dieulafoy: everything that was not my grandmother no longer existed. I remember (and here I anticipate) that at the cemetery, where we saw her, like a supernatural apparition, tremulously approach the grave, her eyes seeming to gaze after a being that had taken wing and was already far away, my father having remarked to her: "Old Norpois came to the house and to the church and on here; he gave up a most important committee meeting to come; you ought really to say a word to him, he'd be very touched," my mother, when the Ambassador bowed to her, could do no more than gently lower her face, which showed no sign of tears. A couple of days earlier— to anticipate still before returning to the bedside of the dying woman—while we were watching over her dead body, Françoise, who, not disbelieving entirely in ghosts, was terrified by the least sound, had said: "I believe that's her." But instead of fear, it was an ineffable sweetness that her words aroused in my mother, who would have dearly wished that the dead could return, so as to have her mother with her sometimes still.

To return now to those last hours, "You heard about the telegram her sisters sent us?" my grandfather asked the cousin.

"Yes, Beethoven, I've been told. It's worth framing. Still, I'm not surprised."

"And my poor wife was so fond of them, too," said my grandfather, wiping away a tear. "We mustn't blame them. They're stark mad, both of them, as I've always said. What's the matter now? Aren't you going on with the oxygen?"

My mother spoke: "Oh, but then Mamma will be having trouble with her breathing again."

The doctor reassured her: "Oh, no! The effect of the oxygen will last a good while yet. We can begin it again presently."

It seemed to me that he would not have said this of a dying woman, that if this good effect was going to last it meant that it was still possible to do something to keep her alive. The hiss of the oxygen ceased for a few moments. But the happy plaint of her breathing still poured forth, light, troubled, unfinished, ceaselessly recommencing. Now and then it seemed that all was over; her breath stopped, whether owing to one of those transpositions to another octave that occur in the respiration of a sleeper, or else from a natural intermittence, an effect of anaesthesia, the progress of asphyxia, some failure of the heart. The doctor stooped to feel my grandmother's pulse, but already, as if a tributary had come to irrigate the dried-up river-bed, a new chant had taken up the interrupted phrase, which resumed in another key with the same inexhaustible momentum. Who knows whether, without my grandmother's even being conscious of them, countless happy and tender memories compressed by suffering were not escaping from her now, like those lighter gases which had long been compressed in the cylinders? It was as though everything that she had to tell us was pouring out, that it was us that she was addressing with this prolixity, this eagerness, this effusion. At the foot of the bed, convulsed by every gasp of this agony, not weeping but at moments drenched with tears, my mother stood with the unheeding desolation of a tree lashed by the rain and shaken by the wind. I was made to dry my eyes before I went up to kiss my grandmother.

"But I thought she could no longer see," said my father.

"One can never be sure," replied the doctor.

When my lips touched her face, my grandmother's hands quivered, and a long shudder ran through her whole body—a reflex, perhaps, or perhaps it is that certain forms of tenderness have, so to speak, a hyperaesthesia which recognises through the veil of unconsciousness what they scarcely need senses to enable them to love. Suddenly my grandmother half rose, made a violent effort, like someone struggling to resist an attempt on his life. Françoise could not withstand this sight and burst out sobbing. Remembering what the doctor had just said I tried to make her leave the room. At that moment my grandmother opened her eyes. I thrust myself hurriedly in front of Françoise to hide her tears, while my parents were speaking to the patient. The hiss of the oxygen had ceased; the doctor moved away from the bed-side. My grandmother was dead.

An hour or two later Françoise was able for the last time, and without causing it any pain, to comb that beautiful hair which was only tinged with grey and hitherto had seemed less old than my grandmother herself. But now, on the contrary, it alone set the crown of age on a face grown young again, from which had vanished the wrinkles, the contractions, the swellings, the strains, the hollows which pain had carved on it over the years. As in the far-off days when her parents had chosen for her a bridegroom, she had the features, delicately traced by purity and submission, the cheeks glowing with a chaste expectation, with a dream of happiness, with an innocent gaiety even, which the years had gradually destroyed. Life in withdrawing from her had taken with it the disillusionments of life. A smile seemed to be hovering on my grandmother's lips. On that funeral couch, death, like a sculptor of the Middle Ages, had laid her down in the form of a young girl.

CHAPTER TWO

ALTHOUGH it was simply a Sunday in autumn, I had been born
again, life lay intact before me, for that morning, after a succession
of mild days, there had been a cold fog which had not cleared until
nearly midday: and a change in the weather is sufficient to create
the world and ourselves anew. Formerly, when the wind howled
in my chimney, I would listen to the blows which it struck on the
iron trap with as keen an emotion as if, like the famous chords with
which the Fifth Symphony opens, they had been the irresistible
calls of a mysterious destiny. Every change in the aspect of nature
offers us a similar transformation by adapting our desires so as to
harmonise with the new form of things. The mist, from the
moment of my awakening, had made of me, instead of the centrifugal being which one is on fine days, a man turned in on
himself, longing for the chimney corner and the shared bed, a
shivering Adam in quest of a sedentary Eve, in this different world.

Between the soft grey tint of a morning landscape and the taste
of a cup of chocolate I incorporated all the originality of
the physical, intellectual and moral life which I had taken with
me to Doncières about a year earlier and which, blazoned with the
oblong form of a bare hillside—always present even when it was
invisible—formed in me a series of pleasures entirely distinct from
all others, incommunicable to my friends in the sense that the
impressions, richly interwoven with one another, which orches-
trated them were a great deal more characteristic of them to my
unconscious mind than any facts that I might have related. From
this point of view the new world in which this morning's fog had
immersed me was a world already known to me (which only made
it more real) and forgotten for some time (which restored all its
novelty). And I was able to look at several of the pictures of misty
landscapes which my memory had acquired, notably a series of
"Mornings at Doncières," including my first morning there in
barracks and another in a neighbouring country house where I had

gone with Saint-Loup to spend the night, from the windows of which, when I had drawn back the curtains at daybreak before getting back into bed, in the first a trooper, in the second (on the thin margin of a pond and a wood, all the rest of which was engulfed in the uniform and liquid softness of the mist) a coachman busy polishing harness, had appeared to me like those rare figures, scarcely visible to the eye that is obliged to adapt itself to the mysterious vagueness of the half-light, which emerge from a faded fresco.

It was from my bed that I was contemplating these memories that afternoon, for I had returned to it to wait until the hour came at which, taking advantage of the absence of my parents who had gone for a few days to Combray, I proposed to get up and go to a little play which was being given that evening in Mme de Villeparisis's drawing-room. Had they been at home I should perhaps not have ventured to do so; my mother, in the delicacy of her respect for my grandmother's memory, wished the tokens of regret that were paid to it to be freely and sincerely given; she would not have forbidden me this outing, but she would have disapproved of it. From Combray, on the other hand, had I consulted her wishes, she would not have replied with a melancholy: "Do just as you like; you're old enough now to know what is right or wrong," but, reproaching herself for having left me alone in Paris, and measuring my grief by her own, would have wished for it distractions of a sort which she herself would have eschewed and which she persuaded herself that my grandmother, solicitous above all things for my health and my nervous equilibrium, would have recommended for me.

That morning the boiler of the new central heating installation had been turned on for the first time. Its disagreeable sound—an intermittent hiccup—had no connexion with my memories of Doncières. But its prolonged encounter with them in my thoughts that afternoon was to give it so lasting an affinity with them that whenever, after succeeding more or less in forgetting it, I heard the central heating again it would bring them back to me.

There was no one else in the house but Françoise. The fog had lifted. The grey light, falling like a fine rain, wove without ceasing a transparent web through which the Sunday strollers appeared in a silvery sheen. I had flung to the foot of my bed the *Figaro*, for which I had been sending out religiously every morning ever since I had sent in an article which it had not yet printed; despite the absence of sun, the intensity of the daylight was an indication that we were still only half-way through the afternoon. The tulle window-curtains, vaporous and friable as they would not have been on a fine day, had that same blend of softness and brittleness that dragonflies' wings have, and Venetian glass. It depressed me all the more that I should be spending this Sunday alone because I had sent a note that morning to Mlle de Stermaria. Robert de Saint-Loup, whom his mother had at length succeeded—after painful abortive attempts—in parting from his mistress, and who immediately afterwards had been sent to Morocco in the hope of forgetting the woman he had already for some time ceased to love, had sent me a line, which had reached me the day before, announcing his imminent arrival in France for a short spell of leave. As he would only be passing through Paris (where his family were doubtless afraid of seeing him renew relations with Rachel), he informed me, to show me that he had been thinking of me, that he had met at Tangier Mlle or rather Mme (for she had divorced her husband after three months of marriage) de Stermaria. And Robert, remembering what I had said to him at Balbec, had asked on my behalf for an assignation with the young woman. She would be delighted to dine with me, she had told him, on one of the evenings which she would be spending in Paris before her return to Brittany. He told me to lose no time in writing to Mme de Stermaria, for she must certainly have arrived.

Saint-Loup's letter had come as no surprise to me, even though I had had no news of him since, at the time of my grandmother's illness, he had accused me of perfidy and treachery. I had grasped at once what must have happened. Rachel, who liked to provoke his jealousy (she also had other causes for resentment against me), had persuaded her lover that I had made sly attempts to have relations with her in his absence. It is probable that he continued to believe in the truth of this allegation, but he had ceased to be in love with her, which meant that its truth or falsehood had become a matter of complete indifference to him, and our friendship alone remained. When, on meeting him again, I tried to talk to him about his accusations, he merely gave me a benign and affectionate smile which seemed to be a sort of apology, and then changed the subject. All this was not to say that he did not, a little later, see Rachel occasionally when he was in Paris. Those who have played a big part in one's life very rarely disappear from it suddenly for good. They return to it at odd moments (so much so that people suspect a renewal of old love) before leaving it for ever. Saint-Loup's breach with Rachel had very soon become less painful to him, thanks to the soothing pleasure that was given him by her incessant demands for money. Jealousy, which prolongs the course of love, is not capable of containing many more ingredients than the other products of the imagination. If one takes with one, when one starts on a journey, three or four images which incidentally one is sure to lose on the way (such as the lilies and anemones heaped on the Ponte Vecchio, or the Persian church shrouded in mist), one's trunk is already pretty full. When one leaves a mistress, one would be just as glad, until one has begun to forget her, that she should not become the property of three or four potential protectors whom one pictures in one's mind's eye, of whom, that is to say, one is jealous: all those whom one does not so picture count for nothing. Now frequent demands for money from a cast-off mistress no more give one a complete idea of her life than charts showing a high temperature would of her illness. But the latter would at any rate be an indication that she was ill, and the former furnish a presumption, vague enough it is true, that the forsaken one or forsaker (whichever she be) cannot have found anything very remarkable in the way of rich protectors. And so each demand is welcomed with the joy which a lull produces in the jealous one's sufferings, and answered with the immediate dispatch of money, for naturally one does not like to think of her being in want of anything except lovers (one of the three lovers one has in one's mind's eye), until time has enabled one to regain one's composure and to learn one's successor's name without wilting. Sometimes Rachel came in so late at night that she could ask her former lover's permission to lie down beside him until the morning. This was a great comfort to Robert, for it reminded him how intimately, after all, they had lived together, simply to see that even if he took the greater part of the bed for himself it did not in the least interfere with her sleep. He realised that she was more comfortable, lying close to his familiar body, than she would have been elsewhere, that she felt herself by his side—even in an hotel—to be in a bedroom known of old in which one has one's habits, in which one sleeps better. He felt that his shoulders, his limbs, all of him, were for her, even when he was unduly restless from insomnia or thinking of the things he had to do, so entirely usual that they could not disturb her and that the perception of them added still further to her sense of repose.

To revert to where we were, I had been all the more excited by Robert's letter in that I could read between the lines what he had not ventured to write more explicitly. "You can most certainly ask her to dine in a private room," he told me. "She is a charming young person, with a delightful nature—you will get on splendidly with her, and I am sure you will have a most enjoyable evening together." As my parents were returning at the end of the week, on Saturday or Sunday, and after that I should be obliged to dine every evening at home, I had written at once to Mme de Stermaria proposing any evening that might suit her up to Friday. A message was brought back that I should hear from her in writing that very evening at about eight o'clock. This time would have passed quickly enough if I had had, during the afternoon that separated me from her letter, the help of a visit from someone else. When the hours are wrapped in conversation one ceases to measure, or indeed to notice them; they vanish, and suddenly it is a long way beyond the point at which it escaped you that the nimble truant time impinges once more on your attention. But if we are alone, our preoccupation, by bringing before us the still distant and incessantly awaited moment with the frequency and uniformity of a ticking pendulum, divides, or rather multiplies, the hours by all the minutes which, had we been with friends, we should not have counted. And confronted, by the incessant return of my desire, with the ardent pleasure which I was to enjoy—not for some days, though, alas!—in Mme de Stermaria's company, this afternoon, which I was going to have to spend alone, seemed to me very empty and very melancholy.

Every now and then I heard the sound of the lift coming up, but it was followed by a second sound, not the one I was hoping for, namely its coming to a halt at our landing, but another very different sound which the lift made in continuing its progress to the floors above and which, because it so often meant the desertion of my floor when I was expecting a visitor, remained for me later, even when I had ceased to wish for visitors, a sound lugubrious in itself, in which there echoed, as it were, a sentence of solitary confinement. Weary, resigned, occupied for several hours still with its immemorial task, the grey day stitched its shimmering needlework of light and shade, and it saddened me to think that I was to be left alone with a thing that knew me no more than would a seamstress who, installed by the window so as to see better while she finishes her work, pays no attention to the person present with her in the room. Suddenly, although I had heard no bell, Françoise opened the door to introduce Albertine, who entered smiling, silent, plump, containing in the plenitude of her body, made ready so that I might continue living them, come to seek me out, the days we had spent together in that Balbec to which I had never since returned. No doubt, whenever we see again a person with whom our relations—however trivial they may be—have now changed, it is like a juxtaposition of two different periods. For this, there is no need for a former mistress to call round to see us as a friend; all that is required is the visit to Paris of someone we have known day by day in a certain kind of life, and that this life should have ceased for us, if only a week ago. On each of Albertine's smiling, questioning, self-conscious features I could read the questions: "And what about Madame de Villeparisis? And the dancing-master? And the pastry-cook?" When she sat down, her back seemed to be saying: "Well, well, there are no cliffs here, but you don't mind if I sit down beside you, all the same, as I used to do at Balbec?" She was like an enchantress offering me a mirror that reflected time. In this she resembled all the people whom we seldom see now but with whom at one time we lived on more intimate terms. With Albertine, however, there was something more than this. True, even in our daily encounters at Balbec, I had always been surprised when I caught sight of her, so changeable was her appearance. But now she was scarcely recognisable. Freed from the pink haze that shrouded them, her features had emerged in sharp relief like those of a statue. She had another face, or rather she had a face at last; her body too had grown. There remained scarcely anything now of the sheath in which she had been enclosed and on the surface of which, at Balbec, her future outline had been barely visible.

This time, Albertine had returned to Paris earlier than usual. As a rule she did not arrive until the spring, so that, already disturbed for some weeks past by the storms that were beating down the first flowers, I did not distinguish, in the pleasure that I felt, the return of Albertine from that of the fine weather. It was enough that I should be told that she was in Paris and that she had called at my house, for me to see her again like a rose flowering by the sea. I cannot say whether it was the desire for Balbec or for her that took possession of me then; perhaps my desire for her was itself a lazy, cowardly, and incomplete form of possessing Balbec, as if to possess a thing materially, to take up residence in a town, were tantamount to possessing it spiritually. Besides, even materially, when she was no longer swaying in my imagination before a horizon of sea, but motionless in a room beside me, she seemed to me often a very poor specimen of a rose, so much so that I wanted to shut my eyes in order not to observe this or that blemish of its petals, and to imagine instead that I was inhaling the salt air on the beach.

I may say all this here, although I was not then aware of what was to happen later on. Certainly, it is more reasonable to devote one's life to women than to postage stamps or old snuff-boxes, even to pictures or statues. But the example of other collections should be a warning to us to diversify, to have not one woman only but several. Those charming associations that a young girl affords with a sea-shore, with the braided tresses of a statue in a church, with an old print, with everything that causes one to love in her, whenever she appears, a delightful picture, those associations are not very stable. When you come to live with a woman you will soon cease to see anything of what made you love her; though it is true that the two sundered elements can be reunited by jealousy. If, after a long period of living together, I was to end by seeing no more in Albertine than an ordinary woman, an intrigue between her and someone she had loved at Balbec would still perhaps have sufficed to reincorporate in her, to amalgamate with her, the beach and the unrolling of the tide. But these secondary associations no longer captivate our eyes; it is to the heart that they are perceptible and fatal. We cannot, under so dangerous a form, regard the renewal of the miracle as a thing to be desired. But I am anticipating the course of years. And here I need only register my regret that I did not have the sense simply to keep my collection of women as people keep their collections of old quizzing-glasses, never so complete, in their cabinet, that there is not room always for another and rarer still.

Contrary to the habitual order of her holiday movements, this year she had come straight from Balbec, where furthermore she had not stayed nearly so late as usual. It was a long time since I had seen her. And since I did not know even by name the people with whom she was in the habit of mixing in Paris, I knew nothing of her life during the periods in which she abstained from coming to see me. These lasted often for quite a time. Then, one fine day, in would burst Albertine whose rosy apparitions and silent visits left me little if any better informed as to what she might have been doing during an interval which remained plunged in that darkness of her hidden life which my eyes felt little anxiety to penetrate.

This time, however, certain signs seemed to indicate that some new experience must have entered into that life. And yet, perhaps, all that one was entitled to conclude from them was that girls change very rapidly at the age which Albertine had now reached. For instance, her intelligence was now more in evidence, and on my reminding her of the day when she had insisted with so much ardour on the superiority of her idea of making Sophocles write "My dear Racine," she was the first to laugh, quite whole-heartedly. "Andrée was quite right, it was stupid of me," she admitted. "Sophocles ought to have begun: 'Sir.'" I replied that Andrée's "Sir" and "Dear Sir" were no less comic than her own "My dear Racine," or Gisèle's "My dear friend," but that after all the really stupid people were the professors for making Sophocles write letters to Racine. Here, however, Albertine was unable to follow me. She could not see what was stupid about it; her intelligence was opening up, but was not fully developed. There were other more attractive novelties in her; I sensed, in this same pretty girl who had just sat down by my bed, something that was different; and in those lines which, in the look and the features of the face, express a person's habitual volition, a change of front, a partial conversion, as though something had happened to break down those resistances I had come up against in Balbec one long-ago evening when we had formed a couple symmetrical with but the converse of our present arrangement, for then it had been she who was lying down and I by her bedside. Wishing and not daring to ascertain whether she would now let herself be kissed, every time that she rose to go I asked her to stay a little longer. This was a concession not very easy to obtain, for although she had nothing to do (otherwise she would have rushed out of the house) she was a person methodical in her habits and moreover not very gracious towards me, seeming no longer to take pleasure in my company. Yet each time, after looking at her watch, she sat down again at my request until finally she had spent several hours with me without my having asked her for anything; the things I said to her were connected with those I had said during the preceding hours, and were totally unconnected with what I was thinking about, what I desired from her, remaining obstinately parallel thereto. There is nothing like desire for preventing the things one says from bearing any resemblance to what one has in one's mind. Time presses, and yet it seems as though we were seeking to gain time by speaking of subjects absolutely alien to the one that preoccupies us. We go on chatting, whereas the sentence we should like to utter would have been accompanied by a gesture, if indeed we have not (to give ourselves the pleasure of immediate action and to gratify the curiosity we feel as to the reactions which will follow it, without saying a word, without a by-your-leave) already made this gesture. Certainly I was not in the least in love with Albertine; child of the mists outside, she could simply satisfy the fanciful desire which the change of weather had awakened in me and which was midway between the desires that are satisfied by the arts of the kitchen and of monumental sculpture respectively, for it made me dream simultaneously of mingling with my flesh a substance different and warm, and of attaching at some point to my recumbent body a divergent one, as the body of Eve barely holds by the feet to the side of Adam, to whose body hers is almost perpendicular, in those Romanesque bas-reliefs in the church at Balbec which represent in so noble and so reposeful a fashion, still almost like a classical frieze, the creation of woman; God in them is everywhere, fol-lowed, as by two ministers, by two little angels in whom one recognises—like those winged, swarming summer creatures which winter has caught by surprise and spared—cupids from Herculaneum still surviving well into the thirteenth century, and winging their last slow flight, weary but never failing in the grace that might be expected of them, over the whole front of the porch.

As for this pleasure which by accomplishing my desire would have released me from these musings and which I should have sought quite as readily from any other pretty woman, had I been asked upon what—in the course of this endless chatter throughout which I was at pains to keep from Albertine the one thing that was in my mind—my optimistic assumption with regard to her poss-ible complaisances was based, I should perhaps have answered that this assumption was due (while the forgotten outlines of Albertine's voice retraced for me the contour of her personality) to the advent of certain words which had not formed part of her vocabulary, or at least not in the acceptation which she now gave them. Thus, when she said to me that Elstir was stupid and I protested: "You don't understand," she replied, smiling, "I mean that he was stupid in that instance, but of course I know he's a very distinguished person, really."

Similarly, wishing to say of the Fontainebleau golf club that it was smart, she declared: "It's really quite a selection."

Speaking of a duel I had fought, she said of my seconds: "What very choice seconds," and looking at my face confessed that she would like to see me "sport a moustache." She even went so far (and at this point my chances appeared to me very great) as to announce, in a phrase of which I would have sworn that she was ignorant a year earlier, that since she had last seen Gisèle there had passed a certain "lapse of time." This was not to say that Albertine had not already possessed, when I was at Balbec, a quite adequate assortment of those expressions which reveal at once that one comes of a well-to-do family and which, year by year, a mother passes on to her daughter just as she gradually bestows on her, as the girl grows up, her own jewels on important occasions. It was evident that Albertine had ceased to be a little girl when one day, to express her thanks for a present which a strange lady had given her, she had said: "I'm quite overcome." Mme Bontemps had been unable to refrain from looking across at her husband, whose comment was: "Well, well, and she's only four-teen."

Her more pronounced nubility had struck home when Albertine, speaking of another girl whom she considered ill-bred, said: "One can't even tell whether she's pretty, because she paints her face a *foot thick*." Finally, though still only a girl, she already displayed the manner of a grown woman of her upbringing and station when she said, of someone whose face twitched: "I can't look at him, because it makes me want to do the same," or, if someone else were being imitated: "The absurd thing about it is that when you imitate her voice you look exactly like her." All this is drawn from the social treasury. But the point was that it did not seem to me possible that Albertine's natural environment could have supplied her with "distinguished" in the sense in which my father would say of a colleague whom he had not actually met but whose intellectual attainments he had heard praised: "It appears he's a very distinguished person." "Selection," even when used of a golf club, struck me as being as incompatible with the Simonet family as it would be, if preceded by the adjective "natural," with a text published centuries before the researches of Darwin. "Lapse of time" seemed to me to augur better still. Finally there appeared the evidence of certain upheavals, the nature of which was unknown to me, but sufficient to justify me in all my hopes, when Albertine observed, with the self-satisfaction of a person whose opinion is by no means to be despised:

"*To my mind*, that is the best thing that could possibly happen. I regard it as the best solution, the stylish way out."

This was so novel, so manifestly an alluvial deposit leading one to suspect such capricious wanderings over ground hitherto unknown to her, that on hearing the words "to my mind" I drew Albertine towards me, and at "I regard" sat her down on my bed.

No doubt it happens that women of moderate culture, on marrying well-read men, receive such expressions as part of their dowry. And shortly after the metamorphosis which follows the wedding night, when they start paying calls and are stand-offish with their old friends, one notices with surprise that they have turned into matrons if, in decreeing that some person is intelligent, they sound both "l"s in the word; but that is precisely the sign of a change of state, and it seemed to me that there was a world of difference between the new expressions and the vocabulary of the Albertine I had known of old—a vocabulary in which the most daring flights were to say of any unusual person: "He's a type," or, if you suggested a game of cards to her: "I don't have money to burn," or again, if any of her friends were to reproach her in terms which she felt to be unjustified: "You really are the limit!"— expressions dictated in such cases by a sort of bourgeois tradition almost as old as the *Magnificat* itself, which a girl slightly out of temper and confident that she is in the right employs, as the saying is, "quite naturally," that is to say because she has learned them from her mother, just as she has learned to say her prayers or to curtsey. All these expressions Mme Bontemps had imparted to her at the same time as a hatred of the Jews and a respect for black because it is always suitable and becoming, even without any formal instruction, but as the piping of the parent goldfinches serves as a model for that of the newborn goldfinches so that they in turn grow into true goldfinches also. But when all was said, "selection" appeared to me of alien growth and "I regard" encouraging. Albertine was no longer the same; therefore she might not perhaps act, might not react in the same way.

Not only did I no longer feel any love for her, but I no longer had to consider, as I might have at Balbec, the risk of shattering in her an affection for myself, since it no longer existed. There could be no doubt that she had long since become quite indifferent to me. I was well aware that to her I was no longer in any sense a member of the "little band" into which I had at one time so anxiously sought and had then been so happy to have secured admission. Besides, since she no longer even had, as in the Balbec days, an air of frank good nature, I felt no serious scruples. However, I think what finally decided me was another philological discovery. As, continuing to add fresh links to the external chain of talk behind which I hid my inner desire, I spoke (having Albertine secure now on the corner of my bed) of one of the girls of the little band who was less striking than the rest but whom nevertheless I had thought quite pretty. "Yes," answered Albertine, "she reminds me of a little *mousmé*."[25] Clearly, when I first knew Albertine the word was unknown to her. It was probable that, had things followed their normal course, she would never have learned it, and for my part I should have seen no cause for regret in that, for there is no more repulsive word in the language. The mere sound of it sets one's teeth on edge as when one has put too large a spoonful of ice in one's mouth. But coming from Albertine, pretty as she was, not even "*mousmé*" could strike me as unpleasing. On the contrary, I felt it to be a revelation, if not of an external initiation, at any rate of an internal evolution. Unfortunately it was now time for me to bid her good-bye if I wished her to reach home in time for her dinner, and myself to be out of bed and dressed in time for my own. It was Françoise who was preparing it; she did not like it to be delayed, and must already have found it an infringement of one of the articles of her code that Albertine, in the absence of my parents, should be paying me so prolonged a visit, and one which was going to make everything late. But before "*mousmé*" all these arguments fell to the ground and I hastened to say:

"You know, I'm not in the least ticklish. You could go on tickling me for a whole hour and I wouldn't feel it."

"Really?"

"I assure you."

She understood, doubtless, that this was the awkward expression of a desire on my part, for, like a person who offers to give you an introduction for which you have not ventured to ask, though what you have said has shown him that it would be of great service to you:

"Would you like me to try?" she inquired with womanly meekness.

"Just as you like, but you would be more comfortable if you lay down properly on the bed."

"Like that?"

"No, further in."

"You're sure I'm not too heavy?"

As she uttered these words the door opened and Françoise walked in carrying a lamp. Albertine just had time to scramble back on to her chair. Perhaps Françoise had chosen this moment to confound us, having been listening at the door or even peeping through the keyhole. But there was no need to suppose anything of the sort; she might well have scorned to assure herself by the use of her eyes of what her instinct must plainly enough have detected, for by dint of living with me and my parents she had succeeded in acquiring, through fear, prudence, alertness and cunning, that instinctive and almost divinatory knowledge of us all that the mariner has of the sea, the quarry has of the hunter, and if not the physician, often at any rate the invalid has of disease. The amount of knowledge that she managed to acquire would have astounded a stranger with as good reason as does the advanced state of certain arts and sciences among the ancients, given the almost non-existent means of information at their disposal (hers were no less exiguous; they consisted of a few casual remarks forming barely a twentieth part of our conversation at dinner, caught on the wing by the butler and inaccurately transmitted to the kitchen). And even her mistakes were due, like theirs, like the fables in which Plato believed, rather to a false conception of the world and to preconceived ideas than to inadequacy of material resources. Thus even in our own day it has been possible for the most important discoveries as to the habits of insects to be made by a scientist who had access to no laboratory and no apparatus of any sort. But if the drawbacks arising from her menial position had not prevented her from acquiring a stock of learning indispensable to the art which was its ultimate goal—and which consisted in putting us to confusion by communicating to us the results of her discoveries—the limitations under which she worked had done more; in this case the impediment, not content with merely not paralysing the flight of her imagination, had powerfully reinforced it. Of course Françoise neglected no artificial aids, those for example of diction and attitude. Since (if she never believed what we said to her in the hope that she would believe it) she accepted without the slightest hesitation the truth of anything, however absurd, that a person of her own condition in life might tell her which might at the same time offend our notions, just as her way of listening to our assertions bore witness to her incredulity, so the accents in which (the use of indirect speech enabling her to hurl the most deadly insults at us with impunity) she reported the narrative of a cook who had told her how she had threatened her employers and, by calling them "dung" in public, had wrung from them any number of privileges and concessions, showed that she regarded the story as gospel. Françoise went so far as to add: "I'm sure if I had been the mistress I should have been quite vexed." In vain might we, despite our original dislike of the lady on the fourth floor, shrug our shoulders, as though at an unlikely fable, at this unedifying report, the teller knew how to invest her tone with the trenchant assertiveness of the most irrefutable and most irritating affirmation.

But above all, just as writers, when they are bound hand and foot by the tyranny of a monarch or of a school of poetry, by the constraints of prosodic laws or of a state religion, often attain a power of concentration from which they would have been dispensed under a system of political liberty or literary anarchy, so Françoise, not being able to reply to us in an explicit fashion, spoke like Tiresias and would have written like Tacitus. She managed to embody everything that she could not express directly in a sentence for which we could not find fault with her without accusing ourselves, indeed in less than a sentence, in a silence, in the way in which she placed an object in a room.

Thus, whenever I inadvertently left on my table, among a pile of other letters, one which it was imperative that she should not see, because, for instance, it referred to her with a malevolence which afforded a presumption of the same feeling towards her in the recipient as in the writer, that evening, if I came home with a feeling of uneasiness and went straight to my room, there on top of my letters, neatly arranged in a symmetrical pile, the compromising document caught my eye as it could not possibly have failed to catch the eye of Françoise, placed by her right at the top, almost apart from the rest, in a prominence that was a form of speech, that had an eloquence all its own, and, as soon as I crossed the threshold, made me start as I would at a cry. She excelled in the preparation of these stage effects, intended to so enlighten the spectator, in her absence, that he already knew that she knew everything when in due course she made her entry. She possessed, for thus making an inanimate object speak, the art, at once inspired and painstaking, of an Irving or a Frédérick Lemaître. On this occasion, holding over Albertine and myself the lighted lamp whose searching beams missed none of the still visible depressions which the girl's body had made in the counterpane, Françoise conjured up a picture of "Justice shedding light upon Crime." Albertine's face did not suffer by this illumination. It revealed on her cheeks the same sunny burnish that had charmed me at Balbec. This face of hers, which sometimes, out of doors, made a general effect of livid pallor, now showed, in the light of the lamp, surfaces so glowingly, so uniformly coloured, so firm and so smooth, that one might have compared them to the sustained flesh tints of certain flowers. Taken aback meanwhile by Françoise's unexpected entry, I exclaimed:

"What, the lamp already? Heavens, how bright it is!"

My object, as may be imagined, was by the second of these ejaculations to dissimulate my confusion, by the first to excuse my lateness in rising. Françoise replied with cruel ambiguity:

"Do you want me to extinglish it?"

"Guish?" Albertine murmured in my ear, leaving me charmed by the familiar quick-wittedness with which, taking me at once for master and accomplice, she insinuated this psychological affirmation in the interrogative tone of a grammatical question.[26]

When Françoise had left the room and Albertine was seated once again on my bed:

"Do you know what I'm afraid of?" I asked her. "It is that if we go on like this I may not be able to resist the temptation to kiss you."

"That would be a happy misfortune."

I did not respond at once to this invitation. Another man might even have found it superfluous, for Albertine's way of pronouncing her words was so carnal, so seductive that merely in speaking to you she seemed to be caressing you. A word from her was a favour, and her conversation covered you with kisses. And yet it was highly gratifying to me, this invitation. It would have been so, indeed, coming from any pretty girl of Albertine's age; but that Albertine should be now so accessible to me gave me more than pleasure, brought before my eyes a series of images fraught with beauty. I remembered Albertine first of all on the beach, almost painted upon a background of sea, having for me no more real an

existence than those theatrical tableaux in which one does not
know whether one is looking at the actress herself who is supposed
to appear, at an understudy who for the moment is taking her
principal's part, or simply at a projection. Then the real woman
had detached herself from the beam of light and had come towards
me, but only for me to perceive that in the real world she had none
of the amorous facility with which one had credited her in the
magic tableau. I had learned that it was not possible to touch her,
to kiss her, that one might only talk to her, that for me she was no
more a woman than jade grapes, an inedible decoration at one
time in fashion on dinner-tables, are really fruit. And now she was
appearing to me on a third plane, real as in the second experience
that I had had of her but available as in the first; available, and all
the more deliciously so in that I had long imagined that she was
not. My surplus of knowledge of life (life as being less uniform, less
simple than I had at first supposed it to be) inclined me provisionally towards agnosticism. What can one positively affirm, when
the thing that one thought probable at first has then shown itself to
be false and in the third instance turns out true? (And alas, I was not
yet at the end of my discoveries with regard to Albertine.) In any
case, even if there had not been the romantic attraction of this
disclosure of a greater wealth of planes revealed one after another
by life (an attraction the opposite of that which Saint-Loup had felt
during our dinners at Rivebelle on recognising, beneath the masks
which life had superimposed on a calm face, features to which his
lips had once been pressed), the knowledge that to kiss Albertine's
cheeks was a possible thing was a pleasure perhaps greater even
than that of kissing them. What a difference there is between
possessing a woman to whom one applies one's body alone,
because she is no more than a piece of flesh, and possessing the
girl whom one used to see on the beach with her friends on certain
days without even knowing why one saw her on those days and
not on others, so that one trembled at the thought that one might
not see her again! Life had obligingly revealed to one in its whole
extent the novel of this little girl's life, had lent one, for the study of
her, first one optical instrument, then another, and had added to
carnal desire the accompaniment, which multiplies and diversifies
it, of those other desires, more spiritual and less easily assuaged,
which do not emerge from their torpor but leave it to carry on
alone when it aims only at the conquest of a piece of flesh, but
which, to gain possession of a whole tract of memories from which

they have felt nostalgically exiled, come surging round it, enlarge and extend it, are unable to follow it to the fulfilment, to the assimilation, impossible in the form in which it is looked for, of an immaterial reality, but wait for this desire half-way and at the moment of return, provide it once more with their escort; to kiss, instead of the cheeks of the first comer, anonymous, without mystery or glamour, however cool and fresh they may be, those of which I had so long been dreaming, would be to know the taste, the savour, of a colour on which I had endlessly gazed. One has seen a woman, a mere image in the decorative setting of life, like Albertine silhouetted against the sea, and then one has been able to take that image, to detach it, to bring it close to oneself, gradually to discern its volume, its colours, as though one had placed it behind the lens of a stereoscope. It is for this reason that women who are to some extent resistant, whom one cannot possess at once, of whom one does not indeed know at first whether one will ever possess them, are alone interesting. For to know them, to approach them, to conquer them, is to make the human image vary in shape, in dimension, in relief, is a lesson in relativity in the appreciation of a woman's body, a woman's life, so delightful to see afresh when it has resumed the slender proportions of a silhouette against the back-drop of life. The women one meets first of all in a brothel are of no interest because they remain invariable.

At the same time, Albertine preserved, inseparably attached to her, all my impressions of a series of sea-scapes of which I was particularly fond. I felt that in kissing her cheeks I should be kissing the whole of Balbec beach.

"If you really don't mind my kissing you, I'd rather put it off for a while and choose a good moment. Only you mustn't forget that you've said I may. I want a voucher: 'Valid for one kiss.'"

"Do I have to sign it?"

"But if I took it now, should I be entitled to another later on?"

"You do make me laugh with your vouchers: I shall issue a new one every now and then."

"Tell me, just one thing more. You know, at Balbec, before I got to know you, you used often to have a hard, calculating look. You couldn't tell me what you were thinking about when you looked like that?"

"No, I don't remember at all."

"Wait, this may remind you: one day your friend Gisèle jumped with her feet together over the chair an old gentleman was sitting in. Try to remember what was in your mind at that moment."

"Gisèle was the one we saw least of. She did belong to the group, I suppose, but not properly. I expect I thought that she was very ill-bred and common."

"Oh, is that all?"

I should have liked, before kissing her, to be able to breathe into her anew the mystery which she had had for me on the beach before I knew her, to discover in her the place where she had lived earlier still; in its stead at least, if I knew nothing of it, I could insinuate all the memories of our life at Balbec, the sound of the waves breaking beneath my window, the shouts of the children. But when I let my eyes glide over the charming pink globe of her cheeks, the gently curving surfaces of which expired beneath the first foothills of her beautiful black hair which ran in undulating ridges, thrust out its escarpments, and moulded the hollows and ripples of its valleys, I could not help saying to myself: "Now at last, after failing at Balbec, I am going to discover the fragrance of the secret rose that blooms in Albertine's cheeks. And, since the cycles through which we are able to make things and people pass in the course of our existence are comparatively few, perhaps I shall be able to consider mine in a certain sense fulfilled when, having taken out of its distant frame the blossoming face that I had chosen from among all others, I shall have brought it on to this new plane, where I shall at last have knowledge of it through my lips."
I told myself this because I believed that there was such a thing as knowledge acquired by the lips; I told myself that I was going to know the taste of this fleshly rose, because I had not stopped to think that man, a creature obviously less rudimentary than the sea-urchin or even the whale, nevertheless lacks a certain number of essential organs, and notably possesses none that will serve for kissing. For this absent organ he substitutes his lips, and thereby arrives perhaps at a slightly more satisfying result than if he were reduced to caressing the beloved with a horny tusk. But a pair of lips, designed to convey to the palate the taste of whatever whets their appetite, must be content, without understanding their mistake or admitting their disappointment, with roaming over the surface and with coming to a halt at the barrier of the impenetrable but irresistible cheek. Moreover at the moment of actual contact with the flesh, the lips, even on the assumption that they might

become more expert and better endowed, would doubtless be unable to enjoy any more fully the savour which nature prevents their ever actually grasping, for in that desolate zone in which they are unable to find their proper nourishment they are alone, the sense of sight, then that of smell, having long since deserted them. At first, as my mouth began gradually to approach the cheeks which my eyes had recommended it to kiss, my eyes, in changing position, saw a different pair of cheeks; the neck, observed at closer range and as though through a magnifying glass, showed in its coarser grain a robustness which modified the character of the face.

Apart from the most recent applications of photography—which huddle at the foot of a cathedral all the houses that so often, from close to, appeared to us to reach almost to the height of the towers, which drill and deploy like a regiment, in file, in extended order, in serried masses, the same monuments, bring together the two columns on the Piazzetta which a moment ago were so far apart, thrust away the adjoining dome of the Salute and in a pale and toneless background manage to include a whole immense horizon within the span of a bridge, in the embrasure of a window, among the leaves of a tree that stands in the foreground and is more vigorous in tone, or frame a single church successively in the arcades of all the others—I can think of nothing that can to so great a degree as a kiss evoke out of what we believed to be a thing with one definite aspect the hundred other things which it may equally well be, since each is related to a no less legitimate perspective. In short, just as at Balbec Albertine had often appeared different to me, so now—as if, prodigiously accelerating the speed of the changes of perspective and changes of colouring which a person presents to us in the course of our various encounters, I had sought to contain them all in the space of a few seconds so as to reproduce experimentally the phenomenon which diversifies the individuality of a fellow-creature, and to draw out one from another, like a nest of boxes, all the possibilities that it contains—so now, during this brief journey of my lips towards her cheek, it was ten Albertines that I saw; this one girl being like a many-headed goddess, the head I had seen last, when I tried to approach it, gave way to another. At least so long as I had not touched that head, I could still see it, and a faint perfume came to me from it. But alas—for in this matter of kissing our nostrils and eyes are as ill-placed as our lips are ill-made—suddenly my eyes ceased to see, then my nose, crushed by the collision, no longer perceived any odour, and, without thereby gaining any clearer idea of the taste of the rose of my desire, I learned, from these obnoxious signs, that at last I was in the act of kissing Albertine's cheek.

Was it because we were enacting (represented by the rotation of a solid body) the converse of our scene together at Balbec, because it was I who was lying in bed and she who was up, capable of evading a brutal attack and of controlling the course of events, that she allowed me to take so easily now what she had refused me on the former occasion with so forbidding a look? (No doubt from that earlier look the voluptuous expression which her face assumed now at the approach of my lips differed only by an infinitesimal deviation of its lines but one in which may be contained all the disparity that there is between the gesture of finishing off a wounded man and that of giving him succour, between a sublime and a hideous portrait.) Not knowing whether I had to give credit and thanks for this change of attitude to some unwitting benefactor who in these last months, in Paris or at Balbec, had been working on my behalf, I supposed that the respective positions in which we were now placed was the principal cause of it. It was quite another explanation, however, that Albertine offered me; precisely this: "Oh, well, you see, that time at Balbec I didn't know you properly. For all I knew, you might have meant mischief." This argument left me perplexed. Albertine was no doubt sincere in advancing it—so difficult is it for a woman to recognise in the movements of her limbs, in the sensations felt by her body, during a tête-à-tête with a male friend, the unknown sin into which she trembled to think that a stranger might be planning her fall!

In any case, whatever the modifications that had occurred recently in her life and that might perhaps have explained why it was that she now so readily accorded to my momentary and purely physical desire what at Balbec she had refused with horror to allow to my love, an even more surprising one manifested itself in Albertine that same evening as soon as her caresses had procured in me the satisfaction which she could not fail to notice and which, indeed, I had been afraid might provoke in her the instinctive movement of revulsion and offended modesty which Gilberte had made at a similar moment behind the laurel shrubbery in the Champs-Elysées.

The exact opposite happened. Already, when I had first made her lie on my bed and had begun to fondle her, Albertine had assumed an air which I did not remember in her, of docile good-will, of an almost childish simplicity. Obliterating every trace of her customary preoccupations and pretensions, the moment preceding pleasure, similar in this respect to the moment that follows death, had restored to her rejuvenated features what seemed like the innocence of earliest childhood. And no doubt everyone whose special talent is suddenly brought into play becomes modest, diligent and charming; especially if by this talent such persons know that they are giving us a great pleasure, are themselves made happy by it, and want us to enjoy it to the full. But in this new expression on Albertine's face there was more than disinterestedness and professional conscientiousness and generosity, there was a sort of conventional and unexpected zeal; and it was further than to her own childhood, it was to the infancy of her race that she had reverted. Very different from myself, who had looked for nothing more than a physical alleviation, which I had finally secured, Albertine seemed to feel that it would indicate a certain coarseness on her part were she to think that this material pleasure could be unaccompanied by a moral sentiment or was to be regarded as terminating anything. She, who had earlier been in so great a hurry, now, doubtless because she felt that kisses implied love and that love took precedence over all other duties, said when I reminded her of her dinner:

"Oh, but that doesn't matter in the least. I've got plenty of time."

She seemed embarrassed at the idea of getting up and going immediately after what had happened, embarrassed from a sense of propriety, just as Françoise when, without feeling thirsty, she had felt herself bound to accept with a seemly gaiety the glass of wine which Jupien offered her, would never have dared to leave him as soon as the last drops were drained, however urgent the call of duty. Albertine—and this was perhaps, with another which the reader will learn in due course, one of the reasons which had made me unconsciously desire her—was one of the incarnations of the little French peasant whose type may be seen in stone at Saint-André-des-Champs. As in Françoise, who presently, however, was to become her deadly enemy, I recognised in her a courtesy towards the host and the stranger, a sense of propriety, a respect for the bedside.

Françoise, who after the death of my aunt felt obliged to speak only in a doleful tone, would, in the months that preceded her daughter's marriage, have been quite shocked if the girl had not taken her lover's arm when the young couple walked out together. Albertine lying motionless beside me said:

"What nice hair you have; what nice eyes—you're sweet."

When, after pointing out to her that it was getting late, I added: "You don't believe me?", she replied, what was perhaps true, but only since the minute before and for the next few hours:

"I always believe you."

She spoke to me of myself, my family, my social background. She said: "Oh, I know your parents know some very nice people. You're a friend of Robert Forestier and Suzanne Delage." For a moment these names conveyed absolutely nothing to me. But suddenly I remembered that I had indeed played as a child in the Champs-Elysées with Robert Forestier, whom I had never seen since. As for Suzanne Delage, she was the great-niece of Mme Blandais, and I had once been due to go to a dancing-lesson, and even to take a small part in a play in her parents' house. But the fear of getting a fit of giggles and a nose-bleed had at the last moment prevented me, so that I had never set eyes on her. I had at the most a vague idea that I had once heard that the Swanns' feather-hatted governess had at one time been with the Delages, but perhaps it was only a sister of this governess, or a friend. I protested to Albertine that Robert Forestier and Suzanne Delage occupied a very small place in my life. "That may be; but your mothers are friends, I can place you by that. I often pass Suzanne Delage in the Avenue de Messine. I admire her style." Our mothers were acquainted only in the imagination of Mme Bontemps, who having heard that I had at one time played with Robert Forestier, to whom, it appeared, I used to recite poetry, had concluded from that that we were bound by family ties. She could never, I gathered, hear my mother's name mentioned without observing: "Oh yes, she belongs to the Delage–Forestier set," giving my parents a good mark which they had done nothing to deserve.

Quite apart from this, Albertine's social notions were fatuous in the extreme. She regarded the Simonnets with a double "n" as inferior not only to the Simonets with a single "n" but to everyone in the world. That someone else should bear the same name as yourself without belonging to your family is an excellent reason for despising him. Of course there are exceptions. It may happen that two Simonnets (introduced to one another at one of those gatherings where one feels the need to talk, no matter what about, and where moreover one is instinctively well disposed towards strangers, for instance in a funeral procession on its way to the cemetery), finding that they have the same name, will seek with mutual affability though without success to discover a possible kinship. But that is only an exception. Plenty of people are disreputable, without our either knowing or caring. If, however, a similarity of names brings to our door letters addressed to them, or vice versa, we at once feel a mistrust, often justified, as to their moral worth. We are afraid of being confused with them, and forestall the mistake by a grimace of disgust when anyone refers to them in our hearing. When we read our own name, as borne by them, in the newspaper, they seem to have usurped it. The transgressions of other members of the social organism are a matter of indifference to us. We lay the burden of them the more heavily upon our namesakes. The hatred which we bear towards the other Simonnets is all the stronger in that it is not a personal feeling but has been transmitted hereditarily. After the second generation we remember only the expression of disgust with which our grand-parents used to refer to the other Simonnets; we know nothing of the reason; we should not be surprised to learn that it had begun with a murder. Until, as is not uncommon, the day comes when a male Simonnet and a female Simonnet who are not in any way related are joined together in matrimony and so repair the breach.

Not only did Albertine speak to me of Robert Forestier and Suzanne Delage, but spontaneously, with that impulse to confide which the juxtaposition of two human bodies creates, at the beginning at least, during a first phase before it has engendered a special duplicity and reticence in one person towards the other, she told me a story about her own family and one of Andrée's uncles, of which, at Balbec, she had refused to say a word; but she now felt that she ought not to appear to have any secrets from me. Now, had her dearest friend said anything to her against me, she would have made a point of repeating it to me.

I insisted on her going home, and finally she did go, but she was so ashamed on my account at my discourtesy that she laughed almost as though to apologise for me, as a hostess to whose party you have gone without dressing makes the best of you but is offended nevertheless.

"What are you laughing at?" I inquired.

"I'm not laughing, I'm smiling at you," she replied tenderly. "When am I going to see you again?" she went on, as though declining to admit that what had just happened between us, since it is generally the consummation of it, might not be at least the prelude to a great friendship, a pre-existent friendship which we owed it to ourselves to discover, to confess, and which alone could account for what we had indulged in.

"Since you give me leave, I shall send for you when I can."

I dared not let her know that I was subordinating everything else to the chance of seeing Mme de Stermaria.

"It will have to be at short notice, unfortunately," I went on, "I never know beforehand. Would it be possible for me to send round for you in the evenings when I'm free?"

"It will be quite possible soon, because I'm going to have an independent entrance. But just at present it's impracticable. Anyhow I shall come round tomorrow or the next day in the afternoon. You needn't see me if you're busy."

On reaching the door, surprised that I had not preceded her, she offered me her cheek, feeling that there was no need now for any coarse physical desire to prompt us to kiss one another. The brief relations in which we had just indulged being of the sort to which a profound intimacy and a heartfelt choice sometimes lead, Albertine had felt it incumbent upon her to improvise and add temporarily to the kisses which we had exchanged on my bed the sentiment of which those kisses would have been the symbol for a knight and his lady such as they might have been conceived by a Gothic minstrel.

When she had left me, this young Picarde who might have been carved on his porch by the sculptor of Saint-André-des-Champs, Françoise brought me a letter which filled me with joy, for it was from Mme de Stermaria, who accepted my invitation to dinner for Wednesday. From Mme de Stermaria—that was to say, for me, not so much from the real Mme de Stermaria as from the one of whom I had been thinking all day before Albertine's arrival. It is the terrible deception of love that it begins by engaging us in play not with a woman of the outside world but with a doll inside our brain—the only woman moreover that we have always at our disposal, the only one we shall ever possess—whom the arbitrary power of memory, almost as absolute as that of the imagination, may have made as different from the real woman as the Balbec of my dreams had been from the real Balbec; an artificial creation which by degrees, and to our own hurt, we shall force the real woman to resemble.

Albertine had made me so late that the play had just finished when I entered Mme de Villeparisis's drawing-room; and having little desire to be caught in the stream of guests who were pouring out, discussing the great piece of news, the separation, which was said to have been already effected, between the Duc de Guermantes and his wife, I had taken a seat on a *bergère* in the outer room while waiting for an opportunity to greet my hostess, when from the inner one, where she had no doubt been sitting in the front row, I saw emerging, majestic, ample and tall in a flowing gown of yellow satin upon which huge black poppies were picked out in relief, the Duchess herself. The sight of her no longer disturbed me in the least. One fine day my mother, laying her hands on my forehead (as was her habit when she was afraid of hurting my feelings) and saying: "You really must stop hanging about trying to meet Mme de Guermantes. You're becoming a laughing-stock. Besides, look how ill your grandmother is, you really have something more serious to think about than waylaying a woman who doesn't care a straw about you," instantaneously— like a hypnotist who brings you back from the distant country in which you imagined yourself to be, and opens your eyes for you, or like the doctor who, by recalling you to a sense of duty and reality, cures you of an imaginary disease in which you have been wallowing—had awakened me from an unduly protracted dream. The rest of the day had been consecrated to a last farewell to this malady which I was renouncing; I had sung, for hours on end and weeping as I sang, the words of Schubert's *Adieu*:

> Farewell, strange voices call thee,
> Sweet sister of the angels, far from me.

And then it was over. I had given up my morning walks, and with so little difficulty that I thought myself justified in the prophecy (which we shall see was to prove false later on) that I should easily grow accustomed, during the course of my life, to no longer seeing a woman. And when, shortly afterwards, Françoise had reported to me that Jupien, anxious to enlarge his business, was looking for a shop in the neighbourhood, wanting to find one for him (delighted, too, while strolling along a street which already from my bed I had heard luminously vociferous like a peopled beach, to see behind the raised iron shutters of the dairies the young milk-maids with their white sleeves), I had been able to begin those outings again. Nor did I feel the slightest constraint; for I was conscious that I was no longer going out with the object of seeing Mme de Guermantes—much as a married woman, who has taken endless precautions so long as she has a lover, from the day she breaks with him leaves his letters lying about, at the risk of disclosing to her husband an infidelity which ceased to alarm her the moment she ceased to be guilty of it.

What troubled me now was the discovery that almost every house sheltered some unhappy person. In one the wife was always in tears because her husband was unfaithful to her. In the next it was the other way about. In another a hard-working mother, beaten black and blue by a drunkard son, tried to conceal her sufferings from the eyes of the neighbours. Quite half of the human race was in tears. And when I came to know it I saw that it was so exasperating that I wondered whether it might not be the adulterous husband and wife (who were unfaithful only because their lawful happiness had been denied them, and showed themselves charming and loyal to everyone but their respective spouses) who were in the right. Presently I ceased to have even the excuse of being useful to Jupien for continuing my morning peregrinations. For we learned that the cabinet-maker in our courtyard, whose workrooms were separated from Jupien's shop only by the flimsiest of partitions, was shortly to be "given notice" by the Duke's agent because his hammering made too much noise. Jupien could have hoped for nothing better. The workrooms had a basement for storing timber, which communicated with our cellars. He could keep his coal there, could knock down the partition, and would then have one huge shop. Indeed, since Jupien, finding the rent that M. de Guermantes was asking him exorbitant, allowed the premises to be inspected in the hope that, discouraged by his failure to find a tenant, the Duke would resign himself to accepting a lower offer, Françoise, noticing that, even at an hour when no prospective tenant was likely to call, the concierge left the door of the empty shop on the latch with the "To let" sign still up, scented a trap laid by him to entice the young woman who was engaged to the Guermantes footman (they would find a lovers' retreat there) and to catch them red-handed.

However that might be, and for all that I had no longer to find Jupien a new shop, I still went out before lunch. Often, on these excursions, I met M. de Norpois. It would happen that, conversing as he walked with a colleague, he cast at me a glance which, after making a thorough scrutiny of my person, turned back towards his companion without his having smiled at me or given me any more sign of recognition than if he had never set eyes on me before. For, with these eminent diplomats, looking at you in a certain way is intended to let you know not that they have seen you but that they have not seen you and that they have some serious matter to discuss with the colleague who is accompanying them. A tall woman whom I frequently encountered near the house was less discreet with me. For although I did not know her, she would turn round to look at me, would wait for me, unavailingly, in front of shop windows, smile at me as though she were going to kiss me, make gestures indicative of complete surrender. She resumed an icy coldness towards me if anyone appeared whom she knew. For a long time now in these morning walks, according to what I had to do, even if it was the most trivial purchase of a newspaper, I chose the shortest way, with no regret if it was off the Duchess's habitual route, and if on the other hand it did lie along that route, without either compunction or concealment, because it no longer appeared to me the forbidden road on which I extorted from an ungrateful woman the favour of setting eyes on her against her will. But it had never occurred to me that my recovery, in restoring me to a normal attitude towards Mme de Guermantes, would have a corresponding effect on her and make possible a friendliness, even a friendship, which no longer mattered to me. Until then, the efforts of the entire world banded together to bring me into touch with her would have been powerless to counteract the evil spell that is cast by an ill-starred love. Fairies more powerful than mankind have decreed that in such cases nothing can avail us until the day we utter sincerely in our hearts the formula: "I am no longer in love." I had been vexed with Saint-Loup for not having taken me to see his aunt. But he was no more capable than anyone else of breaking a spell. So long as I was in love with Mme de Guermantes, the marks of cordiality that I received from others, their compliments, actually distressed me, not only because they did not come from her but because she would never hear of them. And yet even if she had known of them it would not have been of the slightest use to me. But even in the details of an attachment, an absence, the declining of an invitation to dinner, an unintentional, unconscious harshness are of more service than all the cosmetics and fine clothes in the world. There would be plenty of social success if people were taught upon these lines the art of succeeding.

As she swept through the room in which I was sitting, her thoughts filled with the memory of friends whom I did not know and whom she would perhaps be meeting again presently at some other party, the Duchess caught sight of me on my *bergère*, genuinely indifferent and seeking only to be polite whereas while I was in love I had tried so desperately, without ever succeeding, to assume an air of indifference. She swerved aside, came towards me and, reproducing the smile she had worn that evening at the Opéra, which the painful feeling of being loved by someone she did not love no longer obliterated, "No, don't move," she said, gracefully gathering in her immense skirt which otherwise would have occupied the entire *bergère*. "You don't mind if I sit down beside you a moment?"

She was taller than me, and further enlarged by the volume of her dress, and I felt myself almost touching her handsome bare arm, round which a faint and ubiquitous down exhaled as it were a perpetual golden mist, and the blonde coils of her hair which wafted their fragrance over me. Having barely room to sit down, she could not turn easily to face me, and so, obliged to look straight in front of her rather than in my direction, assumed the sort of soft and dreamy expression one sees in a portrait.

"Have you any news of Robert?" she inquired.

At that moment Mme de Villeparisis entered the room.

"Well, what a fine time you arrive when we do see you here for once in a way!"

And noticing that I was talking to her niece, and concluding, perhaps, that we were more intimate than she had supposed: "But don't let me interrupt your conversation with Oriane," she went on (for the good offices of the procuress are part of the duties of the perfect hostess). "You wouldn't care to dine with her here on Wednesday?"

It was the day on which I was to dine with Mme de Stermaria, so I declined.

"Saturday, then?"

As my mother was returning on Saturday or Sunday, it would have been unkind not to stay at home every evening to dine with her. I therefore declined this invitation also.

"Ah, you're not an easy person to get hold of."

"Why do you never come to see me?" inquired Mme de Guermantes when Mme de Villeparisis had left us to go and congratulate the performers and present the leading lady with a bunch of roses upon which the hand that offered it conferred all its value, for it had cost no more than twenty francs. (This, incidentally, was as high as she ever went when an artist had performed only once. Those who gave their services at all her afternoons and evenings throughout the season received roses painted by the Marquise.) "It's such a bore never to see each other except in other people's houses. Since you won't dine with me at my aunt's, why not come and dine at my house?"

Various people who had stayed to the last possible moment on one pretext or another, but were at last preparing to leave, seeing that the Duchess had sat down to talk to a young man on a seat so narrow as just to contain them both, thought that they must have been misinformed, that it was not the Duchess but the Duke who was seeking a separation, on my account. Whereupon they hastened to spread abroad this intelligence. I had better grounds than anyone for being aware of its falsity. But I was myself surprised that at one of those difficult periods in which a separation is being effected but is not yet complete, the Duchess, instead of withdrawing from society, should go out of her way to invite a person whom she knew so slightly. The suspicion crossed my mind that it had been the Duke alone who had been opposed to her having me in the house, and that now that he was leaving her she saw no further obstacle to her surrounding herself with the people she liked.

A few minutes earlier I should have been amazed had anyone told me that Mme de Guermantes was going to ask me to come and see her, let alone to dine with her. However much I might be aware that the Guermantes salon could not present those distinctive features which I had extracted from the name, the fact that it had been forbidden territory to me, by obliging me to give it the same kind of existence that we give to the salons of which we have read the description in a novel or seen the image in a dream, made me, even when I was certain that it was just like any other, imagine it as quite different; between myself and it was the barrier at which reality ends. To dine with the Guermantes was like travelling to a place I had long wished to see, making a desire emerge from my head and take shape before my eyes, making acquaintance with a dream. At least I might have supposed that it would be one of those dinners to which the hosts invite someone by telling him: "Do come; there'll be *absolutely* nobody but ourselves," pretending to attribute to the pariah the alarm which they themselves feel at the thought of his mixing with their friends, and seeking indeed to convert into an enviable privilege, reserved for their intimates alone, the quarantine of the outcast, involuntarily unsociable and favoured. I felt on the contrary that Mme de Guermantes was anxious for me to taste the most delightful society that she had to offer me when she went on to say, projecting before my eyes as it were the violet-hued loveliness of a visit to Fabrice's aunt and the miracle of an introduction to Count Mosca:

"You wouldn't be free on Friday, now, for a small dinner-party? It would be so nice. There'll be the Princesse de Parme, who's charming, not that I'd ask you to meet anyone who wasn't agreeable."

Discarded in the intermediate social grades which are engaged in a perpetual climbing movement, the family still plays an important part in certain stationary grades, such as the middle class and the semi-royal aristocracy, which latter cannot seek to raise itself since above it, from its own special point of view, there exists nothing. The friendship shown me by her "aunt Villeparisis" and Robert had perhaps made me, for Mme de Guermantes and her friends, living always upon themselves and in the same little circle, the object of an attentive curiosity of which I had no suspicion.

With these two kinsfolk she had a familiar, everyday, homely relationship of a sort, very different from what we imagine, in which, if we happen to be included, so far from our actions being ejected therefrom like a speck of dust from the eye or a drop of water from the windpipe, they are capable of remaining engraved, and will still be related and discussed years after we ourselves have forgotten them, in the palace in which we are astonished to find them preserved like a letter in our own handwriting among a priceless collection of autographs.

People who are merely fashionable may close their doors against undue invasion. But the Guermantes door did not suffer from that. Hardly ever did a stranger have occasion to appear at it. If, for once in a way, the Duchess had one pointed out to her, she never dreamed of troubling herself about the social distinction that he might bring, since this was a thing that she conferred and could not receive. She thought only of his real merits. Both Mme de

Villeparisis and Saint-Loup had testified to mine. And doubtless she would not have believed them if she had not at the same time observed that they could never manage to secure me when they wanted me, and that therefore I attached no importance to society, which seemed to the Duchess a sign that a stranger was to be numbered among what she called "agreeable people."

It was worth seeing, when one spoke to her of women for whom she did not care, how her face changed as soon as one named, in connexion with one of these, let us say her sister-in-law. "Oh, she's charming!" the Duchess would say in an assured and judicious tone. The only reason she gave was that this lady had declined to be introduced to the Marquise de Chaussegros and the Princesse de Silistrie. She did not add that the lady had also refused to be introduced to herself, the Duchesse de Guermantes. This had nevertheless been the case, and ever since, the mind of the Duchess had been at work trying to unravel the motives of a woman who was so hard to know. She was dying to be invited to her house. People in society are so accustomed to being sought after that the person who shuns them seems to them a phoenix and at once monopolises their attention.

Was the real motive in the mind of Mme de Guermantes for thus inviting me (now that I was no longer in love with her) that I did not seek the society of her relatives, although apparently sought after by them? I cannot say. In any case, having made up her mind to invite me, she was anxious to do me the honours of her house to the fullest extent and to keep away those of her friends whose presence might have dissuaded me from coming again, those whom she knew to be boring. I had not known to what to attribute her change of direction, when I had seen her diverge from her stellar path, come to sit down beside me, and invite me to dinner, the effect of unexplained causes: for want of a special sense to enlighten us in this respect, we imagine the people we know only slightly—as was my case with the Duchesse de Guermantes—as thinking of us only at the rare moments in which they set eyes on us. Whereas in fact this ideal oblivion in which we picture them as holding us is purely arbitrary. So much so that while in the silence of solitude, reminiscent of a clear and starlit night, we imagine the various queens of society pursuing their course in the heavens at an infinite distance, we cannot help an involuntary start of dismay or pleasure if there falls upon us from that starry height, like a meteorite engraved with our name which we supposed to be unknown on Venus or Cassiopeia, an invitation to dinner or a piece of wicked gossip.

Perhaps from time to time when, following the example of the Persian princes who, according to the Book of Esther, made their scribes read out to them the registers in which were enrolled the names of those of their subjects who had shown zeal in their service, Mme de Guermantes consulted her list of the well-disposed, she had said to herself, on coming to my name: "A man we must ask to dine some day." But other thoughts had distracted her

> (Beset by surging cares, a Prince's mind
> Towards fresh matters ever is inclined)

until the moment she caught sight of me sitting alone like Mordecai at the palace gate; and, the sight of me having refreshed her memory, she wished, like Ahasuerus, to lavish her gifts upon me.

I must however add that a surprise of a totally different sort was to follow the one which I had had on hearing Mme de Guermantes ask me to dine with her. Since I had felt that it would show great modesty on my part, and gratitude also, not to conceal this initial surprise but rather to exaggerate my expression of the delight that it gave me, Mme de Guermantes, who was getting ready to go on to another, final party, had said to me, almost as a justification and for fear of my not being quite certain who she was since I appeared so astonished at being invited to dine with her: "You know I'm the aunt of Robert de Saint-Loup who is very fond of you, and besides, we've already met each other here." In replying that I was aware of this I added that I also knew M. de Charlus, "who had been very kind to me at Balbec and in Paris." Mme de Guermantes appeared surprised and her eyes seemed to turn, as though for a verification of this statement, to some much earlier page of her internal register. "What, so you know Palamède, do you?" This name took on a considerable charm on the lips of Mme de Guermantes because of the instinc-tive simplicity with which she spoke of a man who was socially so brilliant a figure but for her was no more than her brother-in-law and the cousin with whom she had grown up. And on the dim greyness which the life of the Duchesse de Guermantes repre-sented for me this name Palamède shed as it were the radiance of long summer days when she had played with him as a girl in the garden at Guermantes. Moreover, in that long-forgotten period of their lives, Oriane de Guermantes and her cousin Palamède had been very different from what they had since become: M. de Charlus in particular, entirely absorbed in artistic pursuits which he had so effectively curbed in later life that I was amazed to learn that it was he who had painted the huge fan decorated with black and yellow irises which the Duchess was at this moment unfurling. She could also have shown me a little sonatina which he had once composed for her. I was completely unaware that the Baron possessed all these talents, of which he never spoke. Let me remark in passing that M. de Charlus did not at all relish being called "Palamède" by his family. That the form "Mémé" might not please him one could easily understand. These stupid abbreviations are a sign of the utter inability of the aristocracy to appreciate its own poetry (in Jewry, too, we may see the same defect, since a nephew of Lady Israels, whose name was Moses, was commonly known as "Momo") at the same time as its anxiety not to appear to attach any importance to what is aristocratic. Now on this point M. de Charlus had more poetic imagination and a more blatant pride. But the reason for his distaste for "Mémé" could not be this, since it extended also to the fine name Palamède. The truth was that, considering himself, knowing himself, to be of princely stock, he would have liked his brother and sister-in-law to refer to him as "Charlus," just as Queen Marie-Amélie and the Duc d'Orléans might speak of their sons and grandsons, brothers and nephews as "Joinville, Nemours, Chartres, Paris."

"What a humbug Mémé is!" she exclaimed. "We talked to him about you for hours, and he told us he would be delighted to make your acquaintance, just as if he had never set eyes on you. You must admit he's odd, and—though it's not very nice of me to say such a thing about a brother-in-law I'm devoted to and really do admire immensely—a trifle mad at times."

I was struck by the application of this last epithet to M. de Charlus, and thought to myself that this half-madness might perhaps account for certain things, such as his having appeared so delighted with his proposal that I should ask Bloch to beat his own mother. I decided that, by reason not only of the things he said but of the way in which he said them, M. de Charlus must be a little mad. The first time one listens to a barrister or an actor, one is surprised by his tone, so different from the conversational. But, observing that everyone else seems to find this quite natural, one says nothing about it to other people, one says nothing in fact to oneself, one is content to appreciate the degree of talent shown. At the most one may think, of an actor at the Théâtre-Français: "Why, instead of letting his raised arm fall naturally, did he bring it down in a series of little jerks broken by pauses for at least ten minutes?" or of a Labori: "Why, whenever he opened his mouth, did he utter those tragic, unexpected sounds to express the simplest things?" But as everybody accepts these things *a priori* one is not shocked by them. In the same way, on thinking it over, one said to oneself that M. de Charlus spoke of himself very grandiloquently, in a tone which was not in the least that of ordinary speech. One felt that people should have been saying to him every other minute: "But why are you shouting so loud? Why are you so offensive?" But everyone seemed to have tacitly agreed that it was quite all right. And one took one's place in the circle which applauded his perorations. But certainly there were moments when a stranger might have thought that he was listening to the ravings of a maniac.

"But," went on the Duchess with the faint insolence that went with her natural simplicity, "are you absolutely sure you're not thinking of someone else? Do you really mean my brother-in-law Palamède? I know he loves mystery, but this seems a bit much."

I replied that I was absolutely sure, and that M. de Charlus must have misheard my name.

"Well, I must leave you," said Mme de Guermantes, as though with regret. "I have to look in for a moment at the Princesse de Ligne's. You aren't going on there? No? You don't care for parties? You're very wise, they're too boring for words. If only I didn't have to go! But she's my cousin; it wouldn't be polite. I'm sorry, selfishly, for my own sake, because I could have taken you there, and brought you back afterwards, too. Good-bye then; I look forward to seeing you on Friday."

That M. de Charlus should have blushed to be seen with me by M. d'Argencourt was all very well. But that to his own sister-in-law, who had so high an opinion of him besides, he should deny all knowledge of me, a knowledge that was perfectly natural since I was a friend of both his aunt and his nephew, was something I could not understand.

I must end my account of this incident with the remark that from one point of view there was an element of true grandeur in Mme de Guermantes which consisted in the fact that she entirely obliterated from her memory what other people would have only partially forgotten. Had she never seen me waylaying her, follow-ing her, tracking her down on her morning walks, had she never responded to my daily salute with an irritated impatience, had she never sent Saint-Loup about his business when he begged her to invite me to her house, she could not have been more graciously and naturally amiable to me. Not only did she waste no time in retrospective inquiries, in hints, allusions or ambiguous smiles, not only was there in her present affability, without any harking back to the past, without the slightest reticence, something as proudly rectilinear as her majestic stature, but any resentment which she might have felt against someone in the past was so entirely reduced to ashes, and those ashes were themselves cast so utterly from her memory, or at least from her manner, that on studying her face whenever she had occasion to treat with the most exquisite simplicity what in so many other people would have been a pretext for reviving stale antipathies and recriminations, one had the impression of a sort of purification.

But if I was surprised by the modification that had occurred in her opinion of me, how much more did it surprise me to find an even greater change in my feelings for her! Had there not been a time when I could regain life and strength only if—always build-ing new castles in the air!—I had found someone who would obtain for me an invitation to her house and, after this initial boon, would procure many others for my increasingly exacting heart? It was the impossibility of making any headway that had made me leave Paris for Doncières to visit Robert de Saint-Loup. And now it was indeed by the consequence of a letter from him that I was agitated, but on account this time of Mme de Stermaria, not of Mme de Guermantes.

Let me add further, to conclude my account of this evening, that in the course of it there occurred an incident, contradicted a few days later, which surprised me not a little, which caused a breach between myself and Bloch, and which constitutes in itself one of those curious paradoxes the explanation of which will be found in the next part of this work. At this party at Mme de Villeparisis's, Bloch kept on boasting to me about the friendly attentions shown him by M. de Charlus, who, when he passed him in the street, looked him straight in the face as though he recog-nised him, was anxious to know him personally, knew quite well who he was. I smiled at first, Bloch having expressed himself so violently at Balbec on the subject of the said M. de Charlus. And I supposed merely that Bloch, like his father in the case of Bergotte, knew the Baron "without actually knowing him," and that what he took for a friendly glance was an absent-minded stare. But finally Bloch produced such circumstantial details, and appeared so confident that on two or three occasions M. de Charlus had wished to address him that, remembering that I had spoken of my friend to the Baron, who had asked me various questions about him as we walked together from this very house, I came to the conclusion that Bloch was not lying, that M. de Charlus had heard his name, realised that he was my friend, and so forth. And so, some time later, at the theatre one evening, I asked M. de Charlus if I might introduce Bloch to him, and, on his assenting, went in search of my friend. But as soon as M. de Charlus caught sight of him an expression of astonishment, instantly repressed, appeared on his face, where it gave way to a blazing fury. Not only did he not offer Bloch his hand but whenever Bloch spoke to him he replied in the rudest manner, in an irate and wounding tone. So that Bloch, who, according to his version, had received nothing until then from the Baron but smiles, assumed that I had disparaged rather than recommended him during the brief conversation which, knowing M. de Charlus's liking for etiquette, I had had with him about my friend before bringing him up to be introduced. Bloch left us, exhausted and broken, like a man who has been trying to mount a horse which is constantly on the verge of bolting, or to swim against waves which continually fling him back on the shingle, and did not speak to me again for six months.

The days that preceded my dinner with Mme de Stermaria, far from being delightful, were almost unbearable for me. For as a general rule, the shorter the interval that separates us from our planned objective the longer it seems to us, because we apply to it a more minute scale of measurement, or simply because it occurs to us to measure it. The Papacy, we are told, reckons by centuries, and indeed may perhaps not bother to reckon time at all, since its goal is in eternity. Mine being no more than three days off, I counted by seconds, I gave myself up to those imaginings which are the adumbrations of caresses, of caresses which one itches to be able to make the woman herself reciprocate and complete—precisely those caresses, to the exclusion of all others. And on the whole, if it is true that in general the difficulty of attaining the object of a desire enhances that desire (the difficulty, not the impossibility, for that suppresses it altogether), yet in the case of a desire that is purely physical, the certainty that it will be realised at a specific and fairly imminent point in time is not much more stirring than uncertainty; almost as much as anxious doubt, the absence of doubt makes intolerable the period of waiting for the pleasure that is bound to come, because it makes of that suspense an innumerably rehearsed accomplishment and, by the frequency of our proleptic representations, divides time into sections as minute as any that could be carved by anguished uncertainty.

What I wanted was to possess Mme de Stermaria: for several days my desires had been actively and incessantly preparing my imagination for this pleasure, and this pleasure alone; any other pleasure (pleasure with another woman) would not have been ready, pleasure being but the realisation of a prior craving which is not always the same but changes according to the endless variations of one's fancies, the accidents of one's memory, the state of one's sexual disposition, the order of availability of one's desires, the most recently assuaged of which lie dormant until the disillusion of their fulfilment has been to some extent forgotten; I had already turned from the main road of general desires and had ventured along the path of a more particular desire; I should have had—in order to wish for a different assignation—to retrace my steps too far before rejoining the main road and taking another path. To take possession of Mme de Stermaria on the island in the Bois de Boulogne where I had asked her to dine with me: this was the pleasure that I pictured to myself all the time. It would naturally have been destroyed if I had dined on that island without Mme de Stermaria; but perhaps as greatly diminished had I dined, even with her, somewhere else. Besides, the attitudes according to which one envisages a pleasure are prior to the woman, to the type of woman suitable thereto. They dictate the pleasure, and the place as well, and for that reason bring to the fore alternatively, in our capricious fancy, this or that woman, this or that setting, this or that room, which in other weeks we should have dismissed with contempt. Daughters of the attitude that produced them, certain women will not appeal to us without the double bed in which we find peace by their side, while others, to be caressed with a more secret intention, require leaves blown by the wind, water rippling in the dark, things as light and fleeting as they are.

No doubt in the past, long before I received Saint-Loup's letter and when there was as yet no question of Mme de Stermaria, the island in the Bois had seemed to me to be specially designed for pleasure, because I had found myself going there to taste the bitterness of having no pleasure to enjoy there. It is to the shores of the lake from which one goes to that island, and along which, in the last weeks of summer, those ladies of Paris who have not yet left for the country take the air, that, not knowing where to look for her, or whether indeed she has not already left Paris, one wanders in the hope of seeing the girl go by with whom one fell in love at the last ball of the season, whom one will not have a chance of meeting again on any evening until the following spring. Sensing it to be at least the eve, if not the morrow, of the beloved's departure, one follows along the brink of the shimmering water those pleasant paths by which already a first red leaf is blooming like a last rose, one scans that horizon where, by a contrivance the opposite of that employed in those panoramas beneath whose rotundas the wax figures in the foreground impart to the painted canvas beyond them the illusory appearance of depth and mass, our eyes, travelling without transition from the cultivated park to the natural heights of Meudon and the Mont Valérien, do not know where to set the boundary, and make the natural country trespass upon the handiwork of the gardener, the artificial charm of which they project far beyond its own limits; like those rare birds reared in liberty in a botanical garden which every day, wherever their winged excursions may chance to take them, sound an exotic note here or there in the surrounding woods. Between the last festivity of summer and one's winter exile, one anxiously ranges that romantic world of chance encounters and lover's melancholy, and one would be no more surprised to learn that it was situated outside the mapped universe than if, at Versailles, looking down from the terrace, an observatory round which the clouds gather against the blue sky in the manner of Van der Meulen, after having thus risen above the bounds of nature, one were informed that, there where nature begins again at the end of the great canal, the villages which one cannot make out, on a horizon as dazzling as the sea, are called Fleurus or Nijmegen.

And then, the last carriage having rolled by, when one feels with pain that she will not now come, one goes to dine on the island; above the quivering poplars which endlessly recall the mysteries of evening more than they respond to them, a pink cloud puts a last touch of living colour into the tranquil sky. A few drops of rain fall soundlessly on the ancient water which, in its divine infancy, remains always the colour of the weather and continually forgets the reflexions of clouds and flowers. And after the geraniums have vainly striven, by intensifying the brilliance of their scarlet, to resist the gathering twilight, a mist rises to envelop the now slumbering island; one walks in the moist darkness along the water's edge, where at the most the silent passage of a swan startles one like the momentarily wide-open eyes and the swift smile of a child in bed at night whom one did not suppose to be awake. Then one longs all the more to have a lover by one's side because one feels alone and can believe oneself to be far away.

But to this island, where even in summer there was often a mist, how much more gladly would I have brought Mme de Stermaria now that the cold season, the end of autumn had come! If the weather that had prevailed since Sunday had not in itself rendered grey and maritime the scenes in which my imagination was living—as other seasons made them balmy, luminous, Italian— the hope of making Mme de Stermaria mine in a few days' time would have been quite enough to raise, twenty times in an hour, a curtain of mist in my monotonously yearning imagination. In any event the fog which since yesterday had risen even in Paris not only made me think incessantly of the native province of the young woman whom I had invited, but since it was probable that it must after sunset invade the Bois, and especially the shores of the lake, far more thickly than the streets of the town, I felt that for me it would give the Isle of Swans a hint of that Breton island whose marine and misty atmosphere had always enveloped in my mind like a garment the pale silhouette of Mme de Stermaria. Of course when we are young, at the age I had reached at the time of my walks along the Méséglise way, our desires, our beliefs confer on a woman's clothing an individual personality, an irreducible essence. We pursue the reality. But by dint of allowing it to escape we end by noticing that, after all those vain endeavours which have led to nothing, something solid subsists, which is what we have been seeking. We begin to isolate, to identify what we love, we try to procure it for ourselves, if only by a stratagem. Then, in the absence of our vanished faith, costume fills the gap, by means of a deliberate illusion. I knew quite well that within half an hour of home I should not find myself in Brittany. But in walking arm in arm with Mme de Stermaria in the dusk of the island, by the water's edge, I should be acting like other men who, unable to penetrate the walls of a convent, do at least, before enjoying a woman, clothe her in the habit of a nun.

I could even look forward to hearing with her a lapping of waves, for, on the day before our dinner, a storm broke over Paris. I was beginning to shave before going to the island to engage the room (although at this time of year the island was empty and the restaurant deserted) and order the food for our dinner next day when Françoise came in to announce the arrival of Albertine. I had her shown in at once, indifferent to her finding me disfigured by a bristling chin, although at Balbec I had never felt smart enough for her and she had cost me as much agitation and distress as Mme de Stermaria did now. The latter, I was determined, must go away with the best possible impression from our evening together. Accordingly I asked Albertine to come with me there and then to the island to choose the menu. She to whom one gives everything is so quickly replaced by another that one is surprised to find oneself giving all that one has afresh at every moment, without any hope of future reward. At my suggestion the smiling rosy face beneath Albertine's flat toque, which came down very low, over her eyebrows, seemed to hesitate. She had probably other plans; if so she sacrificed them willingly, to my great satisfaction, for I attached the utmost importance to having with me a young housewife who would know a great deal more than me about ordering dinner.

It is certain that she had represented something utterly different for me at Balbec. But our intimacy with a woman with whom we are in love, even when we do not consider it close enough at the time, creates between her and us, in spite of the shortcomings that pain us while our love lasts, social ties which outlast our love and even the memory of our love. Then, in the woman who is now no more to us than a means of approach, an avenue towards others, we are just as astonished and amused to learn from our memory what her name meant originally to that other person we formerly were as if, after giving a cabman an address in the Boulevard des Capucines or the Rue du Bac, thinking only of the person we are going to see there, we remind ourselves that these names were once those of the Capuchin nuns whose convent stood on the site and of the ferry across the Seine.

At the same time, my Balbec desires had so generously ripened Albertine's body, had gathered and stored in it savours so fresh and sweet that, during our expedition to the Bois, while the wind like a careful gardener shook the trees, brought down the fruit, swept up the fallen leaves, I told myself that had there been any risk of Saint-Loup's being mistaken, or of my having misunderstood his letter, so that my dinner with Mme de Stermaria might lead to no satisfactory result, I should have made an appointment for later the same evening with Albertine, in order to forget, during an hour of purely sensual pleasure, holding in my arms a body of which my curiosity had once computed, weighed up all the possible charms in which it now abounded, the emotions and perhaps the regrets of this burgeoning love for Mme de Stermaria. And certainly, if I could have supposed that Mme de Stermaria would grant me none of her favours at our first meeting, I should have formed a slightly depressing picture of my evening with her. I knew only too well from experience how bizarrely the two stages which succeed one another in the first phase of our love for a woman whom we have desired without knowing her, loving in her rather the particular kind of existence in which she is steeped than her still unfamiliar self—how bizarrely those two stages are reflected in the domain of reality, that is to say no longer in ourselves but in our meetings with her. Without ever having talked to her, we have hesitated, tempted as we were by the poetic charm which she represented for us. Shall it be this woman or another? And suddenly our dreams become focused on her, are indistinguishable from her. The first meeting with her which will shortly follow should reflect this dawning love. Nothing of the sort. As if it were necessary for material reality to have its first phase also, loving her already we talk to her in the most trivial fashion: "I asked you to come and dine on this island because I thought the surroundings would amuse you. Mind you, I've nothing particular to say to you. But it's rather damp, I'm afraid, and you may find it cold—" "Oh, no, not at all!" "You just say that out of politeness. Very well, Madame, I shall allow you to battle against the cold for another quarter of an hour, as I don't want to pester you, but in fifteen minutes I shall take you away by force. I don't want to have you catching a chill." And without having said anything to her we take her home, remembering nothing about her, at the most a certain look in her eyes, but thinking only of seeing her again. Then at the second meeting (when we do not even find that look, our sole memory of her, but nevertheless still only thinking—indeed even more so—of seeing her again), the first stage is transcended. Nothing has happened in the interval. And yet, instead of talking about the comfort or want of comfort of the restaurant, we say, without apparently surprising the new person, who seems to us positively plain but to whom we should like to think that people were talking about us at every moment in her life: "We're going to have our work cut out to overcome all the obstacles in our way. Do you think we shall be successful? Do you think we'll get the better of our enemies, live happily ever after?" But these contrasting conversations, trivial to begin with, then hinting at love, would not be required; Saint-Loup's letter was a guarantee of that. Mme de Stermaria would give herself on the very first evening, so that I should have no need to engage Albertine to come to me as a substitute later in the evening. It would be unnecessary; Robert never exaggerated, and his letter was quite clear.

Albertine spoke hardly at all, sensing that my thoughts were elsewhere. We went a little way on foot into the greenish, almost submarine grotto of a dense grove on the dome of which we heard the wind howl and the rain splash. I trod underfoot dead leaves which sank into the soil like sea-shells, and poked with my stick at fallen chestnuts prickly as sea-urchins.

On the boughs of the trees, the last clinging leaves, shaken by the wind, followed it only as far as their stems would allow, but sometimes these broke and they fell to the ground, along which they coursed to overtake it. I thought joyfully how much more remote still, if this weather lasted, the island would be the next day, and in any case quite deserted. We returned to our carriage and, as the squall had subsided, Albertine asked me to take her on to Saint-Cloud. As on the ground the drifting leaves, so up above the clouds were chasing the wind. And a stream of migrant evenings, of which a sort of conic section cut into the sky made visible the successive layers, pink, blue and green, were gathered in readiness for departure to warmer climes. To obtain a closer view of a marble goddess who had been carved in the act of springing from her pedestal and, alone in a great wood which seemed to be consecrated to her, filled it with the mythological terror, half animal, half divine, of her frenzied leaps, Albertine climbed a knoll while I waited for her in the road. She herself, seen thus from below, no longer coarse and plump as a few days earlier on my bed when the grain of her neck appeared under the magnifying glass of my eyes, but delicately chiselled, seemed like a little statue on which our happy hours together at Balbec had left their patina.

When I found myself alone again at home, remembering that I had been for an expedition that afternoon with Albertine, that I was to dine in two days' time with Mme de Guermantes and that I had to answer a letter from Gilberte, three women I had loved, I said to myself that our social existence, like an artist's studio, is filled with abandoned sketches in which we fancied for a moment that we could set down in permanent form our need of a great love, but it did not occur to me that sometimes, if the sketch is not too old, it may happen that we return to it and make of it a wholly different work, and one that is possibly more important than what we had originally planned.

The next day was cold and fine; winter was in the air—indeed the season was so far advanced that it was a miracle that we should have found in the already ravaged Bois a few domes of gilded green. When I awoke I saw, as from the window of the barracks at Doncières, a uniform, dead white mist which hung gaily in the sunlight, thick and soft as a web of spun sugar. Then the sun withdrew, and the mist thickened still further in the afternoon. Night fell early, and I washed and changed, but it was still too soon to start. I decided to send a carriage for Mme de Stermaria. I did not like to go for her in it myself, not wishing to force my company on her, but I gave the driver a note for her in which I asked whether she would mind my coming to call for her. Meanwhile I lay down on my bed, shut my eyes for a moment, then opened them again. Over the top of the curtains there was now only a thin strip of daylight which grew steadily dimmer. I recognised that vacant hour, the vast ante-room of pleasure, the dark, delicious emptiness of which I had learned at Balbec to know and to enjoy when, alone in my room as I was now, while everyone else was at dinner, I saw without regret the daylight fade from above my curtains, knowing that presently, after a night of polar brevity, it was to be resuscitated in a more dazzling brightness in the lighted rooms at Rivebelle. I sprang from my bed, tied my black tie, brushed my hair, final gestures of a belated tidying-up, carried out at Balbec with my mind not on myself but on the women whom I should see at Rivebelle, while I smiled at them in anticipation in the mirror that stood across a corner of my room, gestures which for that reason had remained the harbingers of an entertainment in which music and lights would be mingled. Like magic signs they conjured it up, indeed already brought it into being; thanks to them I had as positive a notion of its reality, as

complete an enjoyment of its intoxicating frivolous charm, as I had
had at Combray, in the month of July, when I heard the hammer-
blows ring on the packing-cases and enjoyed the warmth and the
sunshine in the coolness of my darkened room.

Thus it was no longer entirely Mme de Stermaria that I should
have wished to see. Forced now to spend my evening with her, I
should have preferred, as it was almost the last before the return of
my parents, that it should remain free and that I should be able to
seek out some of the women I had seen at Rivebelle. I gave my
hands one more final wash and, my sense of pleasure keeping me
on the move, dried them as I walked through the shuttered
dining-room. It appeared to be open on to the lighted hall, but
what I had taken for the bright crevice of the door, which in fact
was closed, was only the gleaming reflexion of my towel in a
mirror that had been laid against the wall in readiness to be fixed in
its place before Mamma's return. I thought again of all the other
illusions of the sort which I had discovered in different parts of the
house, and which were not optical only, for when we first came
there I had thought that our next door neighbour kept a dog on
account of the prolonged, almost human, yapping which came
from a kitchen pipe whenever the tap was turned on. And the
door on to the outer landing never closed by itself, very gently,
against the draughts of the staircase, without rendering those
broken, voluptuous, plaintive phrases that overlap the chant of
the pilgrims towards the end of the Overture to *Tannhäuser*. I had
in fact, just as I had put my towel back on its rail, an opportunity of
hearing a fresh rendering of this dazzling symphonic fragment, for
at a peal of the bell I hurried out to open the door to the driver
who had come with Mme de Stermaria's answer. I thought that his
message would be: "The lady is downstairs," or "The lady is
waiting." But he had a letter in his hand. I hesitated for a moment
before looking to see what Mme de Stermaria had written, which
as long as she held the pen in her hand might have been different,
but was now, detached from her, an engine of fate pursuing its
course alone, which she was utterly powerless to alter. I asked the
driver to wait downstairs for a moment, although he grumbled
about the fog. As soon as he had gone I opened the envelope. On
her card, inscribed *Vicomtesse Alix de Stermaria*, my guest had
written: "Am so sorry—am unfortunately prevented from dining
with you this evening on the island in the Bois. Had been so
looking forward to it. Will write you a proper letter from

Stermaria. Very sorry. Kindest regards." I stood motionless,
stunned by the shock that I had received. At my feet lay the card
and envelope, fallen like the spent cartridge from a gun when the
shot has been fired. I picked them up, and tried to analyse her
message. "She says that she cannot dine with me on the island in
the Bois. One might conclude from that she might be able to dine
with me somewhere else. I shall not be so indiscreet as to go and
fetch her, but, after all, that is quite a reasonable interpretation."
And from the island in the Bois, since for the last few days my
thoughts had been installed there in advance with Mme de
Stermaria, I could not succeed in bringing them back to where I
was. My desire continued to respond automatically to the gravitational force which had been impelling it now for so many hours,
and in spite of this message, too recent to counteract that force, I
went on instinctively getting ready to set out, just as a student,
although ploughed by the examiners, tries to answer one question
more. At last I decided to tell Françoise to go down and pay the
driver. I went along the passage, and failing to find her, passed
through the dining-room, where suddenly my feet ceased to ring
out on the bare boards as they had been doing until then and were
hushed to a silence which, even before I had realised the explanation of it, gave me a feeling of suffocation and confinement. It was
the carpets which, with a view to my parents' return, the servants
had begun to put down again, those carpets which look so well on
bright mornings when amid their disorder the sun awaits you like a
friend come to take you out to lunch in the country, and casts over
them the dappled light and shade of the forest, but which now on
the contrary were the first installations of the wintry prison from
which, obliged as I should be to live and take my meals at home, I
should no longer be free to escape when I chose.

"Take care you don't slip, sir; they're not tacked yet," Françoise
called to me. "I ought to have lighted up. Oh, dear, it's the end of
'Sectember' already, the fine days are over."

In no time, winter; at the corner of a window, as in a Gallé glass,
a vein of crusted snow; and even in the Champs-Elysées, instead of
the girls one waits to see, nothing but solitary sparrows.

What added to my despair at not seeing Mme de Stermaria was
that her answer led me to suppose that whereas, hour by hour,
since Sunday, I had been living for this dinner alone, she had
presumably never given it a second thought. Later on I learned
of an absurd love match that she made with a young man whom

she must already have been seeing at this time, and who had presumably made her forget my invitation. For if she had remembered it she would surely never have waited for the carriage, which I had not in fact arranged to send for her, to inform me that she was otherwise engaged. My dreams of a young feudal maiden on a misty island had opened up a path to a still non-existent love. Now my disappointment, my rage, my desperate desire to recapture her who had just refused me, were able, by bringing my sensibility into play, to make definite the possible love which until then my imagination alone had—though more feebly—offered me.

How many they are in our memories, how many more we have forgotten—those faces of girls and young women, all different, on which we have superimposed a certain charm and a frenzied desire to see them again only because at the last moment they eluded us! In the case of Mme de Stermaria there was a good deal more than this, and it was enough now, in order to love her, for me to see her again so that I might refresh those impressions, so vivid but all too brief, which my memory would not otherwise have the strength to keep alive in her absence. Circumstances decided against me; I did not see her again. It was not she that I loved, but it might well have been. And one of the things that made most painful, perhaps, the great love which was presently to come to me was telling myself, when I thought of this evening, that given a slight modification of very simple circumstances, my love might have been transferred elsewhere, on to Mme de Stermaria; that, applied to her who inspired it in me so soon afterwards, it was not therefore—as I longed, so needed to believe—absolutely necessary and predestined.

Françoise had left me by myself in the dining-room with the remark that it was foolish of me to stay there before she had lighted the fire. She went to get me some dinner, for from this very evening, even before the return of my parents, my seclusion was beginning. I caught sight of a huge bundle of carpets, still rolled up, and propped against one end of the sideboard; and burying my head in it, swallowing its dust together with my own tears, as the Jews used to cover their heads with ashes in times of mourning, I began to sob. I shivered, not only because the room was cold, but because a distinct lowering of temperature (against the danger and, it must be said, the by no means disagreeable sensation of which we make no attempt to react) is brought about by a certain kind of tears which fall from our eyes, drop by drop, like a fine, penetrating, icy rain, and seem as though they will never cease to flow. Suddenly I heard a voice:

"May I come in? Françoise told me you might be in the dining-room. I looked in to see whether you would care to come out and dine somewhere, if it isn't bad for your throat—there's a fog outside you could cut with a knife."

It was Robert de Saint-Loup, who had arrived in Paris that morning, when I imagined him to be still in Morocco or on the sea.

I have already said (and it was precisely Robert himself who at Balbec had helped me, quite unwittingly, to arrive at this conclusion) what I think about friendship: to wit, that it is so trivial a thing that I find it hard to understand how men with some claim to genius—Nietzsche, for instance—can have been so ingenuous as to ascribe to it a certain intellectual merit, and consequently to deny themselves friendships in which intellectual esteem would have no part. Yes, it has always been a surprise to me to think that a man who carried honesty with himself to the point of cutting himself off from Wagner's music from scruples of conscience could have imagined that the truth can ever be attained by the mode of expression, by its very nature vague and inadequate, which actions in general and acts of friendship in particular constitute, or that there can be any kind of significance in the fact of one's leaving one's work to go and see a friend and shed tears with him on hearing the false report that the Louvre has been burned down. I had reached the point, at Balbec, of regarding the pleasure of playing with a troop of girls as less destructive of the spiritual life, to which at least it remains alien, than friendship, the whole effort of which is directed towards making us sacrifice the only part of ourselves that is real and incommunicable (otherwise than by means of art) to a superficial self which, unlike the other, finds no joy in its own being, but rather a vague, sentimental glow at feeling itself supported by external props, hospitalised in an extraneous individuality, where, happy in the protection that is afforded it there, it expresses its well-being in warm approval and marvels at qualities which it would denounce as failings and seek to correct in itself. Besides, the scorners of friendship can, without illusion and not without remorse, be the finest friends in the world, in the same way as an artist who is carrying a masterpiece within him and feels it his duty to live and carry on his work, nevertheless, in order not to be thought or to run the risk of being selfish, gives his life for a futile cause, and gives it all the more gallantly in that the reasons for which he would have preferred not to give it were disinterested. But whatever might be my opinion of friendship, to mention only the pleasure that it procured me, of a quality so mediocre as to be like something half-way between physical exhaustion and mental boredom, there is no brew so deadly that it cannot at certain moments become precious and invigorating by giving us just the stimulus that was necessary, the warmth that we cannot generate ourselves.

It never entered my mind of course to ask Saint-Loup to take me to see some of the Rivebelle women, as I had wanted to do an hour ago; the scar left by my regret about Mme de Stermaria was too recent to be so quickly healed, but at the moment when I had ceased to feel in my heart any reason for happiness Saint-Loup's arrival was like a sudden apparition of kindness, gaiety, life, which were external to me, no doubt, but offered themselves to me, asked only to be made mine. He did not himself understand my cry of gratitude, my tears of affection. And is there anything indeed more paradoxically affectionate than one of those friends, be he diplomat, explorer, airman, or soldier like Saint-Loup, who, having to leave next day for the country whence they will go on heaven knows where, seem to derive from the evening they devote to us an impression which we are astonished to find so heart-warming for them, so rare and fleeting is it, and equally astonished, since it delights them so much, not to see them prolong further or repeat more often? A meal with us, an event so natural in itself, gives these travellers the same strange and exquisite pleasure as our boulevards give to an Asiatic.

We set off together to dine, and on the way downstairs I thought of Doncières, where every evening I used to meet Robert at his restaurant, and the little dining-rooms there that I had forgotten. I remembered one of these to which I had never given a thought, and which was not in the hotel where Saint-Loup dined but in another, far humbler, a cross between an inn and a boarding-house, where the waiting was done by the landlady and one of her servants. I had been forced to take shelter there once from a snowstorm. Besides, Robert was not to be dining at the hotel that evening and I had not cared to go any further. My food was brought to me in a little panelled room upstairs. The lamp went out during dinner and the serving-girl lighted a couple of candles. Pretending that I could not see very well as I held out my plate while she helped me to potatoes, I took her bare forearm in my hand, as though to guide her. Seeing that she did not withdraw it, I began to fondle it, then, without saying a word, pulled her towards me, blew out the candles and told her to feel in my pocket for some money. For the next few days physical pleasure seemed to me to require, to be properly enjoyed, not only this serving-girl but the timbered dining-room, so remote and isolated. And yet it was to the other, in which Saint-Loup and his friends dined, that I returned every evening, from force of habit and from friendship, until I left Doncières. But even of this hotel, where he boarded with his friends, I had long ceased to think. We make little use of our experience, we leave unfulfilled on long summer evenings or premature winter nights the hours in which it had seemed to us that there might nevertheless be contained some element of peace or pleasure. But those hours are not altogether wasted. When new moments of pleasure call to us in their turn, moments which would pass by in the same way, equally bare and one-dimensional, the others recur, bringing them the groundwork, the solid con-sistency of a rich orchestration. They thus prolong themselves into one of those classic examples of happiness which we recapture only now and again but which continue to exist; in the present instance it was the abandonment of everything else to dine in comfortable surroundings, which by the help of memory embody in a scene from nature suggestions of the rewards of travel, with a friend who is going to stir our dormant life with all his energy, all his affection, to communicate to us a tender pleasure, very differ-ent from anything that we could derive from our own efforts or from social distractions; we are going to exist solely for him, to make vows of friendship which, born within the confines of the hour, remaining imprisoned in it, will perhaps not be kept on the morrow but which I need have no scruple in making to Saint-Loup since, with a courage that enshrined a great deal of common sense and the presentiment that friendship cannot be very deeply probed, on the morrow he would be gone.

If as I came downstairs I relived those evenings at Doncières, suddenly, when we reached the street, the almost total darkness, in which the fog seemed to have extinguished the lamps, which one could make out, glimmering very faintly, only when close at hand, took me back to a dimly remembered arrival by night at Combray, when the streets there were still lighted only at distant intervals and one groped one's way through a moist, warm, hallowed crib-like darkness in which there flickered here and there a dim light that shone no brighter than a candle. Between that year—to which in any case I could ascribe no precise date—of my Combray life and the evenings at Rivebelle which had, an hour earlier, been reflected above my drawn curtains, what a world of differences! I felt on perceiving them an enthusiasm which might have borne fruit had I remained alone and would thus have saved me the detour of many wasted years through which I was yet to pass before the invisible vocation of which this book is the history declared itself. Had the revelation come to me that evening, the carriage in which I sat would have deserved to rank as more memorable for me than Dr Percepied's, on the box seat of which I had composed that little sketch—which, as it happened, I had recently unearthed, altered and sent in vain to the *Figaro*—of the steeples of Martinville. Is it because we relive our past years not in their continuous sequence, day by day, but in a memory focused upon the coolness or sunshine of some morning or afternoon suffused with the shade of some isolated and enclosed setting, immovable, arrested, lost, remote from all the rest, and thus the changes gradually wrought not only in the world outside but in our dreams and our evolving character (changes which have imperceptibly carried us through life from one time to another, wholly different) are eliminated, that, if we relive another memory taken from a different year, we find between the two, thanks to lacunae, to vast stretches of oblivion, as it were the gulf of a difference in altitude or the incompatibility of two divergent qualities of breathed atmosphere and surrounding coloration? But between the memories that had now come to me in turn of Combray, of Doncières and of Rivebelle, I was conscious at that moment of much more than a distance in time, of the distance that there would be between two separate universes whose substance was not the same. If I had sought to reproduce in a piece of writing the material in which my most insignificant memories of Rivebelle appeared to me to be carved, I should have had to vein with pink, to render at once translucent, compact, cool and resonant, a substance hitherto analogous to the sombre, rugged sandstone of Combray.

But Robert, having finished giving his instructions to the driver, now joined me in the carriage. The ideas that had appeared before me took flight. They are goddesses who deign at times to make themselves visible to a solitary mortal, at a turning in the road, even in his bedroom while he sleeps, when, standing framed in the doorway, they bring him their annunciation. But as soon as a companion joins him they vanish; in the society of his fellows no man has ever beheld them. And I found myself thrown back upon friendship.

Robert on arriving had indeed warned me that there was a good deal of fog outside, but while we were talking it had grown steadily thicker. It was no longer merely the light mist which I had looked forward to seeing rise from the island and envelop Mme de Stermaria and myself. A few feet away from us the street lamps were blotted out and then it was night, as dark as in open fields, in a forest, or rather on a mild Breton island whither I should have liked to go; I felt lost, as on the stark coast of some northern sea where one risks one's life twenty times over before coming to the solitary inn; ceasing to be a mirage for which one seeks, the fog had become one of those dangers against which one has to fight, so that in finding our way and reaching a safe haven, we experienced the difficulties, the anxiety and finally the joy which safety, so little perceived by one who is not threatened with the loss of it, gives to the perplexed and benighted traveller. One thing only came near to destroying my pleasure during our adventurous ride, owing to the angry astonishment into which it flung me for a moment. "You know," Saint-Loup suddenly said to me, "I told Bloch that you didn't like him all that much, that you found him rather vulgar at times. I'm like that, you see, I like clear-cut situations," he wound up with a self-satisfied air and in an unanswerable tone of voice. I was astounded. Not only had I the most absolute confidence in Saint-Loup, in the loyalty of his friendship, and he had betrayed it by what he had said to Bloch, but it seemed to me that he of all men ought to have been restrained from doing so by his defects as well as by his good qualities, by that astonishing veneer of breeding which was capable of carrying politeness to what was positively a want of frankness. Was his triumphant air the sort that we assume to cloak a certain embarrassment in admitting a thing which we know that we ought not to have done? Was it simply the expression of frivolity, stupidity, making a virtue out of a defect which I had not associated with him? Or a passing fit of ill-humour towards me, prompting him to make an end of our friendship, or the registering of a passing fit of ill-humour against Bloch to whom he had wanted to say something disagreeable even though it would compromise me? Whatever it was, his face was seared, while he uttered these vulgar words, by a frightful sinuosity which I saw on it once or twice only in all the time I knew him, and which, beginning by running more or less down the middle of his face, when it came to his lips twisted them, gave them a hideous expression of baseness, almost of bestiality, quite transitory and no doubt inherited. There must have been at such moments, which recurred probably not more than once every other year, a partial eclipse of his true self by the passage across it of the personality of some ancestor reflecting itself upon him. Fully as much as his self-satisfied air, the words "I like clear-cut situations" encouraged the same doubt and should have incurred a similar condemnation. I felt inclined to say to him that if one likes clear-cut situations one ought to confine these outbursts of frankness to one's own affairs and not to acquire a too easy merit at the expense of others. But by this time the carriage had stopped outside the restaurant, the huge front of which, glazed and streaming with light, alone succeeded in piercing the darkness. The fog itself, lit up by the comfortable brightness of the interior, seemed to be waiting outside on the pavement to show one the way in with the joy of servants whose faces reflect the hospitable instincts of their master; shot with the most delicate shades of light, it pointed the way like the pillar of fire which guided the Hebrews. Many of these, as it happened, were to be found inside. For this was the place to which Bloch and his friends, intoxicated by their fast on coffee and political curiosity, a fast as famishing as the ritual fast which occurs only once a year, had long been in the habit of repairing in the evenings. Every mental excitement creating a value that overrides everything else, a quality superior to the habits bound up in it, there is no taste at all keenly developed that does not thus gather round it a society which it unites and in which the esteem of his fellows is what each of its members seeks before anything else from life. Here, in their café, be it in a little provincial town, you will find impassioned music-lovers; the greater part of their time and all their spare cash are spent in chamber-concerts, in meetings for musical discussion, in cafés where they find themselves among music-lovers and rub shoulders with musicians. Others, keen on flying, seek to stand well with the old waiter in the glazed bar perched on top of the aerodrome; sheltered from the wind as in the glass cage of a lighthouse, they can follow in the company of an airman who is not going up that day the gyrations of a pilot looping the loop, while another, invisible a moment ago, comes suddenly swooping down to land with the great winged roar of an Arabian roc. The little group which met to try to grasp and to perpetuate the fugitive emotions aroused by the Zola trial attached a similar importance to this particular café. But they were not viewed with favour by the young nobles who composed the other part of the clientele and had taken over a second room, separated from the other only by a flimsy parapet topped with a row of plants. These looked upon Dreyfus and his supporters as traitors, although twenty-five years later, ideas having had time to settle down and Dreyfusism to acquire a certain glamour in the light of history, the Bolshevistic and dance-mad sons of these same young nobles would declare to the "intellectuals" who questioned them that undoubtedly, had they been alive at the time, they would have been for Dreyfus, without having any clearer idea of what the Affair had been about than Comtesse Edmond de Pourtalès or the Marquise de Galliffet, other luminaries already extinct at the date of their birth. For on the night of the fog the noblemen of the café, who were in due course to become the fathers of these retrospectively Dreyfusard young intellectuals, were still bachelors. Naturally the idea of a rich marriage was present in the minds of all their families, but none of them had yet brought such a marriage off. Still only potential, this rich marriage which was the simultaneous ambition of several of them (there were indeed several "good matches" in view, but after all the number of big dowries was considerably below that of the aspirants to them) merely tended to create among these young men a certain amount of rivalry.

As ill luck would have it, Saint-Loup remaining outside for a few minutes to explain to the driver that he was to call for us again after dinner, I had to go in alone. Now, to begin with, once I had ventured into the turning door, a contrivance to which I was unaccustomed, I began to fear that I should never succeed in getting out again. (Let me note here for the benefit of lovers of verbal accuracy that the contrivance in question, despite its peaceful appearance, is known as a "revolver," from the English "revolving door.") That evening the proprietor, unwilling either to brave the elements outside or to desert his customers, nevertheless remained standing near the entrance so as to have the pleasure of listening to the joyful complaints of the new arrivals, all aglow with the satisfaction of people who had had trouble getting there and been afraid of getting lost. The smiling cordiality of his welcome was, however, dissipated by the sight of a stranger incapable of disengaging himself from the rotating sheets of glass. This flagrant sign of ignorance made him frown like an examiner who has a good mind not to utter the formula: *Dignus est intrare*. As a crowning error I went and sat down in the room set apart for the nobility, from which he came at once to root me out, with a rudeness to which all the waiters immediately conformed, and showed me to a place in the other room. This was all the less to my liking because the seat was in the middle of a crowded bench and I had opposite me the door reserved for the Hebrews which, since it did not revolve, opened and closed every other minute and kept me in a horrible draught. But the proprietor declined to move me, saying: "No, sir, I cannot disturb everybody just for you." Presently, however, he forgot this belated and troublesome guest, captivated as he was by the arrival of each newcomer who, before calling for his beer, his wing of cold chicken, or his hot grog (it was by now long past dinner-time), must first, as in the old romances, sing for his supper by relating his adventure as soon as he entered this asylum of warmth and security where the contrast with the perils just escaped engendered the sort of gaiety and sense of comradeship that create a cheerful harmony round the camp fire.

One reported that his carriage, thinking it had got to the Pont de la Concorde, had circled the Invalides three times, another that his, in trying to make its way down the Avenue des Champs-Elysées, had driven into a clump of trees at the Rond-Point, from which it had taken three-quarters of an hour to extricate itself. Then followed lamentations about the fog, the cold, the deathly silence of the streets, uttered and received with the same exceptionally jovial air that was attributable to the pleasant atmosphere of the room which, except where I sat, was warm, the dazzling light which set blinking eyes already accustomed to not seeing, and the buzz of talk which restored their activity to deafened ears.

The new arrivals had the greatest difficulty in keeping silence. The singularity of the mishaps which each of them thought unique set their tongues on fire, and their eyes roved in search of someone to engage in conversation. The proprietor himself lost all sense of social distinctions: "M. le Prince de Foix lost his way three times coming from the Porte Saint-Martin," he was not afraid to say with a laugh, actually pointing out, as though introducing one to the other, the illustrious nobleman to a Jewish barrister who on any evening but this would have been separated from him by a barrier far harder to surmount than the ledge of greenery. "Three times—fancy that!" said the barrister, touching his hat. This note of friendly interest was not at all to the Prince's liking. He belonged to an aristocratic group for whom the practice of rudeness, even at the expense of their fellow-nobles when these were not of the very highest rank, seemed to be the sole occupation. Not to acknowledge a greeting; if the polite stranger repeated the offence, to laugh with sneering contempt or fling back one's head with a look of fury; to pretend not to recognise some elderly man who had done them a service; to reserve their handshakes for dukes and the really intimate friends of dukes whom the latter introduced to them: such was the attitude of these young men, and especially of the Prince de Foix. Such an attitude was encouraged by the thoughtlessness of youth (a period in which, even in the middle class, one appears ungrateful and behaves boorishly because, having forgotten for months to write to a benefactor who has just lost his wife, one then ceases to greet him in the street so as to simplify matters), but it was inspired above all by an acute caste snobbery. It is true that, after the fashion of certain nervous disorders the symptoms of which grow less pronounced in later life, this snobbishness would generally cease to express itself in so offensive a form in these men who had been so intolerable when young. Once youth is outgrown, it is rare for a man to remain confined in insolence. He had supposed it to be the only thing in the world; suddenly he discovers, prince though he is, that there are also such things as music, literature, even standing for parliament. The scale of human values is correspondingly altered and he engages in conversation with people whom at one time he would have dismissed with a withering glance. Good luck to those of the latter who have had the patience to wait, and who are of such a good disposition—if "good" is the right word—that they accept with pleasure in their forties the civility and welcome that had been coldly withheld from them at twenty.

Since we are on the subject of the Prince de Foix, it may be mentioned here that he belonged to a set of a dozen or fifteen young men and to an inner group of four. The dozen or fifteen shared the characteristic (from which the Prince, I fancy, was exempt) that each of them presented a dual aspect to the world. Up to their eyes in debt, they were regarded as bounders by their tradesmen, notwithstanding the pleasure these took in addressing them as "Monsieur le Comte," "Monsieur le Marquis," "Monsieur le Duc." They hoped to retrieve their fortunes by means of the famous rich marriage ("moneybags" as the expression still was) and, as the fat dowries which they coveted numbered at the most four or five, several of them were secretly setting their sights on the same damsel. And the secret would be so well kept that when one of them, on arriving at the café, announced: "My dear fellows, I'm too fond of you all not to tell you of my engagement to Mlle d'Ambresac," there would be a general outburst, more than one of the others imagining that the marriage was as good as settled already between Mlle d'Ambresac and himself, and not having the self-control to stifle a spontaneous cry of stupefaction and rage. "So you like the idea of marriage, do you, Bibi?" the Prince de Châtellerault could not help exclaiming, dropping his fork in surprise and despair, for he had been fully expecting the engagement of this identical Mlle d'Ambresac to be announced, but with himself, Châtellerault, as her bridegroom. And heaven only knew all that his father had cunningly hinted to the Ambresacs about Bibi's mother. "So you think it'll be fun, being married, do you?" he could not help repeating for the second time to Bibi, who, better prepared because he had had plenty of time to decide on the right attitude to adopt since the engagement had reached the semi-official stage, would reply with a smile: "I'm pleased, not to be getting married, which I didn't particularly want to do, but to be marrying Daisy d'Ambresac whom I find charming." In the time taken up by this response M. de Châtellerault would have recovered his composure, but then he would think that he must at the earliest possible moment execute an about-face in the direction of Mlle de la Canourgue or Miss Foster, numbers two and three on the list of heiresses, pacify somehow the creditors who were expecting the Ambresac marriage, and, finally, explain to the people to whom he too had declared that Mlle de Ambresac was charming that this marriage was all very well for Bibi, but that he himself would have had all his family down on him like a ton of bricks if he had married her. Mme Soléon (he would say) had actually gone so far as to announce that she would not have them in her house.

But if in the eyes of tradesmen, restaurant proprietors and the like they seemed of little account, conversely, being creatures of dual personality, the moment they appeared in society they ceased to be judged by the dilapidated state of their fortunes and the sordid occupations by which they sought to repair them. They became once more M. le Prince this, M. le Duc that, and were judged only by their quarterings. A duke who was practically a multimillionaire and seemed to combine in his person every possible distinction would give precedence to them because, being the heads of their various houses, they were by descent sovereign princes of small territories in which they were entitled to mint money and so forth. Often, in this café, one of them would lower his eyes when another came in so as not to oblige the newcomer to greet him. This was because in his imaginative pursuit of riches he had invited a banker to dine. Every time a man about town enters into relations with a banker in such circumstances, the latter leaves him the poorer by a hundred thousand francs, which does not prevent the man about town from at once repeating the process with another. We continue to burn candles in churches and to consult doctors.

But the Prince de Foix, who was himself rich, belonged not only to this fashionable set of fifteen or so young men, but to a more exclusive and inseparable group of four, which included Saint-Loup. These were never asked anywhere separately, they were known as the four gigolos, they were always to be seen riding together, and in country houses their hostesses gave them communicating bedrooms, with the result that, especially as they were all four extremely good-looking, rumours were current as to the extent of their intimacy. I was in a position to give these the lie direct so far as Saint-Loup was concerned. But the curious thing is that if, later on, it was discovered that these rumours were true of all four, each of the quartet had been entirely in the dark as to the other three. And yet each of them had done his utmost to find out about the others, to gratify a desire or (more probably) a grudge, to prevent a marriage or to secure a hold over the friend whose secret he uncovered. A fifth (for in groups of four there are always more than four) had joined this platonic party who was more so than any of the others. But religious scruples restrained him until long after the group had broken up and he himself was a married man, the father of a family, fervently praying at Lourdes that the next baby might be a boy or a girl, and in the meantime flinging himself upon soldiers.

Despite the Prince's arrogant ways, the fact that the barrister's comment, though uttered in his hearing, had not been directly addressed to him made him less angry than he would otherwise have been. Besides, this evening was somehow exceptional. And in any case the barrister had no more chance of getting to know the Prince de Foix than the cabman who had driven that noble lord to the restaurant. The Prince accordingly felt that he might allow himself to reply—in an arrogant tone, however, and as though to the company at large—to this stranger who, thanks to the fog, was in the position of a travelling companion whom one meets at some seaside place at the ends of the earth, scoured by all the winds of heaven or shrouded in mist: "Losing your way isn't so bad; the trouble is finding it again." The wisdom of this aphorism impressed the proprietor, for he had already heard it several times in the course of the evening.

He was, indeed, in the habit of always comparing what he heard or read with an already familiar canon, and felt his admiration quicken if he could detect no difference. This state of mind is by no means to be ignored, for, applied to political conversations, to the reading of newspapers, it forms public opinion and thereby makes possible the greatest events in history. A large number of German café owners, simply by being impressed by a customer or a newspaper when they said that France, England and Russia were "provoking" Germany, made war possible at the time of Agadir, even if no war occurred. Historians, if they have not been wrong to abandon the practice of attributing the actions of peoples to the will of kings, ought to substitute for the latter the psychology of the individual, the inferior individual at that.

In politics the proprietor of this particular café had for some time now applied his recitation-teacher's mentality to a certain number of set-pieces on the Dreyfus case. If he did not find the terms that were familiar to him in the remarks of a customer or the columns of a newspaper he would pronounce the article boring or the speaker insincere. The Prince de Foix, however, impressed him so forcibly that he barely gave him time to finish his sentence. "Well said, Prince, well said" (which meant, more or less, "fault-lessly recited"), "that's it, that's exactly it," he exclaimed, "swelling up," as they say in the *Arabian Nights*, "to the extreme limit of satisfaction." But the Prince had already vanished into the smaller room. Then, as life resumes its normal course after even the most sensational happenings, those who had emerged from the sea of fog began to order whatever they wanted to eat or drink; among them a party of young men from the Jockey Club who, in view of the abnormality of the occasion, had no hesitation in taking their places at a couple of tables in the big room, and were thus quite close to me. So the cataclysm had established even between the smaller room and the bigger, among all these people stimulated by the comfort of the restaurant after their long wanderings across the ocean of fog, a familiarity from which I alone was excluded and which was not unlike the spirit that must have prevailed in Noah's ark.

Suddenly I saw the landlord bent double, bowing and scraping, and the waiters hurrying to support him in full force, a scene which drew every eye towards the door. "Quick, send Cyprien here, a table for M. le Marquis de Saint-Loup," cried the proprietor, for whom Robert was not merely a great nobleman who enjoyed genuine prestige even in the eyes of the Prince de Foix, but a customer who burned the candle at both ends and spent a great deal of money in this restaurant. The customers in the big room looked on with curiosity, those in the small room vied with one another in hailing their friend as he finished wiping his shoes. But just as he was about to make his way into the small room he caught sight of me in the big one. "Good God," he exclaimed, "what on earth are you doing there? And with the door wide open too?" he added with a furious glance at the proprietor, who ran to shut it, throwing the blame on his staff: "I'm always telling them to keep it shut."

I had been obliged to shift my own table and to disturb others which stood in the way in order to reach him. "Why did you move? Would you sooner dine here than in the little room? Why, my poor fellow, you're freezing. You will oblige me by keeping that door permanently locked," he said to the proprietor. "This very instant, Monsieur le Marquis. The customers who arrive from now on will have to go through the little room, that's all." And the better to prove his zeal, he detailed for this operation a head waiter and several satellites, vociferating the most terrible threats if it were not properly carried out. He proceeded to show me exaggerated marks of respect, to make me forget that these had begun not upon my arrival but only after that of Saint-Loup, while, lest I should think them to have been prompted by the friendliness shown me by this rich and noble client, he gave me now and again a surreptitious little smile which seemed to indicate a regard that was wholly personal.

Something said by one of the diners behind me made me turn my head for a moment. I had caught, instead of the words: "Wing of chicken, excellent; and a glass of champagne, only not too dry," these: "I should prefer glycerine. Yes, hot, excellent." I had wanted to see who the ascetic was who was inflicting upon himself such a diet, but I quickly turned back to Saint-Loup in order not to be recognised by the man of strange appetite. It was simply a doctor whom I happened to know and of whom another customer, taking advantage of the fog to buttonhole him here in the café, was asking his professional advice. Like stockbrokers, doctors employ the first person singular.

Meanwhile I looked at Robert, and my thoughts ran as follows. There were in this café, and I had myself known at other times in my life, plenty of foreigners, intellectuals, budding geniuses of all sorts, resigned to the laughter excited by their pretentious capes, their 1830 ties and still more by the clumsiness of their movements, going so far as to provoke that laughter in order to show that they paid no heed to it, who yet were men of real intellectual and moral worth, of profound sensibility. They repelled—the Jews among them principally, the unassimilated Jews, that is to say, for with the other kind we are not concerned—those who could not endure any oddity or eccentricity of appearance (as Bloch repelled Albertine). Generally speaking, one realised afterwards that, if it could be held against them that their hair was too long, their noses and eyes were too big, their gestures abrupt and theatrical, it was puerile to judge them by this, that they had plenty of wit and good-heartedness, and were men to whom, in the long run, one could become closely attached. Among the Jews especially there were few whose parents and kinsfolk had not a warmth of heart, a breadth of mind, a sincerity, in comparison with which Saint-Loup's mother and the Duc de Guermantes cut the poorest of moral figures by their aridity, their skin-deep religiosity which denounced only the most open scandal, their apology for a Christianity which led invariably (by the unexpected channels of the uniquely prized intellect) to a colossally mercenary marriage. But in Saint-Loup, when all was said, however the faults of his parents had combined to create a new blend of qualities, there reigned the most charming openness of mind and heart. And whenever (it must be allowed to the undying glory of France) these qualities are found in a man who is purely French, whether he belongs to the aristocracy or the people, they flower—flourish would be too strong a word, for moderation persists in this field, as well as restriction—with a grace which the foreigner, however estimable he may be, does not present to us. Of these intellectual and moral qualities others undoubtedly have their share, and, if we have first to overcome what repels us and what makes us smile, they remain no less precious. But it is all the same a pleasant thing, and one which is perhaps exclusively French, that what is fine in all equity of judgment, what is admirable to the mind and the heart, should be first of all attractive to the eyes, pleasingly coloured, consummately chiselled, should express as well in substance as in form an inner perfection. I looked at Saint-Loup, and I said to myself that it is a thing to be glad of when there is no lack of physical grace to serve as vestibule to the graces within, and when the curves of the nostrils are as delicate and as perfectly designed as the wings of the little butterflies that hover over the field-flowers round Combray; and that the true *opus francigenum*, the secret of which was not lost in the thirteenth century, and would not perish with our churches, consists not so much in the stone angels of Saint-André-des-Champs as in the young sons of France, noble, bourgeois or peasant, whose faces are carved with that delicacy and boldness which have remained as traditional as on the famous porch, but are creative still.

After leaving us for a moment in order to supervise personally the barring of the door and the ordering of our dinner (he laid great stress on our choosing "butcher's meat," the fowls being presumably nothing to boast of) the proprietor came back to inform us that M. le Prince de Foix would esteem it a favour if M. le Marquis would allow him to dine at a table next to his. "But they are all taken," objected Robert, casting an eye over the tables which blocked the way to mine. "That doesn't matter in the least. If M. le Marquis is agreeable, I can easily ask these people to move to another table. It is always a pleasure to do anything for M. le Marquis!" "But you must decide," said Saint-Loup to me. "Foix is a good fellow. I don't know whether he'd bore you, but he's not such a fool as most of them." I told Robert that of course I should like to meet his friend but that now that I was dining with him for once in a way and was so happy to be doing so, I should be just as pleased to have him to myself. "He's got a very fine cloak, the Prince has," the proprietor broke in upon our deliberation. "Yes, I know," said Saint-Loup. I wanted to tell Robert that M. de Charlus had concealed from his sister-in-law the fact that he knew me, and ask him what could be the reason for this, but I was prevented from doing so by the arrival of M. de Foix. He had come to see whether his request had been favourably received, and we caught sight of him standing a few feet away. Robert introduced us, but made no secret of the fact that as we had things to talk about he would prefer us to be left alone. The Prince withdrew, adding to the farewell bow which he made me a smile which, pointed at Saint-Loup, seemed to transfer to him the responsibility for the shortness of a meeting which the Prince himself would have liked to see prolonged. But at that moment Robert, apparently struck by a sudden thought, went off with his friend after saying to me: "Do sit down and start your dinner, I shall be back in a moment," and vanished into the smaller room. I was pained to hear the smart young men whom I did not know telling the most absurd and malicious stories about the adoptive Grand Duke of Luxembourg (formerly Comte de Nassau) whom I had met at Balbec and who had given me such delicate proofs of sympathy during my grandmother's illness. According to one of these young men, he had said to the Duchesse de Guermantes: "I expect everyone to get up when my wife comes in," to which the Duchess had retorted (with as little truth, had she said any such thing, as wit, the grandmother of the young Princess having always been the very pink of propriety): "Get up when your wife comes in, do they? Well, that's a change from her grandmother—she expected the gentlemen to lie down." Then someone alleged that, having gone down to see his aunt the Princesse de Luxembourg at Balbec, and put up at the Grand Hotel, he had complained to the manager (my friend) that the royal standard of Luxembourg was not flown in front of the hotel, and that this flag being less familiar and less generally in use than the British or Italian, it had taken him several days to procure one, greatly to the young Grand Duke's annoyance. I did not believe a word of this story, but made up my mind, as soon as I went to Balbec, to question the manager in order to satisfy myself that it was pure invention. While waiting for Saint-Loup to return I asked the restaurant proprietor for some bread. "Certainly, Monsieur le Baron!" "I am not a baron," I told him in a tone of mock sadness. "Oh, beg pardon, Monsieur le Comte!" I had no time to lodge a second protest which would certainly have promoted me to the rank of marquis: faithful to his promise of an immediate return, Saint-Loup reappeared in the doorway carrying over his arm the thick vicuna cloak of the Prince de Foix, from whom I guessed that he had borrowed it in order to keep me warm. He signed to me not to get up, and came towards me, but either my table would have to be moved again, or I must change my seat if he was to get to his. On entering the big room he sprang lightly on to one of the red plush benches which ran round its walls and on which, apart from myself, there were sitting three or four of the young men from the Jockey Club, friends of his, who had not managed to find places in the other room. Between the tables and the wall electric wires were stretched at a certain height; without the slightest hesitation Saint-Loup jumped nimbly over them like a steeplechaser taking a fence; embarrassed that it should be done wholly for my benefit and to save me the trouble of a very minor disturbance, I was at the same time amazed at the precision with which my friend performed this feat of acrobatics; and in this I was not alone; for although they would probably have been only moderately appreciative of a similar display on the part of a more humbly born and less generous client, the proprietor and his staff stood fascinated, like race-goers in the enclosure; one underling, apparently rooted to the ground, stood gaping with a dish in his hand for which a party close beside him were waiting; and when Saint-Loup, having to get past his friends, climbed on to the back of the bench behind them and ran along it, balancing himself like a tight-rope walker, discreet applause broke from the body of the room. On coming to where I was sitting, he checked his momentum with the precision of a tributary chieftain before the throne of a sovereign, and, stooping down, handed to me with an air of courtesy and submission the vicuna cloak which a moment later, having taken his place beside me, without my having to make a single movement, he arranged as a light but warm shawl about my shoulders.

"By the way, while I think of it, my uncle Charlus has something to say to you. I promised I'd send you round to him tomorrow evening."

"I was just going to speak to you about him. But tomorrow evening I'm dining out with your aunt Guermantes."

"Yes, there's a full-scale blow-out tomorrow at Oriane's. I'm not asked. But my uncle Palamède doesn't want you to go there. You can't get out of it, I suppose? Well, anyhow, go on to my uncle's afterwards. I think he's very anxious to see you. Surely you could manage to get there by eleven. Eleven o'clock, don't forget.

I'll let him know. He's very touchy. If you don't turn up he'll never forgive you. And Oriane's parties are always over quite early. If you're only going to dine there you can quite easily be at my uncle's by eleven. Actually I ought to go and see Oriane, about getting a transfer from Morocco. She's so nice about all that sort of thing, and she can get anything she likes out of General de Saint-Joseph, who's the man in charge. But don't say anything about it to her. I've mentioned it to the Princesse de Parme, everything will be all right. Interesting place, Morocco. I could tell you all sorts of things. Very fine lot of men out there. One feels they're on one's own level, mentally."

"You don't think the Germans are going to go to war over it?"

"No, they're annoyed with us, as after all they have every right to be. But the Kaiser is out for peace. They're always making us think they want war, to force us to give in. Pure bluff, you know, like poker. The Prince of Monaco, one of Wilhelm II's agents, comes and tells us in confidence that Germany will attack us if we don't give in. So then we give in. But if we didn't give in, there wouldn't be war in any shape or form. You have only to think what a cosmic thing a war would be today. It'd be a bigger catastrophe than the Flood and the *Götterdämmerung* rolled into one. Only it wouldn't last so long."

He spoke to me of friendship, affection, regret, although like all travellers of his sort he was going off the next morning for some months which he was to spend in the country and would only be staying a couple of nights in Paris on his way back to Morocco (or elsewhere); but the words which he thus let fall into the warm furnace of my heart this evening kindled a pleasant glow there. Our infrequent meetings, and this one in particular, have since assumed epoch-making proportions in my memory. For him, as for me, this was the evening of friendship. And yet the friendship that I felt for him at this moment was scarcely, I feared (and felt therefore some remorse at the thought), what he would have liked to inspire. Suffused still with the pleasure that I had had in seeing him canter towards me and come gracefully to a halt on arriving at his goal, I felt that this pleasure lay in my recognising that each of the movements which he had executed on the bench, along the wall, had its meaning, its cause, in Saint-Loup's own personal nature perhaps, but even more in that which by birth and upbringing he had inherited from his race.

A certainty of taste in the domain not of aesthetics but of behaviour, which when he was faced by a novel combination of circumstances enabled the man of breeding to grasp at once—like a musician who has been asked to play a piece he has never seen—the attitude and the action required and to apply the appropriate mechanism and technique, and then allowed this taste to be exercised without the constraint of any other consideration by which so many young men of the middle class would have been paralysed from fear both of making themselves ridiculous in the eyes of strangers by a breach of propriety and of appearing over-zealous in those of their friends, and which in Robert's case was replaced by a lofty disdain that certainly he had never felt in his heart but had received by inheritance in his body, and that had fashioned the attitudes of his ancestors into a familiarity which, they imagined, could only flatter and enchant those to whom it was addressed; together with a noble liberality which, far from taking undue heed of his boundless material advantages (lavish expenditure in this restaurant had succeeded in making him, here as elsewhere, the most fashionable customer and the general favourite, a position underlined by the deference shown him not only by the waiters but by all its most exclusive young patrons), led him to trample them underfoot, just as he had actually and sym-bolically trodden upon those crimson benches, suggestive of some ceremonial way which pleased my friend only because it enabled him more gracefully and swiftly to arrive at my side: such were the quintessentially aristocratic qualities that shone through the husk of this body—not opaque and dim as mine would have been, but limpid and revealing—as, through a work of art, the industrious, energetic force which has created it, and rendered the movements of that light-footed course which Robert had pursued along the wall as intelligible and charming as those of horsemen on a marble frieze. "Alas!" Robert might have thought, "was it worth while to have grown up despising birth, honouring only justice and intel-lect, choosing, outside the ranks of the friends provided for me, companions who were awkward and ill-dressed but had the gift of eloquence, only to find that the sole personality apparent in me which remains a treasured memory is not the one that my will, with the most praiseworthy effort, has fashioned in my likeness, but one that is not of my making, that is not myself, that I have always despised and striven to overcome; was it worth while to love my chosen friend as I have done, only to find that the greatest pleasure he derives from my company is that of discovering in it something far more general than myself, a pleasure which is not in the least (as he says, though he cannot seriously believe it) the pleasure of friendship, but an intellectual and detached, a sort of artistic pleasure?" This is what I now fear that Saint-Loup may at times have thought. If so, he was mistaken. If he had not (as he steadfastly had) cherished something more lofty than the innate suppleness of his body, if he had not been detached for so long from aristocratic arrogance, there would have been something more studied, more heavy-handed in this very agility, a self-important vulgarity in his manners. Just as a strong vein of serious-ness had been necessary for Mme de Villeparisis to convey in her conversation and in her *Memoirs* a sense of the frivolous, which is intellectual, so, in order that Saint-Loup's body should be imbued with so much nobility, the latter had first to desert his mind, which was straining towards higher things, and, reabsorbed into his body, to establish itself there in unconsciously aristocratic lines. In this way his distinction of mind was not inconsistent with a physical distinction which otherwise would not have been complete. An artist has no need to express his thought directly in his work for the latter to reflect its quality; it has even been said that the highest praise of God consists in the denial of him by the atheist who finds creation so perfect that it can dispense with a creator. And I was well aware, too, that it was not merely a work of art that I was admiring in this young man unfolding along the wall the frieze of his flying course; the young prince (a descendant of Catherine de Foix, Queen of Navarre and granddaughter of Charles VII) whom he had just left for my sake, the endowments of birth and fortune which he was laying at my feet, the proud and shapely ancestors who survived in the assurance, the agility and the courtesy with which he had arranged about my shivering body the warm wool-len cloak—were not all these like friends of longer standing in his life, by whom I might have expected that we should be perman-ently kept apart, and whom, on the contrary, he was sacrificing to me by a choice that can be made only in the loftiest places of the mind, with that sovereign liberty of which Robert's movements were the image and the symbol and in which perfect friendship is enshrined?

The vulgar arrogance that was to be detected in the familiarity of a Guermantes—as opposed to the distinction that it had in Robert, because hereditary disdain was in him only the outer garment, transmuted into an unconscious grace, of a genuine moral humility—had been brought home to me, not by M. de Charlus, in whom certain characteristic faults for which I had so far been unable to account were superimposed on his aristocratic habits, but by the Duc de Guermantes. And yet he too, in the general impression of commonness which had so repelled my grandmother when she had met him years earlier at Mme de Villeparisis's, showed glimpses of ancient grandeur of which I became conscious when I went to dine at his house the following evening.

They had not been apparent to me either in himself or in the Duchess when I had first met them in their aunt's drawing-room, any more than I had discerned, on first seeing her, the differences that set Berma apart from her colleagues, although in her case the distinctive qualities were infinitely more striking than in any social celebrity, since they become more marked in proportion as the objects are more real, more conceivable by the intellect. And yet, however slight the shades of social distinction may be (and so slight are they that when an accurate portrayer like Sainte-Beuve tries to indicate the shades of difference between the salons of Mme Geoffrin, Mme Récamier and Mme de Boigne, they appear so alike that the cardinal truth which, unknown to the author, emerges from his investigations is the vacuity of that form of life), nevertheless, for the same reason as with Berma, when I had ceased to be dazzled by the Guermantes and their droplet of originality was no longer vaporised by my imagination, I was able to distil and analyse it, imponderable as it was.

The Duchess having made no reference to her husband at her aunt's party, I wondered whether, in view of the rumours of divorce, he would be present at the dinner. But I was soon enlightened on that score, for through the crowd of footmen who stood about in the hall and who (since they must until then have regarded me much as they regarded the children of the evicted cabinet-maker, that is to say with more fellow-feeling perhaps than their master but as a person incapable of being admitted to his house) must have been asking themselves to what this social revolution could be due, I caught sight of M. de Guermantes, who had been watching for my arrival so as to receive me on his threshold and take off my overcoat with his own hands.

"Mme de Guermantes will be as pleased as Punch," he said to me in a glibly persuasive tone. "Let me help you off with your duds." (He felt it to be at once companionable and comic to use popular colloquialisms.) "My wife was just the least bit afraid you might defect, although you had fixed a date. We've been saying to each other all day: 'Depend upon it, he'll never turn up.' I'm bound to say that Mme de Guermantes was a better prophet than I was. You are not an easy man to get hold of, and I was quite sure you were going to let us down." And the Duke was such a bad husband, so brutal even (people said), that one felt grateful to him, as one feels grateful to wicked people for their occasional kindness of heart, for those words "Mme de Guermantes" with which he appeared to be spreading a protective wing over the Duchess, so that she might be one with him. Meanwhile, taking me familiarly by the hand, he set about introducing me into his household. Just as some common expression may delight us coming from the lips of a peasant if it points to the survival of a local tradition or shows the trace of some historic event, unknown, it may be, to the person who thus alludes to it, so this politeness on the part of M. de Guermantes, which he was to continue to show me throughout the evening, charmed me as a survival of habits many centuries old, habits of the seventeenth century in particular. The people of bygone ages seem infinitely remote from us. We do not feel justified in ascribing to them any underlying intentions beyond those they formally express; we are amazed when we come upon a sentiment more or less akin to what we feel today in a Homeric hero, or a skilful tactical feint by Hannibal during the battle of Cannae, where he let his flank be driven back in order to take the enemy by surprise and encircle him; it is as though we imagined the epic poet and the Carthaginian general to be as remote from ourselves as an animal seen in a zoo. Even with certain personages of the court of Louis XIV, when we find signs of courtesy in letters written by them to some man of inferior rank who could be of no service to them whatever, these letters leave us astonished because they reveal to us suddenly in these great noblemen a whole world of beliefs which they never directly express but which govern their conduct, and in particular the belief that they are bound in polite- ness to feign certain sentiments and to exercise with the most scrupulous care certain obligations of civility.

This imagined remoteness of the past is perhaps one of the things that may enable us to understand how even great writers have found an inspired beauty in the works of mediocre mystifiers such as Ossian. We are so astonished that bards long dead should have modern ideas that we marvel if in what we believe to be an ancient Gaelic epic we come across one which we should have thought as most ingenious in a contemporary. A translator of talent has only to add to an ancient writer whom he is reconstructing more or less faithfully a few passages which, signed with a contemporary name and published separately, would seem agreeable merely; at once he imparts a moving grandeur to his poet, who is thus made to play upon the keyboards of several ages at once. The translator was capable only of a mediocre book, if that book had been published as his original work. Offered as a translation, it seems a masterpiece. The past is not fugitive, it stays put. It is not only months after the outbreak of a war that laws passed without haste can effectively influence its course, it is not only fifteen years after a crime which has remained obscure that a magistrate can still find the vital evidence which will throw light on it; after hundreds and thousands of years the scholar who has been studying the place-names and the customs of the inhabitants of some remote region may still extract from them some legend long anterior to Christianity, already unintelligible, if not actually forgotten, at the time of Herodotus, which in the name given to a rock, in a religious rite, still dwells in the midst of the present, like a denser emanation, immemorial and stable. There was an emanation too, though far less ancient, of the life of the court, if not in the manners of M. de Guermantes, which were often vulgar, at least in the mind that controlled them. I was to experience it again, like an ancient odour, when I rejoined him a little later in the drawing-room. For I did not go there at once.

As we left the outer hall, I had mentioned to M. de Guermantes that I was extremely anxious to see his Elstirs. "I am at your service. Is M. Elstir a friend of yours, then? I'm mortified not to have known that you were so interested in him. I know him slightly, he's an amiable man, what our fathers used to call an 'honest fellow.' I might have asked him to honour us with his company at dinner tonight. I'm sure he would have been highly flattered at being invited to spend the evening in your company." Very untrue to the old world when he tried thus to assume its manner, the Duke then relapsed into it unconsciously. After inquiring whether I wished him to show me the pictures, he conducted me to them, gracefully standing aside for me at each door, apologising when, to show me the way, he was obliged to precede me, a little scene which (since the time when Saint-Simon relates that an ancestor of the Guermantes did him the honours of his house with the same punctilious exactitude in the performance of the frivolous duties of a gentleman) before reaching our day must have been enacted by many another Guermantes for many another visitor. And as I had said to the Duke that I would like very much to be left alone for a few minutes with the pictures, he discreetly withdrew, telling me that I should find him in the drawing-room when I had finished.

However, once I was face to face with the Elstirs, I completely forgot about dinner and the time; here again as at Balbec I had before me fragments of that world of new and strange colours which was no more than the projection of that great painter's peculiar vision, which his speech in no way expressed. The parts of the walls that were covered by paintings of his, all homogeneous with one another, were like the luminous images of a magic lantern which in this instance was the brain of the artist, and the strangeness of which one could never have suspected so long as one had known only the man, in other words so long as one had only seen the lantern boxing its lamp before any coloured slide had been slid into its groove. Among these pictures, some of those that seemed most absurd to people in fashionable society interested me more than the rest because they re-created those optical illusions which prove to us that we should never succeed in identifying objects if we did not bring some process of reasoning to bear on them. How often, when driving, do we not come upon a bright street beginning a few feet away from us, when what we have actually before our eyes is merely a patch of wall glaringly lit which has given us the mirage of depth. This being the case, it is surely logical, not from any artifice of symbolism but from a sincere desire to return to the very root of the impression, to represent one thing by that other for which, in the flash of a first illusion, we mistook it. Surfaces and volumes are in reality independent of the names of objects which our memory imposes on them after we have recognised them. Elstir sought to wrest from what he had just felt what he already knew; he had often been at pains to break up that medley of impressions which we call vision.

The people who detested these "horrors" were astonished to find that Elstir admired Chardin, Perronneau, and many other painters whom they, the ordinary men and women of society, liked. They did not realise that Elstir for his own part, in striving to reproduce reality (with the particular trademark of his taste for certain experiments), had made the same effort as a Chardin or a Perronneau and that consequently, when he ceased to work for himself, he admired in them attempts of the same kind, anticipatory fragments, so to speak, of works of his own. Nor did these society people add to Elstir's work in their mind's eye that temporal perspective which enabled them to like, or at least to look without discomfort at, Chardin's painting. And yet the older among them might have reminded themselves that in the course of their lives they had gradually seen, as the years bore them away from it, the unbridgeable gulf between what they considered a masterpiece by Ingres and what they had supposed must for ever remain a "horror" (Manet's *Olympia*, for example) shrink until the two canvases seemed like twins. But we never learn, because we lack the wisdom to work backwards from the particular to the general, and imagine ourselves always to be faced with an experience which has no precedents in the past.

I was moved by the discovery in two of the pictures (more realistic, these, and in an earlier manner) of the same person, in one of them in evening dress in his own drawing-room, in the other wearing a frock-coat and tall hat at some popular seaside festival where he had evidently no business to be, which proved that for Elstir he was not only a regular sitter but a friend, perhaps a patron, whom he liked to introduce into his paintings, as Carpaccio introduced—and in the most speaking likenesses—prominent Venetian noblemen into his; in the same way as Beethoven, too, found pleasure in inscribing at the top of a favourite work the beloved name of the Archduke Rudolph. There was something enchanting about this waterside carnival. The river, the women's dresses, the sails of the boats, the innumerable reflexions of one thing and another jostled together enchantingly in this little square panel of beauty which Elstir had cut out of a marvellous afternoon. What delighted one in the dress of a woman who had stopped dancing for a moment because she was hot and out of breath shimmered too, and in the same way, in the cloth of a motionless sail, in the water of the little harbour, in the wooden landing-stage, in the leaves of the trees and in the sky. Just as, in one of the pictures that I had seen at Balbec, the hospital, as beautiful beneath its lapis lazuli sky as the cathedral itself, seemed (more daring than Elstir the theorist, than Elstir the man of taste, the lover of things mediaeval) to be intoning: "There is no such thing as Gothic, there is no such thing as a masterpiece, a hospital with no style is just as good as the glorious porch," so I now heard: "The slightly vulgar lady whom a man of discernment wouldn't bother to look at as he passed her by, whom he would exclude from the poetical composition which nature has set before him—she is beautiful too; her dress is receiving the same light as the sail of that boat, everything is equally precious; the commonplace dress and the sail that is beautiful in itself are two mirrors reflecting the same image; their virtue is all in the painter's eye." This eye had succeeded in arresting for all time the motion of the hours at this luminous instant when the lady had felt hot and had stopped dancing, when the tree was encircled with a perimeter of shadow, when the sails seemed to be gliding over a golden glaze. But precisely because that instant impressed itself on one with such force, this unchanging canvas gave the most fleeting impression: one felt that the lady would presently go home, the boats drift away, the shadow change place, night begin to fall; that pleasure comes to an end, that life passes and that instants, illuminated by the convergence at one and the same time of so many lights, cannot be recaptured. I recognised yet another aspect, quite different it is true, of what the Moment means, in a series of water-colours of mythological subjects, dating from Elstir's first period, which also adorned this room. Society people who held "advanced" views on art went "as far as" this earliest manner, but no further. It was certainly not the best work he had done, but already the sincerity with which the subject had been thought out took away its coldness. Thus the Muses, for instance, were represented as though they were creatures belonging to a species now fossilised, but creatures it would not have been surprising in mythological times to see pass by in the evening, in twos or threes, along some mountain path. Here and there a poet, of a race that would also have been of peculiar interest to a zoologist (characterised by a certain sexlessness), strolled with a Muse, as one sees in nature creatures of different but of kindred species consort together. In one of these water-colours one saw a poet exhausted by a long journey in the mountains, whom a Centaur, meeting him and moved to pity by his weakness, has taken on his back and is carrying home. In others, the vast landscape (in which the mythical scene, the fabulous heroes occupied a minute place and seemed almost lost) was rendered, from the mountain tops to the sea, with an exactitude which told one more than the hour, told one to the very minute what time of day it was, thanks to the precise angle of the setting sun and the fleeting fidelity of the shadows. In this way the artist had managed, by making it instantaneous, to give a sort of lived historical reality to the fable, painted it and related it in the past tense.*

While I was examining Elstir's paintings, the bell, rung by arriving guests, had been pealing uninterruptedly and had lulled me into a pleasing unawareness. But the silence which followed its clangour and had already lasted for some time finally succeeded—less rapidly, it is true—in awakening me from my reverie as the silence that follows Lindor's music arouses Bartolo from his sleep. I was afraid that I might have been forgotten, that they might already have sat down to dinner, and I hurried to the drawing-room. At the door of the Elstir gallery I found a servant waiting for me, white-haired, though whether with age or powder I could not say, and reminiscent of a Spanish minister, though he treated me with the same respect that he would have shown to a king. I felt from his manner that he would have waited for me for another hour, and I thought with alarm of the delay I had caused in the service of dinner, especially as I had promised to be at M. de Charlus's by eleven.

It was the Spanish minister (though I also met on the way the footman persecuted by the porter, who, radiant with delight when I inquired after his fiancée, told me that tomorrow was a "day off" for both of them, so that he would be able to spend the whole day with her, and extolled the kindness of Madame la Duchesse) who conducted me to the drawing-room, where I was afraid of finding M. de Guermantes in a bad humour. He welcomed me, on the contrary, with a joy that was obviously to some extent factitious and dictated by politeness, but was in other respects sincere, prompted both by his stomach which so long a delay had begun to famish, and his consciousness of a similar impatience in all his other guests, who completely filled the room. Indeed I learned afterwards that I had kept them waiting for nearly three-quarters of an hour. The Duc de Guermantes probably thought that to prolong the general torment for two minutes more would make it no worse and that, politeness having driven him to postpone for so long the moment of moving into the dining-room, this politeness would be more complete if, by not having dinner announced immediately, he could succeed in persuading me that I was not late and they had not been waiting for me. And so he asked me, as if we still had an hour before dinner and some of the party had not yet arrived, what I thought of his Elstirs. But at the same time, and without letting the cravings of his stomach become too apparent, in order not to lose another moment he proceeded in concert with the Duchess to the ceremony of introduction. It was only then that I perceived that, having until this evening—save for my novitiate in Mme Swann's salon—been accustomed in my mother's drawing-room, in Combray and in Paris, to the patronising or defensive attitudes of prim bourgeois ladies who treated me as a child, I was now witnessing a change of surroundings comparable to that which introduces Parsifal suddenly into the midst of the flower-maidens. Those who surrounded me now, their necks and shoulders entirely bare (the naked flesh appearing on either side of a sinuous spray of mimosa or the petals of a full-blown rose), accompanied their salutations with long, caressing glances, as though shyness alone restrained them from kissing me. Many of them were nevertheless highly respectable from the moral standpoint; many, not all, for the more virtuous did not feel the same revulsion as my mother would have done for those of easier virtue. The vagaries of conduct, denied by saintlier friends in the face of the evidence, seemed in the Guermantes world to matter far less than the social relations one had been able to maintain. One pretended not to know that the body of a hostess was at the disposal of all comers, provided that her visiting-list showed no gaps.

As the Duke showed very little concern for his other guests (from whom he had for long had as little to learn as they from him), but a great deal for me, whose particular kind of superiority, being outside his experience, inspired in him something akin to the respect which the great noblemen of the court of Louis XIV used to feel for his bourgeois ministers, he evidently considered that the fact of my not knowing his guests mattered not at all—to me at least, though it might to them—and while I was anxious, on his account, as to the impression that I might make on them, he was thinking only of the impression they would make on me.

At the very outset, indeed, there was a little twofold imbroglio. No sooner had I entered the drawing-room than M. de Guermantes, without even allowing me time to shake hands with the Duchess, led me, as though to give a pleasant surprise to the person in question to whom he seemed to be saying: "Here's your friend! You see, I'm bringing him to you by the scruff of the neck," towards a lady of smallish stature. Well before I arrived in her vicinity, the lady had begun to flash at me continuously from her large, soft, dark eyes the sort of knowing smiles which we address to an old friend who perhaps has not recognised us. As this was precisely the case with me and I could not for the life of me remember who she was, I averted my eyes as the Duke propelled me towards her, in order not to have to respond until our introduction should have released me from my predicament. Meanwhile the lady continued to maintain in precarious balance the smile she was aiming at me. She looked as though she was in a hurry to be relieved of it and to hear me say: "Ah, Madame, of course! How delighted Mamma will be to hear that we've met again!" I was as impatient to learn her name as she was to see that I did finally greet her with every indication of recognition, so that her smile, indefinitely prolonged like the note of a tuning-fork, might at length be given a rest. But M. de Guermantes managed things so badly (to my mind, at least) that it seemed to me that only my own name was mentioned and I was given no clue as to the identity of my unknown friend, to whom it never occurred to name herself, so obvious did the grounds of our intimacy, which baffled me completely, seem to her. Indeed, as soon as I had come within reach, she did not offer me her hand, but took mine in a familiar clasp, and spoke to me exactly as though I had been as aware as she was of the pleasant memories to which her mind reverted. She told me how sorry Albert (who I gathered was her son) would be to have missed seeing me. I tried to remember which of my school-friends had been called Albert, and could think only of Bloch, but this could not be Bloch's mother since she had been dead for many years. In vain I struggled to identify the past experience common to herself and me to which her thoughts had been carried back. But I could no more distinguish it through the translucent jet of her large, soft pupils which allowed only her smile to pierce their surface than one can distinguish a landscape that lies on the other side of a pane of smoked glass even when the sun is blazing on it. She asked me whether my father was not working too hard, if I would like to come to the theatre some evening with Albert, if my health was better, and as my replies, stumbling through the mental darkness in which I was plunged, became distinct only to explain that I was not feeling well that evening, she pushed forward a chair for me herself, putting herself out in a way to which I had never been accustomed by my parents' other friends. At length the clue to the riddle was furnished me by the Duke: "She thinks you're charming," he murmured in my ear, which felt somehow that it had heard these words before. They were the words Mme de Villeparisis had spoken to my grandmother and myself after we had made the acquaintance of the Princesse de Luxembourg. Everything was now clear; the present lady had nothing in common with Mme de Luxembourg, but from the language of the man who served her up to me I could discern the nature of the beast. She was a royal personage. She had never before heard of either my family or myself, but, a scion of the noblest race and endowed with the greatest fortune in the world (for, a daughter of the Prince de Parme, she had married an equally princely cousin), she sought always, in gratitude to her Creator, to testify to her neighbour, however poor or lowly he might be, that she did not look down upon him. And indeed I ought to have guessed this from her smile, for I had seen the Princesse de Luxembourg buy little rye-cakes on the beach at Balbec to give to my grandmother, as though to a caged deer in the zoo. But this was only the second princess of the blood royal to whom I had been presented, and I might be excused my failure to discern in her the generic features of the affability of the great. Besides, had not they themselves gone out of their way to warn me not to count too much on this affability, since the Duchesse de Guermantes, who had waved me so effusive a greeting with her gloved hand at the Opéra, had appeared furious when I bowed to her in the street, like the people who, having once given somebody a sovereign, feel that this has released them from any further obligation towards him. As for M. de Charlus, his ups and downs were even more sharply contrasted. And I was later to know, as the reader will learn, highnesses and majesties of another sort altogether, queens who play the queen and speak not after the conventions of their kind but like the queens in Sardou's plays.

If M. de Guermantes had been in such haste to present me, it was because the presence at a gathering of anyone not personally known to a royal personage is an intolerable state of things which must not be prolonged for a single instant. It was similar to the haste which Saint-Loup had shown to be introduced to my grandmother. By the same token, in a fragmentary survival of the old life of the court which is called social etiquette and is by no means superficial, wherein, rather, by a sort of outside-in reversal, it is the surface that becomes essential and profound, the Duc and

Duchesse de Guermantes regarded as a duty more essential and more inflexible than those (all too often neglected by one at least of the pair) of charity, chastity, pity and justice, that of rarely addressing the Princesse de Parme save in the third person.

Failing the visit to Parma which I had never yet made (and which I had wanted to make ever since certain Easter holidays long ago), meeting its Princess—who, I knew, owned the finest palace in that unique city where in any case everything must be homogeneous, isolated as it was from the rest of the world within its polished walls, in the atmosphere, stifling as an airless summer evening on the piazza of a small Italian town, of its compact and almost cloying name—ought to have substituted in a flash, for what I had so often tried to imagine, all that did really exist at Parma, in a sort of fragmentary arrival there without having moved; it was, in the algebra of my imagined journey to the city of Giorgione,[27] a simple equation, so to speak, with that unknown quantity. But if I had for many years past—like a perfumer impregnating a solid block of fat—saturated this name, Princesse de Parme, with the scent of thousands of violets, in return, when I set eyes on the Princess, who until then I would have sworn must be the Sanseverina herself, a second process began which was not, I may say, completed until several months had passed, and consisted in expelling, by means of fresh chemical combinations, all the essential oil of violets and all the Stendhalian fragrance from the name of the Princess, and implanting there in their place the image of a little dark woman taken up with good works and so humbly amiable that one felt at once in how exalted a pride that amiability had its roots. Moreover, while identical, barring a few points of difference, with any other great lady, she was as little Stendhalian as is, for example, in the Europe district of Paris, the Rue de Parme, which bears far less resemblance to the name of Parma than to any or all of the neighbouring streets, and reminds one not nearly so much of the Charterhouse in which Fabrice ends his days as of the concourse in the Gare Saint-Lazare.

Her amiability sprang from two causes. The first and more general was the upbringing which this daughter of kings had received. Her mother (not merely related to all the royal families of Europe but furthermore—in contrast to the ducal house of Parma—richer than any reigning princess) had instilled into her from her earliest childhood the arrogantly humble precepts of an evangelical snobbery; and today every line of the daughter's face, the curve of her shoulders, the movements of her arms, seemed to repeat the lesson: "Remember that if God has caused you to be born on the steps of a throne you ought not to make that a reason for looking down upon those to whom Divine Providence has willed (wherefore His Name be praised) that you should be superior by birth and fortune. On the contrary, you must be kind to the lowly. Your ancestors were Princes of Cleves and Juliers from the year 647; God in His bounty has decreed that you should hold practically all the shares in the Suez Canal and three times as many Royal Dutch as Edmond de Rothschild; your pedigree in a direct line has been established by genealogists from the year 63 of the Christian era; you have as sisters-in-law two empresses. Therefore never seem in your speech to be recalling these great privileges, not that they are precarious (for nothing can alter the antiquity of blood, and the world will always need oil), but because it is unnecessary to point out that you are better born than other people or that your investments are all gilt-edged, since everyone knows these facts already. Be helpful to the needy. Give to all those whom the bounty of heaven has been graciously pleased to put beneath you as much as you can give them without forfeiting your rank, that is to say help in the form of money, even caring for the sick, but of course never any invitations to your soirées, which would do them no possible good and, by diminishing your prestige, would detract from the efficacy of your benevolent activities."

And so, even at moments when she could not do good, the Princess endeavoured to demonstrate, or rather to let it be thought, by all the external signs of dumb-show, that she did not consider herself superior to the people among whom she found herself. She treated each of them with that charming courtesy with which well-bred people treat their inferiors and was continually, to make herself useful, pushing back her chair so as to leave more room, holding my gloves, offering me all those services which would demean the proud spirit of a commoner but are willingly rendered by sovereign ladies or, instinctively and from force of professional habit, by old servants.

The other reason for the amiability shown me by the Princesse de Parme was a more special one, yet in no way dictated by a mysterious liking for me. But for the moment I did not have time to get to the bottom of it. For already the Duke, who seemed in a hurry to complete the round of introductions, had led me off to

another of the flower-maidens. On hearing her name I told her
that I had passed by her country house, not far from Balbec. "Oh, I
should have been so pleased to show you round it," she said to me
almost in a whisper as though to emphasise her modesty, but in a
heartfelt tone filled with regret for the loss of an opportunity to
enjoy a quite exceptional pleasure; and she added with a meaning
look: "I do hope you will come again some day. But I must say that
what would interest you even more would be my aunt Brancas's
place. It was built by Mansard and it's the jewel of the province." It
was not only she herself who would have been glad to show me
over her house, but her aunt Brancas would have been no less
delighted to do me the honours of hers, or so I was assured by this
lady who evidently thought that, especially at a time when the land
showed a tendency to pass into the hands of financiers who had no
idea how to live, it was important that the great should keep up the
lofty traditions of lordly hospitality, by speeches which did not
commit them to anything. It was also because she sought, like
everyone in her world, to say the things that would give most
pleasure to the person she was addressing, to give him the highest
idea of himself, to make him think that he flattered people by
writing to them, that he honoured those who entertained him,
that everyone was longing to know him. The desire to give other
people this comforting idea of themselves does, it is true, sometimes exist even among the middle classes. We find there that
amiable disposition, in the form of an individual quality compensating for some other defect, not alas in the most trusty male friends
but at any rate in the most agreeable female companions. But there
it flourishes only in isolation. In an important section of the
aristocracy, on the other hand, this characteristic has ceased to be
individual; cultivated by upbringing, sustained by the idea of a
personal grandeur that need fear no humiliation, that knows no
rival, is aware that by being gracious it can make people happy and
delights in doing so, it has become the generic feature of a class.
And even those whom personal defects of too incompatible a kind
prevent from keeping it in their hearts bear the unconscious trace
of it in their vocabulary or their gesticulation.

"She's a very kind woman," said the Duc de Guermantes of the
Princesse de Parme, "and she knows how to play the *grande dame*
better than anyone."

While I was being introduced to the ladies, one of the gentlemen of the party had been showing various signs of agitation: this

was Comte Hannibal de Bréauté-Consalvi. Having arrived late, he had not had time to investigate the composition of the party, and when I entered the room, seeing in me a guest who was not one of the Duchess's regular circle and must therefore have some quite extraordinary claim to admission, installed his monocle beneath the groined arch of his eyebrow, thinking that this would help him, far more than to see me, to discern what manner of man I was. He knew that Mme de Guermantes had (the priceless appanage of truly superior women) what was called a "salon," that is to say added occasionally to the people of her own set some celebrity who had recently come into prominence by the discovery of a new cure for something or the production of a masterpiece. The Faubourg Saint-Germain had not yet recovered from the shock of learning that the Duchess had not been afraid to invite M. Detaille[28] to the reception which she had given to meet the King and Queen of England. The clever women of the Faubourg were not easily consolable for not having been invited, so deliciously thrilling would it have been to come into contact with that strange genius. Mme de Courvoisier averred that M. Ribot had been there as well, but this was a pure invention designed to make people believe that Oriane was aiming at an embassy for her husband. To cap it all, M. de Guermantes, with a gallantry that would have done credit to Marshal Saxe, had presented himself at the stage-door of the Comédie-Française and had persuaded Mlle Reichenberg to come and recite before the King, something that constituted an event without precedent in the annals of routs. Remembering all these unexpected happenings, which moreover had his entire approval, his own presence being both an ornament to and, in the same way as that of the Duchesse de Guermantes but in the masculine gender, an endorsement for any salon, M. de Bréauté, when he asked himself who I could be, felt that the field of inquiry was very wide. For a moment the name of M. Widor flashed before his mind, but he decided that I was too young to be an organist, and M. Widor not prominent enough to be "received." It seemed on the whole more plausible to regard me simply as the new attaché at the Swedish Legation of whom he had heard, and he was preparing to ask me for the latest news of King Oscar, by whom he had several times been very hospitably received; but when the Duke, in introducing me, had mentioned my name to M. de Bréauté, the latter, finding the name to be completely unknown to him, had no longer any doubt that, since

I was there, I must be a celebrity of some sort. It was absolutely typical of Oriane, who had the knack of attracting to her salon men who were in the public eye, in a ratio that of course never exceeded one in a hundred, otherwise she would have lowered its tone. Accordingly M. de Bréauté began to lick his chops and to sniff the air greedily, his appetite whetted not only by the good dinner he could count on, but by the character of the party, which my presence could not fail to make interesting and which would furnish him with an intriguing topic of conversation next day at the Duc de Chartres's luncheon-table. He was not yet enlightened as to whether I was the man who had just been making those experiments with a serum against cancer, or the author of the new "curtain-raiser" then in rehearsal at the Théâtre-Français; but, a great intellectual, a great collector of "travellers' tales," he lavished on me an endless series of bows, signs of mutual understanding, smiles filtered through the glass of his monocle, either in the misapprehension that a man of standing would esteem him more highly if he could manage to instil into me the illusion that for him, the Comte de Bréauté-Consalvi, the privileges of the mind were no less deserving of respect than those of birth, or simply from the need to express and the difficulty of expressing his satisfaction, in his ignorance of the language in which he ought to address me, precisely as if he had found himself face to face with one of the "natives" of an undiscovered country on which his raft had landed, from whom, in the hope of ultimate profit, he would endeavour, observing with interest the while their quaint customs and without interrupting his demonstrations of friendship or forgetting to utter loud cries of benevolence like them, to obtain ostrich eggs and spices in exchange for glass beads. Having responded as best I could to his joy, I shook hands with the Duc de Châtellerault, whom I had already met at Mme de Villeparisis's and who observed that she was "a sharp customer." He was typically Guermantes with his fair hair, his aquiline profile, the points where the skin of the cheeks was blemished, all of which may be seen in the portraits of that family which have come down to us from the sixteenth and seventeenth centuries. But, as I was no longer in love with the Duchess, her reincarnation in the person of a young man offered me no attraction. I interpreted the hook made by the Duc de Châtellerault's nose as if it had been the signature of a painter whose work I had long studied but who no longer interested me in the least. Next, I said good evening also to the Prince de Foix, and to the detriment of my knuckles, which emerged crushed and mangled, let them be caught in the vice of a German handclasp, accompanied by an ironical or good-natured smile, from the Prince von Faffenheim, M. de Norpois's friend, who, by virtue of the craze for nicknames which prevailed in this circle, was known so universally as Prince Von that he himself used to sign his letters "Prince Von," or, when he wrote to his intimates, "Von." At least this abbreviation was understandable, in view of his triple-barrelled name. It was less easy to grasp the reasons which caused "Elizabeth" to be replaced, now by "Lili," now by "Bebeth," just as another world swarmed with "Kikis." One can understand how people, idle and frivolous though they in general were, should have come to adopt "Quiou" in order not to waste the precious time that it would have taken them to pronounce "Montesquiou." But it is less easy to see what they gained by nicknaming one of their cousins "Dinand" instead of "Ferdinand." It must not be thought, however, that in the invention of nicknames the Guermantes invariably proceeded by curtailing or duplicating syllables. Thus two sisters, the Comtesse de Montpeyroux and the Vicomtesse de Vélude, who were both of them enormously stout, invariably heard themselves addressed, without the least trace of annoyance on their part or of amusement on other people's, so long established was the custom, as "Petite" and "Mignonne." Mme de Guermantes, who adored Mme de Montpeyroux, would, if the latter had fallen seriously ill, have flown to the sister with tears in her eyes and exclaimed: "I hear Petite is dreadfully bad!" Mme de l'Eclin, who wore her hair in bands that entirely hid her ears, was never called anything but "Hungry belly."[29] In some cases people simply added an "a" to the surname or Christian name of the husband to designate the wife. The most miserly, most sordid, most inhuman man in the Faubourg having been christened Raphael, his charmer, his flower springing also from the rock, always signed herself "Raphaela." But these are merely a few specimens of countless rules to which we can always return later on if the occasion arises, and explain some of them.

I then asked the Duke to introduce me to the Prince d'Agrigente. "What! do you mean to say you don't know the good Gri-gri!" exclaimed M. de Guermantes, and gave M. d'Agrigente my name. His own, so often quoted by Françoise, had always appeared to me like a transparent sheet of

coloured glass through which I beheld, struck by the slanting rays
of a golden sun, on the shore of the violet sea, the pink marble
cubes of an ancient city of which I had not the least doubt that the
Prince—who happened by some brief miracle to be passing
through Paris—was himself, as luminously Sicilian and as glori-
ously weathered, the absolute sovereign. Alas, the vulgar drone to
whom I was introduced, and who wheeled round to bid me good
evening with a ponderous nonchalance which he considered
elegant, was as independent of his name as of a work of art that
he owned without betraying in his person any reflexion of it,
without, perhaps, ever having looked at it. The Prince
d'Agrigente was so entirely devoid of anything princely, anything
remotely reminiscent of Agrigento, that one was led to suppose
that his name, entirely distinct from himself, bound by no ties to
his person, had had the power of attracting to itself every iota of
vague poetry that there might have been in this man, as in any
other, and enclosing it, after this operation, in the enchanted
syllables. If any such operation had been performed, it had certainly been done most efficiently, for there remained not an atom
of charm to be drawn from this kinsman of the Guermantes. With
the result that he found himself at one and the same time the only
man in the world who was Prince d'Agrigente and of all the men
in the world the one who was perhaps least so. He was, for all that,
very glad to be what he was, but as a banker is glad to hold a
number of shares in a mine, without caring whether the said mine
answers to the charming name of Ivanhoe or Primrose, or is called
merely the Premier. Meanwhile, as these introductions which
have taken so long to recount but which, beginning as soon as I
entered the room, had lasted only a few moments, were drawing
to an end at last, and Mme de Guermantes was saying to me in an
almost suppliant tone: "I'm sure Basin is tiring you, dragging you
round like that from one person to the next. We want you to
know our friends, but we're a great deal more anxious not to tire
you, so that you may come again often," the Duke, with a somewhat awkward and timorous wave of the hand, gave the signal
(which he would gladly have given at any time during the hour I
had spent in contemplation of the Elstirs) that dinner might now
be served.

I should add that one of the guests was still missing, M. de
Grouchy, whose wife, a Guermantes by birth, had arrived by
herself, her husband being due to come straight from the country

where he had been shooting all day. This M. de Grouchy, a descendant of his namesake of the First Empire, of whom it has been falsely said that his absence at the start of the Battle of Waterloo was the principal cause of Napoleon's defeat, came of an excellent family which, however, was not good enough in the eyes of certain fanatics for blue blood. Thus the Prince de Guermantes, who was to prove less fastidious in later life as far as he himself was concerned, was in the habit of saying to his nieces: "What a misfortune for that poor Mme de Guermantes" (the Vicomtesse de Guermantes, Mme de Grouchy's mother) "that she has never succeeded in marrying any of her children." "But, uncle, the eldest girl married M. de Grouchy." "I don't call that a husband! However, they say that your uncle François has proposed to the youngest one, so perhaps they won't all die old maids."

No sooner had the order to serve dinner been given than with a vast gyratory whirr, multiple and simultaneous, the double doors of the dining-room swung apart; a butler with the air of a court chamberlain bowed before the Princesse de Parme and announced the tidings "Madame is served," in a tone such as he would have employed to say "Madame is dead," which, however, cast no gloom over the assembly for it was with a sprightly air and as, in summer, at Robinson[30] that the couples advanced one behind the other to the dining-room, separating when they had reached their places, where footmen thrust their chairs in behind them; last of all, Mme de Guermantes advanced towards me to be taken in to dinner, without my feeling the least shadow of the timidity that I might have feared, for, like a huntress whose muscular dexterity has endowed her with natural ease and grace, observing no doubt that I had placed myself on the wrong side of her, she pivoted round me so adroitly that I found her arm resting on mine and was at once naturally attuned to a rhythm of precise and noble movements. I yielded to them all the more readily because the Guermantes attached no more importance to them than does to learning a truly learned man in whose company one is less cowed than in that of a dunce. Other doors opened through which there entered the steaming soup, as though the dinner were being held in a skilfully contrived puppet-theatre, where, at a signal from the puppet-master, the belated arrival of the young guest set all the machinery in motion.

Timid, rather than majestically sovereign, had been this signal from the Duke, to which that vast, ingenious, subservient and sumptuous clockwork, mechanical and human, had responded. The indecisiveness of the gesture did not spoil for me the effect of the spectacle that was attendant upon it. For I sensed that what had made it hesitant and embarrassed was the fear of letting me see that they had been waiting only for me to begin dinner and that they had been waiting for a long time, in the same way as Mme de Guermantes was afraid that, after looking at so many pictures, I would find it tiring and would be hindered from taking my ease among them if her husband engaged me in a continuous flow of introductions. So that it was the absence of grandeur in this gesture that disclosed the true grandeur which lay in the Duke's indifference to the splendour of his surroundings, in contrast to his deference towards a guest, however insignificant in himself, whom he desired to honour.

Not that M. de Guermantes was not in certain aspects thoroughly commonplace, showing indeed some of the absurd weaknesses of a man with too much money, the arrogance of an upstart which he certainly was not. But just as a public official or a priest sees his own humble talents multiplied to infinity (as a wave is by the whole mass of the sea which presses behind it) by the forces that stand behind him, the Government of France or the Catholic Church, so M. de Guermantes was borne up by that other force, aristocratic courtesy in its truest form. This courtesy excluded a large number of people. Mme de Guermantes would not have entertained Mme de Cambremer or M. de Forcheville. But the moment that anyone (as was the case with me) appeared eligible for admission into the Guermantes world, this courtesy disclosed a wealth of hospitable simplicity more splendid still, if possible, than those historic rooms and the marvellous furniture that remained in them.

When he wished to give pleasure to someone, M. de Guermantes went about making him the most important personage on that particular day with an art and a skill that made the most of the circumstances and the place. No doubt at Guermantes his "distinctions" and "favours" would have assumed another form. He would have ordered his carriage to take me for a drive alone with himself before dinner. Such as they were, one could not help feeling touched by his courteous ways, as one is, when one reads the memoirs of the period, by those of Louis XIV when he replies benignly, with a smile and a half-bow, to someone who has come to solicit his favour. It must however, in both instances, be borne in mind that this "politeness" did not go beyond the strict meaning of the word.

Louis XIV (with whom the sticklers for pure nobility of his day nevertheless find fault for his scant regard for etiquette, so much so that, according to Saint-Simon, he was only a very minor king, in terms of rank, by comparison with such monarchs as Philippe de Valois or Charles V) has the most meticulous instructions drawn up so that princes of the blood and ambassadors may know to what sovereigns they ought to give precedence. In certain cases, in view of the impossibility of arriving at an agreement, a compromise is arranged by which the son of Louis XIV, Monseigneur, shall entertain a certain foreign sovereign only out of doors, in the open air, so that it may not be said that in entering the palace one has preceded the other; and the Elector Palatine, entertaining the Duc de Chevreuse to dinner, in order not to have to give way to his guest, pretends to be taken ill and dines with him lying down, thus solving the difficulty. When M. le Duc avoids occasions when he must wait upon Monsieur, the latter, on the advice of the King, his brother, who is incidentally extremely attached to him, seizes an excuse for making his cousin attend his levee and forcing him to put on the royal shirt. But as soon as deeper feelings are involved, matters of the heart, this rule of duty, so inflexible when politeness only is at stake, changes entirely. A few hours after the death of this brother, one of the people whom he most dearly loved, when Monsieur, in the words of the Duc de Montfort, is "still warm," we find Louis XIV singing snatches from operas, astonished that the Duchesse de Bourgogne, who can scarcely conceal her grief, should be looking so woebegone, and, anxious that the gaiety of the court shall be at once resumed, encouraging his courtiers to sit down to the card-tables by ordering the Duc de Bourgogne to start a game of *brelan*. Now, not only in his social or business activities, but in his most spontaneous utterances, his ordinary preoccupations, his daily routine, one found a similar contrast in M. de Guermantes. The Guermantes were no more susceptible to grief than other mortals; it could indeed be said that they had less real sensibility; on the other hand one saw their names every day in the social columns of the *Gaulois* on account of the prodigious number of funerals at which they would have felt it culpable of them not to have their presence recorded. As the traveller discovers, almost unaltered, the houses roofed with turf, the terraces which may have met the eyes of Xenophon or St Paul, so in the manners of M. de Guermantes, a man who was heart-warming in his graciousness and revolting in his hardness, a slave to the pettiest obligations and derelict as regards the most solemn pacts, I found still intact after more than two centuries that aberration, peculiar to the life of the court under Louis XIV, which transfers the scruples of conscience from the domain of the affections and morality to questions of pure form.

The other reason for the friendliness shown me by the Princesse de Parme was that she was convinced beforehand that everything that she saw at the Duchesse de Guermantes's, people and things alike, was of a superior quality to anything she had at home. It is true that in every other house she also behaved as if this was the case; not merely did she go into raptures over the simplest dish, the most ordinary flowers, but she would ask permission to send round next morning, for the purpose of copying the recipe or examining the variety of blossom, her head cook or head gardener, personages with large emoluments who kept their own carriages and above all their professional pretensions, and were deeply humiliated at having to come to inquire after a dish they despised or to take a cutting of a variety of carnation that was not half as fine, as variegated, did not produce as large a blossom as those which they had long been growing for her at home. But if, wherever she went, this astonishment on the part of the Princess at the sight of the most commonplace things was factitious, and intended to show that she did not derive from the superiority of her rank and riches a pride forbidden by her early instructors, habitually dissembled by her mother and intolerable in the sight of her Creator, it was, on the other hand, in all sincerity that she regarded the drawing-room of the Duchesse de Guermantes as a privileged place in which she could progress only from surprise to delight. To a certain extent, it is true, though not nearly enough to justify this state of mind, the Guermantes were different from the rest of society; they were more precious and rare. They had given me at first sight the opposite impression; I had found them vulgar, similar to all other men and women, but this was because before meeting them I had seen them, as I saw Balbec, Florence or Parma, as names. Naturally enough, in this drawing-room, all the women whom I had imagined as being like Dresden figures were after all more like the great majority of women. But, in the same way as

Balbec or Florence, the Guermantes, after first disappointing the imagination because they resembled their fellow-men rather more than their name, could subsequently, though to a lesser degree, hold out to one's intelligence certain distinctive characteristics. Their physique, the colour—a peculiar pink that merged at times into purple—of their skins, a certain almost lustrous blondness of the finely spun hair even in the men, massed in soft golden tufts, half wall-growing lichen, half catlike fur (a luminous brilliance to which corresponded a certain intellectual glitter, for if people spoke of the Guermantes complexion, the Guermantes hair, they spoke also of the Guermantes wit, as of the wit of the Mortemarts), a certain social quality whose superior refinement—pre-Louis XIV—was all the more universally recognised because they promulgated it themselves—all this meant that in the actual substance, however precious it might be, of the aristocratic society in which they were to be found embedded here and there, the Guermantes remained recognisable, easy to detect and to follow, like the veins whose paleness streaks a block of jasper or onyx, or, better still, like the supple undulation of those tresses of light whose loosened hairs run like flexible rays along the sides of a moss-agate.

The Guermantes—those at least who were worthy of the name—were not only endowed with an exquisite quality of flesh, of hair, of transparency of gaze, but had a way of holding themselves, of walking, of bowing, of looking at one before they shook one's hand, of shaking hands, which made them as different in all these respects from an ordinary member of fashionable society as he in turn was from a peasant in a smock. And despite their affability one asked oneself: "Have they not indeed the right, though they waive it, when they see us walk, bow, leave a room, do any of those things which when performed by them become as graceful as the flight of a swallow or the droop of a rose on its stem, to think: 'These people are of a different breed from us, and we are the lords of creation'?" Later on, I realised that the Guermantes did indeed regard me as being of a different breed, but one that aroused their envy because I possessed merits unknown to myself which they professed to prize above all others. Later still I came to feel that this profession of faith was only half sincere and that in them scorn or amazement could co-exist with admiration and envy. The physical flexibility peculiar to the Guermantes was twofold: on the one hand always in action, at every moment, so that if, for example, a male Guermantes were about to salute a lady, he produced a silhouette of himself formed from the tension between a series of asymmetrical and energetically compensated movements, one leg dragging a little, either on purpose or because, having been broken so often in the hunting-field, it imparted to his trunk in its effort to keep pace with the other a curvature to which the upward thrust of one shoulder gave a counterpoise, while the monocle was inserted in the eye and raised an eyebrow just as the tuft of hair on the forehead flopped down-ward in the formal bow; on the other hand, like the shape which wave or wind or wake have permanently imprinted on a shell or a boat, this flexibility was so to speak stylised into a sort of fixed mobility, curving the arched nose which, beneath the blue, pro-truding eyes, above the thin lips from which, in the women, there emerged a husky voice, recalled the fabulous origin attrib-uted in the sixteenth century by the complaisance of parasitic and Hellenising genealogists to this race, ancient beyond dispute, but not to the extent which they claimed when they gave as its source the mythological impregnation of a nymph by a divine Bird.

The Guermantes were no less idiosyncratic from the intellectual than from the physical point of view. With the exception of Prince Gilbert, the husband of "Marie-Gilbert" with the antiquated ideas, who made his wife sit on his left when they drove out together because her blood, though royal, was inferior to his own (but he was an exception and a perpetual laughing-stock, behind his back, to the rest of his family, for whom he provided an endless source of fresh anecdotes), the Guermantes, while living among the cream of the aristocracy, affected to set no store by nobility. The theories of the Duchesse de Guermantes, who, it must be said, by virtue of being a Guermantes, had become to a certain extent something different and more attractive, put intelli-gence so much above everything else and were in politics so socialistic that one wondered where in her mansion could be the hiding-place of the genie whose duty it was to ensure the main-tenance of the aristocratic way of life and who, always invisible but evidently lurking at one moment in the entrance hall, at another in the drawing-room, at a third in her dressing-room, reminded the servants of this woman who did not believe in titles to address her as "Madame la Duchesse," and reminded this woman herself, who cared only for reading and was no respecter of persons, to go out to dinner with her sister-in-law when eight o'clock struck, and to put on a low-necked dress for the occasion.

The same family genie represented to Mme de Guermantes the social duties of duchesses, at least of the foremost among them who like herself were also multimillionaires—the sacrifice to boring tea-parties, grand dinners, routs of every kind, of hours in which she might have read interesting books—as unpleasant necessities like rain, which Mme de Guermantes accepted while bringing her irreverent humour to bear on them, though without going so far as to examine the reasons for her acceptance. The curious coincidence whereby Mme de Guermantes's butler invariably said "Madame la Duchesse" to this woman who believed only in the intellect did not appear to shock her. Never had it entered her head to request him to address her simply as "Madame." Giving her the utmost benefit of the doubt one might have supposed that, being absent-minded, she caught only the word "Madame" and that the suffix appended to it remained unheard. Only, though she might feign deafness, she was not dumb. And the fact was that whenever she had a message to give to her husband she would say to the butler: "Remind Monsieur le Duc——"

The family genie had other occupations as well, one of which was to inspire them to talk morality. It is true that there were Guermantes who went in for intellect and Guermantes who went in for morals, and that these two groups did not as a rule coincide. But the former—including a Guermantes who had forged cheques, who cheated at cards and was the most delightful of them all, with a mind open to every new and sensible idea—spoke even more eloquently about morals than the others, and in the same strain as Mme de Villeparisis, at the moments when the family genie expressed itself through the lips of the old lady. At corresponding moments one saw the Guermantes suddenly adopt a tone almost as antiquated and as affable as, and (since they themselves had more charm) more affecting than that of the Marquise, to say of a servant: "One feels that she has a thoroughly sound nature, she's not at all a common girl, she must come of decent parents, she's certainly a girl who has never gone astray." At such moments the family genie adopted the form of a tone of voice. But at times it could reveal itself in the bearing also, in the expression on the face, the same in the Duchess as in her grandfather the Marshal, a sort of imperceptible convulsion (like that of the Snake, the genius of the Carthaginian family of Barca) by which my heart had more than once been made to throb, on my morning walks, when before I had recognised Mme de Guermantes I felt her eyes fastened upon me from the inside of a little dairy. This family genie had intervened in a situation which was far from immaterial not merely to the Guermantes but to the Courvoisiers, the rival faction of the family and, though of as noble stock as the Guermantes (it was, indeed, through his Courvoisier grand-mother that the Guermantes explained the obsession which led the Prince de Guermantes always to speak of birth and titles as though they were the only things that mattered), their opposite in every respect. Not only did the Courvoisiers not assign to intelli-gence the same importance as the Guermantes, they had a differ-ent notion of it. For a Guermantes (however stupid), to be intelligent meant to have a sharp tongue, to be capable of saying scathing things, to give short shrift; but it meant also the capacity to hold one's own equally in painting, music, architecture, and to speak English. The Courvoisiers had a less favourable notion of intelligence, and unless one belonged to their world, being intel-ligent was almost tantamount to "having probably murdered one's father and mother." For them intelligence was the sort of burglar's jemmy by means of which people one did not know from Adam forced the doors of the most reputable drawing-rooms, and it was common knowledge among the Courvoisiers that you always had to pay in the long run for having "those sort" of people in your house. To the most trivial statements made by intelligent people who were not "in society" the Courvoisiers opposed a systematic distrust. Someone having once remarked: "But Swann is younger than Palamède," Mme de Gallardon had retorted: "So he says, at any rate, and if he says it you may be sure it's because he thinks it's in his interest!" Better still, when someone said of two highly distinguished strangers whom the Guermantes had entertained that one of them had been sent in first because she was the elder: "But is she really the elder?" Mme de Gallardon had inquired, not positively as though that sort of person did not have an age, but as if, being very probably devoid of civil or religious status, of definite traditions, they were both more or less of an age, like two kittens of the same litter between which only a veterinary surgeon would be competent to decide. The Courvoisiers how-ever, more than the Guermantes, maintained in a certain sense the integrity of the titled class thanks at once to the narrowness of their minds and the malevolence of their hearts. Just as the Guermantes (for whom, below the royal families and a few others like the Lignes, the La Trémoïlles and so forth, all the rest were a vague jumble of indistinguishable small-fry) were insolent towards various people of ancient stock who lived round Guermantes, precisely because they paid no attention to those secondary distinctions by which the Courvoisiers set enormous store, so the absence of such distinctions affected them little. Certain women who did not enjoy a very exalted rank in their native provinces but had made glittering marriages and were rich, pretty, beloved of duchesses, were for Paris, where people are never very well up in who one's "father and mother" were, desirable and elegant imports. It might happen, though rarely, that such women were, through the medium of the Princesse de Parme, or by virtue of their own attractions, received by certain Guermantes. But towards these the indignation of the Courvoisiers was unrelenting. Having to meet at their cousin's, between five and six in the afternoon, people with whose relatives their own relatives did not care to be seen mixing down in the Perche became for them an ever-increasing source of rage and an inexhaustible fount of rhetoric. Whenever, for instance, the charming Comtesse G―― entered the Guermantes drawing-room, the face of Mme de Villebon assumed exactly the expression that would have befitted it had she been called upon to recite the line:

And if but one is left, then that one will be me,

a line which for that matter was unknown to her. This Courvoisier had consumed, almost every Monday, éclairs stuffed with cream within a few feet of the Comtesse G――, but to no consequence. And Mme de Villebon confessed in secret that she could not conceive how her cousin Guermantes could allow a woman into her house who was not even in the second-best society of Châteaudun. "I really fail to see why my cousin should make such a fuss about whom she knows; she really has got a nerve!" concluded Mme de Villebon with a change of facial expression, now smilingly sardonic in its despair, to which, in a charade, another line of verse would have been applied, one with which she was no more familiar than with the first:

Thanks to the gods! Mischance outstrips my esperance.

We may here anticipate events to explain that the *perseverance* (which rhymes, in the following line, with *esperance*) shown by Mme de Villebon in snubbing Mme G—— was not entirely wasted. In the eyes of Mme G—— it invested Mme de Villebon with a distinction so supreme, though purely imaginary, that when the time came for Mme G——'s daughter, who was the prettiest girl and the greatest heiress in the ballrooms of that season, to marry, people were astonished to see her refuse all the dukes in succession. The fact was that her mother, remembering the weekly snubs she had to endure in the Rue de Grenelle in memory of Châteaudun, could think of only one possible husband for her daughter—a Villebon son.

A single point at which Guermantes and Courvoisiers converged was the art (one, moreover, of infinite variety) of keeping distances. The Guermantes manners were not absolutely uniform throughout the family. And yet, to take an example, all of them, all those who were genuine Guermantes, when you were introduced to them proceeded to perform a sort of ceremony almost as though the fact that they had held out their hands to you were as significant as if they had been dubbing you a knight. At the moment when a Guermantes, were he no more than twenty, but treading already in the footsteps of his ancestors, heard your name uttered by the person who introduced you, he let fall on you as though he had by no means made up his mind to say "How d'ye do" to you a gaze generally blue and always of the coldness of a steel blade which he seemed ready to plunge into the deepest recesses of your heart. Which was as a matter of fact what the Guermantes imagined themselves to be doing, since they all regarded themselves as psychologists of the first water. They felt moreover that they enhanced by this inspection the affability of the salute which was to follow it, and would not be rendered you without full knowledge of your deserts. All this occurred at a distance from yourself which, little enough had it been a question of a passage of arms, seemed immense for a handclasp and had as chilling an effect in the latter case as it would have had in the former, so that when a Guermantes, after a rapid tour round the last hiding-places of your soul to establish your credentials, had deemed you worthy to consort with him thereafter, his hand, directed towards you at the end of an arm stretched out to its fullest extent, appeared to be presenting a rapier to you for a single combat, and that hand was on the whole placed so far in advance of the Guermantes himself at that moment that when he proceeded to bow his head it was difficult to distinguish whether it was yourself or his own hand that he was saluting. Certain Guermantes, lacking any sense of moderation, or being incapable of refraining from repeating themselves incessantly, went further and repeated this ceremony afresh every time they met you. Seeing that they had no longer any need to conduct the preliminary psychological investigation for which the "family genie" had delegated its powers to them and the result of which they had presumably kept in mind, the insistency of the piercing gaze preceding the handclasp could be explained only by the automatism which their gaze had acquired or by some hypnotic power which they believed themselves to possess. The Courvoisiers, whose physique was different, had tried in vain to acquire that searching gaze and had had to fall back upon a haughty stiffness or a hurried negligence. On the other hand, it was from the Courvoisiers that certain very rare Guermantes of the gentler sex seemed to have borrowed the feminine form of greeting. At the moment when you were presented to one of these, she made you a sweeping bow in which she carried towards you, almost at an angle of forty-five degrees, her head and bust, the rest of her body (which was very tall) up to the belt which formed a pivot, remaining stationary. But no sooner had she projected thus towards you the upper part of her person, than she flung it backwards beyond the vertical with a brusque withdrawal of roughly equal length. This subsequent withdrawal neutralised what appeared to have been conceded to you; the ground which you believed yourself to have gained did not even remain in your possession as in a duel; the original positions were retained. This same annulment of affability by the resumption of distance (which was Courvoisier in origin and intended to show that the advances made in the first movement were no more than a momentary feint) displayed itself equally clearly, in the Courvoisier ladies as in the Guermantes, in the letters which you received from them, at any rate in the first period of your acquaintance. The "body" of the letter might contain sentences such as one writes only (you would suppose) to a friend, but in vain might you have thought yourself entitled to boast of being in that relation to the lady, since the letter would begin with "Monsieur" and end with "Croyez, monsieur, à mes sentiments distingués." After which, between this cold opening and frigid conclusion which altered the meaning of all the rest, there might (were it a reply to a letter of condolence) come a succession of the most touching pictures of the grief which the Guermantes lady had felt on losing her sister, of the intimacy that had existed between them, of the beauty of the place in which she was staying, of the consolation that she found in the charm of her grandchildren, in other words it was simply a letter such as one finds in printed collections, the intimate character of which implied, however, no more intimacy between yourself and the writer than if she had been Pliny the Younger or Mme de Simiane.

It is true that certain Guermantes ladies wrote to you from the first as "My dear friend," or "Dear friend." These were not always the most homely among them, but rather those who, living only in the society of kings and being at the same time "of easy virtue," assumed in their pride the certainty that everything that came from them gave pleasure and in their corruption the habit of not grudging you any of the satisfactions they had to offer. However, since to have had a common great-great-grandmother in the reign of Louis XIII was enough to make a young Guermantes invariably refer to the Marquise de Guermantes as "Aunt Adam," the Guermantes were so numerous a clan that, even with these simple rites, that for example of the form of greeting adopted on introduction to a stranger, there existed a wide divergence. Each sub-group of any refinement had its own, which was handed down from parents to children like the prescription for a liniment or a special way of making jam. Thus we have seen Saint-Loup's handshake unleashed as though involuntarily as soon as he heard one's name, without any participation by his eyes, without the addition of a nod or a bow. Any unfortunate commoner who for a particular reason—which in fact very rarely occurred—was presented to a member of the Saint-Loup subgroup would scratch his head over this abrupt minimum of a greeting, which deliberately assumed the appearance of non-recognition, wondering what in the world the Guermantes—male or female—could have against him. And he was highly surprised to learn that the said Guermantes had thought fit to write specially to the introducer to tell him how delighted he or she had been with the stranger, whom he or she looked forward to meeting again. As characteristic as the mechanical gestures of Saint-Loup were the complicated and rapid capers (which M. de Charlus condemned as ridiculous) of the Marquis de Fierbois, or the grave and measured paces of the Prince de Guermantes. But it is impossible to describe here the richness of this Guermantes choreography because of the sheer extent of the corps de ballet.

To return to the antipathy which animated the Courvoisiers against the Duchesse de Guermantes, the former might have had the consolation of feeling sorry for her so long as she was still unmarried, for she was then of comparatively slender means. Unfortunately, at all times and seasons, a sort of fuliginous emanation, quite *sui generis*, enveloped and concealed from view the wealth of the Courvoisiers which, however great it might be, remained obscure. In vain might a young Courvoisier with an enormous dowry find a most eligible bridegroom; it invariably happened that the young couple had no house of their own in Paris, would "descend on" their parents-in-law, and for the rest of the year lived down in the country in the midst of a society that was unadulterated but undistinguished. Whereas Saint-Loup, who was up to the eyes in debt, dazzled Doncières with his carriage-horses, a Courvoisier who was extremely rich always went by tram. Similarly (though of course many years earlier) Mlle de Guermantes (Oriane), who had scarcely a penny to her name, created more stir with her clothes than all the Courvoisiers put together. The very scandalousness of her remarks was a sort of advertisement for her style of dressing and doing her hair. She had had the audacity to say to the Russian Grand Duke: "Well, sir, it appears you would like to have Tolstoy assassinated?" at a dinner-party to which none of the Courvoisiers, in any case ill-informed about Tolstoy, had been asked. They were no better informed about the Greek authors, if we may judge by the Dowager Duchesse de Gallardon (mother-in-law of the Princesse de Gallardon who at that time was still a girl) who, not having been honoured by Oriane with a single visit in five years, replied to someone who asked her the reason for this abstention: "It seems she recites Aristotle" (meaning Aristophanes) "in society. I won't tolerate that sort of thing in my house!"

One can imagine how greatly this "sally" by Mlle de Guermantes on the subject of Tolstoy, if it enraged the Courvoisiers, delighted the Guermantes, and beyond them everyone who was not merely closely but even remotely attached to them. The Dowager Comtesse d'Argencourt (*née* Seineport), who entertained more or less everyone because she was a blue-stocking and in spite of her son's being a terrible snob, retailed the remark to her literary friends with the comment: "Oriane de Guermantes, you know, she's as sharp as a needle, as mischievous as a monkey, gifted at everything, does water-colours worthy of a great painter, and writes better verses than most of the great poets, and as for family, you couldn't imagine anything better, her grandmother was Mlle de Montpensier, and she's the eighteenth Oriane de Guermantes in succession, without a single misalliance; it's the purest, the oldest blood in the whole of France." And so the sham men of letters, the pseudo-intellectuals whom Mme d'Argencourt entertained, picturing Oriane de Guermantes, whom they would never have an opportunity of knowing personally, as something more wonderful and more extraordinary than Princess Bedr-el-Budur, not only felt ready to die for her on learning that so noble a person glorified Tolstoy above all others, but felt also a quickening in their hearts of their own love of Tolstoy, their longing to resist Tsarism. These liberal ideas might have languished in them, they might have begun to doubt their importance, no longer daring to confess to them, when suddenly from Mlle de Guermantes herself, that is to say from a girl so indisputably cultured and authoritative, who wore her hair flat on her forehead (a thing that no Courvoisier would ever have dreamed of doing), came this vehement support. A certain number of realities, good or bad in themselves, gain enormously in this way by receiving the adhesion of people who are in authority over us. For instance, among the Courvoisiers the rites of civility in a public thoroughfare consisted in a certain form of greeting, very ugly and far from affable in itself, which people nevertheless knew to be the distinguished way of bidding a person good-day, with the result that everyone else, suppressing their instinctive smiles of welcome, endeavoured to imitate these frigid gymnastics. But the Guermantes in general and Oriane in particular, while more conversant than anyone with these rites, did not hesitate, if they caught sight of you from a carriage, to greet you with a friendly wave, and in a drawing-room, leaving the Courvoisiers to give their stiff, self-conscious salutes, offered the most charming bows, held out their hands as though to a comrade with a smile from their blue eyes, so that suddenly, thanks to the Guermantes, there entered into the substance of stylish manners, hitherto rather hollow and dry, everything that one would naturally have liked and had forced oneself to eschew, a genuine welcome, the warmth of true friendliness, spontaneity. It is in a similar fashion (but by a rehabilitation which in this case is less justified) that the people who are most strongly imbued with an instinctive taste for bad music and for melodies, however commonplace, which have something facile and caressing about them, succeed, by dint of education in symphonic culture, in mortifying that appetite. But once they have arrived at this point, when, dazzled—and rightly so—by the brilliant orchestral colouring of Richard Strauss, they see that musician adopt the most vulgar motifs with a self-indulgence worthy of Auber, what those-people originally admired finds suddenly in so high an authority a justification which delights them, and they wallow without qualms and with a twofold gratitude, when they listen to *Salomé*, in what it would have been impossible for them to admire in *Les Diamants de la Couronne*.

Authentic or not, Mlle de Guermantes's apostrophe to the Grand Duke, retailed from house to house, provided an opportunity to relate with what excessive elegance Oriane had been turned out at the dinner-party in question. But if such splendour (and this is precisely what rendered it inaccessible to the Courvoisiers) springs not from wealth but from prodigality, the latter nevertheless lasts longer if it enjoys the constant support of the former, which then allows it to pull out all the stops. Now, given the principles openly paraded not only by Oriane but by Mme de Villeparisis, namely that nobility does not count, that it is ridiculous to bother one's head about rank, that money doesn't bring happiness, that intellect, heart, talent are alone of importance, the Courvoisiers were justified in hoping that, as a result of the training she had received from the Marquise, Oriane would marry someone who was not in society, an artist, an ex-convict, a tramp, a free-thinker, that she would enter for good and all into the category of what the Courvoisiers called "black sheep." They were all the more justified in this hope because, inasmuch as Mme de Villeparisis was at that time going through an awkward crisis from the social point of view (none of the few bright stars whom I was to meet in her drawing-room had as yet reappeared there), she professed an intense horror of the society which thus excluded her. Even when she spoke of her nephew the Prince de Guermantes, whom she did still see, she never ceased mocking him because he was so infatuated with his pedigree. But the moment it became a question of finding a husband for Oriane, it was no longer the principles publicly paraded by aunt and niece that had guided the operation; it was the mysterious "family genie." As unerringly as if Mme de Villeparisis and Oriane had never spoken of anything but rent-rolls and pedigrees instead of literary merit and depth of character, and as if the Marquise, for the space of a few days, had been—as she would ultimately be—dead and in her coffin in the church at Combray, where each member of the family became simply a Guermantes, with a forfeiture of individuality and baptismal names attested on the voluminous black drapery of the pall by the single "G" in purple surmounted by the ducal coronet, it was on the wealthiest and the most nobly born, on the most eligible bachelor of the Faubourg Saint-Germain, on the eldest son of the Duc de Guermantes, the Prince des Laumes, that the family genie had fixed the choice of the intellectual, the rebellious, the evangelical Mme de Villeparisis. And for a couple of hours, on the day of the wedding, Mme de Villeparisis received in her drawing-room all the noble persons whom she had been in the habit of deriding, whom she even derided with the few bourgeois intimates whom she had invited and on whom the Prince des Laumes promptly left cards, preparatory to "cutting the painter" in the following year. And then, making the Courvoisiers' cup of bitterness overflow, the same old maxims according to which intellect and talent were the sole claims to social pre-eminence began once more to be trotted out in the household of the Princesse des Laumes immediately after her marriage. And in this respect, be it said in passing, the point of view which Saint-Loup upheld when he lived with Rachel, frequented the friends of Rachel, would have liked to marry Rachel, entailed—whatever the horror that it inspired in the family—less falsehood than that of the Guermantes young ladies in general, extolling the intellect, barely allowing the poss-ibility that anyone could question the equality of mankind, all of which led, when it came to the point, to the same result as if they had professed the opposite principles, that is to say to marrying an extremely wealthy duke. Saint-Loup, on the contrary, acted in conformity with his theories, which led people to say that he was treading in evil ways. Certainly from the moral standpoint Rachel was not altogether satisfactory. But it is by no means certain that, if she had been no more virtuous but a duchess or the heiress to many millions, Mme de Marsantes would not have been in favour of the match.

However, to return to Mme des Laumes (shortly afterwards Duchesse de Guermantes, on the death of her father-in-law), it was the last agonising straw for the Courvoisiers that the theories of the young Princess, remaining thus confined to her speech, should in no way have guided her conduct; with the result that this philosophy (if one may so call it) did not impair the aristocratic elegance of the Guermantes drawing-room. No doubt all the people whom Mme de Guermantes did not invite imagined that it was because they were not clever enough, and a rich American lady who had never possessed any other book except a little old copy, never opened, of Parny's poems, arranged because it was "of the period" on one of the tables in her small drawing-room, showed how much store she set by the things of the mind by the devouring gaze which she fastened on the Duchesse de Guermantes when that lady made her appearance at the Opéra. No doubt, too, Mme de Guermantes was sincere when she elected a person on account of his or her intelligence. When she said of a woman: "It appears she's quite charming!" or of a man that he was the "cleverest person in the world," she imagined herself to have no other reason for consenting to receive them than this charm or cleverness, the family genie not interposing itself at the last moment; more deeply rooted, stationed at the obscure entrance to the region in which the Guermantes exercised their judgment, this vigilant spirit precluded them from finding the man clever or the woman charming if they had no social merit, actual or potential. The man was pronounced learned, but like a dictionary, or, on the contrary, common, with the mind of a commercial traveller, the woman pretty, but with a terribly bad style, or too talkative. As for the people who had no definite position, they were simply dreadful—such snobs! M. de Bréauté, whose country house was quite close to Guermantes, mixed with no one below the rank of Highness. But he was totally indifferent to them and longed only to spend his days in museums. Accordingly Mme de Guermantes was indignant when anyone spoke of M. de Bréauté as a snob. "Babal a snob! But, my dear man, you must be mad, he's just the opposite. He loathes smart people; he won't let himself be introduced to anyone. Even in my house! If I invite him to meet someone he doesn't know, he never stops grumbling when he comes."

This was not to say that, even in practice, the Guermantes did not set altogether more store by intelligence than the Courvoisiers. In a positive sense, this difference between the Guermantes and the Courvoisiers had already begun to bear very promising fruit. Thus the Duchesse de Guermantes,

enveloped moreover in a mystery which had set so many poets
dreaming of her from afar, had given that ball to which I have
already referred, at which the King of England had enjoyed
himself more thoroughly than anywhere else, for she had had
the idea, which would never have occurred to the Courvoisier
mind, of inviting, and the audacity, from which the Courvoisier
courage would have recoiled, to invite, apart from the personages
already mentioned, the musician Gaston Lemaire and the dramatist Grandmougin. But it was chiefly from the negative point of
view that intellectuality made itself felt. If the necessary coefficient
of cleverness and charm declined steadily as the rank of the person
who sought an invitation from the Duchesse de Guermantes
became more exalted, vanishing to zero when it came to the
principal crowned heads of Europe, conversely the further they
fell below this royal level the higher the coefficient rose. For
instance, at the Princesse de Parme's receptions there were a
number of people whom Her Royal Highness invited because
she had known them as children, or because they were related to
some duchess, or attached to the person of some sovereign, they
themselves being quite possibly ugly, boring or stupid. Now, in
the case of a Courvoisier reasons such as "a favourite of the
Princesse de Parme," or "a half-sister of the Duchesse d'Arpajon
on the mother's side," or "spends three months every year with
the Queen of Spain," would have been sufficient to make her
invite such people to her house, but Mme de Guermantes, who
had politely acknowledged their greetings for ten years at the
Princesse de Parme's, had never once allowed them to cross her
threshold, considering that the same rule applied to a drawing-
room in a social as in a physical sense, where it only needed a few
pieces of furniture which had no particular beauty, but were left
there to fill the room and as a sign of the owner's wealth, to render
it hideous. Such a drawing-room resembled a book in which the
author cannot refrain from the use of language advertising his own
learning, brilliance, fluency. Like a book, like a house, the quality
of a "salon," Mme de Guermantes rightly thought, is based on the
cornerstone of sacrifice.

Many of the friends of the Princesse de Parme, with whom the
Duchesse de Guermantes had confined herself for years past to the
same conventional greeting, or to returning their cards, without
ever inviting them to her house or going to theirs, complained
discreetly of these omissions to Her Highness who, on days when

M. de Guermantes came by himself to see her, dropped a hint of it to him. But the wily nobleman, a bad husband to the Duchess in so far as he kept mistresses, but her most tried and trusty friend in everything that concerned the proper functioning of her salon (and her own wit, which formed its chief attraction), replied: "But does my wife know her? Indeed! Oh, well, I dare say she ought to have. But the truth is, Ma'am, that Oriane doesn't care for women's conversations. She lives surrounded by a court of superior minds—I'm not her husband, I'm only the senior valet. Except for quite a small number, who are all of them very witty indeed, women bore her. Surely, Ma'am, Your Highness with all her fine judgment is not going to tell me that the Marquise de Souvré has any wit. Yes, I quite understand, Your Highness receives her out of kindness. Besides, Your Highness knows her. You tell me that Oriane has met her; it's quite possible, but once or twice at the most, I assure you. And then, I must explain to Your Highness, it's really a little my fault as well. My wife is very easily tired, and she's so anxious to be friendly always that if I allowed her she would never stop going to see people. Only yesterday evening, although she had a temperature, she was afraid of hurting the Duchesse de Bourbon's feelings by not going to see her. I had to show my teeth, I can tell you; I positively forbade them to bring the carriage round. Do you know, Ma'am, I've a very good mind not to mention to Oriane that you've spoken to me about Mme de Souvré. Oriane is so devoted to Your Highness that she'll go round at once to invite Mme de Souvré to the house; that will mean another call to be paid, it will oblige us to make friends with the sister, whose husband I know quite well. I think I shall say nothing at all about it to Oriane, if Your Highness has no objection. We'll save her a great deal of strain and agitation. And I assure you that it will be no loss to Mme de Souvré. She goes everywhere, moves in the most brilliant circles. We scarcely entertain at all, really, just a few little friendly dinners. Mme de Souvré would be bored to death." The Princesse de Parme, innocently convinced that the Duc de Guermantes would not transmit her request to the Duchess, and dismayed by her failure to procure the invitation that Mme de Souvré sought, was all the more flattered to think that she herself was one of the regular frequenters of so exclusive a household. No doubt this satisfaction had its drawbacks also. Thus whenever the Princesse de Parme invited Mme de Guermantes to her own parties she had to rack her brains

to be sure that there was no one else on her list whose presence
might offend the Duchess and make her refuse to come again.

On her habitual evenings, after dinner, to which she always
invited a few people (very early, for she clung to old customs), the
Princesse de Parme's drawing-room was thrown open to her
regular guests and, generally speaking, to the whole of the higher
aristocracy, French and foreign. The order of her receptions was as
follows: on issuing from the dining-room the Princess sat down on
a settee in front of a large round table and chatted with two of the
most important ladies who had dined with her, or else cast her eyes
over a magazine, or sometimes played cards (or pretended to play,
following a German court custom), either a game of patience or
selecting as her real or pretended partner some prominent personage. By nine o'clock the double doors of the big drawing-room
were in constant action, opening and shutting and opening again
to admit the visitors who had dined hurriedly at home (or if they
had dined "out," skipped coffee, promising to return later, having
intended only "to go in at one door and out at the other") in order
to conform with the Princess's time-table. She, meanwhile,
attentive to her game or conversation, made a show of not seeing
the new arrivals, and it was not until they were actually within
reach of her that she rose graciously from her seat, with a benevolent smile for the women. The latter thereupon sank before the
standing Princess in a curtsey which was tantamount to a genuflexion, in such a way as to bring their lips down to the level of the
beautiful hand which hung very low, and to kiss it. But at that
moment the Princess, just as if she had been surprised each time by
a protocol with which nevertheless she was perfectly familiar,
raised the kneeling lady as though by main force, but with incomparable grace and sweetness, and kissed her on both cheeks. A
grace and sweetness that were conditional, you may say, upon the
meekness with which the arriving guest bent her knee. Very
likely; and it would seem that in an egalitarian society social
etiquette would vanish, not, as is generally supposed, from want
of breeding, but because on the one side would disappear the
deference due to a prestige which must be imaginary to be effective, and on the other, more completely still, the affability that is
gracefully and generously dispensed when it is felt to be of infinite
price to the recipient, a price which, in a world based on equality,
would at once fall to nothing like everything that has only a
fiduciary value. But this disappearance of social distinctions in a

reconstructed society is by no means a foregone conclusion, and we are at times too ready to believe that present circumstances are the only ones in which a state of things can survive. People of first-rate intelligence believed that a republic could not have any diplomacy or foreign alliances, and that the peasant class would not tolerate the separation of Church and State. After all, the survival of etiquette in an egalitarian society would be no more miraculous than the practical success of the railways or the use of the aeroplane in war. Besides, even if politeness were to vanish, there is nothing to show that this would be a misfortune. Finally, would not society become secretly more hierarchical as it became outwardly more democratic? Very possibly. The political power of the Popes has grown enormously since they ceased to possess either States or an army; our cathedrals meant far less to a devout Catholic of the seventeenth century than they mean to an atheist of the twentieth, and if the Princesse de Parme had been the sovereign ruler of a State, no doubt I should have felt moved to speak of her about as much as of a President of the Republic, that is to say not at all.

As soon as the postulant had been raised up and embraced by the Princess, the latter resumed her seat and returned to her game of patience, unless the newcomer was a lady of some distinction, in which case she sat her down in an armchair and chatted to her for a while.

When the room became too crowded the lady-in-waiting who had to control the traffic cleared some space by leading the regular guests into an immense hall on to which the drawing-room opened, a hall filled with portraits and minor trophies relating to the House of Bourbon. The intimate friends of the Princess would then volunteer as guides and tell interesting anecdotes, to which the young people had not the patience to listen, more interested in the spectacle of living royalty (with the possibility of getting themselves presented to it by the lady-in-waiting and the maids of honour) than in examining the relics of dead sovereigns. Too occupied with the acquaintances they might be able to make and the invitations they might be able to pick up, they knew absolutely nothing, even after several years, of what there was in this priceless museum of the archives of the monarchy, and could only recall vaguely that it was decorated with cacti and giant palms which gave this centre of social elegance a look of the palmarium in the Zoological Gardens.

Of course the Duchesse de Guermantes, by way of self-morti-
fication, did occasionally appear on these evenings to pay an "after
dinner" call on the Princess, who kept her all the time by her side,
while exchanging pleasantries with the Duke. But on evenings
when the Duchess came to dine, the Princess took care not to
invite her regular party, and closed her doors to the world on rising
from table, for fear lest a too liberal selection of guests might offend
the exacting Duchess. On such evenings, were any of the faithful
who had not received warning to present themselves on the royal
doorstep, they would be informed by the porter: "Her Royal
Highness is not at home this evening," and would turn away.
But many of the Princess's friends would have known in advance
that on the day in question they would not be asked to her house.
These were a special category of parties, a category barred to many
who must have longed for admission. Those who were excluded
could with virtual certainty enumerate the roll of the elect, and
would say irritably among themselves: "You know, of course, that
Oriane de Guermantes never goes anywhere without her entire
general staff." With the help of this body, the Princesse de Parme
sought to surround the Duchess as with a protective rampart
against those persons the chance of whose making a good impression on her was at all doubtful. But there were several of the
Duchess's favourites, several members of this glittering "staff,"
for whom the Princesse de Parme resented having to put herself
out, seeing that they paid little or no attention to herself. No doubt
the Princess was fully prepared to admit that people might derive
more enjoyment from the company of the Duchesse de
Guermantes than from her own. She could not deny that there
was always a "crush" at the Duchess's "at homes," or that she
herself often met there three or four royal personages who thought
it sufficient to leave their cards upon her. And in vain might she
commit to memory Oriane's witty sayings, copy her gowns, serve
at her own tea-parties the same strawberry tarts, there were occasions on which she was left by herself all afternoon with a lady-in-
waiting and some councillor from a foreign legation. And so
whenever (as had been the case with Swann, for instance, at an
earlier period) there was anyone who never let a day pass without
going to spend an hour or two at the Duchess's and paid a call once
every two years on the Princesse de Parme, the latter felt no great
desire, even for the sake of amusing Oriane, to make "advances"
to this Swann or whoever he was by inviting him to dinner. In a

word, having the Duchess in her house was for the Princess a source of endless perplexity, so haunted was she by the fear that Oriane would find fault with everything. But in return, and for the same reason, when the Princesse de Parme came to dine with Mme de Guermantes she could be certain in advance that everything would be perfect, delightful, and she had only one fear, which was that of being unable to understand, remember, give satisfaction, being unable to assimilate new ideas and people. On this score, my presence aroused her attention and excited her cupidity, just as might a new way of decorating the dinner-table with garlands of fruit, uncertain as she was which of the two—the table decorations or my presence—was the more distinctively one of those charms which were the secret of the success of Oriane's receptions, and in her uncertainty firmly resolved to try to have them both at her own next dinner-party. What in fact fully justified the enraptured curiosity which the Princesse de Parme brought to the Duchess's house was that unique, dangerous, exciting element into which the Princess used to plunge with a thrill of anxiety, shock and delight (as at the seaside on one of those days of "heavy seas" of the danger of which the bathing-attendants warn one for the simple reason that none of them can swim), and from which she would emerge feeling braced, happy, rejuvenated—the element known as the wit of the Guermantes. The wit of the Guermantes—a thing as non-existent as the squared circle, according to the Duchess who regarded herself as the sole Guermantes to possess it—was a family reputation like that of the minced pork of Tours or the biscuits of Rheims. However (since an intellectual characteristic does not employ for its propagation the same channels as the colour of hair or complexion) certain intimate friends of the Duchess who were not of her blood were nevertheless endowed with this wit, which on the other hand had failed to inculcate itself into various Guermantes who were all too resistant to wit of any kind. For the most part, the custodians of the Guermantes wit who were not related to the Duchess shared the characteristic feature of having been brilliant men, eminently fitted for a career to which, whether in the arts, diplomacy, parliamentary eloquence or the army, they had preferred the life of society. Possibly this preference could be explained by a certain lack of originality, of initiative, of will-power, of health or of luck, or possibly by snobbishness.

With certain of them (though these, it must be admitted, were the exception), if the Guermantes drawing-room had been the stumbling-block in their careers, it had been against their will. Thus a doctor, a painter and a diplomat of great promise had failed to achieve success in the careers for which they were nevertheless more brilliantly endowed than most because their friendship with the Guermantes had resulted in the first two being regarded as men of fashion and the third as a reactionary, and this had prevented all three from winning the recognition of their peers. The mediaeval gown and red cap which are still donned by the electoral colleges of the Faculties are (or were, at least, not so long since) something more than a purely outward survival from a narrow-minded past, from a rigid sectarianism. Under the cap with its golden tassels, like the high priests in the conical mitre of the Jews, the "professors" were still, in the years that preceded the Dreyfus case, fast rooted in rigorously pharisaical ideas. Du Boulbon was at heart an artist, but was safe because he did not care for society. Cottard was always at the Verdurins', but Mme Verdurin was a patient, he was moreover protected by his vulgarity, and at his own house he entertained no one outside the Faculty, at banquets over which there floated an aroma of carbolic acid. But in strongly corporate bodies, where moreover the rigidity of their prejudices is but the price that must be paid for the noblest integrity, the most lofty conceptions of morality, which wither in more tolerant, more liberal, ultimately more corrupt atmospheres, a professor in his gown of scarlet satin faced with ermine, like that of a Doge (which is to say a Duke) of Venice shut away in the ducal palace, was as virtuous, as deeply attached to noble principles, but as pitiless towards any alien element as that other admirable but fearsome duke, M. de Saint-Simon. The alien, here, was the worldly doctor, with other manners, other social relations. To make good, the unfortunate of whom we are now speaking, so as not to be accused by his colleagues of looking down on them (who but a man of fashion would think of such an idea!) if he concealed the Duchesse de Guermantes from them, hoped to disarm them by giving mixed dinner-parties in which the medical element was merged in the fashionable. He was unaware that in so doing he signed his own death-warrant, or rather he discovered this when the Council of Ten (a little larger in number) had to fill a vacant chair, and it was invariably the name of another doctor, more normal if more mediocre, that emerged from the fatal urn, and the "Veto" thundered round the ancient Faculty, as solemn, as absurd and as terrible as the "Juro" that spelt the death of Molière. So too with the painter permanently labelled man of fashion, when fashionable people who dabbled in art had succeeded in getting themselves labelled artists; so with the diplomat who had too many reactionary associations.

But these cases were rare. The prototype of the distinguished men who formed the main substance of the Guermantes salon was someone who had voluntarily (or at least they supposed) renounced all else, everything that was incompatible with the wit of the Guermantes, with the courtesy of the Guermantes, with that indefinable charm odious to any "body" that is at all "corporate."

And the people who were aware that one of the habitués of the Duchess's drawing-room had once been awarded the gold medal of the Salon, that another, Secretary to the Bar Council, had made a brilliant début in the Chamber, that a third had ably served France as chargé d'affaires, might have been led to regard as "failures" people who had now done nothing for twenty years. But there were few who were thus "in the know," and the persons concerned would themselves have been the last to remind one, finding these old distinctions valueless, precisely by virtue of the Guermantes wit: for did this not encourage them to denounce on the one hand as a bore and a pedant, on the other as a counter-jumper, a pair of eminent ministers, one a trifle solemn, the other addicted to puns, whose praises the newspapers were constantly singing but in whose company Mme de Guermantes would begin to yawn and show signs of impatience if a hostess had rashly placed either of them next to her at the dinner-table? Since being a statesman of the first rank was in no sense a recommendation in the eyes of the Duchess, those of her friends who had abandoned the "Career" or the "Service," who had never stood for parliament, felt, as they came day after day to have lunch and talk with their great friend, or when they met her in the houses of royal personages—incidentally held in low esteem by them (or so they said)—that they had chosen the better part, albeit their melancholy air, even in the midst of the gaiety, seemed somehow to impugn the validity of this judgment.

And it must be acknowledged that the refinement of social life, the sparkle of the conversation at the Guermantes', did have something real about it, however exiguous it may have been.

No official title was worth more than the personal charm of certain of Mme de Guermantes's favourites whom the most powerful ministers would have been unable to attract to their houses. If in this drawing-room so many intellectual ambitions and even noble efforts had been for ever buried, still at least from their dust the rarest flowering of civilised society had sprung to life. Certainly men of wit, such as Swann for instance, regarded themselves as superior to men of merit, whom they despised, but that was because what the Duchess valued above everything else was not intelligence but—a superior form of intelligence, according to her, rarer, more exquisite, raising it up to a verbal variety of talent—wit. And long ago at the Verdurins', when Swann denounced Brichot and Elstir, one as a pedant and the other as an oaf, despite all the learning of the one and the genius of the other, it was the infiltration of the Guermantes spirit that had led him to classify them thus. Never would he have dared to introduce either of them to the Duchess, conscious instinctively of the air with which she would have listened to Brichot's perorations and Elstir's "balderdash," the Guermantes spirit consigning pretentious and prolix speech, whether in a serious or a farcical vein, to the category of the most intolerable imbecility.

As for the Guermantes of the true flesh and blood, if the Guermantes spirit had not infected them as completely as we see occur in, for example, those literary coteries in which everyone has the same way of pronouncing, enunciating and consequently thinking, it was certainly not because originality is stronger in social circles and inhibits imitation therein. But imitation requires not only the absence of any unconquerable originality but also a relative fineness of ear which enables one first of all to discern what one is afterwards to imitate. And there were several Guermantes in whom this musical sense was as entirely lacking as in the Courvoisiers.

To take as an instance what is called, in another sense of the word imitation, "giving imitations" (or among the Guermantes was called "taking off"), for all that Mme de Guermantes could bring these off to perfection, the Courvoisiers were as incapable of appreciating it as if they had been a tribe of rabbits instead of men and women, because they had never managed to observe the particular defect or accent that the Duchess was endeavouring to mimic. When she "imitated" the Duc de Limoges, the Courvoisiers would protest: "Oh, no, he doesn't really speak

like that. I dined with him again at Bebeth's last night; he talked to
me all evening and he didn't speak like that at all!" whereas any
Guermantes who was at all cultivated would exclaim: "Goodness,
how droll Oriane is! The amazing thing is that when she's
mimicking him she looks exactly like him! I feel I'm listening to
him. Oriane, do give us a little more Limoges!" Now these
Guermantes (without even including those absolutely remarkable
members of the clan who, when the Duchess imitated the Duc de
Limoges, would say admiringly: "Oh, you really have got him," or
"You do hit him off!") might be devoid of wit according to Mme
de Guermantes (in this respect she was right), but by dint of
hearing and repeating her sayings they had come to imitate more
or less her way of expressing herself, of criticising people, of what
Swann, like the Duchess herself, would have called her way of
"phrasing" things, so that they presented in their conversation
something which to the Courvoisiers appeared appallingly similar
to Oriane's wit and was treated by them collectively as the
Guermantes wit. As these Guermantes were to her not merely
kinsfolk but admirers, Oriane (who kept the rest of the family
rigorously at arm's-length and now avenged by her disdain the
spitefulness they had shown her in her girlhood) went to call on
them now and then, generally in the company of the Duke, when
she drove out with him in the summer months. These visits were
an event. The Princesse d'Epinay's heart would begin to beat
more rapidly, as she entertained in her big drawing-room on the
ground floor, when she saw from a distance, like the first glow of
an innocuous fire, or the scouting party of an unexpected invasion,
making her way slowly across the courtyard in a diagonal course,
the Duchess wearing a ravishing hat and holding atilt a sunshade
redolent with a summer fragrance. "Why, here comes Oriane,"
she would say, like an "On guard!" intended to convey a prudent
warning to her visitors, so that they should have time to beat an
orderly retreat, to evacuate the rooms without panic. Half of those
present dared not remain, and rose at once to go. "But no, why?
Sit down again, I insist on keeping you a little longer," the Princess
would say in an airy, off-hand manner (to show herself the great
lady) but in a voice that suddenly rang false. "But you may want to
talk to each other." "Really, you're in a hurry? Oh, very well,
I shall come and see you," the lady of the house would reply to
those whom she would just as soon see leave. The Duke and
Duchess would give a very civil greeting to people whom they

had seen there regularly for years though without coming to know them any better, while these in return barely said good-day to them, from discretion. Scarcely had they left the room before the Duke would begin asking good-naturedly who they were, so as to appear to be taking an interest in the intrinsic quality of people whom he never saw in his own house owing to the malevolence of fate or the state of Oriane's nerves which the company of women was bad for:

"Tell me, who was that little woman in the pink hat?"

"Why, my dear cousin, you've seen her hundreds of times, she's the Vicomtesse de Tours, who was a Lamarzelle."

"But, do you know, she's very pretty, and she has a witty look. If it weren't for a little flaw in her upper lip she'd be a regular charmer. If there's a Vicomte de Tours, he can't have any too bad a time. Oriane, do you know who her eyebrows and the way her hair grows reminded me of? Your cousin Hedwige de Ligne."

The Duchesse de Guermantes, who languished whenever people spoke of the beauty of any woman other than herself, let the subject drop. She had reckoned without the weakness of her husband for letting it be seen that he knew all about the people who did not come to his house, whereby he believed that he showed himself to be more "serious" than his wife.

"But," he would suddenly resume with emphasis, "you mentioned the name Lamarzelle. I remember, when I was in the Chamber, hearing a really remarkable speech made. . . "

"That was the uncle of the young woman you saw just now."

"Indeed! What talent! No, my dear girl," he assured the Vicomtesse d'Egremont, whom Mme de Guermantes could not endure but who, refusing to stir from the Princesse d'Epinay's drawing-room where she willingly stooped to the role of parlour-maid (though it did not prevent her from slapping her own on returning home), stayed there, tearful and abashed, but nevertheless stayed, when the ducal couple were there, taking their cloaks, trying to make herself useful, discreetly offering to withdraw into the next room, "you're not to make tea for us, let's just sit and talk quietly, we're simple, homely souls. Besides," he went on, turning to the Princesse d'Epinay (leaving the Egremont lady blushing, humble, ambitious and full of zeal), "we can only spare you a quarter of an hour."

This quarter of an hour would be entirely taken up with a sort of exhibition of the witty things which the Duchess had said during the previous week, and to which she herself would certainly have refrained from alluding had not her husband, with great adroitness, by appearing to be rebuking her with reference to the incidents that had provoked them, obliged her as though against her will to repeat them.

The Princesse d'Epinay, who was fond of her cousin and knew that she had a weakness for compliments, would go into ecstasies over her hat, her sunshade, her wit. "Talk to her as much as you like about her clothes," the Duke would say in the surly tone which he had adopted and now tempered with a mocking smile so that his displeasure should not be taken seriously, "but for heaven's sake don't speak of her wit. I could do without having such a witty wife. You're probably alluding to the shocking pun she made about my brother Palamède," he went on, knowing quite well that the Princess and the rest of the family had not yet heard this pun, and delighted to have an opportunity of showing off his wife. "In the first place I consider it unworthy of a person who has occasionally, I must admit, said some quite good things, to make bad puns, but especially about my brother, who is very touchy, and if it's going to lead to bad blood between us, that would really be too much of a good thing."

"But we've no idea! One of Oriane's puns? It's sure to be delicious. Oh, do tell us!"

"No, no," the Duke went on, still surly though with a broader smile, "I'm delighted you haven't heard it. Seriously, I'm very fond of my brother."

"Look here, Basin," the Duchess would break in, the moment having come for her to take up her husband's cue, "I can't think why you should say that it might annoy Palamède, you know quite well it would do nothing of the sort. He's far too intelligent to be offended by a stupid joke which has nothing offensive about it. You'll make them think I said something nasty; I simply made a remark which wasn't in the least funny, it's you who make it seem important by getting so indignant. I don't understand you."

"You're being horribly tantalising. What's it all about?"

"Oh, obviously nothing serious!" cried M. de Guermantes. "You may have heard that my brother offered to give Brézé, the place he got from his wife, to his sister Marsantes."

"Yes, but we were told she didn't want it, that she didn't care for that part of the country, that the climate didn't suit her."

"Precisely. Well, someone was telling my wife all that and saying that if my brother was giving this place to our sister it wasn't so much to please her as to tease her. 'He's such a teaser, Charlus,' was what they actually said. Well, you know Brézé is really impressive, I should say it's worth millions, it used to be part of the crown lands, it includes one of the finest forests in France. There are plenty of people who would be only too delighted to be teased to that tune. And so when she heard the words 'teaser' applied to Charlus because he was giving away such a magnificent property, Oriane couldn't help exclaiming, quite involuntarily, I must admit, without the slightest suggestion of malice, for it came out like a flash of lightning: 'Teaser, teaser? Then he must be Teaser Augustus!' You understand," he went on, resuming his surly tone, having first cast a sweeping glance round the room in order to judge the effect of his wife's witticism—and in some doubt as to the extent of Mme d'Epinay's acquaintance with ancient history, "you understand, it's an allusion to Augustus Caesar, the Roman Emperor. It's too stupid, a bad play on words, quite unworthy of Oriane. And then, you see, I'm more circumspect than my wife. Even if I haven't her wit, I think of the consequences. If anyone should be so ill-advised as to repeat the remark to my brother there'll be the devil to pay. All the more so," he went on, "because as you know Palamède is very high and mighty, and also very captious, given to tittle-tattle, so that quite apart from the question of his giving away Brézé you must admit that 'Teaser Augustus' suits him down to the ground. That's what justifies my wife's quips; even when she stoops to feeble puns, she's always witty and does really describe people rather well."

And so, thanks on one occasion to "Teaser Augustus," on another to something else, the visits paid by the Duke and Duchess to their kinsfolk replenished the stock of anecdotes, and the excitement they had caused lasted long after the departure of the sparkling lady and her impresario. The hostess would begin by going over again with the privileged persons who had been at the entertainment (those who had remained) the clever things that Oriane had said. "You hadn't heard 'Teaser Augustus'?" the Princesse d'Epinay would ask. "Yes," the Marquise de Baveno would reply, blushing as she spoke, "the Princesse de Sarsina-La Rochefoucauld mentioned it to me, not quite in the same terms. But of course it was far more interesting to hear it repeated like that with my cousin in the room," she went on, as though speaking of a song that had been accompanied by the composer himself. "We were speaking of Oriane's latest—she was here just now," her hostess would greet a visitor who was very disconsolate at not having arrived an hour earlier.

"What! has Oriane been here?"

"Yes, if you'd come a little sooner . . ." the Princesse d'Epinay replied, not in reproach but making it clear how much the blunderer had missed. It was her fault alone if she had not been present at the creation of the world or at Mme Carvalho's last performance. "What do you think of Oriane's latest? I must say I do like 'Teaser Augustus,'" and the quip would be served up again cold next day at lunch before a few intimate friends invited for the purpose, and would reappear under various sauces throughout the week. Indeed Mme d'Epinay happening in the course of that week to pay her annual visit to the Princesse de Parme, seized the opportunity to ask whether Her Royal Highness had heard the pun, and repeated it to her. "Ah! Teaser Augustus," said the Princesse de Parme, wide-eyed with an *a priori* admiration, which begged however for a complementary elucidation which Mme d'Epinay was not loth to furnish. "I must say Teaser Augustus pleases me enormously as a piece of 'phrasing,'" she concluded. As a matter of fact the word "phrasing" was not in the least applicable to this pun, but the Princesse d'Epinay, who claimed to have assimilated her share of the Guermantes wit, had borrowed from Oriane the expressions "phrased" and "phrasing" and employed them without much discrimination. Now the Princesse de Parme, who was not at all fond of Mme d'Epinay, whom she considered plain, knew to be miserly, and believed, on the authority of the Courvoisiers, to be malicious, recognised this word "phrasing" which she had heard on Mme de Guermantes's lips but would not herself have known how or when to apply. She concluded that it must indeed be its "phrasing" that formed the charm of "Teaser Augustus" and, without altogether forgetting her antipathy towards the plain and miserly lady, could not repress an impulse of admiration for a person endowed to such a degree with the Guermantes wit, so much so that she was on the point of inviting the Princesse d'Epinay to the Opéra. She was held in check only by the reflexion that it would be wiser perhaps to consult Mme de Guermantes first. As for Mme d'Epinay, who, unlike the Courvoisiers, was endlessly obliging towards Oriane and was genuinely fond of her, but was jealous of her exalted friends and slightly irritated by the fun which the Duchess used to make of her in front of everyone on account of her meanness, she reported on her return home how much difficulty the Princesse de Parme had had in grasping the point of "Teaser Augustus," and declared what a snob Oriane must be to number such a goose among her friends. "I should never have been able to see much of the Princesse de Parme even if I had wanted to, because M. d'Epinay would never have allowed it on account of her immorality," she told the friends who were dining with her, alluding to certain purely imaginary excesses on the part of the Princess. "But even if I had had a husband less strict in his views, I must say I could never have made friends with her. I don't know how Oriane can bear to see her every other day, as she does. I go there once a year, and it's all I can do to sit out my call."

As for those of the Courvoisiers who happened to be at Victurnienne's on the day of Mme de Guermantes's visit, the arrival of the Duchess generally put them to flight owing to the exasperation they felt at the "ridiculous salaams" that were made to her there. One alone remained on the evening of "Teaser Augustus." He did not entirely see the point, but he half-understood it, being an educated man. And the Courvoisiers went about repeating that Oriane had called uncle Palamède "Caesar Augustus," which was, according to them, a good enough description of him. But why all this endless talk about Oriane, they went on. People couldn't make more fuss about a queen. "After all, what is Oriane? I don't say the Guermantes aren't an old family, but the Courvoisiers are inferior to them in nothing, neither in illustriousness, nor in antiquity, nor in alliances. We mustn't forget that on the Field of the Cloth of Gold, when the King of England asked François I who was the noblest of the lords there present, 'Sire,' said the King of France, 'Courvoisier.'" But even if all the Courvoisiers had stayed in the room to hear them, Oriane's witticisms would have fallen on deaf ears, since the incidents that usually gave rise to them would have been regarded by them from a totally different point of view. If, for instance, a Courvoisier found herself running short of chairs in the middle of a reception she was giving, or if she used the wrong name in greeting a guest whose face she did not remember, or if one of her servants said something stupid, the Courvoisier lady, extremely annoyed, flushed, quivering with agitation, would deplore so unfortunate an occurrence. And when she had a visitor in the room, and Oriane was expected, she would ask in an anxious and imperious tone: "Do you know her?", fearing that if the visitor did not know her his presence might make a bad impression on Oriane. But Mme de Guermantes on the contrary drew from such incidents opportunities for stories which made the Guermantes laugh until the tears streamed down their cheeks, so that one was obliged to envy the lady for having run short of chairs, for having herself made or allowed her servant to make a gaffe, for having had at a party someone whom nobody knew, as one is obliged to be thankful that great writers have been kept at a distance by men and betrayed by women when their humiliations and their sufferings have been if not the direct stimulus of their genius at any rate the subject matter of their works.

The Courvoisiers were equally incapable of rising to the spirit of innovation which the Duchesse de Guermantes introduced into the life of society and which, by adapting it with an unerring instinct to the necessities of the moment, made it into something artistic, where the purely rational application of cut and dried rules would have produced results as unfortunate as would greet a man who, anxious to succeed in love or in politics, reproduced to the letter in his own life the exploits of Bussy d'Amboise. If the Courvoisiers gave a family dinner or a dinner to meet some prince, the addition of a recognised wit, of some friend of their son, seemed to them an anomaly capable of producing the direst consequences. A Courvoisier lady whose father had been a minister under the Empire, having to give an afternoon party in honour of the Princesse Mathilde, deduced with a geometrical logic that she could invite no one but Bonapartists—of whom she knew practically none. All the smart women of her acquaintance, all the amusing men, were ruthlessly barred because, with their Legitimist views or connexions, they might, according to Courvoisier logic, have given offence to the Imperial Highness. The latter, who in her own house entertained the flower of the Faubourg Saint-Germain, was somewhat surprised when she found at Mme de Courvoisier's only a notorious old sponger whose husband had been a prefect under the Empire, the widow of the Director of Posts, and sundry others known for their loyalty to Napoleon III, for their stupidity and for their dullness. The Princesse Mathilde nevertheless in no way constrained the sweet and generous outpouring of her sovereign grace over these calamitous ugly ducklings, whom the Duchesse de Guermantes, for her part, took good care not to invite when it was her turn to entertain the Princess, but substituted for them, without any *a priori* reasoning about Bonapartism, the most brilliant coruscation of all the beauties, all the talents, all the celebrities whom, by some subtle sixth sense, she felt likely to be acceptable to the niece of the Emperor even when they actually belonged to the Royal House. Not even the Duc d'Aumale was excluded, and when, on withdrawing, the Princess, raising Mme de Guermantes from the ground where she had sunk in a curtsey and was about to kiss the august hand, embraced her on both cheeks, it was from the bottom of her heart that she was able to assure the Duchess that never had she spent a happier afternoon nor attended so successful a party. The Princesse de Parme was Courvoisier in her incapacity for innovation in social matters but unlike the Courvoisiers in that the surprise that was perpetually caused her by the Duchesse de Guermantes engendered in her not, as in them, antipathy, but wonderment. This feeling was still further enhanced by the infinitely backward state of the Princess's education. Mme de Guermantes was herself a great deal less advanced than she supposed. But she had only to be a little ahead of Mme de Parme to astound that lady, and, as the critics of each generation confine themselves to maintaining the direct opposite of the truths acknowledged by their predecessors, she had only to say that Flaubert, that arch-enemy of the bourgeoisie, had been bourgeois through and through, or that there was a great deal of Italian music in Wagner, to open before the Princess, at the cost of a nervous exhaustion that was constantly renewed, as before the eyes of a swimmer in a stormy sea, horizons that seemed to her unimaginable and remained for ever dim. A stupefaction caused also by the paradoxes uttered not only in connexion with works of art but with persons of their acquaintance and with current social events. Doubtless the incapacity that prevented Mme de Parme from distinguishing the true wit of the Guermantes from certain rudimentarily acquired forms of that wit (which made her believe in the high intellectual worth of certain Guermantes, especially certain female Guermantes, of whom afterwards she was bewildered to hear the Duchess confide to her with a smile that they were mere nitwits) was one of the causes of the astonishment which the Princess always felt on hearing Mme de Guermantes criticise other people. But there was another cause also, one which I, who knew at that time more books than people and literature better than life, explained to myself by thinking that the Duchess, living this worldly life the idleness and sterility of which are to a true social activity what, in art, criticism is to creation, extended to the persons who surrounded her the instability of viewpoint, the unhealthy thirst, of the caviller who, to slake a mind that has grown too dry, goes in search of no matter what paradox that is still fairly fresh, and will not hesitate to uphold the thirst-quenching opinion that the really great *Iphigenia* is Piccinni's and not Gluck's, and at a pinch that the true *Phèdre* is that of Pradon.

When an intelligent, witty, educated woman had married a shy bumpkin whom one seldom saw and never heard, Mme de Guermantes one fine day would find a rare intellectual pleasure not only in decrying the wife but in "discovering" the husband. In the Cambremer household, for example, if she had lived in that section of society at the time, she would have decreed that Mme de Cambremer was stupid, and on the other hand, that the interesting person, misunderstood, delightful, condemned to silence by a chattering wife but himself worth a thousand of her, was the Marquis, and the Duchess would have felt on declaring this the same kind of refreshment as the critic who, after people have been admiring *Hernani* for seventy years, confesses to a preference for *Le Lion amoureux*. And from this same morbid need of arbitrary novelties, if from her girlhood everyone had been pitying a model wife, a true saint, for being married to a scoundrel, one fine day Mme de Guermantes would assert that this scoundrel was perhaps a frivolous man but one with a heart of gold, whom the implacable harshness of his wife had driven to behave irrationally. I knew that it was not only between the works of different artists, in the long course of the centuries, but between the different works of the same artist, that criticism enjoyed thrusting back into the shade what for too long had been radiant and bringing to the fore what seemed doomed to permanent obscurity. I had not only seen Bellini, Winterhalter, the Jesuit architects, a Restoration cabinet-maker, come to take the place of men of genius who were described as tired simply because idle intellectuals had grown tired of them, as neurasthenics are always tired and fickle; I had seen Sainte-Beuve preferred alternately as critic and as poet, Musset rejected so far as his poetry went save for a few insignificant pieces, and extolled as a story-teller. No doubt certain essayists are mistaken when they set above the most famous scenes in *Le Cid* or *Polyeucte* some speech from *Le Menteur* which, like an old plan, gives us information about the Paris of the day, but their predilection, justified if not by considerations of beauty at least by a documentary interest, is still too rational for our criticism run mad. It will barter the whole of Molière for a line from *L'Etourdi*, and even when it pronounces Wagner's *Tristan* a bore will except a "charming note on the horns" at the point where the hunt goes by. This depravity of taste helped me to understand the similar perversity in Mme de Guermantes that made her decide that a man of their world, who was recognised as a good fellow but a fool, was a monster of egoism, sharper than people thought, that another who was well known for his generosity might be considered the personification of avarice, that a good mother paid no attention to her children, and that a woman generally supposed to be vicious was really actuated by the noblest sentiments. As though corrupted by the nullity of life in society, the intelligence and sensibility of Mme de Guermantes were too vacillating for disgust not to follow pretty swiftly in the wake of infatuation (leaving her still ready to be attracted afresh by the kind of cleverness which she had alternately sought and abandoned) and for the charm which she had found in some warm-hearted man not to change, if he came too often to see her, sought too freely from her a guidance which she was incapable of giving him, into an irritation which she believed to be produced by her admirer but which was in fact due to the utter impossibility of finding pleasure when one spends all one's time seeking it. The Duchess's vagaries of judgment spared no one, except her husband. He alone had never loved her; in him she had always felt an iron character, indifferent to her whims, contemptuous of her beauty, violent, one of those unbreakable wills under whose rule alone highly-strung people can find tranquillity. M. de Guermantes for his part, pursuing a single type of feminine beauty but seeking it in mistresses whom he constantly replaced, had, once he had left them, and to share with him in mocking them, one lasting and identical partner, who irritated him often by her chatter but whom he knew that everyone regarded as the most beautiful, the most virtuous, the cleverest, the best-read member of the aristocracy, as a wife whom he, M. de Guermantes, was only too fortunate to have found, who covered up for all his irregularities, entertained like no one else in the world, and upheld for their salon its position as the premier in the Faubourg Saint-Germain. This common opinion he himself shared; often bad-tempered with his wife, he was proud of her. If, being as niggardly as he was ostentatious, he refused her the most trifling sums for her charities or for the servants, yet he insisted on her having the most sumptuous clothes and the finest equipages in Paris. And finally, he enjoyed bringing out his wife's wit. Now, whenever Mme de Guermantes had just thought up, with reference to the merits and defects, suddenly transposed, of one of their friends, a new and succulent paradox, she longed to try it out on people capable of appreciating it, to bring out the full savour of its psychological originality and the brilliance of its epigrammatic malice. Of course these new opinions contained as a rule no more truth than the old, often less; but this very element of arbitrariness and unexpected-ness conferred on them an intellectual quality which made them exciting to communicate. However, the patient on whom the Duchess was exercising her psychological skill was generally an intimate friend as to whom the people to whom she longed to hand on her discovery were entirely unaware that he was not still at the apex of her favour; thus Mme de Guermantes's reputation for being an incomparable friend, sentimental, tender and devoted, made it difficult for her to launch the attack herself; she could at the most intervene later on, as though under con-straint, by taking up a cue in order to appease, to contradict in appearance but actually to support a partner who had taken it on himself to provoke her; this was precisely the role in which M. de Guermantes excelled.

As for social activities, Mme de Guermantes enjoyed yet another arbitrarily theatrical pleasure in expressing thereon some of those unexpected judgments which whipped the Princesse de Parme into a state of perpetual and delicious surprise. In the case of this particular pleasure of the Duchess's, it was not so much with the help of literary criticism as from the example of political life and the reports of parliamentary debates that I tried to understand in what it might consist. The successive and contradictory edicts by which Mme de Guermantes continually reversed the scale of values among the people of her world no longer sufficing to distract her, she sought also in the manner in which she ordered her own social behaviour, in which she accounted for her own most trifling decisions on points of fashion, to savour those artifi-cial emotions, to fulfil those factitious obligations, which stir the feelings of parliaments and impress themselves on the minds of politicians. We know that when a minister explains to the Chamber that he believed himself to be acting rightly in following a line of conduct which does indeed appear quite straightforward to the commonsense person who reads the report of the sitting in his newspaper next morning, this commonsense reader nevertheless feels suddenly stirred and begins to doubt whether he has been right in approving the minister's conduct when he sees that the latter's speech was listened to in an uproar and punctuated with expressions of condemnation such as: "It's most serious!" pronounced by a Deputy whose name and titles are so long, and followed in the report by reactions so emphatic, that in the whole interruption the words "It's most serious!" occupy less room than a hemistich in an alexandrine. For instance in the days when M. de Guermantes, Prince des Laumes, sat in the Chamber, one used to read now and then in the Paris newspapers, although it was intended primarily for the Méséglise constituency, to show the electors there that they had not given their votes to an inactive or voiceless representative:

MONSIEUR DE GUERMANTES-BOUILLON, PRINCE DES LAUMES: "This is serious!" (*"Hear, hear!" from the centre and some of the benches on the right, loud exclamations from the extreme left.*)

The commonsense reader still retains a glimmer of loyalty to the sage minister, but his heart is convulsed with a fresh palpitation by the first words of the speaker who rises to reply:

"The astonishment, it is not too much to say the stupor" (*keen sensation on the right side of the House*) "that I have felt at the words of one who is still, I presume, a member of the Government..." (*thunderous applause; several Deputies then rush towards the ministerial bench. The Under-Secretary of State for Posts and Telegraphs, without rising from his seat, gives an affirmative nod.*)

This "thunderous applause" carries away the last shred of resistance in the mind of the commonsense reader: he regards as an insult to the Chamber, monstrous in fact, a way of proceeding which in itself is of no great significance. It may be some quite straightforward item, such as wanting to make the rich pay more than the poor, bringing to light some piece of injustice, preferring peace to war, but he will find it scandalous and will see it as an offence to certain principles to which in fact he had never given a thought, which are not engraved in the heart of man, but which move him strongly by reason of the acclamations which they provoke and the majorities which they assemble.

It must at the same time be recognised that this subtlety of the politician which served to explain to me the Guermantes circle, and other groups in society later on, is no more than the perversion of a certain nicety of interpretation often described by the expression "reading between the lines." If in representative assemblies there is absurdity owing to the perversion of this quality, there is equally stupidity, through the lack of it, in the public who take everything literally, who do not suspect a dismissal when a high dignitary is relieved of his office "at his own request," and say: "He cannot have been dismissed, since it was he who asked to go," or a defeat when, in the face of the Japanese advance, the Russians by a strategic manoeuvre fall back on stronger positions, prepared in advance, or a refusal when, a province having demanded its independence from the German Emperor, he grants it religious autonomy. It is possible, moreover (to revert to these sittings of the Chamber), that when they open the Deputies themselves are like the commonsense person who will read the published report. Learning that certain workers on strike have sent their delegates to confer with a minister, they may ask themselves naïvely: "There now, I wonder what they can have been saying; let's hope it's all settled," at the moment when the minister himself rises to address the House in a solemn silence which has already brought artificial emotions into play. The minister's first words: "There is no necessity for me to inform the Chamber that I have too high a sense of what is the duty of the Government to have received a deputation of which the authority entrusted to me could take no cognisance," produce a dramatic effect, for this was the one hypothesis which the commonsense of the Deputies had failed to foresee. But precisely because of its dramatic effect it is greeted with such applause that it is only after several minutes have passed that the minister can succeed in making himself heard, and on returning to his bench he will receive the congratulations of his colleagues. They are as deeply moved as on the day when the same minister failed to invite to a big official reception the chairman of the municipal council who supported the Opposition, and they declare that on this occasion as on the other he has acted with true statesmanship.

M. de Guermantes at this period of his life had, to the great scandal of the Courvoisiers, frequently been among the crowd of Deputies who came forward to congratulate the minister. I later heard it said that even at a time when he was playing a fairly important role in the Chamber and was being thought of in connexion with ministerial office or an embassy, he was, when a friend came to ask a favour of him, infinitely more simple, behaved politically a great deal less like a person of importance, than anyone else who did not happen to be Duc de Guermantes. For if he said that nobility was of no account, that he regarded his colleagues as equals, he did not believe it for a moment. He sought, and pretended to value, but really despised political position, and as he remained in his own eyes M. de Guermantes it did not envelop his person in that starchiness of high office which makes others unapproachable. And in this way his pride protected against every assault not only his manners, which were of an ostentatious familiarity, but also such true simplicity as he might actually possess.

To return to those artificial and dramatic decisions of hers, so like those of politicians, Mme de Guermantes was no less disconcerting to the Guermantes, the Courvoisiers, the Faubourg in general and, more than anyone, the Princesse de Parme, in her habit of issuing unaccountable decrees behind which one sensed latent principles which impressed one all the more the less one was aware of them. If the new Greek Minister gave a fancy dress ball, everyone chose a costume and wondered what the Duchess would wear. One thought that she would appear as the Duchesse de Bourgogne, another suggested as probable the guise of Princess of Deryabar, a third Psyche. Finally a Courvoisier, having asked her: "What are you going as, Oriane?", provoked the one response of which nobody had thought: "Why, nothing at all!", which at once set every tongue wagging, as revealing Oriane's opinion as to the true social position of the new Greek Minister and the proper attitude to adopt towards him, that is to say the opinion which ought to have been foreseen, namely that a duchess "wasn't obliged" to attend the fancy dress ball given by this new minister. "I don't see that there's any necessity to go to the Greek Minister's. I don't know him; I'm not Greek; why should I go to his house? I have nothing to do with him," said the Duchess.

"But everybody will be there, they say it's going to be charming!" cried Mme de Gallardon.

"But it's just as charming sometimes to sit by one's own fireside," replied Mme de Guermantes.

The Courvoisiers could not get over this, but the Guermantes, without copying their cousin, approved: "Naturally, everybody isn't in a position like Oriane to break with all the conventions.

But if you look at it in one way you can't say she's wrong to want to show that we do go rather too far in grovelling before these foreigners who appear from heaven knows where."

Naturally, knowing the stream of comment which one or other attitude would not fail to provoke, Mme de Guermantes took as much pleasure in appearing at a party to which her hostess had not dared to count on her coming as in staying at home or spending the evening at the theatre with her husband on the night of a party to which "everybody was going," or, again, when people imagined that she would eclipse the finest diamonds with some historic diadem, by stealing into the room without a single jewel, and in another style of dress than what had been wrongly supposed to be essential to the occasion. Although she was anti-Dreyfusard (while believing Dreyfus to be innocent, just as she spent her life in the social world while believing only in ideas), she had created an enormous sensation at a party at the Princesse de Ligne's, first of all by remaining seated when all the ladies had risen to their feet as General Mercier entered the room, and then by getting up and asking for her carriage in a loud voice when a nationalist orator had begun to address the gathering, thereby showing that she did not consider that society was meant for talking politics in; and all heads had turned towards her at a Good Friday concert at which, although a Voltairean, she had refused to remain because she thought it indecent to bring Christ on the stage. We know how important, even for the great queens of society, is that moment of the year at which the round of entertainment begins: so much so that the Marquise d'Amoncourt, who, from a need to say something, a psychological quirk, and also from a lack of sensitivity, was always making a fool of herself, had actually replied to somebody who had called to condole with her on the death of her father, M. de Montmorency: "What perhaps makes it still sadder is that it should come at a time when one's mirror is simply stuffed with cards!" Well, at this point in the social year, when people invited the Duchesse de Guermantes to dinner, hurrying so as to make sure that she was not already engaged, she declined for the one reason of which nobody in society would ever have thought: she was just setting off on a cruise in the Norwegian fjords, which were so interesting. The fashionable world was stunned, and, without any thought of following the Duchess's example, derived nevertheless from her action that sense of relief which one has in reading Kant when, after the most rigorous demonstration of determinism, one finds that above the world of necessity there is the world of freedom. Every invention of which no one had ever thought before excites the interest even of people who can derive no benefit from it. That of steam navigation was a small thing compared with the employment of steam navigation at that sedentary time of year called "the season." The idea that anyone could voluntarily renounce a hundred dinners or luncheons, twice as many afternoon teas, three times as many receptions, the most brilliant Mondays at the Opéra and Tuesdays at the Comédie-Française to visit the Norwegian fjords seemed to the Courvoisiers no more explicable than the idea of *Twenty Thousand Leagues under the Sea*, but conveyed to them a similar impression of independence and charm. So that not a day passed on which somebody might not be heard to ask, not merely: "You've heard Oriane's latest joke?" but "You know Oriane's latest?" and on "Oriane's latest" as on "Oriane's latest joke" would follow the comment: "How typical of Oriane!" "Isn't that pure Oriane?" Oriane's latest might be, for instance, that, having to write on behalf of a patriotic society to Cardinal X——, Bishop of Mâcon (whom M. de Guermantes when he spoke of him invariably called "Monsieur de Mascon," thinking this to be "old French"), when everyone was trying to imagine what form the letter would take, and had no difficulty as to the opening words, the choice lying between "Eminence" and "Monseigneur," but was puzzled as to the rest, Oriane's letter, to the general astonishment, began: "Monsieur le Cardinal," following an old academic form, or: "My cousin," this term being in use among the Princes of the Church, the Guermantes and crowned heads, who prayed to God to take each and all of them into "His fit and holy keeping." To start people on the topic of an "Oriane's latest" it was sufficient that at a performance at which all Paris was present and a most charming play was being given, when they looked for Mme de Guermantes in the boxes of the Princesse de Parme, the Princesse de Guermantes, countless other ladies who had invited her, they discovered her sitting by herself, in black, with a tiny hat on her head, in a stall in which she had arrived before the curtain rose. "You hear better, when it's a play that's worth listening to," she explained, to the scandal of the Courvoisiers and the admiring bewilderment of the Guermantes and the Princesse de Parme, who suddenly discovered that the "fashion" of hearing the beginning of a play was more up to date, was a proof of greater

originality and intelligence (which need not astonish them, coming from Oriane) than arriving for the last act after a big dinner-
party and having put in an appearance at a reception. Such were
the various kinds of surprise for which the Princesse de Parme
knew that she ought to be prepared if she put a literary or social
question to Mme de Guermantes, and because of which, during
these dinner-parties at Oriane's, Her Royal Highness never ventured upon the slightest topic save with the uneasy and enraptured
prudence of the bather emerging from between two breakers.

Among the elements which, absent from the three or four other
more or less equivalent salons that set the fashion for the Faubourg
Saint-Germain, differentiated that of the Duchesse de Guermantes
from them, just as Leibniz allows that each monad, while reflecting the entire universe, adds to it something of its own, one of the
least attractive was habitually furnished by one or two extremely
good-looking women who had no other right to be there but their
beauty and the use that M. de Guermantes had made of them, and
whose presence revealed at once, as does in other drawing-rooms
that of certain otherwise unaccountable pictures, that in this
household the husband was an ardent appreciator of feminine
graces. They were all more or less alike, for the Duke had a taste
for tall women, at once statuesque and airy, of a type half-way
between the Venus de Milo and the Winged Victory; often fair,
rarely dark, sometimes auburn, like the most recent, who was at
this dinner, that Vicomtesse d'Arpajon whom he had loved so well
that for a long time he had obliged her to send him as many as ten
telegrams daily (which slightly irritated the Duchess) and corresponded with her by carrier pigeon when he was at Guermantes,
and from whom moreover he had long been so incapable of
tearing himself away that, one winter which he had had to spend
at Parma, he travelled back regularly every week to Paris, spending
two days in the train, in order to see her.

As a rule these handsome supernumeraries had been his mistresses but were no longer (as was Mme d'Arpajon's case) or were
on the point of ceasing to be. It may well have been that the
glamour which the Duchess enjoyed in their eyes and the hope of
being invited to her house, though they themselves came from
thoroughly aristocratic backgrounds, if of the second rank, had
prompted them, even more than the good looks and generosity of
the Duke, to yield to his desires. Not that the Duchess would have
placed any insuperable obstacle in the way of their crossing her

threshold: she was aware that in more than one of them she had found an ally thanks to whom she had obtained countless things which she wanted but which M. de Guermantes pitilessly denied his wife so long as he was not in love with someone else. And so the reason why they were not received by the Duchess until their liaison was already far advanced lay principally in the fact that the Duke, each time he embarked on a love affair, had imagined no more than a brief fling, as a reward for which he considered an invitation from his wife excessive. And yet he found himself offering this as the price for far less, for a first kiss in fact, because he had met with unexpected resistance or, on the contrary, because there had been no resistance. In love it often happens that gratitude, the desire to give pleasure, make us generous beyond the limits of what hope and self-interest had foreseen. But then the realisation of this offer was hindered by conflicting circumstances. In the first place, all the women who had responded to M. de Guermantes's love, and sometimes even when they had not yet given themselves to him, he had one after another kept cut off from the world. He no longer allowed them to see anyone, spent almost all his time in their company, looked after the education of their children, to whom now and again, if one was to judge by certain striking resemblances later on, he had occasion to present a little brother or sister. And then if, at the start of the liaison, the prospect of an introduction to Mme de Guermantes, which had never been envisaged by the Duke, had played a part in the mistress's mind, the liaison in itself had altered the lady's point of view; the Duke was no longer for her merely the husband of the smartest woman in Paris, but a man with whom the new mistress was in love, a man moreover who had given her the means and the inclination for a more luxurious style of living and had transposed the relative importance in her mind of questions of social and of material advantage; while now and then a composite jealousy of Mme de Guermantes, into which all these factors entered, animated the Duke's mistresses. But this case was the rarest of all; besides, when the day appointed for the introduction at length arrived (at a point when as a rule it had more or less become a matter of indifference to the Duke, whose actions, like everyone else's, were more often dictated by previous actions than by the original motive which had ceased to exist), it frequently happened that it was Mme de Guermantes who had sought the acquaintance of the mistress in whom she hoped, and so greatly needed, to find a valuable ally against her dread husband. This is not to say that, except at rare moments, in their own house, when, if the Duchess talked too much, he let fall a few words or, more dreadful still, preserved a silence which petrified her, M. de Guermantes failed in his outward relations with his wife to observe what are called the forms. People who did not know them might easily be taken in. Sometimes in autumn, between racing at Deauville, taking the waters, and returning to Guermantes for the shooting, in the few weeks which people spend in Paris, since the Duchess had a liking for café-concerts, the Duke would go with her to spend the evening at one of these. The audience remarked at once, in one of those little open boxes in which there is just room for two, this Hercules in his "smoking" (for in France we give to everything that is more or less British the one name that it happens not to bear in England), his monocle screwed in his eye, a fat cigar, from which now and then he drew a puff of smoke, in his plump but finely shaped hand, on the ring-finger of which a sapphire glowed, keeping his eyes for the most part on the stage but, when he did let them fall upon the audience in which there was absolutely no one whom he knew, softening them with an air of gentleness, reserve, courtesy and considera-tion. When a song struck him as amusing and not too indecent, the Duke would turn round with a smile to his wife, would share with her, with a twinkle of good-natured complicity, the innocent merriment which the new song had aroused in him. And the spectators might believe that there was no better husband in the world than he, nor anyone more enviable than the Duchess— that woman outside whom every interest in the Duke's life lay, that woman whom he did not love, to whom he had never ceased to be unfaithful; and when the Duchess felt tired, they saw M. de Guermantes rise, put on her cloak with his own hands, arranging her necklaces so that they did not get caught in the lining, and clear a path for her to the exit with an assiduous and respectful attention which she received with the coldness of the woman of the world who sees in such behaviour simply conventional good manners, at times even with the slightly ironical bitterness of the disabused spouse who has no illusion left to shatter. But despite these externals (another element of that politeness which has transferred duty from the inner depths to the surface, at a period already remote but which still continues for its survivors) the life of the Duchess was by no means easy. M. de Guermantes only became generous and human again for a new mistress, who would, as it generally happened, take the Duchess's side; the latter saw the possibility arising for her once again of generosities towards inferiors, charities to the poor, and even for herself, later on, a new and sumptuous motor-car. But from the irritation which was provoked as a rule pretty rapidly in Mme de Guermantes by people whom she found too submissive, the Duke's mistresses were not exempt. Presently the Duchess grew tired of them. As it happened, at that moment too the Duke's liaison with Mme d'Arpajon was drawing to an end. Another mistress was in the offing.

No doubt the love which M. de Guermantes had borne each of them in succession would begin one day to make itself felt anew: in the first place this love, in dying, bequeathed them to the household like beautiful marble statues—beautiful to the Duke, become thus in part an artist, because he had loved them and was appreciative now of lines which he would not have appreciated without love—which brought into juxtaposition in the Duchess's drawing-room their forms that had long been inimical, devoured by jealousies and quarrels, and finally reconciled in the peace of friendship; and then this friendship itself was an effect of the love which had made M. de Guermantes observe in those who had been his mistresses virtues which exist in every human being but are perceptible only to the carnal eye, so much so that the ex-mistress who has become "a good friend" who would do anything in the world for one has become a cliché, like the doctor or father who is not a doctor or a father but a friend. But during a period of transition, the woman whom M. de Guermantes was preparing to abandon bewailed her lot, made scenes, showed herself exacting, appeared indiscreet, became a nuisance. The Duke would begin to take a dislike to her. Then Mme de Guermantes had a chance to bring to light the real or imagined defects of a person who annoyed her. Known to be kind, she would receive the constant telephone calls, the confidences, the tears of the abandoned mistress and make no complaint. She would laugh at them, first with her husband, then with a few chosen friends. And imagining that the pity which she showed for the unfortunate woman gave her the right to make fun of her, even to her face, whatever the lady might say, provided it could be included among the attributes of the ridiculous character which the Duke and Duchess had recently fabricated for her, Mme de Guermantes had no hesitation in exchanging glances of ironical connivance with her husband.

Meanwhile, as she sat down to table, the Princesse de Parme remembered that she had thought of inviting Mme d'Heudicourt to the Opéra, and, wishing to be assured that this would not in any way offend Mme de Guermantes, was preparing to sound her.

At this moment M. de Grouchy entered, his train having been held up for an hour owing to a derailment. He made what excuses he could. His wife, had she been a Courvoisier, would have died of shame. But Mme de Grouchy was not a Guermantes for nothing. As her husband was apologising for being late, "I see," she broke in, "that even in little things arriving late is a tradition in your family."

"Sit down, Grouchy, and don't let them fluster you," said the Duke. "Although I move with the times, I must admit that the Battle of Waterloo had its points, since it brought about the Restoration of the Bourbons, and, better still, in a way that made them unpopular. But you seem to be a regular Nimrod!"

"Well, as a matter of fact, I did get quite a good bag. I shall take the liberty of sending the Duchess six brace of pheasant tomorrow."

An idea seemed to flicker in the eyes of Mme de Guermantes. She insisted that M. de Grouchy must not give himself the trouble of sending the pheasants. And making a sign to the betrothed footman with whom I had exchanged a few words on my way from the Elstir room, "Poullein," she told him, "you will go tomorrow and fetch M. le Comte's pheasants and bring them straight back—you won't mind, will you, Grouchy, if I make a few little presents. Basin and I can't eat a dozen pheasants by ourselves."

"But the day after tomorrow will be soon enough," said M. de Grouchy.

"No, tomorrow suits me better," the Duchess insisted.

Poullein had turned pale; he would miss his rendezvous with his sweetheart. This was quite enough for the diversion of the Duchess, who liked to appear to be taking a human interest in everyone.

"I know it's your day off," she went on to Poullein, "all you've got to do is change with Georges; he can take tomorrow off and stay in the day after."

But the day after, Poullein's sweetheart would not be free. He had no interest in going out then. As soon as he had left the room, everyone complimented the Duchess on her kindness towards her servants.

"But I only behave towards them as I'd like people to behave to me."

"That's just it. They can say they've found a good place with you all right."

"Oh, nothing so very wonderful. But I think they all like me. That one is a little irritating because he's in love. He thinks it incumbent on him to go about with a long face."

At this point Poullein reappeared.

"You're quite right," said M. de Grouchy, "he doesn't look very cheerful. With those fellows one has to be kind but not too kind."

"I admit I'm not a very dreadful mistress. He'll have nothing to do all day but call for your pheasants, sit in the house doing nothing and eat his share of them."

"There are plenty of people who would be glad to be in his place," said M. de Grouchy, for envy makes men blind.

"Oriane," began the Princesse de Parme, "I had a visit the other day from your cousin d'Heudicourt; of course she's a highly intelligent woman; she's a Guermantes—need I say more?—but they tell me she has a spiteful tongue."

The Duke fastened on his wife a slow gaze of feigned stupefaction. Mme de Guermantes began to laugh. Gradually the Princess became aware of their pantomime.

"But . . . do you mean to say . . . you don't agree with me?" she stammered with growing uneasiness.

"Really, Ma'am, it's too good of you to pay any attention to Basin's faces. Now, Basin, you're not to hint nasty things about our cousins."

"Does he think she's too malicious?" inquired the Princess briskly.

"Oh, dear me, no!" replied the Duchess. "I don't know who told Your Highness that she was malicious. On the contrary, she's an excellent creature who never spoke ill of anyone, or did any harm to anyone."

"Ah!" sighed Mme de Parme, greatly relieved. "I must say I'd never noticed it either. But I know it's often difficult not to be a bit malicious when one has a great deal of wit . . . "

"Ah! now that is a quality of which she has even less."

"Less wit?" asked the stupefied Princess.

"Come now, Oriane," broke in the Duke in a plaintive tone, casting to right and left of him a glance of amusement, "you heard the Princess tell you that she was a superior woman."

"But isn't she?"

"Superior in chest measurement, at any rate."

"Don't listen to him, Ma'am, he's having you on; she's as stupid as a (h'm) goose," came in a loud and husky voice from Mme de Guermantes, who, a great deal more "old world" even than the Duke when she wasn't trying, often deliberately sought to be, but in a manner entirely different from the deliquescent, lace jabot style of her husband and in reality far more subtle, with a sort of almost peasant pronunciation which had a harsh and delicious flavour of the soil. "But she's the best woman in the world. Besides, I don't really know that one can call it stupidity when it's carried to such a point as that. I don't believe I ever met anyone quite like her; she's a case for a specialist, there's something pathological about her, she's a sort of 'natural' or cretin or 'mooncalf,' like the people you see in melodramas, or in L'Arlésienne. I always ask myself, when she comes here, whether the moment may not have arrived at which her intelligence is going to dawn, which makes me a little nervous always."

The Princess marvelled at these expressions, but remained astonished by the verdict. "She repeated to me—and so did Mme d'Epinay—your remark about 'Teaser Augustus.' It's delicious," she put in.

M. de Guermantes explained the joke to me. I wanted to tell him that his brother, who pretended not to know me, was expecting me that very evening at eleven o'clock. But I had not asked Robert whether I might mention this assignation, and as the fact that M. de Charlus had practically fixed it with me himself directly contradicted what he had told the Duchess, I judged it more tactful to say nothing.

"'Teaser Augustus' isn't bad," said M. de Guermantes, "but Mme d'Heudicourt probably didn't tell you a far wittier remark Oriane made to her the other day in reply to an invitation to luncheon."

"Oh, no! Do tell me!"

"Now Basin, you keep quiet. In the first place, it was a stupid remark, and it will make the Princess think me inferior even to my nitwit of a cousin. Though I don't know why I should call her my cousin. She's one of Basin's cousins. Still, I believe she is related to me in some sort of way."

"Oh!" cried the Princesse de Parme at the idea that she could possibly think Mme de Guermantes stupid, and protesting desperately that nothing could ever make the Duchess fall from the place she held in her estimation.

"Besides, we've already deprived her of the qualities of the mind, and since the remark in question tends to deny certain qualities of the heart, it seems to me inopportune to repeat it."

"'Deny her!' 'Inopportune!' How well she expresses herself!" said the Duke with a pretence of irony, to win admiration for the Duchess.

"Now, then, Basin, you're not to make fun of your wife."

"I should explain to your Royal Highness," went on the Duke, "that Oriane's cousin may be superior, good, stout, anything you like to mention, but she is not exactly—what shall I say—lavish."

"Yes, I know, she's terribly close-fisted," broke in the Princess.

"I should not have ventured to use the expression, but you have hit on exactly the right word. It's reflected in her housekeeping, and especially in the cooking, which is excellent, but strictly rationed."

"Which gives rise to some quite amusing scenes," M. de Bréauté interrupted him. "For instance, my dear Basin, I was down at Heudicourt one day when you were expected, Oriane and yourself. They had made the most sumptuous preparations when a footman brought in a telegram during the afternoon to say that you weren't coming."

"That doesn't surprise me!" said the Duchess, who not only was difficult to get, but liked people to know as much.

"Your cousin read the telegram, was duly distressed, then immediately, without missing a trick, telling herself that there was no point in going to unnecessary expense for so unimportant a gentleman as myself, called the footman back: 'Tell the cook not to put on the chicken!' she shouted after him. And that evening I heard her asking the butler: 'Well? What about the beef that was left over yesterday? Aren't you going to let us have that?'"

"All the same, one must admit that the fare you get there is of the very best," said the Duke, who fancied that in using this expression he was showing himself to be very old school. "I don't know any house where one eats better."

"Or less," put in the Duchess.

"It's quite wholesome and quite adequate for what you would call a vulgar yokel like myself," went on the Duke. "One doesn't outrun one's appetite."

"Oh, if it's to be taken as a cure, that's another matter. It's certainly more healthy than sumptuous. Not that it's as good as all that," added Mme de Guermantes, who was not at all pleased that the title of "best table in Paris" should be awarded to any but her own. "With my cousin it's just the same as with those costive authors who turn out a one-act play or a sonnet every fifteen years. The sort of thing people call little masterpieces, trifles that are perfect gems, in fact what I loathe most in the world. The cooking at Zénaïde's is not bad, but you would think it more ordinary if she was less parsimonious. There are some things her cook does quite well, and others he doesn't bring off. I've had some thoroughly bad dinners there, as in most houses, only they've done me less harm there because the stomach is, after all, more sensitive to quantity than to quality."

"Well, to get on with the story," the Duke concluded, "Zénaïde insisted that Oriane should go to luncheon there, and as my wife is not very fond of going out anywhere she resisted, wanted to be sure that under the pretence of a quiet meal she was not being trapped into some great junket, and tried in vain to find out who else would be of the party. 'You must come,' Zénaïde insisted, boasting of all the good things there would be to eat. 'You're going to have a purée of chestnuts, I need say no more than that, and there will be seven little *bouchées à la reine*.' 'Seven little *bouchées*!' cried Oriane, 'that means that we shall be at least eight!'"

There was silence for a few seconds, and then the Princess, having seen the point, let her laughter explode like a peal of thunder. "Ah! 'Then we shall be eight'—it's exquisite. How very well phrased!" she said, having by a supreme effort recalled the expression she had heard used by Mme d'Epinay, which this time was more appropriate.

"Oriane, that was very charming of the Princess, she said your remark was well phrased."

"But, my dear, you're telling me nothing new. I know how clever the Princess is," replied Mme de Guermantes, who readily appreciated a remark when it was uttered at once by a royal personage and in praise of her own wit. "I'm very proud that

Ma'am should appreciate my humble phrasings. I don't remember, though, that I ever did say such a thing, and if I did, it must have been to flatter my cousin, for if she had ordered seven 'mouthfuls,' the mouths, if I may so express myself, would have been a round dozen if not more."

During this time the Comtesse d'Arpajon, who, before dinner, had told me that her aunt would have been so happy to show me round her house in Normandy, was saying to me over the Prince d'Agrigente's head that where she would most like to entertain me was in the Côte d'Or, because there, at Pont-le-Duc, she would be at home.

"The archives of the château would interest you. There are some absolutely fascinating correspondences between all the most prominent people of the seventeenth, eighteenth and nineteenth centuries. I've spent many wonderful hours there, living in the past," she declared, and I remembered that M. de Guermantes had told me that she was extremely well up in literature.

"She owns all M. de Bornier's manuscripts," went on the Princess, speaking of Mme d'Heudicourt, and anxious to make the most of the good reasons she might have for befriending that lady.

"She must have dreamed it, I don't believe she ever even knew him," said the Duchess.

"What is especially interesting is that these correspondences are with people of different countries," went on the Comtesse d'Arpajon who, allied to the principal ducal and even reigning families of Europe, was always glad to remind people of the fact.

"Surely, Oriane," said M. de Guermantes, meaningly, "you can't have forgotten that dinner-party where you had M. de Bornier sitting next to you!" "But, Basin," the Duchess interrupted him, "if you mean to inform me that I knew M. de Bornier, why of course I did, he even called upon me several times, but I could never bring myself to invite him to the house because I should always have been obliged to have it disinfected afterwards with formol. As for the dinner you mean, I remember it only too well, but it was certainly not at Zénaïde's, who never set eyes on Bornier in her life and would probably think if you spoke to her of *La Fille de Roland* that you meant a Bonaparte princess who is said to be engaged to the son of the King of Greece;[31] no, it was at the Austrian Embassy. Dear Hoyos imagined he was giving me a great treat by planting that pestiferous academician on the chair next to mine. I quite thought I had a squadron of mounted police sitting beside me. I was obliged to stop my nose as best I could all through dinner; I didn't dare breathe until the gruyère came round."

M. de Guermantes, having achieved his secret objective, made a furtive examination of his guests' faces to judge the effect of the Duchess's pleasantry.

"As a matter of fact I find that old correspondences have a peculiar charm," the lady who was well up in literature and had such fascinating letters in her château went on, in spite of the intervening head of the Prince d'Agrigente. "Have you noticed how often a writer's letters are superior to the rest of his work? What's the name of that author who wrote *Salammbô*?"

I should have liked not to have to reply in order not to prolong this conversation, but I felt it would be disobliging to the Prince d'Agrigente, who had pretended to know perfectly well who *Salammbô* was and out of pure politeness to be leaving it to me to say, but who was now in a painful quandary.

"Flaubert," I ended up by saying, but the vigorous signs of assent that came from the Prince's head smothered the sound of my reply, so that my interlocutress was not exactly sure whether I had said Paul Bert or Fulbert, names which she did not find entirely satisfactory.

"In any case," she went on, "how intriguing his correspondence is, and how superior to his books! It explains him, in fact, because one sees from everything he says about the difficulty he has in writing a book that he wasn't a real writer, a gifted man."

"Talking of correspondence, I must say I find Gambetta's admirable," said the Duchesse de Guermantes, to show that she was not afraid to be found taking an interest in a proletarian and a radical. M. de Bréauté, who fully appreciated the brilliance of this feat of daring, gazed round him with an eye at once tipsy and affectionate, after which he wiped his monocle.

"Gad, it's infernally dull, that *Fille de Roland*," said M. de Guermantes (who was still on the subject of M. de Bornier), with the satisfaction which he derived from the sense of his own superiority over a work which had bored him so much, and perhaps also from the *suave mari magno* feeling one has in the middle of a good dinner, when one recalls such terrible evenings in the past. "Still, there were some quite good lines in it, and a patriotic feeling."

I made a remark that implied that I had no admiration for M. de Bornier.

"Ah! have you got something against him?" the Duke asked with genuine curiosity, for he always imagined when anyone spoke ill of a man that it must be on account of a personal resentment, just as to speak well of a woman marked the beginning of a love affair. "You've obviously got a grudge against him. What did he do to you? You must tell us. Why yes, there must be some skeleton in the cupboard or you wouldn't run him down. It's long-winded, *La Fille de Roland*, but it's quite strong in parts."

"Strong is just the word for such an odorous author," Mme de Guermantes broke in sarcastically. "If this poor boy ever found himself in his company I can quite understand that he got up his nostrils!"

"I must confess, though, Ma'am," the Duke went on, addressing the Princesse de Parme, "that quite apart from *La Fille de Roland*, in literature and even in music I'm terribly old-fashioned; no old junk can be too stale for my taste. You won't believe me, perhaps, but in the evenings, if my wife sits down to the piano, I find myself calling for some old tune by Auber or Boieldieu, or even Beethoven! That's the sort of thing I like. As for Wagner, he sends me to sleep at once."

"You're wrong there," said Mme de Guermantes. "In spite of his insufferable long-windedness, Wagner was a genius. *Lohengrin* is a masterpiece. Even in *Tristan* there are some intriguing passages here and there. And the Spinning Chorus in the *Flying Dutchman* is a perfect marvel."

"Aren't I right, Babal," said M. de Guermantes, turning to M. de Bréauté, "what we like is:

> The gatherings of noble companions
> Are all of them held in this charming haunt.[32]

It's delightful. And *Fra Diavolo* and the *Magic Flute*, and *Le Chalet*, and the *Marriage of Figaro*, and *Les Diamants de la Couronne*—there's music for you! It's the same thing in literature. For instance, I adore Balzac, *Le Bal de Sceaux*, *Les Mohicans de Paris*."

"Ah! my dear man, if you're off on the subject of Balzac we'll be here all night. Keep it for some evening when Mémé's here. He's even better, he knows it all by heart."

Irritated by his wife's interruption, the Duke held her for some seconds under the fire of a menacing silence. Meanwhile Mme d'Arpajon had been exchanging with the Princesse de Parme some remarks about poetry, tragic and otherwise, which did not reach me distinctly until I caught the following from Mme d'Arpajon: "Oh, I quite agree with all that, I admit he makes the world seem ugly because he's unable to distinguish between ugliness and beauty, or rather because his insufferable vanity makes him believe that everything he says is beautiful. I agree with your Highness that in the piece in question there are some ridiculous things, unintelligible, and errors of taste, and that it's difficult to understand, that it's as much trouble to read as if it was written in Russian or Chinese, because obviously it's anything in the world but French; but still, when one has taken the trouble, how richly one is rewarded, it's so full of imagination!"

I had missed the opening sentences of this little lecture. I gathered in the end not only that the poet incapable of distinguishing between beauty and ugliness was Victor Hugo, but furthermore that the poem which was as difficult to understand as Chinese or Russian was

> When the child appears, the family circle
> Applauds with loud cries . . .

a piece dating from the poet's earliest period, and perhaps even nearer to Mme Deshoulières[33] than to the Victor Hugo of the *Légende des Siècles*. Far from thinking Mme d'Arpajon ridiculous, I saw her (the first person at this table, so real and so ordinary, at which I had sat down with such keen disappointment), I saw her in my mind's eye crowned with that lace cap, with the long spiral ringlets falling from it on either side, which was worn by Mme de Rémusat, Mme de Broglie, Mme de Saint-Aulaire, all those distinguished ladies who in their delightful letters quote with such learning and such aptness Sophocles, Schiller and the *Imitation*, but in whom the earliest poetry of the Romantics induced the alarm and exhaustion inseparable for my grandmother from the later verses of Stéphane Mallarmé.

"Mme d'Arpajon is very fond of poetry," said the Princesse de Parme to her hostess, impressed by the ardent tone in which the speech had been delivered.

"No, she doesn't understand the first thing about it," replied Mme de Guermantes in an undertone, taking advantage of the fact that Mme d'Arpajon, who was dealing with an objection raised by General de Beautreillis, was too intent upon what she herself was saying to hear what was being murmured by the Duchess. "She has become literary since she's been forsaken. I may tell your Highness that it's I who have to bear the brunt of it because it's to me that she comes to complain whenever Basin hasn't been to see her, which is practically every day. But it isn't my fault, after all, if she bores him, and I can't force him to go to her, although I'd rather he were a little more faithful, because then I shouldn't see quite so much of her myself. But she drives him mad and I'm not surprised. She isn't a bad sort, but she's boring to a degree you can't imagine. She gives me such a headache every day that I'm obliged to take a pyramidon tablet whenever she comes. And all this because Basin took it into his head for a year or so to go to bed with her. And on top of that to have a footman who's in love with a little tart and goes about with a long face if I don't ask the young person to leave her profitable pavement for half an hour and come to tea with me! Oh! life is really too tedious!" the Duchess languorously concluded.

Mme d'Arpajon bored M. de Guermantes principally because he had recently become the lover of another woman, whom I discovered to be the Marquise de Surgis-le-Duc. As it happened, the footman who had been deprived of his day off was at that moment waiting at table. And it struck me that, still disconsolate, he was doing it with some lack of composure, for I noticed that in handing the dish to M. de Châtellerault he performed his task so awkwardly that the young Duke's elbow came in contact several times with his. The young Duke showed no sign of annoyance with the blushing footman, but on the contrary looked up at him with a smile in his clear blue eyes. This good humour seemed to me to betoken kindness on the guest's part. But the insistency of his smile led me to think that, aware of the servant's discomfiture, what he felt was perhaps a malicious amusement.

"But, my dear, you know you're not revealing any new discovery when you tell us about Victor Hugo," went on the Duchess, this time addressing Mme d'Arpajon whom she had just seen turn round with a worried look. "You mustn't expect to launch that young genius. Everybody knows that he has talent. What is utterly detestable is the Victor Hugo of the last stage, the *Légende des Siècles*, I forget all their names. But in the *Feuilles d'Automne*, the *Chants du Crépuscule*, there's much of a poet, a true poet. Even in the *Contemplations*," went on the Duchess, whom none of her listeners dared to contradict, and with good reason, "there are still some quite pretty things. But I confess that

I prefer not to venture further than the *Crépuscule*! And then in the finer poems of Victor Hugo, and there really are some, one frequently comes across an idea, even a profound idea."

And with just the right shade of feeling, bringing out the sorrowful thought with the full force of her intonation, projecting it somewhere beyond her voice, and fixing straight in front of her a charming, dreamy gaze, the Duchess slowly recited:

> "Sorrow is a fruit, God does not cause it to grow
> On a branch that is still too feeble to bear it.

Or again:

> The dead last so short a time . . .
> Alas, in the coffin they crumble into dust,
> Less quickly than in our hearts!"

And, while a smile of disillusionment puckered her sorrowful lips with a graceful sinuosity, the Duchess fastened on Mme d'Arpajon the dreamy gaze of her lovely clear blue eyes. I was beginning to know them, as well as her voice, with its heavy drawl, its harsh savour. In those eyes and in that voice, I recognised much of the life of nature round Combray. Certainly, in the affectation with which that voice betrayed at times a rudeness of the soil, there was more than one element: the wholly provincial origin of one branch of the Guermantes family, which had for long remained more localised, more hardy, wilder, more combative than the rest; and then the ingrained habit of really distinguished people and people of intelligence who know that distinction does not lie in mincing speech, and the habit of nobles who fraternise more readily with their peasants than with the middle classes; peculiarities all of which the regal position of Mme de Guermantes enabled her to display more freely, to bring out in full fig. It appears that the same voice existed also in some of her sisters, whom she detested, and who, less intelligent than herself and almost humbly married, if one may use this adverb to speak of unions with obscure noblemen, holed up on their provincial estates, or, in Paris, in one of the dimmer reaches of Faubourg society, possessed this voice also but had curbed it, corrected it, softened it so far as lay in their power, just as it is very rarely that any of us has the courage of his own originality and does not apply himself diligently to resembling the most approved models. But Oriane was so much more intelligent, so much richer, above all, so much more in vogue than her sisters, she had, when Princesse des Laumes, cut so successful a figure in the company of the Prince of Wales, that she had realised that this discordant voice was an attraction, and had made it, in the social sphere, with the courage of originality rewarded by success, what in the theatrical sphere a Réjane or a Jeanne Granier (which implies no comparison, naturally, between the respective merits and talents of those two actresses) had made of theirs, something admirable and distinctive which possibly certain Réjane and Granier sisters, whom no one has ever known, strove to conceal as a defect.

To all these reasons for displaying her local originality, Mme de Guermantes's favourite writers—Mérimée, Meilhac and Halévy—had brought in addition, together with a respect for "naturalness," a feeling for the prosaic by which she attained to poetry and a purely society spirit which called up distant landscapes before my eyes. Besides, the Duchess was fully capable, adding to these influences an artful refinement of her own, of having chosen for the majority of her words the pronunciation that seemed to her most "Ile-de-France," most "Champenoise," since, if not quite to the same extent as her sister-in-law Marsantes, she rarely strayed beyond the pure vocabulary that might have been used by an old French writer. And when one was tired of the composite patchwork of modern speech, it was very restful to listen to Mme de Guermantes's talk, even though one knew it could express far fewer things—almost as restful, if one was alone with her and she restrained and clarified the flow of her speech still further, as listening to an old song. Then, as I looked at and listened to Mme de Guermantes, I could see, imprisoned in the perpetual afternoon of her eyes, a sky of the Ile-de-France or of Champagne spread itself, grey-blue, oblique, with the same angle of inclination as in the eyes of Saint-Loup.

Thus, through these diverse influences, Mme de Guermantes expressed at once the most ancient aristocratic France, then, much later, the manner in which the Duchesse de Broglie might have enjoyed and found fault with Victor Hugo under the July Monarchy, and, finally, a keen taste for the literature that sprang from Mérimée and Meilhac. The first of these influences attracted me more than the second, did more to console me for the disappointments of my pilgrimage to and arrival in the Faubourg Saint-Germain, so different from what I had imagined it to be; but even the second I preferred to the last. For, while Mme de

Guermantes was almost involuntarily Guermantes, her Pailleronism,[34] her taste for the younger Dumas were self-conscious and deliberate. As this taste was the opposite of my own, she furnished my mind with literature when she talked to me of the Faubourg Saint-Germain, and never seemed to me so stupidly Faubourg Saint-Germain as when she talked literature.

Moved by this last quotation, Mme d'Arpajon exclaimed: " 'These relics of the heart, they also have their dust!'— Monsieur, you must write that down for me on my fan," she said to M. de Guermantes.

"Poor woman, I feel sorry for her!" said the Princesse de Parme to Mme de Guermantes.

"No, really, Ma'am, you mustn't be soft-hearted, she has only got what she deserves."

"But—you'll forgive my saying this to you—she does really love him all the same!"

"Oh, not at all; she isn't capable of it; she thinks she loves him just as she thought just now she was quoting Victor Hugo when she was reciting a line from Musset. Look," the Duchess went on in a melancholy tone, "nobody would be more touched than myself by a true feeling. But let me give you an example. Only yesterday she made a terrible scene with Basin. Your Highness thinks perhaps that it was because he's in love with other women, because he no longer loves her; not in the least, it was because he won't put her sons up for the Jockey. Is that the behaviour of a woman in love? No! I will go further," Mme de Guermantes added with precision, "she is a person of rare insensitivity."

Meanwhile it was with an eye sparkling with satisfaction that M. de Guermantes had listened to his wife talking about Victor Hugo "point-blank" and quoting those few lines. The Duchess might frequently irritate him, but at moments such as this he was proud of her. "Oriane is really extraordinary. She can talk about anything, she has read everything. She couldn't possibly have guessed that the conversation this evening would turn on Victor Hugo. Whatever subject you take her on at, she's ready for you, she can hold her own with the most learned scholars. This young man must be quite captivated."

"But do let's change the subject," Mme de Guermantes added, "because she's dreadfully susceptible . . . You must think me very old-fashioned," she went on, turning to me, "I know that nowadays it's considered a weakness to care for ideas in poetry, poetry with some thought in it."

"Old-fashioned?" asked the Princesse de Parme, quivering with the slight shock produced by this new wave which she had not expected, although she knew that the Duchess's conversation always held in store for her those continuous and delightful thrills, that breath-catching panic, that wholesome exhaustion after which her thoughts instinctively turned to the necessity of taking a footbath in a dressing-cabin and a brisk walk to "restore her circulation."

"For my part, no, Oriane," said Mme de Brissac, "I don't in the least object to Victor Hugo's having ideas, quite the contrary, but I do object to his seeking them in everything that's monstrous. It was he who accustomed us to ugliness in literature. There's quite enough ugliness in life already. Why can't we be allowed at least to forget it while we're reading? A distressing spectacle from which we should turn away in real life, that's what attracts Victor Hugo."

"Victor Hugo is not so realistic as Zola though, surely?" asked the Princesse de Parme.

The name of Zola did not stir a muscle on the face of M. de Beautreillis. The General's anti-Dreyfusism was too deep-rooted for him to seek to give expression to it. And his benign silence when anyone broached these topics touched the layman's heart as a proof of the same delicacy that a priest shows in avoiding any reference to your religious duties, a financier in taking pains not to recommend the companies which he himself controls, a strong man in behaving with lamblike gentleness and not hitting you in the jaw.

"I know you're related to Admiral Jurien de La Gravière," Mme de Varambon, the lady-in-waiting to the Princesse de Parme, said to me with a knowing look. An excellent but limited woman, she had been procured for the Princess long ago by the Duke's mother. She had not previously addressed me, and I could never afterwards, despite the admonitions of the Princess and my own protestations, get out of her mind the idea that I was in some way connected with the admiral-academician, who was a complete stranger to me. The obstinate persistence of the Princesse de Parme's lady-in-waiting in seeing in me a nephew of Admiral Jurien de La Gravière was in itself quite an ordinary form of silliness. But the mistake she made was only an extreme and desiccated sample of the numberless mistakes, more frivolous, more pointed, unwitting or deliberate, which accompany one's name on the label which the world attaches to one. I remember a friend of the Guermantes who expressed a keen desire to meet me, and gave me as his reason that I was a great friend of his cousin, Mme de Chaussegros. "She's a charming person, and so fond of you." I scrupulously, though quite vainly, insisted on the fact that there must be some mistake, as I did not know Mme de Chaussegros. "Then it's her sister you know; it comes to the same thing. She met you in Scotland." I had never been to Scotland, and took the fruitless trouble, in my honesty, to apprise my interlocutor of the fact. It was Mme de Chaussegros herself who had said that she knew me, and no doubt sincerely believed it, as a result of some initial confusion, for from that time onwards she never failed to greet me whenever she saw me. And since, after all, the world in which I moved was precisely that in which Mme de Chaussegros moved, my humility had neither rhyme nor reason. To say that I was an intimate friend of the Chaussegros family was, literally, a mistake, but from the social point of view it roughly corresponded to my position, if one can speak of the social position of so young a man as I then was. It therefore mattered not in the least that this friend of the Guermantes should tell me things that were untrue about myself, he neither lowered nor raised me (from the social point of view) in the idea which he continued to hold of me. And when all is said, for those of us who are not professional actors, the tedium of living always in the same character is dispelled for a moment, as if we were to go on the boards, when another person forms a false idea of us, imagines that we are friends with a lady whom we do not know and are reported to have met in the course of a delightful journey which we have never made. Errors that multiply themselves and are harmless when they do not have the inflexible rigidity of the one which had been committed, and continued for the rest of her life to be committed, in spite of my denials, by the imbecile lady-in-waiting to Mme de Parme, rooted for all time in the belief that I was related to the tiresome Admiral Jurien de La Gravière. "She's not very strong in the head," the Duke confided to me, "and besides, she ought not to indulge in too many libations. I fancy she's slightly under the influence of Bacchus." As a matter of fact Mme de Varambon had drunk nothing but water, but the Duke liked to seize opportunities for his favourite phrases.

"But Zola is not a realist, Ma'am, he's a poet!" said Mme de Guermantes, drawing inspiration from the critical essays she had read in recent years and adapting them to her own personal genius. Agreeably buffeted hitherto, in the course of the bath of wit, a bath stirred up specially for her, which she was taking this evening and which, she considered, must be particularly good for her health, letting herself be borne up by the waves of paradox which curled and broke one after another, at this, even more enormous than the rest, the Princesse de Parme jumped for fear of being knocked over. And it was with a catch in her voice, as though she had lost her breath, that she now gasped: "Zola a poet!"

"Why, yes," answered the Duchess with a laugh, entranced by this display of suffocation. "Your Highness must have remarked how he magnifies everything he touches. You will tell me that he only touches . . . what brings luck! But he makes it into something colossal. His is the epic dungheap! He is the Homer of the sewers! He hasn't enough capital letters to write the *mot de Cambronne*."[35]

Despite the extreme exhaustion which she was beginning to feel, the Princess was enchanted; never had she felt better. She would not have exchanged for an invitation to Schönbrunn, although that was the one thing that really flattered her, these divine dinner-parties at Mme de Guermantes's, made invigorating by so liberal a dose of Attic salt.

"He writes it with a big 'C,'" exclaimed Mme d'Arpajon.

"Surely with a big 'M,' I think, my dear," replied Mme de Guermantes, exchanging first with her husband a merry glance which implied: "Did you ever hear such an idiot?"

"Wait a minute, now," Mme de Guermantes turned to me, fixing on me a tender, smiling gaze, because, as an accomplished hostess, she was anxious to display her own knowledge of the artist who interested me particularly and to give me, if need be, an opportunity to exhibit mine, "wait now," she said, gently waving her feather fan, so conscious was she at this moment that she was exercising to the full the duties of hospitality, and, that she might be found wanting in none of them, making a sign also to the servants to help me to more of the asparagus with *mousseline* sauce, "wait now, I do believe that Zola has actually written an essay on Elstir, the painter whose paintings you were looking at just now—the only ones of his I care for, incidentally."

As a matter of fact she hated Elstir's work, but found a unique quality in anything that was in her own house. I asked M. de

Guermantes if he knew the name of the gentleman in the tall hat who figured in the picture of the crowd and whom I recognised as the same person whose formal portrait the Guermantes also had and had hung beside the other, both dating more or less from the same early period in which Elstir's personality had not yet completely emerged and he modelled himself a little on Manet.

"Oh, heavens!" he replied, "I know it's a fellow who is quite well-known and no fool either in his own line, but I have no head for names. I have it on the tip of my tongue, Monsieur... Monsieur... oh, well, it doesn't matter, I've forgotten. Swann would be able to tell you. It was he who made Mme de Guermantes buy all that stuff. She's always too good-natured, afraid of hurting people's feelings if she refuses to do things; between ourselves, I believe he's landed us with a lot of daubs. What I *can* tell you is that the gentleman you mean has been a sort of Maecenas to M. Elstir—he launched him and has often helped him out of difficulties by commissioning pictures from him. As a compliment to this man—if you call it a compliment, it's a matter of taste—he painted him standing about among that crowd, where with his Sunday-go-to-meeting look he creates a distinctly odd effect. He may be no end of a pundit but he's evidently not aware of the proper time and place for a top hat. With that thing on his head, among all those bare-headed girls, he looks like a little country lawyer on the spree. But tell me, you seem quite gone on his pictures. If I'd only known, I should have had it all at my fingertips. Not that there's much need to rack one's brains to get to the bottom of M. Elstir's work, as there would be for Ingres's *Source* or the *Princes in the Tower* by Paul Delaroche. What one appreciates in his work is that it's shrewdly observed, amusing, Parisian, and then one passes on to the next thing. One doesn't need to be an expert to look at that sort of thing. I know of course that they're merely sketches, but still, I don't feel myself that he puts enough work into them. Swann had the nerve to try and make us buy a *Bundle of Asparagus*. In fact it was in the house for several days. There was nothing else in the picture, just a bundle of asparagus exactly like the ones you're eating now. But I must say I refused to swallow M. Elstir's asparagus. He wanted three hundred francs for them. Three hundred francs for a bundle of asparagus! A louis, that's as much as they're worth, even early in the season. I thought it a bit stiff. When he puts people into his pictures as well, there's something squalid and depressing about them that I dislike. I'm surprised to see a man of refinement, a superior mind like you, admiring that sort of thing."

"I don't know why you should say that, Basin," interrupted the Duchess, who did not like to hear people run down anything that her rooms contained. "I'm by no means prepared to admit that there's no distinction in Elstir's painting. You have to take it or leave it. But it's not always lacking in talent. And you must admit that the ones I bought are remarkably beautiful."

"Well, Oriane, in that style of thing I'd infinitely prefer to have the little study by M. Vibert we saw at the water-colour exhibition. There's nothing much in it, if you like, you could hold it in the palm of your hand, but you can see the man's got wit to the tips of his fingers: that shabby scarecrow of a missionary standing in front of the sleek prelate who is making his little dog do tricks, it's a perfect little poem of subtlety, and even profundity."

"I believe you know M. Elstir," the Duchess said to me. "As a man, he's quite pleasant."

"He's intelligent," said the Duke. "You're surprised, when you talk to him, that his paintings should be so vulgar."

"He's more than intelligent, he's really quite witty," said the Duchess in the judicious, appraising tone of a person who knew what she was talking about.

"Didn't he once start a portrait of you, Oriane?" asked the Princesse de Parme.

"Yes, in shrimp pink," replied Mme de Guermantes, "but that's not going to make his name live for posterity. It's a ghastly thing; Basin wanted to have it destroyed."

This last statement was one which Mme de Guermantes often made. But at other times her appreciation of the picture was different: "I don't care for his painting, but he did once do a good portrait of me." The first of these judgments was addressed as a rule to people who spoke to the Duchess of her portrait, the other to those who did not refer to it and whom therefore she was anxious to inform of its existence. The first was inspired in her by coquetry, the second by vanity.

"Make a portrait of you look ghastly! Why, then it can't be a portrait, it's a lie. I don't know one end of a brush from the other, but I'm sure if I were to paint you, merely putting you down as I see you, I should produce a masterpiece," said the Princesse de Parme ingenuously.

"He probably sees me as I see myself, bereft of allurements," said the Duchesse de Guermantes, with the look, at once melancholy, modest and winning, which seemed to her best calculated to make her appear different from what Elstir had portrayed.

"That portrait ought to appeal to Mme de Gallardon," said the Duke.

"Because she knows nothing about pictures?" asked the Princesse de Parme, who knew that Mme de Guermantes had an infinite contempt for her cousin. "But she's a very kind woman, isn't she?"

The Duke assumed an air of profound astonishment.

"Why, Basin, don't you see the Princess is making fun of you?" (The Princess had never dreamed of doing such a thing.) "She knows as well as you do that Gallardonette is a poisonous crone," went on Mme de Guermantes, whose vocabulary, habitually limited to all these old expressions, was as richly flavoured as those dishes which it is possible to come across in the delicious books of Pampille, but which have in real life become so rare, dishes in which the jellies, the butter, the gravy, the quenelles are all genuine and unalloyed, in which even the salt is brought specially from the salt-marshes of Brittany: from her accent, her choice of words, one felt that the basis of the Duchess's conversation came directly from Guermantes. In this way, the Duchess differed profoundly from her nephew Saint-Loup, impregnated by so many new ideas and expressions; it is difficult, when one's mind is troubled by the ideas of Kant and the yearnings of Baudelaire, to write the exquisite French of Henri IV, so that the very purity of the Duchess's language was a sign of limitation and that, in her, both intelligence and sensibility had remained closed against innovation. Here again, Mme de Guermantes's mind attracted me just because of what it excluded (which was precisely the substance of my own thoughts) and everything which, by virtue of that exclusion, it had been able to preserve, that seductive vigour of supple bodies which no exhausting reflexion, no moral anxiety or nervous disorder has deformed. Her mind, of a formation so anterior to my own, was for me the equivalent of what had been offered me by the gait and the bearing of the girls of the little band along the sea-shore. Mme de Guermantes offered me, domesticated and subdued by civility, by respect for intellectual values, all the energy and charm of a cruel little girl of one of the noble families round Combray who from her childhood had been brought up in the saddle, had tortured cats, gouged out the eyes of rabbits, and, instead of having remained a pillar of virtue, might equally well have been, a good few years ago now, so much did she have the same dashing style, the most brilliant mistress of the Prince de Sagan. But she was incapable of understanding what I had looked for in her—the charm of her historic name—and the tiny quantity of it that I had found in her, a rustic survival from Guermantes. Our relations were based on a misunderstanding which could not fail to become manifest as soon as my homage, instead of being addressed to the relatively superior woman she believed herself to be, was diverted to some other woman of equal mediocrity and exuding the same unconscious charm. A misunderstanding that is entirely natural, and one that will always exist between a young dreamer and a society woman, but nevertheless profoundly disturbs him, so long as he has not yet discovered the nature of his imaginative faculties and has not yet resigned himself to the inevitable disappointments he is destined to find in people, as in the theatre, in travel and indeed in love.

M. de Guermantes having declared (following upon Elstir's asparagus and those that had just been served after the chicken *financière*) that green asparagus grown in the open air, which, as has been so quaintly said by the charming writer who signs herself E. de Clermont-Tonnerre, "have not the impressive rigidity of their sisters," ought to be eaten with eggs. "One man's meat is another man's poison, as they say," replied M. de Bréauté. "In the province of Canton, in China, the greatest delicacy that can be set before one is a dish of completely rotten ortolan's eggs." M. de Bréauté, the author of an essay on the Mormons which had appeared in the *Revue des Deux Mondes*, moved in none but the most aristocratic circles, but among these only such as had a certain reputation for intellect, with the result that from his presence, if it was at all regular, in a woman's house, one could tell that she had a "salon." He claimed to loathe society, and assured each of his duchesses in turn that it was for the sake of her wit and beauty that he came to see her. They all believed him. Whenever he resigned himself, with a heavy heart, to attending a big reception at the Princesse de Parme's, he collected them all around him to keep up his courage, and thus appeared only to be moving in the midst of an intimate circle. So that his reputation as an intellectual might survive his social activity, applying certain maxims of the Guermantes spirit, he would set out with the ladies of fashion on long scientific expeditions at the height of the dancing-season, and when a snobbish person, in other words a person not yet socially secure, began to be seen everywhere, he would be ferociously obstinate in his refusal to know that person, to allow himself to be introduced to him or her. His hatred of snobs derived from his snobbishness, but made the simple-minded (in other words, everyone) believe that he was immune from snobbishness.

"Babal always knows everything," exclaimed the Duchesse de Guermantes. "I think it must be charming, a country where you can be quite sure that your dairyman will supply you with really rotten eggs, eggs of the year of the comet. I can just see myself dipping my bread and butter in them. I may say that it sometimes happens at aunt Madeleine's" (Mme de Villeparisis's) "that things are served in a state of putrefaction, eggs included." Then, as Mme d'Arpajon protested, "But my dear Phili, you know it as well as I do. You can see the chicken in the egg. In fact I can't think how they can be so well behaved as to stay in. It's not an omelette you get there, it's a regular hen-house, but at least it isn't marked on the menu. You were so wise not to come to dinner there the day before yesterday, there was a brill cooked in carbolic! I assure you, it wasn't hospitality so much as a hospital for contagious diseases. Really, Norpois carries loyalty to the pitch of heroism: he had a second helping!"

"I believe I saw you there the time she lashed out at M. Bloch" (M. de Guermantes, perhaps to give a Jewish name a more foreign sound, pronounced the "ch" in Bloch not like a "k" but as in the German "hoch") "when he said about some poit" (poet) "or other that he was sublime. Châtellerault did his best to break M. Bloch's shins, but the fellow didn't understand and thought my nephew's kicks were aimed at a young woman sitting next to him." (At this point M. de Guermantes coloured slightly.) "He didn't realise that he was irritating our aunt with his 'sublimes' chucked about all over the place like that. Anyhow, aunt Madeleine, who's never at a loss for words, turned on him with: 'Indeed, sir, and what epithet are you going to keep for M. de Bossuet?'" (M. de Guermantes thought that, when one mentioned a famous name, the use of "Monsieur" and a particle was eminently "old school.") "It was absolutely killing."

"And what answer did this M. Bloch make?" came in a careless tone from Mme de Guermantes, who, running short for the moment of original ideas, felt that she must copy her husband's Teutonic pronunciation.

"Ah! I can assure you M. Bloch didn't wait for any more, he fled."

"Yes, I remember very well seeing you there that evening," said Mme de Guermantes with emphasis, as though there must be something highly flattering to myself in this remembrance on her part. "It's always so interesting at my aunt's. At that last party, where I met you, I meant to ask you whether that old gentleman who went past us wasn't François Coppée. You must know who everyone is," she went on, sincerely envious of my relations with poets and poetry, and also out of amiability towards me, the wish to enhance the status, in the eyes of her other guests, of a young man so well versed in literature. I assured the Duchess that I had not observed any celebrities at Mme de Villeparisis's party. "What!" she exclaimed unguardedly, betraying the fact that her respect for men of letters and her contempt for society were more superficial than she said, perhaps even than she thought, "what, no famous authors there! You astonish me! Why, I saw all sorts of quite impossible-looking people!"

I remembered the evening very well on account of an entirely trivial incident. Mme de Villeparisis had introduced Bloch to Mme Alphonse de Rothschild, but my friend had not caught the name and, thinking he was talking to an old English lady who was a trifle mad, had replied only in monosyllables to the garrulous conversation of the historic beauty, when Mme de Villeparisis, introducing her to someone else, had pronounced, quite distinctly this time: "The Baronne Alphonse de Rothschild." Thereupon so many ideas of millions and of glamour, which it would have been more prudent to subdivide and separate, had suddenly and simultaneously coursed through Bloch's arteries that he had had a sort of heart attack and brainstorm combined, and had cried aloud in the dear old lady's presence: "If I'd only known!"—an exclamation the silliness of which kept him awake at nights for a whole week. This remark of Bloch's was of no great interest, but I remembered it as a proof that sometimes in this life, under the stress of an exceptional emotion, people do say what they think.

"I fancy Mme de Villeparisis is not absolutely . . . moral," said the Princesse de Parme, who knew that the best people did not visit the Duchess's aunt, and, from what the Duchess herself had just been saying, that one might speak freely about her. But, Mme de Guermantes not seeming to approve of this criticism, she hastened to add: "Though, of course, intelligence carried to that degree excuses everything."

"You take the same view of my aunt as everyone else," replied the Duchess, "which is, on the whole, quite mistaken. It's just what Mémé was saying to me only yesterday." (She blushed, her eyes clouding with a memory unknown to me. I conjectured that M. de Charlus had asked her to cancel my invitation, as he had sent Robert to ask me not to go to her house. I had the impression that the blush—equally incomprehensible to me—which had tinged the Duke's cheeks when he made some reference to his brother could not be attributed to the same cause.) "My poor aunt—she will always have the reputation of being a lady of the old school, of sparkling wit and uncontrolled passions. And really there's no more middle-class, solemn, drab, commonplace mind in Paris. She will go down as a patron of the arts, which means to say that she was once the mistress of a great painter, though he was never able to make her understand what a picture was; and as for her private life, so far from being a depraved woman, she was so much made for marriage, so conjugal from her cradle that, not having succeeded in keeping a husband, who incidentally was a scoundrel, she has never had a love affair which she hasn't taken just as seriously as if it were holy matrimony, with the same irritations, the same quarrels, the same fidelity. Mind you, those relationships are often the most sincere; on the whole there are more inconsolable lovers than husbands."

"And yet, Oriane, if you take the case of your brother-in-law Palamède whom you were speaking about just now, no mistress in the world could ever dream of being mourned as that poor Mme de Charlus has been."

"Ah!" replied the Duchess, "Your Highness must permit me to be not altogether of her opinion. People don't all like to be mourned in the same way, each of us has his preferences."

"Still, he has made a regular cult of her since her death. It's true that people sometimes do for the dead what they would not have done for the living."

"For one thing," retorted Mme de Guermantes in a dreamy tone which belied her facetious intent, "we go to their funerals, which we never do for the living!" (M. de Guermantes gave M. de Bréauté a sly glance as though to provoke him into laughter at the Duchess's wit.) "At the same time I frankly admit," went on Mme de Guermantes, "that the manner in which I should like to be mourned by a man I loved would not be that adopted by my brother-in-law."

The Duke's face darkened. He did not like to hear his wife utter random judgments, especially about M. de Charlus. "You're very particular. His grief set an edifying example to everyone," he reproved her stiffly. But the Duchess had in dealing with her husband that sort of boldness which animal tamers show, or people who live with a madman and are not afraid of provoking him.

"Well, yes, if you like, I suppose it's edifying—he goes every day to the cemetery to tell her how many people he has had to luncheon, he misses her enormously, but as he'd mourn a cousin, a grandmother, a sister. It isn't the grief of a husband. It's true that they were a pair of saints, which makes it all rather exceptional." (M. de Guermantes, infuriated by his wife's chatter, fixed on her with a terrible immobility a pair of eyes already loaded.) "I don't wish to say anything against poor Mémé, who, by the way, couldn't come this evening," went on the Duchess. "I quite admit there's no one like him, he's kind and sweet, he has a delicacy, a warmth of heart that you don't as a rule find in men. He has a woman's heart, Mémé has!"

"What you say is absurd," M. de Guermantes broke in sharply. "There's nothing effeminate about Mémé. Nobody could be more manly than he is."

"But I'm not suggesting for a moment that he's the least bit effeminate. Do at least take the trouble to understand what I say," retorted the Duchess. "He's always like that the moment he thinks one's getting at his brother," she added, turning to the Princesse de Parme.

"It's very charming, it's a pleasure to hear him. There's nothing so nice as two brothers who are fond of each other," replied the Princess, as many a humbler person might have replied, for it is possible to belong to a princely family by blood and a very plebeian family by intellect.

"While we're on the subject of your family, Oriane," said the Princess, "I saw your nephew Saint-Loup yesterday. I believe he wants to ask you a favour."

The Duc de Guermantes knitted his Olympian brow. When he did not care to do someone a favour, he preferred that his wife should not undertake to do so, knowing that it would come to the same thing in the end and that the people to whom she would be obliged to apply would put it down to the common account of the household, just as much as if it had been requested by the husband alone.

"Why didn't he ask me himself?" said the Duchess, "he was here yesterday and stayed a couple of hours, and I can't tell you how boring he was. He would be no stupider than anyone else if he had only had the sense, like many people we know, to remain a fool. It's his veneer of knowledge that's so terrible. He wants to have an open mind—open to all the things he doesn't understand. The way he goes on about Morocco, it's frightful."

"He doesn't want to go back there, because of Rachel," said the Prince de Foix.

"But I thought they'd broken it off," interrupted M. de Bréauté.

"So far from breaking it off, I found her a couple of days ago in Robert's rooms, and they didn't look at all like people who'd quarrelled, I can assure you," replied the Prince de Foix, who liked to spread every rumour that could damage Robert's chances of marrying, and who might, moreover, have been misled by one of the intermittent resumptions of a liaison that was practically at an end.

"That Rachel was speaking to me about you. I run into her occasionally in the morning in the Champs-Elysées. She's somewhat *flighty* as you say, what you call *unbuttoned*, a kind of 'Dame aux Camélias,' figuratively speaking, of course." (This speech was addressed to me by Prince Von, who liked always to appear conversant with French literature and Parisian refinements.)

"Why, that's just what it was—Morocco!" exclaimed the Princess, flinging herself into this opening.

"What on earth can he want in Morocco?" asked M. de Guermantes sternly. "Oriane can do absolutely nothing for him there, as he knows perfectly well."

"He thinks he invented strategy," Mme de Guermantes pursued the theme, "and then he uses impossible words for the simplest thing, which doesn't prevent him from making blots all over his letters. The other day he announced that he'd been given some *sublime* potatoes, and that he'd taken a *sublime* stage box."

"He speaks Latin," the Duke went one better.

"What! Latin?" the Princess gasped.

"On my word of honour! Your Highness can ask Oriane if I'm not telling the truth."

"Why, yes, Ma'am; the other day he said to us straight out, without stopping to think: 'I know of no more touching example of *sic transit gloria mundi*.' I can repeat the phrase now to Your Highness because, after endless inquiries and by appealing to *linguists*, we succeeded in reconstructing it, but Robert flung it out without pausing for breath, one could hardly make out that there was Latin in it, he was just like a character in the *Malade Imaginaire*. And it was simply to do with the death of the Empress of Austria!"

"Poor woman!" cried the Princess, "what a delicious creature she was!"

"Yes," replied the Duchess, "a trifle mad, a trifle headstrong, but she was a thoroughly good woman, a nice, kind-hearted lunatic; the only thing I could never understand was why she never managed to get a set of false teeth that fitted her; they always came loose half-way through a sentence and she was obliged to stop short or she'd have swallowed them."

"That Rachel was telling me that young Saint-Loup worshipped you, that he was fonder of you than he was of her," said Prince Von to me, devouring his food like an ogre as he spoke, his face scarlet, his teeth bared by his perpetual grin.

"But in that case she must be jealous of me and hate me," said I.

"Not at all, she said all sorts of nice things about you. The Prince de Foix's mistress would perhaps be jealous if he preferred you to her. You don't understand? Come home with me, and I'll explain it all to you."

"I'm afraid I can't, I'm going on to M. de Charlus at eleven."

"Why, he sent round to me yesterday to ask me to dine with him this evening, but told me not to come after a quarter to eleven. But if you insist on going to him, at least come with me as far as the Théâtre-Français, you will be in the periphery," said the Prince, who thought doubtless that this last word meant "proximity" or possibly "centre."

But the bulging eyes in his coarse though handsome red face frightened me and I declined, saying that a friend was coming to call for me. This reply seemed to me in no way offensive. The Prince, however, apparently formed a different impression of it, for he did not say another word to me.

"I really must go and see the Queen of Naples—it must be a great grief to her," said, or at least appeared to me to have said, the Princesse de Parme. For her words had come to me only

indistinctly through the intervening screen of those addressed to
me, albeit in an undertone, by Prince Von, who had doubtless been
afraid of being overheard by the Prince de Foix if he spoke louder.

"Oh, dear, no!" replied the Duchess, "I don't believe she feels
any grief at all."

"None at all! You do always fly to extremes, Oriane," said M. de
Guermantes, resuming his role as the cliff which, by standing up
against the wave, forces it to fling even higher its crest of foam.

"Basin knows even better than I that I'm telling the truth,"
replied the Duchess, "but he thinks he's obliged to look severe
because you are present, Ma'am, and he's afraid of my shocking
you."

"Oh, please no, I beg of you," cried the Princesse de Parme,
dreading the slightest alteration on her account of these delicious
evenings at the Duchesse de Guermantes's, this forbidden fruit
which the Queen of Sweden herself had not yet acquired the right
to taste.

"Why, it was to Basin himself, when he said to her with a duly
sorrowful expression: 'But I see the Queen is in mourning. For
whom, pray? Is it a great grief to Your Majesty?' that she replied:
'No, it's not a deep mourning, it's a light mourning, a very light
mourning, it's my sister.' The truth is, she's delighted about it, as
Basin knows perfectly well. She invited us to a party that very
evening, and gave me two pearls. I wish she could lose a sister
every day! So far from weeping for her sister's death, she was in fits
of laughter over it. She probably says to herself, like Robert, '*sic
transit*——' I forget how it goes on," she added modestly, knowing how it went on perfectly well.

In saying all this Mme de Guermantes was only indulging her
wit, and in the most disingenuous way, for the Queen of Naples,
like the Duchesse d'Alençon, who also died in tragic circumstances, had the warmest heart in the world and sincerely mourned
her kinsfolk. Mme de Guermantes knew these noble Bavarian
sisters, her cousins, too well not to be aware of this. "He is anxious
not to go back to Morocco," said the Princesse de Parme, grasping
once more at the name Robert which Mme de Guermantes had
held out to her, quite unintentionally, like a lifeline. "I believe you
know General de Monserfeuil."

"Very slightly," replied the Duchess, who was an intimate
friend of the officer in question. The Princess explained what it
was that Saint-Loup wanted.

"Oh dear, well, yes, if I see him . . . It's possible that I may run into him," the Duchess replied, so as not to appear to be refusing, her relations with General de Monserfeuil seeming to have grown rapidly more intermittent since it had become a question of her asking him for something. This uncertainty did not, however, satisfy the Duke, who interrupted his wife.

"You know perfectly well you won't be seeing him, Oriane, and besides you've already asked him for two things which he hasn't done. My wife has a passion for doing people good turns," he went on, getting more and more furious in order to force the Princess to withdraw her request without making her doubt his wife's good nature and so that Mme de Parme should throw the blame on his own essentially crotchety character. "Robert could get anything he wanted out of Monserfeuil. Only, as he happens not to know what he wants, he gets us to ask for it because he knows there's no better way of making the whole thing fall through. Oriane has asked too many favours of Monserfeuil. A request from her now would be a reason for him to refuse."

"Oh, in that case, it would be better if the Duchess did nothing," said Mme de Parme.

"Obviously," the Duke concluded.

"That poor General, he's been defeated again at the elections," said the Princess, to change the subject.

"Oh, it's nothing serious, it's only the seventh time," said the Duke, who, having been obliged himself to retire from politics, quite enjoyed hearing of other people's failures at the polls. "He has consoled himself by giving his wife another baby."

"What! Is that poor Mme de Monserfeuil pregnant again?" cried the Princess.

"Why, of course," replied the Duchess, "it's the one *ward* where the poor General has never failed."

In the period that followed I was continually to be invited, however small the party, to these repasts at which I had at one time imagined the guests as seated like the Apostles in the Sainte-Chapelle. They did assemble there indeed, like the early Christians, not to partake merely of a material nourishment, which was incidentally exquisite, but in a sort of social Eucharist; so that in the course of a few dinner-parties I assimilated the acquaintance of all the friends of my hosts, friends to whom they presented me with a tinge of benevolent patronage so marked (as a person for whom they had always had a sort of parental affection) that there was not one among them who would not have felt himself to be somehow failing the Duke and Duchess if he had given a ball without including my name on his list, and at the same time, while I sipped one of those Yquems which lay concealed in the Guermantes cellars, I tasted ortolans dressed according to a variety of recipes judiciously elaborated and modified by the Duke himself. However, for one who had already sat down more than once at the mystic board, the consumption of these latter was not indispensable. Old friends of M. and Mme de Guermantes came in to see them after dinner, "with the tooth-picks" as Mme Swann would have said, without being expected, and took in winter a cup of lime-blossom tea in the lighted warmth of the great drawing-room, in summer a glass of orange-ade in the darkness of the little rectangular strip of garden outside. No one could remember having ever received from the Guermantes, on these evenings in the garden, anything else but orangeade. It had a sort of ritual meaning. To have added other refreshments would have seemed to be falsifying the tradition, just as a big at-home in the Faubourg Saint-Germain ceases to be an at-home if there is a play also, or music. You must be assumed to have come simply—even if there were five hundred of you—to pay a call on, let us say, the Princesse de Guermantes. People marvelled at my influence because I managed to procure the addition to this orangeade of a jug containing the juice of stewed cherries or stewed pears. I took a dislike on this account to the Prince d'Agrigente, who was like all those people who, lacking in ima-gination but not in covetousness, take a keen interest in what one is drinking and ask if they may taste a little of it themselves. Which meant that, every time, M. d'Agrigente, by diminishing my ration, spoiled my pleasure. For this fruit juice can never be provided in sufficient quantities to quench one's thirst. Nothing is less cloying than that transmutation into flavour of the colour of a fruit, which, when cooked, seems to have travelled backwards to the season of its blossoming. Blushing like an orchard in spring, or else colourless and cool like the zephyr beneath the fruit-trees, the juice can be sniffed and gloated over drop by drop, and M. d'Agrigente prevented me, regularly, from taking my fill of it. Despite these distillations, the traditional orangeade persisted like the lime-blossom tea. In these humble kinds, the social com-munion was none the less celebrated. In this respect, doubtless, the friends of M. and Mme de Guermantes had after all, as I had originally imagined them, remained more different from the rest of humanity than their disappointing exterior might have misled me into supposing. Numbers of elderly men came to receive from the Duchess, together with the invariable drink, a welcome that was often far from warm. Now this could not have been due to snobbishness, they themselves being of a rank to which there was none superior; nor to love of luxury: they did love it perhaps, but, in less exalted social conditions, might have been enjoying a glittering example of it, for on those same evenings the charming wife of a colossally rich financier would have given anything in the world to have them among the brilliant shooting-party she was giving for a couple of days for the King of Spain. They had nevertheless declined her invitation, and had come round without fail to see whether Mme de Guermantes was at home. They were not even certain of finding there opinions that conformed entirely with their own, or sentiments of any great cordiality; Mme de Guermantes would throw out from time to time—on the Dreyfus case, on the Republic, on the anti-religious laws, or even, in an undertone, on themselves, their weaknesses, the dullness of their conversation—comments which they had to appear not to notice. No doubt, if they kept up their habit of coming there, it was owing to their consummate training as epicures in things worldly, to their clear consciousness of the prime and perfect quality of the social pabulum, with its familiar, reassuring, sapid flavour, free of admixture or adulteration, with the origin and history of which they were as well acquainted as she who served them with it, remaining more "noble" in this respect than they themselves imagined. Now, on this occasion, among the visitors to whom I was introduced after dinner, it so happened that there was that General de Monserfeuil of whom the Princesse de Parme had spoken and whom Mme de Guermantes, of whose drawing-room he was one of the regular frequenters, had not expected that evening. He bowed before me, on hearing my name, as though I had been the President of the Supreme War Council. I had supposed it to be simply from some deep-rooted unwillingness to oblige, in which the Duke, as in wit if not in love, was his wife's accomplice, that the Duchess had practically refused to recommend her nephew to M. de Monserfeuil. And I saw in this an indifference all the more blameworthy in that I seemed to have gathered from a few words which the Princess had let fall that Robert was in a post of danger from which it would be prudent to have him removed. But it was by the genuine malice of Mme de Guermantes that I was revolted when, the Princesse de Parme having timidly suggested that she might say something herself and on her own initiative to the General, the Duchess did everything in her power to dissuade her.

"But Ma'am," she cried, "Monserfeuil has no sort of standing or influence whatever with the new Government. You would be wasting your breath."

"I think he can hear us," murmured the Princess, as a hint to the Duchess not to speak so loud.

"Your Highness needn't be afraid, he's as deaf as a post," said the Duchess, without lowering her voice, though the General could hear her perfectly.

"The thing is, I believe M. de Saint-Loup is in a place that is not very safe," said the Princess.

"It can't be helped," replied the Duchess, "he's in the same boat as everybody else, the only difference being that it was he who asked to be sent there. Besides, no, it's not really dangerous; if it was, you can imagine how anxious I should be to help. I'd have spoken to Saint-Joseph about it during dinner. He has far more influence, and he's a real worker. But, as you see, he's gone now. Besides, it would be less awkward than going to this one, who has three of his sons in Morocco just now and has refused to apply for them to be transferred; he might raise that as an objection. Since Your Highness insists, I shall speak to Saint-Joseph—if I see him again, or to Beautreillis. But if I don't see either of them, you mustn't waste your pity on Robert. It was explained to us the other day where he is. I don't think he could be anywhere better."

"What a pretty flower, I've never seen one like it; there's no one like you, Oriane, for having such marvellous things in your house," said the Princesse de Parme, who, fearing that General de Monserfeuil might have overheard the Duchess, sought now to change the subject. I looked and recognised a plant of the sort that I had watched Elstir painting.

"I'm so glad you like them; they are charming, do look at their little purple velvet collars; the only thing against them is—as may happen with people who are very pretty and very nicely dressed— they have a hideous name and a horrid smell. In spite of which I'm very fond of them. But what is rather sad is that they're going to die."

"But they're growing in a pot, they aren't cut flowers," said the Princess.

"No," answered the Duchess with a smile, "but it comes to the same thing, as they're all ladies. It's a kind of plant where the ladies and the gentlemen don't both grow on the same stalk. I'm like the people who keep a lady dog. I have to find a husband for my flowers. Otherwise I shan't have any young ones!"

"How very strange. Do you mean to say that in nature . . .?"

"Yes, there are certain insects whose duty it is to bring about the marriage, as with sovereigns, by proxy, without the bride and bridegroom ever having set eyes on one another. And so, I assure you, I always tell my man to put my plant at the open window as often as possible, on the courtyard side and the garden side turn about, in the hope that the necessary insect will arrive. But the odds are so enormous! Just think, he would need to have just visited a person of the same species and the opposite sex, and he must then have taken it into his head to come and leave cards at the house. He hasn't appeared so far—I believe my plant still deserves the name of virgin, but I must say a little more shamelessness would please me better. It's just the same with that fine tree we have in the courtyard—it will die childless because it belongs to a species that's very rare in these latitudes. In its case, it's the wind that's responsible for bringing about the union, but the wall is a trifle high."

"Yes, indeed," said M. de Bréauté, "you ought to have taken just a couple of inches off the top, that would have been quite enough. You have to know all the tricks of the trade. The flavour of vanilla we tasted in the excellent ice you gave us this evening, Duchess, comes from the plant of that name. It produces flowers which are both male and female, but a sort of partition between them prevents any communication. And so one could never get any fruit from them until a young negro, a native of Réunion, by the name of Albins, which by the way is rather a comic name for a black since it means 'white,' had the happy thought of using the point of a needle to bring the separate organs into contact."

"Babal, you're divine, you know everything," cried the Duchess.

"But you yourself, Oriane, have taught me things I had no idea of," the Princesse de Parme assured her.

"I must explain to Your Highness that it's Swann who has always talked to me a great deal about botany. Sometimes when we thought it would be too boring to go to an afternoon party we would set off for the country, and he would show me extraordinary marriages between flowers, which was far more amusing than going to human marriages—no wedding-breakfast and no crowd in the sacristy. We never had time to go very far. Now that motor-cars have come in, it would be delightful. Unfortunately, in the meantime he himself has made an even more astonishing marriage, which makes everything very difficult. Ah, Ma'am, life is a dreadful business, we spend our whole time doing things that bore us, and when by chance we come across somebody with whom we could go and look at something really interesting, he has to make a marriage like Swann's. Faced with the alternatives of giving up my botanical expeditions and being obliged to call upon a degrading person, I chose the first of these two calamities. Actually, though, there's no need to go quite so far. It seems that even here, in my own little bit of garden, more improper things happen in broad daylight than at midnight . . . in the Bois de Boulogne! Only they attract no attention, because between flowers it's all done quite simply—you see a little orange shower, or else a very dusty fly coming to wipe its feet or take a bath before crawling into a flower. And that does the trick!"

"The cabinet the plant is standing on is splendid, too; it's Empire, I believe," said the Princess, who, not being familiar with the works of Darwin and his followers, was unable to grasp the point of the Duchess's pleasantries.

"It's lovely, isn't it? I'm so glad Your Highness likes it," replied the Duchess, "it's a magnificent piece. I must tell you that I've always adored the Empire style, even when it wasn't in fashion. I remember at Guermantes I got into terrible disgrace with my mother-in-law because I told them to bring down from the attics all the splendid Empire furniture Basin had inherited from the Montesquious, and used it to furnish the wing we lived in."

M. de Guermantes smiled. He must nevertheless have remembered that the course of events had been very different. But, the witticisms of the Princesse des Laumes on the subject of her mother-in-law's bad taste having been a tradition during the short time in which the Prince had been in love with his wife, his love for the latter had been outlasted by a certain contempt for the intellectual inferiority of the former, a contempt which, however, went hand in hand with considerable attachment and respect.

"The Iénas have the same armchair with Wedgwood medallions. It's a fine piece, but I prefer mine," said the Duchess, with the same air of impartiality as if she had not been the owner of either of these two pieces of furniture. "I admit, of course, that they've got some marvellous things which I haven't."

The Princesse de Parme remained silent.

"But it's quite true; Your Highness hasn't seen their collection. Oh, you ought really to come there one day with me, it's one of the most magnificent things in Paris. You'd say it was a museum come to life."

And since this suggestion was one of the most "Guermantes" of the Duchess's audacities, inasmuch as the Iénas were for the Princesse de Parme rank usurpers, their son bearing like her own the title of Duc de Guastalla, Mme de Guermantes in thus launching it could not refrain (so much did the love that she bore her own originality prevail over the deference due to the Princesse de Parme) from glancing round at her other guests with an amused smile. They too made an effort to smile, at once alarmed, amazed and above all delighted to think that they were being witnesses of Oriane's very "latest" and could serve it up "piping hot." They were only half shocked, knowing that the Duchess had the knack of throwing all the Courvoisier prejudices to the wind for the sake of a more striking and enjoyable triumph. Had she not, within the last few years, brought together Princesse Mathilde and the Duc d'Aumale, who had written to the Princess's own brother the famous letter: "In my family all the men are brave and the women chaste"? And inasmuch as princes remain princely even at those moments when they appear anxious to forget that they are, the Duc d'Aumale and the Princesse Mathilde had enjoyed themselves so greatly at Mme de Guermantes's that they had afterwards exchanged visits, with that faculty for forgetting the past which Louis XVIII showed when he appointed as a minister Fouché, who had voted the death of his brother. Mme de Guermantes was now nursing a similar project of arranging a reconciliation between the Princesse Murat and the Queen of Naples. In the meantime, the Princesse de Parme appeared as embarrassed as might have been the heirs-apparent to the thrones of the Netherlands and Belgium, styled respectively Prince of Orange and Duke of Brabant, had one offered to present to them M. de Mailly-Nesle, Prince d'Orange, and M. de Charlus, Duc de Brabant. But, before anything further could happen, the

Duchess, in whom Swann and M. de Charlus between them (albeit the latter was resolute in ignoring the Iénas' existence) had with great difficulty succeeded in inculcating a taste for the Empire style, exclaimed:

"Honestly, Ma'am, I can't tell you how beautiful you'll find it! I must confess that the Empire style has always had a fascination for me. But at the Iénas' it really is hallucinating. That sort of—what shall I say—reflux from the Egyptian expedition, and then, too, the sort of upsurge into our own times from Antiquity, all those things invading our houses, the Sphinxes crouching at the feet of the armchairs, the snakes coiled round candelabra, a huge Muse who holds out a little torch for you to play cards under, or has quietly climbed on to the mantelpiece and is leaning against your clock; and then all the Pompeian lamps, the little boat-shaped beds which look as if they had been found floating on the Nile so that you expect to see Moses climb out of them, the classical chariots galloping along the bedside tables . . ."

"They're not very comfortable to sit in, those Empire chairs," the Princess ventured.

"No," the Duchess agreed, "but I love," she at once added, stressing the point with a smile, "I love being uncomfortable on those mahogany seats covered with ruby velvet or green silk. I love that discomfort of warriors who understand nothing but the curule chair and weave their fasces and stack their laurels in the middle of their main living-room. I can assure you that at the Iénas' one doesn't stop to think for a moment of how comfortable one is, when one sees in front of one a great strapping wench of a Victory painted in fresco on the wall. My husband is going to say that I'm a very bad royalist, but I'm terribly wrong-thinking, you know, I can assure you that in those people's house one comes to love all the big N's and all the Napoleonic bees. Good heavens, after all, since we hadn't been exactly surfeited with glory for a good many years under our kings, those warriors who brought home so many crowns that they stuck them even on the arms of the chairs, I must say I think it's all rather fetching! Your Highness really must."

"Why, my dear, if you think so," said the Princess, "but it seems to me that it won't be easy."

"But Your Highness will find that it will all go quite smoothly. They are very kind people, and no fools. We took Mme de Chevreuse there," added the Duchess, knowing the force of this example, "and she was enchanted. The son is really very pleasant... I'm going to tell you something that's not quite proper," she went on, "but he has a bedroom, and more especially a bed, in which I should love to sleep—without him! What is even less proper is that I went to see him once when he was ill and lying in it. By his side, on the frame of the bed, there was a sculpted Siren, stretched out at full length, absolutely ravishing, with a mother-of-pearl tail and some sort of lotus flowers in her hand. I assure you," went on Mme de Guermantes, reducing the speed of her delivery to bring into even bolder relief the words which she seemed to be modelling with the pout of her fine lips, drawing them out with her long expressive hands, directing on the Princess as she spoke a soft, intent, profound gaze, "that with the palm-leaves and the golden crown on one side, it was most moving, it was precisely the same composition as Gustave Moreau's *Death and the Young Man* (Your Highness must know that masterpiece, of course)."

The Princesse de Parme, who did not know so much as the painter's name, nodded her head vehemently and smiled ardently, in order to manifest her admiration for this picture. But the intensity of her mimicry could not fill the place of that light which is absent from our eyes so long as we do not understand what people are talking to us about.

"A good-looking boy, I believe?" she asked.

"No, he's just like a tapir. The eyes are a little those of a Queen Hortense on a lamp-shade. But he probably came to the conclusion that it would be rather absurd for a man to develop such a resemblance, and so it's lost in the encaustic surface of his cheeks which give him really rather a Mameluke appearance. You feel that the polisher must call round every morning. Swann," she went on, reverting to the young duke's bed, "was struck by the resemblance between that Siren and Gustave Moreau's *Death*. But in fact," she added, in a more rapid but still serious tone of voice, in order to provoke more laughter, "there was nothing really to get worked up about, for it was only a cold in the head, and the young man is now as fit as a fiddle."

"They say he's a snob?" put in M. de Bréauté, with a malicious twinkle, expecting to be answered with the same precision as though he had said: "They tell me that he has only four fingers on his right hand; is that so?"

"G—ood g—racious, n—o," replied Mme de Guermantes with a smile of benign tolerance. "Perhaps just the least little bit of a snob in appearance, because he's extremely young, but I should be surprised to hear that he was in reality, for he's intelligent," she added, as though there were to her mind some absolute incompatibility between snobbishness and intelligence. "He has wit, too, I've known him to be quite amusing," she said again, laughing with the air of an epicure and expert, as though the act of declaring that a person could be amusing demanded a certain expression of merriment from the speaker, or as though the Duc de Guastalla's sallies were recurring to her mind as she spoke. "Anyway, as he is never invited anywhere, he can't have much scope for his snobbishness," she wound up, oblivious of the fact that this was hardly an encouragement to the Princesse de Parme.

"I cannot help wondering what the Prince de Guermantes, who calls her Mme Iéna, will say if he hears that I've been to see her."

"What!" cried the Duchess with extraordinary vivacity. "Don't you know that it was we who gave up to Gilbert" (she bitterly regretted that surrender now) "a complete card-room done in the Empire style which came to us from Quiou-Quiou and is an absolute marvel! There was no room for it here, though I think it would look better here than it does in his house. It's a thing of sheer beauty, half Etruscan, half Egyptian . . ."

"Egyptian?" queried the Princess, to whom the word Etruscan conveyed little.

"Well, you know, a little of both. Swann told us that, he explained it all to me, only you know I'm such a dunce. But then, Ma'am, what one has to bear in mind is that the Egypt of the Empire cabinet-makers has nothing to do with the historical Egypt, nor their Romans with the Romans nor their Etruria . . ."

"Indeed," said the Princess.

"No, it's like what they used to call a Louis XV costume under the Second Empire, when Anna de Mouchy and dear Brigode's mother were girls. Basin was talking to you just now about Beethoven. We heard a thing of his played the other day which was really rather fine, though a little stiff, with a Russian theme in it. It's pathetic to think that he believed it to be Russian. In the same way as the Chinese painters believed they were copying Bellini. Besides, even in the same country, whenever anybody begins to look at things in a slightly new way, nine hundred and ninety-nine people out of a thousand are totally incapable of seeing what he puts before them. It takes at least forty years before they can manage to make it out."

"Forty years!" the Princess cried in alarm.

"Why, yes," went on the Duchess, adding more and more to her words (which were practically my own, for I had just been expressing a similar idea to her), thanks to her way of pronouncing them, the equivalent of what on the printed page are called italics, "it's like a sort of first isolated individual of a species which does not yet exist but is going to multiply in the future, an individual endowed with a kind of *sense* which the human race of his generation does not possess. I can hardly give myself as an instance because I, on the contrary, have always loved any interesting artistic offering from the very start, however novel it might be. But anyway the other day I was with the Grand Duchess in the Louvre and we happened to pass Manet's *Olympia*. Nowadays nobody is in the least surprised by it. It looks just like an Ingres! And yet, heaven knows how I had to take up the cudgels on behalf of that picture, which I don't altogether like but which is unquestionably the work of *somebody*. Perhaps the Louvre isn't quite the place for it."

"And is the Grand Duchess well?" inquired the Princesse de Parme, to whom the Tsar's aunt was infinitely more familiar than Manet's model.

"Yes; we talked about you. After all," she resumed, clinging to her idea, "the fact of the matter is, as my brother-in-law Palamède always says, that one has between oneself and the rest of the world the barrier of a strange language.* Though I admit that there's no one it's quite so true of as Gilbert. If it amuses you to go to the Iénas', you have far too much sense to let your actions be governed by what that poor fellow may think—he's a dear, innocent creature, but he really lives in another world. I feel nearer, more akin to my coachman, my horses even, than to a man who keeps on harking back to what people would have thought under Philip the Bold or Louis the Fat. Just fancy, when he goes for a walk in the country, he waves the peasants out of his way with his stick, quite affably, saying 'Get along there, churls!' In fact I'm as amazed when he speaks to me as if I heard myself addressed by a recumbent figure on an old Gothic tomb. It's all very well that animated gravestone's being my cousin; he frightens me, and the only idea that comes into my head is to let him stay in his Middle

Ages. Apart from that, I quite admit that he's never murdered anyone."

"I've just been seeing him at dinner at Mme de Villeparisis's," said the General, but without either smiling at or endorsing the Duchess's pleasantries.

"Was M. de Norpois there?" asked Prince Von, whose mind still ran on the Academy of Moral Sciences.

"Yes," said the General. "In fact he was talking about your Emperor."

"It seems the Emperor William is highly intelligent, but he doesn't care for Elstir's painting. Not that that's anything against him," said the Duchess, "I quite share his point of view. Although Elstir has done a fine portrait of me. You don't know it? It's not in the least like me, but it's an intriguing piece of work. He's most interesting while one's sitting to him. He has made me like a little old woman. It's modelled on *The Women Regents of the Hospice*, by Hals. I expect you know those sublimities, to borrow one of my nephew's favourite expressions," the Duchess turned to me, gently flapping her black feather fan. More than erect on her chair, she flung her head nobly backwards, for, while always a great lady, she was a trifle inclined to act the part of the great lady too. I said that I had been once to Amsterdam and The Hague, but that to avoid getting everything muddled up, since my time was limited, I had left out Haarlem.

"Ah! The Hague! What a gallery!" cried M. de Guermantes. I said to him that he had doubtless admired Vermeer's *View of Delft*. But the Duke was less erudite than arrogant. Accordingly he contented himself with replying in a self-complacent tone, as was his habit whenever anyone spoke to him of a picture in a gallery, or in the Salon, which he did not remember having seen: "If it's to be seen, I saw it!"

"What? You've been to Holland, and you never visited Haarlem!" cried the Duchess. "Why, even if you had only a quarter of an hour to spend in the place, they're an extraordinary thing to have seen, those Halses. I don't mind saying that a person who only caught a passing glimpse of them from the top of a tram without stopping, supposing they were hung out to view in the street, would open his eyes pretty wide."

This remark shocked me as indicating a misconception of the way in which artistic impressions are formed in our minds, and because it seemed to imply that our eye is in that case simply a recording machine which takes snapshots.

M. de Guermantes, rejoicing that she should be speaking to me with so competent a knowledge of the subjects that interested me, appraised his wife's illustrious presence, listened to what she was saying about Franz Hals, and thought: "She's thoroughly at home in everything. Our young friend can go home and say that he's had before his eyes a great lady of the old school, in the full sense of the word, the like of whom couldn't be found anywhere else today." Thus I beheld the pair of them, divorced from that name Guermantes in which long ago I had imagined them leading an unimaginable life, now just like other men and other women, merely lagging a little behind their contemporaries, and that not evenly, as in so many households of the Faubourg Saint-Germain where the wife has had the good taste to stop at the golden, the husband the misfortune to come down to the pinchbeck age of the past, she remaining still Louis XV while her partner is pompously Louis-Philippe. That Mme de Guermantes should be like other women had been for me at first a disappointment; it was now, by a natural reaction, and with the help of so many good wines, almost a miracle. A Don John of Austria, an Isabella d'Este, situated for us in the world of names, have as little communication with the great pages of history as the Méséglise way had with the Guermantes. Isabella d'Este was no doubt in reality a very minor princess, similar to those who under Louis XIV obtained no special place at Court. But because she seems to us to be of a unique and therefore incomparable essence, we cannot conceive of her as being any less great than he, so that a supper-party with Louis XIV would appear to us only to be rather interesting, whereas with Isabella d'Este we should find ourselves miraculously transported into the presence of a heroine of romance. Then, after having studied Isabella d'Este, after having transplanted her patiently from that magic world into the world of history, and discovered that her life, her thought, contained nothing of that mysterious strangeness which had been suggested to us by her name, once we have recovered from our disappointment we feel a boundless gratitude to that princess for having had a knowledge of Mantegna's paintings almost equal to that, hitherto despised by us and put, as Françoise would have said, "lower than the dirt," of M. Lafenestre. After having scaled the inaccessible heights of the name Guermantes, on descending the inner slope of the life of the Duchess, I felt on finding there the names, familiar elsewhere, of Victor Hugo, Franz Hals and, I regret to say, Vibert, the same astonishment that an explorer, after having taken into account, in order to visualise the singularity of the native customs in some wild valley of Central America or Northern Africa, its geographical remoteness, the strangeness of its place-names and its flora, feels on discovering, once he has made his way through a screen of giant aloes or manchineels, inhabitants who (sometimes indeed among the ruins of a Roman theatre and beneath a column dedicated to Venus) are engaged in reading Voltaire's *Mérope* or *Alzire*. And, so remote, so distinct from, so superior to the educated women of the middle classes whom I had known, the similar culture by which Mme de Guermantes had made herself, with no ulterior motive, to gratify no ambition, descend to the level of people whom she would never know, had the praiseworthy character, almost touching in its uselessness, of a knowledge of Phoenician antiquities in a politician or a doctor.

"I might have been able to show you a very fine one," Mme de Guermantes said to me amiably, still speaking of Hals, "the finest in existence, some people say, which was left to me by a German cousin. Unfortunately, it turned out to be 'enfeoffed' in the castle—you don't know the expression? nor do I," she added, with her fondness for jokes (which made her, she thought, seem modern) at the expense of the old customs to which nevertheless she was unconsciously but fiercely attached. "I'm glad you have seen my Elstirs, but I must admit I should have been a great deal more glad if I could have done you the honours of my Hals, of that 'enfeoffed' picture."

"I know the one," said Prince Von, "it's the Grand Duke of Hesse's Hals."

"Quite so; his brother married my sister," said M. de Guermantes, "and his mother and Oriane's were first cousins as well."

"But so far as M. Elstir is concerned," the Prince went on, "I shall take the liberty of saying, without having any opinion of his work, which I do not know, that the hatred with which the Kaiser pursues him ought not, it seems to me, to be counted against him. The Kaiser is a man of marvellous intelligence."

"Yes, I've met him at dinner twice, once at my aunt Sagan's and once at my aunt Radziwill's, and I must say I found him quite unusual. I didn't find him at all simple! But there's something amusing about him, something 'forced'" (she detached the word) "like a green carnation, that is to say a thing that surprises me and doesn't please me enormously, a thing it's surprising that anyone should have been able to create but which I feel would have been just as well left uncreated. I trust I'm not shocking you?"

"The Kaiser is a man of astounding intelligence," resumed the Prince, "he is passionately fond of the arts, he has for works of art a taste that is practically infallible, he never makes a mistake: if a thing is good he spots it at once and takes a dislike to it. If he detests anything, there can be no more doubt about it, the thing is excellent."

Everyone smiled.

"You set my mind at rest," said the Duchess.

"I should be inclined to compare the Kaiser," went on the Prince, who, not knowing how to pronounce the word archaeologist (that is to say, as though it were spelt with a "k"), never missed an opportunity of using it, "to an old archaeologist" (but the Prince said "arsheologist") "we have in Berlin. If you put him in front of a genuine Assyrian antique, he weeps. But if it is a modern fake, if it is not really old, he does not weep. And so, when they want to know whether an arsheological piece is really old, they take it to the old arsheologist. If he weeps, they buy the piece for the Museum. If his eyes remain dry, they send it back to the dealer, and prosecute him for fraud. Well, every time I dine at Potsdam, if the Kaiser says to me of a play: 'Prince, you must see it, it's a work of genius,' I make a note not to go to it; and when I hear him fulminating against an exhibition, I rush to see it at the first possible opportunity."

"Norpois is in favour of an Anglo-French understanding, isn't he?" said M. de Guermantes.

"What good would that do you?" asked Prince Von, who could not endure the English, with an air at once irritated and crafty. "The English are so *schtubid*. I know, of course, that it would not be as soldiers that they would help you. But one can judge them, all the same, by the *schtubidity* of their generals. A friend of mine was talking the other day to Botha, you know, the Boer leader. He said to my friend: 'It's terrible, an army like that. I rather like the English, as a matter of fact, but just imagine that I, a mere *peassant*, have beaten them in every battle. And in the last, when I was overpowered by a force twenty times the strength of my own, even while surrendering because I had to, I managed to take two thousand prisoners! That was all right because I was only a leader of an army of *peassants*, but if those poor fools ever have to stand up against a European army, one trembles to think what may happen to them!' Besides, you have only to see how their King, whom you know as well as I do, passes for a great man in England."

I scarcely listened to these stories, of the kind that M. de Norpois used to tell my father; they supplied no food for my favourite trains of thought; and besides, even had they possessed the elements which they lacked, they would have had to be of a very exciting quality for my inner life to awaken during those hours in which I lived on the surface, my hair well brushed, my shirt-front starched, in which, that is to say, I could feel nothing of what constituted for me the pleasure of life.

"Oh, I don't agree with you at all," said Mme de Guermantes, who felt that the German prince was wanting in tact, "I find King Edward charming, so simple, and much cleverer than people think. And the Queen is, even now, the most beautiful thing I've ever seen in the world."

"But, *Matame* la Duchesse," said the Prince, who was losing his temper and unable to see that he was giving offence, "you must admit that if the Prince of Wales had been an ordinary person there isn't a club that wouldn't have blackballed him, and nobody would have been willing to shake hands with him. The Queen is charming, excessively gentle and dim-witted. But still, there's something shocking about a royal couple who are literally kept by their subjects, who get the big Jewish financiers to foot all the bills they ought to pay themselves, and create them Baronets in return. It's like the Prince of Bulgaria . . ."

"He's our cousin," put in the Duchess, "he's a witty fellow."

"He's mine, too, but we don't think him a good man on that account. No, it is us you ought to make friends with, it's the Kaiser's dearest wish, but he insists on its coming from the heart. He says: 'What I want to see is a hand clasped in mine, not waving a hat in the air.' With that, you would be invincible. It would be more practical than the Anglo-French rapprochement M. de Norpois preaches."*

"You know him, of course," said the Duchess, turning to me, so as not to leave me out of the conversation. Remembering that M. de Norpois had said that I had once looked as though I wanted to kiss his hand, and thinking that he had no doubt repeated this

story to Mme de Guermantes, and in any event could have spoken
of me to her only with malice, since in spite of his friendship with
my father he had not hesitated to make me appear so ridiculous, I
did not do what a man of the world would have done. He would
have said that he detested M. de Norpois, and had let him see it; he
would have said this so as to give himself the appearance of being
the deliberate cause of the Ambassador's slanders, which would
then have been no more than lying and calculated reprisals. I said,
on the contrary, that, to my great regret, I was afraid that M. de
Norpois did not like me.

"You're quite mistaken," replied the Duchess, "he likes you
very much indeed. You can ask Basin, for if people give me the
reputation of only saying nice things, he certainly doesn't. He will
tell you that we've never heard Norpois speak about anyone so
kindly as he spoke about you. And only the other day he was
wanting to give you a fine post at the Ministry. As he knew that
you were not very strong and couldn't accept it, he had the
delicacy not to speak of his kind thought to your father, for
whom he has an unbounded admiration."

M. de Norpois was quite the last person whom I should have
expected to do me any practical service. The truth was that, his
being a mocking and indeed somewhat malicious nature, those
who, like me, had let themselves be taken in by his outward
appearance of a Saint Louis delivering justice beneath an oak-
tree, by the affecting sounds that emerged from his somewhat too
tuneful lips, suspected real treachery when they learned of a
slander uttered at their expense by a man whose words had always
seemed so heartfelt. These slanders were frequent enough with
him. But that did not prevent him from taking a liking to people,
from praising those he liked and taking pleasure in showing willingness to help them.

"Not that I'm in the least surprised at his appreciating you," said
Mme de Guermantes, "he's an intelligent man. And I can quite
understand," she added, for the benefit of the rest of the party,
alluding to a plan of marriage of which I knew nothing, "that my
aunt, who has long ceased to amuse him as an old mistress, may not
seem of very much use to him as a new wife. Especially as
I understand that even as a mistress she hasn't functioned for
years now. Her only relations, if I may say so, are with God.
She is more churchy than you would believe, and Boaz-Norpois
can say, in the words of Victor Hugo:

> How long a time since she with whom I slept,
> O Lord, forsook my bed for yours!

Really, my poor aunt is like those avant-garde artists who have railed against the Academy all their lives, and in the end start a little academy of their own, or those unfrocked priests who fabricate a religion of their own. Might as well stick to the cloth, or not live together. But who knows," went on the Duchess with a meditative air, "it may be in anticipation of widowhood—there's nothing sadder than weeds one's not entitled to wear."

"Ah! if Mme de Villeparisis were to become Mme de Norpois, I really believe our cousin Gilbert would have a fit," said General de Monserfeuil. "The Prince de Guermantes is a charming man, but he really is rather taken up with questions of birth and etiquette," said the Princesse de Parme. "I went to spend a few days with them in the country, when the Princess, unfortunately, was ill in bed. I was accompanied by Petite." (This was a nickname that was given to Mme d'Hunolstein because she was enormously stout.) "The Prince came to meet me at the foot of the steps, and pretended not to see Petite. We went up to the first floor, and then at the entrance to the reception rooms, stepping back to make way for me, he said: 'Oh, how d'ye do, Mme d'Hunolstein' (he always calls her that now, since her separation) pretending to have caught sight of Petite for the first time, so as to show that he didn't have to come down to receive her at the foot of the steps."

"That doesn't surprise me in the least. I don't need to tell you," said the Duke, who regarded himself as extremely modern, more contemptuous than anyone in the world of mere birth, and in fact a Republican, "that I haven't many ideas in common with my cousin. Your Highness can imagine that we are about as much agreed on most subjects as day and night. But I must say that if my aunt were to marry Norpois, for once I should be of Gilbert's opinion. To be the daughter of Florimond de Guise and then to make a marriage like that would be enough, as the saying is, to make a cat laugh, when all's said and done." (These last words, which the Duke uttered as a rule in the middle of a sentence, were here quite superfluous. But he felt a perpetual need to say them which made him shift them to the end of a period if he had found no place for them elsewhere. They were for him, among other things, almost a question of prosody.) "Mind you," he added, "the Norpois are excellent people with a good place, of good stock."

"Listen to me, Basin, it's really not worth your while to poke fun at Gilbert if you're going to speak the same language as he does," said Mme de Guermantes, for whom the "goodness" of a family, no less than that of a wine, consisted in its age. But, less frank than her cousin and more subtle than her husband, she made a point of never in her conversation playing false to the Guermantes spirit, and despised rank in her speech while ready to honour it by her actions.

"But aren't you even some sort of cousins?" asked General de Monserfeuil. "I seem to remember that Norpois married a La Rochefoucauld."

"Not in that way at all, she belonged to the branch of the Ducs de La Rochefoucauld, and my grandmother comes from the Ducs de Doudeauville. She was own grandmother to Edouard Coco, the wisest man in the family," replied the Duke, whose views of wisdom were somewhat superficial, "and the two branches haven't intermarried since Louis XIV's time; the connexion would be rather distant."

"Really, how interesting; I never knew that," said the General.

"However," went on M. de Guermantes, "his mother, I believe, was the sister of the Duc de Montmorency, and had originally been married to a La Tour d'Auvergne. But as those Montmorencys are barely Montmorencys, while those La Tour d'Auvergnes are not La Tour d'Auvergnes at all, I cannot see that it gives him any very great position. He says—and this should be more to the point—that he's descended from Saintrailles, and as we ourselves are in a direct line of descent..."

There was at Combray a Rue de Saintrailles to which I had never given another thought. It led from the Rue de la Bretonnerie to the Rue de l'Oiseau. And as Saintrailles, the companion of Joan of Arc, had, by marrying a Guermantes, brought into the family that county of Combray, his arms were quartered with those of Guermantes at the base of one of the windows in Saint-Hilaire. I saw again a vision of dark sandstone steps, while a modulation of sound brought to my ears that name, Guermantes, in the forgotten tone in which I used to hear it long ago, so different from that in which it simply meant the genial hosts with whom I was dining this evening. If the name, Duchesse de Guermantes, was for me a collective name, it was not so merely in history, by the accumulation of all the women who had successively borne it, but also in the course of my own short life, which had already seen, in this single Duchesse de Guermantes, so many different women superimpose themselves, each one vanishing as soon as the next had acquired sufficient consistency. Words do not change their meaning as much in centuries as names do for us in the space of a few years. Our memories and our hearts are not large enough to be able to remain faithful. We have not room enough, in our present mental field, to keep the dead there as well as the living. We are obliged to build on top of what has gone before and is brought to light only by a chance excavation, such as the name Saintrailles had just opened up. I felt that it would be useless to explain all this, and indeed a little while earlier I had lied by implication in not answering when M. de Guermantes said to me: "You don't know our little corner?" Perhaps he was quite well aware that I did know it, and it was only from good breeding that he did not press the question. Mme de Guermantes drew me out of my meditation.

"Really, I find all that sort of thing too deadly. I say, it's not always as boring as this at my house. I hope you'll soon come and dine again as a compensation, with no pedigrees next time," she said to me in a low voice, incapable both of appreciating the kind of charm which I might find in her house and of having sufficient humility to be content to appeal to me simply as a herbarium filled with plants of another day.

What Mme de Guermantes believed to be disappointing my expectations was on the contrary what in the end—for the Duke and the General went on to discuss pedigrees now without stopping—saved my evening from being a complete disappointment. How could I have felt otherwise until now? Each of my fellow-guests at dinner, decking out the mysterious name under which I had merely known and dreamed of them at a distance in a body and a mind similar or inferior to those of all the people I knew, had given me the impression of a commonplace dullness which the view on entering the Danish port of Elsinore would give to any passionate admirer of *Hamlet*. No doubt these geographical regions and that ancient past which put forest glades and Gothic belfries into their names had in a certain measure formed their faces, their minds and their prejudices, but survived in them only as does the cause in the effect, that is to say as a thing possible for the intelligence to perceive but in no way perceptible to the imagination.

And these old-time prejudices restored in a flash to the friends of M. and Mme de Guermantes their lost poetry. Assuredly, the notions in the possession of the nobility which make them the scholars, the etymologists of the language not of words but of names (and even then only in comparison with the ignorant mass of the middle classes, for if at the same level of mediocrity a devout Catholic would be better able to stand questioning on the details of the liturgy than a free-thinker, on the other hand an anti-clerical archaeologist can often give points to his parish priest on every-thing connected even with the latter's own church), those notions, if we are to keep to the truth, that is to say to the spirit, did not even have for these noblemen the charm that they would have had for a bourgeois. They knew perhaps better than I that the Duchesse de Guise was Princess of Cleves, of Orléans, of Porcien, and all the rest, but they had known, long before they knew all these names, the face of the Duchesse de Guise which thenceforth that name reflected back to them. I had begun with the fairy, even if she was fated soon to perish; they with the woman.

In middle-class families one sometimes sees jealousies spring up if the younger sister marries before the elder. So the aristocratic world, Courvoisiers especially but Guermantes also, reduced its ennobled greatness to simple domestic superiorities, by virtue of a childishness which I had met originally (and this for me was its sole charm) in books. Is it not just as though Tallemant des Réaux were speaking of the Guermantes, and not of the Rohans, when he relates with evident satisfaction how M. de Guéménée cried to his brother: "You can come in here; this is not the Louvre!" and said of the Chevalier de Rohan (because he was a natural son of the Duc de Clermont): "At any rate he's a prince." The only thing that distressed me in all this talk was to find that the absurd stories which were being circulated about the charming adopted Grand Duke of Luxembourg found as much credence in this salon as they had among Saint-Loup's friends. Plainly it was an epidemic that would not last longer than perhaps a year or two but had mean-while infected everyone. People repeated the same old stories, or enriched them with others equally untrue. I gathered that the Princesse de Luxembourg herself, while apparently defending her nephew, supplied weapons for the assault. "You are wrong to stand up for him," M. de Guermantes told me, as Saint-Loup had told me before. "Look, even leaving aside the opinion of our family, which is unanimous, you have only to talk to his servants,

and they, after all, are the people who know us best. Mme de
Luxembourg gave her little negro page to her nephew. The negro
came back in tears: 'Grand Duke beat me, me no bad boy, Grand
Duke naughty man, just fancy!' And I can speak with some
knowledge, he's Oriane's cousin."

I cannot, by the way, say how many times in the course of this
evening I heard the word "cousin" used. On the one hand, M. de
Guermantes, almost at every name that was mentioned,
exclaimed: "But he's Oriane's cousin!" with the sudden delight
of a man who, lost in a forest, reads at the ends of a pair of arrows
pointing in opposite directions on a signpost, and followed by
quite a low number of kilometres, the words: "Belvédère Casimir-
Périer" and "Croix du Grand-Veneur," and gathers from them
that he is on the right road. On the other hand the word cousin
was employed in a wholly different connexion (which was here
the exception to the prevailing rule) by the Turkish Ambassadress,
who had come in after dinner. Devoured by social ambition and
endowed with a real power of assimilating knowledge, she would
pick up with equal facility Xenophon's story of the Retreat of the
Ten Thousand or the details of sexual perversion among birds. It
would have been impossible to catch her out on any of the most
recent German publications, whether they dealt with political
economy, mental aberrations, the various forms of onanism, or
the philosophy of Epicurus. She was, incidentally, a dangerous
person to listen to, for, perpetually in error, she would point out to
you as being of the loosest morals women of irreproachable virtue,
would put you on your guard against a man with the most
honourable intentions, and would tell you anecdotes of the sort
that seem always to have come out of a book, not so much because
they are serious as because they are so wildly improbable.

She was at this period little received in society. For some weeks
now she had been frequenting the houses of women of real social
brilliance, such as the Duchesse de Guermantes, but in general had
confined herself, of necessity, as regards the noblest families, to
obscure scions whom the Guermantes no longer called on. She
hoped to prove her social credentials by quoting the most historic
names of the little-known people who were her friends. At once
M. de Guermantes, thinking that she was referring to people who
frequently dined at his table, quivered with joy at finding himself
once more in sight of a landmark and uttered the rallying-cry:
"But he's Oriane's cousin! I know him as well as I know my own

name. He lives in the Rue Vaneau. His mother was Mlle d'Uzès."
The Ambassadress was obliged to admit that her specimen had
been drawn from smaller game. She tried to connect her friends
with those of M. de Guermantes by means of a detour. "I know
quite well who you mean. No, it's not those ones, they're cousins."
But this reflux launched by the unfortunate Ambassadress ran
but a little way. For M. de Guermantes, losing interest, answered:
"Oh, then I don't know who you're talking about." The
Ambassadress offered no reply, for if she never knew anyone nearer
than the "cousins" of those whom she ought to have known in
person, very often these cousins were not even related at all. Then,
from the lips of M. de Guermantes, would flow a fresh wave
of "But she's Oriane's cousin!"—words which seemed to have
for the Duke the same practical value in each of his sentences as
certain epithets which the Roman poets found convenient
because they provided them with dactyls or spondees for their
hexameters.

At least the explosion of "But she's Oriane's cousin!" appeared
to me quite natural when applied to the Princesse de Guermantes,
who was indeed very closely related to the Duchess. The
Ambassadress did not seem to care for this Princess. She said to
me in an undertone: "She is stupid. No, she's not so beautiful as all
that. That reputation is usurped. Anyhow," she went on, with
an air at once considered, dismissive and decisive, "I find her
extremely antipathetic." But often the cousinship extended a
great deal further, Mme de Guermantes making it a point of
honour to address as "Aunt" ladies with whom it would have been
impossible to find her an ancestress in common without going
back at least to Louis XV; just as, whenever the "hardness" of the
times brought it about that a multimillionairess married a prince
whose great-great-grandfather had married, as had Oriane's also, a
daughter of Louvois, one of the chief joys of the fair American was
to be able, after a first visit to the Hôtel de Guermantes, where she
was, incidentally, somewhat coolly received and critically
dissected, to say "Aunt" to Mme de Guermantes, who allowed
her to do so with a maternal smile. But little did it matter to
me what "birth" meant for M. de Guermantes and M. de
Monserfeuil; in the conversations which they held on the subject
I sought only a poetic pleasure. Without being conscious of it
themselves, they procured me this pleasure as might a couple of
farmers or sailors speaking of the soil or the tides, realities too little

detached from their own lives for them to be capable of enjoying the beauty which personally I undertook to extract from them.

Sometimes, rather than of a race, it was of a particular fact, of a date, that a name reminded me. Hearing M. de Guermantes recall that M. de Bréauté's mother had been a Choiseul and his grandmother a Lucinge, I fancied I could see beneath the commonplace shirt-front with its plain pearl studs, bleeding still in two globes of crystal, those august relics, the hearts of Mme de Praslin and of the Duc de Berry. Others were more voluptuous: the fine and flowing hair of Mme Tallien or Mme de Sabran.

Sometimes it was more than a simple relic that I saw. Better informed than his wife as to what their ancestors had been, M. de Guermantes had at his command memories which gave to his conversation a fine air of an ancient mansion, lacking in real masterpieces but still full of pictures, authentic, indifferent and majestic, which taken as a whole has an air of grandeur. The Prince d'Agrigente having asked why the Prince Von had said, in speaking of the Duc d'Aumale, "my uncle," M. de Guermantes replied: "Because his mother's brother, the Duke of Württemberg, married a daughter of Louis-Philippe." At once I was lost in contemplation of a reliquary such as Carpaccio or Memling used to paint, from its first panel in which the princess, at the wedding festivities of her brother the Duc d'Orléans, appeared wearing a plain garden dress to indicate her ill-humour at having seen her ambassadors, who had been sent to sue on her behalf for the hand of the Prince of Syracuse, return empty-handed, down to the last, in which she has just given birth to a son, the Duke of Württemberg (the uncle of the prince with whom I had just dined), in that castle called Fantaisie, one of those places which are as aristocratic as certain families, for they too, outlasting a single generation, see attached to themselves more than one historical personage: in this one, notably, survive side by side memories of the Margravine of Bayreuth, of that other somewhat fantastic princess (the Duc d'Orléans's sister), to whom, it was said, the name of her husband's castle made a distinct appeal, of the King of Bavaria, and finally of the Prince Von whose address it now in fact was, at which he had just asked the Duc de Guermantes to write to him, for he had succeeded to it and let it only during the Wagner festivals, to the Prince de Polignac, another delightful "fantasist." When M. de Guermantes, to explain how he was related to Mme d'Arpajon, was obliged to go back, so far and so simply, along the chain formed by the joined hands of three or five ancestresses, to Marie-Louise or Colbert, it was the same thing again: in each of these cases, a great historical event appeared only in passing, masked, distorted, reduced, in the name of a property, in the Christian names of a woman, chosen for her because she was the grand-daughter of Louis-Philippe and Marie-Amélie, considered no longer as King and Queen of France but only in so far as, in their capacity as grandparents, they bequeathed a heritage. (We see for other reasons in a glossary to the works of Balzac, where the most illustrious personages figure only according to their connexion with the *Comédie Humaine*, Napoleon occupying a space consid-erably less than that allotted to Rastignac, and occupying that space solely because he once spoke to Mlle de Cinq-Cygne.) Thus does the aristocracy, in its heavy structure, pierced with rare windows, admitting a scanty daylight, showing the same incapacity to soar but also the same massive and blind force as Romanesque architecture, embody all our history, immuring it, beetling over it.

Thus the empty spaces of my memory were covered by degrees with names which in arranging, composing themselves in relation to one another, in linking themselves to one another by increas-ingly numerous connexions, resembled those finished works of art in which there is not one touch that is isolated, in which every part in turn receives from the rest a justification which it confers on them in turn.

M. de Luxembourg's name having been brought up again, the Turkish Ambassadress told us how, the young bride's grandfather (he who had made that immense fortune out of flour and pasta) having invited M. de Luxembourg to lunch, the latter had written to decline, putting on the envelope: "M. So-and-so, miller," to which the grandfather had replied: "I am all the more disappointed that you were unable to come, my dear friend, in that I should have been able to enjoy your society in privacy, for we were an intimate party and there would have been only the miller, his son, and you."[36] This story was not merely utterly distasteful to me, who knew how inconceivable it was that my dear M. de Nassau could write to his wife's grandfather (whose fortune, moreover, he was expecting to inherit) and address him as "miller"; but further-more its stupidity was glaring from the start, the word "miller" having obviously been dragged in only to lead up to the title of La Fontaine's fable. But there is in the Faubourg Saint-Germain a silliness so great, when it is aggravated by malice, that everyone agreed that it was "well said" and that the grandfather, whom at once everyone confidently declared to have been a remarkable man, had shown a prettier wit than his grandson-in-law. The Duc de Châtellerault wanted to take advantage of this story to tell the one I had heard in the café: "Everyone had to lie down!"— but scarcely had he begun, or reported M. de Luxembourg's pretension that in his wife's presence M. de Guermantes ought to stand up, when the Duchess stopped him with the protest: "No, he's very absurd, but not as bad as that." I was privately convinced that all these stories at the expense of M. de Luxembourg were equally untrue, and that whenever I found myself face to face with any of the reputed actors or spectators I should hear the same denial. I wondered, however, whether the denial just uttered by Mme de Guermantes had been inspired by regard for truth or by pride. In any event the latter quality succumbed to malice, for she added with a laugh: "Not that I haven't had my little snub too, for he invited me to luncheon, wishing to introduce me to the Grand Duchess of Luxembourg, which is how he has the good taste to describe his wife when he's writing to his aunt. I sent a reply expressing my regret, and adding: As for the 'Grand Duchess of Luxembourg' (in inverted commas), tell her that if she wants to come to see me I am at home every Thursday after five. I even had another snub. Happening to be in Luxembourg, I telephoned and asked to speak to him. His Highness was going into luncheon, had just risen from luncheon, two hours went by and nothing happened; so then I employed another method: 'Will you tell the Comte de Nassau to come and speak to me?' Cut to the quick, he was at the instrument that very minute." Everyone laughed at the Duchess's story, and at other analogous, that is to say (I am convinced of it) equally untrue stories, for a man more intelligent, kinder, more refined, in a word more exquisite than this Luxembourg-Nassau I have never met. The sequel will show that it was I who was right. I must admit that, in the midst of her scurrilous onslaught, Mme de Guermantes nevertheless did have a kind word for him.

"He wasn't always like that," she informed us. "Before he went off his head, like the man in the story-book who thinks he's become king, he was no fool, and indeed in the early days of his engagement he used to speak of it in really quite a nice way, as an undreamed-of happiness: 'It's just like a fairy-tale; I shall have to make my entry into Luxembourg in a fairy coach,' he said to his uncle d'Ornessan, who answered—for you know it's not a very big place, Luxembourg: 'A fairy coach! I'm afraid, my dear fellow, you'd never get it in. I should suggest that you take a goat-cart.' Not only did this not annoy Nassau, but he was the first to tell us the story, and to laugh at it."

"Ornessan is a witty fellow, and he has every reason to be; his mother was a Montjeu. He's in a very bad way now, poor Ornessan."

This name had the magic virtue of interrupting the flow of stale witticisms which otherwise would have gone on for ever. For M. de Guermantes went on to explain that M. d'Ornessan's great-grandmother had been the sister of Marie de Castille Montjeu, the wife of Timoléon de Lorraine, and consequently Oriane's aunt, with the result that the conversation drifted back to genealogies, while the imbecile Turkish Ambassadress breathed in my ear: "You appear to be very much in the Duke's good books; have a care!" and, on my demanding an explanation: "I mean to say— verb. sap.—he's a man to whom one could safely entrust one's daughter, but not one's son." Now if ever, on the contrary, there was a man who was passionately and exclusively a lover of women, it was certainly the Duc de Guermantes. But error, untruth fatuously believed, were for the Ambassadress like a vital element out of which she could not move. "His brother Mémé, who is, as it happens, for other reasons altogether" (he ignored her) "profoundly uncongenial to me, is genuinely distressed by the Duke's morals. So is their aunt Villeparisis. Ah, now, her I adore! There is a saint of a woman for you, the true type of the great ladies of the past. She's not only virtue itself but reserve itself. She still says 'Monsieur' to the Ambassador Norpois whom she sees every day, and who, by the way, made an excellent impression in Turkey."

I did not even reply to the Ambassadress, in order to listen to the genealogies. They were not all of them important. It happened indeed that one of the alliances about which I learned from M. de Guermantes in the course of the conversation was a mis-alliance, but one not without charm, for, uniting under the July Monarchy the Duc de Guermantes and the Duc de Fezensac with the two irresistible daughters of an eminent navigator, it gave to the two duchesses the unexpected piquancy of an exotically bourgeois, "Louisphilippically" Indian grace. Or else, under Louis

XIV, a Norpois had married the daughter of the Duc de Mortemart, whose illustrious title, in that far-off epoch, struck the name Norpois, which I had found lacklustre and might have supposed to be recent, and engraved it deeply with the beauty of an old medal. And in these cases, moreover, it was not only the less well-known name that benefited by the association; the other, hackneyed by its very glitter, struck me more forcibly in this novel and more obscure aspect, just as among the portraits painted by a brilliant colourist the most striking is sometimes one that is all in black. The sudden mobility with which all these names seemed to me to have been endowed, as they sprang to take their places by the side of others from which I should have supposed them to be remote, was due not to my ignorance alone; the to-ings and fro-ings which they were performing in my mind had been performed no less readily at those epochs in which a title, being always attached to a piece of land, used to follow it from one family to another, so much so that, for example, in the fine feudal structure that is the title of Duc de Nemours or Duc de Chevreuse, I might discover successively, crouching as in the hospitable abode of a hermit-crab, a Guise, a Prince of Savoy, an Orléans, a Luynes. Sometimes several remained in competition for a single shell: for the Principality of Orange the royal house of the Netherlands and MM. de Mailly-Nesle, for the Duchy of Brabant the Baron de Charlus and the royal house of Belgium, various others for the titles of Prince of Naples, Duke of Parma, Duke of Reggio. Sometimes it was the other way; the shell had been so long uninhabited by proprietors long since dead that it had never occurred to me that this or that name of a castle could have been, at an epoch which after all was comparatively recent, the name of a family. Thus, when M. de Guermantes replied to a question put to him by M. de Monserfeuil: "No, my cousin was a fanatical royalist; she was the daughter of the Marquis de Féterne, who played some part in the Chouan rising," on seeing this name Féterne, which to me, since my stay at Balbec, had been the name of a castle, become, what I had never dreamed that it could possibly be, a family name, I felt the same astonishment as in reading a fairy-tale where turrets and a terrace come to life and turn into men and women. In this sense of the words, we may say that history, even mere family history, restores old stones to life. There have been in Parisian society men who played as consider-able a part in it, who were more sought after for their distinction or

for their wit, who were equally well born as the Duc de
Guermantes or the Duc de La Trémoïlle. They have now fallen
into oblivion because, as they left no descendants, their name,
which we no longer hear, has an unfamiliar ring; at most, like the
name of a thing beneath which we never think to discover the
name of any person, it survives in some remote castle or village.
The day is not distant when the traveller who, in the heart of
Burgundy, stops in the little village of Charlus to look at its church,
if he is not studious enough or is in too great a hurry to examine its
tombstones, will go away ignorant of the fact that this name,
Charlus, was that of a man who ranked with the highest in the
land. This thought reminded me that it was time to go, and that
while I listened to M. de Guermantes talking pedigrees, the hour
was approaching at which I had promised to call on his brother.
"Who knows," I continued to muse, "whether one day
Guermantes itself may appear nothing more than a place-name,
save to the archaeologists who, stopping by chance at Combray
and standing beneath the window of Gilbert the Bad, have the
patience to listen to the account given them by Théodore's successor or to read the Curé's guide?" But so long as a great name is
not extinct it keeps the men and women who bear it in the
limelight; and doubtless to some extent the interest which the
illustriousness of these families gave them in my eyes lay in the fact
that one can, starting from today, follow their ascending course,
step by step, to a point far beyond the fourteenth century, and find
the diaries and correspondence of all the forebears of M. de
Charlus, of the Prince d'Agrigente, of the Princesse de Parme, in
a past in which an impenetrable darkness would cloak the origins
of a middle-class family, and in which we make out, in the
luminous backward projection of a name, the origin and persistence of certain nervous characteristics, vices and disorders of one
or another Guermantes. Almost pathologically identical with their
namesakes of the present day, they excite from century to century
the startled interest of their correspondents, whether these be
anterior to the Princess Palatine and Mme de Motteville, or
subsequent to the Prince de Ligne.

However, my historical curiosity was faint in comparison with
my aesthetic pleasure. The names cited had the effect of disem-
bodying the Duchess's guests—for all that they were called
the Prince d'Agrigente or of Cystria—whose masks of flesh and
unintelligence or vulgar intelligence had transformed them into

ordinary mortals, so much so that I had made my landing on the
ducal door-mat not as upon the threshold (as I had supposed) but
as at the terminus of the enchanted world of names. The Prince
d'Agrigente himself, as soon as I heard that his mother had been a
Damas, a granddaughter of the Duke of Modena, was delivered,
as from an unstable chemical alloy, from the face and speech that
prevented one from recognising him, and went to form with
Damas and Modena, which themselves were only titles, an infinitely more seductive combination. Each name displaced by the
attraction of another with which I had never suspected it of having
any affinity left the unalterable position which it had occupied in
my brain, where familiarity had dulled it, and, speeding to join the
Mortemarts, the Stuarts or the Bourbons, traced with them
branches of the most graceful design and ever-changing colour.
The name Guermantes itself received from all the beautiful
names—extinct, and so all the more glowingly rekindled—with
which I learned only now that it was connected, a new and purely
poetic sense and purpose. At the most, at the extremity of each
spray that burgeoned from the exalted stem, I could see it flower in
some face of a wise king or illustrious princess, like the sire of
Henri IV or the Duchesse de Longueville. But as these faces,
different in this respect from those of the party around me, were
not overlaid for me by any residue of physical experience or social
mediocrity, they remained, in their handsome outlines and rainbow iridescence, homogeneous with those names which at regular intervals, each of a different hue, detached themselves from the
genealogical tree of Guermantes, and disturbed with no foreign or
opaque matter the translucent, alternating, multicoloured buds
which like the ancestors of Jesus in the old Jesse windows, blossomed on either side of the tree of glass.

Already I had made several attempts to slip away, on account,
more than for any other reason, of the insignificance which my
presence in it imparted to the gathering, although it was one of
those which I had long imagined as being so beautiful—as it would
doubtless have been had there been no inconvenient witness
present. At least my departure would allow the guests, once the
interloper had gone, to form themselves into a closed group. They
would be free to celebrate the mysteries for which they had
assembled there, since it could obviously not have been to talk
of Franz Hals or of avarice, and to talk of them in the same way as
people talk in bourgeois society. They spoke nothing but

trivialities, doubtless because I was in the room, and I felt with some compunction, on seeing all these pretty women kept apart, that I was preventing them by my presence from carrying on, in the most precious of its drawing-rooms, the mysterious life of the Faubourg Saint-Germain. But M. and Mme de Guermantes carried the spirit of self-sacrifice so far as to keep postponing, by detaining me, this departure which I was constantly trying to effect. A more curious thing still, several of the ladies who had come hurrying, ecstatic, decked out in their finery, bespangled with jewels, only to attend a party which, through my fault, differed in essence from those that are given elsewhere than in the Faubourg Saint-Germain no more than one feels oneself at Balbec to be in a town that differs from what one's eyes are accustomed to see—several of these ladies left, not at all disappointed, as they had every reason to be, but thanking Mme de Guermantes most effusively for the delightful evening which they had spent, as though on other days, those on which I was not present, nothing more occurred.

Was it really for the sake of dinners such as this that all these people dressed themselves up and refused to allow middle-class women to penetrate into their so exclusive drawing-rooms—for dinners such as this, identical had I been absent? The suspicion flashed across my mind for a moment, but it was too absurd. Plain commonsense enabled me to brush it aside. And then, if I had adopted it, what would have been left of the name Guermantes, already so debased since Combray?

It struck me that these flower-maidens were, to a strange extent, easily pleased with another person, or anxious to please that person, for more than one of them, to whom I had not uttered during the whole course of the evening more than two or three casual remarks the stupidity of which had left me blushing, made a point, before leaving the drawing-room, of coming to tell me, fastening on me her fine caressing eyes, straightening as she spoke the garland of orchids that followed the curve of her bosom, what an intense pleasure it had been to her to make my acquaintance, and to speak to me—a veiled allusion to an invitation to dinner— of her desire to "arrange something" after she had "fixed a day" with Mme de Guermantes.

None of these flower-ladies left the room before the Princesse de Parme. The presence of the latter—one must never depart before royalty—was one of the two reasons, neither of which I had guessed, for which the Duchess had insisted so strongly on my remaining. As soon as Mme de Parme had risen, it was like a deliverance. Each of the ladies, having made a genuflexion before the Princess, who then raised her up from the ground, received from her in a kiss, and as it were a benediction which they had craved on their knees, the permission to ask for their cloaks and carriages. With the result that there followed, at the front door, a sort of stentorian recital of great names from the History of France. The Princesse de Parme had forbidden Mme de Guermantes to accompany her downstairs to the hall for fear of her catching cold, and the Duke had added: "There, Oriane, since Ma'am gives you leave, remember what the doctor told you."

"I think the Princesse de Parme was *very pleased* to dine with you." I knew the formula. The Duke had come the whole way across the drawing-room in order to utter it for my benefit with an obliging, earnest air, as though he were handing me a diploma or offering me a plateful of biscuits. And I guessed from the pleasure which he appeared to be feeling as he spoke, and which brought so gentle an expression momentarily into his face, that the duties and concerns which it represented for him were of the kind which he would continue to discharge to the very end of his life, like one of those honorific and easy posts which one is still allowed to retain even when senile.

Just as I was about to leave, the Princess's lady-in-waiting reappeared in the drawing-room, having forgotten to take away some wonderful carnations, sent up from Guermantes, which the Duchess had presented to Mme de Parme. The lady-in-waiting was somewhat flushed, and one felt that she had just been receiving a scolding, for the Princess, so kind to everyone else, could not contain her impatience at the stupidity of her attendant. And so the latter picked up the flowers quickly and ran, but to preserve an air of nonchalance and independence, flung at me as she passed: "The Princess says I'm keeping her waiting; she wants to be gone, and to have the carnations as well. After all, I'm not a little bird, I can't be in several places at once."

Alas! the rule of not leaving before royalty was not the only one. I could not depart at once, for there was another: this was that the famous prodigality, unknown to the Courvoisiers, with which the Guermantes, whether opulent or practically ruined, excelled in entertaining their friends, was not only a material prodigality, of the kind that I had often experienced with Robert de Saint-Loup, but also a prodigality of charming words, of courteous gestures, a whole system of verbal elegance fed by a positive cornucopia within. But as this last, in the idleness of fashionable existence, remains unemployed, it overflowed at times, sought an outlet in a sort of fleeting effusion which was all the more intense, and which might, on the part of Mme de Guermantes, have led one to suppose a genuine affection. She did in fact feel it at the moment when she let it overflow, for she found then, in the society of the friend, man or woman, with whom she happened to be, a sort of intoxication, in no way sensual, similar to that which music produces in certain people; she would suddenly pluck a flower from her bodice, or a medallion, and present it to someone with whom she would have liked to prolong the evening, with a melancholy feeling the while that such a prolongation could have led to nothing but idle talk, into which nothing could have passed of the nervous pleasure, the fleeting emotion, reminiscent of the first warm days of spring in the impression they leave behind them of lassitude and regret. As for the friend, it did not do for him to put too implicit a faith in the promises, more exhilarating than anything he had ever heard, tendered by these women who, because they feel with so much more force the sweetness of a moment, make of it, with a delicacy, a nobility of which normally constituted creatures are incapable, a compelling masterpiece of grace and kindness, and no longer have anything of themselves left to give when the next moment has arrived. Their affection does not outlive the exaltation that has dictated it; and the subtlety of mind which had then led them to divine all the things that you wished to hear, and to say them to you, will enable them just as easily, a few days later, to seize hold of your absurdities and use them to entertain another of their visitors with whom they will then be in the act of enjoying one of those "musical moments" which are so brief.

In the hall where I asked the footmen for my snowboots, which I had brought, not realising how unfashionable they were, as a precaution against the snow, a few flakes of which had already fallen, to be converted rapidly into slush, I felt, at the contemptuous smiles on all sides, a shame which rose to its highest pitch when I saw that Mme de Parme had not yet gone and was watching me put on my American "rubbers." The Princess came towards me. "Oh! what a good idea," she exclaimed, "it's so practical! There's a sensible man for you. Madame, we shall have to get a pair of those," she said to her lady-in-waiting, while the mockery of the footmen turned to respect and the other guests crowded round me to inquire where I had managed to find these marvels. "With those on, you will have nothing to fear even if it starts snowing again and you have a long way to go. You're independent of the weather," the Princess said to me.

"Oh! if it comes to that, Your Royal Highness can rest assured," broke in the lady-in-waiting with a knowing air, "it won't snow again."

"What do you know about it, Madame?" came witheringly from the excellent Princesse de Parme, whose temper only the stupidity of her lady-in-waiting could succeed in ruffling.

"I can assure Your Royal Highness that it can't snow again. It's a physical impossibility."

"But why?"

"It can't snow any more, because they've taken the necessary steps to prevent it: they've sprinkled salt in the streets!"

The simple-minded lady did not notice either the anger of the Princess or the mirth of the rest of her audience, for instead of remaining silent she said to me with a genial smile, paying no heed to my repeated denials of any connexion with Admiral Jurien de La Gravière: "Not that it matters, after all. Monsieur must have stout sea-legs. What's bred in the bone!"

Having escorted the Princesse de Parme to her carriage, M. de Guermantes said to me, taking hold of my greatcoat: "Let me help you into your skin." He had ceased even to smile when he employed this expression, for those that were most vulgar had for that very reason, because of the Guermantes affectation of simplicity, become aristocratic.

An exhilaration relapsing only into melancholy, because it was artificial, was what I also, although quite differently from Mme de Guermantes, felt once I had finally left her house, in the carriage that was to take me to that of M. de Charlus. We can as we choose abandon ourselves to one or other of two forces, of which one rises in ourselves, emanates from our deepest impressions, while the other comes to us from without. The first brings with it naturally a joy, the joy that springs from the life of those who create. The other current, that which endeavours to introduce into us the impulses by which persons external to ourselves are stirred, is not accompanied by pleasure; but we can add a pleasure to it, by a sort of recoil, in an intoxication so artificial that it turns swiftly into boredom, into melancholy—whence the gloomy faces of so many men of the world, and all those nervous conditions which may even lead to suicide. Now, in the carriage which was taking me to M. de Charlus, I was a prey to this second sort of exaltation, very different from that which is given us by a personal impression, such as I had received in other carriages, once at Combray, in Dr Percepied's gig, from which I had seen the spires of Martinville against the setting sun, another day at Balbec, in Mme de Villeparisis's barouche, when I strove to identify the reminiscence that was suggested to me by an avenue of trees. But in this third carriage, what I had before my mind's eye were those conversations that had seemed to me so tedious at Mme de Guermantes's dinner-table, for example Prince Von's stories about the German Emperor, General Botha and the British Army. I had just slid them into the internal stereoscope through the lenses of which, as soon as we are no longer ourselves, as soon as, endowed with a worldly spirit, we wish to receive our life only from other people, we give depth and relief to what they have said and done. Like a tipsy man filled with tender feeling for the waiter who has been serving him, I marvelled at my good fortune, a good fortune not recognised by me, it is true, at the actual moment, in having dined with a person who knew Wilhelm II so well and had told stories about him that were—upon my word—extremely witty. And, as I repeated to myself, with the Prince's German accent, the story of General Botha, I laughed out loud, as though this laugh, like certain kinds of applause which increase one's inward admiration, were necessary to the story as a corroboration of its hilariousness. Through the magnifying lenses, even those of Mme de Guermantes's pronouncements which had struck me as being stupid (as for example the one about the Hals pictures which one ought to see from the top of a tram-car) took on an extraordinary life and depth. And I must say that, even if this exaltation was quick to subside, it was not altogether unreasonable. Just as there may always come a day when we are glad to know the person whom we despise more than anyone in the world because he happens to be connected with a girl with whom we are in love, to whom he can introduce us, and thus offers us both utility and agreeableness, attributes in which we should have supposed him to be permanently lacking, so there is no conversation, any more than there are personal relations, from which we can be certain that we shall not one day derive some benefit. What Mme de Guermantes had said to me about the pictures which it would be interesting to see, even from a tram-car, was untrue, but it contained a germ of truth which was of value to me later on.

Similarly the lines of Victor Hugo which I had heard her quote were, it must be admitted, of a period earlier than that in which he became something more than a new man, in which he brought to light, in the order of evolution, a literary species hitherto unknown, endowed with more complex organs. In these early poems, Victor Hugo is still a thinker, instead of contenting him-self, like Nature, with providing food for thought. His "thoughts" he at that time expressed in the most direct form, almost in the sense in which the Duke understood the word when, feeling it to be "old hat" and otiose for the guests at his big parties at Guermantes to append to their signatures in the visitors' book a philosophico-poetical reflexion, he used to warn newcomers in a beseeching tone: "Your name, my dear fellow, but no 'thoughts,' please!" Now, it was these "thoughts" of Victor Hugo's (almost as absent from the *Légende des Siècles* as "tunes," as "melodies" are from Wagner's later manner) that Mme de Guermantes admired in the early Hugo. Nor was she altogether wrong. They were touch-ing, and already round about them, before their form had yet achieved the depth which it was to acquire only in later years, the rolling tide of words and of richly articulated rhymes rendered them unassimilable to the lines that one can discover in a Corneille, for example, lines in which a romanticism that is inter-mittent, restrained, and thus all the more moving, has nevertheless in no way penetrated to the physical sources of life, modified the unconscious and generalisable organism in which the idea is latent. And so I had been wrong in confining myself, hitherto, to the later volumes of Hugo. Of the earlier ones, of course, it was only with a fractional part that Mme de Guermantes embellished her conver-sation. But it is precisely by thus quoting an isolated line that one multiplies its power of attraction tenfold. The lines that had entered or returned to my mind during this dinner magnetised in turn, summoned to themselves with such force, the poems within which they were normally embedded, that my electrified hands could not hold out for longer than forty-eight hours against the force that drew them towards the volume in which were bound up the *Orientales* and the *Chants du Crépuscule*. I cursed Françoise's footman for having made a present to his native village of my copy of the *Feuilles d'Automne*, and sent him off without a moment's delay to buy me another. I read these volumes from cover to cover and found peace of mind only when I suddenly came across, awaiting me in the light in which she had bathed them, the lines which Mme de Guermantes had quoted to me. For all these reasons, conversations with the Duchess resembled the discoveries that we make in the library of a country house, out of date, incomplete, incapable of forming a mind, lacking in almost everything that we value, but offering us now and then some curious scrap of information, or even a quotation from a fine passage which we did not know and as to which we are glad to remember in after years that we owe our knowledge of it to a stately baronial mansion. We are then, as a result of having found Balzac's preface to the *Chartreuse*, or some unpublished letters of Joubert, tempted to exaggerate the value of the life we led there, the barren frivolity of which we forget for this windfall of a single evening.

From this point of view, if this world had been unable at the outset to respond to what my imagination expected, and was consequently to strike me first of all by what it had in common with every other world rather than by the ways in which it differed from them, it yet revealed itself to me by degrees as something quite distinct. Noblemen are almost the only people from whom one learns as much as one does from peasants; their conversation is adorned with everything that concerns the land, dwellings as people used to live in them long ago, old customs, everything of which the world of money is profoundly ignorant. Even supposing that the aristocrat most moderate in his aspirations has finally caught up with the period in which he lives, his mother, his uncles, his great-aunts keep him in touch, when he recalls his childhood, with the conditions of a life almost unknown today. In the death-chamber of a contemporary corpse Mme de Guermantes would not have pointed out, but would immediately have noticed, all the lapses from traditional customs. She was shocked to see women mingling with the men at a funeral, when there was a particular ceremony which ought to be celebrated for the women. As for the pall, the use of which Bloch would doubtless have believed to be confined to coffins, on account of the pall bearers of whom one reads in the reports of funerals, M. de Guermantes could remember the time when, as a child, he had seen it borne at the wedding of M. de Mailly-Nesle. While Saint-Loup had sold his priceless "genealogical tree," old portraits of the

Bouillons, letters of Louis XIII, in order to buy Carrières and Art Nouveau furniture, M. and Mme de Guermantes, actuated by a sentiment in which a fervent love of art may have played very little part and which left them themselves more commonplace, had kept their marvellous Boulle furniture, which presented an ensemble altogether more seductive to an artist. A literary man would similarly have been enchanted by their conversation, which would have been for him—for a hungry man has no need of another to keep him company—a living dictionary of all those expressions which every day are becoming more and more forgotten: St Joseph ties, children pledged to wear blue for Our Lady, and so forth, which one finds today only among those who have constituted themselves the amiable and benevolent custodians of the past. The pleasure that a writer experiences among them, far more than among other writers, is not without danger, for there is a risk of his coming to believe that the things of the past have a charm in themselves, of his transferring them bodily into his work, still-born in that case, exhaling a tedium for which he consoles himself with the reflexion: "It's attractive because it's true; that's how people do talk." These aristocratic conversations had moreover the charm, in Mme de Guermantes's case, of being couched in excellent French. For this reason they made permissible on the Duchess's part her hilarity at the words "vatic," "cosmic," "pythian," "supereminent," which Saint-Loup used to employ—as well as his Bing furniture.

When all was said, the stories I had heard at Mme de Guermantes's, very different in this respect from what I had felt in the case of the hawthorns, or when I tasted a *madeleine*, remained alien to me. Entering me for a moment and possessing me only physically, it was as though, being of a social, not an individual nature, they were impatient to escape. I writhed in my seat in the carriage like the priestess of an oracle. I looked forward to another dinner-party at which I might myself become a sort of Prince of X . . . , of Mme de Guermantes, and repeat them. In the meantime they made my lips quiver as I stammered them to myself, and I tried in vain to bring back and concentrate a mind that was carried away by a centrifugal force. And so it was with a feverish impatience not to have to bear the whole weight of them any longer by myself in a carriage where indeed I made up for the lack of conversation by soliloquising aloud, that I rang the bell at M. de Charlus's door, and it was in long monologues with myself, in which I rehearsed everything that I was going to tell him and gave scarcely a thought to what he might have to say to me, that I spent the whole of the time during which I was kept waiting in a drawing-room into which a footman showed me and which I was incidentally too excited to inspect. I felt so urgent a need for M. de Charlus to listen to the stories I was burning to tell him that I was bitterly disappointed to think that the master of the house was perhaps in bed, and that I might have to go home to work off by myself my verbal intoxication. I had just noticed, in fact, that I had been twenty-five minutes—that they had perhaps forgotten about me—in this room of which, despite this long wait, I could at the most have said that it was immense, greenish in colour, and contained a large number of portraits. The need to speak prevents one not merely from listening but from seeing, and in this case the absence of any description of external surroundings is tantamount to a description of an internal state. I was about to leave the room to try to get hold of someone, and, if I found no one, to make my way back to the hall and have myself let out, when, just as I had risen from my chair and taken a few steps across the mosaic parquet of the floor, a manservant came in with a troubled expression and said to me: "Monsieur le Baron has been engaged all evening, sir. There are still several people waiting to see him. I shall do everything I possibly can to get him to receive you; I have already telephoned up twice to the secretary."

"No; please don't bother. I had an appointment with M. le Baron, but it's now very late, and if he's busy this evening I can come back another day."

"Oh no, sir, you mustn't go away," cried the servant. "M. le Baron might be vexed. I will try again."

I was reminded of the things I had heard about M. de Charlus's servants and their devotion to their master. One could not quite say of him as of the Prince de Conti that he sought to give pleasure as much to the valet as to the minister, but he had shown such skill in making of the least thing that he asked of them a sort of personal favour that at night, when his body-servants were assembled round him at a respectful distance, and after running his eye over them he said: "Coignet, the candlestick!" or "Ducret, the night-shirt!" it was with an envious murmur that the rest used to with-draw, jealous of him who had been singled out by his master's favour. Two of them, indeed, who could not abide one another, used each to try to snatch the favour from his rival by going on the most flimsy pretext with a message to the Baron, if he had gone upstairs earlier than usual, in the hope of being invested for the evening with the charge of candlestick or nightshirt. If he addressed a few words directly to one of them on some subject outside the scope of his duty, still more if in winter, in the garden, knowing that one of his coachmen had caught cold, he said to him after ten minutes: "Put your cap on!" the others would not speak to the fellow again for a fortnight, in their jealousy of the great distinction that had been conferred on him.

I waited ten minutes more, and then, after requesting me not to stay too long as M. le Baron was tired and had had to send away several most important people who had made appointments with him many days before, they admitted me to his presence. These histrionic trappings with which M. de Charlus surrounded himself seemed to me a great deal less impressive than the simplicity of his brother Guermantes, but already the door stood open, and I could see the Baron, in a Chinese dressing-gown, with his throat bare, lying on a settee. My eye was caught at the same moment by a tall hat, its nap flashing like a mirror, which had been left on a chair with a cape, as though the Baron had but recently come in. The valet withdrew. I supposed that M. de Charlus would rise to greet me. Without moving a muscle he fastened on me a pair of implacable eyes. I went towards him and said good evening; he did not hold out his hand, made no reply, did not ask me to take a chair. After a moment's silence I asked him, as one would ask an ill-mannered doctor, whether it was necessary for me to remain standing. I said this with no ill intent, but my words seemed only to intensify the cold fury on M. de Charlus's face. I was not aware, moreover, that at home, in the country, at the Château de Charlus, he was in the habit after dinner (so much did he love to play the king) of sprawling in an armchair in the smoking-room, letting his guests remain standing round him. He would ask for a light from one, offer a cigar to another and then, after a few minutes' interval, would say: "But Argencourt, why don't you sit down? Take a chair, my dear fellow," and so forth, having made a point of keeping them standing simply to remind them that it was from him that they must receive permission to be seated. "Put yourself in the Louis XIV seat," he answered me with an imperious air, as though rather to force me to move further away from him than to invite me to be seated. I took an armchair which was comparatively near. "Ah! so that is what you call a Louis XIV seat! I can see you are a well-educated young man," he exclaimed in derision. I was so taken aback that I did not move, either to leave the house, as I ought to have done, or to change my seat, as he wished. "Sir," he next said to me, weighing each of his words, to the more insulting of which he prefixed a double yoke of consonants, "the interview which I have condescended to grant you, at the request of a person who desires to remain nameless, will mark the final point in our relations. I make no secret of the fact that I had hoped for better things! I should perhaps be straining the meaning of the words a little—which one ought not to do, even with people who are ignorant of their value, simply out of the respect due to oneself—were I to tell you that I had felt a certain *liking* for you. I think, however, that *benevolence*, in its most effectively patronising sense, would exceed neither what I felt nor what I was proposing to display. I had, immediately on my return to Paris, given you to understand, while you were still at Balbec, that you could count upon me." I who remembered with what a torrent of abuse M. de Charlus had parted from me at Balbec made an instinctive gesture of denial. "What!" he shouted angrily, and indeed his face, convulsed and white, differed as much from his ordinary face as does the sea when, on a stormy morning, one sees instead of its customary smiling surface a myriad writhing snakes of spray and foam, "do you mean to pretend that you did not receive my message—almost a declaration—that you were to remember me? What was there in the way of decoration round the cover of the book that I sent you?"

"Some very pretty plaited garlands with ornaments," I told him.

"Ah!" he replied scornfully, "the young in France know little of the treasures of our land. What would be said of a young Berliner who had never heard of the *Walküre*? Besides, you must have eyes to see and see not, since you yourself told me that you had spent two hours contemplating that particular treasure. I can see that you know no more about flowers than you do about styles. Don't protest that you know about styles," he cried in a shrill scream of rage, "you don't even know what you are sitting on. You offer your hindquarters a Directory fireside chair as a Louis XIV *bergère*. One of these days you'll be mistaking Mme de Villeparisis's lap for the lavatory, and goodness knows what you'll do in it. Similarly, you did not even recognise on the binding of Bergotte's book the lintel of myosotis over the door of Balbec church. Could there have been a clearer way of saying to you: 'Forget me not!'?"

I looked at M. de Charlus. Undoubtedly his magnificent head, though repellent, yet far surpassed that of any of his relatives; he was like an ageing Apollo; but an olive-hued, bilious juice seemed ready to start from the corners of his malevolent mouth; as for intellect, one could not deny that his, over a vast compass, had a grasp of many things which would always remain unknown to his brother Guermantes. But whatever the fine words with which he embellished all his hatreds, one felt that, whether he was moved by offended pride or disappointed love, whether his motivating force was rancour, sadism, teasing or obsession, this man was capable of committing murder, and of proving by dint of logic that he had been right in doing it and was still head and shoulders above his brother, his sister-in-law, or any of the rest.

"As, in Velazquez's *Surrender of Breda*," he went on, "the victor advances towards him who is the humbler in rank, and as is the duty of every noble nature, since I was everything and you were nothing, it was I who took the first steps towards you. You have made an imbecilic reply to what it is not for me to describe as an act of grandeur. But I did not allow myself to be discouraged. Our religion enjoins patience. The patience I have shown towards you will be counted, I hope, to my credit, and also my having only smiled at what might be denounced as impertinence, were it within your power to be impertinent to one who is so infinitely your superior. However, all this is now neither here nor there. I have subjected you to the test which the one eminent man of our world has ingeniously named the test of untoward kindness, and which he rightly declares to be the most terrible of all, the only one that can separate the wheat from the chaff. I can scarcely reproach you for having undergone it without success, for those who emerge from it triumphant are very few. But at least, and this is the conclusion which I am entitled to draw from the last words that we shall exchange on this earth, at least I intend to protect myself against your calumnious fabrications."

So far, I had never dreamed that M. de Charlus's rage could have been caused by an unflattering remark which had been repeated to him; I searched my memory; I had not spoken about him to anyone. Some ill-wisher had invented the whole thing. I protested to M. de Charlus that I had said absolutely nothing about him. "I don't think I can have annoyed you by saying to Mme de Guermantes that I was a friend of yours." He gave a disdainful smile, raised his voice to the supreme pitch of its highest register, and there, softly attacking the shrillest and most contumelious note, "Oh! Sir," he said, returning by the most gradual stages to a natural intonation, and seeming to revel as he went in the oddities of this descending scale, "I think you do yourself an injustice when you accuse yourself of having said that we were *friends*. I do not look for any great verbal accuracy in one who could all too easily mistake a piece of Chippendale for a rococo chair, but really I do not believe," he went on, with vocal caresses that grew more and more sardonically winning until a charming smile actually began to play about his lips, "I do not believe that you can ever have said, or thought, that we were *friends*! As for your having boasted that you had been *presented* to me, had *talked* to me, *knew* me slightly, had obtained, almost without solicitation, the prospect of becoming my *protégé*, I find it on the contrary very natural and intelligent of you to have done so. The extreme difference in age that there is between us enables me to recognise without absurdity that that *presentation*, those *talks*, that vague prospect of future *relations* were for you, it is not for me to say an honour, but still, when all is said and done, an advantage as to which I consider that your folly lay not in divulging it but in not having had the sense to keep it. I will even go so far as to say," he went on, switching suddenly and momentarily from haughty anger to a gentleness so tinged with melancholy that I thought he was going to burst into tears, "that when you left unanswered the proposal I made to you here in Paris, it seemed to me so unbelievable on your part, you who had struck me as well brought up and of a good *bourgeois* family" (on this adjective alone his voice gave a little hiss of impertinence), "that I was ingenuous enough to imagine all the tall stories that never happen, letters miscarrying, addresses misread. I recognise that it was extremely naïve of me, but St Bonaventure preferred to believe that an ox could fly rather than that his brother was capable of lying. However, all that is over: the idea did not appeal to you, there is no more to be said. It seems to me only that you might have brought yourself" (and there were genuine tears in his voice), "were it only out of consideration for my age, to write to me. I had conceived and planned for you infinitely seductive things, which I had taken good care not to divulge to you. You preferred to refuse without knowing what they were; that is your affair. But, as I say, one can always *write*. In your position, and indeed in my own, I should have done so. For that reason I prefer mine to yours—I say 'for that reason,' because I believe that all our positions are equal, and I have more fellow-feeling for an intelligent labourer than for many a duke. But I can say that I prefer my position, because in the whole course of my life, which is beginning now to be a pretty long one, I am conscious that I have never done what you did." (His head was turned away from the light, and I could not see if tears were falling from his eyes, as his voice led one to suppose.) "I said that I had advanced a long way towards you; the effect that had was to make you withdraw twice as far. Now it is for me to withdraw, and we shall know one another no longer. I shall retain not your name but your case, so that at moments when I might be tempted to believe that men have good manners, or simply the intelligence not to let slip an unparalleled opportunity, I may remember that that is ranking them too highly. No, that you should have said that you knew me when it was true—for henceforward it will cease to be true—I regard that as only natural, and I take it as an act of homage, that is to say something agreeable. Unfortunately, elsewhere and in other circumstances, you have uttered remarks of a very different nature."

"Monsieur, I swear to you that I have said nothing that could offend you."

"And who says that I am offended?" he screamed in fury, raising himself into an erect posture on the sofa on which hitherto he had been reclining motionless, while, as the pallid, frothing snakes twisted and stiffened in his face, his voice became alternately shrill and solemn like the deafening onrush of a storm. (The force with which he habitually spoke, which made strangers turn round in the street, was multiplied a hundredfold, as is a musical forte if, instead of being played on the piano, it is played by an orchestra, and changed into a fortissimo as well. M. de Charlus roared.) "Do you suppose that it is within your power to offend me? You are evidently not aware to whom you are speaking? Do you imagine that the envenomed spittle of five hundred little gentlemen of your type, heaped one upon another, would succeed in slobbering so much as the tips of my august toes?"

While he was speaking, my desire to persuade M. de Charlus that I had never spoken or heard anyone else speak ill of him had given place to a wild rage, provoked by the words which, to my mind, were dictated to him solely by his colossal pride. Perhaps they were indeed the effect, in part at any rate, of this pride. Almost all the rest sprang from a feeling of which I was then still

ignorant, and for which I could not therefore be blamed for not
making due allowance. Failing this unknown element, I might,
had I remembered the words of Mme de Guermantes, have been
tempted to assume a trace of madness in his pride. But at that
moment the idea of madness never even entered my head. There
was in him, in my view, only pride, while in me there was only
fury. This fury (at the moment when M. de Charlus ceased to
shout, in order to refer to his august toes, with a majesty that was
accompanied by a grimace, a vomit of disgust at his obscure
blasphemers), this fury could contain itself no longer. I felt a
compulsive desire to strike something, and, a lingering trace of
discernment making me respect the person of a man so much older
than myself, and even, in view of their dignity as works of art, the
pieces of German porcelain that were grouped around him, I
seized the Baron's new silk hat, flung it to the ground, trampled
it, picked it up again, began blindly pulling it to pieces, wrenched
off the brim, tore the crown in two, heedless of the continuing
vociferations of M. de Charlus, and, crossing the room in order to
leave, opened the door. To my intense astonishment, two footmen were standing one on either side of it, who moved slowly
away, so as to appear only to have been casually passing in the
course of their duty. (I afterwards learned their names; one was
called Burnier, the other Charmel.) I was not taken in for a
moment by the explanation which their leisurely gait seemed to
offer me. It was highly improbable; three others appeared to me to
be less so: one was that the Baron sometimes entertained guests
against whom, in case he happened to need assistance (but why?),
he deemed it necessary to keep reinforcements posted close at
hand; the second was that, drawn by curiosity, they had stopped to
listen at the keyhole, not thinking that I should come out so
quickly; the third, that, the whole of the scene which M. de
Charlus had made having been a piece of play-acting rehearsed
in advance, he had himself told them to listen, from a love of
spectacle combined, perhaps, with a *nunc erudimini*, "Be wise
now," by which everyone would profit.

My anger had not calmed that of M. de Charlus, and my
departure from the room seemed to cause him acute distress; he
called me back, shouted to his servants to stop me, and finally,
forgetting that a moment earlier, when he spoke of his "august
toes," he had thought to make me a witness of his own deification,
came running after me at full speed, overtook me in the hall, and

stood barring the door. "Come, now," he said, "don't be childish; come back for a minute; he that loveth well chasteneth well, and if I have chastened you well it is because I love you well." My anger had subsided; I let the word "chasten" pass and followed the Baron who, summoning a footman, ordered him without a trace of self-consciousness to clear away the remains of the shattered hat, which was replaced by another.

"If you will tell me, Monsieur, who it is that has treacherously maligned me," I said to M. de Charlus, "I will stay here to learn his name and to confute the impostor."

"Who? Do you not know? Do you retain no memory of the things you say? Do you think that the people who are so good as to inform me of such things do not begin by demanding secrecy? And do you imagine that I'm going to betray a person to whom I have given my promise?"

"So it's impossible for you to tell me?" I asked, racking my brains in a last fruitless effort to discover to whom I could have spoken about M. de Charlus.

"Did you not hear me say that I had given a promise of secrecy to my informant?" he said in a snarling voice. "I see that with your fondness for abject utterances you combine one for futile persistence. You ought at least to have the intelligence to profit from a final interview with me, and not go on talking for the sake of talking drivel."

"Monsieur," I replied, moving away from him, "you insult me. I am disarmed, because you are several times my age, we are not equally matched. Moreover, I cannot convince you. I have already sworn to you that I have said nothing."

"So I'm lying!" he screamed in a terrifying tone, and with a bound forward that brought him within a yard of me.

"Someone has misinformed you."

Then in a gentle, affectionate, melancholy voice, as in those symphonies which are played without a break between the different movements, in which a graceful scherzo, amiable and idyllic, follows the thunder-peals of the opening part, "It is quite possible," he said. "Generally speaking, a remark repeated at second hand is rarely true. It is your fault if, not having profited by the opportunities of seeing me which I had held out to you, you have not furnished me, by those frank and open words of daily intercourse which create confidence, with the unique and sovereign remedy against a remark which made you out a traitor. Either

way, true or false, the allegation has done its work. I can never rid
myself of the impression it made on me. I cannot even say that he
who chasteneth well loveth well, for I have chastened you well
enough but I no longer love you."

While saying this he had forced me to sit down and had rung the
bell. A different footman appeared. "Bring something to drink and
order the brougham." I said that I was not thirsty, that it was very
late, and that in any case I had a carriage waiting. "They have
probably paid him and sent him away," he told me, "you needn't
worry about that. I'm ordering a carriage to take you home . . . If
you're anxious about the time . . . I could have given you a room
here . . ." I said that my mother would be worried. "Ah! of course,
yes. Well, true or false, the remark has done its work. My affection, a trifle premature, had flowered too soon, and, like those
apple-trees of which you spoke so poetically at Balbec, it has been
unable to withstand the first frost."

If M. de Charlus's affection for me had not been destroyed, he
could hardly have acted differently, since, while assuring me that
we had fallen out, he made me sit down and drink, asked me to
stay the night, and was now going to send me home. He had
indeed an air of dreading the moment at which he must part from
me and find himself alone, that sort of slightly anxious fear which
his sister-in-law and cousin Guermantes had appeared to me to be
feeling when she had tried to force me to stay a little longer, with
something of the same momentary fondness for me, of the same
effort to prolong the passing minute.

"Unfortunately," he went on, "I have not the gift to cause what
has once been destroyed to blossom again. My affection for you is
quite dead. Nothing can revive it. I believe that it is not unworthy
of me to confess that I regret it. I always feel myself to be a little like
Victor Hugo's Boaz: 'I am widowed and alone, and darkness
gathers over me.' "

I walked back through the big green drawing-room with him.
I told him, speaking quite at random, how beautiful I thought it.
"Isn't it?" he replied. "It's a good thing to be fond of something.
The panelling is by Bagard. What is rather charming, d'you see, is
that it was made to match the Beauvais chairs and the consoles.
You observe, it repeats the same decorative design. There used to
be only two places where you could see this, the Louvre and
M. d'Hinnisdal's house. But naturally, as soon as I had decided
to come and live in this street, there cropped up an old family

house of the Chimays which nobody had ever seen before because it came here expressly for *me*. On the whole it's quite good. It might perhaps be better, but after all it's not bad. Some pretty things, are there not? These are portraits of my uncles, the King of Poland and the King of England, by Mignard. But why am I telling you all this? You must know it as well as I do, since you were waiting in this room. No? Ah, then they must have put you in the blue drawing-room," he said with an air that might have been either rudeness, on the score of my lack of curiosity, or personal superiority, in not having taken the trouble to ask where I had been kept waiting. "Look, in this cabinet I have all the hats worn by Madame Elisabeth, by the Princesse de Lamballe, and by Marie-Antoinette. They don't interest you; it's as though you couldn't see. Perhaps you are suffering from an affection of the optic nerve. If you like this kind of beauty better, here is a rainbow by Turner beginning to shine out between these two Rembrandts, as a sign of our reconciliation. You hear: Beethoven has come to join him." And indeed one could hear the first chords of the last movement of the Pastoral Symphony, "Joy after the Storm," performed somewhere not far away, on the first floor no doubt, by a band of musicians. I innocently inquired how they happened to be playing that, and who the musicians were. "Ah, well, one doesn't know. One never does know. It's invisible music. Pretty, isn't it?" he said to me in a slightly insolent tone, which nevertheless suggested somehow the influence and accent of Swann. "But you don't care two hoots about it. You want to go home, even if it means showing disrespect for Beethoven and for me. You are pronouncing judgment on yourself," he added, with an affectionate and mournful air, when the moment had come for me to go. "You will excuse my not accompanying you home, as good manners ordain that I should. Since I have decided not to see you again, spending five minutes more in your company would make very little difference to me. But I am tired, and I have a great deal to do." However, seeing that it was a fine night: "Ah, well, perhaps I will come in the carriage after all," he said. "There's a superb moon which I shall go on to admire from the Bois after I have taken you home. What, you don't know how to shave!— even on a night when you've been dining out, you have still a few hairs here," he said, taking my chin between two fingers which seemed as it were magnetised, and after a moment's resistance ran up to my ears like the fingers of a barber. "Ah! how pleasant it would be to look at the 'blue light of the moon' in the Bois with someone like yourself," he said to me with a sudden and almost involuntary gentleness, and then, sadly: "For you're nice, really; you could be nicer than anyone," he went on, laying his hand in a fatherly way on my shoulder. "Originally, I must confess that I found you quite insignificant." I ought to have reflected that he must find me so still. I had only to recall the rage with which he had spoken to me, barely half an hour before. In spite of this I had the impression that he was, for the moment, sincere, that his kindness of heart was prevailing over what I regarded as an almost frenzied condition of susceptibility and pride. The carriage was waiting beside us, and still he prolonged the conversation. "Come along," he said abruptly, "jump in, in five minutes we shall be at your door. And I shall bid you a good-night which will cut short our relations, for all time. It is better, since we must part for ever, that we should do so, as in music, on a common chord." Despite these solemn affirmations that we should never see one another again, I could have sworn that M. de Charlus, annoyed at having forgotten himself earlier in the evening and afraid of having hurt my feelings, would not have been displeased to see me once again. Nor was I mistaken, for, a moment later: "There, now," he said, "if I hadn't forgotten the most important thing of all. In memory of your grandmother, I have had a rare edition of Mme de Sévigné bound for you. I fear that that will prevent this from being our last meeting. One must console oneself with the reflexion that complicated affairs are rarely settled in a day. Just look how long they took over the Congress of Vienna."

"But I could send round for it without disturbing you," I said obligingly.

"Will you hold your tongue, you little fool," he replied angrily, "and not assume the grotesque air of regarding as a small matter the honour of being probably (I do not say certainly, for it will perhaps be one of my servants who hands you the volumes) received by me."

Then, regaining possession of himself: "I do not wish to part from you on these words. No dissonance; before the eternal silence, the dominant chord!" It was for his own nerves that he seemed to dread an immediate return home after harsh words of dissension. "You would not care to come to the Bois," he said to me in a tone that was not so much interrogative as affirmative, not, it seemed to me, because he did not wish to make me the offer, but because he was afraid that his self-esteem might meet with a refusal. "Ah, well," he went on, still postponing our separation, "it is the moment when, as Whistler says, the *bourgeois* go to bed" (perhaps he wished now to appeal to my self-esteem) "and it is meet to begin to look at things. But you don't even know who Whistler is!" I changed the subject and asked him whether the Princesse d'Iéna was an intelligent person. M. de Charlus stopped me, and, adopting the most contemptuous tone that I had yet heard him use, "Ah! there, sir," he said, "you are alluding to an order of nomenclature with which I do not hold. There is perhaps an aristocracy among the Tahitians, but I must confess that I know nothing about it. The name which you have just pronounced did sound in my ears, strangely enough, only a few days ago. Someone asked me whether I would condescend to allow the young Duc de Guastalla to be presented to me. The request astonished me, for the Duc de Guastalla has no need of an introduction to me, for the simple reason that he is my cousin, and has known me all his life; he is the son of the Princesse de Parme, and, as a well brought-up young kinsman, he never fails to come and pay his respects to me on New Year's Day. But, on making inquiries, I discovered that the young man in question was not my kinsman but the son of the person in whom you are interested. As there exists no princess of that title, I supposed that my friend was referring to some poor wanton sleeping under the Pont d'Iéna, who had picturesquely assumed the title of Princesse d'Iéna, as one talks about the Panther of the Batignolles, or the Steel King. But no, the reference was to a rich person who possesses some remarkable furniture which I had seen and admired at an exhibition, and which enjoys the superiority over the name of its owner of being genuine. As for this self-styled Duc de Guastalla, I supposed him to be my secretary's stockbroker; one can procure so many things with money. But no; it was the Emperor, it appears, who amused himself by conferring on these people a title which simply was not his to bestow. It was perhaps a sign of power, or of ignorance, or of malice, but in any case, I consider that it was an exceedingly scurvy trick to play on these unwitting usurpers. However, I cannot enlighten you on the subject; my knowledge begins and ends with the Faubourg Saint-Germain, where, among all the Courvoisiers and Gallardons, you will find, if you can manage to secure an introduction, plenty of old harridans taken straight out of Balzac who will amuse you. Naturally, all that has nothing to do with the prestige of the Princesse de Guermantes, but without me and my 'Open Sesame' her portals are inaccessible."

"The Princesse de Guermantes's house is really very beautiful."

"Oh, it's not very beautiful. It's the most beautiful thing in the world. Next to the Princess herself, of course."

"Is the Princesse de Guermantes superior to the Duchesse de Guermantes?"

"Oh! there's no comparison." (It is to be observed that, whenever people in society have the least touch of imagination, they will crown or dethrone, at the whim of their affections or their quarrels, those whose position appeared most solid and unalterably fixed.) "The Duchesse de Guermantes" (perhaps in not calling her "Oriane" he wished to set a greater distance between her and myself) "is delightful, far superior to anything you can have guessed. But really she is incommensurable with her cousin. The Princess is exactly what the people in the market-place might imagine Princess Metternich to have been, but *la* Metternich believed she had launched Wagner, because she knew Victor Maurel.[37] The Princesse de Guermantes, or rather her mother, knew the man himself. Which is a distinction, not to mention the incredible beauty of the lady. And the Esther gardens alone!"

"Can one not visit them?"

"No, you would have to be invited, but they never invite *anyone* unless I intercede."

But at once withdrawing the bait of this offer after having dangled it in front of me, he held out his hand, for we had reached my door.

"My role is at an end, sir. I will simply add these few words. Another person will perhaps offer you his affection some day as I have done. Let the present examples serve for your instruction. Do not neglect it. Affection is always precious. What one cannot do alone in this life, because there are things which one cannot ask, or do, or wish, or learn by oneself, one can do in company, and without needing to be thirteen, as in Balzac's *Story of the Thirteen*, or four, as in *The Three Musketeers*. Good-bye."

He must have been feeling tired and have abandoned the idea of going to look at the moonlight, for he asked me to tell his coachman to drive home. At once he made a sharp movement as though he had changed his mind. But I had already given the order, and, so as not to lose any more time, I went and rang my door-bell. It had not recurred to me for a moment that I had been meaning to tell M. de Charlus, on the subject of the German Emperor and General Botha, stories which had been such an obsession an hour ago but which his unexpected and crushing reception had sent flying far from my mind.

On entering my room I saw on my desk a letter which Françoise's young footman had written to one of his friends and had left lying there. Now that my mother was away, there was no liberty that he hesitated to take. I was even more at fault for taking the liberty of reading the letter which lay spread out before me with no envelope and (this was my sole excuse) seemed to be offering itself to my eyes.

Dear Friend and Cousin,

I hope this finds you in good health, and the same with all the young folk, particularily my young godson Joseph who I have not yet had the pleasure of meeting but who I preffer to you all as being my godson, these relics of the heart they also have their dust, upon their blest remains let us not lay our hands. Besides dear friend and cousin who can say that tomorrow you and your dear wife my cousin Marie, will not both be cast hedlong down into the bottom of the sea, like the sailor clinging to the mast on high, for this life is but a dark valley. Dear friend I must tell you that my principal occupation, which will astonish you I'm sure, is now poetry which I love passionately, for we must wile away the time. And so dear friend do not be too surprised if I have not ansered your last letter before now, in place of pardon let oblivion come. As you know, Madame's mother has past away amid unspeakable sufferings which fairly exausted her as she saw as many as three doctors. The day of her intern-ment was a great day for all Monsieur's relations came in crowds as well as several Ministers. It took them more than two hours to get to the cemetry, which will make you all open your eyes pretty wide in your village for they certainly wont do as much for mother Michu. So all my life to come can be but one long sob. I am enjoying myself imensely with the motorcycle which Ive recently learned. What would you say my dear friends if I arrived suddenly like that at full speed at Les Ecorres. But on that head I shall no more keep silence for I feel that the frenzy of grief sweeps its reason away. I am associating with the Duchesse de Guermantes, poeple whose names you have never even heard in our ignorant villages. Therefore it is with pleasure that Im going to send the works of Racine, of Victor Hugo, of Pages Choisies de Chenedollé, of Alfred de Musset, for I would cure the land which give me birth of ignorance which leads innevitably to crime. I cant think of anything more to say to you and send you like the pelican wearied by a long flite my best regards as well as to your wife my godson and your sister Rose. May it never be said of her: And Rose she lived only as live the roses, as has been said by Victor Hugo, the sonnet of Arvers, Alfred de Musset all those great geniuses who because of that were sent to die at the steak like Joan of Arc. Hoping for your next missive soon, your loving cousin Périgot Joseph.

We are attracted by any life which represents for us something unknown and strange, by a last illusion still unshattered. Many of the things that M. de Charlus had told me had given a vigorous spur to my imagination and, making it forget how much the reality had disappointed it at Mme de Guermantes's (people's names are in this respect like the names of places), had swung it towards Oriane's cousin. Moreover, M. de Charlus misled me for some time as to the imaginary worth and variety of society people only because he was himself misled. And this, perhaps, because he did nothing, did not write, did not paint, did not even read anything in a serious and thorough manner. But, superior as he was by several degrees to society people, if it was from them and the spectacle they afforded that he drew the material for his conversation, he was still not understood by them. Speaking as an artist, he could at the most bring out the deceptive charm of society people —but for artists only, in relation to whom he might be said to play the part played by the reindeer among the Eskimos: this precious animal plucks for them from the barren rocks lichens and mosses which they themselves could neither discover nor utilise, but which, once they have been digested by the reindeer, become for the inhabitants of the far North an assimilable form of food.

To which I may add that the pictures which M. de Charlus drew of society were animated with plenty of life by the blend of his ferocious hatreds and his passionate affections—hatreds directed mainly against young men, adoration aroused principally by certain women.

If among these the Princesse de Guermantes was placed by M. de Charlus upon the most exalted throne, his mysterious words about the "inaccessible Aladdin's palace" in which his cousin dwelt were not sufficient to account for my stupefaction, speedily followed by the fear that I might be the victim of some bad joke concocted by someone who wanted to get me thrown out of a house to which I had gone without being invited, when, about two months after my dinner with the Duchess and while she was at Cannes, having opened an envelope the appearance of which had not led me to suppose that it contained anything out of the ordinary, I read the following words engraved on a card: "The Princesse de Guermantes, *née* Duchesse en Bavière, At Home, the——th." No doubt to be invited to the Princesse de Guermantes's was perhaps not, from the social point of view, any more difficult than to dine with the Duchess, and my slight knowledge of heraldry had taught me that the title of Prince is not superior to that of Duke. Besides, I told myself that the intelligence of a society woman could not be essentially so dissimilar from that of the rest of her kind as M. de Charlus made out. But my imagination, like Elstir engaged upon rendering some effect of perspective without reference to the notions of physics which he might quite well possess, depicted for me not what I knew but what it saw; what it saw, that is to say what the name showed it. Now, even before I had met the Duchess, the name Guermantes preceded by the title of Princess, like a note or a colour or a quantity profoundly modified by surrounding values, by the mathematical or aesthetic "sign" that governs it, had always evoked for me something entirely different. With that title, it is to be found chiefly in the memoirs of the days of Louis XIII and Louis XIV; and I imagined the town house of the Princesse de Guermantes as being regularly frequented by the Duchesse de Longueville and the great Condé, whose presence there rendered it highly improbable that I should ever enter it.

In spite of whatever may stem from various subjective points of view, of which I shall have something to say later, in these artificial magnifications, the fact remains that there is a certain objective reality in all these people, and consequently a difference between them.

How, in any case, could it be otherwise? The humanity with which we consort and which bears so little resemblance to our dreams is none the less the same that, in the memoirs and in the letters of eminent persons, we have seen described and have felt a desire to know. The utterly insignificant old man we meet at dinner is the same who wrote that proud letter to Prince Friedrich-Karl which we read with such emotion in a book about the war of 1870. We are bored at the dinner-table because our imagination is absent, and, because it is keeping us company, we are interested in a book. But the people in question are the same. We should like to have known Mme de Pompadour, who was so valuable a patron of the arts, and we should have been as bored in her company as among the modern Egerias at whose houses we cannot bring ourselves to pay a second call, so mediocre do we find them. The fact remains that these differences do exist. People are never completely alike; their behaviour with regard to ourselves, at, one might say, the same level of friendship, reveals differences which, in the end, counter-balance one another. When I knew Mme de Montmorency, she enjoyed saying disagreeable things to me, but if I asked her a favour she would use all her influence as unstintingly and as effectively as possible in order to obtain what I needed. Whereas another woman, Mme de Guermantes for example, would never have wished to hurt my feelings, never said anything about me except what might give me pleasure, showered on me all those tokens of friendship which formed the rich texture of the Guermantes's moral life, but, if I asked her for the smallest thing above and beyond that, would not have moved an inch to procure it for me, as in those country houses where one has at one's disposal a motor-car and a valet but where it is impossible to obtain a glass of cider for which no provision has been made in the arrangements for a party. Which was for me the true friend, Mme de Montmorency, so happy to ruffle my feelings and always so ready to oblige, or Mme de Guermantes, distressed by the slightest offence that might have been given me and incapable of the slightest effort to be of use to me? Similarly, it was said that the Duchesse de Guermantes spoke only about frivolities, and her cousin, intellectually so mediocre, invariably about interesting things. Types of mind are so varied, so conflicting, not only in literature but in society, that Baudelaire and Mérimée are not the only people who have the right to despise one another mutually. These distinctive characteristics form in each person a system of looks, words and actions so coherent, so despotic, that when we are in his or her presence it seems to us superior to the rest. With Mme de Guermantes, her words, deduced like a theorem from her type of mind, seemed to me the only ones that could possibly be said. And at heart I was of her opinion when she told me that Mme de Montmorency was stupid and kept an open mind towards all the things she did not understand, or when, having heard of some malicious remark made by that lady, she said: "So that's what you call a kind woman. I call her a monster." But this tyranny of the reality which confronts us, this self-evidence of the lamp-light which turns the already distant dawn as pale as the faintest memory, disappeared when I was away from Mme de Guermantes and a different lady said to me, putting herself on my level and considering the Duchess as being far below either of us: "Oriane takes no interest, really, in anything or anybody," or even (something that in the presence of Mme de Guermantes it would have seemed impossible to believe, so loudly did she herself proclaim the opposite): "Oriane is a snob." Since no mathematical process would have enabled one to convert Mme d'Arpajon and Mme de Montpensier into commensurable quantities, it would have been impossible for me to answer had anyone asked me which of the two seemed to me superior to the other.

Now, among the characteristics peculiar to the Princesse de Guermantes's salon, the one most generally cited was an exclusiveness due in part to the Princess's royal birth but more especially to the almost fossilised rigidity of the Prince's aristocratic prejudices—which, incidentally, the Duke and Duchess had had no hesitation in deriding in front of me. This exclusiveness made me regard it as even more improbable that I should have been invited by this man who reckoned only in royal personages and dukes and at every dinner-party made a scene because he had not been put in the place to which he would have been entitled under Louis XIV, a place which, thanks to his immense erudition in matters of history and genealogy, he was the only person who knew. For this reason, many society people came down on the side of the Duke and Duchess when discussing the differences that distinguished them from their cousins. "The Duke and Duchess are far more modern, far more intelligent, they aren't simply interested, like the other couple, in how many quarterings one has, their salon is three hundred years in advance of their cousins'," were customary remarks, the memory of which made me tremble as I looked at the invitation card, since they made it all the more probable that it had been sent to me by some practical joker.

If the Duke and Duchess had not been still at Cannes, I might have tried to find out from them whether the invitation I had received was genuine. This state of doubt in which I was plunged is not in fact, as I deluded myself for a time by supposing, a sentiment which a man of fashion would not have felt and which consequently a writer, even if he otherwise belonged to the world of society, ought to reproduce in order to be thoroughly "objective" and to depict each class differently. I happened indeed, only the other day, in a charming volume of memoirs, to come upon the record of uncertainties analogous to those which the Princesse de Guermantes's card engendered in me. "Georges and I" (or "Hély and I"—I haven't the book at hand to verify the reference) "were so longing to be asked to Mme Delessert's that, having received an invitation from her, we thought it prudent, each of us independently, to make certain that we were not the victims of an April fool hoax." And the writer is none other than the Comte d'Haussonville (he who married the Duc de Broglie's daughter), while the other young man who "independently" tries to ascertain whether he is the victim of a hoax is, according to whether he is called Georges or Hély, one or other of the two inseparable friends of M. d'Haussonville, either M. d'Harcourt or the Prince de Chalais.

The day on which the reception at the Princesse de Guermantes's was to be held, I learned that the Duke and Duchess had returned to Paris the night before, and I made up my mind to go and see them that morning. But, having gone out early, they had not yet returned; I watched first of all from a little room, which had seemed to me to be a good look-out post, for the arrival of their carriage. As a matter of fact I had made a singularly bad choice of observatory, for I could scarcely see into our court-yard, but I caught a glimpse of several others, and this, though of no practical use to me, diverted me for a time. It is not only in Venice that one has these views on to several houses at once which have proved so tempting to painters; it is just the same in Paris. Nor do I cite Venice at random. It is of its poorer quarters that certain poor quarters of Paris remind one, in the morning, with their tall, splayed chimneys to which the sun imparts the most vivid pinks, the brightest reds—like a garden flowering above the houses, and flowering in such a variety of tints as to suggest the garden of a tulip-fancier of Delft or Haarlem planted above the town. And then the extreme proximity of the houses, with their windows looking across at one another over a common courtyard, makes of each casement the frame in which a cook sits dreamily gazing down at the ground below, or, further off, a girl is having her hair combed by an old woman with a witchlike face, barely distinguishable in the shadow: thus each courtyard provides the neighbours in the adjoining house, suppressing sound by its width and framing silent gestures in a series of rectangles placed under glass by the closing of the windows, with an exhibition of a hundred Dutch paintings hung in rows. True, from the Hôtel de Guermantes one did not have the same kind of views, but one had curious ones none the less, especially from the strange trigonometrical point at which I had placed myself and from which there was nothing to arrest one's gaze, across the relatively featureless and steeply sloping intervening area, until the distant heights formed by the mansion of the Marquise de Plassac and Mme de Tresmes, extremely noble cousins of M. de Guermantes whom I did not know. Between me and this house (which was that of their father, M. de Bréquigny) nothing but blocks of buildings of low elevation, facing in every conceivable direction, which, without obstructing the view, prolonged the distance with their oblique planes. The red-tiled turret of the coach-house in which the Marquis de Frécourt kept his carriages did indeed end in a spire that rose rather higher, but was so slender that it concealed nothing, and reminded one of those picturesque old buildings in Switzerland which spring up in isolation at the foot of a mountain. All these vague and divergent points on which my eyes came to rest made Mme de Plassac's house, actually quite near but misleadingly distant as in an Alpine landscape, appear as though it were separated from us by several streets or by a series of foothills. When its large rectangular windows, glittering in the sunlight like flakes of rock crystal, were thrown open to air the rooms, one felt, in following from one floor to the next the footmen whom it was impossible to see clearly but who were visibly shaking carpets, the same pleasure as when one sees in a landscape by Turner or Elstir a traveller in a stage-coach, or a guide, at different degrees of altitude on the Saint-Gothard. But from the vantage-point where I had placed myself I should have been in danger of not seeing M. or Mme de Guermantes come in, so that when in the afternoon I was free to resume my watch I simply stood on the staircase, from which the opening of the carriage-gate could not escape my notice, and it was on this staircase that I posted myself, although the Alpine beauties of the Hôtel de Bréquigny, so entrancing with their footmen rendered minute by distance and busily cleaning, were not visible from there. Now this wait on the staircase was to have for me consequences so considerable, and to reveal to me so important a landscape, no longer Turneresque but moral, that it is preferable to postpone the account of it for a little while by interposing first that of my visit to the Guermantes when I knew that they had come home.

It was the Duke alone who received me in his library. As I was approaching the door there emerged a little man with snow-white hair, a rather shabby appearance, a little black tie such as was worn by the Combray notary and by several of my grandfather's friends, but of a more timid aspect than they, who, making me a series of deep bows, refused absolutely to go downstairs until I had passed him. The Duke shouted after him from the library something which I did not understand, and the other responded with further bows, addressed to the wall, for the Duke could not see him, but endlessly repeated nevertheless, like the purposeless smiles on the faces of people who are talking to one on the telephone; he had a falsetto voice, and saluted me afresh with the humility of a steward. And he might indeed have been a steward from Combray, so much was he in the style, provincial, antiquated and mild, of the small folk, the modest elders of those parts.

"You'll see Oriane presently," the Duke said to me when I entered the room. "As Swann is coming round soon with the proofs of his essay on the coinage of the Order of Malta, and, what is worse, an immense photograph he has had taken showing both sides of each of the coins, Oriane decided to get dressed first in order to be able to stay with him until it's time to go out to dinner. We're already so cluttered with things that we don't know where to put them all, and I wonder where on earth we're going to stick this photograph. But my wife's too good-natured—she can't resist obliging people. She thought it would be nice to ask Swann to let her see side by side on one sheet the heads of all those Grand Masters of the Order whose medals he found at Rhodes. I said Malta, didn't I—it's Rhodes, but it's the same Order of St John of Jerusalem. The truth is that she's interested in all that only because Swann makes a hobby of it. Our family is very much mixed up in the whole story; even today, my brother, whom you know, is one of the highest dignitaries in the Order of Malta. But if I'd talked to Oriane about it all she simply wouldn't have listened to me. On the other hand, Swann's researches into the Templars (it's astonishing the passion people of one religion have for studying others) only had to lead him on to the history of the Knights of Rhodes, who succeeded the Templars, for Oriane at once to insist on seeing the heads of these knights. They were very small fry indeed compared with the Lusignans, Kings of Cyprus, from whom we descend in a direct line. But so far Swann hasn't taken them up, so Oriane doesn't care to hear anything about the Lusignans."

I could not at once explain to the Duke why I had come. The fact was that several relatives or friends, including Mme de Silistrie and the Duchesse de Montrose, came to call on the Duchess, who was often at home before dinner, and not finding her, stayed for a short while with the Duke. The first of these ladies (the Princesse de Silistrie), simply attired, with a curt but friendly manner, was carrying a stick. I was afraid at first that she had injured herself, or was a cripple. She was on the contrary most alert. She spoke sadly to the Duke, of a first cousin of his—not on the Guermantes side, but more illustrious still, were that possible—whose health, which had been in a grave condition for some time past, had grown suddenly worse. But it was evident that the Duke, while sympathising with his cousin and repeating "Poor Mama!" (the cousin's nickname in the family) "He's such a good fellow," had formed a favourable prognosis. The fact was that the Duke was looking forward to the dinner-party he was to attend, and far from bored at the prospect of the big reception at the Princesse de Guermantes's, but above all he was to go on at one o'clock in the morning with his wife to a great supper and fancy dress ball, with a view to which a costume as Louis XI for himself, and one as Isabella of Bavaria for the Duchess, were waiting in readiness. And the Duke was determined not to be disturbed amid all these gaieties by the sufferings of the worthy Amanien d'Osmond. Two other ladies carrying sticks, Mme de Plassac and Mme de Tresmes, both daughters of the Comte de Bréquigny, came in next to pay Basin a visit, and declared that cousin Mama's state was now beyond hope. The Duke shrugged his shoulders, and to change the subject asked whether they were going that evening to Marie-Gilbert's. They replied that they were not, in view of the state of Amanien who was *in extremis*, and indeed they had excused themselves from the dinner to which the Duke was going, the other guests at which they proceeded to enumerate to him: the brother of King Theodosius, the Infanta Maria-Concepción, and so forth. As the Marquis d'Osmond was less closely related to them than he was to Basin, their "defection" appeared to the Duke to be a sort of indirect reproach for his own conduct, and he was rather curt with them. And so, although they had come down from the heights of the Hôtel de Bréquigny to see the Duchess (or rather to announce to her the alarming character, incompatible for his relatives with attendance at social gatherings, of their cousin's illness), they did not stay long: each armed with her alpenstock,

Walpurge and Dorothée (such were the names of the two sisters) retraced the craggy path to their citadel. I never thought to ask the Guermantes what was the meaning of these sticks, so common in a certain part of the Faubourg Saint-Germain. Possibly, looking upon the whole parish as their domain, and not caring to hire cabs, they were in the habit of taking long walks, for which some old fracture, due to immoderate indulgence in the chase and to the falls from horseback which are often the fruit of that indulgence, or simply rheumatism caused by the dampness of the left bank and of old country houses, made a stick necessary. Perhaps they had not set out upon any such long expedition through the neighbourhood, but, having merely come down into their garden (which lay at no great distance from that of the Duchess) to pick the fruit required for their compotes, had looked in on their way home to bid good evening to Mme de Guermantes, though without going so far as to bring a pair of secateurs or a watering-can into her house.

The Duke appeared touched that I should have come to see them on the very day of their return to Paris. But his face clouded over when I told him I had come to ask his wife to find out whether her cousin really had invited me. I had touched upon one of those services which M. and Mme de Guermantes were not fond of rendering. The Duke explained to me that it was too late, that if the Princess had not sent me an invitation it would make him appear to be asking her for one, that his cousins had refused him one once before, and he had no wish to appear either directly or indirectly to be interfering with their visiting-list, to be "meddling," that anyhow he could not even be sure that he and his wife, who were dining out that evening, would not come straight home afterwards, that in that case their best excuse for not having gone to the Princess's party would be to conceal from her the fact of their return to Paris, instead of hastening to inform her of it, as they must do if they sent her a note or spoke to her over the telephone about me, and certainly too late to be of any use, since, in all probability, the Princess's list of guests would be closed by now. "You've not fallen foul of her in any way?" he asked in a suspicious tone, the Guermantes living in constant fear of not being informed of the latest society quarrels, and of people's trying to climb back into favour on their shoulders. Finally, as the Duke was in the habit of taking upon himself all decisions that might seem ungracious, "Listen, my boy," he said to me suddenly, as though the idea had just come into his head, "I'd really rather not mention at all to Oriane that you've spoken to me about this. You know how kind-hearted she is, and besides, she's enormously fond of you—she'd insist on sending to ask her cousin, in spite of anything I might say to the contrary, and if she's tired after dinner, there'll be no getting out of it, she'll be forced to go to the party. No, decidedly, I shall say nothing to her about it. Anyhow, you'll see her yourself in a minute. But not a word about this matter, I beg of you. If you decide to go to the party, I've no need to tell you what a pleasure it will be for us to spend the evening there with you."

Humane motives are too sacred for the person before whom they are invoked not to bow to them, whether he believes them to be sincere or not; I did not wish to appear to be weighing in the balance for a moment the relative importance of my invitation and the possible tiredness of Mme de Guermantes, and I promised not to speak to her of the object of my visit, exactly as though I had been taken in by the little farce which M. de Guermantes had performed for my benefit. I asked him if he thought there was any chance of my seeing Mme de Stermaria at the Princess's.

"Why, no," he replied with the air of a connoisseur. "I know the name you mention, from having seen it in club directories—it isn't at all the type of person who goes to Gilbert's. You'll see nobody there who is not excessively well-bred and intensely boring, duchesses bearing titles which one thought were extinct years ago and which have been trotted out for the occasion, all the ambassadors, heaps of Coburgs, foreign royalties, but you mustn't expect even the ghost of a Stermaria. Gilbert would be taken ill at the mere thought of such a thing. Wait now, you're fond of painting, I must show you a superb picture I bought from my cousin, partly in exchange for the Elstirs, which frankly didn't appeal to us. It was sold to me as a Philippe de Champaigne, but I believe myself that it's by someone even greater. Would you like to know what I think? I think it's a Velazquez, and of the best period," said the Duke, looking me boldly in the eyes, either to ascertain my impression or in the hope of enhancing it. A footman came in.

"Mme la Duchesse wishes to know if M. le Duc will be so good as to see M. Swann, as Mme la Duchesse is not quite ready."

"Show M. Swann in," said the Duke, after looking at his watch and seeing that he himself still had a few minutes before he need go to dress. "Naturally my wife, who told him to come, isn't ready.

No point in saying anything in front of Swann about Marie-Gilbert's party," said the Duke. "I don't know whether he's been invited. Gilbert likes him immensely, because he believes him to be the natural grandson of the Duc de Berry, but that's a long story. (Otherwise you can imagine!—my cousin, who has a fit if he sees a Jew a mile off.) But now of course the Dreyfus case has made things more serious. Swann ought to have realised that he more than anyone must drop all connexion with those fellows, instead of which he says the most regrettable things."

The Duke called back the footman to know whether the man who had been sent to inquire at cousin Osmond's had returned. His plan was as follows: since he rightly believed that his cousin was dying, he was anxious to obtain news of him before his death, that is to say before he was obliged to go into mourning. Once covered by the official certainty that Amanien was still alive, he would sneak off to his dinner, to the Prince's reception, to the midnight revel where he was to appear as Louis XI and where he had a most tantalising assignation with a new mistress, and would make no more inquiries until the following day, when his pleasures would be over. Then he would put on mourning if the cousin had passed away in the night. "No, M. le Duc, he is not back yet." "Hell and damnation! Nothing is ever done in this house till the last minute," cried the Duke, at the thought that Amanien might still be in time to "croak" for an evening paper, and to make him miss his revel. He sent for *Le Temps*, in which there was nothing.

I had not seen Swann for a long time, and found myself wondering momentarily whether in the old days he used to clip his moustache, or whether his hair had not been *en brosse*, for I found him somehow changed. It was simply that he was indeed greatly "changed" because he was very ill, and illness produces in the face modifications as profound as are created by growing a beard or by changing one's parting. (Swann's illness was the same that had killed his mother, who had been struck down by it at precisely the age which he had now reached. Our lives are in truth, owing to heredity, as full of cabalistic ciphers, of horoscopic castings as if sorcerers really existed. And just as there is a certain duration of life for humanity in general, so there is one for families in particular, that is to say, in any one family, for the members of it who resemble one another.) Swann was dressed with an elegance which, like that of his wife, associated with what he now was what he once had been. Buttoned up in a pearl-grey frock-coat which emphasised his tall, slim figure, his white gloves stitched in black, he had a grey topper of a flared shape which Delion no longer made except for him, the Prince de Sagan, M. de Charlus, the Marquis de Modène, M. Charles Haas and Comte Louis de Turenne. I was surprised at the charming smile and affectionate handclasp with which he replied to my greeting for I had imagined that after so long an interval he would not recognise me at once; I told him of my astonishment; he received it with a shout of laughter, a trace of indignation and a further squeeze of my hand, as if it were to throw doubt on the soundness of his brain or the sincerity of his affection to suppose that he did not recognise me. And yet that was in fact the case; he did not identify me, as I learned long afterwards, until several minutes later when he heard my name mentioned. But no change in his face, in his speech, in the things he said to me betrayed the discovery which a chance word from M. de Guermantes had enabled him to make, with such mastery, with such absolute sureness did he play the social game. He brought to it, moreover, that spontaneity in manners and that personal enterprise, even in matters of dress, which characterised the Guermantes style. Thus it was that the greeting which the old clubman had given me without recognising me was not the cold, stiff greeting of the purely formalist man of the world, but a greeting full of real friendliness, genuine charm, such as the Duchesse de Guermantes, for instance, possessed (carrying it so far as to smile at you first, before you had bowed to her, if she met you in the street), in contrast to the more mechanical greeting customary among the ladies of the Faubourg Saint-Germain. In the same way, the hat which, in conformity with a custom that was beginning to disappear, he laid on the floor by his feet, was lined with green leather, a thing not usually done, because (he said) it showed the dirt far less, in reality because (but this he did not say) it was highly becoming.

"Now, Charles, you're a great expert, come and see what I've got to show you, after which, my boys, I'm going to ask your permission to leave you together for a moment while I go and change my clothes. Besides, I expect Oriane won't be long now." And he showed his "Velazquez" to Swann. "But it seems to me that I know this," said Swann with the grimace of a sick man for whom the mere act of speaking requires an effort.

"Yes," said the Duke, perturbed by the time which the expert was taking to express his admiration. "You've probably seen it at Gilbert's."

"Oh, yes, of course, I remember."

"What do you suppose it is?"

"Oh, well, if it comes from Gilbert's house it's probably one of your *ancestors*," said Swann with a blend of irony and deference towards a grandeur which he would have felt it impolite and absurd to belittle, but to which for reasons of good taste he preferred to make only a playful reference.

"Of course it is," said the Duke bluntly. "It's Boson, the I forget how manyeth de Guermantes. Not that I care a damn about that. You know I'm not as feudal as my cousin. I've heard the names of Rigaud, Mignard, even Velazquez mentioned," he went on, fastening on Swann the look of both an inquisitor and a torturer in an attempt at once to read into his mind and to influence his response. "Well," he concluded (for when he was led to provoke artificially an opinion which he desired to hear, he had the faculty, after a few moments, of believing that it had been spontaneously uttered), "come, now, none of your flattery. Do you think it's by one of those big guns I've mentioned?"

"Nnnnno," said Swann.

"Well anyway, I know nothing about these things, it's not for me to decide who daubed the canvas. But you're a dilettante, a master of the subject, what would you say it was?"

Swann hesitated for a moment in front of the picture, which obviously he thought atrocious.

"A bad joke!" he replied with a smile at the Duke who could not restrain an impulse of rage. When this had subsided: "Be good fellows, both of you, wait a moment for Oriane, I must go and put on my swallow-tails and then I'll be back. I shall send word to the missus that you're both waiting for her."

I chatted for a minute or two with Swann about the Dreyfus case and asked him how it was that all the Guermantes were anti-Dreyfusards. "In the first place because at heart all these people are anti-semites," replied Swann, who nevertheless knew very well from experience that certain of them were not, but, like everyone who holds a strong opinion, preferred to explain the fact that other people did not share it by imputing to them preconceptions and prejudices against which there was nothing to be done, rather than reasons which might permit of discussion. Besides, having come to the premature term of his life, like a weary animal that is being tormented, he cried out against these persecutions and was returning to the spiritual fold of his fathers.

"Yes, it's true I've been told that the Prince de Guermantes is anti-semitic."

"Oh, that fellow! I don't even bother to consider him. He carries it to such a point that when he was in the army and had a frightful toothache he preferred to grin and bear it rather than go to the only dentist in the district, who happened to be a Jew, and later on he allowed a wing of his castle to be burned to the ground because he would have had to send for extinguishers to the place next door, which belongs to the Rothschilds."

"Are you going to be there this evening, by any chance?"

"Yes," Swann replied, "although I don't really feel up to it. But he sent me a wire to tell me that he has something to say to me. I feel that I shall soon be too unwell to go there or to receive him at my house, it will be too agitating, so I prefer to get it over at once."

"But the Duc de Guermantes is not anti-semitic?"

"You can see quite well that he is, since he's an anti-Dreyfusard," replied Swann, without noticing that he was begging the question. "All the same I'm sorry to have disappointed the fellow—His Grace I should say!—by not admiring his Mignard or whatever he calls it."

"But at any rate," I went on, reverting to the Dreyfus case, "the Duchess, now, is intelligent."

"Yes, she is charming. To my mind, however, she was even more charming when she was still known as the Princesse des Laumes. Her mind has become somehow more angular—it was all much softer in the juvenile great lady. But after all, young or old, men or women, when all's said and done these people belong to a different race, one can't have a thousand years of feudalism in one's blood with impunity. Naturally they imagine that it counts for nothing in their opinions."

"All the same, Robert de Saint-Loup is a Dreyfusard."

"Ah! So much the better, especially as his mother is extremely anti. I had heard that he was, but I wasn't certain of it. That gives me a great deal of pleasure. It doesn't surprise me, he's highly intelligent. It's a great thing, that is."

Swann's Dreyfusism had brought out in him an extraordinary naïvety and imparted to his way of looking at things an impulsiveness, an inconsistency more noticeable even than had been the similar effects of his marriage to Odette; this new "declassing" would have been better described as a "reclassing" and was entirely to his credit, since it made him return to the paths which his forebears had trodden and from which he had been deflected by his aristocratic associations. But precisely at the moment when, with all his clear-sightedness, and thanks to the principles he had inherited from his ancestors, he was in a position to perceive a truth that was still hidden from people of fashion, Swann showed himself nevertheless quite comically blind. He subjected all his admirations and all his contempts to the test of a new criterion, Dreyfusism. That the anti-Dreyfusism of Mme Bontemps should make him think her a fool was no more astonishing than that, when he had got married, he should have thought her intelligent. It was not very serious, either, that the new wave should also affect his political judgments and make him lose all memory of having denounced Clemenceau—whom, he now declared, he had always regarded as a voice of conscience, a man of steel, like Cornély—as a man with a price, a British spy (this latter was an absurdity of the Guermantes set). "No, no, I never told you anything of the sort. You're thinking of someone else." But, sweeping past his political judgments, the wave overturned Swann's literary judgments too, down to his way of expressing them. Barrès was now devoid of talent, and even his early books were feeble, could scarcely bear re-reading. "You try, you'll find you can't struggle to the end. What a difference from Clemenceau! Personally I'm not anti-clerical, but when you compare them together you must see that Barrès is invertebrate. He's a very great man, is old Clemenceau. How he knows the language!" However, the anti-Dreyfusards were in no position to criticise these follies. They explained that one was only a Dreyfusard because one was of Jewish origin. If a practising Catholic like Saniette was also in favour of reconsideration, that was because he was cornered by Mme Verdurin, who behaved like a wild radical. She was first and foremost against the "frocks." Saniette was more fool than knave, and had no idea of the harm that the Mistress was doing him. If you pointed out that Brichot was equally a friend of Mme Verdurin and was a member of the "Patrie Française," that was because he was more intelligent.

"You see him occasionally?" I asked Swann, referring to Saint-Loup.

"No, never. He wrote to me the other day asking me to persuade the Duc de Mouchy and various other people to vote for him at the Jockey, where for that matter he got through like a letter through the post."

"In spite of the Affair!"

"The question was never raised. However I must tell you that since all this business began I never set foot in the place."

M. de Guermantes returned and was presently joined by his wife, all ready now for the evening, tall and proud in a gown of red satin the skirt of which was bordered with sequins. She had in her hair a long ostrich feather dyed purple, and over her shoulders a tulle scarf of the same red as her dress. "How nice it is to have one's hat lined in green," said the Duchess, who missed nothing. "However, with you, Charles, everything is always charming, whether it's what you wear or what you say, what you read or what you do." Swann meanwhile, without apparently listening, was considering the Duchess as he would have studied the canvas of a master, and then sought her eyes, making a face which implied the exclamation "Gosh!" Mme de Guermantes rippled with laughter. "So my clothes please you? I'm delighted. But I must say they don't please me much," she went on with a sulky air. "God, what a bore it is to have to dress up and go out when one would ever so much rather stay at home!"

"What magnificent rubies!"

"Ah! my dear Charles, at least one can see that you know what you're talking about, you're not like that brute Monserfeuil who asked me if they were real. I must say I've never seen anything quite like them. They were a present from the Grand Duchess. They're a little too big for my liking, a little too like claret glasses filled to the brim, but I've put them on because we shall be seeing the Grand Duchess this evening at Marie-Gilbert's," added Mme de Guermantes, never suspecting that this assertion destroyed the force of those previously made by the Duke.

"What's on at the Princess's?" inquired Swann.

"Practically nothing," the Duke hastened to reply, the question having made him think that Swann was not invited.

"What do you mean, Basin? The whole world has been invited. It will be a deathly crush. What will be pretty, though," she went on, looking soulfully at Swann, "if the storm I can feel in the air now doesn't break, will be those marvellous gardens. You know them, of course. I was there a month ago, when the lilacs were in flower. You can't imagine how lovely they were. And then the fountain—really, it's Versailles in Paris."

"What sort of person is the Princess?" I asked.

"Why, you know quite well, since you've seen her here, that she's as beautiful as the day, and also a bit of a fool, but very nice, in spite of all her Germanic high-and-mightiness, full of good-nature and gaffes."

Swann was too shrewd not to perceive that the Duchess was trying to show off the "Guermantes wit," and at no great cost to herself, for she was only serving up in a less perfect form a few of her old quips. Nevertheless, to prove to the Duchess that he appreciated her intention to be funny, and as though she had really succeeded in being funny, he gave a somewhat forced smile, causing me by this particular form of insincerity the same embarrassment as I used to feel long ago when I heard my parents discussing with M. Vinteuil the corruption of certain sections of society (when they knew very well that a corruption far greater reigned at Montjouvain), or simply on hearing Legrandin embellishing his utterances for the benefit of fools, choosing delicate epithets which he knew perfectly well would not be understood by a rich or smart but illiterate audience.

"Come now, Oriane, what on earth are you saying?" broke in M. de Guermantes. "Marie a fool? Why, she's read everything, and she's as musical as a fiddle."

"But, my poor little Basin, you're as innocent as a new-born babe. As if one couldn't be all that, and rather an idiot as well. Idiot is too strong a word; no, she's in the clouds, she's Hesse-Darmstadt, Holy Roman Empire, and wa-wa-wa. Even her pronunciation gets on my nerves. But I quite admit that she's a charming loony. In the first place, the very idea of stepping down from her German throne to go and marry, in the most bourgeois way, a private individual. It's true that she chose him! Ah, but of course," she went on, turning to me, "you don't know Gilbert. Let me give you an idea of him: he took to his bed once because I had left a card on Mme Carnot . . . But, my dear Charles" (the Duchess changed the subject when she saw that the story of the card left on the Carnots appeared to irritate M. de Guermantes), "you know, you've never sent me that photograph of our Knights of Rhodes, whom I've learned to love through you and with whom I'm so anxious to become acquainted." The Duke meanwhile had not taken his eyes from his wife's face: "Oriane, you might at least tell the story properly and not cut out half. I ought to explain," he corrected, addressing Swann, "that the British Ambassadress at that time, who was a very worthy woman but lived rather in the moon and was in the habit of making up these odd combinations, conceived the distinctly quaint idea of inviting us with the President and his wife. Even Oriane was rather surprised, especially as the Ambassadress knew quite enough of the same sort of people as us not to invite us to such an ill-assorted gathering. There was a minister there who's a swindler . . . however I'll draw a veil over all that—the fact was that we hadn't been warned, we were trapped, and to be honest I'm bound to admit that all these people behaved most civilly. Still, that was quite enough of a good thing. But Mme de Guermantes, who does not often do me the honour of consulting me, felt it incumbent upon her to leave a card in the course of the following week at the Elysée. Gilbert may perhaps have gone rather far in regarding it as a stain upon our name. But it must not be forgotten that, politics apart, M. Carnot, who incidentally filled his post quite respectably, was the grandson of a member of the revolutionary tribunal which slaughtered eleven of our people in a single day."

"In that case, Basin, why used you to go every week to dine at Chantilly? The Duc d'Aumale was just as much the grandson of a member of the revolutionary tribunal, with this difference, that Carnot was a decent man and Philippe-Egalité a frightful scoundrel."

"Excuse my interrupting you to explain that I did send the photograph," said Swann. "I can't understand how it hasn't reached you."

"It doesn't altogether surprise me," said the Duchess, "my servants tell me only what they think fit. They probably don't approve of the Order of St John." And she rang the bell.

"You know, Oriane, that when I used to go to Chantilly it was without much enthusiasm."

"Without much enthusiasm, but with a nightshirt in case the Prince asked you to stay the night, which in fact he very rarely did, being a perfect boor like all the Orléans lot . . . Do you know who else we're dining with at Mme de Saint-Euverte's?" Mme de Guermantes asked her husband.

"Besides the people you know already, she's asked King Theodosius's brother at the last moment."

At these tidings the Duchess's features exuded contentment and her speech boredom: "Oh, God, more princes!"

"But that one is amiable and intelligent," Swann remarked.

"Not altogether, though," replied the Duchess, apparently seeking for words that would give more novelty to her thought. "Have you ever noticed with princes that the nicest of them are never entirely nice? They must always have an opinion about everything. And as they have no opinions of their own, they spend the first half of their lives asking us ours and the second half serving them up to us again. They positively must be able to say that this has been well played and that not so well. When there's no difference. Do you know, this little Theodosius junior (I forget his name) asked me once what an orchestral motif was called. I answered" (the Duchess's eyes sparkled and a laugh exploded from her beautiful red lips) " 'It's called an orchestral motif.' I don't think he was any too well pleased, really. Oh, my dear Charles," she went on with a languishing air, "what a bore it can be, dining out. There are evenings when one would sooner die! It's true that dying may be perhaps just as great a bore, because we don't know what it's like."

A servant appeared. It was the young lover who had had a quarrel with the concierge, until the Duchess, out of the kindness of her heart, had brought about an apparent peace between them.

"Am I to go round this evening to inquire after M. le Marquis d'Osmond?" he asked.

"Most certainly not, nothing before tomorrow morning. In fact I don't want you to remain in the house tonight. His footman, whom you know, might very well come and bring you the latest report and send you out after us. Be off with you, go anywhere you like, have a spree, sleep out, but I don't want to see you here before tomorrow morning."

The footman's face glowed with happiness. At last he would be able to spend long hours with his betrothed, whom he had practically ceased to see ever since, after a final scene with the concierge, the Duchess had considerately explained to him that it would be better, to avoid further conflicts, if he did not go out at all. He floated, at the thought of having an evening free at last, on a tide of happiness which the Duchess saw and the reason for which she guessed. She felt a sort of pang and as it were an itching in all her limbs at the thought of this happiness being snatched behind her back, unbeknown to her, and it made her irritated and jealous.

"No, Basin, he must stay here; he's not to stir out of the house."

"But Oriane, that's absurd, the house is crammed with servants, and you have the costumier's people coming as well at twelve to dress us for our ball. There's absolutely nothing for him to do, and he's the only one who's a friend of Mama's footman; I'd much sooner get him right away from the house."

"Listen, Basin, let me do what I want. I shall have a message for him during the evening, as it happens—I'm not yet sure at what time. In any case you're not to budge from here for a single instant, do you hear?" she said to the despairing footman.

If there were continual quarrels, and if servants did not stay long with the Duchess, the person to whose charge this guerrilla warfare was to be laid was indeed irremovable, but it was not the concierge. No doubt for the heavy work, for the martyrdoms it was particularly tiring to inflict, for the quarrels which ended in blows, the Duchess entrusted the blunter instruments to him; but even then he played his role without the least suspicion that he had been cast for it. Like the household servants, he was impressed by the Duchess's kindness, and the imperceptive footmen who came back, after leaving her service, to visit Françoise used to say that the Duke's house would have been the finest "place" in Paris if it had not been for the porter's lodge. The Duchess made use of the lodge in the same way as at different times clericalism, freemasonry, the Jewish peril and so on have been made use of. Another footman came into the room.

"Why haven't they brought up the package M. Swann sent here? And, by the way (you've heard, Charles, that Mama is seriously ill?), Jules went round to inquire for news of M. le Marquis d'Osmond: has he come back yet?"

"He's just arrived this instant, M. le Duc. They're expecting M. le Marquis to pass away at any moment."

"Ah, he's alive!" exclaimed the Duke with a sigh of relief. "They're expecting, are they? Well, they can go on expecting. While there's life there's hope," he added cheerfully for our benefit. "They've been talking to me about him as though he were dead and buried. In a week from now he'll be fitter than I am."

"It's the doctors who said that he wouldn't last out the evening. One of them wanted to call again during the night. The head one said it was no use. M. le Marquis would be dead by then; they've only kept him alive by injecting him with camphorated oil."

"Hold your tongue, you damned fool," cried the Duke in a paroxysm of rage. "Who the devil asked you for your opinion? You haven't understood a word of what they told you."

"It wasn't me they told, it was Jules."

"Will you hold your tongue!" roared the Duke, and, turning to Swann: "What a blessing he's still alive! He'll regain his strength gradually, don't you know. Still alive, after being in such a critical state—that in itself is an excellent sign. One mustn't expect everything at once. It can't be at all unpleasant, a little injection of camphorated oil." He rubbed his hands. "He's alive; what more could anyone want? After all that he's gone through, it's a great step forward. Upon my word, I envy him having such a constitution. Ah! these invalids, you know, people do all sorts of little things for them that they don't do for us. For instance, today some beggar of a chef sent me up a leg of mutton with *béarnaise* sauce—it was done to a turn, I must admit, but just for that very reason I took so much of it that it's still lying on my stomach. However, that doesn't make people come to inquire after me as they do after dear Amanien. We do too much inquiring. It only tires him. We must leave him room to breathe. They're killing the poor fellow by sending round to him all the time."

"Well," said the Duchess to the footman as he was leaving the room, "I gave orders for the envelope containing a photograph which M. Swann sent me to be brought up here."

"Madame la Duchesse, it's so large that I didn't know if I could get it through the door. We've left it in the hall. Does Madame la Duchesse wish me to bring it up?"

"Oh, in that case, no; they ought to have told me, but if it's so big I shall see it in a moment when I come downstairs."

"I forgot to tell Mme la Duchesse that Mme la Comtesse Molé left a card this morning for Mme la Duchesse."

"What, this morning?" said the Duchess with an air of disapproval, feeling that so young a woman ought not to take the liberty of leaving cards in the morning.

"About ten o'clock, Madame la Duchesse."

"Show me the cards."

"In any case, Oriane, when you say that it was a funny idea on Marie's part to marry Gilbert," went on the Duke, reverting to the original topic of conversation, "it's you who have an odd way of writing history. If either of them was a fool, it was Gilbert, for having married of all people a woman so closely related to the

King of the Belgians, who has usurped the name of Brabant which belongs to us. To put it briefly, we are of the same blood as the Hesses, and of the elder branch. It's always stupid to talk about oneself," he apologised to me, "but after all, whenever we've been not only to Darmstadt, but even to Cassel and all over electoral Hesse, all the landgraves have always been most courteous in giving us precedence as being of the elder branch."

"But really, Basin, you don't mean to tell me that a person who was honorary commandant of every regiment in her country, who people thought would become engaged to the King of Sweden ..."

"Oh, Oriane, that's too much; anyone would think you didn't know that the King of Sweden's grandfather was tilling the soil at Pau when we had been ruling the roost for nine hundred years throughout the whole of Europe."

"That doesn't alter the fact that if somebody were to say in the street: 'Hallo, there's the King of Sweden,' everyone would at once rush to see him as far as the Place de la Concorde, and if he said: 'There's M. de Guermantes,' nobody would know who it was."

"What an argument!"

"Besides, I can't understand how, once the title of Duke of Brabant has passed to the Belgian royal family, you can continue to claim it."

The footman returned with the Comtesse Molé's card, or rather what she had left in place of a card. On the pretext that she did not have one with her, she had taken from her pocket a letter addressed to herself, and keeping the contents had handed in the envelope which bore the inscription: "La Comtesse Molé." As the envelope was rather large, following the fashion in notepaper which prevailed that year, this "card" was almost twice the size of an ordinary visiting-card.

"That's what people call Mme Molé's 'simplicity,'" said the Duchess sarcastically. "She wants to make us think that she had no cards on her to show her originality. But we know all about that, don't we, my little Charles, we're quite old enough and quite original enough ourselves to see through the tricks of a little lady who has only been going about for four years. She is charming, but she doesn't seem to me, all the same, to have the weight to imagine that she can stun the world with so little effort as merely by leaving an envelope instead of a card and leaving it at ten o'clock in the morning. Her old mother mouse will show her that she knows a thing or two about that."

Swann could not help smiling at the thought that the Duchess, who was, as it happened, a trifle jealous of Mme Molé's success, would find it quite in accordance with the "Guermantes wit" to make some insolent retort to her visitor.

"So far as the title of Duc de Brabant is concerned, I've told you a hundred times, Oriane ... " the Duke continued, but the Duchess, without listening, cut him short.

"But, my dear Charles, I'm longing to see your photograph."

"Ah! *Extinctor draconis latrator Anubis*," said Swann.

"Yes, it was so charming what you said about that apropos of San Giorgio at Venice. But I don't understand why Anubis?"

"What's the one like who was an ancestor of Babal?" asked M. de Guermantes.

"You want to see his bauble," said his wife drily, to show that she herself despised the pun. "I want to see them all," she added.

"I'll tell you what, Charles, let's go downstairs till the carriage comes," said the Duke. "You can pay your call on us in the hall, because my wife won't let us have any peace until she's seen your photograph. I'm less impatient, I must say," he added complacently. "I'm not easily stirred myself, but she would see us all dead rather than miss it."

"I entirely agree with you, Basin," said the Duchess, "let's go into the hall; we shall at least know why we have come down from your study, whereas we shall never know how we have come down from the Counts of Brabant."

"I've told you a hundred times how the title came into the House of Hesse," said the Duke (while we were going downstairs to look at the photograph, and I thought of those that Swann used to bring me at Combray), "through the marriage of a Brabant in 1241 with the daughter of the last Landgrave of Thuringia and Hesse, so that really it's the title of Prince of Hesse that came to the House of Brabant rather than that of Duke of Brabant to the House of Hesse. You will remember that our battle-cry was that of the Dukes of Brabant: 'Limbourg to her conqueror!' until we exchanged the arms of Brabant for those of Guermantes, in which I think myself that we were wrong, and the example of the Gramonts will not make me change my opinion."

"But," replied Mme de Guermantes, "as it's the King of the Belgians who is the conqueror . . . Besides, the Belgian Crown Prince calls himself Duc de Brabant."

"But, my dear child, your argument will not hold water for a moment. You know as well as I do that there are titles of pretension which can perfectly well survive even if the territory is occupied by usurpers. For instance, the King of Spain describes himself equally as Duke of Brabant, claiming in virtue of a possession less ancient than ours, but more ancient than that of the King of the Belgians. He also calls himself Duke of Burgundy, King of the West and East Indies, and Duke of Milan. Well, he's no more in possession of Burgundy, the Indies or Brabant than I possess Brabant myself, or the Prince of Hesse either, for that matter. The King of Spain likewise proclaims himself King of Jerusalem, as does the Austrian Emperor, and Jerusalem belongs to neither one nor the other."

He stopped for a moment, perturbed by the thought that the mention of Jerusalem might have embarrassed Swann, in view of "current events," but only went on more rapidly: "What you said just now might be said of anyone. We were at one time Dukes of Aumale, a duchy that has passed as regularly to the House of France as Joinville and Chevreuse have to the House of Albert. We make no more claim to those titles than to that of Marquis de Noirmoutiers, which was at one time ours, and became perfectly regularly the appanage of the House of La Trémoïlle, but because certain cessions are valid, it does not follow that they all are. For instance," he went on, turning to me, "my sister-in-law's son bears the title of Prince d'Agrigente, which comes to us from Joan the Mad, as that of Prince de Tarente comes to the La Trémoïlles. Well, Napoleon went and gave this title of Tarente to a soldier, who may have been an excellent campaigner, but in doing so the Emperor was disposing of what belonged to him even less than Napoleon III when he created a Duc de Montmorency, since Périgord had at least a mother who was a Montmorency, while the Tarente of Napoleon I had no more Tarente about him than Napoleon's wish that he should become so. That didn't prevent Chaix d'Est-Ange, alluding to our uncle Condé, from asking the Imperial Attorney if he had picked up the title of Duc de Montmorency in the moat at Vincennes."

"Look, Basin, I ask for nothing better than to follow you to the moat of Vincennes, or even to Taranto. And that reminds me,

Charles, of what I was going to say to you when you were telling me about your San Giorgio of Venice. We have a plan, Basin and I, to spend next spring in Italy and Sicily. If you were to come with us, just think what a difference it would make! I'm not thinking only of the pleasure of seeing you, but imagine, after all you've told me about the remains of the Norman Conquest and of antiquity, imagine what a trip like that would become if you were with us! I mean to say that even Basin—what am I saying, Gilbert!—would benefit by it, because I feel that even his claims to the throne of Naples and all that sort of thing would interest me if they were explained by you in old Romanesque churches in little villages perched on hills as in primitive paintings. But now we're going to look at your photograph. Open the envelope," she said to a footman.

"Please, Oriane, not this evening; you can look at it tomorrow," implored the Duke, who had already been making signs of alarm to me on seeing the enormous size of the photograph.

"But I want to look at it with Charles," said the Duchess, with a smile at once spuriously concupiscent and subtly psychological, for in her desire to be amiable to Swann she spoke of the pleasure which she would derive from looking at the photograph as of the kind an invalid feels he would derive from eating an orange, or as though she had simultaneously contrived an escapade with some friends and informed a biographer of tastes flattering to herself.

"Well, he'll come and see you specially," declared the Duke, to whom his wife was obliged to yield. "You can spend three hours in front of it, if that amuses you," he added sarcastically. "But where are you going to stick a toy that size?"

"In my room, of course. I want to have it before my eyes."

"Oh, just as you please; if it's in your room, there's a chance I shall never see it," said the Duke, oblivious of the revelation he was thus blindly making of the negative character of his conjugal relations.

"Make sure you undo it with the greatest care," Mme de Guermantes told the servant, underlining her instructions out of deference to Swann. "And don't crumple the envelope, either."

"Even the envelope has to be respected!" the Duke murmured to me, raising his eyes to the ceiling. "But, Swann," he added, "what amazes me, a poor prosaic husband, is how you managed to find an envelope that size. Where on earth did you dig it up?"

"Oh, at the photographer's; they're always sending out things like that. But the man is an oaf, for I see he's written on it 'La Duchesse de Guermantes,' without putting 'Madame.'"

"I forgive him," said the Duchess carelessly; then, seeming to be struck by a sudden idea which amused her, repressed a faint smile; but at once returning to Swann: "Well, you don't say whether you're coming to Italy with us?"

"Madame, I'm very much afraid that it won't be possible."

"Indeed! Mme de Montmorency is more fortunate. You went with her to Venice and Vicenza. She told me that with you one saw things one would never see otherwise, things no one had ever thought of mentioning before, that you showed her things she'd never dreamed of, and that even in the well-known things she was able to appreciate details which without you she might have passed by a dozen times without ever noticing. She's certainly been more highly favoured than we are to be ... You will take the big envelope which contained M. Swann's photograph," she said to the servant, "and you will hand it in, from me, the corner turned down, this evening at half-past ten at Mme la Comtesse Molé's."

Swann burst out laughing.

"I should like to know, all the same," Mme de Guermantes asked him, "how you can tell ten months in advance that a thing will be impossible."

"My dear Duchess, I'll tell you if you insist, but, first of all, you can see that I'm very ill."

"Yes, my little Charles, I don't think you look at all well. I'm not pleased with your colour. But I'm not asking you to come with us next week, I'm asking you to come in ten months' time. In ten months one has time to get oneself cured, you know."

At this point a footman came in to say that the carriage was at the door. "Come, Oriane, to horse," said the Duke, already pawing the ground with impatience as though he were himself one of the horses that stood waiting outside.

"Very well, give me in one word the reason why you can't come to Italy," the Duchess put it to Swann as she rose to say good-bye to us.

"But, my dear lady, it's because I shall then have been dead for several months. According to the doctors I've consulted, by the end of the year the thing I've got—which may, for that matter, carry me off at any moment—won't in any case leave me more than three or four months to live, and even that is a generous estimate," replied Swann with a smile, while the footman opened the glazed door of the hall to let the Duchess out.

"What's that you say?" cried the Duchess, stopping for a moment on her way to the carriage and raising her beautiful, melancholy blue eyes, now clouded by uncertainty. Placed for the first time in her life between two duties as incompatible as getting into her carriage to go out to dinner and showing compassion for a man who was about to die, she could find nothing in the code of conventions that indicated the right line to follow; not knowing which to choose, she felt obliged to pretend not to believe that the latter alternative need be seriously considered, in order to comply with the first, which at the moment demanded less effort, and thought that the best way of settling the conflict would be to deny that any existed. "You're joking," she said to Swann.

"It would be a joke in charming taste," he replied ironically. "I don't know why I'm telling you this. I've never said a word to you about my illness before. But since you asked me, and since now I may die at any moment . . . But whatever I do I mustn't make you late; you're dining out, remember," he added, because he knew that for other people their own social obligations took precedence over the death of a friend, and he put himself in their place thanks to his instinctive politeness. But that of the Duchess enabled her also to perceive in a vague way that the dinner-party to which she was going must count for less to Swann than his own death. And so, while continuing on her way towards the carriage, she let her shoulders droop, saying: "Don't worry about our dinner. It's not of any importance!" But this put the Duke in a bad humour and he exclaimed: "Come, Oriane, don't stop there chattering like that and exchanging your jeremiads with Swann; you know very well that Mme de Saint-Euverte insists on sitting down to table at eight o'clock sharp. We must know what you propose to do; the horses have been waiting for a good five minutes. Forgive me, Charles," he went on, turning to Swann, "but it's ten minutes to eight already. Oriane is always late, and it will take us more than five minutes to get to old Saint-Euverte's."

Mme de Guermantes advanced resolutely towards the carriage and uttered a last farewell to Swann. "You know, we'll talk about that another time; I don't believe a word you've been saying, but we must discuss it quietly. I expect they've frightened you quite unnecessarily. Come to luncheon, any day you like" (with Mme de Guermantes things always resolved themselves into luncheons), "just let me know the day and the time," and, lifting her red skirt, she set her foot on the step. She was just getting into the carriage when, seeing this foot exposed, the Duke cried out in a terrifying voice: "Oriane, what have you been thinking of, you wretch? You've kept on your black shoes! With a red dress! Go upstairs quick and put on red shoes, or rather," he said to the footman, "tell Mme la Duchesse's lady's-maid at once to bring down a pair of red shoes."

"But, my dear," replied the Duchess gently, embarrassed to see that Swann, who was leaving the house with me but had stood back to allow the carriage to pass out in front of us, had heard, "seeing that we're late . . . "

"No, no, we have plenty of time. It's only ten to; it won't take us ten minutes to get to the Parc Monceau. And after all, what does it matter? Even if we turn up at half-past eight they'll wait for us, but you can't possibly go there in a red dress and black shoes. Besides, we shan't be the last, I can tell you; the Sassenages are coming, and you know they never arrive before twenty to nine."

The Duchess went up to her room.

"Well," said M. de Guermantes to Swann and myself, "people laugh at us poor downtrodden husbands, but we have our uses. But for me, Oriane would have gone out to dinner in black shoes."

"It's not unbecoming," said Swann, "I noticed the black shoes and they didn't offend me in the least."

"I don't say you're wrong," replied the Duke, "but it looks better to have them to match the dress. Besides, you needn't worry, no sooner had she got there than she'd have noticed them, and I should have been obliged to come home and fetch the others. I should have had my dinner at nine o'clock. Good-bye, my boys," he said, thrusting us gently from the door, "off you go before Oriane comes down again. It's not that she doesn't like seeing you both. On the contrary, she's too fond of your company. If she finds you still here she'll start talking again. She's already very tired, and she'll reach the dinner-table quite dead. Besides, I tell you frankly, I'm dying of hunger. I had a wretched luncheon this morning when I came from the train. There was the devil of a *béarnaise* sauce, I admit, but in spite of that I shan't be sorry, not at all sorry to sit down to dinner. Five minutes to eight! Ah, women! She'll give us both indigestion before tomorrow. She's not nearly as strong as people think."

The Duke felt no compunction in speaking thus of his wife's ailments and his own to a dying man, for the former interested him more and therefore appeared to him more important. And so, after gently showing us out, it was simply from breeding and jollity that in a stentorian voice, as if addressing someone off-stage, he shouted from the gate to Swann, who was already in the court-yard: "You, now, don't let yourself be alarmed by the nonsense of those damned doctors. They're fools. You're as sound as a bell. You'll bury us all!"

NOTES · ADDENDA · SYNOPSIS

NOTES

WITHIN A BUDDING GROVE

PART TWO

1. (p. 12) This is an imaginary work. No such Memoirs exist.
2. (p. 61) Baronne d'Ange: character in *Le Demi-monde* by Alexandre Dumas *fils*—a courtesan who tries to marry into high society without success.
3. (p. 94) *Concours général*: competitive examination open to all secondary schools at *baccalauréat* level. "People's universities" were established between 1898 and 1901 with the object of raising the intellectual level of the workers and bringing different social classes together. They mainly consisted of evening lecture courses.
4. (p. 172) The reference is to Amphion, who, according to Greek legend, rebuilt the walls of Thebes, charming the stones into place with his lyre.
5. (p. 215) Arvède Barine was the pseudonym of Mme Charles Vincens (1840–1908), a French woman writer who published several volumes of critical and historical essays.
6. (p. 262) *Le jeu du furet* is the French equivalent of "hunt-the-slipper".

THE GUERMANTES WAY

7. (p. 311) The French is *s'ennuyer de*, which can mean to miss, to suffer from the absence of.
8. (p. 313) Françoise says *avoir d'argent* instead of *avoir de l'argent*.
9. (p. 313) *Ce n'est pas mon père*: celebrated remark by the *môme* Crevette in Feydeau's *La Dame de chez Maxim*. It became a popular all-purpose catch-phrase. John Mortimer translated it as "How's your father?" in his adaptation of the Feydeau play for the National Theatre.
10. (p. 317) The French is *plaindre*, to pity, which used also to

861

mean to deplore or regret. The sense here is that Mme
Octave did not regret her expenditure on rich fare.

11. (p. 389) A somewhat inaccurate quotation from Pascal's
famous "memorial".

12. (p. 394) The allusion is to the Romanian-born Comtesse
Anna de Noailles (*née* Brancovan), friend and correspondent
of Proust, who was an extravagant admirer of her verse.

13. (p. 432) Popular abbreviation of the newspaper *l'Intransigeant*.

14. (p. 435) The Academy in question is *l'Académie des Sciences
morales et politiques*, one of the five (including the *Académie
Française*) which comprise the *Institut de France*.

15. (p. 436) Jules Méline, Prime Minister for two years during
the Dreyfus Case.

16. (p. 451) Bernard de Jussieu (1699–1777), the best-known
member of an illustrious family of botanists.

17. (p. 462) *La barbe* has the colloquial meaning "tedious" or
"boring".

18. (p. 474) Duc Decazes: minister and favourite of Louis
XVIII.

19. (p. 484) Carmen Sylva was the pen-name of Elizabeth,
Queen of Romania (1843–1916).

20. (p. 510) "*Qu'importe le flacon pourvu qu'on ait l'ivresse!*"—the
line is in fact by Alfred de Musset.

21. (p. 517) *Le Syndicat* was the term used by anti-semites to
describe the secret power of the Jews.

22. (p. 523) Prince Henri d'Orléans, son of the Duc de Chartres,
publicly embraced the notorious Esterhazy after he had
given evidence at the Zola trial.

23. (p. 534) "Quand on parle du Saint-Loup!" is what the
Duchess says. The French for "Talk of the devil" is "Quand
on parle du loup". The pun doesn't work in English.

24. (p. 588) Paraphrase of a famous line from Molière's *Le
Misanthrope*: '*Ah, qu'en termes galants ces choses-là sont mises!*".

25. (p. 633) A word introduced by Pierre Loti from the Japanese
musume, meaning girl or young woman.

26. (p. 636) There is a complicated pun here, impossible to
convey in English. Françoise says: "Faut-il que j'éteinde?"
instead of "éteigne". Albertine's "Teigne?" is not only a
tentative correction of Françoise's faulty subjunctive; it also
suggests that she is an old shrew (a secondary meaning of
teigne = tinea, moth).

27. (p. 698) i.e. Venice. For an elucidation of this passage, see "Place-names · the Name": Volume One, pp. 380–3.

28. (p. 701) A Proustian joke here: Edouard Detaille was a mediocre academic painter known especially for his paintings of military life. Alexandre Ribot was a familiar middle-of-the-road political figure, twice Prime Minister under the Third Republic. Suzanne Reichenberg was for thirty years the principal *ingénue* at the Comédie-Française.

29. (p. 703) *Ventre affamé*—from the expression "Ventre affamé n'a pas d'oreilles", meaning "Words are wasted on a starving man".

30. (p. 705) A riverside restaurant/cabaret with "tree-houses" where, the notion was, patrons could imagine themselves the *Swiss Family Robinson*. It gave its name to the spot where it was situated, now incorporated in the Paris suburb of Le Plessis-Robinson.

31. (p. 756) *La Fille de Roland* was a popular verse drama by Henri de Bornier. The Duchess's joke refers to Princess Marie, daughter of Prince Roland Bonaparte, who married Prince George, second son of King George I of Greece.

32. (p. 758) An aria from Hérold's *Le Pré-aux-Clercs*.

33. (p. 759) A seventeenth-century poetess noted for rather mawkish verses.

34. (p. 763) A reference to the playwright Edouard Pailleron, noted for his quick, sharp-witted, rather shallow comedies.

35. (p. 766) Euphemism for *merde* (shit), hence the joke about capital C or M.

36. (p. 802) A reference to La Fontaine's fable, *The Miller and his Son*, in which the third party is an ass.

37. (p. 828) A well-known French opera singer, who had little connexion with Wagner.

ADDENDA

WITHIN A BUDDING GROVE

PART TWO

Page 110. *The manuscript gives a longer and more detailed version of this passage, reproduced in the Pléiade "Notes and Variants":*

So Mme de Villeparisis, who when I used to hear my grandmother talking about her in my childhood had seemed to me to be an old lady of the same sort as her other friends and had always remained so to me—that person who had once given me a box of chocolates held by a duck and was now going out of her way to be agreeable to us—was a member of the powerful Guermantes clan! This change in the value of what we possess, like those old bundles which turn out to be priceless treasures, is one of the things that introduce most wonder, animation, variety and consequently poetry into one's adolescence (that adolescence which, while gradually dwindling until it becomes no more than a thin trickle that often runs dry, is sometimes prolonged throughout the whole course of one's life). The rise or depreciation of one's wealth, the weirdly unexpected reassessments of one's possessions, the misrepresentations of people we know, which make one's youth as fabulous as the metamorphoses of Ovid or even the metempsychoses of the Hindus, derive in part from ignorance—an ignorance that extends to people's names as to everything else. My great-aunt had bought for one of the rooms at Combray some crude painted canvases (perhaps indeed they were only coloured paper) framed in coffee-coloured wood, which represented scenes by Teniers. I had told Bloch in perfectly good faith that we had a room full of Teniers. In the vague world, innocent of any notion of discrimination, that painting was to me then, I could see no difference between a five-franc reproduction and an original work. Similarly in the Army, where one has a captain called Lévy and another called Lévy-Mirepoix: these two names, though the second is longer than the first and therefore a little more ridiculous, appear otherwise interchangeable. When one is a child, certain words placed in front of a name seem funny, except *M. l'abbé* which is respectable; but if Mme Galopin is called Marie-Euphrosine Galopin, or Mme de Villeparisis the Marquise de Villeparisis, this merely adds something rather heteroclite to persons otherwise of the same ilk. For one starts from the impressions one has received, and not from the preconceptions whereby an educated man knows what a painting is, and a man of the world what the Villeparisis are. People have only to present themselves to our eyes in a particularly simple light—which happens especially often with elegant people, like Swann who pushed the piano for my great-aunt and sent her strawberries, or Mme de Villeparisis who had given me a chocolate duck—while being otherwise indistinguishable from the other modest supernumeraries on the family stage, and they will seem to us if anything of a slightly inferior rank. One fine day we are amazed to hear someone we place very high, someone to whose level we seek to aspire, speak of them as people far superior to himself. Thus to ignorance is added, further to mislead us, the homogeneity in one's memory of impressions belonging to the same category, and their heterogeneousness in relation to impressions of another category. This heterogeneousness, in effect, makes it far more difficult for us to calculate value. In order to compare, to subtract, it is first of all necessary to reduce to qualities of the same kind. Those who start from preconceived notions can do so. Childhood, enclosed in its impressions, cannot. Mme de Villeparisis, an old family acquaintance, less brilliant and intimidating than the optician, was further removed from "the Guermantes way" than if she had been confined to "the Méséglise way". But these differences in kind, if they make the assessment of values impossible, are great sources of poetry (all the more so because those beliefs of our youth, like forces that need room in which to deploy, operate over the great, wide surfaces of time that stretch behind us). When we discover that the easy-going captain whom we treated with less respect than Captain Lévy, and who—not content with being nice to us every day—asked us to dinner before we finished our term of service, was the stepbrother of the Duc de Fezensac (once we have acquired preconceptions and know who the latter is), this sudden displacement—as of a ray of light shifting on the horizon—of a personage who rapidly switches from the vulgar and charming environment in which we have always situated him into a totally different world, acquires a sort of poetic charm. He had become almost unreal, like everything that we once knew in a place to which we have never returned, in a special life intercalated into our very different life for three years, like the officers in our regiment, or long ago the good people of Combray. To learn that these people, as different from real people as pantomime figures, took the train on Saturday, after removing their uniforms or their country clothes, and went to dine with Mme de Pourtalès—how interesting that makes it for us to know Mme de Pourtalès, how we long to get her to talk to us about them! But what she tells us will no more be able to enlighten us than what we ask of people who knew the real people on whom Mme Bovary or Frédéric Moreau were modelled. How could this information elucidate an inner charm which stems from a certain distortion of memory and certain transformations of reality? Thus Saint-Loup could have spoken to me indefinitely about his family without helping me to get to the bottom of the pleasure I had derived from the fact that suddenly, set free from a homely bourgeois prison that had been spirited away as in a fairy tale, Mme de Villeparisis was embarking—or rather (so swift had been the spell) was already awaiting me—on the Guermantes way.

"But how do you know the Château de Guermantes?" Saint-Loup asked me. "Have you visited it—or perhaps you knew my aunt de Guermantes-La Trémoïlle who lived there before?" he added, whether because, finding it quite natural that one should know the same people as he did, he failed to realise that I came from a different background, or because he was pretending not to realise out of politeness.

"No ... but ... I've heard of the château. They have all the busts of the old lords of Guermantes there, haven't they?"

"Yes, it's a fine sight ..."

Page 131. *At this point in the holograph material the Pléiade editors found some loose sheets containing the following passage which Proust failed to complete and incorporate in his novel. (Santois was the name Proust originally gave to the violinist, Morel, who does not make his first appearance until* The Guermantes Way.*):*

N.B. This, which was originally intended for the last Guermantes party, is for the evening in the Casino at Balbec, but may perhaps be changed. I might split it in two, keeping the quintet for the Guermantes party and the organ for Balbec?

At the back of the Casino's dance hall was a stage from which some excessively steep and widely-spaced steps led up to an organ. The "famous Lepic Quintet", composed of women, came in to play *a quintet by Franck (insert another name)*. Although this quintet was her favourite piece, the pianist executed it with the same feverish concentration both on the score and on her fingers as she would have shown had she been sight-reading, and with such a striving towards speed that she seemed not so much to be playing the music as catching up with it as fast as she could go. The piano might perhaps be shattered by the end of it, but she would get there. Since she was a distinguished lady, dressed with studied elegance, she gave her feverish attentiveness a knowing air which from a distance seemed almost mischievous; and indeed whenever she played wrong notes—which happened all the time—she smiled as though she were playing a joke on them, as one laughs when one splashes someone in order to pretend that one has done it on purpose. All the people there were sufficiently elegant and musical not to be paying attention to anything but the music, as would have happened at a bourgeois soirée ... *Put in here the remarks made to me by Mme de Cambremer about the quintet, perhaps even put in here, to vary it a bit, my observations on art and love ... and in that case perhaps bring on the man who says "It's devilish fine", who will be a character already introduced but who has gone grey. Before putting in Mme de Cambremer's reflexions during the interval, say*: Nevertheless the minds of all these people were preoccupied less with what they were listening to than with the way they were listening and the impression they were making all round them. They endeavoured with their boas or their fans to give the appearance of knowing what was being played, of judging the performers and waiting for the extremely difficult *allegro vivace* to compose a satisfying ensemble. The minuet set all their heads nodding and wagging, with knowing smiles which signified both "Isn't it charming!" and "Of course I know it!" Meanwhile my unintentionally ironical smile upset the head-wagging of a few intrepid listeners who replaced the knowing smile with a furious glance and abandoned the head-wagging,

though—in order not to appear to be surrendering to a threat—
not at once but rather as if under the pressure of Westinghouse
brakes, which slow trains down gradually until they come to a
complete stop. An artistic gentleman, anxious to show that he
knew the quintet, shouted "Bravo, bravo" when he judged that
it had reached its conclusion, and began to clap. Unfortunately,
what he had taken for the end of the quintet was not even the
end of one of its movements but simply a two-bar pause. He
consoled himself with the thought that people might imagine
that he knew the pianist and had merely wished to encourage
her. When the end, longed for by the more musical members of
the audience, came at last, I said to Mme de Cambremer...

Meanwhile the organ recital had begun. At that moment a
paralytic old man, who could walk with some difficulty but was
utterly incapable of climbing the steps, conceived the strange
intention of going to sit on a chair right at the top beside the
organ, and three young men pushed him up. But after a while,
as the organ's crisp keyboard notes were executing their pastoral
variations, he got up again, with the three young men in hot
pursuit. I thought he must have had a stroke, and I admired the
obliviousness of the organist who, having ceased to uncoil the
spirals of his rustic pipes, covered the descent of the unfortunate
paralytic with a thunderous noise. Pushed and carried by the
three young men, the old gentleman disappeared into the wings.
The pianist, performer turned critic, had now come to sit on
the stage. In spite of the suffocating heat, she had donned a white
fur coat, of which she was evidently extremely proud. Moreover
her hands, so active on the keyboard only a moment before,
were buried in an immense white fur muff, either because she
simply wanted to show how elegant she was, or in order to
enclose the precious relics of her piano-playing in a shrine
worthy of them, or to exchange the activity of the keyboard for
the motionless but skilful exercise of the muff, which moreover
dispensed her from having to applaud her colleagues. No one
understood the rôle of this muff, about which Saint-Loup interrogated me in vain. But what surprised me more was that scarcely
two minutes had passed before the paralytic old man, evidently
warming to the very exercise of which he was all but incapable,
returned, pushed by the three young men, to take his useless
place beside the organ. He nodded off there for a moment,
then awoke and climbed down again, and since the organist was

invisible behind his instrument, the stage was to all intents and purposes occupied by the perilous exertions of the clumsy quinquagenarian [*sic*] squirrel. When the organist came down in his turn to take his bow, it was to him that the thankless task devolved of helping down the impotent dotard, whose every step made the frail executant stumble. But with a wiliness that is often characteristic of the moribund, the old man clung to the organist in such a way that it was he who appeared to be supporting the man who was more or less carrying him, to be protecting him, to be presenting him to the audience, and to be receiving his share of the applause, which out of pure modesty he seemed not to wish to take for himself by pointing to the organist, who, tottering beneath his human burden and afraid of falling down the steep steps, could not make his bow.

Meanwhile, I was looking at the programme to see what the next piece was to be when I was struck by the name of the soloist: Santois. "He has the same name as the son of my uncle's former valet," I thought to myself. I heard someone say: "Look, a soldier." I raised my eyes and at once recognised the young Santois, who was indeed now a soldier for a year, or rather disguised as a soldier, so much did he give the impression of being in fancy dress.

He played well, looking down at his instrument with that charming Gallic face, the open yet pious demeanour of some contemporary of St Louis or Louis XI, with the defiance of the peasant who feels that there would be little point in having had a revolution if one still had to say "Monsieur le Comte". To these agreeable features there was added, after the first two pieces, as though to complete the picture of the traditional young violinist, a symmetrical adjunct to the redness of the neck at the spot where the instrument rests (the product of the *allegro* although it was *non troppo*), a curvaceous lock of hair, as round as if it had been in a locket, ... charming, belated, perhaps not entirely fortuitous, but activated at the appropriate moment by a virtuoso who knew what a contribution it can make to the seductiveness of a performance.

After he had finished playing, I sent a message round to him asking if I could come and pay my compliments. He replied in a few words scribbled on his card saying that he looked forward to seeing me and assuring me of his "amicable regards". I thought of the indignation Françoise would have felt, she who since she had learned, fairly recently it was true, the use of the third person, had prescribed it to the whole of her family, down to the most remote degrees of kinship or descent, every time a young cousin of hers came "to pay her respects to Monsieur". But if I found this deference towards me of the whole of Françoise's family very traditionally domestic, it seemed to me that, although it was at the opposite extreme, there was something no less characteristically French in the cavalier tone of the young Santois, scion of a race that made the Revolution, implying that a peasant's son, educated or not, considers himself nobody's inferior, and when a prince is mentioned insists on showing by his demeanour that such a person seems to him no better than his father or himself—though with a tinge of hauteur in the way he manifests it that betrays the fact that the age when princes were indeed superior is still fairly recent and that he may be afraid that people still remember it.

After the concert I went round to congratulate him, and recognised him without difficulty, not from the face I remembered, since there is always a certain discrepancy, a certain displacement in the memory, but because his appearance accorded with the impression he had made on me in Paris and which I had forgotten. He was doing his military service near Balbec, and he too had immediately recognised me. We had nothing in common save a few mental images, and the memory of the things we had said to one another during the short visit he had paid to me, and which were of little moment. But it would seem that faces are fairly individual, and moreover that the memory is a pretty faithful organ, since we had remembered each other and our meeting.

Santois was presently joined by his colleagues, the other players, for each of whom, as an aeroplane adds wings to an aviator, his instrument was as it were the beak and the throat of a melodious song-bird; a twittering troupe that had gathered for the summer season at this resort and would shortly, with the first frosts, take off elsewhere. I left Santois with his friends, but when I got back to the hotel I regretted not having asked him who the mountaineering paralytic was who had scaled the heights of the organ so many times, and also whether Santois, his father, had ever told him how my uncle had come to have the portrait of Mme Swann by Elstir. I resolved not to forget to ask him these two questions if I saw him again.

THE GUERMANTES WAY

Page 694. *This passage continues as follows in Proust's manuscript*:

And the legendary scenes depicted in this landscape gave it the curious grandeur of having become contemporaneous with them. The myth dated the landscape; it swept the sky, the sun, the mountains which were its witnesses back with it to a past in the depths of which they already appeared to me to be identical to what they are today. It pushed back through endless time the unfurling of the waves which I had seen at Balbec. I said to myself: that sunset, that ocean which I can contemplate once again, whenever I wish, from the hotel or from the cliff, those identical waves, constitute a setting analogous, especially in the summer when the light orientalises it, to that in which Hercules killed the Hydra of Lerna, in which Orpheus was torn to pieces by the Bacchantes. Already, in those immemorial days of kings whose palaces are unearthed by archaeologists and of whom mythology has made its demi-gods, the sea at evening washed against the shore with that plaint which so often aroused in me a similar vague disquiet. And when I walked along the esplanade at the close of day, the sea which formed such a large part of the picture before my eyes, made up of so many contemporary images such as the band-stand and the casino, was the sea that the Argonauts saw, the sea of pre-history, and it was only by the alien elements I introduced into it that it was of today, it was only because I adjusted it to the hour of my quotidian vision that I found a familiar echo in the melancholy murmur which Theseus heard.

Page 788. *The following development appears in the original manuscript*:

"That is why life is so horrible, since nobody can understand anybody else," Mme de Guermantes concluded with a self-consciously pessimistic air, but also with the animation induced by the pleasure of shining before the Princesse de Parme. And when I saw this woman who was so difficult to please, who had claimed to be bored to death by M. and Mme Ribot [*changed to*: with an extremely impressive minister-academician], going to so much trouble for this uninspiring princess, I understood how a man of such refinement as Swann could have enjoyed the company of M. Bontemps [*changed to*: Mme Bontemps]. Indeed if she had had reasons for adopting the latter, the Duchess might have preferred him to the celebrated statesman, for, outside the ranks of the princely families, only charm and distinction, either proved or imaginary but in the latter case its existence having been decreed in the same way as a monarch ennobles people, counted in the Guermantes circle. Political or professional hierarchies meant nothing. And if Cottard, a professor and an academician, who was not received there, had been called in as a consultant, he might have found there a complete unknown, Dr Percepied, whom for purely self-interested motives it was convenient for the Duchess to have to lunch now and then and whom she declared to be rather distinguished because she received him.

"Really?" replied the Princess, astonished by the assertion that life is horrible. "At least," she added, "one can do a great deal of good."

"Not even that, when you come down to it," said the Duchess, fearful lest the conversation should turn to philanthropy, which she found boring. "How can one do good to people one doesn't understand? And besides, one doesn't know which people to do good to—one tries to do good to the wrong people. That's what is so frightful. But to get back to Gilbert and his being shocked at your visiting the Iénas, Your Highness has far too much sense to let her actions be governed..."

Page 793. *Additional passage of dialogue in the manuscript*:

"I think he's mainly preoccupied by a Villeparisis–Norpois rapprochement," said the Duchess, in order to change the subject.

"But is there any room for a closer rapprochement in that direction?" asked the Prince. "I thought they were already very close."

"Good heavens!" said the Duchess with a gesture of alarm at the image of coupling which the Prince conjured up for her, "I believe at any rate that they have been. But I'm told, ridiculous though it may seem, that my aunt would like to marry him. No, seriously, it seems incredible, but I gather she's the one who wants it, and he doesn't because she already bores him enough as it is. Really, she can't have any sense of the ridiculous. Why,

I wonder, when one has so seldom 'resisted' in the course of one's life, should one suddenly feel the need to sanction a liaison with matrimony, after dispensing with it on so many other occasions? There really isn't much point in having caused every door to be closed to one if one cannot bear the idea of a union remaining illicit, especially when it's as respectable as this one, and, we all hope, as platonic."

SYNOPSIS

WITHIN A BUDDING GROVE

PART TWO

PLACE-NAMES · THE PLACE

Departure for Balbec (3). Subjectiveness of love (4). Contradictory effects of habit (4). Railway-stations (5). Françoise's simple and infallible taste (9). Alcoholic euphoria (11). Mme de Sévigné and Dostoievsky (14). Sunrise from the train (15); the milk-girl (15). Balbec Church (18). "The tyranny of the Particular" (20). Place-names on the way to Balbec-Plage (21).

Arrival at Balbec-Plage (22). The manager of the Grand Hotel (22, 25). My room at the top of the hotel (26; cf. I 10). Attention and habit (26, 30). My grandmother's kindness (27). The sea in the morning (32). Balbec tourists (34). Balbec and Rivebelle (35). Mme de Villeparisis (37). M. and Mlle de Stermaria (38). An actress and three friends (39). The weekly Cambremer garden-party (41). Resemblances (43). Poetic visions of Mlle de Stermaria (47). The general manager (49). Françoise's Grand Hotel connections (50). Meeting of Mme de Villeparisis and my grandmother (52). The "sordid moment" at the end of meals (53; cf. 216). The Princesse de Luxembourg (56). Mme de Villeparisis, M. de Norpois and my father (59). The bourgeoisie and the Faubourg Saint-Germain (61).

Drives with Mme de Villeparisis (62). Different seas (62). The ivy-covered church (66). Mme de Villeparisis's conversation (67, 78). Norman girls (69). The handsome fisher-girl (73). The three trees of Hudimesnil (74; cf. I 177). The fat Duchesse de La Rochefoucauld (82). My grandmother and I: intimations of death (84).

Robert de Saint-Loup (85). My friendship with him (92), but real happiness requires solitude (92; cf. 251). Saint-Loup as a work of art: the "nobleman" (93). A Jewish colony (95). Variety of human failings and similarity of virtues (97). Bloch's bad manners (100). Bloch and his father (101; cf. 125). The stereoscope (104). Mme de Villeparisis is a Guermantes (110).

M. de Charlus's strange behaviour (107). I recognise him as the man in the grounds of Tansonville (111; cf. I 139). Further weird behaviour (114). Mme de Sévigné, La Fontaine and Racine (117). Charlus comes to my room (120).

Dinner at the Blochs' with Saint-Loup (122). To know "without knowing" (124). Bloch's sisters (124). The elegance of "Uncle Solomon" (126). Nissim Bernard (127); his lies (129). Bloch and Mme Swann in the train (132). Françoise's view of Bloch and Saint-Loup (132). Saint-Loup and his mistress (134). My grandmother's inexplicable behaviour (139).

The blossoming girls (141). "Oh the poor old boy ..." (145). The dark-haired cyclist: Albertine (146). The name Simonet (153, 158, 193). Rest before dinner: different aspects of the sea (155). Dinners at Rivebelle (159). The astral tables (161). Euphoria induced by alcohol and music (162). Meeting with Elstir (175). A new aspect of Albertine (179).

Elstir's studio (183); his sea-scapes (184); the painter's "metaphors" (185). Elstir explains to me the beauty of Balbec Church (189). Albertine passes by (192). The portrait of *Miss Sacripant* (195). "My beautiful Gabrielle!" (198). Age and the artist (198). Elstir and the little band (202). Nullity of love (205). *Miss Sacripant* was Mme Swann (208) and M. Biche Elstir! (210). "One must discover wisdom for oneself" (211). My grandmother and Saint-Loup (212). Saint-Loup and Bloch (213). Still lifes (216; cf. 53). Afternoon party at Elstir's (217). Yet another Albertine: a well-brought-up girl (220). Albertine on the esplanade: once more a member of the little band (223). Octave, the gigolo (224). Albertine's antipathy for Bloch (226). Saint-Loup engaged to a Mlle d'Ambresac? (230). Albertine's intelligence and taste (231). Andrée (232). Gisèle (233).

Days with the girls (236). Françoise's bad temper (241). Balbec through Elstir's eyes (242) Fortuny (244). A sketch of Les Creuniers (245). The mobile beauty of youth (249). Friendship: an abdication of oneself (251; cf. 92). Twittering of the girls (252). Letter from Sophocles to Racine (255). A love divided among several girls (258). Albertine is to spend a night at the Grand Hotel (271). The rejected kiss (275) The attraction of Albertine (276). The multiple utilisation of a single action (279). Straying in the budding grove (286). The different Albertines (287).

End of the season (291). Departure (294).

THE GEURMANTES WAY

PART ONE

professed hatred of society (437). Visit to the suburbs to meet Saint-Loup's mistress (439). I recognise her as "Rachel when from the Lord" (441). Pear-trees in blossom (444). Jealous scenes in the restaurant (448). In the theatre after lunch (455). Rachel's cruelty (456). Her transformation on stage (457). Rachel and the dancer (460). Saint-Loup and the journalist (463). Saint-Loup and the passionate stranger (465).

An afternoon party at Mme de Villeparisis's (466). Her social decline (466; cf. III 765); her literary qualities (467). The social kaleido-scope and the Dreyfus case (472). Mme de Villeparisis's *Memoirs* (476). The three Parcae (479). The portrait of the Duchesse de Montmorency (480). Legrandin in society (482). Mme de Guermantes's face and her conversation lack the mysterious glamour of her name (486, 491). Mme de Guermantes's lunch-eons (488); the Mérimée and Meilhac and Halévy type of mind (489). Bloch's bad manners (499). Entry of M. de Norpois (502). Entry of the Duc de Guermantes (504). Norpois and my father's candidature for the Academy (505). Generality of psychological laws (508). Various opinions on Rachel (508; cf. 499, 504, 509), on Odette (509), on Mme de Cambremer (512). Norpois and the Dreyfus case (513, 520). The laws of the imagination and of language (516). Mme de Villeparisis's by-play with Bloch (528). The Comtesse de Marsantes (530). Entry of Robert de Saint-Loup (534). Mme de Guermantes's amiability towards me (535, 543). Norpois and Prince von Faffenheim (537). Oriane refuses to meet Mme Swann (543). Charles Morel pays me a visit (543); Mme Swann and the "Lady in pink" (546). Charlus and Odette (546). Charlus's strange behaviour to his aunt (547). Mme de Marsantes and her son (549, 558). I learn that Charlus is the Duc de Guermantes's brother (556). The affair of the necklace (557, 560). Mme de Villeparisis tries to prevent me from going home with M. de Charlus (562). Charlus offers to guide my life (563). "Terrible, almost insane" remarks about the Bloch family (566). M. d'Argencourt's coldness towards me (569). Strange choice of a cab (573).

The Dreyfus case below-stairs (574). My grandmother's ill-ness (575). The thermometer (576). Dr du Boulbon's diagnosis (579). Expedition to the Champs-Elysées with my grandmother (585). The "marquise" (586). My grandmother has a slight stroke (588).

historic name of Guermantes detectable only in the Duchess's vocal mannerisms: traces of her country childhood (769; cf. 761). Misunderstanding between a young dreamer and a society woman (770). Why Saint-Loup will return to a dangerous post in Morocco (777). The ritual orangeade (779). The Duchess praises the Empire style (783, cf. I 330). The Guermantes divorced from the name Guermantes (790). Norpois at once malicious and obliging (794). The Turkish Ambassadress (799). The poetry of genealogy (800). Exaltation in the cab on the way to M. de Charlus (811).

Waiting in M. de Charlus's drawing-room (816). His strange welcome (817). Gentleness succeeding rage (823). He accompanies me home in his carriage (825).

Letter from the young footman to his cousin (829). Invitation from the Princesse de Guermantes (830). Diversity of society people in spite of their apparently monotonous insignificance (831). Visit to the Duke and Duchess: view of the neighbouring houses (834). Remarkable discovery which will be described later (835; cf. III 3). The Duc de Bouillon (836). The coins of the Order of Malta (836). The Duc de Guermantes's "Philippe de Champaigne" (839). Swann greatly "changed" (840). His Dreyfusism (842). The Duke's ball and Amanien's illness (849). Swann's illness (855). The Duchess's red shoes (857).

ABOUT THE TRANSLATORS

CHARLES KENNETH SCOTT MONCRIEFF was born in Scotland in 1889 and studied Law and English at Edinburgh University. He trained as a professional soldier and spent World War I in France until wounded in 1917. While convalescing he turned to translating, and his English version of the *Chansons de Roland* was published in 1919. He translated Proust during the 1920s, along with Stendhal's *The Charterhouse of Parma*, *Scarlet and Black*, *Armance* and some of the *Chroniques italiennes*. He died in Rome in 1930.

TERENCE KILMARTIN translated selected letters of Proust in four volumes (together with his wife, Joanna), and wrote an exhaustive *Guide to Proust*. His other translations include de Gaulle's memoirs, and works by André Malraux and Henri de Montherlant. He was Literary Editor of the *Observer* from 1952 to 1987. After his death in 1991, the poet and translator D. J. ENRIGHT, who had worked closely with Kilmartin on the Scott Moncrieff version of *À la recherche du temps perdu*, continued the task of revising the translation.

CHINUA ACHEBE
Things Fall Apart

THE ARABIAN NIGHTS
(2 vols, tr. Husain Haddawy)

AUGUSTINE
The Confessions

JANE AUSTEN
Emma
Mansfield Park
Northanger Abbey
Persuasion
Pride and Prejudice
Sanditon and Other Stories
Sense and Sensibility

HONORÉ DE BALZAC
Cousin Bette
Eugénie Grandet
Old Goriot

SIMONE DE BEAUVOIR
The Second Sex

SAUL BELLOW
The Adventures of Augie March

WILLIAM BLAKE
Poems and Prophecies

JORGE LUIS BORGES
Ficciones

JAMES BOSWELL
The Life of Samuel Johnson

CHARLOTTE BRONTË
Jane Eyre
Villette

EMILY BRONTË
Wuthering Heights

MIKHAIL BULGAKOV
The Master and Margarita

SAMUEL BUTLER
The Way of all Flesh

ITALO CALVINO
If on a winter's night a traveler

ALBERT CAMUS
The Outsider

MIGUEL DE CERVANTES
Don Quixote

GEOFFREY CHAUCER
Canterbury Tales

ANTON CHEKHOV
My Life and Other Stories
The Steppe and Other Stories

KATE CHOPIN
The Awakening

CARL VON CLAUSEWITZ
On War

S. T. COLERIDGE
Poems

WILKIE COLLINS
The Moonstone
The Woman in White

CONFUCIUS
The Analects

JOSEPH CONRAD
Heart of Darkness
Lord Jim
Nostromo
The Secret Agent
Typhoon and Other Stories
Under Western Eyes
Victory

THOMAS CRANMER
The Book of Common Prayer

DANTE ALIGHIERI
The Divine Comedy

DANIEL DEFOE
Moll Flanders
Robinson Crusoe

CHARLES DICKENS
Bleak House
David Copperfield
Dombey and Son
Great Expectations
Hard Times
Little Dorrit
Martin Chuzzlewit
Nicholas Nickleby
The Old Curiosity Shop
Oliver Twist
Our Mutual Friend
The Pickwick Papers
A Tale of Two Cities

DENIS DIDEROT
Memoirs of a Nun

JOHN DONNE
The Complete English Poems

FYODOR DOSTOEVSKY
The Brothers Karamazov
Crime and Punishment
Demons

GEORGE ELIOT
Adam Bede
Daniel Deronda
Middlemarch
The Mill on the Floss
Silas Marner

WILLIAM FAULKNER
The Sound and the Fury

HENRY FIELDING
Joseph Andrews and Shamela
Tom Jones

F. SCOTT FITZGERALD
The Great Gatsby
This Side of Paradise

GUSTAVE FLAUBERT
Madame Bovary

FORD MADOX FORD
The Good Soldier
Parade's End

E. M. FORSTER
Howards End
A Passage to India

ELIZABETH GASKELL
Mary Barton

EDWARD GIBBON
The Decline and Fall of the
Roman Empire
Vols 1 to 3: The Western Empire
Vols 4 to 6: The Eastern Empire

J. W. VON GOETHE
Selected Works

IVAN GONCHAROV
Oblomov

GÜNTER GRASS
The Tin Drum

GRAHAM GREENE
Brighton Rock
The Human Factor

DASHIELL HAMMETT
The Maltese Falcon
The Thin Man
Red Harvest
(in 1 vol.)

THOMAS HARDY
Far From the Madding Crowd
Jude the Obscure
The Mayor of Casterbridge
The Return of the Native
Tess of the d'Urbervilles
The Woodlanders

JAROSLAV HAŠEK
The Good Soldier Švejk

NATHANIEL HAWTHORNE
The Scarlet Letter

JOSEPH HELLER
Catch-22

ERNEST HEMINGWAY
A Farewell to Arms
The Collected Stories

GEORGE HERBERT
The Complete English Works

HERODOTUS
The Histories

PATRICIA HIGHSMITH
The Talented Mr. Ripley
Ripley Under Ground
Ripley's Game
(in 1 vol.)

HINDU SCRIPTURES
(tr. R. C. Zaehner)

JAMES HOGG
Confessions of a Justified Sinner

HOMER
The Iliad
The Odyssey

VICTOR HUGO
Les Misérables

HENRY JAMES
The Awkward Age
The Bostonians
The Golden Bowl
The Portrait of a Lady
The Princess Casamassima
The Wings of the Dove
Collected Stories (2 vols)

JAMES JOYCE
Dubliners
A Portrait of the Artist as
a Young Man
Ulysses

This book is set in BEMBO which was cut
by the punch-cutter Francesco Griffo
for the Venetian printer-publisher
Aldus Manutius in early 1495
and first used in a pamphlet
by a young scholar
named Pietro
Bembo.

MARCEL PROUST

*In Search of
Lost Time*

VOLUME 2
Within a Budding Grove (Part Two)
The Guermantes Way

Translated from the French by
C. K. Scott Moncrieff and Terence Kilmartin
Revised by D. J. Enright
with an Introduction by Harold Bloom

EVERYMAN'S LIBRARY

250

This book is one of 250 volumes in Everyman's Library
which have been distributed to 4500 state schools
throughout the United Kingdom.
The project has been supported by a grant of £4 million
from the Millennium Commission.

First included in Everyman's Library, 2001
Translation copyright © Chatto & Windus and Random House, Inc.,
1981
Copyright in the revisions to translation © D. J. Enright, 1992
Introduction originally appeared as 'Proust:
The True Persuasion of Sexual Jealousy' in *The Western Canon* by
Harold Bloom, Macmillan, 1995, and is reprinted by permission of
Macmillan Publishers Ltd.
Bibliography and Chronology © Everyman Publishers plc, 2001
Typography by Peter B. Willberg

ISBN 1-84159-897-6

A CIP catalogue record for this book is available from the
British Library

Published by Everyman Publishers plc,
Gloucester Mansions, 140A Shaftesbury Avenue,
London WC2H 8HD

Distributed by Random House (UK) Ltd.,
20 Vauxhall Bridge Road, London SW1V 2SA